Jules Verne

JULES VERNE

TWENTY THOUSAND LEAGUES UNDER THE SEA

THE MYSTERIOUS ISLAND

JOURNEY TO THE CENTER OF THE EARTH

AROUND THE WORLD IN EIGHTY DAYS

BARNES & NOBLE
BOOKS
NEW YORK

This edition published by Barnes & Noble, Inc.

1994 Barnes & Noble Books

ISBN 1-56619-536-5

Book design by Mario A. Moreno

Printed and bound in the United States of America

M 9 8 7 6 5 4 3 2

Contents

INTRODUCTION

American children growing up in the years following World War II had ample occasion to become aware of Jules Verne. Thanks to his prophetic novels *From the Earth to the Moon* and *Around the Moon*, his name was indissolubly linked to space travel, the great scientific project of that day. Abridgments and comic book versions of his books abounded, and following the lead of Walt Disney's *20,000 Leagues Under the Sea* (1954) and Michael Todd's *Around the World in 80 Days* (1956), filmmakers mined his work enthusiastically, turning out in rapid succession *From the Earth to the Moon* (1958), *Journey to the Center of the Earth* (1959), *The Mysterious Island* (1961), *Master of the World* (1961), *Five Weeks in a Balloon* (1962), and *In Search of the Castaways* (1962, based on *The Children of Captain Grant*). Like television adventure serials or DC comics, Verne's work was the exclusive cultural property of children. If adults thought of him at all, it was as a strictly subliterary phenomenon, a constructor of clever but mechanistic boys' adventures who had fortuitously earned a footnote in the history of technology: he had "foreseen" submarines, high-speed modern travel, the exploration of space.

That was the Verne I absorbed with more or less enthusiasm at an early age, without having had to read a single one of his books in its original form. It was with some surprise that a few years later I came upon a different and unexpected Verne. In 1966, the French publisher Livre de Poche began an ambitious project of reissuing a series of Verne's novels in paperback, accompanied by their original illustrations. The paperbacks' striking cover designs interpolated cut-outs from those engravings—figures of impeccable 19th-century voyagers decked out in top hats, canes, and exquisitely trimmed moustaches—into contemporary color photographs of appropriate natural settings: sea, sky, cavern, harbor, jungle, mountain, glacier. Drawn mostly by the cover, I picked up *Journey to the Center of the Earth* and read it in a single night, entranced above all by the inexorable rhythms of Verne's storytelling voice.

The Livre de Poche covers turned out to be an elegant statement about Verne's aesthetic. Splicing fictitious beings into actual places is his fundamental gesture, a collision that implies others: of dream with waking life, of myth with history, of theater with politics, of magic with science. The substrata through which his subterranean explorers crawl are as real as Verne can make them, a realness certified by an impressive display of scientific terminology. The explorers themselves, by contrast, are puppet figures, and not in any pejorative sense: they have the facile energy and acrobatic grace of performers in the *opera comique* where he labored for years as playwright and librettist before succeeding as a novelist. Verne assumes many roles—scientist, geographer, historian, political polemicist, effusive tour guide, romantic contemplator of the cosmos—but it is the unredeemed vaudevillian in him that keeps his books moving inexhaustibly along.

As Livre de Poche continued to reissue those works, it became clear that Verne's *oeuvre* was considerably more extensive and varied than most English-language readers realized. His life work, grouped under the rubric *Extraordinary Voyages*, began its trajectory in 1863 with *Five Weeks in a Balloon*, written when Verne was already thirty-five and had behind him a long, largely unsuccessful career as playwright and magazine writer; and it continued through sixty-four more novels and story collections, the last published in 1919, fourteen years after Verne's death. It was a project that in its playful fashion embodied the impulses of a half-century of European expansionism in high gear. The voluminousness of Verne's output corresponds to an unbridled spatial reach: around the moon and off on a comet, under the sea and around the world, and into every corner of the globe. The *Voyages* contain novels set in India (*The Steam House*), China (*The Tribulations of a Chinaman in China*), Russia (*Michael Strogoff*), Greece (*The Archipelago On Fire*), Turkey (*Kereban the Inflexible*), Ireland (*Foundling Mick*), Scotland (*The Green Ray*), the Gobi Desert (*Claudius Bombarnac*), the Sahara (*The Invasion of the Sea*), South Africa (*The Southern Star*), Brazil (*The Jangada*), Canada (*Family Without a Name*, whose liberationist sentiments continue to make it a rallying point for Quebec Libre partisans), and the United States (the Civil War novel *North Against South* and the remarkable political fantasy *The Begum's*

Fortune, which pits a French utopia against a German dystopia in the wilds of Oregon): not to mention the ice floes of the Arctic and Antarctic regions, an assortment of far-flung islands, and a number of entirely man-made environments, airborne, afloat, or sunk among the underground networks of an abandoned colliery.

Taken together the novels constitute a 19th-century Book of Knowledge, an encyclopedia of geographic, scientific, and historical monuments, factoids, and stereotypes, methodically laid out like an immense relief map: a map with little people roaming among the landmarks, pausing to smoke under an explication of geology or geography, achieving their melodramatic itineraries by means of elaborately explicated technology either just invented or just about to be invented, or engaging in a life-and-death pursuit in between paragraphs on the discovery of Australia, the opium trade, or the disposition of vowels and consonants in Old Icelandic.

As French scholars have pointed out in tireless detail, it is also an encyclopedia of political concepts jostling each other with their contradictions intact, the conservatism and prejudice of the bourgeois householder side by side with a romantic sympathy for oppressed nationalities, remnants of Saint-Simonian utopianism, visions of future technocratic states, and bursts of the mysterious anarchic rebellion most powerfully expressed in the figure of Captain Nemo.

Verne's literary ambitions were high, nurtured by a deep admiration for Scott, Dumas, Cooper, Defoe, Dickens, Balzac, Sterne, and (crucially) Poe. The only ornaments in his workroom were busts of Molière and Shakespeare. One of his great achievements (which has hitherto tended to elude translation) is a magnificently supple prose style which can accommodate lyrical rhapsody and technical explanation, absurdist comedy and methodical political analysis, frantic action sequences and lush and langorously extended descriptive passages. Nothing is out of place because, after all, it is a model of the whole world that he is constructing: a model, potentially, of all the worlds, "known and unknown," as the series' subtitle proclaimed.

Roland Barthes defined Verne's motive force as the will to appropriate, and indeed his protagonists' overriding goal is to learn how to use the world, how to master and exploit the material universe while remaining in control and protected from its dangers. The travelers in *The Steam House* traverse India in a lavishly appointed, steam-driven house on wheels, so that they can survey the terrors and mysteries of the jungle while calmly sipping tea and reading the newspaper. The luxuriously appointed drawing room which constitutes the interior of the space capsule in *From the Earth to the Moon* anticipates not so much the realities of NASA space capsules as the psychic space of modern motel chains.

The Vernian hero creates a private world within the world, of which the supreme example is Nemo's *Nautilus*, a self-sufficient mobile home equipped with the best in literature and music and art, and invulnerable to penetration from outside. Nemo, its captain and inventor, is at once Verne's supreme creation and a figure standing in dark and singular contrast to his other characters, the isolated genius who will not play ball, the misanthropic freedom fighter almost indifferent to the fate of the humanity he wishes to save. He enjoys perfect freedom under the sign of his slogan "Mobilis in Mobili" ("mobile in the mobile element," or, perhaps, "go with the flow"): but his freedom is exacted at the cost of uncompromising isolation.

Verne's favorite books were *Robinson Crusoe* and *The Swiss Family Robinson*, novels in which castaways create micro-societies superior in many ways to the larger society from which they have been separated. The fascination this theme exerted on him finds its fullest expression in *The Mysterious Island*, a primal epic enabling him to plot a rebuilding of the world from scratch. It is symbolically appropriate that Lincoln Island's settlers, who devote all their efforts to outward expansion in a spirit of teamwork, should find their destiny linked ultimately with that of the dying Captain Nemo, whose life has been dedicated to the creation of a miniaturized, solitary, hermetically sealed universe. The gulf between the hearty cameraderie of the pioneers and the isolated superiority of the embittered genius is the geography that *The Mysterious Island* seeks to chart with its fictional coordinates. The island here is far more than setting; it is an entity far more alive than the people who inhabit it, because it incorporates all their contradictory energies and impulses. Its peaks and caves and subterranean channels exist to provide a unified resolution for human turbulence.

For a writer whose ostensible theme is human mastery over the planet, Verne's characters are dwarfed to a large degree by their surroundings. The real protagonist of *Journey to the Center of the Earth* (and this is the book's originality) is the geological substratum. The professor and his associates are not so much characters as fellow readers; we advance through the book's prose as if it embodied the rock through which they thread their path. Likewise, in 20,000 *Leagues Under the Sea*, the very pages seem steeped in water; from page to page we glide through a teeming natural paradise which Verne's prose represents as a subaqueous jungle of scientific nomenclature, a kind of concrete poetry. His planet is language: it's in the primal material of prose that he goes digging for his lost worlds.

The characters can hardly compete with language and geography. They are toy people running mad races in their balloons and railroads, pathetically tiny by comparison with the oceans and mountain ranges they must contend with. They don't have psychology; they have tics, wardrobes, schedules, methods, projects. They have names, and what names: Nemo, Arronax, Gideon Spillett, Phileas Fogg. Yet however helpless they may appear, they are determined to make an impact on their physical surroundings. They are heroic or obsessive: or, not infrequently, heroic through obsession, possessed by the absurd perseverance of the scholar or the explorer or the avenging outlaw.

Consider only Phileas Fogg of *Around the World in 80 Days*, that ultimate control freak narrowing space and time down to their minutest units of measurement, reducing the earth itself to a hotel or train station set aside for his convenience. Oddly imperturbable in the heart of his own mania, he moves with the calm of a surrealist through every catastrophe, and of course triumphs in the end through an elegant conjunction of coincidences. Professor Lidenbrock* in *Journey to the Center of the Earth* is the absent-minded professor of popular humor, but his fever to descend is anything but a joke; his path leads into visions of horrifying desolation, darkness, silence, culminating in his nephew Axel's dream of immense geological epochs, "the great and wondrous series of terrestrial transformations" in which rocks melt, oceans boil away, and the earth evaporates into a cloud of gas.

The cozy bourgeois interiors where Verne's characters feel so much at home open onto sudden dizzying perspectives: the geological epochs glimpsed by Axel in his reverie, the undersea Atlantean ruins and polar maelstroms to which the *Nautilus* provides access, the frenzy of mechanized high-speed travel to which life is reduced by the voyage of Phileas Fogg. If Cyrus Harding of *The Mysterious Island* is Verne's supreme heroic figure—the engineer as organizer of reality, calm and penetrating—it is because only his sort of phlegmatic practicality can come to grips with a situation of absolute deprivation and abandonment.

Verne's idealization of Harding could not be more serious; but if he takes

* In most English-language editions of Verne's novel, the names of Professor Lidenbrock and Axel have been changed to Professor von Hardwigg and Harry.

pride in delineating the patriarchal and colonizing culture which Harding will plant on Lincoln Island, he is also the barely concealed caricaturist of that culture. Sancho to his own Quixote, he undermines the monuments he so conscientiously erects. There is no certainty that is not undermined, no note of strident grandiloquence that does not have its ironic or sardonic counterpoint. The heroic scientist and the mad scientist stare each other down; the clownish servants cast the pretensions of their masters in a ridiculous light; the sweet humor of the happy endings curdles under the influence of apocalyptic forebodings.

Phileas Fogg's voyage is the trajectory of the industrial West abstracted into farce; only the films of Buster Keaton offer a comparable mix of melancholy and precision and abrupt heartless cataclysm. All the bubbly tricks that Verne acquired from the *opera comique* serve here, as elsewhere, as a sort of anti-gravity device cushioning the very real brutality implied by his fictions. His reservoirs of optimistic exclamation, his unlimited capacity to enlarge on his faith in progress: these are like the twirled cane or the flower in the lapel, the boulevardier's tokens of good form. The consummate showman, he delivers all that his age expects in the way of grand tour, hall of waxworks, geographical survey of the known universe, cyclorama of scientific marvels. One should not be fooled. Beneath the optimism there are deeper reservoirs of sadness. He knows how badly things can go wrong, understands the power of the machines even before they have been invented. The oceanic creatures observed by the passengers of the *Nautilus* little suspect how ill Nemo's technology bodes for them, but Verne is already remarking—in the margins, as it were—on the human capacity to provoke extinctions.

Whatever nostalgia Verne may evoke, it is not simple: his Eden is complex, his desert island already carries within its limits the seeds of a future world. Verne is not so much scientific forecaster—indeed most of the notions he plays with were already in circulation in one form or another—as he is prophet of the future of his own stories: as if, even as he told the tale, it foreshadowed what it would one day become. His structures are so cunningly built that they have room even for what he did not put in them. The toys in his box of marvels are like miniaturized versions of other novels, perhaps darker and more disturbing, that he did not write but which he makes it possible to imagine. What more can one ask for from any toy?

—*Geoffrey O'Brien*

1994

Twenty Thousand Leagues Under the Sea

Contents

Part 1

Part 2

Part 1

A Shifting Reef

The year 1866 was signalized by a remarkable incident, a mysterious and inexplicable phenomenon, which doubtless no one has yet forgotten. Not to mention rumors which agitated the maritime population, and excited the public mind, even in the interior of continents, seafaring men were particularly excited. Merchants, common sailors, captains of vessels, skippers, both of Europe and America, naval officers of all countries, and the governments of several states on the two continents, were deeply interested in the matter.

For some time past, vessels had been met by "an enormous thing," a long object spindle-shaped, occasionally phosphorescent, and infinitely larger and more rapid in its movements than a whale.

The facts relating to this apparition (entered in various log-books) agreed in most respects as to the shape of the object or creature in question, the untiring rapidity of its movements, its surprising power of locomotion, and the peculiar life with which it seemed endowed. If it was a cetacean, it surpassed in size all those hitherto classified in science. Taking into consideration the mean of observations made at divers times—rejecting the timid estimate of those who assigned to this object a length of two hundred feet, equally with the exaggerated opinions which set it down as a mile in width and three in length—we might fairly conclude that this mysterious being surpassed greatly all dimensions admitted by the ichthyologists of the day, if it existed at all. And that it did exist was an undeniable fact; and, with that tendency which disposes the human mind in favor of the marvelous, we can understand the excitement produced in the entire world by this supernatural apparition. As to classing it in the list of fables, the idea was out of the question.

On the 20th of July, 1866, the steamer *Governor Higginson*, of the Calcutta and Burnach Steam Navigation Company, had met this moving mass five miles off the east coast of Australia. Captain Baker thought at first that he was in the presence of an unknown sand-bank; he even prepared to determine its exact position, when two columns of water, projected by the inexplicable object, shot with a hissing noise a hundred and fifty feet up into the air. Now, unless the sand-bank had been submitted to the intermittent eruption of a geyser, the *Governor Higginson* had to do neither more nor less than with an aquatic mammal, unknown till then, which threw up from its blow-holes columns of water mixed with air and vapor.

Similar facts were observed on the 23d of July in the same year, in the Pacific Ocean, by the *Columbus,* of the West India and Pacific Steam Navigation Company. But this extraordinary cetaceous creature could transport itself from one place to another with surprising velocity; as, in an interval of three days, the *Governor Higginson* and the *Columbus* had observed it at two different points of the chart, separated by a distance of more than seven hundred nautical leagues.

Fifteen days later, two thousand miles further off, the *Helvetia,* of the Compagnie-Nationale, and the *Shannon,* of the Royal Mail Steamship Company, sailing to windward in that portion of the Atlantic lying between the United States and Europe, respectively signaled the monster to each other in 42° 15′ N. lat. and 60° 35′ W. long. In these simultaneous observations, they thought themselves justified in estimating the minimum length of the mammal at more than three hundred and fifty feet, as the *Shannon* and *Helvetia* were of smaller dimensions than it, though they measured three hundred feet over all.

Now the largest whales, those which frequent those parts of the sea round the Aleutian, Kulammak, and Umgullich Islands, have never exceeded the length of sixty yards, if they attain that.

These reports arriving one after the other, with fresh observations made on board the transatlantic ship *Pereira,* a collision which occurred between the *Etna* of the Inman line and the monster, a *proces verbal* directed by the officers of the French frigate *Normandie,* a very accurate survey made by the staff of Commodore Fitz-James on board the *Lord Clyde* greatly influenced public opinion. Light-thinking people jested upon the phenomenon, but grave, practical countries, such as England, America, and Germany, treated the matter more seriously.

In every place of great resort the monster was the fashion. They sang of it in the cafés, ridiculed it in the papers, and represented it on the stage. All kinds of stories were circulated regarding it. There appeared in the papers caricatures of every gigantic and imaginary creature, from the white whale, the terrible "Moby Dick" of hyperborean regions, to the immense kraken whose tentacles could entangle a ship of five hundred tons, and hurry it into the abyss of the ocean. The legends of ancient times were even resuscitated, and the opinions of Aristotle and Pliny revived, who admitted the existence of these monsters, as well as the Norwegian tales of Bishop

Pontoppidan, the accounts of Paul Heggede, and, last of all, the reports of Mr. Harrington (whose good faith no one could suspect), who affirmed that, being on board the *Castillan,* in 1857, he had seen this enormous serpent, which had never until that time frequented any other seas but those of the ancient "Constitutionnel."

Then burst forth the interminable controversy between the credulous and the incredulous in the societies of savants and scientific journals. "The question of the monster" inflamed all minds. Editors of scientific journals, quarreling with believers in the supernatural, spilled seas of ink during this memorable campaign, some even drawing blood; for, from the sea-serpent, they came to direct personalities.

For six months war was waged with various fortune in the leading articles of the Geographical Institution of Brazil, the Royal Academy of Science of Berlin, the British Association, the Smithsonian Institution of Washington, in the discussions of the "Indian Archipelago," of the Cosmos of the Abbé Moigno, in the Mittheilungen of Petermann, in the scientific chronicles of the great journals of France and other countries. The cheaper journals replied keenly and with inexhaustible zest. These satirical writers parodied a remark of Linnæus, quoted by the adversaries of the monster, maintaining that "nature did not make fools," and adjured their contemporaries not to give the lie to nature, by admitting the existence of krakens, sea-serpents, "Moby Dicks," and other lucubrations of delirious sailors. At length an article in a well-known satirical journal by a favorite contributor, the chief of the staff, settled the monster, like Hippolytus, giving it the death-blow amid a universal burst of laughter. Wit had conquered science.

During the first months of the year 1867, the question seemed buried never to revive, when new facts were brought before the public. It was then no longer a scientific problem to be solved, but a real danger seriously to be avoided. The question took quite another shape. The monster became a small island, a rock, a reef, but a reef of indefinite and shifting proportions.

On the 5th of March, 1867, the *Moravian,* of the Montreal Ocean Company, finding herself during the night in 27° 30′ lat. and 72° 15′ long., struck on her starboard quarter a rock, marked in no chart for that part of the sea. Under the combined efforts of the wind and its four hundred horsepower, it was going at the rate of thirteen knots. Had it not been for the superior strength of the hull of the *Moravian,* she would have been broken by the shock, and gone down with the 237 passengers she was bringing home from Canada.

The accident happened about five o'clock in the morning, as the day was breaking. The officers of the quarter-deck hurried to the after-part of the vessel. They examined the sea with the most scrupulous attention. They saw nothing but a strong eddy about three cables' length distant, as if the surface had been violently agitated. The bearings of the place were taken exactly, and the *Moravian* continued its route without apparent damage. Had it struck on a submerged rock, or on an enormous wreck? They could not tell; but on examination of the ship's bottom when undergoing repairs, it was found that part of her keel was broken.

This fact, so grave in itself, might perhaps have been forgotten like many others, if, three weeks after, it had not been re-enacted under similar circumstances. But, thanks to the nationality of the victim of the shock, thanks to the reputation of the company to which the vessel belonged, the circumstance became extensively circulated.

The 13th of April, 1867, the sea being beautiful, the breeze favorable, the *Scotia*, of the Cunard Company's line, found herself in 15° 12′ long. and 45° 37′ lat. She was going at the speed of thirteen knots and a half.

At seventeen minutes past four in the afternoon, while the passengers were assembled at lunch in the great saloon, a slight shock was felt on the hull of the *Scotia*, on her quarter, a little aft of the port paddle.

The *Scotia* had not struck, but she had been struck, and seemingly by something rather sharp and penetrating than blunt. The shock had been so light that no one had been alarmed, had it not been for the shouts of the carpenter's watch, who rushed on to the bridge, exclaiming, "We are sinking! We are sinking!" At first the passengers were much frightened, but Captain Anderson hastened to reassure them. The danger could not be imminent. The *Scotia*, divided into seven compartments by strong partitions, could brave with impunity any leak. Captain Anderson went down immediately into the hold. He found that the sea was pouring into the fifth compartment; and the rapidity of the influx proved that the force of the water was considerable. Fortunately this compartment did not hold the boilers, or the fires would have been immediately extinguished. Captain Anderson ordered the engines to be stopped at once, and one of the men went down to ascertain the extent of the injury. Some minutes afterward they discovered the existence of a large hole, of two yards in diameter, in the ship's bottom. Such a leak could not be stopped; and the *Scotia*, her paddles half submerged, was obliged to continue her course. She was then three hundred miles from Cape Clear, and after three days' delay, which caused great uneasiness in Liverpool, she entered the basin of the company.

The engineers visited the *Scotia,* which was put in dry-dock. They could scarcely believe it possible; at two yards and a half below water-mark was a regular rent, in the form of an isosceles triangle. The broken place in the iron plates was so perfectly defined that it could not have been more neatly done by a punch. It was clear, then, that the instrument producing the perforation was not of a common stamp; and after having been driven with prodigious strength, and piercing an iron plate one and three-eighth inches thick, had withdrawn itself by a retrograde motion truly inexplicable.

Such was the last fact, which resulted in exciting once more the torrent of public opinion. From this moment all unlucky casualties which could not be otherwise accounted for were put down to the monster.

Upon this imaginary creature rested the responsibility of all these shipwrecks, which unfortunately were considerable; for of three thousand ships whose loss was annually recorded at Lloyd's, the number of sailing and steamships supposed to be totally lost, from the absence of all news, amounted to not less than two hundred.

Now, it was the "monster" who, justly or unjustly, was accused of their disappearance, and, thanks to it, communication between the different continents became more and more dangerous. The public demanded peremptorily that the seas should at any price be relieved from this formidable cetacean.

Pro and Con

At the period when these events took place, I had just returned from a scientific research in the disagreeable territory of Nebraska, in the United States. In virtue of my office as Assistant Professor in the Museum of Natural History in Paris, the French government had attached me to that expedition. After six months in Nebraska, I arrived in New York toward the end of March, laden with a precious collection. My departure for France was fixed for the first days in May. Meanwhile, I was occupying myself in classifying my mineralogical, botanical, and zoölogical riches, when the accident happened to the *Scotia*.

I was perfectly up in the subject which was the question of the day. How could I be otherwise? I had read and reread all the American and European papers without being any nearer a conclusion. This mystery puzzled me. Under the impossibility of forming an opinion, I jumped from one extreme to the other. That there really was something could not be doubted, and the incredulous were invited to put their finger on the wound of the *Scotia*.

On my arrival at New York, the question was at its height. The hypothesis of the floating island, and the unapproachable sand-bank, supported by minds little competent to form a judgment, was abandoned. And, indeed, unless this shoal had a machine in its stomach, how could it change its position with such astonishing rapidity?

From the same cause, the idea of a floating hull of an enormous wreck was given up.

There remained then only two possible solutions of the question, which created two distinct parties: on one side, those who were for a monster of colossal strength; on the other, those who were for a submarine vessel of enormous motive power.

But this last hypothesis, plausible as it was, could not stand against inquiries made in both worlds. That a private gentleman should have such a machine at his command was not likely. Where, when, and how was it built? And how could its construction have been kept secret? Certainly a government might possess such a destructive machine. And in these disastrous times, when the ingenuity of man has multiplied the power of weapons of war, it was possible that, without the knowledge of others, a state might try to work such a formidable engine. After the chassepots came the torpedoes, after the torpedoes the submarine rams, then—the reaction. At least, I hope so.

But the hypothesis of a war-machine fell before the declaration of governments. As public interest was in question, and transatlantic communications suffered, their veracity could not be doubted. But, how admit that the construction of this submarine boat had escaped the public eye? For a private gentleman to keep the secret under such circumstances would be very difficult, and for a state whose every act is persistently watched by powerful rivals, certainly impossible.

After inquiries made in England, France, Russia, Prussia, Spain, Italy, and America, even in Turkey, the hypothesis of a submarine monitor was definitely rejected.

Upon my arrival in New York several persons did me the honor of consulting me on the phenomenon in question. I had published in France a work in quarto, in two volumes, entitled "Mysteries of the Great Submarine Grounds." This book, highly approved of in the learned world, gained for me a special reputation in this rather obscure branch of Natural History. My advice was asked. As long as I could deny the reality of the fact, I confined myself to a decided negative. But soon finding myself driven into a corner, I was obliged to explain myself categorically. And even "the Honorable Pierre Aronnax, Professor in the Museum of Paris," was called upon by the *New York Herald* to express a definite opinion of some sort. I did something. I spoke for want of power to hold my tongue. I discussed the question in all its forms, politically and scientifically; and I give here an extract from a carefully studied article which I published in the number of the 30th of April. It ran as follows:

"After examining one by one the different hypotheses, rejecting all other suggestions, it becomes necessary to admit the existence of a marine animal of enormous power.

"The great depths of the ocean are entirely unknown to us. Soundings cannot reach them. What passes in those remote depths—what beings live, or can live, twelve or fifteen miles beneath the surface of the waters—what is the organization of these animals—we can scarcely conjecture. However, the solution of the problem submitted to me may modify the form of the dilemma. Either we do know all the varieties of beings which people our planet, or we do not. If we do not know them all, if Nature still has secrets in ichthyology for us, nothing is more conformable to reason than to admit the existence of fishes, or cetaceans of other kinds, or even of new species, of an organization formed to inhabit the strata inaccessible to soundings, and which an accident of some sort, either fantastical or capricious, has brought at long intervals to the upper level of the ocean.

"If, on the contrary, we do know all living kinds, we must necessarily seek for the animal in question among those marine beings already classed; and, in that case, I should be disposed to admit the existence of a gigantic narwhal.

"The common narwhal, or unicorn of the sea, often attains a length of sixty feet. Increase its size fivefold or tenfold, give it strength proportionate to its size, lengthen its destructive weapons, and you obtain the animal required. It will have the proportions determined by the officers of the *Shannon*, the instrument required by the perforation of the *Scotia*, and the power necessary to pierce the hull of the steamer.

"Indeed the narwhal is armed with a sort of ivory sword, a halberd, according to the expression of certain naturalists. The principal tusk has the hardness of steel. Some of these tusks have been found buried in the bodies of whales, which the unicorn always attacks with success. Others have been drawn out, not without trouble, from the bottoms of ships, which they had pierced through and through, as a gimlet pierces a barrel. The Museum of the Faculty of Medicine of Paris possesses one of these defensive weapons, two yards and a quarter in length, and fifteen inches in diameter at the base.

"Very well! Suppose this weapon to be six times stronger, and the animal ten times more powerful; launch it at the rate of twenty miles an hour, and you obtain a shock capable of producing the catastrophe required. Until further information, therefore, I shall maintain it to be a sea-unicorn of colossal dimensions, armed, not with a halberd, but with a real spur, as the armored frigates, or the 'rams' of war, whose massiveness and motive power it would possess at the same time. Thus may this inexplicable phenomenon be explained, unless there be something over and above all that one has ever conjectured, seen, perceived, or experienced; which is just within the bounds of possibility."

These last words were cowardly on my part; but, up to a certain point, I wished to shelter my dignity as professor, and not give too much cause for laughter to the Americans, who laugh well when they do laugh. I reserved for myself a way of escape. In effect, however, I admitted the existence of the "monster." My article was warmly discussed, which procured it a high reputation. It rallied round it a certain number of partisans. The solution it proposed gave, at least, full liberty to the imagination. The human mind delights in grand conceptions of supernatural beings. And the sea is precisely their best vehicle, the only medium through which these giants (against which terrestrial animals, such as elephants or rhinoceroses, are as nothing) can be produced or developed.

The industrial and commercial papers treated the question chiefly from this point of view. The *Shipping and Mercantile Gazette*, the *Lloyds' List*, the *Packet-Boat* and the *Maritime and Colonial Review*, all papers devoted to insurance companies which threatened to raise their rates of premium, were unanimous on this point. Public opinion had been pronounced. The United States was the first in the field; and in New York they made preparations for an expedition destined to pursue this narwhal. A frigate of great speed, the *Abraham Lincoln,* was put in commission, as soon as possible. The arsenals were opened to Commander Farragut, who hastened the arming of his frigate; but, as it always happens, the moment it was decided to pursue the monster, the monster did not appear. For two months no one heard it spoken of. No ship met with it. It seemed as if this unicorn knew of the plots weaving around it. It had been so much talked of, even through the Atlantic cable, that jesters pretended that this slender fly had stopped a telegram on its passage, and was making the most of it.

So when the frigate had been armed for a long campaign, and provided with formidable fishing apparatus, no one could tell what course to pursue. Impatience grew apace, when, on the 2d of June, they learned that a steamer of the line of San Francisco, from California to Shanghai, had seen the animal three weeks before in the North Pacific Ocean. The excitement caused by this news was extreme. The ship was revictualed and well stocked with coal.

Three hours before the *Abraham Lincoln* left Brooklyn pier, I received a letter worded as follows:

To M. Aronnax, Professor in the Museum of Paris,
Fifth Avenue Hotel, New York.

Sir: If you will consent to join the Abraham Lincoln *in this expedition, the government of the United States will with pleasure see France represented in the enterprise. Commander Farragut has a cabin at your disposal.*

Very cordially yours,
J. B. Hobson
Secretary of Marine

I Form My Resolution

Three seconds before the arrival of J. B. Hobson's letter, I no more thought of pursuing the unicorn than of attempting the passage of the North Sea. Three seconds after reading the letter of the Honorable Secretary of Marine, I felt that my true vocation, the sole end of my life, was to chase this disturbing monster, and purge it from the world.

But I had just returned from a fatiguing journey, weary, and longing for repose. I aspired to nothing more than again seeing my country, my friends, my little lodging by the Jardin des Plantes, my dear and precious collections. But nothing could keep me back! I forgot all—fatigue, friends, and collections—and accepted without hesitation the offer of the American government.

"Besides," thought I, "all roads lead back to Europe; and the unicorn may be amiable enough to hurry me toward the coast of France. This worthy animal may allow itself to be caught in the seas of Europe (for my particular benefit), and I will not bring back less than half a yard of his ivory halberd to the Museum of Natural History." But in the meanwhile I must seek this narwhal in the North Pacific Ocean, which, to return to France, was taking the road to the antipodes.

"Conseil," I called in an impatient voice.

Conseil was my servant, a true, devoted Flemish boy, who had accompanied me in all my travels. I liked him, and he returned the liking well. He was phlegmatic by nature, regular from principle, zealous from habit, evincing little disturbance at the different surprises of life, very quick with his hands, and apt at any service required of him; and, despite his name, never giving advice—even when asked for it.

Conseil had followed me for the last ten years wherever science led. Never once did he complain of the length or fatigue of a journey, never make an objection to pack his portmanteau for whatever country it might be, or however far away, whether China or Congo. Besides all this, he had good health, which defied all sickness, and solid muscles, but no nerves; good morals are understood. This boy was thirty years old, and his age to that of his master as fifteen to twenty. May I be excused for saying that I was forty years old?

But Conseil had one fault—he was ceremonious to a degree, and would never speak to me but in the third person, which was sometimes provoking.

"Conseil," said I again, beginning with feverish hands to make preparations for my departure.

Certainly, I was sure of this devoted boy. As a rule, I never asked him if it were convenient for him or not to follow me in my travels; but this time the expedition in question might be prolonged, and the enterprise might be hazardous in pursuit of an animal capable of sinking a frigate as easily as a nutshell. Here there was matter for reflection even to the most impassive man in the world. What would Conseil say?

"Conseil," I called a third time.

Conseil appeared.

"Did you call, sir?" said he, entering.

"Yes, my boy; make preparations for me and yourself too. We leave in two hours."

"As you please, sir," replied Conseil quietly.

"Not an instant to lose; lock in my trunk all traveling utensils, coats, shirts, and stockings—without counting—as many as you can, and make haste."

"And your collections, sir?" observed Conseil.

"We will think of them by and by."

"What! the archiotherium, the hyracotherium, the oreodons, the cheropotamus, and the other skins?"

"They will keep them at the hotel."

"And your live Babiroussa, sir?"

"They will feed it during our absence; besides, I will give orders to forward our menagerie to France."

"We are not returning to Paris, then?" said Conseil.

"Oh! Certainly," I answered evasively, "by making a curve."

"Will the curve please you, sir?"

"Oh! It will be nothing; not quite so direct a road, that is all. We take our passage in the *Abraham Lincoln*."

"As you think proper, sir," coolly replied Conseil.

"You see, my friend, it has to do with the monster—the famous narwhal. We are going to purge it from the seas. The author of a work in quarto, in two volumes, on the 'Mysteries of the Great Submarine Grounds' cannot forbear embarking with Commander Farragut. A glorious mission, but a dangerous one! We cannot tell where we may go; these animals can be very capricious. But we will go whether or no; we have got a captain who is pretty wide awake."

I opened a credit account for Babiroussa, and, Conseil following, I jumped into a cab. Our luggage was transported to the deck of the frigate immediately. I hastened on board and asked for Commander Farragut. One of the sailors conducted me to the poop, where I found myself in the presence of a good-looking officer, who held out his hand to me.

"Monsieur Pierre Aronnax?" said he.

"Himself," replied I. "Commander Farragut?"

"You are welcome, professor; your cabin is ready for you."

I bowed, and desired to be conducted to the cabin destined for me.

The *Abraham Lincoln* had been well chosen and equipped for her new destination. She was a frigate of great speed, fitted with high-pressure engines which admitted a pressure of seven atmospheres. Under this the *Abraham Lincoln* attained the mean speed of nearly eighteen knots and a third an hour—a considerable speed, but, nevertheless, insufficient to grapple with this gigantic cetacean.

The interior arrangements of the frigate corresponded to its nautical qualities. I was well satisfied with my cabin, which was in the after-part, opening upon the gun room.

"We shall be well off here," said I to Conseil.

"As well, by your honor's leave, as a hermit crab in the shell of a whelk," said Conseil.

I left Conseil to stow our trunks conveniently away, and remounted the poop in order to survey the preparations for departure.

At that moment Commander Farragut was ordering the last moorings to be cast loose which held the *Abraham Lincoln* to the pier of Brooklyn. So in a quarter of an hour, perhaps less, the frigate would have sailed without me. I should have missed this extraordinary, supernatural, and incredible expedition, the recital of which may well meet with some skepticism.

But Commander Farragut would not lose a day nor an hour in scouring the seas in which the animal had been sighted. He sent for the engineer.

"Is the steam full on?" asked he.

"Yes, sir," replied the engineer.

"Go ahead," cried Commander Farragut.

The quay of Brooklyn, and all that part of New York bordering on the East River, was crowded with spectators. Three cheers burst successively from five hundred thousand throats; thousands of handkerchiefs were waved above the heads of the compact mass, saluting the *Abraham Lincoln*, until she reached the waters of the Hudson, at the point of that elongated peninsula which forms the town of New York. Then the frigate, following the coast of New Jersey along the right bank of the beautiful river, covered with villas, passed between the forts, which saluted her with their heaviest guns. The *Abraham Lincoln* answered by hoisting the American colors three times, whose thirty-nine stars shone resplendent from the mizzen-peak; then modifying its speed to take the narrow channel marked by buoys placed in the inner bay formed by Sandy Hook Point, it coasted the long sandy beach, where some thousands of spectators gave it one final cheer. The escort of boats and tenders still followed the frigate, and did not leave her until they came abreast of the light-ship whose two lights marked the entrance of New York Channel.

Six bells struck, the pilot got into his boat, and rejoined the little schooner which was waiting under our lee, the fires were made up, the screw beat the waves more rapidly, the frigate skirted the low yellow coast of Long Island; and at eight bells, after having lost sight in the northwest of the lights of Fire Island, she ran at full steam on to the dark waters of the Atlantic.

Ned Land

Captain Farragut was a good seaman, worthy of the frigate he commanded. His vessel and he were one. He was the soul of it. On the question of the cetacean there was no doubt in his mind, and he would not allow the existence of the animal to be disputed on board. He believed in it as certain good women believe in the leviathan—by faith, not by reason. The monster did exist, and he had sworn to rid the seas of it. He was a kind of Knight of Rhodes, a second Dieudonné de Gozon, going to meet the serpent which desolated the island. Either Captain Farragut would kill the narwhal, or the narwhal would kill the captain. There was no third course.

The officers on board shared the opinion of their chief. They were ever chatting, discussing, and calculating the various chances of a meeting, watching narrowly the vast surface of the ocean. More than one took up his quarters voluntarily in the cross-trees, who would have cursed such a berth under any other circumstances. As long as the sun described its daily course, the rigging was crowded with sailors, whose feet were burned to such an extent by the heat of the deck as to render it unbearable; still the *Abraham Lincoln* had not yet breasted the suspected waters of the Pacific. As to the ship's company, they desired nothing better than to meet the unicorn, to harpoon it, hoist it on board, and dispatch it. They watched the sea with eager attention.

Besides, Captain Farragut had spoken of a certain sum of two thousand dollars, set apart for whoever should first sight the monster, were he cabin-boy, common seaman, or officer.

I leave you to judge how eyes were used on board the *Abraham Lincoln*.

For my own part, I was not behind the others, and left to no one my share of daily observations. The frigate might have been called the Argus, for a hundred reasons. Only one among us, Conseil, seemed to protest by his indifference against the question which so interested us all, and seemed to be out of keeping with the general enthusiasm on board.

I have said that Captain Farragut had carefully provided his ship with every apparatus for catching the gigantic cetacean. No whaler had ever been better armed. We possessed every known engine, from the harpoon thrown by the hand to the barbed arrows of the blunderbuss, and the explosive balls of the duck-gun. On the forecastle lay the perfection of a breech-loading gun, very thick at the breech, and very narrow in the bore, the model of which had been in the Exhibition of 1867. This precious weapon of American origin could throw with ease a conical projectile of nine pounds to a mean distance of ten miles.

Thus the *Abraham Lincoln* wanted for no means of destruction; and, what was better still, she had on board Ned Land, the prince of harpooners.

Ned Land was a Canadian, with an uncommon quickness of hand, and who knew no equal in his dangerous occupation. Skill, coolness, audacity, and cunning he possessed in a superior degree, and it must be a cunning whale or a singularly "cute" cachalot to escape the stroke of his harpoon.

Ned Land was about forty years of age; he was a tall man (more than six feet high), strongly built, grave and taciturn, occasionally violent, and very passionate when contradicted. His person attracted attention, but above all the boldness of his look, which gave a singular expression to his face.

Who calls himself Canadian calls himself French; and little communicative as Ned Land was, I must admit that he took a certain liking for me. My nationality drew him to me, no doubt. It was an opportunity for him to talk, and for me to hear, that old language of Rabelais, which is still in use in some Canadian provinces. The harpooner's family was originally from Quebec, and was already a tribe of hardy fishermen when this town belonged to France.

Little by little, Ned Land acquired a taste for chatting, and I loved to hear the recital of his adventures in the polar seas. He related his fishing, and his combats, with natural poetry of expression; his recital took the form of an epic poem, and I seemed to be listening to a Canadian Homer singing the Iliad of the regions of the North.

I am portraying this hardy companion as I really knew him. We are old friends now, united in that unchangeable friendship which is born and cemented amid extreme dangers. Ah, brave Ned! I ask no more than to live a hundred years longer, that I may have more time to dwell the longer on your memory.

Now, what was Ned Land's opinion upon the question of the marine monster? I must admit that he did not believe in the unicorn, and was the only one on board who did not share that universal conviction. He even avoided the subject, which I one day thought it my duty to press upon him. One magnificent evening, the 25th of June—that is to say, three weeks after our departure—the frigate was abreast of Cape Blanc, thirty miles to leeward of the coast of Patagonia. We had crossed the Tropic of Capricorn, and the Straits of Magellan opened less than seven miles to the south. Before eight days were over, the *Abraham Lincoln* would be plowing the waters of the Pacific.

Seated on the poop, Ned Land and I were chatting of one thing and another as we looked at this mysterious sea, whose great depths had up to this time been inaccessible to the eye of man. I naturally led up the conversation to the giant unicorn, and examined the various chances of success or failure of the expedition. But seeing that Ned Land let me speak without saying too much himself, I pressed him more closely.

"Well, Ned," said I, "is it possible that you are not convinced of the existence of this cetacean that we are following? Have you any particular reason for being so incredulous?"

The harpooner looked at me fixedly for some moments before answering, struck his broad forehead with his hand (a habit of his), as if to collect himself, and said at last, "Perhaps I have, Mr. Aronnax."

"But, Ned, you, a whaler by profession, familiarized with all the great marine mammalia—you, whose imagination might easily accept the hypothesis of enormous cetaceans—*you* ought to be the last to doubt under such circumstances!"

"That is just what deceives you, professor," replied Ned. "That the vulgar should believe in extraordinary comets traversing space, and in the existence of antediluvian monsters in the heart of the globe, may well be; but neither astronomers nor geologists believe in such chimeras. As a whaler, I have followed many a cetacean, harpooned a great number, and killed several; but, however strong or well-armed they may have been, neither their tails nor their weapons would have been able even to scratch the iron plates of a steamer."

"But, Ned, they tell of ships which the teeth of the narwhal have pierced through and through."

"Wooden ships—that is possible," replied the Canadian; "but I have never seen it done; and, until further proof, I deny that whales, cetaceans, or sea-unicorns could ever produce the effect you describe."

"Well, Ned, I repeat it with a conviction resting on the logic of facts. I believe in the existence of a mammal powerfully organized, belonging to the branch of vertebrata, like the whales, the cachalots, or the dolphins, and furnished with a horn of defense of great penetrating power."

"Hum!" said the harpooner, shaking his head with the air of a man who would not be convinced.

"Notice one thing, my worthy Canadian," I resumed. "If such an animal is in existence, if it inhabits the depths of the ocean, if it frequents the strata lying miles below the surface of the water, it must necessarily possess an organization the strength of which would defy all comparison."

"And why this powerful organization?" demanded Ned.

"Because it requires incalculable strength to keep one's self in these strata and resist the pressure. Listen to me. Let us admit that the pressure of the atmosphere is represented by the weight of a column of water thirty-two feet high. In reality the column of water would be shorter, as we are speaking of sea-water, the density of which is greater than that of fresh water. Very well, when you dive, Ned, as many times thirty-two feet of water as there are above you, so many times does your body bear a pressure equal to that of the atmosphere, that is to say 15 lbs. for each square inch of its surface. It follows, then, that at 320 feet this pressure equals that of 10 atmospheres, of 100 atmospheres at 3,200 feet, and of 1,000 atmospheres at 32,000 feet, that is, about 6 miles; which is equivalent to saying that, if you could attain this depth in the ocean, each square 3/8 of an inch of the surface of your body would bear a pressure of 5,600 lbs. Ah! my brave Ned, do you know how many square inches you carry on the surface of your body?"

"I have no idea, Mr. Aronnax."

"About 6,500; and, as in reality the atmospheric pressure is about 15 lbs. to the square inch, your 6,500 square inches bear at this moment a pressure of 97,500 lbs."

"Without my perceiving it?"

"Without your perceiving it. And if you are not crushed by such a pressure, it is because the air penetrates the interior of your body with equal pressure. Hence perfect equilibrium between the interior and exterior pressure, which thus neutralize each other, and which allows you to bear it without inconvenience. But in the water it is another thing."

"Yes, I understand," replied Ned, becoming more attentive; "because the water surrounds me, but does not penetrate."

"Precisely, Ned; so that at 32 feet beneath the surface of the sea you would undergo a pressure of 97,500 lbs.; at 320 feet, ten times that pressure; at 3,200 feet, a hundred times that pressure; lastly, at 32,000 feet, a thousand times that pressure would be 97,500,000 lbs.—that is to say, that you would be flattened as if you had been drawn from the plates of an hydraulic machine!"

"The devil!" exclaimed Ned.

"Very well, my worthy harpooner, if some vertebrate, several hundred yards long, and large in proportion, can maintain itself in such depths—of those whose surface is represented by millions of square inches, that is by tens of millions of pounds, we must estimate the pressure they undergo. Consider, then, what must be the resistance of their bony structure, and the strength of their organization to withstand such pressure!"

"Why!" exclaimed Ned Land. "They must be made of iron plates eight inches thick, like the armored frigates."

"As you say, Ned. And think what destruction such a mass would cause if hurled with the speed of an express train against the hull of a vessel."

"Yes—certainly—perhaps," replied the Canadian, shaken by these figures, but not yet willing to give in.

"Well, have I convinced you?"

"You have convinced me of one thing, sir, which is, that if such animals do exist at the bottom of the seas, they must necessarily be as strong as you say."

"But if they do not exist, mine obstinate harpooner, how explain the accident to the *Scotia?*"

At a Venture

The voyage of the *Abraham Lincoln* was for a long time marked by no special incident. But one circumstance happened which showed the wonderful dexterity of Ned Land, and proved what confidence we might place in him.

The 30th of June, the frigate spoke some American whalers, from whom we learned that they knew nothing about the narwhal. But one of them, the captain of the *Monroe,* knowing that Ned Land had shipped on board the *Abraham Lincoln,* begged for his help in chasing a whale they had in sight. Commander Farragut, desirous of seeing Ned Land at work, gave him permission to go on board the *Monroe.* And fate served our Canadian so well that, instead of one whale, he harpooned two with a double blow, striking one straight to the heart and catching the other after some minutes' pursuit.

Decidedly, if the monster ever had to do with Ned Land's harpoon, I would not bet in its favor.

The frigate skirted the southeast coast of America with great rapidity. The 3d of July we were at the opening of the Straits of Magellan, level with Cape Vierges. But Commander Farragut would not take a tortuous passage, but doubled Cape Horn.

The ship's crew agreed with him. And certainly it was possible that they might meet the narwhal in this narrow pass. Many of the sailors affirmed that the monster could not pass there, "that he was too big for that!"

The 6th of July, about three o'clock in the afternoon, the *Abraham Lincoln,* at fifteen miles to the south, doubled the solitary island, this last rock at the extremity of the American continent to which some Dutch sailors gave the name of their native town, Cape Horn. The course was taken toward the northwest, and the next day the screw of the frigate was at last beating the waters of the Pacific.

"Keep your eyes open!" called out the sailors.

And they were opened widely. Both eyes and glasses, a little dazzled, it is true, by the prospect of two thousand dollars, had not an instant's repose. Day and night they watched the surface of the ocean, and even nyctalopes, whose faculty of seeing in the darkness multiplies their chances a hundredfold, would have had enough to do to gain the prize.

I, myself, for whom money had no charms, was not the least attentive on board. Giving but few minutes to my meals, but a few hours to sleep, indifferent to either rain or sunshine, I did not leave the poop of the vessel. Now leaning on the netting of the forecastle, now on the taffrail, I devoured with eagerness the soft foam which whitened the sea as far as the eye could reach; and how often have I shared the emotion of the majority of the crew when some capricious whale raised its black back above the waves! The poop of the vessel was crowded in a moment. The cabins poured forth a torrent of sailors and officers, each with heaving breast and troubled eye watching the course of the cetacean. I looked, and looked, till I was nearly blind, while Conseil, always phlegmatic, kept repeating in a calm voice:

"If, sir, you would not squint so much, you would see better!"

But vain excitement! The *Abraham Lincoln* checked its speed and made for the animal signaled, a simple whale, or common cachalot, which soon disappeared amid a storm of execration.

But the weather was good. The voyage was being accomplished under the most favorable auspices. It was then the bad season in Australia, the July of that zone corresponding to our January in Europe; but the sea was beautiful and easily scanned round a vast circumference.

The 20th of July, the Tropic of Capricorn was cut by 105° of longitude, and the 27th of the same month we crossed the equator on the 110th meridian. This passed, the frigate took a more decided westerly direction, and scoured the central waters of the Pacific. Commander Farragut thought, and with reason, that it was better to remain in deep water, and keep clear of continents or islands, which the beast itself seemed to shun (perhaps because there was not enough water for him! suggested the greater part of the crew). The frigate passed at some distance from the Marquesas and the Sandwich Islands, crossed the Tropic of Cancer, and made for the China Seas. We were on the theater of the last diversions of the monster; and to say truth, we no longer *lived* on board. Hearts palpitated, fearfully preparing themselves for future incurable aneurism. The entire ship's crew were undergoing a nervous excitement, of which I can give no idea; they could not eat, they could not sleep: twenty times a day, a misconception or an optical illusion of some sailor seated on the taffrail would cause dreadful perspirations, and these emotions, twenty times repeated, kept us in a state of excitement so violent that a reaction was unavoidable.

And truly, reaction soon showed itself. For three months, during which a day seemed an age, the *Abraham Lincoln* furrowed all the waters of the Northern Pacific, running at whales, making sharp deviations from her course, veering suddenly from one tack to another, stopping suddenly, putting on steam, and backing ever and anon at the risk of deranging her machinery; and not one point of the Japanese or American coast was left unexplored.

The warmest partisans of the enterprise now became its most ardent detractors. Reaction mounted from the crew to the captain himself, and certainly, had it not been for resolute determination on the part of Captain Farragut, the frigate would have headed due southward. This useless search could not last much longer. The *Abraham Lincoln* had nothing to reproach herself with, she had done her best to succeed. Never had an American ship's crew shown more zeal or patience; its failure could not be placed to their charge—there remained nothing but to return.

This was represented to the commander. The sailors could not hide their discontent, and the service suffered. I will not say there was a mutiny on board, but after a reasonable period of obstinacy, Captain Farragut (as Columbus did) asked for three days' patience. If in three days the monster did not appear, the man at the helm should give three turns of the wheel, and the *Abraham Lincoln* would make for the European seas.

This promise was made on the 2d of November. It had the effect of rallying the ship's crew. The ocean was watched with renewed attention. Each one wished for a last glance in which to sum up his remembrance. Glasses were used with feverish activity. It was a grand defiance given to the giant narwhal, and he could scarcely fail to answer the summons and "appear."

Two days passed, the steam was at half-pressure; a thousand schemes were tried to attract the attention and stimulate the apathy of the animal in case it should be met in those parts. Large quantities of bacon were trailed in the wake of the ship, to the great satisfaction (I must say) of the sharks. Small craft radiated in all directions round the *Abraham Lincoln* as she lay to, and did not leave a spot of the sea unexplored. But the night of the 4th of November arrived without the unveiling of this submarine mystery.

The next day, the 5th of November, at twelve, the delay would (morally speaking) expire; after that time, Commander Farragut, faithful to his promise, was to turn the course to the southeast and abandon forever the northern regions of the Pacific.

The frigate was then in 31° 15′ north latitude and 136° 42′ east longitude. The coast of Japan still remained less than two hundred miles to leeward. Night was approaching. They had just struck eight bells; large clouds veiled the face of the moon, then in its first quarter. The sea undulated peaceably under the stern of the vessel.

At that moment I was leaning forward on the starboard netting. Conseil, standing near me, was looking straight before him. The crew, perched in the ratlines, examined the horizon, which contracted and darkened by degrees. Officers with their night-glasses scoured the growing darkness; sometimes the ocean sparkled under the rays of the moon, which darted between two clouds, then all trace of light was lost in the darkness.

In looking at Conseil, I could see he was undergoing a little of the general influence. At least I thought so. Perhaps for the first time his nerves vibrated to a sentiment of curiosity.

"Come, Conseil," said I, "this is the last chance of pocketing the two thousand dollars."

"May I be permitted to say, sir," replied Conseil, "that I never reckoned on getting the prize; and, had the government of the Union offered a hundred thousand dollars, it would have been none the poorer."

"You are right, Conseil. It is a foolish affair after all, and one upon which we entered too lightly. What time lost, what useless emotions! We should have been back in France six months ago."

"In your little room, sir," replied Conseil, "and in your museum, sir; and I should have already classed all your fossils, sir. And the Babiroussa would have been installed in its cage in the Jardin des Plantes, and have drawn all the curious people of the capital!"

"As you say, Conseil. I fancy we shall run a fair chance of being laughed at for our pains."

"That's tolerably certain," replied Conseil quietly; "I think they will make fun of you, sir. And—must I say it?"

"Go on, my good friend."

"Well, sir, you will only get your deserts."

"Indeed!"

"When one has the honor of being a savant as you are, sir, one should not expose one's self to——"

Conseil had not time to finish his compliment. In the midst of general silence a voice had just been heard. It was the voice of Ned Land shouting:

"Look out there! The very thing we are looking for—on our weather beam!"

At Full Steam

At this cry the whole ship's crew hurried toward the harpooner—commander, officers, masters, sailors, cabin boys; even the engineers left their engines, and the stokers their furnaces.

The order to stop her had been given, and the frigate now simply went on by her own momentum. The darkness was then profound; and however good the Canadian's eyes were, I asked myself how he had managed to see, and what he had been able to see. My heart beat as if it would break. But Ned Land was not mistaken, and we all perceived the object he pointed to. At two cables' length from the *Abraham Lincoln,* on the starboard quarter, the sea seemed to be illuminated all over. It was not a mere phosphoric phenomenon. The monster emerged some fathoms from the water, and then threw out that very intense but inexplicable light mentioned in the report of several captains. This magnificent irradiation must have been produced by an agent of great *shining* power. The luminous part traced on the sea an immense oval, much elongated, the center of which condensed a burning heat, whose overpowering brilliancy died out by successive gradations.

"It is only an agglomeration of phosphoric particles," cried one of the officers.

"No, sir, certainly not," I replied. "Never did pholades or salpæ produce such a powerful light. That brightness is of an essentially electrical nature. Besides, see, see! It moves; it is moving forward, backward, it is darting toward us!"

A general cry arose from the frigate.

"Silence!" said the captain. "Up with the helm, reverse the engines."

The steam was shut off, and the *Abraham Lincoln*, beating to port, described a semicircle.

"Right the helm, go ahead," cried the captain.

These orders were executed, and the frigate moved rapidly from the burning light.

I was mistaken. She tried to sheer off, but the supernatural animal approached with a velocity double her own.

We gasped for breath. Stupefaction more than fear made us dumb and motionless. The animal gained on us, sporting with the waves. It made the round of the frigate, which was then making fourteen knots, and enveloped it with its electric rings like luminous dust. Then it moved away two or three miles, leaving a phosphorescent track, like those volumes of steam that the express trains leave behind. All at once from the dark line of the horizon whither it retired to gain its momentum, the monster rushed suddenly toward the *Abraham Lincoln* with alarming rapidity, stopped suddenly about twenty feet from the hull, and died out—not diving under the water, for its brilliancy did not abate—but suddenly, and as if the source of this brilliant emanation was exhausted. Then it reappeared on the other side of the vessel, as if it had turned and slid under the hull. Any moment a collision might have occurred which would have been fatal to us. However, I was astonished at the maneuvers of the frigate. She fled and did not attack.

On the captain's face, generally so impassive, was an expression of unaccountable astonishment.

"Mr. Aronnax," he said, "I do not know with what formidable being I have to deal, and I will not imprudently risk my frigate in the midst of this darkness. Besides, how attack this unknown thing, how defend one's self from it? Wait for daylight, and the scene will change."

"You have no further doubt, captain, of the nature of the animal?"

"No, sir; it is evidently a gigantic narwhal, and an electric one."

"Perhaps," added I, "one can only approach it with a gymnotus or a torpedo."

"Undoubtedly," replied the captain, "if it possesses such dreadful power, it is the most terrible animal that ever was created. That is why, sir, I must be on my guard."

The crew were on their feet all night. No one thought of sleep. The *Abraham Lincoln*, not being able to struggle with such velocity, had moderated its pace, and sailed at half speed. For its part, the narwhal, imitating the frigate, let the waves rock it at will, and seemed decided not to leave the scene of the struggle. Toward midnight, however, it disappeared, or, to use a more appropriate term, it "died out" like a large glow-worm. Had it fled? One could only fear, not hope it. But at seven minutes to one o'clock in the morning a deafening whistling was heard, like that produced by a body of water rushing with great violence.

The captain, Ned Land, and I were then on the poop, eagerly peering through the profound darkness.

"Ned Land," asked the commander, "you have often heard the roaring of whales?"

"Often, sir; but never such whales the sight of which brought me in two thousand dollars. If I can only approach within four harpoon lengths of it!"

"But to approach it," said the commander, "I ought to put a whaler at your disposal?"

"Certainly, sir."

"That will be trifling with the lives of my men."

"And mine too," simply said the harpooner.

Toward two o'clock in the morning, the burning light reappeared, not less intense, about five miles to windward of the *Abraham Lincoln*. Notwithstanding the distance, and the noise of the wind and sea, one heard distinctly the loud strokes of the animal's tail, and even its panting breath. It seemed that, at the moment that the enormous narwhal had come to take breath at the surface of the water, the air was ingulfed in its lungs, like the steam in the vast cylinders of a machine of two thousand horsepower.

"Hum!" thought I. "A whale with the strength of a cavalry regiment would be a pretty whale!"

We were on the *qui vive* till daylight, and prepared for the combat. The fishing implements were laid along the hammock nettings. The second lieutenant loaded the blunderbusses, which could throw harpoons to the distance of a mile, and long duck-guns, with explosive bullets, which inflicted mortal wounds even to the most terrible animals. Ned Land contented himself with sharpening his harpoon—a terrible weapon in his hands.

At six o'clock, day began to break; and with the first glimmer of light, the electric light of the narwhal disappeared. At seven o'clock the day was sufficiently advanced, but a very thick sea-fog obscured our view, and the best spy-glasses could not pierce it. That caused disappointment and anger.

I climbed the mizzen-mast. Some officers were already perched on the mast-heads. At eight o'clock the fog lay heavily on the waves, and its thick scrolls rose little by little. The horizon grew wider and clearer at the same time. Suddenly, just as on the day before, Ned Land's voice was heard:

"The thing itself on the port quarter!" cried the harpooner.

Every eye was turned toward the point indicated. There, a mile and a half from the frigate, a long blackish body emerged a yard above the waves. Its tail, violently agitated, produced a considerable eddy. Never did a caudal appendage beat the sea with such violence. An immense track, of a dazzling whiteness, marked the passage of the animal, and described a long curve.

The frigate approached the cetacean. I examined it thoroughly.

The reports of the *Shannon* and of the *Helvetia* had rather exaggerated its size, and I estimated its length at only two hundred and fifty feet. As to its dimensions, I could only conjecture them to be admirably proportioned. While I watched this phenomenon, two jets of steam and water were ejected from its vents, and rose to the height of 120 feet; thus I ascertained its way of breathing. I concluded definitely that it belonged to the vertebrate branch, class mammalia.

The crew waited impatiently for their chief's orders. The latter, after having observed the animal attentively, called the engineer. The engineer ran to him.

"Sir," said the commander, "you have steam up?"

"Yes, sir," answered the engineer.

"Well, make up your fires and put on all steam."

Three hurrahs greeted this order. The time for the struggle had arrived. Some moments after, the two funnels of the frigate vomited torrents of black smoke, and the bridge quaked under the trembling of the boilers.

The *Abraham Lincoln*, propelled by her powerful screw, went straight at the animal. The latter allowed it to come within half a cable's length; then, as if disdaining to dive, it took a little turn, and stopped a short distance off.

This pursuit lasted nearly three-quarters of an hour, without the frigate gaining two yards on the cetacean. It was quite evident that at that rate we should never come up with it.

"Well, Mr. Land," asked the captain, "do you advise me to put the boats out to sea?"

"No, sir," replied Ned Land; "because we shall not take that beast easily."

"What shall we do then?"

"Put on more steam if you can, sir. With your leave, I mean to post myself under the bowsprit, and if we get within harpooning distance, I shall throw my harpoon."

"Go, Ned," said the captain. "Engineer, put on more pressure."

Ned Land went to his post. The fires were increased, the screw revolved forty-three times a minute, and the steam poured out of the valves. We heaved the log, and calculated that the *Abraham Lincoln* was going at the rate of 18½ miles an hour.

But the accursed animal swam too at the rate of 18½ miles.

For a whole hour, the frigate kept up this pace, without gaining six feet. It was humiliating for one of the swiftest sailers in the American navy. A stubborn anger seized the crew; the sailors abused the monster, who, as before, disdained to answer them; the captain no longer contented himself with twisting his beard—he gnawed it.

The engineer was again called.

"You have turned full steam on?"

"Yes, sir," replied the engineer.

The speed of the *Abraham Lincoln* increased. Its masts trembled down to their stepping-holes, and the clouds of smoke could hardly find way out of the narrow funnels.

They heaved the log a second time.

"Well?" asked the captain of the man at the wheel.

"Nineteen miles and three-tenths, sir."

"Clap on more steam."

The engineer obeyed. The manometer showed ten degrees. But the cetacean grew warm itself, no doubt; for, without straining itself, it made 19³⁄₁₀ miles.

What a pursuit! No, I cannot describe the emotion that vibrated through me. Ned Land kept his post, harpoon in hand. Several times the animal let us gain upon it. "We shall catch it! We shall catch it!" cried the Canadian. But just as he was going to strike the cetacean stole away with a rapidity that could not be estimated at less than thirty miles an hour, and even during our maximum of speed it bullied the frigate, going round and round it. A cry of fury broke from everyone.

At noon we were no further advanced than at eight o'clock in the morning.

The captain then decided to take more direct means.

"Ah!" said he. "That animal goes quicker than the *Abraham Lincoln*; Very well! We will see whether it will escape these conical bullets. Send your men to the forecastle, sir."

The forecastle gun was immediately loaded and slewed round. But the shot passed some feet above the cetacean, which was half a mile off.

"Another more to the right," cried the commander, "and five dollars to whoever will hit that infernal beast."

An old gunner with a gray beard—that I can see now—with steady eye and grave face, went up to the gun and took a long aim. A loud report was heard, with which were mingled the cheers of the crew.

The bullet did its work; it hit the animal, but not fatally, and, sliding off the rounded surface, was lost in two miles' depth of sea.

The chase began again, and the captain, leaning toward me, said:

"I will pursue that beast till my frigate bursts up."

"Yes," answered I; "and you will be quite right to do it."

I wished the beast would exhaust itself, and not be insensible to fatigue, like a steam-engine! But it was of no use. Hours passed, without its showing any signs of exhaustion.

However, it must be said in praise of the *Abraham Lincoln*, that she struggled on indefatigably. I cannot reckon the distance she made under three hundred miles during this unlucky day, November the 6th. But night came on, and overshadowed the rough ocean.

Now I thought our expedition was at an end, and that we should never again see the extraordinary animal. I was mistaken. At ten minutes to eleven in the evening, the electric light reappeared three miles to windward of the frigate, as pure, as intense as during the preceding night.

The narwhal seemed motionless; perhaps, tired with its day's work, it slept, letting itself float with the undulation of the waves. Now was a chance of which the captain resolved to take advantage.

He gave his orders. The *Abraham Lincoln* kept up half-steam, and advanced cautiously so as not to awake its adversary. It is no rare thing to meet in the middle of the ocean whales so sound asleep that they can be successfully attacked, and Ned Land had harpooned more than one during its sleep. The Canadian went to take his place again under the bowsprit.

The frigate approached noiselessly, stopped at two cables' length from the animal, and following its track. No one breathed; a deep silence reigned on the bridge. We were not a hundred feet from the burning focus, the light of which increased and dazzled our eyes.

At this moment, leaning on the forecastle bulwark, I saw below me Ned Land grappling the martingale in one hand, brandishing his terrible harpoon in the other, scarcely twenty feet from the motionless animal. Suddenly his arm straightened, and the harpoon was thrown; I heard the sonorous stroke of the weapon, which seemed to have struck a hard body. The electric light went out suddenly, and two enormous waterspouts broke over the bridge of the frigate, rushing like a torrent from stem to stern, overthrowing men, and breaking the lashing of the spars. A fearful shock followed, and, thrown over the rail without having time to stop myself, I fell into the sea.

AN UNKNOWN SPECIES OF WHALE

This unexpected fall so stunned me that I have no clear recollection of my sensations at the time. I was at first drawn down to a depth of about twenty feet. I am a good swimmer (though without pretending to rival Byron or Edgar Poe, who were masters of the art), and in that plunge I did not lose my presence of mind. Two vigorous strokes brought me to the surface of the water. My first care was to look for the frigate. Had the crew seen me disappear? Had the *Abraham Lincoln* veered round? Would the captain put out a boat? Might I hope to be saved?

The darkness was intense. I caught a glimpse of a black mass disappearing in the east, its beacon-lights dying out in the distance. It was the frigate! I was lost.

"Help! Help!" I shouted, swimming toward the *Abraham Lincoln* in desperation.

My clothes encumbered me; they seemed glued to my body, and paralyzed my movements.

I was sinking! I was suffocating!

"Help!"

This was my last cry. My mouth filled with water; I struggled against being drawn down the abyss. Suddenly my clothes were seized by a strong hand, and I felt myself quickly drawn up to the surface of the sea; and I heard, yes, I heard these words pronounced in my ear:

"If master would be so good as to lean on my shoulder, master would swim with much greater ease."

I seized with one hand my faithful Conseil's arm.

"Is it you?" said I. "You?"

"Myself," answered Conseil; "and waiting master's orders."

"That shock threw you as well as me into the sea?"

"No; but being in my master's service, I followed him."

The worthy fellow thought that was but natural.

"And the frigate?" I asked.

"The frigate?" replied Conseil, turning on his back. "I think that master had better not count too much on her."

"You think so?"

"I say that, at the time I threw myself into the sea, I heard the men at the wheel say, 'The screw and the rudder are broken.' "

"Broken?"

"Yes, broken by the monster's teeth. It is the only injury the *Abraham Lincoln* has sustained. But it is a bad lookout for us—she no longer answers her helm."

"Then we are lost!"

"Perhaps so," calmly answered Conseil. "However, we have still several hours before us, and one can do a good deal in some hours."

Conseil's imperturbable coolness set me up again. I swam more vigorously; but, cramped by my clothes, which stuck to me like a leaden weight, I felt great difficulty in bearing up. Conseil saw this.

"Will master let me make a slit?" said he; and slipping an open knife under my clothes, he ripped them up from top to bottom very rapidly. Then he cleverly slipped them off me, while I swam for both of us.

Then I did the same for Conseil, and we continued to swim near to each other.

Nevertheless, our situation was no less terrible. Perhaps our disappearance had not been noticed; and if it had been, the frigate could not tack, being without its helm. Conseil argued on this supposition, and laid his plans accordingly. This phlegmatic boy was perfectly self-possessed. We then decided that, as our only chance of safety was being picked up by the *Abraham Lincoln*'s boats, we ought to manage so as to wait for them as long as possible. I resolved then to husband our strength, so that both should not be exhausted at the same time; and this is how we managed: while one of us lay on our back, quite still, with arms crossed, and legs stretched out, the other would swim and push the other on in front. This towing business did not last more than ten minutes each; and relieving each other thus, we could swim on for some hours, perhaps till daybreak. Poor chance! But hope is so firmly rooted in the heart of man! Moreover, there were two of us. Indeed, I declare (though it may seem improbable) if I sought to destroy all hope, if I wished to despair, I could not.

The collision of the frigate with the cetacean had occurred about eleven o'clock the evening before. I reckoned then we should have eight hours to swim before sunrise—an operation quite practicable if we relieved each other. The sea, very calm, was in our favor. Sometimes I tried to pierce the intense darkness that was only dispelled by the phosphorescence caused by our movements. I watched the luminous waves that broke over my hand, whose mirror-like surface was spotted with silvery rings. One might have said that we were in a bath of quicksilver.

Near one o'clock in the morning, I was seized with dreadful fatigue. My limbs stiffened under the strain of violent cramp. Conseil was obliged to keep me up, and our preservation devolved on him alone. I heard the poor boy pant; his breathing became short and hurried. I found that he could not keep up much longer.

"Leave me! Leave me!" I said to him.

"Leave my master? Never!" replied he. "I would drown first."

Just then the moon appeared through the fringes of a thick cloud that the wind was driving to the east. The surface of the sea glittered with its rays. This kindly light reanimated us. My head got better again. I looked at all the points of the horizon. I saw the frigate! She was five miles from us, and looked like a dark mass, hardly discernible. But no boats!

I would have cried out. But what good would it have been at such a distance? My swollen lips could utter no sounds. Conseil could articulate some words, and I heard him repeat at intervals, "Help! Help!"

Our movements were suspended for an instant; we listened. It might be only a singing in the ear, but it seemed to me as if a cry answered the cry from Conseil.

"Did you hear?" I murmured.

"Yes! Yes!"

And Conseil gave one more despairing call.

This time there was no mistake! A human voice responded to ours! Was it the voice of another unfortunate creature, abandoned in the middle of the ocean, some other victim of the shock sustained by the vessel? Or rather was it a boat from the frigate, that was hailing us in the darkness?

Conseil made a last effort, and leaning on my shoulder, while I struck out in a despairing effort, he raised himself half out of the water, then fell back exhausted.

"What did you see?"

"I saw," murmured he—"I saw—but do not talk—reserve all your strength!"

What had he seen? Then, I know not why, the thought of the monster came into my head for the first time! But that voice? The time is past for Jonahs to take refuge in whales' bellies! However, Conseil was towing me again. He raised his head sometimes, looked before us, and uttered a cry of recognition, which was responded to by a voice that came nearer and nearer. I scarcely heard it. My strength was exhausted; my fingers stiffened; my hand afforded me support no longer; my mouth, convulsively opening, filled with salt water. Cold crept over me. I raised my head for the last time, then I sank.

At this moment a hard body struck me. I clung to it, then I felt that I was being drawn up, that I was brought to the surface of the water, that my chest collapsed: I fainted.

It is certain that I soon came to, thanks to the vigorous rubbings that I received. I half opened my eyes.

"Conseil!" I murmured.

"Does master call me?" asked Conseil.

Just then, by the waning light of the moon, which was sinking down to the horizon, I saw a face which was not Conseil's, and which I immediately recognized.

"Ned!" I cried.

"The same, sir, who is seeking his prize!" replied the Canadian.

"Were you thrown into the sea by the shock of the frigate?"

"Yes, professor; but, more fortunate than you, I was able to find a footing almost directly upon a floating island."

"An island?"

"Or, more correctly speaking, on our gigantic narwhal."

"Explain yourself, Ned!"

"Only I soon found out why my harpoon had not entered its skin and was blunted."

"Why, Ned, why?"

"Because, professor, that beast is made of sheet-iron."

The Canadian's last words produced a sudden revolution in my brain. I wriggled myself quickly to the top of the being, or object, half out of the water, which served us for a refuge. I kicked it. It was evidently a hard, impenetrable body, and not the soft substance that forms the bodies of the great marine mammalia. But this hard body might be a bony carapace, like that of the antediluvian animals; and I should be free to class this monster among amphibious reptiles, such as tortoises or alligators.

Well, no! The blackish back that supported me was smooth, polished, without scales. The blow produced a metallic sound; and incredible though it may be, it seemed, I might say, as if it was made of riveted plates.

There was no doubt about it! This monster, this natural phenomenon that had puzzled the learned world, and overthrown and misled the imagination of seamen of both hemispheres, was, it must be owned, a still more astonishing phenomenon, inasmuch as it was simply a human construction.

We had no time to lose, however. We were lying upon the back of a sort of submarine boat, which appeared (as far as I could judge) like a huge fish of steel. Ned Land's mind was made up on this point. Conseil and I could only agree with him.

Just then a bubbling began at the back of this strange thing (which was evidently propelled by a screw), and it began to move. We had only just time to seize hold of the upper part, which rose about seven feet out of the water, and happily its speed was not great.

"As long as it sails horizontally," muttered Ned Land, "I do not mind; but if it takes a fancy to dive, I would not give two straws for my life."

The Canadian might have said still less. It became really necessary to communicate with the beings, whatever they were, shut up inside the machine. I searched all over the outside for an aperture, a panel, or a manhole, to use a technical expression; but the lines of the iron rivets, solidly driven into the joints of the iron plates, were clear and uniform. Besides, the moon disappeared then, and left us in total darkness.

At last this long night passed. My indistinct remembrance prevents my describing all the impressions it made. I can only recall one circumstance. During some lulls of the wind and sea, I fancied I heard several times vague sounds, a sort of fugitive harmony produced by distant words of command. What was then the mystery of this submarine craft of which the whole world vainly sought an explanation? What kind of beings existed in this strange boat? What mechanical agent caused its prodigious speed?

Daybreak appeared. The morning mists surrounded us, but they soon cleared off. I was about to examine the hull, which formed on deck a kind of horizontal platform, when I felt it gradually sinking.

"Oh, confound it!" cried Ned Land, kicking the resounding plate. "Open, you inhospitable rascals!"

Happily the sinking movement ceased. Suddenly a noise, like iron works violently pushed aside, came from the interior of the boat. One iron plate was moved, a man appeared, uttered an odd cry, and disappeared immediately.

Some moments after, eight strong men with masked faces appeared noiselessly, and drew us down into their formidable machine.

Mobilis in Mobili

This forcible abduction, so roughly carried out, was accomplished with the rapidity of lightning. I shivered all over. Whom had we to deal with? No doubt some new sort of pirates, who explored the sea in their own way.

Hardly had the narrow panel closed upon me, when I was enveloped in darkness. My eyes, dazzled with the outer light, could distinguish nothing. I felt my naked feet cling to the rungs of an iron ladder. Ned Land and Conseil, firmly seized, followed me. At the bottom of the ladder, a door opened, and shut after us immediately with a bang.

We were alone. Where, I could not say, hardly imagine. All was black, and such a dense black that, after some minutes, my eyes had not been able to discern even the faintest glimmer.

Meanwhile, Ned Land, furious at these proceedings, gave free vent to his indignation.

"Confound it!" cried he. "Here are people who come up to the Scotch for hospitality. They only just miss being cannibals. I should not be surprised at it, but I declare that they shall not eat me without my protesting."

"Calm yourself, friend Ned, calm yourself," replied Conseil quietly. "Do not cry out before you are hurt. We are not quite done for yet."

"Not quite," sharply replied the Canadian, "but pretty near, at all events. Things look black. Happily my bowie-knife I have still, and I can always see well enough to use it. The first of these pirates who lays a hand on me——"

"Do not excite yourself, Ned," I said to the harpooner, "and do not compromise us by useless violence. Who knows that they will not listen to us? Let us rather try to find out where we are."

I groped about. In five steps I came to an iron wall, made of plates bolted together. Then turning back I struck against a wooden table, near which were ranged several stools. The boards of this prison were concealed under a thick mat of phormium, which deadened the noise of the feet. The bare walls revealed no trace of window or door. Conseil, going round the reverse way, met me, and we went back to the middle of the cabin, which measured about twenty feet by ten. As to its height, Ned Land, in spite of his own great height, could not measure it.

Half an hour had already passed without our situation being bettered, when the dense darkness suddenly gave way to extreme light. Our prison was suddenly lighted—that is to say, it became filled with a luminous matter, so strong that I could not bear it at first. In its whiteness and intensity I recognized the electric light which played round the submarine boat like a magnificent phenomenon of phosphorescence. After shutting my eyes involuntarily, I opened them and saw that this luminous agent came from a half-globe, unpolished, placed in the roof of the cabin.

"At last one can see," cried Ned Land, who, knife in hand, stood on the defensive.

"Yes," said I; "but we are still in the dark about ourselves."

"Let master have patience," said the imperturbable Conseil.

The sudden lighting of the cabin enabled me to examine it minutely. It only contained a table and five stools. The invisible door might be hermetically sealed. No noise was heard. All seemed dead in the interior of this boat. Did it move, did it float on the surface of the ocean, or did it dive into its depths? I could not guess.

A noise of bolts was now heard, the door opened and two men appeared.

One was short, very muscular, broad-shouldered, with robust limbs, strong head, an abundance of black hair, thick mustache, a quick, penetrating look, and the vivacity which characterizes the population of Southern France.

The second stranger merits a more detailed description. A disciple of Gratiolet or Engel would have read his face like an open book. I made out his prevailing qualities directly: self-confidence—because his head was well set on his shoulders, and his black eyes looked around with cold assurance; calmness—for his skin, rather pale, showed his coolness of blood; energy—evinced by the rapid contraction of his lofty brows; and courage—because his deep breathing denoted great power of lungs.

Whether this person was thirty-five or fifty years of age, I could not say. He was tall, had a large forehead, straight nose, a clearly cut mouth, beautiful teeth, with fine tapered hands, indicative of a highly nervous temperament. This man was certainly the most admirable specimen I had ever met. One particular feature was his eyes, rather far from each other, and which could take in nearly a quarter of the horizon at once.

This faculty—I verified it later—gave him a range of vision far superior to Ned Land's. When this stranger fixed upon an object, his eyebrows met, his large eyelids closed around so as to contract the range of his vision, and he looked as if he magnified the objects lessened by distance, as if he pierced those sheets of water so opaque to our eyes, and as if he read the very depths of the seas.

The two strangers, with caps made from the fur of the sea otter and shod with sea boots of seals' skin, were dressed in clothes of a particular texture, which allowed free movement of the limbs. The taller of the two, evidently the chief on board, examined us with great attention, without saying a word; then turning to his companion, talked with him in an unknown tongue. It was a sonorous, harmonious, and flexible dialect, the vowels seeming to admit of very varied accentuation.

The other replied by a shake of the head, and added two or three perfectly incomprehensible words. Then he seemed to question me by a look.

I replied in good French that I did not know his language; but he seemed not to understand me, and my situation became more embarrassing.

"If master were to tell our story," said Conseil, "perhaps these gentlemen may understand some words."

I began to tell our adventures, articulating each syllable clearly, and without omitting one single detail. I announced our names and rank, introducing in person Professor Aronnax, his servant Conseil, and Master Ned Land, the harpooner.

The man with the soft calm eyes listened to me quietly, even politely, and with extreme attention; but nothing in his countenance indicated that he had understood my story. When I finished he said not a word.

There remained one resource, to speak English. Perhaps they would know this almost universal language. I knew it, as well as the German language—well enough to read it fluently, but not to speak it correctly. But anyhow, we must make ourselves understood.

"Go on in your turn," I said to the harpooner; "speak your best Anglo-Saxon, and try to do better than I."

Ned did not beg off, and recommenced our story.

To his great disgust, the harpooner did not seem to have made himself more intelligible than I had. Our visitors did not stir. They evidently understood neither the language of Arago nor of Faraday.

Very much embarrassed, after having vainly exhausted our philological resources, I knew not what part to take, when Conseil said:

"If master will permit me, I will relate it in German."

But in spite of the elegant turns and good accent of the narrator, the German language had no success. At last, nonplussed, I tried to remember my first lessons, and to narrate our adventures in Latin, but with no better success. This last attempt being of no avail, the two strangers exchanged some words in their unknown language and retired.

The door shut.

"It is an infamous shame," cried Ned Land, who broke out for the twentieth time; "we speak to those rogues in French, English, German, and Latin, and not one of them has the politeness to answer!"

"Calm yourself," I said to the impetuous Ned, "anger will do no good."

"But do you see, professor," replied our irascible companion, "that we shall absolutely die of hunger in this iron cage?"

"Bah," said Conseil philosophically; "we can hold out some time yet."

"My friends," I said, "we must not despair. We have been worse off than this. Do me the favor to wait a little before forming an opinion upon the commander and crew of this boat."

"My opinion is formed," replied Ned Land sharply. "They are rascals."

"Good! And from what country?"

"From the land of rogues!"

"My brave Ned, that country is not clearly indicated on the map of the world; but I admit that the nationality of the two strangers is hard to determine. Neither English, French, nor German, that is quite certain. However, I am inclined to think that the commander and his companion were born in low latitudes. There is southern blood in them. But I cannot decide by their appearance whether they are Spaniards, Turks, Arabians, or Indians. As to their language, it is quite incomprehensible."

"There is the disadvantage of not knowing all languages," said Conseil, "or the disadvantage of not having one universal language."

As he said these words, the door opened. A steward entered. He brought us clothes, coats and trousers, made of a stuff I did not know. I hastened to dress myself, and my companions followed my example. During that time, the steward—dumb, perhaps deaf—had arranged the table, and laid three plates.

"This is something like," said Conseil.

"Bah," said the rancorous harpooner, "what do you suppose they eat here? Tortoise liver, filleted shark, and beefsteaks from sea dogs."

"We shall see," said Conseil.

The dishes, of bell metal, were placed on the table, and we took our places. Undoubtedly we had to do with civilized people, and had it not been for the electric light which flooded us, I could have fancied I was in the dining-room of the Adelphi Hotel at Liverpool, or at the Grand Hotel in Paris. I must say, however, that there was neither bread nor wine. The water was fresh and clear, but it was water, and did not suit Ned Land's taste. Among the dishes which were brought to us, I recognized several fish delicately dressed; but of some, although excellent, I could give no opinion, neither could I tell to what kingdom they belonged, whether animal or vegetable. As to the dinner service, it was elegant, and in perfect taste. Each utensil, spoon, fork, knife, plate, had a letter engraved on it, with a motto above it, of which this is an exact facsimile:

MOBILIS IN MOBILI
N.

The letter N was no doubt the initial of the name of the enigmatical person who commanded at the bottom of the seas.

Ned and Conseil did not reflect much. They devoured the food, and I did likewise. I was, besides, reassured as to our fate; and it seemed evident that our hosts would not let us die of want.

However, everything has an end, everything passes away, even the hunger of people who have not eaten for fifteen hours. Our appetites satisfied, we felt overcome with sleep.

"Faith! I shall sleep well," said Conseil.

"So shall I," replied Ned Land.

My two companions stretched themselves on the cabin carpet, and were soon sound asleep. For my own part, too many thoughts crowded my brain, too many insoluble questions pressed upon me, too many fancies kept my eyes half open. Where were we? What strange power carried us on? I felt—or rather fancied I felt—the machine sinking down to the lowest beds of the sea. Dreadful nightmares beset me; I saw in these mysterious asylums a world of unknown animals, among which this submarine boat seemed to be of the same kind, living, moving, and formidable as they. Then my brain grew calmer, my imagination wandered into vague unconsciousness, and I soon fell into a deep sleep.

NED LAND'S TEMPERS

How long we slept I do not know; but our sleep must have lasted long, for it rested us completely from our fatigues. I woke first. My companions had not moved, and were still stretched in their corner.

Hardly roused from my somewhat hard couch, I felt my brain freed, my mind clear. I then began an attentive examination of our cell. Nothing was changed inside. The prison was still a prison; the prisoners, prisoners. However, the steward, during our sleep, had cleared the table. I breathed with difficulty. The heavy air seemed to oppress my lungs. Although the cell was large, we had evidently consumed a great part of the oxygen that it contained. Indeed, each man consumes, in one hour, the oxygen contained in more than 176 pints of air, and this air, charged (as then) with a nearly equal quantity of carbonic acid, becomes unbreathable.

It became necessary to renew the atmosphere of our prison, and no doubt the whole in the submarine boat. That gave rise to a question in my mind. How would the commander of this floating dwelling-place proceed? Would he obtain air by chemical means, in getting by heat the oxygen contained in chlorate of potash, and in absorbing carbonic acid by caustic potash? Or, a more convenient, economical, and consequently more probable alternative, would he be satisfied to rise and take breath at the surface of the water, like a cetacean, and so renew for twenty-four hours the atmospheric provision?

In fact, I was already obliged to increase my respirations to eke out of this cell the little oxygen it contained, when suddenly I was refreshed by a current of pure air, and perfumed with saline emanations. It was an invigorating seabreeze, charged with iodine. I opened my mouth wide, and my lungs saturated themselves with fresh particles.

At the same time I felt the boat rolling. The iron-plated monster had evidently just risen to the surface of the ocean to breathe, after the fashion of whales. I found out from that the mode of ventilating the boat.

When I had inhaled this air freely, I sought the conduit-pipe which conveyed to us the beneficial whiff, and I was not long in finding it. Above the door was a ventilator, through which volumes of fresh air renewed the impoverished atmosphere of the cell.

I was making my observations, when Ned and Conseil awoke almost at the same time, under the influence of this reviving air. They rubbed their eyes, stretched themselves, and were on their feet in an instant.

"Did master sleep well?" asked Conseil, with his usual politeness.

"Very well, my brave boy. And you, Mr. Land?"

"Soundly, professor. But I don't know if I am right or not; there seems to be a sea-breeze!"

A seaman could not be mistaken, and I told the Canadian all that had passed during his sleep.

"Good!" said he. "That accounts for those roarings we heard when the supposed narwhal sighted the *Abraham Lincoln.*"

"Quite so, Master Land; it was taking breath."

"Only, Mr. Aronnax, I have no idea what o'clock it is, unless it is dinner-time."

"Dinner-time! My good fellow? Say rather breakfast-time, for we certainly have begun another day."

"So," said Conseil, "we have slept twenty-four hours?"

"That is my opinion."

"I will not contradict you," replied Ned Land. "But dinner or breakfast, the steward will be welcome, whichever he brings."

"Master Land, we must conform to the rules on board, and I suppose our appetites are in advance of the dinner-hour."

"That is just like you, friend Conseil," said Ned impatiently. "You are never out of temper, always calm; you would return thanks before grace, and die of hunger rather than complain!"

Time was getting on, and we were fearfully hungry; and this time the steward did not appear. It was rather too long to leave us, if they really had good intentions toward us. Ned Land, tormented by the cravings of hunger, got still more angry; and notwithstanding his promise, I dreaded an explosion when he found himself with one of the crew.

For two hours more, New Land's temper increased; he cried, he shouted, but in vain. The walls were deaf. There was no sound to be heard in the boat; all was still as death. It did not move, for I should have felt the trembling motion of the hull under the influence of the screw. Plunged in the depths of the waters, it belonged no longer to earth—this silence was dreadful.

I felt terrified, Conseil was calm, Ned Land roared.

Just then a noise was heard outside. Steps sounded on the metal flags. The locks were turned, the door opened, and the steward appeared.

Before I could rush forward to stop him, the Canadian had thrown him down, and held him by the throat. The steward was choking under the grip of his powerful hand.

Conseil was already trying to unclasp the harpooner's hand from his half-suffocated victim, and I was going to fly to the rescue, when suddenly I was nailed to the spot by hearing these words in French:

"Be quiet, Master Land; and you, professor, will you be so good as to listen to me?"

The Man of the Seas

It was the commander of the vessel who thus spoke.

At these words, Ned Land rose suddenly. The steward, nearly strangled, tottered out on a sign from his master; but such was the power of the commander on board, that not a gesture betrayed the resentment which this man must have felt toward the Canadian. Conseil interested in spite of himself, I stupefied, awaited in silence the result of this scene.

The commander, leaning against a corner of the table with his arms folded, scanned us with profound attention. Did he hesitate to speak? Did he regret the words which he had just spoken in French? One might almost think so.

After some moments of silence, which not one of us dreamed of breaking, "Gentlemen," said he, in a calm and penetrating voice, "I speak French, English, German, and Latin equally well. I could, therefore, have answered you at our first interview, but I wished to know you first, then to reflect. The story told by each one, entirely agreeing in the main points, convinced me of your identity. I know now that chance has brought before me M. Pierre Aronnax, Professor of Natural History at the Museum of Paris, intrusted with a scientific mission abroad; Conseil, his servant; and Ned Land, of Canadian origin, harpooner on board the frigate *Abraham Lincoln* of the navy of the United States of America."

I bowed assent. It was not a question that the commander put to me. Therefore there was no answer to be made. This man expressed himself with perfect ease, without any accent. His sentences were well turned, his words clear, and his fluency of speech remarkable. Yet I did not recognize in him a fellow-countryman.

He continued the conversation in these terms:

"You have doubtless thought, sir, that I have delayed long in paying you this second visit. The reason is that, your identity recognized, I wished to weigh maturely what part to act toward you. I have hesitated much. Most annoying circumstances have brought you into the presence of a man who has broken all the ties of humanity. You have come to trouble my existence."

"Unintentionally!" said I.

"Unintentionally?" replied the stranger, raising his voice a little. "Was it unintentionally that the *Abraham Lincoln* pursued me all over the seas? Was it unintentionally that you took passage in this frigate? Was it unintentionally that your cannon-balls rebounded off the plating of my vessel? Was it unintentionally that Mr. Ned Land struck me with his harpoon?"

I detected a restrained irritation in these words. But to these recriminations I had a very natural answer to make, and I made it.

"Sir," said I, "no doubt you are ignorant of the discussions which have taken place concerning you in America and Europe. You do not know that divers accidents, caused by collisions with your submarine machine, have excited public feeling in the two continents. I omit the hypotheses without number by which it was sought to explain the inexplicable phenomenon of which you alone possess the secret. But you must understand that, in pursuing you over the high seas of the Pacific, the *Abraham Lincoln* believed itself to be chasing some powerful sea-monster, of which it was necessary to rid the ocean at any price."

A half-smile curled the lips of the commander: then, in a calmer tone: "M. Aronnax," he replied, "dare you affirm that your frigate would not as soon have pursued and cannonaded a submarine boat as a monster?"

This question embarrassed me, for certainly Captain Farragut might not have hesitated. He might have thought it his duty to destroy a contrivance of this kind, as he would a gigantic narwhal.

"You understand then, sir," continued the stranger, "that I have the right to treat you as enemies?"

I answered nothing, purposely. For what good would it be to discuss such a proposition, when force could destroy the best arguments?

"I have hesitated for some time," continued the commander; "nothing obliged me to show you hospitality. If I chose to separate myself from you, I should have no interest in seeing you again; I could place you upon the deck of this vessel which has served you as a refuge, I could sink beneath the waters, and forget that you had ever existed. Would not that be my right?"

"It might be the right of a savage," I answered, "but not that of a civilized man."

"Professor," replied the commander quickly, "I am not what you call a civilized man! I have done with society entirely, for reasons which I alone have the right of appreciating. I do not therefore obey its laws, and I desire you never to allude to them before me again!"

This was said plainly. A flash of anger and disdain kindled in the eyes of the Unknown, and I had a glimpse of a terrible past in the life of this man. Not only had he put himself beyond the pale of human laws, but he had made himself independent of them, free in the strictest acceptation of the word, quite beyond their reach! Who then would dare to pursue him at the bottom of the sea, when, on its surface, he defied all attempts made against him? What vessel could resist the shock of his submarine monitor? What cuirass, however thick, could withstand the blows of his spur? No man could demand from him an account of his actions; God, if he believed in one—his conscience, if he had one—were the sole judges to whom he was answerable.

These reflections crossed my mind rapidly, while the stranger personage was silent, absorbed, and as if wrapped up in himself. I regarded him with fear mingled with interest, as, doubtless, Œdipus regarded the Sphinx.

After a rather long silence, the commander resumed the conversation.

"I have hesitated," said he, "but I have thought that my interest might be reconciled with that pity to which every human being has a right. You will remain on board my vessel, since fate has cast you there. You will be free; and in exchange for this liberty, I shall only impose one single condition. Your word of honor to submit to it will suffice."

"Speak, sir," I answered. "I suppose this condition is one which a man of honor may accept?"

"Yes, sir; it is this. It is possible that certain events, unforeseen, may oblige me to consign you to your cabins for some hours or some days, as the case may be. As I desire never to use violence, I expect from you, more than all the others, a passive obedience. In thus acting, I take all the responsibility: I acquit you entirely, for I make it an impossibility for you to see what ought not to be seen. Do you accept this condition?"

Then things took place on board which, to say the least, were singular, and which ought not to be seen by people who were not placed beyond the pale of social laws. Among the surprises which the future was preparing for me, this might not be the least.

"We accept," I answered; "only I will ask your permission, sir, to address one question to you—one only."

"Speak, sir."

"You said that we should be free on board."

"Entirely."

"I ask you, then, what you mean by this liberty?"

"Just the liberty to go, to come, to see, to observe even all that passes here—save under rare circumstances—the liberty, in short, which we enjoy ourselves, my companions and I."

It was evident that we did not understand one another.

"Pardon me, sir," I resumed, "but this liberty is only what every prisoner has of pacing his prison. It cannot suffice us."

"It must suffice you, however."

"What! We must renounce forever seeing our country, our friends, our relations again?"

"Yes, sir. But to renounce that unendurable worldly yoke which men believe to be liberty is not perhaps so painful as you think."

"Well," exclaimed Ned Land, "never will I give my word of honor not to try to escape."

"I did not ask you for your word of honor, Master Land," answered the commander coldly.

"Sir," I replied, beginning to get angry in spite of myself, "you abuse your situation toward us; it is cruelty."

"No, sir, it is clemency. You are my prisoners of war. I keep you, when I could, by a word, plunge you into the depths of the ocean. You attacked me. You came to surprise a secret which no man in the world must penetrate—the secret of my whole existence. And you think that I am going to send you back to that world which must know me no more? Never! In retaining you, it is not you whom I guard—it is myself."

These words indicated a resolution taken on the part of the commander, against which no arguments would prevail.

"So, sir," I rejoined, "you give us simply the choice between life and death?"

"Simply."

"My friends," said I, "to a question thus put, there is nothing to answer. But no word of honor binds us to the master of this vessel."

"None, sir," answered the Unknown.

Then, in a gentler tone, he continued:

"Now, permit me to finish what I have to say to you. I know you, M. Aronnax. You and your companions will not, perhaps, have so much to complain of in the chance which has bound you to my fate. You will find among the books which are my favorite study the work which you have published on 'the depths of the sea.' I have often read it. You have carried your work as far as terrestrial science permitted you. But you do not know all—you have not seen all. Let me tell you then, professor, that you will not regret the time passed on board my vessel. You are going to visit the land of marvels."

These words of the commander had a great effect upon me. I cannot deny it. My weak point was touched; and I forgot, for a moment, that the contemplation of these sublime subjects was not worth the loss of liberty. Besides, I trusted to the future to decide this grave question. So I contented myself with saying:

"By what name ought I to address you?"

"Sir," replied the commander, "I am nothing to you but Captain Nemo;

and you and your companions are nothing to me but the passengers of the *Nautilus.*"

Captain Nemo called. A steward appeared. The captain gave him his orders in that strange language which I did not understand. Then, turning toward the Canadian and Conseil:

"A repast awaits you in your cabin," said he. "Be so good as to follow this man. And now, M. Aronnax, our breakfast is ready. Permit me to lead the way."

"I am at your service, captain."

I followed Captain Nemo; and as soon as I had passed through the door, I found myself in a kind of passage lighted by electricity, similar to the waist of a ship. After we had proceeded a dozen yards, a second door opened before me.

I then entered a dining-room, decorated and furnished in severe taste. High oaken sideboards, inlaid with ebony, stood at the two extremities of the room, and upon their shelves glittered china, porcelain, and glass of inestimable value.

The plate on the table sparkled in the rays which the luminous ceiling shed around while the light was tempered and softened by exquisite paintings.

In the center of the room was a table richly laid out. Captain Nemo indicated the place I was to occupy.

The breakfast consisted of a certain number of dishes, the contents of which were furnished by the sea alone; and I was ignorant of the nature and mode of preparation of some of them. I acknowledged that they were good, but they had a peculiar flavor, which I easily became accustomed to. These different aliments appeared to me to be rich in phosphorus, and I thought they must have a marine origin.

Captain Nemo looked at me. I asked him no questions, but he guessed my thoughts, and answered of his own accord the questions which I was burning to address to him.

"The greater part of these dishes are unknown to you," he said to me. "However, you may partake of them without fear. They are wholesome and nourishing. For a long time I have renounced the food of the earth, and I am never ill now. My crew, who are healthy, are fed on the same food."

"So," said I, "all these eatables are the produce of the sea?"

"Yes, professor, the sea supplies all my wants. Sometimes I cast my nets in tow, and I draw them in ready to break. Sometimes I hunt in the midst of this element, which appears to be inaccessible to man, and quarry the game which dwells in my submarine forests. My flocks, like those of Neptune's old shepherds, graze fearlessly in the immense prairies of the ocean. I have a vast property there, which I cultivate myself, and which is always sown by the hand of the Creator of all things."

"I can understand perfectly, sir, that your nets furnish excellent fish for your table; I can understand also that you hunt aquatic game in your submarine forests; but I cannot understand at all how a particle of meat, no matter how small, can figure in your bill of fare."

"This, which you believe to be meat, professor, is nothing else than fillet of turtle. Here are also some dolphin's livers, which you take to be ragout of pork. My cook is a clever fellow, who excels in dressing these various products of the ocean. Taste all these dishes. Here is a preserve of holothuria, which a Malay would declare to be unrivaled in the world; here is a cream, of which the milk has been furnished by the cetacea, and the sugar by the great fucus of the North Sea; and lastly, permit me to offer you some preserve of anemones, which is equal to that of the most delicious fruits."

I tasted, more from curiosity than as a connoisseur, while Captain Nemo enchanted me with his extraordinary stories.

"You like the sea, captain?"

"Yes, I love it! The sea is everything. It covers seven-tenths of the terrestrial globe. Its breath is pure and healthy. It is an immense desert, where man is never lonely, for he feels life stirring on all sides. The sea is only the embodiment of a supernatural and wonderful existence. It is nothing but love and emotion; it is the 'Living Infinite,' as one of your poets has said. In fact, professor, Nature manifests herself in it by her three kingdoms, mineral, vegetable, and animal. The sea is the vast reservoir of Nature. The globe began with sea, so to speak; and who knows if it will not end with it? In it is supreme tranquillity. The sea does not belong to despots. Upon its surface men can still exercise unjust laws, fight, tear one another to pieces, and be carried away with terrestrial horrors. But at thirty feet below its level, their reign ceases, their influence is quenched, and their power disappears. Ah! sir, live—live in the bosom of the waters! There only is independence! There I recognize no masters! There I am free!"

Captain Nemo suddenly became silent in the midst of this enthusiasm, by which he was quite carried away. For a few moments he paced up and down, much agitated. Then he became more calm, regained his accustomed coldness of expression, and turning toward me:

"Now, professor," said he, "if you wish to go over the *Nautilus*, I am at your service."

Captain Nemo rose. I followed him. A double door, contrived at the back of the dining-room, opened, and I entered a room equal in dimensions to that which I had just quitted.

It was a library. High pieces of furniture, of black violet ebony inlaid with brass, supported upon their wide shelves a great number of books uniformly bound. They followed the shape of the room, terminating at the lower part in huge divans, covered with brown leather, which were curved, to afford the greatest comfort. Light movable desks, made to slide in and out at will, allowed one to rest one's book while reading. In the center stood an immense table, covered with pamphlets, among which were some newspapers, already of old date. The electric light flooded everything; it was shed from four unpolished globes half sunk in the volutes of the ceiling. I looked with real admiration at this room, so ingeniously fitted up, and I could scarcely believe my eyes.

"Captain Nemo," said I to my host, who had just thrown himself on one of the divans, "this is a library which would do honor to more than one of the continental palaces, and I am absolutely astounded when I consider that it can follow you to the bottom of the seas."

"Where could one find greater solitude or silence, professor?" replied Captain Nemo. "Did your study in the Museum afford you such perfect quiet?"

"No, sir; and I must confess that it is a very poor one after yours. You must have six or seven thousand volumes here."

"Twelve thousand, M. Aronnax. These are the only ties which bind me to the earth. But I had done with the world on the day when my *Nautilus* plunged for the first time beneath the waters. That day I bought my last volumes, my last pamphlets, my last papers, and from that time I wish to think that men no longer think or write. These books, professor, are at your service besides, and you can make use of them freely."

I thanked Captain Nemo, and went up to the shelves of the library. Works on science, morals, and literature abounded in every language; but I did not see one single work on political economy; that subject appeared to be strictly proscribed. Strange to say, all these books were irregularly arranged, in whatever language they were written; and this medley proved that the captain of the *Nautilus* must have read indiscriminately the books which he took up by chance.

"Sir," said I to the captain, "I thank you for having placed this library at my disposal. It contains treasures of science, and I shall profit by them."

"This room is not only a library," said Captain Nemo, "it is also a smoking-room."

"A smoking-room!" I cried. "Then one may smoke on board?"

"Certainly."

"Then, sir, I am forced to believe that you have kept up a communication with Havana."

"Not any," answered the captain. "Accept this cigar, M. Aronnax; and though it does not come from Havana, you will be pleased with it, if you are a connoisseur."

I took the cigar which was offered me; its shape recalled the London ones, but it seemed to be made of leaves of gold. I lighted it at a little brazier, which was supported upon an elegant bronze stem, and drew the first whiffs with the delight of a lover of smoking who has not smoked for two days.

"It is excellent," said I, "but it is not tobacco."

"No!" answered the captain. "This tobacco comes neither from Havana nor from the East. It is a kind of seaweed, rich in nicotine, with which the sea provides me, but somewhat sparingly."

At that moment Captain Nemo opened a door which stood opposite to that by which I had entered the library, and I passed into an immense drawing-room splendidly lighted.

It was a vast four-sided room, thirty feet long, eighteen wide, and fifteen high. A luminous ceiling, decorated with light arabesques, shed a soft clear light over all the marvels accumulated in this museum. For it was in fact a museum, in which an intelligent and prodigal hand had gathered all the treasures of nature and art, with the artistic confusion which distinguishes a painter's studio. Thirty first-rate pictures, uniformly framed, separated by bright drapery, ornamented the walls, which were hung with tapestry of severe design. I saw works of great value, the greater part of which I had admired in the special collections of Europe, and in the exhibitions of paintings. The several schools of the old masters were represented by a Madonna of Raphael, a Virgin of Leonardo da Vinci, a nymph of Correggio, a woman of Titian, an Adoration of Veronese, an Assumption of Murillo, a portrait of Holbein, a monk of Velasquez, a martyr of Ribeira, a fair of Rubens, two Flemish landscapes of Teniers, three little "genre" pictures of Gérard Dow, Metsu, and Paul Potter, two specimens of Géricault and Prudhon, and some sea-pieces of Backhuysen and Vernet. Among the works of modern painters were pictures with the signatures of Delacroix, Ingres, Decamp, Troyon, Meissonier, Daubigny, etc.; and some admirable statues in marble and bronze, after the finest antique models, stood upon pedestals in the corners of this magnificent museum. Amazement, as the captain of the *Nautilus* had predicted, had already begun to take possession of me.

"Professor," said this strange man, "you must excuse the unceremonious way in which I receive you, and the disorder of this room."

"Sir," I answered, "without seeking to know who you are, I recognize in you an artist."

"An amateur, nothing more, sir. Formerly I loved to collect these beautiful works created by the hand of man. I sought them greedily and ferreted them out indefatigably, and I have been able to bring together some objects of great value. These are my last souvenirs of that world which is dead to me. In my eyes, your modern artists are already old; they have two or three thousand years of existence; I confound them in my own mind. Masters have no age."

"And these musicians?" said I, pointing out some works of Weber, Rossini, Mozart, Beethoven, Haydn, Meyerbeer, Hérold, Wagner, Auber, Gounod, and a number of others scattered over a large model piano organ which occupied one of the panels of the drawing-room.

"These musicians," replied Captain Nemo, "are the contemporaries of Orpheus; for in the memory of the dead all chronological differences are effaced; and I am dead, professor; as much dead as those of your friends who are sleeping six feet under the earth!"

Captain Nemo was silent, and seemed lost in a profound reverie. I contemplated him with deep interest, analyzing in silence the strange expression of his countenance. Leaning on his elbow against an angle of a costly mosaic table, he no longer saw me—he had forgotten my presence.

I did not disturb this reverie, and continued my observation of the curiosities which enriched this drawing-room.

Under elegant glass cases, fixed by copper rivets, were classed and labeled the most precious productions of the sea which had ever been presented to the eye of a naturalist. My delight as a professor may be conceived.

The division containing the zoöphytes presented the most curious specimens of the two groups of polypi and echinodermes. In the first group, the tubipores, were gorgones arranged like a fan, soft sponges of Syria, ises of the Moluccas, pennatules, an admirable virgularia of the Norwegian seas, variegated umbellulariæ, alcyonariæ, a whole series of madrepores, which my master Milne-Edwards has so cleverly classified, among which I remarked some wonderful flabellinæ, oculinæ of the island of Bourbon, the "Neptune's car" of the Antilles, superb varieties of corals, in short, every species of those curious polypi of which entire islands are formed, which will one day become continents. Of the echinodermes, remarkable for their coating of spines, asteri, sea-stars, pantacrinæ, comatules, astérophons, echini, holothuri, etc., represented individually a complete collection of this group.

A somewhat nervous conchyliologist would certainly have fainted before other more numerous cases, in which were classified the specimens of mollusks. It was a collection of inestimable value, which time fails me to describe minutely. Among these specimens, I will quote from memory only the elegant royal hammer-fish of the Indian Ocean, whose regular white spots stood out brightly on a red and brown ground, an imperial spondyle, bright colored, bristling with spines, a rare specimen in the European museums (I estimated its value at not less than £1,000); a common hammer-fish of the seas of New Holland, which is only procured with difficulty; exotic buccardia of Senegal; fragile white bivalve shells, which a breath might shatter like a soap-bubble; several varieties of the aspirgillum of Java, a kind of calcareous tube, edged with leafy folds, and much debated by amateurs; a whole series of trochi, some a greenish-yellow, found in the American seas, others a reddish-brown, natives of Australian waters; others from the Gulf of Mexico, remarkable for their imbricated shell; stellari found in the Southern Seas; and last, the rarest of all, the magnificent spur of New Zealand; and every description of delicate and fragile shells to which science has given appropriate names.

Apart, in separate compartments, were spread out chaplets of pearls of the greatest beauty, which reflected the electric light in little sparks of fire; pink pearls, torn from the pinna-marina of the Red Sea; green pearls of the haliotyde iris; yellow, blue, and black pearls, the curious productions of the divers mollusks of every ocean, and certain mussels of the watercourses of the North; lastly, several specimens of inestimable value which had been gathered from the rarest pintadines. Some of these pearls were larger than a pigeon's egg, and were worth as much, and more than that which the traveler Tavernier sold to the Shah of Persia for three millions, and surpassed the one in the possession of the Imaum of Muscat, which I had believed to be unrivaled in the world.

Therefore, to estimate the value of this collection was simply impossible. Captain Nemo must have expended millions in the acquirement of these various specimens, and I was thinking what source he could have drawn from, to have been able thus to gratify his fancy for collecting, when I was interrupted by these words:

"You are examining my shells, professor? Unquestionably they must be interesting to a naturalist; but for me they have a far greater charm, for I have collected them all with my own hand, and there is not a sea on the face of the globe which has escaped my researches."

"I can understand, captain, the delight of wandering about in the midst of such riches. You are one of those who have collected their treasures themselves. No museum in Europe possesses such a collection of the produce of the ocean. But if I exhaust all my admiration upon it, I shall have none left for the vessel which carries it. I do not wish to pry into your secrets; but I must confess that this *Nautilus,* with the motive power which is confined in it, the contrivances which enable it to be worked, the powerful agent which propels it, all excite my curiosity to the highest pitch. I see suspended on the walls of this room instruments of whose use I am ignorant."

"You will find these same instruments in my own room, professor, where I shall have much pleasure in explaining their use to you. But first come and inspect the cabin which is set apart for your own use. You must see how you will be accommodated on board the *Nautilus.*"

I followed Captain Nemo, who, by one of the doors opening from each panel of the drawing-room, regained the waist. He conducted me toward the bow, and there I found, not a cabin, but an elegant room, with a bed, dressing-table, and several other pieces of furniture.

I could only thank my host.

"Your room adjoins mine," said he, opening a door, "and mine opens into the drawing-room that we have just quitted."

I entered the captain's room; it had a severe, almost a monkish, aspect. A small iron bedstead, a table, some articles for the toilet; the whole lighted by a skylight. No comforts, the strictest necessaries only.

Captain Nemo pointed to a seat.

"Be so good as to sit down," he said. I seated myself, and he began thus:

All by Electricity

"Sir," said Captain Nemo, showing me the instruments hanging on the walls of his room, "here are the contrivances required for the navigation of the *Nautilus*. Here, as in the drawing-room, I have them always under my eyes, and they indicate my position and exact direction in the middle of the ocean. Some are known to you, such as the thermometer, which gives the internal temperature of the *Nautilus*; the barometer, which indicates the weight of the air and foretells the changes of the weather; the hygrometer, which marks the dryness of the atmosphere; the storm-glass, the contents of which, by decomposing, announce the approach of tempests; the compass, which guides my course; the sextant, which shows the latitude by the altitude of the sun; chronometers, by which I calculate the longitude; and glasses for day and night, which I use to examine the points of the horizon when the *Nautilus* rises to the surface of the waves."

"These are the usual nautical instruments," I replied, "and I know the use of them. But these others, no doubt, answer to the particular requirements of the *Nautilus*. This dial with the movable needle is a manometer, is it not?"

"It is actually a manometer. But by communication with the water, whose external pressure it indicates, it gives our depth at the same time."

"And these other instruments, the use of which I cannot guess?"

"Here, professor, I ought to give you some explanations. Will you be kind enough to listen to me?"

He was silent for a few moments, then he said:

"There is a powerful agent, obedient, rapid, easy, which conforms to every use, and reigns supreme on board my vessel. Everything is done by means of it. It lights it, warms it, and is the soul of my mechanical apparatus. This agent is electricity."

"Electricity?" I cried in surprise.

"Yes, sir."

"Nevertheless, captain, you possess an extreme rapidity of movement, which does not agree well with the power of electricity. Until now its dynamic force has remained under restraint, and has only been able to produce a small amount of power."

"Professor," said Captain Nemo, "my electricity is not everybody's. You know what sea-water is composed of. In a thousand grams are found ninety-six and a half per cent. of water, and about two and two-thirds per cent. of chloride of sodium; then, in a smaller quantity, chlorides of magnesium and of potassium, bromide of magnesium, sulphate of magnesia, sulphate and carbonate of lime. You see, then, that chloride of sodium forms a large part of it. So it is this sodium that I extract from sea-water, and of which I compose my ingredients. I owe all to the ocean; it produces electricity, and electricity gives heat, light, motion, and, in a word, life to the *Nautilus*."

"But not the air you breathe?"

"Oh, I could manufacture the air necessary for my consumption, but it is useless, because I go up to the surface of the water when I please. However, if electricity does not furnish me with air to breath, it works at least the powerful pumps that are stored in spacious reservoirs, and which enable me to prolong at need, and as long as I will, my stay in the depths of the sea. It gives a uniform and unintermittent light, which the sun does not. Now look at this clock; it is electrical, and goes with a regularity that defies the best chronometers. I have divided it into twenty-four hours, like the Italian clocks, because for me there is neither night nor day, sun nor moon, but only the factitious light that I take with me to the bottom of the sea. Look! just now, it is ten o'clock in the morning."

"Exactly."

"Another application of electricity. This dial hanging in front of us indicates the speed of the *Nautilus*. An electric thread puts it in communication with the screw, and the needle indicates the real speed. Look! now we are spinning along with a uniform speed of fifteen miles an hour."

"It is marvelous! and I see, captain, you were right to make use of this agent that takes the place of wind, water, and steam."

"We have not finished, M. Aronnax," said Captain Nemo, rising; "if you will follow me, we will examine the stern of the *Nautilus*."

Really, I knew already the anterior part of this submarine boat, of which this is the exact division, starting from the ship's head: the dining-room, five yards long, separated from the library by a water-tight partition; the library, five yards long; the large drawing-room, ten yards long, separated from the captain's room by a second water-tight partition; the said room, five yards in length; mine, two and half yards; and lastly, a reservoir of air, seven and a half yards, that extended to the bows. Total length thirty-five yards, or one hundred and five feet. The partitions had doors that were shut hermetically by means of India-rubber instruments, and they insured the safety of the *Nautilus* in case of a leak.

I followed Captain Nemo through the waist, and arrived at the center of the boat. There was a sort of well that opened between two partitions. An iron ladder, fastened with an iron hook to the partition, led to the upper end. I asked the captain what the ladder was used for.

"It leads to the small boat," he said.

"What! Have you a boat?" I exclaimed, in surprise.

"Of course; an excellent vessel, light and insubmersible, that serves either as a fishing or as a pleasure boat."

"But then, when you wish to embark, you are obliged to come to the surface of the water?"

"Not at all. This boat is attached to the upper part of the hull of the *Nautilus,* and occupies a cavity made for it. It is decked, quite water-tight, and held together by solid bolts. This ladder leads to a man-hole made in the hull of the *Nautilus,* that corresponds with a similar hole made in the side of the boat. By this double opening I get into the small vessel. They shut the one belonging to the *Nautilus,* I shut the other by means of screw pressure. I undo the bolts, and the little boat goes up to the surface of the sea with prodigious rapidity. I then open the panel of the bridge, carefully shut till then; I mast it, hoist my sail, take my oars, and I'm off."

"But how do you get back on board?"

"I do not come back, M. Aronnax; the *Nautilus* comes to me."

"By your orders?"

"By my orders. An electric thread connects us. I telegraph to it, and that is enough."

"Really," I said, astonished at these marvels, "nothing can be more simple."

After having passed by the cage of the staircase that led to the platform, I saw a cabin six feet long, in which Conseil and Ned Land, enchanted with their repast, were devouring it with avidity. Then a door opened into a kitchen nine feet long, situated between the large storerooms. There electricity, better than gas itself, did all the cooking. The streams under the furnaces gave out to the sponges of platina a heat which was regularly kept up and distributed. They also heated a distilling apparatus, which, by evaporation, furnished excellent drinkable water. Near this kitchen was a bath-room comfortably furnished, with hot and cold water taps.

Next to the kitchen was the berth-room of the vessel, sixteen feet long. But the door was shut, and I could not see the management of it, which might have given me an idea of the number of men employed on board the *Nautilus*.

At the bottom was a fourth partition, that separated this office from the engine-room. A door opened, and I found myself in the compartment where Captain Nemo—certainly an engineer of a very high order—had arranged his locomotive machinery. This engine-room, clearly lighted, did not measure less than sixty-five feet in length. It was divided into two parts; the first contained the materials for producing electricity, and the second the machinery that connected it with the screw. I examined it with great interest, in order to understand the machinery of the *Nautilus*.

"You see," said the captain, "I use Bunsen's contrivances, not Ruhmkorff's. Those would not have been powerful enough. Bunsen's are fewer in number, but strong and large, which experience proves to be the best. The electricity produced passes forward, where it works, by electro-magnets of great size, on a system of levers and cog-wheels that transmit the movement to the axle of the screw. This one, the diameter of which is nineteen feet, and the thread twenty-three feet, performs about a hundred and twenty revolutions in a second."

"And you get then?"

"A speed of fifty miles an hour."

"I have seen the *Nautilus* maneuver before the *Abraham Lincoln*, and I have my own ideas as to its speed. But this is not enough. We must see where we go. We must be able to direct it to the right, to the left, above, below. How do you get to the great depths, where you find an increasing resistance, which is rated by hundreds of atmospheres? How do you return to the surface of the ocean? And how do you maintain yourselves in the requisite medium? Am I asking too much?"

"Not at all, professor," replied the captain with some hesitation; "since you may never leave this submarine boat. Come into the saloon; it is our usual study, and there you will learn all you want to know about the *Nautilus*."

Some Figures

A moment after we were seated on a divan in the saloon smoking. The captain showed me a sketch that gave the plan, section, and elevation of the *Nautilus*. Then he began his description in these words:

"Here, M. Aronnax, are the several dimensions of the boat you are in. It is an elongated cylinder with conical ends. It is very like a cigar in shape, a shape already adopted in London in several constructions of the same sort. The length of this cylinder, from stem to stern, is exactly 232 feet, and its maximum breadth is twenty-six feet. It is not built quite like your long-voyage steamers, but its lines are sufficiently long, and its curves prolonged enough, to allow the water to slide off easily, and oppose no obstacle to its passage. These two dimensions enable you to obtain by a simple calculation the surface and cubic contents of the *Nautilus*. Its area measures 6,032 feet; and its contents about 1,500 cubic yards; that is to say, when completely immersed it displaces 50,000 feet of water, or weighs 1,500 tons.

"When I made the plans for this submarine vessel, I meant that nine-tenths should be submerged; consequently, it ought only to displace nine-tenths of its bulk, that is to say, only to weigh that number of tons. I ought not, therefore, to have exceeded that weight, constructing it on the aforesaid dimensions.

"The *Nautilus* is composed of two hulls, one inside, the other outside, joined by T-shaped irons, which render it very strong. Indeed, owing to this cellular arrangement it resists like a block, as if it were solid. Its sides cannot yield; it coheres spontaneously, and not by the closeness of its rivets; and the homogeneity of its construction, due to the perfect union of the materials, enables it to defy the roughest seas.

"These two hulls are composed of steel plates, whose density is from .07 to .08 that of water. The first is not less than two inches and a half thick, and weighs 394 tons. The second envelope, the keel, twenty inches high and ten thick, weighs alone sixty-two tons. The engine, the ballast, the several accessories and apparatus appendages, the partitions and bulkheads, weigh 961.62 tons. Do you follow all this?"

"I do."

"Then, when the *Nautilus* is afloat under these circumstances, one-tenth is out of the water. Now, if I have made reservoirs of a size equal to this tenth, or capable of holding 150 tons, and if I fill them with water, the boat, weighing then 1,507 tons, will be completely immersed. That would happen, professor. These reservoirs are in the lower parts of the *Nautilus.* I turn on taps and they fill, and the vessel sinks that had just been level with the surface."

"Well, captain, but now we come to the real difficulty. I can understand your rising to the surface; but diving below the surface, does not your submarine contrivance encounter a pressure, and consequently undergo an upward thrust of one atmosphere for every thirty feet of water, just about fifteen pounds per square inch?"

"Just so, sir."

"Then unless you quite fill the *Nautilus,* I do not see how you can draw it down to those depths."

"Professor, you must not confound statics with dynamics, or you will be exposed to grave errors. There is very little labor spent in attaining the lower regions of the ocean, for all bodies have a tendency to sink. When I wanted to find out the necessary increase of weight required to sink the *Nautilus,* I had only to calculate the reduction of volume that sea-water acquires according to the depth."

"That is evident."

"Now, if water is not absolutely incompressible, it is at least capable of very slight compression. Indeed, after the most recent calculations this reduction is only 0.000436 of an atmosphere for each thirty feet of depth. If we want to sink 3,000 feet, I should keep account of the reduction of bulk under a pressure equal to that of a column of water of a thousand feet. The calculation is easily verified. Now, I have supplementary reservoirs capable of holding a hundred tons. Therefore I can sink to a considerable depth. When I wish to rise to the level of the sea, I only let off the water, and empty all the reservoirs if I want the *Nautilus* to emerge from the tenth part of her total capacity."

I had nothing to object to these reasonings.

"I admit your calculations, captain," I replied; "I should be wrong to dispute them since daily experience confirms them; but I foresee a real difficulty in the way."

"What, sir?"

"When you are about 1,000 feet deep, the walls of the *Nautilus* bear a pressure of 100 atmospheres. If, then, just now you were to empty the supplementary reservoirs, to lighten the vessel, and to go up to the surface, the pumps must overcome the pressure of 100 atmospheres, which is 1,500 lbs. per square inch. From that a power——"

"That electricity alone can give," said the captain hastily. "I repeat, sir, that the dynamic power of my engines is almost infinite. The pumps of the *Nautilus* have an enormous power, as you must have observed when their jets of water burst like a torrent upon the *Abraham Lincoln*. Besides, I use subsidiary reservoirs only to attain a mean depth of 750 to 1,000 fathoms, and that with a view of managing my machines. Also, when I have a mind to visit the depths of the ocean five or six miles below the surface, I make use of slower but not less infallible means."

"What are they, captain?"

"That involves my telling you how the *Nautilus* is worked."

"I am impatient to learn."

"To steer this boat to starboard or port, to turn, in a word, following a horizontal plan, I use an ordinary rudder fixed on the back of the stern post, and with one wheel and some tackle to steer by. But I can also make the *Nautilus* rise and sink, and sink and rise, by a vertical movement by means of two inclined planes fastened to its sides, opposite the center of flotation, planes that move in every direction, and that are worked by powerful levers from the interior. If the planes are kept parallel with the boat, it moves horizontally. If slanted, the *Nautilus*, according to this inclination, and under the influence of the screw, either sinks diagonally or rises diagonally as it suits me. And even if I wish to rise more quickly to the surface, I ship the screw, and the pressure of the water causes the *Nautilus* to rise vertically like a balloon filled with hydrogen."

"Bravo, captain! But how can the steersman follow the route in the middle of the waters?"

"The steersman is placed in a glazed box, that is raised above the hull of the *Nautilus*, and furnished with lenses."

"Are these lenses capable of resisting such pressure?"

"Perfectly. Glass, which breaks at a blow, is, nevertheless, capable of offering considerable resistance. During some experiments of fishing by electric light in 1864 in the Northern Seas, we saw plates less than a third of an inch thick resist a pressure of sixteen atmospheres. Now, the glass that I use is not less than thirty times thicker."

"Granted. But, after all, in order to see, the light must exceed the darkness, and in the midst of the darkness in the water, how can you see?"

"Behind the steersman's cage is placed a powerful electric reflector, the rays from which light up the sea for half a mile in front."

"Ah! bravo, bravo, captain! Now I can account for this phosphorescence in the supposed narwhal that puzzled us so. I now ask you if the boarding of the *Nautilus* and of the *Scotia,* that has made such a noise, has been the result of a chance rencounter?"

"Quite accidental, sir. I was sailing only one fathom below the surface of the water when the shock came. It had no bad result."

"None, sir. But now, about your rencounter with the *Abraham Lincoln?*"

"Professor, I am sorry for one of the best vessels in the American navy; but they attacked me, and I was bound to defend myself. I contented myself, however, with putting the frigate *hors de combat:* she will not have any difficulty in getting repaired at the next port."

"Ah, commander! your *Nautilus* is certainly a marvelous boat."

"Yes, professor; and I love it as if it were part of myself. If danger threatens one of your vessels on the ocean, the first impression is the feeling of an abyss above and below. On the *Nautilus,* men's hearts never fail them. No defects to be afraid of, for the double shell is as firm as iron; no rigging to attend to; no sails for the wind to carry away; no boilers to burst; no fire to fear, for the vessel is made of iron, not of wood; no coal to run short, for electricity is the only mechanical agent; no collision to fear, for it alone swims in deep water; no tempest to brave, for when it dives below the water, it reaches absolute tranquillity. There, sir! that is the perfection of vessels! And if it is true that the engineer has more confidence in the vessel than the builder, and the builder than the captain himself, you understand the trust I repose in my *Nautilus;* for I am at once captain, builder, and engineer."

"But how could you construct this wonderful *Nautilus* in secret?"

"Each separate portion, M. Aronnax, was brought from different parts of the globe. The keel was forged at Creusot, the shaft of the screw at Penn & Co.'s, London, the iron plates of the hull at Laird's of Liverpool, the screw itself at Scott's at Glasgow. The reservoirs were made by Cail & Co. at Paris, the engine by Krupp in Prussia, its beak in Motala's workshop in Sweden, its mathematical instruments by Hart Brothers, of New York, etc.; and each of these people had my orders under different names."

"But these parts had to be put together and arranged?"

"Professor, I had set up my workshops upon a desert island in the ocean. There my workmen, that is to say, the brave men that I instructed and educated, and myself have put together our *Nautilus*. Then, when the work was finished fire destroyed all trace of our proceedings on this island, that I could have jumped over if I had liked."

"Then the cost of this vessel is great?"

"M. Aronnax, an iron vessel costs £45 per ton. Now the *Nautilus* weighed 1,500. It came therefore to £67,500 and £80,000 more for fitting it up, and about £200,000 with the works of art and the collections it contains."

"One last question, Captain Nemo."

"Ask it, professor."

"You are rich?"

"Immensely rich, sir; and I could, without missing it, pay the national debt of France."

I stared at the singular person who spoke thus. Was he playing upon my credulity? The future would decide that.

THE BLACK RIVER

The portion of the terrestrial globe which is covered by water is estimated at upward of eighty millions of acres. This fluid mass comprises two billions two hundred and fifty millions of cubic miles, forming a spherical body of a diameter of sixty leagues, the weight of which would be three quintillions of tons. To comprehend the meaning of these figures, it is necessary to observe that a quintillion is to a billion as a billion is to unity; in other words, there are as many billions in a quintillion as there are units in a billion. This mass of fluid is equal to about the quantity of water which would be discharged by all the rivers of the earth in forty thousand years.

During the geological epochs, the igneous period succeeded to the aqueous. The ocean originally prevailed everywhere. Then by degrees, in the silurian period, the tops of the mountains began to appear, the islands emerged, then disappeared in partial deluges, reappeared, became settled, formed continents, till at length the earth became geographically arranged, as we see in the present day. The solid had wrested from the liquid thirty-seven million six hundred and fifty-seven square miles, equal to twelve billions nine hundred and sixty millions of acres.

The shape of continents allows us to divide the waters into five great portions: the Arctic or Frozen Ocean, the Antarctic or Frozen Ocean, the Indian, the Atlantic, and the Pacific Oceans.

The Pacific Ocean extends from north to south between the two polar circles, and from east to west between Asia and America, over an extent of 145 degrees of longitude. It is the quietest of seas; its currents are broad and slow, it has medium tides and abundant rain. Such was the ocean that my fate destined me first to travel over under these strange conditions.

"Sir," said Captain Nemo, "we will, if you please, take our bearings and fix the starting-point of this voyage. It is a quarter to twelve. I will go up again to the surface."

The captain pressed an electric clock three times. The pumps began to drive the water from the tanks; the needle of the manometer marked by a different pressure the ascent of the *Nautilus,* then it stopped.

"We have arrived," said the captain.

I went to the central staircase which opened on to the platform, clambered up the iron steps, and found myself on the upper part of the *Nautilus.*

The platform was only three feet out of water. The front and back of the *Nautilus* was of that spindle-shape which caused it justly to be compared to a cigar. I noticed that its iron plates, slightly overlaying each other, resembled the shell which clothes the bodies of our large terrestrial reptiles. It explained to me how natural it was, in spite of all glasses, that this boat should have been taken for a marine animal.

Toward the middle of the platform the long-boat, half buried in the hull of the vessel, formed a slight excrescence. Fore and aft rose two cages of medium height with inclined sides, and partly closed by thick lenticular glasses; one destined for the steersman who directed the *Nautilus,* the other containing a brilliant lantern to give light on the road.

The sea was beautiful, the sky pure. Scarcely could the long vehicle feel the broad undulations of the ocean. A light breeze from the east rippled the surface of the waters. The horizon, free from fog, made observation easy. Nothing was in sight. Not a quicksand, not an island. A vast desert.

Captain Nemo, by the help of his sextant, took the altitude of the sun, which ought also to give the latitude. He waited for some moments till its disk touched the horizon. While taking observations not a muscle moved; the instrument could not have been more motionless in a hand of marble.

"Twelve o'clock, sir," said he. "When you like——"

I cast a last look upon the sea, slightly yellowed by the Japanese coast, and descended to the saloon.

"And now, sir, I leave you to your studies," added the captain; "our course is E.N.E., our depth is twenty-six fathoms. Here are maps on a large scale by which you may follow it. The saloon is at your disposal, and with your permission I will retire." Captain Nemo bowed, and I remained alone, lost in thoughts all bearing on the commander of the *Nautilus*.

For a whole hour was I deep in these reflections, seeking to pierce this mystery so interesting to me. Then my eyes fell upon the vast planisphere spread upon the table, and I placed my finger on the very spot where the given latitude and longitude crossed.

The sea has its large rivers like the continents. They are special currents known by their temperature and their color. The most remarkable of these is known by the name of the Gulf Stream. Science has decided on the globe the direction of five principal currents: one in the North Atlantic, a second in the South, a third in the North Pacific, a fourth in the South, and a fifth in the Southern Indian Ocean. It is even probable that a sixth current existed at one time or another in the Northern Indian Ocean, when the Caspian and Aral Seas formed but one vast sheet of water.

At this point indicated on the planisphere one of these currents was rolling, the Kuro-Scivo of the Japanese, the Black River, which, leaving the Gulf of Bengal where it is warmed by the perpendicular rays of a tropical sun, crosses the Straits of Malacca along the coast of Asia, turns into the North Pacific to the Aleutian Islands, carrying with it trunks of camphor-trees and other indigenous productions, and edging the waves of the ocean with the pure indigo of its warm water. It was this current that the *Nautilus* was to follow. I followed it with my eye; saw it lose itself in the vastness of the Pacific, and felt myself drawn with it, when Ned Land and Conseil appeared at the door of the saloon.

My two brave companions remained petrified at the sight of the wonders spread before them.

"Where are we—where are we?" exclaimed the Canadian. "In the museum at Quebec?"

"My friends," I answered, making a sign to them to enter, "you are not in Canada, but on board the *Nautilus*, fifty yards below the level of the sea."

"But, M. Aronnax," said Ned Land, "can you tell me how many men there are on board? Ten, twenty, fifty, a hundred?"

"I cannot answer you, Mr. Land; it is better to abandon for a time all idea of seizing the *Nautilus* or escaping from it. This ship is a masterpiece of modern industry, and I should be sorry not to have seen it. Many people would accept the situation forced upon us, if only to move among such wonders. So be quiet and let us try and see what passes around us."

"See!" exclaimed the harpooner. "But we can see nothing in this iron prison! We are walking—we are sailing—blindly."

Ned Land had scarcely pronounced these words when all was suddenly darkness. The luminous ceiling was gone, and so rapidly that my eyes received a painful impression.

We remained mute, not stirring, and not knowing what surprise awaited us, whether agreeable or disagreeable. A sliding noise was heard: one would have said that panels were working at the sides of the *Nautilus*.

"It is the end of the end!" said Ned Land.

Suddenly light broke at each side of the saloon, through two oblong openings. The liquid mass appeared vividly lit up by the electric gleam. Two crystal plates separated us from the sea. At first I trembled at the thought that this frail partition might break, but strong bands of copper bound them, giving an almost infinite power of resistance.

The sea was distinctly visible for a mile all round the *Nautilus*. What a spectacle! What pen can describe it? Who could paint the effects of the light through those transparent sheets of water, and the softness of the successive gradations from the lower to the superior strata of the ocean?

We know the transparency of the sea, and that its clearness is far beyond that of rock water. The mineral and organic substances which it holds in suspension heighten its transparency. In certain parts of the ocean at the Antilles, under seventy-five fathoms of water, can be seen with surprising clearness a bed of sand. The penetrating power of the solar rays does not seem to cease for a depth of one hundred and fifty fathoms. But in this middle fluid traveled over by the *Nautilus* the electric brightness was produced even in the bosom of the waves. It was no longer luminous water, but liquid light.

On each side a window opened into this unexplored abyss. The obscurity of the saloon showed to advantage the brightness outside, and we looked out as if this pure crystal had been the glass of an immense aquarium.

"You wished to see, friend Ned; well, you see now."

"Curious! curious!" muttered the Canadian, who, forgetting his ill-temper, seemed to submit to some irresistible attraction; "and one would come further than this to admire such a sight!"

"Ah!" thought I to myself. "I understand the life of this man; he has made a world apart for himself, in which he treasures all his greatest wonders."

For two whole hours an aquatic army escorted the *Nautilus*. During their games, their bounds, while rivaling each other in beauty, brightness, and velocity, I distinguished the green labre; the banded mullet, marked by a double line of black; the round-tailed goby, of a white color, with violet spots on the back; the Japanese scombrus, a beautiful mackerel of these seas, with a blue body and silvery head; the brilliant azurors, whose name alone defies description; some banded spares, with variegated fins of blue and yellow; some aclostones, the woodcocks of the seas, some specimens of which attain a yard in length; Japanese salamanders, spider lampreys, serpents six feet long, with eyes small and lively, and a huge mouth bristling with teeth; with many other species.

Our imagination was kept at its height; interjections followed quickly on each other. Ned named the fish, and Conseil classed them. I was in ecstasies with the vivacity of their movements and the beauty of their forms. Never had it been given to me to surprise these animals, alive and at liberty, in their natural element. I will not mention all the varieties which passed before my dazzled eyes, all the collection of the seas of China and Japan. These fish, more numerous than the birds of the air, came, attracted, no doubt, by the brilliant focus of the electric light.

Suddenly there was daylight in the saloon, the iron panels closed again, and the enchanting vision disappeared. But for a long time I dreamed on till my eyes fell on the instruments hanging on the partition. The compass still showed the course to be E.N.E., the manometer indicated a pressure of five atmospheres, equivalent to a depth of twenty-five fathoms, and the electric log gave a speed of fifteen miles an hour. I expected Captain Nemo, but he did not appear. The clock marked the hour of five.

Ned Land and Conseil returned to their cabin, and I retired to my chamber. My dinner was ready. It was composed of turtle soup made of the most delicate hawksbills, of a surmullet served with puff paste (the liver of which, prepared by itself, was most delicious), and fillets of the emperor-holocanthus, the savor of which seemed to me superior even to salmon.

I passed the evening reading, writing, and thinking. Then sleep overpowered me, and I stretched myself on my couch of zostera, and slept profoundly, while the *Nautilus* was gliding rapidly through the current of the Black River.

A Note of Invitation

The next day was the 9th of November. I awoke after a long sleep of twelve hours. Conseil came, according to custom, to know "how had I passed the night," and to offer his services. He had left his friend the Canadian sleeping like a man who had never done anything else all his life. I let the worthy fellow chatter as he pleased, without caring to answer him. I was preoccupied by the absence of the captain during our sitting of the day before, and hoping to see him to-day.

As soon as I was dressed I went into the saloon. It was deserted.

I plunged into the study of the conchological treasures hidden behind the glasses. I reveled also in great herbals filled with the rarest marine plants, which, although dried up, retained their lovely colors. Among these precious hydrophytes I remarked some vorticellæ, pavonariæ, delicate ceramies with scarlet tints, some fan-shaped agari, and some natabuli like flat mushrooms, which at one time used to be classed as zoöphytes; in short, a perfect series of algæ.

The whole day passed without my being honored by a visit from Captain Nemo. The panels of the saloon did not open. Perhaps they did not wish us to tire of these beautiful things.

The course of the *Nautilus* was E.N.E., her speed twelve knots, the depth below the surface between twenty-five and thirty fathoms.

The next day, 10th of November, the same desertion, the same solitude. I did not see one of the ship's crew; Ned and Conseil spent the greater part of the day with me. They were astonished at the inexplicable absence of the captain. Was this singular man ill? Had he altered his intentions with regard to us?

After all, as Conseil said, we enjoyed perfect liberty, we were delicately and abundantly fed. Our host kept to his terms of the treaty. We could not complain, and, indeed, the singularity of our fate reserved such wonderful compensation for us that we had no right to accuse it as yet.

That day I commenced the journal of these adventures which has enabled me to relate them with more scrupulous exactitude and minute detail. I wrote it on paper made from the zostera marina.

November 11th, early in the morning. The fresh air spreading over the interior of the *Nautilus* told me that we had come to the surface of the ocean to renew our supply of oxygen. I directed my steps to the central staircase, and mounted the platform.

It was six o'clock, the weather was cloudy, the sea gray but calm. Scarcely a billow. Captain Nemo, whom I hoped to meet, would he be there? I saw no one but the steersman imprisoned in his glass cage. Seated upon the projection formed by the hull of the pinnace, I inhaled the salt breeze with delight.

By degrees the fog disappeared under the action of the sun's rays, the radiant orb rose from behind the eastern horizon. The sea flamed under its glance like a train of gunpowder. The clouds scattered in the heights were colored with lively tints of beautiful shades, and numerous "mare's tails," which betokened wind for that day. But what was wind to this *Nautilus*, which tempests could not frighten!

I was admiring this joyous rising of the sun, so gay, and so life-giving, when I heard steps approaching the platform. I was prepared to salute Captain Nemo, but it was his second (whom I had already seen on the captain's first visit) who appeared. He advanced on the platform, not seeming to see me. With his powerful glass to his eye he scanned every point of the horizon with great attention. This examination over, he approached the panel and pronounced a sentence in exactly these terms. I have remembered it, for every morning it was repeated under exactly the same conditions. It was thus worded:

"Nautron respoc lorni virch."

What it meant I could not say.

These words pronounced, the second descended. I thought that the *Nautilus* was about to return to its submarine navigation. I regained the panel and returned to my chamber.

Five days sped thus, without any change in our situation. Every morning I mounted the platform. The same phrase was pronounced by the same individual. But Captain Nemo did not appear.

I had made up my mind that I should never see him again, when, on the 16th of November, on returning to my room with Ned and Conseil, I found upon my table a note addressed to me. I opened it impatiently. It was written in a bold, clear hand, the characters rather pointed, recalling the German type. The note was worded as follows:

16th of November, 1867

To Professor Aronnax, on board the Nautilus:

Captain Nemo invites Professor Aronnax to a hunting-party, which will take place to-morrow morning in the forests of the island of Crespo. He hopes that nothing will prevent the professor from being present, and he will with pleasure see him joined by his companions.

Captain Nemo, Commander of the Nautilus.

"A hunt!" exclaimed Ned.

"And in the forests of the island of Crespo!" added Conseil.

"Oh, then the gentleman is going on *terra firma?*" replied Ned Land.

"That seems to me to be clearly indicated," said I, reading the letter once more.

"Well, we must accept," said the Canadian. "But once more on dry ground, we shall know what to do. Indeed, I shall not be sorry to eat a piece of fresh venison."

Without seeking to reconcile what was contradictory between Captain Nemo's manifest aversion to islands and continents, and his invitation to hunt in a forest, I contented myself with replying:

"Let us first see where the island of Crespo is."

I consulted the planisphere, and in 32° 40′ north lat., and 157° 50′ west long., I found a small island, recognized in 1801 by Captain Crespo, and marked in the ancient Spanish maps as Rocca de la Plata, the meaning of which is "The Silver Rock." We were then about eighteen hundred miles from our starting-point, and the course of the *Nautilus*, a little changed, was bringing it back toward the southeast.

I showed this little rock lost in the midst of the North Pacific to my companions.

"If Captain Nemo does sometimes go on dry ground," said I, "he at least chooses desert islands."

Ned Land shrugged his shoulders without speaking, and Conseil and he left me.

After supper, which was served by the steward, mute and impassible, I went to bed, not without some anxiety.

The next morning, the 17th of November, on awakening I felt that the *Nautilus* was perfectly still. I dressed quickly and entered the saloon.

Captain Nemo was there, waiting for me. He rose, bowed, and asked me if it was convenient for me to accompany him. As he made no allusion to his absence during the last eight days, I did not mention it, and simply answered that my companions and myself were ready to follow him.

We entered the dining-room, where breakfast was served.

"M. Aronnax," said the captain, "pray share my breakfast without ceremony; we will chat as we eat. For though I promised you a walk in the forest, I did not undertake to find hotels there. So breakfast as a man who will most likely not have his dinner till very late."

I did honor to the repast. It was composed of several kinds of fish, and slices of holothuridæ (excellent zoöphytes), and different sorts of seaweed. Our drink consisted of pure water, to which the captain added some drops of a fermented liquor, extracted by the Kamschatcha method from a seaweed known under the name of Rhodomenia palmata. Captain Nemo ate at first without saying a word. Then he began:

"Sir, when I proposed to you to hunt in my submarine forest of Crespo, you evidently thought me mad. Sir, you should never judge lightly of any man."

"But, captain, believe me——"

"Be kind enough to listen, and you will then see whether you have any cause to accuse me of folly and contradiction."

"I listen."

"You know as well as I do, professor, that man can live under water, providing he carries with him a sufficient supply of breathable air. In submarine works, the workman, clad in an impervious dress, with his head in a metal helmet, receives air from above by means of forcing-pumps and regulators."

"That is a diving apparatus," said I.

"Just so; but under these conditions the man is not at liberty; he is attached to the pump which sends him air through an India-rubber tube, and if we were obliged to be thus held to the *Nautilus*, we could not go far."

"And the means of getting free?" I asked.

"It is to use the Rouquayrol apparatus, invented by two of your own countrymen, which I have brought to perfection for my own use, and which will allow you to risk yourself under these new physiological conditions, without any organ whatever suffering. It consists of a reservoir of thick iron plates, in which I store the air under a pressure of fifty atmospheres. This reservoir is fixed on the back by means of braces, like a soldier's knapsack. Its upper part forms a box in which the air is kept by means of a bellows, and therefore cannot escape unless at its normal tension. In the Rouquayrol apparatus such as we use, two India-rubber pipes leave this box and join a sort of tent which holds the nose and mouth; one is to introduce fresh air, the other to let out the foul, and the tongue closes one or the other according to the wants of the respirator. But I, in encountering great pressures at the bottom of the sea, was obliged to shut my head, like that of a diver, in a ball of copper; and it is to this ball of copper that the two pipes, the inspirator and the expirator, open."

"Perfectly, Captain Nemo; but the air that you carry with you must soon be used; when it only contains fifteen per cent. of oxygen, it is no longer fit to breathe."

"Right! But I told you, M. Aronnax, that the pumps of the *Nautilus* allow me to store the air under considerable pressure; and on those conditions, the reservoir of the apparatus can furnish breathable air for nine or ten hours."

"I have no further objections to make," I answered. "I will only ask you one thing, captain—how can you light your road at the bottom of the sea?"

"With the Ruhmkorff apparatus, M. Aronnax; one is carried on the back, the other is fastened to the waist. It is composed of a Bunsen pile, which I do not work with bichromate of potash, but with sodium. A wire is introduced which collects the electricity produced, and directs it toward a particularly made lantern. In this lantern is a spiral glass which contains a small quantity of carbonic gas. When the apparatus is at work, this gas becomes luminous, giving out a white and continuous light. Thus provided, I can breathe and I can see."

"Captain Nemo, to all my objections you make such crushing answers that I dare no longer doubt. But if I am forced to admit the Rouquayrol and Ruhmkorff apparatus, I must be allowed some reservations with regard to the gun I am to carry."

"But it is not a gun for powder," answered the captain.

"Then it is an air-gun."

"Doubtless! How would you have me manufacture gunpowder on board, without either saltpeter, sulphur, or charcoal?"

"Besides," I added, "to fire under water in a medium eight hundred and fifty-five times denser than the air, we must conquer very considerable resistance."

"That would be no difficulty. There exist guns, according to Fulton, perfected in England by Philip Coles and Burley, in France by Furcy, and in Italy by Landi, which are furnished with a peculiar system of closing, which can fire under these conditions. But I repeat, having no powder, I use air under great pressure, which the pumps of the *Nautilus* furnish abundantly."

"But this air must be rapidly used?"

"Well, have I not my Rouquayrol reservoir, which can furnish it at need? A tap is all that is required. Besides, M. Aronnax, you must see yourself that during our submarine hunt we can spend but little air and but few balls."

"But it seems to me that in this twilight, and in the midst of this fluid, which is very dense compared with the atmosphere, shots could not go far, nor easily prove mortal."

"Sir, on the contrary, with this gun every blow is mortal; and however lightly the animal is touched, it falls as if struck by a thunderbolt."

"Why?"

"Because the balls sent by this gun are not ordinary balls, but little cases of glass (invented by Leniebroek, an Austrian chemist), of which I have a large supply. These glass cases are covered with a case of steel, and weighted with a pellet of lead; they are real Leyden bottles, into which the electricity is forced to a very high tension. With the slightest shock they are discharged, and the animal, however strong it may be, falls dead. I must tell you that these cases are size number four, and that the charge for an ordinary gun would be ten."

"I will argue no longer," I replied, rising from the table; "I have nothing left me but to take my gun. At all events, I will go where you go."

Captain Nemo then led me aft; and in passing before Ned and Conseil's cabin, I called my two companions, who followed immediately. We then came to a kind of cell near the machinery-room, in which we were to put on our walking-dress.

A Walk on the Bottom of the Sea

This cell was, to speak correctly, the arsenal and wardrobe of the *Nautilus*. A dozen diving apparatus hung from the partition, waiting our use.

Ned Land, on seeing them, showed evident repugnance to dress himself in one.

"But, my worthy Ned, the forests of the island of Crespo are nothing but submarine forests."

"Good!" said the disappointed harpooner, who saw his dreams of fresh meat fade away. "And you, M. Aronnax, are you going to dress yourself in those clothes?"

"There is no alternative, Master Ned."

"As you please, sir," replied the harpooner, shrugging his shoulders; "but as for me, unless I am forced, I will never get into one."

"No one will force you, Master Ned," said Captain Nemo.

"Is Conseil going to risk it?" asked Ned.

"I follow my master wherever he goes," replied Conseil.

At the captain's call two of the ship's crew came to help us to dress in these heavy and impervious clothes, made of India-rubber without seam, and constructed expressly to resist considerable pressure. One would have thought it a suit of armor, both supple and resisting. This suit formed trousers and waistcoat. The trousers were finished off with thick boots, weighted with heavy leaden soles. The texture of the waistcoat was held together by bands of copper, which crossed the chest, protecting it from the great pressure of the water, and leaving the lungs free to act; the sleeves ended in gloves, which in no way restrained the movement of the hands. There was a vast difference noticeable between these consummate apparatus and the old cork breastplates, jackets, and other contrivances in vogue during the eighteenth century.

Captain Nemo and one of his companions (a sort of Hercules, who must have possessed great strength), Conseil, and myself, were soon enveloped in the dresses. There remained nothing more to be done but to inclose our heads in the metal box. But before proceeding to this operation, I asked the captain's permission to examine the guns we were to carry.

One of the *Nautilus* men gave me a simple gun, the butt end of which, made of steel hollow in the center, was rather large. It served as a reservoir for compressed air, which a valve worked by a spring allowed to escape into a metal tube. A box of projectiles, in a groove, in the thickness of the butt end, contained about twenty of these electric balls, which by means of a spring were forced into the barrel of the gun. As soon as one shot was fired, another was ready.

"Captain Nemo," said I, "this arm is perfect, and easily handled; I only ask to be allowed to try it. But how shall we gain the bottom of the sea?"

"At this moment, professor, the *Nautilus* is stranded in five fathoms, and we have nothing to do but to start."

"But how shall we get off?"

"You shall see."

Captain Nemo thrust his head into the helmet; Conseil and I did the same, not without hearing an ironical "Good sport!" from the Canadian. The upper part of our dress terminated in a copper collar upon which was screwed the metal helmet. Three holes, protected by thick glass, allowed us to see in all directions, by simply turning our heads in the interior of the head-dress. As soon as it was in position, the Rouquayrol apparatus on our backs began to act; and, for my part, I could breathe with ease.

With the Ruhmkorff lamp hanging from my belt, and the gun in my hand, I was ready to set out. But to speak the truth, imprisoned in these heavy garments, and glued to the deck by my leaden soles, it was impossible for me to take a step.

But this state of things was provided for. I felt myself being pushed into a little room contiguous to the wardrobe-room. My companions followed, towed along in the same way. I heard a water-tight door, furnished with stopper-plates, close upon us, and we were wrapped in profound darkness.

After some minutes, a loud hissing was heard. I felt the cold mount from my feet to my chest. Evidently from some part of the vessel they had by means of a tap given entrance to the water, which was invading us, and with which the room was soon filled. A second door cut in the side of the *Nautilus* then opened. We saw a faint light. In another instant our feet trod the bottom of the sea.

And now, how can I retrace the impression left upon me by that walk under the waters? Words are impotent to relate such wonders! Captain Nemo walked in front, his companion followed some steps behind. Conseil and I remained near each other, as if an exchange of words had been possible through our metallic cases. I no longer felt the weight of my clothing, or of my shoes, of my reservoir of air, or my thick helmet, in the midst of which my head rattled like an almond in its shell.

The light, which lit the soil thirty feet below the surface of the ocean, astonished me by its power. The solar rays shone through the watery mass easily, and dissipated all color, and I clearly distinguished objects at a distance of a hundred and fifty yards. Beyond that the tints darkened into fine gradations of ultramarine, and faded into vague obscurity. Truly this water which surrounded me was but another air denser than the terrestrial atmosphere, but almost as transparent. Above me was the calm surface of the sea. We were walking on fine, even sand, not wrinkled, as on a flat shore, which retains the impression of the billows. This dazzling carpet, really a reflector, repelled the rays of the sun with wonderful intensity, which accounted for the vibration which penetrated every atom of liquid. Shall I be believed when I say that, at the depth of thirty feet, I could see as if I was in broad daylight?

For a quarter of an hour I trod on this sand, sown with the impalpable dust of shells. The hull of the *Nautilus,* resembling a long shoal, disappeared by degrees; but its lantern, when darkness should overtake us in the waters, would help to guide us on board by its distinct rays.

Soon forms of objects outlined in the distance were discernible. I recognized magnificent rocks, hung with a tapestry of zoöphytes of the most beautiful kind, and I was at first struck by the peculiar effect of this medium.

It was then ten in the morning; the rays of the sun struck the surface of the waves at rather an oblique angle, and at the touch of their light, decomposed by refraction as through a prism, flowers, rocks, plants, shells, and polypi were shaded at the edges by the seven solar colors. It was marvelous, a feast for the eyes, this complication of colored tints, a perfect kaleidoscope of green, yellow, orange, violet, indigo, and blue; in one word, the whole palette of an enthusiastic colorist! Why could I not communicate to Conseil the lively sensations which were mounting to my brain, and rival him in expressions of admiration? For aught I knew, Captain Nemo and his companion might be able to exchange thoughts by means of signs previously agreed upon. So for want of better, I talked to myself; I declaimed in the copper box which covered my head, thereby expending more air in vain words than was, perhaps, expedient.

Various kinds of isis, clusters of pure tuft-coral, prickly fungi, and anemones, formed a brilliant garden of flowers, enameled with porphitæ, decked with their collarettes of blue tentacles, sea-stars studding the sandy bottom, together with asterophytons like fine lace embroidered by the hands of naiads, whose festoons were waved by the gentle undulations caused by our walk. It was a real grief to me to crush under my feet the brilliant specimens of mollusks which strewed the ground by thousands, of hammerheads, donaciæ (veritable bounding shells), of staircases, and red helmet-shells, angel-wings, and many others produced by this inexhaustible ocean. But we were bound to walk, so we went on, while above our heads waved shoals of physalides leaving their tentacles to float in their train, medusæ whose umbrellas of opal or rose-pink, escalloped with a band of blue, sheltered us from the rays of the sun, and fiery pelagiæ, which in the darkness would have strewn our path with phosphorescent light.

All these wonders I saw in the space of a quarter of a mile, scarcely stopping, and following Captain Nemo, who beckoned me on by signs. Soon the nature of the soil changed; to the sandy plain succeeded an extent of slimy mud, which the Americans call "ooze," composed of equal parts of silicious and calcareous shells. We then traveled over a plain of seaweed of wild and luxuriant vegetation. This sward was of close texture, and soft to the feet, and rivaled the softest carpet woven by the hand of man. But while verdure was spread at our feet, it did not abandon our heads. A light network of marine plants, of that inexhaustible family of seaweeds of which more than two thousand kinds are known, grew on the surface of the water. I saw long ribbons of fucus floating, some globular, others tuberous; laurenciæ and cladostephi of most delicate foliage, and some rhodomeniæ palmatæ resembling the fan of a cactus. I noticed that the green plants kept nearer the top of the sea, while the red were at a greater depth, leaving to the black or brown hydrophytes the care of forming gardens and parterres in the remote beds of the ocean.

We had quitted the *Nautilus* about an hour and a half. It was near noon; I knew by the perpendicularity of the sun's rays, which were no longer refracted. The magical colors disappeared by degrees, and the shades of emerald and sapphire were effaced. We walked with a regular step, which rang upon the ground with astonishing intensity; the slightest noise was transmitted with a quickness to which the ear is unaccustomed on the earth; indeed, water is a better conductor of sound than air, in the ratio of four to one. At this period the earth sloped downward; the light took a uniform tint. We were at a depth of a hundred and five yards and twenty inches, undergoing a pressure of six atmospheres.

At this depth I could still see the rays of the sun, though feebly; to their intense brilliancy had succeeded a reddish twilight, the lowest state between day and night; but we could still see well enough; it was not necessary to resort to the Ruhmkorff apparatus as yet. At this moment Captain Nemo stopped; he waited till I joined him, and then pointed to an obscure mass, looming in the shadow, at a short distance.

"It is the forest of the island of Crespo," thought I: and I was not mistaken.

A Submarine Forest

We had at last arrived on the borders of this forest, doubtless one of the finest of Captain Nemo's immense domains. He looked upon it as his own, and considered he had the same right over it that the first men had in the first days of the world. And, indeed, who would have disputed with him the possession of this submarine property? What other hardier pioneer would come, hatchet in hand, to cut down the dark copses?

This forest was composed of large tree-plants; and the moment we penetrated under its vast arcades, I was struck by the singular position of their branches—a position I had not yet observed.

Not an herb which carpeted the ground, not a branch which clothed the trees, was either broken or bent, nor did they extend horizontally; all stretched up to the surface of the ocean. Not a filament, not a ribbon, however thin they might be, but kept as straight as a rod of iron. The fuci and llianas grew in rigid perpendicular lines, due to the density of the element which had produced them. Motionless, yet, when bent to one side by the hand, they directly resumed their former position. Truly it was the region of perpendicularity!

I soon accustomed myself to this fantastic position, as well as to the comparative darkness which surrounded us. The soil of the forest seemed covered with sharp blocks, difficult to avoid. The submarine flora struck me as being very perfect, and richer even than it would have been in the arctic or tropical zones, where these productions are not so plentiful. But for some minutes I involuntarily confounded the genera, taking zoöphytes for hydrophytes, animals for plants; and who would not have been mistaken? The fauna and the flora are too closely allied in this submarine world.

These plants are self-propagated, and the principle of their existence is in the water, which upholds and nourishes them. The greater number, instead of leaves, shoot forth blades of capricious shapes comprised within a scale of colors—pink, carmine, green, olive, fawn, and brown. I saw there (but not dried up, as our specimens of the *Nautilus* are) pavonari spread like a fan as if to catch the breeze; scarlet ceramies, whose laminaries extended their edible shoots of fern-shaped nereocysti, which grow to a height of fifteen feet; clusters of acetabuli, whose stems increase in size upward; and numbers of other marine plants, all devoid of flowers!

"Curious anomaly! fantastic element," said an ingenious naturalist, "in which the animal kingdom blossoms, and the vegetable does not!"

Under these numerous shrubs (as large as trees of the temperate zone), and under their damp shadow, were massed together real bushes of living flowers, hedges of zoöphytes, on which blossomed some zebra-meandrines, with crooked grooves; some yellow caryophylliæ; and to complete the illusion, the fish-flies flew from branch to branch like a swarm of humming-birds, while yellow lepisacomthi, with bristling jaws, dactylopteri, and monocentrides rose at our feet like a flight of snipes.

In about an hour Captain Nemo gave the signal to halt. I, for my part, was not sorry, and we stretched ourselves under an arbor of alariæ, the long thin blades of which stood up like arrows.

This short rest seemed delicious to me; there was nothing wanting but the charm of conversation; but, impossible to speak, impossible to answer, I only put my great copper head to Conseil's. I saw the worthy fellow's eyes glistening with delight, and to show his satisfaction he shook himself in his breastplate of air, in the most comical way in the world.

After four hours of this walking I was surprised not to find myself dreadfully hungry. How to account for this state of the stomach I could not tell. But instead I felt an insurmountable desire to sleep, which happens to all divers. And my eyes soon closed behind the thick glasses, and I fell into a heavy slumber, which the movement alone had prevented before. Captain Nemo and his robust companion, stretched in the clear crystal, set us the example.

How long I remained buried in this drowsiness I cannot judge; but when I woke, the sun seemed sinking toward the horizon. Captain Nemo had already risen, and I was beginning to stretch my limbs, when an unexpected apparition brought me briskly to my feet.

A few steps off, a monster sea-spider, about thirty-eight inches high, was watching me with squinting eyes, ready to spring upon me. Though my diver's dress was thick enough to defend me from the bite of this animal, I could not help shuddering with horror. Conseil and the sailor of the *Nautilus* awoke at this moment. Captain Nemo pointed out the hideous crustacean, which a blow from the butt end of the gun knocked over, and I saw the horrible claws of the monster writhe in terrible convulsions. This accident reminded me that other animals more to be feared might haunt these obscure depths, against whose attacks my diving-dress would not protect me. I had never thought of it before, but I now resolved to be upon my guard. Indeed, I thought that this halt would mark the termination of our walk; but I was mistaken, for, instead of returning to the *Nautilus*, Captain Nemo continued his bold excursion. The ground was still on the incline, its declivity seemed to be getting greater, and to be leading us to greater depths. It must have been about three o'clock when we reached a narrow valley, between high perpendicular walls, situated about seventy-five fathoms deep. Thanks to the perfection of our apparatus, we were forty-five fathoms below the limit which nature seems to have imposed on man as to his submarine excursions.

I say seventy-five fathoms, though I had no instrument by which to judge the distance. But I knew that even in the clearest waters the solar rays could not penetrate further. And accordingly the darkness deepened. At ten paces not an object was visible. I was groping my way, when I suddenly saw a brilliant white light. Captain Nemo had just put his electric apparatus into use; his companion did the same, and Conseil and I followed their example. By turning a screw I established a communication between the wire and the spiral glass, and the sea, lit by our four lanterns, was illuminated for a circle of thirty-six yards.

Captain Nemo was still plunging into the dark depths of the forest, whose trees were getting scarcer at every step. I noticed that vegetable life disappeared sooner than animal life. The medusæ had already abandoned the arid soil, from which a great number of animals, zoöphytes, articulata, mollusks, and fishes, still obtained sustenance.

As we walked, I thought the light of our Ruhmkorff apparatus could not fail to draw some inhabitant from its dark couch. But if they did approach us, they at least kept at a respectful distance from the hunters. Several times I saw Captain Nemo stop, put his gun to his shoulder, and after some moments drop it and walk on. At last, after about four hours, this marvelous excursion came to an end. A wall of superb rocks, in an imposing mass, rose before us, a heap of gigantic blocks, an enormous steep granite shore, forming dark grottoes, but which presented no practicable slope; it was the prop of the island of Crespo. It was the earth! Captain Nemo stopped suddenly. A gesture of his brought us all to a halt; and however desirous I might be to scale the wall, I was obliged to stop. Here ended Captain Nemo's domains, and he would not go beyond them. Further on was a portion of the globe he might not trample upon.

The return began. Captain Nemo had returned to the head of his little band, directing their course without hesitation. I thought we were not following the same road to return to the *Nautilus.* The new road was very steep, and consequently very painful. We approached the surface of the sea rapidly. But this return to the upper strata was not so sudden as to cause relief from the pressure too rapidly, which might have produced serious disorder in our organization, and brought on internal lesions, so fatal to divers. Very soon light reappeared and grew, and the sun being low on the horizon, the refraction edged the different objects with a spectral ring. At ten yards and a half deep, we walked amid a shoal of little fishes of all kinds, more numerous than the birds of the air, and also more agile; but no aquatic game worthy of a shot had as yet met our gaze, when at that moment I saw the captain shoulder his gun quickly, and follow a moving object into the shrubs. He fired—I heard a slight hissing, and a creature fell stunned at some distance from us. It was a magnificent sea-otter, an enhydrus, the only exclusively marine quadruped. This otter was five feet long, and must have been very valuable. Its skin, chestnut-brown above and silvery underneath, would have made one of those beautiful furs so sought after in the Russian and Chinese markets; the fineness and the luster of its coat would certainly fetch £80. I admired this curious mammal, with its rounded head ornamented with short ears, its round eyes, and white whiskers like those of a cat, with webbed feet and nails, and tufted tail. This precious animal, hunted and tracked by fishermen, has now become very rare, and taken refuge chiefly in the northern parts of the Pacific, or probably its race would soon become extinct.

Captain Nemo's companion took the beast, threw it over his shoulder, and we continued our journey. For one hour a plain of sand lay stretched before us. Sometimes it rose to within two yards and some inches of the surface of the water. I then saw our image clearly reflected, drawn inversely, and above us appeared an identical group reflecting our movements and our actions; in a word, like us in every point, except that they walked with their heads downward and their feet in the air.

Another effect I noticed, which was the passage of thick clouds, which formed and vanished rapidly; but on reflection I understood that these seeming clouds were due to the varying thickness of the reeds at the bottom, and I could even see the fleecy foam which their broken tops multiplied on the water, and the shadows of large birds passing above our heads, whose rapid flight I could discern on the surface of the sea.

On this occasion I was witness to one of the finest gunshots which ever made the nerves of a hunter thrill. A large bird of great breadth of wing, clearly visible, approached, hovering over us. Captain Nemo's companion shouldered his gun and fired, when it was only a few yards above the waves. The creature fell stunned, and the force of its fall brought it within the reach of the dexterous hunter's grasp. It was an albatross of the finest kind.

Our march had not been interrupted by this incident. For two hours we followed these sandy plains, then fields of algæ very disagreeable to cross. Candidly, I could do no more when I saw a glimmer of light, which for a half-mile broke the darkness of the waters. It was the lantern of the *Nautilus*. Before twenty minutes were over we should be on board, and I should be able to breathe with ease; for it seemed that my reservoir supplied air very deficient in oxygen. But I did not reckon on an accidental meeting, which delayed our arrival for some time.

I had remained some steps behind, when I presently saw Captain Nemo coming hurriedly toward me. With his strong hand he bent me to the ground, his companion doing the same to Conseil. At first I knew not what to think of this sudden attack, but I was soon reassured by seeing the captain lie down beside me, and remain immovable.

I was stretched on the ground, just under shelter of a bush of algæ, when, raising my head, I saw some enormous mass, casting phosphorescent gleams, pass blusteringly by.

My blood froze in my veins as I recognized two formidable sharks which threatened us. It was a couple of tintoreas, terrible creatures, with enormous tails and a dull glassy stare, the phosphorescent matter ejected from holes pierced around the muzzle. Monstrous brutes, which would crush a whole man in their iron jaws! I did not know whether Conseil stopped to classify them; for my part, I noticed their silver bellies, and their huge mouths bristling with teeth, from a very unscientific point of view, and more as a possible victim than as a naturalist.

Happily the voracious creatures do not see well. They passed without seeing us, brushing us with their brownish fins, and we escaped by a miracle from a danger certainly greater than meeting a tiger full-face in the forest. Half an hour after, guided by the electric light, we reached the *Nautilus*. The outside door had been left open, and Captain Nemo closed it as soon as we had entered the first cell. He then pressed a knob. I heard the pumps working in the midst of the vessel. I felt the water sinking from around me, and in a few moments the cell was entirely empty. The inside door then opened, and we entered the vestry.

There our diving-dress was taken off, not without some trouble; and, fairly worn out from want of food and sleep, I returned to my room, in great wonder at this surprising excursion at the bottom of the sea.

FOUR THOUSAND LEAGUES UNDER THE PACIFIC

The next morning, the 18th of November, I had quite recovered from my fatigues of the day before, and I went up on to the platform, just as the second lieutenant was uttering his daily phrase.

I was admiring the magnificent aspect of the ocean when Captain Nemo appeared. He did not seem to be aware of my presence, and began a series of astronomical observations. Then, when he had finished, he went and leaned on the cage of the watchlight, and gazed abstractedly on the ocean. In the meantime, a number of the sailors of the *Nautilus*, all strong and healthy men, had come up on to the platform. They came to draw up the nets that had been laid all night. These sailors were evidently of different nations, although the European type was visible in all of them. I recognized some unmistakable Irishmen, Frenchmen, some Slavs, and a Greek or a Candiote. They were civil, and only used that odd language among themselves, the origin of which I could not guess, neither could I question them.

The nets were hauled in. They were a large kind of "chaluts," like those on the Normandy coast, great pockets that the waves and a chain fixed in the smaller meshes kept open. These pockets, drawn by iron poles, swept through the water, and gathered in everything in their way. That day they brought up curious specimens from those productive coasts—fishing-frogs that, from their comical movements, have acquired the name of buffoons; black commersons, furnished with antennæ; trigger-fish, encircled with red bands; orthragorisci, with very subtle venom; some olive-colored lampreys; macrorhynci, covered with silvery scales; trichiuri, the electric power of which is equal to that of the gymnotus and cramp-fish; scaly notopteri, with transverse brown bands; greenish cod; several varieties of gobies, etc.; also some larger fish; a caranx with a prominent head a yard long; several fine bonitos, streaked with blue and silver; and three splendid tunnies, which, in spite of the swiftness of their motion, had not escaped the net.

I reckoned that the haul had brought in more than nine hundredweight of fish. It was a fine haul, but not to be wondered at. Indeed, the nets are let down for several hours, and inclose in their meshes an infinite variety. We had no lack of excellent food, and the rapidity of the *Nautilus* and the attraction of the electric light could always renew our supply. These several productions of the sea were immediately lowered through the panel to the steward's room, some to be eaten fresh, and others pickled.

The fishing ended, the provision of air renewed, I thought that the *Nautilus* was about to continue its submarine excursion, and was preparing to return to my room, when, without further preamble, the captain turned to me, saying:

"Professor, is not this ocean gifted with real life? It has its tempers and its gentle moods. Yesterday it slept as we did, and now it has woke after a quiet night. Look!" he continued. "It wakes under the caresses of the sun. It is going to renew its diurnal existence. It is an interesting study to watch the play of its organization. It has a pulse, arteries, spasms; and I agree with the learned Maury, who discovered in it a circulation as real as the circulation of blood in animals.

"Yes, the ocean has indeed circulation, and to promote it, the Creator has caused things to multiply in it—caloric, salt, and animalculæ."

When Captain Nemo spoke thus, he seemed altogether changed, and aroused an extraordinary emotion in me.

"Also," he added, "true existence is there; and I can imagine the foundations of nautical towns, clusters of submarine houses, which, like the *Nautilus*, would ascend every morning to breathe at the surface of the water—free towns, independent cities. Yet who knows whether some despot——"

Captain Nemo finished his sentence with a violent gesture. Then, addressing me as if to chase away some sorrowful thought:

"M. Aronnax," he asked, "do you know the depth of the ocean?"

"I only know, captain, what the principal soundings have taught us."

"Could you tell me them, so that I can suit them to my purpose?"

"These are some," I replied, "that I remember. If I am not mistaken, a depth of 8,000 yards has been found in the North Atlantic, and 2,500 yards in the Mediterranean. The most remarkable soundings have been made in the South Atlantic, near the 35th parallel, and they gave 12,000 yards, 14,000 yards, and 15,000 yards. To sum up all, it is reckoned that if the bottom of the sea were leveled, its mean depth would be about one and three-quarter leagues."

"Well, professor," replied the captain, "we shall show you better than that, I hope. As to the mean depth of this part of the Pacific, I tell you it is only 4,000 yards."

Having said this, Captain Nemo went toward the panel, and disappeared down the ladder. I followed him, and went into the large drawing-room. The screw was immediately put in motion, and the log gave twenty miles an hour.

During the days and weeks that passed, Captain Nemo was very sparing of his visits. I seldom saw him. The lieutenant pricked the ship's course regularly on the chart, so I could always tell exactly the route of the *Nautilus*.

Nearly every day, for some time, the panels of the drawing-room were opened, and we were never tired of penetrating the mysteries of the submarine world.

The general direction of the *Nautilus* was southeast, and it kept between 100 and 150 yards of depth. One day, however, I do not know why, being drawn diagonally by means of the inclined planes, it touched the bed of the sea. The thermometer indicated a temperature of 4.25 (Cent.); a temperature that at this depth seemed common to all latitudes.

At three o'clock on the morning of the 26th of November, the *Nautilus* crossed the Tropic of Cancer at 172° longitude. On the 27th instant it sighted the Sandwich Islands, where Cook died, February 14, 1779. We had then gone 4,860 leagues from our starting-point. In the morning, when I went on the platform, I saw, two miles to windward, Hawaii, the largest of the seven islands that form the group. I saw clearly the cultivated ranges, and the several mountain-chains that run parallel with the side, and the volcanoes that overtop Mouna-Rea, which rise 5,000 yards above the level of the sea. Besides other things the nets brought up were several flabellariæ and graceful polypi, that are peculiar to that part of the ocean. The direction of the *Nautilus* was still to the southeast. It crossed the equator December 1, in 142° longitude; and on the 4th of the same month, after crossing rapidly and without anything particular occurring, we sighted the Marquesas group. I saw, three miles off, at 8° 57′ latitude south, and 139° 32′ west longitude, Martin's peak in Nouka-Hiva, the largest of the group that belongs to France. I only saw the woody mountains against the horizon, because Captain Nemo did not wish to bring the ship to the wind. There the nets brought up beautiful specimens of fish: choryphenes, with azure fins and tails like gold, the flesh of which is unrivaled; hologymnoses, nearly destitute of scales, but of exquisite flavor; ostorhyncs, with bony jaws, and yellow-tinged thasards, as good as bonitos; all fish that would be of use to us. After leaving these charming islands protected by the French flag, from the 4th to the 11th of December the *Nautilus* sailed over about 2,000 miles. This navigation was remarkable for the meeting with an immense shoal of calmars, near neighbors to the cuttle. The French fishermen call them *hornets*; they belong to the cephalopod class, and to the dibranchial family, that comprehends the cuttles and the argonauts. These animals were particularly studied by students of antiquity, and they furnished numerous metaphors to the popular orators, as well as excellent dishes for the tables of the rich citizens, if one can believe Athenæus, a Greek doctor, who lived before Galen. It was during the night of the 9th or 10th of December that the *Nautilus* came across this shoal of mollusks, that are peculiarly nocturnal. One could count them by millions. They emigrate from the temperate to the warmer zones, following the track of herrings and sardines. We watched them through the thick crystal panes, swimming down the wind with great rapidity, moving by means of their locomotive tube, pursuing fish and mollusks, eating the little ones, eaten by the big ones, and tossing about in indescribable confusion the ten arms that nature has placed on their heads like a crest of pneumatic serpents. The *Nautilus*, in spite of its speed, sailed for several hours in the midst of these animals, and its nets brought in an enormous quantity, among which I recognized the nine species that D'Orbigny classed for the Pacific. One saw, while crossing, that the sea displays the most wonderful sights. They were in endless variety. The scene changed continually, and we were called upon not only to contemplate the works of the Creator in the midst of the liquid element, but to penetrate the awful mysteries of the ocean.

During the daytime of the 11th of December, I was busy reading in the large drawing-room. Ned Land and Conseil watched the luminous water through the half-open panels. The *Nautilus* was immovable. While its reservoirs were filled, it kept at a depth of 1,000 yards, a region rarely visited in the ocean, and in which large fish were seldom seen.

I was then reading a charming book by Jean Macé, "The Slaves of the Stomach," and I was learning some valuable lessons from it, when Conseil interrupted me.

"Will master come here a moment?" he said in a curious voice.

"What is the matter, Conseil?"

"I want master to look."

I rose, went and leaned on my elbows before the panes, and watched.

In a full electric light, an enormous black mass, quite immovable, was suspended in the midst of the waters. I watched it attentively, seeking to find out the nature of this gigantic cetacean. But a sudden thought crossed my mind. "A vessel!" I said, half aloud.

"Yes," replied the Canadian, "a disabled ship that has sunk perpendicularly."

Ned Land was right; we were close to a vessel of which the tattered shrouds still hung from their chains. The keel seemed to be in good order, and it had been wrecked at most some few hours. Three stumps of masts, broken off about two feet above the bridge, showed that the vessel had had to sacrifice its masts. But, lying on its side, it had filled, and it was heeling over to port. This skeleton of what it had once been was a sad spectacle as it lay lost under the waves; but sadder still was the sight of the bridge, where some corpses, bound with ropes, were still lying. I counted five—four men, one of whom was standing at the helm, and a woman standing by the poop holding an infant in her arms. She was quite young. I could distinguish her features, which the water had not decomposed, by the brilliant light from the *Nautilus*. In one despairing effort, she had raised her infant above her head, poor little thing, whose arms encircled its mother's neck. The attitude of the four sailors was frightful, distorted as they were by their convulsive movements, while making a last effort to free themselves from the cords that bound them to the vessel. The steersman alone, calm, with a grave, clear face, his gray hair glued to his forehead, and his hand clutching the wheel of the helm, seemed even then to be guiding the three broken masts through the depths of the ocean.

What a scene! We were dumb; our hearts beat fast before this shipwreck, taken as it were from life, and photographed in its last moments. And I saw already, coming toward it with hungry eyes, enormous sharks, attracted by the human flesh.

However, the *Nautilus,* turning, went round the submerged vessel, and in one instant I read on the stern—*The Florida, Sunderland.*

Vanikoro

This terrible spectacle was the forerunner of the series of maritime catastrophes that the *Nautilus* was destined to meet with in its route. As long as it went through more frequented waters, we often saw the hulls of shipwrecked vessels that were rotting in the depths, and, deeper down, cannons, bullets, anchors, chains, and a thousand other iron materials eaten up by rust. However, on the 11th of December, we sighted the Pomotou Islands, the old "dangerous group" of Bougainville, that extend over a space of 500 leagues at E.S.E. to W.N.W., from the Island Ducie to that of Lazareff. This group covers an area of 370 square leagues, and it is formed of sixty groups of islands, among which the Gambier group is remarkable, over which France exercises sway. These are coral islands, slowly raised, but continuous, created by the daily work of polypi. Then this new island will be joined later on to the neighboring groups, and a fifth continent will stretch from New Zealand and New Caledonia, and from thence to the Marquesas.

One day, when I was suggesting this theory to Captain Nemo, he replied coldly:

"The earth does not want new continents, but new men."

Chance had conducted the *Nautilus* toward the island of Clermont-Tonnerre, one of the most curious of the group that was discovered in 1822 by Captain Bell of the *Minerva.* I could study now the madreporal system, to which are due the islands in this ocean.

Madrepores (which must not be mistaken for corals) have a tissue lined with a calcareous crust, and the modifications of its structure have induced M. Milne-Edwards, my worthy master, to class them into five sections. The animalculæ that the marine polypus secretes live by millions at the bottom of their cells. Their calcareous deposits become rocks, reefs, and large and small islands. Here they form a ring, surrounding a little inland lake, that communicates with the sea by means of gaps. There they make barriers of reefs like those on the coast of New Caledonia and the various Pomotou islands. In other places, like those at Reunion and at Maurice, they raise fringed reefs, high, straight walls, near which the depth of the ocean is considerable.

Some cable-lengths off the shores of the island of Clermont, I admired the gigantic work accomplished by these microscopical workers. These walls are especially the work of those madrepores known as milleporas, porites, and astræas. These polypi are found particularly in the rough beds of the sea, near the surface; and consequently it is from the upper part that they begin their operations in which they bury themselves by degrees with the debris of the secretions that support them. Such is, at least, Darwin's theory, who thus explains the formation of the *atolls,* a superior theory (to my mind) to that given of the foundation of the madreporical works, summits of mountains or volcanoes, that are submerged some feet below the level of the sea.

I could observe closely these curious walls, for perpendicularly they were more than 300 yards deep, and our electric sheets lighted up this calcareous matter brilliantly. Replying to a question Conseil asked me as to the time these colossal barriers took to be raised, I astonished him much by telling him that learned men reckoned it about the eighth of an inch in a hundred years.

Toward evening Clermont-Tonnerre was lost in the distance, and the route of the *Nautilus* was sensibly changed. After having crossed the Tropic of Capricorn in 135° longitude, it sailed W.N.W., making again for the tropical zone. Although the summer sun was very strong, we did not suffer from heat, for at fifteen or twenty fathoms below the surface the temperature did not rise above from ten to twelve degrees.

On December 15, we left to the east the bewitching group of the Societies and the graceful Tahiti, queen of the Pacific. I saw in the morning, some miles to the windward, the elevated summits of the island. These waters furnished our table with excellent fish, mackerel, bonitos, and albicores, and some varieties of a sea-serpent called munirophis.

On the 25th of December the *Nautilus* sailed into the midst of the New Hebrides, discovered by Quiros in 1606, and that Bougainville explored in 1768, and to which Cook gave its present name in 1773. This group is composed principally of nine large islands, that form a band of 120 leagues N.N.E. to S.S.W., between 15° and 20° south latitude, and 164° and 168° longitude. We passed tolerably near to the island of Aurou, that at noon looked like a mass of green woods surmounted by a peak of great height.

That day being Christmas Day, Ned Land seemed to regret sorely the non-celebration of "Christmas," the family *fête* of which Protestants are so fond. I had not seen Captain Nemo for a week when, on the morning of the 27th, he came into the large drawing-room, always seeming as if he had seen you five minutes before. I was busily tracing the route of the *Nautilus* on the planisphere. The captain came up to me, put his finger on one spot on the chart, and said this single word:

"Vanikoro."

The effect was magical! It was the name of the islands on which La Perouse had been lost! I rose suddenly.

"The *Nautilus* has brought us to Vanikoro?" I asked.

"Yes, professor," said the captain.

"And I can visit the celebrated islands where the *Boussole* and the *Astrolabe* struck?"

"If you like, professor."

"When shall we be there?"

"We are there now."

Followed by Captain Nemo, I went up on to the platform, and greedily scanned the horizon.

To the N.E. two volcanic islands emerged, of unequal size, surrounded by a coral reef that measured forty miles in circumference.

We were close to Vanikoro, really the one to which Dumont d'Urville gave the name of Isle de la Récherché, and exactly facing the little harbor of Vanou, situated in 16° 4′ south latitude, and 164° 32′ east longitude. The earth seemed covered with verdure from the shore to the summits in the interior, that were crowned by Mount Kapogo, 476 feet high. The *Nautilus*, having passed the outer belt of rocks by a narrow strait, found itself among breakers where the sea was from thirty to forty fathoms deep. Under the verdant shade of some mangroves I perceived some savages, who appeared greatly surprised at our approach. In the long black body, moving between wind and water, did they not see some formidable cetacean that they regarded with suspicion?

Just then Captain Nemo asked me what I knew about the wreck of La Perouse.

"Only what everyone knows, captain," I replied.

"And could you tell me what everyone knows about it?" he inquired ironically.

"Easily."

I related to him all that the last works of Dumont d'Urville had made known—works from which the following is a brief account.

La Perouse, and his second, Captain de Langle, were sent by Louis XVI, in 1785, on a voyage of circumnavigation. They embarked in the corvettes the *Boussole* and the *Astrolabe,* neither of which were again heard of. In 1791 the French government, justly uneasy as to the fate of these two sloops, manned two large merchantmen, the *Récherché* and the *Esperance,* which left Brest the 28th of September, under the command of Bruni d'Entrecasteaux.

Two months after, they learned from Bowen, commander of the *Albemarle,* that the debris of shipwrecked vessels had been seen on the coasts of New Georgia. But D'Entrecasteaux, ignoring this communication—rather uncertain besides—directed his course toward the Admiralty Isles, mentioned in a report of Captain Hunter's as being the place where La Perouse was wrecked.

They sought in vain. The *Esperance* and the *Récherché* passed before Vanikoro without stopping there, and in fact this voyage was most disastrous, as it cost D'Entrecasteaux his life, and those of two of his lieutenants, besides several of his crew.

Captain Dillon, a shrewd old Pacific sailor, was the first to find unmistakable traces of the wrecks. On the 15th of May, 1824, his vessel, the *St. Patrick,* passed close to Tikopia, one of the New Hebrides. There a Lascar came alongside in a canoe, sold him the handle of a sword in silver, that bore the print of characters engraved on the hilt. The Lascar pretended that six years before, during a stay at Vanikoro, he had seen two Europeans that belonged to some vessels that had run aground on the reefs some years ago.

Dillon guessed that he meant La Perouse, whose disappearance had troubled the whole world. He tried to get on to Vanikoro, where according to the Lascar he would find numerous debris of the wreck, but winds and tide prevented him.

Dillon returned to Calcutta. There he interested the Asiatic Society and the Indian Company in his discovery. A vessel, to which was given the name of the *Récherché,* was put at his disposal, and he set out, January 23, 1827, accompanied by a French agent.

The *Récherché,* after touching at several points in the Pacific, cast anchor before Vanikoro, July 7, 1827, in this same harbor of Vanou where the *Nautilus* was at this time.

There it collected numerous relics of the wreck—iron utensils, anchors, pulley-strops, swivel-guns, an eighteen-pound shot, fragments of astronomical instruments, a piece of crown-work, and a bronze clock, bearing this inscription: *"Bazin m'a fait,"* the mark of the foundry of the arsenal at Brest about 1785. There could be no further doubt.

Dillon, having made all inquiries, stayed in the unlucky place till October. Then he quitted Vanikoro, and directed his course toward New Zealand; put into Calcutta, April 7, 1828, and returned to France, where he was warmly welcomed by Charles X.

But at the same time, without knowing Dillon's movements, Dumont d'Urville had already set out to find the scene of the wreck. And they had learned from a whaler that some medals and a cross of St. Louis had been found in the hands of some savages of Louisiade and New Caledonia. Dumont d'Urville, commander of the *Astrolabe,* had then sailed, and two months after Dillon had left Vanikoro, he put into Hobart Town. There he learned the results of Dillon's inquiries, and found that a certain James Hobbs, second lieutenant of the *Union,* of Calcutta, after landing on an island situated 8° 18′ south latitude, and 156° 30′ east longitude, had seen some iron bars and red stuffs used by the natives of these parts. Dumont d'Urville, much perplexed, and not knowing how to credit the reports of low-class journals, decided to follow Dillon's track.

On the 10th of February, 1828, the *Astrolabe* appeared off Tikopia, and D'Urville took as guide and interpreter a deserter found on the island; made his way to Vanikoro, sighted it on the 12th inst., lay among the reefs until the 14th, and not until the 20th did he cast anchor within the barrier in the harbor of Vanou.

On the 23d, several officers went round the island, and brought back some unimportant trifles. The natives, adopting a system of denials and evasions, refused to take them to the unlucky place. This ambiguous conduct led them to believe that the natives had ill-treated the castaways, and indeed they seemed to fear that Dumont d'Urville had come to avenge La Perouse and his unfortunate crew.

However, on the 26th, appeased by some presents, and understanding that they had no reprisals to fear, they led M. Jacquireot to the scene of the wreck.

There, in three or four fathoms of water, between the reefs of Pacou and Vanou, lay anchors, cannons, pigs of lead and iron, imbedded in the limy concretions. The large boat and the whaler belonging to the *Astrolabe* were sent to this place, and, not without some difficulty, their crews hauled up an anchor weighing 1,800 pounds, a brass gun, some pigs of iron, and two copper swivel-guns.

Dumont d'Urville, questioning the natives, learned, too, that La Perouse, after losing both his vessels on the reefs of this island, had constructed a smaller boat, only to be lost a second time. Where? No one knew.

But the French government, fearing that Dumont d'Urville was not acquainted with Dillon's movements, had sent the sloop *Bayonnaise*, commanded by Legoarant de Tromelin, to Vanikoro, which had been stationed on the west coast of America. The *Bayonnaise* cast her anchor before Vanikoro some months after the departure of the *Astrolabe*, but found no new document; but stated that the savages had respected the monument to La Perouse. That is the substance of what I told to Captain Nemo.

"So," he said, "no one knows now where the third vessel perished that was constructed by the castaways on the island of Vanikoro?"

"No one knows."

Captain Nemo said nothing, but signed to me to follow him into the large saloon. The *Nautilus* sank several yards below the waves, and the panels were opened.

I hastened to the aperture, and under the crustations of coral, covered with fungi, syphonules, alcyons, madrepores, through myriads of charming fish—girelles, glyphisidri, pompherides, diacopes, and holocentres—I recognized certain debris that the drags had not been able to tear up: iron stirrups, anchors, cannons, bullets, capstan-fittings, the stem of a ship—all objects clearly proving the wreck of some vessel, and now carpeted with living flowers.

While I was looking on this desolate scene, Captain Nemo said, in a sad voice:

"Commander La Perouse set out December 7, 1785, with his vessels *La*

Boussole and the *Astrolabe.* He first cast anchor at Botany Bay, visited the Friendly Isles, New Caledonia, then directed his course toward Santa Cruz, and put into Namouka, one of the Hapaï group. Then his vessel struck on the unknown reefs of Vanikoro. The *Boussole,* which went first, ran aground on the southerly coast. The *Astrolabe* went to its help, and ran aground too. The first vessel was destroyed almost immediately. The second, stranded under the wind, resisted some days. The natives made the castaways welcome. They installed themselves in the island, and constructed a smaller boat with the debris of the two large ones. Some sailors stayed willingly at Vanikoro; the others, weak and ill, set out with La Perouse. They directed their course toward the Solomon Isles, and there perished, with everything, on the westerly coast of the chief island of the group, between Capes Deception and Satisfaction."

"How do you know that?"

"By this, that I found on the spot where was the last wreck."

Captain Nemo showed me a tin-plate box, stamped with the French arms, and corroded by the salt water. He opened it, and I saw a bundle of papers, yellow but still readable.

They were the instructions of the naval minister to Commander La Perouse, annotated in the margin in Louis XVI's handwriting.

"Ah! it is a fine death for a sailor!" said Captain Nemo, at last. "A coral tomb makes a quiet grave; and I trust that I and my comrades will find no other."

Torres Straits

During the night of the 27th or 28th of December, the *Nautilus* left the shores of Vanikoro with great speed. Her course was southwesterly, and in three days she had gone over the 750 leagues that separated it from La Perouse's group and the southeast point of Papua.

Early on the 1st of January, 1863, Conseil joined me on the platform.

"Master, will you permit me to wish you a happy new year?"

"What! Conseil; exactly as if I was at Paris in my study at the Jardin des Plantes? Well, I accept your good wishes, and thank you for them. Only, I will ask you what you mean by a 'happy new year,' under our circumstances? Do you mean the year that will bring us to the end of our imprisonment, or the year that sees us continue this strange voyage?"

"Really, I do not know how to answer, master. We are sure to see curious things, and for the last two months we have not had time for *ennui*. The last marvel is always the most astonishing; and if we continue this progression, I do not know how it will end. It is my opinion that we shall never again see the like. I think, then, with no offense to master, that a happy year would be one in which we could see everything."

On January 2, we had made 11,340 miles, or 5,250 French leagues, since our starting-point in the Japan seas. Before the ship's head stretched the dangerous shores of the coral sea, on the northeast coast of Australia. Our boat lay along some miles from the redoubtable bank on which Cook's vessel was lost, June 10, 1770. The boat in which Cook was struck on a rock, and if it did not sink, it was owing to a piece of the coral that was broken by the shock, and fixed itself in the broken keel.

I had wished to visit the reef, 360 leagues long, against which the sea, always rough, broke with great violence, with a noise like thunder. But just then the inclined planes drew the *Nautilus* down to a great depth, and I could see nothing of the high coral walls. I had to content myself with the different specimens of fish brought up by the nets. I remarked, among others, some germons, a species of mackerel as large as a tunny, with bluish sides, and striped with transverse bands, that disappear with the animal's life. These fish followed us in shoals, and furnished us with very delicate food. We took also a large number of giltheads, about one and a half inches long, tasting like dorys; and flying pyrapeds like submarine swallows, which, in dark nights, light alternately the air and water with their phosphorescent light. Among the mollusks and zoöphytes, I found in the meshes of the net several species of alcyonarians, echini, hammers, spurs, dials, cerites, and hyalleæ. The flora was represented by beautiful floating seaweeds, laminariæ, and macrocystes, impregnated with the mucilage that transudes through their pores; and among which I gathered an admirable *Nemastoma Geliniarois*, that was classed among the natural curiosities of the museum.

Two days after crossing the coral sea, January 4, we sighted the Papuan coasts. On this occasion, Captain Nemo informed me that his intention was to get into the Indian Ocean by the Strait of Torres. His communication ended there.

The Torres Straits are nearly thirty-four leagues wide; but they are obstructed by an innumerable quantity of islands, islets, breakers, and rocks, that make its navigation almost impracticable; so that Captain Nemo took all needful precautions to cross them. The *Nautilus*, floating betwixt wind and water, went at a moderate pace. Her screw, like a cetacean's tail, beat the waves slowly.

Profiting by this, I and my two companions went up on to the deserted platform. Before us was the steersman's cage, and I expected that Captain Nemo was there directing the course of the *Nautilus*. I had before me the excellent charts of the Strait of Torres, made out by the hydrographical engineer Vincendon Dumoulin. These and Captain King's are the best charts that clear the intricacies of this strait, and I consulted them attentively. Round the *Nautilus* the sea dashed furiously. The course of the waves, that went from southeast to northwest at the rate of two and a half miles, broke on the coral that showed itself here and there.

"This is a bad sea!" remarked Ned Land.

"Detestable indeed, and one that does not suit a boat like the *Nautilus*."

"The captain must be very sure of his route, for I see there pieces of coral that would do for its keel if it only touched them slightly."

Indeed the situation was dangerous, but the *Nautilus* seemed to slide like magic off these rocks. It did not follow the routes of the *Astrolabe* and the *Boussole* exactly, for they proved fatal to Dumont d'Urville. It bore more northward, coasted the island of Murray, and came back to the southwest toward Cumberland Passage. I thought it was going to pass it by, when, going back to northwest, it went through a large quantity of islands and islets little known, toward the Island Sound and Canal Mauvais.

I wondered if Captain Nemo, foolishly imprudent, would steer his vessel into that pass where Dumont d'Urville's two corvettes touched; when, swerving again, and cutting straight through to the west, he steered for the island of Gilboa.

It was then three in the afternoon. The tide began to recede, being quite full. The *Nautilus* approached the island, that I still saw, with its remarkable border of screw-pines. He stood off it at about two miles distant. Suddenly a shock overthrew me. The *Nautilus* just touched a rock, and stayed immovable, laying lightly to port side.

When I rose, I perceived Captain Nemo and his lieutenant on the platform. They were examining the situation of the vessel, and exchanging words in their incomprehensible dialect.

She was situated thus: two miles, on the starboard side, appeared Gilboa, stretching from north to west like an immense arm; toward the south and east some coral showed itself, left by the ebb. We had run aground, and in one of those seas where the tides are middling—a sorry matter for the floating of the *Nautilus*. However, the vessel had not suffered, for her keel was solidly joined. But if she could neither glide off nor move, she ran the risk of being forever fastened to these rocks, and then Captain Nemo's submarine vessel would be done for.

I was reflecting thus, when the captain, cool and calm, always master of himself, approached me.

"An accident?" I asked.

"No; an incident."

"But an incident that will oblige you perhaps to become an inhabitant of this land from which you flee?"

Captain Nemo looked at me curiously, and made a negative gesture, as much as to say that nothing would force him to set foot on *terra firma* again. Then he said:

"Besides, M. Aronnax, the *Nautilus* is not lost; it will carry you yet into the midst of the marvels of the ocean. Our voyage is only begun, and I do not wish to be deprived so soon of the honor of your company."

"However, Captain Nemo," I replied, without noticing the ironical turn of his phrase, "the *Nautilus* ran aground in open sea. Now the tides are not strong in the Pacific; and if you cannot lighten the *Nautilus*, I do not see how it will be reinflated."

"The tides are not strong in the Pacific: you are right there, professor; but in Torres Straits, one finds still a difference of a yard and a half between the level of high and low seas. To-day is January 4, and in five days the moon will be full. Now, I shall be very much astonished if that complaisant satellite does not raise these masses of water sufficiently, and render me a service that I should be indebted to her for."

Having said this Captain Nemo, followed by his lieutenant, redescended to the interior of the *Nautilus*. As to the vessel, it moved not, and was immovable, as if the coralline polypi had already walled it up with their indestructible cement.

"Well, sir?" said Ned Land, who came up to me after the departure of the captain.

"Well, friend Ned, we will wait patiently for the tide on the 9th instant; for it appears that the moon will have the goodness to put it off again."

"Really?"

"Really."

"And this captain is not going to cast anchor at all, since the tide will suffice?" said Conseil simply.

The Canadian looked at Conseil, then shrugged his shoulders.

"Sir, you may believe me when I tell you that this piece of iron will navigate neither on nor under the sea again; it is only fit to be sold for its weight. I think, therefore, that the time has come to part company with Captain Nemo."

"Friend Ned; I do not despair of this stout *Nautilus,* as you do; and in four days we shall know what to hold to on the Pacific tides. Besides, flight might be possible if we were in sight of the English or Provençal coasts; but on the Papuan shores, it is another thing; and it will be time enough to come to that extremity if the *Nautilus* does not recover itself again, which I look upon as a grave event."

"But do they know, at least, how to act circumspectly? There is an island; on that island there are trees; under those trees, terrestrial animals, bearers of cutlets and roast-beef, to which I would willingly give a trial."

"In this, friend Ned is right," said Conseil, "and I agree with him. Could not master obtain permission from his friend Captain Nemo to put us on land, if only so as not to lose the habit of treading on the solid parts of our planet?"

"I can ask him, but he will refuse."

"Will master risk it?" asked Conseil. "And we shall know how to rely upon the captain's amiability."

To my great surprise Captain Nemo gave me the permission I asked for, and he gave it very agreeably, without even exacting from me a promise to return to the vessel; but flight across New Guinea might be very perilous, and I should not have counseled Ned Land to attempt it. Better to be a prisoner on board the *Nautilus* than to fall into the hands of the natives.

At eight o'clock, armed with guns and hatchets, we got off the *Nautilus.* The sea was pretty calm; a slight breeze blew on land. Conseil and I rowing, we sped along quickly, and Ned steered in the straight passage that the breakers left between them. The boat was well handled, and moved rapidly.

Ned Land could not restrain his joy. He was like a prisoner that had escaped from prison, and knew not that it was necessary to re-enter it.

"Meat! We are going to eat some meat; and what meat!" he replied. "Real game! No, bread, indeed. I do not say that fish is not good; we must not abuse it; but a piece of fresh venison grilled on live coals will agreeably vary our ordinary course."

"Gourmand!" said Conseil. "He makes my mouth water."

"It remains to be seen," I said, "if these forests are full of game, and if the game is not such as will hunt the hunter himself."

"Well said, M. Aronnax," replied the Canadian, whose teeth seemed sharpened like the edge of a hatchet; "but I will eat tiger—loin of tiger—if there is no other quadruped on this island."

"Friend Ned is uneasy about it," said Conseil.

"Whatever it may be," continued Ned Land, "every animal with four paws without feathers, or with two paws with feathers, will be saluted by my first shot."

"Very well! Master Land's imprudences are beginning."

"Never fear, M. Aronnax," replied the Canadian; "I do not want twenty-five minutes to offer you a dish of my sort."

At half-past eight the *Nautilus'* boat ran softly aground, on a heavy sand, after having happily passed the coral reef that surrounds the island of Gilboa.

A Few Days on Land

I was much impressed on touching land. Ned Land tried the soil with his feet, as if to take possession of it. However, it was only two months before that we had become, according to Captain Nemo, "passengers on board the *Nautilus,*" but, in reality, prisoners of its commander.

In a few minutes we were within musket-shot of the coast. The soil was almost entirely madreporical, but certain beds of dried-up torrents strewn with debris of granite showed that this island was of the primary formation. The whole horizon was hidden behind a beautiful curtain of forests. Enormous trees, the trunks of which attained a height of 200 feet, were tied to each other by garlands of bindweed, real natural hammocks, which a light breeze rocked. They were mimosas, ficuses, casuarinæ, teks, hibisci, and palm trees, mingled together in profusion; and under the shelter of their verdant vault grew orchids, leguminous plants, and ferns.

But without noticing all these beautiful specimens of Papuan flora, the

Canadian abandoned the agreeable for the useful. He discovered a cocoa-tree, beat down some of the fruit, broke them, and we drank the milk and ate the nut with a satisfaction that protested against the ordinary food on the *Nautilus*.

"Excellent!" said Ned Land.

"Exquisite!" replied Conseil.

"And I do not think," said the Canadian, "that he would object to our introducing a cargo of cocoanuts on board."

"I do not think he would, but he would not taste them."

"So much the worse for him," said Conseil.

"And so much the better for us," replied Ned Land. "There will be more for us."

"One word only, Master Land," I said to the harpooner, who was beginning to ravage another cocoanut-tree. "Cocoanuts are good things, but before filling the canoe with them, it would be wise to reconnoiter and see if the island does not produce some substance not less useful. Fresh vegetables would be welcome on board the *Nautilus*."

"Master is right," replied Conseil; "and I propose to reserve three places in our vessel: one for fruits, the other for vegetables, and the third for the venison, of which I have not yet seen the smallest specimen."

"Conseil, we must not despair," said the Canadian.

"Let us continue," I returned, "and lie in wait. Although the island seems uninhabited, it might still contain some individuals that would be less hard than we on the nature of game."

"Ho! ho!" said Ned Land, moving his jaws significantly.

"Well, Ned!" cried Conseil.

"My word!" returned the Canadian, "I begin to understand the charms of anthropophagy."

"Ned! Ned! What are you saying? You, a man-eater? I should not feel safe with you, especially as I share your cabin. I might perhaps wake one day to find myself half-devoured."

"Friend Conseil, I like you much, but not enough to eat you unnecessarily."

"I would not trust you," replied Conseil. "But enough. We must absolutely bring down some game to satisfy this cannibal, or else, one of these fine mornings, master will find only pieces of his servant to serve him."

While we were talking thus, we were penetrating the somber arches of the forest, and for two hours we surveyed it in all directions.

Chance rewarded our search for eatable vegetables, and one of the most useful products of the tropical zones furnished us with precious food that we missed on board. I would speak of the bread-fruit tree, very abundant in the island of Gilboa; and I remarked chiefly the variety destitute of seeds, which bears in Malaya the name of "rima."

Ned Land knew these fruits well. He had already eaten many during his numerous voyages, and he knew how to prepare the eatable substance. Moreover, the sight of them excited him, and he could contain himself no longer.

"Master," he said, "I shall die if I do not taste a little of this bread-fruit pie."

"Taste it, friend Ned, taste it as you want. We are here to make experiments—make them."

"It won't take long," said the Canadian.

And provided with a lentil, he lighted a fire of dead wood, that crackled joyously. During this time, Conseil and I chose the best fruits of the artocarpus. Some had not then attained a sufficient degree of maturity, and their thick skin covered a white but rather fibrous pulp. Others, the greater number yellow and gelatinous, waited only to be picked.

These fruits inclose no kernel. Conseil brought a dozen to Ned Land, who placed them on a coal fire, after having cut them in thick slices, and while doing this repeating:

"You will see, master, how good this bread is. More so when one has been deprived of it so long. It is not even bread," added he, "but a delicate pastry. You have eaten none, master?"

"No, Ned."

"Very well, prepare yourself for a juicy thing. If you do not come for more, I am no longer the king of harpooners."

After some minutes, the part of the fruits that was exposed to the fire was completely roasted. The interior looked like a white pastry, a sort of soft crumb, the flavor of which was like that of an artichoke.

It must be confessed this bread was excellent, and I ate of it with great relish.

"What time is it now?" asked the Canadian.

"Two o'clock at least," replied Conseil.

"How time flies on firm ground!" sighed Ned Land.

"Let us be off," replied Conseil.

We returned through the forest, and completed our collection by a raid upon the cabbage-palms, that we gathered from the tops of the trees, little beans that I recognized as the "abrou" of the Malays, and yams of a superior quality.

We were loaded when we reached the boat. But Ned Land did not find his provision sufficient. Fate, however, favored us. Just as we were pushing off, he perceived several trees, from twenty-five to thirty feet high, a species of palm tree. These trees, as valuable as the artocarpus, justly are reckoned among the most useful products of Malaya.

At last, at five o'clock in the evening, loaded with our riches, we quitted the shore, and half an hour after we hailed the *Nautilus*. No one appeared on our arrival. The enormous iron-plated cylinder seemed deserted. The provisions embarked, I descended to my chamber, and after supper slept soundly.

The next day, January 6, nothing new on board. Not a sound inside, not a sign of life. The boat rested along the edge, in the same place in which we had left it. We resolved to return to the island. Ned Land hoped to be more fortunate than on the day before with regard to the hunt, and wished to visit another part of the forest.

At dawn we set off. The boat, carried on by the waves that flowed to shore, reached the island in a few minutes.

We landed, and thinking that it was better to give in to the Canadian, we followed Ned Land, whose long limbs threatened to distance us. He wound up the coast toward the west; then, fording some torrents, he gained the high plain that was bordered with admirable forests. Some kingfishers were rambling along the water-courses, but they would not let themselves be approached. Their circumspection proved to me that these birds knew what to expect from bipeds of our species, and I concluded that, if the island was not inhabited, at least human beings occasionally frequented it.

After crossing a rather large prairie, we arrived at the skirts of a little wood that was enlivened by the songs and flight of a large number of birds.

"There are only birds!" said Conseil.

"But they are eatable," replied the harpooner.

"I do not agree with you, friend Ned, for I see only parrots there."

"Friend Conseil," said Ned gravely, "the parrot is like pheasant to those who have nothing else."

"And," I added, "this bird, suitably prepared, is worth knife and fork."

Indeed, under the thick foliage of this wood, a world of parrots were flying from branch to branch, only needing a careful education to speak the human language. For the moment, they were chattering with parrots of all colors, and grave cockatoos, who seemed to meditate upon some philosophical problem, while brilliant red lories passed like a piece of bunting carried away by the breeze; Papuans, with the finest azure colors, and in all a variety of winged things most charming to behold, but few eatable.

However, a bird peculiar to these lands, and which has never passed the limits of the Arrow and Papuan islands, was wanting in this collection. But fortune reserved it for me before long.

After passing through a moderately thick copse, we found a plain obstructed with bushes. I saw then those magnificent birds, the disposition of whose long feathers obliges them to fly against the wind. Their undulating flight, graceful aërial curves, and the shading of their colors, attracted and charmed one's looks. I had no trouble in recognizing them.

"Birds of paradise!" I exclaimed.

The Malays, who carry on a great trade in these birds with the Chinese, have several means that we could not employ for taking them. Sometimes they put snares at the top of high trees that the birds of paradise prefer to frequent. Sometimes they catch them with a viscous birdlime that paralyzes their movements. They even go so far as to poison the fountain that the birds generally drink from. But we were obliged to fire at them during flight, which gave us few chances to bring them down; and indeed, we vainly exhausted one-half of our ammunition.

About eleven o'clock in the morning, the first range of mountains that form the center of the island was traversed, and we had killed nothing. Hunger drove us on. The hunters had relied on the products of the chase, and they were wrong. Happily Conseil, to his great surprise, made a double shot and secured breakfast. He brought down a white pigeon and a wood-pigeon, which, cleverly plucked and suspended from a skewer, were roasted before a red fire of dead wood. While those interesting birds were cooking, Ned prepared the fruit of the artocarpus. Then the wood-pigeons were devoured to the bones, and declared excellent. The nutmeg, with which they are in the habit of stuffing their crops, flavors their flesh and renders it delicious eating.

"Now, Ned, what do you miss now?"

"Some four-footed game, M. Aronnax. All these pigeons are only side-dishes and trifles; and until I have killed an animal with cutlets, I shall not be content."

"Nor I, Ned, if I do not catch a bird of paradise."

"Let us continue hunting," replied Conseil. "Let us go toward the sea. We have arrived at the first declivities of the mountains, and I think we had better regain the region of forests."

That was sensible advice, and was followed out. After walking for one hour, we had attained a forest of sago trees. Some inoffensive serpents glided away from us. The birds of paradise fled at our approach, and truly I despaired of getting near one, when Conseil, who was walking in front, suddenly bent down, uttered a triumphal cry, and came back to me bringing a magnificent specimen.

"Ah! bravo, Conseil!"

"Master is very good."

"No, my boy; you have made an excellent stroke. Take one of these living birds, and carry it in your hand."

"If master will examine it, he will see that I have not deserved great merit."

"Why, Conseil?"

"Because this bird is as drunk as a quail."

"Drunk!"

"Yes, sir; drunk with the nutmegs that it devoured under the nutmeg-tree under which I found it. See, friend Ned, see the monstrous effects of intemperance!"

"By Jove!" exclaimed the Canadian. "Because I have drunk gin for two months, you must needs reproach me!"

However, I examined the curious bird. Conseil was right. The bird, drunk with the juice, was quite powerless. It could not fly; it could hardly walk.

This bird belonged to the most beautiful of the eight species that are found in Papua and in the neighboring islands. It was the "large emerald bird, the most rare kind." It measured three feet in length. Its head was comparatively small, its eyes placed near the opening of the beak, and also small. But the shades of color were beautiful, having a yellow beak, brown feet and claws, nut-colored wings with purple tips, pale yellow at the back of the neck and head, and emerald color at the throat, chestnut on the breast and belly. Two horned downy nets rose from below the tail, that prolonged the long light feathers of admirable fineness, and they completed the whole of this marvelous bird, that the natives have poetically named the "bird of the sun."

But if my wishes were satisfied by the possession of the bird of paradise, the Canadian's were not yet. Happily about two o'clock Ned Land brought down a magnificent hog, from the brood of those the natives call "bari-outang." The animal came in time for us to procure real quadruped meat, and he was well received. Ned Land was very proud of his shot. The hog, hit by the electric ball, fell stone dead. The Canadian skinned and cleaned it properly, after having taken half a dozen cutlets, destined to furnish us with a grilled repast in the evening. Then the hunt was resumed, which was still more marked by Ned and Conseil's exploits.

Indeed, the two friends, beating the bushes, roused a herd of kangaroos, that fled and bounded along on their elastic paws. But these animals did not take flight so rapidly but what the electric capsule could stop their course.

"Ah, professor!" cried Ned Land, who was carried away by the delights of the chase. "What excellent game! and stewed too! What a supply for the *Nautilus!* two! three! five down! And to think that we shall eat that flesh, and that the idiots on board shall not have a crumb!"

I think that, in the excess of his joy, the Canadian, if he had not talked so much, would have killed them all. But he contented himself with a single dozen of these interesting marsupians. These animals were small. They were a species of those "kangaroo rabbits" that live habitually in the hollows of trees, and whose speed is extreme; but they are moderately fat, and furnish, at least, estimable food. We were very satisfied with the results of the hunt. Happy Ned proposed to return to this enchanting island the next day, for he wished to depopulate it of all the eatable quadrupeds. But he reckoned without his host.

At six o'clock in the evening we had regained the shore; our boat was moored to the usual place. The *Nautilus*, like a long rock, emerged from the waves two miles from the beach. Ned Land, without waiting, occupied himself about the important dinner business. He understood all about cooking well. The "bari-outang," grilled on the coals, soon scented the air with a delicious odor.

Indeed, the dinner was excellent. Two wood-pigeons completed this extraordinary *menu*. The sago pasty, the artocarpus bread, some mangoes, half a dozen pineapples, and the liquor fermented from some cocoanuts, overjoyed us. I even think that my worthy companions' ideas had not all the plainness desirable.

"Suppose we do not return to the *Nautilus* this evening?" said Conseil.

"Suppose we never return?" added Ned Land.

Just then a stone fell at our feet, and cut short the harpooner's proposition.

Captain Nemo's Thunderbolt

We looked at the edge of the forest without rising, my hand stopping in the action of putting it to my mouth, Ned Land's completing its office.

"Stones do not fall from the sky," remarked Conseil, "or they would merit the name of aërolites."

A second stone, carefully aimed, that made a savory pigeon's leg fall from Conseil's hand, gave still more weight to his observation. We all three arose, shouldered our guns, and were ready to reply to any attack.

"Are they apes?" cried Ned Land.

"Very nearly—they are savages."

"To the boat!" I said, hurrying to the sea.

It was indeed necessary to beat a retreat, for about twenty natives, armed with bows and slings, appeared on the skirts of a copse that masked the horizon to the right, hardly a hundred steps from us.

Our boat was moored about sixty feet from us. The savages approached us, not running, but making hostile demonstrations. Stones and arrows fell thickly.

Ned Land had not wished to leave his provisions; and, in spite of his imminent danger, his pig on one side, and kangaroos on the other, he went tolerably fast. In two minutes we were on the shore. To load the boat with provisions and arms, to push it out to sea, and ship the oars, was the work of an instant. We had not gone two cables' lengths when a hundred savages, howling and gesticulating, entered the water up to their waists. I watched to see if their apparition would attract some men from the *Nautilus* on to the platform. But no. The enormous machine, lying off, was absolutely deserted.

Twenty minutes later we were on board. The panels were open. After making the boat fast, we entered into the interior of the *Nautilus*.

I descended to the drawing-room, from whence I heard some chords.

Captain Nemo was there, bending over his organ, and plunged in a musical ecstasy.

"Captain!"

He did not hear me.

"Captain!" I said again, touching his hand.

He shuddered, and, turning round, said: "Ah! it is you, professor? Well, have you had a good hunt? Have you botanized successfully?"

"Yes, captain; but we have unfortunately brought a troop of bipeds, whose vicinity troubles me."

"What bipeds?"

"Savages."

"Savages!" he echoed ironically. "So you are astonished, professor, at having set foot on a strange land and finding savages? Savages! Where are there not any? Besides, are they worse than others, these whom you call savages?"

"But, captain——"

"How many have you counted?"

"A hundred at least."

"M. Aronnax," replied Captain Nemo, placing his fingers on the organ stops, "when all the natives of Papua are assembled on this shore, the *Nautilus* will have nothing to fear from their attacks."

The captain's fingers were then running over the keys of the instrument, and I remarked that he touched only the black keys, which gave to his melodies an essentially Scotch character. Soon he had forgotten my presence, and had plunged into a reverie that I did not disturb. I went up again on to the platform—night had already fallen; for, in this low latitude, the sun sets rapidly and without twilight. I could only see the island indistinctly; but the numerous fires lighted on the beach showed that the natives did not think of leaving it. I was alone for several hours, sometimes thinking of the natives—but without any dread of them, for the imperturbable confidence of the captain was catching—sometimes forgetting them to admire the splendors of the night in the tropics. My remembrances went to France, in the train of those zodiacal stars that would shine in some hours' time. The moon shone in the midst of the constellations of the zenith.

The night slipped away without any mischance, the islanders frightened, no doubt, at the sight of a monster aground in the bay. The panels were open, and would have offered an easy access to the interior of the *Nautilus*.

At six o'clock in the morning of the 8th of January, I went up on to the platform. The dawn was breaking. The island soon showed itself through the dissipating fogs—first the shore, then the summits.

The natives were there, more numerous than on the day before—500 or 600 perhaps—some of them, profiting by the low water, had come on to the coral, at less than two cables' lengths from the *Nautilus*. I distinguished them easily; they were true Papuans, with athletic figures; men of good race, large high foreheads—large, but not broad, and flat—and white teeth. Their woolly hair, with a reddish tinge, showed off on their black, shining bodies like those of the Nubians. From the lobes of their ears, cut and distended, hung chaplets of bones. Most of these savages were naked. Among them I remarked some women dressed from the hips to the knees in quite a crinoline of herbs, that sustained a vegetable waistband. Some chiefs had ornamented their necks with a crescent and collars of glass beads, red and white; nearly all were armed with bows, arrows, and shields, and carried on their shoulders a sort of net containing those round stones which they cast from their slings with great skill. One of these chiefs, rather near to the *Nautilus*, examined it attentively. He was, perhaps, a "mado" of high rank, for he was draped in a mat of banana leaves notched round the edges, and set off with brilliant colors.

I could easily have knocked down this native, who was within a short length; but I thought that it was better to wait for real hostile demonstrations. Between Europeans and savages, it is proper for the Europeans to parry sharply, not to attack.

During low water the natives roamed about near the *Nautilus*, but were not troublesome; I heard them frequently repeat the word "Assai," and by their gestures I understood that they invited me to go on land, an invitation that I declined.

So that, on that day, the boat did not push off, to the great displeasure of Master Land, who could not complete his provisions.

This adroit Canadian employed his time in preparing the viands and meat that he had brought off the island. As for the savages, they returned to the shore about eleven o'clock in the morning, as soon as the coral tops began to disappear under the rising tide; but I saw their numbers had increased considerably on the shore. Probably they came from the neighboring islands, or very likely from Papua. However, I had not seen a single native canoe. Having nothing better to do, I thought of dragging these beautiful limpid waters, under which I saw a profusion of shells, zoöphytes, and marine plants. Moreover, it was the last day that the *Nautilus* would pass in these parts, if it float in open sea the next day, according to Captain Nemo's promise.

I therefore called Conseil, who brought me a little light drag, very like those for the oyster fishery. Now to work! For two hours we fished unceasingly, but without bringing up any rarities. The drag was filled with midas-ears, harps, melames, and particularly the most beautiful hammers I have ever seen. We also brought up some holothurias, pearl oysters, and a dozen little turtles, that were reserved for the pantry on board.

But just when I expected it least, I put my hand on a wonder, I might say a natural deformity, very rarely met with. Conseil was just dragging, and his net came up filled with divers ordinary shells, when, all at once, he saw me plunge my arm quickly into the net, to draw out a shell, and heard me utter a conchological cry, that is to say, the most piercing cry that human throat can utter.

"What is the matter, sir?" he asked, in surprise. "Has master been bitten?"

"No, my boy; but I would willingly have given a finger for my discovery."

"What discovery?"

"This shell," I said, holding up the object of my triumph.

"It is simply an olive porphyry, genus olive, order of the pectinibranchidæ, class of gasteropods, sub-class of molluska."

"Yes, Conseil; but instead of being rolled from right to left, this olive turns from left to right."

"Is it possible?"

"Yes, my boy; it is a left shell."

Shells are all right-handed, with rare exceptions; and when by chance their spiral is left, amateurs are ready to pay their weight in gold.

Conseil and I were absorbed in the contemplation of our treasure, and I was promising myself to enrich the museum with it, when a stone, unfortunately thrown by a native, struck against and broke the precious object in Conseil's hand. I uttered a cry of despair! Conseil took up his gun, and aimed at a savage who was poising his sling at ten yards from him. I would have stopped him, but his blow took effect, and broke the bracelet of amulets which encircled the arm of the savage.

"Conseil!" cried I; "Conseil!"

"Well, sir! do you not see that the cannibal has commenced the attack?"

"A shell is not worth the life of a man," said I.

"Ah! the scoundrel!" cried Conseil; "I would rather he had broken my shoulder!"

Conseil was in earnest, but I was not of his opinion. However, the situation had changed some minutes before, and we had not perceived. A score of canoes surrounded the *Nautilus*. These canoes, scooped out of the trunk of a tree, long, narrow, well adapted for speed, were balanced by means of a long bamboo pole, which floated on the water. They were managed by skillful, half-naked paddlers, and I watched their advance with some uneasiness. It was evident that these Papuans had already had dealings with the Europeans, and knew their ships. But this long iron cylinder anchored in the bay, without masts or chimney, what could they think of it? Nothing good, for at first they kept at a respectful distance. However, seeing it motionless, by degrees they took courage, and sought to familiarize themselves with it. Now this familiarity was precisely what it was necessary to avoid. Our arms, which were noiseless, could only produce a moderate effect on the savages, who have little respect for aught but blustering things. The thunderbolt without the reverberations of thunder would frighten man but little, though the danger lies in the lightning, not in the noise.

At this moment the canoes approached the *Nautilus*, and a shower of arrows alighted on her.

I went down to the saloon, but found no one there. I ventured to knock at the door that opened into the captain's room. "Come in," was the answer.

I entered, and found Captain Nemo deep in algebraical calculations of x and other quantities.

"I am disturbing you," said I, for courtesy's sake.

"That is true, M. Aronnax," replied the captain; "but I think you have serious reasons for wishing to see me?"

"Very grave ones; the natives are surrounding us in their canoes, and in a few minutes we shall certainly be attacked by many hundreds of savages."

"Ah!" said Captain Nemo quietly. "They are come with their canoes?"

"Yes, sir."

"Well, sir, we must close the hatches."

"Exactly, and I came to say to you—"

"Nothing can be more simple," said Captain Nemo. And pressing an electric button, he transmitted an order to the ship's crew.

"It is all done, sir," said he, after some moments. "The pinnace is ready, and the hatches are closed. You do not fear, I imagine, that these gentlemen could stave in walls on which the balls of your frigate have had no effect?"

"No, captain; but a danger still exists."

"What is that, sir?"

"It is that to-morrow, at about this hour, we must open the hatches to renew the air of the *Nautilus*. Now if, at this moment, the Papuans should occupy the platform, I do not see how you could prevent them from entering."

"Then, sir, you suppose that they will board us?"

"I am certain of it."

"Well, sir, let them come. I see no reason for hindering them. After all, these Papuans are poor creatures, and I am unwilling that my visit to the island of Gueberoan should cost the life of a single one of these wretches."

Upon that I was going away; but Captain Nemo detained me, and asked me to sit down by him. He questioned me with interest about our excursions on shore, and our hunting, and seemed not to understand the craving for meat that possessed the Canadian. Then the conversation turned on various subjects, and without being more communicative, Captain Nemo showed himself more amiable.

Among other things, we happened to speak of the situation of the *Nautilus,* run aground in exactly the same spot in this strait where Dumont d'Urville was nearly lost. Apropos of this:

"This D'Urville was one of your great sailors," said the captain to me; "one of your most intelligent navigators. He is the Captain Cook of you Frenchmen. Unfortunate man of science, after having braved the icebergs of the South Pole, the coral reefs of Oceania, the cannibals of the Pacific, to perish miserably in a railway train! If this energetic man could have reflected during the last moments of his life, what must have been uppermost in his last thoughts, do you suppose?"

So speaking, Captain Nemo seemed moved, and his emotion gave me a better opinion of him. Then, chart in hand, we reviewed the travels of the French navigator, his voyages of circumnavigation, his double detention at the South Pole, which led to the discovery of Adelaide and Louis Philippe, and fixing the hydrographical bearings of the principal islands of Oceania.

"That which your D'Urville has done on the surface of the seas," said Captain Nemo, "that have I done under them, and more easily, more completely than he. The *Astrolabe* and the *Boussole,* incessantly tossed about by the hurricanes, could not be worth the *Nautilus,* quiet repository of labor that she is, truly motionless in the midst of the waters."

"To-morrow," added the captain, rising, "to-morrow, at twenty minutes to three P.M., the *Nautilus* shall float, and leave the Strait of Torres uninjured."

Having curtly pronounced these words, Captain Nemo bowed slightly. This was to dismiss me, and I went back to my room.

There I found Conseil, who wished to know the result of my interview with the captain.

"My boy," said I, "when I feigned to believe that his *Nautilus* was threatened by the natives of Papua, the captain answered me very sarcastically. I have but one thing to say to you: Have confidence in him, and go to sleep in peace."

"Have you no need of my services, sir?"

"No, my friend. What is Ned Land doing?"

"If you will excuse me, sir," answered Conseil, "friend Ned is busy making a kangaroo-pie, which will be a marvel."

I remained alone, and went to bed, but slept indifferently. I heard the noise of the savages, who stamped on the platform, uttering deafening cries. The night passed thus, without disturbing the ordinary repose of the crew. The presence of these cannibals affected them no more than the soldiers of a masked battery care for the ants that crawl over its front.

At six in the morning I rose. The hatches had not been opened. The inner air was not renewed, but the reservoirs, filled ready for any emergency, were now resorted to, and discharged several cubic feet of oxygen into the exhausted atmosphere of the *Nautilus*.

I worked in my room till noon, without having seen Captain Nemo, even for an instant. On board no preparations for departure were visible. I waited still some time, then went into the large saloon. The clock marked half-past two. In ten minutes it would be high tide, and if Captain Nemo had not made a rash promise, the *Nautilus* would be immediately detached. If not, many months would pass ere she could leave her bed of coral.

However, some warning vibrations began to be felt in the vessel. I heard the keel grating against the rough, calcareous bottom of the coral reef.

At five-and-twenty minutes to three, Captain Nemo appeared in the saloon.

"We are going to start," said he.

"Ah!" replied I.

"I have given the order to open the hatches."

"And the Papuans?"

"The Papuans?" answered Captain Nemo, slightly shrugging his shoulders.

"Will they not come inside the *Nautilus?*"

"How?"

"Only by leaping over the hatches you have opened."

"M. Aronnax," quietly answered Captain Nemo, "they will not enter the hatches of the *Nautilus* in that way, even if they were open."

I looked at the captain.

"You do not understand?" said he.

"Hardly."

"Well, come and you will see."

I directed my steps toward the central staircase. There Ned Land and Conseil were slyly watching some of the ship's crew, who were opening the hatches, while cries of rage and fearful vociferations resounded outside.

The port lids were pulled down outside. Twenty horrible faces appeared. But the first native who placed his hand on the stair-rail, struck from behind by some invisible force, I know not what, fled, uttering the most fearful cries, and making the wildest contortions.

Ten of his companions followed him. They met with the same fate.

Conseil was in ecstasy. Ned Land, carried away by his violent instincts, rushed on to the staircase. But the moment he seized the rail with both hands, he, in his turn, was overthrown.

"I am struck by a thunderbolt," cried he, with an oath.

This explained all. It was no rail, but a metallic cable, charged with electricity from the deck, communicating with the platform. Whoever touched it felt a powerful shock—and this shock would have been mortal, if Captain Nemo had discharged into the conductor the whole force of the current. It might truly be said that between his assailants and himself he had stretched a network of electricity which none could pass with impunity.

Meanwhile, the exasperated Papuans had beaten a retreat, paralyzed with terror. As for us, half-laughing, we consoled and rubbed the unfortunate Ned Land, who swore like one possessed.

But, at this moment, the *Nautilus,* raised by the last waves of the tide, quitted her coral bed exactly at the fortieth minute fixed by the captain. Her screw swept the waters slowly and majestically. Her speed increased gradually, and sailing on the surface of the ocean, she quitted safe and sound the dangerous passes of the Straits of Torres.

"Ægri Somnia"

The following day, 10th of January, the *Nautilus* continued her course between two seas, but with such remarkable speed that I could not estimate it at less than thirty-five miles an hour. The rapidity of her screw was such that I could neither follow nor count its evolutions. When I reflected that this marvelous electric agent, after having afforded motion, heat, and light to the *Nautilus,* still protected her from outward attack, and transformed her into an ark of safety which no profane hand might touch without being thunderstricken, my admiration was unbounded, and from the structure it extended to the engineer who had called it into existence.

Our course was directed to the west, and on the 11th of January we doubled Cape Wessel, situated in 135° longitude and 10° north latitude, which forms the east point of the Gulf of Carpentaria. The reefs were still numerous, but more equalized, and marked on the chart with extreme precision. The *Nautilus* easily avoided the breakers of Money to port, and the Victoria reefs to starboard, placed at 130° longitude, and on the tenth parallel which we strictly followed.

On the 13th of January, Captain Nemo arrived in the Sea of Timor, and recognized the island of that name in 122° longitude.

From this point the direction of the *Nautilus* inclined toward the southwest. Her head was set for the Indian Ocean. Where would the fancy of Captain Nemo carry us next? Would he return to the coast of Asia, or would he approach again the shores of Europe? Improbable conjectures both, for a man who fled from inhabited continents. Then, would he descend to the south? Was he going to double the Cape of Good Hope, then Cape Horn, and finally go as far as the antarctic pole? Would he come back at last to the Pacific, where his *Nautilus* could sail free and independently? Time would show.

After having skirted the sands of Cartier, of Hibernia, Seringapatam, and Scott, last efforts of the solid against the liquid element, on the 14th of January we lost sight of land altogether. The speed of the *Nautilus* was considerably abated, and with irregular course she sometimes swam in the bosom of the waters, sometimes floated on their surface.

During this period of the voyage, Captain Nemo made some interesting experiments on the varied temperature of the sea, in different beds. Under ordinary conditions, these observations are made by means of rather complicated instruments, and with somewhat doubtful results, by means of thermometrical sounding-leads, the glasses often breaking under the pressure of the water, or an apparatus grounded on the variations of the resistance of metals to the electric currents. Results so obtained could not be correctly calculated. On the contrary, Captain Nemo went himself to test the temperature in the depths of the sea, and his thermometer, placed in communication with the different sheets of water, gave him the required degree immediately and accurately.

It was thus that, either by overloading her reservoirs, or by descending obliquely by means of her inclined planes the *Nautilus* successively attained the depth of three, four, five, seven, nine, and ten thousand yards, and the definite result of this experience was, that the sea preserved an average temperature of four degrees and a half, at a depth of five thousand fathoms, under all latitudes.

On the 16th of January, the *Nautilus* seemed becalmed, only a few yards beneath the surface of the waves. Her electric apparatus remained inactive, and her motionless screw left her to drift at the mercy of the currents. I supposed that the crew was occupied with interior repairs, rendered necessary by the violence of the mechanical movements of the machine.

My companions and I then witnessed a curious spectacle. The hatches of the saloon were open, and as the beacon-light of the *Nautilus* was not in action, a dim obscurity reigned, in the midst of the waters. I observed the state of the sea under these conditions, and the largest fish appeared to me no more than scarcely defined shadows, when the *Nautilus* found herself suddenly transported into full light. I thought at first that the beacon had been lighted, and was casting its electric radiance into the liquid mass. I was mistaken, and after a rapid survey perceived my error.

The *Nautilus* floated in the midst of a phosphorescent bed, which, in this obscurity, became quite dazzling. It was produced by myriads of luminous animalculæ, whose brilliancy was increased as they glided over the metallic hull of the vessel. I was surprised by lightning in the midst of these luminous sheets, as though they had been rivulets of lead melted in an ardent furnace, or metallic masses brought to a white heat, so that, by force of contrast, certain portions of light appeared to cast a shade in the midst of the general ignition, from which all shade seemed banished. No; this was not the calm irradiation of our ordinary lightning. There was unusual life and vigor; this was truly living light!

In reality, it was an infinite agglomeration of colored infusoria, of veritable globules of diaphanous jelly, provided with a thread-like tentacle, and of which as many as twenty-five thousand have been counted in less than two cubic half-inches of water; and their light was increased by the glimmering peculiar to the medusæ, starfish, aurelia, and other phosphorescent zoöphytes, impregnated by the grease of the organic matter decomposed by the sea, and, perhaps, the mucus secreted by the fish.

During several hours the *Nautilus* floated in these brilliant waves, and our admiration increased as we watched the marine monsters disporting themselves like salamanders. I saw there, in the midst of this fire that burns not, the swift and elegant porpoise (the indefatigable clown of the ocean), and some sword-fish ten feet long, those prophetic heralds of the hurricane, whose formidable sword would now and then strike the glass of the saloon. Then appeared the smaller fish, the variegated balista, the leaping mackerel, wolfthorn-tails, and a hundred others which striped the luminous atmosphere as they swam. This dazzling spectacle was enchanting! Perhaps some atmospheric condition increased the intensity of this phenomenon. Perhaps some storm agitated the surface of the waves. But, at this depth of some yards, the *Nautilus* was unmoved by its fury, and reposed peacefully in still water.

So we progressed, incessantly charmed by some new marvel. Conseil arranged and classed his zoöphytes, his articulata, his mollusks, his fishes. The days passed rapidly away, and I took no account of them. Ned, according to habit, tried to vary the diet on board. Like snails, we were fixed to our shells, and I declare it is easy to lead a snail's life.

Thus this life seemed easy and natural, and we thought no longer of the life we led on land; but something happened to recall us to the strangeness of our situation.

On the 18th of January, the *Nautilus* was in 105° longitude and 15°

south latitude. The weather was threatening, the sea rough and rolling. There was a strong east wind. The barometer, which had been going down for some days, foreboded a coming storm. I went up on the platform just as the second lieutenant was taking the measure of the horary angles, and waited, according to habit, till the daily phrase was said. But, on this day, it was exchanged for another phrase not less incomprehensible. Almost directly, I saw Captain Nemo appear, with a glass, looking toward the horizon.

For some minutes he was immovable, without taking his eye off the point of observation. Then he lowered his glass, and exchanged a few words with his lieutenant. The latter seemed to be a victim to some emotion that he tried in vain to repress. Captain Nemo, having more command over himself, was cool. He seemed, too, to be making some objections, to which the lieutenant replied by formal assurances; at least I concluded so by the difference of their tones and gestures. For myself, I had looked carefully in the direction indicated without seeing anything. The sky and water were lost in the clear line of the horizon.

However, Captain Nemo walked from one end of the platform to the other, without looking at me, perhaps without seeing me. His step was firm, but less regular than usual. He stopped sometimes, crossed his arms, and observed the sea. What could he be looking for on that immense expanse?

The *Nautilus* was then some hundreds of miles from the nearest coast.

The lieutenant had taken up the glass and examined the horizon steadfastly, going and coming, stamping his foot and showing more nervous agitation than his superior officer. Besides, this mystery must necessarily be solved, and before long; for, upon an order from Captain Nemo, the engine, increasing its propelling power, made the screw turn more rapidly.

Just then the lieutenant drew the captain's attention again. The latter stopped walking and directed his glass toward the place indicated. He looked long. I felt very much puzzled, and descended to the drawing-room and took out an excellent telescope that I generally used. Then, leaning on the cage of the watch-light, that jutted out from the front of the platform, set myself to look over all the line of the sky and sea.

But my eye was no sooner applied to the glass, than it was quickly snatched out of my hands.

I turned round. Captain Nemo was before me, but I did not know him. His face was transfigured. His eyes flashed sullenly; his teeth were set; his stiff body, clinched fists, and head shrunk between his shoulders, betrayed the violent agitation that pervaded his whole frame. He did not move. My glass, fallen from his hands, had rolled at his feet.

Had I unwittingly provoked this fit of anger? Did this incomprehensible person imagine that I had discovered some forbidden secret? No; I was not the object of this hatred, for he was not looking at me, his eye was steadily fixed upon the impenetrable point of the horizon. At last Captain Nemo recovered himself. His agitation subsided. He addressed some words in a foreign language to his lieutenant, then turned to me. "M. Aronnax," he said, in rather an imperious tone, "I require you to keep one of the conditions that bind you to me."

"What is it, captain?"

"You must be confined, with your companions, until I think fit to release you."

"You are the master," I replied, looking steadily at him. "But may I ask you one question?"

"None, sir."

There was no resisting this imperious command; it would have been useless. I went down to the cabin occupied by Ned Land and Conseil, and told them the captain's determination. You may judge how this communication was received by the Canadian.

But there was no time for altercation. Four of the crew waited at the door, and conducted us to that cell where we had passed our first night on board the *Nautilus*.

Ned Land would have remonstrated, but the door was shut upon him.

"Will master tell me what this means?" asked Conseil.

I told my companions what had passed. They were as much astonished as I, and equally at a loss how to account for it.

Meanwhile, I was absorbed in my own reflections, and could think of nothing but the strange fear depicted in the captain's countenance. I was utterly at a loss to account for it, when my cogitations were disturbed by these words from Ned Land:

"Hallo! Breakfast is ready!"

And indeed the table was laid. Evidently Captain Nemo had given this order at the same time that he had hastened the speed of the *Nautilus*.

"Will master permit me to make a recommendation?" asked Conseil.

"Yes, my boy."

"Well, it is that master breakfast. It is prudent, for we do not know what may happen."

"You are right, Conseil."

"Unfortunately," said Ned Land, "they have only given us the ship's fare."

"Friend Ned," asked Conseil, "what would you have said if the breakfast had been entirely forgotten?"

This argument cut short the harpooner's recriminations.

We sat down to table. The meal was eaten in silence.

Just then, the luminous globe that lighted the cell went out, and left us in total darkness. Ned Land was soon asleep, and what astonished me was that Conseil went off into a heavy sleep. I was thinking what could have caused his irresistible drowsiness, when I felt my brain becoming stupefied. In spite of my efforts to keep my eyes open, they would close. A painful suspicion seized me. Evidently soporific substances had been mixed with the food we had just taken. Imprisonment was not enough to conceal Captain Nemo's projects from us; sleep was more necessary.

I then heard the panels shut. The undulations of the sea, which caused a slight rolling motion, ceased. Had the *Nautilus* quitted the surface of the ocean? Had it gone back to the motionless bed of water? I tried to resist sleep. It was impossible. My breathing grew weak. I felt a mortal cold freeze my stiffened and half-paralyzed limbs. My eyelids, like leaden caps, fell over my eyes. I could not raise them; a morbid sleep, full of hallucinations, bereft me of my being. Then the visions disappeared, and left me in complete insensibility.

The Coral Kingdom

The next day I woke with my head singularly clear. To my great surprise I was in my own room. My companions, no doubt, had been reinstated in their cabin, without having perceived it any more than I. Of what had passed during the night they were as ignorant as I was, and to penetrate this mystery I only reckoned upon the chances of the future.

I then thought of quitting my room. Was I free again, or a prisoner? Quite free. I opened the door, went to the half-deck, went up the central stairs. The panels, shut the evening before, were open. I went on to the platform.

Ned Land and Conseil waited there for me. I questioned them; they knew nothing. Lost in a heavy sleep in which they had been totally unconscious, they had been astonished at finding themselves in their cabin.

As for the *Nautilus*, it seemed quiet and mysterious as ever. It floated on the surface of the waves at a moderate pace. Nothing seemed changed on board.

The second lieutenant then came on to the platform, and gave the usual order below.

As for Captain Nemo, he did not appear.

Of the people on board I only saw the impassive steward, who served me with his usual dumb regularity.

About two o'clock, I was in the drawing-room, busied in arranging my notes, when the captain opened the door and appeared. I bowed. He made a slight inclination in return, without speaking. I resumed my work, hoping that he would perhaps give me some explanation of the events of the preceding night. He made none. I looked at him. He seemed fatigued; his heavy eyes had not been refreshed by sleep; his face looked very sorrowful. He walked to and fro, sat down and got up again, took up a chance book, put it down, consulted his instruments without taking his habitual notes, and seemed restless and uneasy. At last he came up to me, and said:

"Are you a doctor, M. Aronnax?"

I so little expected such a question that I stared some time at him without answering.

"Are you a doctor?" he repeated. "Several of your colleagues have studied medicine."

"Well," said I, "I am a doctor and resident surgeon to the hospital. I practiced several years before entering the museum."

"Very well, sir."

My answer had evidently satisfied the captain. But not knowing what he would say next, I waited for other questions, reserving my answers according to circumstances.

"M. Aronnax, will you consent to prescribe for one of my men?" he asked.

"Is he ill?"

"Yes."

"I am ready to follow you."

"Come then."

I own my heart beat, I do not know why. I saw a certain connection between the illness of one of the crew and the events of the day before; and this mystery interested me at least as much as the sick man.

Captain Nemo conducted me to the poop of the *Nautilus,* and took me into a cabin situated near the sailors' quarters.

There, on a bed, lay a man about forty years of age, with a resolute expression of countenance, a true type of an Anglo-Saxon.

I leaned over him. He was not only ill, he was wounded. His head, swathed in bandages covered with blood, lay on a pillow. I undid the bandages, and the wounded man looked at me with his large eyes and gave no sign of pain as I did it. It was a horrible wound. The skull, shattered by some deadly weapon, left the brain exposed, which was much injured. Clots of blood had formed in the bruised and broken mass, in color like the dregs of wine.

There was both contusion and suffusion of the brain. His breathing was slow, and some spasmodic movements of the muscles agitated his face. I felt his pulse. It was intermittent. The extremities of the body were growing cold already, and I saw death must inevitably ensue. After dressing the unfortunate man's wounds, I readjusted the bandages on his head, and turned to Captain Nemo.

"What caused this wound?" I asked.

"What does it signify?" he replied evasively. "A shock has broken one of the levers of the engine, which struck myself. But your opinion as to his state?"

I hesitated before giving it.

"You may speak," said the captain. "This man does not understand French."

I gave a last look at the wounded man.

"He will be dead in two hours."

"Can nothing save him?"

"Nothing."

Captain Nemo's hand contracted, and some tears glistened in his eyes, which I thought incapable of shedding any.

For some moments I still watched the dying man, whose life ebbed slowly. His pallor increased under the electric light that was shed over his deathbed. I looked at his intelligent forehead, furrowed with premature wrinkles, produced probably by misfortune and sorrow. I tried to learn the secret of his life from the last words that escaped his lips.

"You can go now, M. Aronnax," said the captain.

I left him in the dying man's cabin, and returned to my room, much affected by this scene. During the whole day, I was haunted by uncomfortable suspicions, and at night I slept badly, and, between my broken dreams, I fancied I heard distant sighs like the notes of a funeral psalm. Were they the prayers of the dead, murmured in that language that I could not understand?

The next morning I went on to the bridge. Captain Nemo was there before me. As soon as he perceived me he came to me.

"Professor, will it be convenient to you to make a submarine excursion to-day?"

"With my companions?" I asked.

"If they like."

"We obey your orders, captain."

"Will you be so good, then, as to put on your cork-jackets?"

It was not a question of dead or dying. I rejoined Ned Land and Conseil, and told them of Captain Nemo's proposition. Conseil hastened to accept it, and this time the Canadian seemed quite willing to follow our example.

It was eight o'clock in the morning. At half-past eight we were equipped for this new excursion, and provided with two contrivances for light and breathing. The double door was open; and accompanied by Captain Nemo, who was followed by a dozen of the crew, we set foot, at a depth of about thirty feet, on the solid bottom on which the *Nautilus* rested.

A slight declivity ended in an uneven bottom, at fifteen fathoms depth. This bottom differed entirely from the one I had visited on my first excursion under the waters of the Pacific Ocean. Here, there was no fine sand, no submarine prairies, no sea-forest. I immediately recognized that marvelous region in which, on that day, the captain did the honors to us. It was the coral kingdom. In the zoöphyte branch and in the alcyon class I noticed the gorgoneæ, the isidiæ, and the corollariæ.

The light produced a thousand charming varieties, playing in the midst of the branches that were so vividly colored. I seemed to see the membranous and cylindrical tubes tremble beneath the undulation of the waters. I was tempted to gather their fresh petals, ornamented with delicate tentacles, some just blown, the others budding, while small fish, swimming swiftly, touched them slightly like flights of birds. But if my hand approached these living flowers, these animated sensitive plants, the whole colony took alarm. The white petals reentered their red cases, the flowers faded as I looked, and the bush changed into a block of stony knobs.

Chance had thrown me just by the most precious specimens of this zoöphyte. This coral was more valuable than that found in the Mediterranean, on the coasts of France, Italy, and Barbary. Its tints justified the poetical names of "Flower of Blood" and "Froth of Blood" that trade has given to its most beautiful productions. Coral is sold for £20 per ounce, and in this place the watery beds would make the fortunes of a company of coral-divers. This precious matter, often confounded with other polypi, formed then the inextricable plots called "macciota," and on which I noticed several beautiful specimens of pink coral.

But soon the bushes contract, and the arborizations increase. Real petrified thickets, long joists of fantastic architecture, were disclosed before us. Captain Nemo placed himself under a dark gallery, where by a slight declivity we reached a depth of 100 yards. The light from our lamps produced sometimes magical effects, following the rough outlines of the natural arches, and pendants disposed like lusters, that were tipped with points of fire. Between the coralline shrubs I noticed other polypi not less curious—melites, and irises with articulated ramifications; also some tufts of coral, some green, others red, like seaweed incrusted in their calcareous salts, that naturalists, after long discussion, have definitely classed in the vegetable kingdom. But following the remark of a thinking man, "there is perhaps the real point where life rises obscurely from the sleep of a stone, without detaching itself from the rough point of departure."

At last, after walking two hours, we had attained a depth of about 300 yards, that is to say, the extreme limit on which coral begins to form. But there was no isolated bush, nor modest brushwood, at the bottom of lofty trees. It was an immense forest of large mineral vegetations, enormous petrified trees, united by garlands of elegant plumarias, sea bindweed, all adorned with clouds and reflections. We passed freely under their high branches, lost in the shade of the waves, while at our feet, tubipores, meandrines, stars, fungi, and caryophyllidæ formed a carpet of flowers sown with dazzling gems. What an indescribable spectacle!

Captain Nemo had stopped. I and my companions halted, and turning round, I saw his men were forming a semicircle round their chief. Watching attentively, I observed that four of them carried on their shoulders an object of an oblong shape.

We occupied in this place the center of a vast glade surrounded by the lofty foliage of the submarine forest. Our lamps threw over the place a sort of clear twilight that singularly elongated the shadows on the ground. At the end of the glade the darkness increased, and was only relieved by little sparks reflected by the points of coral.

Ned Land and Conseil were near me. We watched, and I thought I was going to witness a strange scene. On observing the ground, I saw that it was raised in certain places by slight excrescences incrusted with limy deposits, and disposed with a regularity that betrayed the hand of man.

In the midst of the glade, on a pedestal of rocks roughly piled up, stood a cross of coral, that extended its long arms that one might have thought were made of petrified blood.

Upon a sign from Captain Nemo, one of the men advanced; and at some feet from the cross, he began to dig a hole with a pickaxe that he took from his belt. I understood all! This glade was a cemetery, this hole a tomb, this oblong object the body of the man who had died in the night! The captain and his men had come to bury their companion in this general resting-place, at the bottom of this inaccessible ocean!

The grave was being dug slowly; the fish fled on all sides while their retreat was being thus disturbed; I heard the strokes of the pickaxe, which sparkled when it hit upon some flint lost at the bottom of the waters. The hole was soon large and deep enough to receive the body. Then the bearers approached; the body, enveloped in a tissue of white byssus, was lowered into the damp grave. Captain Nemo, with his arms crossed on his breast, and all the friends of he who had loved them, knelt in prayer.

The grave was then filled in with the rubbish taken from the ground, which formed a slight mound. When this was done, Captain Nemo and his men rose; then, approaching the grave, they knelt again, and all extended their hands in sign of a last adieu. Then the funeral procession returned to the *Nautilus,* passing under the arches of the forest, in the midst of thickets, along the coral bushes, and still on the ascent. At last the fires on board appeared, and their luminous track guided us to the *Nautilus.* At one o'clock we had returned.

As soon as I had changed my clothes, I went up on to the platform, and, a prey to conflicting emotions, I sat down near the binnacle. Captain Nemo joined me. I rose and said to him:

"So, as I said he would, this man died in the night?"

"Yes, M. Aronnax."

"And he rests now, near his companions, in the coral cemetery?"

"Yes, forgotten by all else, but not by us. We dug the grave, and the polypi undertake to seal our dead for eternity." And burying his face quickly in his hands, he tried in vain to suppress a sob. Then he added: "Our peaceful cemetery is there, some hundred feet below the surface of the waves."

"Your dead sleep quietly, at least, captain, out of the reach of sharks."

"Yes, sir, of sharks and men," gravely replied the captain.

PART 2

The Indian Ocean

We now come to the second part of our journey under the sea. The first ended with the moving scene in the coral cemetery, which left such a deep impression on my mind. Thus, in the midst of this great sea, Captain Nemo's life was passing even to his grave, which he had prepared in one of its deepest abysses. There, not one of the ocean's monsters could trouble the last sleep of the crew of the *Nautilus,* of those friends riveted to each other in death as in life. "Nor any man either," had added the captain. Still the same fierce, implacable defiance toward human society!

I could no longer content myself with the hypothesis which satisfied Conseil.

That worthy fellow persisted in seeing in the commander of the *Nautilus* one of those unknown savants who return mankind contempt for indifference. For him, he was a misunderstood genius, who, tired of earth's deceptions, had taken refuge in this inaccessible medium, where he might follow his instincts freely. To my mind, this hypothesis explained but one side of Captain Nemo's character.

Indeed, the mystery of that last night, during which we had been chained in prison, the sleep, and the precaution so violently taken by the captain of snatching from my eyes the glass I had raised to sweep the horizon, the mortal wound of the man, due to an unaccountable shock of the *Nautilus,* all put me on a new track. No; Captain Nemo was not satisfied with shunning man. His formidable apparatus not only suited his instinct of freedom, but, perhaps, also the design of some terrible retaliation.

At this moment nothing is clear to me; I catch but a glimpse of light amid all the darkness, and I must confine myself to writing as events shall dictate.

That day, the 24th of January, 1868, at noon, the second officer came to take the altitude of the sun. I mounted the platform, lit a cigar, and watched the operation. It seemed to me that the man did not understand French; for several times I made remarks in a loud voice, which must have drawn from him some involuntary sign of attention, if he had understood them; but he remained undisturbed and dumb.

As he was taking observations with the sextant, one of the sailors of the *Nautilus* (the strong man who had accompanied us on our first submarine excursion to the island of Crespo) came to clean the glasses of the lantern. I examined the fittings of the apparatus, the strength of which was increased a hundredfold by lenticular rings, placed similar to those in a lighthouse, and which projected their brilliance in a horizontal plane. The electric lamp was combined in such a way as to give its most powerful light. Indeed it was produced in *vacuo*, which insured both its steadiness and its intensity. This vacuum economized the graphite points, between which the luminous arc was developed—an important point of economy for Captain Nemo, who could not easily have replaced them; and under these conditions their waste was imperceptible. When the *Nautilus* was ready to continue its submarine journey, I went down to the saloon. The panels were closed and the course marked direct west.

We were furrowing the waters of the Indian Ocean, a vast liquid plain with a surface of 1,200,000,000 acres, and whose waters are so clear and transparent that anyone leaning over them would turn giddy. The *Nautilus* usually floated between fifty and a hundred fathoms deep. We went on so for some days. To anyone but myself, who had a great love for the sea, the hours would have seemed long and monotonous; but the daily walks on the platform, when I steeped myself in the reviving air of the ocean, the sight of the rich waters through the windows of the saloon, the books in the library, the compiling of my memoirs, took up all my time, and left me not a moment of *ennui* or weariness.

For some days we saw a great number of aquatic birds, sea-mews or gulls. Some were cleverly killed, and, prepared in a certain way, made very acceptable water game. Among large-winged birds, carried a long distance from all lands, and resting upon the waves from the fatigue of their flight, I saw some magnificent albatrosses, uttering discordant cries like the braying of an ass, and birds belonging to the family of the longipennates. The family of the totipalmates was represented by the sea-swallows, which caught the fish from the surface, and by numerous phaetons, or lepturi; among others, the phaeton with red lines, as large as a pigeon, whose white plumage, tinted with pink, shows off to advantage the blackness of its wings.

As to the fish, they always provoked our admiration when we surprised the secrets of their aquatic life through the open panels. I saw many kinds which I never before had a chance of observing.

I shall notice chiefly ostracions peculiar to the Red Sea, the Indian Ocean, and that part which washes the coast of tropical America. These fishes, like the tortoise, the armadillo, the sea hedgehog, and the crustacea, are protected by a breastplate which is neither chalky nor stony, but real bone. In some it takes the form of a solid triangle, in others of a solid quadrangle. Among the triangular I saw some an inch and a half in length, with wholesome flesh and a delicious flavor; they are brown at the tail and yellow at the fins, and I recommend their introduction into fresh water, to which a certain number of sea-fish easily accustom themselves. I would also mention quadrangular ostracions, having on the back four large tubercles; some dotted over with white spots on the lower part of the body, and which may be tamed like birds; trigons provided with spikes formed by the lengthening of their bony shell, and which from their strange gruntings are called "sea-pigs"; also dromedaries with large humps in the shape of a cone, whose flesh is very tough and leathery.

I now borrow from the daily notes of Master Conseil. "Certain fish of the genus petrodon peculiar to those seas, with red backs and white chests, which are distinguished by three rows of longitudinal filaments; and some electrical, seven inches long, decked in the liveliest colors. Then, as specimens of other kinds, some ovoides, resembling an egg of a dark brown color, marked with white bands and without tails; diodons, real sea porcupines, furnished with spikes, and capable of swelling in such a way as to look like cushions bristling with darts; hippocampi, common to every ocean; some pegasi with lengthened snouts, which their pectoral fins, being much elongated and formed in the shape of wings, allow, if not to fly, at least to shoot into the air; pigeon spatulæ, with tails covered with many rings of shell; macrognathi with long jaws, an excellent fish, nine inches long, and bright with most agreeable colors; pale-colored calliomores, with rugged heads; and plenty of chætodons, with long and tubular muzzles, which kill insects by shooting them, as from an air-gun, with a single drop of water. These we may call the fly-catchers of the seas.

"In the eighty-ninths genus of fishes, classed by Lacépède, belonging to the second lower class of bony, characterized by opercules and bronchial membranes, I remarked the scorpæna, the head of which is furnished with spikes, and which has but one dorsal fin; these creatures are covered or not, with little shells, according to the sub-class to which they belong. The second sub-class gives us specimens of didactyles fourteen or fifteen inches in length, with yellow rays, and heads of a most fantastic appearance. As to the first sub-class, it gives several specimens of that singular-looking fish appropriately called a 'sea-frog,' with large head, sometimes swollen with protuberances, bristling with spikes, and covered with tubercles; it has irregular and hideous horns; its body and tail are covered with callosities; its sting makes a dangerous wound; it is both repugnant and horrible to look at."

From the 21st to the 23d of January, the *Nautilus* went at the rate of two hundred and fifty leagues in twenty-four hours, being five hundred and forty miles, or twenty-two miles an hour. If we recognized so many different varieties of fish, it was because, attracted by the electric light, they tried to follow us; the greater part, however, were soon distanced by our speed, though some kept their place in the waters of the *Nautilus* for a time. The morning of the 24th, in 12° 5′ south latitude, and 94° 33′ longitude, we observed Keeling Island, a madrepore formation, planted with magnificent cocoas, and which had been visited by Mr. Darwin and Captain Fitzroy. The *Nautilus* skirted the shores of this desert island for a little distance. Its nets brought up numerous specimens of polypi, and curious shells of molluska. Some precious productions of the species of delphinulæ enriched the treasures of Captain Nemo, to which I added an astræa punctifera, a kind of parasite polypus often found fixed to a shell. Soon Keeling Island disappeared from the horizon, and our course was directed to the northwest in the direction of the Indian Peninsula.

From Keeling Island our course was slower and more variable, often taking us into great depths. Several times they made use of the inclined planes, which certain internal levers placed obliquely to the water-line. In that way we went about two miles, but without ever obtaining the greatest depths of the Indian Sea, which soundings of seven thousand fathoms have never reached. As to the temperature of the lower strata, the thermometer invariably indicated 4° above zero. I only observed that, in the upper regions, the water was always colder in the high levels than at the surface of the sea.

On the 25th of January, the ocean was entirely deserted; the *Nautilus* passed the day on the surface, beating the waves with its powerful screw, and making them rebound to a great height. Who under such circumstances would not have taken it for a gigantic cetacean? Three parts of this day I spent on the platform. I watched the sea. Nothing on the horizon, till about four o'clock a steamer running west on our counter. Her masts were visible for an instant, but she could not see the *Nautilus*, being too low in the water. I fancied this steamboat belonged to the P. O. Company, which runs from Ceylon to Sydney, touching at King George's Point and Melbourne.

At five o'clock in the evening, before that fleeting twilight which binds night to day in tropical zones, Conseil and I were astonished by a curious spectacle.

It was a shoal of argonauts traveling along on the surface of the ocean. We could count several hundreds. They belonged to the tubercle kind which are peculiar to the Indian seas.

These graceful mollusks moved backward by means of their locomotive tube, through which they propelled the water already drawn in. Of their eight tentacles, six were elongated, and stretched out floating on the water, while the other two, rolled up flat, were spread to the wind like a light sail. I saw their spiral-shaped and fluted shells, which Cuvier justly compares to an elegant skiff. A boat indeed! It bears the creature which secretes it without its adhering to it.

For nearly an hour the *Nautilus* floated in the midst of this shoal of mollusks. Then I know not what sudden fright they took; but as if at a signal every sail was furled, the arms folded, the body drawn in, the shells turned over, changing their center of gravity, and the whole fleet disappeared under the waves. Never did the ships of a squadron maneuver with more unity.

At that moment night fell suddenly, and the reeds, scarcely raised by the breeze, lay peaceably under the sides of the *Nautilus*.

The next day, 26th of January, we cut the equator at the eighty-second meridian, and entered the northern hemisphere. During the day, a formidable troop of sharks accompanied us, terrible creatures, which multiply in these seas, and make them very dangerous. They were "cestracio philippi" sharks, with brown backs and whitish bellies, armed with eleven rows of teeth—eyed sharks—their throat being marked with a large black spot surrounded with white like an eye. There were also some Isabella sharks, with rounded snouts marked with dark spots. These powerful creatures often hurled themselves at the windows of the saloon with such violence as to make us feel very insecure. At such times Ned Land was no longer master of himself. He wanted to go to the surface and harpoon the monsters, particularly certain smooth-hound sharks, whose mouth is studded with teeth like a mosaic; and large tiger-sharks nearly six yards long, the last-named of which seemed to excite him more particularly. But the *Nautilus*, accelerating her speed, easily left the most rapid of them behind.

The 27th of January, at the entrance of the vast Bay of Bengal, we met repeatedly a forbidding spectacle—dead bodies floating on the surface of the water. They were the dead of the Indian villages, carried by the Ganges to the level of the sea, and which the vultures, the only undertakers of the country, had not been able to devour. But the sharks did not fail to help them at their funereal work.

About seven o'clock in the evening, the *Nautilus,* half immersed, was sailing in a sea of milk. At first sight the ocean seemed lactified. Was it the effect of the lunar rays? No; for the moon, scarcely two days old, was still lying hidden under the horizon in the rays of the sun. The whole sky, though lit by the sidereal rays, seemed black by contrast with the whiteness of the waters.

Conseil could not believe his eyes, and questioned me as to the cause of this strange phenomenon. Happily I was able to answer him.

"It is called a milk sea," I explained; "a large extent of white wavelets often to be seen on the coasts of Amboyna, and in these parts of the sea."

"But, sir," said Conseil, "can you tell me what causes such an effect, for I suppose the water is not really turned into milk?"

"No, my boy; and the whiteness which surprises you is caused only by the presence of myriads of infusoria, a sort of luminous little worm, gelatinous and without color, of the thickness of a hair, and whose length is not more than the seven-one-thousandths of an inch. These insects adhere to one another sometimes for several leagues."

"Several leagues!" exclaimed Conseil.

"Yes, my boy; and you need not try to compute the number of these infusoria. You will not be able; for, if I am not mistaken, ships have floated on these milk seas for more than forty miles."

Toward midnight the sea suddenly resumed its usual color; but behind us, even to the limits of the horizon, the sky reflected the whitened waves, and for a long time seemed impregnated with the vague glimmerings of an aurora borealis.

A Novel Proposal of Captain Nemo's

On the 28th of February, when at noon the *Nautilus* came to the surface of the sea, in 9° 4′ north latitude, there was land in sight about eight miles to westward. The first thing I noticed was a range of mountains about two thousand feet high, the shapes of which were most capricious. On taking the bearings, I knew that we were nearing the island of Ceylon, the pearl which hangs from the lobe of the Indian Peninsula.

Captain Nemo and his second appeared at this moment. The captain glanced at the map. Then, turning to me, said:

"The island of Ceylon, noted for its pearl-fisheries. Would you like to visit one of them, M. Aronnax?"

"Certainly, captain."

"Well, the thing is easy. Though if we see the fisheries, we shall not see the fishermen. The annual exportation has not yet begun. Never mind, I will give orders to make for the Gulf of Manaar, where we shall arrive in the night."

The captain said something to his second, who immediately went out. Soon the *Nautilus* returned to her native element, and the manometer showed that she was about thirty feet deep.

"Well, sir," said Captain Nemo, "you and your companions shall visit the Bank of Manaar, and if by chance some fisherman should be there, we shall see him at work."

"Agreed, captain!"

"By the bye, M. Aronnax, you are not afraid of sharks?"

"Sharks!" exclaimed I.

This question seemed a very hard one.

"Well?" continued Captain Nemo.

"I admit, captain, that I am not yet very familiar with that kind of fish."

"*We* are accustomed to them," replied Captain Nemo, "and in time you will be too. However, we shall be armed, and on the road we may be able to hunt some of the tribe. It is interesting. So, till to-morrow, sir, and early."

This said in a careless tone, Captain Nemo left the saloon. Now, if you were invited to hunt the bear in the mountains of Switzerland, what would you say? "Very well! To-morrow we will go and hunt the bear." If you were asked to hunt the lion in the plains of Atlas, or the tiger in the Indian jungles, what would you say? "Ha! ha! it seems we are going to hunt the tiger or the lion!" But when you are invited to hunt the shark in its natural element, you would perhaps reflect before accepting the invitation. As for myself, I passed my hand over my forehead, on which stood large drops of cold perspiration. "Let us reflect," said I, "and take our time. Hunting otters in submarine forests, as we did in the island of Crespo, will pass; but going up and down at the bottom of the sea, where one is almost certain to meet sharks, is quite another thing! I know well that in certain countries, particularly in the Andaman Islands, the Negroes never hesitate to attack them with a dagger in one hand and a running noose in the other; but I also know that few who affront those creatures ever return alive. However, I am not a negro, and, if I were, I think a little hesitation in this case would not be ill-timed."

At this moment, Conseil and the Canadian entered, quite composed, and even joyous. They knew not what awaited them.

"Faith, sir," said Ned Land, "your Captain Nemo—the devil take him—has just made us a very pleasant offer!"

"Ah!" said I. "You know?"

"If agreeable to you, sir," interrupted Conseil, "the commander of the *Nautilus* has invited us to visit the magnificent Ceylon fisheries to-morrow, in your company; he did it kindly, and behaved like a real gentleman."

"He said nothing more?"

"Nothing more, sir, except that he had already spoken to you of this little walk."

"Sir," said Conseil, "would you give us some details of the pearl-fishery?"

"As to the fishing itself," I asked, "or the incidents—which?"

"On the fishing," replied the Canadian; "before entering upon the ground, it is as well to know something about it."

"Very well; sit down, my friends, and I will teach you."

Ned and Conseil seated themselves on an ottoman, and the first thing the Canadian asked was:

"Sir, what is a pearl?"

"My worthy Ned," I answered, "to the poet, a pearl is a tear of the sea; to the Orientals, it is a drop of dew solidified; to the ladies, it is a jewel of an oblong shape, of a brilliancy of mother-of-pearl substance, which they wear on their fingers, their necks, or their ears; for the chemist, it is a mixture of phosphate and carbonate of lime, with a little gelatine; and lastly, for naturalists, it is simply a morbid secretion of the organ that produces the mother-of-pearl among certain bivalves."

"Branch of molluska," said Conseil, "class of acephali, order of testacea."

"Precisely so, my learned Conseil; and, among these testacea, the ear-shell, the tridacnæ, the turbots—in a word, all those which secrete mother-of-pearl, that is, the blue, bluish, violet, or white substance which lines the interior of their shells, are capable of producing pearls."

"Mussels too?" asked the Canadian.

"Yes, mussels of certain waters in Scotland, Wales, Ireland, Saxony, Bohemia, and France."

"Good! For the future I shall pay attention," replied the Canadian.

"But," I continued, "the particular mollusk which secretes the pearl is the *pearl-oyster,* the *Meleagrina margaritifera,* that precious pintadine. The pearl is nothing but a nacreous formation, deposited in a globular form, either adhering to the oyster shell, or buried in the folds of the creature. On the shell it is fast; in the flesh it is loose; but always has for a kernel a small, hard substance, maybe a barren egg, maybe a grain of sand, around which the pearly matter deposits itself year after year successively, and by thin concentric layers."

"Are many pearls found in the same oyster?" asked Conseil.

"Yes, my boy. There are some pintadines a perfect casket. One oyster has been mentioned, though I allow myself to doubt it, as having contained no less than a hundred and fifty sharks."

"A hundred and fifty sharks!" exclaimed Ned Land.

"Did I say sharks?" said I hurriedly. "I meant to say a hundred and fifty pearls. Sharks would not be sense."

"Certainly not," said Conseil; "but will you tell us now by what means they extract these pearls?"

"They proceed in various ways. When they adhere to the shell, the fishermen often pull them off with pinchers; but the most common way is to lay the pintadines on mats of the seaweed which covers the banks. Thus they die in the open air; and at the end of ten days they are in a forward state of decomposition. They are then plunged into large reservoirs of sea-water; then they are opened and washed. Now begins the double work of the sorters. First they separate the layers of pearls, known in commerce by the name of bastard whites and bastard blacks, which are delivered in boxes of two hundred and fifty and three hundred pounds each. Then they take the parenchyma of the oyster, boil it, and pass it through a sieve in order to extract the very smallest pearls."

"The price of these pearls varies according to their size?" asked Conseil.

"Not only according to their size," I answered, "but also according to their shape, their water (that is, their color), and their luster; that is, that bright and diapered sparkle which make them so charming to the eye. The most beautiful are called virgin pearls or paragons. They are formed alone in the tissue of the mollusk, are white, often opaque, and sometimes have the transparency of an opal; they are generally round or oval. The round are made into bracelets, the oval into pendants; and, being more precious, are sold singly. Those adhering to the shell of the oyster are more irregular in shape, and are sold by weight. Lastly, in a lower order are classed those small pearls known under the name of seed-pearls; they are sold by measure, and are especially used in embroidery for church ornaments."

"But," said Conseil, "is this pearl-fishing dangerous?"

"No," I answered quickly; "particularly if certain precautions are taken."

"What does one risk in such a calling?" said Ned Land. "The swallowing of some mouthfuls of sea-water?"

"As you say, Ned. By the bye," said I, trying to take Captain Nemo's careless tone, "are you afraid of sharks, brave Ned?"

"I!" replied the Canadian. "A harpooner by profession! It is my trade to make light of them."

"But," said I, "it is not a question of fishing for them with an iron swivel, hoisting them into the vessel, cutting off their tails with a blow of the chopper, ripping them up, and throwing their hearts into the sea!"

"Then, it is a question of——"

"Precisely."

"In the water?"

"In the water."

"Faith, with a good harpoon! You know, sir, these sharks are ill-fashioned beasts. They must turn on their bellies to seize you, and in that time——"

Ned Land had a way of saying "seize" which made my blood run cold.

"Well, and you, Conseil, what do you think of sharks?"

"Me!" said Conseil. "I will be frank, sir."

"So much the better," thought I.

"If you, sir, mean to face the sharks, I do not see why your faithful servant should not face them with you."

A Pearl of Ten Millions

The next morning at four o'clock I was awakened by the steward, whom Captain Nemo had placed at my service. I rose hurriedly, dressed, and went into the saloon.

Captain Nemo was awaiting me.

"M. Aronnax," said he, "are you ready to start?"

"I am ready."

"Then, please to follow me."

"And my companions, captain?"

"They have been told, and are waiting."

"Are we not to put on our diver's dresses?" asked I.

"Not yet. I have not allowed the *Nautilus* to come too near this coast, and we are some distance from the Manaar Bank; but the boat is ready, and will take us to the exact point of disembarking, which will save us a long way. It carries our diving apparatus, which we will put on when we begin our submarine journey."

Captain Nemo conducted me to the central staircase, which led on to the platform. Ned and Conseil were already there, delighted at the idea of the "pleasure party" which was preparing. Five sailors from the *Nautilus*, with their oars, waited in the boat, which had been made fast against the side.

The night was still dark. Layers of clouds covered the sky, allowing but few stars to be seen. I looked on the side where the land lay, and saw nothing but a dark line inclosing three parts of the horizon, from south-west to northwest. The *Nautilus*, having returned during the night up the western coast of Ceylon, was now west of the bay, or rather gulf, formed by the mainland and the island of Manaar. There, under the dark waters, stretched the pintadine bank, an inexhaustible field of pearls, the length of which is more than twenty miles.

Captain Nemo, Ned Land, Conseil, and I took our places in the stern of the boat. The master went to the tiller; his four companions leaned on their oars, the painter was cast off, and we sheered off.

The boat went toward the south; the oarsmen did not hurry. I noticed that their strokes, strong in the water, only followed each other every ten seconds, according to the method generally adopted in the navy. While the craft was running by its own velocity, the liquid drops struck the dark depths of the waves crisply like spats of melted lead. A little billow, spreading wide, gave a slight roll to the boat, and some samphire reeds flapped before it.

We were silent. What was Captain Nemo thinking of? Perhaps of the land he was approaching, and which he found too near to him, contrary to the Canadian's opinion, who thought it too far off. As to Conseil, he was merely there from curiosity.

About half-past five, the first tints on the horizon showed the upper line of coast more distinctly. Flat enough in the east, it rose a little to the south. Five miles still lay between us, and it was indistinct, owing to the mist on the water. At six o'clock it became suddenly daylight, with that rapidity peculiar to tropical regions, which know neither dawn nor twilight. The solar rays pierced the curtain of clouds piled up on the eastern horizon, and the radiant orb rose rapidly. I saw land distinctly, with a few trees scattered here and there. The boat neared Manaar Island, which was rounded to the south. Captain Nemo rose from his seat and watched the sea.

At a sign from him the anchor was dropped, but the chain scarcely ran, for it was little more than a yard deep, and this spot was one of the highest points of the bank of pintadines.

"Here we are, M. Aronnax," said Captain Nemo. "You see that inclosed bay? Here, in a month, will be assembled the numerous fishing-boats of the exporters, and these are the waters their divers will ransack so boldly. Happily, this bay is well situated for that kind of fishing. It is sheltered from the strongest winds; the sea is never very rough here, which makes it favorable for the diver's work. We will now put on our dresses, and begin our walk."

I did not answer, and while watching the suspected waves, began with the help of the sailors to put on my heavy sea-dress. Captain Nemo and my companions were also dressing. None of the *Nautilus* men were to accompany us on this new excursion.

Soon we were enveloped to the throat in India-rubber clothing; the air apparatus fixed to our backs by braces. As to the Ruhmkorff apparatus, there was no necessity for it. Before putting my head into the copper cap, I had asked the question of the captain.

"They would be useless," he replied. "We are going to no great depth, and the solar rays will be enough to light our walk. Besides, it would not be prudent to carry the electric light in these waters; its brilliancy might attract some of the dangerous inhabitants of the coast most inopportunely."

As Captain Nemo pronounced these words, I turned to Conseil and Ned Land. But my two friends had already incased their heads in the metal cap, and they could neither hear nor answer.

One last question remained to ask of Captain Nemo.

"And our arms?" asked I. "Our guns?"

"Guns! What for? Do not mountaineers attack the bear with a dagger in their hand, and is not steel surer than lead? Here is a strong blade; put it in your belt, and we start."

I looked at my companions; they were armed like us, and, more than that, Ned Land was brandishing an enormous harpoon, which he had placed in the boat before leaving the *Nautilus*.

Then, following the captain's example, I allowed myself to be dressed in the heavy copper helmet, and our reservoirs of air were at once in activity. An instant after, we were landed, one after the other, in about two feet of water upon an even sand. Captain Nemo made a sign with his hand, and we followed him by a gentle declivity till we disappeared under the waves.

Over our feet, like coveys of snipe in a bog, rose shoals of fish, of the genus monoptera, which have no other fins but their tail. I recognized the Javanese, a real serpent two and a half feet long, of a livid color underneath, and which might easily be mistaken for a conger eel if it was not for the golden stripes on its sides. In the genus stromateus, whose bodies are very flat and oval, I saw some of the most brilliant colors, carrying their dorsal fin like a scythe; an excellent eating fish, which, dried and pickled, is known by the name of karawade; then some tranquebars, belonging to the genus apsiphoroides, whose body is covered with a shell cuirass of eight longitudinal plates.

The heightening sun lit the mass of waters more and more. The soil changed by degrees. To the fine sand succeeded a perfect causeway of boulders, covered with a carpet of mollusks and zoöphytes. Among the specimens of these branches I noticed some placenæ, with thin, unequal shells, a kind of ostracion peculiar to the Red Sea and the Indian Ocean; some orange lucinæ with rounded shells; rock-fish three feet and a half long, which raised themselves under the waves like hands ready to seize one. There were also some panopyres, slightly luminous; and lastly, some oculines, like magnificent fans, forming one of the richest vegetations of these seas.

In the midst of these living plants, and under the arbors of the hydrophytes, were layers of clumsy articulates, particularly some raninæ, whose carapace formed a slightly rounded triangle; and some horrible-looking parthenopes.

At about seven o'clock we found ourselves at last surveying the oyster-banks, on which the pearl-oysters are reproduced by millions.

Captain Nemo pointed with his hand to the enormous heap of oysters; and I could well understand that this mine was inexhaustible, for nature's creative power is far beyond man's instinct of destruction. Ned Land, faithful to his instinct, hastened to fill a net which he carried by his side with some of the finest specimens. But we could not stop. We must follow the captain, who seemed to guide himself by paths known only to himself. The ground was sensibly rising, and sometimes, on holding up my arm, it was above the surface of the sea. Then the level of the bank would sink capriciously. Often we rounded high rocks scarped into pyramids. In their dark fractures huge crustacea, perched upon their high claws like some war-machine, watched us with fixed eyes, and under our feet crawled various kinds of annelides.

At this moment there opened before us a large grotto, dug in a picturesque heap of rocks, and carpeted with all the thick warp of the submarine flora. At first it seemed very dark to me. The solar rays seemed to be extinguished by successive gradations, until its vague transparency became nothing more than drowned light. Captain Nemo entered; we followed. My eyes soon accustomed themselves to this relative state of darkness. I could distinguish the arches springing capriciously from natural pillars, standing broad upon their granite base, like the heavy columns of Tuscan architecture. Why had our incomprehensible guide led us to the bottom of this submarine crypt? I was soon to know. After descending a rather sharp declivity, our feet trod the bottom of a kind of circular pit. There Captain Nemo stopped, and with his hand indicated an object I had not yet perceived. It was an oyster of extraordinary dimensions, a gigantic tridacne, a goblet which could have contained a whole lake of holy water, a basin the breadth of which was more than two yards and a half, and consequently larger than that ornamenting the saloon of the *Nautilus.* I approached this extraordinary mollusk. It adhered by its byssus to a table of granite, and there, isolated, it developed itself in the calm waters of the grotto. I estimated the weight of this tridacne at 600 pounds. Such an oyster would contain thirty pounds of meat; and one must have the stomach of a Gargantua to demolish some dozens of them.

Captain Nemo was evidently acquainted with the existence of this bivalve, and seemed to have a particular motive in verifying the actual state of this tridacne. The shells were a little open; the captain came near, and put his dagger between to prevent them from closing; then with his hand he raised the membrane with its fringed edges, which formed a cloak for the creature. There, between the folded plaits, I saw a loose pearl, whose size equaled that of a cocoanut. Its globular shape, perfect clearness, and admirable luster made it altogether a jewel of inestimable value. Carried away by my curiosity I stretched out my hand to seize it, weigh it, and touch it; but the captain stopped me, made a sign of refusal, and quickly withdrew his dagger, and the two shells closed suddenly. I then understood Captain Nemo's intention. In leaving this pearl hidden in the mantle of the tridacne, he was allowing it to grow slowly. Each year the secretions of the mollusk would add new concentric circles. I estimated its value at £500,000 at least.

After ten minutes Captain Nemo stopped suddenly. I thought he had halted previously to returning. No; by a gesture he bade us crouch beside him in a deep fracture of the rock, his hand pointed to one part of the liquid mass, which I watched attentively.

About five yards from me a shadow appeared and sank to the ground. The disquieting idea of sharks shot through my mind, but I was mistaken; and once again it was not a monster of the ocean that we had anything to do with.

It was a man, a living man, an Indian, a fisherman, a poor devil, who, I suppose, had come to glean before the harvest. I could see the bottom of his canoe anchored some feet above his head. He dived and went up successively. A stone held between his feet, cut in the shape of a sugar-loaf, while a rope fastened him to his boat, helped him to descend more rapidly. This was all his apparatus. Reaching the bottom about five yards deep, he went on his knees and filled his bag with oysters picked up at random. Then he went up, emptied it, pulled up his stone, and began the operation once more, which lasted thirty seconds.

The diver did not see us. The shadow of the rock hid us from sight. And how should this poor Indian ever dream that men, beings like himself, should be there under the water watching his movements, and losing no detail of the fishing? Several times he went up in this way, and dived again.

He did not carry away more than ten at each plunge, for he was obliged to pull them from the bank to which they adhered by means of their strong byssus. And how many of those oysters for which he risked his life had no pearl in them! I watched him closely; his maneuvers were regular, and for the space of half an hour, no danger appeared to threaten him.

I was beginning to accustom myself to the sight of this interesting fishing, when suddenly, as the Indian was on the ground, I saw him make a gesture of terror, rise, and make a spring to return to the surface of the sea.

I understood his dread. A gigantic shadow appeared just above the unfortunate diver. It was a shark of enormous size advancing diagonally, his eyes on fire, and his jaws open. I was mute with horror and unable to move.

The voracious creature shot toward the Indian, who threw himself on one side in order to avoid the shark's fins; but not its tail, for it struck his chest, and stretched him on the ground.

This scene lasted but a few seconds; the shark returned, and, turning on his back, prepared himself for cutting the Indian in two, when I saw Captain Nemo rise suddenly, and then, dagger in hand, walk straight to the monster, ready to fight face to face with him. The very moment the shark was going to snap the unhappy fisherman in two, he perceived his new adversary, and, turning over, made straight toward him.

I can still see Captain Nemo's position. Holding himself well together, he waited for the shark with admirable coolness; and, when it rushed at him, threw himself on one side with wonderful quickness, avoiding the shock, and burying his dagger deep into its side. But it was not all over. A terrible combat ensued.

The shark had seemed to roar, if I might say so. The blood rushed in torrents from its wound. The sea was dyed red, and through the opaque liquid I could distinguish nothing more. Nothing more, until the moment when, like lightning, I saw the undaunted captain hanging on to one of the creature's fins, struggling, as it were, hand to hand with the monster, and dealing successive blows at his enemy, yet still unable to give a decisive one.

The shark's struggles agitated the water with such fury that the rocking threatened to upset me.

I wanted to go to the captain's assistance, but, nailed to the spot with horror, I could not stir.

I saw the haggard eye; I saw the different phases of the fight. The captain fell to the earth, upset by the enormous mass which leaned upon him. The shark's jaws opened wide, like a pair of factory shears, and it would have been all over with the captain; but, quick as thought, harpoon in hand, Ned Land rushed toward the shark and struck it with its sharp point.

The waves were impregnated with a mass of blood. They rocked under the shark's movements, which beat them with indescribable fury. Ned Land had not missed his aim. It was the monster's death-rattle. Struck to the heart, it struggled in dreadful convulsions, the shock of which overthrew Conseil.

But Ned Land had disentangled the captain, who, getting up without any wound, went straight to the Indian, quickly cut the cord which held him to the stone, took him in his arms, and, with a sharp blow of his heel, mounted to the surface.

We all three followed in a few seconds, saved by a miracle, and reached the fisherman's boat.

Captain Nemo's first care was to recall the unfortunate man to life again. I did not think he could succeed. I hoped so, for the poor creature's immersion was not long; but the blow from the shark's tail might have been his death-blow.

Happily, with the captain's and Conseil's sharp friction, I saw consciousness return by degrees. He opened his eyes. What was his surprise, his terror even, at seeing four great copper heads leaning over him! And, above all, what must he have thought when Captain Nemo, drawing from the pocket of his dress a bag of pearls, placed it in his hand! This munificent charity from the man of the waters to the poor Cingalese was accepted with a trembling hand. His wondering eyes showed that he knew not to what superhuman beings he owed both fortune and life.

At a sign from the captain we regained the bank, and following the road already traversed, came in about half an hour to the anchor which held the canoe of the *Nautilus* to the earth.

Once on board, we each, with the help of the sailors, got rid of the heavy copper helmets.

Captain Nemo's first word was to the Canadian.

"Thank you, Master Land," said he.

"It was in revenge, captain," replied Ned Land. "I owed you that."

A ghastly smile passed across the captain's lips, and that was all.

"To the *Nautilus*," said he.

The boat flew over the waves. Some minutes after we met the shark's dead body floating. By the black marking of the extremity of its fins, I recognized the terrible melanopteron of the Indian seas, of the species of shark properly so called. It was more than twenty-five feet long; its enormous mouth occupied one-third of its body. It was an adult, as was known by its six rows of teeth placed in an isosceles triangle in the upper jaw.

Conseil looked at it with scientific interest, and I am sure that he placed it, and not without reason, in the cartilaginous class, of the chondropterygian order, with fixed gills, of the selacian family, in the genus of the sharks.

While I was contemplating this inert mass, a dozen of these voracious beasts appeared round the boat; and, without noticing us, threw themselves upon the dead body and fought with one another for the pieces.

At half-past eight we were again on board the *Nautilus*. There I reflected on the incidents which had taken place in our excursion to the Manaar Bank.

Two conclusions I must inevitably draw from it—one bearing upon the unparalleled courage of Captain Nemo, the other upon his devotion to a human being, a representative of that race from which he fled beneath the sea. Whatever he might say, this strange man had not yet succeeded in entirely crushing his heart.

When I made this observation to him, he answered in a slightly moved tone:

"That Indian, sir, is an inhabitant of an oppressed country; and I am still, and shall be, to my last breath, one of them!"

THE RED SEA

In the course of the day of the 29th of January, the island of Ceylon disappeared under the horizon, and the *Nautilus*, at a speed of twenty miles an hour, slid into the labyrinth of canals which separate the Maldives from the Laccadives. It coasted even the island of Kiltan, a land originally madreporic, discovered by Vasco da Gama in 1499, and one of the nineteen principal islands of the Laccadive Archipelago, situated between 10° and 14° 30′ north latitude, and 69° 50′ 72″ east longitude.

We had made 16,220 miles, or 7,500 (French) leagues, from our starting-point in the Japanese seas.

The next day (30th of January), when the *Nautilus* went to the surface of the ocean, there was no land in sight. Its course was N.N.E., in the direction of the Sea of Oman, between Arabia and the Indian Peninsula, which serves as an outlet to the Persian Gulf. It was evidently a block without any possible egress. Where was Captain Nemo taking us to? I could not say. This, however, did not satisfy the Canadian, who that day came to me asking where we were going.

"We are going where our captain's fancy takes us, Master Ned."

"His fancy cannot take us far, then," said the Canadian. "The Persian Gulf has no outlet; and if we do go in, it will not be long before we are out again."

"Very well, then, we will come out again, Master Land; and if after the Persian Gulf the *Nautilus* would like to visit the Red Sea, the Straits of Bab-el-mandeb are there to give us entrance."

"I need not tell you, sir," said Ned Land, "that the Red Sea is as much closed as the gulf, as the Isthmus of Suez is not yet cut; and if it was, a boat as mysterious as ours would not risk itself in a canal cut with sluices. And again the Red Sea is not the road to take us back to Europe."

"But I never said we were going back to Europe."

"What do you suppose, then?"

"I suppose that after visiting the curious coasts of Arabia and Egypt, the *Nautilus* will go down the Indian Ocean again, perhaps cross the Channel of Mozambique, perhaps off the Mascarenhas, so as to gain the Cape of Good Hope."

"And once at the Cape of Good Hope?" asked the Canadian, with peculiar emphasis.

"Well, we shall penetrate into that Atlantic which we do not yet know. Ah! friend Ned, you are getting tired of this journey under the sea: you are surfeited with the incessantly varying spectacle of submarine wonders. For my part, I shall be sorry to see the end of a voyage which it is given to so few men to make."

For four days, till the 3d of February, the *Nautilus* scoured the Sea of Oman, at various speeds and at various depths. It seemed to go at random, as if hesitating as to which road it should follow, but we never passed the Tropic of Cancer.

In quitting this sea we sighted Muscat for an instant, one of the most important towns of the country of Oman. I admired its strange aspect, surrounded by black rocks upon which its white houses and forts stood in relief. I saw the rounded domes of its mosques, the elegant points of its minarets, its fresh and verdant terraces. But it was only a vision! The *Nautilus* soon sank under the waves of that part of the sea.

We passed along the Arabian coast of Mahrah and Hadramaut, for a distance of six miles, its undulating line of mountains being occasionally relieved by some ancient ruin. The 5th of February we at last entered the Gulf of Aden, a perfect funnel introduced into the neck of Bab-el-mandeb, through which the Indian waters entered the Red Sea.

The 6th of February, the *Nautilus* floated in sight of Aden, perched upon a promontory which a narrow isthmus joins to the mainland, a kind of inaccessible Gibraltar, the fortifications of which were rebuilt by the English after taking possession in 1839. I caught a glimpse of the octagon minarets of this town, which was at one time, according to the historian Edrisi, the richest commercial magazine on the coast.

I certainly thought that Captain Nemo, arrived at this point, would back out again; but I was mistaken, for he did no such thing, much to my surprise.

The next day, the 7th of February, we entered the Straits of Bab-el-mandeb, the name of which, in the Arab tongue, means "The gate of tears."

To twenty miles in breadth, it is only thirty-two in length. And for the *Nautilus,* starting at full speed, the crossing was scarcely the work of an hour. But I saw nothing, not even the island of Perim, with which the British government has fortified the position of Aden. There were too many English or French steamers of the line of Suez to Bombay, Calcutta to Melbourne, and from Bourbon to the Mauritius, furrowing this narrow passage, for the *Nautilus* to venture to show itself. So it remained prudently below. At last, about noon, we were in the waters of the Red Sea.

I would not even seek to understand the caprice which had decided Captain Nemo upon entering the gulf. But I quite approved of the *Nautilus* entering it. Its speed was lessened: sometimes it kept on the surface, sometimes it dived to avoid a vessel, and thus I was able to observe the upper and lower parts of this curious sea.

The 8th of February, from the first dawn of day, Mocha came in sight, now a ruined town, whose walls would fall at a gunshot, yet which shelters here and there some verdant date-trees; once an important city, containing six public markets and twenty-six mosques, and whose walls, defended by fourteen forts, formed a girdle of two miles in circumference.

The *Nautilus* then approached the African shore, where the depth of the sea was greater. There, between two waters clear as crystal, through the open panels we were allowed to contemplate the beautiful bushes of brilliant coral, and large blocks of rock clothed with a splendid fur of green algæ and fuci. What an indescribable spectacle, and what variety of sites and landscapes along these sand-banks and volcanic islands which bound the Lybian coast! But where these shrubs appeared in all their beauty was on the eastern coast, which the *Nautilus* soon gained. It was on the coast of Tehama, for there not only did this display of zoöphytes flourish beneath the level of the sea, but they also formed picturesque interlacings which unfolded themselves about sixty feet above the surface, more capricious but less highly colored than those whose freshness was kept up by the vital power of the waters.

What charming hours I passed thus at the window of the saloon! What new specimens of submarine flora and fauna did I admire under the brightness of our electric lantern!

There grew sponges of all shapes, pediculated, foliated, globular, and digital. They certainly justified the names of baskets, cups, distaffs, elk's-horns, lion's-feet, peacock's-tails, and Neptune's-gloves, which have been given to them by the fishermen, greater poets than the savants.

Other zoöphytes which multiply near the sponges consist principally of medusæ of a most elegant kind. The mollusks were represented by varieties of the calmar (which, according to Orbigny, are peculiar to the Red Sea); and reptiles by the virgata turtle, of the genus of cheloniæ, which furnished a wholesome and delicate food for our table.

As to the fish, they were abundant and often remarkable. The following are those which the nets of the *Nautilus* brought more frequently on board:

Rays of a red-brick color, with bodies marked with blue spots, and easily recognizable by their double spikes; some superb caranxes, marked with seven transverse bands of jet-black, blue and yellow fins, and gold and silver scales; mullets with yellow heads; gobies, and a thousand other species, common to the ocean which we had just traversed.

The 9th of February, the *Nautilus* floated in the broadest part of the Red Sea, which is comprised between Souakin, on the west coast, and Koomfidah, on the east coast, with a diameter of ninety miles.

That day at noon, after the bearings were taken, Captain Nemo mounted the platform, where I happened to be, and I was determined not to let him go down again without at least pressing him regarding his ulterior projects. As soon as he saw me he approached, and graciously offered me a cigar.

"Well, sir, does this Red Sea please you? Have you sufficiently observed the wonders it covers, its fishes, its zoöphytes, its parterres of sponges, and its forests of coral? Did you catch a glimpse of the towns on its borders?"

"Yes, Captain Nemo," I replied; "and the *Nautilus* is wonderfully fitted for such a study. Ah! it is an intelligent boat!"

"Yes, sir, intelligent and invulnerable. It fears neither the terrible tempests of the Red Sea, nor its currents, nor its sand-banks."

"Certainly," said I, "this sea is quoted as one of the worst, and in the time of the ancients, if I am not mistaken, its reputation was detestable."

"Detestable, M. Aronnax. The Greek and Latin historians do not speak favorably of it, and Strabo says it is very dangerous during the Etesian winds, and in the rainy season. The Arabian Edrisi portrays it under the name of the Gulf of Colzoum, and relates that vessels perished there in great numbers on the sand-banks, and that no one would risk sailing in the night. It is, he pretends, a sea subject to fearful hurricanes, strewn with inhospitable islands, and 'which offers nothing good either on its surface or in its depths.' Such, too, is the opinion of Arrian, Agatharcides, and Artemidorus."

"One may see," I replied, "that these historians never sailed on board the *Nautilus*."

"Just so," replied the captain, smiling; "and in that respect moderns are not more advanced than the ancients. It required many ages to find out the mechanical power of steam. Who knows if, in another hundred years, we may not see a second *Nautilus*? Progress is slow, M. Aronnax."

"It is true," I answered; "your boat is at least a century before its time, perhaps an era. What a misfortune that the secret of such an invention should die with its inventor!"

Captain Nemo did not reply. After some minutes' silence he continued: "You were speaking of the opinions of ancient historians upon the dangerous navigation of the Red Sea."

"It is true," said I; "but were not their fears exaggerated?"

"Yes and no, M. Aronnax," replied Captain Nemo, who seemed to know the Red Sea by heart. "That which is no longer dangerous for a modern vessel, well rigged, strongly built, and master of its own course, thanks to obedient steam, offered all sorts of perils to the ships of the ancients. Picture to yourself those first navigators venturing in ships made of planks sewn with the cords of the palm trees, saturated with the grease of the sea-dog, and covered with powdered resin! They had not even instruments wherewith to take their bearings, and they went by guess among currents of which they scarcely knew anything. Under such conditions shipwrecks were, and must have been, numerous. But in our time, steamers running between Suez and the South Seas have nothing more to fear from the fury of this gulf, in spite of contrary trade winds. The captain and passengers do not prepare for their departure by offering propitiatory sacrifices; and, on their return, they no longer go ornamented with wreaths and gilt fillets to thank the gods in the neighboring temple."

"I agree with you," said I; "and steam seems to have killed all gratitude in the hearts of sailors. But, captain, since you seem to have especially studied this sea, can you tell me the origin of its name?"

"There exist several explanations on the subject, M. Aronnax. Would you like to know the opinion of a chronicler of the fourteenth century?"

"Willingly."

"This fanciful writer pretends that its name was given to it after the passage of the Israelites, when Pharaoh perished in the waves which closed at the voice of Moses."

"A poet's explanation, Captain Nemo," I replied; "but I cannot content myself with that. I ask you for your personal opinion."

"Here it is, M. Aronnax. According to my idea, we must see in this appellation of the Red Sea a translation of the Hebrew word 'Edom'; and if the ancients gave it that name, it was on account of the particular color of its waters."

"But up to this time I have seen nothing but transparent waves and without any particular color."

"Very likely; but as we advance to the bottom of the gulf, you will see this singular appearance. I remember seeing the Bay of Tor entirely red, like a sea of blood."

"And you attribute this color to the presence of a microscopic seaweed?"

"Yes; it is a mucilaginous purple matter, produced by the restless little plants known by the name of trichodesmia, and of which it requires 40,000 to occupy the space of a square 0.04 of an inch. Perhaps we shall meet some when we get to Tor."

"So, Captain Nemo, it is not the first time you have overrun the Red Sea on board the *Nautilus?"*

"No, sir."

"As you spoke a while ago of the passage of the Israelites and of the catastrophe to the Egyptians, I will ask whether you have met with traces under the water of this great historical fact?"

"No, sir; and for a very good reason."

"What is it?"

"It is, that the spot where Moses and his people passed is now so blocked up with sand that the camels can barely bathe their legs there. You can well understand that there would not be water enough for my *Nautilus."*

"And the spot?" I asked.

"The spot is situated a little above the Isthmus of Suez, in the arm which formerly made a deep estuary when the Red Sea extended to the Salt Lakes. Now, whether this passage were miraculous or not, the Israelites, nevertheless, crossed there to reach the Promised Land, and Pharaoh's army perished precisely on that spot; and I think that excavations made in the middle of the sand would bring to light a large number of arms and instruments of Egyptian origin."

"That is evident," I replied; "and for the sake of archæologists let us hope that these excavations will be made sooner or later, when new towns are established on the isthmus, after the construction of the Suez Canal; a canal, however, very useless to a vessel like the *Nautilus."*

"Very likely; but useful to the whole world," said Captain Nemo. "The ancients well understood the utility of a communication between the Red Sea and the Mediterranean for their commercial affairs; but they did not think of digging a canal direct, and took the Nile as an intermediate. Very probably the canal which united the Nile to the Red Sea was begun by Sesostris, if we may believe tradition. One thing is certain, that in the year 615 before Jesus Christ, Necos undertook the works of an alimentary canal to the waters of the Nile, across the plain of Egypt, looking toward Arabia. It took four days to go up this canal, and it was so wide that two triremes could go abreast. It was carried on by Darius, the son of Hystaspes, and probably finished by Ptolemy II. Strabo saw it navigated; but its decline from the point of departure, near Bubastes, to the Red Sea was so slight that it was only navigable for a few months in the year. This canal answered all commercial purposes to the age of Antoninus, when it was abandoned and blocked up with sand. Restored by order of the Caliph

Omar, it was definitively destroyed in 761 or 762 by Caliph Al-Mansor, who wished to prevent the arrival of provisions to Mohammed-ben-Abdallah, who had revolted against him. During the expedition into Egypt, your General Bonaparte discovered traces of the works in the Desert of Suez; and, surprised by the tide, he nearly perished before regaining Hadjaroth, at the very place where Moses had encamped three thousand years before him."

"Well, captain, what the ancients dared not undertake, this junction between the two seas, which will shorten the road from Cadiz to India, M. Lesseps has succeeded in doing; and before long he will have changed Africa into an immense island."

"Yes, M. Aronnax; you have the right to be proud of your countryman. Such a man brings more honor to a nation than great captains. He began, like so many others, with disgust and rebuffs; but he has triumphed, for he has the genius of will. And it is sad to think that a work like that, which ought to have been an international work, and which would have sufficed to make a reign illustrious, should have succeeded by the energy of one man. All honor to M. Lesseps!"

"Yes, honor to the great citizen!" I replied, surprised by the manner in which Captain Nemo had just spoken.

"Unfortunately," he continued, "I cannot take you through the Suez Canal; but you will be able to see the long jetty of Port Said after to-morrow, when we shall be in the Mediterranean."

"The Mediterranean!" I exclaimed.

"Yes, sir; does that astonish you?"

"What astonishes me is to think that we shall be there the day after to-morrow."

"Indeed?"

"Yes, captain, although by this time I ought to have accustomed myself to be surprised at nothing since I have been on board your boat."

"But the cause of this surprise?"

"Well! it is the fearful speed you will have to put on the *Nautilus,* if the day after to-morrow she is to be in the Mediterranean, having made the round of Africa, and doubled the Cape of Good Hope!"

"Who told you that she would make the round of Africa, and double the Cape of Good Hope, sir?"

"Well, unless the *Nautilus* sails on dry land, and passes above the isthmus——"

"Or beneath it, M. Aronnax."

"Beneath it!"

"Certainly," replied Captain Nemo quietly. "A long time ago nature made under this tongue of land what man has this day made on its surface."

"What! Such a passage exists?"

"Yes; a subterranean passage, which I have named the Arabian Tunnel. It takes us beneath Suez, and opens into the Gulf of Pelusium."

"But this isthmus is composed of nothing but quicksands."

"To a certain depth. But at fifty-five yards only, there is a solid layer of rock."

"Did you discover this passage by chance?" I asked, more and more surprised.

"Chance and reasoning, sir; and by reasoning even more than by chance. Not only does this passage exist, but I have profited by it several times. Without that I should not have ventured this day into the impassable Red Sea. I noticed that in the Red Sea and in the Mediterranean there existed a certain number of fishes of a kind perfectly identical—ophidia, fiatoles, girelles, and exocœti. Certain of that fact, I asked myself, was it possible that there was no communication between the two seas? If there was, the subterranean current must necessarily run from the Red Sea to the Mediterranean, from the sole cause of difference of level. I caught a large number of fishes in the neighborhood of Suez. I passed a copper ring through their tails, and threw them back into the sea. Some months later, on the coast of Syria, I caught some of my fish ornamented with the ring. Thus the communication between the two was proved. I then sought for it with my *Nautilus*; I discovered it, ventured into it, and before long, sir, you too will have passed through my Arabian Tunnel!"

THE ARABIAN TUNNEL

That same evening, in 21° 30′ north latitude, the *Nautilus* floated on the surface of the sea, approaching the Arabian coast. I saw Djeddah, the most important counting-house of Egypt, Syria, Turkey, and India. I distinguished clearly enough its buildings, the vessels anchored at the quays, and those whose draught of water obliged them to anchor in the roads. The sun, rather low on the horizon, struck full on the houses of the town, bringing out their whiteness. Outside, some wooden cabins, and some made of reeds, showed the quarter inhabited by the Bedouins. Soon Djeddah was shut out from view by the shadows of night, and the *Nautilus* found herself under water slightly phosphorescent.

The next day, the 10th of February, we sighted several ships running to windward. The *Nautilus* returned to its submarine navigation; but at noon, when her bearings were taken, the sea being deserted, she rose again to her waterline.

Accompanied by Ned and Conseil, I seated myself on the platform. The coast on the eastern side looked like a mass faintly printed upon a damp fog.

We were leaning on the sides of the pinnace, talking of one thing and another, when Ned Land, stretching out his hand toward a spot on the sea, said:

"Do you see anything there, sir?"

"No, Ned," I replied; "but I have not your eyes, you know."

"Look well," said Ned, "there, on the starboard beam, about the height of the lantern! Do you not see a mass which seems to move?"

"Certainly," said I, after close attention; "I see something like a long black body on the top of the water."

And certainly before long the black object was not more than a mile from us. It looked like a great sand-bank deposited in the open sea. It was a gigantic dugong!

Ned Land looked eagerly. His eyes shone with covetousness at the sight of the animal. His hand seemed ready to harpoon it. One would have thought he was waiting the moment to throw himself into the sea, and attack it in its element.

At this instant Captain Nemo appeared on the platform. He saw the dugong, understood the Canadian's attitude, and addressing him, said:

"If you held a harpoon just now, Master Land, would it not burn your hand?"

"Just so, sir."

"And you would not be sorry to go back, for one day, to your trade of a fisherman, and to add this cetacean to the list of those you have already killed?"

"I should not, sir."

"Well, you can try."

"Thank you, sir," said Ned Land, his eyes flaming.

"Only," continued the captain, "I advise you for your own sake not to miss the creature."

"Is the dugong dangerous to attack?" I asked, in spite of the Canadian's shrug of the shoulders.

"Yes," replied the captain; "sometimes the animal turns upon its assailants and overturns their boat. But for Master Land, this danger is not to be feared. His eye is prompt, his arm sure."

At this moment seven men of the crew, mute and immovable as ever, mounted the platform. One carried a harpoon and a line similar to those employed in catching whales. The pinnace was lifted from the bridge, pulled from its socket, and let down into the sea. Six oarsmen took their seats, and the coxswain went to the tiller. Ned, Conseil, and I went to the back of the boat.

"You are not coming, captain?" I asked.

"No, sir; but I wish you good sport."

The boat put off, and lifted by the six rowers, drew rapidly toward the dugong, which floated about two miles from the *Nautilus*.

Arrived some cables' length from the cetacean, the speed slackened, and the oars dipped noiselessly into the quiet waters. Ned Land, harpoon in hand, stood in the fore part of the boat. The harpoon used for striking the whale is generally attached to a very long cord, which runs out rapidly as the wounded creature draws it after him. But here the cord was not more than ten fathoms long, and the extremity was attached to a small barrel, which, by floating, was to show the course the dugong took under the water.

I stood, and carefully watched the Canadian's adversary. This dugong, which also bears the name of the halicore, closely resembles the manatee; its oblong body terminated in a lengthened tail, and its lateral fins in perfect fingers. Its difference from the manatee consisted in its upper jaw, which was armed with two long and pointed teeth, which formed on each side diverging tusks.

This dugong, which Ned Land was preparing to attack, was of colossal dimensions; it was more than seven yards long. It did not move, and seemed to be sleeping on the waves, which circumstance made it easier to capture.

The boat approached within six yards of the animal. The oars rested on the rowlocks. I half rose. Ned Land, his body thrown a little back, brandished the harpoon in his experienced hand.

Suddenly a hissing noise was heard, and the dugong disappeared. The harpoon, although thrown with great force, had apparently only struck the water.

"Curse it!" exclaimed the Canadian furiously; "I have missed it!"

"No," said I; "the creature is wounded—look at the blood; but your weapon has not stuck in his body."

"My harpoon! My harpoon!" cried Ned Land.

The sailors rowed on, and the coxswain made for the floating barrel. The harpoon regained, we followed in pursuit of the animal.

The latter came now and then to the surface to breathe. Its wound had not weakened it, for it shot onward with great rapidity.

The boat, rowed by strong arms, flew on its track. Several times it approached within some few yards, and the Canadian was ready to strike, but the dugong made off with a sudden plunge, and it was impossible to reach it.

Imagine the passion which excited impatient Ned Land! He hurled at the unfortunate creature the most energetic expletives in the English tongue. For my part I was only vexed to see the dugong escape all our attacks.

We pursued it without relaxation for an hour, and I began to think it would prove difficult to capture, when the animal, possessed with the perverse idea of vengeance, of which he had cause to repent, turned upon the pinnace and assailed us in its turn.

This maneuver did not escape the Canadian.

"Look out!" he cried.

The coxswain said some words in his outlandish tongue, doubtless warning the men to keep on their guard.

The dugong came within twenty feet of the boat, stopped, sniffed the air briskly with its large nostrils (not pierced at the extremity, but in the upper part of its muzzle). Then taking a spring he threw himself upon us.

The pinnace could not avoid the shock, and half upset, shipped at least two tons of water, which had to be emptied; but thanks to the coxswain, we caught it sideways, not full front, so we were not quite overturned. While Ned Land, clinging to the bows, belabored the gigantic animal with blows from his harpoon, the creature's teeth were buried in the gunwale, and it lifted the whole thing out of the water, as a lion does a roebuck. We were upset over one another, and I know not how the adventure would have ended, if the Canadian, still enraged with the beast, had not struck it to the heart.

I heard its teeth grind on the iron plate, and the dugong disappeared, carrying the harpoon with him. But the barrel soon returned to the surface, and shortly after the body of the animal, turned on its back. The boat came up with it, took it in tow, and made straight for the *Nautilus*.

It required tackle of enormous strength to hoist the dugong on to the platform. It weighed 10,000 lbs.

The next day, February 11th, the larder of the *Nautilus* was enriched by some more delicate game. A flight of sea-swallows rested on the *Nautilus*. It was a species of the *Sterna nilotica*, peculiar to Egypt; its beak is black, head gray and pointed, the eye surrounded by white spots, the back, wings, and tail of a grayish color, the belly and throat white, and claws red. They also took some dozen of Nile ducks, a wild bird of high flavor, its throat and upper part of the head white with black spots.

About five o'clock in the evening we sighted to the north the Cape of Ras-Mohammed. This cape forms the extremity of Arabia Petræa, comprised between the Gulf of Suez and the Gulf of Acabah.

The *Nautilus* penetrated into the Strait of Jubal, which leads to the Gulf of Suez. I distinctly saw a high mountain, towering between the two gulfs of Ras-Mohammed. It was Mount Horeb, that Sinai at the top of which Moses saw God face to face.

At six o'clock the *Nautilus*, sometimes floating, sometimes immersed, passed some distance from Tor, situated at the end of the bay, the waters of which seemed tinted with red, an observation already made by Captain Nemo. Then night fell in the midst of a heavy silence, sometimes broken by the cries of the pelican and other night-birds, and the noise of the waves breaking upon the shore, chafing against the rocks, or the panting of some far-off steamer beating the waters of the gulf with its noisy paddles.

From eight to nine o'clock the *Nautilus* remained some fathoms under the water. According to my calculation we must have been very near Suez. Through the panel of the saloon I saw the bottom of the rocks brilliantly lit up by our electric lamp. We seemed to be leaving the straits behind us more and more.

At a quarter past nine, the vessel having returned to the surface, I mounted the platform. Most impatient to pass through Captain Nemo's tunnel, I could not stay in one place, so came to breathe the fresh night-air.

Soon in the shadow I saw a pale light, half discolored by the fog, shining about a mile from us.

"A floating lighthouse!" said someone near me.

I turned, and saw the captain.

"It is the floating light of Suez," he continued. "It will not be long before we gain the entrance of the tunnel."

"The entrance cannot be easy?"

"No, sir; and for that reason I am accustomed to go into the steersman's cage, and myself direct our course. And now if you will go down, M. Aronnax, the *Nautilus* is going under the waves, and will not return to the surface until we have passed through the Arabian Tunnel."

Captain Nemo led me toward the central staircase; halfway down he opened a door, traversed the upper deck, and landed in the pilot's cage, which it may be remembered rose at the extremity of the platform. It was a cabin measuring six feet square, very much like that occupied by the pilot on the steamboats of the Mississippi or Hudson. In the midst worked a wheel, placed vertically, and caught to the tiller-rope, which ran to the back of the *Nautilus*. Four light-ports with lenticular glasses, let in a groove in the partition of the cabin, allowed the man at the wheel to see in all directions.

This cabin was dark, but soon my eyes accustomed themselves to the obscurity, and I perceived the pilot, a strong man, with his hands resting on the spokes of the wheel. Outside, the sea appeared vividly lit up by the lantern, which shed its rays from the back of the cabin to the other extremity of the platform.

"Now," said Captain Nemo, "let us try to make our passage."

Electric wires connected the pilot's cage with the machinery-room, and from there the captain could communicate simultaneously to his *Nautilus* the direction and the speed. He pressed a metal knob, and at once the speed of the screw diminished.

I looked in silence at the high straight wall we were running by at this moment, the immovable base of a massive sandy coast. We followed it thus for an hour only some few yards off.

Captain Nemo did not take his eye from the knob, suspended by its two concentric circles in the cabin. At a simple gesture the pilot modified the course of the *Nautilus* every instant.

I had placed myself at the port scuttle, and saw some magnificent substructures of coral, zoöphytes, seaweed, and fucus, agitating their enormous claws, which stretched out from the fissures of the rock.

At a quarter past ten, the captain himself took the helm. A large gallery, black and deep, opened before us. The *Nautilus* went boldly into it. A strange roaring was heard round its sides. It was the waters of the Red Sea, which the incline of the tunnel precipitated violently toward the Mediterranean. The *Nautilus* went with the torrent, rapid as an arrow, in spite of the efforts of the machinery, which, in order to offer more effective resistance, beat the waves with reversed screw.

On the walls of the narrow passage I could see nothing but brilliant rays, straight lines, furrows of fire, traced by the great speed, under the brilliant electric light. My heart beat fast.

At thirty-five minutes past ten, Captain Nemo quitted the helm; and, turning to me, said:

"The Mediterranean!"

In less than twenty minutes, the *Nautilus*, carried along by the torrent, had passed through the Isthmus of Suez.

THE GRECIAN ARCHIPELAGO

The next day, the 12th of February, at the dawn of day, the *Nautilus* rose to the surface. I hastened on to the platform. Three miles to the south the dim outline of Pelusium was to be seen. A torrent had carried us from one sea to the other. About seven o'clock Ned and Conseil joined me.

"Well, Sir Naturalist," said the Canadian, in a slightly jovial tone, "and the Mediterranean?"

"We are floating on its surface, friend Ned."

"What!" said Conseil. "This very night?"

"Yes, this very night; in a few minutes we have passed this impassable isthmus."

"I do not believe it," replied the Canadian.

"Then you are wrong, Master Land," I continued; "this low coast which rounds off to the south is the Egyptian coast. And you, who have such good eyes, Ned, you can see the jetty of Port Said stretching into the sea."

The Canadian looked attentively.

"Certainly you are right, sir, and your captain is a first-rate man. We are in the Mediterranean. Good! Now, if you please, let us talk of our own little affair, but so that no one hears us."

I saw what the Canadian wanted, and, in my case, I thought it better to let him talk, as he wished it; so we all three went and sat down near the lantern, where we were less exposed to the spray of the blades.

"Now, Ned, we listen; what have you to tell us?"

"What I have to tell you is very simple. We are in Europe; and before Captain Nemo's caprices drag us once more to the bottom of the Polar seas, or lead us into Oceania, I ask to leave the *Nautilus*."

I wished in no way to shackle the liberty of my companions, but I certainly felt no desire to leave Captain Nemo.

Thanks to him, and thanks to his apparatus, I was each day nearer the completion of my submarine studies; and I was rewriting my book of submarine depths in its very element. Should I ever again have such an opportunity of observing the wonders of the ocean? No, certainly not! And I could not bring myself to the idea of abandoning the *Nautilus* before the cycle of investigation was accomplished.

"Friend Ned, answer me frankly, are you tired of being on board? Are you sorry that destiny has thrown us into Captain Nemo's hands?"

The Canadian remained some moments without answering. Then crossing his arms, he said:

"Frankly, I do not regret this journey under the seas. I shall be glad to have made it; but now that it is made, let us have done with it. That is my idea."

"It will come to an end, Ned."

"Where and when?"

"Where I do not know, when I cannot say; or, rather, I suppose it will end when these seas have nothing more to teach us."

"Then what do you hope for?" demanded the Canadian.

"That circumstances may occur as well six months hence as now by which we may and ought to profit."

"Oh," said Ned Land, "and where shall we be in six months, if you please, Sir Naturalist?"

"Perhaps in China; you know the *Nautilus* is a rapid traveler. It goes through water as swallows through the air, or as an express on the land. It does not fear frequented seas; who can say that it may not beat the coasts of France, England, or America, on which flight may be attempted as advantageously as here."

"M. Aronnax," replied the Canadian, "your arguments are rotten at the foundation. You speak in the future, 'We shall be there! We shall be here!' I speak in the present, 'We are here, and we must profit by it.'"

Ned Land's logic pressed me hard, and I felt myself beaten on that ground. I knew not what argument would now tell in my favor.

"Sir," continued Ned, "let us suppose an impossibility; if Captain Nemo should this day offer you your liberty, would you accept it?"

"I do not know," I answered.

"And if," he added, "the offer he made you this day was never to be renewed, would you accept it?"

"Friend Ned, this is my answer. Your reasoning is against me. We must not rely on Captain Nemo's goodwill. Common prudence forbids him to set us at liberty. On the other side, prudence bids us profit by the first opportunity to leave the *Nautilus*."

"Well, M. Aronnax, that is wisely said."

"Only one observation—just one. The occasion must be serious, and our first attempt must succeed; if it fails, we shall never find another, and Captain Nemo will never forgive us."

"All that is true," replied the Canadian. "But your observation applies equally to all attempts at flight, whether in two years' time, or in two days. But the question is still this: if a favorable opportunity presents itself, it must be seized."

"Agreed! And now, Ned, will you tell me what you mean by a favorable opportunity?"

"It will be that which, on a dark night, will bring the *Nautilus* a short distance from some European coast."

"And you will try and save yourself by swimming?"

"Yes, if we were near enough to the bank, and if the vessel was floating at the time. Not if the bank was far away, and the boat was under the water."

"And in that case?"

"In that case, I should seek to make myself master of the pinnace. I know how it is worked. We must get inside, and the bolts once drawn, we shall come to the surface of the water, without even the pilot, who is in the bows, perceiving our flight."

"Well, Ned, watch for the opportunity; but do not forget that a hitch will ruin us."

"I will not forget, sir."

"And now, Ned, would you like to know what I think of your project?"

"Certainly, M. Aronnax."

"Well, I think—I do not say I hope—I think that this favorable opportunity will never present itself."

"Why not?"

"Because Captain Nemo cannot hide from himself that we have not given up all hope of regaining our liberty, and he will be on his guard, above all, in the seas, and in the sight of European coasts."

"We shall see," replied Ned Land, shaking his head determinedly.

"And now, Ned Land," I added, "let us stop here. Not another word on the subject. The day that you are ready, come and let us know, and we will follow you. I rely entirely upon you."

Thus ended a conversation which, at no very distant time, led to such grave results. I must say here that facts seemed to confirm my foresight, to the Canadian's great despair. Did Captain Nemo distrust us in these frequented seas, or did he only wish to hide himself from the numerous vessels of all nations, which plowed the Mediterranean? I could not tell; but we were oftener between waters, and far from the coast. Or, if the *Nautilus* did emerge, nothing was to be seen but the pilot's cage; and sometimes it went to great depths, for, between the Grecian Archipelago and Asia Minor, we could not touch the bottom by more than a thousand fathoms.

Thus I only knew we were near the island of Carpathos, one of the Sporades, by Captain Nemo reciting these lines from Virgil:

Est in Carpathio Neptuni gurgite vates,
Cæruleus Proteus,

as he pointed to a spot on the planisphere.

It was indeed the ancient abode of Proteus, the old shepherd of Neptune's flocks, now the island of Scarpanto, situated between Rhodes and Crete. I saw nothing but the granite base through the glass panels of the saloon.

The next day, the 14th of February, I resolved to employ some hours in studying the fishes of the archipelago; but for some reason or other, the panels remained hermetically sealed. Upon taking the course of the *Nautilus* I found that we were going toward Candia, the ancient isle of Crete. At the time I embarked on the *Abraham Lincoln,* the whole of this island had risen in insurrection against the despotism of the Turks. But how the insurgents had fared since that time I was absolutely ignorant, and it was not Captain Nemo, deprived of all land communications, who could tell me.

I made no allusion to this event when that night I found myself alone with him in the saloon. Besides, he seemed to be taciturn and preoccupied. Then, contrary to his custom, he ordered both panels to be opened, and going from one to the other, observed the mass of waters attentively. To what end I could not guess; so, on my side, I employed my time in studying the fish passing before my eyes.

Among others, I remarked some gobies, mentioned by Aristotle, and commonly known by the name of sea-braches which are more particularly met with in the salt waters lying near the Delta of the Nile. Near them rolled some seabream, half-phosphorescent, a kind of sparus, which the Egyptians ranked among their sacred animals, whose arrival in the waters of their river announced a fertile overflow, and was celebrated by religious ceremonies. I also noticed some cheilines about nine inches long, a bony fish with transparent shell, whose livid color is mixed with red spots; they are great eaters of marine vegetation, which gives them an exquisite flavor. These cheilines were much sought after by the epicures of ancient Rome; the inside, dressed with the soft roe of the lamprey, peacocks' brains, and tongues of the phenicoptera, composed that divine dish of which Vitellius was so enamored.

Another inhabitant of these seas drew my attention, and led my mind back to recollections of antiquity. It was the remora, that fastens on to the shark's belly. This little fish, according to the ancients, hooking on to the ship's bottom, could stop its movements; and one of them, by keeping back Antony's ship during the battle of Actium, helped Augustus to gain the victory. On how little hangs the destiny of nations! I observed some fine anthiæ, which belong to the order of lutjans, a fish held sacred by the Greeks, who attributed to them the power of hunting the marine monsters from waters they frequented. Their name signifies *flower,* and they justify their appellation by their shaded colors, their shades comprising the whole gamut of reds, from the paleness of the rose to the brightness of the ruby, and the fugitive tints that clouded their dorsal fin. My eyes could not leave these wonders of the sea, when they were suddenly struck by an unexpected apparition.

In the midst of the waters a man appeared, a diver, carrying at his belt a leathern purse. It was not a body abandoned to the waves; it was a living man, swimming with a strong hand, disappearing occasionally to take breath at the surface.

I turned toward Captain Nemo, and in an agitated voice exclaimed:

"A man shipwrecked! He must be saved at any price!"

The captain did not answer me, but came and leaned against the panel.

The man had approached, and with his face flattened against the glass, was looking at us.

To my great amazement, Captain Nemo signed to him. The diver answered with his hand, mounted immediately to the surface of the water, and did not appear again.

"Do not be uncomfortable," said Captain Nemo. "It is Nicholas of Cape Matapan; surnamed Pesca. He is well known in all the Cyclades. A bold diver! Water is his element, and he lives more in it than on land, going continually from one island to another, even as far as Crete."

"You know him, captain?"

"Why not, M. Aronnax?"

Saying which, Captain Nemo went toward a piece of furniture standing near the left panel of the saloon. Near this piece of furniture, I saw a chest bound with iron, on the cover of which was a copper plate, bearing the cipher of the *Nautilus* with its device.

At that moment, the captain, without noticing my presence, opened the piece of furniture, a sort of strong box, which held a great many ingots.

They were ingots of gold. From whence came this precious metal, which represented an enormous sum? Where did the captain gather this gold from and what was he going to do with it?

I did not say one word. I looked. Captain Nemo took the ingots one by one, and arranged them methodically in the chest, which he filled entirely. I estimated the contents at more than 4,000 lbs. weight of gold, that is to say, nearly £200,000.

The chest was securely fastened, and the captain wrote an address on the lid, in characters which must have belonged to Modern Greece.

This done, Captain Nemo pressed a knob, the wire of which communicated with the quarters of the crew. Four men appeared, and, not without some trouble, pushed the chest out of the saloon. Then I heard them hoisting it up the iron staircase by means of pulleys.

At that moment, Captain Nemo turned to me.

"And you were saying, sir?" said he.

"I was saying nothing, captain."

"Then, sir, if you will allow me, I will wish you good-night."

Whereupon he turned and left the saloon.

I returned to my room much troubled, as one may believe. I vainly tried to sleep—I sought the connecting link between the apparition of the diver and the chest filled with gold. Soon, I felt by certain movements of pitching and tossing that the *Nautilus* was leaving the depths and returning to the surface.

Then I heard steps upon the platform; and I knew they were unfastening the pinnace, and launching it upon the waves. For one instant it struck the side of the *Nautilus*, then all noise ceased.

Two hours after, the same noise, the same going and coming was renewed; the boat was hoisted on board, replaced in its socket, and the *Nautilus* again plunged under the waves.

So these millions had been transported to their address. To what point of the continent? Who was Captain Nemo's correspondent?

The next day, I related to Conseil and the Canadian the events of the night, which had excited my curiosity to the highest degree. My companions were not less surprised than myself.

"But where does he take his millions to?" asked Ned Land.

To that there was no possible answer. I returned to the saloon after having breakfast, and set to work. Till five o'clock in the evening, I employed myself in arranging my notes. At that moment (ought I to attribute it to some peculiar idiosyncrasy?) I felt so great a heat that I was obliged to take off my coat of byssus! It was strange, for we were not under low latitudes; and even then, the *Nautilus*, submerged as it was, ought to experience no change of temperature. I looked at the manometer; it showed a depth of sixty feet, to which atmospheric heat could never attain.

I continued my work, but the temperature rose to such a pitch as to be intolerable.

"Could there be fire on board?" I asked myself.

I was leaving the saloon, when Captain Nemo entered; he approached the thermometer, consulted it, and turning to me, said:

"Forty-two degrees."

"I have noticed it, captain," I replied; "and if it gets much hotter we cannot bear it."

"Oh, sir, it will not get hotter if we do not wish it!"

"You can reduce it as you please, then?"

"No; but I can go further from the stove which produces it."

"It is outward then!"

"Certainly; we are floating in a current of boiling water."

"Is it possible!" I exclaimed.

"Look."

The panels opened, and I saw the sea entirely white all round. A sulphurous smoke was curling amid the waves, which boiled like water in a copper. I placed my hand on one of the panes of glass, but the heat was so great that I quickly took it off again.

"Where are we?" I asked.

"Near the island of Santorin, sir," replied the captain, "and just in the canal which separates Nea Kamenni from Pali Kamenni. I wished to give you a sight of the curious spectacle of a submarine eruption."

"I thought," said I, "that the formation of these new islands was ended."

"Nothing is ever ended in the volcanic parts of the sea," replied Captain Nemo; "and the globe is always being worked by subterranean fires. Already, in the nineteenth year of our era, according to Cassiodorus and Pliny, a new island, Theia (the divine), appeared in the very place where these islets have recently been formed. Then they sank under the waves, to rise again in the year 69, when they again subsided. Since that time to our days, the Plutonian work has been suspended. But, on the 3d of February, 1866, a new island, which they named George Island, emerged from the midst of the sulphurous vapor near Nea Kamenni, and settled again the 6th of the same month. Seven days after, the 13th of February, the island of Aphroessa appeared, leaving between Nea Kamenni and itself a canal ten yards broad. I was in these seas when the phenomenon occurred, and I was able therefore to observe all the different phases. The island of Aphroessa, of round form, measured 300 feet in diameter, and thirty feet in height. It was composed of black and vitreous lava, mixed with fragments of felspar. And lastly, on the 10th of March, a smaller island, called Reka, showed itself near Nea Kamenni, and since then these three have joined together, forming but one and the same island."

"And the canal in which we are at this moment?" I asked.

"Here it is," replied Captain Nemo, showing me a map of the archipelago. "You see I have marked the new islands."

I returned to the glass. The *Nautilus* was no longer moving, the heat was becoming unbearable. The sea, which till now had been white, was red, owing to the presence of salts of iron. In spite of the ship's being hermetically sealed, an insupportable smell of sulphur filled the saloon, and the brilliancy of the electricity was entirely extinguished by bright scarlet flames. I was in a bath, I was choking, I was broiled.

"We can remain no longer in this boiling water," said I to the captain.

"It would not be prudent," replied the impassive Captain Nemo.

An order was given; the *Nautilus* tacked about and left the furnace it could not brave with impunity. A quarter of an hour after we were breathing fresh air on the surface. The thought then struck me that, if Ned Land had chosen this part of the sea for our flight, we should never have come alive out of this sea of fire.

The next day, the 16th of February, we left the basin which, between Rhodes and Alexandria, is reckoned about 1,500 fathoms in depth, and the *Nautilus,* passing some distance from Cerigo, quitted the Grecian Archipelago, after having doubled Cape Matapan.

The Mediterranean in Forty-eight Hours

The Mediterranean, the blue sea *par excellence,* "the great sea" of the Hebrews, "the sea" of the Greeks, the "mare nostrum" of the Romans, bordered by orange trees, aloes, cacti, and sea-pines; embalmed with the perfume of the myrtle, surrounded by rude mountains, saturated with pure and transparent air, but incessantly worked by underground fires, a perfect battlefield in which Neptune and Pluto still dispute the empire of the world!

It is upon these banks, and on these waters, says Michelet, that man is renewed in one of the most powerful climates of the globe. But, beautiful as it was, I could only take a rapid glance at the basin whose superficial area is two millions of square yards. Even Captain Nemo's knowledge was lost to me, for this enigmatical person did not appear once during our passage at full speed. I estimated the course which the *Nautilus* took under the waves of the sea at about six hundred leagues, and it was accomplished in forty-eight hours. Starting on the morning of the 16th of February from the shores of Greece, we had crossed the Straits of Gibraltar by sunrise on the 18th.

It was plain to me that this Mediterranean, inclosed in the midst of those countries which he wished to avoid, was distasteful to Captain Nemo. Those waves and those breezes brought back too many remembrances, if not too many regrets. Here he had no longer that independence and that liberty of gait which he had when in the open seas, and his *Nautilus* felt itself cramped between the close shores of Africa and Europe.

Our speed was now twenty-five miles an hour. It may be well understood that Ned Land, to his great disgust, was obliged to renounce his intended flight. He could not launch the pinnace, going at the rate of twelve or thirteen yards every second. To quit the *Nautilus* under such conditions would be as bad as jumping from a train going at full speed—an imprudent thing, to say the least of it. Besides, our vessel only mounted to the surface of the waves at night to renew its stock of air; it was steered entirely by the compass and the log.

I saw no more of the interior of this Mediterranean than a traveler by express train perceives of the landscape which flies before his eyes; that is to say, the distant horizon, and not the nearer objects which pass like a flash of lightning.

In the midst of the mass of waters brightly lit up by the electric light glided some of those lampreys, more than a yard long, common to almost every climate. Some of the oxyrhynchi, a kind of ray five feet broad, with white belly and gray spotted back, spread out like a large shawl carried along by the current. Other rays passed so quickly that I could not see if they deserved the name of eagles which was given to them by the ancient Greeks, or the qualification of rats, toads, and bats, with which modern fishermen have loaded them. A few milander sharks, twelve feet long, and much feared by divers, struggled among them. Sea foxes eight feet long, endowed with wonderful fineness of scent, appeared like large blue shadows. Some dorades of the shark kind, some of which measured seven feet and a half, showed themselves in their dress of blue and silver, encircled by small bands which struck sharply against the somber tints of their fins, a fish consecrated to Venus, the eyes of which are incased in a socket of gold, a precious species, friend of all waters, fresh or salt, an inhabitant of rivers, lakes, and oceans, living in all climates, and bearing all temperatures; a race belonging to the geological era of the earth, and which has preserved all the beauty of its first days. Magnificent sturgeons, nine or ten yards long, creatures of great speed, striking the panes of glass with their strong tails, displayed their bluish backs with small brown spots; they resemble the sharks, but are not equal to them in strength, and are to be met with in all seas. But of all the diverse inhabitants of the Mediterranean, those I observed to the greatest advantage, when the *Nautilus* approached the surface, belonged to the sixty-third genus of bony fish. They were a kind of tunny, with bluish-black backs, and silvery breastplates, whose dorsal fins threw out sparkles of gold. They are said to follow in the wake of vessels, whose refreshing shade they seek from the fire of a tropical sky, and they did not belie the saying, for they accompanied the *Nautilus* as they did in former times the vessel of La Perouse. For many a long hour they struggled to keep up with our vessel. I was never tired of admiring these creatures really built for speed—their small heads, their bodies lithe and cigar-shaped, which in some were more than three yards long, their pectoral fins, and forked tail endowed with remarkable strength. They swam in a triangle, like certain flocks of birds, whose rapidity they equaled, and of which the ancients used to say that they understood geometry and strategy. But still they do not escape the pursuit of the provençals, who esteem them as highly as the inhabitants of the Propontis and of Italy used to do; and these precious but blind and foolhardy creatures perish by millions in the nets of the Marseillaise.

With regard to the species of fish common to the Atlantic and the Mediterranean, the giddy speed of the *Nautilus* prevented me from observing them with any degree of accuracy.

As to marine mammals, I thought, in passing the entrance of the Adriatic, that I saw two or three cachalots, furnished with one dorsal fin, of the genus physetera, some dolphins of the genus globicephala, peculiar to the Mediterranean, the back part of the head being marked like a zebra with small lines; also, a dozen of seals, with white bellies and black hair, known by the name of *monks,* and which really have the air of a Dominican; they are about three yards in length.

As to zoöphytes, for some instants I was able to admire a beautiful orange galeolaria, which had fastened itself to the port panel; it held on by a long filament, and was divided into an infinity of branches, terminated by the finest lace which could ever have been woven by the rivals of Arachne herself. Unfortunately, I could not take this admirable specimen; and doubtless no other Mediterranean zoöphyte would have offered itself to my observation, if, on the night of the 16th, the *Nautilus* had not, singularly enough, slackened its speed, under the following circumstances.

We were then passing between Sicily and the coast of Tunis. In the narrow space between Cape Bon and the Straits of Messina the bottom of the sea rose almost suddenly. There was a perfect bank, on which there was not more than nine fathoms of water, while on either side the depth was ninety fathoms.

The *Nautilus* had to maneuver very carefully so as not to strike against this submarine barrier.

I showed Conseil on the map of the Mediterranean the spot occupied by this reef.

"But if you please, sir," observed Conseil, "it is like a real isthmus joining Europe to Africa."

"Yes, my boy; it forms a perfect bar to the Straits of Lybia, and the soundings of Smith have proved that in former times the continents between Cape Boco and Cape Furina were joined."

"I can well believe it," said Conseil.

"I will add," I continued, "that a similar barrier exists between Gibraltar and Ceuta, which in geological times formed the entire Mediterranean."

"What if some volcanic burst should one day raise these two barriers above the waves?"

"It is not probable, Conseil."

"Well, but allow me to finish, please, sir; if this phenomenon should take place, it will be troublesome for M. Lesseps, who has taken so much pains to pierce the isthmus."

"I agree with you; but I repeat, Conseil, this phenomenon will never happen. The violence of subterranean force is ever diminishing. Volcanoes, so plentiful in the first days of the world, are being extinguished by degrees; the internal heat is weakened; the temperature of the lower strata of the globe is lowered by a perceptible quantity every century to the detriment of our globe, for its heat is its life."

"But the sun?"

"The sun is not sufficient, Conseil. Can it give heat to a dead body?"

"Not that I know of."

"Well, my friend, this earth will one day be that cold corpse; it will become uninhabitable and uninhabited like the moon, which has long since lost all its vital heat."

"In how many centuries?"

"In some hundreds of thousands of years, my boy."

"Then," said Conseil, "we shall have time to finish our journey, that is, if Ned Land does not interfere with it."

And Conseil, reassured, returned to the study of the bank, which the *Nautilus* was skirting at a moderate speed.

There, beneath the rocky and volcanic bottom, lay outspread a living flora of sponges and reddish cydippes, which emitted a slight phosphorescent light, commonly known by the name of sea-cucumbers; and walking comatulæ more than a yard long, the purple of which completely colored the water around.

The *Nautilus* having now passed the high bank in the Lybian Straits returned to the deep waters and its accustomed speed.

From that time no more mollusks, no more articulates, no more zoöphytes; barely a few large fish passing like shadows.

During the night of the 16th and 17th of February, we had entered the second Mediterranean basin, the greatest depth of which was 1,450 fathoms. The *Nautilus,* by the action of its screw, slid down the inclined planes, and buried itself in the lowest depths of the sea.

On the 18th of February, about three o'clock in the morning, we were at the entrance of the Straits of Gibraltar. There once existed two currents—an upper one, long since recognized, which conveys the waters of the ocean into the basin of the Mediterranean; and a lower counter-current, which reasoning has now shown to exist. Indeed, the volume of water in the Mediterranean, incessantly added to by the waves of the Atlantic, and by rivers falling into it, would each year raise the level of this sea, for its evaporation is not sufficient to restore the equilibrium. As it is not so, we must necessarily admit the existence of an under-current, which empties into the basin of the Atlantic, through the Straits of Gibraltar, the surplus waters of the Mediterranean. A fact, indeed; and it was this counter-current by which the *Nautilus* profited. It advanced rapidly by the narrow pass. For one instant I caught a glimpse of the beautiful ruins of the temple of Hercules, buried in the ground, according to Pliny, and with the low island which supports it; and a few minutes later we were floating on the Atlantic.

Vigo Bay

The Atlantic! A vast sheet of water, whose superficial area covers twenty-five millions of square miles, the length of which is nine thousand miles, with a mean breadth of two thousand seven hundred—an ocean whose parallel winding shores embrace an immense circumference, watered by the largest rivers of the world, the St. Lawrence, the Mississippi, the Amazon, the Plata, the Orinoco, the Niger, the Senegal, the Elbe, the Loire, and the Rhine, which carry water from the most civilized, as well as from the most savage countries! Magnificent field of water, incessantly plowed by vessels of every nation, sheltered by the flags of every nation, and which terminates in those two terrible points so dreaded by mariners, Cape Horn, and the Cape of Tempests!

The *Nautilus* was piercing the water with its sharp spur, after having accomplished nearly ten thousand leagues in three months and a half, a distance greater than the great circle of the earth. Where were we going now, and what was reserved for the future? The *Nautilus,* leaving the Straits of Gibraltar, had gone far out. It returned to the surface of the waves, and our daily walks on the platform were restored to us.

I mounted at once, accompanied by Ned Land and Conseil. At a distance of about twelve miles, Cape St. Vincent was dimly to be seen, forming the southwestern point of the Spanish peninsula. A strong southerly gale was blowing. The sea was swollen and billowy; it made the *Nautilus* rock violently. It was almost impossible to keep one's footing on the platform, which the heavy rolls of the sea beat over every instant. So we descended after inhaling some mouthfuls of fresh air.

I returned to my room, Conseil to his cabin; but the Canadian, with a preoccupied air, followed me. Our rapid passage across the Mediterranean had not allowed him to put his project into execution, and he could not help showing his disappointment. When the door of my room was shut, he sat down and looked at me silently.

"Friend Ned," said I, "I understand you; but you cannot reproach yourself. To have attempted to leave the *Nautilus* under the circumstances would have been folly."

Ned Land did not answer; his compressed lips and frowning brow showed with him the violent possession this fixed idea had taken of his mind.

"Let us see," I continued; "we need not despair yet. We are going up the coast of Portugal again; France and England are not far off, where we can easily find refuge. Now, if the *Nautilus,* on leaving the Straits of Gibraltar, had gone to the south, if it had carried us toward regions where there were no continents, I should share your uneasiness. But we know now that Captain Nemo does not fly from civilized seas, and in some days I think you can act with security."

Ned Land still looked at me fixedly; at length his fixed lips parted, and he said, "It is for to-night."

I drew myself up suddenly. I was, I admit, little prepared for this communication. I wanted to answer the Canadian, but words would not come.

"We agreed to wait for an opportunity," continued Ned Land, "and the opportunity has arrived. This night we shall be but a few miles from the Spanish coast. It is cloudy. The wind blows freely. I have your word, M. Aronnax, and I rely upon you."

As I was still silent, the Canadian approached me.

"To-night, at nine o'clock," said he. "I have warned Conseil. At that moment, Captain Nemo will be shut up in his room, probably in bed. Neither the engineers nor the ship's crew can see us. Conseil and I will gain the central staircase, and you, M. Aronnax, will remain in the library, two steps from us, waiting my signal. The oars, the mast, and the sail are in the canoe. I have even succeeded in getting in some provisions. I have procured an English wrench, to unfasten the bolts which attach it to the shell of the *Nautilus.* So all is ready, till to-night."

"The sea is bad."

"That I allow," replied the Canadian; "but we must risk that. Liberty is worth paying for; besides, the boat is strong, and a few miles with a fair wind to carry us is no great thing. Who knows but by to-morrow we may be a hundred leagues away? Let circumstances only favor us, and by ten or eleven o'clock we shall have landed on some spot of *terra firma,* alive or dead. But adieu now till to-night."

With these words, the Canadian withdrew, leaving me almost dumb. I had imagined that, the chance gone, I should have time to reflect and discuss the matter. My obstinate companion had given me no time; and, after all, what could I have said to him? Ned Land was perfectly right. There was almost the opportunity to profit by. Could I retract my word, and take upon myself the responsibility of compromising the future of my companions? To-morrow Captain Nemo might take us far from all land.

At that moment a rather loud hissing told me that the reservoirs were filling, and that the *Nautilus* was sinking under the waves of the Atlantic.

A sad day I passed, between the desire of regaining my liberty of action, and of abandoning the wonderful *Nautilus*, and leaving my submarine studies incomplete.

What dreadful hours I passed thus, sometimes seeing myself and companions safely landed, sometimes wishing, in spite of my reason, that some unforeseen circumstances would prevent the realization of Ned Land's project.

Twice I went to the saloon. I wished to consult the compass. I wished to see if the direction the *Nautilus* was taking was bringing us nearer or taking us further from the coast. But no; the *Nautilus* kept in Portuguese waters.

I must therefore take my part, and prepare for flight. My luggage was not heavy; my notes, nothing more.

As to Captain Nemo, I asked myself what he would think of our escape; what trouble, what wrong it might cause him, and what he might do in case of its discovery or failure. Certainly I had no cause to complain of him; on the contrary, never was hospitality freer than his. In leaving him I could not be taxed with ingratitude. No oath bound us to him. It was on the strength of circumstances he relied, and not upon our word, to fix us forever.

I had not seen the captain since our visit to the island of Santorin. Would chance bring me to his presence before our departure? I wished it, and I feared it at the same time. I listened if I could hear him walking in the room contiguous to mine. No sound reached my ear. I felt an unbearable uneasiness. This day of waiting seemed eternal. Hours struck too slowly to keep pace with my impatience.

My dinner was served in my room as usual. I ate but little, I was too preoccupied. I left the table at seven o'clock. A hundred and twenty minutes (I counted them) still separated me from the moment in which I was to join Ned Land. My agitation redoubled. My pulse beat violently. I could not remain quiet. I went and came, hoping to calm my troubled spirit by constant movement. The idea of failure in our bold enterprise was the least painful of my anxieties; but the thought of seeing our project discovered before leaving the *Nautilus*, of being brought before Captain Nemo, irritated, or (what was worse) saddened at my desertion, made my heart beat.

I wanted to see the saloon for the last time. I descended the stairs, and arrived in the museum where I had passed so many useful and agreeable hours. I looked at all its riches, all its treasures, like a man on the eve of an eternal exile who was leaving never to return. These wonders of nature, these masterpieces of art, among which, for so many days, my life had been concentrated, I was going to abandon them forever! I should like to have taken a last look through the windows of the saloon into the waters of the Atlantic; but the panels were hermetically closed, and a cloak of steel separated me from that ocean which I had not yet explored.

In passing through the saloon, I came near the door, let into the angle, which opened into the captain's room. To my great surprise this door was ajar. I drew back, involuntarily. If Captain Nemo should be in his room, he could see me. But, hearing no noise, I drew nearer. The room was deserted. I pushed open the door, and took some steps forward. Still the same monk-like severity of aspect.

Suddenly the clock struck eight. The first beat of the hammer on the bell awoke me from my dreams. I trembled as if an invisible eye had plunged into my most secret thoughts, and I hurried from the room.

There my eye fell upon the compass. Our course was still north. The log indicated moderate speed, the manometer a depth of about sixty feet.

I returned to my room, clothed myself warmly—sea boots, an otterskin cap, a great-coat of byssus, lined with sealskin; I was ready, I was waiting. The vibration of the screw alone broke the deep silence which reigned on board. I listened attentively. Would no loud voice suddenly inform me that Ned Land had been surprised in his projected flight? A mortal dread hung over me, and I vainly tried to regain my accustomed coolness.

At a few minutes to nine, I put my ear to the captain's door. No noise. I left my room and returned to the saloon, which was half in obscurity, but deserted.

I opened the door communicating with the library. The same insufficient light, the same solitude. I placed myself near the door leading to the central staircase, and there waited for Ned Land's signal.

At that moment the trembling of the screw sensibly diminished, then it stopped entirely. The silence was now only disturbed by the beatings of my own heart. Suddenly a slight shock was felt; and I knew that the *Nautilus* had stopped at the bottom of the ocean. My uneasiness increased. The Canadian's signal did not come. I felt inclined to join Ned Land and beg of him to put off his attempt. I felt that we were not sailing under our usual conditions.

At this moment the door of the large saloon opened, and Captain Nemo appeared. He saw me, and, without further preamble, began in an amiable tone of voice:

"Ah, sir! I have been looking for you. Do you know the history of Spain?"

Now, one might know the history of one's own country by heart; but in the condition I was at the time, with troubled mind and head quite lost, I could not have said a word of it.

"Well," continued Captain Nemo, "you heard my question? Do you know the history of Spain?"

"Very slightly," I answered.

"Well, here are learned men having to learn," said the captain. "Come, sit down, and I will tell you a curious episode in this history. Sir, listen well," said he; "this history will interest you on one side, for it will answer a question which doubtless you have not been able to solve."

"I listen, captain," said I, not knowing what my interlocutor was driving at, and asking myself if this incident was bearing on our projected flight.

"Sir, if you have no objection, we will go back to 1702. You cannot be ignorant that your king, Louis XIV, thinking that the gesture of a potentate was sufficient to bring the Pyrenees under his yoke, had imposed the Duke of Anjou, his grandson, on the Spaniards. This prince reigned more or less badly under the name of Philip V, and had a strong party against him abroad. Indeed, the preceding year, the royal houses of Holland, Austria, and England had concluded a treaty of alliance at the Hague, with the intention of plucking the crown of Spain from the head of Philip V, and placing it on that of an archduke to whom they prematurely gave the title of Charles III.

"Spain must resist this coalition; but she was almost entirely unprovided with either soldiers or sailors. However, money would not fail them, provided that their galleons, laden with gold and silver from America, once entered their ports. And about the end of 1702 they expected a rich convoy which France was escorting with a fleet of twenty-three vessels, commanded by Admiral Château-Renaud, for the ships of the coalition were already beating the Atlantic. This convoy was to go to Cadiz, but the admiral, hearing that an English fleet was cruising in those waters, resolved to make for a French port.

"The Spanish commanders of the convoy objected to this decision. They wanted to be taken to a Spanish port, and if not to Cadiz, into Vigo Bay, situated on the northwest coast of Spain, and which was not blocked.

"Admiral Château-Renaud had the rashness to obey this injunction, and the galleons entered Vigo Bay.

"Unfortunately, it formed an open road which could not be defended in any way. They must therefore hasten to unload the galleons before the arrival of the combined fleet; and time would not have failed them had not a miserable question of rivalry suddenly arisen.

"You are following the chain of events?" asked Captain Nemo.

"Perfectly," said I, not knowing the end proposed by this historical lesson.

"I will continue. This is what passed. The merchants of Cadiz had a privilege by which they had the right of receiving all merchandise coming from the West Indies. Now, to disembark these ingots at the port of Vigo was depriving them of their rights. They complained at Madrid, and obtained the consent of the weak-minded Philip that the convoy, without discharging its cargo, should remain sequestered in the roads of Vigo until the enemy had disappeared.

"But while coming to this decision, on the 22d of October, 1702, the English vessels arrived in Vigo Bay, when Admiral Château-Renaud, in spite of inferior forces, fought bravely. But seeing that the treasure must fall into the enemy's hands, he burned and scuttled every galleon, which went to the bottom with their immense riches."

Captain Nemo stopped. I admit I could not yet see why this history should interest me.

"Well?" I asked.

"Well, M. Aronnax," replied Captain Nemo, "we are in that Vigo Bay; and it rests with yourself whether you will penetrate its mysteries."

The captain rose, telling me to follow him. I had had time to recover. I obeyed. The saloon was dark, but through the transparent glass the waves were sparkling. I looked.

For half a mile around the *Nautilus* the waters seemed bathed in electric light. The sandy bottom was clean and bright. Some of the ship's crew in their diving-dresses were clearing away half-rotten barrels and empty cases from the midst of the blackened wrecks. From these cases and from these barrels escaped ingots of gold and silver, cascades of piastres and jewels. The sand was heaped up with them. Laden with their precious booty the men returned to the *Nautilus*, disposed of their burden, and went back to this inexhaustible fishery of gold and silver.

I understood now. This was the scene of the battle of the 22d of October, 1702. Here on this very spot the galleons laden for the Spanish government had sunk. Here Captain Nemo came, according to his wants, to pack up those millions with which he burdened the *Nautilus*. It was for him and him alone America had given up her precious metals. He was heir direct, without anyone to share in those treasures torn from the Incas and from the conquered of Ferdinand Cortez.

"Did you know, sir," he asked, smiling, "that the sea contained such riches?"

"I knew," I answered, "that they value the money held in suspension in these waters at two millions."

"Doubtless; but to extract this money the expense would be greater than the profit. Here, on the contrary, I have but to pick up what man has lost; and not only in Vigo Bay, but in a thousand other spots where shipwrecks have happened, and which are marked on my submarine map. Can you understand now the source of the millions I am worth?"

"I understand, captain. But allow me to tell you that in exploring Vigo Bay you have only been beforehand with a rival society."

"And which?"

"A society which has received from the Spanish government the privilege of seeking these buried galleons. The shareholders are led on by the allurement of an enormous bounty, for they value these rich shipwrecks at five hundred millions."

"Five hundred millions they were," answered Captain Nemo, "but they are so no longer."

"Just so," said I; "and a warning to those shareholders would be an act of charity. But who knows if it would be well received? What gamblers usually regret above all is less the loss of their money, than of their foolish hopes. After all, I pity them less than the thousands of unfortunates to whom so much riches well distributed would have been profitable, while for them they will be forever barren."

I had no sooner expressed this regret than I felt that it must have wounded Captain Nemo.

"Barren!" he exclaimed, with animation. "Do you think then, sir, that these riches are lost because I gather them? Is it for myself alone, according to your idea, that I take the trouble to collect these treasures? Who told you that I did not make a good use of it? Do you think I am ignorant that there are suffering beings and oppressed races on this earth, miserable creatures to console, victims to avenge? Do you not understand?"

Captain Nemo stopped at these last words, regretting perhaps that he had spoken so much. But I had guessed that, whatever the motive which had forced him to seek independence under the sea, it had left him still a man, that his heart still beat for the sufferings of humanity, and that his immense charity was for oppressed races as well as individuals. And I then understood for whom those millions were destined, which were forwarded by Captain Nemo when the *Nautilus* was cruising in the waters of Crete.

A Vanished Continent

The next morning, the 19th of February, I saw the Canadian enter my room. I expected this visit. He looked very disappointed.

"Well, sir?" said he.

"Well, Ned, fortune was against us yesterday."

"Yes; that captain must needs stop exactly at the hour we intended leaving his vessel."

"Yes, Ned, he had business at his banker's."

"His banker's!"

"Or rather his banking-house; by that I mean the ocean, where his riches are safer than in the chests of the state."

I then related to the Canadian the incidents of the preceding night, hoping to bring him back to the idea of not abandoning the captain; but my recital had no other result than an energetically expressed regret from Ned, that he had not been able to take a walk on the battlefield of Vigo on his own account.

"However," said he, "all is not ended. It is only a blow of the harpoon lost. Another time we must succeed; and to-night, if necessary—"

"In what direction is the *Nautilus* going?" I asked.

"I do not know," replied Ned.

"Well, at noon we shall see the point."

The Canadian returned to Conseil. As soon as I was dressed, I went into the saloon. The compass was not reassuring. The course of the *Nautilus* was S.S.W. We were turning our backs on Europe.

I waited with some impatience till the ship's place was pricked on the chart. At about half-past eleven the reservoirs were emptied, and our vessel rose to the surface of the ocean. I rushed toward the platform. Ned Land had preceded me. No more land in sight. Nothing but an immense sea. Some sails on the horizon, doubtless those going to San Roque in search of favorable winds for doubling the Cape of Good Hope. The weather was cloudy. A gale of wind was preparing. Ned raved, and tried to pierce the cloudy horizon. He still hoped that behind all that fog stretched the land he so longed for.

At noon the sun showed itself for an instant. The second profited by this brightness to take its height. Then the sea becoming more billowy, we descended, and the panel closed.

An hour after, upon consulting the chart, I saw the position of the *Nautilus* was marked at 16° 17′ longitude, and 33° 22′ latitude, at 150 leagues from the nearest coast. There was no means of flight, and I leave you to imagine the rage of the Canadian, when I informed him of our situation.

For myself, I was not particularly sorry. I felt lightened of the load which had oppressed me, and was able to return with some degree of calmness to my accustomed work.

That night, about eleven o'clock, I received a most unexpected visit from Captain Nemo. He asked me very graciously if I felt fatigued from my watch of the preceding night. I answered in the negative.

"Then, M. Aronnax, I propose a curious excursion."

"Propose, captain."

"You have hitherto only visited the submarine depths by daylight, under the brightness of the sun. Would it suit you to see them in the darkness of the night?"

"Most willingly."

"I warn you, the way will be tiring. We shall have far to walk, and must climb a mountain. The roads are not well kept."

"What you say, captain, only heightens my curiosity; I am ready to follow you."

"Come, then, sir, we will put on our diving-dresses."

Arrived at the robing-room, I saw that neither of my companions nor any of the ship's crew were to follow us on this excursion. Captain Nemo had not even proposed my taking with me either Ned or Conseil.

In a few moments we had put on our diving-dresses; they placed on our backs the reservoirs, abundantly filled with air, but no electric lamps were prepared. I called the captain's attention to the fact.

"They will be useless," he replied.

I thought I had not heard aright, but I could not repeat my observation, for the captain's head had already disappeared in its metal case. I finished harnessing myself, I felt them put an iron-pointed stick into my hand, and some minutes later, after going through the usual form, we set foot on the bottom of the Atlantic, at a depth of 150 fathoms. Midnight was near. The waters were profoundly dark, but Captain Nemo pointed out in the distance a reddish spot, a sort of large light shining brilliantly, about two miles from the *Nautilus*. What this fire might be, what could feed it, why and how it lit up the liquid mass, I could not say. In any case, it did light our way, vaguely, it is true, but I soon accustomed myself to the peculiar darkness, and I understood, under such circumstances, the uselessness of the Ruhmkorff apparatus.

As we advanced, I heard a kind of pattering above my head. The noise redoubling, sometimes producing a continual shower, I soon understood the cause. It was rain falling violently, and crisping the surface of the waves. Instinctively the thought flashed across my mind that I should be wet through! By the water! In the midst of the water! I could not help laughing at the odd idea. But indeed, in the thick diving-dress, the liquid element is no longer felt, and one only seems to be in an atmosphere somewhat denser than the terrestrial atmosphere. Nothing more.

After half an hour's walk the soil became stony. Medusæ, microscopic crustacea, and pennatules lit it slightly with their phosphorescent gleam. I caught a glimpse of pieces of stone covered with millions of zoöphytes and masses of seaweed. My feet often slipped upon this viscous carpet of seaweed, and without my iron-tipped stick I should have fallen more than once. In turning round I could still see the whitish lantern of the *Nautilus* beginning to pale in the distance.

But the rosy light which guided us increased and lit up the horizon. The presence of this fire under water puzzled me in the highest degree. Was it some electric effulgence? Was I going toward a natural phenomenon as yet unknown to the savants of the earth? Or even (for this thought crossed my brain) had the hand of man aught to do with this conflagration? Had he fanned this flame? Was I to meet in these depths companions and friends of Captain Nemo whom he was going to visit, and who, like him, led this strange existence? Should I find down there a whole colony of exiles, who, weary of the miseries of this earth, had sought and found independence in the deep ocean? All these foolish and unreasonable ideas pursued me. And in this condition of mind, overexcited by the succession of wonders continually passing before my eyes, I should not have been surprised to meet at the bottom of the sea one of those submarine towns of which Captain Nemo dreamed.

Our road grew lighter and lighter. The white glimmer came in rays from the summit of a mountain of about 800 feet high. But what I saw was simply a reflection, developed by the clearness of the waters. The source of this inexplicable light was a fire on the opposite side of the mountain.

In the midst of this stony maze, furrowing the bottom of the Atlantic, Captain Nemo advanced without hesitation. He knew this dreary road. Doubtless he had often traveled over it, and could not lose himself. I followed him with unshaken confidence. He seemed to me like a genie of the sea; and, as he walked before me, I could not help admiring his stature, which was outlined in black on the luminous horizon.

It was one in the morning when we arrived at the first slopes of the mountain; but to gain access to them we must venture through the difficult paths of a vast copse.

Yes; a copse of dead trees, without leaves, without sap, trees petrified by the action of the water, and here and there overtopped by gigantic pines. It was like a coal pit, still standing, holding by the roots to the broken soil, and whose branches, like fine black paper cuttings, showed distinctly on the watery ceiling. Picture to yourself a forest in the Hartz, hanging on to the sides of the mountain, but a forest swallowed up. The paths were encumbered with seaweed and fucus, between which groveled a whole world of crustacea. I went along, climbing the rocks, striding over extended trunks, breaking the sea bind-weed which hung from one tree to the other, and frightening the fishes, which flew from branch to branch. Pressing onward, I felt no fatigue. I followed my guide, who was never tired. What a spectacle! How can I express it? How paint the aspect of those woods and rocks in this medium—their under parts dark and wild, the upper colored with red tints, by that light which the reflecting powers of the waters doubled? We climbed rocks, which fell directly after with gigantic bounds, and the low growling of an avalanche. To right and left ran long, dark galleries, where sight was lost. Here opened vast glades which the hand of man seemed to have worked; and I sometimes asked myself if some inhabitant of these submarine regions would not suddenly appear to me.

But Captain Nemo was still mounting. I could not stay behind. I followed boldly. My stick gave me good help. A false step would have been dangerous on the narrow passes sloping down to the sides of the gulfs; but I walked with firm step, without feeling any giddiness. Now I jumped a crevice the depth of which would have made me hesitate had it been among the glaciers on the land; now I ventured on the unsteady trunk of a tree, thrown across from one abyss to the other, without looking under my feet, having only eyes to admire the wild sights of this region.

There, monumental rocks, leaning on their regularly cut bases, seemed to defy all laws of equilibrium. From between their stony knees, trees sprang, like a jet under heavy pressure, and upheld others which upheld them. Natural towers, large scarps, cut perpendicularly, like a "curtain," inclined at an angle which the laws of gravitation could never have tolerated in terrestrial regions.

Two hours after quitting the *Nautilus,* we had crossed the line of trees, and a hundred feet above our heads rose the top of the mountain, which cast a shadow on the brilliant irradiation of the opposite slope. Some petrified shrubs ran fantastically here and there. Fishes got up under our feet like birds in the long grass. The massive rocks were rent with impenetrable fractures, deep grottoes, and unfathomable holes, at the bottom of which formidable creatures might be heard moving. My blood curdled when I saw enormous antennæ blocking my road, or some frightful claw closing with a noise in the shadow of some cavity. Millions of luminous spots shone brightly in the midst of the darkness. They were the eyes of giant crustacea crouched in their holes; giant lobsters setting them selves up like halberdiers, and moving their claws with the clicking sound of pinchers; titanic crabs, pointed like a gun on its carriage; and frightful-looking poulps, interweaving their tentacles like a living nest of serpents.

We had now arrived on the first platform, where other surprises awaited me. Before us lay some picturesque ruins which betrayed the hand of man and not that of the Creator. There were vast heaps of stone, among which might be traced the vague and shadowy forms of castles and temples clothed with a world of blossoming zoöphytes, and over which, instead of ivy, seaweed and fucus threw a thick vegetable mantle. But what was this portion of the globe which had been swallowed by cataclysms? Who had placed those rocks and stones like cromlechs of prehistoric times? Where was I? Whither had Captain Nemo's fancy hurried me?

I would fain have asked him; not being able to, I stopped him—I seized his arm. But shaking his head, and pointing to the highest point of the mountain, he seemed to say:

"Come, come along; come higher!"

I followed, and in a few minutes I had climbed to the top, which for a circle of ten yards commanded the whole mass of rock.

I looked down the side we had just climbed. The mountain did not rise more than seven or eight hundred feet above the level of the plain; but on the opposite side it commanded from twice that height the depths of this part of the Atlantic. My eyes ranged far over a large space lit by a violent fulguration. In fact, the mountain was a volcano.

At fifty feet above the peak, in the midst of a rain of stones and scoriæ, a large crater was vomiting forth torrents of lava which fell in a cascade of fire into the bosom of the liquid mass. Thus situated, this volcano lit the lower plain like an immense torch, even to the extreme limits of the horizon. I said that the submarine crater threw up lava, but no flames. Flames require the oxygen of the air to feed upon, and cannot be developed underwater; but streams of lava, having in themselves the principles of their incandescence, can attain a white heat, fight vigorously against the liquid element, and turn it to vapor by contact.

Rapid currents bearing all these gases in diffusion, and torrents of lava, slid to the bottom of the mountain like an eruption of Vesuvius on another Terra del Greco.

There indeed, under my eyes, ruined, destroyed, lay a town—its roofs open to the sky, its temples fallen, its arches dislocated, its columns lying on the ground, from which one could still recognize the massive character of Tuscan architecture. Further on, some remains of a gigantic aqueduct; here the high base of an Acropolis, with the floating outline of a Parthenon; there traces of a quay, as if an ancient port had formerly abutted on the borders of the ocean, and disappeared with its merchant vessels and its war galleys. Further on again, long lines of sunken walls and broad deserted streets—a perfect Pompeii escaped beneath the waters. Such was the sight that Captain Nemo brought before my eyes.

Where was I? Where was I? I must know at any cost. I tried to speak, but Captain Nemo stopped me by a gesture, and picking up a piece of chalk stone advanced to a rock of black basalt, and traced the one word,

ATLANTIS

What a light shot through my mind! Atlantis, the ancient Meropis of Theopompus, the Atlantis of Plato, that continent denied by Origen, Jamblichus, D'Anville, Malte-Brun, and Humboldt, who placed its disappearance among the legendary tales admitted by Posidonius, Pliny, Ammianus Marcellinus, Tertullian, Engel, Buffon, and D'Avezac. I had it there now before my eyes, bearing upon it the unexceptionable testimony of its catastrophe. The region thus ingulfed was beyond Europe, Asia, and Lybia, beyond the columns of Hercules, where those powerful people, the Atlantides, lived, against whom the first wars of ancient Greece were waged.

Thus, led by the strangest destiny, I was treading underfoot the mountains of this continent, touching with my hand those ruins a thousand generations old, and contemporary with the geological epochs. I was walking on the very spot where the contemporaries of the first man had walked.

While I was trying to fix in my mind every detail of this grand landscape Captain Nemo remained motionless, as if petrified in mute ecstasy, leaning on a mossy stone. Was he dreaming of those generations long since disappeared? Was he asking them the secret of human destiny? Was it here this strange man came to steep himself in historical recollections and live again this ancient life—he who wanted no modern one? What would I not have given to know his thoughts, to share them, to understand them! We remained for an hour at this place, contemplating the vast plain under the brightness of the lava, which was sometimes wonderfully intense. Rapid tremblings ran along the mountain caused by internal bubblings, deep noises distinctly transmitted through the liquid medium were echoed with majestic grandeur. At this moment the moon appeared through the mass of waters and threw her pale rays on the buried continent. It was but a gleam, but what an indescribable effect! The captain rose, cast one last look on the immense plain, and then bade me follow him.

We descended the mountain rapidly, and the mineral forest once passed, I saw the lantern of the *Nautilus* shining like a star. The captain walked straight to it, and we got on board as the first rays of light whitened the surface of the ocean.

The Submarine Coal Mines

The next day, the 20th of February, I awoke very late; the fatigues of the previous night had prolonged my sleep until eleven o'clock. I dressed quickly and hastened to find the course the *Nautilus* was taking. The instruments showed it to be still toward the south, with a speed of twenty miles an hour and a depth of fifty fathoms.

The species of fishes here did not differ much from those already noticed. There were rays of giant size, five yards long and endowed with great muscular strength, which enabled them to shoot above the waves; sharks of many kinds, among others a glaucus fifteen feet long, with triangular sharp teeth, and whose transparency rendered it almost invisible in the water; brown sagræ; humantins, prism-shaped and clad with a tuberculous hide; sturgeons, resembling their congeners of the Mediterranean; trumpet syngnathes a foot and a half long, furnished with grayish bladders, without teeth or tongue, and as supple as snakes.

Among bony fish Conseil noticed some blackish makairas about three yards long, armed at the upper jaw with a piercing sword; other bright-colored creatures, known in the time of Aristotle by the name of the sea-dragon, which are dangerous to capture on account of the spikes on their back; also some coryphænes with brown backs marked with little blue stripes and surrounded with a gold border; some beautiful dorades, and swordfish four-and-twenty feet long, swimming in troops, fierce animals, but rather herbivorous than carnivorous.

About four o'clock the soil, generally composed of a thick mud mixed with petrified wood, changed by degrees, and it became more stony and seemed strewn with conglomerate and pieces of basalt, with a sprinkling of lava and sulphurous obsidian. I thought that a mountainous region was succeeding the long plains, and accordingly, after a few evolutions of the *Nautilus,* I saw the southerly horizon blocked by a high wall which seemed to close all exit. Its summit evidently passed the level of the ocean. It must be a continent, or at least an island—one of the Canaries, or of the Cape Verde Islands. The bearings not being yet taken, perhaps designedly, I was ignorant of our exact position. In any case, such a wall seemed to me to mark the limits of that Atlantis of which we had in reality passed over only the smallest part.

Much longer should I have remained at the window, admiring the beauties of sea and sky, but the panels closed. At this moment the *Nautilus* arrived at the side of this high perpendicular wall. What it would do I could not guess. I returned to my room; it no longer moved. I laid myself down with the full intention of waking after a few hours' sleep, but it was eight o'clock the next day when I entered the saloon. I looked at the manometer. It told me that the *Nautilus* was floating on the surface of the ocean. Besides, I heard steps on the platform. I went to the panel. It was open; but instead of broad daylight, as I expected, I was surrounded by profound darkness. Where were we? Was I mistaken? Was it still night? No; not a star was shining, and night has not that utter darkness.

I knew not what to think, when a voice near me said:

"Is that you, professor?"

"Ah! Captain," I answered, "where are we?"

"Underground, sir."

"Underground!" I exclaimed. "And the *Nautilus* floating still?"

"It always floats."

"But I do not understand."

"Wait a few minutes, our lantern will be lit, and if you like light places, you will be satisfied."

I stood on the platform and waited. The darkness was so complete that I could not even see Captain Nemo; but looking to the zenith, exactly above my head, I seemed to catch an undecided gleam, a kind of twilight filling a circular hole. At this instant the lantern was lit, and its vividness dispelled the faint light. I closed my dazzled eyes for an instant, and then looked again. The *Nautilus* was stationary, floating near a mountain which formed a sort of quay. The lake then supporting it was a lake imprisoned by a circle of walls, measuring two miles in diameter and six in circumference. Its level (the manometer showed) could only be the same as the outside level, for there must necessarily be a communication between the lake and the sea. The high partitions, leaning forward on their base, grew into a vaulted roof bearing the shape of an immense funnel turned upside down, the height being about five or six hundred yards. At the summit was a circular orifice, by which I had caught the slight gleam of light, evidently daylight.

"Where are we?" I asked.

"In the very heart of an extinct volcano, the interior of which has been invaded by the sea, after some great convulsion of the earth. While you were sleeping, professor, the *Nautilus* penetrated to this lagoon by a natural canal, which opens about ten yards beneath the surface of the ocean. This is its harbor of refuge, a sure, commodious, and mysterious one, sheltered from all gales. Show me, if you can, on the coasts of any of your continents or islands, a road which can give such perfect refuge from all storms."

"Certainly," I replied, "you are in safety here, Captain Nemo. Who could reach you in the heart of a volcano? But did I not see an opening at its summit?"

"Yes; its crater, formerly filled with lava, vapor, and flames, and which now gives entrance to the life-giving air we breathe."

"But what is this volcanic mountain?"

"It belongs to one of the numerous islands with which this sea is strewn —to vessels a simple sand-bank—to us an immense cavern. Chance led me to discover it, and chance led me well."

"But of what use is this refuge, captain? The *Nautilus* wants no port."

"No, sir; but it wants electricity to make it move, and the wherewithal to make the electricity—sodium to feed the elements, coal from which to get the sodium, and a coal mine to supply the coal. And exactly on this spot the sea covers entire forests imbedded during the geological periods, now mineralized, and transformed into coal; for me they are an inexhaustible mine."

"Your men follow the trade of miners here, then, captain?"

"Exactly so. These mines extend under the waves like the mines of Newcastle. Here, in their diving-dresses, pickaxe and shovel in hand, my men extract the coal, which I do not even ask from the mines of the earth. When I burn this combustible for the manufacture of sodium, the smoke, escaping from the crater of the mountain, gives it the appearance of a still active volcano."

"And we shall see your companions at work?"

"No; not this time at least; for I am in a hurry to continue our submarine tour of the earth. So I shall content myself with drawing from the reserve of sodium I already possess. The time for loading is one day only, and we continue our voyage. So if you wish to go over the cavern, and make the round of the lagoon, you must take advantage of to-day, M. Aronnax."

I thanked the captain, and went to look for my companions, who had not yet left their cabin. I invited them to follow me without saying where we were. They mounted the platform. Conseil, who was astonished at nothing, seemed to look upon it as quite natural that he should wake under a mountain, after having fallen asleep under the waves. But Ned Land thought of nothing but finding whether the cavern had any exit. After breakfast, about ten o'clock, we went down on to the mountain.

"Here we are, once more on land," said Conseil.

"I do not call this land," said the Canadian. "And besides, we are not on it, but beneath it."

Between the walls of the mountain and the waters of the lake lay a sandy shore, which, at its greatest breadth, measured five hundred feet. On this soil one might easily make the tour of the lake. But the base of the high partitions was stony ground, with volcanic blocks and enormous pumice-stones lying in picturesque heaps. All these detached masses, covered with enamel, polished by the action of the subterraneous fires, shone resplendent by the light of our electric lantern. The mica-dust from the shore, rising under our feet, flew like a cloud of sparks. The bottom now rose sensibly, and we soon arrived at long circuitous slopes, or inclined planes, which took us higher by degrees; but we were obliged to walk carefully among these conglomerates, bound by no cement, the feet slipping on the glassy trachyte, composed of crystal, felspar, and quartz.

The volcanic nature of this enormous excavation was confirmed on all sides, and I pointed it out to my companions.

"Picture to yourselves," said I, "what this crater must have been when filled with boiling lava, and when the level of the incandescent liquid rose to the orifice of the mountain, as though melted on the top of a hot plate."

"I can picture it perfectly," said Conseil. "But, sir, will you tell me why the Great Architect has suspended operations, and how it is that the furnace is replaced by the quiet waters of the lake?"

"Most probably, Conseil, because some convulsion beneath the ocean produced that very opening which has served as a passage for the *Nautilus*. Then the waters of the Atlantic rushed into the interior of the mountain. There must have been a terrible struggle between the two elements, a struggle which ended in the victory of Neptune. But many ages have run out since then, and the submerged volcano is now a peaceable grotto."

"Very well," replied Ned Land; "I accept the explanation, sir; but, in our own interests, I regret that the opening of which you speak was not made above the level of the sea."

"But, friend Ned," said Conseil, "if the passage had not been under the sea, the *Nautilus* could not have gone through it."

We continued ascending. The steps became more and more perpendicular and narrow. Deep excavations, which we were obliged to cross, cut them here and there; sloping masses had to be turned. We slid upon our knees and crawled along. But Conseil's dexterity and the Canadian's strength surmounted all obstacles. At a height of about thirty-one feet, the nature of the ground changed without becoming more practicable. To the conglomerate and trachyte succeeded black basalt, the first dispread in layers full of bubbles, the latter forming regular prisms, placed like a colonnade supporting the spring of the immense vault, an admirable specimen of natural architecture. Between the blocks of basalt wound long streams of lava, long since grown cold, encrusted with bituminous rays; and in some places there were spread large carpets of sulphur. A more powerful light shone through the upper crater, shedding a vague glimmer over these volcanic depressions forever buried in the bosom of this extinguished mountain. But our upward march was soon stopped at a height of about two hundred and fifty feet by impassable obstacles. There was a complete vaulted arch overhanging us, and our ascent was changed to a circular walk. At the last change vegetable life began to struggle with the mineral. Some shrubs, and even some trees, grew from the fractures of the walls. I recognized some euphorbias, with the caustic sugar coming from them; heliotropes, quite incapable of justifying their name, sadly drooped their clusters of flowers, both their color and perfume half gone. Here and there some chrysanthemums grew timidly at the foot of an aloe with long sickly looking leaves. But between the streams of lava, I saw some little violets still slightly perfumed, and I admit that I smelt them with delight. Perfume is the soul of the flower, and sea-flowers, those splendid hydrophytes, have no soul.

We had arrived at the foot of some sturdy dragon trees, which had pushed aside the rocks with their strong roots, when Ned Land exclaimed:

"Ah! sir, a hive! A hive!"

"A hive!" I replied with a gesture of incredulity.

"Yes, a hive," repeated the Canadian; "and bees humming round it."

I approached, and was bound to believe my own eyes. There, at a hole bored in one of the dragon trees, were some thousands of these ingenious insects, so common in all the Canaries, and whose produce is so much esteemed. Naturally enough, the Canadian wished to gather the honey, and I could not well oppose his wish. A quantity of dry leaves, mixed with sulphur, he lit with a spark from his flint, and he began to smoke out the bees. The humming ceased by degrees, and the hive eventually yielded several pounds of the sweetest honey, with which Ned Land filled his haversack.

"When I have mixed this honey with the paste of the artocarpus," said he, "I shall be able to offer you a succulent cake."

"Upon my word," said Conseil, "it will be gingerbread."

"Never mind the gingerbread," said I; "let us continue our interesting walk."

At every turn of the path we were following, the lake appeared in all its length and breadth. The lantern lit up the whole of its peaceable surface which knew neither ripple nor wave. The *Nautilus* remained perfectly immovable. On the platform, and on the mountain, the ship's crew were working like black shadows clearly carved against the luminous atmosphere. We were now going round the highest crest of the first layers of rock which upheld the roof. I then saw that bees were not the only representatives of the animal kingdom in the interior of this volcano. Birds of prey hovered here and there in the shadows, or fled from their nests on the top of the rocks. There were sparrow-hawks with white breasts, and kestrels, and down the slopes scampered, with their long legs, several fine fat bustards. I leave anyone to imagine the covetousness of the Canadian at the sight of this savory game, and whether he did not regret having no gun. But he did his best to replace the lead by stones, and after several fruitless attempts, he succeeded in wounding a magnificent bird. To say that he risked his life twenty times before reaching it, is but the truth; but he managed so well that the creature joined the honey cakes in his bag. We were now obliged to descend toward the shore, the crest becoming impracticable. Above us the crater seemed to gape like the mouth of a well. From this place the sky could be clearly seen, and clouds, dissipated by the west wind, leaving behind them, even on the summit of the mountain, their misty remnants—certain proof that they were only moderately high, for the volcano did not rise more than eight hundred feet above the level of the ocean. Half an hour after the Canadian's last exploit we had regained the inner shore. Here the flora was represented by large carpets of marine crystal, a little umbelliferous plant very good to pickle, which also bears the name of pierce-stone and sea-fennel. Conseil gathered some bundles of it. As to the fauna, it might be counted by thousands of crustacea of all sorts, lobsters, crabs, palæmons, spider crabs, chameleon shrimps, and a large number of shells, rockfish, and limpets. Three-quarters of an hour later, we had finished our circuitous walk, and were on board.

The crew had just finished loading the sodium, and the *Nautilus* could have left that instant. But Captain Nemo gave no order. Did he wish to wait until night, and leave the submarine passage secretly? Perhaps so. Whatever it might be, the next day, the *Nautilus*, having left its port, steered clear of all land at a few yards beneath the waves of the Atlantic.

The Sargasso Sea

That day the *Nautilus* crossed a singular part of the Atlantic Ocean. No one can be ignorant of the existence of a current of warm water, known by the name of the Gulf Stream. After leaving the Gulf of Mexico, about the twenty-fifth degree of north latitude, this current divides into two arms, the principal one going toward the coast of Ireland and Norway, while the second bends to the south about the height of the Azores; then, touching the African shore, and describing a lengthened oval, returns to the Antilles. This second arm—it is rather a collar than an arm—surrounds with its circles of warm water that portion of the cold, quiet, immovable ocean called the Sargasso Sea, a perfect lake in the open Atlantic: it takes no less than three years for the great current to pass round it. Such was the region the *Nautilus* was now visiting, a perfect meadow, a close carpet of seaweed, fucus, and tropical berries, so thick and so compact that the stem of a vessel could hardly tear its way through it. And Captain Nemo, not wishing to entangle his screw in this herbaceous mass, kept some yards beneath the surface of the waves. The name Sargasso comes from the Spanish word *sargazzo* which signifies kelp. This kelp or varech, or berry-plant, is the principal formation of this immense bank. And this is the reason, according to the learned Maury, the author of *The Physical Geography of the Globe,* why these hydrophytes unite in the peaceful basin of the Atlantic. The only explanation which can be given, he says, seems to me to result from the experience known to all the world. Place in a vase some fragments of cork or other floating body, and give to the water in the vase a circular movement the scattered fragments will unite in a group in the center of the liquid surface, that is to say, in the part least agitated. In the phenomenon we are considering, the Atlantic is the vase, the Gulf Stream the circular current, and the Sargasso Sea the central point at which the floating bodies unite.

I share Maury's opinion, and I was able to study the phenomenon in the very midst, where vessels rarely penetrate. Above us floated products of all kinds, heaped up among these brownish plants; trunks of trees torn from the Andes or the Rocky Mountains, and floated by the Amazon or the Mississippi; numerous wrecks, remains of keels, or ships' bottoms, side planks stove in, and so weighted with shells and barnacles that they could not again rise to the surface. And time will one day justify Maury's other opinion, that these substances thus accumulated for ages will become petrified by the action of the water, and will then form inexhaustible coal mines—a precious reserve prepared by far-seeing nature for the moment when men shall have exhausted the mines of continents.

In the midst of this inextricable mass of plants and seaweed, I noticed some charming pink halcyons and actiniæ, with their long tentacles trailing after them; medusæ, green, red, and blue, and the great rhyostoms of Cuvier, the large umbrella of which was bordered and festooned with violet.

All the day of the 22d of February we passed in the Sargasso Sea, where such fish as are partial to marine plants and fuci find abundant nourishment. The next, the ocean had returned to its accustomed aspect. From this time for nineteen days, from the 23d of February to the 12th of March, the *Nautilus* kept in the middle of the Atlantic, carrying us at a constant speed of a hundred leagues in twenty-four hours. Captain Nemo evidently intended accomplishing his submarine programme, and I imagined that he intended, after doubling Cape Horn, to return to the Australian seas of the Pacific. Ned Land had cause for fear. In these large seas, void of islands, we could not attempt to leave the boat. Nor had we any means of opposing Captain Nemo's will. Our only course was to submit; but what we could neither gain by force nor cunning, I liked to think might be obtained by persuasion. This voyage ended, would he not consent to restore our liberty, under an oath never to reveal his existence—an oath of honor which we should have religiously kept? But we must consider that delicate question with the captain. But was I free to claim this liberty? Had he not himself said from the beginning, in the firmest manner, that the secret of his life exacted from him our lasting imprisonment on board the *Nautilus*? And would not my four months' silence appear to him a tacit acceptance of our situation? And would not a return to the subject result in raising suspicions which might be hurtful to our projects if at some future time a favorable opportunity offered to return to them?

During the nineteen days mentioned above, no incident of any note happened to signalize our voyage. I saw little of the captain; he was at work. In the library I often found his books left open, especially those on natural history. My work on submarine depths, conned over by him, was covered with marginal notes, often contradicting my theories and systems; but the captain contented himself with thus purging my work; it was very rare for him to discuss it with me. Sometimes I heard the melancholy tones of his organ; but only at night, in the midst of the deepest obscurity, when the *Nautilus* slept upon the deserted ocean. During this part of our voyage we sailed whole days on the surface of the waves. The sea seemed abandoned. A few sailing-vessels, on the road to India, were making for the Cape of Good Hope. One day we were followed by the boats of a whaler, who, no doubt, took us for some enormous whale of great price; but Captain Nemo did not wish the worthy fellows to lose their time and trouble, so ended the chase by plunging under the water. Our navigation continued until the 13th of March; that day the *Nautilus* was employed in taking soundings, which greatly interested me. We had then made about 13,000 leagues since our departure from the high seas of the Pacific. The bearings gave us 45° 37′ south latitude, and 37° 53′ west longitude. It was the same water in which Captain Denham, of the *Herald*, sounded 7,000 fathoms without finding the bottom. There, too, Lieutenant Parker, of the American frigate *Congress*, could not touch the bottom with 15,140 yards. Captain Nemo intended seeking the bottom of the ocean by a diagonal sufficiently lengthened by means of lateral planes, placed at an angle of forty-five degrees with the water-line of the *Nautilus*. Then the screw set to work at its maximum speed, its four blades beating the waves with indescribable force. Under this powerful pressure the hull of the *Nautilus* quivered like a sonorous chord, and sank regularly under the water.

At 7,000 fathoms I saw some blackish tops rising from the midst of the waters; but these summits might belong to high mountains like the Himalayas or Mount Blanc, even higher; and the depth of the abyss remained incalculable. The *Nautilus* descended still lower, in spite of the great pressure. I felt the steel plates tremble at the fastenings of the bolts; its bars bent, its partitions groaned; the windows of the saloon seemed to curve under the pressure of the waters. And this firm structure would doubtless have yielded, if, as its captain had said, it had not been capable of resistance like a solid block. In skirting the declivity of these rocks, lost under the water, I still saw some shells, some serpulæ and spinorbes, still living, and some specimens of asteriads. But soon this last representative of animal life disappeared; and at the depth of more than three leagues, the *Nautilus* had passed the limits of submarine existence, even as a balloon does when it rises above the respirable atmosphere. We had attained a depth of 16,000 yards (four leagues), and the sides of the *Nautilus* then bore a pressure of 1,600 atmospheres, that is to say, 3,200 pounds to each square two-fifths of an inch of its surface.

"What a situation to be in!" I exclaimed. "To overrun these deep regions where man has never trod! Look, captain, look at these magnificent rocks, these uninhabited grottoes, these lowest receptacles of the globe, where life is no longer possible! What unknown sights are here! Why should we be unable to preserve a remembrance of them?"

"Would you like to carry away more than the remembrance?" said Captain Nemo.

"What do you mean by those words?"

"I mean to say that nothing is easier than to take a photographic view of this submarine region."

I had not time to express my surprise at this new proposition, when, at Captain Nemo's call, an objective was brought into the saloon. Through the widely opened panel, the liquid mass was bright with electricity, which was distributed with such uniformity that not a shadow, not a gradation, was to be seen in our manufactured light. The *Nautilus* remained motionless, the force of its screw subdued by the inclination of its planes: the instrument was propped on the bottom of the oceanic site, and in a few seconds we had obtained a perfect negative. I here give the positive, from which may be seen those primitive rocks, which have never looked upon the light of heaven; that lowest granite which forms the foundation of the globe; those deep grottoes, woven in the stony mass whose outlines were of such sharpness, and the border lines of which are marked in black, as if done by the brush of some Flemish artist. Beyond that again a horizon of mountains, an admirable undulating line, forming the prospective of the landscape. I cannot describe the effect of these smooth, black, polished rocks, without moss, without a spot, and of strange forms, standing solidly on the sandy carpet, which sparkled under the jets of our electric light.

But the operation being over, Captain Nemo said: "Let us go up; we must not abuse our position, nor expose the *Nautilus* too long to such great pressure."

"Go up again!" I exclaimed.

"Hold well on."

I had not time to understand why the captain cautioned me thus, when I was thrown forward on to the carpet. At a signal from the captain, its screw was shipped, and its blades raised vertically; the *Nautilus* shot into the air like a balloon, rising with stunning rapidity, and cutting the mass of waters with a sonorous agitation. Nothing was visible; and in four minutes it had shot through the four leagues which separated it from the ocean, and, after emerging like a flying-fish, fell, making the waves rebound to an enormous height.

Cachalots and Whales

During the nights of the 13th and 14th of March, the *Nautilus* returned to its southerly course. I fancied that, when on a level with Cape Horn, he would turn the helm westward, in order to beat the Pacific seas, and so complete the tour of the world. He did nothing of the kind, but continued on his way to the southern regions. Where was he going to? To the pole? It was madness! I began to think that the captain's temerity justified Ned Land's fears. For some time past the Canadian had not spoken to me of his projects of flight; he was less communicative, almost silent. I could see that this lengthened imprisonment was weighing upon him, and I felt that rage was burning within him. When he met the captain, his eyes lit up with suppressed anger; and I feared that his natural violence would lead him into some extreme. That day, the 14th of March, Conseil and he came to me in my room. I inquired the cause of their visit.

"A simple question to ask you, sir," replied the Canadian.

"Speak, Ned."

"How many men are there on board the *Nautilus*, do you think?"

"I cannot tell, my friend."

"I should say that its working does not require a large crew."

"Certainly, under existing conditions, ten men, at the most, ought to be enough."

"Well, why should there be any more?"

"Why?" I replied, looking fixedly at Ned Land, whose meaning was easy to guess. "Because," I added, "if my surmises are correct, and if I have well understood the captain's existence, the *Nautilus* is not only a vessel, it is also a place of refuge for those who, like its commander, have broken every tie upon earth."

"Perhaps so," said Conseil; "but, in any case, the *Nautilus* can only contain a certain number of men. Could not you, sir, estimate their maximum?"

"How, Conseil?"

"By calculation; given the size of the vessel, which you know, sir, and consequently the quantity of air it contains, knowing also how much each man expends at a breath, and comparing these results with the fact that the *Nautilus* is obliged to go to the surface every twenty-four hours."

Conseil had not finished the sentence before I saw what he was driving at.

"I understand," said I; "but that calculation, though simple enough, can give but a very uncertain result."

"Never mind," said Ned Land urgently.

"Here it is, then," said I. "In one hour each man consumes the oxygen contained in twenty gallons of air; and in twenty-four, that contained in 480 gallons. We must, therefore, find how many times 480 gallons of air the *Nautilus* contains."

"Just so," said Conseil.

"Or," I continued, "the size of the *Nautilus* being 1,500 tons, and one ton holding 200 gallons, it contains 300,000 gallons of air, which, divided by 480, gives a quotient of 625. Which means to say, strictly speaking, that the air contained in the *Nautilus* would suffice for 625 men for twenty-four hours."

"Six hundred and twenty-five!" repeated Ned.

"But remember, that all of us, passengers, sailors, and officers included, would not form a tenth part of that number."

"Still too many for three men," murmured Conseil.

The Canadian shook his head, passed his hand across his forehead, and left the room without answering.

"Will you allow me to make one observation, sir?" said Conseil. "Poor Ned is longing for everything that he cannot have. His past life is always present to him; everything that we are forbidden he regrets. His head is full of old recollections. And we must understand him. What has he to do here? Nothing; he is not learned like you, sir; and has not the same taste for the beauties of the sea that we have. He would risk everything to be able to go once more into a tavern in his own country."

Certainly the monotony on board must seem intolerable to the Canadian, accustomed as he was to a life of liberty and activity. Events were rare which could rouse him to any show of spirit; but that day an event did happen which recalled the bright days of the harpooner. About eleven in the morning, being on the surface of the ocean, the *Nautilus* fell in with a troop of whales—an encounter which did not astonish me, knowing that these creatures, hunted to the death, had taken refuge in high latitudes.

We were seated on the platform, with a quiet sea. The month of October in those latitudes gave us some lovely autumnal days. It was the Canadian—he could not be mistaken—who signaled a whale on the eastern horizon. Looking attentively one might see its black back rise and fall with the waves five miles from the *Nautilus*.

"Ah!" exclaimed Ned Land, "if I was on board a whaler now, such a meeting would give me pleasure. It is one of large size. See with what strength its blow-holes throw up columns of air and steam! Confound it, why am I bound to these steel plates?"

"What, Ned," said I, "you have not forgotten your old ideas of fishing!"

"Can a whale-fisher ever forget his old trade, sir? Can he ever tire of the emotions caused by such a chase?"

"You have never fished in these seas, Ned?"

"Never, sir; in the northern only, and as much in Behring as in Davis Straits."

"Then the southern whale is still unknown to you. It is the Greenland whale you have hunted up to this time, and that would not risk passing through the warm waters of the equator. Whales are localized according to their kinds, in certain seas which they never leave. And if one of these creatures went from Behring to Davis Straits, it must be simply because there is a passage from one sea to the other, either on the American or the Asiatic side."

"In that case, as I have never fished in these seas, I do not know the kind of whale frequenting them."

"I have told you, Ned."

"A greater reason for making their acquaintance," said Conseil.

"Look! Look!" exclaimed the Canadian. "They approach; they aggravate me; they know that I cannot get at them!"

Ned stamped his feet. His hand trembled as he grasped an imaginary harpoon.

"Are these cetacea as large as those of the northern seas?" asked he.

"Very nearly, Ned."

"Because I have seen large whales, sir, whales measuring a hundred feet. I have been even told that those of Hullamoch and Umgallick, of the Aleutian Islands, are sometimes a hundred and fifty feet long."

"That seems to me exaggeration. These creatures are only balænopterons, provided with dorsal fins; and, like the cachalots, are generally much smaller than the Greenland whale."

"Ah!" exclaimed the Canadian, whose eyes had never left the ocean. "They are coming nearer; they are in the same water as the *Nautilus!*"

Then returning to the conversation, he said:

"You spoke of the cachalot as a small creature. I have heard of gigantic ones. They are intelligent cetacea. It is said of some that they cover themselves with seaweed and fucus, and then are taken for islands. People encamp upon them, and settle there; light a fire—"

"And build houses," said Conseil.

"Yes, joker," said Ned Land. "And one fine day the creature plunges, carrying with it all the inhabitants to the bottom of the sea."

"Something like the travels of Sindbad the Sailor," I replied, laughing.

"Ah!" suddenly exclaimed Ned Land. "It is not one whale; there are ten —there are twenty—it is a whole troop! And I not able to do anything! Hands and feet tied!"

"But, friend Ned," said Conseil, "why do you not ask Captain Nemo's permission to chase them?"

Conseil had not finished his sentence when Ned Land had lowered himself through the panel to seek the captain. A few minutes afterward the two appeared together on the platform.

Captain Nemo watched the troop of cetacea playing on the waters about a mile from the *Nautilus.*

"They are southern whales," said he; "there goes the fortune of a whole fleet of whalers."

"Well, sir," asked the Canadian, "can I not chase them, if only to remind me of my old trade of harpooner?"

"And to what purpose?" replied Captain Nemo. "Only to destroy! We have nothing to do with whale-oil on board."

"But, sir," continued the Canadian, "in the Red Sea you allowed us to follow the dugong."

"Then it was to procure fresh meat for my crew. Here it would be killing for killing's sake. I know that is a privilege reserved for man, but I do not approve of such murderous pastime. In destroying the southern whale (like the Greenland whale, an inoffensive creature), your traders do a culpable action, Master Land. They have already depopulated the whole of Baffin's Bay, and are annihilating a class of useful animals. Leave the unfortunate cetacea alone. They have plenty of natural enemies—cachalots, swordfish, and sawfish—without *your* troubling them."

The captain was right. The barbarous and inconsiderate greed of these fishermen will one day cause the disappearance of the last whale in the ocean. Ned Land whistled "Yankee Doodle" between his teeth, thrust his hands into his pockets, and turned his back upon us. But Captain Nemo watched the troop of cetacea, and addressing me said:

"I was right in saying that whales had natural enemies enough, without counting man. These will have plenty to do before long. Do you see, M. Aronnax, about eight miles to leeward, those blackish moving points?"

"Yes, captain," I replied.

"Those are cachalots—terrible animals, which I have sometimes met in troops of two or three hundred. As to *those,* they are cruel, mischievous creatures; they would be right in exterminating them."

The Canadian turned quickly at the last words.

"Well, captain," said he, "it is still time, in the interest of the whales."

"It is useless to expose one's self, professor. The *Nautilus* will disperse them. It is armed with a steel spur as good as Master Land's harpoon, I imagine."

The Canadian did not put himself out enough to shrug his shoulders. Attack cetacea with blows of a spur! Who had ever heard of such a thing?

"Wait, M. Aronnax," said Captain Nemo. "We will show you something you have never yet seen. We have no pity for these ferocious creatures. They are nothing but mouth and teeth."

Mouth and teeth! No one could better describe the macrocephalous cachalot, which is sometimes more than seventy-five feet long. Its enormous head occupies one-third of its entire body. Better armed than the whale, whose upper jaw is furnished only with whalebone, it is supplied with twenty-five large tusks, about eight inches long, cylindrical and conical at the top, each weighing two pounds. It is in the upper part of this enormous head, in great cavities divided by cartilages, that is to be found from six to eight hundred pounds of that precious oil called spermaceti. The cachalot is a disagreeable creature, more tadpole than fish, according to Fredol's description. It is badly formed, the whole of its left side being (if we may say it) a "failure," and being only able to see with its right eye. But the formidable troop was nearing us. They had seen the whales and were preparing to attack them. One could judge beforehand that the cachalots would be victorious, not only because they were better built for attack than their inoffensive adversaries, but also because they could remain longer underwater without coming to the surface. There was only just time to go to the help of the whales. The *Nautilus* went underwater. Conseil, Ned Land, and I took our places before the window in the saloon, and Captain Nemo joined the pilot in his cage to work his apparatus as an engine of destruction. Soon I felt the beatings of the screw quicken, and our speed increased. The battle between the cachalots and the whales had already begun when the *Nautilus* arrived. They did not at first show any fear at the sight of this new monster joining in the conflict. But they soon had to guard against its blows. What a battle! The *Nautilus* was nothing but a formidable harpoon, brandished by the hand of its captain. It hurled itself against the fleshy mass, passing through from one part to the other, leaving behind it two quivering halves of the animal. It could not feel the formidable blows from their tails upon its sides, nor the shock which it produced itself, much more. One cachalot killed, it ran at the next, tacked on the spot that it might not miss its prey, going forward and backward, answering to its helm, plunging when the cetacean dived into the deep waters, coming up with it when it returned to the surface, striking it front or sideways, cutting or tearing in all directions, and at any pace, piercing it with its terrible spur. What carnage! What a noise on the surface of the waves! What sharp hissing, and what snorting peculiar to these enraged animals! In the midst of these waters generally so peaceful their tails made perfect billows. For one hour this wholesale massacre continued, from which the cachalots could not escape. Several times ten or twelve united tried to crush the *Nautilus* by their weight. From the window we could see their enormous mouths studded with tusks, and their formidable eyes. Ned Land could not contain himself, he threatened and swore at them. We could feel them clinging to our vessel like dogs worrying a wild boar in a copse. But the *Nautilus*, working its screw, carried them here and there, or to the upper levels of the ocean, without caring for their enormous weight, nor the powerful strain on the vessel. At length, the mass of cachalots broke up, the waves became quiet, and I felt that we were rising to the surface. The panel opened, and we hurried on to the platform. The sea was covered with mutilated bodies. A formidable explosion could not have divided and torn this fleshy mass with more violence. We were floating amid gigantic bodies, bluish on the back and white underneath, covered with enormous protuberances. Some terrified cachalots were flying toward the horizon. The waves were dyed red for several miles, and the *Nautilus* floated in a sea of blood. Captain Nemo joined us.

"Well, Master Land?" said he.

"Well, sir," replied the Canadian, whose enthusiasm had somewhat calmed; "it is a terrible spectacle, certainly. But I am not a butcher. I am a hunter, and I call this a butchery."

"It is a massacre of mischievous creatures," replied the captain; "and the *Nautilus* is not a butcher's knife."

"I like my harpoon better," said the Canadian.

"Everyone to his own," answered the captain, looking fixedly at Ned Land.

I feared he would commit some act of violence, which would end in sad consequences. But his anger was turned by the sight of a whale which the *Nautilus* had just come up with. The creature had not quite escaped from the cachalot's teeth. I recognized the southern whale by its flat head, which is entirely black. Anatomically, it is distinguished from the white whale and the North Cape whale by the seven cervical vertebræ, and it has two more ribs than its congeners. The unfortunate cetacean was lying on its side, riddled with holes from the bites, and quite dead. From its mutilated fin still hung a young whale which it could not save from the massacre. Its open mouth let the water flow in and out, murmuring like the waves breaking on the shore. Captain Nemo steered close to the corpse of the creature. Two of his men mounted its side, and I saw, not without surprise, that they were drawing from its breasts all the milk which they contained, that is to say, about two or three tons. The captain offered me a cup of the milk, which was still warm. I could not help showing my repugnance to the drink; but he assured me that it was excellent, and not to be distinguished from cow's milk. I tasted it, and was of his opinion. It was a useful reserve to us, for in the shape of salt butter or cheese it would form an agreeable variety from our ordinary food. From that day I noticed with uneasiness that Ned Land's ill-will toward Captain Nemo increased, and I resolved to watch the Canadian's gestures closely.

THE ICEBERG

The *Nautilus* was steadily pursuing its southerly course, following the fiftieth meridian with considerable speed. Did he wish to reach the pole? I did not think so, for every attempt to reach that point had hitherto failed. Again the season was far advanced; for in the antarctic regions the 13th of March corresponds with the 13th of September of northern regions, which begins at the equinoctial season. On the 14th of March I saw floating ice in latitude 55°, merely pale bits of debris from twenty to twenty-five feet long, forming banks over which the sea curled. The *Nautilus* remained on the surface of the ocean. Ned Land, who had fished in the arctic seas, was familiar with its icebergs; but Conseil and I admired them for the first time. In the atmosphere toward the southern horizon stretched a white dazzling band. English whalers had given it the name of "ice blink." However thick the clouds may be, it is always visible, and announces the presence of an ice-pack or bank. Accordingly, larger blocks soon appeared, whose brilliancy changed with the caprices of the fog. Some of these masses showed green veins, as if long undulating lines had been traced with sulphate of copper; others resembled enormous amethysts with the light shining through them. Some reflected the light of day upon a thousand crystal facets. Others shaded with vivid calcareous reflections resembled a perfect town of marble. The more we neared the south the more these floating islands increased both in number and importance.

At the sixtieth degree of latitude, every pass had disappeared. But seeking carefully, Captain Nemo soon found a narrow opening, through which he boldly slipped, knowing, however, that it would close behind him. Thus, guided by this clever hand, the *Nautilus* passed through all the ice with a precision which quite charmed Conseil; icebergs or mountains, ice-fields or smooth plains, seeming to have no limits, drift ice or floating ice-packs, or plains broken up, called palches when they are circular, and streams when they are made up of long strips. The temperature was very low; the thermometer exposed to the air marked two or three degrees below zero, but we were warmly clad with fur, at the expense of the sea bear and seal. The interior of the *Nautilus,* warmed regularly by its electric apparatus, defied the most intense cold. Besides, it would only have been necessary to go some yards beneath the waves to find a more bearable temperature. Two months earlier we should have had perpetual daylight in these latitudes; but already we had three or four hours night, and by and by there would be six months of darkness in these circumpolar regions. On the 15th of March we were in the latitude of New Shetland and South Orkney. The captain told me that formerly numerous tribes of seals inhabited them; but that English and American whalers, in their rage for destruction, massacred both old and young; thus where there was once life and animation, they had left silence and death.

About eight o'clock on the morning of the 16th of March, the *Nautilus,* following the fifty-fifth meridian, cut the antarctic polar circle. Ice surrounded us on all sides, and closed the horizon. But Captain Nemo went from one opening to another, still going higher. I cannot express my astonishment at the beauties of these new regions. The ice took most surprising forms. Here the grouping formed an Oriental town, with innumerable mosques and minarets; there a fallen city thrown to the earth, as it were, by some convulsion of nature. The whole aspect was constantly changed by the oblique rays of the sun, or lost in the grayish fog amid hurricanes of snow. Detonations and falls were heard on all sides, great overthrows of icebergs, which altered the whole landscape like a diorama. Often seeing no exit, I thought we were definitively prisoners; but instinct guiding him at the slightest indication, Captain Nemo would discover a new pass. He was never mistaken when he saw the thin threads of bluish water trickling along the ice-fields; and I had no doubt that he had already ventured into the midst of these antarctic seas before. On the 16th of March, however, the ice-fields absolutely blocked our road. It was not the iceberg itself, as yet, but vast fields cemented by the cold. But this obstacle could not stop Captain Nemo: he hurled himself against it with frightful violence. The *Nautilus* entered the brittle mass like a wedge, and split it with frightful crackings. It was the battering-ram of the ancients hurled by infinite strength. The ice, thrown high in the air, fell like hail around us. By its own power of impulsion our apparatus made a canal for itself; sometimes carried away by its own impetus, it lodged on the ice-field, crushing it with its weight, and sometimes buried beneath it, dividing it by a simple pitching movement, producing large rents in it. Violent gales assailed us at this time, accompanied by thick fogs, through which, from one end of the platform to the other, we could see nothing. The wind blew sharply from all points of the compass, and the snow lay in such hard heaps that we had to break it with blows of a pickaxe. The temperature was always at five degrees below zero; every outward part of the *Nautilus* was covered with ice. A rigged vessel could never have worked its way there, for all the rigging would have been entangled in the blocked-up gorges. A vessel without sails, with electricity for its motive-power, and wanting no coal, could alone brave such high latitudes. At length, on the 18th of March, after many useless assaults, the *Nautilus* was positively blocked. It was no longer either streams, packs, or ice-fields, but an interminable and immovable barrier, formed by mountains soldered together.

"An iceberg!" said the Canadian to me.

I knew that to Ned Land, as well as to all other navigators who had preceded us, this was an inevitable obstacle. The sun appearing for an instant at noon, Captain Nemo took an observation as near as possible, which gave our situation at 51° 30′ longitude and 67° 39′ of south latitude. We had advanced one degree more in this antarctic region. Of the liquid surface of the sea there was no longer a glimpse. Under the spur of the *Nautilus* lay stretched a vast plain, entangled with confused blocks. Here and there sharp points, and slender needles rising to a height of 200 feet; further on a steep shore, hewn as it were with an axe, and clothed with grayish tints; huge mirrors, reflecting a few rays of sunshine, half drowned in the fog. And over this desolate face of nature a stern silence reigned, scarcely broken by the flapping of the wings of petrels and puffins. Everything was frozen—even the noise. The *Nautilus* was then obliged to stop in its adventurous course amid these fields of ice. In spite of our efforts, in spite of the powerful means employed to break up the ice, the *Nautilus* remained immovable. Generally, when we can proceed no further, we have return still open to us; but here return was as impossible as advance, for every pass had closed behind us; and for the few moments when we were stationary, we were likely to be entirely blocked, which did, indeed, happen about two o'clock in the afternoon, the fresh ice forming around its sides with astonishing rapidity. I was obliged to admit that Captain Nemo was more than imprudent. I was on the platform at that moment. The captain had been observing our situation for some time past, when he said to me:

"Well, sir, what do you think of this?"

"I think that we are caught, captain."

"So, M. Aronnax, you really think that the *Nautilus* cannot disengage itself?"

"With difficulty, captain; for the season is already too far advanced for you to reckon on the breaking up of the ice."

"Ah! sir," said Captain Nemo, in an ironical tone, "you will always be the same. You see nothing but difficulties and obstacles. I affirm that not only can the *Nautilus* disengage itself, but also that it can go further still."

"Further to the south?" I asked, looking at the captain.

"Yes, sir; it shall go to the pole."

"To the pole!" I exclaimed, unable to repress a gesture of incredulity.

"Yes," replied the captain coldly, "to the antarctic pole, to that unknown point from whence springs every meridian of the globe. *You* know whether I can do as I please with the *Nautilus!*"

Yes, I knew that. I knew that this man was bold, even to rashness. But to conquer those obstacles which bristled round the South Pole, rendering it more inaccessible than the north, which had not yet been reached by the boldest navigators—was it not a mad enterprise, one which only a maniac would have conceived? It then came into my head to ask Captain Nemo if he had ever discovered that pole which had never yet been trodden by a human creature.

"No, sir," he replied; "but we will discover it together. Where others have failed, *I* will not fail. I have never yet led my *Nautilus* so far into southern seas; but I repeat, it shall go further yet."

"I can well believe you, captain," said I, in a slightly ironical tone. "I believe you! Let us go ahead! There are no obstacles for us! Let us smash this iceberg! Let us blow it up; and if it resists, let us give the *Nautilus* wings to fly over it!"

"Over it, sir!" said Captain Nemo quietly. "No, not *over* it, but *under* it!"

"Under it!" I exclaimed, a sudden idea of the captain's projects flashing upon my mind. I understood the wonderful qualities of the *Nautilus* were going to serve us in this super-human enterprise.

"I see we are beginning to understand one another, sir," said the captain, half smiling. "You begin to see the possibility—I should say the success—of this attempt. That which is impossible for an ordinary vessel, is easy to the *Nautilus*. If a continent lies before the pole, it must stop before the continent; but, if, on the contrary, the pole is washed by open sea, it will go even to the pole."

"Certainly," said I, carried away by the captain's reasoning; "if the surface of the sea is solidified by the ice, the lower depths are free by the providential law which has placed the maximum of density of the waters of the ocean one degree higher than freezing-point; and, if I am not mistaken, the portion of this iceberg which is above the water is as one to four to that which is below."

"Very nearly, sir; for one foot of iceberg above the sea there are three below it. If these ice mountains are not more than 300 feet above the surface, they are not more than 900 beneath. And what are 900 feet to the *Nautilus?*"

"Nothing, sir."

"It could even seek at greater depths that uniform temperature of sea-water, and there brave with impunity the thirty or forty degrees of surface cold."

"Just so, sir—just so," I replied, getting animated.

"The only difficulty," continued Captain Nemo, "is that of remaining several days without renewing our provision of air."

"Is that all? The *Nautilus* has vast reservoirs; we can fill them, and they will supply us with all the oxygen we want."

"Well thought of, M. Aronnax," replied the captain, smiling. "But not wishing you to accuse me of rashness, I will first give you all my objections."

"Have you any more to make?"

"Only one. It is possible, if the sea exists at the South Pole, that it may be covered; and, consequently, we shall be unable to come to the surface."

"Good, sir! but do you forget that the *Nautilus* is armed with a powerful spur, and could we not send it diagonally against these fields of ice, which would open at the shock?"

"Ah! sir, you are full of ideas to-day."

"Besides, captain," I added enthusiastically, "why should we not find the sea open at the South Pole as well as at the North? The frozen poles and the poles of the earth do not coincide, either in the southern or in the northern regions; and, until it is proved to the contrary, we may suppose either a continent or an ocean free from ice at these two points of the globe."

"I think so, too, M. Aronnax," replied Captain Nemo. "I only wish you to observe that, after having made so many objections to my project, you are now crushing me with arguments in its favor!"

The preparations for this audacious attempt now began. The powerful pumps of the *Nautilus* were working air into the reservoirs and storing it at high pressure. About four o'clock, Captain Nemo announced the closing of the panels on the platform. I threw one last look at the massive iceberg which we were going to cross. The weather was clear, the atmosphere was pure enough, the cold very great, being twelve degrees below zero; but the wind having gone down, this temperature was not so unbearable. About ten men mounted the sides of the *Nautilus,* armed with pickaxes to break the ice around the vessel, which was soon free. The operation was quickly performed, for the fresh ice was still very thin. We all went below. The usual reservoirs were filled with the newly liberated water, and the *Nautilus* soon descended. I had taken my place with Conseil in the saloon; through the open window we could see the lower beds of the Southern Ocean. The thermometer went up, the needle of the compass deviated on the dial. At about 900 feet, as Captain Nemo had foreseen, we were floating beneath the undulating bottom of the iceberg. But the *Nautilus* went lower still—it went to the depth of four hundred fathoms. The temperature of the water at the surface showed twelve degrees, it was now only ten; we had gained two. I need not say the temperature of the *Nautilus* was raised by its heating apparatus to a much higher degree; every maneuver was accomplished with wonderful precision.

"We shall pass it, if you please, sir," said Conseil.

"I believe we shall," I said in a tone of firm conviction.

In this open sea, the *Nautilus* had taken its course direct to the pole, without leaving the fifty-second meridian. From 67° 30′ to 90°, twenty-two degrees and a half of latitude remained to travel; that is, about five hundred leagues. The *Nautilus* kept up a mean speed of twenty-six miles an hour—the speed of an express train. If that was kept up, in forty hours we should reach the pole.

For a part of the night the novelty of the situation kept us at the window. The sea was lit with the electric lantern; but it was deserted; fishes did not sojourn in these imprisoned waters; they only found there a passage to take them from the Antarctic Ocean to the open polar sea. Our progress was rapid; we could feel it by the quivering of the long steel body. About two in the morning, I took some hours' repose, and Conseil did the same. In crossing the waist I did not meet Captain Nemo: I supposed him to be in the pilot's cage. The next morning, the 19th of March, I took my post once more in the saloon. The electric log told me that the speed of the *Nautilus* had been slackened. It was then going toward the surface, but prudently emptying its reservoirs very slowly. My heart beat fast. Were we going to emerge and regain the open polar atmosphere? No! A shock told me that the *Nautilus* had struck the bottom of the iceberg, still very thick, judging from the deadened sound. We had indeed "struck," to use a sea expression, but in an inverse sense, and at a thousand feet deep. This would give three thousand feet of ice above us; one thousand being above the water-mark. The iceberg was then higher than at its borders—not a very reassuring fact. Several times that day the *Nautilus* tried again, and every time it struck the wall which lay like a ceiling above it. Sometimes it met with but 900 yards, only 200 of which rose above the surface. It was twice the height it was when the *Nautilus* had gone under the waves. I carefully noted the different depths, and thus obtained a submarine profile of the chain as it was developed under the water. That night no change had taken place in our situation. Still ice between four and five hundred yards in depth! It was evidently diminishing, but still what a thickness between us and the surface of the ocean! It was then eight. According to the daily custom on board the *Nautilus*, its air should have been renewed four hours ago; but I did not suffer much, although Captain Nemo had not yet made any demand upon his reserve of oxygen. My sleep was painful that night; hope and fear besieged me by turns: I rose several times. The groping of the *Nautilus* continued. About three in the morning, I noticed that the lower surface of the iceberg was only about fifty feet deep. One hundred and fifty feet now separated us from the surface of the waters. The iceberg was by degrees becoming an ice-field, the mountain a plain. My eyes never left the manometer. We were still rising diagonally to the surface, which sparkled under the electric rays. The iceberg was stretching both above and beneath into lengthening slopes; mile after mile it was getting thinner. At length, at six in the morning of that memorable day, the 19th of March, the door of the saloon opened, and Captain Nemo appeared.

"The sea is open!" was all he said.

The South Pole

I rushed on to the platform. Yes! the open sea, with but a few scattered pieces of ice and moving icebergs—a long stretch of sea; a world of birds in the air, and myriads of fishes under those waters, which varied from intense blue to olive-green, according to the bottom. The thermometer marked three degrees centigrade above zero. It was comparatively spring, shut up as we were behind this iceberg, whose lengthened mass was dimly seen on our northern horizon.

"Are we at the pole?" I asked the captain, with a beating heart.

"I do not know," he replied. "At noon I will take our bearings."

"But will the sun show himself through this fog?" said I, looking at the leaden sky.

"However little it shows, it will be enough," replied the captain.

About ten miles south, a solitary island rose to a height of one hundred and four yards. We made for it, but carefully, for the sea might be strewn with banks. One hour afterward we had reached it, two hours later we had made the round of it. It measured four or five miles in circumference. A narrow canal separated it from a considerable stretch of land, perhaps a continent, for we could not see its limits. The existence of this land seemed to give some color to Maury's hypothesis. The ingenious American has remarked that between the South Pole and the sixtieth parallel, the sea is covered with floating ice of enormous size, which is never met with in the North Atlantic. From this fact he has drawn the conclusion that the Antarctic Circle incloses considerable continents, as icebergs cannot form in open sea, but only on the coasts. According to these calculations, the mass of ice surrounding the southern pole forms a vast cap, the circumference of which must be, at least, 2,500 miles. But the *Nautilus,* for fear of running aground, had stopped about three cables' length from a strand over which reared a superb heap of rocks. The boat was launched; the captain, two of his men bearing instruments, Conseil, and myself were in it. It was ten in the morning. I had not seen Ned Land. Doubtless the Canadian did not wish to admit the presence of the South Pole. A few strokes of the oar brought us to the sand, where we ran ashore. Conseil was going to jump on to the land, when I held him back.

"Sir," said I to Captain Nemo, "to you belongs the honor of first setting foot on this land."

"Yes, sir," said the captain; "and if I do not hesitate to tread this South Pole, it is because, up to this time, no human being has left a trace there."

Saying this, he jumped lightly on to the sand. His heart beat with emotion. He climbed a rock, sloping to a little promontory; and there, with his arms crossed, mute and motionless, and with an eager look, he seemed to take possession of these southern regions. After five minutes passed in this ecstasy, he turned to us.

"When you like, sir."

I landed, followed by Conseil, leaving the two men in the boat. For a long way the soil was composed of a reddish, sandy stone, something like crushed brick, scoriæ, streams of lava, and pumice-stones. One could not mistake its volcanic origin. In some parts, slight curls of smoke emitted a sulphurous smell, proving that the internal fires had lost nothing of their expansive powers, though, having climbed a high acclivity, I could see no volcano for a radius of several miles. We know that in those antarctic countries, James Ross found two craters, the Erebus and Terror, in full activity, on the 167th meridian, latitude 77° 32′. The vegetation of this desolate continent seemed to me much restricted. Some lichens of the species usnea melanoxantha lay upon the black rocks; some microscopic plants, rudimentary diatomas, a kind of cells, placed between two quartz shells; long purple and scarlet fucus, supported on little swimming bladders, which the breaking of the waves brought to the shore. These constituted the meager flora of this region. The shore was strewn with mollusks, little mussels, limpets, smooth bucards in the shape of a heart, and particularly some clios, with oblong membranous bodies, the head of which was formed of two rounded lobes. I also saw myriads of northern clios, one and a quarter inches long, of which a whale would swallow a whole world at a mouthful; and some charming pteropods, perfect sea-butterflies, animating the waters on the skirts of the shore.

Among other zoöphytes, there appeared on the high bottoms some coral shrubs, of that kind which, according to James Ross, live in the antarctic seas to the depth of more than 1,000 yards. Then there were little kingfishers, belonging to the species procellaria pelagica, as well as a large number of asteriads, peculiar to these climates, and starfish studding the soil. But where life abounded most was in the air. There thousands of birds fluttered and flew of all kinds, deafening us with their cries; others crowded the rocks, looking at us as we passed by without fear, and pressing familiarly close by our feet. There were penguins, so agile in the water that they have been taken for the rapid bonitos, heavy and awkward as they are on the ground; they were uttering harsh cries, a large assembly, sober in gesture, but extravagant in clamor. Among the birds I noticed the chionis, of the long-legged family, as large as pigeons, white, with a short conical beak, and the eye framed in a red circle. Conseil laid in a stock of them, for these winged creatures, properly prepared, make an agreeable meat. Albatrosses passed in the air (the expanse of their wings being at least four yards and a half), and justly called the vultures of the ocean; some gigantic petrels, and some damiers, a kind of small duck, the underpart of whose body is black and white; then there were a whole series of petrels, some whitish with brown-bordered wings, others blue, peculiar to the antarctic seas, and so oily, as I told Conseil, that the inhabitants of the Ferroe Islands had nothing to do before lighting them, but to put a wick in.

"A little more," said Conseil, "and they would be perfect lamps! After that, we cannot expect nature to have previously furnished them with wicks!"

About half a mile further on, the soil was riddled with ruff's nests, a sort of laying ground, out of which many birds were issuing. Captain Nemo had some hundreds hunted. They uttered a cry like the braying of an ass, were about the size of a goose, slate color on the body, white beneath, with a yellow line round their throats; they allowed themselves to be killed with a stone, never trying to escape. But the fog did not lift, and at eleven the sun had not yet shown itself. Its absence made me uneasy. Without it no observations were possible. How then could we decide whether we had reached the pole? When I rejoined Captain Nemo, I found him leaning on a piece of rock, silently watching the sky. He seemed impatient and vexed. But what was to be done? This rash and powerful man could not command the sun as he did the sea. Noon arrived without the orb of day showing itself for an instant. We could not even tell its position behind the curtain of fog; and soon the fog turned to snow.

"Till to-morrow," said the captain quietly, and we returned to the *Nautilus* amid these atmospheric disturbances.

The tempest of snow continued till the next day. It was impossible to remain on the platform. From the saloon, where I was taking notes of incidents happening during this excursion to the polar continent, I could hear the cries of petrels and albatrosses sporting in the midst of this violent storm. The *Nautilus* did not remain motionless, but skirted the coast, advancing ten miles more to the south in the half-light left by the sun as it skirted the edge of the horizon. The next day, the 20th of March, the snow had ceased. The cold was a little greater, the thermometer showing two degrees below zero. The fog was rising, and I hoped that that day our observations might be taken. Captain Nemo not having yet appeared, the boat took Conseil and myself to land. The soil was still of the same volcanic nature; everywhere were traces of lava, scoriæ, and basalt; but the crater which had vomited them I could not see. Here, as lower down, this continent was alive with myriads of birds; but their rule was now divided with large troops of sea-mammals, looking at us with their soft eyes. There were several kinds of seals, some stretched on the earth, some on flakes of ice, many going in and out of the sea. They did not flee at our approach, never having had anything to do with man; and I reckoned that there were provisions there for hundreds of vessels.

"Sir," said Conseil, "will you tell me the names of these creatures?"

"They are seals and morses."

It was now eight in the morning. Four hours remained to us before the sun could be observed with advantage. I directed our step toward a vast bay cut in the steep granite shore. There, I can aver that earth and ice were lost to sight by the numbers of sea-mammals covering them, and I involuntarily sought for old Proteus, the mythological shepherd who watched these immense flocks of Neptune. There were more seals than anything else, forming distinct groups, male and female, the father watching over his family, the mother suckling her little ones, some already strong enough to go a few steps. When they wished to change their place, they took little jumps, made by the contraction of their bodies, and helped awkwardly enough by their imperfect fin, which, as with the lamantin, their congener, forms a perfect forearm. I should say that in the water, which is their element—the spine of these creatures is flexible—with smooth and close skin and webbed feet, they swim admirably. In resting on the earth they take the most graceful attitudes. Thus the ancients, observing their soft and expressive looks, which cannot be surpassed by the most beautiful look a woman can give, their clear voluptuous eyes, their charming positions, and the poetry of their manners, metamorphosed them, the male into a triton and the female into a mermaid. I made Conseil notice the considerable development of the lobes of the brain in these interesting cetaceans. No mammal, except man, has such a quantity of cerebral matter; they are also capable of receiving a certain amount of education, are easily domesticated, and I think, with other naturalists, that, if properly taught, they would be of great service as fishing-dogs. The greater part of them slept on the rocks or on the sand. Among these seals, properly so called, which have no external ears (in which they differ from the otter, whose ears are prominent), I noticed several varieties of stenorhynchi about three yards long, with a white coat, bulldog heads, armed with teeth in both jaws, four incisors at the top and four at the bottom, and two large canine teeth in the shape of a "fleur de lis." Among them glided sea-elephants, a kind of seal, with short flexible trunks. The giants of this species measured twenty feet round, and ten yards and a half in length; but they did not move as we approached.

"These creatures are not dangerous?" asked Conseil.

"No; not unless you attack them. When they have to defend their young, their rage is terrible, and it is not uncommon for them to break the fishing-boats to pieces."

"They are quite right," said Conseil.

"I do not say they are not."

Two miles further on we were stopped by the promontory which shelters the bay from the southerly winds. Beyond it we heard loud bellowings such as a troop of ruminants would produce.

"Good!" said Conseil. "A concert of bulls!"

"No; a concert of morses."

"They are fighting!"

"They are either fighting or playing."

We now began to climb the blackish rocks, amid unforeseen stumbles, and over stones which the ice made slippery. More than once I rolled over, at the expense of my loins. Conseil, more prudent or more steady, did not stumble, and helped me up, saying:

"If, sir, you would have the kindness to take wider steps, you would preserve your equilibrium better."

Arrived at the upper ridge of the promontory, I saw a vast white plain covered with morses. They were playing among themselves, and what we heard were bellowings of pleasure, not of anger.

As I passed near these curious animals, I could examine them leisurely, for they did not move. Their skins were thick and rugged, of a yellowish tint, approaching to red; their hair was short and scant. Some of them were four yards and a quarter long. Quieter and less timid than their congeners of the north, they did not, like them, place sentinels round the outskirts of their encampment. After examining this city of morses, I began to think of returning. It was eleven o'clock, and if Captain Nemo found the conditions favorable for observations, I wished to be present at the operation. We followed a narrow pathway running along the summit of the steep shore. At half-past eleven we had reached the place where we landed. The boat had run aground bringing the captain. I saw him standing on a block of basalt, his instruments near him, his eyes fixed on the northern horizon, near which the sun was then describing a lengthened curve. I took my place beside him, and waited without speaking. Noon arrived, and, as before, the sun did not appear. It was a fatality. Observations were still wanting. If not accomplished to-morrow, we must give up all idea of taking any. We were indeed exactly at the 20th of March. To-morrow, the 21st, would be the equinox: the sun would disappear behind the horizon for six months, and with its disappearance the long polar night would begin. Since the September equinox it had emerged from the northern horizon, rising by lengthened spirals up to the 21st of December. At this period, the summer solstice of the northern regions, it had begun to descend, and to-morrow was to shed its last rays upon them. I communicated my fears and observations to Captain Nemo.

"You are right, M. Aronnax," said he; "if to-morrow I cannot take the altitude of the sun, I shall not be able to do it for six months. But precisely because chance has led me into these seas on the 21st of March, my bearings will be easy to take, if at twelve we can see the sun."

"Why, captain?"

"Because then the orb of day describes such lengthened curves, that it is difficult to measure exactly its height above the horizon, and grave errors may be made with instruments."

"What will you do then?"

"I shall only use my chronometer," replied Captain Nemo. "If to-morrow, the 21st of March, the disk of the sun, allowing for refraction, is exactly cut by the northern horizon, it will show that I am at the South Pole."

"Just so," said I. "But this statement is not mathematically correct, because the equinox does not necessarily begin at noon."

"Very likely, sir; but the error will not be a hundred yards, and we do not want more. Till to-morrow then!"

Captain Nemo returned on board. Conseil and I remained to survey the shore, observing and studying until five o'clock. Then I went to bed, not, however, without invoking, like the Indian, the favor of the radiant orb.

The next day, the 21st of March, at five in the morning, I mounted the platform. I found Captain Nemo there.

"The weather is lightening a little," said he. "I have some hope. After breakfast we will go on shore, and choose a post for observation."

That point settled, I sought Ned Land. I wanted to take him with me. But the obstinate Canadian refused, and I saw that his taciturnity and his bad humor grew day by day. After all I was not sorry for his obstinacy under the circumstances. Indeed, there were too many seals on shore, and we ought not to lay such temptations in this unreflecting fisherman's way. Breakfast over, we went on shore. The *Nautilus* had gone some miles further up in the night. It was a whole league from the coast, above which reared a sharp peak about five hundred yards high. The boat took with me Captain Nemo, two men of the crew, and the instruments, which consisted of a chronometer, a telescope, and a barometer. While crossing, I saw numerous whales belonging to the three kinds peculiar to the southern seas: the whale, or the English "right whale," which has no dorsal fin; the "hump-back," or balænopteron, with reeved chest, and large whitish fins, which, in spite of its name, do not form wings; and the finback, of a yellowish-brown, the liveliest of all the cetacea. This powerful creature is heard a long way off when he throws to a great height columns of air and vapor, which look like whirlwinds of smoke. These different mammals were disporting themselves in troops in the quiet waters; and I could see that this basin of the Antarctic Pole served as a place of refuge to the cetacea too closely tracked by the hunters. I also noticed long whitish lines of salpæ, a kind of gregarious mollusk, and large medusæ floating between the reeds.

At nine we landed; the sky was brightening, the clouds were flying to the south, and the fog seemed to be leaving the cold surface of the waters. Captain Nemo went toward the peak, which he doubtless meant to be his observatory. It was a painful ascent over the sharp lava and the pumice-stones, in an atmosphere often impregnated with a sulphurous smell from the smoking cracks. For a man unaccustomed to walk on land, the captain climbed the steep slopes with an agility I never saw equaled, and which a hunter would have envied. We were two hours getting to the summit of this peak, which was half porphyry and half basalt. From thence we looked upon a vast sea, which, toward the north, distinctly traced its boundary line upon the sky. At our feet lay fields of dazzling whiteness. Over our heads a pale azure, free from fog. To the north the disk of the sun seemed like a ball of fire, already horned by the cutting of the horizon. From the bosom of the water rose sheaves of liquid jets by hundreds. In the distance lay the *Nautilus* like a cetacean asleep on the water. Behind us, to the south and east, an immense country, and a chaotic heap of rocks and ice, the limits of which were not visible. On arriving at the summit, Captain Nemo carefully took the mean height of the barometer, for he would have to consider that in taking his observations. At a quarter to twelve, the sun, then seen only by refraction, looked like a golden disk shedding its last rays upon this deserted continent, and seas which never man had yet plowed. Captain Nemo, furnished with a lenticular glass, which, by means of a mirror, corrected the refraction, watched the orb sinking below the horizon by degrees, following a lengthened diagonal. I held the chronometer. My heart beat fast. If the disappearance of the half-disk of the sun coincided with twelve o'clock on the chronometer, we were at the pole itself.

"Twelve!" I exclaimed.

"The South Pole!" replied Captain Nemo, in a grave voice, handing me the glass, which showed the orb cut in exactly equal parts by the horizon.

I looked at the last rays crowning the peak, and the shadows mounting by degrees up its slopes. At that moment Captain Nemo, resting with his hand on my shoulder, said:

"I, Captain Nemo, on this 21st day of March, 1868, have reached the South Pole on the ninetieth degree; and I take possession of this part of the globe, equal to one-sixth of the known continents."

"In whose name, captain?"

"In my own, sir!"

Saying which, Captain Nemo unfurled a black banner, bearing an N in gold quartered on its bunting. Then turning toward the orb of day, whose last rays lapped the horizon of the sea, he exclaimed:

"Adieu, sun! Disappear, thou radiant orb! Rest beneath this open sea, and let a night of six months spread its shadows over my new domains!"

Accident or Incident?

The next day, the 22d of March, at six in the morning, preparations for departure were begun. The last gleams of twilight were melting into night. The cold was great; the constellations shone with wonderful intensity. In the zenith glittered that wondrous Southern Cross—the polar bear of antarctic regions. The thermometer showed twelve degrees below zero, and when the wind freshened, it was most biting. Flakes of ice increased on the open water. The sea seemed everywhere alike. Numerous blackish patches spread on the surface, showing the formation of fresh ice. Evidently the southern basin, frozen during the six winter months, was absolutely inaccessible. What became of the whales in that time? Doubtless they went beneath the icebergs, seeking more practicable seas. As to the seals and morses, accustomed to live in a hard climate, they remained on these icy shores. These creatures have the instinct to break holes in the ice-fields, and to keep them open. To these holes they come for breath; when the birds, driven away by the cold, have emigrated to the north, these sea mammals remain sole masters of the polar continent. But the reservoirs were filling with water, and the *Nautilus* was slowly descending. At 1,000 feet deep it stopped; its screw beat the waves, and it advanced straight toward the north, at a speed of fifteen miles an hour. Toward night it was already floating under the immense body of an iceberg. At three in the morning I was awakened by a violent shock. I sat up in my bed and listened in the darkness, when I was thrown into the middle of the room. The *Nautilus,* after having struck, had rebounded violently. I groped along the partition, and by the staircase to the saloon, which was lit by the luminous ceiling. The furniture was upset. Fortunately the windows were firmly set, and had held fast. The pictures on the starboard side, from being no longer vertical, were clinging to the paper, while those of the port side were hanging at least a foot from the wall. The *Nautilus* was lying on its starboard side perfectly motionless. I heard footsteps, and a confusion of voices; but Captain Nemo did not appear. As I was leaving the saloon, Ned Land and Conseil entered.

"What is the matter?" said I, at once.

"I came to ask you, sir," said Conseil.

"Confound it!" exclaimed the Canadian, "I know well enough! The *Nauti-*

lus has struck; and judging by the way she lies, I do not think she will right herself as she did the first time in Torres Straits."

"But," I asked, "has she at least come to the surface of the sea?"

"We do not know," said Conseil.

"It is easy to decide," I answered. I consulted the manometer. To my great surprise it showed a depth of more than 180 fathoms. "What does that mean?" I exclaimed.

"We must ask Captain Nemo," said Conseil.

"But where shall we find him?" said Ned Land.

"Follow me," said I to my companions.

We left the saloon. There was no one in the library. At the center staircase, by the berths of the ship's crew, there was no one. I thought that Captain Nemo must be in the pilot's cage. It was best to wait. We all returned to the saloon. For twenty minutes we remained thus, trying to hear the slightest noise which might be made on board the *Nautilus*, when Captain Nemo entered. He seemed not to see us; his face, generally so impassive, showed signs of uneasiness. He watched the compass silently, then the manometer; and going to the planisphere, placed his finger on the spot representing the southern seas. I would not interrupt him; but, some minutes later, when he turned toward me, I said, using one of his own expressions in the Torres Straits:

"An incident, captain?"

"No, sir; an accident this time."

"Serious?"

"Perhaps."

"Is the danger immediate?"

"No."

"The *Nautilus* has stranded?"

"Yes."

"And this has happened—how?"

"From a caprice of nature, not from the ignorance of man. Not a mistake has been made in the working. But we cannot prevent equilibrium from producing its effects. We may brave human laws, but we cannot resist natural ones."

Captain Nemo had chosen a strange moment for uttering this philosophical reflection. On the whole, his answer helped me little.

"May I ask, sir, the cause of this accident?"

"An enormous block of ice, a whole mountain, has turned over," he replied. "When icebergs are undermined at their base by warmer water or reiterated shocks, their center of gravity rises, and the whole thing turns over. This is what has happened; one of these blocks, as it fell, struck the *Nautilus,* then, gliding under its hull, raised it with irresistible force, bringing it into beds which are not so thick, where it is lying on its side."

"But can we not get the *Nautilus* off by emptying its reservoirs, that it may regain its equilibrium?"

"That, sir, is being done at this moment. You can hear the pump working. Look at the needle of the manometer; it shows that the *Nautilus* is rising, but the block of ice is rising with it; and, until some obstacle stops its ascending motion, our position cannot be altered."

Indeed, the *Nautilus* still held the same position to starboard; doubtless it would right itself when the block stopped. But at this moment who knows if we may not strike the upper part of the iceberg, and if we may not be frightfully crushed between the two glassy surfaces? I reflected on all the consequences of our position. Captain Nemo never took his eyes off the manometer. Since the fall of the iceberg, the *Nautilus* had risen about a hundred and fifty feet, but it still made the same angle with the perpendicular. Suddenly a slight movement was felt in the hold. Evidently it was righting a little. Things hanging in the saloon were sensibly returning to their normal position. The partitions were nearing the upright. No one spoke. With beating hearts we watched and felt the straightening. The boards became horizontal under our feet. Ten minutes passed.

"At last we have righted!" I exclaimed.

"Yes," said Captain Nemo, going to the door of the saloon.

"But are we floating?" I asked.

"Certainly," he replied; "since the reservoirs are not empty; and, when empty, the *Nautilus* must rise to the surface of the sea."

We were in open sea; but at a distance of about ten yards, on either side of the *Nautilus,* rose a dazzling wall of ice. Above and beneath the same wall: above, because the lower surface of the iceberg stretched over us like an immense ceiling: beneath, because the overturned block, having slid by degrees, had found a resting-place on the lateral walls, which kept it in that position. The *Nautilus* was really imprisoned in a perfect tunnel of ice more than twenty yards in breadth, filled with quiet water. It was easy to get out of it by going either forward or backward, and then make a free passage under the iceberg, some hundreds of yards deeper. The luminous ceiling had been extinguished, but the saloon was still resplendent with intense light. It was the powerful reflection from the glass partition sent violently back to the sheets of the lantern. I cannot describe the effect of the voltaic rays upon the great blocks so capriciously cut; upon every angle, every ridge, every facet, was thrown a different light, according to the nature of the veins running through the ice; a dazzling mine of gems, particularly of sapphires, their blue rays crossing with the green of the emerald. Here and there were opal shades of wonderful softness, running through bright spots like diamonds of fire, the brilliancy of which the eye could not bear. The power of the lantern seemed increased a hundredfold, like a lamp through the lenticular plates of a first-class lighthouse.

"How beautiful! How beautiful!" cried Conseil.

"Yes," I said, "it is a wonderful sight. Is it not, Ned?"

"Yes, confound it! Yes," answered Ned Land, "it is superb! I am mad at being obliged to admit it. No one has ever seen anything like it; but the sight may cost us dear. And if I must say all, I think we are seeing here things which God never intended man to see."

Ned was right, it was too beautiful. Suddenly a cry from Conseil made me turn.

"What is it?" I asked.

"Shut your eyes, sir! Do not look, sir!" Saying which, Conseil clapped his hands over his eyes.

"But what is the matter, my boy?"

"I am dazzled, blinded."

My eyes turned involuntarily toward the glass, but I could not stand the fire which seemed to devour them. I understood what had happened. The *Nautilus* had put on full speed. All the quiet luster of the ice-walls was at once changed into flashes of lightning. The fire from these myriads of diamonds was blinding. It required some time to calm our troubled looks. At last the hands were taken down.

"Faith, I should never have believed it," said Conseil.

It was then five in the morning; and at that moment a shock was felt at the bows of the *Nautilus*. I knew that its spur had struck a block of ice. It must have been a false maneuver, for this submarine tunnel, obstructed by blocks, was not very easy navigation. I thought that Captain Nemo, by changing his course, would either turn these obstacles, or else follow the windings of the tunnel. In any case, the road before us could not be entirely blocked. But, contrary to my expectations, the *Nautilus* took a decided retrograde motion.

"We are going backward?" said Conseil.

"Yes," I replied. "This end of the tunnel can have no egress."

"And then?"

"Then," said I, "the working is easy. We must go back again, and go out at the southern opening. That is all."

In speaking thus, I wished to appear more confident than I really was. But the retrograde motion of the *Nautilus* was increasing: and, reversing the screw, it carried us at great speed.

"It will be a hindrance," said Ned.

"What does it matter, some hours more or less, provided we get out at last?"

"Yes," repeated Ned Land, "provided we do get out at last!"

For a short time I walked from the saloon to the library. My companions were silent. I soon threw myself on an ottoman, and took a book, which my eyes overran mechanically. A quarter of an hour after, Conseil, approaching me, said, "Is what you are reading very interesting, sir?"

"Very interesting!" I replied.

"I should think so, sir. It is your own book you are reading."

"My book?"

And indeed I was holding in my hand the work on the *Great Submarine Depths*. I did not even dream of it. I closed the book, and returned to my walk. Ned and Conseil rose to go.

"Stay here, my friends," said I, detaining them. "Let us remain together until we are out of this block."

"As you please, sir," Conseil replied.

Some hours passed. I often looked at the instruments hanging from the partition. The manometer showed that the *Nautilus* kept at a constant depth of more than three hundred yards; the compass still pointed to the south; the log indicated a speed of twenty miles an hour, which, in such a cramped space, was very great. But Captain Nemo knew that he could not hasten too much, and that minutes were worth ages to us. At twenty-five minutes past eight a second shock took place, this time from behind. I turned pale. My companions were close by my side. I seized Conseil's hand. Our looks expressed our feelings better than words. At this moment the captain entered the saloon. I went up to him.

"Our course is barred southward?" I asked.

"Yes, sir. The iceberg has shifted, and closed every outlet."

"We are blocked up, then?"

"Yes."

WANT OF AIR

Thus, around the *Nautilus*, above and below, was an impenetrable wall of ice. We were prisoners to the iceberg. I watched the captain. His countenance had resumed its habitual imperturbability.

"Gentlemen," he said calmly, "there are two ways of dying in the circumstances in which we are placed." (This inexplicable person had the air of a mathematical professor lecturing to his pupils.) "The first is to be crushed; the second is to die of suffocation. I do not speak of the possibility of dying of hunger, for the supply of provisions in the *Nautilus* will certainly last longer than we shall. Let us then calculate our chances."

"As to suffocation, captain," I replied, "that is not to be feared, because our reservoirs are full."

"Just so; but they will only yield two days' supply of air. Now, for thirty-six hours we have been hidden under the water, and already the heavy atmosphere of the *Nautilus* requires renewal. In forty-eight hours our reserve will be exhausted."

"Well, captain, can we be delivered before forty-eight hours?"

"We will attempt it, at least, by piercing the wall that surrounds us."

"On which side?"

"Sound will tell us. I am going to run the *Nautilus* aground on the lower bank, and my men will attack the iceberg on the side that is least thick."

Captain Nemo went out. Soon I discovered by a hissing noise that the water was entering the reservoirs. The *Nautilus* sank slowly, and rested on the ice at a depth of 350 yards, the depth at which the lower bank was immersed.

"My friends," I said, "our situation is serious, but I rely on your courage and energy."

"Sir," replied the Canadian, "I am ready to do anything for the general safety."

"Good, Ned!" and I held out my hand to the Canadian.

"I will add," he continued, "that being as handy with the pickaxe as with the harpoon, if I can be useful to the captain, he can command my services."

"He will not refuse your help. Come, Ned!"

I led him to the room where the crew of the *Nautilus* were putting on their cork-jackets. I told the captain of Ned's proposal, which he accepted. The Canadian put on his sea-costume, and was ready as soon as his companions. When Ned was dressed, I reentered the drawing-room, where the panes of glass were open, and, posted near Conseil, I examined the ambient beds that supported the *Nautilus.* Some instants after, we saw a dozen of the crew set foot on the bank of ice, and among them Ned Land, easily known by his stature. Captain Nemo was with them. Before proceeding to dig the walls, he took the soundings, to be sure of working in the right direction. Long sounding-lines were sunk in the side walls, but after fifteen yards they were again stopped by the thick wall. It was useless to attack it on the ceiling-like surface, since the iceberg itself measured more than 400 yards in height. Captain Nemo then sounded the lower surface. There ten yards of wall separated us from the water, so great was the thickness of the ice-field. It was necessary, therefore, to cut from it a piece equal in extent to the water-line of the *Nautilus.* There was about 6,000 cubic yards to detach, so as to dig a hole by which we could descend to the ice-field. The work was begun immediately, and carried on with indefatigable energy. Instead of digging round the *Nautilus,* which would have involved greater difficulty, Captain Nemo had an immense trench made at eight yards from the port quarter. Then the men set to work simultaneously with their screws on several points of its circumference. Presently the pickaxe attacked this compact matter vigorously, and large blocks were detached from the mass. By a curious effect of specific gravity, these blocks, lighter than water, fled, so to speak, to the vault of the tunnel, that increased in thickness at the top in proportion as it diminished at the base. But that mattered little, so long as the lower part grew thinner. After two hours' hard work, Ned Land came in exhausted. He and his comrades were replaced by new workers, whom Conseil and I joined. The second lieutenant of the *Nautilus* superintended us. The water seemed singularly cold, but I soon got warm handling the pickaxe. My movements were free enough, although they were made under a pressure of thirty atmospheres. When I reentered, after working two hours, to take some food and rest, I found a perceptible difference between the pure fluid with which the Rouquayrol engine supplied me, and the atmosphere of the *Nautilus*, already charged with carbonic acid. The air had not been renewed for forty-eight hours, and its vivifying qualities were considerably enfeebled. However, after a lapse of twelve hours, we had only raised a block of ice one yard thick, on the marked surface, which was about 600 cubic yards! Reckoning that it took twelve hours to accomplish this much, it would take five nights and four days to bring this enterprise to a satisfactory conclusion. Five nights and four days! And we have only air enough for two days in the reservoirs! "Without taking into account," said Ned, "that, even if we get out of this infernal prison, we shall also be imprisoned under the iceberg, shut out from all possible communication with the atmosphere." True enough! Who could then foresee the minimum of time necessary for our deliverance? We might be suffocated before the *Nautilus* could regain the surface of the waves! Was it destined to perish in this ice-tomb, with all those it inclosed? The situation was terrible. But everyone had looked the danger in the face, and each was determined to do his duty to the last.

As I expected, during the night a new block a yard square was carried away, and still further sank the immense hollow. But in the morning when, dressed in my cork-jacket, I traversed the slushy mass at a temperature of six or seven degrees below zero, I remarked that the side walls were gradually closing in. The beds of water furthest from the trench, that were not warmed by the men's mere work, showed a tendency to solidification. In presence of this new and imminent danger, what would become of our chances of safety, and how hinder the solidification of this liquid medium, that would burst the partitions of the *Nautilus* like glass?

I did not tell my companions of this new danger. What was the good of damping the energy they displayed in the painful work of escape? But when I went on board again, I told Captain Nemo of this grave complication.

"I know it," he said, in that calm tone which could counteract the most terrible apprehensions. "It is one danger more; but I see no way of escaping it; the only chance of safety is to go quicker than solidification. We must be beforehand with it, that is all."

On this day for several hours I used my pickaxe vigorously. The work kept me up. Besides, to work was to quit the *Nautilus*, and breathe directly the pure air drawn from the reservoirs, and supplied by our apparatus, and to quit the impoverished and vitiated atmosphere. Toward evening the trench was dug one yard deeper. When I returned on board, I was nearly suffocated by the carbonic acid with which the air was filled—ah! if we had only the chemical means to drive away this deleterious gas! We had plenty of oxygen; all this water contained a considerable quantity, and by dissolving it with our powerful piles, it would restore the vivifying fluid. I had thought well over it; but of what good was that, since the carbonic acid produced by our respiration had invaded every part of the vessel? To absorb it, it was necessary to fill some jars with caustic potash, and to shake them incessantly. Now this substance was wanting on board, and nothing could replace it. On that evening, Captain Nemo ought to open the taps of his reservoirs, and let some pure air into the interior of the *Nautilus*; without this precaution, we could not get rid of the sense of suffocation. The next day, March 26th, I resumed my miner's work in beginning the fifth yard. The side walls and the lower surface of the iceberg thickened visibly. It was evident that they would meet before the *Nautilus* was able to disengage itself. Despair seized me for an instant, my pickaxe nearly fell from my hands. What was the good of digging if I must be suffocated, crushed by the water that was turning into stone—a punishment that the ferocity of the savages even would not have invented! Just then Captain Nemo passed near me. I touched his hand and showed him the walls of our prison. The wall to port had advanced to at least four yards from the hull of the *Nautilus*. The captain understood me, and signed to me to follow him. We went on board. I took off my cork-jacket, and accompanied him into the drawing-room.

"M. Aronnax, we must attempt some desperate means, or we shall be sealed up in this solidified water as in cement."

"Yes; but what is to be done?"

"Ah! if my *Nautilus* were strong enough to bear this pressure without being crushed!"

"Well?" I asked, not catching the captain's idea.

"Do you not understand," he replied, "that this congelation of water will help us? Do you not see that, by its solidification, it would burst through this field of ice that imprisons us, as, when it freezes, it bursts the hardest stones? Do you not perceive that it would be an agent of safety instead of destruction?"

"Yes, captain, perhaps. But whatever resistance to crushing the *Nautilus* possesses, it could not support this terrible pressure, and would be flattened like an iron plate."

"I know it, sir. Therefore we must not reckon on the aid of nature, but on our own exertions. We must stop this solidification. Not only will the side walls be pressed together; but there is not ten feet of water before or behind the *Nautilus*. The congelation gains on us on all sides."

"How long will the air in the reservoirs last for us to breathe on board?"

The captain looked in my face. "After to-morrow they will be empty!"

A cold sweat came over me. However, ought I to have been astonished at the answer? On March 22, the *Nautilus* was in the open polar seas. We were at 26°. For five days we had lived on the reserve on board. And what was left of the respirable air must be kept for the workers. Even now, as I write, my recollection is still so vivid that an involuntary terror seizes me, and my lungs seem to be without air. Meanwhile Captain Nemo reflected silently, and evidently an idea had struck him; but he seemed to reject it. At last, these words escaped his lips:

"Boiling water!" he muttered.

"Boiling water?" I cried.

"Yes, sir. We are inclosed in a space that is relatively confined. Would not jets of boiling water, constantly injected by the pumps, raise the temperature in this part, and stay the congelation?"

"Let us try it," I said resolutely.

"Let us try, professor."

The thermometer then stood at seven degrees outside. Captain Nemo took me to the galleys, where the vast distillatory machines stood that furnished the drinkable water by evaporation. They filled these with water, and all the electric heat from the piles was thrown through the worms bathed in the liquid. In a few minutes this water reached a hundred degrees. It was directed toward the pumps, while fresh water replaced it in proportion. The heat developed by the troughs was such that cold water, drawn up from the sea, after only having gone through the machines, came boiling into the body of the pump. The injection was begun, and three hours after the thermometer marked six degrees below zero outside. One degree was gained. Two hours later, the thermometer only marked four degrees.

"We shall succeed," I said to the captain, after having anxiously watched the result of the operation.

"I think," he answered, "that we shall not be crushed. We have no more suffocation to fear."

During the night the temperature of the water rose to one degree below zero. The injections could not carry it to a higher point. But as the congelation of the sea-water produces at least two degrees, I was at last reassured against the dangers of solidification.

The next day, March 27, six yards of ice had been cleared, four yards only remaining to be cleared away. There was yet forty-eight hours' work. The air could not be renewed in the interior of the *Nautilus*. And this day would make it worse. An intolerable weight oppressed me. Toward three o'clock in the evening, this feeling rose to a violent degree. Yawns dislocated my jaws. My lungs panted as they inhaled this burning fluid, which became rarefied more and more. A moral torpor took hold of me. I was powerless, almost unconscious. My brave Conseil, though exhibiting the same symptoms and suffering in the same manner, never left me. He took my hand and encouraged me, and I heard him murmur, "Oh, if I could only not breathe, so as to leave more air for my master!"

Tears came into my eyes on hearing him speak thus. If our situation to all was intolerable in the interior, with what haste and gladness would we put on our cork-jackets to work in our turn! Pickaxes sounded on the frozen ice-beds. Our arms ached, the skin was torn off our hands. But what were these fatigues, what did the wounds matter? Vital air came to the lungs! We breathed! We breathed!

All this time no one prolonged his voluntary task beyond the prescribed time. His task accomplished, each one handed in turn to his panting companions the apparatus that supplied him with life. Captain Nemo set the example, and submitted first to this severe discipline. When the time came he gave up his apparatus to another, and returned to the vitiated air on board, calm, unflinching, unmurmuring.

On that day the ordinary work was accomplished with unusual vigor. Only two yards remained to be raised from the surface. Two yards only separated us from the open sea. But the reservoirs were nearly emptied of air. The little that remained ought to be kept for the workers; not a particle for the *Nautilus*. When I went back on board, I was half-suffocated. What a night! I know not how to describe it. The next day my breathing was oppressed. Dizziness accompanied the pain in my head, and made me like a drunken man. My companions showed the same symptoms. Some of the crew had rattling in the throat.

On that day, the sixth of our imprisonment, Captain Nemo, finding the pickaxes work too slowly, resolved to crush the ice-bed that still separated us from the liquid sheet. This man's coolness and energy never forsook him. He subdued his physical pains by moral force.

By his orders the vessel was lightened, that is to say, raised from the ice-bed by a change of specific gravity. When it floated they towed it so as to bring it above the immense trench made on the level of the water-line. Then filling his reservoirs of water, he descended and shut himself up in the hole.

Just then all the crew came on board, and the double door of communication was shut. The *Nautilus* then rested on the bed of ice, which was not one yard thick, and which the sounding leads had perforated in a thousand places. The taps of the reservoirs were then opened, and a hundred cubic yards of water was let in, increasing the weight of the *Nautilus* to 1,800 tons. We waited, we listened, forgetting our sufferings in hope. Our safety depended on this last chance. Notwithstanding the buzzing in my head, I soon heard the humming sound under the hull of the *Nautilus*. The ice cracked with a singular noise, like tearing paper, and the *Nautilus* sank.

"We are off!" murmured Conseil in my ear.

I could not answer him. I seized his hand, and pressed it convulsively. All at once, carried away by its frightful overcharge, the *Nautilus* sank like a bullet under the waters, that is to say, it fell as if it was in a vacuum. Then all the electric force was put on the pumps, that soon began to let the water out of the reservoirs. After some minutes, our fall was stopped. Soon, too, the manometer indicated an ascending movement. The screw, going at full speed, made the iron hull tremble to its very bolts, and drew us toward the north. But if this floating under the iceberg is to last another day before we reach the open sea, I shall be dead first.

Half stretched upon a divan in the library, I was suffocating. My face was purple, my lips blue, my faculties suspended. I neither saw nor heard. All notion of time had gone from my mind. My muscles could not contract. I do not know how many hours passed thus, but I was conscious of the agony that was coming over me. I felt as if I was going to die. Suddenly I came to. Some breaths of air penetrated my lungs. Had we risen to the surface of the waves? Were we free of the iceberg? No; Ned and Conseil, my two brave friends, were sacrificing themselves to save me. Some particles of air still remained at the bottom of one apparatus. Instead of using it, they had kept it for me, and while they were being suffocated, they gave me life drop by drop. I wanted to push back the thing; they held my hands, and for some moments I breathed freely. I looked at the clock; it was eleven in the morning. It ought to be the 28th of March. The *Nautilus* went at a frightful pace, forty miles an hour. It literally tore through the water.

Where was Captain Nemo? Had he succumbed? Were his companions dead with him? At the moment, the manometer indicated that we were not more than twenty feet from the surface. A mere plate of ice separated us from the atmosphere; could we not break it? Perhaps. In any case the *Nautilus* was going to attempt it. I felt that it was in an oblique position, lowering the stern, and raising the bows. The introduction of water had been the means of disturbing its equilibrium. Then, impelled by its powerful screw, it attacked the ice-field from beneath like a formidable battering-ram. It broke it by backing and then rushing forward against the field, which gradually gave way; and at last, dashing suddenly against it, shot forward on the icy field, that crushed beneath its weight. The panel was opened—one might say torn off—and the pure air came in in abundance to all parts of the *Nautilus*.

From Cape Horn to the Amazon

How I got on to the platform, I have no idea; perhaps the Canadian had carried me there. But I breathed, I inhaled the vivifying sea-air. My two companions were getting drunk with the fresh particles. The other unhappy men had been so long without food that they could not with impunity indulge in the simplest aliments that were given them. We, on the contrary, had no need to restrain ourselves; we could draw this air freely into our lungs, and it was the breeze, the breeze alone, that filled us with this keen enjoyment.

"Ah!" said Conseil. "How delightful this oxygen is! Master need not fear to breathe it. There is enough for everybody."

Ned Land did not speak, but he opened his jaws wide enough to frighten a shark. Our strength soon returned, and when I looked round me, I saw we were alone on the platform. The foreign seamen in the *Nautilus* were contented with the air that circulated in the interior; none of them had come to drink in the open air.

The first words I spoke were words of gratitude and thankfulness to my two companions. Ned and Conseil had prolonged my life during the last hours of this long agony. All my gratitude could not repay such devotion.

"My friends," said I, "we are bound one to the other forever, and I am under infinite obligations to you."

"Which I shall take advantage of," exclaimed the Canadian.

"What do you mean?" said Conseil.

"I mean that I shall take you with me when I leave this infernal *Nautilus*."

"Well," said Conseil, "after all this, are we going right?"

"Yes," I replied, "for we are going the way of the sun, and here the sun is in the north."

"No doubt," said Ned Land, "but it remains to be seen whether he will bring the ship into the Pacific or the Atlantic Ocean, that is, into frequented or deserted seas."

I could not answer that question, and I feared that Captain Nemo would rather take us to the vast ocean that touches the coasts of Asia and America at the same time. He would thus complete the tour round the submarine world, and return to those waters in which the *Nautilus* could sail freely. We ought, before long, to settle this important point. The *Nautilus* went at a rapid pace. The polar circle was soon passed, and the course shaped for Cape Horn. We were off the American point, March 31, at seven o'clock in the evening. Then all our past sufferings were forgotten. The remembrance of that imprisonment in the ice was effaced from our minds. We only thought of the future. Captain Nemo did not appear again either in the drawing-room or on the platform. The point shown each day on the planisphere, and marked by the lieutenant, showed me the exact direction of the *Nautilus*. Now, on that evening, it was evident, to my great satisfaction, that we were going back to the north by the Atlantic. The next day, April 1, when the *Nautilus* ascended to the surface, some minutes before noon, we sighted land to the west. It was Terra del Fuego, which the first navigators named thus from seeing the quantity of smoke that rose from the natives' huts. The coast seemed low to me, but in the distance rose high mountains. I even thought I had a glimpse of Mount Sarmiento, that rises 2,070 yards above the level of the sea, with a very pointed summit, which, according as it is misty or clear, is a sign of fine or of wet weather. At this moment, the peak was clearly defined against the sky. The *Nautilus*, diving again under the water, approached the coast, which was only some few miles off. From the glass windows in the drawing-room, I saw long seaweeds, and gigantic fuci, and varech, of which the open polar sea contains so many specimens, with their sharp polished filaments; they measured about 300 yards in length—real cables, thicker than one's thumb; and having great tenacity, they are often used as ropes for vessels. Another weed known as velp, with leaves four feet long, buried in the coral concretions, hung at the bottom. It served as nest and food for myriads of crustacea and mollusks, crabs and cuttlefish. There seals and otters had splendid repasts, eating the flesh of fish with sea-vegetables, according to the English fashion. Over this fertile and luxuriant ground the *Nautilus* passed with great rapidity. Toward evening it approached the Falkland group, the rough summits of which I recognized the following day. The depth of the sea was moderate. On the shores, our nets brought in beautiful specimens of seaweed, and particularly a certain fucus, the roots of which were filled with the best mussels in the world. Geese and ducks fell by dozens on the platform, and soon took their places in the pantry on board. With regard to fish, I observed especially specimens of the goby species, some two feet long, all over white and yellow spots. I admired also numerous medusæ, and the finest of the sort, the crysaora, peculiar to the sea about the Falkland Isles. I should have liked to preserve some specimens of these delicate zoöphytes; but they are only like clouds, shadows, apparitions, that sink and evaporate, when out of their native element.

When the last heights of the Falklands had disappeared from the horizon, the *Nautilus* sank to between twenty and twenty-five yards, and followed the American coast. Captain Nemo did not show himself. Until the 3d of April we did not quit the shores of Patagonia, sometimes under the ocean, sometimes at the surface. The *Nautilus* passed beyond the large estuary formed by the mouth of the Plata, and was, on the 4th of April, fifty-six miles off Uruguay. Its direction was northward, and followed the long windings of the coast of South America. We had then made 16,000 miles since our embarkation in the seas of Japan. About eleven o'clock in the morning the Tropic of Capricorn was crossed on the thirty-seventh meridian, and we passed Cape Frio standing out to sea. Captain Nemo, to Ned Land's great displeasure, did not like the neighborhood of the inhabited coasts of Brazil, for we went at a giddy speed. Not a fish, not a bird of the swiftest kind could follow us, and the natural curiosities of these seas escaped all observation.

This speed was kept up for several days, and in the evening of the 9th of April we sighted the most easterly point of South America that forms Cape San Roque. But then the *Nautilus* swerved again, and sought the lowest depth of a submarine valley, which is between this cape and Sierra Leone on the African coast. This valley bifurcates to the parallel of the Antilles, and terminates at the north by the enormous depression of 9,000 yards. In this place, the geological basin of the ocean forms, as far as the Lesser Antilles, a cliff of three and a half miles perpendicular in height, and at the parallel of the Cape Verde Islands, another wall not less considerable, that incloses thus all the sunk continent of the Atlantic. The bottom of this immense valley is dotted with some mountains, that give to these submarine places a picturesque aspect. I speak, moreover, from the manuscript charts that were in the library of the *Nautilus*—charts evidently due to Captain Nemo's hand, and made after his personal observations. For two days the desert and deep waters were visited by means of the inclined planes. The *Nautilus* was furnished with long diagonal broadsides, which carried it to all elevations. But, on the 11th of April, it rose suddenly, and land appeared at the mouth of the Amazon River, a vast estuary, the embouchure of which is so considerable that it freshens the sea-water for the distance of several leagues.

The equator was crossed. Twenty miles to the west were the Guianas, a French territory, on which we could have found an easy refuge; but a stiff breeze was blowing, and the furious waves would not have allowed a single boat to face them. Ned Land understood that, no doubt, for he spoke not a word about it. For my part, I made no allusion to his schemes of flight, for I would not urge him to make an attempt that must inevitably fail. I made the time pass pleasantly by interesting studies. During the days of April 11th and 12th the *Nautilus* did not leave the surface of the sea, and the net brought in a marvelous haul of zoöphytes, fish, and reptiles. Some zoöphytes had been fished up by the chain of the nets; they were for the most part beautiful phyctallines, belonging to the actinidian family, and among other species the phyctalis protexta, peculiar to that part of the ocean, with a little cylindrical trunk, ornamented with vertical lines, speckled with red dots, crowning a marvelous blossoming of tentacles. As to the mollusks, they consisted of some I had already observed—turritellas, olive porphyras, with regular lines intercrossed, with red spots standing out plainly against the flesh; odd peteroceras, like petrified scorpions; translucid hyaleas, argonauts, cuttle-fish (excellent eating), and certain species of calmars that naturalists of antiquity have classed among the flying-fish, and that serve principally for bait for cod fishing. I had not an opportunity of studying several species of fish on these shores. Among the cartilaginous ones, petromyzons-pricka, a sort of eel, fifteen inches long, with a greenish head, violet fins, gray-blue back, brown belly, silvered and sown with bright spots, the pupil of the eye encircled with gold—a curious animal that the current of the Amazon had drawn to the sea, for they inhabit fresh waters—tuberculated streaks, with pointed snouts, and a long loose tail, armed with a long jagged sting; little sharks, a yard long, gray and whitish skin, and several rows of teeth, bent back, that are generally known by the name of pantouffles; vespertilios, a kind of red isosceles triangle, half a yard long, to which pectorals are attached by fleshy prolongations that make them look like bats, but that their horny appendage, situated near the nostrils, has given them the name of sea-unicorns; lastly, some species of balistæ, the curassavian, whose spots were of a brilliant gold color, and the capriscus of clear violet, and with varying shades like a pigeon's throat.

I end here this catalogue, which is somewhat dry, perhaps, but very exact, with a series of bony fish that I observed in passing, belonging to the apteronotes, and whose snout is white as snow, the body of a beautiful black, marked with a very long loose fleshy strip; odontognathes, armed with spikes; sardines, nine inches long, glittering with a bright silver light; a species of mackerel provided with two anal fins; centronotes of a blackish tint, that are fished for with torches, long fish, two yards in length, with fat flesh, white and firm, which, when they are fresh, taste like eel, and when dry, like smoked salmon; labres, half red, covered with scales only at the bottom of the dorsal and anal fins; chrysoptera, on which gold and silver blend their brightness with that of the ruby and topaz; golden-tailed spares, the flesh of which is extremely delicate, and whose phosphorescent properties betray them in the midst of the waters; orange-colored spares with a long tongue; maigres, with gold caudal fins, dark thorn-tails, anableps of Surinam, etc.

Notwithstanding this "et cetera," I must not omit to mention fish that Conseil will long remember, and with good reason. One of our nets had hauled up a sort of very flat ray-fish, which, with the tail cut off, formed a perfect disk, and weighed twenty ounces. It was white underneath, red above, with large round spots of dark blue encircled with black, very glossy skin, terminating in a bilobed fin. Laid out on the platform, it struggled, tried to turn itself by convulsive movements, and made so many efforts that one last turn had nearly sent it into the sea. But Conseil, not wishing to let the fish go, rushed to it, and, before I could prevent him, had seized it with both hands. In a moment he was overthrown, his legs in the air, and half his body paralyzed, crying:

"Oh, master, master! Come to me!"

It was the first time the poor boy had not spoken to me in the third person. The Canadian and I took him up, and rubbed his contracted arms till he became sensible. The unfortunate Conseil had attacked a crampfish of the most dangerous kind, the cumana. This odd animal, in a medium conductor like water, strikes fish at several yards' distance, so great is the power of its electric organ, the two principal surfaces of which do not measure less than twenty-seven square feet. The next day, April 12, the *Nautilus* approached the Dutch coast, near the mouth of the Maroni. There several groups of sea-cows herded together; they were manatees, that, like the dugong and the stellera, belong to the sirenian order. These beautiful animals, peaceable and inoffensive, from eighteen to twenty-one feet in length, weigh at least sixteen hundredweight. I told Ned Land and Conseil that provident nature had assigned an important *rôle* to these mammalia. Indeed, they, like the seals, are designed to graze on the submarine prairies, and thus destroy the accumulation of weed that obstructs the tropical rivers.

"And do you know," I added, "what has been the result since men have almost entirely annihilated this useful race? That the putrified weeds have poisoned the air, and the poisoned air causes the yellow fever, that desolates these beautiful countries. Enormous vegetations are multiplied under the torrid seas, and the evil is irresistibly developed from the mouth of the Rio de la Plata to Florida. If we are to believe Toussenel, this plague is nothing to what it would be if the seas were cleared of whales and seals. Then, infested with poulps, medusæ, and cuttle-fish, they would become immense centers of infection, since their waves would not possess 'these vast stomachs that God had charged to infest the surface of the seas.' "

However, without disputing these theories, the crew of the *Nautilus* took possession of half a dozen manatees. They provisioned the larders with excellent flesh, superior to beef and veal. This sport was not interesting. The manatees allowed themselves to be hit without defending themselves. Several thousand pounds of meat were stored up on board to be dried. On this day, a successful haul of fish increased the stores of the *Nautilus*, so full of game were these seas. They were echeneides belonging to the third family of the malacopterygiens; their flattened disks were composed of transverse movable cartilaginous plates, by which the animal was enabled to create a vacuum, and so to adhere to any object like a cupping-glass. The remora that I had observed in the Mediterranean belongs to this species. But the one of which we are speaking was the echeneis osteochera, peculiar to this sea.

The fishing over, the *Nautilus* neared the coast. About here a number of sea-turtles were sleeping on the surface of the water. It would have been difficult to capture these precious reptiles, for the least noise awakens them, and their solid skull is proof against the harpoon. But the echeneis effects their capture with extraordinary precision and certainty. This animal is, indeed, a living fishhook, which would make the fortune of an inexperienced fisherman. The crew of the *Nautilus* tied a ring to the tail of these fish, so large as not to encumber their movements, and to this ring a long cord, lashed to the ship's side by the other end. The echeneids, thrown into the sea, directly began their game, and fixed themselves to the breastplate of the turtles. Their tenacity was such that they were torn rather than let go their hold. The men hauled them on board, and with them the turtles to which they adhered. They took also several cacouannes a yard long, which weighed 400 lbs. Their carapace covered with large horny plates, thin, transparent, brown, with white and yellow spots, fetch a good price in the market. Besides, they were excellent in an edible point of view, as well as the fresh turtles, which have an exquisite flavor. This day's fishing brought to a close our stay on the shores of the Amazon, and by nightfall the *Nautilus* had regained the high seas.

The Poulps

For several days the *Nautilus* kept off from the American coast. Evidently it did not wish to risk the tides of the Gulf of Mexico, or of the sea of the Antilles. April 16th, we sighted Martinique and Guadaloupe from a distance of about thirty miles. I saw their tall peaks for an instant. The Canadian, who counted on carrying out his projects in the Gulf, by either landing, or hailing one of the numerous boats that coast from one island to another, was quite disheartened. Flight would have been quite practicable, if Ned Land had been able to take possession of the boat without the captain's knowledge. But in the open sea it could not be thought of. The Canadian, Conseil, and I had a long conversation on this subject. For six months we had been prisoners on board the *Nautilus*. We had traveled 17,000 leagues; and, as Ned Land said, there was no reason why it should not come to an end. We could hope nothing from the captain of the *Nautilus*, but only from ourselves. Besides, for some time past he had become graver, more retired, less sociable. He seemed to shun me. I met him rarely. Formerly, he was pleased to explain the submarine marvels to me; now, he left me to my studies, and came no more to the saloon. What change had come over him? For what cause? For my part, I did not wish to bury with me my curious and novel studies. I had now the power to write the true book of the sea; and this book, sooner or later, I wished to see daylight. Then again, in the water by the Antilles, ten yards below the surface of the waters, by the open panels, what interesting products I had to enter on my daily notes! There were, among other zoöphytes, those known under the name of physalis pelagica, a sort of large oblong bladder with mother-of-pearl rays, holding out their membranes to the wind, and letting their blue tentacles float like threads of silk; charming medusæ to the eye, real nettles to the touch, that distill a corrosive fluid. There were also annelides, a yard and a half long, furnished with a pink horn, and with 1,700 locomotive organs that wind through the waters, and throw out in passing all the light of the solar spectrum. There were, in the fish category, some Malabar rays, enormous gristly things, ten feet long, weighing 600 pounds, the pectoral fin triangular in the midst of a slightly humped back, the eyes fixed in the extremities of the face, beyond the head, and which floated like weft, and looked sometimes like an opaque shutter on our glass window. There were American balistæ, which nature has only dressed in black and white; gobies, with yellow fins and prominent jaw; mackerel sixteen feet long, with short pointed teeth, covered with small scales, belonging to the albicore species. Then, in swarms, appeared gray mullet, covered with stripes of gold from the head to the tail, beating their resplendent fins, like masterpieces of jewelry, consecrated formerly to Diana, particularly sought after by rich Romans, and of which the proverb says, "Whoever takes them does not eat them." Lastly, pomacanthe dorees, ornamented with emerald bands, dressed in velvet and silk, passed before our eyes like Veronese lords; spurred spari passed with their pectoral fins; clupanodons, fifteen inches long, enveloped in their phosphorescent light; mullet beat the sea with their large jagged tails; red vendaces seemed to mow the waves with their showy pectoral fins; and silvery selenes, worthy of their name, rose on the horizon of the waters like so many moons with whitish rays. April 20th, we had risen to a mean height of 1,500 yards. The land nearest us then was the archipelago of the Bahamas. There rose high submarine cliffs covered with large weeds, giant laminariæ and fuci, a perfect espalier of hydrophytes worthy of a Titan world. It was about eleven o'clock when Ned Land drew my attention to a formidable pricking, like the sting of an ant, which was produced by means of large seaweeds.

"Well," I said, "these are proper caverns for poulps, and I should not be astonished to see some of these monsters."

"What!" said Conseil. "Cuttle-fish, real cuttle-fish, of the cephalopod class?"

"No," I said; "poulps of huge dimensions."

"I will never believe that such animals exist," said Ned.

"Well," said Conseil, with the most serious air in the world, "I remember perfectly to have seen a large vessel drawn under the waves by a cephalopod's arm."

"You saw that?" said the Canadian.

"Yes, Ned."

"With your own eyes?"

"With my own eyes."

"Where, pray, might that be?"

"At St. Malo," answered Conseil.

"In the port?" said Ned ironically.

"No; in a church," replied Conseil.

"In a church!" cried the Canadian.

"Yes; friend Ned. In a picture representing the poulp in question."

"Good!" said Ned Land, bursting out laughing.

"He is quite right," I said. "I have heard of this picture; but the subject represented is taken from a legend, and you know what to think of legends in the matter of natural history. Besides, when it is a question of monsters, the imagination is apt to run wild. Not only is it supposed that these poulps can draw down vessels, but a certain Olaüs Magnus speaks of a cephalopod a mile long, that is more like an island than an animal. It is also said that the Bishop of Nidros was building an altar on an immense rock. Mass finished, the rock began to walk, and returned to the sea. The rock was a poulp. Another bishop, Pontoppidan, speaks also of a poulp on which a regiment of cavalry could maneuver. Lastly, the ancient naturalists speak of monsters whose mouths were like gulfs, and which were too large to pass through the Straits of Gibraltar."

"But how much is true of these stories?" asked Conseil.

"Nothing, my friends; at least of that which passes the limit of truth to get to fable or legend. Nevertheless, there must be some ground for the imagination of the story-tellers. One cannot deny that poulps and cuttle-fish exist of a large species, inferior, however, to the cetaceans. Aristotle has stated the dimensions of a cuttle-fish as five cubits, or nine feet two inches. Our fishermen frequently see some that are more than four feet long. Some skeletons of poulps are preserved in the museums of Trieste and Montpellier, that measure two yards in length. Besides, according to the calculations of some naturalists, one of these animals, only six feet long, would have tentacles twenty-seven feet long. That would suffice to make a formidable monster."

"Do they fish for them in these days?" asked Ned.

"If they do not fish for them, sailors see them at least. One of my friends, Captain Paul Bos of Havre, has often affirmed that he met one of these monsters, of colossal dimensions, in the Indian seas. But the most astonishing fact, and which does not permit of the denial of the existence of these gigantic animals, happened some years ago, in 1861."

"What is the fact?" asked Ned Land.

"This is it. In 1861, to the northeast of Teneriffe, very nearly in the same latitude we are in now, the crew of the dispatch-boat Alector perceived a monstrous cuttle-fish swimming in the waters. Captain Bouguer went near to the animal, and attacked it with harpoons and guns, without much success, for balls and harpoons glided over the soft flesh. After several fruitless attempts, the crew tried to pass a slip-knot round the body of the mollusk. The noose slipped as far as the caudal fins, and there stopped. They tried then to haul it on board, but its weight was so considerable that the tightness of the cord separated the tail from the body, and, deprived of this ornament, he disappeared under the water."

"Indeed! Is that a fact?"

"An indisputable fact, my good Ned. They proposed to name this poulp 'Bouguer's cuttle-fish.' "

"What length was it?" asked the Canadian.

"Did it not measure about six yards?" said Conseil, who, posted at the window, was examining again the irregular windings of the cliff.

"Precisely," I replied.

"Its head," rejoined Conseil, "was it not crowned with eight tentacles, that beat the water like a nest of serpents?"

"Precisely."

"Had not its eyes, placed at the back of its head, considerable development?"

"Yes, Conseil."

"And was not its mouth like a parrot's beak?"

"Exactly, Conseil."

"Very well! No offense to master," he replied quietly; "if this is not Bouguer's cuttle-fish, it is, at least, one of its brothers."

I looked at Conseil. Ned Land hurried to the window.

"What a horrible beast!" he cried.

I looked in my turn, and could not repress a gesture of disgust. Before my eyes was a horrible monster, worthy to figure in the legends of the marvelous. It was an immense cuttle-fish, being eight yards long. It swam crossways in the direction of the *Nautilus* with great speed, watching us with its enormous staring green eyes. Its eight arms, or rather feet, fixed to its head, that have given the name of cephalopod to these animals, were twice as long as its body, and were twisted like the Furies' hair. One could see the 250 air-holes on the inner side of the tentacles. The monster's mouth, a horned beak like a parrot's, opened and shut vertically. Its tongue, a horned substance, furnished with several rows of pointed teeth, came out quivering from this veritable pair of shears. What a freak of nature—a bird's beak on a mollusk! Its spindle-like body formed a fleshy mass that might weigh 4,000 to 5,000 lbs.; the varying color changing with great rapidity, according to the irritation of the animal, passed successively from livid gray to reddish-brown. What irritated this mollusk? No doubt the presence of the *Nautilus*, more formidable than itself, and on which its suckers or its jaws had no hold. Yet, what monsters these poulps are! What vitality the Creator has given them! What vigor in their movements! And they possess three hearts! Chance had brought us in presence of this cuttle-fish, and I did not wish to lose the opportunity of carefully studying this specimen of cephalopods. I overcame the horror that inspired me; and, taking a pencil, began to draw it.

"Perhaps this is the same which the Alector saw," said Conseil.

"No," replied the Canadian; "for this is whole, and the other had lost its tail."

"That is no reason," I replied. "The arms and tails of these animals are reformed by redintegration; and, in seven years, the tail of Bouguer's cuttle-fish has no doubt had time to grow."

By this time other poulps appeared at the port light. I counted seven.

They formed a procession after the *Nautilus,* and I heard their beaks gnashing against the iron hull. I continued my work. These monsters kept in the water with such precision that they seemed immovable. Suddenly the *Nautilus* stopped. A shock made it tremble in every plate.

"Have we struck anything?" I asked.

"In any case," replied the Canadian, "we shall be free, for we are floating."

The *Nautilus* was floating, no doubt, but it did not move. A minute passed. Captain Nemo, followed by his lieutenant, entered the drawing-room. I had not seen him for some time. He seemed dull. Without noticing or speaking to us, he went to the panel, looked at the poulps, and said something to his lieutenant. The latter went out. Soon the panels were shut. The ceiling was lighted. I went toward the captain.

"A curious collection of poulps?" I said.

"Yes, indeed, Mr. Naturalist," he replied; "and we are going to fight them, man to beast."

I looked at him. I thought I had not heard aright.

"Man to beast?" I repeated.

"Yes, sir. The screw is stopped. I think that the horny jaw of one of the cuttle-fish is entangled in the blades. That is what prevents our moving."

"What are you going to do?"

"Rise to the surface, and slaughter this vermin."

"A difficult enterprise."

"Yes, indeed. The electric bullets are powerless against the soft flesh, where they do not find resistance enough to go off. But we shall attack them with the hatchet."

"And the harpoon, sir," said the Canadian, "if you do not refuse my help."

"I will accept it, Master Land."

"We will follow you," I said; and following Captain Nemo, we went toward the central staircase.

There, about ten men with boarding hatchets were ready for the attack. Conseil and I took two hatchets; Ned Land seized a harpoon. The *Nautilus* had then risen to the surface. One of the sailors, posted on the top ladder-step, unscrewed the bolts of the panels. But hardly were the screws loosed, when the panel rose with great violence, evidently drawn by the suckers of a poulp's arm. Immediately one of these arms slid like a serpent down the opening, and twenty others were above. With one blow of the axe, Captain Nemo cut this formidable tentacle, that slid wriggling down the ladder. Just as were pressing one on the other to reach the platform, two other arms, lashing the air, came down on the seaman placed before Captain Nemo and lifted him up with irresistible power. Captain Nemo uttered a cry, and rushed out. We hurried after him.

What a scene! The unhappy man, seized by the tentacle, and fixed to the suckers, was balanced in the air at the caprice of this enormous trunk. He rattled in his throat, he was stifled, he cried, "Help! Help!" These words, *spoken in French*, startled me! I had a fellow-countryman on board, perhaps several! That heartrending cry! I shall hear it all my life. The unfortunate man was lost. Who could rescue him from that powerful pressure? However, Captain Nemo had rushed to the poulp, and with one blow of the axe had cut through one arm. His lieutenant struggled furiously against other monsters that crept on the flanks of the *Nautilus*. The crew fought with their axes. The Canadian, Conseil, and I buried our weapons in the fleshy masses; a strong smell of musk penetrated the atmosphere. It was horrible!

For one instant, I thought the unhappy man entangled with the poulp would be torn from its powerful suction. Seven of the eight arms had been cut off. One only wriggled in the air, brandishing the victim like a feather. But just as Captain Nemo and his lieutenant threw themselves on it, the animal ejected a stream of black liquid. We were blinded with it. When the cloud dispersed, the cuttle-fish had disappeared, and my unfortunate countryman with it. Ten or twelve poulps now invaded the platform and sides of the *Nautilus*. We rolled pell-mell into the midst of this nest of serpents, that wriggled on the platform in the waves of blood and ink. It seemed as though these slimy tentacles sprang up like the hydra's heads. Ned Land's harpoon, at each stroke, was plunged into the staring eyes of the cuttle-fish. But my bold companion was suddenly overturned by the tentacles of a monster he had not been able to avoid.

Ah! how my heart beat with emotion and horror! The formidable beak of a cuttle-fish was open over Ned Land. The unhappy man would be cut in two. I rushed to his succor. But Captain Nemo was before me; his axe disappeared between the two enormous jaws, and, miraculously saved, the Canadian, rising, plunged his harpoon deep into the triple heart of the poulp.

"I owed myself this revenge!" said the captain to the Canadian.

Ned bowed without replying. The combat had lasted a quarter of an hour. The monsters, vanquished and mutilated, left us at last, and disappeared under the waves. Captain Nemo, covered with blood, nearly exhausted, gazed upon the sea that had swallowed up one of his companions, and great tears gathered in his eyes.

THE GULF STREAM

This terrible scene of the 20th of April none of us can ever forget. I have written it under the influence of violent emotion. Since then I have revised the recital; I have read it to Conseil and to the Canadian. They found it exact as to facts, but insufficient as to effect. To paint such pictures, one must have the pen of the most illustrious of our poets, the author of "The Toilers of the Deep."

I have said that Captain Nemo wept while watching the waves; his grief was great. It was the second companion he had lost since our arrival on board, and what a death! That friend, crushed, stifled, bruised by the dreadful arms of a poulp, pounded by his iron jaws, would not rest with his comrades in the peaceful coral cemetery! In the midst of the struggle, it was the despairing cry uttered by the unfortunate man that had torn my heart. The poor Frenchman, forgetting his conventional language, had taken to his own mother tongue, to utter a last appeal! Among the crew of the *Nautilus*, associated with the body and soul of the captain, recoiling like him from all contact with men, I had a fellow-countryman. Did he alone represent France in this mysterious association, evidently composed of individuals of divers nationalities? It was one of these insoluble problems that rose up unceasingly before my mind!

Captain Nemo entered his room, and I saw him no more for some time. But that he was sad and irresolute I could see by the vessel, of which he was the soul, and which received all his impressions. The *Nautilus* did not keep on in its settled course; it floated about like a corpse at the will of the waves. It went at random. He could not tear himself away from the scene of the last struggle, from this sea that had devoured one of his men. Ten days passed thus. It was not till the 1st of May that the *Nautilus* resumed its northerly course, after having sighted the Bahamas at the mouth of the Bahama Canal. We were then following the current from the largest river to the sea, that has its banks, its fish, and its proper temperatures. I mean the Gulf Stream. It is really a river, that flows freely to the middle of the Atlantic, and whose waters do not mix with the ocean waters. It is a salt river, saltier than the surrounding sea. Its mean depth is 1,500 fathoms, its mean breadth ten miles. In certain places the current flows with the speed of two miles and a half an hour. The body of its waters is more considerable than that of all the rivers on the globe. It was on this ocean river that the *Nautilus* then sailed.

This current carried with it all kinds of living things. Argonauts, so common in the Mediterranean, were there in quantities. Of the gristly sort, the most remarkable were the turbot, whose slender tails form nearly the third part of the body, and that looked like large lozenges twenty-five feet long; also, small sharks a yard long, with large heads, short rounded muzzles, pointed teeth in several rows, and whose bodies seemed covered with scales. Among the bony fish I noticed some gray gobies, peculiar to these waters; black giltheads, whose iris shone like fire; sirenes a yard long, with large snouts thickly set with little teeth, that uttered little cries; blue coryphænes, in gold and silver; parrots, like the rainbows of the ocean, that could rival in color the most beautiful tropical birds; blennies with triangular heads; bluish rhombs destitute of scales; batrachoides covered with yellow transversal bands like a Greek τ; heaps of little gobies spotted with yellow; dipterodons with silvery heads and yellow tails; several specimens of salmon, mugilomores slender in shape, shining with a soft light that Lacépède consecrated to the service of his wife; and lastly, a beautiful fish, the American-knight, that, decorated with all the orders and ribbons, frequents the shores of this great nation, that esteems orders and ribbons so little.

I must add that, during the night, the phosphorescent waters of the Gulf Stream rivaled the electric power of our watch-light, especially in the stormy weather that threatened us so frequently. May 8th, we were still crossing Cape Hatteras, at the height of North Carolina. The width of the Gulf Stream there is seventy-five miles, and its depth 210 yards. The *Nautilus* still went at random; all supervision seemed abandoned. I thought that, under these circumstances, escape would be possible. Indeed, the inhabited shores offered anywhere an easy refuge. The sea was incessantly plowed by the steamers that ply between New York or Boston and the Gulf of Mexico, and overrun day and night by the little schooners coasting about the several parts of the American coast. We could hope to be picked up. It was a favorable opportunity, notwithstanding the thirty miles that separated the *Nautilus* from the coasts of the Union. One unfortunate circumstance thwarted the Canadian's plans. The weather was very bad. We were nearing those shores where tempests are so frequent, that country of waterspouts and cyclones actually engendered by the current of the Gulf Stream. To tempt the sea in a frail boat was certain destruction! Ned Land owned this himself. He fretted, seized with nostalgia that flight only could cure.

"Master," he said that day to me, "this must come to an end. I must make a clean breast of it. This Nemo is leaving land and going up to the north. But I declare to you, I have had enough of the South Pole, and I will not follow him to the north."

"What is to be done, Ned, since flight is impracticable just now?"

"We must speak to the captain," said he; "you said nothing when we were in your native seas. I will speak, now we are in mine. When I think that before long the *Nautilus* will be by Nova Scotia, and that there near Newfoundland is a large bay, and into that bay the St. Lawrence empties itself, and that the St. Lawrence is my river, the river by Quebec, my native town—when I think of this I feel furious, it makes my hair stand on end. Sir, I would rather throw myself into the sea! I will not stay here! I am stifled!"

The Canadian was evidently losing all patience. His vigorous nature could not stand this prolonged imprisonment. His face altered daily; his temper became more surly. I knew what he must suffer, for I was seized with nostalgia myself. Nearly seven months had passed without our having had any news from land; Captain Nemo's isolation, his altered spirits, especially since the fight with the poulps, his taciturnity, all made me view things in a different light.

"Well, sir?" said Ned, seeing I did not reply.

"Well, Ned! Do you wish me to ask Captain Nemo his intentions concerning us?"

"Yes, sir."

"Although he has already made them known?"

"Yes; I wish it settled finally. Speak for me, in my name only, if you like."

"But I so seldom meet him. He avoids me."

"That is all the more reason for you to go to see him."

I went to my room. From thence I meant to go to Captain Nemo's. It would not do to let this opportunity of meeting him slip. I knocked at the door. No answer. I knocked again, then turned the handle. The door opened, I went in. The captain was there. Bending over his work-table, he had not heard me. Resolved not to go without having spoken, I approached him. He raised his head quickly, frowned, and said roughly, "You here! What do you want?"

"To speak to you, captain."

"But I am busy, sir; I am working. I leave you at liberty to shut yourself up; cannot I be allowed the same?"

This reception was not encouraging; but I was determined to hear and answer everything.

"Sir," I said coldly, "I have to speak to you on a matter that admits of no delay."

"What is that, sir?" he replied ironically. "Have you discovered something that has escaped me, or has the sea delivered up any new secrets?"

We were at cross-purposes. But before I could reply, he showed me an open manuscript on his table, and said, in a more serious tone, "Here, M. Aronnax, is a manuscript written in several languages. It contains the sum of my studies of the sea; and, if it please God, it shall not perish with me. This manuscript, signed with my name, completed with the history of my life, will be shut up in a little insubmersible case. The last survivor of all of us on board the *Nautilus* will throw this case into the sea, and it will go whither it is borne by the waves."

This man's name! his history written by himself! His mystery would then be revealed some day.

"Captain," I said, "I can but approve of the idea that makes you act thus. The result of your studies must not be lost. But the means you employ seem to me to be primitive. Who knows where the winds will carry this case, and in whose hands it will fall? Could you not use some other means? Could not you, or one of yours—"

"Never, sir!" he said, hastily interrupting me.

"But I and my companions are ready to keep this manuscript in store; and, if you will put us at liberty—"

"At liberty?" said the captain, rising.

"Yes, sir; that is the subject on which I wish to question you. For seven months we have been here on board, and I ask you to-day, in the name of my companions, and in my own, if your intention is to keep us here always?"

"M. Aronnax, I will answer you to-day as I did seven months ago; whoever enters the *Nautilus* must never quit it."

"You impose actual slavery on us!"

"Give it what name you please."

"But everywhere the slave has the right to regain his liberty."

"Who denies you this right? Have I ever tried to chain you with an oath?"

He looked at me with his arms crossed.

"Sir," I said, "to return a second time to this subject will be neither to your nor to my taste; but as we have entered upon it, let us go through with it. I repeat, it is not only myself whom it concerns. Study is to me a relief, a diversion, a passion that could make me forget everything. Like you, I am willing to live obscure in the frail hope of bequeathing one day, to future time, the result of my labors. But it is otherwise with Ned Land. Every man, worthy of the name, deserves some consideration. Have you thought that love of liberty, hatred of slavery, can give rise to schemes of revenge in a nature like the Canadian's; that he could think, attempt, and try—"

I was silenced; Captain Nemo rose.

"Whatever Ned Land thinks of, attempts, or tries, what does it matter to me? I did not seek him! It is not for my pleasure that I keep him on board! As for you, M. Aronnax, you are one of those who can understand everything, even silence. I have nothing more to say to you. Let this first time you have come to treat of this subject be the last; for a second time I will not listen to you."

I retired. Our situation was critical. I related my conversation to my two companions.

"We know now," said Ned, "that we can expect nothing from this man. The *Nautilus* is nearing Long Island. We will escape, whatever the weather may be."

But the sky became more and more threatening. Symptoms of a hurricane became manifest. The atmosphere was becoming white and misty. On the horizon fine streaks of cirrhous clouds were succeeded by masses of cumuli. Other low clouds passed swiftly by. The swollen sea rose in huge billows. The birds disappeared, with the exception of the petrels, those friends of the storm. The barometer fell sensibly, and indicated an extreme tension of the vapors. The mixture of the storm-glass was decomposed under the influence of the electricity that pervaded the atmosphere.

The tempest burst on the 18th of May, just as the *Nautilus* was floating off Long Island, some miles from the port of New York. I can describe this strife of the elements! For, instead of fleeing to the depths of the sea, Captain Nemo, by an unaccountable caprice, would brave it at the surface. The wind blew from the southwest at first. Captain Nemo, during the squalls, had taken his place on the platform. He had made himself fast, to prevent being washed overboard by the monstrous waves. I had hoisted myself up, and made myself fast also, dividing my admiration between the tempest and this extraordinary man who was coping with it. The raging sea was swept by huge cloud-drifts, which were actually saturated with the waves. The *Nautilus,* sometimes lying on its side, sometimes standing up like a mast, rolled and pitched terribly. About five o'clock a torrent of rain fell, that lulled neither sea nor wind. The hurricane blew nearly forty leagues an hour. It is under these conditions that it overturns houses, breaks iron gates, displaces twenty-four-pounders. However, the *Nautilus,* in the midst of the tempest, confirmed the words of a clever engineer: "There is no well-constructed hull that cannot defy the sea." This was not a resisting rock; it was a steel spindle, obedient and movable, without rigging or masts, that braved its fury with impunity. However, I watched these raging waves attentively. They measured fifteen feet in height, and 150 to 175 yards long, and their speed of propagation was thirty feet per second. Their bulk and power increased with the depth of the water. Such waves as these at the Hebrides have displaced a mass weighing 8,400 lbs. They are they which, in the tempest of December 23, 1864, after destroying the town of Yeddo, in Japan, broke the same day on the shores of America. The intensity of the tempest increased with the night. The barometer, as in 1860 at Reunion during a cyclone, fell seven-tenths at the close of day. I saw a large vessel pass the horizon struggling painfully. She was trying to lie to under half steam, to keep up above the waves. It was probably one of the steamers of the line from New York to Liverpool or Havre. It soon disappeared in the gloom. At ten o'clock in the evening the sky was on fire. The atmosphere was streaked with vivid lightning. I could not bear the brightness of it; while the captain, looking at it, seemed to envy the spirit of the tempest. A terrible noise filled the air, a complex noise, made up of the howls of the crushed waves, the roaring of the wind, and the claps of thunder. The wind veered suddenly to all points of the horizon; and the cyclone, rising in the east, returned after passing by the north, west, and south, in the inverse course pursued by the circular storms of the southern hemisphere. Ah, that Gulf Stream! It deserves its name of the King of Tempests. It is that which causes those formidable cyclones, by the difference of temperature between its air and its currents. A shower of fire had succeeded the rain. The drops of water were changed to sharp spikes. One would have thought that Captain Nemo was courting a death worthy of himself, a death by lightning. As the *Nautilus,* pitching dreadfully, raised its steel spur in the air, it seemed to act as a conductor, and I saw long sparks burst from it. Crushed and without strength, I crawled to the panel, opened it, and descended to the saloon. The storm was then at its height. It was impossible to stand upright in the interior of the *Nautilus.* Captain Nemo came down about twelve. I heard the reservoirs filling by degrees, and the *Nautilus* sank slowly beneath the waves. Through the open windows in the saloon I saw large fish, terrified, passing like phantoms in the water. Some were struck before my eyes. The *Nautilus* was still descending. I thought that at about eight fathoms deep we should find a calm. But no! The upper beds were too violently agitated for that. We had to seek repose at more than twenty-five fathoms in the bowels of the deep. But there, what quiet, what silence, what peace! Who could have told that such a hurricane had been let loose on the surface of that ocean?

FROM LATITUDE 47° 24′ TO LONGITUDE 17° 28′

In consequence of the storm, we had been thrown eastward once more. All hope of escape on the shores of New York or St. Lawrence had faded away; and poor Ned, in despair, had isolated himself like Captain Nemo. Conseil and I, however, never left each other. I said that the *Nautilus* had gone aside to the east. I should have said (to be more exact) the northeast. For some days it wandered, first on the surface and then beneath it, amid those fogs so dreaded by sailors. What accidents are due to these thick fogs! What shocks upon these reefs when the wind drowns the breaking of the waves! What collisions between vessels, in spite of their warning lights, whistles, and alarm-bells! And the bottoms of these seas look like a field of battle, where still lie all the conquered of the ocean; some old and already incrusted, others fresh and reflecting from their iron bands and copper plates the brilliancy of our lantern.

On the 15th of May we were at the extreme south of the Bank of Newfoundland. This bank consists of alluvia, or large heaps of organic matter, brought either from the equator by the Gulf Stream, or from the North Pole by the counter-current of cold water which skirts the American coast. There also are heaped up those erratic blocks which are carried along by the broken ice; and close by, a vast charnel-house of mollusks or zoöphytes, which perish here by millions. The depth of the sea is not great at Newfoundland—not more than some hundreds of fathoms; but toward the south is a depression of 1,500 fathoms. There the Gulf Stream widens. It loses some of its speed and some of its temperature, but it becomes a sea.

It was on the 17th of May, about 500 miles from Heart's Content, at a depth of more than 1,400 fathoms, that I saw the electric cable lying on the bottom. Conseil, to whom I had not mentioned it, thought at first that it was a gigantic sea-serpent. But I undeceived the worthy fellow, and by way of consolation related several particulars in the laying of this cable. The first one was laid in the years 1857 and 1858; but after transmitting about 400 telegrams, would not act any longer. In 1863, the engineers constructed another one, measuring 2,000 miles in length, and weighing 4,500 tons, which was embarked on the Great Eastern. This attempt also failed.

On the 25th of May, the *Nautilus*, being at a depth of more than 1,918 fathoms, was on the precise spot where the rupture occurred which ruined the enterprise. It was within 638 miles of the coast of Ireland; and at half-past two in the afternoon they discovered that communication with Europe had ceased. The electricians on board resolved to cut the cable before fishing it up, and at eleven o'clock at night they had recovered the damaged part. They made another point and spliced it, and it was once more submerged. But some days after it broke again, and in the depths of the ocean could not be recaptured. The Americans, however, were not discouraged. Cyrus Field, the bold promoter of the enterprise, as he had sunk all his own fortune, set a new subscription on foot, which was at once answered, and another cable was constructed on better principles. The bundles of conducting wires were each enveloped in gutta-percha, and protected by a wadding of hemp, contained in a metallic covering. The Great Eastern sailed on the 13th of July, 1866. The operation worked well. But one incident occurred. Several times in unrolling the cable they observed that nails had been recently forced into it, evidently with the motive of destroying it. Captain Anderson, the officers and engineers, consulted together, and had it posted up that if the offender was surprised on board, he would be thrown without further trial into the sea. From that time the criminal attempt was never repeated.

On the 23d of July the Great Eastern was not more than 500 miles from Newfoundland, when they telegraphed from Ireland news of the armistice concluded between Prussia and Austria after Sadowa. On the 27th, in the midst of heavy fogs, they reached the port of Heart's Content. The enterprise was successfully terminated; and for its first dispatch young America addressed old Europe in these words of wisdom so rarely understood: "Glory to God in the highest, and on earth peace, good-will toward men."

I did not expect to find the electric cable in its primitive state, such as it was on leaving the manufactory. The long serpent, covered with the remains of shells, bristling with foraminiferæ, was incrusted with a strong coating which served as a protection against all boring mollusks. It lay quietly sheltered from the motions of the sea, and under a favorable pressure for the transmission of the electric spark which passes from Europe to America in 0.32 of a second. Doubtless this cable will last for a great length of time, for they find that the gutta-percha covering is improved by the sea-water. Besides, on this level, so well chosen, the cable is never so deeply submerged as to cause it to break. The *Nautilus* followed it to the lowest depth, which was more than 2,212 fathoms, and there it lay without any anchorage and then we reached the spot where the accident had taken place in 1863. The bottom of the ocean then formed a valley about 100 miles broad, in which Mont Blanc might have been placed without its summit appearing above the waves. This valley is closed at the east by a perpendicular wall more than 2,000 yards high. We arrived there on the 28th of May, and the *Nautilus* was then not more than 120 miles from Ireland.

Was Captain Nemo going to land on the British Isles? No. To my great surprise he made for the south, once more coming back toward European seas. In rounding the Emerald Isle, for one instant I caught sight of Cape Clear, and the light which guides the thousands of vessels leaving Glasgow or Liverpool. An important question then arose in my mind. Did the *Nautilus* dare entangle itself in the Mauch? Ned Land, who had reappeared since we had been nearing land, did not cease to question me. How could I answer? Captain Nemo remained invisible. After having shown the Canadian a glimpse of American shores, was he going to show me the coast of France?

But the *Nautilus* was still going southward. On the 30th of May, it passed in sight of Land's End, between the extreme point of England and the Scilly Isles, which were left to starboard. If he wished to enter the Mauch he must go straight to the east. He did not do so.

During the whole of the 31st of May, the *Nautilus* described a series of circles on the water, which greatly interested me. It seemed to be seeking a spot it had some trouble in finding. At noon, Captain Nemo himself came to work the ship's log. He spoke no word to me, but seemed gloomier than ever. What could sadden him thus? Was it his proximity to European shores? Had he some recollections of his abandoned country? If not, what did he feel? Remorse or regret? For a long while this thought haunted my mind, and I had a kind of presentiment that before long chance would betray the captain's secrets.

The next day, the 1st of June, the *Nautilus* continued the same process. It was evidently seeking some particular spot in the ocean. Captain Nemo took the sun's altitude as he had done the day before. The sea was beautiful, the sky clear. About eight miles to the east, a large steamvessel could be discerned on the horizon. No flag fluttered from its mast, and I could not discover its nationality. Some minutes before the sun passed the meridian, Captain Nemo took his sextant, and watched with great attention. The perfect rest of the water greatly helped the operation. The *Nautilus* was motionless; it neither rolled nor pitched.

I was on the platform when the altitude was taken, and the captain pronounced these words—"It is here."

He turned and went below. Had he seen the vessel which was changing its course and seemed to be nearing us? I could not tell. I returned to the saloon. The panels closed, I heard the hissing of the water in the reservoirs. The *Nautilus* began to sink, following a vertical line, for its screw communicated no motion to it. Some minutes later it stopped at a depth of more than 420 fathoms, resting on the ground. The luminous ceiling was darkened, then the panels were opened, and through the glass I saw the sea brilliantly illuminated by the rays of our lantern for at least half a mile round us.

I looked to the port side, and saw nothing but an immensity of quiet waters. But to starboard, on the bottom appeared a large protuberance, which at once attracted my attention. One would have thought it a ruin buried under a coating of white shells, much resembling a covering of snow. Upon examining the mass attentively, I could recognize the ever-thickening form of a vessel bare of its masts, which must have sunk. It certainly belonged to past times. This wreck, to be thus incrusted with the lime of the water, must already be able to count many years passed at the bottom of the ocean.

What was this vessel? Why did the *Nautilus* visit its tomb? Could it have been aught but a shipwreck which had drawn it under the water? I knew not what to think, when near me in a slow voice I heard Captain Nemo say:

"At one time this ship was called the *Marseillais.* It carried seventy-four guns, and was launched in 1762. In 1778, the 13th of August, commanded by La Poype-Vertrieux, it fought boldly against the *Preston.* In 1779, on the 4th of July, it was at the taking of Grenada, with the squadron of Admiral Estaing. In 1781, on the 5th of September, it took part in the battle of Comte de Grasse, in Chesapeake Bay. In 1794, the French Republic changed its name. On the 16th of April, in the same year, it joined the squadron of Villaret Joyeuse, at Brest, being intrusted with the escort of a cargo of corn coming from America, under the command of Admiral Van Stabel. On the 11th and 12th Prairal of the second year, this squadron fell in with an English vessel. Sir, to-day is the 13th Prairal, the 1st of June, 1868. It is now seventy-four years ago, day for day, on this very spot, in latitude 47° 24′, longitude 17° 28′, that this vessel, after fighting heroically, losing its three masts, with the water in its hold, and the third of its crew disabled, preferred sinking with its 356 sailors to surrendering; and nailing its colors to the poop, disappeared under the waves to the cry of 'Long live the Republic!' "

"The *Avenger!*" I exclaimed.

"Yes, sir, the *Avenger!* A good name!" muttered Captain Nemo, crossing his arms.

A Hecatomb

The way of describing this unlooked-for scene, the history of the patriot ship, told at first so coldly, and the emotion with which this strange man pronounced the last words, the name of the *Avenger,* the significance of which could not escape me, all impressed itself deeply on my mind. My eyes did not leave the captain; who, with his hand stretched out to sea, was watching with a glowing eye the glorious wreck. Perhaps I was never to know who he was, from whence he came, or where he was going to, but I saw the man move, and apart from the savant. It was no common misanthropy which had shut Captain Nemo and his companions within the *Nautilus,* but a hatred, either monstrous or sublime, which time could never weaken. Did this hatred still seek for vengeance? The future would soon teach me that. But the *Nautilus* was rising slowly to the surface of the sea, and the form of the *Avenger* disappeared by degrees from my sight. Soon a slight rolling told me that we were in the open air. At that moment a dull boom was heard. I looked at the captain. He did not move.

"Captain!" said I.

He did not answer. I left him and mounted the platform. Conseil and the Canadian were already there.

"Where did that sound come from?" I asked.

"It was a gunshot," replied Ned Land.

I looked in the direction of the vessel I had already seen. It was nearing the *Nautilus,* and we could see that it was putting on steam. It was within six miles of us.

"What is that ship, Ned?"

"By its rigging, and the height of its lower masts," said the Canadian, "I bet she is a ship of war. May it reach us; and, if necessary, sink this cursed *Nautilus.*"

"Friend Ned," replied Conseil, "what harm can it do to the *Nautilus?* Can it attack it beneath the waves? Can it cannonade us at the bottom of the sea?"

"Tell me, Ned," said I, "can you recognize what country she belongs to?"

The Canadian knitted his eyebrows, dropped his eyelids, and screwed up the corners of his eyes, and for a few moments fixed a piercing look upon the vessel.

"No, sir," he replied; "I cannot tell what nation she belongs to, for she shows no colors. But I can declare she is a man-of-war, for a long pennant flutters from her mainmast."

For a quarter of an hour we watched the ship which was steaming toward us. I could not, however, believe that she could see the *Nautilus* from that distance, and still less that she could know what this submarine engine was. Soon the Canadian informed me that she was a large armored two-decker ram. A thick black smoke was pouring from her two funnels.

Her closely furled sails were stopped to her yards. She hoisted no flag at her mizzen-peak. The distance prevented us from distinguishing the colors of her pennant, which floated like a thin ribbon. She advanced rapidly. If Captain Nemo allowed her to approach, there was a chance of salvation for us.

"Sir," said Ned Land, "if that vessel passes within a mile of us, I shall throw myself into the sea, and I should advise you to do the same."

I did not reply to the Canadian's suggestion, but continued watching the ship. Whether English, French, American, or Russian, she would be sure to take us in if we could only reach her. Presently a white smoke burst from the forepart of the vessel; some seconds after the water, agitated by the fall of a heavy body, splashed the stern of the *Nautilus*, and shortly afterward a loud explosion struck my ear.

"What! They are firing at us!" I exclaimed.

"So please you, sir," said Ned, "they have recognized the unicorn, and they are firing at us."

"But," I exclaimed, "surely they can see that there are men in the case?"

"It is, perhaps, because of that," replied Ned Land, looking at me.

A whole flood of light burst upon my mind. Doubtless they knew now how to believe the stories of the pretended monster. No doubt, on board the *Abraham Lincoln*, when the Canadian struck it with the harpoon, Commander Farragut had recognized in the supposed narwhal a submarine vessel, more dangerous than a supernatural cetacean. Yes, it must have been so; and on every sea they were now seeking this engine of destruction. Terrible indeed if, as we supposed, Captain Nemo employed the *Nautilus* in works of vengeance! On the night when we were imprisoned in that cell, in the midst of the Indian Ocean, had he not attacked some vessel? The man buried in the coral cemetery, had he not been a victim to the shock caused by the *Nautilus*? Yes, I repeat it, it must be so. One part of the mysterious existence of Captain Nemo had been unveiled; and, if his identity had not been recognized, at least, the nations united against him were no longer hunting a chimerical creature, but a man who had vowed a deadly hatred against them. All the formidable past rose before me. Instead of meeting friends on board the approaching ship, we could only expect pitiless enemies. But the shot rattled about us. Some of them struck the sea and ricochetted, losing themselves in the distance. But none touched the *Nautilus*. The vessel was not more than three miles from us. In spite of the serious cannonade, Captain Nemo did not appear on the platform; but, if one of the conical projectiles had struck the shell of the *Nautilus,* it would have been fatal. The Canadian then said, "Sir, we must do all we can to get out of this dilemma. Let us signal them. They will then, perhaps, understand that we are honest folks."

Ned Land took his handkerchief to wave in the air; but he had scarcely displayed it, when he was struck down by an iron hand, and fell, in spite of his great strength, upon the deck.

"Fool!" exclaimed the captain. "Do you wish to be pierced by the spur of the *Nautilus* before it is hurled at this vessel?"

Captain Nemo was terrible to hear; he was still more terrible to see. His face was deadly pale, with a spasm at his heart. For an instant it must have ceased to beat. His pupils were fearfully contracted. He did not *speak,* he *roared,* as, with his body thrown forward, he wrung the Canadian's shoulders. Then, leaving him, and turning to the ship of war, whose shot was still raining around him, he exclaimed, with a powerful voice, "Ah, ship of an accursed nation, you know who I am! I do not want your colors to know you by. Look and I will show you mine!"

And on the forepart of the platform Captain Nemo unfurled a black flag, similar to the one he had placed at the South Pole. At that moment a shot struck the shell of the *Nautilus* obliquely, without piercing it; and, rebounding near the captain, was lost in the sea. He shrugged his shoulders; and addressing me, said shortly, "Go down, you and your companions, go down!"

"Sir," I exclaimed, "are you going to attack this vessel?"

"Sir, I am going to sink it."

"You will not do that?"

"I shall do it," he replied coldly. "And I advise you not to judge me, sir. Fate has shown you what you ought not to have seen. The attack has begun; go down."

"What is this vessel?"

"You do not know? Very well! So much the better! Its nationality to you, at least, will be a secret. Go down!"

We could but obey. About fifteen of the sailors surrounded the captain, looking with implacable hatred at the vessel nearing them. One could feel that the same desire of vengeance animated every soul. I went down at the moment another projectile struck the *Nautilus,* and I heard the captain exclaim:

"Strike, mad vessel! Shower your useless shot! And then, you will not escape the spur of the *Nautilus.* But it is not here that you shall perish! I would not have your ruins mingle with those of the *Avenger!*"

I reached my room. The captain and his second had remained on the platform. The screw was set in motion, and the *Nautilus,* moving with speed, was soon beyond the reach of the ship's guns. But the pursuit continued, and Captain Nemo contented himself with keeping his distance.

About four in the afternoon, being no longer able to contain my impatience, I went to the central staircase. The panel was open, and I ventured on to the platform. The captain was still walking up and down with an agitated step. He was looking at the ship, which was five or six miles to leeward.

He was going round it like a wild beast, and drawing it eastward, he allowed them to pursue. But he did not attack. Perhaps he still hesitated? I wished to mediate once more. But I had scarcely spoken, when Captain Nemo imposed silence, saying:

"I am the law, and I am the judge! I am the oppressed, and there is the oppressor! Through him I have lost all that I loved, cherished, and venerated—country, wife, children, father, and mother. I saw all perish! All that I hate is there! Say no more!"

I cast a last look at the man-of-war, which was putting on steam, and rejoined Ned and Conseil.

"We will fly!" I exclaimed.

"Good!" said Ned. "What is this vessel?"

"I do not know; but whatever it is, it will be sunk before night. In any case, it is better to perish with it, than be made accomplices in a retaliation, the justice of which we cannot judge."

"That is my opinion too," said Ned Land coolly. "Let us wait for night."

Night arrived. Deep silence reigned on board. The compass showed that the *Nautilus* had not altered its course. It was on the surface, rolling slightly. My companions and I resolved to fly when the vessel should be near enough either to hear us or to see us; for the moon, which would be full in two or three days, shone brightly. Once on board the ship, if we could not prevent the blow which threatened it, we could, at least we would, do all that circumstances would allow. Several times I thought the *Nautilus* was preparing for attack; but Captain Nemo contented himself with allowing his adversary to approach, and then fled once more before it.

Part of the night passed without any incident. We watched the opportunity for action. We spoke little, for we were too much moved. Ned Land would have thrown himself into the sea, but I forced him to wait. According to my idea, the *Nautilus* would attack the ship at her water-line, and then it would not only be possible, but easy to fly.

At three in the morning, full of uneasiness, I mounted the platform. Captain Nemo had not left it. He was standing at the forepart near his flag, which a slight breeze displayed above his head. He did not take his eyes from the vessel. The intensity of his look seemed to attract, and fascinate, and draw it onward more surely than if he had been towing it. The moon was then passing the meridian. Jupiter was rising in the east. Amid this peaceful scene of nature, sky and ocean rivaled each other in tranquillity, the sea offering to the orbs of night the finest mirror they could ever have in which to reflect their image. As I thought of the deep calm of these elements, compared with all those passions brooding imperceptibly within the *Nautilus,* I shuddered.

The vessel was within two miles of us. It was ever nearing that phosphorescent light which showed the presence of the *Nautilus.* I could see its green and red lights, and its white lantern hanging from the large mizzenmast. An indistinct vibration quivered through its rigging, showing that the furnaces were heated to the uttermost. Sheaves of sparks and red ashes flew from the funnels, shining in the atmosphere like stars.

I remained thus until six in the morning, without Captain Nemo noticing me. The ship stood about a mile and a half from us, and with the first dawn of day the firing began afresh. The moment could not be far off when, the *Nautilus* attacking its adversary, my companions and myself should forever leave this man. I was preparing to go down to remind them when the second mounted the platform, accompanied by several sailors. Captain Nemo either did not or would not see them. Some steps were taken which might be called the signal for action. They were very simple. The iron balustrade around the platform was lowered, and the lantern and pilot cages were pushed within the shell until they were flush with the deck. The long surface of the steel cigar no longer offered a single point to check its maneuvers. I returned to the saloon. The *Nautilus* still floated; some streaks of light were filtering through the liquid beds. With the undulations of the waves the windows were brightened by the red streaks of the rising sun, and this dreadful day of the 2d of June had dawned.

At five o'clock, the log showed that the speed of the *Nautilus* was slackening, and I knew that it was allowing them to draw nearer. Besides, the reports were heard more distinctly, and the projectiles, laboring through the ambient water, were extinguished with a strange hissing noise.

"My friends," said I, "the moment is come. One grasp of the hand, and may God protect us!"

Ned Land was resolute, Conseil calm, myself so nervous that I knew not how to contain myself. We all passed into the library; but the moment I pushed the door opening on the central staircase, I heard the upper panel close sharply. The Canadian rushed on to the stairs, but I stopped him. A well-known hissing noise told me that the water was running into the reservoirs, and in a few minutes the *Nautilus* was some yards beneath the surface of the waves. I understood the maneuver. It was too late to act. The *Nautilus* did not wish to strike at the impenetrable cuirass, but below the water-line, where the metallic covering no longer protected it.

We were again imprisoned, unwilling witnesses of the dreadful drama that was preparing. We had scarcely time to reflect; taking refuge in my room, we looked at each other without speaking. A deep stupor had taken hold of my mind; thought seemed to stand still. I was in that painful state of expectation preceding a dreadful report. I waited, I listened; every sense was merged in that of hearing! The speed of the *Nautilus* was accelerated. It was preparing to rush. The whole ship trembled. Suddenly I screamed. I felt the shock, but comparatively light. I felt the penetrating power of the steel spur. I heard rattlings and scrapings. But the *Nautilus*, carried along by its propelling power, passed through the mass of the vessel, like a needle through sail-cloth!

I could stand it no longer. Mad, out of my mind, I rushed from my room into the saloon. Captain Nemo was there, mute, gloomy, implacable; he was looking through the port panel. A large mass cast a shadow on the water; and that it might lose nothing of her agony, the *Nautilus* was going down into the abyss with her. Ten yards from me I saw the open shell through which the water was rushing with the noise of thunder, then the double line of guns and the netting. The bridge was covered with black agitated shadows.

The water was rising. The poor creatures were crowding the ratlings, clinging to the masts, struggling underwater. It was a human ant-heap ovetaken by the sea. Paralyzed, stiffened with anguish, my hair standing on end, with eyes wide open, panting, without breath and without voice, I too was watching! An irresistible attraction glued me to the glass! Suddenly an explosion took place. The compressed air blew up her decks, as if the magazines had caught fire. Then the unfortunate vessel sank more rapidly. Her topmast, laden with victims, now appeared; then her spars, bending under the weight of men; and last of all, the top of her mainmast. Then the dark mass disappeared, and with it the dead crew, drawn down by the strong eddy.

I turned to Captain Nemo. That terrible avenger, a perfect archangel of hatred, was still looking. When all was over, he turned to his room, opened the door, and entered. I followed him with my eyes. On the end wall beneath his heroes, I saw the portrait of a woman still young, and two little children. Captain Nemo looked at them for some moments, stretched his arms toward them, and kneeling down burst into deep sobs.

The Last Words of Captain Nemo

The panels had closed on this dreadful vision, but light had not returned to the saloon: all was silence and darkness within the *Nautilus*. At wonderful speed, a hundred feet beneath the water, it was leaving this desolate spot. Whither was it going? To the north or south? Where was the man flying to after such dreadful retaliation? I had returned to my room, where Ned and Conseil had remained silent enough. I felt an insurmountable horror for Captain Nemo. Whatever he had suffered at the hands of these men, he had no right to punish thus. He had made me, if not an accomplice, at least a witness of his vengeance. At eleven the electric light reappeared. I passed into the saloon. It was deserted. I consulted the different instruments. The *Nautilus* was flying northward at the rate of twenty-five miles an hour, now on the surface, and now thirty feet below it. On taking the bearings by the chart, I saw that we were passing the mouth of the Manche, and that our course was hurrying us toward the northern seas at a frightful speed. That night we had crossed two hundred leagues of the Atlantic. The shadows fell, and the sea was covered with darkness until the rising of the moon. I went to my room, but could not sleep. I was troubled with a dreadful nightmare. The horrible scene of destruction was continually before my eyes. From that day, who could tell into what part of the North Atlantic basin the *Nautilus* would take us? Still with unaccountable speed, still in the midst of these northern fogs, would it touch at Spitzbergen, or on the shores of Nova Zembla? Should we explore those unknown seas, the White Sea, the Sea of Kara, the Gulf of Obi, the Archipelago of Liarrov, and the unknown coast of Asia? I could not say. I could no longer judge of the time that was passing. The clocks had been stopped on board. It seemed, as in polar countries, that night and day no longer followed their regular course. I felt myself being drawn into that strange region where the foundered imagination of Edgar Poe roamed at will. Like the fabulous Gordon Pym, at every moment I expected to see "that veiled human figure, of larger proportions than those of any inhabitant of the earth, thrown across the cataract which defends the approach to the pole." I estimated (though perhaps I may be mistaken)—I estimated this adventurous course of the *Nautilus* to have lasted fifteen or twenty days. And I know not how much longer it might have lasted, had it not been for the catastrophe which ended this voyage. Of Captain Nemo I saw nothing whatever now, nor of his second. Not a man of the crew was visible for an instant. The *Nautilus* was almost incessantly underwater. When we came to the surface to renew the air, the panels opened and shut mechanically. There were no more marks on the planisphere. I knew not where we were. And the Canadian, too, his strength and patience at an end, appeared no more. Conseil could not draw a word from him, and fearing that, in a dreadful fit of madness, he might kill himself, watched him with constant devotion. One morning (what date it was I could not say), I had fallen into a heavy sleep toward the early hours, a sleep both painful and unhealthy, when I suddenly awoke. Ned Land was leaning over me, saying in a low voice, "We are going to fly."

I sat up.

"When shall we go?" I asked.

"To-night. All inspection on board the *Nautilus* seems to have ceased. All appear to be stupefied. You will be ready, sir?"

"Yes; where are we?"

"In sight of land. I took the reckoning this morning in the fog—twenty miles to the east."

"What country is it?"

"I do not know, but whatever it is we will take refuge there."

"Yes, Ned, yes. We will fly to-night, even if the sea should swallow us up."

"The sea is bad, the wind violent, but twenty miles in that light boat of the *Nautilus* does not frighten me. Unknown to the crew I have been able to procure food and some bottles of water."

"I will follow you."

"But," continued the Canadian, "if I am surprised I will defend myself; I will force them to kill me."

"We will die together, friend Ned."

I had made up my mind to all. The Canadian left me. I reached the platform, on which I could with difficulty support myself against the shock of the waves. The sky was threatening, but as land was in those thick brown shadows we must fly. I returned to the saloon, fearing and yet hoping to see Captain Nemo, wishing and yet not wishing to see him. What could I have said to him? Could I hide the involuntary horror with which he inspired me? No. It was better that I should not meet him face to face; better to forget him. And yet—How long seemed that day, the last that I should pass in the *Nautilus*. I remained alone. Ned Land and Conseil avoided speaking, for fear of betraying themselves. At six I dined, but I was not hungry; I forced myself to eat in spite of my disgust, that I might not weaken myself. At half-past six Ned Land came to my room saying, "We shall not see each other again before our departure. At ten the moon will not be risen. We will profit by the darkness. Come to the boat; Conseil and I will wait for you."

The Canadian went out without giving me time to answer. Wishing to verify the course of the *Nautilus*, I went to the saloon. We were running N.N.E. at frightful speed and more than fifty yards deep. I cast a last look on these wonders of nature, on the riches of art heaped up in this museum, upon the unrivaled collection destined to perish at the bottom of the sea with him who had formed it. I wished to fix an indelible impression of it in my mind. I remained an hour thus, bathed in the light of that luminous ceiling, and passing in review those treasures shining under their glasses. Then I returned to my room.

I dressed myself in strong sea clothing. I collected my notes, placing them carefully about me. My heart beat loudly. I could not check its pulsations. Certainly my trouble and agitation would have betrayed me to Captain Nemo's eyes. What was he doing at this moment? I listened at the door of his room. I heard steps. Captain Nemo was there. He had not gone to rest. At every moment I expected to see him appear and ask me why I wished to fly. I was constantly on the alert. My imagination magnified everything. The impression became at last so poignant that I asked myself if it would not be better to go to the captain's room, see him face to face, and brave him with look and gesture.

It was the inspiration of a madman; fortunately I resisted the desire, and stretched myself on my bed to quiet my bodily agitation. My nerves were somewhat calmer, but in my excited brain I saw over again all my existence on board the *Nautilus*; every incident, either happy or unfortunate, which had happened since my disappearance from the *Abraham Lincoln*—the submarine hunt, the Torres Straits, the savages of Papua, the running ashore, the coral cemetery, the passage of Suez, the island of Santorin, the Cretan diver, Vigo Bay, Atlantis, the iceberg, the South Pole, the imprisonment in the ice, the fight among the poulps, the storm in the Gulf Stream, the *Avenger*, and the horrible scene of the vessel sunk with all her crew. All these events passed before my eyes like scenes in a drama. Then Captain Nemo seemed to grow enormously, his features to assume superhuman proportions. He was no longer my equal, but a man of the waters, the genie of the sea.

It was then half-past nine. I held my head between my hands to keep it from bursting. I closed my eyes, I would not think any longer. There was another half-hour to wait, another half-hour of a nightmare, which might drive me mad.

At that moment I heard the distant strains of the organ, a sad harmony to an undefinable chant, the wail of a soul longing to break these earthly bonds. I listened with every sense, scarcely breathing; plunged, like Captain Nemo, in that musical ecstasy, which was drawing him in spirit to the end of life.

Then a sudden thought terrified me. Captain Nemo had left his room. He was in the saloon, which I must cross to fly. There I should meet him for the last time. He would see me, perhaps speak to me. A gesture of his might destroy me, a single word chain me on board.

But ten was about to strike. The moment had come for me to leave my room and join my companions.

I must not hesitate, even if Captain Nemo himself should rise before me. I opened my door carefully; and even then, as it turned on its hinges, it seemed to me to make a dreadful noise. Perhaps it only existed in my own imagination.

I crept along the dark stairs of the *Nautilus*, stopping at each step to check the beating of my heart. I reached the door of the saloon, and opened it gently. It was plunged in profound darkness. The strains of the organ sounded faintly. Captain Nemo was there. He did not see me. In the full light I do not think he would have noticed me, so entirely was he absorbed in the ecstasy.

I crept along the carpet, avoiding the slightest sound which might betray my presence. I was at least five minutes reaching the door, at the opposite side, opening into the library.

I was going to open it, when a sigh from Captain Nemo nailed me to the spot. I knew that he was rising. I could even see him, for the light from the library came through to the saloon. He came toward me silently, with his arms crossed, gliding like a specter rather than walking. His breast was swelling with sobs; and I heard him murmur these words (the last which ever struck my ear):

"Almighty God! Enough! Enough!"

Was it a confession of remorse which thus escaped from this man's conscience?

In desperation I rushed through the library, mounted the central staircase, and following the upper flight reached the boat. I crept through the opening, which had already admitted my two companions.

"Let us go! Let us go!" I exclaimed.

"Directly!" replied the Canadian.

The orifice in the plates of the *Nautilus* was first closed, and fastened down by means of a false key, with which Ned Land had provided himself; the opening in the boat was also closed. The Canadian began to loosen the bolts which still held us to the submarine boat.

Suddenly a noise within was heard. Voices were answering each other loudly. What was the matter? Had they discovered our flight? I felt Ned Land slipping a dagger into my hand.

"Yes," I murmured, "we know how to die!"

The Canadian had stopped in his work. But one word many times repeated, a dreadful word, revealed the cause of the agitation spreading on board the *Nautilus.* It was not we the crew were looking after!

"The Maëlstrom! The Maëlstrom!" I exclaimed.

The Maëlstrom! Could a more dreadful word in a more dreadful situation have sounded in our ears! We were then upon the dangerous coast of Norway. Was the *Nautilus* being drawn into this gulf at the moment our boat was going to leave its sides? We knew that at the tide the pent-up waters between the islands of Ferroe and Lofoten rush with irresistible violence, forming a whirlpool from which no vessel ever escapes. From every point of the horizon enormous waves were meeting, forming a gulf justly called the "Navel of the Ocean," whose power of attraction extends to a distance of twelve miles. There, not only vessels, but whales, are sacrificed, as well as white bears from the northern regions.

It is thither that the *Nautilus*, voluntarily or involuntarily, had been run by the captain.

It was describing a spiral, the circumference of which was lessening by degrees, and the boat, which was still fastened to its side, was carried along with giddy speed. I felt that sickly giddiness which arises from long-continued whirling round.

We were in dread. Our horror was at its height, circulation had stopped, all nervous influence was annihilated, and we were covered with cold sweat, like a sweat of agony! And what noise around our frail bark! What roarings repeated by the echo miles away! What an uproar was that of the waters broken on the sharp rocks at the bottom, where the hardest bodies are crushed, and trees worn away, "with all the fur rubbed off," according to the Norwegian phrase!

What a situation to be in! We rocked frightfully. The *Nautilus* defended itself like a human being. Its steel muscles cracked. Sometimes it seemed to stand upright, and we with it!

"We must hold on," said Ned, "and look after the bolts. We may still be saved if we stick to the *Nautilus*—"

He had not finished the words when we heard a crashing noise, the bolts gave way, and the boat, torn from its groove, was hurled like a stone from a sling into the midst of the whirlpool.

My head struck on a piece of iron, and with the violent shock I lost all consciousness.

CONCLUSION

Thus ends the voyage under the seas. What passed during that night—how the boat escaped from the eddies of the Maëlstrom, how Ned Land, Conseil, and myself ever came out of the gulf—I cannot tell.

But when I returned to consciousness, I was lying in a fisherman's hut, on the Lofoten Isles. My two companions, safe and sound, were near me holding my hands. We embraced each other heartily.

At that moment we could not think of returning to France. The means of communication between the north of Norway and the south are rare, and I am therefore obliged to wait for the steamboat running monthly from Cape North.

And among the worthy people who have so kindly received us I revise my record of these adventures once more. Not a fact has been omitted, not a detail exaggerated. It is a faithful narrative of this incredible expedition in an element inaccessible to man, but to which Progress will one day open a road.

Shall I be believed? I do not know. And it matters little, after all. What I now affirm is, that I have a right to speak of these seas, under which, in less than ten months, I have crossed 20,000 leagues in that submarine tour of the world which has revealed so many wonders.

But what has become of the *Nautilus*? Did it resist the pressure of the Maëlstrom? Does Captain Nemo still live? And does he still follow under the ocean those frightful retaliations? Or did he stop after that last hecatomb?

Will the waves one day carry to him this manuscript containing the history of his life? Shall I ever know the name of this man? Will the missing vessel tell us by its nationality that of Captain Nemo?

I hope so. And I also hope that his powerful vessel has conquered the sea at its most terrible gulf, and that the *Nautilus* has survived where so many other vessels have been lost! If it be so, if Captain Nemo still inhabits the ocean, his adopted country, may hatred be appeased in that savage heart! May the contemplation of so many wonders extinguish forever the spirit of vengeance! May the judge disappear, and the philosopher continue the peaceful exploration of the sea! If his destiny be strange, it is also sublime. Have I not understood it myself? Have I not lived ten months of this unnatural life? And to the question asked by Ecclesiastes 3,000 years ago, "That which is far off and exceeding deep, who can find it out?" two men alone of all now living have the right to give an answer:

CAPTAIN NEMO AND MYSELF.

The Mysterious Island

Part 1

Dropped from the Clouds

I

"Are we rising again?" "No. On the contrary." "Are we descending?" "Worse than that, captain! we are falling!" "For Heaven's sake heave out the ballast!" "There! the last sack is empty!" "Does the balloon rise?" "No!" "I hear a noise like the dashing of waves!" "The sea is below the car! It cannot be more than 500 feet from us!" "Overboard with every weight! . . . . everything!"

Such were the loud and startling words which resounded through the air, above the vast watery desert of the Pacific, about four o'clock in the evening of the 23rd of March, 1865.

Few can possibly have forgotten the terrible storm from the northeast, in the middle of the equinox of that year. The tempest raged without intermission from the 18th to the 26th of March. Its ravages were terrible in America, Europe, and Asia, covering a distance of eighteen hundred miles, and extending obliquely to the equator from the thirty-fifth north parallel to the fortieth south parallel. Towns were overthrown, forests uprooted, coasts devastated by the mountains of water which were precipitated on them, vessels cast on the shore, which the published accounts numbered by hundreds, whole districts leveled by waterspouts which destroyed everything they passed over, several thousand people crushed on land or drowned at sea; such were the traces of its fury, left by this devastating tempest. It surpassed in disasters those which so frightfully ravaged Havana and Guadalupe, one on the 25th of October, 1810, the other on the 26th of July, 1825.

But while so many catastrophes were taking place on land and at sea, a drama not less exciting was being enacted in the agitated air.

In fact, a balloon, as a ball might be carried on the summit of a waterspout, had been taken into the circling movement of a column of air and had traversed space at the rate of ninety miles an hour, turning around and around as if seized by some aerial maëlstrom.

Beneath the lower point of the balloon swung a car, containing five passengers, scarcely visible in the midst of the thick vapor mingled with spray which hung over the surface of the ocean.

Whence, it may be asked, had come that plaything of the tempest? From what part of the world did it rise? It surely could not have started during the storm. But the storm had raged five days already, and the first symptoms were manifested on the 18th. It cannot be doubted that the balloon came from a great distance, for it could not have traveled less than two thousand miles in twenty-four hours.

At any rate the passengers, destitute of all marks for their guidance, could not have possessed the means of reckoning the route traversed since their departure. It was a remarkable fact that, although in the very midst of the furious tempest, they did not suffer from it. They were thrown about and whirled around and around without feeling the rotation in the slightest degree, or being sensible that they were removed from a horizontal position.

Their eyes could not pierce through the thick mist which had gathered beneath the car. Dark vapor was all around them. Such was the density of the atmosphere that they could not be certain whether it was day or night. No reflection of light, no sound from inhabited land, no roaring of the ocean could have reached them, through the obscurity, while suspended in those elevated zones. Their rapid descent alone had informed them of the dangers which they ran from the waves. However, the balloon, lightened of heavy articles, such as ammunition, arms, and provisions, had risen into the higher layers of the atmosphere, to a height of 4,500 feet. The voyagers, after having discovered that the sea extended beneath them, and thinking the dangers above less dreadful than those below, did not hesitate to throw overboard even their most useful articles, while they endeavored to lose no more of that fluid, the life of their enterprise, which sustained them above the abyss.

The night passed in the midst of alarms which would have been death to less energetic souls. Again the day appeared and with it the tempest began to moderate. From the beginning of that day, the 24th of March, it showed symptoms of abating. At dawn, some of the lighter clouds had risen into the more lofty regions of the air. In a few hours the wind had changed from a hurricane to a fresh breeze, that is to say, the rate of the transit of the atmospheric layers was diminished by half. It was still what sailors call "a close-reefed topsail breeze," but the commotion in the elements had none the less considerably diminished.

Toward eleven o'clock, the lower region of the air was sensibly clearer. The atmosphere threw off that chilly dampness which is felt after the passage of a great meteor. The storm did not seem to have gone farther to the west. It appeared to have exhausted itself. Could it have passed away in electric sheets, as is sometimes the case with regard to the typhoons of the Indian Ocean?

But at the same time, it was also evident that the balloon was again slowly descending with a regular movement. It appeared as if it were, little by little, collapsing, and that its case was lengthening and extending, passing from a spherical to an oval form. Toward midday the balloon was hovering above the sea at a height of only 2,000 feet. It contained 50,000 cubic feet of gas, and, thanks to its capacity, it could maintain itself a long time in the air, although it should reach a great altitude or might be thrown into a horizontal position.

Perceiving their danger, the passengers cast away the last articles which still weighed down the car, the few provisions they had kept, everything, even to their pocket-knives, and one of them, having hoisted himself on to the circles which united the cords of the net, tried to secure more firmly the lower point of the balloon.

It was, however, evident to the voyagers that the gas was failing, and that the balloon could no longer be sustained in the higher regions. They must infallibly perish!

There was not a continent, nor even an island, visible beneath them. The watery expanse did not present a single speck of land, not a solid surface upon which their anchor could hold.

It was the open sea, whose waves were still dashing with tremendous violence! It was the ocean, without any visible limits, even for those whose gaze, from their commanding position, extended over a radius of forty miles. The vast liquid plain, lashed without mercy by the storm, appeared as if covered with herds of furious chargers, whose white and disheveled crests were streaming in the wind. No land was in sight, not a solitary ship could be seen. It was necessary at any cost to arrest their downward course, and to prevent the balloon from being engulfed in the waves. The voyagers directed all their energies to this urgent work. But, notwithstanding their efforts, the balloon still fell, and at the same time shifted with the greatest rapidity, following the direction of the wind, that is to say, from the northeast to the southwest.

Frightful indeed was the situation of these unfortunate men. They were evidently no longer masters of the machine. All their attempts were useless. The case of the balloon collapsed more and more. The gas escaped without any possibility of retaining it. Their descent was visibly accelerated, and soon after midday the car hung within 600 feet of the ocean.

It was impossible to prevent the escape of gas, which rushed through a large rent in the silk. By lightening the car of all the articles which it contained, the passengers had been able to prolong their suspension in the air for a few hours. But the inevitable catastrophe could only be retarded, and if land did not appear before night, voyagers, car, and balloon must to a certainty vanish beneath the waves.

They now resorted to the only remaining expedient. They were truly dauntless men, who knew how to look death in the face. Not a single murmur escaped from their lips. They were determined to struggle to the last minute, to do anything to retard their fall. The car was only a sort of willow basket, unable to float, and there was not the slightest possibility of maintaining it on the surface of the sea.

Two more hours passed and the balloon was scarcely 400 feet above the water.

At that moment a loud voice, the voice of a man whose heart was inaccessible to fear, was heard. To this voice responded others not less determined. "Is everything thrown out?" "No, here are still 2,000 dollars in gold." A heavy bag immediately plunged into the sea. "Does the balloon rise?" "A little, but it will not be long before it falls again." "What still remains to be thrown out?" "Nothing." "Yes! the car!" "Let us catch hold of the net, and into the sea with the car."

This was, in fact, the last and only mode of lightening the balloon. The ropes which held the car were cut, and the balloon, after its fall, mounted 2,000 feet. The five voyagers had hoisted themselves into the net, and clung to the meshes, gazing at the abyss.

The delicate sensibility of balloons is well known. It is sufficient to throw out the lightest article to produce a difference in its vertical position. The apparatus in the air is like a balance of mathematical precision. It can be thus easily understood that when it is lightened of any considerable weight its movement will be impetuous and sudden. So it happened on this occasion. But after being suspended for an instant aloft, the balloon began to redescend, the gas escaping by the rent which it was impossible to repair.

The men had done all that men could do. No human efforts could save them now.

They must trust to the mercy of Him who rules the elements.

At four o'clock the balloon was only 500 feet above the surface of the water.

A loud barking was heard. A dog accompanied the voyagers, and was held pressed close to his master in the meshes of the net.

"Top has seen something," cried one of the men. Then immediately a loud voice shouted,

"Land! land!" The balloon, which the wind still drove toward the southwest, had since daybreak gone a considerable distance, which might be reckoned by hundreds of miles, and a tolerably high land had, in fact, appeared in that direction. But this land was still thirty miles off. It would not take less than an hour to get to it, and then there was the chance of falling to leeward.

An hour! Might not the balloon before that be emptied of all the fluid it yet retained?

Such was the terrible question! The voyagers could distinctly see that solid spot which they must reach at any cost. They were ignorant of what it was, whether an island or a continent, for they did not know to what part of the world the hurricane had driven them. But they must reach this land, whether inhabited or desolate, whether hospitable or not.

It was evident that the balloon could no longer support itself! Several times already had the crests of the enormous billows licked the bottom of the net, making it still heavier, and the balloon only half rose, like a bird with a wounded wing. Half an hour later the land was not more than a mile off, but the balloon, exhausted, flabby, hanging in great folds, had gas in its upper part alone. The voyagers, clinging to the net, were still too heavy for it, and soon, half plunged into the sea, they were beaten by the furious waves. The balloon-case bulged out again, and the wind, taking it, drove it along like a vessel. Might it not possibly thus reach the land?

But, when only two fathoms off, terrible cries resounded from four pairs of lungs at once. The balloon, which had appeared as if it would never again rise, suddenly made an unexpected bound, after having been struck by a tremendous sea. As if it had been at that instant relieved of a new part of its weight, it mounted to a height of 1,500 feet, and here it met a current of wind, which instead of taking it directly to the coast, carried it in a nearly parallel direction.

At last, two minutes later, it reapproached obliquely, and finally fell on a sandy beach, out of the reach of the waves.

The voyagers, aiding each other, managed to disengage themselves from the meshes of the net. The balloon, relieved of their weight, was taken by the wind, and like a wounded bird which revives for an instant, disappeared into space.

But the car had contained five passengers, with a dog, and the balloon only left four on the shore.

The missing person had evidently been swept off by the sea, which had just struck the net, and it was owing to this circumstance that the lightened balloon rose the last time, and then soon after reached the land. Scarcely had the four castaways set foot on firm ground, than they all, thinking of the absent one, simultaneously exclaimed, "Perhaps he will try to swim to land! Let us save him! let us save him!"

II

Those whom the hurricane had just thrown on this coast were neither aeronauts by profession nor amateurs. They were prisoners of war whose boldness had induced them to escape in this extraordinary manner.

A hundred times they had almost perished! A hundred times had they almost fallen from their torn balloon into the depths of the ocean. But Heaven had reserved them for a strange destiny, and after having, on the 20th of March, escaped from Richmond, besieged by the troops of General Ulysses Grant, they found themselves seven thousand miles from the capital of Virginia, which was the principal stronghold of the South, during the terrible War of Secession. Their aerial voyage had lasted five days.

The curious circumstances which led to the escape of the prisoners were as follows:

That same year, in the month of February, 1865, in one of the coups de main by which General Grant attempted, though in vain, to possess himself of Richmond, several of his officers fell into the power of the enemy and were detained in the town. One of the most distinguished was Captain Cyrus Harding. He was a native of Massachusetts, a first-class engineer, to whom the government had confided, during the war, the direction of the railways, which were so important at that time. A true Northerner, thin, bony, lean, about forty-five years of age; his close-cut hair and his beard, of which he only kept a thick mustache, were already getting gray. He had one of those finely-developed heads which appear made to be struck on a medal, piercing eyes, a serious mouth, the physiognomy of a clever man of the military school. He was one of those engineers who began by handling the hammer and pickaxe, like generals who first act as common soldiers. Besides mental power, he also possessed great manual dexterity. His muscles exhibited remarkable proofs of tenacity. A man of action as well as a man of thought, all he did was without effort to one of his vigorous and sanguine temperament. Learned, clear-headed, and practical, he fulfilled in all emergencies those three conditions which united ought to ensure human success—activity of mind and body, impetuous wishes, and powerful will. He might have taken for his motto that of William of Orange in the 17th century: "I can undertake and persevere even without hope of success." Cyrus Harding was courage personified. He had been in all the battles of that war. After having begun as a volunteer at Illinois, under Ulysses Grant, he fought at Paducah, Belmont, Pittsburg Landing, at the siege of Corinth, Port Gibson, Black River, Chattanooga, the Wilderness, on the Potomac, everywhere and valiantly, a soldier worthy of the general who said, "I never count my dead!" And hundreds of times Captain Harding had almost been among those who were not counted by the terrible Grant; but in these combats where he never spared himself, fortune favored him till the moment when he was wounded and taken prisoner on the field of battle near Richmond. At the same time and on the same day another important personage fell into the hands of the Southerners. This was no other than Gideon Spilett, a reporter for the *New York Herald*, who had been ordered to follow the changes of the war in the midst of the Northern armies.

Gideon Spilett was one of that race of indomitable English or American chroniclers, like Stanley and others, who stop at nothing to obtain exact information, and transmit it to their journal in the shortest possible time. The newspapers of the Union, such as the *New York Herald*, are genuine powers, and their reporters are men to be reckoned with. Gideon Spilett ranked among the first of those reporters: a man of great merit, energetic, prompt and ready for anything, full of ideas, having traveled over the whole world, soldier and artist, enthusiastic in council, resolute in action, caring neither for trouble, fatigue, nor danger, when in pursuit of information, for himself first, and then for his journal, a perfect treasury of knowledge on all sorts of curious subjects, of the unpublished, of the unknown, and of the impossible. He was one of those intrepid observers who write under fire, "reporting" among bullets, and to whom every danger is welcome.

He also had been in all the battles, in the first rank, revolver in one hand, notebook in the other; grape-shot never made his pencil tremble. He did not fatigue the wires with incessant telegrams, like those who speak when they have nothing to say, but each of his notes, short, decisive, and clear, threw light on some important point. Besides, he was not wanting in humor. It was he who, after the affair of the Black River, determined at any cost to keep his place at the wicket of the telegraph office, and after having announced to his journal the result of the battle, telegraphed for two hours the first chapters of the Bible. It cost the *New York Herald* two thousand dollars, but the *New York Herald* published the first intelligence.

Gideon Spilett was tall. He was rather more than forty years of age. Light whiskers bordering on red surrounded his face. His eye was steady, lively, rapid in its changes. It was the eye of a man accustomed to take in at a glance all the details of a scene. Well built, he was inured to all climates, like a bar of steel hardened in cold water.

For ten years Gideon Spilett had been the reporter of the *New York Herald,* which he enriched by his letters and drawings, for he was as skillful in the use of the pencil as of the pen. When he was captured, he was in the act of making a description and sketch of the battle. The last words in his notebook were these: "A Southern rifleman has just taken aim at me, but—" The Southerner notwithstanding missed Gideon Spilett, who, with his usual fortune, came out of this affair without a scratch.

Cyrus Harding and Gideon Spilett, who did not know each other except by reputation, had both been carried to Richmond. The engineer's wounds rapidly healed, and it was during his convalescence that he made acquaintance with the reporter. The two men then learned to appreciate each other. Soon their common aim had but one object, that of escaping, rejoining Grant's army, and fighting together in the ranks of the Federals.

The two Americans had from the first determined to seize every chance; but although they were allowed to wander at liberty in the town, Richmond was so strictly guarded, that escape appeared impossible. In the meanwhile Captain Harding was rejoined by a servant who was devoted to him in life and in death. This intrepid fellow was a Negro born on the engineer's estate, of a slave father and mother, but to whom Cyrus, who was an Abolitionist from conviction and heart, had long since given his freedom. The once slave, though free, would not leave his master. He would have died for him. He was a man of about thirty, vigorous, active, clever, intelligent, gentle, and calm, sometimes naive, always merry, obliging, and honest. His name was Nebuchadnezzar, but he only answered to the familiar abbreviation of Neb.

When Neb heard that his master had been made prisoner, he left Massachusetts without hesitating an instant, arrived before Richmond, and by dint of stratagem and shrewdness, after having risked his life twenty times over, managed to penetrate into the besieged town. The pleasure of Harding on seeing his servant, and the joy of Neb at finding his master, can scarcely be described.

But though Neb had been able to make his way into Richmond, it was quite another thing to get out again, for the Northern prisoners were very strictly watched. Some extraordinary opportunity was needed to make the attempt with any chance of success, and this opportunity not only did not present itself, but was very difficult to find.

Meanwhile Grant continued his energetic operations. The victory of Petersburg had been very dearly bought. His forces, united to those of Butler, had as yet been unsuccessful before Richmond, and nothing gave the prisoners any hope of a speedy deliverance.

The reporter, to whom his tedious captivity did not offer a single incident worthy of note, could stand it no longer. His usually active mind was occupied with one sole thought—how he might get out of Richmond at any cost. Several times had he even made the attempt, but was stopped by some insurmountable obstacle. However, the siege continued; and if the prisoners were anxious to escape and join Grant's army, certain of the besieged were no less anxious to join the Southern forces. Among them was one Jonathan Forster, a determined Southerner. The truth was, that if the prisoners of the Secessionists could not leave the town, neither could the Secessionists themselves while the Northern army invested it. The Governor of Richmond for a long time had been unable to communicate with General Lee, and he very much wished to make known to him the situation of the town, so as to hasten the march of the army to their relief. Thus Jonathan Forster accordingly conceived the idea of rising in a balloon, so as to pass over the besieging lines, and in that way reach the Secessionist camp.

The Governor authorized the attempt. A balloon was manufactured and placed at the disposal of Forster, who was to be accompanied by five other persons. They were furnished with arms in case they might have to defend themselves when they alighted, and provisions in the event of their aerial voyage being prolonged.

The departure of the balloon was fixed for the 18th of March. It should be effected during the night, with a northwest wind of moderate force, and the aeronauts calculated that they would reach General Lee's camp in a few hours.

But this northwest wind was not a simple breeze. From the 18th it was evident that it was changing to a hurricane. The tempest soon became such that Forster's departure was deferred, for it was impossible to risk the balloon and those whom it carried in the midst of the furious elements.

The balloon, inflated on the great square of Richmond, was ready to depart on the first abatement of the wind, and, as may be supposed, the impatience among the besieged to see the storm moderate was very great.

The 18th, the 19th of March passed without any alteration in the weather. There was even great difficulty in keeping the balloon fastened to the ground, as the squalls dashed it furiously about.

The night of the 19th passed, but the next morning the storm blew with redoubled force. The departure of the balloon was impossible.

On that day the engineer, Cyrus Harding, was accosted in one of the streets of Richmond by a person whom he did not in the least know. This was a sailor named Pencroft, a man of about thirty-five or forty years of age, strongly built, very sunburnt, and possessed of a pair of bright sparkling eyes and a remarkably good physiognomy. Pencroft was an American from the North, who had sailed all the ocean over, and who had gone through every possible and almost impossible adventure that a being with two feet and no wings would encounter. It is needless to say that he was a bold, dashing fellow, ready to dare anything and was astonished at nothing. Pencroft at the beginning of the year had gone to Richmond on business, with a young boy of fifteen from New Jersey, son of a former captain, an orphan, whom he loved as if he had been his own child. Not having been able to leave the town before the first operations of the siege, he found himself shut up, to his great disgust; but, not accustomed to succumb to difficulties, he resolved to escape by some means or other. He knew the engineer-officer by reputation; he knew with what impatience that determined man chafed under his restraint. On this day he did not, therefore, hesitate to accost him, saying, without circumlocution, "Have you had enough of Richmond, captain?"

The engineer looked fixedly at the man who spoke, and who added, in a low voice,

"Captain Harding, will you try to escape?"

"When?" asked the engineer quickly, and it was evident that this question was uttered without consideration, for he had not yet examined the stranger who addressed him. But after having with a penetrating eye observed the open face of the sailor, he was convinced that he had before him an honest man.

"Who are you?" he asked briefly.

Pencroft made himself known.

"Well," replied Harding, "and in what way do you propose to escape?"

"By that lazy balloon which is left there doing nothing, and which looks to me as if it was waiting on purpose for us—"

There was no necessity for the sailor to finish his sentence. The engineer understood him at once. He seized Pencroft by the arm, and dragged him to his house. There the sailor developed his project, which was indeed extremely simple. They risked nothing but their lives in its execution. The hurricane was in all its violence, it is true, but so clever and daring an engineer as Cyrus Harding knew perfectly well how to manage a balloon. Had he himself been as well acquainted with the art of sailing in the air as he was with the navigation of a ship, Pencroft would not have hesitated to set out, of course taking his young friend Herbert with him; for, accustomed to brave the fiercest tempests of the ocean, he was not to be hindered on account of the hurricane.

Captain Harding had listened to the sailor without saying a word, but his eyes shone with satisfaction. Here was the long-sought-for opportunity —he was not a man to let it pass. The plan was feasible, though, it must be confessed, dangerous in the extreme. In the night, in spite of their guards, they might approach the balloon, slip into the car, and then cut the cords which held it. There was no doubt that they might be killed, but on the other hand they might succeed, and without this storm!—Without this storm the balloon would have started already and the looked-for opportunity would not have then presented itself.

"I am not alone!" said Harding at last.

"How many people do you wish to bring with you?" asked the sailor.

"Two; my friend Spilett, and my servant Neb."

"That will be three," replied Pencroft; "and with Herbert and me five. But the balloon will hold six—"

"That will be enough, we will go," answered Harding in a firm voice.

This "we" included Spilett, for the reporter, as his friend well knew, was not a man to draw back, and when the project was communicated to him he approved of it unreservedly. What astonished him was, that so simple an idea had not occurred to him before. As to Neb, he followed his master wherever his master wished to go.

"This evening, then," said Pencroft, "we will all meet out there."

"This evening, at ten o'clock," replied Captain Harding; "and Heaven grant that the storm does not abate before our departure."

Pencroft took leave of the two friends, and returned to his lodging, where young Herbert Brown had remained. The courageous boy knew of the sailor's plan, and it was not without anxiety that he awaited the result of the proposal being made to the engineer. Thus five determined persons were about to abandon themselves to the mercy of the tempestuous elements!

No! the storm did not abate, and neither Jonathan Forster nor his companions dreamed of confronting it in that frail car.

It would be a terrible journey. The engineer only feared one thing; it was that the balloon, held to the ground and dashed about by the wind, would be torn into shreds. For several hours he roamed around the nearly-deserted square, surveying the apparatus. Pencroft did the same on his side, his hands in his pockets, yawning now and then like a man who did not know how to kill the time, but really dreading, like his friend, either the escape or destruction of the balloon. Evening arrived. The night was dark in the extreme. Thick mists passed like clouds close to the ground. Rain fell mingled with snow. It was very cold. A mist hung over Richmond. It seemed as if the violent storm had produced a truce between the besiegers and the besieged, and that the cannon were silenced by the louder detonations of the storm. The streets of the town were deserted. It had not even appeared necessary in that horrible weather to place a guard in the square, in the midst of which plunged the balloon. Everything favored the departure of the prisoners, but what might possibly be the termination of the hazardous voyage they contemplated in the midst of the furious elements?

"Dirty weather!" exclaimed Pencroft, fixing his hat firmly on his head with a blow of his fist; "but pshaw, we shall succeed all the same!"

At half-past nine, Harding and his companions glided from different directions into the square, which the gas-lamps, extinguished by the wind, had left in total obscurity. Even the enormous balloon, almost beaten to the ground, could not be seen. Independently of the sacks of ballast, to which the cords of the net were fastened, the car was held by a strong cable passed through a ring in the pavement. The five prisoners met by the car. They had not been perceived, and such was the darkness that they could not even see each other.

Without speaking a word, Harding, Spilett, Neb, and Herbert took their places in the car, while Pencroft by the engineer's order detached successively the bags of ballast. It was the work of a few minutes only, and the sailor rejoined his companions.

The balloon was then only held by the cable, and the engineer had nothing to do but to give the word.

At that moment a dog sprang with a bound into the car. It was Top, a favorite of the engineer. The faithful creature, having broken his chain, had followed his master. He, however, fearing that its additional weight might impede their ascent, wished to send away the animal.

"One more will make but little difference, poor beast!" exclaimed Pencroft, heaving out two bags of sand, and as he spoke letting go the cable; the balloon ascending in an oblique direction, disappeared, after having dashed the car against two chimneys, which it threw down as it swept by them.

Then, indeed, the full rage of the hurricane was exhibited to the voyagers. During the night the engineer could not dream of descending, and when day broke, even a glimpse of the earth below was intercepted by fog.

Five days had passed when a partial clearing allowed them to see the wide extending ocean beneath their feet, now lashed into the maddest fury by the gale.

Our readers will recollect what befell these five daring individuals who set out on their hazardous expedition in the balloon on the 20th of March. Five days afterward four of them were thrown on a desert coast, seven thousand miles from their country! But one of their number was missing, the man who was to be their guide, their leading spirit, the engineer, Captain Harding! The instant they had recovered their feet, they all hurried to the beach in the hopes of rendering him assistance.

III

The engineer, the meshes of the net having given way, had been carried off by a wave. His dog also had disappeared. The faithful animal had voluntarily leaped out to help his master. "Forward," cried the reporter; and all four, Spilett, Herbert, Pencroft, and Neb, forgetting their fatigue, began their search. Poor Neb shed bitter tears, giving way to despair at the thought of having lost the only being he loved on earth.

Only two minutes had passed from the time when Cyrus Harding disappeared to the moment when his companions set foot on the ground. They had hopes therefore of arriving in time to save him. "Let us look for him! let us look for him!" cried Neb.

"Yes, Neb," replied Gideon Spilett, "and we will find him too!"

"Living, I trust!"

"Still living!"

"Can he swim?" asked Pencroft.

"Yes," replied Neb, "and besides, Top is there."

The sailor, observing the heavy surf on the shore, shook his head.

The engineer had disappeared to the north of the shore, and nearly half a mile from the place where the castaways had landed. The nearest point of the beach he could reach was thus fully that distance off.

It was then nearly six o'clock. A thick fog made the night very dark. The castaways proceeded toward the north of the land on which chance had thrown them, an unknown region, the geographical situation of which they could not even guess. They were walking upon a sandy soil, mingled with stones, which appeared destitute of any sort of vegetation. The ground, very unequal and rough, was in some places perfectly riddled with holes, making walking extremely painful. From these holes escaped every minute great birds of clumsy flight, which flew in all directions. Others, more active, rose in flocks and passed in clouds over their heads. The sailor thought he recognized gulls and cormorants, whose shrill cries rose above the roaring of the sea.

From time to time the castaways stopped and shouted, then listened for some response from the ocean, for they thought that if the engineer had landed, and they had been near to the place, they would have heard the barking of the dog Top, even should Harding himself have been unable to give any sign of existence. They stopped to listen, but no sound arose above the roaring of the waves and the dashing of the surf. The little band then continued their march forward, searching into every hollow of the shore.

After walking for twenty minutes, the four castaways were suddenly brought to a standstill by the sight of foaming billows close to their feet. The solid ground ended here. They found themselves at the extremity of a sharp point on which the sea broke furiously.

"It is a promontory," said the sailor; "we must retrace our steps, holding toward the right, and we shall thus gain the mainland."

"But if he is there," said Neb, pointing to the ocean, whose waves shone of a snowy white in the darkness. "Well, let us call again," and all uniting their voices, they gave a vigorous shout, but there came no reply. They waited for a lull, then began again; still no reply.

The castaways accordingly returned, following the opposite side of the promontory, over a soil equally sandy and rugged. However, Pencroft observed that the shore was more equal, that the ground rose, and he declared that it was joined by a long slope to a hill, whose massive front he thought that he could see looming indistinctly through the mist. The birds were less numerous on this part of the shore; the sea was also less tumultuous, and they observed that the agitation of the waves was diminished. The noise of the surf was scarcely heard. This side of the promontory evidently formed a semicircular bay, which the sharp point sheltered from the breakers of the open sea. But to follow this direction was to go south, exactly opposite to that part of the coast where Harding might have landed. After a walk of a mile and a half, the shore presented no curve which would permit them to return to the north. This promontory, of which they had turned the point, must be attached to the mainland. The castaways, although their strength was nearly exhausted, still marched courageously forward, hoping every moment to meet with a sudden angle which would set them in the first direction. What was their disappointment, when, after trudging nearly two miles, having reached an elevated point composed of slippery rocks, they found themselves again stopped by the sea.

"We are on an islet," said Pencroft, "and we have surveyed it from one extremity to the other."

The sailor was right; they had been thrown, not on a continent, not even on an island, but on an islet which was not more than two miles in length, with even a less breadth.

Was this barren spot the desolate refuge of sea-birds, strewn with stones and destitute of vegetation, attached to a more important archipelago? It was impossible to say. When the voyagers from their car saw the land through the mist, they had not been able to reconnoiter it sufficiently. However, Pencroft, accustomed with his sailor eyes to piece through the gloom, was almost certain that he could clearly distinguish in the west confused masses which indicated an elevated coast. But they could not in the dark determine whether it was a single island, or connected with others. They could not leave it either, as the sea surrounded them; they must therefore put off till the next day their search for the engineer, from whom, alas! not a single cry had reached them to show that he was still in existence.

"The silence of our friend proves nothing," said the reporter. "Perhaps he has fainted or is wounded, and unable to reply directly, so we will not despair."

The reporter then proposed to light a fire on a point of the islet, which would serve as a signal to the engineer. But they searched in vain for wood or dry brambles; nothing but sand and stones were to be found. The grief of Neb and his companions, who were all strongly attached to the intrepid Harding, can be better pictured than described. It was too evident that they were powerless to help him. They must wait with what patience they could for daylight. Either the engineer had been able to save himself, and had already found a refuge on some point of the coast, or he was lost for ever! The long and painful hours passed by. The cold was intense. The castaways suffered cruelly, but they scarcely perceived it. They did not even think of taking a minute's rest. Forgetting everything but their chief, hoping or wishing to hope on, they continued to walk up and down on this sterile spot, always returning to its northern point, where they could approach nearest to the scene of the catastrophe. They listened, they called, and then uniting their voices, they endeavored to raise even a louder shout than before, which would be transmitted to a great distance. The wind had now fallen almost to a calm, and the noise of the sea began also to subside. One of Neb's shouts even appeared to produce an echo. Herbert directed Pencroft's attention to it, adding, "That proves that there is a coast to the west, at no great distance." The sailor nodded; besides, his eyes could not deceive him. If he had discovered land, however indistinct it might appear, land was sure to be there. But that distant echo was the only response produced by Neb's shouts, while a heavy gloom hung over all the part east of the island.

Meanwhile, the sky was clearing little by little. Toward midnight the stars shone out, and if the engineer had been there with his companions he would have remarked that these stars did not belong to the Northern Hemisphere. The Polar Star was not visible, the constellations were not those which they had been accustomed to see in the United States; the Southern Cross glittered brightly in the sky.

The night passed away. Toward five o'clock in the morning of the 25th of March, the sky began to lighten; the horizon still remained dark, but with daybreak a thick mist rose from the sea, so that the eye could scarcely penetrate beyond twenty feet or so from where they stood. At length the fog gradually unrolled itself in great heavily moving waves.

It was unfortunate, however, that the castaways could distinguish nothing around them. While the gaze of the reporter and Neb were cast upon the ocean, the sailor and Herbert looked eagerly for the coast in the west. But not a speck of land was visible. "Never mind," said Pencroft, "though I do not see the land, I feel it . . . it is there . . . there . . . as sure as the fact that we are no longer at Richmond." But the fog was not long in rising. It was only a fine-weather mist. A hot sun soon penetrated to the surface of the island. About half-past six, three-quarters of an hour after sunrise, the mist became more transparent. It grew thicker above, but cleared away below. Soon the isle appeared as if it had descended from a cloud, then the sea showed itself around them, spreading far away toward the east, but bounded on the west by an abrupt and precipitous coast.

Yes! the land was there. Their safety was at least provisionally ensured. The islet and the coast were separated by a channel about half a mile in breadth, through which rushed an extremely rapid current.

However, one of the castaways, following the impulse of his heart, immediately threw himself into the current, without consulting his companions, without saying a single word. It was Neb. He was in haste to be on the other side, and to climb toward the north. It had been impossible to hold him back. Pencroft called him in vain. The reporter prepared to follow him, but Pencroft stopped him. "Do you want to cross the channel?" he asked. "Yes," replied Spilett. "All right!" said the seaman; "wait a bit; Neb is well able to carry help to his master. If we venture into the channel, we risk being carried into the open sea by the current, which is running very strong; but, if I'm not wrong, it is ebbing. See, the tide is going down over the sand. Let us have patience, and at low water it is possible we may find a fordable passage." "You are right," replied the reporter, "we will not separate more than we can help."

During this time Neb was struggling vigorously against the current. He was crossing in an oblique direction. His black shoulders could be seen emerging at each stroke. He was carried down very quickly, but he also made way toward the shore. It took more than half an hour to cross from the islet to the land, and he reached the shore several hundred feet from the place which was opposite to the point from which he had started.

Landing at the foot of a high wall of granite, he shook himself vigorously; and then, setting off running, soon disappeared behind a rocky point, which projected to nearly the height of the northern extremity of the islet.

Neb's companions had watched his daring attempt with painful anxiety, and when he was out of sight, they fixed their attention on the land where their hope of safety lay, while eating some shell-fish with which the sand was strewn. It was a wretched repast, but still it was better than nothing. The opposite coast formed one vast bay, terminating on the south by a very sharp point, which was destitute of all vegetation, and was of a very wild aspect. This point abutted on the shore in a grotesque outline of high granite rocks. Toward the north, on the contrary, the bay widened, and a more rounded coast appeared, trending from the southwest to the northeast, and terminating in a slender cape. The distance between these two extremities, which made the bow of the bay, was about eight miles. Half a mile from the shore rose the islet, which somewhat resembled the carcass of a gigantic whale. Its extreme breadth was not more than a quarter of a mile.

Opposite the islet, the beach consisted first of sand, covered with black stones, which were now appearing little by little above the retreating tide. The second level was separated by a perpendicular granite cliff, terminated at the top by an unequal edge at a height of at least 300 feet. It continued thus for a length of three miles, ending suddenly on the right with a precipice which looked as if cut by the hand of man. On the left, above the promontory, this irregular and jagged cliff descended by a long slope of conglomerated rocks till it mingled with the ground of the southern point. On the upper plateau of the coast not a tree appeared. It was a flat tableland like that above Cape Town at the Cape of Good Hope, but of reduced proportions; at least so it appeared seen from the islet. However, verdure was not wanting to the right beyond the precipice. They could easily distinguish a confused mass of great trees, which extended beyond the limits of their view. This verdure relieved the eye, so long wearied by the continued ranges of granite. Lastly, beyond and above the plateau, in a northwesterly direction and at a distance of at least seven miles, glittered a white summit which reflected the sun's rays. It was that of a lofty mountain, capped with snow.

The question could not at present be decided whether this land formed an island, or whether it belonged to a continent. But on beholding the convulsed masses heaped up on the left, no geologist would have hesitated to give them a volcanic origin, for they were unquestionably the work of subterranean convulsions.

Gideon Spilett, Pencroft, and Herbert attentively examined this land, on which they might perhaps have to live many long years; on which indeed they might even die, should it be out of the usual track of vessels, as was likely to be the case.

"Well," asked Herbert, "what do you say, Pencroft?"

"There is some good and some bad, as in everything," replied the sailor. "We shall see. But now the ebb is evidently making. In three hours we will attempt the passage, and once on the other side, we will try to get out of this scrape, and I hope may find the captain." Pencroft was not wrong in his anticipations. Three hours later at low tide, the greater part of the sand forming the bed of the channel was uncovered. Between the islet and the coast there only remained a narrow channel which would no doubt be easy to cross.

About ten o'clock, Gideon Spilett and his companions stripped themselves of their clothes, which they placed in bundles on their heads, and then ventured into the water, which was not more than five feet deep. Herbert, for whom it was too deep, swam like a fish, and got through capitally. All three arrived without difficulty on the opposite shore. Quickly drying themselves in the sun, they put on their clothes, which they had preserved from contact with the water, and sat down to take counsel together what to do next.

IV

All at once the reporter sprang up, and telling the sailor that he would rejoin them at that same place, he climbed the cliff in the direction which the Negro Neb had taken a few hours before. Anxiety hastened his steps, for he longed to obtain news of his friend, and he soon disappeared around an angle of the cliff. Herbert wished to accompany him.

"Stop here, my boy," said the sailor; "we have to prepare an encampment, and to try and find rather better grub than these shell-fish. Our friends will want something when they come back. There is work for everybody."

"I am ready," replied Herbert.

"All right," said the sailor; "that will do. We must set about it regularly. We are tired, cold, and hungry; therefore we must have shelter, fire, and food. There is wood in the forest, and eggs in nests; we have only to find a house."

"Very well," returned Herbert, "I will look for a cove among the rocks, and I shall be sure to discover some hole into which we can creep."

"All right," said Pencroft; "go on, my boy."

They both walked to the foot of the enormous wall over the beach, far from which the tide had now retreated; but instead of going toward the north, they went southward. Pencroft had remarked, several hundred feet from the place at which they landed, a narrow cutting, out of which he thought a river or stream might issue. Now, on the one hand it was important to settle themselves in the neighborhood of a good stream of water, and on the other it was possible that the current had thrown Cyrus Harding on the shore there.

The cliff, as has been said, rose to a height of three hundred feet, but the mass was unbroken throughout, and even at its base, scarcely washed by the sea, it did not offer the smallest fissure which would serve as a dwelling. It was a perpendicular wall of very hard granite, which even the waves had not worn away. Toward the summit fluttered myriads of sea-fowl, and especially those of the web-footed species with long, flat, pointed beaks—a clamorous tribe, bold in the presence of man, who probably for the first time thus invaded their domains. Pencroft recognized the skua and other gulls among them, the voracious little sea-mew, which in great numbers nestled in the crevices of the granite. A shot fired among this swarm would have killed a great number, but to fire a shot a gun was needed, and neither Pencroft nor Herbert had one; besides this, gulls and sea-mews are scarcely eatable, and even their eggs have a detestable taste. However, Herbert, who had gone forward a little more to the left, soon came upon rocks covered with sea-weed, which, some hours later, would be hidden by the high tide. On these rocks, in the midst of slippery wrack, abounded bivalve shell-fish, not to be despised by starving people. Herbert called Pencroft, who ran up hastily.

"Here are mussels!" cried the sailor; "these will do instead of eggs!"

"They are not mussels," replied Herbert, who was attentively examining the molluscs attached to the rocks; "they are lithodomes."

"Are they good to eat?" asked Pencroft.

"Perfectly so."

"Then let us eat some lithodomes."

The sailor could rely upon Herbert; the young boy was well up in natural history, and always had had quite a passion for the science. His father had encouraged him in it, by letting him attend the lectures of the best professors in Boston, who were very fond of the intelligent, industrious lad. And his turn for natural history was, more than once in the course of time, of great use, and he was not mistaken in this instance. These lithodomes were oblong shells, suspended in clusters and adhering very tightly to the rocks. They belong to that species of molluscous perforators which excavate holes in the hardest stone; their shell is rounded at both ends, a feature which is not remarked in the common mussel.

Pencroft and Herbert made a good meal of the lithodomes, which were then half opened to the sun. They ate them as oysters, and as they had a strong peppery taste, they were palatable without condiments of any sort.

Their hunger was thus appeased for the time, but not their thirst, which increased after eating these naturally-spiced molluscs. They had then to find fresh water, and it was not likely that it would be wanting in such a capriciously uneven region. Pencroft and Herbert, after having taken the precaution of collecting an ample supply of lithodomes, with which they filled their pockets and handkerchiefs, regained the foot of the cliff.

Two hundred paces farther they arrived at the cutting, through which, as Pencroft had guessed, ran a stream of water, whether fresh or not was to be ascertained. At this place the wall appeared to have been separated by some violent subterranean force. At its base was hollowed out a little creek, the farthest part of which formed a tolerably sharp angle. The watercourse at that part measured one hundred feet in breadth, and its two banks on each side were scarcely twenty feet high. The river became strong almost directly between the two walls of granite, which began to sink above the mouth; it then suddenly turned and disappeared beneath a wood of stunted trees half a mile off.

"Here is the water, and yonder is the wood we require!" said Pencroft. "Well, Herbert, now we only want the house."

The water of the river was limpid. The sailor ascertained that at this time—that is to say, at low tide, when the rising floods did not reach it—it was sweet. This important point established, Herbert looked for some cavity which would serve them as a retreat, but in vain; everywhere the wall appeared smooth, plain, and perpendicular.

However, at the mouth of the watercourse and above the reach of the high tide, the convulsions of nature had formed, not a grotto, but a pile of enormous rocks, such as are often met with in granite countries and which bear the name of "chimneys."

Pencroft and Herbert penetrated quite far in among the rocks, by sandy passages in which light was not wanting, for it entered through the openings which were left between the blocks, of which some were only sustained by a miracle of equilibrium; but with the light came also air—a regular corridor-gale—and with the wind the sharp cold from the exterior. However, the sailor thought that by stopping-up some of the openings with a mixture of stones and sand, the Chimneys could be rendered habitable. Their geometrical plan represented the typographical sign "&," which signifies "et cetera" abridged, but by isolating the upper mouth of the sign, through which the south and west winds blew so strongly, they could succeed in making the lower part of use.

"Here's our work," said Pencroft, "and if we ever see Captain Harding again, he will know how to make something of this labyrinth."

"We shall see him again, Pencroft," cried Herbert, "and when he returns he must find a tolerable dwelling here. It will be so, if we can make a fireplace in the left passage and keep an opening for the smoke."

"So we can, my boy," replied the sailor, "and these chimneys will serve our turn. Let us set to work, but first come and get a store of fuel. I think some branches will be very useful in stopping up these openings, through which the wind shrieks like so many fiends."

Herbert and Pencroft left the Chimneys, and, turning the angle, they began to climb the left bank of the river. The current here was quite rapid, and drifted down some dead wood. The rising tide—and it could already be perceived—must drive it back with force to a considerable distance. The sailor then thought that they could utilize this ebb and flow for the transport of heavy objects.

After having walked for a quarter of an hour, the sailor and the boy arrived at the angle which the river made in turning toward the left. From this point its course was pursued through a forest of magnificent trees. These trees still retained their verdure, notwithstanding the advanced season, for they belonged to the family of coniferae, which is spread over all the regions of the globe, from northern climates to the tropics. The young naturalist recognized especially the deodara, which are very numerous in the Himalayan zone, and which spread around them a most agreeable odor. Between these beautiful trees sprang up clusters of firs, whose opaque open parasol boughs spread wide around. Among the long grass, Pencroft felt that his feet were crushing dry branches which crackled like fireworks.

"Well, my boy," said he to Herbert, "if I don't know the name of these trees, at any rate I reckon that we may call them 'burning wood,' and just now that's the chief thing we want."

"Let us get a supply," replied Herbert, who immediately set to work.

The collection was easily made. It was not even necessary to lop the trees, for enormous quantities of dead wood were lying at their feet; but if fuel was not wanting, the means of transporting it was not yet found. The wood, being very dry, would burn rapidly; it was therefore necessary to carry to the Chimneys a considerable quantity, and the loads of two men would not be sufficient. Herbert remarked this.

"Well, my boy," replied the sailor, "there must be some way of carrying this wood; there is always a way of doing everything. If we had a cart or a boat, it would be easy enough."

"But we have the river," said Herbert.

"Right," replied Pencroft; "the river will be to us like a road which carries of itself, and rafts have not been invented for nothing."

"Only," observed Herbert, "at this moment our road is going the wrong way, for the tide is rising!"

"We shall be all right if we wait till it ebbs," replied the sailor, "and then we will trust it to carry our fuel to the Chimneys. Let us get the raft ready."

The sailor, followed by Herbert, directed his steps toward the river. They both carried, each in proportion to his strength, a load of wood bound in fagots. They found on the bank also a great quantity of dead branches in the midst of grass, among which the foot of man had probably never before trod. Pencroft began directly to make his raft. In a kind of little bay, created by a point of the shore which broke the current, the sailor and the lad placed some good-sized pieces of wood, which they had fastened together with dry creepers. A raft was thus formed, on which they stacked all they had collected, sufficient, indeed, to have loaded at least twenty men. In an hour the work was finished, and the raft moored to the bank, awaited the turning of the tide.

There were still several hours to be occupied, and with one consent Pencroft and Herbert resolved to gain the upper plateau, so as to have a more extended view of the surrounding country.

Exactly two hundred feet behind the angle formed by the river, the wall, terminated by a fall of rocks, died away in a gentle slope to the edge of the forest. It was a natural staircase. Herbert and the sailor began their ascent; thanks to the vigor of their muscles they reached the summit in a few minutes; and proceeded to the point above the mouth of the river.

On attaining it, their first look was cast upon the ocean which not long before they had traversed in such a terrible condition. They observed, with emotion, all that part to the north of the coast on which the catastrophe had taken place. It was there that Cyrus Harding had disappeared. They looked to see if some portion of their balloon, to which a man might possibly cling, yet existed. Nothing! The sea was but one vast watery desert. As to the coast, it was solitary also. Neither the reporter nor Neb could be anywhere seen. But it was possible that at this time they were both too far away to be perceived.

"Something tells me," cried Herbert, "that a man as energetic as Captain Harding would not let himself be drowned like other people. He must have reached some point of the shore; don't you think so, Pencroft?"

The sailor shook his head sadly. He little expected ever to see Cyrus Harding again; but wishing to leave some hope to Herbert: "Doubtless, doubtless," said he; "our engineer is a man who would get out of a scrape to which any one else would yield."

In the meantime he examined the coast with great attention. Stretched out below them was the sandy shore, bounded on the right of the river's mouth by lines of breakers. The rocks which were visible appeared like amphibious monsters reposing in the surf. Beyond the reef, the sea sparkled beneath the sun's rays. To the south a sharp point closed the horizon, and it could not be seen if the land was prolonged in that direction, or if it ran southeast and southwest, which would have made this coast a very long peninsula. At the northern extremity of the bay the outline of the shore was continued to a great distance in a wider curve. There the shore was low, flat, without cliffs, and with great banks of sand, which the tide left uncovered. Pencroft and Herbert then returned toward the west. Their attention was first arrested by the snow-topped mountain which rose at a distance of six or seven miles. From its first declivities to within two miles of the coast were spread vast masses of wood, relieved by large green patches, caused by the presence of evergreen trees. Then, from the edge of this forest to the shore extended a plain, scattered irregularly with groups of trees. Here and there on the left sparkled through glades the waters of the little river; they could trace its winding course back toward the spurs of the mountain, among which it seemed to spring. At the point where the sailor had left his raft of wood, it began to run between the two high granite walls; but if on the left bank the wall remained clear and abrupt, on the right bank, on the contrary, it sank gradually, the massive sides changed to isolated rocks, the rocks to stones, the stones to shingle running to the extremity of the point.

"Are we on an island?" murmured the sailor.

"At any rate, it seems to be big enough," replied the lad.

"An island, ever so big, is an island all the same!" said Pencroft.

But this important question could not yet be answered. A more perfect survey had to be made to settle the point. As to the land itself, island or continent, it appeared fertile, agreeable in its aspect, and varied in its productions.

"This is satisfactory," observed Pencroft; "and in our misfortune, we must thank Providence for it."

"God be praised!" responded Herbert, whose pious heart was full of gratitude to the Author of all things.

Pencroft and Herbert examined for some time the country on which they had been cast; but it was difficult to guess after so hasty an inspection what the future had in store for them.

They then returned, following the southern crest of the granite platform, bordered by a long fringe of jagged rocks, of the most whimsical shapes. Some hundreds of birds lived there nestled in the holes of the stone; Herbert, jumping over the rocks, startled a whole flock of these winged creatures.

"Oh!" cried he, "those are not gulls nor sea-mews!"

"What are they then?" asked Pencroft.

"Upon my word, one would say they were pigeons!"

"Just so, but these are wild or rock pigeons. I recognize them by the double band of black on the wing, by the white tail, and by their slate-colored plumage. But if the rock-pigeon is good to eat, its eggs must be excellent, and we will soon see how many they may have left in their nests!"

"We will not give them time to hatch, unless it is in the shape of an omelet!" replied Pencroft merrily.

"But what will you make your omelet in?" asked Herbert; "in your hat?"

"Well!" replied the sailor, "I am not quite conjuror enough for that; we must come down to eggs in the shell, my boy, and I will undertake to dispatch the hardest!"

Pencroft and Herbert attentively examined the cavities in the granite, and they really found eggs in some of the hollows. A few dozen being collected, were packed in the sailor's handkerchief, and as the time when the tide would be full was approaching, Pencroft and Herbert began to redescend toward the watercourse. When they arrived there, it was an hour after midday. The tide had already turned. They must now avail themselves of the ebb to take the wood to the mouth. Pencroft did not intend to let the raft go away in the current without guidance, neither did he mean to embark on it himself to steer it. But a sailor is never at a loss when there is a question of cables or ropes, and Pencroft rapidly twisted a cord, a few fathoms long, made of dry creepers. This vegetable cable was fastened to the after-part of the raft, and the sailor held it in his hand while Herbert, pushing off the raft with a long pole, kept it in the current. This succeeded capitally. The enormous load of wood drifted down the current. The bank was very equal; there was no fear that the raft would run aground, and before two o'clock they arrived at the river's mouth, a few paces from the Chimneys.

V

Pencroft's first care, after unloading the raft, was to render the cave habitable by stopping up all the holes which made it drafty. Sand, stones, twisted branches, wet clay, closed up the galleries open to the south winds. One narrow and winding opening at the side was kept, to lead out the smoke and to make the fire draw. The cave was thus divided into three or four rooms, if such dark dens with which a donkey would scarcely have been contented deserved the name. But they were dry, and there was space to stand upright, at least in the principal room, which occupied the center. The floor was covered with fine sand, and taking all in all they were well pleased with it for want of a better.

"Perhaps," said Herbert, while he and Pencroft were working, "our companions have found a superior place to ours."

"Very likely," replied the seaman; "but, as we don't know, we must work all the same. Better to have two strings to one's bow than no string at all!"

"Oh!" exclaimed Herbert, "how jolly it will be if they were to find Captain Harding and were to bring him back with them!"

"Yes, indeed!" said Pencroft, "that was a man of the right sort."

"Was!" exclaimed Herbert, "do you despair of ever seeing him again?"

"God forbid!" replied the sailor. Their work was soon done, and Pencroft declared himself very well satisfied.

"Now," said he, "our friends can come back when they like. They will find a good enough shelter."

They now had only to make a fireplace and to prepare the supper—an easy task. Large flat stones were placed on the ground at the opening of the narrow passage which had been kept. This, if the smoke did not take the heat out with it, would be enough to maintain an equal temperature inside. Their wood was stowed away in one of the rooms, and the sailor laid in the fireplace some logs and brushwood. The seaman was busy with this, when Herbert asked him if he had any matches.

"Certainly," replied Pencroft, "and I may say happily, for without matches or tinder we should be in a fix."

"Still we might get fire as the savages do," replied Herbert, "by rubbing two bits of dry stick one against the other."

"All right; try, my boy, and let's see if you can do anything besides exercising your arms."

"Well, it's a very simple proceeding, and much used in the islands of the Pacific."

"I don't deny it," replied Pencroft, "but the savages must know how to do it or employ a peculiar wood, for more than once I have tried to get fire in that way, but I could never manage it. I must say I prefer matches. By the bye, where are my matches?"

Pencroft searched in his waistcoat for the box, which was always there, for he was a confirmed smoker. He could not find it; he rummaged the pockets of his trousers, but, to his horror, he could nowhere discover the box.

"Here's a go!" said he, looking at Herbert. "The box must have fallen out of my pocket and got lost! Surely, Herbert, you must have something—a tinder-box—anything that can possibly make fire!"

"No, I haven't, Pencroft."

The sailor rushed out, followed by the boy. On the sand, among the rocks, near the river's bank, they both searched carefully, but in vain. The box was of copper, and therefore would have been easily seen.

"Pencroft," asked Herbert, "didn't you throw it out of the car?"

"I knew better than that," replied the sailor; "but such a small article could easily disappear in the tumbling about we have gone through. I would rather even have lost my pipe! Confound the box! Where can it be?"

"Look here, the tide is going down," said Herbert; "let's run to the place where we landed."

It was scarcely probable that they would find the box, which the waves had rolled about among the pebbles, at high tide, but it was as well to try. Herbert and Pencroft walked rapidly to the point where they had landed the day before, about two hundred feet from the cave. They hunted there, among the shingle, in the clefts of the rocks, but found nothing. If the box had fallen at this place it must have been swept away by the waves. As the sea went down, they searched every little crevice with no result. It was a grave loss in their circumstances, and for the time irreparable. Pencroft could not hide his vexation; he looked very anxious, but said not a word. Herbert tried to console him by observing, that if they had found the matches, they would, very likely, have been wetted by the sea and useless.

"No, my boy," replied the sailor; "they were in a copper box which shut very tightly; and now what are we to do?"

"We shall certainly find some way of making a fire," said Herbert. "Captain Harding or Mr. Spilett will not be without them."

"Yes," replied Pencroft; "but in the meantime we are without fire, and our companions will find but a sorry repast on their return."

"But," said Herbert quickly, "do you think it possible that they have no tinder or matches?"

"I doubt it," replied the sailor, shaking his head, "for neither Neb nor Captain Harding smoke, and I believe that Mr. Spilett would rather keep his note-book than his match-box."

Herbert did not reply. The loss of the box was certainly to be regretted, but the boy was still sure of procuring fire in some way or other. Pencroft, more experienced, did not think so, although he was not a man to trouble himself about a small or great grievance. At any rate, there was only one thing to be done—to await the return of Neb and the reporter; but they must give up the feast of hard eggs which they had meant to prepare, and a meal of raw flesh was not an agreeable prospect either for themselves or for the others.

Before returning to the cave, the sailor and Herbert, in the event of fire being positively unattainable, collected some more shell-fish, and then silently retraced their steps to their dwelling.

Pencroft, his eyes fixed on the ground, still looked for his box. He even climbed up the left bank of the river from its mouth to the angle where the raft had been moored. He returned to the plateau, went over it in every direction, searched among the high grass on the border of the forest, all in vain.

It was five in the evening when he and Herbert re-entered the cave. It is useless to say that the darkest corners of the passages were ransacked before they were obliged to give it up in despair. Toward six o'clock, when the sun was disappearing behind the high lands of the west, Herbert, who was walking up and down on the strand, signalized the return of Neb and Spilett.

They were returning alone! . . . The boy's heart sank; the sailor had not been deceived in his forebodings; the engineer, Cyrus Harding, had not been found!

The reporter, on his arrival, sat down on a rock, without saying anything. Exhausted with fatigue, dying of hunger, he had not strength to utter a word.

As to Neb, his red eyes showed how he had cried, and the tears which he could not restrain told too clearly that he had lost all hope.

The reporter recounted all that they had done in their attempt to recover Cyrus Harding. He and Neb had surveyed the coast for a distance of eight miles and consequently much beyond the place where the balloon had fallen the last time but one, a fall which was followed by the disappearance of the engineer and the dog Top. The shore was solitary; not a vestige of a mark. Not even a pebble recently displaced; not a trace on the sand; not a human footstep on all that part of the beach. It was clear that that portion of the shore had never been visited by a human being. The sea was as deserted as the land, and it was there, a few hundred feet from the coast, that the engineer must have found a tomb.

As Spilett ended his account, Neb jumped up, exclaiming in a voice which showed how hope struggled within him, "No! he is not dead! he can't be dead! It might happen to any one else, but never to him! He could get out of anything!" Then his strength forsaking him, "Oh! I can do no more!" he murmured.

"Neb," said Herbert, running to him, "we will find him! God will give him back to us! But in the meantime you are hungry, and you must eat something."

So saying, he offered the poor Negro a few handfuls of shell-fish, which was indeed wretched and insufficient food. Neb had not eaten anything for several hours, but he refused them. He could not, would not live without his master.

As to Gideon Spilett, he devoured the shell-fish, then he laid himself down on the sand, at the foot of a rock. He was very weak, but calm. Herbert went up to him, and taking his hand, "Sir," said he, "we have found a shelter which will be better than lying here. Night is advancing. Come and rest! To-morrow we will search farther."

The reporter got up, and guided by the boy went toward the cave. On the way, Pencroft asked him in the most natural tone, if by chance he happened to have a match or two.

The reporter stopped, felt in his pockets, but finding nothing said, "I had some, but I must have thrown them away."

The seaman then put the same question to Neb and received the same answer.

"Confound it!" exclaimed the sailor.

The reporter heard him and seizing his arm, "Have you no matches?" he asked.

"Not one, and no fire in consequence."

"Ah!" cried Neb, "if my master was here, he would know what to do!"

The four castaways remained motionless, looking uneasily at each other. Herbert was the first to break the silence by saying, "Mr. Spilett, you are a smoker and always have matches about you; perhaps you haven't looked well, try again, a single match will be enough!"

The reporter hunted again in the pockets of his trousers, waistcoat, and great-coat, and at last to Pencroft's great joy, no less to his extreme surprise, he felt a tiny piece of wood entangled in the lining of his waistcoat. He seized it with his fingers through the stuff, but he could not get it out. If this was a match and a single one, it was of great importance not to rub off the phosphorus.

"Will you let me try?" said the boy, and very cleverly, without breaking it, he managed to draw out the wretched yet precious little bit of wood which was of such great importance to these poor men. It was unused.

"Hurrah!" cried Pencroft; "it is as good as having a whole cargo!" He took the match, and, followed by his companions, entered the cave.

This small piece of wood, of which so many in an inhabited country are wasted with indifference and are of no value, must here be used with the greatest caution.

The sailor first made sure that it was quite dry; that done, "We must have some paper," said he.

"Here," replied Spilett, after some hesitation tearing a leaf out of his notebook.

Pencroft took the piece of paper which the reporter held out to him, and knelt down before the fireplace. Some handfuls of grass, leaves, and dry moss were placed under the fagots and disposed in such a way that the air could easily circulate, and the dry wood would rapidly catch fire.

Pencroft then twisted the piece of paper into the shape of a cone, as smokers do in a high wind, and poked it in among the moss. Taking a small, rough stone, he wiped it carefully, and with a beating heart, holding his breath, he gently rubbed the match. The first attempt did not produce any effect. Pencroft had not struck hard enough, fearing to rub off the phosphorus.

"No, I can't do it," said he, "my hand trembles, the match has missed fire; I cannot, I will not!" and rising, he told Herbert to take his place.

Certainly the boy had never in all his life been so nervous. Prometheus going to steal the fire from Heaven could not have been more anxious. He did not hesitate, however, but struck the match directly.

A little spluttering was heard and a tiny blue flame sprang up, making a choking smoke. Herbert quickly turned the match so as to augment the flame, and then slipped it into the paper cone, which in a few seconds too caught fire, and then the moss.

A minute later the dry wood crackled and a cheerful flame, assisted by the vigorous blowing of the sailor, sprang up in the midst of the darkness.

"At last!" cried Pencroft, getting up; "I was never so nervous before in all my life!"

The flat stones made a capital fireplace. The smoke went quite easily out at the narrow passage, the chimney drew, and an agreeable warmth was not long in being felt.

They must now take great care not to let the fire go out, and always to keep some embers alight. It only needed care and attention, as they had plenty of wood and could renew their store at any time.

Pencroft's first thought was to use the fire by preparing a more nourishing supper than a dish of shell-fish. Two dozen eggs were brought by Herbert. The reporter, leaning up in a corner, watched these preparations without saying anything. A threefold thought weighed on his mind. Was Cyrus still alive? If he was alive, where was he? If he had survived from his fall, how was it that he had not found some means of making known his existence? As to Neb, he was roaming about the shore. He was like a body without a soul.

Pencroft knew fifty ways of cooking eggs, but this time he had no choice, and was obliged to content himself with roasting them under the hot cinders. In a few minutes the cooking was done, and the seaman invited the reporter to take his share of the supper. Such was the first repast of the castaways on this unknown coast. The hard eggs were excellent, and as eggs contain everything indispensable to man's nourishment, these poor people thought themselves well off, and were much strengthened by them. Oh! if only one of them had not been missing at this meal! If the five prisoners who escaped from Richmond had been all there, under the piled-up rocks, before this clear, crackling fire on the dry sand, what thanksgiving must they have rendered to Heaven! But the most ingenious, the most learned, he who was their unquestioned chief, Cyrus Harding, was, alas! missing, and his body had not even obtained a burial-place.

Thus passed the 25th of March. Night had come on. Outside could be heard the howling of the wind and the monotonous sound of the surf breaking on the shore. The waves rolled the shingle backward and forward with a deafening noise.

The reporter retired into a dark corner after having shortly noted down the occurrences of the day; the first appearance of this new land, the loss of their leader, the exploration of the coast, the incident of the matches, etc.; and then overcome by fatigue, he managed to forget his sorrows in sleep. Herbert went to sleep directly. As to the sailor, he passed the night with one eye on the fire, on which he did not spare fuel. But one of the castaways did not sleep in the cave. The inconsolable, despairing Neb, notwithstanding all that his companions could say to induce him to take some rest, wandered all night long on the shore calling on his master.

VI

The inventory of the articles possessed by these castaways from the clouds, thrown upon a coast which appeared to be uninhabited, was soon made out. They had nothing, save the clothes which they were wearing at the time of the catastrophe. We must mention, however, a note-book and a watch which Gideon Spilett had kept, doubtless by inadvertence, not a weapon, not a tool, not even a pocket-knife; for while in the car they had thrown out everything to lighten the balloon. The imaginary heroes of Daniel Defoe or of Wyss, as well as Selkirk and Raynal shipwrecked on Juan Fernandez and on the archipelago of the Aucklands, were never in such absolute destitution. Either they had abundant resources from their stranded vessels, in grain, cattle, tools, ammunition, or else some things were thrown up on the coast which supplied them with all the first necessities of life. But here, not any instrument whatever, not a utensil. From nothing they must supply themselves with everything.

And yet, if Cyrus Harding had been with them, if the engineer could have brought his practical science, his inventive mind to bear on their situation, perhaps all hope would not have been lost. Alas! they must hope no longer again to see Cyrus Harding. The castaways could expect nothing but from themselves and from that Providence which never abandons those whose faith is sincere.

But ought they to establish themselves on this part of the coast, without trying to know to what continent it belonged, if it was inhabited, or if they were on the shore of a desert island?

It was an important question, and should be solved with the shortest possible delay. From its answer they would know what measures to take. However, according to Pencroft's advice, it appeared best to wait a few days before commencing an exploration. They must, in fact, prepare some provisions and procure more strengthening food than eggs and molluscs. The explorers, before undertaking new fatigues, must first of all recruit their strength.

The Chimneys offered a retreat sufficient for the present. The fire was lighted, and it was easy to preserve some embers. There were plenty of shell-fish and eggs among the rocks and on the beach. It would be easy to kill a few of the pigeons which were flying by hundreds about the summit of the plateau, either with sticks or stones. Perhaps the trees of the neighboring forest would supply them with eatable fruit. Lastly, the sweet water was there.

It was accordingly settled that for a few days they would remain at the Chimneys so as to prepare themselves for an expedition, either along the shore or into the interior of the country. This plan suited Neb particularly. As obstinate in his ideas as in his presentiments, he was in no haste to abandon this part of the coast, the scene of the catastrophe. He did not, he would not believe in the loss of Cyrus Harding. No, it did not seem to him possible that such a man had ended in this vulgar fashion, carried away by a wave, drowned in the floods, a few hundred feet from a shore. As long as the waves had not cast up the body of the engineer, as long as he, Neb, had not seen with his eyes, touched with his hands the corpse of his master, he would not believe in his death! And this idea rooted itself deeper than ever in his determined heart. An illusion perhaps, but still an illusion to be respected, and one which the sailor did not wish to destroy. As for him, he hoped no longer, but there was no use in arguing with Neb. He was like the dog who will not leave the place where his master is buried, and his grief was such that most probably he would not survive him.

This same morning, the 26th of March, at daybreak, Neb had set out on the shore in a northerly direction, and he had returned to the spot where the sea, no doubt, had closed over the unfortunate Harding.

That day's breakfast was composed solely of pigeon's eggs and lithodomes. Herbert had found some salt deposited by evaporation in the hollows of the rocks, and this mineral was very welcome.

The repast ended, Pencroft asked the reporter if he wished to accompany Herbert and himself to the forest, where they were going to try to hunt. But on consideration, it was thought necessary that someone should remain to keep in the fire, and to be at hand in the highly improbable event of Neb requiring aid. The reporter accordingly remained behind.

"To the chase, Herbert," said the sailor. "We shall find ammunition on our way, and cut our weapons in the forest." But at the moment of starting, Herbert observed, that since they had no tinder, it would perhaps be prudent to replace it by another substance.

"What?" asked Pencroft.

"Burnt linen," replied the boy. "That could in case of need serve for tinder."

The sailor thought it very sensible advice. Only it had the inconvenience of necessitating the sacrifice of a piece of handkerchief. Notwithstanding, the thing was well worth while trying, and a part of Pencroft's large checked handkerchief was soon reduced to the state of a half-burnt rag. This inflammable material was placed in the central chamber at the bottom of a little cavity in the rock, sheltered from all wind and damp.

It was nine o'clock in the morning. The weather was threatening and the breeze blew from the southeast. Herbert and Pencroft turned the angle of the Chimneys, not without having cast a look at the smoke which, just at that place, curled round a point of rock: they ascended the left bank of the river.

Arrived at the forest, Pencroft broke from the first tree two stout branches which he transformed into clubs, the ends of which Herbert rubbed smooth on a rock. Oh! what would they not have given for a knife!

The two hunters now advanced among the long grass, following the bank. From the turning which directed its course to the southwest, the river narrowed gradually and the channel lay between high banks, over which the trees formed a double arch. Pencroft, lest they should lose themselves, resolved to follow the course of the stream, which would always lead them back to the point from which they started. But the bank was not without some obstacles: here, the flexible branches of the trees bent level with the current; there, creepers and thorns which they had to break down with their sticks. Herbert often glided among the broken stumps with the agility of a young cat, and disappeared in the underwood. But Pencroft called him back directly, begging him not to wander away. Meanwhile, the sailor attentively observed the disposition and nature of the surrounding country. On the left bank, the ground, which was flat and marshy, rose imperceptibly toward the interior. It looked there like a network of liquid threads which doubtless reached the river by some underground drain. Sometimes a stream ran through the underwood, which they crossed without difficulty. The opposite shore appeared to be more uneven, and the valley of which the river occupied the bottom was more clearly visible. The hill, covered with trees disposed in terraces, intercepted the view. On the right bank walking would have been difficult, for the declivities fell suddenly, and the trees bending over the water were only sustained by the strength of their roots.

It is needless to add that this forest, as well as the coast already surveyed, was destitute of any sign of human life. Pencroft only saw traces of quadrupeds, fresh footprints of animals, of which he could not recognize the species. In all probability, and such was also Herbert's opinion, some had been left by formidable wild beasts which doubtless would give them some trouble; but nowhere did they observe the mark of an axe on the trees, nor the ashes of a fire, nor the impression of a human foot. On this they might probably congratulate themselves, for on any land in the middle of the Pacific the presence of man was perhaps more to be feared than desired. Herbert and Pencroft speaking little, for the difficulties of the way were great, advanced very slowly, and after walking for an hour they had scarcely gone more than a mile. As yet the hunt had not been successful. However, some birds sang and fluttered in the foliage, and appeared very timid, as if man had inspired them with an instinctive fear. Among others, Herbert described, in a marshy part of the forest, a bird with a long pointed beak, closely resembling the king-fisher, but its plumage was not fine, though of a metallic brilliancy.

"That must be a jacamar," said Herbert, trying to get nearer.

"This will be a good opportunity to taste jacamar," replied the sailor, "if that fellow is in a humor to be roasted!"

Just then, a stone cleverly thrown by the boy, struck the creature on the wing, but the blow did not disable it, and the jacamar ran off and disappeared in an instant.

"How clumsy I am!" cried Herbert.

"No, no, my boy!" replied the sailor. "The blow was well aimed; many a one would have missed it altogether! Come, don't be vexed with yourself. We shall catch it another day!"

As the hunters advanced, the trees were found to be more scattered, many being magnificent, but none bore eatable fruit. Pencroft searched in vain for some of those precious palm-trees which are employed in so many ways in domestic life, and which have been found as far as the fortieth parallel in the Northern Hemisphere, and to the thirty-fifth only in the Southern Hemisphere. But this forest was only composed of coniferae, such as deodaras, already recognized by Herbert, and Douglas pine, similar to those which grow on the northwest coast of America, and splendid firs, measuring a hundred and fifty feet in height.

At this moment a flock of birds, of a small size and pretty plumage, with long glancing tails, dispersed themselves among the branches strewing their feathers, which covered the ground as with fine down. Herbert picked up a few of these feathers, and after having examined them,

"These are couroucous," said he.

"I should prefer a moor-cock or guinea-fowl," replied Pencroft, "still, if they are good to eat—"

"They are good to eat, and also their flesh is very delicate," replied Herbert. "Besides, if I don't mistake, it is easy to approach and kill them with a stick."

The sailor and the lad, creeping among the grass, arrived at the foot of a tree, whose lower branches were covered with little birds. The couroucous were waiting the passage of insects which served for their nourishment. Their feathery feet could be seen clasping the slender twigs which supported them.

The hunters then rose, and using their sticks like scythes, they mowed down whole rows of these couroucous, who never thought of flying away, and stupidly allowed themselves to be knocked off. A hundred were already heaped on the ground, before the others made up their minds to fly.

"Well," said Pencroft, "here is game, which is quite within the reach of hunters like us. We have only to put out our hands and take it!"

The sailor having strung the couroucous like larks on flexible twigs, they then continued their exploration. The stream here made a bend toward the south, but this detour was probably not prolonged for the river must have its source in the mountain, and be supplied by the melting of the snow which covered the sides of the central cone.

The particular object of their expedition was, as has been said, to procure the greatest possible quantity of game for the inhabitants of the Chimneys. It must be acknowledged that as yet this object had not been attained. So the sailor actively pursued his researches, though he exclaimed, when some animal which he had not even time to recognize fled into the long grass, "If only we had had the dog Top!" But Top had disappeared at the same time as his master, and had probably perished with him.

Toward three o'clock new flocks of birds were seen through certain trees, at whose aromatic berries they were pecking, those of the juniper-tree among others. Suddenly a loud trumpet call resounded through the forest. This strange and sonorous cry was produced by a game bird called grouse in the United States. They soon saw several couples, whose plumage was rich chestnut-brown mottled with dark brown, and tail of the same color. Herbert recognized the males by the two wing-like appendages raised on the neck. Pencroft determined to get hold of at least one of these gallinaceae, which were as large as a fowl, and whose flesh is better than that of a pullet. But it was difficult, for they would not allow themselves to be approached. After several fruitless attempts, which resulted in nothing but scaring the grouse, the sailor said to the lad,

"Decidedly, since we can't kill them on the wing, we must try to take them with a line."

"Like a fish?" cried Herbert, much surprised at the proposal.

"Like a fish," replied the sailor quite seriously. Pencroft had found among the grass half a dozen grouse nests, each having three or four eggs. He took great care not to touch these nests, to which their proprietors would not fail to return. It was around these that he meant to stretch his lines, not snares, but real fishing-lines. He took Herbert to some distance from the nests, and there prepared his singular apparatus with all the care which a disciple of Izaak Walton would have used. Herbert watched the work with great interest, though rather doubting its success. The lines were made of fine creepers, fastened one to the other, of the length of fifteen or twenty feet. Thick, strong thorns, the points bent back (which were supplied from a dwarf acacia bush) were fastened to the ends of the creepers, by way of hooks. Large red worms, which were crawling on the ground, furnished bait.

This done, Pencroft, passing among the grass and concealing himself skillfully, placed the end of his lines armed with hooks near the grouse nests; then he returned, took the other ends, and hid with Herbert behind a large tree. There they both waited patiently; though, it must be said, that Herbert did not reckon much on the success of the inventive Pencroft.

A whole half-hour passed, but then, as the sailor had surmised, several couple of grouse returned to their nests. They walked along, pecking the ground, and not suspecting in any way the presence of the hunters, who, besides, had taken care to place themselves to leeward of the gallinaceae.

The lad felt at this moment highly interested. He held his breath, and Pencroft, his eyes staring, his mouth open, his lips advanced, as if about to taste a piece of grouse, scarcely breathed.

Meanwhile, the birds walked about the hooks, without taking any notice of them. Pencroft then gave little tugs which moved the bait as if the worms had been still alive.

The sailor undoubtedly felt much greater anxiety than does the fisherman, for he does not see his prey coming through the water. The jerks attracted the attention of the gallinaceae, and they attacked the hooks with their beaks. Three voracious grouse swallowed at the same moment bait and hook. Suddenly with a smart jerk, Pencroft "struck" his line, and a flapping of wings showed that the birds were taken.

"Hurrah!" he cried, rushing toward the game, of which he made himself master in an instant.

Herbert clapped his hands. It was the first time that he had ever seen birds taken with a line, but the sailor modestly confessed that it was not his first attempt, and that besides he could not claim the merit of invention.

"And at any rate," added he, "situated as we are, we must hope to hit upon many other contrivances."

The grouse were fastened by their claws, and Pencroft, delighted at not having to appear before their companions with empty hands, and observing that the day had begun to decline, judged it best to return to their dwelling.

The direction was indicated by the river, whose course they had only to follow, and, toward six o'clock, tired enough with their excursion, Herbert and Pencroft arrived at the Chimneys.

VII

Gideon Spilett was standing motionless on the shore, his arms crossed, gazing over the sea, the horizon of which was lost toward the east in a thick black cloud which was spreading rapidly toward the zenith. The wind was already strong, and increased with the decline of day. The whole sky was of a threatening aspect, and the first symptoms of a violent storm were clearly visible.

Herbert entered the Chimneys, and Pencroft went toward the reporter. The latter, deeply absorbed, did not see him approach.

"We are going to have a dirty night, Mr. Spilett!" said the sailor: "Petrels delight in wind and rain."

The reporter, turning at the moment, saw Pencroft, and his first words were,

"At what distance from the coast would you say the car was, when the waves carried off our companion?"

The sailor had not expected this question. He reflected an instant and replied,

"Two cables' lengths at the most."

"But what is a cable's length?" asked Gideon Spilett.

"About a hundred and twenty fathoms, or six hundred feet."

"Then," said the reporter, "Cyrus Harding must have disappeared twelve hundred feet at the most from the shore?"

"About that," replied Pencroft.

"And his dog also?"

"Also."

"What astonishes me," rejoined the reporter, "while admitting that our companion has perished, is that Top has also met his death, and that neither the body of the dog nor of his master has been cast on the shore!"

"It is not astonishing, with such a heavy sea," replied the sailor. "Besides, it is possible that currents have carried them farther down the coast."

"Then, it is your opinion that our friend has perished in the waves?" again asked the reporter.

"That is my opinion."

"My own opinion," said Gideon Spilett, "with due deference to your experience, Pencroft, is that in the double fact of the absolute disappearance of Cyrus and Top, living or dead, there is something unaccountable and unlikely."

"I wish I could think like you, Mr. Spilett," replied Pencroft; "unhappily, my mind is made up on this point." Having said this, the sailor returned to the Chimneys. A good fire crackled on the hearth. Herbert had just thrown on an armful of dry wood, and the flame cast a bright light into the darkest parts of the passage.

Pencroft immediately began to prepare the dinner. It appeared best to introduce something solid into the bill of fare, for all needed to get up their strength. The strings of couroucous were kept for the next day, but they plucked a couple of grouse, which were soon spitted on a stick, and roasting before a blazing fire.

At seven in the evening Neb had not returned. The prolonged absence of the Negro made Pencroft very uneasy. It was to be feared that he had met with an accident on this unknown land, or that the unhappy fellow had been driven to some act of despair. But Herbert drew very different conclusions from this absence. According to him, Neb's delay was caused by some new circumstances which had induced him to prolong his search. Also, everything new must be to the advantage of Cyrus Harding. Why had Neb not returned unless hope still detained him? Perhaps he had found some mark, a footstep, a trace which had put him in the right path. Perhaps he was at this moment on a certain track. Perhaps even he was near his master.

Thus the lad reasoned. Thus he spoke. His companions let him talk. The reporter alone approved with a gesture. But what Pencroft thought most probable was, that Neb had pushed his researches on the shore farther than the day before, and that he had not as yet had time to return.

Herbert, however, agitated by vague presentiments, several times manifested an intention to go to meet Neb. But Pencroft assured him that that would be a useless course, that in the darkness and deplorable weather he could not find any traces of Neb, and that it would be much better to wait. If Neb had not made his appearance by the next day, Pencroft would not hesitate to join him in his search.

Gideon Spilett approved of the sailor's opinion that it was best not to divide, and Herbert was obliged to give up his project; but two large tears fell from his eyes.

The reporter could not refrain from embracing the generous boy.

Bad weather now set in. A furious gale from the southeast passed over the coast. The sea roared as it beat over the reef. Heavy rain was dashed by the storm into particles like dust. Ragged masses of vapor drove along the beach, on which the tormented shingles sounded as if poured out in cartloads, while the sand raised by the wind added as it were mineral dust to that which was liquid, and rendered the united attack insupportable. Between the river's mouth and the end of the cliff, eddies of wind whirled and gusts from this maëlstrom lashed the water which ran through the narrow valley. The smoke from the fireplace was also driven back through the opening, filling the passages and rendering them uninhabitable.

Therefore, as the grouse were cooked, Pencroft let the fire die away, and only preserved a few embers buried under the ashes.

At eight o'clock Neb had not appeared, but there was no doubt that the frightful weather alone hindered his return, and that he must have taken refuge in some cave, to await the end of the storm or at least the return of day. As to going to meet him, or attempting to find him, it was impossible.

The game constituted the only dish at supper; the meat was excellent, and Pencroft and Herbert, whose long excursion had rendered them very hungry, devoured it with infinite satisfaction.

Their meal concluded, each retired to the corner in which he had rested the preceding night, and Herbert was not long in going to sleep near the sailor, who had stretched himself beside the fireplace.

Outside, as the night advanced, the tempest also increased in strength, until it was equal to that which had carried the prisoners from Richmond to this land in the Pacific. The tempests which are frequent during the seasons of the equinox, and which are so prolific in catastrophes, are above all terrible over this immense ocean, which opposes no obstacle to their fury. No description can give an idea of the terrific violence of the gale as it beat upon the unprotected coast.

Happily the pile of rocks which formed the Chimneys was solid. It was composed of enormous blocks of granite, a few of which, insecurely balanced, seemed to tremble on their foundations, and Pencroft could feel rapid quiverings under his head as it rested on the rock. But he repeated to himself, and rightly, that there was nothing to fear, and that their retreat would not give way. However he heard the noise of stones torn from the summit of the plateau by the wind, falling down on to the beach. A few even rolled on to the upper part of the Chimneys, or flew off in fragments when they were projected perpendicularly. Twice the sailor rose and entrenched himself at the opening of the passage, so as to take a look in safety at the outside. But there was nothing to be feared from these showers, which were not considerable, and he returned to his couch before the fireplace, where the embers glowed beneath the ashes.

Notwithstanding the fury of the hurricane, the uproar of the tempest, the thunder, and the tumult, Herbert slept profoundly. Sleep at last took possession of Pencroft, whom a seafaring life had habituated to anything. Gideon Spilett alone was kept awake by anxiety. He reproached himself with not having accompanied Neb. It was evident that he had not abandoned all hope. The presentiments which had troubled Herbert did not cease to agitate him also. His thoughts were concentrated on Neb. Why had Neb not returned? He tossed about on his sandy couch, scarcely giving a thought to the struggle of the elements. Now and then, his eyes, heavy with fatigue, closed for an instant, but some sudden thought reopened them almost immediately.

Meanwhile the night advanced, and it was perhaps two hours from morning, when Pencroft, then sound asleep, was vigorously shaken.

"What's the matter?" he cried, rousing himself, and collecting his ideas with the promptitude usual to seamen.

The reporter was leaning over him, and saying,

"Listen, Pencroft, listen!"

The sailor strained his ears, but could hear no noise beyond those caused by the storm.

"It is the wind," said he.

"No," replied Gideon Spilett, listening again, "I thought I heard—"

"What?"

"The barking of a dog!"

"A dog!" cried Pencroft, springing up.

"Yes—barking—"

"It's not possible!" replied the sailor. "And besides, how, in the roaring of the storm—"

"Stop—listen—" said the reporter.

Pencroft listened more attentively, and really thought he heard, during a lull, distant barking.

"Well!" said the reporter, pressing the sailor's hand.

"Yes—yes!" replied Pencroft.

"It is Top! It is Top!" cried Herbert, who had just awoke; and all three rushed toward the opening of the Chimneys. They had great difficulty in getting out. The wind drove them back. But at last they succeeded, and could only remain standing by leaning against the rocks. They looked about, but could not speak. The darkness was intense. The sea, the sky, the land were all mingled in one black mass. Not a speck of light was visible.

The reporter and his companions remained thus for a few minutes, overwhelmed by the wind, drenched by the rain, blinded by the sand.

Then, in a pause of the tumult, they again heard the barking, which they found must be at some distance.

It could only be Top! But was he alone or accompanied? He was most probably alone, for, if Neb had been with him, he would have made his way more directly toward the Chimneys. The sailor squeezed the reporter's hand, for he could not make himself heard, in a way which signified "Wait!" then he re-entered the passage.

An instant after he issued with a lighted fagot, which he threw into the darkness, whistling shrilly.

It appeared as if this signal had been waited for; the barking immediately came nearer, and soon a dog bounded into the passage. Pencroft, Herbert, and Spilett entered after him.

An armful of dry wood was thrown on the embers. The passage was lighted up with a bright flame.

"It is Top!" cried Herbert.

It was indeed Top, a magnificent Anglo-Norman, who derived from these two races, crossed the swiftness of foot and the acuteness of smell which are the pre-eminent qualities of coursing dogs. It was the dog of the engineer, Cyrus Harding. But he was alone! Neither Neb nor his master accompanied him!

How was it that his instinct had guided him straight to the Chimneys, which he did not know? It appeared inexplicable, above all, in the midst of this black night and in such a tempest! But what was still more inexplicable was, that Top was neither tired, nor exhausted, nor even soiled with mud or sand!—Herbert had drawn him toward him, and was patting his head, the dog rubbing his neck against the lad's hands.

"If the dog is found, the master will be found also!" said the reporter.

"God grant it!" responded Herbert. "Let us set off! Top will guide us!"

Pencroft did not make any objection. He felt that Top's arrival contradicted his conjectures. "Come along then!" said he.

Pencroft carefully covered the embers on the hearth. He placed a few pieces of wood among them, so as to keep in the fire until their return. Then, preceded by the dog, who seemed to invite them by short barks to come with him, and followed by the reporter and the boy, he dashed out, after having put up in his handkerchief the remains of the supper.

The storm was then in all its violence, and perhaps at its height. Not a single ray of light from the moon pierced through the clouds. To follow a straight course was difficult. It was best to rely on Top's instinct. They did so. The reporter and Herbert walked behind the dog, and the sailor brought up the rear. It was impossible to exchange a word. The rain was not very heavy, but the wind was terrific.

However, one circumstance favored the seaman and his two companions. The wind being southeast, consequently blew on their backs. The clouds of sand, which otherwise would have been insupportable, from being received behind, did not in consequence impede their progress. In short, they sometimes went faster than they liked, and had some difficulty in keeping their feet; but hope gave them strength, for it was not at random that they made their way along the shore. They had no doubt that Neb had found his master, and that he had sent them the faithful dog. But was the engineer living, or had Neb only sent for his companions that they might render the last duties to the corpse of the unfortunate Harding?

After having passed the precipice, Herbert, the reporter, and Pencroft prudently stepped aside to stop and take breath. The turn of the rocks sheltered them from the wind, and they could breathe after this walk or rather run of a quarter of an hour.

They could now hear and reply to each other, and the lad having pronounced the name of Cyrus Harding, Top gave a few short barks, as much as to say that his master was saved.

"Saved, isn't he?" repeated Herbert; "saved, Top?"

And the dog barked in reply.

They once more set out. The tide began to rise, and urged by the wind it threatened to be unusually high, as it was a spring tide. Great billows thundered against the reef with such violence that they probably passed entirely over the islet, then quite invisible. The mole no longer protected the coast, which was directly exposed to the attacks of the open sea.

As soon as the sailor and his companions left the precipice, the wind struck them again with renewed fury. Though bent under the gale they walked very quickly, following Top, who did not hesitate as to what direction to take.

They ascended toward the north, having on their left an interminable extent of billows, which broke with a deafening noise, and on their right a dark country, the aspect of which it was impossible to guess. But they felt that it was comparatively flat, for the wind passed completely over them, without being driven back as it was when it came in contact with the cliff.

At four o'clock in the morning, they reckoned that they had cleared about five miles. The clouds were slightly raised, and the wind, though less damp, was very sharp and cold. Insufficiently protected by their clothing,

Pencroft, Herbert, and Spilett suffered cruelly, but not a complaint escaped their lips. They were determined to follow Top, wherever the intelligent animal wished to lead them.

Toward five o'clock day began to break. At the zenith, where the fog was less thick, gray shades bordered the clouds; under an opaque belt, a luminous line clearly traced the horizon. The crests of the billows were tipped with a wild light, and the foam regained its whiteness. At the same time on the left the hilly parts of the coast could be seen, though very indistinctly.

At six o'clock day had broken. The clouds rapidly lifted. The seaman and his companions were then about six miles from the Chimneys. They were following a very flat shore bounded by a reef of rocks, whose heads scarcely emerged from the sea, for they were in deep water. On the left, the country appeared to be one vast extent of sandy downs, bristling with thistles. There was no cliff, and the shore offered no resistance to the ocean but a chain of irregular hillocks. Here and there grew two or three trees, inclined toward the west, their branches projecting in that direction. Quite behind, in the southwest, extended the border of the forest.

At this moment, Top became very excited. He ran forward, then returned, and seemed to entreat them to hasten their steps. The dog then left the beach, and guided by his wonderful instinct, without showing the least hesitation, went straight in among the downs. They followed him. The country appeared an absolute desert. Not a living creature was to be seen.

The downs, the extent of which was large, were composed of hillocks and even of hills, very irregularly distributed. They resembled a Switzerland modeled in sand, and only an amazing instinct could have possibly recognized the way.

Five minutes after having left the beach, the reporter and his two companions arrived at a sort of excavation, hollowed out at the back of a high mound. There Top stopped, and gave a loud, clear bark. Spilett, Herbert, and Pencroft dashed into the cave.

Neb was there, kneeling beside a body extended on a bed of grass—

The body was that of the engineer, Cyrus Harding.

VIII

Neb did not move. Pencroft only uttered one word.

"Living?" he cried.

Neb did not reply. Spilett and the sailor turned pale. Herbert clasped his hands, and remained motionless. The poor Negro, absorbed in his grief, evidently had neither seen his companions nor heard the sailor speak.

The reporter knelt down beside the motionless body, and placed his ear to the engineer's chest, having first torn open his clothes.

A minute—an age!—passed, during which he endeavored to catch the faintest throb of the heart.

Neb had raised himself a little and gazed without seeing. Despair had completely changed his countenance. He could scarcely be recognized, exhausted with fatigue, broken with grief. He believed his master was dead.

Gideon Spilett at last rose, after a long and attentive examination.

"He lives!" said he.

Pencroft knelt in his turn beside the engineer; he also heard a throbbing, and even felt a slight breath on his cheek.

Herbert at a word from the reporter ran out to look for water. He found, a hundred feet off, a limpid stream, which seemed to have been greatly increased by the rains, and which filtered through the sand; but nothing in which to put the water, not even a shell among the downs. The lad was obliged to content himself with dipping his handkerchief in the stream, and with it hastened back to the grotto.

Happily the wet handkerchief was enough for Gideon Spilett, who only wished to wet the engineer's lips. The cold water produced an almost immediate effect. His chest heaved and he seemed to try to speak.

"We will save him!" exclaimed the reporter.

At these words hope revived in Neb's heart. He undressed his master to see if he was wounded, but not so much as a bruise was to be found, either on the head, body, or limbs, which was surprising, as he must have been dashed against the rocks; even the hands were uninjured, and it was difficult to explain how the engineer showed no traces of the efforts which he must have made to get out of reach of the breakers.

But the explanation would come later. When Cyrus was able to speak he would say what had happened. For the present the question was, how to recall him to life, and it appeared likely that rubbing would bring this about; so they set to work with the sailor's jersey.

The engineer, revived by this rude shampooing, moved his arm slightly and began to breathe more regularly. He was sinking from exhaustion, and certainly, had not the reporter and his companions arrived, it would have been all over with Cyrus Harding.

"You thought your master was dead, didn't you?" said the seaman to Neb.

"Yes! quite dead!" replied Neb, "and if Top had not found you, and brought you here, I should have buried my master, and then have lain down on his grave to die!"

It had indeed been a narrow escape for Cyrus Harding!

Neb then recounted what had happened. The day before, after having left the Chimneys at daybreak, he had ascended the coast in a northerly direction, and had reached that part of the shore which he had already visited.

There, without any hope he acknowledged, Neb had searched the beach, among the rocks, on the sand, for the smallest trace to guide him. He examined particularly that part of the beach which was not covered by the high tide, for near the sea the water would have obliterated all marks. Neb did not expect to find his master living. It was for a corpse that he searched, a corpse which he wished to bury with his own hands!

He sought long in vain. This desert coast appeared never to have been visited by a human creature. The shells, those which the sea had not reached, and which might be met with by millions above high-water mark, were untouched. Not a shell was broken.

Neb then resolved to walk along the beach for some miles. It was possible that the waves had carried the body to quite a distant point. When a corpse floats a little distance from a low shore, it rarely happens that the tide does not throw it up, sooner or later. This Neb knew, and he wished to see his master again for the last time.

"I went along the coast for another two miles, carefully examining the beach, both at high and low water, and I had despaired of finding anything, when yesterday, above five in the evening, I saw footprints on the sand."

"Footprints?" exclaimed Pencroft.

"Yes!" replied Neb.

"Did these footprints begin at the water's edge?" asked the reporter.

"No," replied Neb, "only above high-water mark, for the others must have been washed out by the tide."

"Go on, Neb," said Spilett.

"I went half crazy when I saw these footprints. They were very clear and went toward the downs. I followed them for a quarter of a mile, running, but taking care not to destroy them. Five minutes after, as it was getting dark, I heard the barking of a dog. It was Top, and Top brought me here, to my master!"

Neb ended his account by saying what had been his grief at finding the inanimate body, in which he vainly sought for the least sign of life. Now that he had found him dead he longed for him to be alive. All his efforts were useless! Nothing remained to be done but to render the last duties to the one whom he had loved so much! Neb then thought of his companions. They, no doubt, would wish to see the unfortunate man again. Top was there. Could he not rely on the sagacity of the faithful animal? Neb several times pronounced the name of the reporter, the one among his companions whom Top knew best.

Then he pointed to the south, and the dog bounded off in the direction indicated to him.

We have heard how, guided by an instinct which might be looked upon almost as supernatural, Top had found them.

Neb's companions had listened with great attention to this account.

It was unaccountable to them how Cyrus Harding, after the efforts which he must have made to escape from the waves by crossing the rocks, had not received even a scratch. And what could not be explained either was how the engineer had managed to get to this cave in the downs, more than a mile from the shore.

"So, Neb," said the reporter, "it was not you who brought your master to this place."

"No, it was not I," replied the Negro.

"It's very clear that the captain came here by himself," said Pencroft.

"It is clear in reality," observed Spilett, "but it is not credible!"

The explanation of this fact could only be produced from the engineer's own lips, and they must wait for that till speech returned. Rubbing had re-established the circulation of the blood. Cyrus Harding moved his arm again, then his head, and a few incomprehensible words escaped him.

Neb, who was bending over him, spoke, but the engineer did not appear to hear, and his eyes remained closed. Life was only exhibited in him by movement, his senses had not as yet been restored.

Pencroft much regretted not having either fire, or the means of procuring it, for he had, unfortunately, forgotten to bring the burnt linen, which would easily have ignited from the sparks produced by striking together two flints. As to the engineer's pockets, they were entirely empty, except that of his waistcoat, which contained his watch. It was necessary to carry Harding to the Chimneys, and that as soon as possible. This was the opinion of all.

Meanwhile, the care which was lavished on the engineer brought him back to consciousness sooner than they could have expected. The water with which they wetted his lips revived him gradually. Pencroft also thought of mixing with the water some moisture from the tétra's flesh which he had brought. Herbert ran to the beach and returned with two large bivalve shells. The sailor concocted something which he introduced between the lips of the engineer, who eagerly drinking it opened his eyes.

Neb and the reporter were leaning over him.

"My master! my master!" cried Neb.

The engineer heard him. He recognized Neb and Spilett, then his other two companions, and his hand slightly pressed theirs.

A few words again escaped him, which showed what thoughts were, even then, troubling his brain. This time he was understood. Undoubtedly they were the same words he had before attempted to utter.

"Island or continent?" he murmured.

"Bother the continent," cried Pencroft hastily; "there is time enough to see about that, captain! we don't care for anything, provided you are living."

The engineer nodded faintly, and then appeared to sleep.

They respected this sleep, and the reporter began immediately to make arrangements for transporting Harding to a more comfortable place. Neb, Herbert, and Pencroft left the cave and directed their steps toward a high mound crowned with a few distorted trees. On the way the sailor could not help repeating,

"Island or continent! To think of that, when at one's last gasp! What a man!"

Arrived at the summit of the mound, Pencroft and his two companions set to work, with no other tools than their hands, to despoil of its principal branches a rather sickly tree, a sort of marine fir; with these branches they made a litter, on which, covered with grass and leaves, they could carry the engineer.

This occupied them nearly forty minutes, and it was ten o'clock when they returned to Cyrus Harding whom Spilett had not left.

The engineer was just awaking from the sleep, or rather from the drowsiness, in which they had found him. The color was returning to his cheeks, which till now had been as pale as death. He raised himself a little, looked around him, and appeared to ask where he was.

"Can you listen to me without fatigue, Cyrus?" asked the reporter.

"Yes," replied the engineer.

"It's my opinion," said the sailor, "that Captain Harding will be able to listen to you still better, if he will have some more grouse jelly—for we have grouse, captain," added he, presenting him with a little of this jelly, to which he this time added some of the flesh.

Cyrus Harding ate a little of the grouse, and the rest was divided among his companions, who found it but a meager breakfast, for they were suffering extremely from hunger.

"Well!" said the sailor, "there is plenty of food at the Chimneys, for you must know, captain, that down there, in the south, we have a house, with rooms, beds, and fireplace, and in the pantry, several dozen of birds, which our Herbert calls couroucous. Your litter is ready, and as soon as you feel strong enough we will carry you home."

"Thanks, my friend," replied the engineer; "wait another hour or two, and then we will set out. And now speak, Spilett."

The reporter then told him all that had occurred. He recounted all the events with which Cyrus was unacquainted, the last fall of the balloon, the landing on this unknown land, which appeared a desert (whatever it was, whether island or continent), the discovery of the Chimneys, the search for him, not forgetting of course Neb's devotion, the intelligence exhibited by the faithful Top, as well as many other matters.

"But," asked Harding, in a still feeble voice, "you did not, then, pick me up on the beach?"

"No," replied the reporter.

"And did you not bring me to this cave?"

"No."

"At what distance is this cave from the sea?"

"About a mile," replied Pencroft; "and if you are astonished, captain, we are not less surprised ourselves at seeing you in this place!"

"Indeed," said the engineer, who was recovering gradually, and who took great interest in these details, "indeed it is very singular!"

"But," resumed the sailor, "can you tell us what happened after you were carried off by the sea?"

Cyrus Harding considered. He knew very little. The wave had torn him from the balloon net. He sank at first several fathoms. On returning to the surface, in the half-light, he felt a living creature struggling near him. It was Top, who had sprung to his help. He saw nothing of the balloon, which, lightened both of his weight and that of the dog, had darted away like an arrow.

There he was, in the midst of the angry sea, at a distance which could not be less than half a mile from the shore. He attempted to struggle against the billows by swimming vigorously. Top held him up by his clothes; but a strong current seized him and drove him toward the north, and after half an hour of exertion, he sank, dragging Top with him into the depths. From that moment to the moment in which he recovered to find himself in the arms of his friends he remembered nothing.

"However," remarked Pencroft, "you must have been thrown on to the beach, and you must have had strength to walk here, since Neb found your footmarks!"

"Yes . . . of course . . ." replied the engineer, thoughtfully; "and you found no traces of human beings on this coast?"

"Not a trace," replied the reporter; "besides, if by chance you had met with some deliverer there, just in the nick of time, why should he have abandoned you after having saved you from the waves?"

"You are right, my dear Spilett. Tell me, Neb," added the engineer, turning to his servant, "it was not you who . . . you can't have had a moment of unconsciousness . . . during which . . . no, that's absurd. . . . Do any of the footsteps still remain?" asked Harding.

"Yes, master," replied Neb; "here, at the entrance, at the back of the mound, in a place sheltered from the rain and wind. The storm has destroyed the others."

"Pencroft," said Cyrus Harding, "will you take my shoe and see if it fits exactly to the footprints?"

The sailor did as the engineer requested. While he and Herbert, guided by Neb, went to the place where the footprints were to be found, Cyrus remarked to the reporter,

"It is a most extraordinary thing!"

"Perfectly inexplicable!" replied Gideon Spilett.

"But do not dwell upon it just now, my dear Spilett, we will talk about it by-and-by."

A moment after the others entered.

There was no doubt about it. The engineer's shoe fitted exactly to the footmarks. It was therefore Cyrus Harding who had left them on the sand.

"Come," said he, "I must have experienced this unconsciousness which I attributed to Neb. I must have walked like a somnambulist, without any knowledge of my steps, and Top must have guided me here, after having dragged me from the waves. . . . Come, Top! Come, old dog!"

The magnificent animal bounded barking to his master, and caresses were lavished on him. It was agreed that there was no other way of accounting for the rescue of Cyrus Harding, and that Top deserved all the honor of the affair.

Toward twelve o'clock, Pencroft having asked the engineer if they could now remove him, Harding, instead of replying, and by an effort which exhibited the most energetic will, got up. But he was obliged to lean on the sailor, or he would have fallen.

"Well done!" cried Pencroft; "bring the captain's litter."

The litter was brought; the transverse branches had been covered with leaves and long grass. Harding was laid on it, and Pencroft, having taken his place at one end and Neb at the other, they started toward the coast. There was a distance of eight miles to be accomplished; but, as they could not go fast, and it would perhaps be necessary to stop frequently, they reckoned that it would take at least six hours to reach the Chimneys. The wind was still strong, but fortunately it did not rain. Although lying down, the engineer, leaning on his elbow, observed the coast, particularly inland. He did not speak, but he gazed; and, no doubt, the appearance of the country, with its inequalities of ground, its forests, its various productions, were impressed on his mind. However, after traveling for two hours, fatigue overcame him, and he slept.

At half-past five the little band arrived at the precipice, and a short time after at the Chimneys.

They stopped, and the litter was placed on the sand; Cyrus Harding was sleeping profoundly, and did not awake.

Pencroft, to his extreme surprise, found that the terrible storm had quite altered the aspect of the place. Important changes had occurred; great blocks of stone lay on the beach, which was also covered with a thick carpet of sea-weed, algae, and wrack. Evidently the sea, passing over the islet, had been carried right up to the foot of the enormous curtain of granite. The soil in front of the cave had been torn away by the violence of the waves. A horrid presentiment flashed across Pencroft's mind. He rushed into the passage, but returned almost immediately, and stood motionless, staring at his companions. . . . The fire was out; the drowned cinders were nothing but mud; the burnt linen, which was to have served as tinder, had disappeared! The sea had penetrated to the end of the passages, and everything was overthrown and destroyed in the interior of the Chimneys!

IX

In a few words, Gideon Spilett, Herbert, and Neb were made acquainted with what had happened. This accident, which appeared so very serious to Pencroft, produced different effects on the companions of the honest sailor.

Neb, in his delight at having found his master, did not listen, or rather, did not care to trouble himself with what Pencroft was saying.

Herbert shared in some degree the sailor's feelings.

As to the reporter, he simply replied,

"Upon my word, Pencroft, it's perfectly indifferent to me!"

"But, I repeat, that we haven't any fire!"

"Pooh!"

"Nor any means of relighting it!"

"Nonsense!"

"But I say, Mr. Spilett—"

"Isn't Cyrus here?" replied the reporter. "Is not our engineer alive? He will soon find some way of making fire for us!"

"With what?"

"With nothing."

What had Pencroft to say? He could say nothing, for, in the bottom of his heart he shared the confidence which his companions had in Cyrus Harding. The engineer was to them a microcosm, a compound of every science, a possessor of all human knowledge. It was better to be with Cyrus in a desert island, than without him in the most flourishing town in the United States. With him they could want nothing; with him they would never despair. If these brave men had been told that a volcanic eruption would destroy the land, that this land would be engulfed in the depths of the Pacific, they would have imperturbably replied,

"Cyrus is here!"

While in the palanquin, however, the engineer had again relapsed into unconsciousness, which the jolting to which he had been subjected during his journey had brought on, so that they could not now appeal to his ingenuity. The supper must necessarily be very meager. In fact, all the grouse flesh had been consumed, and there no longer existed any means of cooking more game. Besides, the couroucous which had been reserved had disappeared. They must consider what was to be done.

First of all, Cyrus Harding was carried into the central passage. There they managed to arrange for him a couch of sea-weed which still remained almost dry. The deep sleep which had overpowered him would no doubt be more beneficial to him than any nourishment.

Night had closed in, and the temperature, which had modified when the wind shifted to the northwest, again became extremely cold. Also, the sea having destroyed the partitions which Pencroft had put up in certain places in the passages, the Chimneys, on account of the drafts, had become scarcely habitable. The engineer's condition would, therefore, have been bad enough, if his companions had not carefully covered him with their coats and waistcoats.

Supper, this evening, was of course composed of the inevitable lithodomes, of which Herbert and Neb picked up a plentiful supply on the beach. However, to these molluscs, the lad added some edible sea-weed, which he gathered on high rocks, whose sides were only washed by the sea at the time of high tides. This sea-weed, which belongs to the order of Fucacae, of the genus Sargassum, produces, when dry, a gelatinous matter, rich and nutritious. The reporter and his companions, after having eaten a quantity of lithodomes, sucked the sargassum, of which the taste was very tolerable. It is used in parts of the East very considerably by the natives. "Never mind!" said the sailor, "the captain will help us soon." Meanwhile the cold became very severe, and unhappily they had no means of defending themselves from it.

The sailor, extremely vexed, tried in all sorts of ways to procure fire. Neb helped him in this work. He found some dry moss, and by striking together two pebbles he obtained some sparks, but the moss, not being inflammable enough, did not take fire, for the sparks were really only incandescent, and not at all of the same consistency as those which are emitted from flint when struck in the same manner. The experiment, therefore, did not succeed.

Pencroft, although he had no confidence in the proceeding, then tried rubbing two pieces of dry wood together, as savages do. Certainly, the movement which he and Neb exhibited, if it had been transformed into heat, according to the new theory, would have been enough to heat the boiler of a steamer! It came to nothing. The bits of wood became hot, to be sure, but much less so than the operators themselves.

After working an hour, Pencroft, who was in a complete state of perspiration, threw down the pieces of wood in disgust.

"I can never be made to believe that savages light their fires in this way, let them say what they will," he exclaimed. "I could sooner light my arms by rubbing them against each other!"

The sailor was wrong to despise the proceeding. Savages often kindle wood by means of rapid rubbing. But every sort of wood does not answer for the purpose, and besides, there is "the knack," following the usual expression, and it is probable that Pencroft had not "the knack."

Pencroft's ill humor did not last long. Herbert had taken the bits of wood which he had thrown down, and was exerting himself to rub them. The hardy sailor could not restrain a burst of laughter on seeing the efforts of the lad to succeed where he had failed.

"Rub, my boy, rub!" said he.

"I am rubbing," replied Herbert, laughing, "but I don't pretend to do anything else but warm myself instead of shivering, and soon I shall be as hot as you are, my good Pencroft!"

This soon happened. However, they were obliged to give up, for this night at least, the attempt to procure fire. Gideon Spilett repeated, for the twentieth time, that Cyrus Harding would not have been troubled for so small a difficulty. And, in the meantime, he stretched himself in one of the passages on his bed of sand. Herbert, Neb, and Pencroft did the same, while Top slept at his master's feet.

Next day, the 28th of March, when the engineer awoke, about eight in the morning, he saw his companions around him watching his sleep, and, as on the day before, his first words were:

"Island or continent?" This was his uppermost thought.

"Well!" replied Pencroft, "we don't know anything about it, captain!"

"You don't know yet?"

"But we shall know," rejoined Pencroft, "when you have guided us into the country."

"I think I am able to try it," replied the engineer, who, without much effort, rose and stood upright.

"That's capital!" cried the sailor.

"I feel dreadfully weak," replied Harding. "Give me something to eat, my friends, and it will soon go off. You have fire, haven't you?"

This question was not immediately replied to. But, in a few seconds—

"Alas! we have no fire," said Pencroft, "or rather, captain, we have it no longer!"

And the sailor recounted all that had passed the day before. He amused the engineer by the history of the single match, then his abortive attempt to procure fire in the savages' way.

"We shall consider," replied the engineer, "and if we do not find some substance similar to tinder—"

"Well?" asked the sailor.

"Well, we will make matches."

"Chemicals?"

"Chemicals!"

"It is not more difficult than that," cried the reporter, striking the sailor on the shoulder.

The latter did not think it so simple, but he did not protest. All went out. The weather had become very fine. The sun was rising from the sea's horizon, and touched with golden spangles the prismatic rugosities of the huge precipice.

Having thrown a rapid glance around him, the engineer seated himself on a block of stone. Herbert offered him a few handfuls of shell-fish and sargassum, saying,

"It is all that we have, Captain Harding."

"Thanks, my boy," replied Harding; "it will do—for this morning at least."

He ate the wretched food with appetite, and washed it down with a little fresh water, drawn from the river in an immense shell.

His companions looked at him without speaking. Then, feeling somewhat refreshed, Cyrus Harding crossed his arms, and said,

"So, my friends, you do not know yet whether fate has thrown us on an island, or on a continent?"

"No, captain," replied the boy.

"We shall know to-morrow," said the engineer; "till then, there is nothing to be done."

"Yes," replied Pencroft.

"What?"

"Fire," said the sailor, who, also, had a fixed idea.

"We will make it, Pencroft," replied Harding.

"While you were carrying me yesterday, did I not see in the west a mountain which commands the country?"

"Yes," replied Spilett, "a mountain which must be rather high—"

"Well," replied the engineer, "we will climb to the summit to-morrow, and then we shall see if this land is an island or a continent. Till then, I repeat, there is nothing to be done."

"Yes, fire!" said the obstinate sailor again.

"But he will make us a fire!" replied Gideon Spilett, "only have a little patience, Pencroft!"

The seaman looked at Spilett in a way which seemed to say, "If it depended upon you to do it, we wouldn't taste roast meat very soon"; but he was silent.

Meanwhile Captain Harding had made no reply. He appeared to be very little troubled by the question of fire. For a few minutes he remained absorbed in thought; then again speaking,

"My friends," said he, "our situation is, perhaps, deplorable; but, at any rate, it is very plain. Either we are on a continent, and then, at the expense of greater or less fatigue, we shall reach some inhabited place, or we are on an island. In the latter case, if the island is inhabited, we will try to get out of the scrape with the help of its inhabitants; if it is desert, we will try to get out of the scrape by ourselves."

"Certainly, nothing could be plainer," replied Pencroft.

"But, whether it is an island or a continent," asked Gideon Spilett, "whereabouts do you think, Cyrus, this storm has thrown us?"

"I cannot say exactly," replied the engineer, "but I presume it is some land in the Pacific. In fact, when we left Richmond, the wind was blowing from the northeast, and its very violence greatly proves that it could not have varied. If the direction has been maintained from the northeast to the southwest, we have traversed the States of North Carolina, of South Carolina, of Georgia, the Gulf of Mexico, Mexico itself, in its narrow part, then a part of the Pacific Ocean. I cannot estimate the distance traversed by the balloon at less than six to seven thousand miles, and, even supposing that the wind had varied half a quarter, it must have brought us either to the archipelago of Mendava, either on the Pomotous, or even, if it had a greater strength than I suppose, to the land of New Zealand. If the last hypothesis is correct, it will be easy enough to get home again. English or Maoris, we shall always find some one to whom we can speak. If, on the contrary, this is the coast of a desert island in some tiny archipelago, perhaps we shall be able to reconnoiter it from the summit of that peak which overlooks the country, and then we shall see how best to establish ourselves here as if we are never to go away."

"Never?" cried the reporter. "You say 'Never,' my dear Cyrus?"

"Better to put things at the worst at first," replied the engineer, "and reserve the best for a surprise."

"Well said," remarked Pencroft. "It is to be hoped, too, that this island, if it be one, is not situated just out of the course of ships; that would be really unlucky!"

"We shall not know what we have to rely on until we have first made the ascent of the mountain," replied the engineer.

"But to-morrow, captain," asked Herbert, "shall you be in a state to bear the fatigue of the ascent?"

"I hope so," replied the engineer, "provided you and Pencroft, my boy, show yourselves quick and clever hunters."

"Captain," said the sailor, "since you are speaking of game, if on my return, I was as certain of roasting it as I am of bringing it back—"

"Bring it back all the same, Pencroft," replied Harding.

It was then agreed that the engineer and the reporter were to pass the day at the Chimneys, so as to examine the shore and the upper plateau. Neb, Herbert, and the sailor were to return to the forest, renew their store of wood, and lay violent hands on every creature, feathered or hairy, which might come within their reach.

They set out accordingly about ten o'clock in the morning, Herbert confident, Neb joyous, Pencroft murmuring aside,

"If, on my return, I find a fire at the house, I shall believe that the thunder itself came to light it." All three climbed the bank; and arrived at the angle made by the river, the sailor, stopping, said to his two companions,

"Shall we begin by being hunters or wood-men?"

"Hunters," replied Herbert. "There is Top already in quest."

"We will hunt, then," said the sailor, "and afterward we can come back and collect our wood."

This agreed to, Herbert, Neb, and Pencroft, after having torn three sticks from the trunk of a young fir, followed Top, who was bounding about among the long grass.

This time, the hunters, instead of following the course of the river, plunged straight into the heart of the forest. There were still the same trees, belonging, for the most part, to the pine family. In certain places, less crowded, growing in clumps, these pines exhibited considerable dimensions, and appeared to indicate, by their development, that the country was situated in a higher latitude than the engineer had supposed. Glades, bristling with stumps worn away by time, were covered with dry wood, which formed an inexhaustible store of fuel. Then, the glade passed, the underwood thickened again, and became almost impenetrable.

It was difficult enough to find the way among the groups of trees, without any beaten track. So the sailor from time to time broke off branches which might be easily recognized. But, perhaps, he was wrong not to follow the watercourse, as he and Herbert had done on their first excursion, for after walking an hour not a creature had shown itself. Top, running under the branches, only roused birds which could not be approached. Even the couroucous were invisible, and it was probable that the sailor would be obliged to return to the marshy part of the forest, in which he had so happily performed his grouse fishing.

"Well, Pencroft," said Neb, in a slightly sarcastic tone, "if this is all the game which you promised to bring back to my master, it won't need a large fire to roast it!"

"Have patience," replied the sailor, "it isn't the game which will be wanting on our return."

"Have you not confidence in Captain Harding?"

"Yes."

"But you don't believe that he will make fire?"

"I shall believe it when the wood is blazing in the fireplace."

"It will blaze, since my master has said so."

"We shall see!"

Meanwhile, the sun had not reached the highest point in its course above the horizon. The exploration, therefore, continued, and was usefully marked by a discovery which Herbert made of a tree whose fruit was edible. This was the stone-pine, which produces an excellent almond, very much esteemed in the temperate regions of America and Europe. These almonds were in a perfect state of maturity, and Herbert described them to his companions, who feasted on them.

"Come," said Pencroft, "sea-weed by way of bread, raw mussels for meat, and almonds for dessert, that's certainly a good dinner for those who have not a single match in their pocket!"

"We mustn't complain," said Herbert.

"I am not complaining, my boy," replied Pencroft, "only I repeat, that meat is a little too much economized in this sort of meal."

"Top has found something!" cried Neb, who ran toward a thicket, in the midst of which the dog had disappeared, barking. With Top's barking were mingled curious gruntings.

The sailor and Herbert had followed Neb. If there was game there this was not the time to discuss how it was to be cooked, but rather, how they were to get hold of it.

The hunters had scarcely entered the bushes when they saw Top engaged in a struggle with an animal which he was holding by the ear. This quadruped was a sort of pig nearly two feet and a half long, of a blackish brown color, lighter below, having hard scanty hair; its toes, then strongly fixed in the ground, seemed to be united by a membrane. Herbert recognized in this animal the capybara, that is to say, one of the largest members of the rodent order.

Meanwhile, the capybara did not struggle against the dog. It stupidly rolled its eyes, deeply buried in a thick bed of fat. Perhaps it saw men for the first time.

However, Neb having tightened his grasp on his stick, was just going to fell the pig, when the latter, tearing itself from Top's teeth, by which it was only held by the tip of its ear, uttered a vigorous grunt, rushed upon Herbert, almost overthrew him, and disappeared in the wood.

"The rascal!" cried Pencroft.

All three directly darted after Top, but at the moment when they joined him the animal had disappeared under the waters of a large pond shaded by venerable pines.

Neb, Herbert, and Pencroft stopped, motionless. Top plunged into the water, but the capybara, hidden at the bottom of the pond, did not appear.

"Let us wait," said the boy, "for he will soon come to the surface to breathe."

"Won't he drown?" asked Neb.

"No," replied Herbert, "since he has webbed feet, and is almost an amphibious animal. But watch him."

Top remained in the water. Pencroft and his two companions went to different parts of the bank, so as to cut off the retreat of the capybara, which the dog was looking for beneath the water.

Herbert was not mistaken. In a few minutes the animal appeared on the surface of the water. Top was upon it in a bound, and kept it from plunging again. An instant later the capybara, dragged to the bank, was killed by a blow from Neb's stick.

"Hurrah!" cried Pencroft, who was always ready with this cry of triumph.

"Give me but a good fire, and this pig shall be gnawed to the bones!"

Pencroft hoisted the capybara on his shoulders, and judging by the height of the sun that it was about two o'clock, he gave the signal to return.

Top's instinct was useful to the hunters, who, thanks to the intelligent animal, were enabled to discover the road by which they had come. Half an hour later they arrived at the river.

Pencroft soon made a raft of wood, as he had done before, though if there was no fire it would be a useless task, and the raft following the current, they returned toward the Chimneys.

But the sailor had not gone fifty paces when he stopped, and again uttering a tremendous hurrah, pointed toward the angle of the cliff,

"Herbert! Neb! Look!" he shouted.

Smoke was escaping and curling up among the rocks.

X

In a few minutes the three hunters were before a crackling fire. The captain and the reporter were there. Pencroft looked from one to the other, his capybara in his hand, without saying a word.

"Well, yes, my brave fellow," cried the reporter.

"Fire, real fire, which will roast this splendid pig perfectly, and we will have a feast presently!"

"But who lighted it?" asked Pencroft.

"The sun!"

Gideon Spilett was quite right in his reply. It was the sun which had furnished the heat which so astonished Pencroft. The sailor could scarcely believe his eyes, and he was so amazed that he did not think of questioning the engineer.

"Had you a burning-glass, sir?" asked Herbert of Harding.

"No, my boy," replied he, "but I made one."

And he showed the apparatus which served for a burning-glass. It was simply two glasses which he had taken from his own and the reporter's watches. Having filled them with water and rendered their edges adhesive by means of a little clay, he thus fabricated a regular burning-glass, which, concentrating the solar rays on some very dry moss, soon caused it to blaze.

The sailor considered the apparatus; then he gazed at the engineer without saying a word, only a look plainly expressed his opinion that if Cyrus Harding was not a magician, he was certainly no ordinary man. At last speech returned to him, and he cried,

"Note that, Mr. Spilett, note that down on your paper!"

"It is noted," replied the reporter.

Then, Neb helping him, the seaman arranged the spit, and the capybara, properly cleaned, was soon roasting like a suckling-pig before a clear, crackling fire.

The Chimneys had again become more habitable, not only because the passages were warmed by the fire, but because the partitions of wood and mud had been re-established.

It was evident that the engineer and his companions had employed their day well. Cyrus Harding had almost entirely recovered his strength, and had proved it by climbing to the upper plateau. From this point his eye, accustomed to estimate heights and distances, was fixed for a long time on the cone, the summit of which he wished to reach the next day. The mountain, situated about six miles to the northwest, appeared to him to measure 3,500 feet above the level of the sea. Consequently the gaze of an observer posted on its summit would extend over a radius of at least fifty miles. Therefore it was probable that Harding could easily solve the question of "island or continent," to which he attached so much importance.

They supped capitally. The flesh of the capybara was declared excellent. The sargassum and the almonds of the stone-pine completed the repast, during which the engineer spoke little. He was preoccupied with projects for the next day.

Once or twice Pencroft gave forth some ideas upon what it would be best to do; but Cyrus Harding, who was evidently of a methodical mind, only shook his head without uttering a word.

"To-morrow," he repeated, "we shall know what we have to depend upon, and we will act accordingly."

The meal ended, fresh armfuls of wood were thrown on the fire, and the inhabitants of the Chimneys, including the faithful Top, were soon buried in a deep sleep.

No incident disturbed this peaceful night, and the next day, the 29th of March, fresh and active they awoke, ready to undertake the excursion which must determine their fate.

All was ready for the start. The remains of the capybara would be enough to sustain Harding and his companions for at least twenty-four hours.

Besides, they hoped to find more food on the way. As the glasses had been returned to the watches of the engineer and reporter, Pencroft burned a little linen to serve as tinder. As to flint, that would not be wanting in these regions of Plutonic origin. It was half-past seven in the morning when the explorers, armed with sticks, left the Chimneys. Following Pencroft's advice, it appeared best to take the road already traversed through the forest, and to return by another route. It was also the most direct way to reach the mountain. They turned the south angle and followed the left bank of the river, which was abandoned at the point where it formed an elbow toward the southwest. The path, already trodden under the evergreen trees, was found, and at nine o'clock Cyrus Harding and his companions had reached the western border of the forest. The ground, till then, very little undulated, boggy at first, dry and sandy afterward, had a gentle slope, which ascended from the shore toward the interior of the country. A few very timid animals were seen under the forest-trees. Top quickly started them, but his master soon called him back, for the time had not come to commence hunting; that would be attended to later. The engineer was not a man who would allow himself to be diverted from his fixed idea. It might even have been said that he did not observe the country at all, either in its configuration or in its natural productions, his great aim being to climb the mountain before him, and therefore straight toward it he went. At ten o'clock a halt of a few minutes was made. On leaving the forest, the mountain system of the country appeared before the explorers. The mountain was composed of two cones; the first, truncated at a height of about two thousand five hundred feet, was sustained by buttresses, which appeared to branch out like the talons of an immense claw set on the ground. Between these were narrow valleys, bristling with trees, the last clumps of which rose to the top of the lowest cone. There appeared to be less vegetation on that side of the mountain which was exposed to the northeast, and deep fissures could be seen which, no doubt, were watercourses.

On the first cone rested a second, slightly rounded, and placed a little on one side, like a great round hat cocked over the ear. A Scotchman would have said, "His bonnet was a thocht ajee." It appeared formed of bare earth, here and there pierced by reddish rocks.

They wished to reach the second cone, and proceeding along the ridge of the spurs seemed to be the best way by which to gain it.

"We are on volcanic ground," Cyrus Harding had said, and his companions following him began to ascend by degrees on the back of a spur, which, by a winding and consequently more accessible path, joined the first plateau.

The ground had evidently been convulsed by subterranean force. Here and there stray blocks, numerous debris of basalt and pumice-stone, were met with. In isolated groups rose fir-trees, which, some hundred feet lower, at the bottom of the narrow gorges, formed massive shades almost impenetrable to the sun's rays.

During the first part of the ascent, Herbert remarked on the footprints which indicated the recent passage of large animals.

"Perhaps these beasts will not let us pass by willingly," said Pencroft.

"Well," replied the reporter, who had already hunted the tiger in India, and the lion in Africa, "we shall soon learn how successfully to encounter them. But in the meantime we must be upon our guard!"

They ascended but slowly.

The distance, increased by detours and obstacles which could not be surmounted directly, was long. Sometimes, too, the ground suddenly fell, and they found themselves on the edge of a deep chasm which they had to go round. Thus, in retracing their steps so as to find some practicable path, much time was employed and fatigue undergone for nothing. At twelve o'clock, when the small band of adventurers halted for breakfast at the foot of a large group of firs, near a little stream which fell in cascades, they found themselves still half way from the first plateau, which most probably they would not reach till nightfall. From this point the view of the sea was much extended, but on the right the high promontory prevented their seeing whether there was land beyond it. On the left, the sight extended several miles to the north; but, on the northwest, at the point occupied by the explorers, it was cut short by the ridge of a fantastically-shaped spur, which formed a powerful support of the central cone.

At one o'clock the ascent was continued. They slanted more toward the southwest and again entered among thick bushes. There under the shade of the trees fluttered several couples of gallinaceae belonging to the pheasant species. They were tragopans, ornamented by a pendant skin which hangs over their throats, and by two small, round horns, planted behind the eyes. Among these birds, which were about the size of a fowl, the female was uniformly brown, while the male was gorgeous in his red plumage, decorated with white spots. Gideon Spilett, with a stone cleverly and vigorously thrown, killed one of these tragopans, on which Pencroft, made hungry by the fresh air, had cast greedy eyes.

After leaving the region of bushes, the party, assisted by resting on each other's shoulders, climbed for about a hundred feet up a steep acclivity and reached a level place, with very few trees, where the soil appeared volcanic. It was necessary to ascend by zigzags to make the slope more easy, for it was very steep, and the footing being exceedingly precarious required the greatest caution. Neb and Herbert took the lead, Pencroft the rear, the captain and the reporter between them. The animals which frequented these heights—and there were numerous traces of them—must necessarily belong to those races of sure foot and supple spine, chamois or goat. Several were seen, but this was not the name Pencroft gave them, for all of a sudden—"Sheep!" he shouted.

All stopped about fifty feet from half a dozen animals of a large size, with strong horns bent back and flattened toward the point, with a woolly fleece, hidden under long silky hair of a tawny color.

They were not ordinary sheep, but a species usually found in the mountainous regions of the temperate zone, to which Herbert gave the name of the musmon.

"Have they legs and chops?" asked the sailor.

"Yes," replied Herbert.

"Well, then, they are sheep!" said Pencroft.

The animals, motionless among the blocks of basalt, gazed with an astonished eye, as if they saw human bipeds for the first time. Then their fears suddenly aroused, they disappeared, bounding over the rocks.

"Good-bye, till we meet again," cried Pencroft, as he watched them, in such a comical tone that Cyrus Harding, Gideon Spilett, Herbert, and Neb could not help laughing.

The ascent was continued. Here and there were traces of lava. Sulphur springs sometimes stopped their way, and they had to go round them. In some places the sulphur had formed crystals among other substances, such as whitish cinders made of an infinity of little feldspar crystals.

In approaching the first plateau formed by the truncating of the lower cone, the difficulties of the ascent were very great. Toward four o'clock the extreme zone of the trees had been passed. There only remained here and there a few twisted, stunted pines, which must have had a hard life in resisting at this altitude the high winds from the open sea. Happily for the engineer and his companions the weather was beautiful, the atmosphere tranquil; for a high breeze at an elevation of three thousand feet would have hindered their proceedings. The purity of the sky at the zenith was felt through the transparent air. A perfect calm reigned around them. They could not see the sun, then hid by the vast screen of the upper cone, which masked the half-horizon of the west, and whose enormous shadow stretching to the shore increased as the radiant luminary sank in its diurnal course. Vapors—mist rather than clouds—began to appear in the east, and assume all the prismatic colors under the influence of the solar rays.

Five hundred feet only separated the explorers from the plateau, which they wished to reach so as to establish there an encampment for the night, but these five hundred feet were increased to more than two miles by the zigzags which they had to describe. The soil, as it were, slid under their feet.

The slope often presented such an angle that they slipped when the stones worn by the air did not give a sufficient support. Evening came on by degrees, and it was almost night when Cyrus Harding and his companions, much fatigued by an ascent of seven hours, arrived at the plateau of the first cone. It was then necessary to prepare an encampment, and to restore their strength by eating first and sleeping afterward. This second stage of the mountain rose on a base of rocks, among which it would be easy to find a retreat. Fuel was not abundant. However, a fire could be made by means of the moss and dry brushwood, which covered certain parts of the plateau. While the sailor was preparing his hearth with stones which he put to this use, Neb and Herbert occupied themselves with getting a supply of fuel. They soon returned with a load of brushwood. The steel was struck, the burnt linen caught the sparks of flint, and, under Neb's breath, a crackling fire showed itself in a few minutes under the shelter of the rocks. Their object in lighting a fire was only to enable them to withstand the cold temperature of the night, as it was not employed in cooking the bird, which Neb kept for the next day. The remains of the capybara and some dozens of the stone-pine almonds formed their supper. It was not half-past six when all was finished.

Cyrus Harding then thought of exploring in the half-light the large circular layer which supported the upper cone of the mountain. Before taking any rest, he wished to know if it was possible to get around the base of the cone in the case of its sides being too steep and its summit being inaccessible. This question preoccupied him, for it was possible that from the way the hat inclined, that is to say, toward the north, the plateau was not practicable. Also, if the summit of the mountain could not be reached on one side, and if, on the other, they could not get around the base of the cone, it would be impossible to survey the western part of the country, and their object in making the ascent would in part be altogether unattained.

The engineer, accordingly, regardless of fatigue, leaving Pencroft and Neb to arrange the beds, and Gideon Spilett to note the incidents of the day, began to follow the edge of the plateau, going toward the north. Herbert accompanied him.

The night was beautiful and still, the darkness was not yet deep. Cyrus Harding and the boy walked near each other, without speaking. In some places the plateau opened before them, and they passed without hindrance. In others, obstructed by rocks, there was only a narrow path, in which two persons could not walk abreast. After a walk of twenty minutes, Cyrus Harding and Herbert were obliged to stop. From this point the slope of the two cones became one. No shoulder here separated the two parts of the mountain. The slope, being inclined almost seventy degrees, the path became impracticable.

But if the engineer and the boy were obliged to give up thoughts of following a circular direction, in return an opportunity was given for ascending the cone.

In fact, before them opened a deep hollow. It was the rugged mouth of the crater, by which the eruptive liquid matter had escaped at the periods when the volcano was still in activity. Hardened lava and crusted scoria formed a sort of natural staircase of large steps, which would greatly facilitate the ascent to the summit of the mountain.

Harding took all this in at a glance, and without hesitating, followed by the lad, he entered the enormous chasm in the midst of an increasing obscurity.

There was still a height of a thousand feet to overcome. Would the interior acclivities of the crater be practicable? It would soon be seen. The persevering engineer resolved to continue his ascent until he was stopped. Happily these acclivities wound up the interior of the volcano and favored their ascent.

As to the volcano itself, it could not be doubted that it was completely extinct. No smoke escaped from its sides; not a flame could be seen in the dark hollows; not a roar, not a mutter, no trembling even issued from this black well, which perhaps reached far into the bowels of the earth. The atmosphere inside the crater was filled with no sulphurous vapor. It was more than the sleep of a volcano; it was its complete extinction. Cyrus Harding's attempt would succeed.

Little by little, Herbert and he climbing up the sides of the interior, saw the crater widen above their heads. The radius of this circular portion of the sky, framed by the edge of the cone, increased obviously. At each step, as it were, that the explorers made, fresh stars entered the field of their vision. The magnificent constellations of the southern sky shone resplendently. At the zenith glittered the splendid Antares in the Scorpion, and not far was Alpha Centauri, which is believed to be the nearest star to the terrestrial globe. Then, as the crater widened, appeared Fomalhaut of the Fish, the Southern Triangle, and lastly, nearly at the Antarctic Pole, the glittering Southern Cross, which replaces the Polar Star of the Northern Hemisphere.

It was nearly eight o'clock when Cyrus Harding and Herbert set foot on the highest ridge of the mountain at the summit of the cone.

It was then perfectly dark, and their gaze could not extend over a radius of two miles. Did the sea surround this unknown land, or was it connected in the west with some continent of the Pacific? It could not yet be made out. Toward the west, a cloudy belt, clearly visible at the horizon, increased the gloom, and the eye could not discover if the sky and water were blended together in the same circular line.

But at one point of the horizon a vague light suddenly appeared, which descended slowly in proportion as the cloud mounted to the zenith.

It was the slender crescent moon, already almost disappearing; but its light was sufficient to show clearly the horizontal line, then detached from the cloud, and the engineer could see its reflection trembling for an instant on a liquid surface. Cyrus Harding seized the lad's hand, and in a grave voice,

"An island!" said he, at the moment when the lunar crescent disappeared beneath the waves.

XI

Half an hour later Cyrus Harding and Herbert had returned to the encampment. The engineer merely told his companions that the land upon which fate had thrown them was an island, and that the next day they would consult. Then each settled himself as well as he could to sleep, and in that rocky hole, at a height of two thousand five hundred feet above the level of the sea, through a peaceful night, the islanders enjoyed profound repose.

The next day, the 30th of March, after a hasty breakfast, which consisted solely of the roasted tragopan, the engineer wished to climb again to the summit of the volcano, so as more attentively to survey the island upon which he and his companions were imprisoned for life perhaps, should the island be situated at a great distance from any land, or if it was out of the course of vessels which visited the archipelagoes of the Pacific Ocean. This time his companions followed him in the new exploration. They also wished to see the island, on the productions of which they must depend for the supply of all their wants.

It was about seven o'clock in the morning when Cyrus Harding, Herbert, Pencroft, Gideon Spilett, and Neb quitted the encampment. No one appeared to be anxious about their situation. They had faith in themselves, doubtless, but it must be observed that the basis of this faith was not the same with Harding as with his companions. The engineer had confidence, because he felt capable of extorting from this wild country everything necessary for the life of himself and his companions; the latter feared nothing, just because Cyrus Harding was with them. Pencroft especially, since the incident of the relighted fire, would not have despaired for an instant, even if he was on a bare rock, if the engineer was with him on the rock.

"Pshaw," said he, "we left Richmond without permission from the authorities! It will be hard if we don't manage to get away some day or other from a place where certainly no one will detain us!"

Cyrus Harding followed the same road as the evening before. They went round the cone by the plateau which formed the shoulder, to the mouth of the enormous chasm. The weather was magnificent. The sun rose in a pure sky and flooded with his rays all the eastern side of the mountain.

The crater was reached. It was just what the engineer had made it out to be in the dark; that is to say, a vast funnel which extended, widening, to a height of a thousand feet above the plateau. Below the chasm, large thick streaks of lava wound over the sides of the mountain, and thus marked the course of the eruptive matter to the lower valleys which furrowed the northern part of the island.

The interior of the crater, whose inclination did not exceed thirty-five to forty degrees, presented no difficulties nor obstacles to the ascent. Traces of very ancient lava were noticed, which probably had overflowed the summit of the cone, before this lateral chasm had opened a new way to it.

As to the volcanic chimney which established a communication between the subterranean layers and the crater, its depth could not be calculated with the eye, for it was lost in obscurity. But there was no doubt as to the complete extinction of the volcano.

Before eight o'clock Harding and his companions were assembled at the summit of the crater, on a conical mound which swelled the northern edge.

"The sea, the sea everywhere!" they cried, as if their lips could not restrain the words which made islanders of them.

The sea, indeed, formed an immense circular sheet of water all around them! Perhaps, on climbing again to the summit of the cone, Cyrus Harding had had a hope of discovering some coast, some island shore, which he had not been able to perceive in the dark the evening before. But nothing appeared on the farthest verge of the horizon, that is to say over a radius of more than fifty miles. No land in sight. Not a sail. Over all this immense space the ocean alone was visible—the island occupied the center of a circumference which appeared to be infinite.

The engineer and his companions, mute and motionless, surveyed for some minutes every point of the ocean, examining it to its most extreme limits. Even Pencroft, who possessed a marvelous power of sight, saw nothing; and certainly if there had been land at the horizon, if it appeared only as an indistinct vapor, the sailor would undoubtedly have found it out, for nature had placed regular telescopes under his eyebrows.

From the ocean their gaze returned to the island which they commanded entirely, and the first question was put by Gideon Spilett in these terms:

"About what size is this island?"

Truly, it did not appear large in the midst of the immense ocean.

Cyrus Harding reflected a few minutes; he attentively observed the perimeter of the island, taking into comsideration the height at which he was placed; then,

"My friends," said he, "I do not think I am mistaken in giving to the shore of the island a circumference of more than a hundred miles."

"And consequently an area?"

"That is difficult to estimate," replied the engineer, "for it is so uneven."

If Cyrus Harding was not mistaken in his calculation, the island had almost the extent of Malta or Zante, in the Mediterranean, but it was at the same time much more irregular and less rich in capes, promontories, points, bays, or creeks. Its strange form caught the eye, and when Gideon Spilett, on the engineer's advice, had drawn the outline, they found that it resembled some fantastic animal, a monstrous leviathan, which lay sleeping on the surface of the Pacific.

This was in fact the exact shape of the island, which it is of consequence to know, and a tolerably correct map of it was immediately drawn by the reporter.

The east part of the shore, where the castaways had landed, formed a wide bay, terminated by a sharp cape, which had been concealed by a high point from Pencroft on his first exploration. At the northeast two other capes closed the bay, and between them ran a narrow gulf, which looked like the half-open jaws of a formidable dog-fish.

From the northeast to the southwest the coast was rounded, like the flattened cranium of an animal, rising again, forming a sort of protuberance which did not give any particular shape to this part of the island, of which the center was occupied by the volcano.

From this point the shore ran pretty regularly north and south, broken at two-thirds of its perimeter by a narrow creek, from which it ended in a long tail, similar to the caudal appendage of a gigantic alligator.

This tail formed a regular peninsula, which stretched more than thirty miles into the sea, reckoning from the cape southeast of the island, already mentioned; it curled around, making an open roadstead, which marked out the lower shore of this strangely-formed land.

At the narrowest part, that is to say between the Chimneys and the creek on the western shore, which corresponded to it in latitude, the island only measured ten miles; but its greatest length, from the jaws at the northeast to the extremity of the tail of the southwest, was not less than thirty miles.

As to the interior of the island, its general aspect was this—very woody throughout the southern part from the mountain to the shore, and arid and sandy in the northern part. Between the volcano and the east coast Cyrus Harding and his companions were surprised to see a lake, bordered with green trees, the existence of which they had not suspected. Seen from this height, the lake appeared to be on the same level as the ocean, but, on reflection, the engineer explained to his companions that the altitude of this little sheet of water must be about three hundred feet, because the plateau, which was its basin, was but a prolongation of the coast.

"Is it a freshwater lake?" asked Pencroft.

"Certainly," replied the engineer, "for it must be fed by the water which flows from the mountain."

"I see a little river which runs into it," said Herbert, pointing out a narrow stream, which evidently took its source somewhere in the west.

"Yes," said Harding, "and since this stream feeds the lake, most probably on the side near the sea there is an outlet by which the surplus water escapes. We shall see that on our return."

This little winding watercourse and the river already mentioned constituted the water-system, at least such as it was displayed to the eyes of the explorers. However, it was possible that under the masses of trees which covered two-thirds of the island, forming an immense forest, other rivers ran toward the sea. It might even be inferred that such was the case, so rich did this region appear in the most magnificent specimens of the flora of the temperate zones. There was no indication of running water in the north, though perhaps there might be stagnant water among the marshes in the northeast; but that was all, in addition to the downs, sand, and aridity which contrasted so strongly with the luxuriant vegetation of the rest of the island.

The volcano did not occupy the central part; it rose, on the contrary, in the northwestern region, and seemed to mark the boundary of the two zones. At the southwest, at the south, and the southeast, the first part of the spurs were hidden under masses of verdure. At the north, on the contrary, one could follow their ramifications, which died away on the sandy plains. It was on this side that, at the time when the mountain was in a state of eruption, the discharge had worn away a passage, and a large heap of lava had spread to the narrow jaw which formed the northeastern gulf.

Cyrus Harding and his companions remained an hour at the top of the mountain. The island was displayed under their eyes, like a plan in relief with different tints, green for the forests, yellow for the sand, blue for the water. They viewed it in its tout-ensemble, nothing remained concealed but the ground hidden by verdure, the hollows of the valleys, and the interior of the volcanic chasms.

One important question remained to be solved, and the answer would have a great effect upon the future of the castaways.

Was the island inhabited?

It was the reporter who put this question, to which after the close examination they had just made, the answer seemed to be in the negative.

Nowhere could the work of a human hand be perceived. Not a group of huts, not a solitary cabin, not a fishery on the shore. No smoke curling in the air betrayed the presence of man. It is true, a distance of nearly thirty miles separated the observers from the extreme points, that is, of the tail which extended to the southwest, and it would have been difficult, even to Pencroft's eyes, to discover a habitation there. Neither could the curtain of verdure, which covered three-quarters of the island, be raised to see if it did not shelter some straggling village. But in general the islanders live on the shores of the narrow spaces which emerge above the waters of the Pacific, and this shore appeared to be an absolute desert.

Until a more complete exploration, it might be admitted that the island was uninhabited. But was it frequented, at least occasionally, by the natives of neighboring islands? It was difficult to reply to this question. No land appeared within a radius of fifty miles. But fifty miles could be easily crossed, either by Malay proas or by the large Polynesian canoes. Everything depended on the position of the island, of its isolation in the Pacific, or of its proximity to archipelagoes. Would Cyrus Harding be able to find out their latitude and longitude without instruments? It would be difficult. Since he was in doubt, it was best to take precautions against a possible descent of neighboring natives.

The exploration of the island was finished, its shape determined, its features made out, its extent calculated, the water and mountain systems ascertained. The disposition of the forests and plains had been marked in a general way on the reporter's plan. They had now only to descend the mountain slopes again, and explore the soil, in the triple point of view, of its mineral, vegetable, and animal resources.

But before giving his companions the signal for departure, Cyrus Harding said to them in a calm, grave voice,

"Here, my friends, is the small corner of land upon which the hand of the Almighty has thrown us. We are going to live here; a long time, perhaps. Perhaps, too, unexpected help will arrive, if some ship passes by chance. I say by chance, because this is an unimportant island; there is not even a port in which ships could anchor, and it is to be feared that it is situated out of the route usually followed, that is to say, too much to the south for the ships which frequent the archipelagoes of the Pacific, and too much to the north for those which go to Australia by doubling Cape Horn. I wish to hide nothing of our position from you—"

"And you are right, my dear Cyrus," replied the reporter, with animation. "You have to deal with men. They have confidence in you, and you can depend upon them. Is it not so, my friends?"

"I will obey you in everything, captain," said Herbert, seizing the engineer's hand.

"My master always, and everywhere!" cried Neb.

"As for me," said the sailor, "if I ever grumble at work, my name's not Jack Pencroft, and if you like, captain, we will make a little America of this island! We will build towns, we will establish railways, start telegraphs, and one fine day, when it is quite changed, quite put in order and quite civilized, we will go and offer it to the government of the Union. Only, I ask one thing."

"What is that?" said the reporter.

"It is, that we do not consider ourselves castaways, but colonists, who have come here to settle." Harding could not help smiling, and the sailor's idea was adopted. He then thanked his companions, and added, that he would rely on their energy and on the aid of Heaven.

"Well, now let us set off to the Chimneys!" cried Pencroft.

"One minute, my friends," said the engineer. "It seems to me it would be a good thing to give a name to this island, as well as to the capes, promontories, and watercourses, which we can see."

"Very good," said the reporter. "In the future, that will simplify the instructions which we shall have to give and follow."

"Indeed," said the sailor, "already it is something to be able to say where one is going, and where one has come from. At least, it looks like somewhere."

"The Chimneys, for example," said Herbert.

"Exactly!" replied Pencroft. "That name was the most convenient, and it came to me quite of myself. Shall we keep the name of the Chimneys for our first encampment, captain?"

"Yes, Pencroft, since you have so christened it."

"Good! as for the others, that will be easy," returned the sailor, who was in high spirits. "Let us give them names, as the Robinsons did, whose story Herbert has often read to me; Providence Bay, Whale Point, Cape Disappointment!"

"Or, rather, the names of Captain Harding," said Herbert, "of Mr. Spilett, of Neb!—"

"My name!" cried Neb, showing his sparkling white teeth.

"Why not?" replied Pencroft. "Port Neb, that would do very well! And Cape Gideon—"

"I should prefer borrowing names from our country," said the reporter, "which would remind us of America."

"Yes, for the principal ones," then said Cyrus Harding; "for those of the bays and seas, I admit it willingly. We might give to that vast bay on the east the name of Union Bay, for example; to that large hollow on the south, Washington Bay; to the mountain upon which we are standing, that of Mount Franklin; to that lake which is extended under our eyes, that of Lake Grant; nothing could be better, my friends. These names will recall our country, and those of the great citizens who have honored it; but for the rivers, gulfs, capes, and promontories, which we perceive from the top of this mountain, rather let us choose names which will recall their particular shape. They will impress themselves better on our memory, and at the same time will be more practical. The shape of the island is so strange that we shall not be troubled to imagine what it resembles. As to the streams which we do not know as yet, in different parts of the forest which we shall explore later, the creeks which afterward will be discovered, we can christen them as we find them. What do you think, my friends?"

The engineer's proposal was unanimously agreed to by his companions. The island was spread out under their eyes like a map, and they had only to give names to all its angles and points. Gideon Spilett would write them down, and the geographical nomenclature of the island would be definitely adopted. First, they named the two bays and the mountain, Union Bay, Washington Bay, and Mount Franklin, as the engineer had suggested.

"Now," said the reporter, "to this peninsula at the southwest of the island, I propose to give the name of Serpentine Peninsula, and that of Reptile End to the bent tail which terminates it, for it is just like a reptile's tail."

"Adopted," said the engineer.

"Now," said Herbert, pointing to the other extremity of the island, "let us call this gulf which is so singularly like a pair of open jaws, Shark Gulf."

"Capital!" cried Pencroft, "and we can complete the resemblance by naming the two parts of the jaws Mandible Cape."

"But there are two capes," observed the reporter.

"Well," replied Pencroft, "we can have North Mandible Cape and South Mandible Cape."

"They are inscribed," said Spilett.

"There is only the point at the southeastern extremity of the island to be named," said Pencroft.

"That is, the extremity of Union Bay?" asked Herbert.

"Claw Cape," cried Neb directly, who also wished to be godfather to some part of his domain.

In truth, Neb had found an excellent name, for this cape was very like the powerful claw of the fantastic animal which this singularly-shaped island represented.

Pencroft was delighted at the turn things had taken, and their imaginations soon gave to the river which furnished the settlers with drinking water and near which the balloon had thrown them, the name of the Mercy, in true gratitude to Providence. To the islet upon which the castaways had first landed, the name of Safety Islet; to the plateau which crowned the high granite precipice above the Chimneys, and from whence the gaze could embrace the whole of the vast bay, the name of Prospect Heights.

Lastly, all the masses of impenetrable wood which covered the Serpentine Peninsula were named the Forests of the Far West.

The nomenclature of the visible and known parts of the island was thus finished, and later, they would complete it as they made fresh discoveries.

As to the points of the compass, the engineer had roughly fixed them by the height and position of the sun, which placed Union Bay and Prospect Heights to the east. But the next day, by taking the exact hour of the rising and setting of the sun, and by marking its position between this rising and setting, he reckoned to fix the north of the island exactly, for, in consequence of its situation in the Southern Hemisphere, the sun, at the precise moment of its culmination, passed in the north and not in the south, as, in its apparent movement, it seems to do, to those places situated in the Northern Hemisphere.

Everything was finished, and the settlers had only to descend Mount Franklin to return to the Chimneys, when Pencroft cried out,

"Well! we are preciously stupid!"

"Why?" asked Gideon Spilett, who had closed his notebook and risen to depart.

"Why! our island! we have forgotten to christen it!"

Herbert was going to propose to give it the engineer's name and all his companions would have applauded him, when Cyrus Harding said simply,

"Let us give it the name of a great citizen, my friend; of him who now struggles to defend the unity of the American Republic! Let us call it Lincoln Island!"

The engineer's proposal was replied to by three hurrahs.

And that evening, before sleeping, the new colonists talked of their absent country; they spoke of the terrible war which stained it with blood; they could not doubt that the South would soon be subdued, and that the cause of the North, the cause of justice, would triumph, thanks to Grant, thanks to Lincoln!

Now this happened the 30th of March, 1865. They little knew that sixteen days afterward a frightful crime would be committed in Washington, and that on Good Friday Abraham Lincoln would fall by the hand of a fanatic.

XII

They now began the descent of the mountain. Climbing down the crater, they went around the cone and reached their encampment of the previous night. Pencroft thought it must be breakfasttime, and the watches of the reporter and engineer were therefore consulted to find out the hour.

That of Gideon Spilett had been preserved from the sea-water, as he had been thrown at once on the sand out of reach of the waves. It was an instrument of excellent quality, a perfect pocket chronometer, which the reporter had not forgotten to wind up carefully every day.

As to the engineer's watch, it, of course, had stopped during the time which he had passed on the downs.

The engineer now wound it up, and ascertaining by the height of the sun that it must be about nine o'clock in the morning, he put his watch at that hour.

"No, my dear Spilett, wait. You have kept the Richmond time, have you not?"

"Yes, Cyrus."

"Consequently, your watch is set by the meridian of that town, which is almost that of Washington?"

"Undoubtedly."

"Very well, keep it thus. Content yourself with winding it up very exactly, but do not touch the hands. This may be of use to us."

"What will be the good of that?" thought the sailor.

They ate, and so heartily, that the store of game and almonds was totally exhausted. But Pencroft was not at all uneasy, they would supply themselves on the way. Top, whose share had been very much to his taste, would know how to find some fresh game among the brushwood. Moreover, the sailor thought of simply asking the engineer to manufacture some powder and one or two fowling-pieces; he supposed there would be no difficulty in that.

On leaving the plateau, the captain proposed to his companions to return to the Chimneys by a new way. He wished to reconnoiter Lake Grant, so magnificently framed in trees. They therefore followed the crest of one of the spurs, between which the creek that supplied the lake probably had its source. In talking, the settlers already employed the names which they had just chosen, which singularly facilitated the exchange of their ideas. Herbert and Pencroft—the one young and the other very boyish—were enchanted, and while walking, the sailor said,

"Hey, Herbert! how capital it sounds! It will be impossible to lose ourselves, my boy, since, whether we follow the way to Lake Grant, or whether we join the Mercy through the woods of the Far West, we shall be certain to arrive at Prospect Heights, and, consequently, at Union Bay!"

It had been agreed, that without forming a compact band, the settlers should not stray away from each other. It was very certain that the thick forests of the island were inhabited by dangerous animals, and it was prudent to be on their guard. In general, Pencroft, Herbert, and Neb walked first, preceded by Top, who poked his nose into every bush. The reporter and the engineer went together, Gideon Spilett ready to note every incident, the engineer silent for the most part, and only stepping aside to pick up one thing or another, a mineral or vegetable substance, which he put into his pocket, without making any remark.

"What can he be picking up?" muttered Pencroft. "I have looked in vain for anything that's worth the trouble of stooping for."

Toward ten o'clock the little band descended the last declivities of Mount Franklin. As yet the ground was scantily strewn with bushes and trees. They were walking over yellowish calcinated earth, forming a plain of nearly a mile long, which extended to the edge of the wood. Great blocks of that basalt, which, according to Bischof, takes three hundred and fifty millions of years to cool, strewed the plain, very confused in some places. However, there were here no traces of lava, which was spread more particularly over the northern slopes.

Cyrus Harding expected to reach, without incident, the course of the creek, which he supposed flowed under the trees at the border of the plain, when he saw Herbert running hastily back, while Neb and the sailor were hiding behind the rocks.

"What's the matter, my boy?" asked Spilett.

"Smoke," replied Herbert. "We have seen smoke among the rocks, a hundred paces from us."

"Men in this place?" cried the reporter.

"We must avoid showing ourselves before knowing with whom we have to deal," replied Cyrus Harding. "I trust that there are no natives on this island; I dread them more than anything else. Where is Top?"

"Top is on before."

"And he doesn't bark?"

"No."

"That is strange. However, we must try to call him back."

In a few moments, the engineer, Gideon Spilett, and Herbert had rejoined their two companions, and like them, they kept out of sight behind the heaps of basalt.

From thence they clearly saw smoke of a yellowish color rising in the air.

Top was recalled by a slight whistle from his master, and the latter, signing to his companions to wait for him, glided away among the rocks. The colonists, motionless, anxiously awaited the result of this exploration, when a shout from the engineer made them hasten forward. They soon joined him, and were at once struck with a disagreeable odor which impregnated the atmosphere.

The odor, easily recognized, was enough for the engineer to guess what the smoke was which at first, not without cause, had startled him.

"This fire," said he, "or rather, this smoke is produced by nature alone. There is a sulphur spring there, which will cure all our sore throats."

"Captain!" cried Pencroft. "What a pity that I haven't got a cold!"

The settlers then directed their steps toward the place from which the smoke escaped. They there saw a sulphur spring which flowed abundantly between the rocks, and its waters discharged a strong sulphuric acid odor, after having absorbed the oxygen of the air.

Cyrus Harding, dipping in his hand, felt the water oily to the touch. He tasted it and found it rather sweet. As to its temperature, that he estimated at ninety-five degrees Fahrenheit. Herbert having asked on what he based this calculation,

"It's quite simple, my boy," said he, "for, in plunging my hand into the water, I felt no sensation either of heat or cold. Therefore it has the same temperature as the human body, which is about ninety-five degrees."

The sulphur spring not being of any actual use to the settlers, they proceeded toward the thick border of the forest, which began some hundred paces off.

There, as they had conjectured, the waters of the stream flowed clear and limpid between high banks of red earth, the color of which betrayed the presence of oxide of iron. From this color, the name of Red Creek was immediately given to the watercourse.

It was only a large stream, deep and clear, formed of the mountain water, which, half river, half torrent, here rippling peacefully over the sand, there chafing against the rocks or dashing down in a cascade, ran toward the lake, over a distance of a mile and a half, its breadth varying from thirty to forty feet. Its waters were sweet, and it was supposed that those of the lake were so also. A fortunate circumstance, in the event of their finding on its borders a more suitable dwelling than the Chimneys.

As to the trees, which some hundred feet downward shaded the banks of the creek, they belonged, for the most part, to the species which abound in the temperate zone of America and Tasmania, and no longer to those coniferae observed in that portion of the island already explored to some miles from Prospect Heights. At this time of the year, the commencement of the month of April, which represents the month of October, in this hemisphere, that is, the beginning of autumn, they were still in full leaf. They consisted principally of casuarinas and eucalypti, some of which next year would yield a sweet manna, similar to the manna of the East. Clumps of Australian cedars rose on the sloping banks, which were also covered with the high grass called tussac in New Holland; but the cocoanut, so abundant in the archipelagoes of the Pacific, seemed to be wanting in the island, the latitude, doubtless, being too low.

"What a pity!" said Herbert, "such a useful tree, and which has such beautiful nuts!"

As to the birds, they swarmed among the scanty branches of the eucalypti and casuarinas, which did not hinder the display of their wings. Black, white, or gray cockatoos, paroquets, with plumage of all colors, kingfishers of a sparkling green and crowned with red, blue lories, and various other birds appeared on all sides, as through a prism, fluttering about and producing a deafening clamor. Suddenly, a strange concert of discordant voices resounded in the midst of a thicket. The settlers heard successively the song of birds, the cry of quadrupeds, and a sort of clacking which they might have believed to have escaped from the lips of a native. Neb and Herbert rushed toward the bush, forgetting even the most elementary principles of prudence. Happily, they found there, neither a formidable wild beast nor a dangerous native, but merely half a dozen mocking and singing birds, known as mountain pheasants. A few skillful blows from a stick soon put an end to their concert, and procured excellent food for the evening's dinner.

Herbert also discovered some magnificent pigeons with bronzed wings, some superbly crested, others draped in green, like their congeners at Port-

Macquarie; but it was impossible to reach them, or the crows and magpies which flew away in flocks.

A charge of small shot would have made great slaughter among these birds, but the hunters were still limited to sticks and stones, and these primitive weapons proved very insufficient.

Their insufficiency was still more clearly shown when a troop of quadrupeds, jumping, bounding, making leaps of thirty feet, regular flying mammiferae, fled over the thickets, so quickly and at such a height, that one would have thought that they passed from one tree to another like squirrels.

"Kangaroos!" cried Herbert.

"Are they good to eat?" asked Pencroft.

"Stewed," replied the reporter, "their flesh is equal to the best venison!—"

Gideon Spilett had not finished this exciting sentence when the sailor, followed by Neb and Herbert, darted on the kangaroos' tracks. Cyrus Harding called them back in vain. But it was in vain too for the hunters to pursue such agile game, which went bounding away like balls. After a chase of five minutes, they lost their breath, and at the same time all sight of the creatures, which disappeared in the wood. Top was not more successful than his masters.

"Captain," said Pencroft, when the engineer and the reporter had rejoined them, "Captain, you see quite well we can't get on unless we make a few guns. Will that be possible?"

"Perhaps," replied the engineer, "but we will begin by first manufacturing some bows and arrows, and I don't doubt that you will become as clever in the use of them as the Australian hunters."

"Bows and arrows!" said Pencroft scornfully. "That's all very well for children!"

"Don't be proud, friend Pencroft," replied the reporter. "Bows and arrows were sufficient for centuries to stain the earth with blood. Powder is but a thing of yesterday, and war is as old as the human race—unhappily."

"Faith, that's true, Mr. Spilett," replied the sailor, "and I always speak too quickly. You must excuse me!"

Meanwhile, Herbert constant to his favorite science, natural history, reverted to the kangaroos, saying,

"Besides, we had to deal just now with the species which is most difficult to catch. They were giants with long gray fur; but if I am not mistaken, there exist black and red kangaroos, rock kangaroos, and rat kangaroos, which are more easy to get hold of. It is reckoned that there are about a dozen species—"

"Herbert," replied the sailor sententiously, "there is only one species of kangaroos to me, that is 'kangaroo on the spit,' and it's just the one we haven't got this evening!"

They could not help laughing at Master Pencroft's new classification. The honest sailor did not hide his regret at being reduced for dinner to the singing pheasants, but fortune once more showed itself obliging to him.

In fact, Top, who felt that his interest was concerned, went and ferreted everywhere with an instinct doubled by a ferocious appetite. It was even probable that if some piece of game did fall into his clutches, none would be left for the hunters, if Top was hunting on his own account; but Neb watched him and he did well.

Toward three o'clock the dog disappeared in the brushwood and gruntings showed that he was engaged in a struggle with some animal. Neb rushed after him, and soon saw Top eagerly devouring a quadruped, which ten seconds later would have been past recognizing in Top's stomach. But fortunately the dog had fallen upon a brood, and besides the victim he was devouring, two other rodents—the animals in question belonged to that order—lay strangled on the turf.

Neb reappeared triumphantly holding one of the rodents in each hand. Their size exceeded that of a rabbit, their hair was yellow, mingled with green spots, and they had the merest rudiments of tails.

The citizens of the Union were at no loss for the right name of these rodents. They were maras, a sort of agouti, a little larger than their congeners of tropical countries, regular American rabbits, with long ears, jaws armed on each side with five molars, which distinguish the agouti.

"Hurrah!" cried Pencroft, "the roast has arrived! and now we can go home."

The walk, interrupted for an instant, was resumed. The limpid waters of the Red Creek flowed under an arch of casuarinas, banksias, and gigantic gum-trees. Superb lilacs rose to a height of twenty feet. Other arborescent species, unknown to the young naturalist, bent over the stream, which could be heard murmuring beneath the bowers of verdure.

Meanwhile the stream grew much wider, and Cyrus Harding supposed that they would soon reach its mouth. In fact, on emerging from beneath a thick clump of beautiful trees, it suddenly appeared before their eyes.

The explorers had arrived on the western shore of Lake Grant. The place was well worth looking at. This extent of water, of a circumference of nearly seven miles and an area of two hundred and fifty acres, reposed in a border of diversified trees. Toward the east, through a curtain of verdure, picturesquely raised in some places, sparkled a horizon of sea. The lake was curved at the north, which contrasted with the sharp outline of its lower part. Numerous aquatic birds frequented the shores of this little Ontario, in which the thousand isles of its American namesake were represented by a rock which emerged from its surface, some hundred feet from the southern shore. There lived in harmony several couples of kingfishers perched on a stone, grave, motionless, watching for fish, then darting down, they plunged in with a sharp cry, and reappeared with their prey in their beaks. On the shores and on the islets, strutted wild ducks, pelicans, water-hens, red-beaks, philedons, furnished with a tongue like a brush, and one or two specimens of the splendid menura, the tail of which expands gracefully like a lyre.

As to the water of the lake, it was sweet, limpid, rather dark, and from certain bubblings, and the concentric circles which crossed each other on the surface, it could not be doubted that it abounded in fish.

"This lake is really beautiful!" said Gideon Spilett. "We could live on its borders!"

"We will live there!" replied Harding.

The settlers, wishing to return to the Chimneys by the shortest way, descended toward the angle formed on the south by the junction of the lake's bank. It was not without difficulty that they broke a path through the thickets and brushwood which had never been put aside by the hand of man, and they thus went toward the shore, so as to arrive at the north of Prospect Heights. Two miles were cleared in this direction, and then, after they had passed the last curtain of trees, appeared the plateau, carpeted with thick turf, and beyond that the infinite sea.

To return to the Chimneys, it was enough to cross the plateau obliquely for the space of a mile, and then to descend to the elbow formed by the first detour of the Mercy. But the engineer desired to know how and where the overplus of the water from the lake escaped, and the exploration was prolonged under the trees for a mile and a half toward the north. It was most probable that an overfall existed somewhere, and doubtless through a cleft in the granite. This lake was only, in short, an immense center basin, which was filled by degrees by the creek, and its waters must necessarily pass to the sea by some fall. If it was so, the engineer thought that it might perhaps be possible to utilize this fall and borrow its power, actually lost without profit to any one. They continued then to follow the shores of Lake Grant by climbing the plateau; but, after having gone a mile in this direction, Cyrus Harding had not been able to discover the overfall, which, however, must exist somewhere.

It was then half-past four. In order to prepare for dinner it was necessary that the settlers should return to their dwelling. The little band retraced their steps, therefore, and by the left bank of the Mercy, Cyrus Harding and his companions arrived at the Chimneys.

The fire was lighted, and Neb and Pencroft, on whom the functions of cooks naturally devolved, to the one in his quality of Negro, to the other in that of sailor, quickly prepared some broiled agouti, to which they did great justice.

The repast at length terminated; at the moment when each one was about to give himself up to sleep, Cyrus Harding drew from his pocket little specimens of different sorts of minerals, and just said,

"My friends, this is iron mineral, this a pyrite, this is clay, this is lime, and this is coal. Nature gives us these things. It is our business to make a right use of them. To-morrow we will commence operations."

XIII

"Well, captain, where are we going to begin?" asked Pencroft next morning of the engineer.

"At the beginning," replied Cyrus Harding.

And in fact, the settlers were compelled to begin "at the very beginning." They did not possess even the tools necessary for making tools, and they were not even in the condition of nature, who, "having time, husbands her strength." They had no time, since they had to provide for the immediate wants of their existence, and though, profiting by acquired experience, they had nothing to invent, still they had everything to make; their iron and their steel were as yet only in the state of minerals, their earthenware in the state of clay, their linen and their clothes in the state of textile material.

It must be said, however, that the settlers were "men" in the complete and higher sense of the word. The engineer Harding could not have been seconded by more intelligent companions, nor with more devotion and zeal. He had tried them. He knew their abilities.

Gideon Spilett, a talented reporter, having learned everything so as to be able to speak of everything, would contribute largely with his head and hands to the colonization of the island. He would not draw back from any task: a determined sportsman, he would make a business of what till then had only been a pleasure to him.

Herbert, a gallant boy, already remarkably well informed in the natural sciences, would render greater service to the common cause.

Neb was devotion personified. Clever, intelligent, indefatigable, robust, with iron health, he knew a little about the work of the forge, and could not fail to be very useful in the colony.

As to Pencroft, he had sailed over every sea, a carpenter in the dock-yards in Brooklyn, assistant tailor in the vessels of the state, gardener, cultivator, during his holidays, etc., and like all seamen, fit for anything, he knew how to do everything.

It would have been difficult to unite five men, better fitted to struggle against fate, more certain to triumph over it.

"At the beginning," Cyrus Harding had said. Now this beginning of which the engineer spoke was the construction of an apparatus which would serve to transform the natural substances. The part which heat plays in these transformations is known. Now fuel, wood or coal, was ready for immediate use, an oven must be built to use it.

"What is this oven for?" asked Pencroft.

"To make the pottery which we have need of," replied Harding.

"And of what shall we make the oven?"

"With bricks."

"And the bricks?"

"With clay. Let us start, my friends. To save trouble, we will establish our manufactory at the place of production. Neb will bring provisions, and there will be no lack of fire to cook the food."

"No," replied the reporter; "but if there is a lack of food for want of instruments for the chase?"

"Ah, if we only had a knife!" cried the sailor.

"Well?" asked Cyrus Harding.

"Well! I would soon make a bow and arrows, and then there could be plenty of game in the larder!"

"Yes, a knife, a sharp blade—" said the engineer, as if he was speaking to himself.

At this moment his eyes fell upon Top, who was running about on the shore. Suddenly Harding's face became animated.

"Top, here," said he.

The dog came at his master's call. The latter took Top's head between his hands, and unfastening the collar which the animal wore around his neck, he broke it in two, saying,

"There are two knives, Pencroft!"

Two hurrahs from the sailor was the reply. Top's collar was made of a thin piece of tempered steel. They had only to sharpen it on a piece of sandstone, then to raise the edge on a finer stone. Now sandstone was abundant on the beach, and two hours after the stock of tools in the colony consisted of two sharp blades, which were easily fixed in solid handles.

The production of these their first tools was hailed as a triumph. It was indeed a valuable result of their labor, and a very opportune one. They set out.

Cyrus Harding proposed that they should return to the western shore of the lake, where the day before he had noticed the clayey ground of which he possessed a specimen. They therefore followed the bank of the Mercy, traversed Prospect Heights, and after a walk of five miles or more they reached a glade, situated two hundred feet from Lake Grant.

On the way Herbert had discovered a tree, the branches of which the Indians of South America employ for making their bows. It was the crejimba, of the palm family, which does not bear edible fruit. Long straight branches were cut, the leaves stripped off; it was shaped, stronger in the middle, more slender at the extremities, and nothing remained to be done but to find a plant fit to make the bow-string. This was the hibiscus heterophyllus, which furnishes fibers of such remarkable tenacity that they have been compared to the tendons of animals. Pencroft thus obtained bows of tolerable strength, for which he only wanted arrows. These were easily made with straight stiff branches, without knots, but the points with which they must be armed, that is to say, a substance to serve in lieu of iron, could not be met with so easily. But Pencroft said, that having done his part of the work, chance would do the rest.

The settlers arrived on the ground which had been discovered the day before. Being composed of the sort of clay which is used for making bricks and tiles, it was very useful for the work in question. There was no great difficulty in it. It was enough to scour the clay with sand, then to mold the bricks and bake them by the heat of a wood fire.

Generally bricks are formed in molds, but the engineer contented himself with making them by hand. All that day and the day following were employed in this work. The clay, soaked in water, was mixed by the feet and hands of the manipulators, and then divided into pieces of equal size. A practiced workman can make, without a machine, about ten thousand bricks in twelve hours; but in their two days' work the five brickmakers on Lincoln Island had not made more than three thousand, which were ranged near each other, until the time when their complete desiccation would permit them to be used in building the oven, that is to say, in three or four days.

It was on the 2nd of April that Harding had employed himself in fixing the orientation of the island, or, in other words, the precise spot where the sun rose. The day before he had noted exactly the hour when the sun disappeared beneath the horizon, making allowance for the refraction. This morning he noted, no less exactly, the hour at which it reappeared. Between this setting and rising twelve hours, twenty-four minutes passed. Then, six hours, twelve minutes after its rising, the sun on this day would exactly pass the meridian and the point of the sky which it occupied at this moment would be the north.

At the said hour, Cyrus marked this point, and putting in a line with the sun two trees which would serve him for marks, he thus obtained an invariable meridian for his ulterior operations.

The settlers employed the two days before the oven was built in collecting fuel. Branches were cut all round the glade, and they picked up all the fallen wood under the trees. They were also able to hunt with greater success, since Pencroft now possessed some dozen arrows armed with sharp points. It was Top who had furnished these points, by bringing in a porcupine, rather inferior eating, but of great value, thanks to the quills with which it bristled. These quills were fixed firmly at the ends of the arrows, the flight of which was made more certain by some cockatoos' feathers. The reporter and Herbert soon became very skillful archers. Game of all sorts in consequence abounded at the Chimneys, capybaras, pigeons, agouties, grouse, etc. The greater part of these animals were killed in the part of the forest on the left bank of the Mercy, to which they gave the name of Jacamar Wood, in remembrance of the bird which Pencroft and Herbert had pursued when on their first exploration.

This game was eaten fresh, but they preserved some capybara hams, by smoking them above a fire of green wood, after having perfumed them with sweet-smelling leaves. However, this food, although very strengthening, was always roast upon roast, and the party would have been delighted to hear some soup bubbling on the hearth, but they must wait till a pot could be made, and, consequently, till the oven was built.

During these excursions, which were not extended far from the brick-field, the hunters could discern the recent passage of animals of a large size, armed with powerful claws, but they could not recognize the species. Cyrus Harding advised them to be very careful, as the forest probably enclosed many dangerous beasts.

And he did right. Indeed, Gideon Spilett and Herbert one day saw an animal which resembled a jaguar. Happily the creature did not attack them, or they might not have escaped without a severe wound. As soon as he could get a regular weapon, that is to say, one of the guns which Pencroft begged for, Gideon Spilett resolved to make desperate war against the ferocious beasts, and exterminate them from the island.

The Chimneys during these few days was not made more comfortable, for the engineer hoped to discover, or build if necessary, a more convenient dwelling. They contented themselves with spreading moss and dry leaves on the sand of the passages, and on these primitive couches the tired workers slept soundly.

They also reckoned the days they had passed on Lincoln Island, and from that time kept a regular account. The 5th of April, which was Wednesday, was twelve days from the time when the wind threw the castaways on this shore.

On the 6th of April, at daybreak, the engineer and his companions were collected in the glade, at the place where they were going to perform the operation of baking the bricks. Naturally this had to be in the open air, and not in a kiln, or rather, the agglomeration of bricks made an enormous kiln, which would bake itself. The fuel, made of well-prepared fagots, was laid on the ground and surrounded with several rows of dried bricks, which soon formed an enormous cube, to the exterior of which they contrived air-holes. The work lasted all day, and it was not till the evening that they set fire to the fagots. No one slept that night, all watching carefully to keep up the fire.

The operation lasted forty-eight hours, and succeeded perfectly. It then became necessary to leave the smoking mass to cool, and during this time Neb and Pencroft, guided by Cyrus Harding, brought, on a hurdle made of interlaced branches, loads of carbonate of lime and common stones, which were very abundant, to the north of the lake. These stones, when decomposed by heat, made a very strong quicklime, greatly increased by slacking, at least as pure as if it had been produced by the calcination of chalk or marble. Mixed with sand the lime made excellent mortar.

The result of these different works was, that, on the 9th of April, the engineer had at his disposal a quantity of prepared lime and some thousands of bricks.

Without losing an instant, therefore, they began the construction of a kiln to bake the pottery, which was indispensable for their domestic use. They succeeded without much difficulty. Five days after, the kiln was supplied with coal, which the engineer had discovered lying open to the sky toward the mouth of the Red Creek, and the first smoke escaped from a chimney twenty feet high. The glade was transformed into a manufactory, and Pencroft was not far wrong in believing that from this kiln would issue all the products of modern industry.

In the meantime what the settlers first manufactured was a common pottery in which to cook their food. The chief material was clay, to which Harding added a little lime and quartz. This paste made regular "pipe-clay," with which they manufactured bowls, cups molded on stones of a proper size, great jars and pots to hold water, etc. The shape of these objects was clumsy and defective, but after they had been baked in a high temperature, the kitchen of the Chimneys was provided with a number of utensils, as precious to the settlers as the most beautifully enameled china. We must mention here that Pencroft, desirous to know if the clay thus prepared was worthy of its name of pipe-clay, made some large pipes, which he thought charming, but for which, alas! he had no tobacco, and that was a great privation to Pencroft. "But tobacco will come, like everything else!" he repeated, in a burst of absolute confidence.

This work lasted till the 15th of April, and the time was well employed. The settlers, having become potters, made nothing but pottery. When it suited Cyrus Harding to change them into smiths, they would become smiths. But the next day being Sunday, and also Easter Sunday, all agreed to sanctify the day by rest. These Americans were religious men, scrupulous observers of the precepts of the Bible, and their situation could not but develop sentiments of confidence toward the Author of all things.

On the evening of the 15th of April they returned to the Chimneys, carrying with them the pottery, the furnace being extinguished until they could put it to a new use. Their return was marked by a fortunate incident; the engineer discovered a substance which replaced tinder. It is known that a spongy, velvety flesh is procured from a certain mushroom of the genus polyporous. Properly prepared, it is extremely inflammable, especially when it has been previously saturated with gunpowder, or boiled in a solution of nitrate or chlorate of potash. But, till then, they had not found any of these polypores or even any of the morels which could replace them. On this day, the engineer, seeing a plant belonging to the wormwood genus, the principal species of which are absinthe, balm-mint, tarragon, etc., gathered several tufts, and, presenting them to the sailor, said,

"Here, Pencroft, this will please you."

Pencroft looked attentively at the plant, covered with long silky hair, the leaves being clothed with soft down.

"What's that, captain?" asked Pencroft. "Is it tobacco?"

"No," replied Harding, "it is wormwood; Chinese wormwood to the learned, but to us it will be tinder."

When the wormwood was properly dried it provided them with a very inflammable substance, especially afterward when the engineer had impregnated it with nitrate of potash, of which the island possessed several beds, and which is in truth saltpeter.

The colonists had a good supper that evening. Neb prepared some agouti soup, a smoked capybara ham, to which was added the boiled tubercules of the caladium macrorhizum, an herbaceous plant of the arum family. They had an excellent taste, and were very nutritious, being something similar to the substance which is sold in England under the name of "Portland sago"; they were also a good substitute for bread, which the settlers in Lincoln Island did not yet possess.

When supper was finished, before sleeping, Harding and his companions went to take the air on the beach. It was eight o'clock in the evening; the night was magnificent. The moon, which had been full five days before, had not yet risen, but the horizon was already silvered by those soft, pale shades which might be called the dawn of the moon. At the southern zenith glittered the circumpolar constellations, and above all the Southern

Cross, which some days before the engineer had greeted on the summit of Mount Franklin.

Cyrus Harding gazed for some time at this splendid constellation, which has at its summit and at its base two stars of the first magnitude, at its left arm a star of the second, and at its right arm a star of the third magnitude.

Then, after some minutes' thought,

"Herbert," he asked of the lad, "is not this the 15th of April?"

"Yes, captain," replied Herbert.

"Well, if I am not mistaken, to-morrow will be one of the four days in the year in which the real time is identical with average time; that is to say, my boy, that to-morrow, to within some seconds, the sun will pass the meridian just at midday by the clocks. If the weather is fine I think that I shall obtain the longitude of the island with an approximation of some degrees."

"Without instruments, without sextant?" asked Gideon Spilett.

"Yes," replied the engineer. "Also, since the night is clear, I will try, this very evening, to obtain our latitude by calculating the height of the Southern Cross, that is, from the southern pole above the horizon. You understand, my friends, that before undertaking the work of installation in earnest it is not enough to have found out that this land is an island; we must, as nearly as possible, know at what distance it is situated, either from the American continent or Australia, or from the principal archipelagoes of the Pacific."

"In fact," said the reporter, "instead of building a house it would be more important to build a boat, if by chance we are not more than a hundred miles from an inhabited coast."

"That is why," returned Harding, "I am going to try this evening to calculate the latitude of Lincoln Island, and to-morrow, at midday, I will try to calculate the longitude."

If the engineer had possessed a sextant, an apparatus with which the angular distance of objects can be measured with great precision, there would have been no difficulty in the operation. This evening by the height of the pole, the next day by the passing of the sun at the meridian, he would obtain the position of the island. But as they had not one he would have to supply the deficiency.

Harding then entered the Chimneys. By the light of the fire he cut two little flat rulers, which he joined together at one end so as to form a pair of compasses, whose legs could separate or come together. The fastening was fixed with a strong acacia thorn which was found in the wood pile. This instrument finished, the engineer returned to the beach, but as it was necessary to take the height of the pole from above a clear horizon, that is, a sea horizon, and as Claw Cape hid the southern horizon, he was obliged to look for a more suitable station. The best would evidently have been the shore exposed directly to the south; but the Mercy would have to be crossed, and that was a difficulty. Harding resolved, in consequence, to make his observation from Prospect Heights, taking into consideration its height above the level of the sea—a height which he intended to calculate next day by a simple process of elementary geometry.

The settlers, therefore, went to the plateau, ascending the left bank of the Mercy, and placed themselves on the edge which looked northwest and southeast, that is, above the curiously-shaped rocks which bordered the river.

This part of the plateau commanded the heights of the left bank, which sloped away to the extremity of Claw Cape, and to the southern side of the island. No obstacle intercepted their gaze, which swept the horizon in a semicircle from the cape to Reptile End. To the south the horizon, lighted by the first rays of the moon, was very clearly defined against the sky.

At this moment the Southern Cross presented itself to the observer in an inverted position, the star Alpha marking its base, which is nearer to the southern pole.

This constellation is not situated as near to the antarctic pole as the Polar Star is to the arctic pole. The star Alpha is about twenty-seven degrees from it, but Cyrus Harding knew this and made allowance for it in his calculation. He took care also to observe the moment when it passed the meridian below the pole, which would simplify the operation.

Cyrus Harding pointed one leg of the compasses to the horizon, the other to Alpha, and the space between the two legs gave him the angular distance which separated Alpha from the horizon. In order to fix the angle obtained, he fastened with thorns the two pieces of wood on a third placed transversely, so that their separation should be properly maintained.

That done, there was only the angle to calculate by bringing back the observation to the level of the sea, taking into consideration the depression of the horizon, which would necessitate measuring the height of the cliff. The value of this angle would give the height of Alpha, and consequently that of the pole above the horizon, that is to say, the latitude of the island, since the latitude of a point of the globe is always equal to the height of the pole above the horizon of this point.

The calculations were left for the next day, and at ten o'clock every one was sleeping soundly.

XIV

The next day, the 16th of April, and Easter Sunday, the settlers issued from the Chimneys at daybreak, and proceeded to wash their linen. The engineer intended to manufacture soap as soon as he could procure the necessary materials—soda or potash, fat or oil. The important question of renewing their wardrobe would be treated of in the proper time and place. At any rate their clothes would last at least six months longer, for they were strong, and could resist the wear of manual labor. But all would depend on the situation of the island with regard to inhabited land. This would be settled to-day if the weather permitted.

The sun rising above a clear horizon, announced a magnificent day, one of those beautiful autumn days which are like the last farewells of the warm season.

It was now necessary to complete the observations of the evening before by measuring the height of the cliff above the level of the sea.

"Shall you not need an instrument similar to the one which you used yesterday?" said Herbert to the engineer.

"No, my boy," replied the latter, "we are going to proceed differently, but in as precise a way."

Herbert, wishing to learn everything he could, followed the engineer to the beach. Pencroft, Neb, and the reporter remained behind and occupied themselves in different ways.

Cyrus Harding had provided himself with a straight stick, twelve feet long, which he had measured as exactly as possible by comparing it with his own height, which he knew to a hair. Herbert carried a plumb-line which Harding had given him, that is to say, a simple stone fastened to the end of a flexible fiber. Having reached a spot about twenty feet from the edge of the beach, and nearly five hundred feet from the cliff, which rose perpendicularly, Harding thrust the pole two feet into the sand, and wedging it up carefully, he managed, by means of the plumb-line, to erect it perpendicularly with the plane of the horizon.

That done, he retired the necessary distance, when, lying on the sand, his eye glanced at the same time at the top of the pole and the crest of the cliff. He carefully marked the place with a little stick.

Then addressing Herbert,

"Do you know the first principles of geometry?" he asked.

"Slightly, captain," replied Herbert, who did not wish to put himself forward.

"You remember what are the properties of two similar triangles?"

"Yes," replied Herbert; "their homologous sides are proportional."

"Well, my boy, I have just constructed two similar right-angled triangles; the first, the smallest, has for its sides the perpendicular pole, the distance which separates the little stick from the foot of the pole and my visual ray for hypothenuse; the second has for its sides the perpendicular cliff, the height of which we wish to measure, the distance which separates the little stick from the bottom of the cliff, and my visual ray also forms its hypothenuse, which proves to be prolongation of that of the first triangle."

"Ah, captain, I understand!" cried Herbert. "As the distance from the stick to the pole is to the distance from the stick to the base of the cliff, so is the height of the pole to the height of the cliff."

"Just so, Herbert," replied the engineer; "and when we have measured the two first distances, knowing the height of the pole, we shall only have a sum in proportion to do, which will give us the height of the cliff, and will save us the trouble of measuring it directly."

The two horizontal distances were found out by means of the pole, whose length above the sand was exactly ten feet.

The first distance was fifteen feet between the stick and the place where the pole was thrust into the sand.

The second distance between the stick and the bottom of the cliff was five hundred feet.

These measurements finished, Cyrus Harding and the lad returned to the Chimneys.

The engineer then took a flat stone which he had brought back from one of his previous excursions, a sort of slate, on which it was easy to trace figures with a sharp shell. He then proved the following proportions:

$$15:500::10:x$$
$$500 \times 10 = 5000$$
$$\frac{5000}{15} = 333.3$$

From which it was proved that the granite cliff measured 333 feet in height.

Cyrus Harding then took the instrument which he had made the evening before, the space between its two legs giving the angular distance between the star Alpha and the horizon. He measured, very exactly, the opening of this angle on a circumference which he divided into 360 equal parts. Now, this angle by adding to it the twenty-seven degrees which separated Alpha from the antarctic pole, and by reducing to the level of the sea the height of the cliff on which the observation had been made, was found to be fifty-three degrees. These fifty-three degrees being subtracted from ninety degrees—the distance from the pole to the equator—there remained thirty-seven degrees. Cyrus Harding concluded, therefore, that Lincoln Island was situated on the thirty-seventh degree of the southern latitude, or taking into consideration through the imperfection of the performance, an error of five degrees, that it must be situated between the thirty-fifth and the fortieth parallel.

There was only the longitude to be obtained, and the position of the island would be determined. The engineer hoped to attempt this the same day, at twelve o'clock, at which moment the sun would pass the meridian.

It was decided that Sunday should be spent in a walk, or rather an exploring expedition, to that side of the island between the north of the lake and Shark Gulf, and if there was time they would push their discoveries to the northern side of South Mandible Cape. They would breakfast on the downs, and not return till evening.

At half-past eight the little band was following the edge of the channel. On the other side, on Safety Islet, numerous birds were gravely strutting. They were divers, easily recognized by their cry, which much resembles the braying of a donkey. Pencroft only considered them in an eatable point of view, and learnt with some satisfaction that their flesh, though blackish, is not bad food.

Great amphibious creatures could also be seen crawling on the sand; seals, doubtless, who appeared to have chosen the islet for a place of refuge. It was impossible to think of those animals in an alimentary point of view, for their oily flesh is detestable; however, Cyrus Harding observed them attentively, and without making known his idea, he announced to his companions that very soon they would pay a visit to the islet. The beach was strewn with innumerable shells, some of which would have rejoiced the heart of a conchologist; there were, among others, the phasianella, the terebratual, etc. But what would be of more use, was the discovery, by Neb, at low tide, of a large oyster-bed among the rocks, nearly five miles from the Chimneys.

"Neb will not have lost his day," cried Pencroft, looking at the spacious oyster-bed.

"It is really a fortunate discovery," said the reporter, "and as it is said that each oyster produces yearly from fifty to sixty thousand eggs, we shall have an inexhaustible supply there."

"Only I believe that the oyster is not very nourishing," said Herbert.

"No," replied Harding. "The oyster contains very little nitrogen, and if a man lived exclusively on them, he would have to eat not less than fifteen to sixteen dozen a day."

"Capital!" replied Pencroft. "We might swallow dozens and dozens without exhausting the bed. Shall we take some for breakfast?"

And without waiting for a reply to this proposal, knowing that it would be approved of, the sailor and Neb detached a quantity of the molluscs. They put them in a sort of net of hibiscus fiber, which Neb had manufactured, and which already contained food; they then continued to climb the coast between the downs and the sea.

From time to time Harding consulted his watch, so as to be prepared in time for the solar observation, which had to be made exactly at midday.

All that part of the island was very barren as far as the point which closed Union Bay, and which had received the name of South Mandible Cape. Nothing could be seen there but sand and shells, mingled with debris of lava. A few sea-birds frequented this desolate coast, gulls, great albatrosses, as well as wild duck, for which Pencroft had a great fancy. He tried to knock some over with an arrow, but without result, for they seldom perched, and he could not hit them on the wing.

This led the sailor to repeat to the engineer,

"You see, captain, so long as we have not one or two fowling-pieces, we shall never get anything!"

"Doubtless, Pencroft," replied the reporter, "but it depends on you. Procure us some iron for the barrels, steel for the hammers, saltpeter, coal and sulphur for powder, mercury and nitric acid for the fulminate, and lead for the shot, and the captain will make us first-rate guns."

"Oh!" replied the engineer, "we might, no doubt, find all these substances on the island, but a gun is a delicate instrument, and needs very particular tools. However, we shall see later!"

"Why," cried Pencroft, "were we obliged to throw overboard all the weapons we had with us in the car, all our implements, even our pocket-knives?"

"But if we had not thrown them away, Pencroft, the balloon would have thrown us to the bottom of the sea!" said Herbert.

"What you say is true, my boy," replied the sailor.

Then passing to another idea,

"Think," said he, "how astounded Jonathan Forster and his companions must have been when, next morning, they found the place empty, and the machine flown away!"

"I am utterly indifferent about knowing what they may have thought," said the reporter.

"It was all my idea, that!" said Pencroft, with a satisfied air.

"A splendid idea, Pencroft!" replied Gideon Spilett, laughing, "and which has placed us where we are."

"I would rather be here than in the hands of the Southerners," cried the sailor, "especially since the captain has been kind enough to come and join us again."

"So would I, truly!" replied the reporter. "Besides, what do we want? Nothing."

"If that is not—everything!" replied Pencroft, laughing and shrugging his shoulders. "But, some day or other, we shall find means of going away!"

"Sooner, perhaps, than you imagine, my friends," remarked the engineer, "if Lincoln Island is but a medium distance from an inhabited island, or from a continent. We shall know in an hour. I have not a map of the Pacific, but my memory has preserved a very clear recollection of its southern part. The latitude which I obtained yesterday placed New Zealand to the west of Lincoln Island, and the coast of Chile to the east. But between these two countries, there is a distance of at least six thousand miles. It has, therefore, to be determined what point in this great space the island occupies, and this the longitude will give us presently, with a sufficient approximation, I hope."

"Is not the archipelago of the Pomoutous the nearest point to us in latitude?" asked Herbert.

"Yes," replied the engineer, "but the distance which separates us from it is more than twelve hundred miles."

"And that way?" asked Neb, who followed the conversation with extreme interest, pointing to the south.

"That way, nothing," replied Pencroft.

"Nothing, indeed," added the engineer.

"Well, Cyrus," asked the reporter, "if Lincoln Island is not more than two or three thousand miles from New Zealand or Chile?"

"Well," replied the engineer, "instead of building a house we will build a boat, and Master Pencroft shall be put in command—"

"Well then," cried the sailor, "I am quite ready to be captain—as soon as you can make a craft that's able to keep at sea!"

"We shall do it, if it is necessary," replied Cyrus Harding.

But while these men, who really hesitated at nothing, were talking, the hour approached at which the observation was to be made. What Cyrus Harding was to do to ascertain the passage of the sun at the meridian of the island, without an instrument of any sort, Herbert could not guess.

The observers were then about six miles from the Chimneys, not far from that part of the downs in which the engineer had been found after his enigmatical preservation. They halted at this place and prepared for breakfast, for it was half-past eleven. Herbert went for some fresh water from a stream which ran near, and brought it back in a jug, which Neb had provided.

During these preparations Harding arranged everything for his astronomical observation. He chose a clear place on the shore, which the ebbing tide had left perfectly level. This bed of fine sand was as smooth as ice, not a grain out of place. It was of little importance whether it was horizontal or not, and it did not matter much whether the stick six feet high, which was planted there, rose perpendicularly. On the contrary, the engineer inclined it toward the south, that is to say, in the direction of the coast opposite to the sun, for it must not be forgotten that the settlers in Lincoln Island, as the island was situated in the Southern Hemisphere, saw the radiant planet describe its diurnal arc above the northern, and not above the southern horizon.

Herbert now understood how the engineer was going to proceed to ascertain the culmination of the sun, that is to say its passing the meridian of the island or, in other words, determine due south. It was by means of the shadow cast on the sand by the stick, a way which, for want of an instrument, would give him a suitable approach to the result which he wished to obtain.

In fact, the moment when this shadow would reach its minimum of length would be exactly twelve o'clock, and it would be enough to watch the extremity of the shadow, so as to ascertain the instant when, after having successively diminished, it began to lengthen. By inclining his stick to the side opposite to the sun, Cyrus Harding made the shadow longer, and consequently its modifications would be more easily ascertained. In fact, the longer the needle of a dial is, the more easily can the movement of its point be followed. The shadow of the stick was nothing but the needle of a dial. The moment had come, and Cyrus Harding knelt on the sand, and with little wooden pegs, which he stuck into the sand, he began to mark the successive diminutions of the stick's shadow. His companions, bending over him, watched the operation with extreme interest. The reporter held his chronometer in his hand, ready to tell the hour which it marked when the shadow would be at its shortest. Moreover, as Cyrus Harding was working on the 16th of April, the day on which the true and the average time are identical, the hour given by Gideon Spilett would be the true hour then at Washington, which would simplify the calculation. Meanwhile as the sun slowly advanced, the shadow slowly diminished, and when it appeared to Cyrus Harding that it was beginning to increase, he asked, "What o'clock is it?"

"One minute past five," replied Gideon Spilett directly. They had now only to calculate the operation. Nothing could be easier. It could be seen that there existed, in around numbers, a difference of five hours between the meridian of Washington and that of Lincoln Island, that is to say, it was midday in Lincoln Island when it was already five o'clock in the evening in Washington. Now the sun, in its apparent movement around the earth, traverses one degree in four minutes, or fifteen degrees an hour. Fifteen degrees multiplied by five hours give seventy-five degrees.

Then, since Washington is 77° 3′11″ as much as to say seventy-seven degrees counted from the meridian of Greenwich—which the Americans take for their starting-point for longitudes concurrently with the English—it followed that the island must be situated seventy-seven and seventy-five degrees west of the meridian of Greenwich, that is to say, on the hundred and fifty-second degree of west longitude.

Cyrus Harding announced this result to his companions, and taking into consideration errors of observation, as he had done for the latitude, he believed he could positively affirm that the position of Lincoln Island was between the thirty-fifth and the thirty-seventh parallel, and between the hundred and fiftieth and the hundred and fifty-fifth meridian to the west of the meridian of Greenwich.

The possible fault which he attributed to errors in the observation was, it may be seen, of five degrees on both sides, which, at sixty miles to a degree, would give an error of three hundred miles in latitude and longitude for the exact position.

But this error would not influence the determination which it was necessary to take. It was very evident that Lincoln Island was at such a distance from every country or island that it would be too hazardous to attempt to reach one in a frail boat.

In fact, this calculation placed it at least twelve hundred miles from Tahiti and the islands of the archipelago of the Pomoutous, more than eighteen hundred miles from New Zealand, and more than four thousand five hundred miles from the American coast!

And when Cyrus Harding consulted his memory, he could not remember in any way that such an island occupied, in that part of the Pacific, the situation assigned to Lincoln Island.

XV

The next day, the 17th of April, the sailor's first words were addressed to Gideon Spilett.

"Well, sir," he asked, "what shall we do to-day?"

"What the captain pleases," replied the reporter.

Till then the engineer's companions had been brickmakers and potters, now they were to become metallurgists.

The day before, after breakfast, they had explored as far as the point of Mandible Cape, seven miles distant from the Chimneys. There, the long series of downs ended, and the soil had a volcanic appearance. There were no longer high cliffs as at Prospect Heights, but a strange and capricious border which surrounded the narrow gulf between the two capes, formed of mineral matter, thrown up by the volcano. Arrived at this point the settlers retraced their steps, and at nightfall entered the Chimneys; but they did not sleep before the question of knowing whether they could think of leaving Lincoln Island or not was definitely settled.

The twelve hundred miles which separated the island from the Pomoutous Island was a considerable distance. A boat could not cross it, especially at the approach of the bad season. Pencroft had expressly declared this. Now, to construct a simple boat even with the necessary tools, was a difficult work, and the colonists not having tools they must begin by making hammers, axes, adzes, saws, augers, planes, etc., which would take some time. It was decided, therefore, that they would winter at Lincoln Island, and that they would look for a more comfortable dwelling than the Chimneys, in which to pass the winter months.

Before anything else could be done it was necessary to make the iron ore, of which the engineer had observed some traces in the northwest part of the island, fit for use by converting it either into iron or into steel.

Metals are not generally found in the ground in a pure state. For the most part they are combined with oxygen or sulphur. Such was the case with the two specimens which Cyrus Harding had brought back, one of magnetic iron, not carbonated, the other a pyrite, also called sulphuret of iron. It was, therefore the first, the oxide of iron, which they must reduce with coal, that is to say, get rid of the oxygen, to obtain it in a pure state. This reduction is made by subjecting the ore with coal to a high temperature, either by the rapid and easy Catalan method, which has the advantage of transforming the ore into iron in a single operation, or by the blast furnace, which first smelts the ore, then changes it into iron, by carrying away the three to four per cent. of coal, which is combined with it.

Now Cyrus Harding wanted iron, and he wished to obtain it as soon as possible. The ore which he had picked up was in itself very pure and rich. It was the oxydulous iron, which is found in confused masses of a deep gray color; it gives a black dust, crystallized in the form of the regular octahedron. Native lodestones consist of this ore, and iron of the first quality is made in Europe from that with which Sweden and Norway are so abundantly supplied. Not far from this vein was the vein of coal already made use of by the settlers. The ingredients for the manufacture being close together would greatly facilitate the treatment of the ore. This is the cause of the wealth of the mines in Great Britain, where the coal aids the manufacture of the metal extracted from the same soil at the same time as itself.

"Then, captain," said Pencroft, "we are going to work iron ore?"

"Yes, my friend," replied the engineer, "and for that—something which will please you—we must begin by having a seal hunt on the islet."

"A seal hunt!" cried the sailor, turning toward Gideon Spilett. "Are seals needed to make iron?"

"Since Cyrus has said so!" replied the reporter.

But the engineer had already left the Chimneys, and Pencroft prepared for the seal hunt, without having received any other explanation.

Cyrus Harding, Herbert, Gideon Spilett, Neb, and the sailor were soon collected on the shore, at a place where the channel left a ford passable at low tide. The hunters could therefore traverse it without getting wet higher than the knee.

Harding then put his foot on the islet for the first, and his companions for the second time.

On their landing some hundreds of penguins looked fearlessly at them. The hunters, armed with sticks, could have killed them easily, but they were not guilty of such useless massacre, as it was important not to frighten the seals, who were lying on the sand several cable lengths off. They also respected certain innocent-looking birds, whose wings were reduced to the state of stumps, spread out like fins, ornamented with feathers of a scaly appearance. The settlers, therefore, prudently advanced toward the north point, walking over ground riddled with little holes, which formed nests for the sea-birds. Toward the extremity of the islet appeared great black heads floating just above the water, having exactly the appearance of rocks in motion.

These were the seals which were to be captured. It was necessary, however, first to allow them to land, for with their close, short hair, and their fusiform conformation, being excellent swimmers, it is difficult to catch them in the sea, while on land their short, webbed feet prevent their having more than a slow, waddling movement.

Pencroft knew the habits of these creatures, and he advised waiting till they were stretched on the sand, when the sun, before long, would send them to sleep. They must then manage to cut off their retreat and knock them on the head.

The hunters, having concealed themselves behind the rocks, waited silently.

An hour passed before the seals came to play on the sand. They could count half a dozen. Pencroft and Herbert then went round the point of the islet, so as to take them in the rear, and cut off their retreat. During this time Cyrus Harding, Spilett, and Neb, crawling behind the rocks, glided toward the future scene of combat.

All at once the tall figure of the sailor appeared. Pencroft shouted. The engineer and his two companions threw themselves between the sea and the seals. Two of the animals soon lay dead on the sand, but the rest regained the sea in safety.

"Here are the seals required, captain!" said the sailor, advancing toward the engineer.

"Capital," replied Harding. "We will make bellows of them!"

"Bellows!" cried Pencroft. "Well! these are lucky seals!"

It was, in fact, a blowing-machine, necessary for the treatment of the ore that the engineer wished to manufacture with the skins of the amphibious creatures. They were of a medium size, for their length did not exceed six feet. They resembled a dog about the head.

As it was useless to burden themselves with the weight of both the animals, Neb and Pencroft resolved to skin them on the spot, while Cyrus Harding and the reporter continued to explore the islet.

The sailor and the Negro cleverly performed the operation, and three hours afterward Cyrus Harding had at his disposal two seals' skins, which he intended to use in this state, without subjecting them to any tanning process.

The settlers waited till the tide was again low, and crossing the channel they entered the Chimneys.

The skins had then to be stretched on a frame of wood and sewn by means of fibers so as to preserve the air without allowing too much to escape. Cyrus Harding had nothing but the two steel blades from Top's collar, and yet he was so clever, and his companions aided him with so much intelligence, that three days afterward the little colony's stock of tools was augmented by a blowing-machine, destined to inject the air into the midst of the ore when it should be subjected to heat—an indispensable condition to the success of the operation.

On the morning of the 20th of April began the "metallic period," as the reporter called it in his notes. The engineer had decided, as has been said, to operate near the veins both of coal and ore. Now, according to his observations, these veins were situated at the foot of the northeast spurs of

Mount Franklin, that is to say, a distance of six miles from their home. It was impossible, therefore, to return every day to the Chimneys, and it was agreed that the little colony should camp under a hut of branches, so that the important operation could be followed night and day.

This settled, they set out in the morning. Neb and Pencroft dragged the bellows on a hurdle; also a quantity of vegetables and animals, which they besides could renew on the way.

The road led through Jacamar Wood, which they traversed obliquely from southeast to northwest, and in the thickest part. It was necessary to beat a path, which would in the future form the most direct road to Prospect Heights and Mount Franklin. The trees, belonging to the species already discovered, were magnificent. Herbert found some new ones, among others some which Pencroft called "sham leeks"; for, in spite of their size, they were of the same liliaceous family as the onion, chive, shallot, or asparagus. These trees produce ligneous roots which, when cooked, are excellent; from them, by fermentation, a very agreeable liquor is made. They therefore made a good store of the roots.

The journey through the wood was long; it lasted the whole day, and so allowed plenty of time for examining the flora and fauna. Top, who took special charge of the fauna, ran through the grass and brushwood, putting up all sorts of game. Herbert and Gideon Spilett killed two kangaroos with bows and arrows, and also an animal which strongly resembled both a hedgehog and an ant-eater. It was like the first because it rolled itself into a ball, and bristled with spines, and the second because it had sharp claws, a long slender snout which terminated in a bird's beak, and an extendible tongue, covered with little thorns which served to hold the insects.

"And when it is in the pot," asked Pencroft naturally, "what will it be like?"

"An excellent piece of beef," replied Herbert.

"We will not ask more from it," replied the sailor.

During this excursion they saw several wild boars, which however, did not offer to attack the little band, and it appeared as if they would not meet with any dangerous beasts; when, in a thick part of the wood, the reporter thought he saw, some paces from him, among the lower branches of a tree, an animal which he took for a bear, and which he very tranquilly began to draw. Happily for Gideon Spilett, the animal in question did not belong to the redoubtable family of the plantigrades. It was only a koala, better known under the name of the sloth, being about the size of a large dog, and having stiff hair of a dirty color, the paws armed with strong claws, which enabled it to climb trees and feed on the leaves. Having identified the animal, which they did not disturb, Gideon Spilett erased "bear" from the title of his sketch, putting koala in its place, and the journey was resumed.

At five o'clock in the evening, Cyrus Harding gave the signal to halt. They were now outside the forest, at the beginning of the powerful spurs which supported Mount Franklin toward the west. At a distance of some hundred feet flowed the Red Creek, and consequently plenty of fresh water was within their reach.

The camp was soon organized. In less than an hour, on the edge of the forest, among the trees, a hut of branches interlaced with creepers, and pasted over with clay, offered a tolerable shelter. Their geological researches were put off till the next day. Supper was prepared, a good fire blazed before the hut, the roast turned, and at eight o'clock, while one of the settlers watched to keep up the fire, in case any wild beasts should prowl in the neighborhood, the others slept soundly.

The next day, the 21st of April, Cyrus Harding accompanied by Herbert, went to look for the soil of ancient formation, on which he had already discovered a specimen of ore. They found the vein above ground, near the source of the creek, at the foot of one of the northeastern spurs. This ore, very rich in iron, enclosed in its fusible veinstone, was perfectly suited to the mode of reduction which the engineer intended to employ; that is, the Catalan method, but simplified, as it is used in Corsica. In fact, the Catalan method, properly so called, requires the construction of kilns and crucibles, in which the ore and the coal, placed in alternate layers, are transformed and reduced. But Cyrus Harding intended to economize these constructions, and wished simply to form, with the ore and the coal, a cubic mass, to the center of which he would direct the wind from his bellows. Doubtless, it was the proceeding employed by Tubalcain, and the first metallurgists of the inhabited world. Now that which had succeeded with the grandson of Adam, and which still yielded good results in countries rich in ore and fuel, could not but succeed with the settlers in Lincoln Island.

The coal, as well as the ore, was collected without trouble on the surface of the ground. They first broke the ore into little pieces, and cleansed them with the hand from the impurities which soiled their surface. Then coal and ore were arranged in heaps and in successive layers, as the charcoal-burner does with the wood which he wishes to carbonize. In this way, under the influence of the air projected by the blowing-machine, the coal would be transformed into carbonic acid, then into oxide of carbon, its use being to reduce the oxide of iron, that is to say, to rid it of the oxygen.

Thus the engineer proceeded. The bellows of sealskin, furnished at its extremity with a nozzle of clay, which had been previously fabricated in the pottery kiln, was established near the heap of ore. Using the mechanism which consisted of a frame, cords of fiber and counterpoise, he threw into the mass an abundance of air, which by raising the temperature also concurred with the chemical transformation to produce in time pure iron.

The operation was difficult. All the patience, all the ingenuity of the settlers was needed; but at last it succeeded, and the result was a lump of iron, reduced to a spongy state, which it was necessary to shingle and fagot, that is to say, to forge so as to expel from it the liquefied veinstone. These amateur smiths had, of course, no hammer; but they were in no worse a situation than the first metallurgist, and therefore did what, no doubt, he had to do.

A handle was fixed to the first lump, and was used as a hammer to forge the second on a granite anvil, and thus they obtained a coarse but useful metal. At length, after many trials and much fatigue, on the 25th of April several bars of iron were forged, and transformed into tools, crowbars, pincers, pickaxes, spades, etc., which Pencroft and Neb declared to be real jewels.

But the metal was not yet in its most serviceable state, that is, of steel. Now steel is a combination of iron and coal, which is extracted, either from the liquid ore, by taking from it the excess of coal, or from the iron by adding to it the coal which was wanting. The first, obtained by the decarburation of the metal, gives natural or puddled steel; the second, produced by the carburation of the iron, gives steel of cementation.

It was the last which Cyrus Harding intended to forge, as he possessed iron in a pure state. He succeeded by heating the metal with powdered coal in a crucible which had previously been manufactured from clay suitable for the purpose.

He then worked this steel, which is malleable both when hot or cold, with the hammer. Neb and Pencroft, cleverly directed, made hatchets, which, heated red-hot, and plunged suddenly into cold water, acquired an excellent temper.

Other instruments, of course roughly fashioned, were also manufactured; blades for planes, axes, hatchets, pieces of steel to be transformed into saws, chisels; then iron for spades, pickaxes, hammers, nails, etc. At last, on the 5th of May, the metallic period ended, the smiths returned to the Chimneys, and new work would soon authorize them to take a fresh title.

XVI

It was the 6th of May, a day which corresponds to the 6th of November in the countries of the Northern Hemisphere. The sky had been obscured for some days, and it was of importance to make preparations for the winter. However, the temperature was not as yet much lower, and a centigrade thermometer, transported to Lincoln Island, would still have marked an average of ten to twelve degrees above zero. This was not surprising, since Lincoln Island, probably situated between the thirty-fifth and fortieth parallel, would be subject, in the Southern Hemisphere, to the same climate as Sicily or Greece in the Northern Hemisphere. But as Greece and Sicily have severe cold, producing snow and ice, so doubtless would Lincoln Island in the severest part of the winter, and it was advisable to provide against it.

In any case if cold did not yet threaten them, the rainy season would begin, and on this lonely island, exposed to all the fury of the elements, in mid-ocean, bad weather would be frequent, and probably terrible. The question of a more comfortable dwelling than the Chimneys must therefore be seriously considered and promptly resolved on.

Pencroft, naturally, had some predilection for the retreat which he had discovered, but he well understood that another must be found. The Chimneys had been already visited by the sea, under circumstances which are known, and it would not do to be exposed again to a similar accident.

"Besides," added Cyrus Harding, who this day was talking of these things with his companions, "we have some precautions to take."

"Why? The island is not inhabited," said the reporter.

"That is probable," replied the engineer, "although we have not yet explored the interior; but if no human beings are found, I fear that dangerous animals may abound. It is necessary to guard against a possible attack, so that we shall not be obliged to watch every night, or to keep up a fire. And then, my friends, we must foresee everything. We are here in a part of the Pacific often frequented by Malay pirates—"

"What!" said Herbert, "at such a distance from land?"

"Yes, my boy," replied the engineer. "These pirates are bold sailors as well as formidable enemies, and we must take measures accordingly."

"Well," replied Pencroft, "we will fortify ourselves against savages with two legs as well as against savages with four. But, captain, will it not be best to explore every part of the island before undertaking anything else?"

"That would be best," added Gideon Spilett.

"Who knows if we might not find on the opposite side one of the caverns which we have searched for in vain here?"

"That is true," replied the engineer, "but you forget, my friends, that it will be necessary to establish ourselves in the neighborhood of a water-course, and that, from the summit of Mount Franklin, we could not see toward the west, either stream or river. Here, on the contrary, we are placed between the Mercy and Lake Grant, an advantage which must not be neglected. And, besides, this side, looking toward the east, is not exposed as the other is to the trade-winds, which in this hemisphere blow from the northwest."

"Then, captain," replied the sailor, "let us build a house on the edge of the lake. Neither bricks nor tools are wanting now. After having been brickmakers, potters, smelters, and smiths, we shall surely know how to be masons!"

"Yes, my friend; but before coming to any decision we must consider the matter thoroughly. A natural dwelling would spare us much work, and would be a surer retreat, for it would be as well defended against enemies from the interior as those from outside."

"That is true, Cyrus," replied the reporter, "but we have already examined all that mass of granite, and there is not a hole, not a cranny!"

"No, not one!" added Pencroft. "Ah, if we were able to dig out a dwelling in that cliff, at a good height, so as to be out of the reach of harm, that would be capital! I can see that on the front which looks seaward, five or six rooms—"

"With windows to light them!" said Herbert, laughing.

"And a staircase to climb up to them!" added Neb.

"You are laughing," cried the sailor, "and why? What is there impossible in what I propose? Haven't we got pickaxes and spades? Won't Captain

Harding be able to make powder to blow up the mine? Isn't it true, captain, that you will make powder the very day we want it?"

Cyrus Harding listened to the enthusiastic Pencroft developing his fanciful projects. To attack this mass of granite, even by a mine, was Herculean work, and it was really vexing that nature could not help them at their need. But the engineer did not reply to the sailor except by proposing to examine the cliff more attentively, from the mouth of the river to the angle which terminated it on the north.

They went out, therefore, and the exploration was made with extreme care, over an extent of nearly two miles. But in no place in the bare, straight cliff, could any cavity be found. The nests of the rock pigeons which fluttered at its summit were only, in reality, holes bored at the very top, and on the irregular edge of the granite.

It was a provoking circumstance, and as to attacking this cliff, either with pickaxe or with powder, so as to effect a sufficient excavation, it was not to be thought of. It so happened that, on all this part of the shore, Pencroft had discovered the only habitable shelter, that is to say, the Chimneys, which now had to be abandoned.

The exploration ended, the colonists found themselves at the north angle of the cliff, where it terminated in long slopes which died away on the shore. From this place, to its extreme limit in the west, it only formed a sort of declivity, a thick mass of stones, earth, and sand, bound together by plants, bushes, and grass inclined at an angle of only forty-five degrees. Clumps of trees grew on these slopes, which were also carpeted with thick grass. But the vegetation did not extend far, and a long, sandy plain, which began at the foot of these slopes, reached to the beach.

Cyrus Harding thought, not without reason, that the overplus of the lake must overflow on this side. The excess of water furnished by the Red Creek must also escape by some channel or other. Now the engineer had not yet found this channel on any part of the shore already explored, that is to say, from the mouth of the stream on the west of Prospect Heights.

The engineer now proposed to his companions to climb the slope, and to return to the Chimneys by the heights, while exploring the northern and eastern shores of the lake. The proposal was accepted, and in a few minutes Herbert and Neb were on the upper plateau. Cyrus Harding, Gideon Spilett, and Pencroft followed with more sedate steps.

The beautiful sheet of water glittered through the trees under the rays of the sun. In this direction the country was charming. The eye feasted on the groups of trees. Some old trunks, bent with age, showed black against the verdant grass which covered the ground. Crowds of brilliant cockatoos screamed among the branches, moving prisms, hopping from one bough to another.

The settlers instead of going directly to the north bank of the lake, made a circuit around the edge of the plateau, so as to join the mouth of the creek on its left bank. It was a detour of more than a mile and a half. Walking was easy, for the trees widely spread, left a considerable space between them. The fertile zone evidently stopped at this point, and vegetation would be less vigorous in the part between the course of the creek and the Mercy.

Cyrus Harding and his companions walked over this new ground with great care. Bows, arrows, and sticks with sharp iron points were their only weapons. However, no wild beast showed itself, and it was probable that these animals frequented rather the thick forests in the south; but the settlers had the disagreeable surprise of seeing Top stop before a snake of great size, measuring from fourteen to fifteen feet in length. Neb killed it by a blow from his stick. Cyrus Harding examined the reptile, and declared it not venomous, for it belonged to that species of diamond serpents which the natives of New South Wales rear. But it was possible that others existed whose bite was mortal such as the deaf vipers with forked tails, which rise up under the feet, or those winged snakes, furnished with two ears, which enable them to proceed with great rapidity. Top, the first moment of surprise over, began a reptile chase with such eagerness, that they feared for his safety. His master called him back directly.

The mouth of the Red Creek, at the place where it entered into the lake, was soon reached. The explorers recognized on the opposite shore the point which they had visited on their descent from Mount Franklin. Cyrus Harding ascertained that the flow of water into it from the creek was considerable. Nature must therefore have provided some place for the escape of the overplus. This doubtless formed a fall, which, if it could be discovered, would be of great use.

The colonists, walking apart, but not straying far from each other, began to skirt the edge of the lake, which was very steep. The water appeared to be full of fish, and Pencroft resolved to make some fishing-rods, so as to try and catch some.

The northeast point was first to be doubled. It might have been supposed that the discharge of water was at this place, for the extremity of the lake was almost on a level with the edge of the plateau. But no signs of this were discovered, and the colonists continued to explore the bank, which, after a slight bend, descended parallel to the shore.

On this side the banks were less woody, but clumps of trees, here and there, added to the picturesqueness of the country. Lake Grant was viewed from thence in all its extent, and no breath disturbed the surface of its waters. Top, in beating the bushes, put up flocks of birds of different kinds, which Gideon Spilett and Herbert saluted with arrows. One was hit by the lad, and fell into some marshy grass. Top rushed forward, and brought a beautiful swimming bird, of a slate color, short beak, very developed frontal plate, and wings edged with white. It was a "coot," the size of a large partridge, belonging to the group of macrodactyls which form the transition between the order of wading birds and that of palmipeds. Sorry game, in truth, and its flavor is far from pleasant. But Top was not so particular in these things as his masters, and it was agreed that the coot should be for his supper.

The settlers were now following the eastern bank of the lake, and they would not be long in reaching the part which they already knew. The engineer was much surprised at not seeing any indication of the discharge of water. The reporter and the sailor talked with him, and he could not conceal his astonishment.

At this moment Top, who had been very quiet till then, gave signs of agitation. The intelligent animal went backward and forward on the shore, stopped suddenly, and looked at the water, one paw raised, as if he was pointing at some invisible game; then he barked furiously, and was suddenly silent.

Neither Cyrus Harding nor his companions had at first paid any attention to Top's behavior; but the dog's barking soon became so frequent that the engineer noticed it.

"What is there, Top?" he asked.

The dog bounded toward his master, seeming to be very uneasy, and then rushed again toward the bank. Then, all at once, he plunged into the lake.

"Here, Top!" cried Cyrus Harding, who did not like his dog to venture into the treacherous water.

"What's happening down there?" asked Pencroft, examining the surface of the lake.

"Top smells some amphibious creature," replied Herbert.

"An alligator, perhaps," said the reporter.

"I do not think so," replied Harding. "Alligators are only met with in regions less elevated in latitude."

Meanwhile Top had returned at his master's call, and had regained the shore: but he could not stay quiet; he plunged in among the tall grass, and guided by instinct, he appeared to follow some invisible being which was slipping along under the surface of the water. However the water was calm; not a ripple disturbed its surface. Several times the settlers stopped on the bank, and observed it attentively. Nothing appeared. There was some mystery there.

The engineer was puzzled.

"Let us pursue this exploration to the end," said he.

Half an hour after they had all arrived at the southeast angle of the lake, on Prospect Heights. At this point the examination of the banks of the lake was considered finished, and yet the engineer had not been able to discover how and where the waters were discharged. "There is no doubt this overflow exists," he repeated, and since it is not visible it must go through the granite cliff at the west!"

"But what importance do you attach to knowing that, my dear Cyrus?" asked Gideon Spilett.

"Considerable importance," replied the engineer; "for if it flows through the cliff there is probably some cavity, which it would be easy to render habitable after turning away the water."

"But is it not possible, captain, that the water flows away at the bottom of the lake," said Herbert, "and that it reaches the sea by some subterranean passage?"

"That might be," replied the engineer, "and should it be so we shall be obliged to build our house ourselves, since nature has not done it for us."

The colonists were about to begin to traverse the plateau to return to the Chimneys, when Top gave new signs of agitation. He barked with fury, and before his master could restrain him, he had plunged a second time into the lake.

All ran toward the bank. The dog was already more than twenty feet off, and Cyrus was calling him back, when an enormous head emerged from the water, which did not appear to be deep in that place.

Herbert recognized directly the species of amphibian to which the tapering head, with large eyes, and adorned with long silky mustaches, belonged.

"A lamantin!" he cried.

It was not a lamantin, but one of that species of the order of cetaceans, which bear the name of the "dugong," for its nostrils were open at the upper part of its snout. The enormous animal rushed on the dog, who tried to escape by returning toward the shore. His master could do nothing to save him, and before Gideon Spilett or Herbert thought of bending their bows, Top, seized by the dugong, had disappeared beneath the water.

Neb, his iron-tipped spear in his hand, wished to go to Top's help, and attack the dangerous animal in its own element.

"No, Neb," said the engineer, restraining his courageous servant.

Meanwhile, a struggle was going on beneath the water, an inexplicable struggle, for in his situation Top could not possibly resist; and judging by the bubbling of the surface it must be also a terrible struggle, and could not but terminate in the death of the dog! But suddenly, in the middle of a foaming circle, Top reappeared. Thrown in the air by some unknown power, he rose ten feet above the surface of the lake, fell again into the midst of the agitated waters, and then soon gained the shore, without any severe wounds, miraculously saved.

Cyrus Harding and his companions could not understand it. What was not less inexplicable was that the struggle still appeared to be going on. Doubtless, the dugong, attacked by some powerful animal, after having released the dog, was fighting on its own account. But it did not last long. The water became red with blood, and the body of the dugong, emerging from the sheet of scarlet which spread around, soon stranded on a little beach at the south angle of the lake. The colonists ran toward it. The dugong was dead. It was an enormous animal, fifteen or sixteen feet long, and must have weighed from three to four thousand pounds. At its neck was a wound, which appeared to have been produced by a sharp blade.

What could the amphibious creature have been, who, by this terrible blow had destroyed the formidable dugong? No one could tell, and much interested in this incident, Harding and his companions returned to the Chimneys.

XVII

The next day, the 7th of May, Harding and Gideon Spilett, leaving Neb to prepare breakfast, climbed Prospect Heights, while Herbert and Pencroft ascended by the river, to renew their store of wood.

The engineer and the reporter soon reached the little beach on which the dugong had been stranded. Already flocks of birds had attacked the mass of flesh, and had to be driven away with stones, for Cyrus wished to keep the fat for the use of the colony. As to the animal's flesh it would furnish excellent food, for in the islands of the Malay Archipelago and elsewhere, it is especially reserved for the table of the native princes. But that was Neb's affair.

At this moment Cyrus Harding had other thoughts. He was much interested in the incident of the day before. He wished to penetrate the mystery of that submarine combat, and to ascertain what monster could have given the dugong so strange a wound. He remained at the edge of the lake, looking, observing; but nothing appeared under the tranquil waters, which sparkled in the first rays of the rising sun.

At the beach, on which lay the body of the dugong, the water was tolerably shallow, but from this point the bottom of the lake sloped gradually, and it was probable that the depth was considerable in the center. The lake might be considered as a large center basin, which was filled by the water from the Red Creek.

"Well, Cyrus," said the reporter, "there seems to be nothing suspicious in this water."

"No, my dear Spilett," replied the engineer, "and I really do not know how to account for the incident of yesterday."

"I acknowledge," returned Spilett, "that the wound given this creature is, at least, very strange, and I cannot explain either how Top was so vigorously cast up out of the water. One could have thought that a powerful arm hurled him up, and that the same arm with a dagger killed the dugong!"

"Yes," replied the engineer, who had become thoughtful; "there is something there that I cannot understand. But do you better understand either, my dear Spilett, in what way I was saved myself—how I was drawn from the waves, and carried to the downs? No! Is it not true? Now, I feel sure that there is some mystery there, which, doubtless, we shall discover some day. Let us observe, but do not dwell on these singular incidents before our companions. Let us keep our remarks to ourselves, and continue our work."

It will be remembered that the engineer had not as yet been able to discover the place where the surplus water escaped, but he knew it must exist somewhere. He was much surprised to see a strong current at this place. By throwing in some bits of wood he found that it set toward the southern angle. He followed the current, and arrived at the south point of the lake.

There was there a sort of depression in the water, as if it was suddenly lost in some fissure in the ground.

Harding listened; placing his ear to the level of the lake, he very distinctly heard the noise of a subterranean fall.

"There," said he, rising, "is the discharge of the water; there, doubtless, by a passage in the granite cliff, it joins the sea, through cavities which we can use to our profit. Well, I can find it!"

The engineer cut a long branch, stripped it of its leaves, and plunging it into the angle between the two banks, he found that there was a large hole one foot only beneath the surface of the water. This hole was the opening so long looked for in vain, and the force of the current was such that the branch was torn from the engineer's hands and disappeared.

"There is no doubt about it now," repeated Harding. "There is the outlet, and I will lay it open to view!"

"How?" asked Gideon Spilett.

"By lowering the level of the water of the lake three feet."

"And how will you lower the level?"

"By opening another outlet larger than this."

"At what place, Cyrus?"

"At the part of the bank nearest the coast."

"But it is a mass of granite!" observed Spilett.

"Well," replied Cyrus Harding, "I will blow up the granite, and the water escaping, will subside, so as to lay bare this opening—"

"And make a waterfall, by falling on to the beach," added the reporter.

"A fall that we shall make use of!" replied Cyrus. "Come, come!"

The engineer hurried away his companion, whose confidence in Harding was such that he did not doubt the enterprise would succeed. And yet, how was this granite wall to be opened without powder, and with imperfect instruments? Was not this work upon which the engineer was so bent above their strength?

When Harding and the reporter entered the Chimneys, they found Herbert and Pencroft unloading their raft of wood.

"The woodmen have just finished, captain," said the sailor, laughing, "and when you want masons—"

"Masons—no, but chemists," replied the engineer.

"Yes," added the reporter, "we are going to blow up the island—"

"Blow up the island?" cried Pencroft.

"Part of it, at least," replied Spilett.

"Listen to me, my friends," said the engineer. And he made known to them the result of his observations.

According to him, a cavity, more or less considerable, must exist in the mass of granite which supported Prospect Heights, and he intended to penetrate into it. To do this, the opening through which the water rushed must first be cleared, and the level lowered by making a larger outlet. Therefore an explosive substance must be manufactured, which would make a deep trench in some other part of the shore. This was what Harding was going to attempt with the minerals which nature placed at his disposal.

It is useless to say with what enthusiasm all, especially Pencroft, received this project. To employ great means, open the granite, create a cascade, that suited the sailor. And he would just as soon be a chemist as a mason or bootmaker, since the engineer wanted chemicals. He would be all that they liked, "even a professor of dancing and deportment," said he to Neb, if that was ever necessary.

Neb and Pencroft were first of all told to extract the grease from the dugong, and to keep the flesh, which was destined for food. Such perfect confidence had they in the engineer, that they set out directly, without even asking a question. A few minutes after them, Cyrus Harding, Herbert, and Gideon Spilett, dragging the hurdle, went toward the vein of coals, where those shistose pyrites abound which are met with in the most recent transition soil, and of which Harding had already found a specimen. All the day being employed in carrying a quantity of these stones to the Chimneys, by evening they had several tons.

The next day, the 8th of May, the engineer began his manipulations. These shistose pyrites being composed principally of coal, flint, alumina, and sulphuret of iron—the latter in excess—it was necessary to separate the sulphuret of iron, and transform it into sulphate as rapidly as possible. The sulphate obtained, the sulphuric acid could then be extracted.

This was the object to be attained. Sulphuric acid is one of the agents the most frequently employed, and the manufacturing importance of a nation can be measured by the consumption which is made of it. This acid would later be of great use to the settlers, in the manufacturing of candles, tanning skins, etc., but this time the engineer reserved it for another use.

Cyrus Harding chose, behind the Chimneys, a site where the ground was perfectly level. On this ground he placed a layer of branches and chopped wood, on which were piled some pieces of shistose pyrites, buttressed one against the other, the whole being covered with a thin layer of pyrites, previously reduced to the size of a nut.

This done, they set fire to the wood, the heat was communicated to the shist, which soon kindled, since it contains coal and sulphur. Then new layers of bruised pyrites were arranged so as to form an immense heap, the exterior of which was covered with earth and grass, several air-holes being left, as if it was a stack of wood which was to be carbonized to make charcoal.

They then left the transformation to complete itself, and it would not take less than ten or twelve days for the sulphuret of iron to be changed to sulphate of iron and the alumina into sulphate of alumina, two equally soluble substances, the others, flint, burnt coal, and cinders, not being so.

While this chemical work was going on, Cyrus Harding proceeded with other operations, which were pursued with more than zeal—it was eagerness.

Neb and Pencroft had taken away the fat from the dugong, and placed it in large earthen pots. It was then necessary to separate the glycerine from the fat by saponifying it. Now, to obtain this result, it had to be treated either with soda or lime. In fact, one or other of these substances, after having attacked the fat, would form a soap by separating the glycerine, and it was just this glycerine which the engineer wished to obtain. There was no want of lime, only treatment by lime would give calcareous soap, insoluble, and consequently useless, while treatment by soda would furnish, on the contrary, a soluble soap, which could be put to domestic use. Now, a practical man, like Cyrus Harding, would rather try to obtain soda. Was this difficult? No; for marine plants abounded on the shore, glass-wort, ficoides, and all those fucaceae which form wrack. A large quantity of these plants was collected, first dried, then burnt in holes in the open air. The combustion of these plants was kept up for several days, and the result was a compact gray mass, which has been long known under the name of natural soda.

This obtained, the engineer treated the fat with soda, which gave both a soluble soap and that neutral substance, glycerine.

But this was not all. Cyrus Harding still needed, in view of his future preparation, another substance, nitrate of potash, which is better known under the name of salt niter, or of saltpeter.

Cyrus Harding could have manufactured this substance by treating the carbonate of potash, which would be easily extracted from the cinders of the vegetables, by azotic acid. But this acid was wanting, and he would have been in some difficulty, if nature had not happily furnished the saltpeter, without giving them any other trouble than that of picking it up. Herbert found a vein of it at the foot of Mount Franklin, and they had nothing to do but purify this salt.

These different works lasted a week. They were finished before the transformation of the sulphuret into sulphate of iron had been accomplished. During the following days the settlers had time to construct a furnace of bricks of a particular arrangement, to serve for the distillation of the sulphate or iron when it had been obtained. All this was finished about the 18th of May, nearly at the time when the chemical transformation terminated. Gideon Spilett, Herbert, Neb, and Pencroft, skillfully directed by the engineer, had become most clever workmen. Before all masters, necessity is the one most listened to, and who teaches the best.

When the heap of pyrites had been entirely reduced by fire, the result of the operation, consisting of sulphate of iron, sulphate of alumina, flint, remains of coal, and cinders, was placed in a basinful of water. They stirred this mixture, let it settle, then decanted it, and obtained a clear liquid containing in solution sulphate of iron and sulphate of alumina, the other matters remaining solid, since they are insoluble. Lastly, this liquid being partly evaporated, crystals of sulphate of iron were deposited, and the not evaporated liquid, which contained the sulphate of alumina, was thrown away.

Cyrus Harding had now at his disposal a large quantity of these sulphate of iron crystals, from which the sulphuric acid had to be extracted. The making of sulphuric acid is a very expensive manufacture. Considerable works are necessary—a special set of tools, an apparatus of platina, leaden chambers, unassailable by the acid, and in which the transformation is performed, etc. The engineer had none of these at his disposal, but he knew that, in Bohemia especially, sulphuric acid is manufactured by very simple means, which have also the advantage of producing it to a superior degree of concentration. It is thus that the acid known under the name of Nordhausen acid is made.

To obtain sulphuric acid, Cyrus Harding had only one operation to make, to calcine the sulphate of iron crystals in a closed vase, so that the sulphuric acid should distil in vapor, which vapor, by condensation, would produce the acid.

The crystals were placed in pots, and the heat from the furnace would distil the sulphuric acid. The operation was successfully completed, and on the 20th of May, twelve days after commencing it, the engineer was the possessor of the agent which later he hoped to use in so many different ways.

Now, why did he wish for this agent? Simply to produce azotic acid; and that was easy, since saltpeter, attacked by sulphuric acid, gives azotic, or nitric, acid by distillation.

But, after all, how was he going to employ this azotic acid? His companions were still ignorant of this, for he had not informed them of the result at which he aimed.

However, the engineer had nearly accomplished his purpose, and by a last operation he would procure the substance which had given so much trouble.

Taking some azotic acid, he mixed it with glycerine, which had been previously concentrated by evaporation, subjected to the water-bath, and he obtained, without even employing a refrigerant mixture, several pints of an oily yellow mixture.

This last operation Cyrus Harding had made alone, in a retired place, at a distance from the Chimneys, for he feared the danger of an explosion, and when he showed a bottle of this liquid to his friends, he contented himself with saying,

"Here is nitro-glycerine!"

It was really this terrible production, of which the explosive power is perhaps tenfold that of ordinary powder, and which has already caused so many accidents. However, since a way has been found to transform it into dynamite, that is to say, to mix with it some solid substance, clay or sugar, porous enough to hold it, the dangerous liquid has been used with some security. But dynamite was not yet known at the time when the settlers worked on Lincoln Island.

"And is it that liquid that is going to blow up our rocks?" said Pencroft incredulously.

"Yes, my friend," replied the engineer, "and this nitro-glycerine will produce so much the more effect, as the granite is extremely hard, and will oppose a greater resistance to the explosion."

"And when shall we see this, captain?"

"To-morrow, as soon as we have dug a hole for the mine," replied the engineer.

The next day, the 21st of May, at daybreak, the miners went to the point which formed the eastern shore of Lake Grant, and was only five hundred feet from the coast. At this place, the plateau inclined downward from the waters, which were only restrained by their granite case. Therefore, if this case was broken, the water would escape by the opening and form a stream, which, flowing over the inclined surface of the plateau, would rush on to the beach. Consequently, the level of the lake would be greatly lowered, and the opening where the water escaped would be exposed, which was their final aim.

Under the engineer's directions, Pencroft, armed with a pickaxe, which he handled skillfully and vigorously, attacked the granite. The hole was made on the point of the shore, slanting, so that it should meet a much lower level than that of the water of the lake. In this way the explosive force, by scattering the rock, would open a large place for the water to rush out.

The work took some time, for the engineer, wishing to produce a great effect, intended to devote not less than seven quarts of nitro-glycerine to the operation. But Pencroft, relieved by Neb, did so well, that toward four o'clock in the evening, the mine was finished.

Now the question of setting fire to the explosive substance was raised. Generally, nitro-glycerine is ignited by caps of fulminate, which in bursting cause the explosion. A shock is therefore needed to produce the explosion, for, simply lighted, this substance would burn without exploding.

Cyrus Harding could certainly have fabricated a percussion cap. In default of fulminate, he could easily obtain a substance similar to guncotton, since he had azotic acid at his disposal. This substance, pressed in a cartridge, and introduced among the nitro-glycerine, would burst by means of a fuse, and cause the explosion.

But Cyrus Harding knew that nitro-glycerine would explode by a shock.

He resolved to employ this means, and try another way, if this did not succeed.

In fact, the blow of a hammer on a few drops of nitro-glycerine, spread out on a hard surface, was enough to create an explosion. But the operator could not be there to give the blow, without becoming a victim to the operation. Harding, therefore, thought of suspending a mass of iron, weighing several pounds, by means of a fiber, to an upright just above the mine. Another long fiber, previously impregnated with sulphur, was attached to the middle of the first, by one end, while the other lay on the ground several feet distant from the mine. The second fiber being set on fire, it would burn till it reached the first. This catching fire in its turn, would break, and the mass of iron would fall on the nitro-glycerine. This apparatus being then arranged, the engineer, after having sent his companions to a distance, filled the hole, so that the nitro-glycerine was on a level with the opening; then he threw a few drops of it on the surface of the rock, above which the mass of iron was already suspended.

This done, Harding lit the end of the sulphured fiber, and leaving the place, he returned with his companions to the Chimneys.

The fiber was intended to burn five and twenty minutes, and, in fact, five and twenty minutes afterward a most tremendous explosion was heard. The island appeared to tremble to its very foundation. Stones were projected in the air as if by the eruption of a volcano. The shock produced by the displacing of the air was such, that the rocks of the Chimneys shook. The settlers, although they were more than two miles from the mine, were thrown on the ground.

They rose, climbed the plateau, and ran toward the place where the bank of the lake must have been shattered by the explosion.

A cheer escaped them! A large rent was seen in the granite! A rapid stream of water rushed foaming across the plateau and dashed down a height of three hundred feet on to the beach!

XVIII

Cyrus Harding's project had succeeded, but, according to his usual habit he showed no satisfaction; with closed lips and a fixed look, he remained motionless. Herbert was in ecstasies, Neb bounded with joy, Pencroft nodded his great head, murmuring these words,

"Come, our engineer gets on capitally!"

The nitro-glycerine had indeed acted powerfully. The opening which it had made was so large that the volume of water which escaped through this new outlet was at least treble that which before passed through the old one. The result was, that a short time after the operation the level of the lake would be lowered two feet, or more.

The settlers went to the Chimneys to take some pickaxes, iron-tipped spears, string made of fibers, flint and steel; they then returned to the plateau, Top accompanying them.

On the way the sailor could not help saying to the engineer,

"Don't you think, captain, that by means of that charming liquid you have made, one could blow up the whole of our island?"

"Without any doubt, the island, continents, and the world itself," replied the engineer. "It is only a question of quantity."

"Then could you not use this nitro-glycerine for loading fire-arms?" asked the sailor.

"No, Pencroft; for it is too explosive a substance. But it would be easy to make some guncotton, or even ordinary powder, as we have azotic acid, saltpeter, sulphur, and coal. Unhappily, it is the guns which we have not got."

"Oh, captain," replied the sailor, "with a little determination—"

Pencroft had erased the word "impossible" from the dictionary of Lincoln Island.

The settlers, having arrived at Prospect Heights, went immediately toward that point of the lake near which was the old opening now uncovered. This outlet had now become practicable, since the water no longer rushed through it, and it would doubtless be easy to explore the interior.

In a few minutes the settlers had reached the lower point of the lake, and a glance showed them that the object had been attained.

In fact, in the side of the lake, and now above the surface of the water, appeared the long-looked-for opening. A narrow ridge, left bare by the retreat of the water, allowed them to approach it. This orifice was nearly twenty feet in width, but scarcely two in height. It was like the mouth of a drain at the edge of the pavement, and therefore did not offer an easy passage to the settlers; but Neb and Pencroft, taking their pickaxes, soon made it of a suitable height.

The engineer then approached, and found that the sides of the opening, in its upper part at least, had not a slope of more than from thirty to thirty-five degrees. It was therefore practicable, and, provided that the declivity did not increase, it would be easy to descend even to the level of the sea. If then, as was probable, some vast cavity existed in the interior of the granite, it might, perhaps, be of great use.

"Well, captain, what are we stopping for?" asked the sailor, impatient to enter the narrow passage. "You see Top has got before us!"

"Very well," replied the engineer. "But we must see our way. Neb, go and cut some resinous branches."

Neb and Herbert ran to the edge of the lake, shaded with pines and other green trees, and soon returned with some branches, which they made into torches. The torches were lighted with flint and steel, and Cyrus Harding leading, the settlers ventured into the dark passage, which the overplus of the lake had formerly filled.

Contrary to what might have been supposed, the diameter of the passage increased as the explorers proceeded, so that they very soon were able to stand upright. The granite, worn by the water for an infinite time, was very slippery, and falls were to be dreaded. But the settlers were all attached to each other by a cord, as is frequently done in ascending mountains. Happily some projections of the granite, forming regular steps, made the descent less perilous. Drops, still hanging from the rocks, shone here and there under the light of the torches, and the explorers guessed that the sides were clothed with innumerable stalactites. The engineer examined this black granite. There was not a stratum, not a break in it. The mass was compact, and of an extremely close grain. The passage dated, then, from the very origin of the island. It was not the water which little by little had hollowed it. Pluto and not Neptune had bored it with his own hand, and on the wall traces of an eruptive work could be distinguished, which all the washing of the water had not been able totally to efface.

The settlers descended very slowly. They could not but feel a certain awe, in this venturing into these unknown depths, for the first time visited by human beings. They did not speak, but they thought; and the thought came to more than one, that some polypus or other gigantic cephalopod might inhabit the interior cavities, which were in communication with the sea. However, Top kept at the head of the little band, and they could rely on the sagacity of the dog, who would not fail to give the alarm if there was any need for it.

After having descended about a hundred feet, following a winding road, Harding who was walking on before, stopped, and his companions came up with him. The place where they had halted was wider, so as to form a cavern of moderate dimensions. Drops of water fell from the vault, but that did not prove that they oozed through the rock. They were simply the last traces left by the torrent which had so long thundered through this cavity, and the air there was pure though slightly damp, but producing no mephitic exhalation.

"Well, my dear Cyrus," said Gideon Spilett, "here is a very secure retreat, well hid in the depths of the rock, but it is, however, uninhabitable."

"Why uninhabitable?" asked the sailor.

"Because it is too small and too dark."

"Couldn't we enlarge it, hollow it out, make openings to let in light and air?" replied Pencroft, who now thought nothing impossible.

"Let us go on with our exploration," said Cyrus Harding. "Perhaps lower down, nature will have spared us this labor."

"We have only gone a third of the way," observed Herbert.

"Nearly a third," replied Harding, "for we have descended a hundred feet from the opening, and it is not impossible that a hundred feet farther down—"

"Where is Top?" asked Neb, interrupting his master.

They searched the cavern, but the dog was not there.

"Most likely he has gone on," said Pencroft.

"Let us join him," replied Harding.

The descent was continued. The engineer carefully observed all the deviations of the passage, and notwithstanding so many detours, he could easily have given an account of its general direction, which went toward the sea.

The settlers had gone some fifty feet farther, when their attention was attracted by distant sounds which came up from the depths. They stopped and listened. These sounds, carried through the passage as through an acoustic tube, came clearly to the ear.

"That is Top barking!" cried Herbert.

"Yes," replied Pencroft, "and our brave dog is barking furiously!"

"We have our iron-tipped spears," said Cyrus Harding. "Keep on your guard, and forward!"

"It is becoming more and more interesting," murmured Gideon Spilett in the sailor's ear, who nodded. Harding and his companions rushed to the help of their dog. Top's barking became more and more perceptible, and it seemed strangely fierce. Was he engaged in a struggle with some animal whose retreat he had disturbed? Without thinking of the danger to which they might be exposed, the explorers were now impelled by an irresistible curiosity, and in a few minutes, sixteen feet lower they rejoined Top.

There the passage ended in a vast and magnificent cavern.

Top was running backward and forward, barking furiously. Pencroft and Neb, waving their torches, threw the light into every crevice; and at the same time, Harding, Gideon Spilett, and Herbert, their spears raised, were ready for any emergency which might arise. The enormous cavern was empty. The settlers explored it in every direction. There was nothing there, not an animal, not a human being; and yet Top continued to bark. Neither caresses nor threats could make him be silent.

"There must be a place somewhere, by which the waters of the lake reached the sea," said the engineer.

"Of course," replied Pencroft, "and we must take care not to tumble into a hole."

"Go, Top, go!" cried Harding.

The dog, excited by his master's words, ran toward the extremity of the cavern, and there redoubled his barking.

They followed him, and by the light of the torches, perceived the mouth of a regular well in the granite. It was by this that the water escaped; and this time it was not an oblique and practicable passage, but a perpendicular well, into which it was impossible to venture.

The torches were held over the opening: nothing could be seen. Harding took a lighted branch, and threw it into the abyss. The blazing resin, whose illuminating power increased still more by the rapidity of its fall, lighted up the interior of the well, but yet nothing appeared. The flame then went out with a slight hiss, which showed that it had reached the water, that is to say, the level of the sea.

The engineer, calculating the time employed in its fall, was able to calculate the depth of the well, which was found to be about ninety feet.

The floor of the cavern must thus be situated ninety feet above the level of the sea.

"Here is our dwelling," said Cyrus Harding.

"But it was occupied by some creature," replied Gideon Spilett, whose curiosity was not yet satisfied.

"Well, the creature, amphibious or otherwise, has made off through this opening," replied the engineer, "and has left the place for us."

"Never mind," added the sailor, "I should like very much to be Top, just for a quarter of an hour, for he doesn't bark for nothing!"

Cyrus Harding looked at his dog, and those of his companions who were near him might have heard him murmur these words,

"Yes, I believe that Top knows more than we do about a great many things."

However, the wishes of the settlers were for the most part satisfied. Chance, aided by the marvelous sagacity of their leader, had done them great service. They had now at their disposal a vast cavern, the size of which could not be properly calculated by the feeble light of their torches, but it would certainly be easy to divide it into rooms, by means of brick partitions, or to use it, if not as a house, at least as a spacious apartment. The water which had left it could not return. The place was free.

Two difficulties remained; firstly, the possibility of lighting this excavation in the midst of solid rock; secondly, the necessity of rendering the means of access more easy. It was useless to think of lighting it from above, because of the enormous thickness of the granite which composed the ceiling; but perhaps the outer wall next to the sea might be pierced. Cyrus Harding, during the descent, had roughly calculated its obliqueness, and consequently the length of the passage, and was therefore led to believe that the outer wall could not be very thick. If light was thus obtained, so would a means of access, for it would be as easy to pierce a door as windows, and to establish an exterior ladder.

Harding made known his ideas to his companions.

"Then, captain, let us set to work!" replied Pencroft. "I have my pickaxe, and I shall soon make my way through this wall. Where shall I strike?"

"Here," replied the engineer, showing the sturdy sailor a considerable recess in the side, which would much diminish the thickness.

Pencroft attacked the granite, and for half an hour, by the light of the torches, he made the splinters fly around him. Neb relieved him, then Spilett took Neb's place.

This work had lasted two hours, and they began to fear that at this spot the wall would not yield to the pickaxe, when at a last blow given by Gideon Spilett, the instrument, passing through the rock, fell outside.

"Hurrah! hurrah!" cried Pencroft.

The wall only measured there three feet in thickness.

Harding applied his eye to the aperture, which overlooked the ground from a height of eighty feet. Before him was extended the sea-coast, the islet, and beyond the open sea.

Floods of light entered by this hole, inundating the splendid cavern and producing a magic effect! On its left side it did not measure more than thirty feet in height and breadth, but on the right it was enormous, and its vaulted roof rose to a height of more than eighty feet.

In some places granite pillars, irregularly disposed, supported the vaulted roof, as those in the nave of a cathedral, here forming lateral piers, there elliptical arches, adorned with pointed moldings, losing themselves in dark bays, amid the fantastic arches of which glimpses could be caught in the shade, covered with a profusion of projections formed like so many pendants. This cavern was a picturesque mixture of all the styles of Byzantine, Roman, or Gothic architecture ever produced by the hand of man. And yet this was only the work of nature. She alone had hollowed this fairy Alhambra in a mass of granite.

The settlers were overwhelmed with admiration. Where they had only expected to find a narrow cavity, they had found a sort of marvelous palace, and Neb had taken off his hat, as if he had been transported into a temple!

Cries of admiration issued from every mouth. Hurrahs resounded, and the echo was repeated again and again till it died away in the dark naves.

"Ah, my friends!" exclaimed Cyrus Harding, "when we have lighted the interior of this place, and have arranged our rooms and storehouses in the left part, we shall still have this splendid cavern, which we will make our study and our museum!"

"And we will call it?—" asked Herbert.

"Granite House," replied Harding; a name which his companions again saluted with a cheer.

The torches were now almost consumed, and as they were obliged to return by the passage to reach the summit of the plateau, it was decided to put off the work necessary for the arrangement of their new dwelling till the next day.

Before departing, Cyrus Harding leaned once more over the dark well, which descended perpendicularly to the level of the sea. He listened attentively. No noise was heard, not even that of the water, which the undulations of the surge must sometimes agitate in its depths. A flaming branch was again thrown in. The sides of the well were lighted up for an instant, but as at the first time, nothing suspicious was seen.

If some marine monster had been surprised unawares by the retreat of the water, he would by this time have regained the sea by the subterranean passage, before the new opening had been offered to him.

Meanwhile, the engineer was standing motionless, his eyes fixed on the gulf, without uttering a word.

The sailor approached him, and touching his arm, "Captain!" said he.

"What do you want, my friend?" asked the engineer, as if he had returned from the land of dreams.

"The torches will soon go out."

"Forward!" replied Cyrus Harding.

The little band left the cavern and began to ascend through the dark passage. Top closed the rear, still growling every now and then. The ascent was painful enough. The settlers rested a few minutes in the upper grotto, which made a sort of landing-place halfway up the long granite staircase. Then they began to climb again.

Soon fresher air was felt. The drops of water, dried by evaporation, no longer sparkled on the walls. The flaring torches began to grow dim. The one which Neb carried went out, and if they did not wish to find their way in the dark, they must hasten.

This was done, and a little before four o'clock, at the moment when the sailor's torch went out in its turn, Cyrus Harding and his companions passed out of the passage.

XIX

The next day, the 22nd of May, the arrangement of their new dwelling was commenced. In fact, the settlers longed to exchange the insufficient shelter of the Chimneys for this large and healthy retreat, in the midst of solid rock, and sheltered from the water both of the sea and sky.

Their former dwelling was not, however, to be entirely abandoned, for the engineer intended to make a manufactory of it for important works. Cyrus Harding's first care was to find out the position of the front of Granite House from the outside. He went to the beach, and as the pickaxe when it escaped from the hands of the reporter must have fallen perpendicularly to the foot of the cliff, the finding of it would be sufficient to show the place where the hole had been pierced in the granite.

The pickaxe was easily found, and the hole could be seen in a perpendicular line above the spot where it was stuck in the sand. Some rock pigeons were already flying in and out of the narrow opening; they evidently thought that Granite House had been discovered on purpose for them. It was the engineer's intention to divide the right portion of the cavern into several rooms, preceded by an entrance passage, and to light it by means of five windows and a door, pierced in the front. Pencroft was much pleased with the five windows, but he could not understand the use of the door, since the passage offered a natural staircase, through which it would always be easy to enter Granite House.

"My friend," replied Harding, "if it is easy for us to reach our dwelling by this passage, it will be equally easy for others besides us. I mean, on the contrary, to block up that opening, to seal it hermetically, and, if it is necessary, to completely hide the entrance by making a dam, and thus causing the water of the lake to rise."

"And how shall we get in?" asked the sailor.

"By an outside ladder," replied Cyrus Harding, "a rope ladder, which, once drawn up, will render access to our dwelling impossible."

"But why so many precautions?" asked Pencroft. "As yet we have seen no dangerous animals. As to our island being inhabited by natives, I don't believe it!"

"Are you quite sure of that, Pencroft?" asked the engineer, looking at the sailor.

"Of course we shall not be quite sure, till we have explored it in every direction," replied Pencroft.

"Yes," said Harding, "for we know only a small portion of it as yet. But at any rate, if we have no enemies in the interior, they may come from the exterior, for parts of the Pacific are very dangerous. We must be provided against every contingency."

Cyrus Harding spoke wisely; and without making any further objection, Pencroft prepared to execute his orders.

The front of Granite House was then to be lighted by five windows and a door, besides a large bay window and some smaller oval ones, which would admit plenty of light to enter into the marvelous nave which was to be their chief room. This façade, situated at a height of eighty feet above the ground, was exposed to the east, and the rising sun saluted it with its first rays. It was found to be just at that part of the cliff which was between the projection at the mouth of the Mercy and a perpendicular line traced above the heap of rocks which formed the Chimneys. Thus the winds from the northeast would only strike it obliquely, for it was protected by the projection. Besides, until the window-frames were made, the engineer meant to close the openings with thick shutters, which would prevent either wind or rain from entering, and which could be concealed in need.

The first work was to make the openings. This would have taken too long with the pickaxe alone, and it is known that Harding was an ingenious man. He had still a quantity of nitro-glycerine at his disposal, and he employed it usefully. By means of this explosive substance the rock was broken open at the very places chosen by the engineer. Then, with the pickaxe and spade, the windows and doors were properly shaped, the jagged edges were smoothed off, and a few days after the beginning of the work, Granite House was abundantly lighted by the rising sun, whose rays penetrated into its most secret recesses. Following the plan proposed by Cyrus Harding, the space was to be divided into five compartments looking out on the sea; to the right, an entry with a door, which would meet the ladder; then a kitchen, thirty feet long; a dining-room, measuring forty feet; a sleeping-room, of equal size; and lastly, a "visitor's room," petitioned for by Pencroft, and which was next to the great hall. These rooms, or rather this suite of rooms, would not occupy all the depth of the cave. There would be also a corridor and a storehouse, in which their tools, provisions, and stores would be kept. All the productions of the island, the flora as well as the fauna, were to be there in the best possible state of preservation, and completely sheltered from the damp. There was no want of space, so that each object could be methodically arranged. Besides, the colonists had still at their disposal the little grotto above the great cavern, which was like the garret of the new dwelling.

This plan settled, it had only to be put into execution. The miners became brickmakers again, then the bricks were brought to the foot of Granite House. Till then, Harding and his companions had only entered the cavern by the long passage. This mode of communication obliged them first to climb Prospect Heights, making a detour by the river's bank, and then to descend two hundred feet through the passage, having to climb as far when they wished to return to the plateau. This was a great loss of time, and was also very fatiguing. Cyrus Harding, therefore, resolved to proceed without any further delay to the fabrication of a strong rope ladder, which, once raised, would render Granite House completely inaccessible.

This ladder was manufactured with extreme care, and its uprights, formed of the twisted fibers of a species of cane, had the strength of a thick cable. As to the rounds, they were made of a sort of red cedar, with light, strong branches; and this apparatus was wrought by the masterly hand of Pencroft.

Other ropes were made with vegetable fibers, and a sort of crane with a tackle was fixed at the door. In this way bricks could easily be raised into Granite House. The transport of the materials being thus simplified, the arrangement of the interior could begin immediately. There was no want of lime, and some thousands of bricks were there ready to be used. The framework of the partitions was soon raised, very roughly at first, and in a short time, the cave was divided into rooms and storehouses, according to the plan agreed upon.

These different works progressed rapidly under the direction of the engineer, who himself handled the hammer and the trowel. No labor came amiss to Cyrus Harding, who thus set an example to his intelligent and zealous companions. They worked with confidence, even gaily, Pencroft always having some joke to crack, sometimes carpenter, sometimes rope-maker, sometimes mason, while he communicated his good humor to all the members of their little world. His faith in the engineer was complete; nothing could disturb it. He believed him capable of undertaking anything and succeeding in everything. The question of boots and clothes—assuredly a serious question—that of light during the winter months, utilizing the fertile parts of the island, transforming the wild flora into cultivated flora, it all appeared easy to him; Cyrus Harding helping, everything would be done in time. He dreamed of canals facilitating the transport of the riches of the ground; workings of quarries and mines; machines for every industrial manufacture; railroads; yes, railroads! of which a network would certainly one day cover Lincoln Island.

The engineer let Pencroft talk. He did not put down the aspirations of this brave heart. He knew how communicable confidence is; he even smiled to hear him speak, and said nothing of the uneasiness for the future which he felt. In fact, in that part of the Pacific, out of the course of vessels, it was to be feared that no help would ever come to them. It was on themselves, on themselves alone, that the settlers must depend, for the distance of Lincoln Island from all other land was such, that to hazard themselves in a boat, of a necessarily inferior construction, would be a serious and perilous thing.

"But," as the sailor said, "they quite took the wind out of the sails of the Robinsons, for whom everything was done by a miracle."

In fact, they were energetic; an energetic man will succeed where an indolent one would vegetate and inevitably perish.

Herbert distinguished himself in these works. He was intelligent and active; understanding quickly, he performed well; and Cyrus Harding became more and more attached to the boy. Herbert had a lively and reverent love for the engineer. Pencroft saw the close sympathy which existed between the two, but he was not in the least jealous. Neb was Neb: he was what he would be always, courage, zeal, devotion, self-denial personified. He had the same faith in his master that Pencroft had, but he showed it less vehemently. When the sailor was enthusiastic, Neb always looked as if he would say, "Nothing could be more natural." Pencroft and he were great friends.

As to Gideon Spilett, he took part in the common work, and was not less skillful in it than his companions, which always rather astonished the sailor. A "journalist," clever, not only in understanding, but in performing everything.

The ladder was finally fixed on the 28th of May. There were not less than a hundred rounds in this perpendicular height of eighty feet. Harding had been able, fortunately, to divide it in two parts, profiting by an overhanging of the cliff which made a projection forty feet above the ground. This projection, carefully leveled by the pickaxe, made a sort of platform, to which they fixed the first ladder, of which the oscillation was thus diminished one-half, and a rope permitted it to be raised to the level of Granite House. As to the second ladder, it was secured both at its lower part, which rested on the projection, and at its upper end, which was fastened to the door. In short the ascent had been made much easier. Besides, Cyrus Harding hoped later to establish a hydraulic apparatus, which would avoid all fatigue and loss of time, for the inhabitants of Granite House.

The settlers soon became habituated to the use of this ladder. They were light and active, and Pencroft, as a sailor, accustomed to run up the masts and shrouds, was able to give them lessons. But it was also necessary to give them to Top. The poor dog, with his four paws, was not formed for this sort of exercise. But Pencroft was such a zealous master, that Top ended by properly performing his ascents, and soon mounted the ladder as readily as his brethren in the circus. It need not be said that the sailor was proud of his pupil. However, more than once Pencroft hoisted him on his back, which Top never complained of.

It must be mentioned here, that during these works, which were actively conducted, for the bad season was approaching, the alimentary question was not neglected. Every day, the reporter and Herbert, who had been voted purveyors to the colony, devoted some hours to the chase. As yet, they only hunted in Jacamar Wood, on the left of the river, because, for want of a bridge or boat, the Mercy had not yet been crossed. All the immense woods, to which the name of the Forests of the Far West had been given, were not explored. They reserved this important excursion for the first fine days of the next spring. But Jacamar Wood was full of game; kangaroos and boars abounded, and the hunters' iron-tipped spears and bows and arrows did wonders. Besides, Herbert discovered toward the southwest point of the lagoon a natural warren, a slightly damp meadow, covered with willows and aromatic herbs which scented the air, such as thyme, basil, savory, all the sweet-scented species of the labiated plants, which the rabbits appeared to be particularly fond of.

On the reporter observing that since the table was spread for the rabbits, it was strange that the rabbits themselves should be wanting, the two sportsmen carefully explored the warren. At any rate, it produced an abundance of useful plants, and a naturalist would have had a good opportunity of studying many specimens of the vegetable kingdom. Herbert gathered several shoots of the basil, rosemary, balm, betony, etc., which possess different medicinal properties, some pectoral, astringent, febrifuge, others anti-spasmodic, or anti-rheumatic. When, afterward, Pencroft asked the use of this collection of herbs,

"For medicine," replied the lad, "to treat us when we are ill."

"Why should we be ill, since there are no doctors in the island?" asked Pencroft quite seriously.

There was no reply to be made to that, but the lad went on with his collection all the same, and it was well received at Granite House. Besides these medicinal herbs, he added a plant known in North America as Oswego tea, which made an excellent beverage.

At last, by searching thoroughly, the hunters arrived at the real site of the warren. There the ground was perforated like a sieve.

"Here are the burrows!" cried Herbert.

"Yes," replied the reporter, "so I see."

"But are they inhabited?"

"That is the question."

This was soon answered. Almost immediately, hundreds of little animals, similar to rabbits, fled in every direction, with such rapidity that even Top could not overtake them. Hunters and dog ran in vain; these rodents escaped them easily. But the reporter resolved not to leave the place, until he had captured at least half a dozen of the quadrupeds. He wished to stock their larder first, and domesticate those which they might take later. It would not have been difficult to do this, with a few snares stretched at the openings of the burrows. But at this moment they had neither snares, nor anything to make them of. They must, therefore, be satisfied with visiting each hole, and rummaging in it with a stick, hoping by dint of patience to do what could not be done in any other way.

At last, after half an hour, four rodents were taken in their holes. They were similar to their European brethren, and are commonly known by the name of American rabbits.

This produce of the chase was brought back to Granite House, and figured at the evening repast. The tenants of the warren were not at all to be despised, for they were delicious. It was a valuable resource of the colony, and it appeared to be inexhaustible.

On the 31st of May the partitions were finished. The rooms had now only to be furnished, and this would be work for the long winter days. A chimney was established in the first room, which served as a kitchen. The pipe destined to conduct the smoke outside gave some trouble to these amateur bricklayers. It appeared simplest to Harding to make it of brick clay; as creating an outlet for it to the upper plateau was not to be thought of, a hole was pierced in the granite above the window of the kitchen, and the pipe met it like that of an iron stove. Perhaps the winds which blew directly against the façade would make the chimney smoke, but these winds were rare, and besides, Master Neb, the cook, was not so very particular about that.

When these interior arrangements were finished, the engineer occupied himself in blocking up the outlet by the lake, so as to prevent any access by that way. Masses of rock were rolled to the entrance and strongly cemented together. Cyrus Harding did not yet realize his plan of drowning this opening under the waters of the lake, by restoring them to their former level by means of a dam. He contented himself with hiding the obstruction with grass and shrubs, which were planted in the interstices of the rocks, and which next spring would sprout thickly. However, he used the waterfall so as to lead a small stream of fresh water to the new dwelling. A little trench, made below their level, produced this result; and this derivation from a pure and inexhaustible source yielded twenty-five or thirty gallons a day. There would never be any want of water at Granite House. At last all was finished, and it was time, for the bad season was near. Thick shutters closed the windows of the façade, until the engineer had time to make glass.

Gideon Spilett had very artistically arranged on the rocky projections around the windows plants of different kinds, as well as long streaming grass, so that the openings were picturesquely framed in green, which had a pleasing effect.

The inhabitants of this solid, healthy, and secure dwelling, could not but be charmed with their work. The view from the windows extended over a boundless horizon, which was closed by the two Mandible Capes on the north, and Claw Cape on the south. All Union Bay was spread before them. Yes, our brave settlers had reason to be satisfied, and Pencroft was lavish in his praise of what he humorously called, "his apartments on the fifth floor above the ground!"

XX

The winter season set in with the month of June, which corresponds with the month of December in the Northern Hemisphere. It began with showers and squalls, which succeeded each other without intermission. The tenants of Granite House could appreciate the advantages of a dwelling which sheltered them from the inclement weather. The Chimneys would have been quite insufficient to protect them against the rigor of winter, and it was to be feared that the high tides would make another irruption. Cyrus Harding had taken precautions against this contingency, so as to preserve as much as possible the forge and furnace which were established there.

During the whole of the month of June the time was employed in different occupations, which excluded neither hunting nor fishing, the larder being, therefore, abundantly supplied. Pencroft, so soon as he had leisure, proposed to set some traps, from which he expected great results. He soon made some snares with creepers, by the aid of which the warren henceforth every day furnished its quota of rodents. Neb employed nearly all his time in salting or smoking meat, which ensured their always having plenty of provisions. The question of clothes was now seriously discussed, the settlers having no other garments than those they wore when the balloon threw them on the island. These clothes were warm and good; they had taken great care of them as well as of their linen, and they were perfectly whole, but they would soon need to be replaced. Moreover, if the winter was severe, the settlers would suffer greatly from cold.

On this subject the ingenuity of Harding was at fault. They must provide for their most pressing wants, settle their dwelling, and lay in a store of food; thus the cold might come upon them before the question of clothes had been settled. They must therefore make up their minds to pass this first winter without additional clothing. When the fine season came around again, they would regularly hunt those musmons which had been seen on the expedition to Mount Franklin, and the wool once collected, the engineer would know how to make it into strong warm stuff. . . . How? He would consider.

"Well, we are free to roast ourselves at Granite House!" said Pencroft. "There are heaps of fuel, and no reason for sparing it."

"Besides," added Gideon Spilett, "Lincoln Island is not situated under a very high latitude, and probably the winters here are not severe. Did you not say, Cyrus, that this thirty-fifth parallel corresponded to that of Spain in the other hemisphere?"

"Doubtless," replied the engineer, "but some winters in Spain are very cold! No want of snow and ice; and perhaps Lincoln Island is just as rigourously tried. However, it is an island, and as such, I hope that the temperature will be more moderate."

"Why, captain?" asked Herbert.

"Because the sea, my boy, may be considered as an immense reservoir, in which is stored the heat of the summer. When winter comes, it restores this heat, which ensures for the regions near the ocean a medium temperature, less high in summer, but less low in winter."

"We shall prove that," replied Pencroft. "But I don't want to bother myself about whether it will be cold or not. One thing is certain, that is that the days are already short, and the evenings long. Suppose we talk about the question of light."

"Nothing is easier," replied Harding.

"To talk about?" asked the sailor.

"To settle."

"And when shall we begin?"

"To-morrow, by having a seal hunt."

"To make candles?"

"Yes."

Such was the engineer's project; and it was quite feasible, since he had lime and sulphuric acid, while the amphibians of the islet would furnish the fat necessary for the manufacture.

They were now at the 4th of June. It was Whit Sunday and they agreed to observe this feast. All work was suspended, and prayers were offered to Heaven. But these prayers were now thanksgivings. The settlers in Lincoln Island were no longer the miserable castaways thrown on the islet. They asked for nothing more—they gave thanks. The next day, the 5th of June, in rather uncertain weather, they set out for the islet. They had to profit by the low tide to cross the channel, and it was agreed that they would construct, for this purpose, as well as they could, a boat which would render communication so much easier, and would also permit them to ascend the Mercy, at the time of their grand exploration of the southwest of the island, which was put off till the first fine days.

The seals were numerous, and the hunters, armed with their iron-tipped spears, easily killed half a dozen. Neb and Pencroft skinned them, and only brought back to Granite House their fat and skin, this skin being intended for the manufacture of boots.

The result of the hunt was this: nearly three hundred pounds of fat, all to be employed in the fabrication of candles.

The operation was extremely simple, and if it did not yield absolutely perfect results, they were at least very useful. Cyrus Harding would only have had at his disposal sulphuric acid, but by heating this acid with the neutral fatty bodies, he could separate the glycerine; then from this new combination, he easily separated the olein, the margarin, and the stearin, by employing boiling water. But to simplify the operation, he preferred to saponify the fat by means of lime. By this he obtained a calcareous soap, easy to decompose by sulphuric acid, which precipitated the lime into the state of sulphate, and liberated the fatty acids.

From these three acids—oleic, margaric, and stearic—the first, being liquid, was driven out by a sufficient pressure. As to the two others, they formed the very substance of which the candles were to be molded.

This operation did not last more than four and twenty hours. The wicks, after several trials, were made of vegetable fibers, and dipped in the liquefied substance, they formed regular stearic candles, molded by the hand, which only wanted whiteness and polish. They would not doubtless have the advantages of the wicks which are impregnated with boracic acid, and which vitrify as they burn and are entirely consumed, but Cyrus Harding having manufactured a beautiful pair of snuffers, these candles would be greatly appreciated during the long evenings in Granite House.

During this month there was no want of work in the interior of their new dwelling. The joiners had plenty to do. They improved their tools, which were very rough, and added others also.

Scissors were made among other things, and the settlers were at last able to cut their hair, and also to shave, or at least trim their beards. Herbert had none, Neb but little, but their companions were bristling in a way which justified the making of the said scissors.

The manufacture of a hand-saw cost infinite trouble, but at last an instrument was obtained which, when vigorously handled, could divide the ligneous fibers of the wood. They then made tables, seats, cupboards, to furnish the principal rooms, and bedsteads, of which all the bedding consisted of grass mattresses. The kitchen, with its shelves, on which rested the cooking utensils, its brick stove, looked very well, and Neb worked away there as earnestly as if he was in a chemist's laboratory.

But the joiners had soon to be replaced by carpenters. In fact, the waterfall created by the explosion rendered the construction of two bridges necessary, one on Prospect Heights, the other on the shore. Now the plateau and the shore were transversely divided by a watercourse, which had to be crossed to reach the northern part of the island. To avoid it the colonists had been obliged to make a considerable detour, by climbing up to the source of the Red Creek. The simplest thing was to establish on the plateau, and on the shore, two bridges from twenty to five and twenty feet in length. All the carpenter's work that was needed was to clear some trees of their branches: this was a business of some days. Directly the bridges were established, Neb and Pencroft profited by them to go to the oyster-bed which had been discovered near the downs. They dragged with them a sort of rough cart, which replaced the former inconvenient hurdle, and brought back some thousands of oysters, which soon increased among the rocks and formed a bed at the mouth of the Mercy. These molluscs were of excellent quality, and the colonists consumed some daily.

It has been seen that Lincoln Island, although its inhabitants had as yet only explored a small portion of it, already contributed to almost all their wants. It was probable that if they hunted into its most secret recesses, in all the wooded part between the Mercy and Reptile End, they would find new treasures.

The settlers in Lincoln Island had still one privation. There was no want of meat, nor of vegetable products; those ligneous roots which they had found, when subjected to fermentation, gave them an acid drink, which was preferable to cold water; they also made sugar, without canes or beet-roots, by collecting the liquor which distils from the acer saccharinum, a sort of maple-tree, which flourishes in all the temperate zones, and of which the island possessed a great number; they made a very agreeable tea by employing the herbs brought from the warren; lastly, they had an abundance of salt, the only mineral which is used in food, . . . but bread was wanting.

Perhaps in time the settlers could replace this want by some equivalent, it was possible that they might find the sago or the breadfruit tree among the forests of the south, but they had not as yet met with these precious trees. However, Providence came directly to their aid, in an infinitesimal proportion it is true, but Cyrus Harding, with all his intelligence, all his ingenuity, would never have been able to produce that which, by the greatest chance, Herbert one day found in the lining of his waistcoat, which he was occupied in setting to rights.

On this day, as it was raining in torrents, the settlers were assembled in the great hall in Granite House, when the lad cried out all at once,

"Look here, captain—a grain of corn!"

And he showed his companions a grain—a single grain—which from a hole in his pocket had got into the lining of his waistcoat.

The presence of this grain was explained by the fact that Herbert, when at Richmond, used to feed some pigeons, of which Pencroft had made him a present.

"A grain of corn?" said the engineer quickly.

"Yes, captain; but one, only one!"

"Well, my boy," said Pencroft, laughing, "we're getting on capitally, upon my word! What shall we make with one grain of corn?"

"We will make bread of it," replied Cyrus Harding.

"Bread, cakes, tarts!" replied the sailor. "Come, the bread that this grain of corn will make won't choke us very soon!"

Herbert, not attaching much importance to his discovery, was going to throw away the grain in question; but Harding took it, examined it, found that it was in good condition, and looking the sailor full in the face,

"Pencroft," he asked quietly, "do you know how many ears one grain of corn can produce?"

"One, I suppose!" replied the sailor, surprised at the question.

"Ten, Pencroft! And do you know how many grains one ear bears?"

"No, upon my word."

"About eighty!" said Cyrus Harding. "Then, if we plant this grain, at the first crop we shall reap eight hundred grains which at the second will produce six hundred and forty thousand; at the third, five hundred and twelve millions; at the fourth, more than four hundred thousands of millions! There is the proportion."

Harding's companions listened without answering. These numbers astonished them. They were exact, however.

"Yes, my friends," continued the engineer, "such are the arithmetical progressions of prolific nature; and yet what is this multiplication of the grain of corn, of which the ear only bears eight hundred grains, compared to the poppy-plant, which bears thirty-two thousand seeds; to the tobacco-plant, which produces three hundred and sixty thousand? In a few years, without the numerous causes of destruction, which arrests their fecundity, these plants would overrun the earth."

But the engineer had not finished his lecture.

"And now, Pencroft," he continued, "do you know how many bushels four hundred thousand millions of grains would make?"

"No," replied the sailor; "but what I do know is, that I am nothing better than a fool!"

"Well, they would make more than three millions, at a hundred and thirty thousand a bushel, Pencroft."

"Three millions!" cried Pencroft.

"Three millions."

"In four years?"

"In four years," replied Cyrus Harding, "and even in two years, if, as I hope, in this latitude we can obtain two crops a year."

At that, according to his usual custom, Pencroft could not reply otherwise than by a tremendous hurrah.

"So, Herbert," added the engineer, "you have made a discovery of great importance to us. Everything, my friends, everything can serve us in the condition in which we are. Do not forget that, I beg of you."

"No, captain, no, we shan't forget it," replied Pencroft; "and if ever I find one of those tobacco-seeds, which multiply by three hundred and sixty thousand, I assure you I won't throw it away! And now, what must we do?"

"We must plant this grain," replied Herbert.

"Yes," added Gideon Spilett, "and with every possible care, for it bears in itself our future harvests."

"Provided it grows!" cried the sailor.

"It will grow," replied Cyrus Harding.

This was the 20th of June. The time was then propitious for sowing this single precious grain of corn. It was first proposed to plant it in a pot, but upon reflection it was decided to leave it to nature, and confide it to the earth. This was done that very day, and it is needless to add, that every precaution was taken that the experiment might succeed.

The weather having cleared, the settlers climbed the height above Granite House. There, on the plateau, they chose a spot, well sheltered from the wind, and exposed to all the heat of the midday sun. The place was cleared, carefully weeded, and searched for insects and worms; then a bed of good earth, improved with a little lime, was made; it was surrounded by a railing; and the grain was buried in the damp earth.

Did it not seem as if the settlers were laying the first stone of some edifice? It recalled to Pencroft the day on which he lighted his only match, and all the anxiety of the operation. But this time the thing was more serious. In fact, the castaways would have been always able to procure fire, in some mode or other, but no human power could supply another grain of corn, if unfortunately this should be lost!

XXI

From this time Pencroft did not let a single day pass without going to visit what he gravely called his "corn-field." And woe to the insects which dared to venture there! No mercy was shown them.

Toward the end of the month of June, after incessant rain, the weather became decidedly colder, and on the 29th a Fahrenheit thermometer would certainly have announced only twenty degrees above zero, that is considerably below the freezing-point. The next day, the 30th of June, the day which corresponds to the 31st of December in the northern year, was a Friday. Neb remarked that the year finished on a bad day, but Pencroft replied that naturally the next would begin on a good one, which was better.

At any rate it commenced by very severe cold. Ice accumulated at the mouth of the Mercy, and it was not long before the whole expanse of the lake was frozen.

The settlers had frequently been obliged to renew their store of wood. Pencroft also had wisely not waited till the river was frozen, but had brought enormous rafts of wood to their destination. The current was an indefatigable moving power, and it was employed in conveying the floating wood to the moment when the frost enchained it. To the fuel which was so abundantly supplied by the forest, they added several cartloads of coal, which had to be brought from the foot of the spurs of Mount Franklin. The powerful heat of the coal was greatly appreciated in the low temperature, which on the 4th of July fell to eight degrees of Fahrenheit, that is, thirteen degrees below zero. A second fireplace had been established in the dining-room, where they all worked together at their different avocations. During this period of cold, Cyrus Harding had great cause to congratulate himself on having brought to Granite House the little stream of water from Lake Grant. Taken below the frozen surface, and conducted through the passage, it preserved its fluidity, and arrived at an interior reservoir which had been hollowed out at the back part of the storeroom, while the overflow ran through the well to the sea.

About this time, the weather being extremely dry, the colonists, clothed as warmly as possible, resolved to devote a day to the exploration of that part of the island between the Mercy and Claw Cape. It was a wide extent of marshy land, and they would probably find good sport, for water-birds ought to swarm there.

They reckoned that it would be about eight or nine miles to go there, and as much to return, so that the whole of the day would be occupied. As an unknown part of the island was about to be explored, the whole colony took part in the expedition. Accordingly, on the 5th of July, at six o'clock in the morning, when day had scarcely broken, Cyrus Harding, Gideon Spilett, Herbert, Neb, and Pencroft, armed with spears, snares, bows and arrows, and provided with provisions, left Granite House, preceded by Top, who bounded before them.

Their shortest way was to cross the Mercy on the ice, which then covered it.

"But," as the engineer justly observed, "that could not take the place of a regular bridge!" So, the construction of a regular bridge was noted in the list of future works.

It was the first time that the settlers had set foot on the right bank of the Mercy, and ventured into the midst of those gigantic and superb coniferae now sprinkled over with snow.

But they had not gone half a mile when from a thicket a whole family of quadrupeds, who had made a home there, disturbed by Top, rushed forth into the open country.

"Ah! I should say those are foxes!" cried Herbert, when he saw the troop rapidly decamping.

They were foxes, but of a very large size, who uttered a sort of barking, at which Top seemed to be very much astonished, for he stopped short in the chase, and gave the swift animals time to disappear.

The dog had reason to be surprised, as he did not know natural history. But, by their barking, these foxes, with reddish-gray hair, black tails terminating in a white tuft, had betrayed their origin. So Herbert was able, without hesitating, to give them their real name of Arctic foxes. They are frequently met with in Chile, in the Falkland Islands, and in all parts of America traversed by the thirtieth and fortieth parallels. Herbert much regretted that Top had not been able to catch one of these carnivora.

"Are they good to eat?" asked Pencroft, who only regarded the representatives of the fauna in the island from one special point of view.

"No," replied Herbert; "but zoologists have not yet found out if the eye of these foxes is diurnal or nocturnal, or whether it is correct to class them in the genus dog, properly so called."

Harding could not help smiling on hearing the lad's reflection, which showed a thoughtful mind. As to the sailor, from the moment when he found that the foxes were not classed in the genus eatable, they were nothing to him. However, when a poultry-yard was established at Granite House, he observed that it would be best to take some precautions against a probable visit from these four-legged plunderers, and no one disputed this.

After having turned the point, the settlers saw a long beach washed by the open sea. It was then eight o'clock in the morning. The sky was very clear, as it often is after prolonged cold; but warmed by their walk, neither Harding nor his companions felt the sharpness of the atmosphere too severely. Besides there was no wind, which made it much more bearable. A brilliant sun, but without any calorific action, was just issuing from the ocean. The sea was as tranquil and blue as that of a Mediterranean gulf, when the sky is clear. Claw Cape, bent in the form of a yataghan, tapered away nearly four miles to the southeast. To the left the edge of the marsh was abruptly ended by a little point. Certainly, in this part of Union Bay, which nothing sheltered from the open sea, not even a sandbank, ships beaten by the east winds would have found no shelter. They perceived by the tranquillity of the sea, in which no shallows troubled the waters, by its uniform color, which was stained by no yellow shades, by the absence of even a reef, that the coast was steep and that the ocean there covered a deep abyss. Behind in the west, but at a distance of four miles, rose the first trees of the Forests of the Far West. They might have believed themselves to be on the desolate coast of some island in the Antarctic regions which the ice had invaded. The colonists halted at this place for breakfast. A fire of brushwood and dried seaweed was lighted, and Neb prepared the breakfast of cold meat, to which he added some cups of Oswego tea.

While eating they looked around them. This part of Lincoln Island was very sterile, and contrasted with all the western part. The reporter was thus led to observe that if chance had thrown them at first on the shore, they would have had but a deplorable idea of their future domain.

"I believe that we should not have been able to reach it," replied the engineer, "for the sea is deep, and there is not a rock on which we could have taken refuge. Before Granite House, at least, there were sandbanks, an islet, which multiplied our chances of safety. Here, nothing but the depths!"

"It is singular enough," remarked Spilett, "that this comparatively small island should present such varied ground. This diversity of aspect, logically only belongs to continents of a certain extent. One would really say, that the western part of Lincoln Island, so rich and so fertile, is washed by the warm waters of the Gulf of Mexico, and that its shores to the north and the southeast extend over a sort of Arctic sea."

"You are right, my dear Spilett," replied Cyrus Harding, "I have also observed this. I think the form and also the nature of this island strange. It is a summary of all the aspects which a continent presents, and I should not be surprised if it was a continent formerly."

"What! a continent in the middle of the Pacific?" cried Pencroft.

"Why not?" replied Cyrus Harding. "Why should not Australia, New Ireland, Australasia, united to the archipelagoes of the Pacific, have once formed a sixth part of the world, as important as Europe or Asia, as Africa or the two Americas? To my mind, it is quite possible that all these islands, emerging from this vast ocean, are but the summits of a continent, now submerged, but which was above the waters at a prehistoric period."

"As the Atlantis was formerly," replied Herbert.

"Yes, my boy . . . if, however, it existed."

"And would Lincoln Island have been a part of that continent?" asked Pencroft.

"It is probable," replied Cyrus Harding, "and that would sufficiently explain the variety of productions which are seen on its surface."

"And the great number of animals which still inhabit it," added Herbert.

"Yes, my boy," replied the engineer, "and you furnish me with an argument to support my theory. It is certain, after what we have seen, that animals are numerous in this island, and what is more strange, that the species are extremely varied. There is a reason for that, and to me it is that Lincoln Island may have formerly been a part of some vast continent which had gradually sunk below the Pacific."

"Then, some fine day," said Pencroft, who did not appear to be entirely convinced, "the rest of this ancient continent may disappear in its turn, and there will be nothing between America and Asia."

"Yes," replied Harding, "there will be new continents which millions and millions of animalculae are building at this moment."

"And what are these masons?" asked Pencroft.

"Coral insects," replied Cyrus Harding. "By constant work they made the island of Clermont-Tonnerre, and numerous other coral islands in the Pacific Ocean. Forty-seven millions of these insects are needed to weigh a grain, and yet, with the sea-salt they absorb, the solid elements of water which they assimilate, these animalculae produce limestone, and this limestone forms enormous submarine erections, of which the hardness and solidity equal granite. Formerly, at the first periods of creation, nature employing fire, heaved up the land, but now she entrusts to these microscopic creatures the task of replacing this agent, of which the dynamic power in the interior of the globe has evidently diminished—which is proved by the number of volcanoes on the surface of the earth, now actually extinct. And I believe that centuries succeeding to centuries, and insects to insects, this Pacific may one day be changed into a vast continent, which new generations will inhabit and civilize in their turn."

"That will take a long time," said Pencroft.

"Nature has time for it," replied the engineer.

"But what would be the use of new continents?" asked Herbert. "It appears to me that the present extent of habitable countries is sufficient for humanity. Yet nature does nothing uselessly."

"Nothing uselessly, certainly," replied the engineer, "but this is how the necessity of new continents for the future, and exactly on the tropical zone occupied by the coral islands, may be explained. At least to me this explanation appears plausible."

"We are listening, captain," said Herbert.

"This is my idea: philosophers generally admit that some day our globe will end, or rather that animal and vegetable life will no longer be possible, because of the intense cold to which it will be subjected. What they are not agreed upon, is the cause of this cold. Some think that it will arise from the falling of the temperature, which the sun will experience after millions of years; others, from the gradual extinction of the fires in the interior of our globe, which have a greater influence on it than is generally supposed. I hold to this last hypothesis, grounding it on the fact that the moon is really a cold star, which is no longer habitable, although the sun continues to throw on its surface the same amount of heat. If, then, the moon has become cold, it is because the interior fires to which, as do all the stars of the stellar world, it owes its origin, are completely extinct. Lastly, whatever may be the cause, our globe will become cold some day, but this cold will only operate gradually. What will happen, then? The temperate zones, at a more or less distant period, will not be more habitable than the polar regions now are. Then the population of men, as well as the animals, will flow toward the latitudes which are more directly under the solar influence.

An immense emigration will take place. Europe, Central Asia, North America, will gradually be abandoned, as well as Australasia and the lower parts of South America. The vegetation will follow the human emigration. The flora will retreat toward the Equator at the same time as the fauna. The central parts of South America and Africa will be the continents chiefly inhabited. The Laplanders and the Samoides will find the climate of the polar regions on the shores of the Mediterranean. Who can say, that at this period, the equatorial regions will not be too small, to contain and nourish terrestrial humanity? Now, may not provident nature, so as to give refuge to all the vegetable and animal emigration, be at present laying the foundation of a new continent under the Equator, and may she not have entrusted these insects with the construction of it? I have often thought of all these things, my friends, and I seriously believe that the aspect of our globe will some day be completely changed; that by the raising of new continents the sea will cover the old, and that, in future ages, a Columbus will go to discover the islands of Chimborazo, of the Himalayas, or of Mont Blanc, remains of a submerged America, Asia, and Europe. Then these new continents will become, in their turn, uninhabitable; heat will die away, as does the heat from a body when the soul has left it; and life will disappear from the globe, if not for ever, at least for a period. Perhaps then, our spheroid will rest—will be left to death—to revive some day under superior conditions! But all that, my friends, is the secret of the Author of all things; and beginning by the work of the insects, I have perhaps let myself be carried too far, in investigating the secrets of the future."

"My dear Cyrus," replied Spilett, "these theories are prophecies to me, and they will be accomplished some day."

"That is the secret of God," said the engineer.

"All that is well and good," then said Pencroft, who had listened with all his might, "but will you tell me, captain, if Lincoln Island has been made by your insects?"

"No," replied Harding; "it is of a purely volcanic origin."

"Then it will disappear some day?"

"That is probable."

"I hope we won't be here then."

"No, don't be uneasy, Pencroft; we shall not be here then, as we have no wish to die here, and hope to get away some time."

"In the meantime," replied Gideon Spilett, "let us establish ourselves here as if forever. There is no use in doing things by halves."

This ended the conversation. Breakfast was finished, the exploration was continued, and the settlers arrived at the border of the marshy region. It was a marsh of which the extent, to the rounded coast which terminated the island at the southeast, was about twenty square miles. The soil was formed of clayey flint-earth, mingled with vegetable matter, such as the remains of rushes, reeds, grass, etc. Here and there beds of grass, thick as a carpet, covered it. In many places icy pools sparkled in the sun. Neither rain nor any river, increased by a sudden swelling, could supply these ponds. They therefore naturally concluded that the marsh was fed by the infiltrations of the soil and it was really so. It was also to be feared that during the heat miasmas would arise, which might produce fevers.

Above the aquatic plants, on the surface of the stagnant water, fluttered numbers of birds. Wild duck, teal, snipe lived there in flocks, and those fearless birds allowed themselves to be easily approached.

One shot from a gun would certainly have brought down some dozen of the birds, they were so close together. The explorers were, however, obliged to content themselves with bows and arrows. The result was less, but the silent arrow had the advantage of not frightening the birds, while the noise of firearms would have dispersed them to all parts of the marsh. The hunters were satisfied, for this time, with a dozen ducks, which had white bodies with a band of cinnamon, a green head, wings black, white, and red, and flattened beak. Herbert called them tadorns. Top helped in the capture of these birds, whose name was given to this marshy part of the island. The settlers had here an abundant reserve of aquatic game. At some future time they meant to explore it more carefully, and it was probable that some of the birds there might be domesticated, or at least brought to the shores of the lake, so that they would be more within their reach.

About five o'clock in the evening Cyrus Harding and his companions retraced their steps to their dwelling by traversing Tadorn's Fens, and crossed the Mercy on the ice-bridge.

At eight in the evening they all entered Granite House.

XXII

This intense cold lasted till the 15th of August, without, however, passing the degree of Fahrenheit already mentioned. When the atmosphere was calm, the low temperature was easily borne, but when the wind blew, the poor settlers, insufficiently clothed, felt it severely. Pencroft regretted that Lincoln Island was not the home of a few families of bears rather than of so many foxes and seals.

"Bears," said he, "are generally very well dressed, and I ask no more than to borrow for the winter the warm cloaks which they have on their backs."

"But," replied Neb, laughing, "perhaps the bears would not consent to give you their cloaks, Pencroft. These beasts are not St. Martins."

"We would make them do it, Neb, we would make them," replied Pencroft, in quite an authoritative tone.

But these formidable carnivora did not exist in the island, or at any rate they had not as yet shown themselves.

In the meanwhile, Herbert, Pencroft, and the reporter occupied themselves with making traps on Prospect Heights and at the border of the forest.

According to the sailor, any animal, whatever it was, would be a lawful prize, and the rodents or carnivora which might get into the new snares would be well received at Granite House.

The traps were besides extremely simple; being pits dug in the ground, a platform of branches and grass above, which concealed the opening, and at the bottom some bait, the scent of which would attract animals. It must be mentioned also, that they had not been dug at random, but at certain places where numerous footprints showed that quadrupeds frequented the ground. They were visited every day, and at three different times, during the first days, specimens of those Antarctic foxes which they had already seen on the right bank of the Mercy were found in them.

"Why, there are nothing but foxes in this country!" cried Pencroft, when for the third time he drew one of the animals out of the pit. Looking at it in great disgust, he added, "beasts which are good for nothing!"

"Yes," said Gideon Spilett, "they are good for something!"

"And what is that?"

"To make bait to attract other creatures!"

The reporter was right, and the traps were henceforward baited with the foxes' carcasses.

The sailor had also made snares from the long tough fibers of a certain plant, and they were even more successful than the traps. Rarely a day passed without some rabbits from the warren being caught. It was always rabbit, but Neb knew how to vary his sauces and the settlers did not think of complaining.

However, once or twice in the second week of August, the traps supplied the hunters with other animals more useful than foxes, namely, several of those small wild boars which had already been seen to the north of the lake. Pencroft had no need to ask if these beasts were eatable. He could see that by their resemblance to the pig of America and Europe.

"But these are not pigs," said Herbert to him, "I warn you of that, Pencroft."

"My boy," replied the sailor, bending over the trap and drawing out one of these representatives of the family of sus by the little appendage which served it as a tail. "Let me believe that these are pigs."

"Why?"

"Because that pleases me!"

"Are you very fond of pig then, Pencroft?"

"I am very fond of pig," replied the sailor, "particularly of its feet, and if it had eight instead of four, I should like it twice as much!"

As to the animals in question, they were peccaries belonging to one of the four species which are included in the family, and they were also of the species of tajacu, recognizable by their deep color and the absence of those long teeth with which the mouths of their congeners are armed. These peccaries generally live in herds, and it was probable that they abounded in the woody parts of the island.

At any rate, they were eatable from head to foot, and Pencroft did not ask more from them.

Toward the 15th of August, the state of the atmosphere was suddenly moderated by the wind shifting to the northwest. The temperature rose some degrees, and the accumulated vapor in the air was not long in resolving into snow. All the island was covered with a sheet of white, and showed itself to its inhabitants under a new aspect. The snow fell abundantly for several days, and it soon reached a thickness of two feet.

The wind also blew with great violence, and at the height of Granite House the sea could be heard thundering against the reefs. In some places, the wind, eddying around the corners, formed the snow into tall whirling columns, resembling those waterspouts which turn around on their base, and which vessels attack with a shot from a gun. However, the storm, coming from the northwest, blew across the island, and the position of Granite House preserved it from a direct attack.

But in the midst of this snow-storm, as terrible as if it had been produced in some polar country, neither Cyrus Harding nor his companions could, notwithstanding their wish for it, venture forth, and they remained shut up for five days, from the 20th to the 25th of August. They could hear the tempest raging in Jacamar Wood, which would surely suffer from it. Many of the trees would no doubt be torn up by the roots, but Pencroft consoled himself by thinking that he would not have the trouble of cutting them down.

"The wind is turning woodman, let it alone," he repeated.

Besides, there was no way of stopping it, if they had wished to do so.

How grateful the inhabitants of Granite House then were to Heaven for having prepared for them this solid and immovable retreat! Cyrus Harding had also his legitimate share of thanks, but after all, it was nature who had hollowed out this vast cavern, and he had only discovered it. There all were in safety, and the tempest could not reach them. If they had constructed a house of bricks and wood on Prospect Heights, it certainly would not have resisted the fury of this storm. As to the Chimneys, it must have been absolutely uninhabitable, for the sea, passing over the islet, would beat furiously against it. But here, in Granite House, in the middle of a solid mass, over which neither the sea nor air had any influence, there was nothing to fear.

During these days of seclusion the settlers did not remain inactive.

There was no want of wood, cut up into planks, in the storeroom, and little by little they completed their furnishing; constructing the most solid of tables and chairs, for material was not spared. Neb and Pencroft were very proud of this rather heavy furniture, which they would not have changed on any account.

Then the carpenters became basket-makers, and they did not succeed badly in this new manufacture. At the point of the lake which projected to the north, they had discovered an osier-bed in which grew a large number of purple osiers. Before the rainy season, Pencroft and Herbert had cut down these useful shrubs, and their branches, well prepared, could now be effectively employed. The first attempts were somewhat crude, but in consequence of the cleverness and intelligence of the workmen, by consulting, and recalling the models which they had seen, and by emulating each other, the possessions of the colony were soon increased by several baskets of different sizes. The storeroom was provided with them, and in special baskets Neb placed his collection of rhizomes, stone-pine almonds, etc.

During the last week of the month of August the weather moderated again. The temperature fell a little, and the tempest abated. The colonists sallied out directly. There was certainly two feet of snow on the shore, but they were able to walk without much difficulty on the hardened surface. Cyrus Harding and his companions climbed Prospect Heights.

What a change! The woods, which they had left green, especially in the part at which the firs predominated, had disappeared under a uniform color. All was white, from the summit of Mount Franklin to the shore, the forests, the plains, the lake, the river. The waters of the Mercy flowed under a roof of ice, which, at each rising and ebbing of the tide, broke up with loud crashes. Numerous birds fluttered over the frozen surface of the lake. Ducks and snipe, teal and guillemots were assembled in thousands. The rocks among which the cascade flowed were bristling with icicles. One might have said that the water escaped by a monstrous gargoyle, shaped with all the imagination of an artist of the Renaissance. As to the damage caused by the storm in the forest, that could not as yet be ascertained; they would have to wait till the snowy covering was dissipated.

Gideon Spilett, Pencroft, and Herbert did not miss this opportunity of going to visit their traps. They did not find them easily, under the snow with which they were covered. They had also to be careful not to fall into one or other of them, which would have been both dangerous and humiliating; to be taken in their own snares! But happily they avoided this unpleasantness, and found their traps perfectly intact. No animal had fallen into them, and yet the footprints in the neighborhood were very numerous, among others, certain very clear marks of claws. Herbert did not hesitate to affirm that some animal of the feline species had passed there, which justified the engineer's opinion that dangerous beasts existed in Lincoln Island. These animals doubtless generally lived in the Forests of the Far West, but pressed by hunger, they had ventured as far as Prospect Heights. Perhaps they had smelled out the inhabitants of Granite House.

"Now, what are these feline creatures?" asked Pencroft.

"They are tigers," replied Herbert.

"I thought those beasts were only found in hot countries?"

"On the new continent," replied the lad, "they are found from Mexico to the Pampas of Buenos Aires. Now, as Lincoln Island is nearly under the same latitude as the provinces of La Plata, it is not surprising that tigers are to be met with in it."

"Well, we must look out for them," replied Pencroft.

However, the snow soon disappeared, quickly dissolving under the influence of the rising temperature. Rain fell, and the sheet of white soon vanished. Notwithstanding the bad weather, the settlers renewed their stores of different things, stone-pine almonds, rhizomes, syrup from the maple-tree, for the vegetable part; rabbits from the warren, agouties, and kangaroos for the animal part. This necessitated several excursions into the forest, and they found that a great number of trees had been blown down by the last hurricane. Pencroft and Neb also pushed with the cart as far as the vein of coal, and brought back several tons of fuel. They saw in passing that the pottery kiln had been severely damaged by the wind, at least six feet of it having been blown off.

At the same time as the coal, the store of wood was renewed at Granite House, and they profited by the current of the Mercy having again become free, to float down several rafts. They could see that the cold period was not ended.

A visit was also paid to the Chimneys, and the settlers could not but congratulate themselves on not having been living there during the hurricane. The sea had left unquestionable traces of its ravages. Sweeping over the islet, it had furiously assailed the passages, half filling them with sand, while thick beds of seaweed covered the rocks. While Neb, Herbert, and Pencroft hunted or collected wood, Cyrus Harding and Gideon Spilett busied themselves in putting the Chimneys to rights, and they found the forge and the bellows almost unhurt, protected as they had been from the first by the heaps of sand.

The store of fuel had not been made uselessly. The settlers had not done with the rigorous cold. It is known that, in the Northern Hemisphere, the month of February is principally distinguished by rapid fallings of the temperature. It is the same in the Southern Hemisphere, and the end of the month of August, which is the February of North America, does not escape this climatic law.

About the 25th, after another change from snow to rain, the wind shifted to the southeast, and the cold became, suddenly, very severe. According to the engineer's calculation, the mercurial column of a Fahrenheit thermometer would not have marked less than eight degrees below zero, and this intense cold, rendered still more painful by a sharp gale, lasted for several days. The colonists were again shut up in Granite House, and as it was necessary to hermetically seal all the openings of the façade, only leaving a narrow passage for renewing the air, the consumption of candles was considerable. To economize them, the cavern was often only lighted by the blazing hearths, on which fuel was not spared. Several times, one or other of the settlers descended to the beach in the midst of ice which the waves heaped up at each tide, but they soon climbed up again to Granite House, and it was not without pain and difficulty that their hands could hold to the rounds of the ladder. In consequence of the intense cold, their fingers felt as if burned when they touched the rounds. To occupy the leisure hours, which the tenants of Granite House now had at their disposal, Cyrus Harding undertook an operation which could be performed indoors.

We know that the settlers had no other sugar at their disposal than the liquid substance which they drew from the maple, by making deep incisions in the tree. They contented themselves with collecting this liquor in jars and employing it in this state for different culinary purposes, and the more so, as on growing old, this liquid began to become white and to be of a syrupy consistence.

But there was something better to be made of it, and one day Cyrus Harding announced that they were going to turn into refiners.

"Refiners!" replied Pencroft. "That is rather a warm trade, I think."

"Very warm," answered the engineer.

"Then it will be seasonable!" said the sailor.

This word refining need not awake in the mind thoughts of an elaborate manufactory with apparatus and numerous workmen. No! to crystallize this liquor, only an extremely easy operation is required. Placed on the fire in large earthen pots, it was simply subjected to evaporation, and soon a scum arose to its surface. As soon as this began to thicken, Neb carefully removed it with a wooden spatula; this accelerated the evaporation, and at the same time prevented it from contracting an empyreumatic flavor.

After boiling for several hours on a hot fire, which did as much good to the operators as the substance operated upon, the latter was transformed into a thick syrup. This syrup was poured into clay molds, previously fabricated in the kitchen stove, and to which they had given various shapes. The next day this syrup had become cold, and formed cakes and tablets. This was sugar of rather a reddish color, but nearly transparent and of a delicious taste.

The cold continued to the middle of September, and the prisoners in Granite House began to find their captivity rather tedious. Nearly every day they attempted sorties which they could not prolong. They constantly worked at the improvement of their dwelling. They talked while working. Harding instructed his companions in many things, principally explaining to them the practical applications of science. The colonists had no library at their disposal; but the engineer was a book which was always at hand, always open at the page which one wanted, a book which answered all their questions, and which they often consulted. The time thus passed away pleasantly, these brave men not appearing to have any fears for the future.

However, all were anxious to see, if not the fine season, at least the cessation of the insupportable cold. If only they had been clothed in a way to meet it, how many excursions they would have attempted, either to the downs or to Tadorn's Fens! Game would have been easily approached, and the chase would certainly have been most productive. But Cyrus Harding considered it of importance that no one should injure his health, for he had need of all his hands, and his advice was followed.

But it must be said, that the one who was most impatient of this imprisonment, after Pencroft perhaps, was Top. The faithful dog found Granite House very narrow. He ran backward and forward from one room to another, showing in his way how weary he was of being shut up. Harding often remarked that when he approached the dark well which communicated with the sea, and of which the orifice opened at the back of the storeroom, Top uttered singular growlings. He ran around and around this hole, which had been covered with a wooden lid. Sometimes even he tried to put his paws under the lid, as if he wished to raise it. He then yelped in a peculiar way, which showed at once anger and uneasiness.

The engineer observed this maneuver several times.

What could there be in this abyss to make such an impression on the intelligent animal? The well led to the sea, that was certain. Could narrow passages spread from it through the foundations of the island? Did some marine monster come from time to time, to breathe at the bottom of this well? The engineer did not know what to think, and could not refrain from dreaming of many strange improbabilities. Accustomed to go far into the regions of scientific reality, he would not allow himself to be drawn into the regions of the strange and almost of the supernatural; but yet how to explain why Top, one of those sensible dogs who never waste their time in barking at the moon, should persist in trying with scent and hearing to fathom this abyss, if there was nothing there to cause his uneasiness? Top's conduct puzzled Cyrus Harding even more than he cared to acknowledge to himself.

At all events, the engineer only communicated his impressions to Gideon Spilett, for he thought it useless to explain to his companions the suspicions which arose from what perhaps was only Top's fancy.

At last the cold ceased. There had been rain, squalls mingled with snow, hailstorms, gusts of wind, but these inclemencies did not last. The ice melted, the snow disappeared; the shore, the plateau, the banks of the Mercy, the forest, again became practicable. This return of spring delighted the tenants of Granite House, and they soon only passed in it the hours necessary for eating and sleeping.

They hunted much in the second part of September, which led Pencroft to again entreat for the firearms, which he asserted had been promised by Cyrus Harding. The latter, knowing well that without special tools it would be nearly impossible for him to manufacture a gun which would be of any use, still drew back and put off the operation to some future time, observing in his usual dry way, that Herbert and Spilett had become very skillful archers, so that many sorts of excellent animals, agouties, kangaroos, capybaras, pigeons, bustards, wild ducks, snipes, in short, game both with fur and feathers, fell victims to their arrows, and that, consequently, they could wait. But the obstinate sailor would listen to nothing of this, and he would give the engineer no peace till he promised to satisfy his desire. Gideon Spilett, however, supported Pencroft.

"If, which may be doubted," said he, "the island is inhabited by wild beasts, we must think how to fight with and exterminate them. A time may come when this will be our first duty."

But at this period, it was not the question of firearms which occupied Harding, but that of clothes. Those which the settlers wore had passed this winter, but they would not last until next winter. Skins of carnivora or the wool of ruminants must be procured at any price, and since there were plenty of musmons, it was agreed to consult on the means of forming a flock which might be brought up for the use of the colony. An enclosure for the domestic animals, a poultry-yard for the birds, in a word to establish a sort of farm in the island, such were the two important projects for the fine season.

In consequence and in view of these future establishments, it became of much importance that they should penetrate into all the yet unknown parts of Lincoln Island, that is to say, through that thick forest which extended on the right bank of the Mercy, from its mouth to the extremity of the Serpentine Peninsula, as well as on the whole of its western side. But this needed settled weather, and a month must pass before this exploration could be profitably undertaken.

They therefore waited with some impatience, when an incident occurred which increased the desire the settlers had to visit the whole of their domain.

It was the 24th of October. On this day, Pencroft had gone to visit his traps, which he always kept properly baited. In one of them he found three animals which would be very welcome for the larder. They were a female peccary and her two young ones.

Pencroft then returned to Granite House, enchanted with his capture, and, as usual, he made a great show of his game.

"Come, we shall have a grand feast, captain!" he exclaimed. "And you too, Mr. Spilett, you will eat some!"

"I shall be very happy," replied the reporter; "but what is it that I am going to eat?"

"Suckling-pig."

"Oh, indeed, suckling-pig, Pencroft? To hear you, I thought that you were bringing back a young partridge stuffed with truffles!"

"What?" cried Pencroft. "Do you mean to say that you turn up your nose at suckling-pig?"

"No," replied Gideon Spilett, without showing any enthusiasm; "provided one doesn't eat too much—"

"That's right, that's right," returned the sailor, who was not pleased whenever he heard his chase made light of. "You like to make objections. Seven months ago, when we landed on the island, you would have been only too glad to have met with such game!"

"Well, well," replied the reporter, "man is never perfect, nor contented."

"Now," said Pencroft, "I hope that Neb will distinguish himself. Look here! These two little peccaries are not more than three months old! They will be as tender as quails! Come along, Neb, come! I will look after the cooking myself."

And the sailor, followed by Neb, entered the kitchen, where they were soon absorbed in their culinary labors.

They were allowed to do it in their own way. Neb, therefore, prepared a magnificent repast—the two little peccaries, kangaroo soup, a smoked ham, stone-pine almonds, Oswego tea; in fact, all the best that they had, but among all the dishes figured in the first rank the savory peccaries.

At five o'clock dinner was served in the dining-room of Granite House. The kangaroo soup was smoking on the table. They found it excellent.

To the soup succeeded the peccaries, which Pencroft insisted on carving himself, and of which he served out monstrous portions to each of the guests.

These suckling-pigs were really delicious, and Pencroft was devouring his share with great gusto, when all at once a cry and an oath escaped him.

"What's the matter?" asked Cyrus Harding.

"The matter? the matter is that I have just broken a tooth!" replied the sailor.

"What, are there pebbles in your peccaries?" said Gideon Spilett.

"I suppose so," replied Pencroft, drawing from his lips the object which had cost him a grinder!

It was not a pebble—it was a leaden bullet.

Part 2

Abandoned

I

It was now exactly seven months since the balloon voyagers had been thrown on Lincoln Island. During that time, notwithstanding the researches they had made, no human being had been discovered. No smoke even had betrayed the presence of man on the surface of the island. No vestiges of his handiwork showed that either at an early or at a late period had man lived there. Not only did it now appear to be uninhabited by any but themselves, but the colonists were compelled to believe that it never had been inhabited. And now, all this scaffolding of reasonings fell before a simple ball of metal, found in the body of an inoffensive rodent! In fact, this bullet must have issued from a firearm, and who but a human being could have used such a weapon?

When Pencroft had placed the bullet on the table, his companions looked at it with intense astonishment. All the consequences likely to result from this incident, notwithstanding its apparent insignificance, immediately took possession of their minds. The sudden apparition of a supernatural being could not have startled them more completely.

Cyrus Harding did not hesitate to give utterance to the suggestions which this fact, at once surprising and unexpected, could not fail to raise in his mind. He took the bullet, turned it over and over, rolled it between his finger and thumb; then, turning to Pencroft, he asked,

"Are you sure that the peccary wounded by this bullet was not more than three months old?"

"Not more, captain," replied Pencroft. "It was still sucking its mother when I found it in the trap."

"Well," said the engineer, "that proves that within three months a gunshot was fired in Lincoln Island."

"And that a bullet," added Gideon Spilett, "wounded, though not mortally, this little animal."

"That is unquestionable," said Cyrus Harding, "and these are the deductions which must be drawn from this incident: that the island was inhabited before our arrival, or that men have landed here within three months. Did these men arrive here voluntarily or involuntarily, by disembarking on the shore or by being wrecked? This point can only be cleared up later. As to what they were, Europeans or Malays, enemies or friends of our race, we cannot possibly guess; and if they still inhabit the island, or if they have left it, we know not. But these questions are of too much importance to be allowed to remain long unsettled."

"No! a hundred times no! a thousand times no!" cried the sailor, springing up from the table. "There are no other men than ourselves on Lincoln Island! By my faith! The island isn't large and if it had been inhabited, we should have seen some of the inhabitants long before this!"

"In fact, the contrary would be very astonishing," said Herbert.

"But it would be much more astonishing, I should think," observed the reporter, "if this peccary had been born with a bullet in its inside!"

"At least," said Neb seriously, "if Pencroft has not had—"

"Look here, Neb," burst out Pencroft. "Do you think I could have a bullet in my jaw for five or six months without finding it out? Where could it be hidden?" he asked, opening his mouth to show the two-and-thirty teeth with which it was furnished. "Look well, Neb, and if you find one hollow tooth in this set, I will let you pull out half a dozen!"

"Neb's supposition is certainly inadmissible," replied Harding, who, notwithstanding the gravity of his thoughts, could not restrain a smile. "It is certain that a gun has been fired in the island, within three months at most. But I am inclined to think that the people who landed on this coast were only here a very short time ago, or that they just touched here; for if, when we surveyed the island from the summit of Mount Franklin, it had been inhabited, we should have seen them or we should have been seen ourselves. It is therefore probable that within only a few weeks castaways have been thrown by a storm on some part of the coast. However that may be, it is of consequence to us to have this point settled."

"I think that we should act with caution," said the reporter.

"Such is my advice," replied Cyrus Harding, "for it is to be feared that Malay pirates have landed on the island!"

"Captain," asked the sailor, "would it not be a good plan, before setting out, to build a canoe in which we could either ascend the river, or, if we liked, coast around the inland? It will not do to be unprovided."

"Your idea is good, Pencroft," replied the engineer, "but we cannot wait for that. It would take at least a month to build a boat."

"Yes, a real boat," replied the sailor; "but we do not want one for a sea voyage, and in five days at the most, I will undertake to construct a canoe fit to navigate the Mercy."

"Five days," cried Neb, "to build a boat?"

"Yes, Neb; a boat in the Indian fashion."

"Of wood?" asked the Negro, looking still unconvinced.

"Of wood," replied Pencroft, "or rather of bark. I repeat, captain, that in five days the work will be finished!"

"In five days, then, be it," replied the engineer.

"But till that time we must be very watchful," said Herbert.

"Very watchful indeed, my friends," replied Harding; "and I beg you to confine your hunting excursions to the neighborhood of Granite House."

The dinner ended less gaily than Pencroft had hoped.

So, then, the island was, or had been, inhabited by others than the settlers. Proved as it was by the incident of the bullet, it was hereafter an unquestionable fact, and such a discovery could not but cause great uneasiness among the colonists.

Cyrus Harding and Gideon Spilett, before sleeping, conversed long about the matter. They asked themselves if by chance this incident might not have some connection with the inexplicable way in which the engineer had been saved, and the other peculiar circumstances which had struck them at different times. However, Cyrus Harding, after having discussed the pros and cons of the question, ended by saying,

"In short, would you like to know my opinion, my dear Spilett?"

"Yes, Cyrus."

"Well, then, it is this: however minutely we explore the island, we shall find nothing."

The next day Pencroft set to work. He did not mean to build a boat with boards and planking, but simply a flat-bottomed canoe, which would be well suited for navigating the Mercy—above all, for approaching its source, where the water would naturally be shallow. Pieces of bark, fastened one to the other, would form a light boat; and in case of natural obstacles, which would render a portage necessary, it would be easily carried. Pencroft intended to secure the pieces of bark by means of nails, to ensure the canoe being water-tight.

It was first necessary to select the trees which would afford a strong and supple bark for the work. Now the last storm had brought down a number of large birch-trees, the bark of which would be perfectly suited for their purpose. Some of these trees lay on the ground, and they had only to be barked, which was the most difficult thing of all, owing to the imperfect tools which the settlers possessed. However, they overcame all difficulties.

While the sailor, seconded by the engineer, thus occupied himself without losing an hour, Gideon Spilett and Herbert were not idle.

They were made purveyors to the colony. The reporter could not but admire the boy, who had acquired great skill in handling the bow and spear. Herbert also showed great courage and much of that presence of mind which may justly be called "the reasoning of bravery." These two companions of the chase, remembering Cyrus Harding's recommendations, did not go beyond a radius of two miles around Granite House; but the borders of the forest furnished a sufficient tribute of agoutis, capybaras, kangaroos, peccaries, etc.; and if the result from the traps was less than during the cold, still the warren yielded its accustomed quota, which might have fed all the colony in Lincoln Island.

Often during these excursions, Herbert talked with Gideon Spilett on the incident of the bullet, and the deductions which the engineer drew from it, and one day—it was the 26th of October—he said,

"But, Mr. Spilett, do you not think it very extraordinary that, if any castaways have landed on the island, they have not yet shown themselves near Granite House?"

"Very astonishing if they are still here," replied the reporter, "but not astonishing at all if they are here no longer!"

"So you think that these people have already quitted the island?" returned Herbert.

"It is more than probable, my boy; for if their stay was prolonged, and above all, if they were still here, some accident would have at last betrayed their presence."

"But if they were able to go away," observed the lad, "they could not have been castaways."

"No, Herbert; or, at least, they were what might be called provisional castaways. It is very possible that a storm may have driven them to the island without destroying their vessel, and that, the storm over, they went away again."

"I must acknowledge one thing," said Herbert, "it is that Captain Harding appears rather to fear than desire the presence of human beings on our island."

"In short," responded the reporter, "there are only Malays who frequent these seas, and those fellows are ruffians which it is best to avoid."

"It is not impossible, Mr. Spilett," said Herbert, "that some day or other we may find traces of their landing."

"I do not say no, my boy. A deserted camp, the ashes of a fire, would put us on the track, and this is what we will look for in our next expedition."

The day on which the hunters spoke thus, they were in a part of the forest near the Mercy, remarkable for its beautiful trees. There, among others, rose, to a height of nearly 200 feet above the ground, some of those superb coniferae, to which, in New Zealand, the natives give the name of kauris.

"I have an idea, Mr. Spilett," said Herbert. "If I were to climb to the top of one of these kauris, I could survey the country for an immense distance around."

"The idea is good," replied the reporter; "but could you climb to the top of those giants?"

"I can at least try," replied Herbert.

The light and active boy then sprang on the first branches, the arrangement of which made the ascent of the kauri easy, and in a few minutes he arrived at the summit, which emerged from the immense plain of verdure.

From this elevated situation his gaze extended over all the southern portion of the island, from Claw Cape on the southeast, to Reptile End on the southwest. To the northwest rose Mount Franklin, which concealed a great part of the horizon.

But Herbert, from the height of his observatory, could examine all the yet unknown portion of the island, which might have given shelter to the strangers whose presence they suspected.

The lad looked attentively. There was nothing in sight on the sea, not a sail, neither on the horizon nor near the island. However, as the bank of trees hid the shore, it was possible that a vessel, especially if deprived of her masts, might lie close to the land and thus be invisible to Herbert.

Neither in the Forests of the Far West was anything to be seen. The wood formed an impenetrable screen, measuring several square miles, without a break or an opening. It was impossible even to follow the course of the Mercy, or to ascertain in what part of the mountain it took its source. Perhaps other creeks also ran toward the west, but they could not be seen.

But at last, if all indication of an encampment escaped Herbert's sight could he not even catch a glimpse of smoke, the faintest trace of which would be easily discernible in the pure atmosphere?

For an instant Herbert thought he could perceive a slight smoke in the west, but a more attentive examination showed that he was mistaken. He strained his eyes in every direction, and his sight was excellent. No, decidedly there was nothing there.

Herbert descended to the foot of the kauri, and the two sportsmen returned to Granite House. There Cyrus Harding listened to the lad's account, shook his head, and said nothing. It was very evident that no decided opinion could be pronounced on this question until after a complete exploration of the island.

Two days after—the 28th of October—another incident occurred, for which an explanation was again required.

While strolling along the shore about two miles from Granite House, Herbert and Neb were fortunate enough to capture a magnificent specimen of the order of chelonia. It was a turtle of the species Midas, the edible green turtle, so called from the color both of its shell and fat.

Herbert caught sight of this turtle as it was crawling among the rocks to reach the sea.

"Help, Neb, help!" he cried.

Neb ran up.

"What a fine animal!" said Neb; "but how are we to catch it?"

"Nothing is easier, Neb," replied Herbert. "We have only to turn the turtle on its back, and it cannot possibly get away. Take your spear and do as I do."

The reptile, aware of danger, had retired between its carapace and plastron. They no longer saw its head or feet, and it was motionless as a rock.

Herbert and Neb then drove their sticks underneath the animal, and by their united efforts managed without difficulty to turn it on its back. The turtle, which was three feet in length, would have weighed at least four hundred pounds.

"Capital!" cried Neb; "this is something which will rejoice friend Pencroft's heart."

In fact, the heart of friend Pencroft could not fail to be rejoiced, for the flesh of the turtle, which feeds on wrack-grass, is extremely savory. At this moment the creature's head could be seen, which was small, flat, but widened behind by the large temporal fossae hidden under the long roof.

"And now, what shall we do with our prize?" said Neb. "We can't drag it to Granite House!"

"Leave it here, since it cannot turn over," replied Herbert, "and we will come back with the cart to fetch it."

"That is the best plan."

However, for greater precaution, Herbert took the trouble, which Neb deemed superfluous, to wedge up the animal with great stones; after which the two hunters returned to Granite House, following the beach, which the tide had left uncovered. Herbert, wishing to surprise Pencroft, said nothing about the "superb specimen of a chelonian" which they had turned over on the sand; but, two hours later, he and Neb returned with the cart to the place where they had left it. The "superb specimen of a chelonian" was no longer there!

Neb and Herbert stared at each other first; then they stared about them. It was just at this spot that the turtle had been left. The lad even found the stones which he had used, and therefore he was certain of not being mistaken.

"Well!" said Neb, "these beasts can turn themselves over, then?"

"It appears so," replied Herbert, who could not understand it at all, and was gazing at the stones scattered on the sand.

"Well, Pencroft will be disgusted!"

"And Captain Harding will perhaps be very perplexed how to explain this disappearance," thought Herbert.

"Look here," said Neb, who wished to hide his ill-luck, "we won't speak about it."

"On the contrary, Neb, we must speak about it," replied Herbert.

And the two, taking the cart, which there was now no use for, returned to Granite House.

Arrived at the dockyard, where the engineer and the sailor were working together, Herbert recounted what had happened.

"Oh! the stupids!" cried the sailor, "to have let at least fifty meals escape!"

"But, Pencroft," replied Neb, "it wasn't our fault that the beast got away; as I tell you, we had turned it over on its back!"

"Then you didn't turn it over enough!" returned the obstinate sailor.

"Not enough!" cried Herbert.

And he told how he had taken care to wedge up the turtle with stones.

"It is a miracle, then!" replied Pencroft.

"I thought, captain," said Herbert, "that turtles, once placed on their backs, could not regain their feet, especially when they are of a large size?"

"That is true, my boy," replied Cyrus Harding.

"Then how did it manage?"

"At what distance from the sea did you leave this turtle?" asked the engineer, who, having suspended his work, was reflecting on this incident.

"Fifteen feet at the most," replied Herbert.

"And the tide was low at the time?"

"Yes, captain."

"Well," replied the engineer, "what the turtle could not do on the sand it might have been able to do in the water. It turned over when the tide overtook it, and then quietly returned to the deep sea."

"Oh! what stupids we were!" cried Neb.

"That is precisely what I had the honor of telling you before!" returned the sailor.

Cyrus Harding had given this explanation, which, no doubt, was admissible. But was he himself convinced of the accuracy of this explanation? It cannot be said that he was.

II

On the 9th of October the bark canoe was entirely finished. Pencroft had kept his promise, and a light boat, the shell of which was joined together by the flexible twigs of the crejimba, had been constructed in five days. A seat in the stern, a second seat in the middle to preserve the equilibrium, a third seat in the bows, rowlocks for the two oars, a scull to steer with, completed the little craft, which was twelve feet long, and did not weigh more than two hundred pounds. The operation of launching it was extremely simple. The canoe was carried to the beach and laid on the sand before Granite House, and the rising tide floated it. Pencroft, who leaped in directly, maneuvered it with the scull and declared it to be just the thing for the purpose to which they wished to put it.

"Hurrah!" cried the sailor, who did not disdain to celebrate thus his own triumph. "With this we could go around—"

"The world?" asked Gideon Spilett.

"No, the island. Some stones for ballast, a mast and a sail, which the captain will make for us some day, and we shall go splendidly! Well, captain—and you, Mr. Spilett; and you, Herbert; and you, Neb—aren't you coming to try our new vessel? Come along! we must see if it will carry all five of us!"

This was certainly a trial which ought to be made. Pencroft soon brought the canoe to the shore by a narrow passage among the rocks, and it was agreed that they should make a trial of the boat that day by following the shore as far as the first point at which the rocks of the south ended.

As they embarked, Neb cried,

"But your boat leaks rather, Pencroft."

"That's nothing, Neb," replied the sailor; "the wood will get seasoned. In two days there won't be a single leak, and our boat will have no more water in her than there is in the stomach of a drunkard. Jump in!"

They were soon all seated, and Pencroft shoved off. The weather was magnificent, the sea as calm as if its waters were contained within the narrow limits of a lake. Thus the boat could proceed with as much security as if it was ascending the tranquil current of the Mercy.

Neb took one of the oars, Herbert the other, and Pencroft remained in the stern in order to use the scull.

The sailor first crossed the channel, and steered close to the southern point of the islet. A light breeze blew from the south. No roughness was found either in the channel or the green sea. A long swell, which the canoe scarcely felt, as it was heavily laden, rolled regularly over the surface of the water. They pulled out about half a mile distant from the shore, that they might have a good view of Mount Franklin.

Pencroft afterward returned toward the mouth of the river. The boat then skirted the shore, which, extending to the extreme point, hid all Tadorn's Fens.

This point, of which the distance was increased by the irregularity of the coast, was nearly three miles from the Mercy. The settlers resolved to go to its extremity, and only go beyond it as much as was necessary to take a rapid survey of the coast as far as Claw Cape.

The canoe followed the windings of the shore, avoiding the rocks which fringed it, and which the rising tide began to cover. The cliff gradually sloped away from the mouth of the river to the point. This was formed of granite rocks, capriciously distributed, very different from the cliff at Prospect Heights, and of an extremely wild aspect. It might have been said that an immense cartload of rocks had been emptied out there. There was no vegetation on this sharp promontory, which projected two miles from the forest, and it thus represented a giant's arm stretched out from a leafy sleeve.

The canoe, impelled by the two oars, advanced without difficulty. Gideon Spilett, pencil in one hand and notebook in the other, sketched the coast in bold strokes. Neb, Herbert, and Pencroft chatted, while examining this part of their domain, which was new to them, and, in proportion as the canoe proceeded toward the south, the two Mandible Capes appeared to move, and surround Union Bay more closely.

As to Cyrus Harding, he did not speak; he simply gazed, and by the mistrust which his look expressed, it appeared that he was examining some strange country.

In the meantime, after a voyage of three-quarters of an hour, the canoe reached the extremity of the point, and Pencroft was preparing to return, when Herbert, rising, pointed to a black object, saying,

"What do I see down there on the beach?"

All eyes turned toward the point indicated.

"Why," said the reporter, "there is something. It looks like part of a wreck half buried in the sand."

"Ah!" cried Pencroft, "I see what it is!"

"What?" asked Neb.

"Barrels, barrels, which perhaps are full," replied the sailor.

"Pull to the shore, Pencroft!" said Cyrus.

A few strokes of the oar brought the canoe into a little creek, and its passengers leaped on shore.

Pencroft was not mistaken. Two barrels were there, half buried in the sand, but still firmly attached to a large chest, which, sustained by them, had floated to the moment when it stranded on the beach.

"There has been a wreck, then, in some part of the island," said Herbert.

"Evidently," replied Spilett.

"But what's in this chest?" cried Pencroft, with very natural impatience. "What's in this chest? It is shut up, and nothing to open it with! Well, perhaps a stone—"

And the sailor, raising a heavy block, was about to break in one of the sides of the chest, when the engineer arrested his hand.

"Pencroft," said he, "can you restrain your impatience for one hour only?"

"But, captain, just think! Perhaps there is everything we want in there!"

"We shall find that out, Pencroft," replied the engineer; "but trust to me, and do not break the chest, which may be useful to us. We must convey it to Granite House, where we can open it easily, and without breaking it. It is quite prepared for a voyage; and since it has floated here, it may just as well float to the mouth of the river."

"You are right, captain, and I was wrong, as usual," replied the sailor.

The engineer's advice was good. In fact, the canoe probably would not have been able to contain the articles possibly enclosed in the chest, which doubtless was heavy, since two empty barrels were required to buoy it up. It was, therefore, much better to tow it to the beach at Granite House.

And now, whence had this chest come? That was the important question. Cyrus Harding and his companions looked attentively around them, and examined the shore for several hundred steps. No other articles or pieces of wreck could be found. Herbert and Neb climbed a high rock to survey the sea, but there was nothing in sight—neither a dismasted vessel nor a ship under sail.

However, there was no doubt that there had been a wreck. Perhaps this incident was connected with that of the bullet? Perhaps strangers had landed on another part of the island? Perhaps they were still there? But the thought which came naturally to the settlers was, that these strangers could not be Malay pirates, for the chest was evidently of American or European make.

All the party returned to the chest, which was of an unusually large size. It was made of oak wood, very carefully closed and covered with a thick hide, which was secured by copper nails. The two great barrels, hermetically sealed, but which sounded hollow and empty, were fastened to its sides by strong ropes, knotted with a skill which Pencroft directly pronounced sailors alone could exhibit. It appeared to be in a perfect state of preservation, which was explained by the fact that it had stranded on a sandy beach, and not among rocks. They had no doubt whatever, on examining it carefully, that it had not been long in the water, and that its arrival on this coast was recent. The water did not appear to have penetrated to the inside, and the articles which it contained were no doubt uninjured.

It was evident that this chest had been thrown overboard from some dismasted vessel driven toward the island, and that, in the hope that it would reach the land, where they might afterward find it, the passengers had taken the precaution to buoy it up by means of this floating apparatus.

"We will tow this chest to Granite House," said the engineer, "where we can make an inventory of its contents; then, if we discover any of the survivors from the supposed wreck, we can return it to those to whom it belongs. If we find no one—"

"We will keep it for ourselves!" cried Pencroft. "But what in the world can there be in it?"

The sea was already approaching the chest, and the high tide would evidently float it. One of the ropes which fastened the barrels was partly unlashed and used as a cable to unite the floating apparatus with the canoe. Pencroft and Neb then dug away the sand with their oars, so as to facilitate the moving of the chest, towing which the boat soon began to double the point, to which the name of Flotsam Point was given.

The chest was heavy, and the barrels were scarcely sufficient to keep it above water. The sailor also feared every instant that it would get loose and sink to the bottom of the sea. But happily his fears were not realized, and an hour and a half after they set out—all that time had been taken up in going a distance of three miles—the boat touched the beach below Granite House.

Canoe and chest were then hauled up on the sands; and as the tide was then going out, they were soon left high and dry. Neb, hurrying home, brought back some tools with which to open the chest in such a way that it might be injured as little as possible, and they proceeded to its inventory. Pencroft did not try to hide that he was greatly excited.

The sailor began by detaching the two barrels, which, being in good condition, would of course be of use. Then the locks were forced with a cold chisel and hammer, and the lid thrown back. A second casing of zinc lined the interior of the chest, which had been evidently arranged that the articles which it enclosed might under any circumstances be sheltered from damp.

"Oh!" cried Neb, "suppose it's jam!"

"I hope not," replied the reporter.

"If only there was—" said the sailor in a low voice.

"What?" asked Neb, who overheard him.

"Nothing!"

The covering of zinc was torn off and thrown back over the sides of the chest, and by degrees numerous articles of very varied character were produced and strewn about on the sand. At each new object Pencroft uttered fresh hurrahs, Herbert clapped his hands, and Neb danced up and down. There were books which made Herbert wild with joy, and cooking utensils which Neb covered with kisses!

In short, the colonists had reason to be extremely satisfied, for this chest contained tools, weapons, instruments, clothes, books; and this is the exact list of them as stated in Gideon Spilett's notebook:

Tools: 3 knives with several blades, 2 woodmen's axes, 2 carpenter's hatchets, 3 planes, 2 adzes, 1 twibil or mattock, 6 chisels, 2 files, 3 hammers, 3 gimlets, 2 augers, 10 bags of nails and screws, 3 saws of different sizes, 2 boxes of needles.

Weapons: 2 flint-lock guns, 2 for percussion caps, 2 breach-loader carbines, 5 boarding cutlasses, 4 sabers, 2 barrels of powder, each containing twenty-five pounds; 12 boxes of percussion caps.

Instruments: 1 sextant, 1 double opera-glass, 1 telescope, 1 box of mathematical instruments, 1 mariner's compass, 1 Fahrenheit thermometer, 1 aneroid barometer, 1 box containing a photographic apparatus, object-glass, plates, chemicals, etc.

Clothes: 2 dozen shirts of a peculiar material resembling wool, but evidently of a vegetable origin; 3 dozen stockings of the same material.

Utensils: 1 iron pot, 6 copper saucepans, 3 iron dishes, 10 metal plates, 2 kettles, 1 portable stove, 6 table-knives.

Books: 1 Bible, 1 atlas, 1 dictionary of the different Polynesian idioms, 1 dictionary of natural science, in six volumes; 3 reams of white paper, 2 books with blank pages.

"It must be allowed," said the reporter, after the inventory had been made, "that the owner of this chest was a practical man! Tools, weapons, instruments, clothes, utensils, books—nothing is wanting! It might really be said that he expected to be wrecked, and had prepared for it beforehand."

"Nothing is wanting, indeed," murmured Cyrus Harding thoughtfully.

"And for a certainty," added Herbert, "the vessel which carried this chest and its owner was not a Malay pirate!"

"Unless," said Pencroft, "the owner had been taken prisoner by pirates—"

"That is not admissible," replied the reporter. "It is more probable that an American or European vessel has been driven into this quarter, and that her passengers, wishing to save necessaries at least, prepared this chest and threw it overboard."

"Is that your opinion, captain?" asked Herbert.

"Yes, my boy," replied the engineer, "that may have been the case. It is possible that at the moment, or in expectation of a wreck, they collected into this chest different articles of the greatest use in hopes of finding it again on the coast—"

"Even the photographic box!" exclaimed the sailor incredulously.

"As to that apparatus," replied Harding, "I do not quite see the use of it; and a more complete supply of clothes or more abundant ammunition would have been more valuable to us as well as to any other castaways!"

"But isn't there any mark or direction on these instruments, tools, or books, which would tell us something about them?" asked Gideon Spilett.

That might be ascertained. Each article was carefully examined, especially the books, instruments, and weapons. Neither the weapons nor the instruments, contrary to the usual custom, bore the name of the maker; they were, besides, in a perfect state, and did not appear to have been used. The same peculiarity marked the tools and utensils; all were new, which proved that the articles had not been taken by chance and thrown into the chest, but, on the contrary, that the choice of things had been well considered and arranged with care. This was also indicated by the second case of metal which had preserved them from damp, and which could not have been soldered in a moment of haste.

As to the dictionaries of natural science and Polynesian idioms, both were English; but they neither bore the name of the publisher nor the date of publication.

The same with the Bible printed in English, in quarto, remarkable from a typographic point of view, and which appeared to have been often used.

The atlas was a magnificent work, comprising maps of every country in the world, and several planispheres arranged upon Mercator's projection, and of which the nomenclature was in French—but which also bore neither date nor name of publisher.

There was nothing, therefore, on these different articles by which they could be traced, and nothing consequently of a nature to show the nationality of the vessel which must have recently passed these shores.

But, wherever the chest might have come from, it was a treasure to the settlers on Lincoln Island. Till then, by making use of the productions of nature, they had created everything for themselves, and, thanks to their intelligence, they had managed without difficulty. But did it not appear as if Providence had wished to reward them by sending them these productions of human industry? Their thanks rose unanimously to Heaven.

However, one of them was not quite satisfied: it was Pencroft. It appeared that the chest did not contain something which he evidently held in great esteem, for in proportion as they approached the bottom of the box, his hurrahs diminished in heartiness, and, the inventory finished, he was heard to mutter these words: "That's all very fine, but you can see that there is nothing for me in that box!"

This led Neb to say,

"Why, friend Pencroft, what more do you expect?"

"Half a pound of tobacco," replied Pencroft seriously, "and nothing would have been wanting to complete my happiness!"

No one could help laughing at this speech of the sailor's.

But the result of this discovery of the chest was, that it was now more than ever necessary to explore the island thoroughly. It was therefore agreed that the next morning at break of day, they should set out, by ascending the Mercy so as to reach the western shore. If any castaways had landed on the coast, it was to be feared they were without resources, and it was therefore the more necessary to carry help to them without delay.

During the day the different articles were carried to Granite House, where they were methodically arranged in the great hall.

This day—the 29th of October—happened to be a Sunday, and, before going to bed, Herbert asked the engineer if he would not read them something from the Gospel.

"Willingly," replied Cyrus Harding.

He took the sacred volume, and was about to open it, when Pencroft stopped him, saying,

"Captain, I am superstitious. Open at random and read the first verse which your eye falls upon. We will see if it applies to our situation."

Cyrus Harding smiled at the sailor's idea, and, yielding to his wish, he opened exactly at a place where the leaves were separated by a marker.

Immediately his eyes were attracted by a cross which, made with a pencil, was placed against the eighth verse of the seventh chapter of the Gospel of St. Matthew. He read the verse, which was this:

"For every one that asketh receiveth; and he that seeketh findeth."

III

The next day, the 30th of October, all was ready for the proposed exploring expedition, which recent events had rendered so necessary. In fact, things had so come about that the settlers in Lincoln Island no longer needed help for themselves, but were even able to carry it to others.

It was therefore agreed that they should ascend the Mercy as far as the river was navigable. A great part of the distance would thus be traversed without fatigue, and the explorers could transport their provisions and arms to an advanced point in the west of the island.

It was necessary to think not only of the things which they should take with them, but also of those which they might have by chance to bring back to Granite House. If there had been a wreck on the coast, as was supposed, there would be many things cast up, which would be lawfully their prizes. In the event of this, the cart would have been of more use than the light canoe, but it was heavy and clumsy to drag, and therefore more difficult to use; this led Pencroft to express his regret that the chest had not contained, besides "his halfpound of tobacco," a pair of strong New Jersey horses, which would have been very useful to the colony!

The provisions, which Neb had already packed up, consisted of a store of meat and of several gallons of beer, that is to say enough to sustain them for three days, the time which Harding assigned for the expedition. They hoped besides to supply themselves on the road, and Neb took care not to forget the portable stove.

The only tools the settlers took were the two woodmen's axes, which they could use to cut a path through the thick forests, as also the instruments, the telescope, and pocket-compass.

For weapons they selected the two flint-lock guns, which were likely to be more useful to them than the percussion fowling-pieces, the first only requiring flints which could be easily replaced, and the latter needing fulminating caps, a frequent use of which would soon exhaust their limited stock. However, they took also one of the carbines and some cartridges. As to the powder, of which there was about fifty pounds in the barrel, a small supply of it had to be taken, but the engineer hoped to manufacture an explosive substance which would allow them to husband it. To the firearms were added the five cutlasses well sheathed in leather, and, thus supplied, the settlers could venture into the vast forest with some chance of success.

It is useless to add that Pencroft, Herbert, and Neb, thus armed, were at the summit of their happiness, although Cyrus Harding made them promise not to fire a shot unless it was necessary.

At six in the morning the canoe put off from the shore; all had embarked, including Top, and they proceeded to the mouth of the Mercy.

The tide had begun to come up half an hour before. For several hours, therefore, there would be a current, which it was well to profit by, for later the ebb would make it difficult to ascend the river. The tide was already strong, for in three days the moon would be full, and it was enough to keep the boat in the center of the current, where it floated swiftly along between the high banks without its being necessary to increase its speed by the aid of the oars. In a few minutes the explorers arrived at the angle formed by the Mercy and exactly at the place where, seven months before, Pencroft had made his first raft of wood.

After this sudden angle the river widened and flowed under the shade of great evergreen firs.

The aspect of the banks was magnificent. Cyrus Harding and his companions could not but admire the lovely effects so easily produced by nature with water and trees. As they advanced the forest element diminished. On the right bank of the river grew magnificent specimens of the ulmaceae tribe, the precious elm, so valuable to builders, and which withstands well the action of water. Then there were numerous groups belonging to the same family, among others one in particular, the fruit of which produces a very useful oil. Farther on, Herbert remarked the lardizabala, a twining shrub which, when bruised in water, furnishes excellent cordage; and two or three ebony trees of a beautiful black, crossed with capricious veins.

From time to time, in certain places where the landing was easy, the canoe was stopped, when Gideon Spilett, Herbert, and Pencroft, their guns in their hands, and preceded by Top, jumped on shore. Without expecting game, some useful plant might be met with, and the young naturalist was delighted with discovering a sort of wild spinach, belonging to the order of chenopodiaceae, and numerous specimens of cruciferae, belonging to the cabbage tribe, which it would certainly be possible to cultivate by transplanting. There were cresses, horseradish, turnips, and lastly, little branching hairy stalks, scarcely more than three feet high, which produced brownish grains.

"Do you know what this plant is?" asked Herbert of the sailor.

"Tobacco!" cried Pencroft, who evidently had never seen his favorite plant except in the bowl of his pipe.

"No, Pencroft," replied Herbert; "this is not tobacco, it is mustard."

"Mustard be hanged!" returned the sailor; "but if by chance you happen to come across a tobacco-plant, my boy, pray don't scorn that!"

"We shall find it some day!" said Gideon Spilett.

"Well!" exclaimed Pencroft, "when that day comes, I do not know what more will be wanting in our island!"

These different plants, which had been carefully rooted up, were carried to the canoe, where Cyrus Harding had remained buried in thought.

The reporter, Herbert, and Pencroft in this manner frequently disembarked, sometimes on the right bank, sometimes on the left bank of the Mercy.

The latter was less abrupt, but the former more wooded. The engineer ascertained by consulting his pocket-compass that the direction of the river from the first turn was obviously southwest and northeast, and nearly straight for a length of about three miles. But it was to be supposed that this direction changed beyond that point, and that the Mercy continued to the northwest, toward the spurs of Mount Franklin, among which the river rose.

During one of these excursions, Gideon Spilett managed to get hold of two couples of living gallinaceae. They were birds with long, thin beaks, lengthened necks, short wings, and without any appearance of a tail. Herbert rightly gave them the name of tinamous, and it was resolved that they should be the first tenants of their future poultry-yard.

But till then the guns had not spoken, and the first report which awoke the echoes of the Forests of the Far West was provoked by the appearance of a beautiful bird, resembling the kingfisher.

"I recognize him!" cried Pencroft, and it seemed as if his gun went off by itself.

"What do you recognize?" asked the reporter.

"The bird which escaped us on our first excursion, and from which we gave the name to that part of the forest."

"A jacamar!" cried Herbert.

It was indeed a jacamar, of which the plumage shines with a metallic luster. A shot brought it to the ground, and Top carried it to the canoe. At the same time half a dozen lories were brought down. The lory is of the size of a pigeon, the plumage dashed with green, part of the wings crimson, and its crest bordered with white. To the young boy belonged the honor of this shot, and he was proud enough of it. Lories are better food than the jacamar, the flesh of which is rather tough, but it was difficult to persuade Pencroft that he had not killed the king of eatable birds. It was ten o'clock in the morning when the canoe reached a second angle of the Mercy, nearly five miles from its mouth. Here a halt was made for breakfast under the shade of some splendid trees. The river still measured from sixty to seventy feet in breadth, and its bed from five to six feet in depth. The engineer had observed that it was increased by numerous affluents, but they were unnavigable, being simply little streams. As to the forest, including Jacamar Wood, as well as the Forests of the Far West, it extended as far as the eye could reach. In no place, either in the depths of the forests or under the trees on the banks of the Mercy, was the presence of man revealed. The explorers could not discover one suspicious trace. It was evident that the woodman's axe had never touched these trees, that the pioneer's knife had never severed the creepers hanging from one trunk to another in the midst of tangled brushwood and long grass. If castaways had landed on the island, they could not have yet quitted the shore, and it was not in the woods that the survivors of the supposed shipwreck should be sought.

The engineer therefore manifested some impatience to reach the western coast of Lincoln Island, which was at least five miles distant according to his estimation.

The voyage was continued, and as the Mercy appeared to flow not toward the shore, but rather toward Mount Franklin, it was decided that they should use the boat as long as there was enough water under its keel to float it. It was both fatigue spared and time gained, for they would have been obliged to cut a path through the thick wood with their axes. But soon the flow completely failed them, either the tide was going down, and it was about the hour, or it could no longer be felt at this distance from the mouth of the Mercy. They had therefore to make use of the oars. Herbert and Neb each took one, and Pencroft took the scull. The forest soon became less dense, the trees grew farther apart and often quite isolated. But the farther they were from each other the more magnificent they appeared, profiting, as they did, by the free, pure air which circulated around them.

What splendid specimens of the flora of this latitude! Certainly their presence would have been enough for a botanist to name without hesitation the parallel which traversed Lincoln Island.

"Eucalypti!" cried Herbert.

They were, in fact, those splendid trees, the giants of the extratropical zone, the congeners of the Australian and New Zealand eucalyptus, both situated under the same latitude as Lincoln Island. Some rose to a height of two hundred feet. Their trunks at the base measured twenty feet in circumference, and their bark was covered by a network of furrows containing a red, sweet-smelling gum. Nothing is more wonderful or more singular than those enormous specimens of the order of the myrtaceae, with their leaves placed vertically and not horizontally, so that an edge and not a surface looks upward, the effect being that the sun's rays penetrate more freely among the trees.

The ground at the foot of the eucalypti was carpeted with grass, and from the bushes escaped flights of little birds, which glittered in the sunlight like winged rubies.

"These are something like trees!" cried Neb; "but are they good for anything?"

"Pooh!" replied Pencroft. "Of course there are vegetable giants as well as human giants, and they are no good, except to show themselves at fairs!"

"I think that you are mistaken, Pencroft," replied Gideon Spilett, "and that the wood of the eucalyptus has begun to be very advantageously employed in cabinet-making."

"And I may add," said Herbert, "that the eucalyptus belongs to a family which comprises many useful members; the guava-tree, from whose fruit guava jelly is made; the clove-tree, which produces the spice; the pomegranate-tree, which bears pomegranates; the eugeacia cauliflora, the fruit of which is used in making a tolerable wine; the Ugui myrtle, which contains an excellent alcoholic liquor; the caryophyllus myrtle, of which the bark forms an esteemed cinnamon; the eugenia pimenta, from whence comes Jamaica pepper; the common myrtle, from whose buds and berries spice is sometimes made; the eucalyptus manifera, which yields a sweet sort of manna; the Guinea eucalyptus, the sap of which is transformed into beer by fermentation; in short, all those trees known under the name of gum-trees or iron-bark trees in Australia, belong to this family of the myrtaceae, which contains forty-six genera and thirteen hundred species!"

The lad was allowed to run on, and he delivered his little botanical lecture with great animation. Cyrus Harding listened smiling, and Pencroft with an indescribable feeling of pride.

"Very good, Herbert," replied Pencroft, "but I could swear that all those useful specimens you have just told us about are none of them giants like these!"

"That is true, Pencroft."

"That supports what I said," returned the sailor, "namely, that these giants are good for nothing!"

"There you are wrong, Pencroft," said the engineer; "these gigantic eucalypti, which shelter us, are good for something."

"And what is that?"

"To render the countries which they inhabit healthy. Do you know what they are called in Australia and New Zealand?"

"No, captain."

"They are called 'fever trees.' "

"Because they give fevers?"

"No, because they prevent them!"

"Good. I must note that," said the reporter.

"Note it then, my dear Spilett; for it appears proved that the presence of the eucalyptus is enough to neutralize miasmas. This natural antidote has been tried in certain countries in the middle of Europe and the north of Africa where the soil was absolutely unhealthy, and the sanitary condition of the inhabitants has been gradually ameliorated. No more intermittent fevers prevail in the regions now covered with forests of the myrtaceae. This fact is now beyond doubt, and it is a happy circumstance for us settlers in Lincoln Island."

"Ah! what an island! What a blessed island!" cried Pencroft. "I tell you, it wants nothing—unless it is—"

"That will come, Pencroft, that will be found," replied the engineer; "but now we must continue our voyage and push on as far as the river will carry our boat!"

The exploration was therefore continued for another two miles in the midst of country covered with eucalypti, which predominated in the woods of this portion of the island. The space which they occupied extended as far as the eye could reach on each side of the Mercy, which wound along between high green banks. The bed was often obstructed by long weeds, and even by pointed rocks, which rendered the navigation very difficult. The action of the oars was prevented, and Pencroft was obliged to push with a pole. They found also that the water was becoming shallower and shallower, and that the canoe must soon stop. The sun was already sinking toward the horizon, and the trees threw long shadows on the ground. Cyrus Harding, seeing that he could not hope to reach the western coast of the island in one journey, resolved to camp at the place where any further navigation was prevented by want of water. He calculated that they were still five or six miles from the coast, and this distance was too great for them to attempt during the night in the midst of unknown woods.

The boat was pushed on through the forest, which gradually became thicker again, and appeared also to have more inhabitants; for if the eyes of the sailor did not deceive him, he thought he saw bands of monkeys springing among the trees. Sometimes even two or three of these animals stopped at a little distance from the canoe and gazed at the settlers without manifesting any terror, as if, seeing men for the first time, they had not yet learned to fear them. It would have been easy to bring down one of these quadrumani with a gunshot, and Pencroft was greatly tempted to fire, but Harding opposed so useless a massacre. This was prudent, for the monkeys, or apes rather, appearing to be very powerful and extremely active, it was useless to provoke an unnecessary aggression, and the creatures might, ignorant of the power of the explorers' firearms, have attacked them. It is true that the sailor considered the monkeys from a purely alimentary point of view, for those animals which are herbivorous make very excellent game; but since they had an abundant supply of provisions, it was a pity to waste their ammunition.

Toward four o'clock, the navigation of the Mercy became exceedingly difficult, for its course was obstructed by aquatic plants and rocks. The banks rose higher and higher, and already they were approaching the spurs of Mount Franklin. The source could not be far off, since it was fed by the water from the southern slopes of the mountain.

"In a quarter of an hour," said the sailor, "we shall be obliged to stop, captain."

"Very well, we will stop, Pencroft, and we will make our encampment for the night."

"At what distance are we from Granite House?" asked Herbert.

"About seven miles," replied the engineer, "taking into calculation, however, the detours of the river, which has carried us to the northwest."

"Shall we go on?" asked the reporter.

"Yes, as long as we can," replied Cyrus Harding. "To-morrow, at break of day, we will leave the canoe, and in two hours I hope we shall cross the distance which separates us from the coast, and then we shall have the whole day in which to explore the shore."

"Go ahead!" replied Pencroft.

But soon the boat grated on the stony bottom of the river, which was now not more than twenty feet in breadth. The trees met like a bower overhead, and caused a half-darkness. They also heard the noise of a waterfall, which showed that a few hundred feet up the river there was a natural barrier.

Presently, after a sudden turn of the river, a cascade appeared through the trees. The canoe again touched the bottom, and in a few minutes it was moored to a trunk near the right bank.

It was nearly five o'clock. The last rays of the sun gleamed through the thick foliage and glanced on the little waterfall, making the spray sparkle with all the colors of the rainbow. Beyond that, the Mercy was lost in the brushwood, where it was fed from some hidden source. The different streams which flowed into it increased it to a regular river farther down, but here it was simply a shallow, limpid brook.

It was agreed to camp here, as the place was charming. The colonists disembarked, and a fire was soon lighted under a clump of trees, among the branches of which Cyrus Harding and his companions could, if it was necessary, take refuge for the night.

Supper was quickly devoured, for they were very hungry, and then there was only sleeping to think of. But, as roarings of rather a suspicious nature had been heard during the evening, a good fire was made up for the night, so as to protect the sleepers with its crackling flames. Neb and Pencroft also watched by turns, and did not spare fuel. They thought they saw the dark forms of some wild animals prowling round the camp among the bushes, but the night passed without incident, and the next day, the 31st of October, at five o'clock in the morning, all were on foot, ready for a start.

IV

It was six o' clock in the morning when the settlers, after a hasty breakfast, set out to reach by the shortest way, the western coast of the island. And how long would it take to do this? Cyrus Harding had said two hours, but of course that depended on the nature of the obstacles they might meet with. As it was probable that they would have to cut a path through the grass, shrubs, and creepers, they marched axe in hand, and with guns also ready, wisely taking warning from the cries of the wild beasts heard in the night.

The exact position of the encampment could be determined by the bearing of Mount Franklin, and as the volcano arose in the north at a distance of less than three miles, they had only to go straight toward the southwest to reach the western coast. They set out, having first carefully secured the canoe. Pencroft and Neb carried sufficient provision for the little band for at least two days. It would not thus be necessary to hunt. The engineer advised his companions to refrain from firing, that their presence might not be betrayed to any one near the shore. The first hatchet blows were given among the brushwood in the midst of some mastic-trees, a little above the cascade; and his compass in his hand, Cyrus Harding led the way.

The forest here was composed for the most part of trees which had already been met with near the lake and on Prospect Heights. There were deodars, Douglas firs, casuarinas, gum-trees, eucalypti, hibiscus, cedars, and other trees, generally of a moderate size, for their number prevented their growth.

Since their departure, the settlers had descended the slopes which constituted the mountain system of the island, on to a dry soil, but the luxuriant vegetation of which indicated it to be watered either by some subterranean marsh or by some stream. However, Cyrus Harding did not remember having seen, at the time of his excursion to the crater, any other watercourses but the Red Creek and the Mercy.

During the first part of their excursion, they saw numerous troops of monkeys who exhibited great astonishment at the sight of men, whose appearance was so new to them. Gideon Spilett jokingly asked whether these active and merry quadrupeds did not consider him and his companions as degenerate brothers.

And certainly, pedestrians, hindered at each step by bushes, caught by creepers, barred by trunks of trees, did not shine beside those supple animals, who, bounding from branch to branch, were hindered by nothing on their course. The monkeys were numerous, but happily they did not manifest any hostile disposition.

Several pigs, agoutis, kangaroos, and other rodents were seen, also two or three koalas, at which Pencroft longed to have a shot.

"But," said he, "you may jump and play just now; we shall have one or two words to say to you on our way back!"

At half-past nine the way was suddenly found to be barred by an unknown stream, from thirty to forty feet broad, whose rapid current dashed foaming over the numerous rocks which interrupted its course. This creek was deep and clear, but it was absolutely unnavigable.

"We are cut off!" cried Neb.

"No," replied Herbert, "it is only a stream, and we can easily swim over."

"What would be the use of that?" returned Harding. "This creek evidently runs to the sea. Let us remain on this side and follow the bank, and I shall be much astonished if it does not lead us very quickly to the coast. Forward!"

"One minute," said the reporter. "The name of this creek, my friends? Do not let us leave our geography incomplete."

"All right!" said Pencroft.

"Name it, my boy," said the engineer, addressing the lad.

"Will it not be better to wait until we have explored it to its mouth?" answered Herbert.

"Very well," replied Cyrus Harding. "Let us follow it as fast as we can without stopping."

"Still another minute!" said Pencroft.

"What's the matter?" asked the reporter.

"Though hunting is forbidden, fishing is allowed, I suppose," said the sailor.

"We have no time to lose," replied the engineer.

"Oh! five minutes!" replied Pencroft, "I only ask for five minutes to use in the interest of our breakfast!"

And Pencroft, lying down on the bank, plunged his arm into the water, and soon pulled up several dozen of fine crayfish from among the stones.

"These will be good!" cried Neb, going to the sailor's aid.

"As I said, there is everything in this island, except tobacco!" muttered Pencroft with a sigh.

The fishing did not take five minutes, for the crayfish were swarming in the creek. A bag was filled with the crustaceae, whose shells were of a cobalt blue. The settlers then pushed on.

They advanced more rapidly and easily along the bank of the river than in the forest. From time to time they came upon the traces of animals of a large size who had come to quench their thirst at the stream, but none were actually seen, and it was evidently not in this part of the forest that the peccary had received the bullet which had cost Pencroft a grinder.

In the meanwhile, considering the rapid current, Harding was led to suppose that he and his companions were much farther from the western coast than they had at first supposed. In fact, at this hour, the rising tide would have turned back the current of the creek, if its mouth had only been a few miles distant. Now, this effect was not produced, and the water pursued its natural course. The engineer was much astonished at this, and frequently consulted his compass, to assure himself that some turn of the river was not leading them again into the Far West.

However, the creek gradually widened and its waters became less tumultuous. The trees on the right bank were as close together as on the left bank, and it was impossible to distinguish anything beyond them; but these masses of wood were evidently uninhabited, for Top did not bark, and the intelligent animal would not have failed to signal the presence of any stranger in the neighborhood.

At half-past ten, to the great surprise of Cyrus Harding, Herbert, who was a little in front, suddenly stopped and exclaimed,

"The sea!"

In a few minutes more, the whole western shore of the island lay extended before the eyes of the settlers.

But what a contrast between this and the eastern coast, upon which chance had first thrown them. No granite cliff, no rocks, not even a sandy beach. The forest reached the shore, and the tall trees bending over the water were beaten by the waves. It was not such a shore as is usually formed by nature, either by extending a vast carpet of sand, or by grouping masses of rock, but a beautiful border consisting of the most splendid trees. The bank was raised a little above the level of the sea, and on this luxuriant soil, supported by a granite base, the fine forest trees seemed to be as firmly planted as in the interior of the island.

The colonists were then on the shore of an unimportant little harbor, which would scarcely have contained even two or three fishing-boats. It served as a neck to the new creek, of which the curious thing was that its waters, instead of joining the sea by a gentle slope, fell from a height of more than forty feet, which explained why the rising tide was not felt up the stream. In fact, the tides of the Pacific, even at their maximum elevation, could never reach the level of the river, and, doubtless, millions of years would pass before the water would have worn away the granite and hollowed a practicable mouth.

It was settled that the name of Falls River should be given to this stream. Beyond, toward the north, the forest border was prolonged for a space of nearly two miles; then the trees became scarcer, and beyond that again the picturesque heights described a nearly straight line, which ran north and south. On the contrary, all the part of the shore between Falls River and Reptile End was a mass of wood, magnificent trees, some straight, others bent, so that the long sea-swell bathed their roots. Now, it was this coast, that is, all the Serpentine Peninsula, that was to be explored, for this part of the shore offered a refuge to castaways, which the other wild and barren side must have refused.

The weather was fine and clear, and from a height of a hillock on which Neb and Pencroft had arranged breakfast, a wide view was obtained. There was, however, not a sail in sight; nothing could be seen along the shore as far as the eye could reach. But the engineer would take nothing for granted until he had explored the coast to the very extremity of the Serpentine Peninsula.

Breakfast was soon dispatched, and at half-past eleven the captain gave the signal for departure. Instead of proceeding over the summit of a cliff or along a sandy beach, the settlers were obliged to remain under cover of the trees so that they might continue on the shore.

The distance which separated Falls River from Reptile End was about twelve miles. It would have taken the settlers four hours to do this, on a clear ground and without hurrying themselves; but as it was they needed double the time, for what with trees to go around, bushes to cut down, and creepers to chop away, they were impeded at every step, these obstacles greatly lengthening their journey.

There was, however, nothing to show that a shipwreck had taken place recently. It is true that, as Gideon Spilett observed, any remains of it might have drifted out to sea, and they must not take it for granted that because they could find no traces of it, a ship had not been castaway on the coast.

The reporter's argument was just, and besides, the incident of the bullet proved that a shot must have been fired in Lincoln Island within three months.

It was already five o'clock, and there were still two miles between the settlers and the extremity of the Serpentine Peninsula. It was evident that after having reached Reptile End, Harding and his companions would not have time to return before dark to their encampment near the source of the Mercy. It would therefore be necessary to pass the night on the promontory. But they had no lack of provisions, which was lucky, for there were no animals on the shore, though birds, on the contrary, abounded—jacamars, couroucous, tragopans, grouse, lories, parrots, cockatoos, pheasants, pigeons, and a hundred others. There was not a tree without a nest, and not a nest which was not full of flapping wings.

Toward seven o'clock the weary explorers arrived at Reptile End. Here the seaside forest ended, and the shore resumed the customary appearance of a coast, with rocks, reefs, and sands. It was possible that something might be found here, but darkness came on, and the further exploration had to be put off to the next day.

Pencroft and Herbert hastened on to find a suitable place for their camp. Among the last trees of the Forests of the Far West, the boy found several thick clumps of bamboos.

"Good," said he; "this is a valuable discovery."

"Valuable?" returned Pencroft.

"Certainly," replied Herbert. "I may say, Pencroft, that the bark of the bamboo, cut into flexible laths, is used for making baskets; that the bark, mashed into a paste, is used for the manufacture of Chinese paper; that the stalks furnish, according to their size, canes and pipes and are used for conducting water; that large bamboos make excellent material for building, being light and strong, and being never attacked by insects. I will add that by sawing the bamboo in two at the joint, keeping for the bottom the part of the transverse film which forms the joint, useful cups are obtained, which are much in use among the Chinese. No! you don't care for that. But—"

"But what?"

"But I can tell you, if you are ignorant of it, that in India these bamboos are eaten like asparagus."

"Asparagus thirty feet high!" exclaimed the sailor. "And are they good?"

"Excellent," replied Herbert. "Only it is not the stems of thirty feet high which are eaten, but the young shoots."

"Perfect, my boy, perfect!" replied Pencroft.

"I will also add that the pith of the young stalks, preserved in vinegar, makes a good pickle."

"Better and better, Herbert!"

"And lastly, that the bamboos exude a sweet liquor which can be made into a very agreeable drink."

"Is that all?" asked the sailor.

"That is all!"

"And they don't happen to do for smoking?"

"No, my poor Pencroft."

Herbert and the sailor had not to look long for a place in which to pass the night. The rocks, which must have been violently beaten by the sea under the influence of the winds of the southwest, presented many cavities in which shelter could be found against the night air. But just as they were about to enter one of these caves a loud roaring arrested them.

"Back!" cried Pencroft. "Our guns are only loaded with small shot, and beasts which can roar as loud as that would care no more for it than for grains of salt!" And the sailor, seizing Herbert by the arm, dragged him behind a rock, just as a magnificent animal showed itself at the entrance of the cavern.

It was a jaguar of a size at least equal to its Asiatic congeners, that is to say, it measured five feet from the extremity of its head to the beginning of its tail. The yellow color of its hair was relieved by streaks and regular oblong spots of black, which contrasted with the white of its chest. Herbert recognized it as the ferocious rival of the tiger, as formidable as the puma, which is the rival of the largest wolf!

The jaguar advanced and gazed around him with blazing eyes, his hair bristling as if this was not the first time he had scented men.

At this moment the reporter appeared around a rock, and Herbert, thinking that he had not seen the jaguar, was about to rush toward him, when Gideon Spilett signed to him to remain where he was. This was not his first tiger, and advancing to within ten feet of the animal he remained motionless, his gun to his shoulder, without moving a muscle. The jaguar collected itself for a spring, but at that moment a shot struck it in the eyes, and it fell dead.

Herbert and Pencroft rushed toward the jaguar. Neb and Harding also ran up, and they remained for some instants contemplating the animal as it lay stretched on the ground, thinking that its magnificent skin would be a great ornament to the hall at Granite House.

"Oh, Mr. Spilett, how I admire and envy you!" cried Herbert, in a fit of very natural enthusiasm.

"Well, my boy," replied the reporter, "you could have done the same."

"I! with such coolness!—"

"Imagine to yourself, Herbert, that the jaguar is only a hare, and you would fire as quietly as possible."

"That is," rejoined Pencroft, "that it is not more dangerous than a hare!"

"And now," said Gideon Spilett, "since the jaguar has left its abode, I do not see, my friends, why we should not take possession of it for the night."

"But others may come," said Pencroft.

"It will be enough to light a fire at the entrance of the cavern," said the reporter, "and no wild beasts will dare to cross the threshold."

"Into the jaguar's house, then!" replied the sailor, dragging after him the body of the animal.

While Neb skinned the jaguar, his companions collected an abundant supply of dry wood from the forest, which they heaped up at the cave.

Cyrus Harding, seeing the clump of bamboos, cut a quantity, which he mingled with the other fuel.

This done, they entered the grotto, of which the floor was strewn with bones; the guns were carefully loaded, in case of a sudden attack; they had supper; and then just before they lay down to rest, the heap of wood piled at the entrance was set fire to. Immediately, a regular explosion, or rather a series of reports, broke the silence! The noise was caused by the bamboos, which, as the flames reached them, exploded like fireworks. The noise was enough to terrify even the boldest of wild beasts.

It was not the engineer who had invented this way of causing loud explosions, for, according to Marco Polo, the Tatars have employed it for many centuries to drive away from their encampments the formidable wild beasts of Central Asia.

V

Cyrus Harding and his companions slept like innocent marmots in the cave which the jaguar had so politely left at their disposal.

At sunrise all were on the shore at the extremity of the promontory, and their gaze was directed toward the horizon, of which two-thirds of the circumference were visible. For the last time the engineer could ascertain that not a sail nor the wreck of a ship was on the sea, and even with the telescope nothing suspicious could be discovered.

There was nothing either on the shore, at least, in the straight line of three miles which formed the south side of the promontory, for beyond that, rising ground had the rest of the coast, and even from the extremity of the Serpentine Peninsula, Claw Cape could not be seen.

The southern coast of the island still remained to be explored. Now should they undertake it immediately, and devote this day to it?

This was not included in their first plan. In fact, when the boat was abandoned at the sources of the Mercy, it had been agreed that after having surveyed the west coast, they should go back to it, and return to Granite House by the Mercy. Harding then thought that the western coast would have offered refuge, either to a ship in distress, or to a vessel in her regular course; but now, as he saw that this coast presented no good anchorage, he wished to seek on the south what they had not been able to find on the west.

Gideon Spilett proposed to continue the exploration, that the question of the supposed wreck might be completely settled, and he asked at what distance Claw Cape might be from the extremity of the peninsula.

"About thirty miles," replied the engineer, "if we take into consideration the curvings of the coast."

"Thirty miles!" returned Spilett. "That would be a long day's march. Nevertheless, I think that we should return to Granite House by the south coast."

"But," observed Herbert, "from Claw Cape to Granite House there must be at least another ten miles."

"Make it forty miles in all," replied the engineer, "and do not hesitate to do it. At least we should survey the unknown shore, and then we shall not have to begin the exploration again."

"Very good," said Pencroft. "But the boat?"

"The boat has remained by itself for one day at the sources of the Mercy," replied Gideon Spilett; "it may just as well stay there two days! As yet, we have had no reason to think that the island is infested by thieves!"

"Yet," said the sailor, "when I remember the history of the turtle, I am far from confident of that."

"The turtle! the turtle!" replied the reporter. "Don't you know that the sea turned it over?"

"Who knows?" murmured the engineer.

"But—" said Neb.

Neb had evidently something to say, for he opened his mouth to speak and yet said nothing.

"What do you want to say, Neb?" asked the engineer.

"If we return by the shore to Claw Cape," replied Neb, "after having doubled the Cape, we shall be stopped—"

"By the Mercy! of course," replied Herbert, "and we shall have neither bridge nor boat by which to cross."

"But, captain," added Pencroft, "with a few floating trunks we shall have no difficulty in crossing the river."

"Never mind," said Spilett, "it will be useful to construct a bridge if we wish to have an easy access to the Far West!"

"A bridge!" cried Pencroft. "Well, is not the captain the best engineer in his profession? He will make us a bridge when we want one. As to transporting you this evening to the other side of the Mercy, and that without wetting one thread of your clothes, I will take care of that. We have provisions for another day, and besides we can get plenty of game. Forward!"

The reporter's proposal, so strongly seconded by the sailor, received general approbation, for each wished to have their doubts set at rest, and by returning by Claw Cape the exploration would be ended. But there was not an hour to lose, for forty miles was a long march, and they could not hope to reach Granite House before night.

At six o'clock in the morning the little band set out. As a precaution the guns were loaded with ball, and Top, who led the van, received orders to beat about the edge of the forest.

From the extremity of the promontory which formed the tail of the peninsula, the coast was rounded for a distance of five miles, which was rapidly passed over, without even the most minute investigations bringing to light the least trace of any old or recent landings; no debris, no mark of an encampment, no cinders of a fire, nor even a footprint!

From the point of the peninsula on which the settlers now were, their gaze could extend along the southwest. Twenty-five miles off the coast terminated in the Claw Cape, which loomed dimly through the morning mists, and which, by the phenomenon of the mirage, appeared as if suspended between land and water.

Between the place occupied by the colonists and the other side of the immense bay, the shore was composed, first, of a tract of low land, bordered in the background by trees; then the shore became more irregular, projecting sharp points into the sea, and finally ended in the black rocks which, accumulated in picturesque disorder, formed Claw Cape.

Such was the development of this part of the island, which the settlers took in at a glance, while stopping for an instant.

"If a vessel ran in here," said Pencroft, "she would certainly be lost. Sandbanks and reefs everywhere! Bad quarters!"

"But at least something would be left of the ship," observed the reporter.

"There might be pieces of wood on the rocks, but nothing on the sands," replied the sailor.

"Why?"

"Because the sands are still more dangerous than the rocks, for they swallow up everything that is thrown on them. In a few days the hull of a ship of several hundred tons would disappear entirely in there!"

"So, Pencroft," asked the engineer, "if a ship has been wrecked on these banks, is it not astonishing that there is now no trace of her remaining?"

"No, captain, with the aid of time and tempest. However, it would be surprising, even in this case, that some of the masts or spars should not have been thrown on the beach, out of reach of the waves."

"Let us go on with our search, then," returned Cyrus Harding.

At one o'clock the colonists arrived at the other side of Washington Bay, they having now gone a distance of twenty miles.

They then halted for breakfast.

Here began the irregular coast, covered with lines of rocks and sandbanks. The long sea-swell could be seen breaking over the rocks in the bay, forming a foamy fringe. From this point to Claw Cape the beach was very narrow between the edge of the forest and the reefs.

Walking was now more difficult, on account of the numerous rocks which encumbered the beach. The granite cliff also gradually increased in height, and only the green tops of the trees which crowned it could be seen.

After half an hour's rest, the settlers resumed their journey, and not a spot among the rocks was left unexamined. Pencroft and Neb even rushed into the surf whenever any object attracted their attention. But they found nothing, some curious formations of the rocks having deceived them. They ascertained, however, that eatable shell-fish abounded there, but these could not be of any great advantage to them until some easy means of communication had been established between the two banks of the Mercy, and until the means of transport had been perfected.

Nothing therefore which threw any light on the supposed wreck could be found on this shore, yet an object of any importance, such as the hull of a ship, would have been seen directly, or any of her masts and spars would have been washed on shore, just as the chest had been, which was found twenty miles from here. But there was nothing.

Toward three o'clock Harding and his companions arrived at a snug little creek. It formed quite a natural harbor, invisible from the sea, and was entered by a narrow channel.

At the back of this creek some violent convulsion had torn up the rocky border, and a cutting, by a gentle slope, gave access to an upper plateau, which might be situated at least ten miles from Claw Cape, and consequently four miles in a straight line from Prospect Heights. Gideon Spilett proposed to his companions that they should make a halt here. They agreed readily, for their walk had sharpened their appetites; and although it was not their usual dinner-hour, no one refused to strengthen himself with a piece of venison. This luncheon would sustain them until their supper, which they intended to take at Granite House. In a few minutes the settlers, seated under a clump of fine sea-pines, were devouring the provisions which Neb produced from his bag.

This spot was raised from fifty to sixty feet above the level of the sea. The view was very extensive, but beyond the cape it ended in Union Bay. Neither the islet nor Prospect Heights was visible, and could not be from thence, for the rising ground and the curtain of trees closed the northern horizon.

It is useless to add that notwithstanding the wide extent of sea which the explorers could survey, and though the engineer swept the horizon with his glass, no vessel could be found.

The shore was of course examined with the same care from the edge of the water to the cliff, and nothing could be discovered even with the aid of the instrument.

"Well," said Gideon Spilett, "it seems we must make up our minds to console ourselves with thinking that no one will come to dispute with us the possession of Lincoln Island!"

"But the bullet," cried Herbert. "That was not imaginary, I suppose!"

"Hang it, no!" exclaimed Pencroft, thinking of his absent tooth.

"Then what conclusion may be drawn?" asked the reporter.

"This," replied the engineer, "that three months or more ago, a vessel, either voluntarily or not, came here."

"What! then you admit, Cyrus, that she was swallowed up without leaving any trace?" cried the reporter.

"No, my dear Spilett; but you see that if it is certain that a human being set foot on the island, it appears no less certain that he has now left it."

"Then, if I understand you right, captain," said Herbert, "the vessel has left again?"

"Evidently."

"And we have lost an opportunity to get back to our country?" said Neb.

"I fear so."

"Very well, since the opportunity is lost, let us go on; it can't be helped," said Pencroft, who felt home-sickness for Granite House.

But just as they were rising, Top was heard loudly barking; and the dog issued from the wood, holding in his mouth a rag soiled with mud.

Neb seized it. It was a piece of strong cloth!

Top still barked, and by his going and coming, seemed to invite his master to follow him into the forest.

"Now there's something to explain the bullet!" exclaimed Pencroft.

"A castaway!" replied Herbert.

"Wounded, perhaps!" said Neb.

"Or dead!" added the reporter.

All ran after the dog, among the tall pines on the border of the forest. Harding and his companions made ready their firearms, in case of an emergency.

They advanced some way into the wood, but to their great disappointment, they as yet saw no signs of any human being having passed that way. Shrubs and creepers were uninjured, and they had even to cut them away with the axe, as they had done in the deepest recesses of the forest. It was difficult to fancy that any human creature had ever passed there, but yet

Top went backward and forward, not like a dog who searches at random, but like a dog being endowed with a mind, who is following up an idea.

In about seven or eight minutes Top stopped in a glade surrounded with tall trees. The settlers gazed around them, but saw nothing, neither under the bushes nor among the trees.

"What is the matter, Top?" said Cyrus Harding.

Top barked louder, bounding about at the foot of a gigantic pine. All at once Pencroft shouted, "Ho, splendid! capital!"

"What is it?" asked Spilett.

"We have been looking for a wreck at sea or on land!"

"Well?"

"Well; and here we've found one in the air!"

And the sailor pointed to a great white rag, caught in the top of the pine, a fallen scrap of which the dog had brought to them.

"But that is not a wreck!" cried Gideon Spilett.

"I beg your pardon!" returned Pencroft.

"Why? is it—?"

"It is all that remains of our airy boat, of our balloon, which has been caught up aloft there, at the top of that tree!"

Pencroft was not mistaken, and he gave vent to his feelings in a tremendous hurrah, adding,

"There is good cloth! There is what will furnish us with linen for years. There is what will make us handkerchiefs and shirts! Ha, ha, Mr. Spilett, what do you say to an island where shirts grow on the trees?"

It was certainly a lucky circumstance for the settlers in Lincoln Island that the balloon, after having made its last bound into the air, had fallen on the island and thus given them the opportunity of finding it again, whether they kept the case under its present form, or whether they wished to attempt another escape by it, or whether they usefully employed the several hundred yards of cotton, which was of fine quality. Pencroft's joy was therefore shared by all.

But it was necessary to bring down the remains of the balloon from the tree, to place it in security, and this was no slight task. Neb, Herbert, and the sailor, climbing to the summit of the tree, used all their skill to disengage the now reduced balloon.

The operation lasted two hours, and then not only the case, with its valve, its springs, its brasswork, lay on the ground, but the net, that is to say a considerable quantity of ropes and cordage, and the circle and the anchor. The case, except for the fracture, was in good condition, only the lower portion being torn.

It was a fortune which had fallen from the sky.

"All the same, captain," said the sailor, "if we ever decide to leave the island, it won't be in a balloon, will it? These airboats won't go where we want them to go, and we have had some experience in that way! Look here, we will build a craft of some twenty tons, and then we can make a main-sail, a foresail, and a jib out of that cloth. As to the rest of it, that will help to dress us."

"We shall see, Pencroft," replied Cyrus Harding; "we shall see."

"In the meantime, we must put it in a safe place," said Neb.

They certainly could not think of carrying this load of cloth, ropes, and cordage, to Granite House, for the weight of it was very considerable, and while waiting for a suitable vehicle in which to convey it, it was of importance that this treasure should not be left longer exposed to the mercies of the first storm. The settlers, uniting their efforts, managed to drag it as far as the shore, where they discovered a large rocky cavity, which owing to its position could not be visited either by the wind or rain.

"We needed a locker, and now we have one," said Pencroft; "but as we cannot lock it up, it will be prudent to hide the opening. I don't mean from two-legged thieves, but from those with four paws!"

At six o'clock, all was stowed away, and after having given the creek the very suitable name of Port Balloon, the settlers pursued their way along Claw Cape. Pencroft and the engineer talked of the different projects which it was agreed to put into execution with the briefest possible delay. It was necessary first of all to throw a bridge over the Mercy, so as to establish an easy communication with the south of the island; then the cart must be taken to bring back the balloon, for the canoe alone could not carry it, then they would build a decked boat, and Pencroft would rig it as a cutter, and they would be able to undertake voyages of circumnavigation around the island, etc.

In the meanwhile night came on, and it was already dark when the settlers reached Flotsam Point, where they had found the precious chest.

The distance between Flotsam Point and Granite House was another four miles, and it was midnight when, after having followed the shore to the mouth of the Mercy, the settlers arrived at the first angle formed by the Mercy.

There the river was eighty feet in breadth, which was awkward to cross, but as Pencroft had taken upon himself to conquer this difficulty, he was compelled to do it. The settlers certainly had reason to be pretty tired. The journey had been long, and the task of getting down the balloon had not rested either their arms or legs. They were anxious to reach Granite House to eat and sleep, and if the bridge had been constructed, in a quarter of an hour they would have been at home.

The night was very dark. Pencroft prepared to keep his promise by constructing a sort of raft, on which to make the passage of the Mercy. He and Neb, armed with axes, chose two trees near the water, and began to attack them at the base.

Cyrus Harding and Spilett, seated on the bank, waited till their companions were ready for their help, while Herbert roamed about, though without going to any distance. All at once, the lad, who had strolled by the river, came running back, and, pointing up the Mercy, exclaimed,

"What is floating there?"

Pencroft stopped working, and seeing an indistinct object moving through the gloom,

"A canoe!" cried he.

All approached, and saw to their extreme surprise, a boat floating down the current.

"Boat ahoy!" shouted the sailor, without thinking that perhaps it would be best to keep silence.

No reply. The boat still drifted onward, and it was not more than twelve feet off, when the sailor exclaimed,

"But it is our own boat! she has broken her moorings, and floated down the current. I must say she has arrived very opportunely."

"Our boat?" murmured the engineer.

Pencroft was right. It was indeed the canoe, of which the rope had undoubtedly broken, and which had come alone from the sources of the Mercy. It was very important to seize it before the rapid current should have swept it away out of the mouth of the river, but Neb and Pencroft cleverly managed this by means of a long pole.

The canoe touched the shore. The engineer leaped in first, and found, on examining the rope, that it had been really worn through by rubbing against the rocks.

"Well," said the reporter to him, in a low voice, "this is a strange thing."

"Strange indeed!" returned Cyrus Harding.

Strange or not, it was very fortunate. Herbert, the reporter, Neb, and

Pencroft, embarked in turn. There was no doubt about the rope having been worn through, but the astonishing part of the affair was, that the boat should arrive just at the moment when the settlers were there to seize it on its way, for a quarter of an hour earlier or later it would have been lost in the sea.

If they had been living in the time of genii, this incident would have given them the right to think that the island was haunted by some supernatural being, who used his power in the service of the castaways!

A few strokes of the oar brought the settlers to the mouth of the Mercy. The canoe was hauled up on the beach near the Chimneys, and all proceeded toward the ladder of Granite House.

But at that moment, Top barked angrily, and Neb, who was looking for the first steps, uttered a cry.

There was no longer a ladder!

VI

Cyrus Harding stood still, without saying a word. His companions searched in the darkness on the wall, in case the wind should have moved the ladder, and on the ground, thinking that it might have fallen down. . . . But the ladder had quite disappeared. As to ascertaining if a squall had blown it on the landing-place, halfway up, that was impossible in the dark.

"If it is a joke," cried Pencroft, "it is a very stupid one! To come home and find no staircase to go up to your room by—that's nothing for weary men to laugh at."

Neb could do nothing but cry out "Oh! oh! oh!"

"I begin to think that very curious things happen in Lincoln Island!" said Pencroft.

"Curious?" replied Gideon Spilett, "not at all, Pencroft, nothing can be more natural. Some one has come during our absence, taken possession of our dwelling and drawn up the ladder."

"Some one," cried the sailor. "But who?"

"Who but the hunter who fired the bullet?" replied the reporter.

"Well, if there is any one up there," replied Pencroft, who began to lose patience, "I will give them a hail, and they must answer."

And in a stentorian voice the sailor gave a prolonged "Halloo!" which was echoed again and again from the cliff and rocks.

The settlers listened and they thought they heard a sort of chuckling laugh, of which they could not guess the origin. But no voice replied to Pencroft, who in vain repeated his vigorous shouts.

There was something indeed in this to astonish the most apathetic of men, and the settlers were not men of that description. In their situation every incident had its importance, and, certainly, during the seven months which they had spent on the island, they had not before met with anything of so surprising a character.

Be that as it may, forgetting their fatigue in the singularity of the event, they remained below Granite House, not knowing what to think, not knowing what to do, questioning each other without any hope of a satisfactory reply, every one starting some supposition each more unlikely than the last. Neb bewailed himself, much disappointed at not being able to get into his kitchen, for the provisions which they had had on their expedition were exhausted, and they had no means of renewing them.

"My friends," at last said Cyrus Harding, "there is only one thing to be done at present; wait for day, and then act according to circumstances. But let us go to the Chimneys. There we shall be under shelter, and if we cannot eat, we can at least sleep."

"But who is it that has played us this cool trick?" again asked Pencroft, unable to make up his mind to retire from the spot.

Whoever it was, the only thing practicable was to do as the engineer proposed, to go to the Chimneys and there wait for day. In the meanwhile Top was ordered to mount guard below the windows of Granite House, and when Top received an order he obeyed it without any questioning. The brave dog therefore remained at the foot of the cliff while his master with his companions sought a refuge among the rocks.

To say that the settlers, notwithstanding their fatigue, slept well on the sandy floor of the Chimneys would not be true. It was not only that they were extremely anxious to find out the cause of what had happened, whether it was the result of an accident which would be discovered at the return of day, or whether on the contrary it was the work of a human being; but they also had very uncomfortable beds. That could not be helped, however, for in some way or other at that moment their dwelling was occupied, and they could not possibly enter it.

Now Granite House was more than their dwelling, it was their warehouse. There were all the stores belonging to the colony, weapons, instruments, tools, ammunition, provisions, etc. To think that all that might be pillaged and that the settlers would have all their work to do over again, fresh weapons and tools to make, was a serious matter. Their uneasiness led one or other of them also to go out every few minutes to see if Top was keeping good watch. Cyrus Harding alone waited with his habitual patience, although his strong mind was exasperated at being confronted with such an inexplicable fact, and he was provoked at himself for allowing a feeling to which he could not give a name, to gain an influence over him. Gideon Spilett shared his feelings in this respect, and the two conversed together in whispers of the inexplicable circumstance which baffled even their intelligence and experience.

"It is a joke," said Pencroft; "it is a trick some one has played us. Well, I don't like such jokes, and the joker had better look out for himself, if he falls into my hands, I can tell him."

As soon as the first gleam of light appeared in the east, the colonists, suitably armed, repaired to the beach under Granite House. The rising sun now shone on the cliff and they could see the windows, the shutters of which were closed, through the curtains of foliage.

All here was in order; but a cry escaped the colonists when they saw that the door, which they had closed on their departure, was now wide open.

Some one had entered Granite House—there could be no more doubt about that.

The upper ladder, which generally hung from the door to the landing, was in its place, but the lower ladder was drawn up and raised to the threshold. It was evident that the intruders had wished to guard themselves against a surprise.

Pencroft hailed again.

No reply.

"The beggars," exclaimed the sailor. "There they are sleeping quietly as if they were in their own house. Halloo there, you pirates, brigands, robbers, sons of John Bull!"

When Pencroft, being a Yankee, treated any one to the epithet of "son of John Bull," he considered he had reached the last limits of insult.

The sun had now completely risen, and the whole façade of Granite House became illuminated by its rays; but in the interior as well as on the exterior all was quiet and calm.

The settlers asked if Granite House was inhabited or not, and yet the position of the ladder was sufficient to show that it was; it was also certain that the inhabitants, whoever they might be, had not been able to escape. But how were they to be got at?

Herbert then thought of fastening a cord to an arrow, and shooting the arrow so that it should pass between the first rounds of the ladder which hung from the threshold. By means of the cord they would then be able to draw down the ladder to the ground, and so re-establish the communication between the beach and Granite House. There was evidently nothing else to be done, and, with a little skill, this method might succeed. Very fortunately bows and arrows had been left at the Chimneys, where they also found a quantity of light hibiscus cord. Pencroft fastened this to a well-feathered arrow. Then Herbert, fixing it to his bow, took a careful aim for the lower part of the ladder.

Cyrus Harding, Gideon Spilett, Pencroft, and Neb drew back, so as to see if anything appeared at the windows. The reporter lifted his gun to his shoulder and covered the door.

The bow was bent, the arrow flew, taking the cord with it, and passed between the two last rounds.

The operation had succeeded.

Herbert immediately seized the end of the cord, but, at that moment when he gave it a pull to bring down the ladder, an arm, thrust suddenly out between the wall and the door, grasped it and dragged it inside Granite House.

"The rascals!" shouted the sailor. "If a ball can do anything for you, you shall not have long to wait for it."

"But who was it?" asked Neb.

"Who was it? Didn't you see?"

"No."

"It was a monkey, a sapajou, an orang-outang, a baboon, a gorilla, a sagoin. Our dwelling has been invaded by monkeys, who climbed up the ladder during our absence."

And, at this moment, as if to bear witness to the truth of the sailor's words, two or three quadrumana showed themselves at the windows, from which they had pushed back the shutters, and saluted the real proprietors of the place with a thousand hideous grimaces.

"I knew that it was only a joke," cried Pencroft; "but one of the jokers shall pay the penalty for the rest."

So saying, the sailor, raising his piece, took a rapid aim at one of the monkeys and fired. All disappeared, except one who fell mortally wounded on the beach. This monkey, which was of a large size, evidently belonged to the first order of the quadrumana. Whether this was a chimpanzee, an orang-outang, or a gorilla, he took rank among the anthropoid apes, who are so called from their resemblance to the human race. However, Herbert declared it to be an orang-outang.

"What a magnificent beast!" cried Neb.

"Magnificent, if you like," replied Pencroft; "but still I do not see how we are to get into our house."

"Herbert is a good marksman," said the reporter, "and his bow is here. He can try again."

"Why, these apes are so cunning," returned Pencroft; "they won't show themselves again at the windows and so we can't kill them; and when I think of the mischief they may do in the rooms and storehouse—"

"Have patience," replied Harding; "these creatures cannot keep us long at bay."

"I shall not be sure of that till I see them down here," replied the sailor. "And now, captain, do you know how many dozens of these fellows are up there?"

It was difficult to reply to Pencroft, and as for the young boy making another attempt, that was not easy; for the lower part of the ladder had been drawn again into the door, and when another pull was given, the line broke and the ladder remained firm. The case was really perplexing. Pencroft stormed. There was a comic side to the situation, but he did not think it funny at all. It was certain that the settlers would end by reinstating themselves in their domicile and driving out the intruders, but when and how? this is what they were not able to say.

Two hours passed, during which the apes took care not to show themselves, but they were still there, and three or four times a nose or a paw was poked out at the door or windows, and was immediately saluted by a gunshot.

"Let us hide ourselves," at last said the engineer. "Perhaps the apes will think we have gone quite away and will show themselves again. Let Spilett and Herbert conceal themselves behind those rocks and fire on all that may appear."

The engineer's orders were obeyed, and while the reporter and the lad, the best marksmen in the colony, posted themselves in a good position, but out of the monkeys' sight, Neb, Pencroft, and Cyrus climbed the plateau and entered the forest in order to kill some game, for it was now time for breakfast and they had no provisions remaining.

In half an hour the hunters returned with a few rock pigeons, which they roasted as well as they could. Not an ape had appeared. Gideon Spilett and Herbert went to take their share of the breakfast, leaving Top to watch under the windows. They then, having eaten, returned to their post.

Two hours later, their situation was in no degree improved. The quadrumana gave no sign of existence, and it might have been supposed that they had disappeared; but what seemed more probable was that, terrified by the death of one of their companions, and frightened by the noise of the firearms, they had retreated to the back part of the house or probably even into the storeroom. And when they thought of the valuables which this storeroom contained, the patience so much recommended by the engineer, fast changed into great irritation, and there certainly was room for it.

"Decidedly it is too bad," said the reporter; "and the worst of it is, there is no way of putting an end to it."

"But we must drive these vagabonds out somehow," cried the sailor. "We could soon get the better of them, even if there are twenty of the rascals; but for that, we must meet them hand to hand. Come now, is there no way of getting at them?"

"Let us try to enter Granite House by the old opening at the lake," replied the engineer.

"Oh!" shouted the sailor, "and I never thought of that."

This was in reality the only way by which to penetrate into Granite House so as to fight with and drive out the intruders. The opening was, it is true, closed up with a wall of cemented stones, which it would be necessary to sacrifice, but that could easily be rebuilt. Fortunately, Cyrus Harding had not as yet effected his project of hiding this opening by raising the waters of the lake, for the operation would then have taken some time.

It was already past twelve o'clock, when the colonists, well armed and provided with picks and spades, left the Chimneys, passed beneath the windows of Granite House, after telling Top to remain at his post, and began to ascend the left bank of the Mercy, so as to reach Prospect Heights.

But they had not made fifty steps in this direction, when they heard the dog barking furiously.

And all rushed down the bank again.

Arrived at the turning, they saw that the situation had changed.

In fact, the apes, seized with a sudden panic, from some unknown cause, were trying to escape. Two or three ran and clambered from one window to another with the agility of acrobats. They were not even trying to replace the ladder, by which it would have been easy to descend; perhaps in their terror they had forgotten this way of escape. The colonists, now being able to take aim without difficulty, fired. Some, wounded or killed, fell back into the rooms, uttering piercing cries. The rest, throwing themselves out, were dashed to pieces in their fall, and in a few minutes, so far as they knew, there was not a living quadrumana in Granite House.

At this moment the ladder was seen to slip over the threshold, then unroll and fall to the ground.

"Hullo!" cried the sailor, "this is queer!"

"Very strange!" murmured the engineer, leaping first up the ladder.

"Take care, captain!" cried Pencroft, "perhaps there are still some of these rascals. . . ."

"We shall soon see," replied the engineer, without stopping however.

All his companions followed him, and in a minute they had arrived at the threshold. They searched everywhere. There was no one in the rooms nor in the storehouse, which had been respected by the band of quadrumana.

"Well now, and the ladder," cried the sailor; "who can the gentleman have been who sent us that down?"

But at that moment a cry was heard, and a great orang, who had hidden himself in the passage, rushed into the room, pursued by Neb.

"Ah, the robber!" cried Pencroft.

And hatchet in hand, he was about to cleave the head of the animal, when Cyrus Harding seized his arm, saying,

"Spare him, Pencroft."

"Pardon this rascal?"

"Yes! it was he who threw us the ladder!"

And the engineer said this in such a peculiar voice that it was difficult to know whether he spoke seriously or not.

Nevertheless, they threw themselves on the orang, who defended himself gallantly, but was soon overpowered and bound.

"There!" said Pencroft. "And what shall we make of him, now we've got him?"

"A servant!" replied Herbert.

The lad was not joking in saying this, for he knew how this intelligent race could be turned to account.

The settlers then approached the ape and gazed at it attentively. He belonged to the family of anthropoid apes, of which the facial angle is not much inferior to that of the Australians and Hottentots. It was an orang-outang, and as such, had neither the ferocity of the gorilla, nor the stupidity of the baboon. It is to this family of the anthropoid apes that so many characteristics belong which prove them to be possessed of an almost human intelligence. Employed in houses, they can wait at table, sweep rooms, brush clothes, clean boots, handle a knife, fork, and spoon properly, and even drink wine, . . . doing everything as well as the best servant that ever walked upon two legs. Buffon possessed one of these apes, who served him for a long time as a faithful and zealous servant.

The one which had been seized in the hall of Granite House was a great fellow, six feet high, with an admirably proportioned frame, a broad chest, head of a moderate size, the facial angle reaching sixty-five degrees, round skull, projecting nose, skin covered with soft glossy hair, in short, a fine specimen of the anthropoids. His eyes, rather smaller than human eyes, sparkled with intelligence; his white teeth glittered under his mustache, and he wore a little curly brown beard.

"A handsome fellow!" said Pencroft; "if we only knew his language, we could talk to him."

"But, master," said Neb, "are you serious? Are we going to take him as a servant?"

"Yes, Neb," replied the engineer, smiling. "But you must not be jealous."

"And I hope he will make an excellent servant," added Herbert. "He appears young, and will be easy to educate, and we shall not be obliged to use force to subdue him, nor draw his teeth, as is sometimes done. He will soon grow fond of his masters if they are kind to him."

"And they will be," replied Pencroft, who had forgotten all his rancor against "the jokers."

Then, approaching the orang,

"Well, old boy!" he asked, "how are you?"

The orang replied by a little grunt which did not show any anger.

"You wish to join the colony?" again asked the sailor. "You are going to enter the service of Captain Cyrus Harding?"

Another respondent grunt was uttered by the ape.

"And you will be satisfied with no other wages than your food?"

Third affirmative grunt.

"This conversation is slightly monotonous," observed Gideon Spilett.

"So much the better," replied Pencroft; "the best servants are those who talk the least. And then, no wages, do you hear, my boy? We will give you no wages at first, but we will double them afterward if we are pleased with you."

Thus the colony was increased by a new member. As to his name the sailor begged that in memory of another ape which he had known, he might be called Jupiter, and Jup for short.

And so, without more ceremony, Master Jup was installed in Granite House.

VII

The settlers in Lincoln Island had now regained their dwelling, without having been obliged to reach it by the old opening, and were therefore spared the trouble of mason's work. It was certainly lucky, that at the moment they were about to set out to do so, the apes had been seized with that terror, no less sudden than inexplicable, which had driven them out of Granite House. Had the animals discovered that they were about to be attacked from another direction? This was the only explanation of their sudden retreat.

During the day the bodies of the apes were carried into the wood, where they were buried; then the settlers busied themselves in repairing the disorder caused by the intruders, disorder but not damage, for although they had turned everything in the rooms topsy-turvy, yet they had broken nothing. Neb relighted his stove, and the stores in the larder furnished a substantial repast, to which all did ample justice.

Jup was not forgotten, and he ate with relish some stone-pine almonds and rhizome roots, with which he was abundantly supplied. Pencroft had unfastened his arms, but judged it best to have his legs tied until they were more sure of his submission.

Then, before retiring to rest, Harding and his companions seated around their table, discussed those plans, the execution of which was most pressing. The most important and most urgent was the establishment of a bridge over the Mercy, so as to form a communication with the southern part of the island and Granite House; then the making of an enclosure for the musmons or other woolly animals which they wished to capture.

These two projects would help to solve the difficulty as to their clothing, which was now serious. The bridge would render easy the transport of the balloon case, which would furnish them with linen, and the inhabitants of the enclosure would yield wool which would supply them with winter clothes.

As to the enclosure, it was Cyrus Harding's intention to establish it at the sources of the Red Creek, where the ruminants would find fresh and abundant pasture. The road between Prospect Heights and the sources of the stream was already partly beaten, and with a better cart than the first, the material could be easily conveyed to the spot, especially if they could manage to capture some animals to draw it.

But though there might be no inconvenience in the enclosure being so far from Granite House, it would not be the same with the poultry-yard, to which Neb called the attention of the colonists. It was indeed necessary that the birds should be close within reach of the cook, and no place appeared more favorable for the establishment of the said poultry-yard than that portion of the banks of the lake which was close to the old opening.

Water-birds would prosper there as well as others, and the couple of tinamous taken in their last excursion would be the first to be domesticated.

The next day, the 3rd of November, the new works were begun by the construction of the bridge, and all hands were required for this important task. Saws, hatchets, and hammers were shouldered by the settlers, who, now transformed into carpenters, descended to the shore.

There Pencroft observed,

"Suppose, that during our absence, Master Jup takes it into his head to draw up the ladder which he so politely returned to us yesterday?"

"Let us tie its lower end down firmly," replied Cyrus Harding.

This was done by means of two stakes securely fixed in the sand. Then the settlers, ascending the left bank of the Mercy, soon arrived at the angle formed by the river.

There they halted, in order to ascertain if the bridge could be thrown across. The place appeared suitable.

In fact, from this spot to Port Balloon, discovered the day before on the southern coast, there was only a distance of three miles and a half, and from the bridge to the Port, it would be easy to make a good cart-road which would render the communication between Granite House and the south of the island extremely easy.

Cyrus Harding now imparted to his companions a scheme for completely isolating Prospect Heights so as to shelter it from the attacks both of quadrupeds and quadrumana. In this way, Granite House, the Chimneys, the poultry-yard, and all the upper part of the plateau which was to be used for cultivation, would be protected against the depredations of animals. Nothing could be easier than to execute this project, and this is how the engineer intended to set to work.

The plateau was already defended on three sides by water-courses, either artificial or natural. On the northwest, by the shores of Lake Grant, from the entrance of the passage to the breach made in the banks of the lake for the escape of the water.

On the north, from this breach to the sea, by the new watercourse which had hollowed out a bed for itself across the plateau and shore, above and below the fall, and it would be enough to dig the bed of this creek a little deeper to make it impracticable for animals, on all the eastern border by the sea itself, from the mouth of the aforesaid creek to the mouth of the Mercy.

Lastly, on the south, from the mouth to the turn of the Mercy where the bridge was to be established.

The western border of the plateau now remained between the turn of the river and the southern angle of the lake, a distance of about a mile, which was open to all comers. But nothing could be easier than to dig a broad deep ditch, which could be filled from the lake, and the overflow of which would throw itself by a rapid fall into the bed of the Mercy. The level of the lake would, no doubt, be somewhat lowered by this fresh discharge of its waters, but Cyrus Harding had ascertained that the volume of water in the Red Creek was considerable enough to allow of the execution of this project.

"So then," added the engineer, "Prospect Heights will become a regular island, being surrounded with water on all sides, and only communicating with the rest of our domain by the bridge which we are about to throw across the Mercy, the two little bridges already established above and below the fall; and, lastly, two other little bridges which must be constructed, one over the canal which I propose to dig, the other across to the left bank of the Mercy. Now, if these bridges can be raised at will, Prospect Heights will be guarded from any surprise."

The bridge was the most urgent work. Trees were selected, cut down, stripped of their branches, and cut into beams, joists, and planks. The end of the bridge which rested on the right bank of the Mercy was to be firm, but the other end on the left bank was to be movable, so that it might be raised by means of a counterpoise, as some canal bridges are managed.

This was certainly a considerable work, and though it was skillfully conducted, it took some time, for the Mercy at this place was eighty feet wide. It was therefore necessary to fix piles in the bed of the river so as to sustain the floor of the bridge and establish a pile-driver to act on the tops of these piles, which would thus form two arches and allow the bridge to support heavy loads.

Happily there was no want of tools with which to shape the wood, nor of iron-work to make it firm, nor of the ingenuity of a man who had a marvelous knowledge of the work, nor lastly, the zeal of his companions, who in seven months had necessarily acquired great skill in the use of their tools; and it must be said that not the least skillful was Gideon Spilett, who in dexterity almost equaled the sailor himself. "Who would ever have expected so much from a newspaper man!" thought Pencroft.

The construction of the Mercy bridge lasted three weeks of regular hard work. They even breakfasted on the scene of their labors, and the weather being magnificent, they only returned to Granite House to sleep.

During this period it may be stated that Master Jup grew more accustomed to his new masters, whose movements he always watched with very inquisitive eyes. However, as a precautionary measure, Pencroft did not as yet allow him complete liberty, rightly wishing to wait until the limits of the plateau should be settled by the projected works. Top and Jup were good friends and played willingly together, but Jup did everything solemnly.

On the 20th of November the bridge was finished. The movable part, balanced by the counterpoise, swung easily, and only a slight effort was needed to raise it; between its hinge and the last cross-bar on which it rested when closed, there existed a space of twenty feet, which was sufficiently wide to prevent any animals from crossing.

The settlers now began to talk of fetching the balloon-case, which they were anxious to place in perfect security; but to bring it, it would be necessary to take a cart to Port Balloon, and consequently, necessary to beat a road through the dense Forests of the Far West. This would take some time. Also, Neb and Pencroft having gone to examine into the state of things at Port Balloon, and reported that the stock of cloth would suffer no damage in the grotto where it was stored, it was decided that the work at Prospect Heights should not be discontinued.

"That," observed Pencroft, "will enable us to establish our poultry-yard under better conditions, since we need have no fear of visits from foxes nor the attacks of other beasts."

"Then," added Neb, "we can clear the plateau, and transplant wild plants to it."

"And prepare our second corn-field!" cried the sailor with a triumphant air.

In fact, the first corn-field sown with a single grain had prospered admirably, thanks to Pencroft's care. It had produced the ten ears foretold by the engineer, and each ear containing eighty grains, the colony found itself in possession of eight hundred grains, in six months, which promised a double harvest each year.

These eight hundred grains, except fifty, which were prudently reserved, were to be sown in a new field, but with no less care than was bestowed on the single grain.

The field was prepared, then surrounded with a strong palisade, high and pointed, which quadrupeds would have found difficulty in leaping. As to birds, some scarecrows, due to Pencroft's ingenious brain, were enough to frighten them. The seven hundred and fifty grains deposited in very regular furrows were then left for nature to do the rest.

On the 21st of November, Cyrus Harding began to plan the canal which was to close the plateau on the west, from the south angle of Lake Grant to the angle of the Mercy. There was there two or three feet of vegetable earth, and below that granite. It was therefore necessary to manufacture some more nitro-glycerine, and the nitro-glycerine did its accustomed work. In less than a fortnight a ditch, twelve feet wide and six deep, was dug out in the hard ground of the plateau. A new trench was made by the same means in the rocky border of the lake, forming a small stream, to which they gave the name of Creek Glycerine, and which was thus an affluent of the Mercy. As the engineer had predicted, the level of the lake was lowered, though very slightly. To complete the enclosure the bed of the stream on the beach was considerably enlarged, and the sand supported by means of stakes.

By the end of the first fortnight of December these works were finished, and Prospect Heights—that is to say, a sort of irregular pentagon, having a perimeter of nearly four miles, surrounded by a liquid belt—was completely protected from depredators of every description.

During the month of December, the heat was very great. In spite of it, however, the settlers continued their work, and as they were anxious to possess a poultry-yard, they forthwith commenced it.

It is useless to say that since the enclosing of the plateau had been completed, Master Jup had been set at liberty. He did not leave his masters, and evinced no wish to escape. He was a gentle animal, though very powerful and wonderfully active. He was already taught to make himself useful by drawing loads of wood and carting away the stones which were extracted from the bed of Creek Glycerine.

The poultry-yard occupied an area of two hundred square yards, on the southeastern bank of the lake. It was surrounded by a palisade, and in it were constructed various shelters for the birds which were to populate it. These were simply built of branches and divided into compartments, made ready for the expected guests.

The first were the two tinamous, which were not long in having a number of young ones; they had for companions half a dozen ducks, accustomed to the borders of the lake. Some belonged to the Chinese species, of which the wings open like a fan, and which by the brilliancy of their plumage rival the golden pheasants. A few days afterward, Herbert snared a couple of gallinaceae, with spreading tails composed of long feathers, magnificent alectors, which soon became tame. As to pelicans, kingfishers, water-hens, they came of themselves to the shores of the poultry-yard, and this little community, after some disputes, cooing, screaming, clucking, ended by settling down peacefully, and increased in encouraging proportion for the future use of the colony.

Cyrus Harding, wishing to complete his performance, established a pigeon-house in a corner of the poultry-yard. There he lodged a dozen of those pigeons which frequented the rocks of the plateau. These birds soon became accustomed to returning every evening to their new dwelling, and showed more disposition to domesticate themselves than their congeners, the wood-pigeons.

Lastly, the time had come for turning the balloon-case to use, by cutting it up to make shirts and other articles; for as to keeping it in its present form, and risking themselves in a balloon filled with gas, above a sea of the limits of which they had no idea, it was not to be thought of.

It was necessary to bring the case to Granite House, and the colonists employed themselves in rendering their heavy cart lighter and more manageable. But though they had a vehicle, the moving power was yet to be found.

But did there not exist in the island some animal which might supply the place of the horse, ass, or ox? That was the question.

"Certainly," said Pencroft, "a beast of burden would be very useful to us until the captain has made a steam cart, or even an engine, for some day we shall have a railroad from Granite House to Port Balloon, with a branch line to Mount Franklin!"

One day, the 23rd of December, Neb and Top were heard shouting and barking, each apparently trying to see who could make the most noise. The settlers, who were busy at the Chimneys, ran, fearing some vexatious incident.

What did they see? Two fine animals of a large size that had imprudently ventured on the plateau, when the bridges were open. One would have said they were horses, or at least donkeys, male and female, of a fine shape, dove-colored, the legs and tail white, striped with black on the head and neck. They advanced quietly without showing any uneasiness, and gazed at the men, in whom they could not as yet recognize their future masters.

"These are onagers!" cried Herbert, "animals something between the zebra and the quagga!"

"Why not donkeys?" asked Neb.

"Because they have not long ears, and their shape is more graceful!"

"Donkeys or horses," interrupted Pencroft, "they are 'moving powers,' as the captain would say, and as such must be captured!"

The sailor, without frightening the animals, crept through the grass to the bridge over Creek Glycerine, lowered it, and the onagers were prisoners.

Now, should they seize them with violence and master them by force? No. It was decided that for a few days they should be allowed to roam freely about the plateau, where there was an abundance of grass, and the engineer immediately began to prepare a stable near the poultry-yard, in which the onagers might find food, with a good litter, and shelter during the night.

This done, the movements of the two magnificent creatures were left entirely free, and the settlers avoided even approaching them so as to terrify them. Several times, however, the onagers appeared to wish to leave the plateau, too confined for animals accustomed to the plains and forests. They were then seen following the water-barrier which everywhere presented itself before them, uttering short neighs, then galloping through the grass, and becoming calmer, they would remain entire hours gazing at the woods, from which they were cut off for ever!

In the meantime harness of vegetable fiber had been manufactured, and some days after the capture of the onagers, not only the cart was ready, but a straight road, or rather a cutting, had been made through the Forests of the Far West, from the angle of the Mercy to Port Balloon. The cart might then be driven there, and toward the end of December they tried the onagers for the first time.

Pencroft had already coaxed the animals to come and eat out of his hand, and they allowed him to approach without making any difficulty, but once harnessed they reared and could with difficulty be held in. However, it was not long before they submitted to this new service, for the onager, being less refractory than the zebra, is frequently put in harness in the mountainous regions of Southern Africa, and it has even been acclimatized in Europe, under zones of a relative coolness.

On this day all the colony, except Pencroft who walked at the animals' heads, mounted the cart, and set out on the road to Port Balloon.

Of course they were jolted over the somewhat rough road, but the vehicle arrived without any accident, and was soon loaded with the case and rigging of the balloon.

At eight o'clock that evening the cart, after passing over the Mercy bridge, descended the left bank of the river, and stopped on the beach.

The onagers being unharnessed, were thence led to their stable, and Pencroft before going to sleep gave vent to his feelings in a deep sigh of satisfaction that awoke all the echoes of Granite House.

VIII

The first week of January was devoted to the manufacture of the linen garments required by the colony. The needles found in the box were used by sturdy if not delicate fingers, and we may be sure that what was sewn was sewn firmly.

There was no lack of thread, thanks to Cyrus Harding's idea of re-employing that which had been already used in the covering of the balloon. This with admirable patience was all unpicked by Gideon Spilett and Herbert, for Pencroft had been obliged to give this work up, as it irritated him beyond measure; but he had no equal in the sewing part of the business. Indeed, everybody knows that sailors have a remarkable aptitude for tailoring.

The cloth of which the balloon-case was made was then cleaned by means of soda and potash, obtained by the incineration of plants, in such a way that the cotton, having got rid of the varnish, resumed its natural softness and elasticity; then, exposed to the action of the atmosphere, it soon became perfectly white. Some dozen shirts and socks—the latter not knitted, of course, but made of cotton—were thus manufactured. What a comfort it was to the settlers to clothe themselves again in clean linen, which was doubtless rather rough, but they were not troubled about that! and then to go to sleep between sheets, which made the couches at Granite House into quite comfortable beds!

It was about this time also that they made boots of seal-leather, which were greatly needed to replace the shoes and boots brought from America. We may be sure that these new shoes were large enough and never pinched the feet of the wearers.

With the beginning of the year 1866 the heat was very great, but the hunting in the forests did not stand still. Agouties, peccaries, capybaras, kangaroos, game of all sorts, actually swarmed there, and Spilett and Herbert were too good marksmen ever to throw away their shot uselessly.

Cyrus Harding still recommended them to husband the ammunition, and he took measures to replace the powder and shot which had been found in the box, and which he wished to reserve for the future. How did he know where chance might one day cast his companions and himself in the event of their leaving their domain? They should, then, prepare for the unknown future by husbanding their ammunition and by substituting for it some easily renewable substance.

To replace lead, of which Harding had found no traces in the island, he employed granulated iron, which was easy to manufacture. These bullets, not having the weight of leaden bullets, were made larger, and each charge contained less, but the skill of the sportsmen made up this deficiency. As to powder, Cyrus Harding would have been able to make that also, for he had at his disposal saltpeter, sulphur, and coal; but this preparation requires extreme care, and without special tools it is difficult to produce it of a good quality. Harding preferred, therefore, to manufacture pyroxyle, that is to say gun-cotton, a substance in which cotton is not indispensable, as the elementary tissue of vegetables may be used, and this is found in an almost pure state, not only in cotton, but in the textile fibers of hemp and flax, in paper, the pith of the elder, etc. Now, the elder abounded in the island toward the mouth of Red Creek, and the colonists had already made coffee of the berries of these shrubs, which belong to the family of the caprifoliaceae.

The only thing to be collected, therefore, was elder-pith, for as to the other substance necessary for the manufacture of pyroxyle, it was only fuming azotic acid. Now, Harding having sulphuric acid at his disposal, had already been easily able to produce azotic acid by attacking the saltpeter with which nature supplied him. He accordingly resolved to manufacture and employ pyroxyle, although it has some inconveniences, that is to say, a great inequality of effect, an excessive inflammability, since it takes fire at one hundred and seventy degrees instead of two hundred and forty, and lastly, an instantaneous deflagration which might damage the firearms. On the other hand, the advantages of pyroxyle consist in this, that it is not injured by damp, that it does not make the gun-barrels dirty, and that its force is four times that of ordinary powder.

To make pyroxyle, the cotton must be immersed in the fuming azotic acid for a quarter of an hour, then washed in cold water and dried. Nothing could be more simple.

Cyrus Harding had only at his disposal the ordinary azotic acid and not the fuming or monohydrate azotic acid, that is to say, acid which emits white vapors when it comes in contact with damp air; but by substituting for the latter ordinary azotic acid, mixed, in the proportion of from three to five volumes of concentrated sulphuric acid, the engineer obtained the same result. The sportsmen of the island therefore soon had a perfectly prepared substance, which, employed discreetly, produced admirable results.

About this time the settlers cleared three acres of the plateau, and the rest was preserved in a wild state, for the benefit of the onagers. Several excursions were made into the Jacamar Wood and the Forests of the Far West, and they brought back from thence a large collection of wild vegetables, spinach, cress, radishes, and turnips, which careful culture would soon improve, and which would temper the regimen on which the settlers had till then subsisted. Supplies of wood and coal were also carted. Each excursion was at the same time a means of improving the roads, which gradually became smoother under the wheels of the cart.

The rabbit-warren still continued to supply the larder of Granite House. As fortunately it was situated on the other side of Creek Glycerine, its inhabitants could not reach the plateau nor ravage the newly-made plantation. The oyster-bed among the rocks was frequently renewed and furnished excellent molluscs. Besides that, the fishing, either in the lake or the Mercy, was very profitable, for Pencroft had made some lines, armed with iron hooks, with which they frequently caught fine trout, and a species of fish whose silvery sides were speckled with yellow, and which were also extremely savory. Master Neb, who was skilled in the culinary art, knew how to vary agreeably the bill of fare. Bread alone was wanting at the table of the settlers, and as has been said, they felt this privation greatly.

The settlers hunted too the turtles which frequented the shores of Mandible Cape. At this place the beach was covered with little mounds, concealing perfectly spherical turtles' eggs, with white hard shells, the albumen of which does not coagulate as that of birds' eggs. They were hatched by the sun, and their number was naturally considerable, as each turtle can lay annually two hundred and fifty.

"A regular egg-field," observed Gideon Spilett, "and we have nothing to do but to pick them up."

But not being contented with simply the produce, they made chase after the producers, the result of which was that they were able to bring back to Granite House a dozen of these chelonians, which were really valuable from an alimentary point of view. The turtle soup, flavored with aromatic herbs, often gained well-merited praises for its preparer, Neb.

We must here mention another fortunate circumstance by which new stores for the winter were laid in. Shoals of salmon entered the Mercy, and ascended the country for several miles. It was the time at which the females, going to find suitable places in which to spawn, precede the males and make a great noise through the fresh water. A thousand of these fish, which measured about two feet and a half in length, came up the river, and a large quantity were retained by fixing dams across the stream. More than a hundred were thus taken, which were salted and stored for the time when winter, freezing up the streams, would render fishing impracticable. By this time the intelligent Jup was raised to the duty of valet. He had been dressed in a jacket, white linen breeches, and an apron, the pockets of which were his delight. The clever orang had been marvelously trained by Neb, and any one would have said that the Negro and the ape understood each other when they talked together. Jup had besides a real affection for Neb, and Neb returned it. When his services were not required, either for carrying wood or for climbing to the top of some tree, Jup passed the greatest part of his time in the kitchen, where he endeavored to imitate Neb in all that he saw him do. The black showed the greatest patience and even extreme zeal in instructing his pupil, and the pupil exhibited remarkable intelligence in profiting by the lessons he received from his master.

Judge then of the pleasure Master Jup gave to the inhabitants of Granite House when, without thei: having had any idea of it, he appeared one day, napkin on his arm, ready to wait at table. Quick, attentive, he acquitted himself perfectly, changing the plates, bringing dishes, pouring out water, all with a gravity which gave intense amusement to the settlers, and which enraptured Pencroft.

"Jup, some soup!"

"Jup, a little agouti!"

"Jup, a plate!"

"Jup! Good Jup! Honest Jup!"

Nothing was heard but that, and Jup without ever being disconcerted, replied to every one, watched for everything, and he shook his head in a knowing way when Pencroft, referring to his joke of the first day, said to him,

"Decidedly, Jup, your wages must be doubled."

It is useless to say that the orang was now thoroughly domesticated at

Granite House, and that he often accompanied his masters to the forest without showing any wish to leave them. It was most amusing to see him walking with a stick which Pencroft had given him, and which he carried on his shoulder like a gun. If they wished to gather some fruit from the summit of a tree, how quickly he climbed for it. If the wheel of the cart stuck in the mud, with what energy did Jup with a single heave of his shoulder put it right again.

"What a jolly fellow he is!" cried Pencroft often. "If he was as mischievous as he is good, there would be no doing anything with him!"

It was toward the end of January the colonists began their labors in the center of the island. It had been decided that a corral should be established near the sources of the Red Creek, at the foot of Mount Franklin, destined to contain the ruminants, whose presence would have been troublesome at Granite House, and especially for the musmons, who were to supply the wool for the settlers' winter garments.

Each morning, the colony, sometimes entire, but more often represented only by Harding, Herbert, and Pencroft, proceeded to the sources of the creek, a distance of not more than five miles, by the newly beaten road to which the name of Corral Road had been given.

There a site was chosen, at the back of the southern ridge of the mountain. It was a meadow land, dotted here and there with clumps of trees, and watered by a little stream, which sprung from the slopes which closed it in on one side. The grass was fresh, and it was not too much shaded by the trees which grew about it. This meadow was to be surrounded by a palisade, high enough to prevent even the most agile animals from leaping over. This enclosure would be large enough to contain a hundred musmons and wild goats, with all the young ones they might produce.

The perimeter of the corral was then traced by the engineer, and they would then have proceeded to fell the trees necessary for the construction of the palisade, but as the opening up of the road had already necessitated the sacrifice of a considerable number, those were brought and supplied a hundred stakes, which were firmly fixed in the ground.

The construction of this corral did not take less than three weeks, for besides the palisade, Cyrus Harding built large sheds, in which the animals could take shelter. These buildings had also to be made very strong, for musmons are powerful animals, and their first fury was to be feared. The stakes, sharpened at their upper end and hardened by fire, had been fixed by means of cross-bars, and at regular distances props assured the solidity of the whole.

The corral finished, a raid had to be made on the pastures frequented by the ruminants. This was done on the 7th of February, on a beautiful summer's day, and every one took part in it. The onagers, already well trained, were ridden by Spilett and Herbert, and were of great use.

The maneuver consisted simply in surrounding the musmons and goats, and gradually narrowing the circle around them. Cyrus Harding, Pencroft, Neb, and Jup, posted themselves in different parts of the wood, while the two cavaliers and Top galloped in a radius of half a mile around the corral.

The musmons were very numerous in this part of the island. These fine animals were as large as deer; their horns were stronger than those of the ram, and their gray-colored fleece was mixed with long hair.

This hunting day was very fatiguing. Such going and coming, and running and riding and shouting! Of a hundred musmons which had been surrounded, more than two-thirds escaped, but at last, thirty of these animals and ten wild goats were gradually driven back toward the corral, the open door of which appearing to offer a means of escape, they rushed in and were prisoners.

In short, the result was satisfactory, and the settlers had no reason to complain. There was no doubt that the flock would prosper, and that at no distant time not only wool but hides would be abundant.

That evening the hunters returned to Granite House quite exhausted. However, notwithstanding their fatigue, they returned the next day to visit the corral. The prisoners had been trying to overthrow the palisade, but of course had not succeeded, and were not long in becoming more tranquil.

During the month of February, no event of any importance occurred. The daily labors were pursued methodically, and, as well as improving the roads to the corral and to Port Balloon, a third was commenced, which, starting from the enclosure, proceeded toward the western coast. The yet unknown portion of Lincoln Island was that of the wood-covered Serpentine Peninsula, which sheltered the wild beasts, from which Gideon Spilett was so anxious to clear their domain.

Before the cold season should appear, the most assiduous care was given to the cultivation of the wild plants which had been transplanted from the forest to Prospect Heights. Herbert never returned from an excursion without bringing home some useful vegetable. One day, it was some specimens of the chicory tribe, the seeds of which by pressure yield an excellent oil; another, it was some common sorrel, whose antiscorbutic qualities were not to be despised; then, some of those precious tubers, which have at all times been cultivated in South America, potatoes, of which more than two hundred species are now known. The kitchen garden, now well stocked and carefully defended from the birds, was divided into small beds, where grew lettuces, kidney potatoes, sorrel, turnips, radishes, and other cruciferae. The soil on the plateau was particularly fertile, and it was hoped that the harvests would be abundant.

They had also a variety of different beverages, and so long as they did not demand wine, the most hard to please would have had no reason to complain. To the Oswego tea, and the fermented liquor extracted from the roots of the dragonnier, Harding had added a regular beer, made from the young shoots of the spruce-fir, which, after having been boiled and fermented, made that agreeable drink called by the Anglo-Americans spring-beer.

Toward the end of the summer, the poultry-yard was possessed of a couple of fine bustards, which belonged to the houbara species, characterized by a sort of feathery mantle; a dozen shovelers, whose upper mandible was prolonged on each side by a membranous appendage; and also some magnificent cocks, similar to the Mozambique cocks, the comb, caruncle, and epidermis being black. So far, everything had succeeded, thanks to the activity of these courageous and intelligent men. Nature did much for them, doubtless; but faithful to the great precept, they made a right use of what a bountiful Providence gave them.

After the heat of these warm summer days, in the evening when their work was finished and the sea-breeze began to blow, they liked to sit on the edge of Prospect Heights, in a sort of veranda, covered with creepers, which Neb had made with his own hands. There they talked, they instructed each other, they made plans, and the rough good-humor of the sailor always amused this little world, in which the most perfect harmony had never ceased to reign.

They often spoke of their country, of their dear and great America. What was the result of the War of Secession? It could not have been greatly prolonged. Richmond had doubtless soon fallen into the hands of General Grant. The taking of the capital of the Confederates must have been the last action of this terrible struggle. Now the North had triumphed in the good cause, how welcome would have been a newspaper to the exiles in Lincoln Island! For eleven months all communication between them and the rest of their fellow-creatures had been interrupted, and in a short time the 24th of March would arrive, the anniversary of the day on which the balloon had thrown them on this unknown coast. They were then mere castaways, not even knowing how they should preserve their miserable lives from the fury of the elements! And now, thanks to the knowledge of their captain, and their own intelligence, they were regular colonists, furnished with arms, tools, and instruments; they had been able to turn to their profit the animals, plants, and minerals of the island, that is to say, the three kingdoms of nature.

Yes; they often talked of all these things and formed still more plans.

As to Cyrus Harding he was for the most part silent, and listened to his companions more often than he spoke to them. Sometimes he smiled at Herbert's ideas or Pencroft's nonsense, but always and everywhere he pondered over those inexplicable facts, that strange enigma, of which the secret still escaped him!

IX

The weather changed during the first week of March. There had been a full moon at the commencement of the month, and the heat was excessive. The atmosphere was felt to be full of electricity, and a period of some length of tempestuous weather was to be feared.

Indeed, on the 2nd, peals of thunder were heard, the wind blew from the east, and hail rattled against the façade of Granite House like volleys of grape-shot. The door and windows were immediately closed, or everything in the rooms would have been drenched. On seeing these hailstones, some of which were the size of a pigeon's egg, Pencroft's first thought was that his corn-field was in serious danger.

He directly rushed to his field, where little green heads were already appearing, and by means of a great cloth, he managed to protect his crop.

This bad weather lasted a week, during which time the thunder rolled without cessation in the depths of the sky.

The colonists, not having any pressing work out of doors, profited by the bad weather to work at the interior of Granite House, the arrangement of which was becoming more complete from day to day. The engineer made a turning-lathe, with which he turned several articles both for the toilet and the kitchen, particularly buttons, the want of which was greatly felt. A gunrack had been made for the firearms, which were kept with extreme care, and neither tables nor cupboards were left incomplete. They sawed, they planed, they filed, they turned; and during the whole of this bad season, nothing was heard but the grinding of tools or the humming of the turning-lathe which responded to the growling of the thunder.

Master Jup had not been forgotten, and he occupied a room at the back, near the storeroom, a sort of cabin with a cot always full of good litter, which perfectly suited his taste.

"With good old Jup there is never any quarreling," often repeated Pencroft, "never any improper reply. What a servant, Neb, what a servant!"

Of course Jup was now well used to service. He brushed their clothes, he turned the spit, he waited at table, he swept the rooms, he gathered wood, and he performed another admirable piece of service which delighted Pencroft—he never went to sleep without first coming to tuck up the worthy sailor in his bed.

As to the health of the members of the colony, bipeds or bimana, quadrumana or quadrupeds, it left nothing to be desired. With their life in the open air, on this salubrious soil, under that temperate zone, working both with head and hands, they could not suppose that illness would ever attack them.

All were indeed wonderfully well. Herbert had already grown two inches in the year. His figure was forming and becoming more manly, and he promised to be an accomplished man, physically as well as morally. Besides he improved himself during the leisure hours which manual occupations left to him; he read the books found in the case; and after the practical lessons which were taught by the very necessity of their position, he found in the engineer for science, and the reporter for languages, masters who were delighted to complete his education.

The tempest ended about the 9th of March, but the sky remained covered with clouds during the whole of this last summer month. The atmosphere, violently agitated by the electric commotions, could not recover its former purity, and there was almost invariably rain and fog, except for three or four fine days on which several excursions were made. About this time the female onager gave birth to a young one which belonged to the same sex as its mother, and which throve capitally. In the corral, the flock of musmons had also increased, and several lambs already bleated in the sheds, to the great delight of Neb and Herbert, who had each their favorite among these newcomers. An attempt was also made for the domestication of the peccaries, which succeeded well. A sty was constructed under the poultry-yard, and soon contained several young ones in the way to become civilized, that is to say, to become fat under Neb's care. Master Jup, entrusted with carrying them their daily nourishment, leavings from the kitchen, etc., acquitted himself conscientiously of his task. He sometimes amused himself at the expense of his little pensioners by tweaking their tails; but this was mischief, and not wickedness, for these little twisted tails amused him like a plaything, and his instinct was that of a child. One day in this month of March, Pencroft, talking to the engineer, reminded Cyrus Harding of a promise which the latter had not as yet had time to fulfill.

"You once spoke of an apparatus which would take the place of the long ladders at Granite House, captain," said he; "won't you make it some day?"

"Nothing will be easier; but is this a really useful thing?"

"Certainly, captain. After we have given ourselves necessaries, let us think a little of luxury. For us it may be luxury, if you like, but for things it is necessary. It isn't very convenient to climb up a long ladder when one is heavily loaded."

"Well, Pencroft, we will try to please you," replied Cyrus Harding.

"But you have no machine at your disposal."

"We will make one."

"A steam machine?"

"No, a water machine."

And, indeed, to work his apparatus there was already a natural force at the disposal of the engineer which could be used without great difficulty. For this, it was enough to augment the flow of the little stream which supplied the interior of Granite House with water. The opening among the stones and grass was then increased, thus producing a strong fall at the bottom of the passage, the overflow from which escaped by the inner well. Below this fall the engineer fixed a cylinder with paddles, which was joined on the exterior with a strong cable rolled on a wheel, supporting a basket. In this way, by means of a long rope reaching to the ground, which enabled them to regulate the motive power, they could rise in the basket to the door of Granite House.

It was on the 17th of March that the lift acted for the first time, and gave universal satisfaction. Henceforward all the loads, wood, coal, provisions, and even the settlers themselves, were hoisted by this simple system, which replaced the primitive ladder, and, as may be supposed, no one thought of regretting the change. Top particularly was enchanted with this improvement, for he had not, and never could have possessed Master Jup's skill in climbing ladders, and often it was on Neb's back, or even on that of the orang that he had been obliged to make the ascent to Granite House. About this time, too, Cyrus Harding attempted to manufacture glass, and he at first put the old pottery-kiln to this new use. There were some difficulties to be encountered; but, after several fruitless attempts, he succeeded in setting up a glass manufactory, which Gideon Spilett and Herbert, his usual assistants, did not leave for several days. As to the substances used in the composition of glass, they are simply sand, chalk, and soda, either carbonate or sulphate. Now the beach supplied sand, lime supplied chalk, sea-weeds supplied soda, pyrites supplied sulphuric acid, and the ground supplied coal to heat the kiln to the wished-for temperature. Cyrus Harding thus soon had everything ready for setting to work.

The tool, the manufacture of which presented the most difficulty, was the pipe of the glass-maker, an iron tube, five or six feet long, which collects on one end the material in a state of fusion. But by means of a long, thin piece of iron rolled up like the barrel of a gun, Pencroft succeeded in making a tube soon ready for use.

On the 28th of March the tube was heated. A hundred parts of sand, thirty-five of chalk, forty of sulphate of soda, mixed with two or three parts of powdered coal, composed the substance, which was placed in crucibles. When the high temperature of the oven had reduced it to a liquid, or rather a pasty state, Cyrus Harding collected with the tube a quantity of the paste: he turned it about on a metal plate, previously arranged, so as to give it a form suitable for blowing, then he passed the tube to Herbert, telling him to blow at the other extremity.

And Herbert, swelling out his cheeks, blew so much and so well into the tube—taking care to twirl it round at the same time—that his breath dilated the glassy mass. Other quantities of the substance in a state of fusion were added to the first, and in a short time the result was a bubble which measured a foot in diameter. Harding then took the tube out of Herbert's hands, and, giving it a pendulous motion, he ended by lengthening the malleable bubble so as to give it a cylindro-conic shape.

The blowing operation had given a cylinder of glass terminated by two hemispheric caps, which were easily detached by means of a sharp iron dipped in cold water; then, by the same proceeding, this cylinder was cut lengthways, and after having been rendered malleable by a second heating, it was extended on a plate and spread out with a wooden roller.

The first pane was thus manufactured, and they had only to perform this operation fifty times to have fifty panes. The windows at Granite House were soon furnished with panes; not very white, perhaps, but still sufficiently transparent.

As to bottles and tumblers, that was only play. They were satisfied with them, besides, just as they came from the end of the tube. Pencroft had asked to be allowed to "blow" in his turn, and it was great fun for him; but he blew so hard that his productions took the most ridiculous shapes, which he admired immensely.

Cyrus Harding and Herbert, while hunting one day, had entered the Forests of the Far West, on the left bank of the Mercy, and, as usual, the lad was asking a thousand questions of the engineer, who answered them heartily. Now, as Harding was not a sportsman, and as, on the other side, Herbert was talking chemistry and natural philosophy, numbers of kangaroos, capybaras, and agouties came within range, which, however, escaped the lad's gun; the consequence was that the day was already advanced, and the two hunters were in danger of having made a useless excursion, when Herbert, stopping, and uttering a cry of joy, exclaimed,

"Oh, Captain Harding, do you see that tree?" and he pointed to a shrub, rather than a tree, for it was composed of a single stem, covered with a scaly bark, which bore leaves streaked with little parallel veins.

"And what is this tree which resembles a little palm?" asked Harding.

"It is a cycas revoluta, of which I have a picture in our dictionary of natural history!" said Herbert.

"But I can't see any fruit on this shrub!" observed his companion.

"No, captain," replied Herbert; "but its stem contains a flour with which nature has provided us all ready ground."

"It is, then, the bread-tree?"

"Yes, the bread-tree."

"Well, my boy," replied the engineer, "this is a valuable discovery, since our wheat harvest is not yet ripe; I hope that you are not mistaken!"

Herbert was not mistaken: he broke the stem of a cycas, which was composed of a glandulous tissue, containing a quantity of floury pith, traversed with woody fiber, separated by rings of the same substance, arranged concentrically. With this fecula was mingled a mucilaginous juice of disagreeable flavor, but which it would be easy to get rid of by pressure. This cellular substance was regular flour of a superior quality, extremely nourishing; its exportation was formerly forbidden by the Japanese laws.

Cyrus Harding and Herbert, after having examined that part of the Far West where the cycas grew, took their bearings, and returned to Granite House, where they made known their discovery.

The next day the settlers went to collect some, and returned to Granite House with an ample supply of cycas stems. The engineer constructed a press, with which to extract the mucilaginous juice mingled with the fecula, and he obtained a large quantity of flour, which Neb soon transformed into cakes and puddings. This was not quite real wheaten bread, but it was very like it.

Now, too, the onager, the goats, and the sheep in the corral furnished daily the milk necessary to the colony. The cart, or rather a sort of light carriole which had replaced it, made frequent journeys to the corral, and when it was Pencroft's turn to go he took Jup, and let him drive, and Jup, cracking his whip, acquitted himself with his customary intelligence.

Everything prospered, as well in the corral as in Granite House, and certainly the settlers, if it had not been that they were so far from their native land, had no reason to complain. They were so well suited to this life, and were, besides, so accustomed to the island, that they could not have left its hospitable soil without regret!

And yet so deeply is the love of his country implanted in the heart of man, that if a ship had unexpectedly come in sight of the island, the colonists would have made signals, would have attracted her attention, and would have departed!

It was the 1st of April, a Sunday, Easter Day, which Harding and his companions sanctified by rest and prayer. The day was fine, such as an October day in the Northern Hemisphere might be.

All, toward the evening after dinner, were seated under the veranda on the edge of Prospect Heights, and they were watching the darkness creeping up from the horizon. Some cups of the infusion of elder-berries, which took the place of coffee, had been served by Neb. They were speaking of the island and of its isolated situation in the Pacific, which led Gideon Spilett to say,

"My dear Cyrus, have you ever, since you possessed the sextant found in the case, again taken the position of our island?"

"No," replied the engineer.

"But it would perhaps be a good thing to do it with this instrument, which is more perfect than that which you before used."

"What is the good?" said Pencroft. "The island is quite comfortable where it is!"

"Well, who knows," returned the reporter, "who knows but that we may be much nearer inhabited land than we think?"

"We shall know to-morrow," replied Cyrus Harding, "and if it had not been for the occupations which left me no leisure, we should have known it already."

"Good!" said Pencroft. "The captain is too good an observer to be mistaken, and, if it has not moved from its place, the island is just where he put it."

"We shall see."

On the next day, therefore, by means of the sextant, the engineer made the necessary observations to verify the position which he had already obtained, and this was the result of his operation. His first observation had given him the situation of Lincoln Island,

In west longitude: from 150° to 155°;

In south latitude: from 35° to 40°.

The second gave exactly:

In west longitude: 150° 30′;

In south latitude: 35° 57′.

So then, notwithstanding the imperfection of his apparatus, Cyrus Harding had operated with so much skill that his error did not exceed five degrees.

"Now," said Gideon Spilett, "since we possess an atlas as well as a sextant, let us see, my dear Cyrus, the exact position which Lincoln Island occupies in the Pacific."

Herbert fetched the atlas, and the map of the Pacific was opened, and the engineer, compass in hand, prepared to determine their position.

Suddenly the compasses stopped, and he exclaimed,

"But an island exists in this part of the Pacific already!"

"An island?" cried Pencroft.

"Tabor Island."

"An important island?"

"No, an islet lost in the Pacific, and which perhaps has never been visited."

"Well, we will visit it," said Pencroft.

"We?"

"Yes, captain. We will build a decked boat, and I will undertake to steer her. At what distance are we from this Tabor Island?"

"About a hundred and fifty miles to the northeast," replied Harding.

"A hundred and fifty miles! And what's that?" returned Pencroft. "In forty-eight hours, with a good wind, we should sight it!"

And, on this reply, it was decided that a vessel should be constructed in time to be launched toward the month of next October, on the return of the fine season.

X

When Pencroft had once got a plan in his head, he had no peace till it was executed. Now he wished to visit Tabor Island, and as a boat of a certain size was necessary for this voyage, he determined to build one.

What wood should he employ? Elm or fir, both of which abounded in the island? They decided for the fir, as being easy to work, but which stands water as well as the elm.

These details settled, it was agreed that since the fine season would not return before six months, Cyrus Harding and Pencroft should work alone at the boat. Gideon Spilett and Herbert were to continue to hunt, and neither Neb nor Master Jup, his assistant, were to leave the domestic duties which had devolved upon them.

Directly the trees were chosen, they were felled, stripped of their branches, and sawn into planks as well as sawyers would have been able to do it. A week after, in the recess between the Chimneys and the cliff, a dockyard was prepared, and a keel five-and-thirty feet long, furnished with a stern-post at the stern and a stem at the bows, lay along the sand.

Cyrus Harding was not working in the dark at this new trade. He knew as much about ship-building as about nearly everything else, and he had at first drawn the model of his ship on paper. Besides, he was ably seconded by Pencroft, who, having worked for several years in a dockyard in Brooklyn, knew the practical part of the trade. It was not until after careful calculation and deep thought that the timbers were laid on the keel.

Pencroft, as may be believed, was all eagerness to carry out his new enterprise, and would not leave his work for an instant.

A single thing had the honor of drawing him, but for one day only, from his dockyard. This was the second wheat-harvest, which was gathered in on the 15th of April. It was as much a success as the first, and yielded the number of grains which had been predicted.

"Five bushels, captain," said Pencroft, after having scrupulously measured his treasure.

"Five bushels," replied the engineer; "and a hundred and thirty thousand grains a bushel will make six hundred and fifty thousand grains."

"Well, we will sow them all this time," said the sailor, "except a little in reserve."

"Yes, Pencroft, and if the next crop gives a proportionate yield, we shall have four thousand bushels."

"And shall we eat bread?"

"We shall eat bread."

"But we must have a mill."

"We will make one."

The third corn-field was very much larger than the two first, and the soil, prepared with extreme care, received the precious seed. That done, Pencroft returned to his work.

During this time Spilett and Herbert hunted in the neighborhood, and they ventured deep into the still unknown parts of the Far West, their guns loaded with ball, ready for any dangerous emergency. It was a vast thicket of magnificent trees, crowded together as if pressed for room. The exploration of these dense masses of wood was difficult in the extreme, and the reporter never ventured there without the pocket-compass, for the sun scarcely pierced through the thick foliage, and it would have been very difficult for them to retrace their way. It naturally happened that game was more rare in those situations where there was hardly sufficient room to move; two or three large herbivorous animals were however killed during the last fortnight of April. These were koalas, specimens of which the settlers had already seen to the north of the lake, and which stupidly allowed themselves to be killed among the thick branches of the trees in which they took refuge. Their skins were brought back to Granite House, and there, by the help of sulphuric acid, they were subjected to a sort of tanning process which rendered them capable of being used.

On the 30th of April, the two sportsmen were in the depth of the Far

West, when the reporter, preceding Herbert a few paces, arrived in a sort of clearing, into which the trees more sparsely scattered had permitted a few rays to penetrate. Gideon Spilett was at first surprised at the odor which exhaled from certain plants with straight stalks, round and branchy, bearing grape-like clusters of flowers and very small berries. The reporter broke off one or two of these stalks and returned to the lad, to whom he said,

"What can this be, Herbert?"

"Well, Mr. Spilett," said Herbert, "this is a treasure which will secure you Pencroft's gratitude forever."

"Is it tobacco?"

"Yes, and though it may not be of the first quality, it is none the less tobacco!"

"Oh, good old Pencroft! Won't he be pleased! But we must not let him smoke it all, he must give us our share."

"Ah! an idea occurs to me, Mr. Spilett," replied Herbert. "Don't let us say anything to Pencroft yet; we will prepare these leaves, and one fine day we will present him with a pipe already filled!"

"All right, Herbert, and on that day our worthy companion will have nothing left to wish for in this world."

The reporter and the lad secured a good store of the precious plant, and then returned to Granite House, where they smuggled it in with as much precaution as if Pencroft had been the most vigilant and severe of custom-house officers.

Cyrus Harding and Neb were taken into confidence, and the sailor suspected nothing during the whole time, necessarily somewhat long, which was required in order to dry the small leaves, chop them up, and subject them to a certain torrefaction on hot stones. This took two months; but all these manipulations were successfully carried on unknown to Pencroft, for, occupied with the construction of his boat, he only returned to Granite House at the hour of rest.

For some days they had observed an enormous animal two or three miles out in the open sea swimming around Lincoln Island. This was a whale of the largest size, which apparently belonged to the southern species, called the cape whale.

"What a lucky chance it would be if we could capture it!" cried the sailor. "Ah! if we only had a proper boat and a good harpoon, I would say 'After the beast,' for he would be well worth the trouble of catching!"

"Well, Pencroft," observed Harding, "I should much like to watch you handling a harpoon. It would be very interesting."

"I am astonished," said the reporter, "to see a whale in this comparatively high latitude."

"Why so, Mr. Spilett?" replied Herbert. "We are exactly in that part of the Pacific which English and American whalemen call the whale-field, and it is here, between New Zealand and South America, that the whales of the Southern Hemisphere are met with in the greatest numbers."

And Pencroft returned to his work, not without uttering a sigh of regret, for every sailor is a born fisherman, and if the pleasure of fishing is in exact proportion to the size of the animal, one can judge how a whaler feels in sight of a whale. And if this had only been for pleasure! But they could not help feeling how valuable such a prize would have been to the colony, for the oil, fat, and bones would have been put to many uses.

Now it happened that this whale appeared to have no wish to leave the waters of the island. Therefore, whether from the windows of Granite House, or from Prospect Heights, Herbert and Gideon Spilett, when they were not hunting, or Neb, unless presiding over his fires, never left the telescope, but watched all the animal's movements. The cetacean, having entered far into Union Bay, made rapid furrows across it from Mandible Cape to Claw Cape, propelled by its enormously powerful flukes, on which it supported itself, and making its way through the water at the rate little short of twelve knots an hour. Sometimes also it approached so near to the island that it could be clearly distinguished. It was the southern whale, which is completely black, the head being more depressed than that of the northern whale.

They could also see it throwing up from its air-holes to a great height a cloud of vapor, or of water, for, strange as it may appear, naturalists and whalers are not agreed on this subject. Is it air or is it water which is thus driven out? It is generally admitted to be vapor, which, condensing suddenly by contact with the cold air, falls again as rain.

However, the presence of this mammifer preoccupied the colonists. It irritated Pencroft especially, as he could think of nothing else while at work. He ended by longing for it, like a child for a thing which it has been denied. At night he talked about it in his sleep, and certainly if he had had the means of attacking it, if the sloop had been in a fit state to put to sea, he would not have hesitated to set out in pursuit.

But what the colonists could not do for themselves chance did for them, and on the 3rd of May shouts from Neb, who had stationed himself at the kitchen window, announced that the whale was stranded on the beach of the island.

Herbert and Gideon Spilett, who were just about to set out hunting, left their guns, Pencroft threw down his ax, and Harding and Neb joining their companions, all rushed toward the scene of action.

The stranding had taken place on the beach of Flotsam Point, three miles from Granite House, and at high tide. It was therefore probable that the cetacean would not be able to extricate itself easily; at any rate it was best to hasten, so as to cut off its retreat if necessary. They ran with pick-axes and iron-tipped poles in their hands, passed over the Mercy bridge, descended the right bank of the river, along the beach, and in less than twenty minutes the settlers were close to the enormous animal, above which flocks of birds already hovered.

"What a monster!" cried Neb.

And the exclamation was natural, for it was a southern whale, eighty feet long, a giant of the species, probably not weighing less than a hundred and fifty thousand pounds!

In the meanwhile, the monster thus stranded did not move, nor attempt by struggling to regain the water while the tide was still high.

It was dead, and a harpoon was sticking out of its left side.

"There are whalers in these quarters, then?" said Gideon Spilett directly.

"Oh, Mr. Spilett, that doesn't prove anything!" replied Pencroft. "Whales have been known to go thousands of miles with a harpoon in the side, and this one might even have been struck in the north of the Atlantic and come to die in the south of the Pacific, and it would be nothing astonishing."

Pencroft, having torn the harpoon from the animal's side, read this inscription on it:

MARIA STELLA, VINEYARD

"A vessel from the Vineyard! A ship from my country!" he cried. "The *Maria Stella*! A fine whaler, 'pon my word; I know her well! Oh, my friends, a vessel from the Vineyard!—a whaler from the Vineyard!"

And the sailor brandishing the harpoon, repeated, not without emotion, the name which he loved so well—the name of his birthplace.

But as it could not be expected that the *Maria Stella* would come to reclaim the animal harpooned by her, they resolved to begin cutting it up before decomposition should commence. The birds, who had watched this rich prey for several days, had determined to take possession of it without further delay, and it was necessary to drive them off by firing at them repeatedly.

The whale was a female, and a large quantity of milk was taken from it, which, according to the opinion of the naturalist Duffenbach, might pass for cow's milk, and, indeed, it differs from it neither in taste, color, nor density.

Pencroft had formerly served on board a whaling-ship, and he could methodically direct the operation of cutting up—a sufficiently disagreeable operation lasting three days, but from which the settlers did not flinch, not even Gideon Spilett, who, as the sailor said, would end by making a "real good castaway."

The blubber, cut in parallel slices of two feet and a half in thickness, then divided into pieces which might weigh about a thousand pounds each, was melted down in large earthen pots brought to the spot, for they did not wish to taint the environs of Granite House, and in this fusion it lost nearly a third of its weight.

But there was an immense quantity of it; the tongue alone yielded six thousand pounds of oil, and the lower lip four thousand. Then, besides the fat, which would ensure for a long time a store of stearine and glycerine, there were still the bones, for which a use could doubtless be found, although there were neither umbrellas nor stays used at Granite House. The upper part of the mouth of the cetacean was, indeed, provided on both sides with eight hundred horny blades, very elastic, of a fibrous texture, and fringed at the edge like great combs, at which the teeth, six feet long, served to retain the thousands of animalculae, little fish, and molluscs, on which the whale fed.

The operation finished, to the great satisfaction of the operators, the remains of the animal were left to the birds, who would soon make every vestige of it disappear, and their usual daily occupations were resumed by the inmates of Granite House.

However, before returning to the dockyard, Cyrus Harding conceived the idea of fabricating certain machines, which greatly excited the curiosity of his companions. He took a dozen of the whale's bones, cut them into six equal parts, and sharpened their ends.

"This machine is not my own invention, and it is frequently employed by the Aleutian hunters in Russian America. You see these bones, my friends; well, when it freezes, I will bend them, and then wet them with water till they are entirely covered with ice, which will keep them bent, and I will strew them on the snow, having previously covered them with fat. Now, what will happen if a hungry animal swallows one of these baits? Why, the heat of his stomach will melt the ice, and the bone, springing straight, will pierce him with its sharp points."

"Well! I do call that ingenious!" said Pencroft.

"And it will spare the powder and shot," rejoined Cyrus Harding.

"That will be better than traps!" added Neb.

In the meanwhile the boat-building progressed, and toward the end of the month half the planking was completed. It could already be seen that her shape was excellent, and that she would sail well.

Pencroft worked with unparalleled ardor, and only a sturdy frame could have borne such fatigue; but his companions were preparing in secret a reward for his labors, and on the 31st of May he was to meet with one of the greatest joys of his life.

On that day, after dinner, just as he was about to leave the table, Pencroft felt a hand on his shoulder.

It was the hand of Gideon Spilett, who said,

"One moment, Master Pencroft, you mustn't sneak off like that! You've forgotten your dessert."

"Thank you, Mr. Spilett," replied the sailor, "I am going back to my work."

"Well, a cup of coffee, my friend?"

"Nothing more."

"A pipe, then?"

Pencroft jumped up, and his great good-natured face grew pale when he saw the reporter presenting him with a ready-filled pipe, and Herbert with a glowing coal.

The sailor endeavored to speak, but could not get out a word; so, seizing the pipe, he carried it to his lips, then applying the coal, he drew five or six great whiffs. A fragrant blue cloud soon arose, and from its depths a voice was heard repeating excitedly,

"Tobacco! real tobacco!"

"Yes, Pencroft," returned Cyrus Harding, "and very good tobacco too!"

"O, divine Providence; sacred Author of all things!" cried the sailor. "Nothing more is now wanting to our island."

And Pencroft smoked, and smoked, and smoked.

"And who made this discovery?" he asked at length. "You, Herbert, no doubt?"

"No, Pencroft, it was Mr. Spilett."

"Mr. Spilett!" exclaimed the sailor, seizing the reporter, and clasping him to his breast with such a squeeze that he had never felt anything like it before.

"Oh Pencroft," said Spilett, recovering his breath at last, "a truce for one moment. You must share your gratitude with Herbert, who recognized the plant, with Cyrus, who prepared it, and with Neb, who took a great deal of trouble to keep our secret."

"Well, my friends, I will repay you some day," replied the sailor. "Now we are friends for life."

XI

Winter arrived with the month of June, which is the December of the northern zones, and the great business was the making of warm and solid clothing.

The musmons in the corral had been stripped of their wool, and this precious textile material was now to be transformed into stuff.

Of course Cyrus Harding, having at his disposal neither carders, combers, polishers, stretchers, twisters, mule-jenny, nor self-acting machine to spin the wool, nor loom to weave it, was obliged to proceed in a simpler way, so as to do without spinning and weaving. And indeed he proposed to make use of the property which the filaments of wool possess when subjected to a powerful pressure of mixing together, and of manufacturing by this simple process the material called felt. This felt could then be obtained by a simple operation which, if it diminished the flexibility of the stuff, increased its power of retaining heat in proportion. Now the wool furnished by the musmons was composed of very short hairs, and was in a good condition to be felted.

The engineer, aided by his companions, including Pencroft, who was once more obliged to leave his boat, commenced the preliminary operations, the subject of which was to rid the wool of that fat and oily substance with which it is impregnated, and which is called grease. This cleaning was done in vats filled with water, which was maintained at the temperature of seventy degrees, and in which the wool was soaked for four-and-twenty hours; it was then thoroughly washed in baths of soda, and, when sufficiently dried by pressure, it was in a state to be compressed, that is to say, to produce a solid material, rough, no doubt, and such as would have no value in a manufacturing center of Europe or America, but which would be highly esteemed in the Lincoln Island markets.

This sort of material must have been known from the most ancient times, and, in fact, the first woolen stuffs were manufactured by the process which Harding was now about to employ. Where Harding's engineering qualifications now came into play was in the construction of the machine for pressing the wool; for he knew how to turn ingeniously to profit the mechanical force, hitherto unused, which the waterfall on the beach possessed to move a fulling-mill.

Nothing could be more rudimentary. The wool was placed in troughs, and upon it fell in turns heavy wooden mallets; such was the machine in question, and such it had been for centuries until the time when the mallets were replaced by cylinders of compression, and the material was no longer subjected to beating, but to regular rolling.

The operation, ably directed by Cyrus Harding, was a complete success. The wool, previously impregnated with a solution of soap, intended on the one hand to facilitate the interlacing, the compression, and the softening of the wool, and on the other to prevent its diminution by the beating, issued from the mill in the shape of thick felt cloth. The roughnesses with which the staple of wool is naturally filled were so thoroughly entangled and interlaced together that a material was formed equally suitable either for garments or bedclothes. It was certainly neither merino, muslin, cashmere, rep, satin, alpaca, cloth, nor flannel. It was "Lincolnian felt," and Lincoln Island possessed yet another manufacture. The colonists had now warm garments and thick bedclothes, and they could without fear await the approach of the winter of 1866–67.

The severe cold began to be felt about the 20th of June, and, to his great regret, Pencroft was obliged to suspend his boat-building, which he hoped to finish in time for next spring.

The sailor's great idea was to make a voyage of discovery to Tabor Island, although Harding could not approve of a voyage simply for curiosity's sake, for there was evidently nothing to be found on this desert and almost arid rock. A voyage of a hundred and fifty miles in a comparatively small vessel, over unknown seas, could not but cause him some anxiety. Suppose that their vessel, once out at sea, should be unable to reach Tabor Island, and could not return to Lincoln Island, what would become of her in the midst of the Pacific, so fruitful of disasters?

Harding often talked over this project with Pencroft, and he found him strangely bent upon undertaking this voyage, for which determination he himself could give no sufficient reason.

"Now," said the engineer one day to him, "I must observe, my friend, that after having said so much, in praise of Lincoln Island, after having spoken so often of the sorrow you would feel if you were obliged to forsake it, you are the first to wish to leave it."

"Only to leave it for a few days," replied Pencroft, "only for a few days, captain. Time to go and come back, and see what that islet is like!"

"But it is not nearly as good as Lincoln Island."

"I know that beforehand."

"Then why venture there?"

"To know what is going on in Tabor Island."

"But nothing is going on there; nothing could happen there."

"Who knows?"

"And if you are caught in a hurricane?"

"There is no fear of that in the fine season," replied Pencroft. "But, captain, as we must provide against everything, I shall ask your permission to take Herbert only with me on this voyage."

"Pencroft," replied the engineer, placing his hand on the sailor's shoulder, "if any misfortune happens to you, or to this lad, whom chance has made our child, do you think we could ever cease to blame ourselves?"

"Captain Harding," replied Pencroft, with unshaken confidence, "we shall not cause you that sorrow. Besides, we will speak further of this voyage, when the time comes to make it. And I fancy, when you have seen our tight-rigged little craft, when you have observed how she behaves at sea, when we sail around our island, for we will do so together—I fancy, I say, that you will no longer hesitate to let me go. I don't conceal from you that your boat will be a masterpiece."

"Say 'our' boat, at least, Pencroft," replied the engineer, disarmed for the moment. The conversation ended thus, to be resumed later on, without convincing either the sailor or the engineer.

The first snow fell toward the end of the month of June. The corral had previously been largely supplied with stores, so that daily visits to it were not requisite; but it was decided that more than a week should never be allowed to pass without someone going to it.

Traps were again set, and the machines manufactured by Harding were tried. The bent whalebones, imprisoned in a case of ice, and covered with a thick outer layer of fat, were placed on the border of the forest at a spot where animals usually passed on their way to the lake.

To the engineer's great satisfaction, this invention, copied from the Aleutian fishermen, succeeded perfectly. A dozen foxes, a few wild boars, and even a jaguar, were taken in this way, the animals being found dead, their stomachs pierced by the unbent bones.

An incident must here be related, not only as interesting in itself, but because it was the first attempt made by the colonists to communicate with the rest of mankind.

Gideon Spilett had already several times pondered whether to throw into the sea a letter enclosed in a bottle, which currents might perhaps carry to an inhabited coast, or to confide it to pigeons.

But how could it be seriously hoped that either pigeons or bottles could cross the distance of twelve hundred miles which separated the island from any inhabited land? It would have been pure folly.

But on the 30th of June the capture was effected, not without difficulty, of an albatross, which a shot from Herbert's gun had slightly wounded in the foot. It was a magnificent bird, measuring ten feet from wing to wing, and which could traverse seas as wide as the Pacific.

Herbert would have liked to keep this superb bird, as its wound would soon heal, and he thought he could tame it; but Spilett explained to him that they should not neglect this opportunity of attempting to communicate by this messenger with the lands of the Pacific; for if the albatross had come from some inhabited region, there was no doubt but that it would return there so soon as it was set free.

Perhaps in his heart Gideon Spilett, in whom the journalist sometimes came to the surface, was not sorry to have the opportunity of sending forth to take its chance an exciting article relating the adventures of the settlers in Lincoln Island. What a success for the authorized reporter of the *New York Herald*, and for the number which should contain the article, if it should ever reach the address of its editor, the Honorable James Bennett!

Gideon Spilett then wrote out a concise account, which was placed in a strong waterproof bag, with an earnest request to whoever might find it to forward it to the office of the *New York Herald*. This little bag was fastened to the neck of the albatross, and not to its foot, for these birds are in the habit of resting on the surface of the sea; then liberty was given to this swift courier of the air, and it was not without some emotion that the colonists watched it disappear in the misty west.

"Where is he going to?" asked Pencroft.

"Toward New Zealand," replied Herbert.

"A good voyage to you," shouted the sailor, who himself did not expect any great result from this mode of correspondence.

With the winter, work had been resumed in the interior of Granite House, mending clothes and different occupations, among others making the sails for their vessel, which were cut from the inexhaustible balloon-case.

During the month of July the cold was intense, but there was no lack of either wood or coal. Cyrus Harding had established a second fireplace in the dining-room, and there the long winter evenings were spent. Talking while they worked, reading when the hands remained idle, the time passed with profit to all.

It was real enjoyment to the settlers when in their room, well lighted with candles, well warmed with coal, after a good dinner, elderberry coffee smoking in the cups, the pipes giving forth an odoriferous smoke, they could hear the storm howling without. Their comfort would have been complete, if complete comfort could ever exist for those who are far from their fellow-creatures, and without any means of communication with them. They often talked of their country, of the friends whom they had left, of the grandeur of the American Republic, whose influence could not but increase; and Cyrus Harding, who had been much mixed up with the affairs of the Union, greatly interested his auditors by his recitals, his views, and his prognostics.

It chanced one day that Spilett was led to say,

"But now, my dear Cyrus, all this industrial and commercial movement to which you predict a continual advance, does it not run the danger of being sooner or later completely stopped?"

"Stopped! And by what?"

"By the want of coal, which may justly be called the most precious of minerals."

"Yes, the most precious indeed," replied the engineer; "and it would seem that nature wished to prove that it was so by making the diamond, which is simply pure carbon crystallized."

"You don't mean to say, captain," interrupted Pencroft, "that we burn diamonds in our stoves in the shape of coal?"

"No, my friend," replied Harding.

"However," resumed Gideon Spilett, "you do not deny that some day the coal will be entirely consumed?"

"Oh! the veins of coal are still considerable, and the hundred thousand miners who annually extract from them a hundred millions of hundredweights have not nearly exhausted them."

"With the increasing consumption of coal," replied Gideon Spilett, "it can be foreseen that the hundred thousand workmen will soon become two hundred thousand, and that the rate of extraction will be doubled."

"Doubtless; but after the European mines, which will be soon worked more thoroughly with new machines, the American and Australian mines will for a long time yet provide for the consumption in trade."

"For how long a time?" asked the reporter.

"For at least two hundred and fifty or three hundred years."

"That is reassuring for us, but a bad look-out for our great-grandchildren!" observed Pencroft.

"They will discover something else," said Herbert.

"It is to be hoped so," answered Spilett, "for without coal there would be no machinery, and without machinery there would be no railways, no steamers, no manufactories, nothing of that which is indispensable to modern civilization!"

"But what will they find?" asked Pencroft. "Can you guess, captain?"

"Nearly, my friend."

"And what will they burn instead of coal?"

"Water," replied Harding.

"Water!" cried Pencroft, "water as fuel for steamers and engines! water to heat water!"

"Yes, but water decomposed into its primitive elements," replied Cyrus Harding, "and decomposed doubtless, by electricity, which will then have become a powerful and manageable force, for all great discoveries, by some inexplicable laws, appear to agree and become complete at the same time. Yes, my friends, I believe that water will one day be employed as fuel, that hydrogen and oxygen which constitute it, used singly or together, will furnish an inexhaustible source of heat and light, of an intensity of which coal is not capable. Some day the coalrooms of steamers and the tenders of locomotives will, instead of coal, be stored with these two condensed gases, which will burn in the furnaces with enormous calorific power. There is, therefore, nothing to fear. As long as the earth is inhabited it will supply the wants of its inhabitants, and there will be no want of either light or heat as long as the productions of the vegetable, mineral, or animal kingdoms do not fail us. I believe, then, that when the deposits of coal are exhausted we shall heat and warm ourselves with water. Water will be the coal of the future."

"I should like to see that," observed the sailor.

"You were born too soon, Pencroft," returned Neb, who only took part in the discussion by these words.

However, it was not Neb's speech which interrupted the conversation, but Top's barking, which broke out again with that strange intonation which had before perplexed the engineer. At the same time Top began to run around the mouth of the well, which opened at the extremity of the interior passage.

"What can Top be barking in that way for?" asked Pencroft.

"And Jup be growling like that?" added Herbert.

In fact the orang, joining the dog, gave unequivocal signs of agitation, and, singular to say, the two animals appeared more uneasy than angry.

"It is evident," said Gideon Spilett, "that this well is in direct communication with the sea, and that some marine animal comes from time to time to breathe at the bottom."

"That's evident," replied the sailor, "and there can be no other explanation to give. Quiet there, Top!" added Pencroft, turning to the dog, "and you, Jup, be off to your room!"

The ape and the dog were silent. Jup went off to bed, but Top remained in the room, and continued to utter low growls at intervals during the rest of the evening. There was no further talk on the subject, but the incident, however, clouded the brow of the engineer.

During the remainder of the month of July there was alternate rain and frost. The temperature was not so low as during the preceding winter, and its maximum did not exceed eight degrees Fahrenheit. But although this winter was less cold, it was more troubled by storms and squalls; the sea besides often endangered the safety of the Chimneys. At times it almost seemed as if an under-current raised these monstrous billows which thundered against the wall of Granite House.

When the settlers, leaning from their windows, gazed on the huge watery masses breaking beneath their eyes, they could not but admire the magnificent spectacle of the ocean in its impotent fury. The waves rebounded in dazzling foam, the beach entirely disappearing under the raging flood, and the cliff appearing to emerge from the sea itself, the spray rising to a height of more than a hundred feet.

During these storms it was difficult and even dangerous to venture out, owing to the frequently falling trees; however, the colonists never allowed a week to pass without having paid a visit to the corral. Happily, this enclosure, sheltered by the southeastern spur of Mount Franklin, did not greatly suffer from the violence of the hurricanes, which spared its trees, sheds, and palisades; but the poultry-yard on Prospect Heights, being directly exposed to the gusts of wind from the east, suffered considerable damage. The pigeon-house was twice unroofed and the paling blown down. All this required to be remade more solidly than before, for, as may be clearly seen, Lincoln Island was situated in one of the most dangerous parts of the Pacific. It really appeared as if it formed the central point of vast cyclones, which beat it perpetually as the whip does the top, only here it was the top which was motionless and the whip which moved. During the first week of the month of August the weather became more moderate, and the atmosphere recovered the calm which it appeared to have lost forever. With the calm the cold again became intense, and the thermometer fell to eight degrees Fahrenheit, below zero.

On the 3rd of August an excursion which had been talked of for several days was made into the southeastern part of the island, toward Tadorn's Fens. The hunters were tempted by the aquatic game which took up their winter quarters there. Wild duck, snipe, teal, and grebe abounded there, and it was agreed that a day should be devoted to an expedition against these birds.

Not only Gideon Spilett and Herbert, but Pencroft and Neb also took part in this excursion. Cyrus Harding alone, alleging some work as an excuse, did not join them, but remained at Granite House.

The hunters proceeded in the direction of Port Balloon, in order to reach the marsh, after having promised to be back by the evening. Top and Jup accompanied them. As soon as they had passed over the Mercy Bridge, the engineer raised it and returned, intending to put into execution a project for the performance of which he wished to be alone.

Now this project was to minutely explore the interior well, the mouth of which was on a level with the passage of Granite House, and which communicated with the sea, since it formerly supplied a way to the waters of the lake.

Why did Top so often run round this opening? Why did he utter such strange barks when a sort of uneasiness seemed to draw him toward this well? Why did Jup join Top in a sort of common anxiety? Had this well branches besides the communication with the sea? Did it spread toward other parts of the island? This is what Cyrus Harding wished to know. He had resolved, therefore, to attempt the exploration of the well during the absence of his companions, and an opportunity for doing so had now presented itself.

It was easy to descend to the bottom of the well by employing the rope ladder which had not been used since the establishment of the lift. The engineer drew the ladder to the hole, the diameter of which measured nearly six feet, and allowed it to unroll itself after having securely fastened its upper extremity. Then, having lighted a lantern, taken a revolver, and placed a cutlass in his belt, he began the descent.

The sides were everywhere entire; but points of rock jutted out here and there, and by means of these points it would have been quite possible for an active creature to climb to the mouth of the well.

The engineer remarked this; but although he carefully examined these points by the light of his lantern, he could find no impression, no fracture which could give any reason to suppose that they had either recently or at any former time been used as a staircase. Cyrus Harding descended deeper, throwing the light of his lantern on all sides.

He saw nothing suspicious.

When the engineer had reached the last rounds he came upon the water, which was then perfectly calm. Neither at its level nor in any other part of the well, did any passage open, which could lead to the interior of the cliff. The wall which Harding struck with the hilt of his cutlass sounded solid. It was compact granite, through which no living being could force a way. To arrive at the bottom of the well and then climb up to its mouth it was necessary to pass through the channel under the rocky subsoil of the beach, which placed it in communication with the sea, and this was only possible for marine animals. As to the question of knowing where this channel ended, at what point of the shore, and at what depth beneath the water, it could not be answered.

Then Cyrus Harding, having ended his survey, re-ascended, drew up the ladder, covered the mouth of the well, and returned thoughtfully to the dining-room, saying to himself,

"I have seen nothing, and yet there *is* something there!"

XII

In the evening the hunters returned, having enjoyed good sport, and being literally loaded with game; indeed, they had as much as four men could possibly carry. Top wore a necklace of teal and Jup wreaths of snipe around his body.

"Here, master," cried Neb; "here's something to employ our time! Preserved and made into pies we shall have a welcome store! But I must have some one to help me. I count on you, Pencroft."

"No, Neb," replied the sailor; "I have the rigging of the vessel to finish and to look after, and you will have to do without me."

"And you, Mr. Herbert?"

"I must go to the corral to-morrow, Neb," replied the lad.

"It will be you then, Mr. Spilett, who will help me?"

"To oblige you, Neb, I will," replied the reporter; "but I warn you that if you disclose your receipts to me, I shall publish them."

"Whenever you like, Mr. Spilett," replied Neb; "whenever you like."

And so the next day Gideon Spilett became Neb's assistant and was installed in his culinary laboratory. The engineer had previously made known to him the result of the exploration which he had made the day before, and on this point the reporter shared Harding's opinion, that although he had found nothing, a secret still remained to be discovered!

The frost continued for another week, and the settlers did not leave Granite House unless to look after the poultry-yard. The dwelling was filled with appetizing odors, which were emitted from the learned manipulation of Neb and the reporter. But all the results of the chase were not made into preserved provisions; and as the game kept perfectly in the intense cold, wild duck and other fowl were eaten fresh, and declared superior to all other aquatic birds in the known world.

During this week, Pencroft, aided by Herbert, who handled the sailmaker's needle with much skill, worked with such energy that the sails of the vessel were finished. There was no want of cordage. Thanks to the rigging which had been discovered with the case of the balloon, the ropes and cables from the net were all of good quality, and the sailor turned them all to account. To the sails were attached strong bolt ropes, and there still remained enough from which to make the halyards, shrouds, and sheets, etc. The blocks were manufactured by Cyrus Harding under Pencroft's directions by means of the turning lathe. It therefore happened that the rigging was entirely prepared before the vessel was finished. Pencroft also manufactured a flag, that flag so dear to every true American, containing the stars and stripes of their glorious Union. The colors for it were supplied from certain plants used in dyeing, and which were very abundant in the island; only to the thirty-seven stars, representing the thirty-seven States of the Union, which shine on the American flag, the sailor added a thirty-eighth, the star of "the State of Lincoln," for he considered his island as already united to the great republic. "And," said he, "it is so already in heart, if not in deed!"

In the meantime, the flag was hoisted at the central window of Granite House, and the settlers saluted it with three cheers.

The cold season was now almost at an end, and it appeared as if this second winter was to pass without any unusual occurrence, when on the night of the 11th of August, the plateau of Prospect Heights was menaced with complete destruction.

After a busy day the colonists were sleeping soundly, when toward four o'clock in the morning they were suddenly awakened by Top's barking.

The dog was not this time barking near the mouth of the well, but at the threshold of the door, at which he was scratching as if he wished to burst it open. Jup was also uttering piercing cries.

"Hello, Top!" cried Neb, who was the first awake. But the dog continued to bark more furiously than ever.

"What's the matter now?" asked Harding.

And all dressing in haste rushed to the windows, which they opened.

Beneath their eyes was spread a sheet of snow which looked gray in the dim light. The settlers could see nothing, but they heard a singular yelping noise away in the darkness. It was evident that the beach had been invaded by a number of animals which could not be seen.

"What are they?" cried Pencroft.

"Wolves, jaguars, or apes?" replied Neb.

"They have nearly reached the plateau," said the reporter.

"And our poultry-yard," exclaimed Herbert, "and our garden!"

"Where can they have crossed?" asked Pencroft.

"They must have crossed the bridge on the shore," replied the engineer, "which one of us must have forgotten to close."

"True," said Spilett, "I remember having left it open."

"A fine job you have made of it, Mr. Spilett," cried the sailor.

"What is done cannot be undone," replied Cyrus Harding. "We must consult what it will now be best to do."

Such were the questions and answers which were rapidly exchanged between Harding and his companions. It was certain that the bridge had been crossed, that the shore had been invaded by animals, and that whatever they might be they could by ascending the left bank of the Mercy reach Prospect Heights. They must therefore be advanced against quickly and fought with if necessary.

"But what are these beasts?" was asked a second time, as the yelpings were again heard more loudly than before. These yelps made Herbert start, and he remembered having heard them before during his first visit to the sources of the Red Creek.

"They are colpeos—foxes!" he exclaimed.

"Forward!" shouted the sailor.

And all arming themselves with hatchets, carbines, and revolvers, threw themselves into the lift and soon set foot on the shore.

Colpeos are dangerous animals when in great numbers and irritated by hunger, nevertheless the colonists did not hesitate to throw themselves into the midst of the troop, and their first shots vividly lighting up the darkness made their assailants draw back.

The chief thing was to hinder these plunderers from reaching the plateau, for the garden and the poultry-yard would then have been at their mercy, and immense, perhaps irreparable mischief, would inevitably be the result, especially with regard to the corn-field. But as the invasion of the plateau could only be made by the left bank of the Mercy, it was sufficient to oppose the colpeos on the narrow bank between the river and the cliff of granite.

This was plain to all, and, by Cyrus Harding's orders, they reached the spot indicated by him, while the colpeos rushed fiercely through the gloom. Harding, Gideon Spilett, Herbert, Pencroft and Neb posted themselves in impregnable line. Top, his formidable jaws open, preceded the colonists, and he was followed by Jup, armed with knotty cudgel, which he brandished like a club.

The night was extremely dark, it was only by the flashes from the revolvers as each person fired that they could see their assailants, who were at least a hundred in number, and whose eyes were glowing like hot coals.

"They must not pass!" shouted Pencroft.

"They shall not pass!" returned the engineer.

But if they did not pass it was not for want of having attempted it. Those in the rear pushed on the foremost assailants, and it was an incessant struggle with revolvers and hatchets. Several colpeos already lay dead on the ground, but their number did not appear to diminish, and it might have been supposed that reinforcements were continually arriving over the bridge.

The colonists were soon obliged to fight at close quarters, not without receiving some wounds, though happily very slight ones. Herbert had, with a shot from his revolver, rescued Neb, on whose back a colpeo had sprung like a tiger cat. Top fought with actual fury, flying at the throats of the foxes and strangling them instantaneously. Jup wielded his weapon valiantly, and it was in vain that they endeavored to keep him in the rear. Endowed doubtless with sight which enabled him to pierce the obscurity, he was always in the thick of the fight uttering from time to time a sharp hissing sound, which was with him the sign of great rejoicing.

At one moment he advanced so far, that by the light from a revolver he was seen surrounded by five or six large colpeos, with whom he was coping with great coolness.

However, the struggle was ended at last, and victory was on the side of the settlers, but not until they had fought for two long hours! The first signs of the approach of day doubtless determined the retreat of their assailants, who scampered away toward the north, passing over the bridge, which Neb ran immediately to raise. When day had sufficiently lighted up the field of battle, the settlers counted as many as fifty dead bodies scattered about on the shore.

"And Jup!" cried Pencroft; "where is Jup?" Jup had disappeared. His friend Neb called him, and for the first time Jup did not reply to his friend's call.

Everyone set out in search of Jup, trembling lest he should be found among the slain; they cleared the place of the bodies which stained the snow with their blood. Jup was found in the midst of a heap of colpeos whose broken jaws and crushed bodies showed that they had to do with the terrible club of the intrepid animal.

Poor Jup still held in his hand the stump of his broken cudgel, but deprived of his weapon he had been overpowered by numbers, and his chest was covered with severe wounds.

"He is living," cried Neb, who was bending over him.

"And we will save him," replied the sailor. "We will nurse him as if he was one of ourselves."

It appeared as if Jup understood, for he leaned his head on Pencroft's shoulder as if to thank him. The sailor was wounded himself, but his wound was insignificant, as were those of his companions; for thanks to their firearms they had been almost always able to keep their assailants at a distance. It was therefore only the orang whose condition was serious.

Jup, carried by Neb and Pencroft, was placed in the lift, and only a slight moan now and then escaped his lips. He was gently drawn up to Granite House. There he was laid on a mattress taken from one of the beds, and his wounds were bathed with the greatest care. It did not appear that any vital part had been reached, but Jup was very weak from loss of blood, and a high fever soon set in after his wounds had been dressed. He was laid down, strict diet was imposed, "just like a real person," as Neb said, and they made him swallow several cups of a cooling drink, for which the ingredients were supplied from the vegetable medicine chest of Granite House. Jup was at first restless, but his breathing gradually became more regular, and he was left sleeping quietly. From time to time Top, walking on tip-toe, as one might say, came to visit his friend, and seemed to approve of all the care that had been taken of him. One of Jup's hands hung over the side of his bed, and Top licked it with a sympathizing air.

They employed the day in interring the dead, who were dragged to the Forests of the Far West, and there buried deep.

This attack, which might have had such serious consequences, was a lesson to the settlers, who from this time never went to bed until one of their number had made sure that all the bridges were raised, and that no invasion was possible.

However, Jup, after having given them serious anxiety for several days, began to recover. His constitution brought him through, the fever gradually subsided, and Gideon Spilett, who was a bit of a doctor, pronounced him quite out of danger. On the 16th of August, Jup began to eat. Neb made him nice little sweet dishes, which the invalid devoured with great relish, for if he had a pet failing it was that of being somewhat of a gourmand, and Neb had never done anything to cure him of this fault.

"What would you have?" said he to Gideon Spilett, who sometimes expostulated with him for spoiling the ape. "Poor Jup has no other pleasure than that of the palate, and I am only too glad to be able to reward his services in this way!"

Ten days after taking to his bed, on the 21st of August, Master Jup arose. His wounds were healed, and it was evident that he would not be long in regaining his usual strength and agility. Like all convalescents, he was tremendously hungry, and the reporter allowed him to eat as much as he liked, for he trusted to that instinct, which is too often wanting in reasoning beings, to keep the orang from any excess. Neb was delighted to see his pupil's appetite returning.

"Eat away, my Jup," said he, "and don't spare anything; you have shed your blood for us, and it is the least I can do to make you strong again!"

On the 25th of August Neb's voice was heard calling to his companions, "Captain, Mr. Spilett, Mr. Herbert, Pencroft, come! come!"

The colonists, who were together in the dining-room, rose at Neb's call, who was then in Jup's room.

"What's the matter?" asked the reporter.

"Look," replied Neb, with a shout of laughter. And what did they see? Master Jup smoking calmly and seriously, sitting cross-legged like a Turk at the entrance to Granite House!

"My pipe," cried Pencroft. "He has taken my pipe! Hello, my honest Jup, I make you a present of it! Smoke away, old boy, smoke away!"

And Jup gravely puffed out clouds of smoke which seemed to give him great satisfaction. Harding did not appear to be much astonished at this incident, and he cited several examples of tame apes, to whom the use of tobacco had become quite familiar.

But from this day Master Jup had a pipe of his own, the sailor's ex-pipe, which was hung in his room near his store of tobacco. He filled it himself, lighted it with a glowing coal, and appeared to be the happiest of quadrumana. It may readily be understood that this similarity of tastes of Jup and Pencroft served to tighten the bonds of friendship which already existed between the honest ape and the worthy sailor.

"Perhaps he is really a man," said Pencroft sometimes to Neb. "Should you be surprised to hear him beginning to speak to us some day?"

"My word, no," replied Neb. "What astonishes me is that he hasn't spoken to us before, for now he wants nothing but speech!"

"It would amuse me all the same," resumed the sailor, "if some fine day he said to me, 'Suppose we change pipes, Pencroft.' "

"Yes," replied Neb, "what a pity he was born dumb!"

With the month of September the winter ended, and the works were again eagerly commenced. The building of the vessel advanced rapidly, she was already completely decked over, and all the inside parts of the hull were firmly united with ribs bent by means of steam, which answered all the purposes of a mold.

As there was no want of wood, Pencroft proposed to the engineer to give a double lining to the hull, to ensure the strength of the vessel.

Harding, not knowing what the future might have in store for them, approved the sailor's idea of making the craft as strong as possible. The interior and deck of the vessel was entirely finished toward the 15th of September. For calking the seams they made oakum of dry seaweed, which was hammered in between the planks; then these seams were covered with boiling tar, which was obtained in great abundance from the pines in the forest.

The management of the vessel was very simple. She had from the first been ballasted with heavy blocks of granite walled up, in a bed of lime, twelve thousand pounds of which they stowed away.

A deck was placed over this ballast, and the interior was divided into two cabins; two benches extended along them and served also as lockers. The foot of the mast supported the partition which separated the two cabins, which were reached by two hatchways let into the deck.

Pencroft had no trouble in finding a tree suitable for the mast. He chose a straight young fir, with no knots, and which he had only to square at the step, and round off at the top. The ironwork of the mast, the rudder and the hull had been roughly but strongly forged at the Chimneys. Lastly, yards, masts, boom, spars, oars, etc., were all finished by the first week in October, and it was agreed that a trial trip should be taken around the island, so as to ascertain how the vessel would behave at sea, and how far they might depend upon her.

During all this time the necessary works had not been neglected. The corral was enlarged, for the flock of musmons and goats had been increased by a number of young ones, who had to be housed and fed. The colonists had paid visits also to the oyster-bed, the warren, the coal and iron mines, and to the till then unexplored districts of the Far West forests, which abounded in game. Certain indigenous plants were discovered, and those fit for immediate use contributed to vary the vegetable stores of Granite House.

They were a species of ficoide, some similar to those of the cape, with eatable fleshy leaves, others bearing seeds containing a sort of flour.

On the 10th of October the vessel was launched. Pencroft was radiant with joy, the operation was perfectly successful; the boat completely rigged, having been pushed on rollers to the water's edge, was floated by the rising tide, amid the cheers of the colonists, particularly of Pencroft, who showed no modesty on this occasion. Besides his importance was to last beyond the finishing of the vessel, since, after having built her, he was to command her. The grade of captain was bestowed upon him with the approbation of all. To satisfy Captain Pencroft, it was now necessary to give a name to the vessel, and, after many propositions had been discussed, the votes were all in favor of the *Bonadventure.* As soon as the *Bonadventure* had been lifted by the rising tide, it was seen that she lay evenly in the water, and would be easily navigated. However, the trial trip was to be made that very day, by an excursion off the coast. The weather was fine, the breeze fresh, and the sea smooth, especially toward the south coast, for the wind was blowing from the northwest.

"All hands on board," shouted Pencroft; but breakfast was first necessary, and it was thought best to take provisions on board, in the event of their excursion being prolonged until the evening.

Cyrus Harding was equally anxious to try the vessel, the model of which had originated with him, although on the sailor's advice he had altered some parts of it, but he did not share Pencroft's confidence in her, and as the latter had not again spoken of the voyage to Tabor Island, Harding hoped he had given it up. He would have indeed great reluctance in letting two or three of his companions venture so far in so small a boat, which was not of more than fifteen tons' burden.

At half-past ten everybody was on board, even Top and Jup, and Herbert weighed the anchor, which was fast in the sand near the mouth of the Mercy. The sail was hoisted, the Lincolnian flag floated from the masthead, and the *Bonadventure,* steered by Pencroft, stood out to sea.

The wind blowing out of Union Bay she ran before it, and thus showed her owners, much to their satisfaction, that she possessed a remarkably fast pair of heels, according to Pencroft's mode of speaking. After having doubled Flotsam Point and Claw Cape, the captain kept her close hauled, so as to sail along the southern coast of the island, when it was found she sailed admirably within five points of the wind. All hands were enchanted, they had a good vessel, which, in case of need, would be of great service to them, and with fine weather and a fresh breeze the voyage promised to be charming.

Pencroft now stood off the shore, three or four miles across from Port Balloon. The island then appeared in all its extent and under a new aspect, with the varied panorama of its shore from Claw Cape to Reptile End, the forests in which dark firs contrasted with the young foliage of other trees and overlooked the whole, and Mount Franklin whose lofty head was still whitened with snow.

"How beautiful it is!" cried Herbert.

"Yes, our island is beautiful and good," replied Pencroft. "I love it as I loved my poor mother. It received us poor and destitute, and now what is wanting to us five fellows who fell on it from the sky?"

"Nothing," replied Neb; "nothing, captain."

And the two brave men gave three tremendous cheers in honor of their island!

During all this time Gideon Spilett, leaning against the mast, sketched the panorama which was developed before his eyes.

Cyrus Harding gazed on it in silence.

"Well, Captain Harding," asked Pencroft, "what do you think of our vessel?"

"She appears to behave well," replied the engineer.

"Good! And do you think now that she could undertake a voyage of some extent?"

"What voyage, Pencroft?"

"One to Tabor Island, for instance."

"My friend," replied Harding, "I think that in any pressing emergency we need not hesitate to trust ourselves to the *Bonadventure* even for a longer voyage; but you know I should see you set off to Tabor Island with great uneasiness, since nothing obliges you to go there."

"One likes to know one's neighbors," returned the sailor, who was obstinate in his idea. "Tabor Island is our neighbor, and the only one! Politeness requires us to go at least to pay a visit."

"By Jove," said Spilett, "our friend Pencroft has become very particular about the proprieties all at once!"

"I am not particular about anything at all," retorted the sailor, who was rather vexed by the engineer's opposition, but who did not wish to cause him anxiety.

"Consider, Pencroft," resumed Harding, "you cannot go alone to Tabor Island."

"One companion will be enough for me."

"Even so," replied the engineer, "you will risk depriving the colony of Lincoln Island of two settlers out of five."

"Out of six," answered Pencroft; "you forget Jup."

"Out of seven," added Neb; "Top is quite worth another."

"There is no risk at all in it, captain," replied Pencroft.

"That is possible, Pencroft; but I repeat it is to expose ourselves uselessly."

The obstinate sailor did not reply, and let the conversation drop, quite determined to resume it again. But he did not suspect that an incident would come to his aid and change into an act of humanity that which was at first only a doubtful whim.

After standing off the shore the *Bonadventure* again approached it in the direction of Port Balloon. It was important to ascertain the channels between the sandbanks and reefs, that buoys might be laid down since this little creek was to be the harbor.

They were not more than half a mile from the coast, and it was necessary to tack to beat against the wind. The *Bonadventure* was then going at a very moderate rate, as the breeze, partly intercepted by the high land, scarcely swelled her sails, and the sea, smooth as glass, was only rippled now and then by passing gusts.

Herbert had stationed himself in the bows that he might indicate the course to be followed among the channels, when all at once he shouted,

"Luff, Pencroft, luff!"

"What's the matter," replied the sailor; "a rock?"

"No—wait," said Herbert; "I don't quite see. Luff again—right—now."

So saying, Herbert, leaning over the side, plunged his arm into the water, and pulled it out, exclaiming,

"A bottle!"

He held in his hand a corked bottle which he had just seized a few cables' length from the shore.

Cyrus Harding took the bottle. Without uttering a single word he drew the cork, and took from it a damp paper, on which were written these words:

"Castaway . . . Tabor Island: 153° W. long., 37° 11′ S. lat."

XIII

A castaway!" exclaimed Pencroft; "left on this Tabor Island not two hundred miles from us! Ah, Captain Harding, you won't now oppose my going."

"No, Pencroft," replied Cyrus Harding; "and you shall set out as soon as possible."

"To-morrow?"

"To-morrow!"

The engineer still held in his hand the paper which he had taken from the bottle. He contemplated it for some instants, then resumed,

"From this document, my friends, from the way in which it is worded, we may conclude this: first, that the castaway on Tabor Island is a man possessing a considerable knowledge of navigation, since he gives the latitude and longitude of the island exactly as we ourselves found it, and to a second of approximation; secondly, that he is either English or American, as the document is written in the English language."

"That is perfectly logical," answered Spilett; "and the presence of this castaway explains the arrival of the case on the shores of our island. There must have been a wreck, since there is a castaway. As to the latter, whoever he may be, it is lucky for him that Pencroft thought of building this boat and of trying her this very day, for a day later and this bottle might have been broken on the rocks."

"Indeed," said Herbert, "it is a fortunate chance that the *Bonadventure* passed exactly where the bottle was still floating!"

"Does not this appear strange to you?" asked Harding of Pencroft.

"It appears fortunate, that's all," answered the sailor. "Do you see anything extraordinary in it, captain? The bottle must go somewhere, and why not here as well as anywhere else?"

"Perhaps you are right, Pencroft," replied the engineer; "and yet—"

"But," observed Herbert, "there's nothing to prove that this bottle has been floating long in the sea."

"Nothing," replied Gideon Spilett, "and the document appears even to have been recently written. What do you think about it, Cyrus?"

During this conversation Pencroft had not remained inactive. He had put the vessel about, and the *Bonadventure*, all sails set, was running rapidly toward Claw Cape.

Every one was thinking of the castaway on Tabor Island. Should they be in time to save him? This was a great event in the life of the colonists! They themselves were but castaways, but it was to be feared that another might not have been so fortunate, and their duty was to go to his succor.

Claw Cape was doubled, and about four o'clock the *Bonadventure* dropped her anchor at the mouth of the Mercy.

That same evening the arrangements for the new expedition were made. It appeared best that Pencroft and Herbert, who knew how to work the vessel, should undertake the voyage alone. By setting out the next day, the 10th of October, they would arrive on the 13th, for with the present wind it would not take more than forty-eight hours to make this passage of a hundred and fifty miles. One day in the island, three or four to return, they might hope therefore that on the 17th they would again reach Lincoln Island. The weather was fine, the barometer was rising, the wind appeared settled; everything then was in favor of these brave men whom an act of humanity was taking far from their island.

Thus it had been agreed that Cyrus Harding, Neb, and Gideon Spilett should remain at Granite House, but an objection was raised, and Spilett, who had not forgotten his business as reporter to the *New York Herald*, having declared that he would go by swimming rather than lose such an opportunity, was admitted to take a part in the voyage.

The evening was occupied in transporting on board the *Bonadventure*, articles of bedding, utensils, arms, ammunition, a compass, provisions for a week; this being rapidly done, the colonists ascended to Granite House.

The next day, at five o'clock in the morning, the farewells were said, not without some emotion on both sides, and Pencroft setting sail made toward Claw Cape, which had to be doubled in order to proceed to the southwest.

The *Bonadventure* was already a quarter of a mile from the coast when the passengers perceived on the heights of Granite House two men waving their farewells; they were Cyrus Harding and Neb.

"Our friends," exclaimed Spilett, "this is our first separation in fifteen months."

Pencroft, the reporter, and Herbert waved in return, and Granite House soon disappeared behind the high rocks of the cape.

During the first part of the day the *Bonadventure* was still in sight of the southern coast of Lincoln Island, which soon appeared just like a green basket, with Mount Franklin rising from the center. The heights, diminished by distance, did not present an appearance likely to tempt vessels to touch there. Reptile End was passed in about an hour, though at a distance of about ten miles.

At this distance it was no longer possible to distinguish anything of the western coast, which stretched away to the ridges of Mount Franklin, and three hours after the last of Lincoln Island sank below the horizon.

The *Bonadventure* behaved capitally. Bounding over the waves she proceeded rapidly on her course. Pencroft had hoisted the foresail, and steering by the compass followed a rectilinear direction. From time to time Herbert relieved him at the helm, and the lad's hand was so firm that the sailor had not a point to find fault with.

Gideon Spilett chatted sometimes with one, sometimes with the other, if wanted he lent a hand with the ropes, and Captain Pencroft was perfectly satisfied with his crew.

In the evening the crescent moon, which would not be in its first quarter until the 16th, appeared in the twilight and soon set again. The night was dark but starry, and the next day again promised to be fine.

Pencroft prudently lowered the foresail, not wishing to be caught by a sudden gust while carrying too much canvas; it was perhaps an unnecessary precaution on such a calm night, but Pencroft was a prudent sailor and cannot be blamed for it.

The reporter slept part of the night. Pencroft and Herbert took turns for a spell of two hours each at the helm. The sailor trusted Herbert as he would himself, and his confidence was justified by the coolness and judgment of the lad. Pencroft gave him his directions as a commander to his steersman, and Herbert never allowed the *Bonadventure* to swerve even a point. The night passed quickly, as did the day of the 12th of October. A southeasterly direction was strictly maintained. Unless the *Bonadventure* fell in with some unknown current, she would come exactly within sight of Tabor island.

As to the sea over which the vessel was then sailing, it was absolutely deserted. Now and then a great albatross or frigate bird passed within gunshot, and Gideon Spilett wondered if it was to one of them that he had confided his last letter addressed to the *New York Herald*. These birds were the only beings that appeared to frequent this part of the ocean between Tabor and Lincoln islands.

"And yet," observed Herbert, "this is the time that whalers usually proceed toward the southern part of the Pacific. Indeed I do not think there could be a more deserted sea than this."

"It is not quite so deserted as all that," replied Pencroft.

"What do you mean?" asked the reporter.

"We are on it. Do you take our vessel for a wreck and us for porpoises?"

And Pencroft laughed at his joke.

By the evening, according to calculation, it was thought that the *Bonadventure* had accomplished a distance of a hundred and twenty miles since her departure from Lincoln Island, that is to say in thirty-six hours, which would give her a speed of between three and four knots an hour. The breeze was very slight and might soon drop altogether. However, it was hoped that the next morning by break of day, if the calculation had been correct and the course true, they would sight Tabor Island.

Neither Gideon Spilett, Herbert, nor Pencroft slept that night. In the expectation of the next day they could not but feel some emotion. There was so much uncertainty in their enterprise! Were they near Tabor Island? Was the island still inhabited by the castaway to whose succor they had come? Who was this man? Would not his presence disturb the little colony till then so united? Besides, would he be content to exchange his prison for another? All these questions, which would no doubt be answered the next day, kept them in suspense, and at the dawn of day they all fixed their gaze on the western horizon.

"Land!" shouted Pencroft at about six o'clock in the morning.

And it was impossible that Pencroft should be mistaken, it was evident that land was there. Imagine the joy of the little crew of the *Bonadventure*. In a few hours they would land on the beach of the island!

The low coast of Tabor Island, scarcely emerging from the sea, was not more than fifteen miles distant.

The head of the *Bonadventure*, which was a little to the south of the island, was set directly toward it, and as the sun mounted in the east, its rays fell upon one or two headlands.

"This is a much less important isle than Lincoln Island," observed Herbert, "and is probably due like ours to some submarine convulsion."

At eleven o'clock the *Bonadventure* was not more than two miles off, and Pencroft, while looking for a suitable place at which to land, proceeded very cautiously through the unknown waters. The whole of the island could now be surveyed, and on it could be seen groups of gum and other large trees, of the same species as those growing on Lincoln Island. But the astonishing thing was that no smoke arose to show that the island was inhabited, no signal whatever appeared on the shore!

And yet the document was clear enough; there was a castaway, and this castaway should have been on the watch.

In the meanwhile the *Bonadventure* entered the winding channels among the reefs, and Pencroft observed every turn with extreme care. He had put Herbert at the helm, posting himself in the bows, inspecting the water, while he held the halyard in his hand, ready to lower the sail at a moment's notice. Gideon Spilett with his glass eagerly scanned the shore, though without perceiving anything.

However, at about twelve o'clock the keel of the *Bonadventure* grated on the bottom. The anchor was let go, the sails furled, and the crew of the little vessel landed.

And there was no reason to doubt that this was Tabor Island, since according to the most recent charts there was no island in this part of the Pacific between New Zealand and the American coast.

The vessel was securely moored, so that there should be no danger of her being carried away by the receding tide; then Pencroft and his companions, well armed, ascended the shore, so as to gain an elevation of about two hundred and fifty or three hundred feet which rose at a distance of half a mile.

"From the summit of that hill," said Spilett, "we can no doubt obtain a complete view of the island, which will greatly facilitate our search."

"So as to do here," replied Herbert, "that which Captain Harding did the very first thing on Lincoln Island, by climbing Mount Franklin."

"Exactly so," answered the reporter, "and it is the best plan."

While thus talking the explorers had advanced along a clearing which terminated at the foot of the hill. Flocks of rock-pigeons and sea-swallows, similar to those of Lincoln Island, fluttered around them. Under the woods which skirted the glade on the left they could hear the bushes rustling and see the grass waving, which indicated the presence of timid animals, but still nothing to show that the island was inhabited.

Arrived at the foot of the hill, Pencroft, Spilett, and Herbert climbed it in a few minutes, and gazed anxiously around the horizon.

They were on an islet, which did not measure more than six miles in circumference, its shape not much bordered by capes or promontories, bays or creeks, being a lengthened oval. All around, the lonely sea extended to the limits of the horizon. No land nor even a sail was in sight.

This woody islet did not offer the varied aspects of Lincoln Island, arid and wild in one part, but fertile and rich in the other. On the contrary this was a uniform mass of verdure, out of which rose two or three hills of no great height. Obliquely to the oval of the island ran a stream through a wide meadow falling into the sea on the west by a narrow mouth.

"The domain is limited," said Herbert.

"Yes," rejoined Pencroft, "it would have been too small for us."

"And moreover," said the reporter, "it appears to be uninhabited."

"Indeed," answered Herbert, "nothing here betrays the presence of man."

"Let us go down," said Pencroft, "and search."

The sailor and his two companions returned to the shore, to the place where they had left the *Bonadventure.*

They had decided to make the tour of the island on foot, before exploring the interior, so that not a spot should escape their investigations. The beach was easy to follow, and only in some places was their way barred by large rocks, which, however, they easily passed around. The explorers proceeded toward the south, disturbing numerous flocks of sea-birds and herds of seals, which threw themselves into the sea as soon as they saw the strangers at a distance.

"Those beasts yonder," observed the reporter, "do not see men for the first time. They fear them, therefore they must know them."

An hour after their departure they arrived on the southern point of the islet, terminated by a sharp cape, and proceeded toward the north along the western coast, equally formed by sand and rocks, the background bordered with thick woods.

There was not a trace of a habitation in any part, not the print of a human foot on the shore of the island, which after four hours' walking had been gone completely around.

It was to say the least very extraordinary, and they were compelled to believe that Tabor Island was not or was no longer inhabited. Perhaps, after all, the document was already several months or several years old, and it was possible in this case, either that the castaway had been enabled to return to his country, or that he had died of misery.

Pencroft, Spilett, and Herbert, forming more or less probable conjectures, dined rapidly on board the *Bonadventure* so as to be able to continue their excursion until nightfall. This was done at five o'clock in the evening, at which hour they entered the wood.

Numerous animals fled at their approach, being principally, one might say, only goats and pigs, which were obviously European species.

Doubtless some whaler had landed them on the island, where they had rapidly increased. Herbert resolved to catch one or two living, and take them back to Lincoln Island.

It was no longer doubtful that men at some period or other had visited this islet, and this became still more evident when paths appeared trodden through the forest, felled trees, and everywhere traces of the hand of man; but the trees were becoming rotten, and had been felled many years ago; the marks of the axe were velveted with moss, and the grass grew long and thick on the paths, so that it was difficult to find them.

"But," observed Gideon Spilett, "this not only proves that men have landed on the island, but also that they lived on it for some time. Now, who were these men? How many of them remain?"

"The document," said Herbert, "only spoke of one castaway."

"Well, if he is still on the island," replied Pencroft, "it is impossible but that we shall find him."

The exploration was continued. The sailor and his companions naturally followed the route which cut diagonally across the island, and they were thus obliged to follow the stream which flowed toward the sea.

If the animals of European origin, if works due to a human hand, showed incontestably that men had already visited the island, several specimens of the vegetable kingdom did not prove it less. In some places, in the midst of clearings, it was evident that the soil had been planted with culinary plants, at probably the same distant period.

What, then, was Herbert's joy, when he recognized potatoes, chicory, sorrel, carrots, cabbages, and turnips, of which it was sufficient to collect the seed to enrich the soil of Lincoln Island.

"Capital, jolly!" exclaimed Pencroft. "That will suit Neb as well as us. Even if we do not find the castaway, at least our voyage will not have been useless, and God will have rewarded us."

"Doubtless," replied Gideon Spilett, "but to see the state in which we find these plantations, it is to be feared that the island has not been inhabited for some time."

"Indeed," answered Herbert, "an inhabitant, whoever he was, could not have neglected such an important culture!"

"Yes," said Pencroft, "the castaway has gone."

"We must suppose so."

"It must then be admitted that the document has already a distant date?"

"Evidently."

"And that the bottle only arrived at Lincoln Island after having floated in the sea a long time."

"Why not?" returned Pencroft. "But night is coming on," added he, "and I think that it will be best to give up the search for the present."

"Let us go on board, and to-morrow we will begin again," said the reporter.

This was the wisest course, and it was about to be followed when Herbert, pointing to a confused mass among the trees, exclaimed,

"A hut!"

All three immediately ran toward the dwelling. In the twilight it was just possible to see that it was built of planks and covered with a thick tarpaulin.

The half-closed door was pushed open by Pencroft, who entered with a rapid step.

The hut was empty!

XIV

Pencroft, Herbert, and Gideon Spilett remained silent in the midst of the darkness.

Pencroft shouted loudly.

No reply was made.

The sailor then struck a light and set fire to a twig. This lighted for a minute a small room, which appeared perfectly empty. At the back was a rude fireplace, with a few cold cinders, supporting an armful of dry wood.

Pencroft threw the blazing twig on it; the wood crackled and gave forth a bright light.

The sailor and his two companions then perceived a disordered bed, of which the damp and yellow coverlets proved that it had not been used for a long time. In the corner of the fireplace were two kettles, covered with rust, and an overthrown pot. A cupboard, with a few moldy sailor's clothes; on the table a tin plate and a Bible, eaten away by damp; in a corner a few tools, a spade, pickaxe, two fowling-pieces, one of which was broken; on a plank, forming a shelf, stood a barrel of powder, still untouched, a barrel of shot, and several boxes of caps, all thickly covered with dust, accumulated, perhaps, by many long years.

"There is no one here," said the reporter.

"No one," replied Pencroft.

"It is a long time since this room has been inhabited," observed Herbert.

"Yes, a very long time!" answered the reporter.

"Mr. Spilett," then said Pencroft, "instead of returning on board, I think that it would be well to pass the night in this hut."

"You are right, Pencroft," answered Gideon Spilett, "and if its owner returns, well! perhaps he will not be sorry to find the place taken possession of."

"He will not return," said the sailor, shaking his head.

"You think that he has quitted the island?" asked the reporter.

"If he had quitted the island he would have taken away his weapons and his tools," replied Pencroft. "You know the value which castaways set on such articles as these, the last remains of a wreck. No! no!" repeated the sailor, in a tone of conviction; "no, he has not left the island! If he had escaped in a boat made by himself, he would still less have left these indispensable and necessary articles. No! he is on the island!"

"Living?" asked Herbert.

"Living or dead. But if he is dead, I suppose he has not buried himself, and so we shall at least find his remains!"

It was then agreed that the night should be passed in the deserted dwelling, and a store of wood found in a corner was sufficient to warm it. The door closed, Pencroft, Herbert and Spilett remained there, seated on a bench, talking little but wondering much. They were in a frame of mind to imagine anything or expect anything. They listened eagerly for sounds outside. The door might have opened suddenly, and a man presented himself to them without their being in the least surprised, notwithstanding all that the hut revealed of abandonment, and they had their hands ready to press the hands of this man, this castaway, this unknown friend, for whom friends were waiting.

But no voice was heard, the door did not open. The hours thus passed away.

How long the night appeared to the sailor and his companions! Herbert alone slept for two hours, for at his age sleep is a necessity. They were all three anxious to continue their exploration of the day before, and to search the most secret recesses of the islet! The inferences deduced by Pencroft were perfectly reasonable, and it was nearly certain that, as the hut was deserted, and the tools, utensils, and weapons were still there, the owner had succumbed. It was agreed, therefore, that they should search for his remains, and give them at least Christian burial.

Day dawned; Pencroft and his companions immediately proceeded to survey the dwelling. It had certainly been built in a favorable situation, at the back of a little hill, sheltered by five or six magnificent gum-trees. Before its front and through the trees the axe had prepared a wide clearing, which allowed the view to extend to the sea. Beyond a lawn, surrounded by a wooden fence falling to pieces, was the shore, on the left of which was the mouth of the stream.

The hut had been built of planks, and it was easy to see that these planks had been obtained from the hull or deck of a ship. It was probable that a disabled vessel had been cast on the coast of the island, that one at least of the crew had been saved, and that by means of the wreck this man, having tools at his disposal, had built the dwelling.

And this became still more evident when Gideon Spilett, after having walked around the hut, saw on a plank, probably one of those which had formed the armor of the wrecked vessel, these letters already half effaced:

BR—TAN—A

"Britannia," exclaimed Pencroft, whom the reporter had called; "it is a common name for ships, and I could not say if she was English or American!"

"It matters very little, Pencroft!"

"Very little indeed," answered the sailor, "and we will save the survivor of her crew if he is still living, to whatever country he may belong. But before beginning our search again let us go on board the *Bonadventure*."

A sort of uneasiness had seized Pencroft upon the subject of his vessel. Should the island be inhabited after all, and should some one have taken possession of her? But he shrugged his shoulders at such an unreasonable supposition. At any rate the sailor was not sorry to go to breakfast on board. The road already trodden was not long, scarcely a mile. They set out on their walk, gazing into the wood and thickets through which goats and pigs fled in hundreds.

Twenty minutes after leaving the hut Pencroft and his companions reached the western coast of the island, and saw the *Bonadventure* held fast by her anchor, which was buried deep in the sand.

Pencroft could not restrain a sigh of satisfaction. After all this vessel was his child, and it is the right of fathers to be often uneasy when there is no occasion for it.

They returned on board, breakfasted, so that it should not be necessary to dine until very late; then the repast being ended, the exploration was continued and conducted with the most minute care. Indeed, it was very probable that the only inhabitant of the island had perished. It was therefore more for the traces of a dead than of a living man that Pencroft and his companions searched. But their searches were vain, and during the half of that day they sought to no purpose among the thickets of trees which covered the islet. There was then scarcely any doubt that, if the castaway was dead, no trace of his body now remained, but that some wild beast had probably devoured it to the last bone.

"We will set off to-morrow at daybreak," said Pencroft to his two companions, as about two o'clock they were resting for a few minutes under the shade of a clump of firs.

"I should think that we might without scruple take the utensils which belonged to the castaway," added Herbert.

"I think so, too," returned Gideon Spilett, "and these arms and tools will make up the stores of Granite House. The supply of powder and shot is also most important."

"Yes," replied Pencroft, "but we must not forget to capture a couple or two of those pigs, of which Lincoln Island is destitute—"

"Nor to gather those seeds," added Herbert, "which will give us all the vegetables of the Old and the New Worlds."

"Then perhaps it would be best," said the reporter, "to remain a day longer on Tabor Island, so as to collect all that may be useful to us."

"No, Mr. Spilett," answered Pencroft, "I will ask you to set off to-morrow at daybreak. The wind seems to me to be likely to shift to the west, and after having had a fair wind for coming we shall have a fair wind for going back."

"Then do not let us lose time," said Herbert, rising.

"We won't waste time," returned Pencroft. "You, Herbert, go and gather the seeds, which you know better than we do. While you do that, Mr. Spilett and I will go and have a pig hunt, and even without Top I hope we shall manage to catch a few!"

Herbert accordingly took the path which led toward the cultivated part of the islet, while the sailor and the reporter entered the forest.

Many specimens of the porcine race fled before them, and these animals, which were singularly active, did not appear to be in a humor to allow themselves to be approached.

However, after an hour's chase, the hunters had just managed to get hold of a couple lying in a thicket, when cries were heard resounding from the north part of the island. With the cries were mingled terrible yells, in which there was nothing human.

Pencroft and Gideon Spilett were at once on their feet, and the pigs by this movement began to run away, at the moment when the sailor was getting ready the rope to bind them.

"That's Herbert's voice," said the reporter.

"Run!" exclaimed Pencroft.

And the sailor and Spilett immediately ran at full speed toward the spot from whence the cries proceeded.

They did well to hasten, for at a turn of the path near a clearing they saw the lad thrown on the ground and in the grasp of a savage being, apparently a gigantic ape, who was about to do him some great harm.

To rush on this monster, throw him on the ground in his turn, snatch Herbert from him, then bind him securely, was the work of a minute for Pencroft and Gideon Spilett. The sailor was of Herculean strength, the reporter also very powerful, and in spite of the monster's resistance he was firmly tied so that he could not even move.

"You are not hurt, Herbert?" asked Spilett.

"No, no!"

"Oh, if this ape had wounded him!" exclaimed Pencroft.

"But he is not an ape," answered Herbert.

At these words Pencroft and Gideon Spilett looked at the singular being who lay on the ground. Indeed it was not an ape; it was a human being, a man. But what a man! A savage in all the horrible acceptation of the word, and so much the more frightful that he seemed fallen to the lowest degree of brutishness!

Shaggy hair, untrimmed beard descending to the chest, the body almost naked except a rag round the waist, wild eyes, enormous hands with immensely long nails, skin the color of mahogany, feet as hard as if made of horn—such was the miserable creature who yet had a claim to be called a man. But it might justly be asked if there were yet a soul in this body, or if the brute instinct alone survived in it!

"Are you quite sure that this is a man, or that he has ever been one?" said Pencroft to the reporter.

"Alas! there is no doubt about it," replied Spilett.

"Then this must be the castaway?" asked Herbert.

"Yes," replied Gideon Spilett, "but the unfortunate man has no longer anything human about him!"

The reporter spoke the truth. It was evident that if the castaway had ever been a civilized being, solitude had made him a savage, or worse, perhaps a regular man of the woods. Hoarse sounds issued from his throat between his teeth, which were sharp as the teeth of a wild beast made to tear raw flesh.

Memory must have deserted him long before, and for a long time also he had forgotten how to use his gun and tools, and he no longer knew how to make a fire! It could be seen that he was active and powerful, but the physical qualities had been developed in him to the injury of the moral qualities. Gideon Spilett spoke to him. He did not appear to understand or even to hear. And yet on looking into his eyes, the reporter thought he could see that all reason was not extinguished in him. However, the prisoner did not struggle, nor even attempt to break his bonds. Was he overwhelmed by the presence of men whose fellow he had once been? Had he found in some corner of his brain a fleeting remembrance which recalled him to humanity? If free, would he attempt to fly, or would he remain? They could not tell, but they did not make the experiment; and after gazing attentively at the miserable creature,

"Whoever he may be," remarked Gideon Spilett, "whoever he may have been, and whatever he may become, it is our duty to take him with us to Lincoln Island."

"Yes, yes!" replied Herbert, "and perhaps with care we may arouse in him some gleam of intelligence."

"The soul does not die," said the reporter, "and it would be a great satisfaction to rescue one of God's creatures from brutishness."

Pencroft shook his head doubtfully.

"We must try at any rate," returned the reporter; "humanity commands us."

It was indeed their duty as Christians and civilized beings. All three felt this, and they well knew that Cyrus Harding would approve of their acting thus.

"Shall we leave him bound?" asked the sailor.

"Perhaps he would walk if his feet were unfastened," said Herbert.

"Let us try," replied Pencroft.

The cords which shackled the prisoner's feet were cut off, but his arms remained securely fastened. He got up by himself and did not manifest any desire to run away. His hard eyes darted a piercing glance at the three men, who walked near him, but nothing denoted that he recollected being their fellow, or at least having been so. A continual hissing sound issued from his lips, his aspect was wild, but he did not attempt to resist.

By the reporter's advice the unfortunate man was taken to the hut. Perhaps the sight of the things that belonged to him would make some impression on him! Perhaps a spark would be sufficient to revive his obscured intellect, to rekindle his dulled soul. The dwelling was not far off. In a few minutes they arrived there, but the prisoner remembered nothing, and it appeared that he had lost consciousness of everything.

What could they think of the degree of brutishness into which this miserable being had fallen, unless that his imprisonment on the islet dated from a very distant period and after having arrived there a rational being, solitude had reduced him to this condition.

The reporter then thought that perhaps the sight of fire would have some effect on him, and in a moment one of those beautiful flames, that attract even animals, blazed up on the hearth. The sight of the flame seemed at first to fix the attention of the unhappy object, but soon he turned away and the look of intelligence faded. Evidently there was nothing to be done, for the time at least, but to take him on board the *Bonadventure.* This was done, and he remained there in Pencroft's charge.

Herbert and Spilett returned to finish their work; and some hours after, they came back to the shore, carrying the utensils and guns, a store of vegetables, of seeds, some game, and two couple of pigs.

All was embarked, and the *Bonadventure* was ready to weigh anchor and sail with the morning tide.

The prisoner had been placed in the fore-cabin, where he remained quiet, silent, apparently deaf and dumb.

Pencroft offered him something to eat, but he pushed away the cooked meat that was presented to him and which doubtless did not suit him. But on the sailor showing him one of the ducks which Herbert had killed, he pounced on it like a wild beast, and devoured it greedily.

"You think that he will recover his senses?" asked Pencroft. "It is not impossible that our care will have an effect upon him, for it is solitude that has made him what he is, and from this time forward he will be no longer alone."

"The poor man must no doubt have been in this state for a long time," said Herbert.

"Perhaps," answered Gideon Spilett.

"About what age is he?" asked the lad.

"It is difficult to say," replied the reporter, "for it is impossible to see his features under the thick beard which covers his face, but he is no longer young, and I suppose he might be about fifty."

"Have you noticed, Mr. Spilett, how deeply sunk his eyes are?" asked Herbert.

"Yes, Herbert, but I must add that they are more human than one could expect from his appearance."

"However, we shall see," replied Pencroft, "and I am anxious to know what opinion Captain Harding will have of our savage. We went to look for a human creature, and we are bringing back a monster! After all, we did what we could."

The night passed, and whether the prisoner slept or not could not be known, but at any rate, although he had been unbound, he did not move. He was like a wild animal, which appears stunned at first by its capture, and becomes wild again afterward.

At daybreak the next morning, the 15th of October, the change of weather predicted by Pencroft occurred. The wind having shifted to the northwest favored the return of the *Bonadventure,* but at the same time it freshened, which might render navigation more difficult.

At five o'clock in the morning the anchor was weighed. Pencroft took a reef in the mainsail, and steered toward the northeast, so as to sail straight for Lincoln Island.

The first day of the voyage was not marked by any incident. The prisoner remained quiet in the fore-cabin, and as he had been a sailor it appeared that the motion of the vessel might produce on him a salutary reaction. Did some recollection of his former calling return to him? However that might be, he remained tranquil, astonished rather than depressed.

The next day the wind increased, blowing more from the north, consequently in a less favorable direction for the *Bonadventure*. Pencroft was soon obliged to sail close-hauled, and without saying anything about it he began to be uneasy at the state of the sea, which frequently broke over the bows. Certainly, if the wind did not moderate, it would take a longer time to reach Lincoln Island than it had taken to make Tabor Island.

Indeed, on the morning of the 17th, the *Bonadventure* had been forty-eight hours at sea, and nothing showed that she was near the island. It was impossible, besides, to estimate the distance traversed, or to trust to the reckoning for the direction, as the speed had been very irregular.

Twenty-four hours after there was yet no land in sight. The wind was right ahead and the sea very heavy. The sails were close-reefed, and they tacked frequently. On the 18th, a wave swept completely over the *Bonadventure*; and if the crew had not taken the precaution of lashing themselves to the deck, they would have been carried away.

On this occasion Pencroft and his companions, who were occupied with loosing themselves, received unexpected aid from the prisoner, who emerged from the hatchway as if his sailor's instinct had suddenly returned, broke a piece out of the bulwarks with a spar so as to let the water which filled the deck escape. Then the vessel being clear, he descended to his cabin without having uttered a word. Pencroft, Gideon Spilett, and Herbert, greatly astonished, let him proceed.

Their situation was truly serious, and the sailor had reason to fear that he was lost on the wide sea without any possibility of recovering his course.

The night was dark and cold. However, about eleven o'clock, the wind fell, the sea went down, and the speed of the vessel, as she labored less, greatly increased.

Neither Pencroft, Spilett, nor Herbert thought of taking an hour's sleep. They kept a sharp look-out, for either Lincoln Island could not be far distant and would be sighted at daybreak, or the *Bonadventure*, carried away by currents, had drifted so much that it would be impossible to rectify her course. Pencroft, uneasy to the last degree, yet did not despair, for he had a gallant heart, and grasping the tiller he anxiously endeavored to pierce the darkness which surrounded them.

About two o'clock in the morning he started forward,

"A light! a light!" he shouted.

Indeed, a bright light appeared twenty miles to the northeast. Lincoln Island was there, and this fire, evidently lighted by Cyrus Harding, showed them the course to be followed. Pencroft, who was bearing too much to the north, altered his course and steered toward the fire, which burned brightly above the horizon like a star of the first magnitude.

XV

The next day, the 20th of October, at seven o'clock in the morning, after a voyage of four days, the *Bonadventure* gently glided up to the beach at the mouth of the Mercy.

Cyrus Harding and Neb, who had become very uneasy at the bad weather and the prolonged absence of their companions, had climbed at daybreak to the plateau of Prospect Heights, and they had at last caught sight of the vessel which had been so long in returning.

"God be praised! there they are!" exclaimed Cyrus Harding.

As to Neb in his joy, he began to dance, to twirl around, clapping his hands and shouting, "Oh! my master!" A more touching pantomime than the finest discourse.

The engineer's first idea, on counting the people on the deck of the *Bonadventure,* was that Pencroft had not found the castaway of Tabor Island, or at any rate that the unfortunate man had refused to leave his island and change one prison for another.

Indeed Pencroft, Gideon Spilett, and Herbert were alone on the deck of the *Bonadventure.*

The moment the vessel touched, the engineer and Neb were waiting on the beach, and before the passengers had time to leap on to the sand, Harding said: "We have been very uneasy at your delay, my friends! Did you meet with any accident?"

"No," replied Gideon Spilett; "on the contrary, everything went wonderfully well. We will tell you all about it."

"However," returned the engineer, "your search has been unsuccessful, since you are only three, just as you went!"

"Excuse me, captain," replied the sailor, "we are four."

"You have found the castaway?"

"Yes."

"And you have brought him?"

"Yes."

"Living?"

"Yes."

"Where is he? Who is he?"

"He is," replied the reporter, "or rather he was a man! There, Cyrus, that is all we can tell you!"

The engineer was then informed of all that had passed during the voyage, and under what conditions the search had been conducted; how the only dwelling in the island had long been abandoned; how at last a castaway had been captured, who appeared no longer to belong to the human species.

"And that's just the point," added Pencroft; "I don't know if we have done right to bring him here."

"Certainly you have, Pencroft," replied the engineer quickly.

"But the wretched creature has no sense!"

"That is possible at present," replied Cyrus Harding, "but only a few months ago the wretched creature was a man like you and me. And who knows what will become of the survivor of us after a long solitude on this island? It is a great misfortune to be alone, my friends; and it must be believed that solitude can quickly destroy reason, since you have found this poor creature in such a state!"

"But, captain," asked Herbert, "what leads you to think that the brutishness of the unfortunate man began only a few months back?"

"Because the document we found had been recently written," answered the engineer, "and the castaway alone can have written it."

"Always supposing," observed Gideon Spilett, "that it had not been written by a companion of this man, since dead."

"That is impossible, my dear Spilett."

"Why so?" asked the reporter.

"Because the document would then have spoken of two castaways," replied Harding, "and it mentioned only one."

Herbert then in a few words related the incidents of the voyage, and dwelt on the curious fact of the sort of passing gleam in the prisoner's mind, when for an instant in the height of the storm he had become a sailor.

"Well, Herbert," replied the engineer, "you are right to attach great importance to this fact. The unfortunate man cannot be incurable, and despair has made him what he is; but here he will find his fellow-men, and since there is still a soul in him, this soul we shall save!"

The castaway of Tabor Island, to the great pity of the engineer and the great astonishment of Neb, was then brought from the cabin which he occupied in the fore part of the *Bonadventure*; when once on land he manifested a wish to run away.

But Cyrus Harding approaching, placed his hand on his shoulder with a gesture full of authority, and looked at him with infinite tenderness. Immediately the unhappy man, submitting to a superior will, gradually became calm, his eyes fell, his head bent, and he made no more resistance.

"Poor fellow!" murmured the engineer.

Cyrus Harding had attentively observed him. To judge by his appearance this miserable being had no longer anything human about him, and yet Harding, as had the reporter already, observed in his look an indefinable trace of intelligence.

It was decided that the castaway, or rather the stranger as he was thenceforth termed by his companions, should live in one of the rooms of Granite House, from which, however, he could not escape. He was led there without difficulty, and with careful attention, it might, perhaps, be hoped that some day he would be a companion to the settlers in Lincoln Island.

Cyrus Harding, during breakfast, which Neb had hastened to prepare, as the reporter, Herbert, and Pencroft were dying of hunger, heard in detail all the incidents which had marked the voyage of exploration to the islet. He agreed with his friends on this point, that the stranger must be either English or American, the name *Britannia* leading them to suppose this, and, besides, through the bushy beard, and under the shaggy, matted hair, the engineer thought he could recognize the characteristic features of the Anglo-Saxon.

"But, by the bye," said Gideon Spilett, addressing Herbert, "you never told us how you met this savage, and we know nothing, except that you would have been strangled, if we had not happened to come up in time to help you!"

"Upon my word," answered Herbert, "it is rather difficult to say how it happened. I was, I think, occupied in collecting my plants, when I heard a noise like an avalanche falling from a very tall tree. I scarcely had time to look around. This unfortunate man, who was without doubt concealed in a tree, rushed upon me in less time than I take to tell you about it, and unless Mr. Spilett and Pencroft—"

"My boy!" said Cyrus Harding, "you ran a great danger, but, perhaps, without that, the poor creature would have still hidden himself from your search, and we should not have had a new companion."

"You hope, then, Cyrus, to succeed in reforming the man?" asked the reporter.

"Yes," replied the engineer.

Breakfast over, Harding and his companions left Granite House and returned to the beach. They there occupied themselves in unloading the *Bonadventure,* and the engineer, having examined the arms and tools, saw nothing which could help them to establish the identity of the stranger.

The capture of pigs, made on the islet, was looked upon as being very profitable to Lincoln Island, and the animals were led to the sty, where they soon became at home.

The two barrels, containing the powder and shot, as well as the box of caps, were very welcome. It was agreed to establish a small powder-magazine, either outside Granite House or in the Upper Cavern, where there would be no fear of explosion. However, the use of pyroxyle was to be continued, for this substance giving excellent results, there was no reason for substituting ordinary powder.

When the unloading of the vessel was finished,

"Captain," said Pencroft, "I think it would be prudent to put our *Bonadventure* in a safe place."

"Is she not safe at the mouth of the Mercy?" asked Cyrus Harding.

"No, captain," replied the sailor. "Half of the time she is stranded on the sand, and that works her. She is a famous craft, you see, and she behaved admirably during the squall which struck us on our return."

"Could she not float in the river?"

"No doubt, captain, she could; but there is no shelter there, and in the east winds, I think that the *Bonadventure* would suffer much from the surf."

"Well, where would you put her, Pencroft?"

"In Port Balloon," replied the sailor. "That little creek, shut in by rocks, seems to me to be just the harbor we want."

"Is it not rather far?"

"Pooh! it is not more than three miles from Granite House, and we have a fine straight road to take us there!"

"Do it then, Pencroft, and take your *Bonadventure* there," replied the engineer, "and yet I would rather have her under our more immediate protection. When we have time, we must make a little harbor for her."

"Famous!" exclaimed Pencroft. "A harbor with a lighthouse, a pier, and dock! Ah! really with you, captain, everything becomes easy."

"Yes, my brave Pencroft," answered the engineer, "but on condition, however, that you help me, for you do as much as three men in all our work."

Herbert and the sailor then re-embarked on board the *Bonadventure,* the anchor was weighed, the sail hoisted, and the wind drove her rapidly toward Claw Cape. Two hours after, she was reposing on the tranquil waters of Port Balloon.

During the first days passed by the stranger in Granite House, had he already given them reason to think that his savage nature was becoming tamed? Did a brighter light burn in the depths of that obscured mind? In short, was the soul returning to the body?

Yes, to a certainty, and to such a degree, that Cyrus Harding and the reporter wondered if the reason of the unfortunate man had ever been totally extinguished. At first, accustomed to the open air, to the unrestrained liberty which he had enjoyed on Tabor Island, the stranger manifested a sullen fury, and it was feared that he might throw himself onto the beach, out of one of the windows of Granite House. But gradually he became calmer, and more freedom was allowed to his movements.

They had reason to hope, and to hope much. Already, forgetting his carnivorous instincts, the stranger accepted a less bestial nourishment than that on which he fed on the islet, and cooked meat did not produce in him the same sentiment of repulsion which he had showed on board the *Bonadventure.* Cyrus Harding had profited by a moment when he was sleeping, to cut his hair and matted beard, which formed a sort of mane and gave him such a savage aspect. He had also been clothed more suitably, after having got rid of the rag which covered him. The result was that, thanks to these attentions, the stranger resumed a more human appearance, and it even seemed as if his eyes had become milder. Certainly, when formerly lighted up by intelligence, this man's face must have had a sort of beauty.

Every day, Harding imposed on himself the task of passing some hours in his company. He came and worked near him, and occupied himself in different things, so as to fix his attention. A spark, indeed, would be sufficient to reillumine that soul, a recollection crossing that brain to recall reason. That had been seen, during the storm, on board the *Bonadventure!* The engineer did not neglect either to speak aloud, so as to penetrate at the same time by the organs of hearing and sight the depths of that torpid intelligence. Sometimes one of his companions, sometimes another, sometimes all joined him. They spoke most often of things belonging to the navy, which must interest a sailor.

At times, the stranger gave some slight attention to what was said, and the settlers were soon convinced that he partly understood them. Sometimes the expression of his countenance was deeply sorrowful, a proof that he suffered mentally, for his face could not be mistaken; but he did not speak, although at different times, however, they almost thought that words were about to issue from his lips. At all events, the poor creature was quite quiet and sad!

But was not his calm only apparent? Was not his sadness only the result of his seclusion? Nothing could yet be ascertained. Seeing only certain objects and in a limited space, always in contact with the colonists, to whom he would soon become accustomed, having no desires to satisfy, better fed, better clothed, it was natural that his physical nature should gradually improve; but was he penetrated with the sense of a new life? or rather, to employ a word which would be exactly applicable to him, was he not becoming tamed, like an animal in company with his master? This was an important question, which Cyrus Harding was anxious to answer, and yet he did not wish to treat his invalid roughly! would he ever be a convalescent?

How the engineer observed him every moment! How he was on the watch for his soul, if one may use the expression! How he was ready to grasp it! The settlers followed with real sympathy all the phases of the cure undertaken by Harding. They aided him also in this work of humanity, and all, except perhaps the incredulous Pencroft, soon shared both his hope and his faith.

The calm of the stranger was deep, as has been said, and he even showed a sort of attachment for the engineer, whose influence he evidently felt. Cyrus Harding resolved then to try him, by transporting him to another scene, from that ocean which formerly his eyes had been accustomed to contemplate, to the border of the forest, which might perhaps recall those where so many years of his life had been passed!

"But," said Gideon Spilett, "can we hope that he will not escape, if once set at liberty?"

"The experiment must be tried," replied the engineer.

"Well!" said Pencroft. "When that fellow is outside, and feels the fresh air, he will be off as fast as his legs can carry him!"

"I do not think so," returned Harding.

"Let us try," said Spilett.

"We will try," replied the engineer.

This was on the 30th of October, and consequently the castaway of Tabor Island had been a prisoner in Granite House for nine days. It was warm, and a bright sun darted its rays on the island. Cyrus Harding and Pencroft went to the room occupied by the stranger, who was found lying near the window and gazing at the sky.

"Come, my friend," said the engineer to him.

The stranger rose immediately. His eyes were fixed on Cyrus Harding, and he followed him, while the sailor marched behind them, little confident as to the result of the experiment.

Arrived at the door, Harding and Pencroft made him take his place in the lift, while Neb, Herbert, and Gideon Spilett waited for them before Granite House. The lift descended, and in a few moments all were united on the beach.

The settlers went a short distance from the stranger, so as to leave him at liberty.

He then made a few steps toward the sea, and his look brightened with extreme animation, but he did not make the slightest attempt to escape. He was gazing at the little waves which, broken by the islet, rippled on the sand.

"This is only the sea," observed Gideon Spilett, "and possibly it does not inspire him with any wish to escape!"

"Yes," replied Harding, "we must take him to the plateau, on the border of the forest. There the experiment will be more conclusive."

"Besides, he could not run away," said Neb, "since the bridge is raised."

"Oh!" said Pencroft, "that isn't a man to be troubled by a stream like Creek Glycerine! He could cross it directly, at a single bound!"

"We shall soon see," Harding contented himself with replying, his eyes not quitting those of his patient.

The latter was then led toward the mouth of the Mercy, and all climbing the left bank of the river, reached Prospect Heights.

Arrived at the spot on which grew the first beautiful trees of the forest, their foliage slightly agitated by the breeze, the stranger appeared greedily to drink in the penetrating odor which filled the atmosphere, and a long sigh escaped from his chest.

The settlers kept behind him, ready to seize him if he made any movement to escape!

And, indeed, the poor creature was on the point of springing into the creek which separated him from the forest, and his legs were bent for an instant as if for a spring, but almost immediately he stepped back, half sank down, and a large tear fell from his eyes.

"Ah!" exclaimed Cyrus Harding, "you have become a man again, for you can weep!"

XVI

Yes! the unfortunate man had wept! Some recollection doubtless had flashed across his brain, and to use Cyrus Harding's expression, by those tears he was once more a man.

The colonists left him for some time on the plateau, and withdrew themselves to a short distance, so that he might feel himself free; but he did not think of profiting by this liberty, and Harding soon brought him back to Granite House. Two days after this occurrence, the stranger appeared to wish gradually to mingle with their common life. He evidently heard and understood, but no less evidently was he strangely determined not to speak to the colonists; for one evening, Pencroft, listening at the door of his room, heard these words escape from his lips:

"No! here! I! never!"

The sailor reported these words to his companions.

"There is some painful mystery there!" said Harding.

The stranger had begun to use the laboring tools, and he worked in the garden. When he stopped in his work, as was often the case, he remained retired within himself, but on the engineer's recommendation, they respected the reserve which he apparently wished to keep. If one of the settlers approached him, he drew back, and his chest heaved with sobs, as if overburdened!

Was it remorse that overwhelmed him thus? They were compelled to believe so, and Gideon Spilett could not help one day making this observation,

"If he does not speak it is because he has, I fear, things too serious to be told!"

They must be patient and wait.

A few days later, on the 3rd of November, the stranger, working on the plateau, had stopped, letting his spade drop to the ground, and Harding, who was observing him from a little distance, saw that tears were again flowing from his eyes. A sort of irresistible pity led him toward the unfortunate man, and he touched his arm lightly.

"My friend!" said he.

The stranger tried to avoid his look, and Cyrus Harding having endeavored to take his hand, he drew back quickly.

"My friend," said Harding in a firmer voice, "look at me, I wish it!"

The stranger looked at the engineer, and seemed to be under his power, as a subject under the influence of a mesmerist. He wished to run away. But then his countenance suddenly underwent a transformation. His eyes flashed. Words struggled to escape from his lips. He could no longer contain himself! . . . At last he folded his arms; then, in a hollow voice,

"Who are you?" he asked Cyrus Harding.

"Castaways, like you," replied the engineer, whose emotion was deep. "We have brought you here, among your fellow-men."

"My fellow-men! . . . I have none!"

"You are in the midst of friends."

"Friends!—for me! friends!" exclaimed the stranger, hiding his face in his hands. "No—never—leave me! leave me!"

Then he rushed to the side of the plateau which overlooked the sea, and remained there a long time motionless.

Harding rejoined his companions and related to them what had just happened.

"Yes! there is some mystery in that man's life," said Gideon Spilett, "and it appears as if he had only re-entered society by the path of remorse."

"I don't know what sort of a man we have brought here," said the sailor. "He has secrets—"

"Which we will respect," interrupted Cyrus Harding quickly. "If he has committed any crime, he has most fearfully expiated it, and in our eyes he is absolved."

For two hours the stranger remained alone on the shore, evidently under the influence of recollections which recalled all his past life—a melancholy life doubtless—and the colonists, without losing sight of him, did not attempt to disturb his solitude. However, after two hours, appearing to have formed a resolution, he came to find Cyrus Harding. His eyes were red with the tears he had shed, but he wept no longer. His countenance expressed deep humility. He appeared anxious, timorous, ashamed, and his eyes were constantly fixed on the ground.

"Sir," said he to Harding, "your companions and you, are you English?"

"No," answered the engineer, "we are Americans."

"Ah!" said the stranger, and he murmured, "I prefer that!"

"And you, my friend?" asked the engineer.

"English," replied he hastily.

And as if these few words had been difficult to say, he retreated to the beach, where he walked up and down between the cascade and the mouth of the Mercy, in a state of extreme agitation.

Then, passing one moment close to Herbert, he stopped and in a stifled voice,

"What month?" he asked.

"December," replied Herbert.

"What year?"

"1866."

"Twelve years! twelve years!" he exclaimed.

Then he left him abruptly.

Herbert reported to the colonists the questions and answers which had been made.

"This unfortunate man," observed Gideon Spilett, "was no longer acquainted with either months or years!"

"Yes!" added Herbert, "and he had been twelve years already on the islet when we found him there!"

"Twelve years!" rejoined Harding. "Ah! twelve years of solitude, after a wicked life, perhaps, may well impair a man's reason!"

"I am induced to think," said Pencroft, "that this man was not wrecked on Tabor Island, but that in consequence of some crime he was left there."

"You must be right, Pencroft," replied the reporter, "and if it is so it is not impossible that those who left him on the island may return to fetch him some day!"

"And they will no longer find him," said Herbert.

"But then," added Pencroft, "they must return, and—"

"My friends," said Cyrus Harding, "do not let us discuss this question until we know more about it. I believe that the unhappy man has suffered, that he has severely expiated his faults, whatever they may have been, and that the wish to unburden himself stifles him. Do not let us press him to tell us his history! He will tell it to us doubtless, and when we know it, we shall see what course it will be best to follow. He alone besides can tell us, if he has more than a hope, a certainty, of returning some day to his country, but I doubt it!"

"And why?" asked the reporter.

"Because that, in the event of his being sure of being delivered at a certain time, he would have waited the hour of his deliverance and would not have thrown this document into the sea. No, it is more probable that he was condemned to die on that islet, and that he never expected to see his fellow-creatures again!"

"But," observed the sailor, "there is one thing which I cannot explain."

"What is it?"

"If this man had been left for twelve years on Tabor Island, one may well suppose that he had been several years already in the wild state in which we found him!"

"That is probable," replied Cyrus Harding.

"It must then be many years since he wrote that document!"

"No doubt, and yet the document appears to have been recently written!"

"Besides, how do you know that the bottle which enclosed the document may not have taken several years to come from Tabor Island to Lincoln Island?"

"That is not absolutely impossible," replied the reporter.

"Might it not have been a long time already on the coast of the island?"

"No," answered Pencroft, "for it was still floating. We could not even suppose that after it had stayed for any length of time on the shore, it would have been swept off by the sea, for the south coast is all rocks, and it would certainly have been smashed to pieces there!"

"That is true," rejoined Cyrus Harding thoughtfully.

"And then," continued the sailor, "if the document was several years old, if it had been shut up in that bottle for several years, it would have been injured by damp. Now, there is nothing of the kind, and it was found in a perfect state of preservation."

The sailor's reasoning was very just, and pointed out an incomprehensible fact, for the document appeared to have been recently written, when the colonists found it in the bottle. Moreover, it gave the latitude and longitude of Tabor Island correctly, which implied that its author had a more complete knowledge of hydrography than could be expected of a common sailor.

"There is in this, again, something unaccountable," said the engineer, "but we will not urge our companions to speak. When he likes, my friends, then we shall be ready to hear him!"

During the following days the stranger did not speak a word, and did not once leave the precincts of the plateau. He worked away, without losing a moment, without taking a minute's rest, but always in a retired place. At meal times he never came to Granite House, although invited several times to do so, but contented himself with eating a few raw vegetables. At nightfall he did not return to the room assigned to him, but remained under some clump of trees, or when the weather was bad crouched in some cleft of the rocks. Thus he lived in the same manner as when he had no other shelter than the forests of Tabor Island, and as all persuasion to induce him to improve his life was in vain, the colonists waited patiently. And the time was near, when, as it seemed, almost involuntarily urged by his conscience, a terrible confession escaped him.

On the 10th of November, about eight o'clock in the evening, as night was coming on, the stranger appeared unexpectedly before the settlers, who were assembled under the veranda. His eyes burned strangely, and he had quite resumed the wild aspect of his worst days.

Cyrus Harding and his companions were astounded on seeing that, overcome by some terrible emotion, his teeth chattered like those of a person in a fever. What was the matter with him? Was the sight of his fellow-creatures insupportable to him? Was he weary of this return to a civilized mode of existence? Was he pining for his former savage life? It appeared so, as soon he was heard to express himself in these incoherent sentences:

"Why am I here? . . . By what right have you dragged me from my islet? . . . Do you think there could be any tie between you and me? . . . Do you know who I am—what I have done—why I was there—

alone? And who told you that I was not abandoned there—that I was not condemned to die there? . . . Do you know my past? . . . How do you know that I have not stolen, murdered—that I am not a wretch—an accursed being—only fit to live like a wild beast, far from all—speak—do you know it?"

The colonists listened without interrupting the miserable creature, from whom these broken confessions escaped, as it were, in spite of himself. Harding wishing to calm him, approached him, but he hastily drew back.

"No! no!" he exclaimed; "one word only—am I free?"

"You are free," answered the engineer.

"Farewell, then!" he cried, and fled like a madman.

Neb, Pencroft, and Herbert ran also toward the edge of the wood—but they returned alone.

"We must let him alone!" said Cyrus Harding.

"He will never come back!" exclaimed Pencroft.

"He will come back," replied the engineer.

Many days passed; but Harding—was it a sort of presentiment?—persisted in the fixed idea that sooner or later the unhappy man would return.

"It is the last revolt of his wild nature," said he, "which remorse has touched, and which renewed solitude will terrify."

In the meanwhile, works of all sorts were continued, as well on Prospect Heights as at the corral, where Harding intended to build a farm. It is unnecessary to say that the seeds collected by Herbert on Tabor Island had been carefully sown. The plateau thus formed one immense kitchen-garden, well laid out and carefully tended, so that the arms of the settlers were never in want of work. There was always something to be done. As the esculents increased in number, it became necessary to enlarge the simple beds, which threatened to grow into regular fields and replace the meadows. But grass abounded in other parts of the island, and there was no fear of the onagers being obliged to go on short allowance. It was well worth while, besides, to turn Prospect Heights into a kitchen-garden, defended by its deep belt of creeks, and to remove them to the meadows, which had no need of protection against the depredations of quadrumana and quadrupeds.

On the 15th of November, the third harvest was gathered in. How wonderfully had the field increased in extent, since eighteen months ago, when the first grain of wheat was sown! The second crop of six hundred thousand grains produced this time four thousand bushels, or five hundred millions of grains!

The colony was rich in corn, for ten bushels alone were sufficient for sowing every year to produce an ample crop for the food both of men and beasts. The harvest was completed, and the last fortnight of the month of November was devoted to the work of converting it into food for man. In fact, they had corn, but not flour, and the establishment of a mill was necessary. Cyrus Harding could have utilized the second fall which flowed into the Mercy to establish his motive power, the first being already occupied with moving the felting mill, but, after some consultation, it was decided that a simple windmill should be built on Prospect Heights. The building of this presented no more difficulty than the building of the former, and it was moreover certain that there would be no want of wind on the plateau, exposed as it was to the sea-breezes.

"Not to mention," said Pencroft, "that the windmill will be more lively and will have a good effect in the landscape!"

They set to work by choosing timber for the frame and machinery of the mill. Some large stones, found at the north of the lake, could be easily transformed into millstones, and as to the sails, the inexhaustible case of the balloon furnished the necessary material.

Cyrus Harding made his model, and the site of the mill was chosen a little to the right of the poultry-yard, near the shore of the lake. The frame was to rest on a pivot supported with strong timbers, so that it could turn with all the machinery it contained according as the wind required it. The work advanced rapidly. Neb and Pencroft had become very skillful carpenters, and had nothing to do but to copy the models provided by the engineer.

Soon a sort of cylindrical box, in shape like a pepper-pot, with a pointed roof, rose on the spot chosen. The four frames which formed the sails had been firmly fixed in the center beam, so as to form a certain angle with it, and secured with iron clamps. As to the different parts of the internal mechanism, the box destined to contain the two millstones, the fixed stone and the moving stone, the hopper, a sort of large square trough, wide at the top, narrow at the bottom, which would allow the grain to fall on the stones, the oscillating spout intended to regulate the passing of the grain, and lastly the bolting machine, which by the operation of sifting, separates the bran from the flour, were made without difficulty. The tools were good, and the work not difficult, for in reality, the machinery of a mill is very simple. This was only a question of time.

Every one had worked at the construction of the mill, and on the 1st of December it was finished. As usual, Pencroft was delighted with his work, and had no doubt that the apparatus was perfect.

"Now for a good wind," said he, "and we shall grind our first harvest splendidly!"

"A good wind, certainly," answered the engineer, "but not too much, Pencroft."

"Pooh! our mill would only go the faster!"

"There is no need for it to go so very fast," replied Cyrus Harding. "It is known by experience that the greatest quantity of work is performed by a mill when the number of turns made by the sails in a minute is six times the number of feet traversed by the wind in a second. A moderate breeze, which passes over twenty-four feet to the second, will give sixteen turns to the sails during a minute, and there is no need of more."

"Exactly!" cried Herbert, "a fine breeze is blowing from the northeast, which will soon do our business for us."

There was no reason for delaying the inauguration of the mill, for the settlers were eager to taste the first piece of bread in Lincoln Island. On this morning two or three bushels of wheat were ground, and the next day at breakfast a magnificent loaf, a little heavy perhaps, although raised with yeast, appeared on the table at Granite House. Every one munched away at it with a pleasure which may be easily understood.

In the meanwhile, the stranger had not reappeared. Several times Gideon Spilett and Herbert searched the forest in the neighborhood of Granite House, without meeting or finding any trace of him. They became seriously uneasy at this prolonged absence. Certainly, the former savage of Tabor Island could not be perplexed how to live in the forest, abounding in game, but was it not to be feared that he had resumed his habits, and that this freedom would revive in him his wild instincts? However, Harding, by a sort of presentiment, doubtless, always persisted in saying that the fugitive would return.

"Yes, he will return!" he repeated with a confidence which his companions could not share. "When this unfortunate man was on Tabor Island, he knew himself to be alone! Here, he knows that fellow-men are awaiting him! Since he has partially spoken of his past life, the poor penitent will return to tell the whole, and from that day he will belong to us!"

The event justified Cyrus Harding's predictions. On the 3rd of December, Herbert had left the plateau to go and fish on the southern bank of the lake. He was unarmed, and till then had never taken any precautions for defense, as dangerous animals had not shown themselves on that part of the island.

Meanwhile, Pencroft and Neb were working in the poultry-yard, while Harding and the reporter were occupied at the Chimneys in making soda, the store of soap being exhausted.

Suddenly cries resounded,

"Help! help!"

Cyrus Harding and the reporter, being at too great a distance, had not been able to hear the shouts. Pencroft and Neb, leaving the poultry-yard in all haste, rushed toward the lake.

But before then, the stranger, whose presence at this place no one had suspected, crossed Creek Glycerine, which separated the plateau from the forest, and bounded up the opposite bank.

Herbert was there face to face with a fierce jaguar, similar to the one which had been killed on Reptile End. Suddenly surprised, he was standing with his back against a tree, while the animal gathering itself together was about to spring.

But the stranger, with no other weapon than a knife, rushed on the formidable animal, who turned to meet this new adversary.

The struggle was short. The stranger possessed immense strength and activity. He seized the jaguar's throat with one powerful hand, holding it as in a vise, without heeding the beast's claws which tore his flesh, and with the other he plunged his knife into its heart.

The jaguar fell. The stranger kicked away the body, and was about to fly at the moment when the settlers arrived on the field of battle, but Herbert, clinging to him, cried,

"No, no! you shall not go!"

Harding advanced toward the stranger, who frowned when he saw him approaching. The blood flowed from his shoulder under his torn shirt, but he took no notice of it.

"My friend," said Cyrus Harding, "we have just contracted a debt of gratitude to you. To save our boy you have risked your life!"

"My life!" murmured the stranger. "What is that worth? Less than nothing!"

"You are wounded?"

"It is no matter."

"Will you give me your hand?"

And as Herbert endeavored to seize the hand which had just saved him, the stranger folded his arms, his chest heaved, his look darkened, and he appeared to wish to escape, but making a violent effort over himself, and in an abrupt tone,

"Who are you?" he asked, "and what do you claim to be to me?"

It was the colonists' history which he thus demanded, and for the first time. Perhaps this history recounted, he would tell his own.

In a few words Harding related all that had happened since their departure from Richmond; how they had managed, and what resources they now had at their disposal.

The stranger listened with extreme attention.

Then the engineer told who they all were, Gideon Spilett, Herbert, Pencroft, Neb, himself, and, he added, that the greatest happiness they had felt since their arrival in Lincoln Island was on the return of the vessel from Tabor Island, when they had been able to include among them a new companion.

At these words the stranger's face flushed, his head sunk on his breast, and confusion was depicted on his countenance.

"And now that you know us," added Cyrus Harding, "will you give us your hand?"

"No," replied the stranger in a hoarse voice; "no! You are honest men! And I—"

XVII

These last words justified the colonists' presentiment. There had been some mournful past, perhaps expiated in the sight of men, but from which his conscience had not yet absolved him. At any rate the guilty man felt remorse, he repented, and his new friends would have cordially pressed the hand which they sought; but he did not feel himself worthy to extend it to honest men! However, after the scene with the jaguar, he did not return to the forest, and from that day did not go beyond the enclosure of Granite House.

What was the mystery of his life? Would the stranger one day speak of it? Time alone could show. At any rate, it was agreed that his secret should never be asked from him, and that they would live with him as if they suspected nothing.

For some days their life continued as before. Cyrus Harding and Gideon Spilett worked together, sometimes chemists, sometimes experimentalists. The reporter never left the engineer except to hunt with Herbert, for it would not have been prudent to allow the lad to ramble alone in the forest; and it was very necessary to be on their guard. As to Neb and Pencroft, one day at the stables and poultry-yard, another at the corral, without reckoning work in Granite House, they were never in want of employment.

The stranger worked alone, and he had resumed his usual life, never appearing at meals, sleeping under the trees in the plateau, never mingling with his companions. It really seemed as if the society of those who had saved him was insupportable to him!

"But then," observed Pencroft, "why did he entreat the help of his fellow-creatures? Why did he throw that paper into the sea?"

"He will tell us why," invariably replied Cyrus Harding.

"When?"

"Perhaps sooner than you think, Pencroft."

And, indeed, the day of confession was near.

On the 10th of December, a week after his return to Granite House, Harding saw the stranger approaching, who, in a calm voice and humble tone, said to him: "Sir, I have a request to make of you."

"Speak," answered the engineer, "but first let me ask you a question."

At these words the stranger reddened, and was on the point of withdrawing. Cyrus Harding understood what was passing in the mind of the guilty man, who doubtless feared that the engineer would interrogate him on his past life.

Harding held him back.

"Comrade," said he, "we are not only your companions but your friends. I wish you to believe that, and now I will listen to you."

The stranger pressed his hand over his eyes. He was seized with a sort of trembling, and remained a few moments without being able to articulate a word.

"Sir," said he at last, "I have come to beg you to grant me a favor."

"What is it?"

"You have, four or five miles from here, a corral for your domesticated animals. These animals need to be taken care of. Will you allow me to live there with them?"

Cyrus Harding gazed at the unfortunate man for a few moments with a feeling of deep commiseration; then,

"My friend," said he, "the corral has only stables hardly fit for animals."

"It will be good enough for me, sir."

"My friend," answered Harding, "we will not constrain you in anything. You wish to live at the corral, so be it. You will, however, be always welcome at Granite House. But since you wish to live at the corral we will make the necessary arrangements for your being comfortably established there."

"Never mind that, I shall do very well."

"My friend," answered Harding, who always intentionally made use of this cordial appellation, "you must let us judge what it will be best to do in this respect."

"Thank you, sir," replied the stranger as he withdrew.

The engineer then made known to his companions the proposal which had been made to him, and it was agreed that they should build a wooden house at the corral, which they would make as comfortable as possible.

That very day the colonists repaired to the corral with the necessary tools, and a week had not passed before the house was ready to receive its tenant. It was built about twenty feet from the sheds, and from there it was easy to overlook the flock of sheep, which then numbered more than eighty. Some furniture, a bed, table, bench, cupboard, and chest were manufactured, and a gun, ammunition, and tools were carried to the corral.

The stranger, however, had seen nothing of his new dwelling, and he had allowed the settlers to work there without him, while he occupied himself on the plateau, wishing, doubtless, to put the finishing stroke to his work. Indeed, thanks to him, all the ground was dug up and ready to be sowed when the time came.

It was on the 20th of December that all the arrangements at the corral were completed. The engineer announced to the stranger that his dwelling was ready to receive him, and the latter replied that he would go and sleep there that very evening.

On this evening the colonists were gathered in the dining-room of Granite House. It was then eight o'clock, the hour at which their companion was to leave them. Not wishing to trouble him by their presence, and thus imposing on him the necessity of saying farewells which might perhaps be painful to him, they had left him alone and ascended to Granite House.

Now, they had been talking in the room for a few minutes, when a light knock was heard at the door. Almost immediately the stranger entered, and without any preamble,

"Gentlemen," said he, "before I leave you, it is right that you should know my history. I will tell it you."

These simple words profoundly impressed Cyrus Harding and his companions. The engineer rose.

"We ask you nothing, my friend," said he; "it is your right to be silent."

"It is my duty to speak."

"Sit down, then."

"No, I will stand."

"We are ready to hear you," replied Harding.

The stranger remained standing in a corner of the room, a little in the shade. He was bareheaded, his arms folded across his chest, and it was in this posture that in a hoarse voice, speaking like some one who obliges himself to speak, he gave the following recital, which his auditors did not once interrupt:

"On the 20th of December, 1854, a steam-yacht, belonging to a Scotch nobleman, Lord Glenarvan, anchored off Cape Bernouilli, on the western coast of Australia, in the thirty-seventh parallel. On board this yacht were Lord Glenarvan and his wife, a major in the English army, a French geographer, a young girl, and a young boy. These two last were the children of Captain Grant, whose ship, the *Britannia,* had been lost, crew and cargo, a year before. The *Duncan* was commanded by Captain John Mangles, and manned by a crew of fifteen men.

"This is the reason the yacht at this time lay off the coast of Australia. Six months before, a bottle, enclosing a document written in English, German, and French, had been found in the Irish Sea, and picked up by the *Duncan.* This document stated in substance that there still existed three survivors from the wreck of the *Britannia,* that these survivors were Captain Grant and two of his men, and that they had found refuge on some land, of which the document gave the latitude, but of which the longitude, effaced by the sea, was no longer legible.

"This latitude was 37° 11′ south; therefore, the longitude being unknown, if they followed the thirty-seventh parallel over continents and seas, they would be certain to reach the spot inhabited by Captain Grant and his two companions. The English Admiralty having hesitated to undertake this search, Lord Glenarvan resolved to attempt everything to find the captain. He communicated with Mary and Robert Grant, who joined him. The *Duncan* yacht was equipped for the distant voyage, in which the nobleman's family and the captain's children wished to take part, and the *Duncan,* leaving Glasgow, proceeded toward the Atlantic, passed through the Straits of Magellan, and ascended the Pacific as far as Patagonia, where, according to a previous interpretation of the document, they supposed that Captain Grant was a prisoner among the Indians.

"The *Duncan* disembarked her passengers on the western coast of Patagonia, and sailed to pick them up again on the eastern coast at Cape Corrientes. Lord Glenarvan traversed Patagonia, following the thirty-seventh parallel, and having found no trace of the captain, he re-embarked on the 13th of November, so as to pursue his search through the ocean.

"After having unsuccessfully visited the islands of Tristan d'Acunha and Amsterdam, situated in her course, the *Duncan,* as I have said, arrived at Cape Bernouilli, on the Australian coast, on the 20th of December, 1854.

"It was Lord Glenarvan's intention to traverse Australia as he had traversed America, and he disembarked. A few miles from the coast was established a farm, belonging to an Irishman, who offered hospitality to the travelers. Lord Glenarvan made known to the Irishman the cause which had brought him to these parts, and asked if he knew whether a three-masted English vessel, the *Britannia,* had been lost less than two years before on the west coast of Australia.

"The Irishman had never heard of this wreck, but, to the great surprise of the bystanders, one of his servants came forward and said,

" 'My lord, praise and thank God! If Captain Grant is still living, he is living on the Australian shores.'

" 'Who are you?' asked Lord Glenarvan.

" 'A Scotchman like yourself, my lord,' replied the man; "I am one of Captain Grant's crew—one of the castaways of the *Britannia.*"

"This man was called Ayrton. He was, in fact, the boatswain's mate of the *Britannia,* as his papers showed. But, separated from Captain Grant at the moment when the ship struck upon the rocks, he had till then believed that the captain with all his crew had perished, and that he, Ayrton, was the sole survivor of the *Britannia.*

" 'Only,' he added, 'it was not on the west coast, but on the east coast of

Australia that the vessel was lost, and if Captain Grant is still living, as his document indicates, he is a prisoner among the natives, and it is on the other coast that he must be looked for.'

"This man spoke in a frank voice and with a confident look; his words could not be doubted. The Irishman, in whose service he had been for more than a year, answered for his trustworthiness. Lord Glenarvan, therefore, believed in the fidelity of this man and, by his advice, resolved to cross Australia, following the thirty-seventh parallel. Lord Glenarvan, his wife, the two children, the major, the Frenchman, Captain Mangles, and a few sailors composed the little band under the command of Ayrton, while the *Duncan*, under charge of the mate, Tom Austin, proceeded to Melbourne, there to await Lord Glenarvan's instructions.

"They set out on the 23rd of December, 1854.

"It is time to say that Ayrton was a traitor. He was, indeed, the boatswain's mate of the *Britannia*, but, after some dispute with his captain, he endeavored to incite the crew to mutiny and seize the ship, and Captain Grant had landed him, on the 8th of April, 1852, on the west coast of Australia, and then sailed, leaving him there, as was only just.

"Therefore this wretched man knew nothing of the wreck of the *Britannia*; he had just heard of it from Glenarvan's account. Since his abandonment, he had become, under the name of Ben Joyce, the leader of the escaped convicts; and if he boldly maintained that the wreck had taken place on the east coast, and led Lord Glenarvan to proceed in that direction, it was that he hoped to separate him from his ship, seize the *Duncan*, and make the yacht a pirate in the Pacific."

Here the stranger stopped for a moment. His voice trembled, but he continued,

"The expedition set out and proceeded across Australia. It was inevitably unfortunate, since Ayrton, or Ben Joyce, as he may be called, guided it, sometimes preceded, sometimes followed by his band of convicts, who had been told what they had to do.

"Meanwhile, the *Duncan* had been sent to Melbourne for repairs. It was necessary, then, to get Lord Glenarvan to order her to leave Melbourne and go to the east coast of Australia, where it would be easy to seize her. After having led the expedition near enough to the coast, in the midst of vast forests with no resources, Ayrton obtained a letter, which he was charged to carry to the mate of the *Duncan*—a letter which ordered the yacht to repair immediately to the east coast, to Twofold Bay, that is to say a few days' journey from the place where the expedition had stopped. It was there that Ayrton had agreed to meet his accomplices, and two days after gaining possession of the letter, he arrived at Melbourne.

"So far the villain had succeeded in his wicked design. He would be able to take the *Duncan* into Twofold Bay, where it would be easy for the convicts to seize her, and her crew massacred, Ben Joyce would become master of the seas. . . . But it pleased God to prevent the accomplishment of these terrible projects.

"Ayrton, arrived at Melbourne, delivered the letter to the mate, Tom Austin, who read it and immediately set sail, but judge of Ayrton's rage and disappointment, when the next day he found that the mate was taking the vessel, not to the east coast of Australia, to Twofold Bay, but to the east coast of New Zealand. He wished to stop him, but Austin showed him the letter! . . . And indeed, by a providential error of the French geographer, who had written the letter, the east coast of New Zealand was mentioned as the place of destination.

"All Ayrton's plans were frustrated! He became outrageous. They put him in irons. He was then taken to the coast of New Zealand, not knowing what would become of his accomplices, or what would become of Lord Glenarvan.

"The *Duncan* cruised about on this coast until the 3rd of March. On that day Ayrton heard the report of guns. The guns on the *Duncan* were being fired, and soon Lord Glenarvan and his companions came on board.

"This is what had happened.

"After a thousand hardships, a thousand dangers, Lord Glenarvan had accomplished his journey, and arrived on the east coast of Australia, at Twofold Bay. 'No *Duncan!*' He telegraphed to Melbourne. They answered, '*Duncan* sailed on the 18th instant. Destination unknown.'

"Lord Glenarvan could only arrive at one conclusion; that his honest yacht had fallen into the hands of Ben Joyce, and had become a pirate vessel!

"However, Lord Glenarvan would not give up. He was a bold and generous man. He embarked in a merchant vessel, sailed to the west coast of New Zealand, traversed it along the thirty-seventh parallel, without finding any trace of Captain Grant; but on the other side, to his great surprise, and by the will of Heaven, he found the *Duncan*, under command of the mate, who had been waiting for him for five weeks!

"This was on the 3rd of March, 1855. Lord Glenarvan was now on board the *Duncan,* but Ayrton was there also. He appeared before the nobleman, who wished to extract from him all that the villain knew about Captain Grant. Ayrton refused to speak. Lord Glenarvan then told him, that at the first port they put into, he would be delivered up to the English authorities. Ayrton remained mute.

"The *Duncan* continued her voyage along the thirty-seventh parallel. In the meanwhile, Lady Glenarvan undertook to vanquish the resistance of the ruffian.

"At last, her influence prevailed, and Ayrton, in exchange for what he could tell, proposed that Lord Glenarvan should leave him on some island in the Pacific, instead of giving him up to the English authorities. Lord Glenarvan, resolving to do anything to obtain information about Captain Grant, consented.

"Ayrton then related all his life, and it was certain that he knew nothing from the day on which Captain Grant had landed him on the Australian coast.

"Nevertheless, Lord Glenarvan kept the promise which he had given. The *Duncan* continued her voyage and arrived at Tabor Island. It was there that Ayrton was to be landed, and it was there also that, by a veritable miracle, they found Captain Grant and two men, exactly on the thirty-seventh parallel.

"The convict, then, went to take their place on this desert islet, and at the moment he left the yacht these words were pronounced by Lord Glenarvan:

" 'Here, Ayrton, you will be far from any land, and without any possible communication with your fellow-creatures. You cannot escape from this islet on which the *Duncan* leaves you. You will be alone, under the eye of a God who reads the depths of the heart, but you will be neither lost nor forgotten, as was Captain Grant. Unworthy as you are to be remembered by men, men will remember you. I know where you are, Ayrton, and I know where to find you. I will never forget it!'

"And the *Duncan,* making sail, soon disappeared. This was on the 18th of March, 1855.

"Ayrton was alone, but he had no want of either ammunition, weapons, tools, or seeds.

"At his, the convict's disposal, was the house built by honest Captain Grant. He had only to live and expiate in solitude the crimes which he had committed.

"Gentlemen, he repented, he was ashamed of his crimes and was very miserable! He said to himself, that if men came some day to take him from that islet, he must be worthy to return among them! How he suffered, that wretched man! How he labored to recover himself by work! How he prayed to be reformed by prayer! For two years, three years, this went on, but Ayrton, humbled by solitude, always looking for some ship to appear on the horizon, asking himself if the time of expiation would soon be complete, suffered as none other suffered! Oh! how dreadful was this solitude, to a heart tormented by remorse!

"But doubtless Heaven had not sufficiently punished this unhappy man, for he felt that he was gradually becoming a savage! He felt that brutishness was gradually gaining on him!

"He could not say if it was after two or three years of solitude, but at last he became the miserable creature you found!

"I have no need to tell you, gentlemen, that Ayrton, Ben Joyce, and I, are the same."

Cyrus Harding and his companions rose at the end of this account. It is impossible to say how much they were moved! What misery, grief, and despair lay revealed before them!

"Ayrton," said Harding, rising, "you have been a great criminal, but Heaven must certainly think that you have expiated your crimes! That has been proved by your having been brought again among your fellow-creatures. Ayrton, you are forgiven! And now you will be our companion?"

Ayrton drew back.

"Here is my hand!" said the engineer.

Ayrton grasped the hand which Harding extended to him, and great tears fell from his eyes.

"Will you live with us?" asked Cyrus Harding.

"Captain Harding, leave me some time longer," replied Ayrton, "leave me alone in the hut in the corral!"

"As you like, Ayrton," answered Cyrus Harding. Ayrton was going to withdraw, when the engineer addressed one more question to him:

"One word more, my friend. Since it was your intention to live alone, why did you throw into the sea the document which put us on your track?"

"A document?" repeated Ayrton, who did not appear to know what he meant.

"Yes, the document which we found enclosed in a bottle, giving us the exact position of Tabor Island!"

Ayrton passed his hand over his brow, then after having thought, "I never threw any document into the sea!" he answered.

"Never?" exclaimed Pencroft.

"Never!"

And Ayrton, bowing, reached the door and departed.

XVIII

Poor man!" said Herbert, who had rushed to the door, but returned, having seen Ayrton slide down the rope on the lift and disappear in the darkness.

"He will come back," said Cyrus Harding.

"Come, now, captain," exclaimed Pencroft, "what does that mean? What! wasn't it Ayrton who threw that bottle into the sea? Who was it then?"

Certainly, if ever a question was necessary to be made, it was that one!

"It was he," answered Neb, "only the unhappy man was half-mad."

"Yes!" said Herbert, "and he was no longer conscious of what he was doing."

"It can only be explained in that way, my friends," replied Harding quickly, "and I understand now how Ayrton was able to point out exactly the situation of Tabor Island, since the events which had preceded his being left on the island had made it known to him."

"However," observed Pencroft, "if he was not yet a brute when he wrote that document, and if he threw it into the sea seven or eight years ago, how is it that the paper has not been injured by damp?"

"That proves," answered Cyrus Harding, "that Ayrton was deprived of intelligence at a more recent time than he thinks."

"Of course it must be so," replied Pencroft, "without that the fact would be unaccountable."

"Unaccountable indeed," answered the engineer, who did not appear desirous to prolong the conversation.

"But has Ayrton told the truth?" asked the sailor.

"Yes," replied the reporter. "The story which he has told is true in every point. I remember quite well the account in the newspapers of the yacht expedition undertaken by Lord Glenarvan, and its result."

"Ayrton has told the truth," added Harding. "Do not doubt it, Pencroft, for it was painful to him. People tell the truth when they accuse themselves like that!"

The next day—the 21st of December—the colonists descended to the beach, and having climbed the plateau they found nothing of Ayrton. He had reached his house in the corral during the night and the settlers judged it best not to agitate him by their presence. Time would doubtless perform what sympathy had been unable to accomplish.

Herbert, Pencroft, and Neb resumed their ordinary occupations. On this day the same work brought Harding and the reporter to the workshop at the Chimneys.

"Do you know, my dear Cyrus," said Gideon Spilett, "that the explanation you gave yesterday on the subject of the bottle has not satisfied me at all! How can it be supposed that the unfortunate man was able to write that document and throw the bottle into the sea without having the slightest recollection of it?"

"Nor was it he who threw it in, my dear Spilett."

"You think then—"

"I think nothing, I know nothing!" interrupted Cyrus Harding. "I am content to rank this incident among those which I have not been able to explain to this day!"

"Indeed, Cyrus," said Spilett, "these things are incredible! Your rescue, the case stranded on the sand, Top's adventure, and lastly this bottle . . . Shall we never have the answer to these enigmas?"

"Yes!" replied the engineer quickly, "yes, even if I have to penetrate into the bowels of this island!"

"Chance will perhaps give us the key to this mystery!"

"Chance! Spilett! I do not believe in chance, any more than I believe in mysteries in this world. There is a reason for everything unaccountable which has happened here, and that reason I shall discover. But in the meantime we must work and observe."

The month of January arrived. The year 1867 commenced. The summer occupations were assiduously continued. During the days which followed, Herbert and Spilett having gone in the direction of the corral, ascertained that Ayrton had taken possession of the habitation which had been prepared for him. He busied himself with the numerous flock confided to his care, and spared his companions the trouble of coming every two or three days to visit the corral. Nevertheless, in order not to leave Ayrton in solitude for too long a time, the settlers often paid him a visit.

It was not unimportant either, in consequence of some suspicions entertained by the engineer and Gideon Spilett, that this part of the island should be subject to a surveillance of some sort, and that Ayrton, if any incident occurred unexpectedly, should not neglect to inform the inhabitants of Granite House of it.

Nevertheless it might happen that something would occur which it would be necessary to bring rapidly to the engineer's knowledge. Independently of facts bearing on the mystery of Lincoln Island, many others might happen, which would call for the prompt interference of the colonists—such as the sighting of a vessel, a wreck on the western coast, the possible arrival of pirates, etc.

Therefore Cyrus Harding resolved to put the corral in instantaneous communication with Granite House.

It was on the 10th of January that he made known his project to his companions.

"Why! how are you going to manage that, captain?" asked Pencroft. "Do you by chance happen to think of establishing a telegraph?"

"Exactly so," answered the engineer.

"Electric?" cried Herbert.

"Electric," replied Cyrus Harding. "We have all the necessary materials for making a battery, and the most difficult thing will be to stretch the wires, but by means of a drawplate I think we shall manage it."

"Well, after that," returned the sailor, "I shall never despair of seeing ourselves some day rolling along on a railway!"

They then set to work, beginning with the most difficult thing, for, if they failed in that, it would be useless to manufacture the battery and other accessories.

The iron of Lincoln Island, as has been said, was of excellent quality, and consequently very fit for being drawn out. Harding commenced by manufacturing a drawplate, that is to say, a plate of steel, pierced with conical holes of different sizes, which would successively bring the wire to the wished-for tenacity. This piece of steel, after having been tempered, was fixed in as firm a way as possible in a solid framework planted in the ground, only a few feet from the great fall, the motive power of which the engineer intended to utilize. In fact as the fulling-mill was there, although not then in use, its beam moved with extreme power would serve to stretch out the wire by rolling it around itself. It was a delicate operation, and required much care. The iron, prepared previously in long thin rods, the ends of which were sharpened with the file, having been introduced into the largest hole of the drawplate, was drawn out by the beam which wound it around itself, to a length of twenty-five or thirty feet, then unrolled, and the same operation was performed successively through the holes of a less size. Finally, the engineer obtained wires from forty to fifty feet long, which could be easily fastened together and stretched over the distance of five miles, which separated the corral from the bounds of Granite House.

It did not take more than a few days to perform this work, and indeed as soon as the machine had been commenced, Cyrus Harding left his companions to follow the trade of wiredrawers, and occupied himself with manufacturing his battery.

It was necessary to obtain a battery with a constant current. It is known that the elements of modern batteries are generally composed of retort coal, zinc, and copper. Copper was absolutely wanting to the engineer, who, notwithstanding all his researches, had never been able to find any trace of it in Lincoln Island, and was therefore obliged to do without it. Retort coal, that is to say, the hard graphite which is found in the retorts of gas manufactories, after the coal has been dehydrogenized, could have been obtained, but it would have been necessary to establish a special apparatus, involving great labor. As to zinc, it may be remembered that the case found at Flotsam Point was lined with this metal, which could not be better utilized than for this purpose.

Cyrus Harding, after mature consideration, decided to manufacture a very simple battery, resembling as nearly as possible that invented by Becquerel in 1820, and in which zinc only is employed. The other substances, azotic acid and potash, were all at his disposal.

The way in which the battery was composed was as follows, and the results were to be attained by the reaction of acid and potash on each other. A number of glass bottles were made and filled with azotic acid. The engineer corked them by means of a stopper through which passed a glass tube, bored at its lower extremity, and intended to be plunged into the acid by means of a clay stopper secured by a rag. Into this tube, through its upper extremity, he poured a solution of potash, previously obtained by burning and reducing to ashes various plants, and in this way the acid and potash could act on each other through the clay.

Cyrus Harding then took two slips of zinc, one of which was plunged into azotic acid, the other into a solution of potash. A current was immediately produced, which was transmitted from the slip of zinc in the bottle to that in the tube, and the two slips having been connected by a metallic wire, the slip in the tube became the positive pole, and that in the bottle the negative pole of the apparatus. Each bottle, therefore, produced as many currents as united would be sufficient to produce all the phenomena of the electric telegraph. Such was the ingenious and very simple apparatus constructed by Cyrus Harding, an apparatus which would allow them to establish a telegraphic communication between Granite House and the corral.

On the 6th of February was commenced the planting along the road to the corral, of posts furnished with glass insulators, and intended to support the wire. A few days after, the wire was extended, ready to produce the electric current at a rate of twenty thousand miles a second.

Two batteries had been manufactured, one for Granite House, the other for the corral; for if it was necessary the corral should be able to communicate with Granite House, it might also be useful that Gramite House should be able to communicate with the corral.

As to the receiver and manipulator, they were very simple. At the two stations the wire was wound around a magnet, that is to say, around a piece of soft iron surrounded with a wire. The communication was thus established between the two poles; the current, starting from the positive pole, traversed the wire, passed through the magnet which was temporarily magnetized, and returned through the earth to the negative pole. If the current was interrupted, the magnet immediately became unmagnetized. It was sufficient to place a plate of soft iron before the magnet, which, attracted during the passage of the current, would fall back when the current was interrupted. This movement of the plate thus obtained, Harding could easily fasten to it a needle arranged on a dial, bearing the letters of the alphabet, and in this way communicate from one station to the other.

All was completely arranged by the 12th of February. On this day, Harding, having sent the current through the wire, asked if all was going on well at the corral, and received in a few moments a satisfactory reply from Ayrton. Pencroft was wild with joy, and every morning and evening he sent a telegram to the corral, which always received an answer.

This mode of communication presented two very real advantages:

firstly, because it enabled them to ascertain that Ayrton was at the corral; and secondly, that he was thus not left completely isolated. Besides, Cyrus Harding never allowed a week to pass without going to see him, and Ayrton came from time to time to Granite House, where he always found a cordial welcome.

The fine season passed away in the midst of the usual work. The resources of the colony, particularly in vegetables and corn, increased from day to day, and the plants brought from Tabor Island had succeeded perfectly.

The plateau of Prospect Heights presented an encouraging aspect. The fourth harvest had been admirable and it may be supposed that no one thought of counting whether the four hundred thousand millions of grains duly appeared in the crop. However, Pencroft had thought of doing so, but Cyrus Harding having told him that even if he managed to count three hundred grains a minute, or nine thousand an hour, it would take him nearly five thousand five-hundred years to finish his task, the honest sailor considered it best to give up the idea.

The weather was splendid, the temperature very warm in the day time, but in the evening the sea-breezes tempered the heat of the atmosphere and procured cool nights for the inhabitants of Granite House. There were, however, a few storms, which, although they were not of long duration, swept over Lincoln Island with extraordinary fury. The lightning blazed and the thunder continued to roll for some hours.

At this period the little colony was extremely prosperous.

The tenants of the poultry-yard swarmed, and they lived on the surplus, but it became necessary to reduce the population to a more moderate number. The pigs had already produced young, and it may be understood that their care for these animals absorbed a great part of Neb and Pencroft's time. The onagers, who had two pretty colts, were most often mounted by Gideon Spilett and Herbert, who had become an excellent rider under the reporter's instruction, and they also harnessed them to the cart either for carrying wood and coal to Granite House, or different mineral productions required by the engineer.

Several expeditions were made about this time into the depths of the Far West forests. The explorers could venture there without having anything to fear from the heat, for the sun's rays scarcely penetrated through the thick foliage spreading above their heads. They thus visited all the left bank of the Mercy, along which ran the road from the corral to the mouth of Falls River.

But in these excursions the settlers took care to be well armed, for they met with savage wild boars, with which they often had a tussle. They also, during this season, made fierce war against the jaguars. Gideon Spilett had vowed a special hatred against them, and his pupil Herbert seconded him well. Armed as they were, they no longer feared to meet one of those beasts. Herbert's courage was superb, and the reporter's sang-froid astonishing. Already twenty magnificent skins ornamented the dining-room of Granite House, and if this continued, the jaguar race would soon be extinct in the island, the object aimed at by the hunters.

The engineer sometimes took part in the expeditions made to the unknown parts of the island, which he surveyed with great attention. It was for other traces than those of animals that he searched the thickets of the vast forest, but nothing suspicious ever appeared. Neither Top nor Jup, who accompanied him, ever betrayed by their behavior that there was anything strange there, and yet more than once again the dog barked at the mouth of the well, which the engineer had before explored without result.

At this time Gideon Spilett, aided by Herbert, took several views of the most picturesque parts of the island, by means of the photographic apparatus found in the cases, and of which they had not as yet made any use.

This apparatus, provided with a powerful object-glass, was very complete. Substances necessary for the photographic reproduction, collodion for preparing the glass plate, nitrate of silver to render it sensitive, hyposulphate of soda to fix the prints obtained, chloride of ammonium in which to soak the paper destined to give the positive proof, acetate of soda and chloride of gold in which to immerse the paper, nothing was wanting. Even the papers were there, all prepared, and before laying in the printing-frame upon the negatives, it was sufficient to soak them for a few minutes in the solution of nitrate of silver.

The reporter and his assistant became in a short time very skillful operators, and they obtained fine views of the country, such as the island, taken from Prospect Heights with Mount Franklin in the distance, the mouth of the Mercy, so picturesquely framed in high rocks, the glade and the corral, with the spurs of the mountain in the background, the curious development of Claw Cape, Flotsam Point, etc.

Nor did the photographers forget to take the portraits of all the inhabitants of the island, leaving out no one.

"It multiplies us," said Pencroft.

And the sailor was enchanted to see his own countenance, faithfully reproduced, ornamenting the walls of Granite House, and he stopped as willingly before this exhibition as he would have done before the richest shop-windows in Broadway.

But it must be acknowledged that the most successful portrait was incontestably that of Master Jup. Master Jup had sat with a gravity not to be described, and his portrait was lifelike!

"He looks as if he was just going to grin!" exclaimed Pencroft.

And if Master Jup had not been satisfied, he would have been very difficult to please; but he was quite contented and contemplated his own countenance with a sentimental air which expressed some small amount of conceit.

The summer heat ended with the month of March. The weather was sometimes rainy, but still warm. The month of March, which corresponds to the September of northern latitudes, was not so fine as might have been hoped. Perhaps it announced an early and rigorous winter.

It might have been supposed one morning—the 21st—that the first snow had already made its appearance. In fact Herbert looking early from one of the windows of Granite House, exclaimed,

"Hallo! the islet is covered with snow!"

"Snow at this time?" answered the reporter, joining the boy.

Their companions were soon beside them, but could only ascertain one thing, that not only the islet but all the beach below Granite House was covered with one uniform sheet of white.

"It must be snow!" said Pencroft.

"Or rather it's very like it!" replied Neb.

"But the thermometer marks fifty-eight degrees!" observed Gideon Spilett.

Cyrus Harding gazed at the sheet of white without saying anything, for he really did not know how to explain this phenomenon, at this time of year and in such a temperature.

"By Jove!" exclaimed Pencroft, "all our plants will be frozen!"

And the sailor was about to descend, when he was preceded by the nimble Jup, who slid down to the sand.

But the orang had not touched the ground, when the snowy sheet arose and dispersed in the air in such innumerable flakes that the light of the sun was obscured for some minutes.

"Birds!" cried Herbert.

They were indeed swarms of sea-birds, with dazzling white plumage. They had perched by thousands on the islet and on the shore, and they disappeared in the distance, leaving the colonists amazed as if they had been present at some transformation scene, in which summer succeeded winter at the touch of a fairy's wand. Unfortunately the change had been so sudden, that neither the reporter nor the lad had been able to bring down one of these birds, of which they could not recognize the species.

A few days after came the 26th of March, the day on which, two years before, the castaways from the air had been thrown upon Lincoln Island.

XIX

Two years already! and for two years the colonists had had no communication with their fellow-creatures! They were without news from the civilized world, lost on this island, as completely as if they had been on the most minute star of the celestial hemisphere!

What was now happening in their country? The picture of their native land was always before their eyes, the land torn by civil war at the time they left it, and which the Southern rebellion was perhaps still staining with blood! It was a great sorrow to them, and they often talked together of these things, without ever doubting however that the cause of the North must triumph, for the honor of the American Confederation.

During these two years not a vessel had passed in sight of the island; or, at least, not a sail had been seen. It was evident that Lincoln Island was out of the usual track, and also that it was unknown—as was besides proved by the maps—for though there was no port, vessels might have visited it for the purpose of renewing their store of water. But the surrounding ocean was deserted as far as the eye could reach, and the colonists must rely on themselves for regaining their native land.

However, one chance of rescue existed, and this chance was discussed one day on the first week of April, when the colonists were gathered together in the dining-room of Granite House.

They had been talking of America, of their native country, which they had so little hope of ever seeing again.

"Decidedly we have only one way," said Spilett, "one single way for leaving Lincoln Island, and that is, to build a vessel large enough to sail several hundred miles. It appears to me, that when one has built a boat it is just as easy to build a ship!"

"And in which we might go to the Pomoutous," added Herbert, "just as easily as we went to Tabor Island."

"I do not say no," replied Pencroft, who had always the casting vote in maritime questions; "I do not say no, although it is not exactly the same thing to make a long as a short voyage! If our little craft had been caught in any heavy gale of wind during the voyage to Tabor Island, we should have known that land was at no great distance either way; but twelve hundred miles is a pretty long way, and the nearest land is at least that distance!"

"Would you not, in that case, Pencroft, attempt the adventure?" asked the reporter.

"I will attempt anything that is desired, Mr. Spilett," answered the sailor, "and you know well that I am not a man to flinch!"

"Remember, besides, that we number another sailor amongst us now," remarked Neb.

"Who is that?" asked Pencroft.

"Ayrton."

"If he will consent to come," said Pencroft.

"Nonsense!" returned the reporter; "do you think that if Lord Glenarvan's yacht had appeared at Tabor Island, while he was still living there, Ayrton would have refused to depart?"

"You forget, my friends," then said Cyrus Harding, "that Ayrton was not in possession of his reason during the last years of his stay there. But that is not the question. The point is to know if we may count among our chances of being rescued, the return of the Scotch vessel. Now, Lord Glenarvan promised Ayrton that he would return to take him off from Tabor Island when he considered that his crimes were expiated, and I believe that he will return."

"Yes," said the reporter, "and I will add that he will return soon, for it is twelve years since Ayrton was abandoned."

"Well!" answered Pencroft, "I agree with you that the nobleman will return, and soon too. But where will he touch? At Tabor Island, and not at Lincoln Island."

"That is the more certain," replied Herbert, "as Lincoln Island is not even marked on the map."

"Therefore, my friends," said the engineer, "we ought to take the necessary precautions for making our presence and that of Ayrton on Lincoln Island known at Tabor Island."

"Certainly," answered the reporter, "and nothing is easier than to place in the hut, which was Captain Grant's and Ayrton's dwelling, a notice which Lord Glenarvan and his crew cannot help finding, giving the position of our island."

"It is a pity," remarked the sailor, "that we forgot to take that precaution on our first visit to Tabor Island."

"And why should we have done it?" asked Herbert. "At that time we did not know Ayrton's history; we did not know that any one was likely to come some day to fetch him, and when we did know his history, the season was too advanced to allow us to return then to Tabor Island."

"Yes," replied Harding, "it was too late, and we must put off the voyage until next spring."

"But suppose the Scotch yacht comes before that," said Pencroft.

"That is not probable," replied the engineer, "for Lord Glenarvan would not choose the winter season to venture into these seas. Either he has already returned to Tabor Island, since Ayrton has been with us, that is to say, during the last five months and has left again; or he will not come till later, and it will be time enough in the first fine October days to go to Tabor Island, and leave a notice there."

"We must allow," said Neb, "that it will be very unfortunate if the *Duncan* has returned to these parts only a few months ago!"

"I hope that it is not so," replied Cyrus Harding, "and that Heaven has not deprived us of the best chance which remains to us."

"I think," observed the reporter, "that at any rate we shall know what we have to depend on when we have been to Tabor Island, for if the yacht has returned there, they will necessarily have left some traces of their visit."

"That is evident," answered the engineer. "So then, my friends, since we have this chance of returning to our country, we must wait patiently, and if it is taken from us we shall see what will be best to do."

"At any rate," remarked Pencroft, "it is well understood that if we do leave Lincoln Island, it will not be because we were uncomfortable there!"

"No, Pencroft," replied the engineer, "it will be because we are far from all that a man holds dearest in the world, his family, his friends, his native land!"

Matters being thus decided, the building of a vessel large enough to sail either to the archipelagoes in the north, or to New Zealand in the west, was no longer talked of, and they busied themselves in their accustomed occupations, with a view to wintering a third time in Granite House.

However, it was agreed that before the stormy weather came on, their little vessel should be employed in making a voyage around the island. A complete survey of the coast had not yet been made, and the colonists had but an imperfect idea of the shore to the west and north, from the mouth of Falls River to the Mandible capes, as well as of the narrow bay between them, which opened like a shark's jaws.

The plan of this excursion was proposed by Pencroft, and Cyrus Harding fully acquiesced in it, for he himself wished to see this part of his domain.

The weather was variable, but the barometer did not fluctuate by sudden movements, and they could therefore count on tolerable weather. However, during the first week of April, after a sudden barometrical fall, a renewed rise was marked by a heavy gale of wind, lasting five or six days; then the needle of the instrument remained stationary at a height of twenty-nine inches and nine-tenths, and the weather appeared propitious for an excursion.

The departure was fixed for the 16th of April, and the *Bonadventure*, anchored in Port Balloon, was provisioned for a voyage which might be of some duration.

Cyrus Harding informed Ayrton of the projected expedition, and proposed that he should take part in it, but Ayrton preferring to remain on shore, it was decided that he should come to Granite House during the absence of his companions. Master Jup was ordered to keep him company, and made no remonstrance.

On the morning of the 16th of April all the colonists, including Top, embarked. A fine breeze blew from the southwest, and the *Bonadventure* tacked on leaving Port Balloon so as to reach Reptile End. Of the ninety miles which the perimeter of the island measured, twenty included the south coast between the port and the promontory. The wind being right ahead it was necessary to hug the shore.

It took the whole day to reach the promontory, for the vessel on leaving port had only two hours of ebb tide and had therefore to make way for six hours against the flood. It was nightfall before the promontory was doubled.

The sailor then proposed to the engineer that they should continue sailing slowly with two reefs in the sail. But Harding preferred to anchor a few cables' lengths from the shore, so as to survey that part of the coast during the day. It was agreed also that as they were anxious for a minute exploration of the coast, they should not sail during the night, but would always, when the weather permitted it, be at anchor near the shore.

The night was passed under the promontory, and the wind having fallen, nothing disturbed the silence. The passengers, with the exception of the sailor, scarcely slept as well on board the *Bonadventure* as they would have done in their rooms at Granite House, but they did sleep however. Pencroft set sail at break of day, and by going on the larboard tack they could keep close to the shore.

The colonists knew this beautiful wooded coast, since they had already explored it on foot, and yet it again excited their admiration. They coasted along as close in as possible, so as to notice everything, avoiding always the trunks of trees which floated here and there. Several times also they anchored, and Gideon Spilett took photographs of the superb scenery.

About noon the *Bonadventure* arrived at the mouth of Falls River. Beyond, on the left bank, a few scattered trees appeared, and three miles farther even these dwindled into solitary groups among the western spurs of the mountain, whose arid ridge sloped down to the shore.

What a contrast between the northern and southern part of the coast! In proportion as one was woody and fertile so was the other rugged and barren! It might have been designated as one of those iron coasts, as they are called in some countries, and its wild confusion appeared to indicate that a sudden crystallization had been produced in the yet liquid basalt of some distant geological sea. These stupendous masses would have terrified the settlers if they had been cast at first on this part of the island! They had not been able to perceive the sinister aspect of this shore from the summit of Mount Franklin, for they overlooked it from too great a height, but viewed from the sea it presented a wild appearance which could not perhaps be equaled in any corner of the globe.

The *Bonadventure* sailed along this coast for the distance of half a mile. It was easy to see that it was composed of blocks of all sizes, from twenty to three hundred feet in height, and of all shapes, round like towers, prismatic like steeples, pyramidal like obelisks, conical like factory chimneys. An iceberg of the polar seas could not have been more capricious in its terrible sublimity! Here, bridges were thrown from one rock to another; there, arches like those of a wave, into the depths of which the eye could not penetrate; in one place, large vaulted excavations presented a monumental aspect; in another, a crowd of columns, spires, and arches, such as no Gothic cathedral ever possessed. Every caprice of nature, still more varied than those of the imagination, appeared on this grand coast, which extended over a length of eight or nine miles.

Cyrus Harding and his companions gazed, with a feeling of surprise bordering on stupefaction. But, although they remained silent, Top, not being troubled with feelings of this sort, uttered barks which were repeated by the thousand echoes of the basaltic cliff. The engineer even observed that these barks had something strange in them, like those which the dog had uttered at the mouth of the well in Granite House.

"Let us go close in," said he.

And the *Bonadventure* sailed as near as possible to the rocky shore. Perhaps some cave, which it would be advisable to explore, existed there? But Harding saw nothing, not a cavern, not a cleft which could serve as a retreat to any being whatever, for the foot of the cliff was washed by the surf. Soon Top's barks ceased, and the vessel continued her course at a few cables' lengths from the coast.

In the northwest part of the island the shore became again flat and sandy. A few trees here and there rose above a low, marshy ground, which the colonists had already surveyed, and in violent contrast to the other desert shore, life was again manifested by the presence of myriads of water-fowl. That evening the *Bonadventure* anchored in a small bay to the north of the island, near the land, such was the depth of water there. The night passed quietly, for the breeze died away with the last light of day, and only rose again with the first streaks of dawn.

As it was easy to land, the usual hunters of the colony, that is to say, Herbert and Gideon Spilett, went for a ramble of two hours or so, and returned with several strings of wild duck and snipe. Top had done wonders, and not a bird had been lost, thanks to his zeal and cleverness.

At eight o'clock in the morning the *Bonadventure* set sail, and ran rapidly toward North Mandible Cape, for the wind was right astern and freshening rapidly.

"However," observed Pencroft, "I should not be surprised if a gale came up from the west. Yesterday the sun set in a very red-looking horizon, and now, this morning, those mare's-tails don't forbode anything good."

These mare's-tails are cirrus clouds, scattered in the zenith, their height from the sea being less than five thousand feet. They look like light pieces of cotton wool, and their presence usually announces some sudden change in the weather.

"Well," said Harding, "let us carry as much sail as possible, and run for shelter into Shark Gulf. I think that the *Bonadventure* will be safe there."

"Perfectly," replied Pencroft, "and besides, the north coast is merely sand, very uninteresting to look at."

"I shall not be sorry," resumed the engineer, "to pass not only to-night but to-morrow in that bay, which is worth being carefully explored."

"I think that we shall be obliged to do so, whether we like it or not," answered Pencroft, "for the sky looks very threatening toward the west. Dirty weather is coming on!"

"At any rate we have a favorable wind for reaching Mandible Cape," observed the reporter.

"A very fine wind," replied the sailor; "but we must tack to enter the gulf, and I should like to see my way clear in these unknown quarters."

"Quarters which appear to be filled with rocks," added Herbert, "if we judge by what we saw on the south coast of Shark Gulf."

"Pencroft," said Cyrus Harding, "do as you think best, we will leave it to you."

"Don't make your mind uneasy, captain," replied the sailor, "I shall not expose myself needlessly! I would rather a knife were run into my ribs than a sharp rock into those of my *Bonadventure!*"

That which Pencroft called ribs was the part of his vessel under water, and he valued it more than his own skin.

"What o'clock is it?" asked Pencroft.

"Ten o'clock," replied Gideon Spilett.

"And what distance is it to the cape, captain?"

"About fifteen miles," replied the engineer.

"That's a matter of two hours and a half," said the sailor, "and we shall be off the cape between twelve and one o'clock. Unluckily, the tide will be turning at that moment, and will be ebbing out of the gulf. I am afraid that it will be very difficult to get in, having both wind and tide against us."

"And the more so that it is a full moon to-day," remarked Herbert, "and these April tides are very strong."

"Well, Pencroft," asked Harding, "can you not anchor off the cape?"

"Anchor near land, with bad weather coming on!" exclaimed the sailor. "What are you thinking of, captain? We should run aground, of a certainty!"

"What will you do then?"

"I shall try to keep in the offing until the flood, that is to say, till about seven in the evening, and if there is still light enough I will try to enter the gulf; if not, we must stand off and on during the night, and we will enter to-morrow at sunrise."

"As I told you, Pencroft, we will leave it to you," answered Harding.

"Ah!" said Pencroft, "if there was only a lighthouse on the coast, it would be much more convenient for sailors."

"Yes," replied Herbert, "and this time we shall have no obliging engineer to light a fire to guide us into port!"

"Why, indeed, my dear Cyrus," said Spilett, "we have never thanked you; but frankly, without that fire we should never have been able—"

"A fire?" asked Harding, much astonished at the reporter's words.

"We mean, captain," answered Pencroft, "that on board the *Bonadventure* we were very anxious during the few hours before our return, and we should have passed to windward of the island, if it had not been for the precaution you took of lighting a fire the night of the 19th of October, on Prospect Heights."

"Yes, yes! That was a lucky idea of mine!" replied the engineer.

"And this time," continued the sailor, "unless the idea occurs to Ayrton, there will be no one to do us that little service!"

"No! No one!" answered Cyrus Harding.

A few minutes after, finding himself alone in the bows of the vessel, with the reporter, the engineer bent down and whispered,

"If there is one thing certain in this world, Spilett, it is that I never lighted any fire during the night of the 19th of October, neither on Prospect Heights nor on any other part of the island!"

XX

Things happened as Pencroft had predicted, he being seldom mistaken in his prognostications. The wind rose, and from a fresh breeze it soon increased to a regular gale; that is to say, it acquired a speed of from forty to forty-five miles an hour, before which a ship in the open sea would have run under close-reefed topsails. Now, as it was nearly six o'clock when the *Bonadventure* reached the gulf, and as at that moment the tide turned, it was impossible to enter. They were therefore compelled to stand off, for even if he had wished to do so, Pencroft could not have gained the mouth of the Mercy. Hoisting the jib to the mainmast by way of a storm-sail, he hove to, putting the head of the vessel toward the land.

Fortunately, although the wind was strong the sea, being sheltered by the land, did not run very high. They had then little to fear from the waves, which always endanger small craft. The *Bonadventure* would doubtlessly not have capsized, for she was well ballasted, but enormous masses of water falling on the deck might injure her if her timbers could not sustain them. Pencroft, as a good sailor, was prepared for anything. Certainly, he had great confidence in his vessel, but nevertheless he awaited the return of day with some anxiety.

During the night, Cyrus Harding and Gideon Spilett had no opportunity for talking together, and yet the words pronounced in the reporter's ear by the engineer were well worth being discussed, together with the mysterious influence which appeared to reign over Lincoln Island. Gideon Spilett did not cease from pondering over this new and inexplicable incident—the appearance of a fire on the coast of the island. The fire had actually been seen! His companions, Herbert and Pencroft, had seen it with him! The fire had served to signalize the position of the island during that dark night, and they had not doubted that it was lighted by the engineer's hand; and here was Cyrus Harding expressly declaring that he had never done anything of the sort! Spilett resolved to recur to this incident as soon as the *Bonadventure* returned, and to urge Cyrus Harding to acquaint their companions with these strange facts. Perhaps it would be decided to make in common a complete investigation of every part of Lincoln Island.

However that might be, on this evening no fire was lighted on these yet unknown shores, which formed the entrance to the gulf, and the little vessel stood off during the night.

When the first streaks of dawn appeared in the western horizon, the wind, which had slightly fallen, shifted two points, and enabled Pencroft to enter the narrow gulf with greater ease. Toward seven o'clock in the morning, the *Bonadventure,* weathering the North Mandible Cape, entered the strait and glided on to the waters, so strangely enclosed in the frame of lava.

"Well," said Pencroft, "this bay would make admirable roads, in which a whole fleet could lie at their ease!"

"What is especially curious," observed Harding, "is that the gulf has been formed by two rivers of lava, thrown out by the volcano, and accumulated by successive eruptions. The result is that the gulf is completely sheltered on all sides, and I believe that even in the stormiest weather, the sea here must be as calm as a lake."

"No doubt," returned the sailor, "since the wind has only that narrow entrance between the two capes to get in by, and, besides, the north cape protects that of the south in a way which would make the entrance of gusts very difficult. I declare our *Bonadventure* could stay here from one end of the year to the other, without even dragging at her anchor!"

"It is rather large for her!" observed the reporter.

"Well! Mr. Spilett," replied the sailor, "I agree that it is too large for the *Bonadventure,* but if the fleets of the Union were in want of a harbor in the Pacific, I don't think they would ever find a better place than this!"

"We are in the shark's mouth," remarked Neb, alluding to the form of the gulf.

"Right into its mouth, my honest Neb!" replied Herbert, "but you are not afraid that it will shut upon us, are you?"

"No, Mr. Herbert," answered Neb, "and yet this gulf here doesn't please me much! It has a wicked look!"

"Hallo!" cried Pencroft, "here is Neb turning up his nose at my gulf, just as I was thinking of presenting it to America!"

"But, at any rate, is the water deep enough?" asked the engineer, "for a depth sufficient for the keel of the *Bonadventure* would not be enough for those of our iron-clads."

"That is easily found out," replied Pencroft.

And the sailor sounded with a long cord, which served him as a lead-line, and to which was fastened a lump of iron. This cord measured nearly fifty fathoms, and its entire length was unrolled without finding any bottom.

"There," exclaimed Pencroft, "our iron-clads can come here after all! They would not run aground!"

"Indeed," said Gideon Spilett, "this gulf is a regular abyss, but, taking into consideration the volcanic origin of the island, it is not astonishing that the sea should offer similar depressions."

"One would say too," observed Herbert, "that these cliffs were perfectly perpendicular; and I believe that at their foot, even with a line five or six times longer, Pencroft would not find bottom."

"That is all very well," then said the reporter, "but I must point out to Pencroft that his harbor is wanting in one very important respect!"

"And what is that, Mr. Spilett?"

"An opening, a cutting of some sort, to give access to the interior of the island. I do not see a spot on which we could land." And, in fact, the steep lava cliffs did not afford a single place suitable for landing. They formed an insuperable barrier, recalling, but with more wildness, the fiords of Norway. The *Bonadventure,* coasting as close as possible along the cliffs, did not discover even a projection which would allow the passengers to leave the deck.

Pencroft consoled himself by saying that with the help of a mine they could soon open out the cliff when that was necessary, and then, as there was evidently nothing to be done in the gulf, he steered his vessel toward the strait and passed out at about two o'clock in the afternoon.

"Ah!" said Neb, uttering a sigh of satisfaction.

One might really say that the honest Negro did not feel at his ease in those enormous jaws.

The distance from Mandible Cape to the mouth of the Mercy was not more than eight miles. The head of the *Bonadventure* was put toward Granite House, and a fair wind filling her sails, she ran rapidly along the coast.

To the enormous lava rocks succeeded soon those capricious sand dunes, among which the engineer had been so singularly recovered, and which sea-birds frequented in thousands.

About four o'clock, Pencroft leaving the point of the islet on his left, entered the channel which separated it from the coast, and at five o'clock the anchor of the *Bonadventure* was buried in the sand at the mouth of the Mercy.

The colonists had been absent three days from their dwelling. Ayrton was waiting for them on the beach, and Jup came joyously to meet them, giving vent to deep grunts of satisfaction.

A complete exploration of the coast of the island had now been made, and no suspicious appearances had been observed. If any mysterious being resided on it, it could only be under cover of the impenetrable forest of the Serpentine Peninsula, to which the colonists had not yet directed their investigations.

Gideon Spilett discussed these things with the engineer, and it was agreed that they should direct the attention of their companions to the strange character of certain incidents which had occurred on the island, and of which the last was the most unaccountable.

However, Harding, returning to the fact of a fire having been kindled on the shore by an unknown hand, could not refrain from repeating for the twentieth time to the reporter,

"But are you quite sure of having seen it? Was it not a partial eruption of the volcano, or perhaps some meteor?"

"No, Cyrus," answered the reporter, "it was certainly a fire lighted by the hand of man. Besides; question Pencroft and Herbert. They saw it as I saw it myself, and they will confirm my words."

In consequence, therefore, a few days after, on the 25th of April, in the evening, when the settlers were all collected on Prospect Heights, Cyrus Harding began by saying,

"My friends, I think it my duty to call your attention to certain incidents which have occurred in the island, on the subject of which I shall be happy to have your advice. These incidents are, so to speak, supernatural—"

"Supernatural!" exclaimed the sailor, emitting a volume of smoke from his mouth. "Can it be possible that our island is supernatural?"

"No, Pencroft, but mysterious, most certainly," replied the engineer; "unless you can explain that which Spilett and I have until now failed to understand."

"Speak away, captain," answered the sailor.

"Well, have you understood," then said the engineer, "how was it that after falling into the sea, I was found a quarter of a mile into the interior of the island, and that, without my having any consciousness of my removal there?"

"Unless, being unconscious—" said Pencroft.

"That is not admissible," replied the engineer. "But to continue. Have you understood how Top was able to discover your retreat five miles from the cave in which I was lying?"

"The dog's instinct—" observed Herbert.

"Singular instinct!" returned the reporter, "since notwithstanding the storm of rain and wind which was raging during that night, Top arrived at the Chimneys, dry and without a speck of mud!"

"Let us continue," resumed the engineer. "Have you understood how our dog was so strangely thrown up out of the water of the lake, after his struggle with the dugong?"

"No! I confess, not at all," replied Pencroft, "and the wound which the dugong had in its side, a wound which seemed to have been made with a sharp instrument; that can't be understood, either."

"Let us continue again," said Harding. "Have you understood, my friends, how that bullet got into the body of the young peccary; how that case happened to be so fortunately stranded, without there being any trace of a wreck; how that bottle containing the document presented itself so opportunely, during our first sea-excursion; how our canoe, having broken its moorings, floated down the current of the Mercy and rejoined us at the very moment we needed it; how after the ape invasion the ladder was so obligingly thrown down from Granite House; and lastly, how the document, which Ayrton asserts was never written by him, fell into our hands?"

As Cyrus Harding thus enumerated, without forgetting one, the singular incidents which had occurred in the island, Herbert, Neb, and Pencroft stared at each other, not knowing what to reply, for this succession of incidents, grouped thus for the first time, could not but excite their surprise to the highest degree.

" 'Pon my word," said Pencroft at last, "you are right, captain, and it is difficult to explain all these things!"

"Well, my friends," resumed the engineer, "a last fact has just been added to these, and it is no less incomprehensible than the others!"

"What is it, captain?" asked Herbert quickly.

"When you were returning from Tabor Island, Pencroft," continued the engineer, "you said that a fire appeared on Lincoln Island?"

"Certainly," answered the sailor.

"And you are quite certain of having seen this fire?"

"As sure as I see you now."

"You also, Herbert?"

"Why, captain," cried Herbert, "that fire was blazing like a star of the first magnitude!"

"But was it not a star?" urged the engineer.

"No," replied Pencroft, "for the sky was covered with thick clouds, and at any rate a star would not have been so low on the horizon. But Mr. Spilett saw it as well as we, and he will confirm our words."

"I will add," said the reporter, "that the fire was very bright, and that it shot up like a sheet of lightning."

"Yes, yes! exactly," added Herbert, "and it was certainly placed on the heights of Granite House."

"Well, my friends," replied Cyrus Harding, "during the night of the 19th of October, neither Neb nor I lighted any fire on the coast."

"You did not!" exclaimed Pencroft, in the height of his astonishment, not being able to finish his sentence.

"We did not leave Granite House," answered Cyrus Harding, "and if a fire appeared on the coast, it was lighted by another hand than ours!"

Pencroft, Herbert, and Neb were stupefied. No illusion could be possible, and a fire had actually met their eyes during the night of the 19th of October. Yes! they had to acknowledge it, a mystery existed! An inexplicable influence, evidently favorable to the colonists, but very irritating to their curiosity, was executed always in the nick of time on Lincoln Island. Could there be some being hidden in its profoundest recesses? It was necessary at any cost to ascertain this.

Harding also reminded his companions of the singular behavior of Top and Jup when they prowled around the mouth of the well, which placed Granite House in communication with the sea, and he told them that he had explored the well, without discovering anything suspicious. The final resolve taken, in consequence of this conversation, by all the members of the colony, was that as soon as the fine season returned they would thoroughly search the whole of the island.

But from that day Pencroft appeared to be anxious. He felt as if the island which he had made his own personal property belonged to him entirely no longer, and that he shared it with another master, to whom, willing or not, he felt subject. Neb and he often talked of those unaccountable things, and both, their natures inclining them to the marvelous, were not far from believing that Lincoln Island was under the dominion of some supernatural power.

In the meanwhile, the bad weather came with the month of May, the

November of the northern zones. It appeared that the winter would be severe and forward. The preparations for the winter season were therefore commenced without delay.

Nevertheless, the colonists were well prepared to meet the winter, however hard it might be. They had plenty of felt clothing, and the musmons, very numerous by this time, had furnished an abundance of wool necessary for the manufacture of this warm material.

It is unnecessary to say that Ayrton had been provided with this comfortable clothing. Cyrus Harding proposed that he should come to spend the bad season with them in Granite House, where he would be better lodged than at the corral, and Ayrton promised to do so, as soon as the last work at the corral was finished. He did this toward the middle of April. From that time Ayrton shared the common life, and made himself useful on all occasions; but still humble and sad, he never took part in the pleasures of his companions.

For the greater part of this, the third winter which the settlers passed in Lincoln Island, they were confined to Granite House. There were many violent storms and frightful tempests, which appeared to shake the rocks to their very foundations. Immense waves threatened to overwhelm the island, and certainly any vessel anchored near the shore would have been dashed to pieces. Twice, during one of these hurricanes, the Mercy swelled to such a degree as to give reason to fear that the bridges would be swept away, and it was necessary to strengthen those on the shore, which disappeared under the foaming waters, when the sea beat against the beach.

It may well be supposed that such storms, comparable to waterspouts in which were mingled rain and snow, would cause great havoc on the plateau of Prospect Heights. The mill and the poultry-yard particularly suffered. The colonists were often obliged to make immediate repairs, without which the safety of the birds would have been seriously threatened.

During the worst weather, several jaguars and troops of quadrumana ventured to the edge of the plateau, and it was always to be feared that the most active and audacious would, urged by hunger, manage to cross the stream, which besides, when frozen, offered them an easy passage. Plantations and domestic animals would then have been infallibly destroyed, without a constant watch, and it was often necessary to make use of the guns to keep those dangerous visitors at a respectful distance. Occupation was not wanting to the colonists, for without reckoning their outdoor cares, they had always a thousand plans for the fitting up of Granite House.

They had also some fine sporting excursions, which were made during the frost in the vast Tadorn's Fens. Gideon Spilett and Herbert, aided by Jup and Top, did not miss a shot in the midst of myriads of wild-duck, snipe, teal, and others. The access to these hunting-grounds was easy; besides, whether they reached them by the road to Port Balloon, after having passed the Mercy Bridge, or by turning the rocks from Flotsam Point, the hunters were never distant from Granite House more than two or three miles.

Thus passed the four winter months, which were really rigorous, that is to say, June, July, August, and September. But, in short, Granite House did not suffer much from the inclemency of the weather, and it was the same with the corral, which, less exposed than the plateau, and sheltered partly by Mount Franklin, only received the remains of the hurricanes, already broken by the forests and the high rocks of the shore. The damages there were consequently of small importance, and the activity and skill of Ayrton promptly repaired them, when some time in October he returned to pass a few days in the corral.

During this winter, no fresh inexplicable incident occurred. Nothing strange happened, although Pencroft and Neb were on the watch for the most insignificant facts to which they attached any mysterious cause. Top and Jup themselves no longer growled around the well or gave any signs of uneasiness. It appeared, therefore, as if the series of supernatural incidents was interrupted, although they often talked of them during the evenings in Granite House, and they remained thoroughly resolved that the island should be searched, even in those parts the most difficult to explore. But an event of the highest importance, and of which the consequences might be terrible, momentarily diverted from their projects Cyrus Harding and his companions.

It was the month of October. The fine season was swiftly returning. Nature was reviving; and among the evergreen foliage of the coniferae which formed the border of the wood, already appeared the young leaves of the banksias, deodars, and other trees.

It may be remembered that Gideon Spilett and Herbert had, at different times, taken photographic views of Lincoln Island.

Now, on the 17th of this month of October, toward three o'clock in the afternoon, Herbert, enticed by the charms of the sky, thought of reproducing Union Bay, which was opposite to Prospect Heights, from Mandible Cape to Claw Cape.

The horizon was beautifully clear, and the sea, undulating under a soft breeze, was as calm as the waters of a lake, sparkling here and there under the sun's rays.

The apparatus had been placed at one of the windows of the dining-room at Granite House, and consequently overlooked the shore and the bay. Herbert proceeded as he was accustomed to do, and the negative obtained, he went away to fix it by means of the chemicals deposited in a dark nook of Granite House.

Returning to the bright light, and examining it well, Herbert perceived on his negative an almost imperceptible little spot on the sea horizon. He endeavored to make it disappear by reiterated washing, but could not accomplish it.

"It is a flaw in the glass," he thought.

And then he had the curiosity to examine this flaw with a strong magnifier which he unscrewed from one of the telescopes.

But he had scarcely looked at it, when he uttered a cry, and the glass almost fell from his hands.

Immediately running to the room in which Cyrus Harding then was, he extended the negative and magnifier toward the engineer, pointing out the little spot.

Harding examined it; then seizing his telescope he rushed to the window.

The telescope, after having slowly swept the horizon, at last stopped on the looked-for spot, and Cyrus Harding, lowering it, pronounced one word only,

"A vessel!"

And in fact a vessel was in sight, off Lincoln Island!

Part 3

The Secret of the Island

I

It was now two years and a half since the castaways from the balloon had been thrown on Lincoln Island, and during that period there had been no communication between them and their fellow-creatures. Once the reporter had attempted to communicate with the inhabited world by confiding to a bird a letter which contained the secret of their situation, but that was a chance on which it was impossible to reckon seriously. Ayrton, alone, under the circumstances which have been related, had come to join the little colony. Now, suddenly, on this day, the 17th of October, other men had unexpectedly appeared in sight of the island, on that deserted sea!

There could be no doubt about it! A vessel was there! But would she pass on, or would she put into port? In a few hours the colonists would definitely know what to expect.

Cyrus Harding and Herbert having immediately called Gideon Spilett, Pencroft, and Neb into the dining-room of Granite House, told them what had happened. Pencroft, seizing the telescope, rapidly swept the horizon, and stopping on the indicated point, that is to say, on that which had made the almost imperceptible spot on the photographic negative,

"I'm blessed but it is really a vessel!" he exclaimed, in a voice which did not express any great amount of satisfaction.

"Is she coming here?" asked Gideon Spilett.

"Impossible to say anything yet," answered Pencroft, "for her rigging alone is above the horizon, and not a bit of her hull can be seen."

"What is to be done?" asked the lad.

"Wait," replied Harding.

And for a considerable time the settlers remained silent, given up to all the thoughts, and the emotions, all the fears, all the hopes, which were aroused by this incident—the most important which had occurred since their arrival in Lincoln Island. Certainly, the colonists were not in the situation of castaways abandoned on a sterile islet, constantly contending against a cruel nature for their miserable existence, and incessantly tormented by the longing to return to inhabited countries. Pencroft and Neb, especially, who felt themselves at once so happy and so rich, would not have left their island without regret. They were accustomed, besides, to this new life in the midst of the domain which their intelligence had as it were civilized. But at any rate this ship brought news from the world, perhaps even from their native land. It was bringing fellow-creatures to them, and it may be conceived how deeply their hearts were moved at the sight!

From time to time Pencroft took the glass and rested himself at the window. From thence he very attentively examined the vessel, which was at a distance of twenty miles to the east. The colonists had as yet, therefore, no means of signalizing their presence. A flag would not have been perceived; a gun would not have been heard; a fire would not have been visible. However, it was certain that the island, overtopped by Mount Franklin, could not escape the notice of the vessel's look-out. But why was the ship coming there? Was it simple chance which brought it to that part of the Pacific, where the maps mentioned no land except Tabor Island, which itself was out of the route usually followed by vessels from the Polynesian Archipelagoes, from New Zealand, and from the American coast? To this question, which each one asked himself, a reply was suddenly made by Herbert.

"Can it be the *Duncan*?" he cried.

The *Duncan*, as has been said, was Lord Glenarvan's yacht, which had left Ayrton on the islet, and which was to return there someday to fetch him. Now, the islet was not so far distant from Lincoln Island, but that a vessel, standing for the one, could pass in sight of the other. A hundred and fifty miles only separated them in longitude, and seventy in latitude.

"We must tell Ayrton," said Gideon Spilett, "and send for him immediately. He alone can say if it is the *Duncan*."

This was the opinion of all, and the reporter, going to the telegraphic apparatus which placed the corral in communication with Granite House, sent this telegram: "Come with all possible speed."

In a few minutes the bell sounded.

"I am coming," replied Ayrton.

Then the settlers continued to watch the vessel.

"If it is the *Duncan*," said Herbert, "Ayrton will recognize her without difficulty, since he sailed on board her for some time."

"And if he recognizes her," added Pencroft, "it will agitate him exceedingly!"

"Yes," answered Cyrus Harding; "but now Ayrton is worthy to return on board the *Duncan*, and pray Heaven that it is indeed Lord Glenarvan's yacht, for I should be suspicious of any other vessel. These are ill-famed seas, and I have always feared a visit from Malay pirates to our island."

"We could defend it," cried Herbert.

"No doubt, my boy," answered the engineer smiling, "but it would be better not to have to defend it."

"A useless observation," said Spilett. "Lincoln Island is unknown to navigators, since it is not marked even on the most recent maps. Do you think, Cyrus, that that is a sufficient motive for a ship, finding herself unexpectedly in sight of new land, to try and visit rather than avoid it?"

"Certainly," replied Pencroft.

"I think so too," added the engineer. "It may even be said that it is the duty of a captain to come and survey any land or island not yet known, and Lincoln Island is in this position."

"Well," said Pencroft, "suppose this vessel comes and anchors there a few cables' lengths from our island, what shall we do?"

This sudden question remained at first without any reply. But Cyrus Harding, after some moments' thought, replied in the calm tone which was usual to him,

"What we shall do, my friends? What we ought to do is this: we will communicate with the ship, we will take our passage on board her, and we will leave our island, after having taken possession of it in the name of the United States. Then we will return with any who may wish to follow us to colonize it definitely, and endow the American Republic with a useful station in this part of the Pacific Ocean!"

"Hurrah!" exclaimed Pencroft, "and that will be no small present which we shall make to our country! The colonization is already almost finished; names are given to every part of the island; there is a natural port, fresh water, roads, a telegraph, a dockyard, and manufactories; and there will be nothing to be done but to inscribe Lincoln Island on the maps!"

"But if anyone seizes it in our absence?" observed Gideon Spilett.

"Hang it!" cried the sailor. "I would rather remain all alone to guard it: and trust to Pencroft, they shouldn't steal it from him, like a watch from the pocket of a swell!"

For an hour it was impossible to say with any certainty whether the vessel was or was not standing toward Lincoln Island. She was nearer, but in what direction was she sailing? This Pencroft could not determine. However, as the wind was blowing from the northeast, in all probability the vessel was sailing on the starboard tack. Besides, the wind was favorable for bringing her toward the island, and, the sea being calm, she would not be afraid to approach although the shallows were not marked on the chart.

Toward four o'clock—an hour after he had been sent for—Ayrton arrived at Granite House. He entered the dining-room saying,

"At your service, gentlemen."

Cyrus Harding gave him his hand, as was his custom to do, and, leading him to the window,

"Ayrton," said he, "we have begged you to come here for an important reason. A ship is in sight of the island."

Ayrton at first paled slightly, and for a moment his eyes became dim; then, leaning out the window, he surveyed the horizon, but could see nothing.

"Take this telescope," said Spilett, "and look carefully, Ayrton, for it is possible that this ship may be the *Duncan* come to these seas for the purpose of taking you home again."

"The *Duncan!*" murmured Ayrton. "Already?" This last word escaped Ayrton's lips as if involuntarily, and his head drooped upon his hands.

Did not twelve years' solitude on a desert island appear to him a sufficient expiation? Did not the penitent yet feel himself pardoned, either in his own eyes or in the eyes of others?

"No," said he, "no! it cannot be the *Duncan!*"

"Look, Ayrton," then said the engineer, "for it is necessary that we should know beforehand what to expect."

Ayrton took the glass and pointed it in the direction indicated. During some minutes he examined the horizon without moving, without uttering a word. Then,

"It is indeed a vessel," said he, "but I do not think she is the *Duncan.*"

"Why do you not think so?" asked Gideon Spilett.

"Because the *Duncan* is a steam-yacht, and I cannot perceive any trace of smoke either above or near that vessel."

"Perhaps she is simply sailing," observed Pencroft. "The wind is favorable for the direction which she appears to be taking, and she may be anxious to economize her coal, being so far from land."

"It is possible that you may be right, Mr. Pencroft," answered Ayrton, "and that the vessel has extinguished her fires. We must wait until she is nearer, and then we shall soon know what to expect."

So saying, Ayrton sat down in a corner of the room and remained silent. The colonists again discussed the strange ship, but Ayrton took no part in the conversation. All were in such a mood that they found it impossible to continue their work. Gideon Spilett and Pencroft were particularly nervous, going, coming, not able to remain still in one place. Herbert felt more curiosity. Neb alone maintained his usual calm manner. Was not his country that where his master was? As to the engineer, he remained plunged in deep thought, and in his heart feared rather than desired the arrival of the ship. In the meanwhile, the vessel was a little nearer the island. With the aid of the glass, it was ascertained that she was a brig, and not one of those Malay proas, which are generally used by the pirates of the Pacific. It was, therefore, reasonable to believe that the engineer's apprehensions would not be justified, and that the presence of this vessel in the vicinity of the island was fraught with no danger.

Pencroft, after a minute examination, was able positively to affirm that the vessel was rigged as a brig, and that she was standing obliquely toward the coast, on the starboard tack, under her topsails and top-gallant-sails. This was confirmed by Ayrton. But by continuing in this direction she must soon disappear behind Claw Cape, as the wind was from the southwest, and to watch her it would be then necessary to ascend the height of Washington Bay, near Port Balloon—a provoking circumstance, for it was already five o'clock in the evening, and the twilight would soon make any observation extremely difficult.

"What shall we do when night comes on?" asked Gideon Spilett. "Shall we light a fire, so as to signal our presence on the coast?"

This was a serious question, and yet, although the engineer still retained some of his presentiments, it was answered in the affirmative. During the night the ship might disappear and leave for ever, and, this ship gone, would another ever return to the waters of Lincoln Island? Who could foresee what the future would then have in store for the colonists?

"Yes," said the reporter, "we ought to make known to that vessel, whoever she may be, that the island is inhabited. To neglect the opportunity which is offered to us might be to create everlasting regrets."

It was therefore decided that Neb and Pencroft should go to Port Balloon, and that there, at nightfall, they should light an immense fire, the blaze of which would necessarily attract the attention of the brig.

But at the moment when Neb and the sailor were preparing to leave Granite House, the vessel suddenly altered her course, and stood directly for Union Bay. The brig was a good sailer, for she approached rapidly. Neb and Pencroft put off their departure, therefore, and the glass was put into Ayrton's hands, that he might ascertain for certain whether the ship was or was not the *Duncan.* The Scotch yacht was also rigged as a brig. The question was, whether a chimney could be discerned between the two masts of the vessel, which was now at a distance of only five miles.

The horizon was still very clear. The examination was easy, and Ayrton soon let the glass fall again, saying—

"It is not the *Duncan!* It could not be!"

Pencroft again brought the brig within the range of the telescope, and could see that she was of between three and four hundred tons burden, wonderfully narrow, well-masted, admirably built, and must be a very rapid sailer. But to what nation did she belong? That was difficult to say.

"And yet," added the sailor, "a flag is floating from her peak, but I cannot distinguish the colors of it."

"In half an hour we shall be certain about that," answered the reporter. "Besides, it is very evident that the intention of the captain of this ship is to land, and, consequently, if not today, to-morrow at the latest, we shall make his acquaintance."

"Never mind!" said Pencroft. "It is best to know whom we have to deal with, and I shall not be sorry to recognize that fellow's colors!"

And, while thus speaking, the sailor never left the glass. The day began to fade, and with the day the breeze fell also. The brig's ensign hung in folds, and it became more and more difficult to observe it.

"It is not the American flag," said Pencroft from time to time, "nor the English, the red of which could be easily seen, nor the French or German colors, nor the white flag of Russia, nor the yellow of Spain. One would say it was all one color. Let's see: in these seas, what do we generally meet with? The Chilean flag?—but that is tri-color. Brazilian?—it is green. Japanese?—it is yellow and black, while this—"

At that moment the breeze blew out the unknown flag. Ayrton seizing the telescope which the sailor had put down, put it to his eye, and in a hoarse voice,

"The black flag!" he exclaimed.

And indeed the somber bunting was floating from the mast of the brig, and they had now good reason for considering her to be a suspicious vessel!

Had the engineer, then, been right in his presentiments? Was this a pirate vessel? Did she scour the Pacific, competing with the Malay proas which still infest it? For what had she come to look at the shores of Lincoln

Island? Was it to them an unknown island, ready to become a magazine for stolen cargoes? Had she come to find on the coast a sheltered port for the winter months? Was the settlers' honest domain destined to be transformed into an infamous refuge—the headquarters of the piracy of the Pacific?

All these ideas instinctively presented themselves to the colonists' imaginations. There was no doubt, besides, of the signification which must be attached to the color of the hoisted flag. It was that of pirates! It was that which the *Duncan* would have carried, had the convicts succeeded in their criminal design! No time was lost before discussing it.

"My friends," said Cyrus Harding, "perhaps this vessel only wishes to survey the coast of the island. Perhaps her crew will not land. There is a chance of it. However that may be, we ought to do everything we can to hide our presence here. The windmill on Prospect Heights is too easily seen. Let Ayrton and Neb go and take down the sails. We must also conceal the windows of Granite House with thick branches. All the fires must be extinguished, so that nothing may betray the presence of men on the island."

"And our vessel?" said Herbert.

"Oh," answered Pencroft, "she is sheltered in Port Balloon, and I defy any of those rascals there to find her!"

The engineer's orders were immediately executed. Neb and Ayrton ascended the plateau, and took the necessary precautions to conceal any indication of a settlement. While they were thus occupied, their companions went to the border of Jacamar Wood, and brought back a large quantity of branches and creepers, which would at some distance appear as natural foliage, and thus disguise the windows in the granite cliff. At the same time, the ammunition and guns were placed ready so as to be at hand in case of an unexpected attack.

When all these precautions had been taken,

"My friends," said Harding, and his voice betrayed some emotion, "if the wretches endeavor to seize Lincoln Island, we shall defend it—shall we not?"

"Yes, Cyrus," replied the reporter, "and if necessary we will die to defend it!"

The engineer extended his hand to his companions, who pressed it warmly. Ayrton remained in his corner, not joining the colonists. Perhaps he, the former convict, still felt himself unworthy to do so!

Cyrus Harding understood what was passing in Ayrton's mind, and going to him,

"And you, Ayrton," he asked, "what will you do?"

"My duty," answered Ayrton.

He then took up his station near the window and gazed through the foliage.

It was now half-past seven. The sun had disappeared twenty minutes ago behind Granite House. Consequently the eastern horizon was becoming obscured. In the meanwhile the brig continued to advance toward Union Bay. She was now not more than two miles off, and exactly opposite the plateau of Prospect Heights, for after having tacked off Claw Cape, she had drifted toward the north in the current of the rising tide. One might have said that at this distance she had already entered the vast bay, for a straight line drawn from Claw Cape to Mandible Cape would have rested on her starboard quarter.

Was the brig about to penetrate far into the bay? That was the first question. When once in the bay, would she anchor there? That was the second. Would she not content herself with only surveying the coast, and stand out to sea again without landing her crew? They would know this in an hour. The colonists could do nothing but wait.

Cyrus Harding had not seen the suspected vessel hoist the black flag without deep anxiety. Was it not a direct menace against the work which he and his companions had till now conducted so successfully? Had these pirates—for the sailors of the brig could be nothing else—already visited the island, since on approaching it they had hoisted their colors. Had they formerly invaded it, so that certain unaccountable peculiarities might be explained in this way? Did there exist in the as yet unexplored parts some accomplice ready to enter into communication with them?

To all these questions which he mentally asked himself, Harding knew not what to reply; but he felt that the safety of the colony could not but be seriously threatened by the arrival of the brig.

However, he and his companions were determined to fight to the last gasp. It would have been very important to know if the pirates were numerous and better armed than the colonists. But how was this information to be obtained?

Night fell. The new moon had disappeared. Profound darkness enveloped the island and the sea. No light could pierce through the heavy piles of clouds on the horizon. The wind had died away completely with the twilight. Not a leaf rustled on the trees, not a ripple murmured on the shore. Nothing could be seen of the ship, all her lights being extinguished, and if she was still in sight of the island, her whereabouts could not be discovered.

"Well! who knows?" said Pencroft. "Perhaps that cursed craft will stand off during the night, and we shall see nothing of her at daybreak."

As if in reply to the sailor's observation, a bright light flashed in the darkness, and a cannon-shot was heard.

The vessel was still there and had guns on board.

Six seconds elapsed between the flash and the report.

Therefore the brig was about a mile and a quarter from the coast.

At the same time, the chains were heard rattling through the hawse-holes.

The vessel had just anchored in sight of Granite House!

II

There was no longer any doubt as to the pirates' intentions. They had dropped anchor at a short distance from the island, and it was evident that the next day by means of their boats they purposed to land on the beach!

Cyrus Harding and his companions were ready to act, but, determined though they were, they must not forget to be prudent. Perhaps their presence might still be concealed in the event of the pirates contenting themselves with landing on the shore without examining the interior of the island. It might be, indeed, that their only intention was to obtain fresh water from the Mercy, and it was not impossible that the bridge, thrown across a mile and a half from the mouth, and the manufactory at the Chimneys might escape their notice.

But why was that flag hoisted at the brig's peak? What was that shot fired for? Pure bravado doubtless, unless it was a sign of the act of taking possession. Harding knew now that the vessel was well armed. And what had the colonists of Lincoln Island to reply to the pirates' guns? A few muskets only.

"However," observed Cyrus Harding, "here we are in an impregnable position. The enemy cannot discover the mouth of the outlet, now that it is hidden under reeds and grass, and consequently it would be impossible for them to penetrate into Granite House."

"But our plantations, our poultry-yard, our corral, all, everything!" exclaimed Pencroft, stamping his foot. "They may spoil everything, destroy everything in a few hours!"

"Everything, Pencroft," answered Harding, "and we have no means of preventing them."

"Are they numerous? that is the question," said the reporter. "If they are not more than a dozen, we shall be able to stop them, but forty, fifty, more perhaps!"

"Captain Harding," then said Ayrton, advancing toward the engineer, "will you give me leave?"

"For what, my friend?"

"To go to that vessel to find out the strength of her crew."

"But Ayrton—" answered the engineer, hesitating, "you will risk your life—"

"Why not, sir?"

"That is more than your duty."

"I have more than my duty to do," replied Ayrton.

"Will you go to the ship in the boat?" asked Gideon Spilett.

"No, sir, but I will swim. A boat would be seen where a man may glide between wind and water."

"Do you know that the brig is a mile and a quarter from the shore?" said Herbert.

"I am a good swimmer, Mr. Herbert."

"I tell you it is risking your life," said the engineer.

"That is no matter," answered Ayrton. "Captain Harding, I ask this as a favor. Perhaps it will be a means of raising me in my own eyes!"

"Go, Ayrton," replied the engineer, who felt sure that a refusal would have deeply wounded the former convict, now become an honest man.

"I will accompany you," said Pencroft.

"You mistrust me!" said Ayrton quickly.

Then more humbly,

"Alas!"

"No! no!" exclaimed Harding with animation, "no, Ayrton, Pencroft does not mistrust you. You interpret his words wrongly."

"Indeed," returned the sailor, "I only propose to accompany Ayrton as far as the islet. It may be, although it is scarcely possible, that one of these villains has landed, and in that case two men will not be too many to hinder him from giving the alarm. I will wait for Ayrton on the islet, and he shall go alone to the vessel, since he has proposed to do so." These things agreed to, Ayrton made preparations for his departure. His plan was bold, but it might succeed, thanks to the darkness of the night. Once arrived at the vessel's side, Ayrton, holding on to the main chains, might reconnoiter the number and perhaps overhear the intentions of the pirates.

Ayrton and Pencroft, followed by their companions, descended to the beach. Ayrton undressed and rubbed himself with grease, so as to suffer less from the temperature of the water, which was still cold. He might, indeed, be obliged to remain in it for several hours.

Pencroft and Neb, during this time, had gone to fetch the boat, moored a few hundred feet higher up, on the bank of the Mercy, and by the time they returned, Ayrton was ready to start. A coat was thrown over his shoulders, and the settlers all came around him to press his hand.

Ayrton then shoved off with Pencroft in the boat.

It was half-past ten in the evening when the two adventurers disappeared in the darkness. Their companions returned to wait at the Chimneys.

The channel was easily traversed, and the boat touched the opposite shore of the islet. This was not done without precaution, for fear lest the pirates might be roaming about there. But after a careful survey, it was evident that the islet was deserted. Ayrton then, followed by Pencroft, crossed it with a rapid step, scaring the birds nestled in the holes of the rocks; then, without hesitating, he plunged into the sea, and swam noiselessly in the direction of the ship, in which a few lights had recently appeared, showing her exact situation. As to Pencroft, he crouched down in a cleft of the rock, and awaited the return of his companion.

In the meanwhile, Ayrton, swimming with a vigorous stroke, glided through the sheet of water without producing the slightest ripple. His head just emerged above it and his eyes were fixed on the dark hull of the brig, from which the lights were reflected in the water. He thought only of the duty which he had promised to accomplish, and nothing of the danger which he ran, not only on board the ship, but in the sea, often frequented by sharks. The current bore him along and he rapidly receded from the shore.

Half an hour afterward, Ayrton, without having been either seen or heard, arrived at the ship and caught hold of the main-chains. He took breath, then, hoisting himself up, he managed to reach the extremity of the cutwater. There were drying several pairs of sailors' trousers. He put on a pair. Then settling himself firmly, he listened. They were not sleeping on board the brig. On the contrary, they were talking, singing, laughing. And these were the sentences, accompanied with oaths, which principally struck Ayrton:

"Our brig is a famous acquisition."

"She sails well, and merits her name of the *Speedy*."

"She would show all the navy of Norfolk a clean pair of heels."

"Hurrah for her captain!"

"Hurrah for Bob Harvey!"

What Ayrton felt when he overheard this fragment of conversation may be understood when it is known that in this Bob Harvey he recognized one of his old Australian companions, a daring sailor, who had continued his criminal career. Bob Harvey had seized, on the shores of Norfolk Island, this brig, which was loaded with arms, ammunition, utensils, and tools of all sorts, destined for one of the Sandwich Islands. All his gang had gone on board, and pirates after having been convicts, these wretches, more ferocious than the Malays themselves, scoured the Pacific, destroying vessels, and massacring their crews.

The convicts spoke loudly, they recounted their deeds, drinking deeply at the same time, and this is what Ayrton gathered. The actual crew of the *Speedy* was composed solely of English prisoners, escaped from Norfolk Island.

Here it may be well to explain what this island was. In 29° 2′ south latitude, and 165° 42′ east longitude, to the east of Australia, is found a little island, six miles in circumference, overlooked by Mount Pitt, which rises to a height of 1,100 feet above the level of the sea. This is Norfolk Island, once the seat of an establishment in which were lodged the most intractable convicts from the English penitentiaries. They numbered 500, under an iron discipline, threatened with terrible punishments, and were guarded by 150 soldiers, and 150 employed under the orders of the governor. It would be difficult to imagine a collection of greater ruffians. Sometimes—although very rarely—notwithstanding the extreme surveillance of which they were the object, many managed to escape, and seizing vessels which they surprised, they infested the Polynesian archipelagoes.

Thus had Bob Harvey and his companions done. Thus had Ayrton formerly wished to do. Bob Harvey had seized the brig *Speedy*, anchored in sight of Norfolk Island; the crew had been massacred; and for a year this ship had scoured the Pacific, under the command of Harvey, now a pirate, and well known to Ayrton!

The convicts were, for the most part, assembled under the poop; but a few, stretched on the deck, were talking loudly.

The conversation still continued amid shouts and libations. Ayrton learned that chance alone had brought the *Speedy* in sight of Lincoln Island; Bob Harvey had never yet set foot on it; but, as Cyrus Harding had conjectured, finding this unknown land in his course, its position being marked on no chart, he had formed the project of visiting it, and, if he found it suitable, of making it the brig's headquarters.

As to the black flag hoisted at the *Speedy*'s peak, and the gun which had been fired, in imitation of men-of-war when they lower their colors, it was pure piratical bravado. It was in no way a signal, and no communication yet existed between the convicts and Lincoln Island.

The settlers' domain was now menaced with terrible danger. Evidently the island, with its water, its harbor, its resources of all kinds so increased in value by the colonists, and the concealment afforded by Granite House, could not but be convenient for the convicts; in their hands it would become an excellent place of refuge, and, being unknown, it would assure them, for a long time perhaps, impunity and security. Evidently, also, the lives of the settlers would not be respected, and Bob Harvey and his accomplices' first care would be to massacre them without mercy. Harding and his companions had, therefore, not even the choice of flying and hiding themselves in the island, since the convicts intended to reside there, and since, in the event of the *Speedy* departing on an expedition, it was probable that some of the crew would remain on shore, so as to settle themselves there. Therefore, it would be necessary to fight, to destroy every one of these scoundrels, unworthy of pity, and against whom any means would be right. So thought Ayrton, and he well knew that Cyrus Harding would be of his way of thinking.

But was resistance and, in the last place, victory possible? That would depend on the equipment of the brig, and the number of men which she carried.

This Ayrton resolved to learn at any cost, and as an hour after his arrival the vociferations had begun to die away, and as a large number of the convicts were already buried in a drunken sleep, Ayrton did not hesitate to venture onto the *Speedy*'s deck, which the extinguished lanterns now left in total darkness. He hoisted himself onto the cutwater, and by the bowsprit arrived at the forecastle. Then, gliding among the convicts stretched here and there, he made the round of the ship, and found that the *Speedy* carried four guns, which would throw shot of from eight to ten pounds in weight. He found also, on touching them that these guns were breech-loaders. They were therefore of modern make, easily used, and of terrible effect.

As to the men lying on the deck, they were about ten in number, but it was to be supposed that more were sleeping down below. Besides, by listening to them, Ayrton had understood that there were fifty on board. That was a large number for the six settlers of Lincoln Island to contend with! But now, thanks to Ayrton's devotion, Cyrus Harding would not be surprised, he would know the strength of his adversaries, and would make his arrangements accordingly.

There was nothing more for Ayrton to do but to return, and render to his companions an account of the mission with which he had charged himself, and he prepared to regain the bows of the brig, so that he might let himself down into the water.

But to this man, whose wish was, as he had said, to do more than his duty, there came an heroic thought. This was to sacrifice his own life, but save the island and the colonists. Cyrus Harding evidently could not resist fifty ruffians, all well armed, who, either by penetrating by main force into Granite House, or by starving out the besieged, could obtain from them what they wanted. And then he thought of his preservers—those who had made him again a man, and an honest man, those to whom he owed all—murdered without pity, their works destroyed, their island turned into a pirates' den! He said to himself that he, Ayrton, was the principal cause of so many disasters, since his old companion, Bob Harvey, had but realized his own plans, and a feeling of horror took possession of him. Then he was seized with an irresistible desire to blow up the brig and with her, all whom she had on board. He would perish in the explosion, but he would have done his duty.

Ayrton did not hesitate. To reach the powder-room, which is always situated in the after-part of a vessel, was easy. There would be no want of powder in a vessel which followed such a trade, and a spark would be enough to destroy it in an instant.

Ayrton stole carefully along the between-decks, strewn with numerous sleepers, overcome more by drunkenness than sleep. A lantern was lighted at the foot of the mainmast, around which was hung a gun-rack, furnished with weapons of all sorts.

Ayrton took a revolver from the rack, and assured himself that it was loaded and primed. Nothing more was needed to accomplish the work of destruction. He then glided toward the stern, so as to arrive under the brig's poop at the powder-magazine.

It was difficult to proceed along the dimly lighted deck without stumbling over some half-sleeping convict, who retorted by oaths and kicks. Ayrton was, therefore, more than once obliged to halt. But at last he arrived at the partition dividing the after-cabin, and found the door opening into the magazine itself.

Ayrton, compelled to force it open, set to work. It was a difficult operation to perform without noise, for he had to break a padlock. But under his vigorous hand, the padlock broke, and the door was open.

At that moment a hand was laid on Ayrton's shoulder.

"What are you doing here?" asked a tall man, in a harsh voice, who, standing in the shadow, quickly threw the light of a lantern in Ayrton's face.

Ayrton drew back. In the rapid flash of the lantern, he had recognized his former accomplice, Bob Harvey, who could not have known him, as he must have thought Ayrton long since dead.

"What are you doing here?" again said Bob Harvey, seizing Ayrton by the waistband.

But Ayrton, without replying, wrenched himself from his grasp and attempted to rush into the magazine. A shot fired into the midst of the powder-casks, and all would be over!

"Help, lads!" shouted Bob Harvey.

At his shout two or three pirates awoke, jumped up, and, rushing on Ayrton, endeavored to throw him down. He soon extricated himself from their grasp. He fired his revolver, and two of the convicts fell, but a blow from a knife which he could not ward off made a gash in his shoulder.

Ayrton perceived that he could no longer hope to carry out his project. Bob Harvey had reclosed the door of the powder-magazine, and a movement on the deck indicated a general awakening of the pirates. Ayrton must reserve himself to fight at the side of Cyrus Harding. There was nothing for him but flight!

But was flight still possible? It was doubtful, yet Ayrton resolved to dare everything in order to rejoin his companions.

Four barrels of the revolver were still undischarged. Two were fired—one, aimed at Bob Harvey, did not wound him, or at any rate only slightly, and Ayrton, profiting by the momentary retreat of his adversaries, rushed toward the companion-ladder to gain the deck. Passing before the lantern, he smashed it with a blow from the butt of his revolver. A profound darkness ensued, which favored his flight. Two or three pirates, awakened by the noise, were descending the ladder at the same moment.

A fifth shot from Ayrton laid one low, and the others drew back, not understanding what was going on. Ayrton was on deck in two bounds, and three seconds later, having discharged his last barrel in the face of a pirate who was about to seize him by the throat, he leaped over the bulwarks into the sea.

Ayrton had not made six strokes before shots were splashing around him like hail.

What were Pencroft's feelings, sheltered under a rock on the islet! What were those of Harding, the reporter, Herbert, and Neb, crouched in the Chimneys, when they heard the reports on board the brig! They rushed out on to the beach, and, their guns shouldered, they stood ready to repel any attack.

They had no doubt about it themselves! Ayrton, surprised by the pirates, had been murdered, and, perhaps, the wretches would profit by the night to make a descent on the island!

Half an hour was passed in terrible anxiety. The firing had ceased, and yet neither Ayrton nor Pencroft had reappeared. Was the islet invaded? Ought they not to fly to the help of Ayrton and Pencroft? But how? The tide being high at that time, rendered the channel impassable. The boat was not there! We may imagine the horrible anxiety which took possession of Harding and his companions!

At last, toward half-past twelve, a boat, carrying two men, touched the beach. It was Ayrton, slightly wounded in the shoulder, and Pencroft, safe and sound, whom their friends received with open arms.

All immediately took refuge in the Chimneys. There Ayrton recounted all that had passed, even to his plan for blowing up the brig, which he had attempted to put into execution.

All hands were extended to Ayrton, who did not conceal from them that their situation was serious. The pirates had been alarmed. They knew that Lincoln Island was inhabited. They would land upon it in numbers and well armed. They would respect nothing. Should the settlers fall into their hands, they must expect no mercy!

"Well, we shall know how to die!" said the reporter.

"Let us go in and watch," answered the engineer.

"Have we any chance of escape, captain?" asked the sailor.

"Yes, Pencroft."

"Hum! six against fifty!"

"Yes! six! without counting—"

"Who?" asked Pencroft.

Cyrus did not reply, but pointed upward.

III

The night passed without incident. The colonists were on the qui vive, and did not leave their post at the Chimneys. The pirates, on their side, did not appear to have made any attempt to land. Since the last shots fired at Ayrton not a report, not even a sound, had betrayed the presence of the brig in the neighborhood of the island. It might have been fancied that she had weighed anchor, thinking that she had to deal with her match, and had left the coast.

But it was no such thing, and when day began to dawn the settlers could see a confused mass through the morning mist. It was the *Speedy*.

"These, my friends," said the engineer, "are the arrangements which appear to me best to make before the fog completely clears away. It hides us from the eyes of the pirates, and we can act without attracting their attention. The most important thing is, that the convicts should believe that the inhabitants of the island are numerous, and consequently capable of resisting them. I therefore propose that we divide into three parties. The first of which shall be posted at the Chimneys, the second at the mouth of the Mercy. As to the third, I think it would be best to place it on the islet, so as to prevent, or at all events delay, any attempt at landing. We have the use of two rifles and four muskets. Each of us will be armed, and, as we are amply provided with powder and shot, we need not spare our fire. We have nothing to fear from the muskets nor even from the guns of the brig. What can they do against these rocks? And, as we shall not fire from the windows of Granite House, the pirates will not think of causing irreparable damage by throwing shell against it. What is to be feared is, the necessity of meeting hand-to-hand, since the convicts have numbers on their side. We must therefore try to prevent them from landing, but without discovering ourselves. Therefore, do not economize the ammunition. Fire often, but with a sure aim. We have each eight or ten enemies to kill, and they must be killed!"

Cyrus Harding had clearly represented their situation, although he spoke in the calmest voice, as if it was a question of directing a piece of work and not ordering a battle. His companions approved these arrangements without even uttering a word. There was nothing more to be done but for each to take his place before the fog should be completely dissipated. Neb and Pencroft immediately ascended to Granite House and brought back a sufficient quantity of ammunition. Gideon Spilett and Ayrton, both very good marksmen, were armed with the two rifles, which carried nearly a mile. The four other muskets were divided among Harding, Neb, Pencroft, and Herbert.

The posts were arranged in the following manner:

Cyrus Harding and Herbert remained in ambush at the Chimneys, thus commanding the shore to the foot of Granite House.

Gideon Spilett and Neb crouched among the rocks at the mouth of the Mercy, from which the drawbridges had been raised, so as to prevent any one from crossing in a boat or landing on the opposite shore.

As to Ayrton and Pencroft, they shoved off in the boat, and prepared to cross the channel and to take up two separate stations on the islet. In this way, shots being fired from four different points at once, the convicts would be led to believe that the island was both largely peopled and strongly defended.

In the event of a landing being effected without their having been able to prevent it, and also if they saw that they were on the point of being cut off by the brig's boat, Ayrton and Pencroft were to return in their boat to the shore and proceed toward the threatened spot.

Before starting to occupy their posts, the colonists for the last time wrung each other's hands.

Pencroft succeeded in controlling himself sufficiently to suppress his emotion when he embraced Herbert, his boy! and then they separated.

In a few moments Harding and Herbert on one side, the reporter and Neb on the other, had disappeared behind the rocks, and five minutes later

Ayrton and Pencroft, having without difficulty crossed the channel, disembarked on the islet and concealed themselves in the clefts of its eastern shore.

None of them could have been seen, for they themselves could scarcely distinguish the brig in the fog.

It was half-past six in the morning.

Soon the fog began to clear away, and the topmasts of the brig issued from the vapor. For some minutes great masses rolled over the surface of the sea, then a breeze sprang up, which rapidly dispelled the mist.

The *Speedy* now appeared in full view, with a spring on her cable, her head to the north, presenting her larboard side to the island. Just as Harding had calculated, she was not more than a mile and a quarter from the coast.

The sinister black flag floated from the peak.

The engineer, with his telescope, could see that the four guns on board were pointed at the island. They were evidently ready to fire at a moment's notice.

In the meanwhile the *Speedy* remained silent. About thirty pirates could be seen moving on the deck. A few more on the poop; two others posted in the shrouds, and armed with spy-glasses, were attentively surveying the island.

Certainly, Bob Harvey and his crew would not be able easily to give an account of what had happened during the night on board the brig. Had this half-naked man, who had forced the door of the powder-magazine, and with whom they had struggled, who had six times discharged his revolver at them, who had killed one and wounded two others, escaped their shot? Had he been able to swim to shore? Whence did he come? What had been his object? Had his design really been to blow up the brig, as Bob Harvey had thought? All this must be confused enough to the convicts' minds. But what they could no longer doubt was that the unknown island before which the *Speedy* had cast anchor was inhabited, and that there was, perhaps, a numerous colony ready to defend it. And yet no one was to be seen, neither on the shore, nor on the heights. The beach appeared to be absolutely deserted. At any rate, there was no trace of dwellings. Had the inhabitants fled into the interior? Thus probably the pirate captain reasoned, and doubtless, like a prudent man, he wished to reconnoiter the locality before he allowed his men to venture there.

During an hour and a half, no indication of attack or landing could be observed on board the brig. Evidently Bob Harvey was hesitating. Even with his strongest telescopes he could not have perceived one of the settlers crouched among the rocks. It was not even probable that his attention had been awakened by the screen of green branches and creepers hiding the windows of Granite House, and showing rather conspicuously on the bare rock. Indeed, how could he imagine that a dwelling was hollowed out, at that height, in the solid granite? From Claw Cape to the Mandible capes, in all the extent of Union Bay, there was nothing to lead him to suppose that the island was or could be inhabited.

At eight o'clock, however, the colonists observed a movement on board the *Speedy*. A boat was lowered, and seven men jumped into her. They were armed with muskets; one took the yoke-lines, four others the oars, and the two others, kneeling in the bows, ready to fire, reconnoitered the island. Their object was no doubt to make an examination but not to land, for in the latter case they would have come in larger numbers. The pirates from their look-out could have seen that the coast was sheltered by an islet, separated from it by a channel half a mile in width. However, it was soon evident to Cyrus Harding, on observing the direction followed by the boat, that they would not attempt to penetrate into the channel, but would land on the islet.

Pencroft and Ayrton, each hidden in a narrow cleft of the rock, saw them coming directly toward them, and waited till they were within range.

The boat advanced with extreme caution. The oars only dipped into the water at long intervals. It could now be seen that one of the convicts held a lead-line in his hand, and that he wished to fathom the depth of the channel hollowed out by the current of the Mercy. This showed that it was Bob Harvey's intention to bring his brig as near as possible to the coast. About thirty pirates, scattered in the rigging, followed every movement of the boat, and took the bearings of certain landmarks which would allow them to approach without danger. The boat was not more than two cables' lengths off the islet when she stopped. The man at the tiller stood up and looked for the best place at which to land.

At that moment two shots were heard. Smoke curled up from among the rocks of the islet. The man at the helm and the man with the lead-line fell backward into the boat. Ayrton's and Pencroft's balls had struck them both at the same moment.

Almost immediately a louder report was heard, a cloud of smoke issued from the brig's side, and a ball, striking the summit of the rock which sheltered Ayrton and Pencroft, made it fly in splinters, but the two marksmen remained unhurt.

Horrible imprecations burst from the boat, which immediately continued its way. The man who had been at the tiller was replaced by one of his comrades, and the oars were rapidly plunged into the water. However, instead of returning on board as might have been expected, the boat coasted along the islet, so as to round its southern point. The pirates pulled vigorously at their oars that they might get out of range of the bullets.

They advanced to within five cables' lengths of that part of the shore terminated by Flotsam Point, and after having rounded it in a semicircular line, still protected by the brig's guns, they proceeded toward the mouth of the Mercy.

Their evident intention was to penetrate into the channel, and cut off the colonists posted on the islet, in such a way, that whatever their number might be, being placed between the fire from the boat and the fire from the brig, they would find themselves in a very disadvantageous position.

A quarter of an hour passed while the boat advanced in this direction. Absolute silence, perfect calm reigned in the air and on the water.

Pencroft and Ayrton, although they knew they ran the risk of being cut off, had not left their post, both that they did not wish to show themselves as yet to their assailants, and expose themselves to the *Speedy*'s guns, and that they relied on Neb and Gideon Spilett, watching at the mouth of the river, and on Cyrus Harding and Herbert, in ambush among the rocks at the Chimneys.

Twenty minutes after the first shots were fired, the boat was less than two cables' lengths off the Mercy. As the tide was beginning to rise with its accustomed violence, caused by the narrowness of the straits, the pirates were drawn toward the river, and it was only by dint of hard rowing that they were able to keep in the middle of the channel. But, as they were passing within good range of the mouth of the Mercy, two balls saluted them, and two more of their number were laid in the bottom of the boat. Neb and Spilett had not missed their aim.

The brig immediately sent a second ball on the post betrayed by the smoke, but without any other result than that of splintering the rock.

The boat now contained only three able men. Carried on by the current, it shot through the channel with the rapidity of an arrow, passed before Harding and Herbert, who, not thinking it within range, withheld their fire, then, rounding the northern point of the islet with the two remaining oars, they pulled toward the brig.

Hitherto the settlers had nothing to complain of. Their adversaries had certainly had the worst of it. The latter already counted four men seriously wounded if not dead; they, on the contrary, unwounded, had not missed a shot. If the pirates continued to attack them in this way, if they renewed their attempt to land by means of a boat, they could be destroyed one by one.

It was now seen how advantageous the engineer's arrangements had been. The pirates would think that they had to deal with numerous and well-armed adversaries, whom they could not easily get the better of.

Half an hour passed before the boat, having to pull against the current, could get alongside the *Speedy*. Frightful cries were heard when they returned on board with the wounded, and two or three guns were fired with no results.

But now about a dozen other convicts, maddened with rage, and possibly by the effect of the evening's potations, threw themselves into the boat. A second boat was also lowered, in which eight men took their places, and while the first pulled straight for the islet, to dislodge the colonists from thence the second maneuvered so as to force the entrance of the Mercy.

The situation was evidently becoming very dangerous for Pencroft and Ayrton, and they saw that they must regain the mainland.

However, they waited till the first boat was within range, when two well-directed balls threw its crew into disorder. Then, Pencroft and Ayrton, abandoning their posts, under fire from the dozen muskets, ran across the islet at full speed, jumped into their boat, crossed the channel at the moment the second boat reached the southern end, and ran to hide themselves in the Chimneys.

They had scarcely rejoined Cyrus Harding and Herbert, before the islet was overrun with pirates in every direction. Almost at the same moment, fresh reports resounded from the Mercy station, to which the second boat was rapidly approaching. Two, out of the eight men who manned her, were mortally wounded by Gideon Spilett and Neb, and the boat herself, carried irresistibly onto the reefs, was stove in at the mouth of the Mercy. But the six survivors, holding their muskets above their heads to preserve them from contact with the water, managed to land on the right bank of the river. Then, finding they were exposed to the fire of the ambush there, they fled in the direction of Flotsam Point, out of range of the balls.

The actual situation was this: on the islet were a dozen convicts, of whom some were no doubt wounded, but who had still a boat at their disposal; on the island were six, but who could not by any possibility reach Granite House, as they could not cross the river, all the bridges being raised.

"Hallo," exclaimed Pencroft as he rushed into the Chimneys, "hallo, captain! What do you think of it, now?"

"I think," answered the engineer, "that the combat will now take a new form, for it cannot be supposed that the convicts will be so foolish as to remain in a position so unfavorable for them!"

"They won't cross the channel," said the sailor. "Ayrton and Mr. Spilett's rifles are there to prevent them. You know that they carry more than a mile!"

"No doubt," replied Herbert; "but what can two rifles do against the brig's guns?"

"Well, the brig isn't in the channel yet, I fancy!" said Pencroft.

"But suppose she does come there?" said Harding.

"That's impossible, for she would risk running aground and being lost!"

"It is possible," said Ayrton. "The convicts might profit by the high tide to enter the channel, with the risk of grounding at low tide, it is true; but then, under the fire from her guns, our posts would be no longer tenable."

"Confound them!" exclaimed Pencroft, "it really seems as if the blackguards were preparing to weigh anchor."

"Perhaps we shall be obliged to take refuge in Granite House!" observed Herbert.

"We must wait!" answered Cyrus Harding.

"But Mr. Spilett and Neb?" said Pencroft.

"They will know when it is best to rejoin us. Be ready, Ayrton. It is yours and Spilett's rifles which must speak now."

It was only too true. The *Speedy* was beginning to weigh her anchor, and her intention was evidently to approach the islet. The tide would be rising for an hour and a half, and the ebb current being already weakened, it would be easy for the brig to advance. But as to entering the channel, Pencroft, contrary to Ayrton's opinion, could not believe that she would dare to attempt it.

In the meanwhile, the pirates who occupied the islet had gradually advanced to the opposite shore, and were now only separated from the mainland by the channel.

Being armed with muskets alone, they could do no harm to the settlers, in ambush at the Chimneys and the mouth of the Mercy; but, not knowing the latter to be supplied with long-range rifles, they on their side did not believe themselves to be exposed. Quite uncovered, therefore, they surveyed the islet, and examined the shore.

Their illusion was of short duration. Ayrton's and Gideon Spilett's rifles then spoke, and no doubt imparted some very disagreeable intelligence to two of the convicts, for they fell backward.

Then there was a general helter-skelter. The ten others, not even stopping to pick up their dead or wounded companions, fled to the other side of the islet, tumbled into the boat which had brought them, and pulled away with all their strength.

"Eight less!" exclaimed Pencroft. "Really, one would have thought that Mr. Spilett and Ayrton had given the word to fire together!"

"Gentlemen," said Ayrton, as he reloaded his gun, "this is becoming more serious. The brig is making sail!"

"The anchor is weighed!" exclaimed Pencroft.

"Yes, and she is already moving."

In fact, they could distinctly hear the creaking of the windlass. The *Speedy* was at first held by her anchor; then, when that had been raised, she began to drift toward the shore. The wind was blowing from the sea; the jib and the foretopsail were hoisted, and the vessel gradually approached the island.

From the two posts of the Mercy and the Chimneys they watched her without giving a sign of life, but not without some emotion. What could be more terrible for the colonists than to be exposed, at a short distance, to the brig's guns, without being able to reply with any effect? How could they then prevent the pirates from landing?

Cyrus Harding felt this strongly, and he asked himself what it would be possible to do. Before long, he would be called upon for his determination. But what was it to be? To shut themselves up in Granite House, to be besieged there, to remain there for weeks, for months even, since they had an abundance of provisions? So far good! But after that? The pirates would not the less be masters of the island, which they would ravage at their pleasure, and in time, they would end by having their revenge on the prisoners in Granite House.

However, one chance yet remained; it was that Bob Harvey, after all, would not venture his ship into the channel, and that he would keep outside the islet. He would be still separated from the coast by half a mile, and at that distance his shot could not be very destructive.

"Never!" repeated Pencroft, "Bob Harvey will never, if he is a good seaman, enter that channel! He knows well that it would risk the brig, if the sea got up ever so little! And what would become of him without his vessel?"

In the meanwhile the brig approached the islet, and it could be seen that she was endeavoring to make the lower end. The breeze was light, and as the current had then lost much of its force, Bob Harvey had absolute command over his vessel.

The route previously followed by the boats had allowed her to reconnoiter the channel, and she boldly entered it.

The pirate's design was now only too evident; he wished to bring her broadside to bear on the Chimneys and from there to reply with shell and ball to the shot which had till then decimated her crew.

Soon the *Speedy* reached the point of the islet; she rounded it with ease; the mainsail was braced up, and the brig hugging the wind, stood across the mouth of the Mercy.

"The scoundrels! they are coming!" said Pencroft.

At that moment, Cyrus Harding, Ayrton, the sailor, and Herbert, were rejoined by Neb and Gideon Spilett.

The reporter and his companion had judged it best to abandon the post at the Mercy, from which they could do nothing against the ship, and they had acted wisely. It was better that the colonists should be together at the moment when they were about to engage in a decisive action. Gideon Spilett and Neb had arrived by dodging behind the rocks, though not without attracting a shower of bullets, which had not, however, reached them.

"Spilett! Neb!" cried the engineer. "You are not wounded?"

"No," answered the reporter, "a few bruises only from the ricochet! But that cursed brig has entered the channel!"

"Yes," replied Pencroft, "and in ten minutes she will have anchored before Granite House!"

"Have you formed any plan, Cyrus?" asked the reporter.

"We must take refuge in Granite House while there is still time, and the convicts cannot see us."

"That is my opinion, too," replied Gideon Spilett, "but once shut up—"

"We must be guided by circumstances," said the engineer.

"Let us be off, then, and make haste!" said the reporter.

"Would you not wish, captain, that Ayrton and I should remain here?" asked the sailor.

"What would be the use of that, Pencroft?" replied Harding. "No. We will not separate!"

There was not a moment to be lost. The colonists left the Chimneys. A bend of the cliff prevented them from being seen by those in the brig, but two or three reports, and the crash of bullets on the rock, told them that the *Speedy* was at no great distance.

To spring into the lift, hoist themselves up to the door of Granite House, where Top and Jup had been shut up since the evening before, to rush into the large room, was the work of a minute only.

It was quite time, for the settlers, through the branches, could see the *Speedy*, surrounded with smoke, gliding up the channel. The firing was incessant, and shot from the four guns struck blindly, both on the Mercy post, although it was not occupied, and on the Chimneys. The rocks were splintered, and cheers accompanied each discharge. However, they were hoping that Granite House would be spared, thanks to Harding's precaution of concealing the windows when a shot, piercing the door, penetrated into the passage.

"We are discovered!" exclaimed Pencroft.

The colonists had not, perhaps, been seen, but it was certain that Bob Harvey had thought proper to send a ball through the suspected foliage which concealed that part of the cliff. Soon he redoubled his attack, when another ball having torn away the leafy screen, disclosed a gaping aperture in the granite.

The colonists' situation was desperate. Their retreat was discovered. They could not oppose any obstacle to these missiles, nor protect the stone, which flew in splinters around them. There was nothing to be done but to take refuge in the upper passage of Granite House, and leave their dwelling to be devastated, when a deep roar was heard, followed by frightful cries!

Cyrus Harding and his companions rushed to one of the windows—

The brig, irresistibly raised on a sort of waterspout, had just split in two, and in less than ten seconds she was swallowed up with all her criminal crew!

IV

She has blown up!" cried Herbert.

"Yes! blown up, just as if Ayrton had set fire to the powder!" returned Pencroft, throwing himself into the lift together with Neb and the lad.

"But what has happened?" asked Gideon Spilett, quite stunned by this unexpected catastrophe.

"Oh! this time, we shall know—" answered the engineer quickly.

"What shall we know?—"

"Later! later! Come, Spilett. The main point is that these pirates have been exterminated!"

And Cyrus Harding, hurrying away the reporter and Ayrton, joined Pencroft, Neb, and Herbert on the beach.

Nothing could be seen of the brig, not even her masts. After having been raised by the waterspout, she had fallen on her side, and had sunk in that position, doubtless in consequence of some enormous leak. But as in that place the channel was not more than twenty feet in depth, it was certain that the sides of the submerged brig would reappear at low water.

A few things from the wreck floated on the surface of the water, a raft could be seen consisting of spare spars, coops of poultry with their occupants still living, boxes and barrels, which gradually came to the surface, after having escaped through the hatchways, but no pieces of the wreck appeared, neither planks from the deck, nor timber from the hull—which rendered the sudden disappearance of the *Speedy* perfectly inexplicable.

However, the two masts, which had been broken and escaped from the shrouds and stays, came up, and with their sails, some furled and the others spread. But it was not necessary to wait for the tide to bring up these riches, and Ayrton and Pencroft jumped into the boat with the intention of towing the pieces of wreck either to the beach or to the islet. But just as they were shoving off, an observation from Gideon Spilett arrested them.

"What about those six convicts who disembarked on the right bank of the Mercy?" said he.

In fact, it would not do to forget that the six men whose boat had gone to pieces on the rocks had landed at Flotsam Point.

They looked in that direction. None of the fugitives were visible. It was probable that, having seen their vessel engulfed in the channel, they had fled into the interior of the island.

"We will deal with them later," said Harding. "As they are armed, they will still be dangerous; but as it is six against six, the chances are equal. To the most pressing business first."

Ayrton and Pencroft pulled vigorously toward the wreck.

The sea was calm and the tide very high, as there had been a new moon but two days before. A whole hour at least would elapse before the hull of the brig could emerge from the water of the channel.

Ayrton and Pencroft were able to fasten the masts and spars by means of ropes, the ends of which were carried to the beach. There, by the united efforts of the settlers the pieces of wreck were hauled up. Then the boat picked up all that was floating, coops, barrels, and boxes, which were immediately carried to the Chimneys.

Several bodies floated also. Among them, Ayrton recognized that of Bob Harvey, which he pointed out to his companion, saying with some emotion,

"That is what I have been, Pencroft."

"But what you are no longer, brave Ayrton!" returned the sailor warmly.

It was singular enough that so few bodies floated. Only five or six were counted, which were already being carried by the current toward the open sea. Very probably the convicts had not had time to escape, and the ship lying over on her side, the greater number of them had remained below. Now the current, by carrying the bodies of these miserable men out to sea, would spare the colonists the sad task of burying them in some corner of their island.

For two hours, Cyrus Harding and his companions were solely occupied in hauling up the spars on to the sand, and then in spreading the sails which were perfectly uninjured, to dry. They spoke little, for they were absorbed in their work, but what thoughts occupied their minds!

The possession of this brig, or rather all that she contained, was a perfect mine of wealth. In fact, a ship is like a little world in miniature, and the stores of the colony would be increased by a large number of useful articles. It would be, on a large scale, equivalent to the chest found at Flotsam Point.

"And besides," thought Pencroft, "why should it be impossible to refloat the brig? If she has only a leak, that may be stopped up; a vessel from three to four hundred tons, why she is a regular ship compared to our *Bonadven-*

ture! And we could go a long distance in her! We could go anywhere we liked! Captain Harding, Ayrton and I must examine her! She would be well worth the trouble!"

In fact, if the brig was still fit to navigate, the colonists' chances of returning to their native land were singularly increased. But, to decide this important question, it was necessary to wait until the tide was quite low, so that every part of the brig's hull might be examined.

When their treasures had been safely conveyed on shore, Harding and his companions agreed to devote some minutes to breakfast. They were almost famished; fortunately, the larder was not far off, and Neb was noted for being an expeditious cook. They breakfasted, therefore, near the Chimneys, and during their repast, as may be supposed, nothing was talked of but the event which had so miraculously saved the colony.

"Miraculous is the word," repeated Pencroft, "for it must be acknowledged that those rascals blew up just at the right moment! Granite House was beginning to be uncomfortable as a habitation!"

"And can you guess, Pencroft," asked the reporter, "how it happened, or what can have occasioned the explosion?"

"Oh! Mr. Spilett, nothing is more simple," answered Pencroft. "A convict vessel is not disciplined like a man-of-war! Convicts are not sailors. Of course the powder-magazine was open, and as they were firing incessantly, some careless or clumsy fellow just blew up the vessel!"

"Captain Harding," said Herbert, "what astonishes me is that the explosion has not produced more effect. The report was not loud, and besides there are so few planks and timbers torn out. It seems as if the ship had rather foundered than blown up."

"Does that astonish you, my boy?" asked the engineer.

"Yes, captain."

"And it astonishes me also, Herbert," replied he, "but when we visit the hull of the brig, we shall no doubt find the explanation of the matter."

"Why, captain," said Pencroft, "you don't suppose that the *Speedy* simply foundered like a ship which has struck on a rock?"

"Why not," observed Neb, "if there are rocks in the channel?"

"Nonsense, Neb," answered Pencroft, "you did not look at the right moment. An instant before she sank, the brig, as I saw perfectly well, rose on an enormous wave, and fell back on her larboard side. Now, if she had only struck, she would have sunk quietly and gone to the bottom like an honest vessel."

"It was just because she was not an honest vessel!" returned Neb.

"Well, we shall soon see, Pencroft," said the engineer.

"We shall soon see," rejoined the sailor, "but I would wager my head there are no rocks in the channel. Look here, captain, to speak candidly, do you mean to say that there is anything marvelous in the occurrence?"

Cyrus Harding did not answer.

"At any rate," said Gideon Spilett, "whether rock or explosion, you will agree, Pencroft, that it occurred just in the nick of time!"

"Yes! yes!" replied the sailor, "but that is not the question. I ask Captain Harding if he sees anything supernatural in all this."

"I cannot say, Pencroft," said the engineer. "That is all the answer I can make."

A reply which did not satisfy Pencroft at all. He stuck to "an explosion," and did not wish to give it up. He would never consent to admit that in that channel, with its fine sandy bed, just like the beach, which he had often crossed at low water, there could be an unknown rock.

And besides, at the time the brig foundered, it was high water, that is to say, there was enough water to carry the vessel clear over any rocks which would not be uncovered at low tide. Therefore, there could not have been a collision. Therefore, the vessel had not struck. So she had blown up.

And it must be confessed that the sailor's arguments were reasonable.

Toward half-past one, the colonists embarked in the boat to visit the wreck. It was to be regretted that the brig's two boats had not been saved; but one, as has been said, had gone to pieces at the mouth of the Mercy, and was absolutely useless; the other had disappeared when the brig went down, and had not again been seen, having doubtless been crushed.

The hull of the *Speedy* was just beginning to issue from the water. The brig was lying right over on her side, for her masts being broken, pressed down by the weight of the ballast displaced by the shock, the keel was visible along her whole length. She had been regularly turned over by the inexplicable but frightful submarine action, which had been at the same time manifested by an enormous waterspout.

The settlers rowed round the hull, and in proportion as the tide went down, they could ascertain, if not the cause which had occasioned the catastrophe, at least the effect produced.

Toward the bows, on both sides of the keel, seven or eight feet from the beginning of the stem, the sides of the brig were frightfully torn. Over a length of at least twenty feet there opened two large leaks, which would be impossible to stop up. Not only had the copper sheathing and the planks disappeared, reduced, no doubt, to powder, but also the ribs, the iron bolts, and treenails which united them. From the entire length of the hull to the stern the false keel had been separated with an unaccountable violence, and the keel itself, torn from the car-line in several places, was split in all its length.

"I've a notion!" exclaimed Pencroft, "that this vessel will be difficult to get afloat again."

"It will be impossible," said Ayrton.

"At any rate," observed Gideon Spilett to the sailor, "the explosion, if there has been one, has produced singular effects! It has split the lower part of the hull, instead of blowing up the deck and topsides! These great rents appear rather to have been made by a rock than by the explosion of a powder-magazine."

"There is not a rock in the channel!" answered the sailor. "I will admit anything you like, except the rock."

"Let us try to penetrate into the interior of the brig," said the engineer; "perhaps we shall then know what to think of the cause of her destruction."

This was the best thing to be done, and it was agreed, besides, to take an inventory of all the treasures on board, and to arrange their preservation.

Access to the interior of the brig was now easy. The tide was still going down and the deck was practicable. The ballast, composed of heavy masses of iron, had broken through in several places. The noise of the sea could be heard as it rushed out at the holes in the hull.

Cyrus Harding and his companions, hatchets in hand, advanced along the shattered deck. Cases of all sorts encumbered it, and, as they had been but a very short time in the water, their contents were perhaps uninjured.

They then busied themselves in placing all this cargo in safety. The water would not return for several hours, and these hours must be employed in the most profitable way. Ayrton and Pencroft had, at the entrance made in the hull, discovered tackle, which would serve to hoist up the barrels and chests. The boat received them and transported them to the shore. They took the articles as they came, intending to sort them afterward.

At any rate, the settlers saw at once, with extreme satisfaction, that the brig possessed a very varied cargo—an assortment of all sorts of articles, utensils, manufactured goods, and tools—such as the ships which make the great coasting-trade of Polynesia are usually laden with. It was probable that they would find a little of everything, and they agreed that it was exactly what was necessary for the colony of Lincoln Island.

However—and Cyrus Harding observed it in silent astonishment—not only, as has been said, had the hull of the brig enormously suffered from the shock, whatever it was, that had occasioned the catastrophe, but the interior arrangements had been destroyed, especially toward the bows. Partitions and stanchions were smashed, as if some tremendous shell had burst in the interior of the brig. The colonists could easily go fore and aft, after having removed the cases as they were extricated. They were not heavy bales, which would have been difficult to remove, but simple packages, of which the stowage, besides, was no longer recognizable.

The colonists then reached the stern of the brig—the part formerly surmounted by the poop. It was there that, following Ayrton's directions, they must look for the powder-magazine. Cyrus Harding thought that it had not exploded; that it was possible some barrels might be saved, and that the powder, which is usually enclosed in metal coverings, might not have suffered from contact with the water.

This, in fact, was just what had happened. They extricated from among a large number of shot twenty barrels, the insides of which were lined with copper. Pencroft was convinced by the evidence of his own eyes that the destruction of the *Speedy* could not be attributed to an explosion. That part of the hull in which the magazine was situated was, moreover, that which had suffered least.

"It may be so," said the obstinate sailor; "but as to a rock, there is not one in the channel!"

"Then, how did it happen?" asked Herbert.

"I don't know," answered Pencroft, "Captain Harding doesn't know, and nobody knows or ever will know!"

Several hours had passed during these researches, and the tide began to flow. Work must be suspended for the present. There was no fear of the brig being carried away by the sea, for she was already fixed as firmly as if moored by her anchors.

They could, therefore, without inconvenience, wait until the next day to resume operations; but, as to the vessel itself, she was doomed, and it would be best to hasten to save the remains of her hull, as she would not be long in disappearing in the quicksands of the channel.

It was now five o'clock in the evening. It had been a hard day's work for the men. They ate with good appetite, and notwithstanding their fatigue, they could not resist, after dinner, their desire of inspecting the cases which composed the cargo of the *Speedy*.

Most of them contained clothes, which, as may be believed, was well received. There were enough to clothe a whole colony—linen for every one's use, shoes for every one's feet.

"We are too rich!" exclaimed Pencroft, "But what are we going to do with all this?"

And every moment burst forth the hurrahs of the delighted sailor when he caught sight of the barrels of gunpowder, firearms and sidearms, balls of cotton, implements of husbandry, carpenter's, joiner's, and blacksmith's tools, and boxes of all kinds of seeds, not in the least injured by their short sojourn in the water. Ah, two years before, how these things would have been prized! And now, even though the industrious colonists had provided themselves with tools, these treasures would find their use.

There was no want of space in the storerooms of Granite House, but that daytime would not allow them to stow away the whole. It would not do also to forget that the six survivors of the *Speedy*'s crew had landed on the island, for they were in all probability scoundrels of the deepest dye, and it was necessary that the colonists should be on their guard against them. Although the bridges over the Mercy were raised, the convicts would not be stopped by a river or a stream and, rendered desperate, these wretches would be capable of anything.

They would see later what plan it would be best to follow; but in the meantime it was necessary to mount guard over cases and packages heaped up near the Chimneys, and thus the settlers employed themselves in turn during the night.

The morning came, however, without the convicts having attempted any attack. Master Jup and Top, on guard at the foot of Granite House, would have quickly given the alarm. The three following days—the 19th, 20th, and 21st of October—were employed in saving everything of value, or of any use whatever, either from the cargo or rigging of the brig. At low tide they overhauled the hold—at high tide they stowed away the rescued articles. A great part of the copper sheathing had been torn from the hull, which every day sank lower. But before the sand had swallowed the heavy things which had fallen through the bottom, Ayrton and Pencroft, diving to the bed of the channel, recovered the chains and anchors of the brig, the iron of her ballast, and even four guns, which, floated by means of empty casks, were brought to shore.

It may be seen that the arsenal of the colony had gained by the wreck, as well as the storerooms of Granite House. Pencroft, always enthusiastic in his projects, already spoke of constructing a battery to command the channel and the mouth of the river. With four guns, he engaged to prevent any fleet, "however powerful it might be," from venturing into the waters of Lincoln Island!

In the meantime, when nothing remained of the brig but a useless hulk, bad weather came on, which soon finished her. Cyrus Harding had intended to blow her up, so as to collect the remains on the shore, but a strong gale from the northeast and a heavy sea compelled him to economize his powder.

In fact, on the night of the 23rd, the hull entirely broke up, and some of the wreck was cast up on the beach.

As to the papers on board, it is useless to say that, although he carefully searched the lockers of the poop, Harding did not discover any trace of them. The pirates had evidently destroyed everything that concerned either the captain or the owners of the *Speedy*, and, as the name of her port was not painted on her counter, there was nothing which would tell them her nationality. However, by the shape of her boats Ayrton and Pencroft believed that the brig was of English build.

A week after the catastrophe—or, rather, after the fortunate, though inexplicable, event to which the colony owed its preservation—nothing more could be seen of the vessel, even at low tide. The wreck had disappeared, and Granite House was enriched by nearly all it had contained.

However, the mystery which enveloped its strange destruction would doubtless never have been cleared away if, on the 30th of November, Neb, strolling on the beach, had not found a piece of a thick iron cylinder, bearing traces of explosion. The edges of this cylinder were twisted and broken, as if they had been subjected to the action of some explosive substance.

Neb brought this piece of metal to his master, who was then occupied with his companions in the workshop of the Chimneys.

Cyrus Harding examined the cylinder attentively, then, turning to Pencroft,

"You persist, my friend," said he, "in maintaining that the *Speedy* was not lost in consequence of a collision?"

"Yes, captain," answered the sailor. "You know as well as I do that there are no rocks in the channel."

"But suppose she had run against this piece of iron?" said the engineer, showing the broken cylinder.

"What, that bit of pipe!" exclaimed Pencroft in a tone of perfect incredulity.

"My friends," resumed Harding, "you remember that before she foundered the brig rose on the summit of a regular waterspout?"

"Yes, captain," replied Herbert.

"Well, would you like to know what occasioned that waterspout? It was this," said the engineer, holding up the broken tube.

"That?" returned Pencroft.

"Yes! This cylinder is all that remains of a torpedo!"

"A torpedo!" exclaimed the engineer's companions.

"And who put the torpedo there?" demanded Pencroft, who did not like to yield.

"All that I can tell you is, that it was not I," answered Cyrus Harding; "but it was there, and you have been able to judge of its incomparable power!"

V

So, then, all was explained by the submarine explosion of this torpedo. Cyrus Harding could not be mistaken, as, during the war of the Union, he had had occasion to try these terrible engines of destruction. It was under the action of this cylinder, charged with some explosive substance, nitro-glycerine, picrate, or some other material of the same nature, that the water of the channel had been raised like a dome, the bottom of the brig crushed in, and she had sunk instantly, the damage done to her hull being so considerable that it was impossible to refloat her. The *Speedy* had not been able to withstand a torpedo that would have destroyed an ironclad as easily as a fishing-boat!

Yes! all was explained, everything—except the presence of the torpedo in the waters of the channel!

"My friends, then," said Cyrus Harding, "we can no longer be in doubt as to the presence of a mysterious being, a castaway like us, perhaps, abandoned on our island, and I say this in order that Ayrton may be acquainted with all the strange events which have occurred during these two years. Who this beneficent stranger is, whose intervention has, so fortunately for us, been manifested on many occasions, I cannot imagine. What his object can be in acting thus, in concealing himself after rendering us so many services, I cannot understand: But his services are not the less real, and are of such a nature that only a man possessed of prodigious power, could render them. Ayrton is indebted to him as much as we are, for, if it was the stranger who saved me from the waves after the fall from the balloon, evidently it was he who wrote the document, who placed the bottle in the channel, and who has made known to us the situation of our companion. I will add that it was he who guided that chest, provided with everything we wanted, and stranded it on Flotsam Point; that it was he who lighted that fire on the heights of the island, which permitted you to land; that it was he who fired that bullet found in the body of the peccary; that it was he who plunged that torpedo into the channel, which destroyed the brig; in a word, that all those inexplicable events, for which we could not assign a reason, are due to this mysterious being. Therefore, whoever he may be, whether shipwrecked, or exiled on our island, we shall be ungrateful, if we think ourselves freed from gratitude toward him. We have contracted a debt, and I hope that we shall one day pay it."

"You are right in speaking thus, my dear Cyrus," replied Gideon Spilett. "Yes, there is an almost all-powerful being, hidden in some part of the island, and whose influence has been singularly useful to our colony. I will add that the unknown appears to possess means of action which border on the supernatural, if in the events of practical life the supernatural were recognizable. Is it he who is in secret communication with us by the well in Granite House, and has he thus a knowledge of all our plans? Was it he who threw us that bottle, when the vessel made her first cruise? Was it he who threw Top out of the lake, and killed the dugong? Was it he, who as everything leads us to believe, saved you from the waves, and that under circumstances in which any one else would not have been able to act? If it was he, he possesses a power which renders him master of the elements."

The reporter's reasoning was just, and every one felt it to be so.

"Yes," rejoined Cyrus Harding, "if the intervention of a human being is not more questionable for us, I agree that he has at his disposal means of action beyond those possessed by humanity. There is a mystery still, but if we discover the man, the mystery will be discovered also. The question, then, is, ought we to respect the incognito of this generous being, or ought we to do everything to find him out? What is your opinion on the matter?"

"My opinion," said Pencroft, "is that, whoever he may be, he is a brave man, and he has my esteem!"

"Be it so," answered Harding, "but that is not an answer, Pencroft."

"Master," then said Neb, "my idea is, that we may search as long as we like for this gentleman whom you are talking about, but that we shall not discover him till he pleases."

"That's not bad, what you say, Neb," observed Pencroft.

"I am of Neb's opinion," said Gideon Spilett, "but that is no reason for not attempting the adventure. Whether we find this mysterious being or not, we shall at least have fulfilled our duty toward him."

"And you, my boy, give us your opinion," said the engineer, turning to Herbert.

"Oh," cried Herbert, his countenance full of animation, "how I should like to thank him, he who saved you first, and who has now saved us!"

"Of course, my boy," replied Pencroft, "so would I and all of us. I am not inquisitive, but I would give one of my eyes to see this individual face to face! It seems to me that he must be handsome, tall, strong, with a splendid beard, radiant hair, and that he must be seated on clouds, a great ball in his hands!"

"But, Pencroft," answered Spilett, "you are describing a picture of the Creator."

"Possibly, Mr. Spilett," replied the sailor, "but that is how I imagine him!"

"And you, Ayrton?" asked the engineer.

"Captain Harding," replied Ayrton, "I can give you no better advice in this matter. Whatever you do will be best; when you wish me to join you in your researches, I am ready to follow you."

"I thank you, Ayrton," answered Cyrus Harding, "but I should like a more direct answer to the question I put to you. You are our companion; you have already endangered your life several times for us, and you, as well as the rest, ought to be consulted in the matter of any important decision. Speak, therefore."

"Captain Harding," replied Ayrton, "I think that we ought to do everything to discover this unknown benefactor. Perhaps he is alone. Perhaps he is suffering. Perhaps he has a life to be renewed. I, too, as you said, have a debt of gratitude to pay him. It was he, it could be only he who must have come to Tabor Island, who found there the wretch you knew, and who made known to you that there was an unfortunate man there to be saved. Therefore it is, thanks to him, that I have become a man again. No, I will never forget him!"

"That is settled, then," said Cyrus Harding. "We will begin our researches as soon as possible. We will not leave a corner of the island unexplored. We will search into its most secret recesses, and will hope that our unknown friend will pardon us in consideration of our intentions!"

For several days the colonists were actively employed in haymaking and the harvest. Before putting their project of exploring the yet unknown parts of the island into execution, they wished to get all possible work finished. It was also the time for collecting the various vegetables from the Tabor Island plants. All was stowed away, and happily there was no want of room in Granite House, in which they might have housed all the treasures of the island. The products of the colony were there, methodically arranged, and in a safe place, as may be believed, sheltered as much from animals as from man.

There was no fear of damp in the middle of that thick mass of granite. Many natural excavations situated in the upper passage were enlarged either by pickaxe or mine, and Granite House thus became a general warehouse, containing all the provisions, arms, tools, and spare utensils—in a word, all the stores of the colony.

As to the guns obtained from the brig, they were pretty pieces of ordnance, which, at Pencroft's entreaty, were hoisted by means of tackle and pulleys, right up into Granite House; embrasures were made between the windows, and the shining muzzles of the guns could soon be seen through the granite cliff. From this height they commanded all Union Bay. It was like a little Gibraltar, and any vessel anchored off the islet would inevitably be exposed to the fire of this aerial battery.

"Captain," said Pencroft one day, it was the 8th of November, "now that our fortifications are finished, it would be a good thing if we tried the range of our guns."

"Do you think that is useful?" asked the engineer.

"It is more than useful, it is necessary! Without that how are we to know to what distance we can send one of those pretty shot with which we are provided?"

"Try them, Pencroft," replied the engineer. "However, I think that in making the experiment, we ought to employ, not the ordinary powder, the supply of which, I think, should remain untouched, but the pyroxyle which will never fail us."

"Can the cannon support the shock of the pyroxyle?" asked the reporter, who was not less anxious than Pencroft to try the artillery of Granite House.

"I believe so. However," added the engineer, "we will be prudent."

The engineer was right in thinking that the guns were of excellent make. Made of forged steel, and breech-loaders, they ought consequently to be able to bear a considerable charge, and also have an enormous range. In fact, as regards practical effect, the transit described by the ball ought to be as extended as possible, and this tension could only be obtained under the condition that the projectile should be impelled with a very great initial velocity.

"Now," said Harding to his companions, "the initial velocity is in proportion to the quantity of powder used. In the fabrication of these pieces, everything depends on employing a metal with the highest possible power of resistance, and steel is incontestably that metal of all others which resists the best. I have, therefore, reason to believe that our guns will bear without risk the expansion of the pyroxyle gas, and will give excellent results."

"We shall be a great deal more certain of that when we have tried them!" answered Pencroft.

It is unnecessary to say that the four cannons were in perfect order. Since they had been taken from the water, the sailor had bestowed great care upon them. How many hours he had spent, in rubbing, greasing, and polishing them, and in cleaning the mechanism! And now the pieces were as brilliant as if they had been on board a frigate of the United States Navy.

On this day, therefore, in presence of all the members of the colony, including Master Jup and Top, the four cannon were successively tried. They were charged with pyroxyle, taking into consideration its explosive power, which, as has been said, is four times that of ordinary powder: the projectile to be fired was cylindroconic.

Pencroft, holding the end of the quick-match, stood ready to fire.

At Harding's signal, he fired. The shot, passing over the islet, fell into the sea at a distance which could not be calculated with exactitude.

The second gun was pointed at the rocks at the end of Flotsam Point, and the shot striking a sharp rock nearly three miles from Granite House, made it fly into splinters. It was Herbert who had pointed this gun and fired it, and very proud he was of his first shot. Pencroft only was prouder than he! Such a shot, the honor of which belonged to his dear boy.

The third shot, aimed this time at the downs forming the upper side of Union Bay, struck the sand at a distance of four miles, then having ricocheted, was lost in the sea in a cloud of spray.

For the fourth piece Cyrus Harding slightly increased the charge, so as to try its extreme range. Then, all standing aside for fear of its bursting, the match was lighted by means of a long cord.

A tremendous report was heard, but the piece had held good, and the colonists rushing to the windows, saw the shot graze the rocks of Mandible Cape, nearly five miles from Granite House, and disappear in Shark Gulf.

"Well, captain," exclaimed Pencroft, whose cheers might have rivaled the reports themselves, "what do you say of our battery? All the pirates in the Pacific have only to present themselves before Granite House! Not one can land there now without our permission!"

"Believe me, Pencroft," replied the engineer, "it would be better not to have to make the experiment."

"Well," said the sailor, "what ought to be done with regard to those six villains who are roaming about the island? Are we to leave them to overrun our forests, our fields, our plantations? These pirates are regular jaguars, and it seems to me we ought not to hesitate to treat them as such! What do you think, Ayrton?" added Pencroft, turning to his companion.

Ayrton hesitated at first to reply, and Cyrus Harding regretted that Pencroft had so thoughtlessly put this question. And he was much moved when Ayrton replied in a humble tone,

"I have been one of those jaguars, Mr. Pencroft. I have no right to speak."

And with a slow step he walked away.

Pencroft understood.

"What a brute I am!" he exclaimed. "Poor Ayrton! He has as much right to speak here as any one!"

"Yes," said Gideon Spilett, "but his reserve does him honor, and it is right to respect the feeling which he has about his sad past."

"Certainly, Mr. Spilett," answered the sailor, "and there is no fear of my doing so again. I would rather bite my tongue off than cause Ayrton any pain! But to return to the question. It seems to me that these ruffians have no right to any pity, and that we ought to rid the island of them as soon as possible."

"Is that your opinion, Pencroft?" asked the engineer.

"Quite my opinion."

"And before hunting them mercilessly, you would not wait until they had committed some fresh act of hostility against us?"

"Isn't what they have done already enough?" asked Pencroft, who did not understand these scruples.

"They may adopt other sentiments!" said Harding, "and perhaps repent."

"They repent!" exclaimed the sailor, shrugging his shoulders.

"Pencroft, think of Ayrton!" said Herbert, taking the sailor's hand. "He became an honest man again!"

Pencroft looked at his companions one after the other. He had never thought of his proposal being met with any objection. His rough nature could not allow that they ought to come to terms with the rascals who had landed on the island with Bob Harvey's accomplices, the murderers of the crew of the *Speedy*, and he looked upon them as wild beasts which ought to be destroyed without delay and without remorse.

"Come!" said he. "Everybody is against me! You wish to be generous to those villains! Very well; I hope we mayn't repent it!"

"What danger shall we run," said Herbert, "if we take care to be always on our guard?"

"Hum!" observed the reporter, who had not given any decided opinion. "They are six and well armed. If they each lay hid in a corner, and each fired at one of us, they would soon be masters of the colony!"

"Why have they not done so?" said Herbert. "No doubt because it was not their interest to do it. Besides, we are six also."

"Well, well!" replied Pencroft, whom no reasoning could have convinced. "Let us leave these good people to do what they like, and don't think anything more about them!"

"Come, Pencroft," said Neb, "don't make yourself out so bad as all that! Suppose one of these unfortunate men were here before you, within good range of your guns, you would not fire."

"I would fire on him as I would on a mad dog, Neb," replied Pencroft coldly.

"Pencroft," said the engineer, "you have always shown much deference to my advice; will you, in this matter, yield to me?"

"I will do as you please, Captain Harding," answered the sailor, who was not at all convinced.

"Very well, wait, and we will not attack them unless we are attacked first."

Thus their behavior toward the pirates was agreed upon, although Pencroft augured nothing good from it. They were not to attack them, but were to be on their guard. After all, the island was large and fertile. If any sentiment of honesty yet remained in the bottom of their hearts, these wretches might perhaps be reclaimed. Was it not their interest in the situation in which they found themselves to begin a new life? At any rate, for humanity's sake alone, it would be right to wait. The colonists would no longer as before, be able to go and come without fear. Hitherto they had only wild beasts to guard against, and now six convicts of the worst description, perhaps, were roaming over their island. It was serious, certainly, and to less brave men, it would have been security lost! No matter! At present, the colonists had reason on their side against Pencroft. Would they be right in the future? That remained to be seen.

VI

However, the chief business of the colonists was to make that complete exploration of the island which had been decided upon, and which would have two objects: to discover the mysterious being whose existence was now indisputable, and at the same time to find out what had become of the pirates, what retreat they had chosen, what sort of life they were leading, and what was to be feared from them. Cyrus Harding wished to set out without delay; but as the expedition would be of some days' duration, it appeared best to load the cart with different materials and tools in order to facilitate the organization of the encampments. One of the onagers, however, having hurt its leg, could not be harnessed at present, and a few days' rest was necessary. The departure was, therefore, put off for a week, until the 20th of November. The month of November in this latitude corresponds to the month of May in the northern zones. It was, therefore, the fine season. The sun was entering the Tropic of Capricorn, and gave the longest days in the year. The time was, therefore, very favorable for the projected expedition, which, if it did not accomplish its principal object, would at any rate be fruitful in discoveries, especially of natural productions, since Harding proposed to explore those dense Forests of the Far West, which stretched to the extremity of the Serpentine Peninsula.

During the nine days which preceded their departure, it was agreed that the work on Prospect Heights should be finished off.

Moreover, it was necessary for Ayrton to return to the corral, where the domesticated animals required his care. It was decided that he should spend two days there, and return to Granite House after having liberally supplied the stables.

As he was about to start, Harding asked him if he would not like one of them to accompany him, observing that the island was less safe than formerly. Ayrton replied that this was unnecessary, as he was enough for the work, and that besides he apprehended no danger. If anything occurred at the corral, or in the neighborhood, he could instantly warn the colonists by sending a telegram to Granite House.

Ayrton departed at dawn on the 9th, taking the cart drawn by one onager, and two hours after, the electric wire announced that he had found all in order at the corral.

During these two days Harding busied himself in executing a project which would completely guard Granite House against any surprise. It was necessary to completely conceal the opening of the old outlet, which was already walled up and partly hidden under grass and plants, at the southern angle of Lake Grant. Nothing was easier, since if the level of the lake was raised two or three feet, the opening would be quite beneath it. Now, to raise this level they had only to establish a dam at the two openings made by the lake, and by which were fed Creek Glycerine and Falls River.

The colonists worked with a will, and the two dams which besides did not exceed eight feet in width by three in height, were rapidly erected by means of well-cemented blocks of stone.

This work finished, it would have been impossible to guess that at that part of the lake, there existed a subterranean passage through which the overflow of the lake formerly escaped.

Of course the little stream which fed the reservoir of Granite House and worked the lift, had been carefully preserved, and the water could not fail. The lift once raised, this sure and comfortable retreat would be safe from any surprise.

This work had been so quickly done, that Pencroft, Gideon Spilett, and Herbert found time to make an expedition to Port Balloon. The sailor was very anxious to know if the little creek in which the *Bonadventure* was moored, had been visited by the convicts.

"These gentlemen," he observed, "landed on the south coast, and if they followed the shore, it is to be feared that they may have discovered the little harbor, and in that case, I wouldn't give half-a-dollar for our *Bonadventure.*"

Pencroft's apprehensions were not without foundation, and a visit to Port Balloon appeared to be very desirable. The sailor and his companions set off on the 10th of November, after dinner, well armed. Pencroft, ostentatiously slipping two bullets into each barrel of his rifle, shook his head in a way which betokened nothing good to any one who approached too near him, whether "man or beast," as he said. Gideon Spilett and Herbert also took their guns, and about three o'clock all three left Granite House.

Neb accompanied them to the turn of the Mercy, and after they had crossed, he raised the bridge. It was agreed that a gunshot should announce the colonists' return, and that at the signal Neb should return and re-establish the communication between the two banks of the river.

The little band advanced directly along the road which led to the southern coast of the island. This was only a distance of three miles and a half, but Gideon Spilett and his companions took two hours to traverse it. They examined all the border of the road, the thick forest, as well as Tadorn's Fens. They found no trace of the fugitives who, no doubt, not having yet discovered the number of the colonists, or the means of defense which they had at their disposal, had gained the less accessible parts of the island.

Arrived at Port Balloon, Pencroft saw with extreme satisfaction that the *Bonadventure* was tranquilly floating in the narrow creek. However, Port Balloon was so well hidden among high rocks, that it could scarcely be discovered either from the land or the sea.

"Come," said Pencroft, "the blackguards have not been there yet. Long grass suits reptiles best, and evidently we shall find them in the Far West."

"And it's very lucky, for if they had found the *Bonadventure,*" added Herbert, "they would have gone off in her, and we should have been prevented from returning to Tabor Island."

"Indeed," remarked the reporter, "it will be important to take a document there which will make known the situation of Lincoln Island, and Ayrton's new residence, in case the Scotch yacht returns to fetch him."

"Well, the *Bonadventure* is always there, Mr. Spilett," answered the sailor. "She and her crew are ready to start at a moment's notice!"

"I think, Pencroft, that that is a thing to be done after our exploration of the island is finished. It is possible after all that the stranger, if we manage to find him, may know as much about Tabor Island as about Lincoln Island. Do not forget that he is certainly the author of the document, and he may, perhaps, know how far we may count on the return of the yacht!"

"But!" exclaimed Pencroft, "who in the world can he be? The fellow knows us and we know nothing about him! If he is a simple castaway, why should he conceal himself! We are honest men, I suppose, and the society of honest men isn't unpleasant to any one. Did he come here voluntarily? Can he leave the island if he likes? Is he here still? Will he remain any longer?"

Chatting thus, Pencroft, Gideon Spilett, and Herbert got on board and looked about the deck of the *Bonadventure*. All at once, the sailor having examined the bitts to which the cable of the anchor was secured,

"Hallo," he cried, "this is queer!"

"What is the matter, Pencroft?" asked the reporter.

"The matter is, that it was not I who made this knot!"

And Pencroft showed a rope which fastened the cable to the bitt itself.

"What, it was not you?" asked Gideon Spilett.

"No! I can swear to it. This is a reef knot, and I always make a running bowline."

"You must be mistaken, Pencroft."

"I am not mistaken!" declared the sailor. "My hand does it so naturally, and one's hand is never mistaken!"

"Then can the convicts have been on board?" asked Herbert.

"I know nothing about that," answered Pencroft, "but what is certain, is that some one has weighed the *Bonadventure*'s anchor and dropped it again! And look here, here is another proof! The cable of the anchor has been run out, and its service is no longer at the hawse-hole. I repeat that some one has been using our vessel!"

"But if the convicts had used her, they would have pillaged her, or rather gone off with her."

"Gone off! where to—to Tabor Island?" replied Pencroft. "Do you think they would risk themselves in a boat of such small tonnage?"

"We must, besides, be sure that they know of the islet," rejoined the reporter.

"However that may be," said the sailor, "as sure as my name is Bonadventure Pencroft, of the Vineyard, our *Bonadventure* has sailed without us!"

The sailor was positive that neither Gideon Spilett nor Herbert could dispute his statement. It was evident that the vessel had been moved, more or less, since Pencroft had brought her to Port Balloon. As to the sailor, he had not the slightest doubt that the anchor had been raised and then dropped again. Now, what was the use of these two maneuvers, unless the vessel had been employed in some expedition?

"But how was it we did not see the *Bonadventure* pass in the sight of the island?" observed the reporter, who was anxious to bring forward every possible objection.

"Why, Mr. Spilett," replied the sailor, "they would only have to start in the night with a good breeze, and they would be out of sight of the island in two hours."

"Well," resumed Gideon Spilett, "I ask again, what object could the convicts have had in using the *Bonadventure,* and why, after they had made use of her, should they have brought her back to port?"

"Why, Mr. Spilett," replied the sailor, "we must put that among the unaccountable things, and not think anything more about it. The chief thing is that the *Bonadventure* was there, and she is there now. Only, unfortunately, if the convicts take her a second time, we shall very likely not find her again in her place!"

"Then, Pencroft," said Herbert, "would it not be wisest to bring the *Bonadventure* off to Granite House?"

"Yes and no," answered Pencroft, "or rather no. The mouth of the Mercy is a bad place for a vessel, and the sea is heavy there."

"But by hauling her up on the sand, to the foot of the Chimneys?"

"Perhaps yes," replied Pencroft. "At any rate, since we must leave Granite House for a long expedition, I think the *Bonadventure* will be safer here during our absence, and we shall do best to leave her here until the island is rid of these blackguards."

"That is exactly my opinion," said the reporter. "At any rate in the event of bad weather, she will not be exposed here as she would be at the mouth of the Mercy."

"But suppose the convicts pay her another visit," said Herbert.

"Well, my boy," replied Pencroft, "not finding her here, they would not be long in finding her on the sands of Granite House, and, during our absence, nothing could hinder them from seizing her! I agree, therefore, with Mr. Spilett, that she must be left in Port Balloon. But, if on our return we have not rid the island of those rascals, it will be prudent to bring our boat to Granite House, until the time when we need not fear any unpleasant visits."

"That's settled. Let us be off," said the reporter.

Pencroft, Herbert, and Gideon Spilett, on their return to Granite House, told the engineer all that had passed, and the latter approved of their arrangements both for the present and the future. He also promised the sailor that he would study that part of the channel situated between the islet and the coast, so as to ascertain if it would not be possible to make an artificial harbor there by means of dams. In this way, the *Bonadventure* would be always within reach, under the eyes of the colonists, and if necessary, under lock and key.

That evening a telegram was sent to Ayrton, requesting him to bring from the corral a couple of goats, which Neb wished to acclimatize to the plateau. Singularly enough, Ayrton did not acknowledge the receipt of the dispatch, as he was accustomed to do. This could not but astonish the engineer. But it might be that Ayrton was not at that moment in the corral, or even that he was on his way back to Granite House. In fact, two days had already passed since his departure, and it had been decided that on the evening of the 10th or at the latest the morning of the 11th, he should return. The colonists waited, therefore, for Ayrton to appear on Prospect Heights. Neb and Herbert even watched at the bridge so as to be ready to lower it the moment their companion presented himself.

But up to ten in the evening, there were no signs of Ayrton. It was, therefore, judged best to send a fresh dispatch, requiring an immediate reply.

The bell of the telegraph at Granite House remained mute.

The colonists' uneasiness was great. What had happened? Was Ayrton no longer at the corral, or if he was still there, had he no longer control over his movements? Could they go to the corral in this dark night?

They consulted. Some wished to go, the others to remain.

"But," said Herbert, "perhaps some accident has happened to the telegraphic apparatus, so that it works no longer?"

"That may be," said the reporter.

"Wait till to-morrow," replied Cyrus Harding. "It is possible, indeed, that Ayrton has not received our dispatch, or even that we have not received his."

They waited, of course not without some anxiety.

At dawn of day, the 11th of November, Harding again sent the electric current along the wire and received no reply.

He tried again: the same result.

"Off to the corral," said he.

"And well armed!" added Pencroft.

It was immediately decided that Granite House should not be left alone and that Neb should remain there. After having accompanied his friends to Creek Glycerine, he raised the bridge; and waiting behind a tree, he watched for the return of either his companions or Ayrton.

In the event of the pirates presenting themselves and attempting to force the passage, he was to endeavor to stop them by firing on them, and as a last resource he was to take refuge in Granite House, where, the lift once raised, he would be in safety.

Cyrus Harding, Gideon Spilett, Herbert, and Pencroft were to repair to the corral, and if they did not find Ayrton, search the neighboring woods.

At six o'clock in the morning, the engineer and his three companions had passed Creek Glycerine, and Neb posted himself behind a small mound crowned by several dragon-trees, on the left bank of the stream.

The colonists, after leaving the plateau of Prospect Heights, immediately took the road to the corral. They shouldered their guns, ready to fire on the slightest hostile demonstration. The two rifles and the two guns had been loaded with ball.

The wood was thick on each side of the road and might easily have concealed the convicts, who owing to their weapons would have been really formidable.

The colonists walked rapidly and in silence. Top preceded them, sometimes running on the road, sometimes taking a ramble into the wood, but always quiet and not appearing to fear anything unusual. And they could be sure that the faithful dog would not allow them to be surprised, but would bark at the least appearance of danger.

Cyrus Harding and his companions followed beside the road the wire which connected the corral with Granite House. After walking for nearly two miles, they had not as yet discovered any explanation of the difficulty. The posts were in good order, the wire regularly extended. However, at that moment the engineer observed that the wire appeared to be slack, and on arriving at post No. 74, Herbert, who was in advance, stopped, exclaiming,

"The wire is broken!"

His companions hurried forward and arrived at the spot where the lad was standing. The post was rooted up and lying across the path. The unexpected explanation of the difficulty was here, and it was evident that the dispatches from Granite House had not been received at the corral, nor those from the corral at Granite House.

"It wasn't the wind that blew down this post," observed Pencroft.

"No," replied Gideon Spilett. "The earth has been dug up around its foot, and it has been torn up by the hand of man."

"Besides, the wire is broken," added Herbert, showing that the wire had been snapped.

"Is the fracture recent?" asked Harding.

"Yes," answered Herbert, "it has certainly been done quite lately."

"To the corral! to the corral!" exclaimed the sailor.

The colonists were now halfway between Granite House and the corral, having still two miles and a half to go. They pressed forward with redoubled speed.

Indeed, it was to be feared that some serious accident had occurred in the corral. No doubt, Ayrton might have sent a telegram which had not arrived, but this was not the reason why his companions were so uneasy, for, a more unaccountable circumstance, Ayrton, who had promised to return the evening before, had not reappeared. In short, it was not without a motive that all communication had been stopped between the corral and Granite House, and who but the convicts could have any interest in interrupting this communication?

The settlers hastened on, their hearts oppressed with anxiety. They were sincerely attached to their new companion. Were they to find him struck down by the hands of those of whom he was formerly the leader?

Soon they arrived at the place where the road led along the side of the little stream which flowed from the Red Creek and watered the meadows of the corral. They then moderated their pace so that they should not be out of breath at the moment when a struggle might be necessary. Their guns were in their hands ready cocked. The forest was watched on every side. Top uttered sullen groans which were rather ominous.

At last the palisade appeared through the trees. No trace of any damage could be seen. The gate was shut as usual. Deep silence reigned in the corral. Neither the accustomed bleating of the sheep nor Ayrton's voice could be heard.

"Let us enter," said Cyrus Harding.

And the engineer advanced, while his companions, keeping watch about twenty paces behind him, were ready to fire at a moment's notice.

Harding raised the inner latch of the gate and was about to push it back, when Top barked loudly. A report sounded and was responded to by a cry of pain.

Herbert, struck by a bullet, lay stretched on the ground.

VII

At Herbert's cry, Pencroft, letting his gun fall, rushed toward him.

"They have killed him!" he cried. "My boy! They have killed him!"

Cyrus Harding and Gideon Spilett ran to Herbert.

The reporter listened to ascertain if the poor lad's heart was still beating.

"He lives," said he, "but he must be carried—"

"To Granite House? that is impossible!" replied the engineer.

"Into the corral, then!" said Pencroft.

"In a moment," said Harding.

And he ran around the left corner of the palisade. There he found a convict, who aiming at him, sent a ball through his hat. In a few seconds, before he had even time to fire his second barrel, he fell, struck to the heart by Harding's dagger, more sure even than his gun.

During this time, Gideon Spilett and the sailor hoisted themselves over the palisade, leaped into the enclosure, threw down the props which supported the inner door, ran into the empty house, and soon, poor Herbert was lying on Ayrton's bed. In a few moments, Harding was by his side.

On seeing Herbert senseless, the sailor's grief was terrible.

He sobbed, he cried, he tried to beat his head against the wall.

Neither the engineer nor the reporter could calm him. They themselves were choked with emotion. They could not speak.

However, they knew that it depended on them to rescue from death the poor boy who was suffering beneath their eyes. Gideon Spilett had not passed through the many incidents by which his life had been checkered without acquiring some slight knowledge of medicine. He knew a little of everything, and several times he had been obliged to attend to wounds produced either by a sword-bayonet or shot. Assisted by Cyrus Harding, he proceeded to render the aid Herbert required.

The reporter was immediately struck by the complete stupor in which Herbert lay, a stupor owing either to the hemorrhage, or to the shock, the ball having struck a bone with sufficient force to produce a violent concussion.

Herbert was deadly pale, and his pulse so feeble that Spilett only felt it beat at long intervals, as if it was on the point of stopping.

These symptoms were very serious.

Herbert's chest was laid bare, and the blood having been stanched with handkerchiefs, it was bathed with cold water.

The contusion, or rather the contused wound, appeared—an oval below the chest between the third and fourth ribs. It was there that Herbert had been hit by the bullet.

Cyrus Harding and Gideon Spilett then turned the poor boy over; as they did so, he uttered a moan so feeble that they almost thought it was his last sigh.

Herbert's back was covered with blood from another contused wound, by which the ball had immediately escaped.

"God be praised!" said the reporter, "the ball is not in the body, and we shall not have to extract it."

"But the heart?" asked Harding.

"The heart has not been touched; if it had been, Herbert would be dead!"

"Dead!" exclaimed Pencroft, with a groan.

The sailor had only heard the last words uttered by the reporter.

"No, Pencroft," replied Cyrus Harding, "no! He is not dead. His pulse still beats. He has even uttered a moan. But for your boy's sake, calm yourself. We have need of all our self-possession. Do not make us lose it, my friend."

Pencroft was silent, but a reaction set in, and great tears rolled down his cheeks.

In the meanwhile, Gideon Spilett endeavored to collect his ideas, and proceed methodically. After his examination he had no doubt that the ball, entering in front, between the seventh and eighth ribs, had issued behind between the third and fourth. But what mischief had the ball committed in its passage? What important organs had been reached? A professional surgeon would have had difficulty in determining this at once, and still more so the reporter.

However, he knew one thing, this was that he would have to prevent the inflammatory strangulation of the injured parts, then to contend with the local inflammation and fever which would result from the wound, perhaps mortal! Now, what styptics, what anti-phlogistics ought to be employed? By what means could inflammation be prevented?

At any rate, the most important thing was that the two wounds should be dressed without delay. It did not appear necessary to Gideon Spilett that a fresh flow of blood should be caused by bathing them in tepid water, and compressing their lips. The hemorrhage had been very abundant, and Herbert was already too much enfeebled by the loss of blood.

The reporter, therefore, thought it best to simply bathe the two wounds with cold water.

Herbert was placed on his left side, and was maintained in that position.

"He must not be moved," said Gideon Spilett. "He is in the most favorable position for the wounds in his back and chest to suppurate easily, and absolute rest is necessary."

"What! can't we carry him to Granite House?" asked Pencroft.

"No, Pencroft," replied the reporter.

"I'll pay the villains off!" cried the sailor, shaking his fist in a menacing manner.

"Pencroft!" said Cyrus Harding.

Gideon Spilett had resumed his examination of the wounded boy. Herbert was still so frightfully pale, that the reporter felt anxious.

"Cyrus," said he, "I am not a surgeon. I am in terrible perplexity. You must aid me with your advice, your experience!"

"Take courage, my friend," answered the engineer, pressing the reporter's hand. "Judge coolly. Think only of this: Herbert must be saved!"

These words restored to Gideon Spilett that self-possession which he had lost in a moment of discouragement on feeling his great responsibility. He seated himself close to the bed. Cyrus Harding stood near. Pencroft had torn up his shirt, and was mechanically making lint.

Spilett then explained to Cyrus Harding that he thought he ought first of all to stop the hemorrhage, but not close the two wounds, or cause their immediate cicatrization, for there had been internal perforation, and the suppuration must not be allowed to accumulate in the chest.

Harding approved entirely, and it was decided that the two wounds should be dressed without attempting to close them by immediate coaptation.

And now did the colonists possess an efficacious agent to act against the inflammation which might occur?

Yes. They had one, for nature had generously lavished it. They had cold water, that is to say, the most powerful sedative that can be employed against inflammation of wounds, the most efficacious therapeutic agent in grave cases, and the one which is now adopted by all physicians. Cold water has, moreover, the advantage of leaving the wound in absolute rest, and preserving it from all premature dressing, a considerable advantage, since it has been found by experience that contact with the air is dangerous during the first days.

Gideon Spilett and Cyrus Harding reasoned thus with their simple good sense, and they acted as the best surgeon would have done. Compresses of linen were applied to poor Herbert's two wounds, and were kept constantly wet with cold water.

The sailor had at first lighted a fire in the hut, which was not wanting in things necessary for life. Maple sugar, medicinal plants, the same which the lad had gathered on the banks of Lake Grant, enabled them to make some refreshing drinks, which they gave him without his taking any notice of it. His fever was extremely high, and all that day and night passed without his becoming conscious.

Herbert's life hung on a thread, and this thread might break at any moment. The next day, the 12th of November, the hopes of Harding and his companions slightly revived. Herbert had come out of his long stupor. He opened his eyes, he recognized Cyrus Harding, the reporter, and Pencroft. He uttered two or three words. He did not know what had happened. They told him, and Spilett begged him to remain perfectly still, telling him that his life was not in danger, and that his wounds would heal in a few days. However, Herbert scarcely suffered at all, and the cold water with which they were constantly bathed, prevented any inflammation of the wounds. The suppuration was established in a regular way, the fever did not increase, and it might now be hoped that this terrible wound would not involve any catastrophe. Pencroft felt the swelling of his heart gradually subside. He was like a sister of mercy. Like a mother by the bed of her child.

Herbert dozed again, but his sleep appeared more natural.

"Tell me again that you hope, Mr. Spilett," said Pencroft. "Tell me again that you will save Herbert!"

"Yes, we will save him!" replied the reporter. "The wound is serious, and, perhaps, even the ball has traversed the lungs, but the perforation of this organ is not fatal."

"God bless you!" answered Pencroft.

As may be believed, during the four-and-twenty hours they had been in the corral, the colonists had no other thought than that of nursing Herbert. They did not think either of the danger which threatened them should the convicts return, or of the precautions to be taken for the future.

But on this day, while Pencroft watched by the sick-bed, Cyrus Harding and the reporter consulted as to what it would be best to do.

First of all they examined the corral. There was not a trace of Ayrton. Had the unhappy man been dragged away by his former accomplices? Had he resisted, and been overcome in the struggle? This last supposition was only too probable. Gideon Spilett, at the moment he scaled the palisade, had clearly seen some one of the convicts running along the southern spur of Mount Franklin, toward whom Top had sprung. It was one of those whose object had been so completely defeated by the rocks at the mouth of the Mercy. Besides, the one killed by Harding, and whose body was found outside the enclosure, of course belonged to Bob Harvey's crew.

As to the corral, it had not suffered any damage. The gates were closed, and the animals had not been able to disperse in the forest. Nor could they see traces of any struggle, any devastation, either in the hut, or in the palisade. The ammunition only, with which Ayrton had been supplied, had disappeared with him.

"The unhappy man has been surprised," said Harding, "and as he was a man to defend himself, he must have been overpowered."

"Yes, that is to be feared!" said the reporter. "Then, doubtless, the convicts installed themselves in the corral where they found plenty of everything, and only fled when they saw us coming. It is very evident, too, that at this moment Ayrton, whether living or dead, is not here!"

"We shall have to beat the forest," said the engineer, "and rid the island of these wretches. Pencroft's presentiments were not mistaken, when he wished to hunt them as wild beasts. That would have spared us all these misfortunes!"

"Yes," answered the reporter, "but now we have the right to be merciless!"

"At any rate," said the engineer, "we are obliged to wait some time, and to remain at the corral until we can carry Herbert without danger to Granite House."

"But Neb?" asked the reporter.

"Neb is in safety."

"But if, uneasy at our absence, he would venture to come?"

"He must not come!" returned Cyrus Harding quickly. "He would be murdered on the road!"

"It is very probable, however, that he will attempt to rejoin us!"

"Ah, if the telegraph still acted, he might be warned! But that is impossible now! As to leaving Pencroft and Herbert here alone, we could not do it! Well, I will go alone to Granite House."

"No, no! Cyrus," answered the reporter, "you must not expose yourself! Your courage would be of no avail. The villains are evidently watching the corral, they are hidden in the thick woods which surround it, and if you go we shall soon have to regret two misfortunes instead of one!"

"But Neb?" repeated the engineer. "It is now four-and-twenty hours since he has had any news of us! He will be sure to come!"

"And as he will be less on his guard than we should be ourselves," added Spilett, "he will be killed!"

"Is there really no way of warning him?"

While the engineer thought, his eyes fell on Top, who, going backward and forward seemed to say,

"Am not I here?"

"Top!" exclaimed Cyrus Harding.

The animal sprang at his master's call.

"Yes, Top will go," said the reporter, who had understood the engineer. "Top can go where we cannot! He will carry to Granite House the news of the corral, and he will bring back to us that from Granite House!"

"Quick!" said Harding. "Quick!"

Spilett rapidly tore a leaf from his notebook, and wrote these words:

"Herbert wounded. We are at the corral. Be on your guard. Do not leave Granite House. Have the convicts appeared in the neighborhood? Reply by Top."

This laconic note contained all that Neb ought to know, and at the same time asked all that the colonists wished to know. It was folded and fastened to Top's collar in a conspicuous position.

"Top, my dog," said the engineer, caressing the animal, "Neb, Top! Neb! Go, go!"

Top bounded at these words. He understood, he knew what was expected of him. The road to the corral was familiar to him. In less than an hour he could clear it, and it might be hoped that where neither Cyrus Harding nor the reporter could have ventured without danger, Top, running among the grass or in the wood, would pass unperceived.

The engineer went to the gate of the corral and opened it.

"Neb, Top! Neb!" repeated the engineer, again pointing in the direction of Granite House.

Top sprang forward, then almost immediately disappeared.

"He will get there!" said the reporter.

"Yes, and he will come back, the faithful animal!"

"What o'clock is it?" asked Gideon Spilett.

"Ten."

"In an hour he may be here. We will watch for his return."

The gate of the corral was closed. The engineer and the reporter reentered the house. Herbert was still in a sleep. Pencroft kept the compresser always wet. Spilett, seeing there was nothing he could do at that moment, busied himself in preparing some nourishment, while attentively watching that part of the enclosure against the hill, at which an attack might be expected.

The settlers awaited Top's return with much anxiety. A little before eleven o'clock, Cyrus Harding and the reporter, rifle in hand, were behind the gate, ready to open it at the first bark of their dog.

They did not doubt that if Top had arrived safely at Granite House, Neb would have sent him back immediately.

They had both been there for about ten minutes, when a report was heard, followed by repeated barks.

The engineer opened the gate, and seeing smoke a hundred feet off in the wood, he fired in that direction.

Almost immediately Top bounded into the corral, and the gate was quickly shut.

"Top, Top!" exclaimed the engineer, taking the dog's great honest head between his hands.

A note was fastened to his neck, and Cyrus Harding read these words, traced in Neb's large writing: "No pirates in the neighborhood of Granite House. I will not stir. Poor Mr. Herbert!"

VIII

So the convicts were still there, watching the corral, and determined to kill the settlers one after the other. There was nothing to be done but to treat them as wild beasts. But great precautions must be taken, for just now the wretches had the advantage on their side, seeing, and not being seen, being able to surprise by the suddenness of their attack, yet not to be surprised themselves. Harding made arrangements, therefore, for living in the corral, of which the provisions would last for a tolerable length of time. Ayrton's house had been provided with all that was necessary for existence, and the convicts, scared by the arrival of the settlers, had not had time to pillage it. It was probable, as Gideon Spilett observed, that things had occurred as follows: The six convicts, disembarking on the island, had followed the southern shore, and after having traversed the double shore of the Serpentine Peninsula, not being inclined to venture into the Far West woods, they had reached the mouth of Falls River. From this point, by following the right bank of the watercourse, they would arrive at the spurs of Mount Franklin, among which they would naturally seek a retreat, and they could not have been long in discovering the corral, then uninhabited. There they had regularly installed themselves, awaiting the moment to put their abominable schemes into execution. Ayrton's arrival had surprised them, but they had managed to overpower the unfortunate man, and—the rest may be easily imagined!

Now, the convicts—reduced to five, it is true, but well armed—were roaming the woods, and to venture there was to expose themselves to their attacks, which could be neither guarded against nor prevented.

"Wait! There is nothing else to be done!" repeated Cyrus Harding. "When Herbert is cured, we can organize a general battue of the island, and have satisfaction of these convicts. That will be the object of our grand expedition at the same time—"

"As the search for our mysterious protector," added Gideon Spilett, finishing the engineer's sentence. "Ah, it must be acknowledged, my dear Cyrus, that this time his protection was wanting at the very moment when it was most necessary to us!"

"Who knows?" replied the engineer.

"What do you mean?" asked the reporter.

"That we are not at the end of our trouble yet, my dear Spilett, and that his powerful intervention may have another opportunity of exercising itself. But that is not the question now. Herbert's life before everything."

This was the colonists' saddest thought. Several days passed, and the poor boy's state was happily no worse. Cold water, always kept at a suitable temperature, had completely prevented the inflammation of the wounds. It even seemed to the reporter that this water, being slightly sulphurous—which was explained by the neighborhood of the volcano—had a more direct action on the healing. The suppuration was much less abundant, and—thanks to the incessant care by which he was surrounded! —Herbert returned to life, and his fever abated. He was besides subjected to a severe diet, and consequently his weakness was and would be extreme; but there was no want of refreshing drinks, and absolute rest was of the greatest benefit to him. Cyrus Harding, Gideon Spilett, and Pencroft had become very skillful in dressing the lad's wounds. All the linen in the house had been sacrificed. Herbert's wounds, covered with compresses and lint, were pressed neither too much nor too little, so as to cause their cicatrization without effecting any inflammatory reaction. The reporter used extreme care in the dressing, knowing well the importance of it, and repeating to his companions that which most surgeons willingly admit, that it is perhaps rarer to see a dressing well done than an operation well performed.

In ten days, on the 22nd of November, Herbert was considerably better. He had begun to take some nourishment.

The color was returning to his cheeks, and his bright eyes smiled at his nurses. He talked a little, notwithstanding Pencroft's efforts, who talked incessantly to prevent him from beginning to speak, and told him the most improbable stories. Herbert had questioned him on the subject of Ayrton, whom he was astonished not to see near him, thinking that he was at the corral. But the sailor, not wishing to distress Herbert, contented himself by replying that Ayrton had rejoined Neb, so as to defend Granite House.

"Humph!" said Pencroft, "these pirates! they are gentlemen who have no right to any consideration! And the captain wanted to win them by kindness! I'll send them some kindness, but in the shape of a good bullet!"

"And have they not been seen again?" asked Herbert.

"No, my boy," answered the sailor, "but we shall find them, and when you are cured we shall see if the cowards who strike us from behind will dare to meet us face to face!"

"I am still very weak, my poor Pencroft!"

"Well! your strength will return gradually! What's a ball through the chest? Nothing but a joke! I've seen many, and I don't think much of them!"

At last things appeared to be going on well, and if no complication occurred, Herbert's recovery might be regarded as certain. But what would have been the condition of the colonists if his state had been aggravated—if, for example, the ball had remained in his body, if his arm or his leg had had to be amputated?

"No," said Spilett more than once, "I have never thought of such a contingency without shuddering!"

"And yet, if it had been necessary to operate," said Harding one day to him, "You would not have hesitated?"

"No, Cyrus!" said Gideon Spilett, "but thank God that we have been spared this complication!"

As in so many other conjectures, the colonists had appealed to the logic of that simple good sense of which they had made use so often, and once more, thanks to their general knowledge, it had succeeded! But might not a time come when all their science would be at fault? They were alone on the island. Now, men in all states of society are necessary to each other. Cyrus Harding knew this well, and sometimes he asked if some circumstance might not occur which they would be powerless to surmount. It appeared to him besides, that he and his companions, till then so fortunate, had entered into an unlucky period. During the two years and a half which had elapsed since their escape from Richmond, it might be said that they had had everything their own way. The island had abundantly supplied them with minerals, vegetables, animals, and as nature had constantly loaded them, their science had known how to take advantage of what she offered them.

The well-being of the colony was therefore complete. Moreover, in certain occurrences an inexplicable influence had come to their aid! . . . But all that could only be for a time.

In short, Cyrus Harding believed that fortune had turned against them.

In fact, the convicts' ship had appeared in the waters of the island, and if the pirates had been, so to speak, miraculously destroyed, six of them, at least, had escaped the catastrophe. They had disembarked on the island, and it was almost impossible to get at the five who survived. Ayrton had no doubt been murdered by these wretches, who possessed firearms, and at the first use that they had made of them, Herbert had fallen, wounded almost mortally. Were these the first blows aimed by adverse fortune at the colonists? This was often asked by Harding. This was often repeated by the reporter; and it appeared to him also that the intervention, so strange, yet so efficacious, which till then had served them so well, had now failed them. Had this mysterious being, whatever he was, whose existence could not be denied, abandoned the island? Had he in his turn succumbed?

No reply was possible to these questions. But it must not be imagined that because Harding and his companions spoke of these things, they were men to despair. Far from that. They looked their situation in the face, they analyzed the chances, they prepared themselves for any event, they stood firm and straight before the future, and if adversity was at last to strike them, it would find in them men prepared to struggle against it.

IX

The convalescence of the young invalid was regularly progressing. One thing only was now to be desired, that his state would allow him to be brought to Granite House. However well built and supplied the corral house was, it could not be so comfortable as the healthy granite dwelling. Besides, it did not offer the same security, and its tenants, notwithstanding their watchfulness, were here always in fear of some shot from the convicts. There, on the contrary, in the middle of that impregnable and inaccessible cliff, they would have nothing to fear, and any attack on their persons would certainly fail. They therefore waited impatiently for the moment when Herbert might be moved without danger from his wound, and they were determined to make this move, although the communication through Jacamar Wood was very difficult.

They had no news from Neb, but were not uneasy on that account. The courageous Negro, well entrenched in the depths of Granite House, would not allow himself to be surprised. Top had not been sent again to him, as it appeared useless to expose the faithful dog to some shot which might deprive the settlers of their most useful auxiliary.

They waited, therefore, although they were anxious to be reunited at Granite House. It pained the engineer to see his forces divided, for it gave great advantage to the pirates. Since Ayrton's disappearance they were only four against five, for Herbert could not yet be counted, and this was not the least care of the brave boy, who well understood the trouble of which he was the cause.

The question of knowing how, in their condition, they were to act against the pirates, was thoroughly discussed on the 29th of November by Cyrus Harding, Gideon Spilett, and Pencroft, at a moment when Herbert was asleep and could not hear them.

"My friends," said the reporter, after they had talked of Neb and of the impossibility of communicating with him, "I think, like you, that to venture on the road to the corral would be to risk receiving a gunshot without being able to return it. But do you not think that the best thing to be done now is to openly give chase to these wretches?"

"That is just what I was thinking," answered Pencroft. "I believe we're not fellows to be afraid of a bullet, and as for me, if Captain Harding approves, I'm ready to dash into the forest! Why, hang it, one man is equal to another!"

"But is he equal to five?" asked the engineer.

"I will join Pencroft," said the reporter, "and both of us, well armed and accompanied by Top—"

"My dear Spilett, and you, Pencroft," answered Harding, "let us reason coolly. If the convicts were hid in one spot of the island, if we knew that spot, and had only to dislodge them, I would undertake a direct attack; but is there not occasion to fear, on the contrary, that they are sure to fire the first shot?"

"Well, captain," cried Pencroft, "a bullet does not always reach its mark."

"That which struck Herbert did not miss, Pencroft," replied the engineer. "Besides, observe that if both of you left the corral I should remain here alone to defend it. Do you imagine that the convicts will not see you leave it, that they will not allow you to enter the forest, and that they will not attack it during your absence, knowing that there is no one here but a wounded boy and a man?"

"You are right, captain," replied Pencroft, his chest swelling with sullen anger. "You are right; they will do all they can to retake the corral, which they know to be well stored; and alone you could not hold it against them."

"Oh, if we were only at Granite House!"

"If we were at Granite House," answered the engineer, "the case would be very different. There I should not be afraid to leave Herbert with one, while the other three went to search the forests of the island. But we are at the corral, and it is best to stay here until we can leave it together."

Cyrus Harding's reasoning was unanswerable, and his companions understood it well.

"If only Ayrton was still one of us!" said Gideon Spilett. "Poor fellow! his return to social life will have been but of short duration."

"If he is dead," added Pencroft, in a peculiar tone.

"Do you hope, then, Pencroft, that the villains have spared him?" asked Gideon Spilett.

"Yes, if they had any interest in doing so."

"What! you suppose that Ayrton, finding his old companions, forgetting all that he owes us—"

"Who knows?" answered the sailor, who did not hazard this shameful supposition without hesitating.

"Pencroft," said Harding, taking the sailor's arm, "that is a wicked idea of yours, and you will distress me much if you persist in speaking thus. I will answer for Ayrton's fidelity."

"And I also," added the reporter quickly.

"Yes, yes, captain, I was wrong," replied Pencroft; "it was a wicked idea indeed that I had, and nothing justifies it. But what can I do? I'm not in my senses. This imprisonment in the corral wearies me horribly, and I have never felt so excited as I do now."

"Be patient, Pencroft," replied the engineer. "How long will it be, my dear Spilett, before you think Herbert may be carried to Granite House?"

"That is difficult to say, Cyrus," answered the reporter, "for any imprudence might involve terrible consequences. But his convalescence is progressing, and if he continues to gain strength, in eight days from now—well, we shall see."

Eight days! That would put off the return to Granite House until the first days of December. At this time two months of spring had already passed. The weather was fine, and the heat began to be great. The forests of the island were in full leaf, and the time was approaching when the usual crops ought to be gathered. The return to the plateau of Prospect Heights would, therefore, be followed by extensive agricultural labors, interrupted only by the projected expedition through the island.

It can, therefore, be well understood how injurious this seclusion in the corral must have been to the colonists.

But if they were compelled to bow before necessity, they did not do so without impatience.

Once or twice the reporter ventured out into the road and made the tour of the palisade. Top accompanied him, and Gideon Spilett, his gun cocked, was ready for any emergency.

He met with no misadventure and found no suspicious traces. His dog would have warned him of any danger, and, as Top did not bark, it might be concluded that there was nothing to fear at the moment at least, and that the convicts were occupied in another part of the island.

However, on his second sortie, on the 27th of November, Gideon Spilett, who had ventured a quarter of a mile into the woods, toward the south of the mountain, remarked that Top scented something. The dog had no longer his unconcerned manner; he went backward and forward, ferreting among the grass and bushes as if his smell had revealed some suspicious object to him.

Gideon Spilett followed Top, encouraged him, excited him by his voice, while keeping a sharp look-out, his gun ready to fire, and sheltering himself behind the trees. It was not probable that Top scented the presence of man, for in that case, he would have announced it by half-uttered, sullen, angry barks. Now, as he did not growl, it was because danger was neither near nor approaching.

Nearly five minutes passed thus, Top rummaging, the reporter following him prudently when, all at once, the dog rushed toward a thick bush, and drew out a rag.

It was a piece of cloth, stained and torn, which Spilett immediately brought back to the corral. There it was examined by the colonists, who found that it was a fragment of Ayrton's waistcoat, a piece of that felt, manufactured solely by the Granite House factory.

"You see, Pencroft," observed Harding, "there has been resistance on the part of the unfortunate Ayrton. The convicts have dragged him away in spite of himself! Do you still doubt his honesty?"

"No, captain," answered the sailor, "and I repented of my suspicion a long time ago! But it seems to me that something may be learned from the incident."

"What is that?" asked the reporter.

"It is that Ayrton was not killed at the corral! That they dragged him away living, since he has resisted. Therefore, perhaps, he is still living!"

"Perhaps, indeed," replied the engineer, who remained thoughtful.

This was a hope, to which Ayrton's companions could still hold. Indeed, they had before believed that, surprised in the corral, Ayrton had fallen by a bullet, as Herbert had fallen. But if the convicts had not killed him at first, if they had brought him living to another part of the island, might it not be admitted that he was still their prisoner? Perhaps, even, one of them had found in Ayrton his old Australian companion Ben Joyce, the chief of the escaped convicts. And who knows but that they had conceived the impossible hope of bringing back Ayrton to themselves? He would have been very useful to them, if they had been able to make him turn traitor!

This incident was, therefore, favorably interpreted at the corral, and it no longer appeared impossible that they should find Ayrton again. On his side, if he was only a prisoner, Ayrton would no doubt do all he could to escape from the hands of the villains, and this would be a powerful aid to the settlers!

"At any rate," observed Gideon Spilett, "if happily Ayrton did manage to escape, he would go directly to Granite House, for he could not know of the attempted assassination of which Herbert has been a victim, and consequently would never think of our being imprisoned in the corral."

"Oh! I wish that he was there, at Granite House!" cried Pencroft, "and that we were there, too! For, although the rascals can do nothing to our house, they may plunder the plateau, our plantations, our poultry-yard!"

Pencroft had become a thorough farmer, heartily attached to his crops. But it must be said that Herbert was more anxious than any to return to Granite House, for he knew how much the presence of the settlers was needed there. And it was he who was keeping them at the corral! Therefore, one idea occupied his mind—to leave the corral, and when! He believed he could bear removal to Granite House. He was sure his strength would return more quickly in his room, with the air and sight of the sea!

Several times he pressed Gideon Spilett, but the latter, fearing, with good reason, that Herbert's wounds, half healed, might reopen on the way, did not give the order to start.

However, something occurred which compelled Cyrus Harding and his two friends to yield to the lad's wish, and God alone knew that this determination might cause them grief and remorse.

It was the 29th of November, seven o'clock in the evening. The three settlers were talking in Herbert's room, when they heard Top utter quick barks.

Harding, Pencroft, and Spilett seized their guns and ran out of the house. Top, at the foot of the palisade, was jumping, barking, but it was with pleasure, not anger.

"Some one is coming."

"Yes."

"It is not an enemy!"

"Neb, perhaps?"

"Or Ayrton?"

These words had hardly been exchanged between the engineer and his two companions when a body leaped over the palisade and fell on the ground inside the corral.

It was Jup, Master Jup in person, to whom Top immediately gave a most cordial reception.

"Jup!" exclaimed Pencroft.

"Neb has sent him to us," said the reporter.

"Then," replied the engineer, "he must have some note on him."

Pencroft rushed up to the orang. Certainly if Neb had any important matter to communicate to his master he could not employ a more sure or more rapid messenger, who could pass where neither the colonists could, nor even Top himself.

Cyrus Harding was not mistaken. At Jup's neck hung a small bag, and in this bag was found a little note traced by Neb's hand.

The despair of Harding and his companions may be imagined when they read these words:

Friday, six o'clock in the morning.
Plateau invaded by convicts.
Neb.

They gazed at each other without uttering a word, then they re-entered the house. What were they to do? The convicts on Prospect Heights! that was disaster, devastation, ruin.

Herbert, on seeing the engineer, the reporter, and Pencroft re-enter, guessed that their situation was aggravated, and when he saw Jup, he no longer doubted that some misfortune menaced Granite House.

"Captain Harding," said he, "I must go; I can bear the journey. I must go."

Gideon Spilett approached Herbert; then, having looked at him,

"Let us go, then!" said he.

The question was quickly decided whether Herbert should be carried on a litter or in the cart which had brought Ayrton to the corral. The motion of the litter would have been more easy for the wounded lad, but it would have necessitated two bearers, that is to say, there would have been two guns less for defense if an attack was made on the road. Would they not, on the contrary, by employing the cart, leave every arm free? Was it impossible to place the mattress on which Herbert was lying in it, and to advance with so much care that any jolt should be avoided? It could be done.

The cart was brought. Pencroft harnessed the onager. Cyrus Harding and the reporter raised Herbert's mattress and placed it on the bottom of the cart. The weather was fine. The sun's bright rays glanced through the trees.

"Are the guns ready?" asked Cyrus Harding.

They were. The engineer and Pencroft, each armed with a double-barreled gun, and Gideon Spilett carrying his rifle, had nothing to do but start.

"Are you comfortable, Herbert?" asked the engineer.

"Ah, captain," replied the lad, "don't be uneasy, I shall not die on the road!"

While speaking thus, it could be seen that the poor boy had called up all his energy, and by the energy of a powerful will had collected his failing strength.

The engineer felt his heart sink painfully. He still hesitated to give the signal for departure; but that would have driven Herbert to despair—killed him perhaps.

"Forward!" said Harding.

The gate of the corral was opened. Jup and Top, who knew when to be silent, ran in advance. The cart came out, the gate was reclosed, and the onager, led by Pencroft, advanced at a slow pace.

Certainly, it would have been safer to have taken a different road than that which led straight from the corral to Granite House, but the cart would have met with great difficulties in moving under the trees. It was necessary, therefore, to follow this way, although it was well known to the convicts.

Cyrus Harding and Gideon Spilett walked one on each side of the cart, ready to answer to any attack. However, it was not probable that the convicts would have yet left the plateau of Prospect Heights.

Neb's note had evidently been written and sent as soon as the convicts had shown themselves there. Now, this note was dated six o'clock in the morning, and the active orang, accustomed to come frequently to the corral, had taken scarcely three quarters of an hour to cross the five miles which separated it from Granite House. They would, therefore, be safe at that time, and if there was any occasion for firing, it would probably not be until they were in the neighborhood of Granite House. However, the colonists kept a strict watch. Top and Jup, the latter armed with his club, sometimes in front, sometimes beating the wood at the sides of the road, signalized no danger.

The cart advanced slowly under Pencroft's guidance. It had left the corral at half-past seven. An hour after, four out of the five miles had been cleared, without any incident having occurred. The road was as deserted as all that part of the Jacamar Wood which lay between the Mercy and the lake. There was no occasion for any warning. The wood appeared as deserted as on the day when the colonists first landed on the island.

They approached the plateau. Another mile and they would see the bridge over Creek Glycerine. Cyrus Harding expected to find it in its place; supposing that the convicts would have crossed it, and that, after having passed one of the streams which enclosed the plateau, they would have taken the precaution to lower it again, so as to keep open a retreat.

At length an opening in the trees allowed the sea-horizon to be seen. But the cart continued its progress, for not one of its defenders thought of abandoning it.

At that moment Pencroft stopped the onager, and in a hoarse voice,

"Oh! the villains!" he exclaimed.

And he pointed to a thick smoke rising from the mill, the sheds, and the buildings at the poultry-yard.

A man was moving about in the midst of the smoke. It was Neb.

His companions uttered a shout. He heard, and ran to meet them.

The convicts had left the plateau nearly half an hour before, having devastated it!

"And Mr. Herbert?" asked Neb.

Gideon Spilett returned to the cart.

Herbert had lost consciousness!

X

Of the convicts, the dangers which menaced Granite House, the ruins with which the plateau was covered, the colonists thought no longer. Herbert's critical state outweighed all other considerations. Would the removal prove fatal to him by causing some internal injury? The reporter could not affirm it, but he and his companions almost despaired of the result. The cart was brought to the bend of the river. There some branches, disposed as a litter, received the mattress on which lay the unconscious Herbert. Ten minutes after, Cyrus Harding, Spilett, and Pencroft were at the foot of the cliff, leaving Neb to take the cart on to the plateau of Prospect Heights. The lift was put in motion, and Herbert was soon stretched on his bed in Granite House.

What cares were lavished on him to bring him back to life! He smiled for a moment on finding himself in his room, but could scarcely even murmur a few words, so great was his weakness. Gideon Spilett examined his wounds. He feared to find them reopened, having been imperfectly healed. There was nothing of the sort. From whence, then, came this prostration? Why was Herbert so much worse? The lad then fell into a kind of feverish sleep, and the reporter and Pencroft remained near the bed. During this time, Harding told Neb all that had happened at the corral, and Neb recounted to his master the events of which the plateau had just been the theater.

It was only during the preceding night that the convicts had appeared on the edge of the forest, at the approaches to Creek Glycerine. Neb, who was watching near the poultry-yard, had not hesitated to fire at one of the pirates, who was about to cross the stream; but in the darkness he could not tell whether the man had been hit or not. At any rate, it was not enough to frighten away the band, and Neb had only just time to get up to Granite House, where at least he was in safety.

But what was he to do there? How prevent the devastations with which the convicts threatened the plateau? Had Neb any means by which to warn his master? And, besides, in what situation were the inhabitants of the corral themselves? Cyrus Harding and his companions had left on the 11th of November, and it was now the 29th. It was, therefore, nineteen days since Neb had had other news than that brought by Top—disastrous news:

Ayrton disappeared, Herbert severely wounded, the engineer, reporter, and sailor, as it were, imprisoned in the corral!

What was he to do? asked poor Neb. Personally he had nothing to fear, for the convicts could not reach him in Granite House. But the buildings, the plantations, all their arrangements at the mercy of the pirates! Would it not be best to let Cyrus Harding judge of what he ought to do, and to warn him, at least, of the danger which threatened him?

Neb then thought of employing Jup, and confiding a note to him. He knew the orang's great intelligence, which had been often put to the proof. Jup understood the word corral, which had been frequently pronounced before him, and it may be remembered, too, that he had often driven the cart thither in company with Pencroft. Day had not yet dawned. The active orang would know how to pass unperceived through the woods, of which the convicts, besides, would think he was a native.

Neb did not hesitate. He wrote the note, he tied it to Jup's neck, he brought the ape to the door of Granite House, from which he let down a long cord to the ground; then, several times he repeated these words,

"Jup Jup! corral, corral!"

The creature understood, seized the cord, glided rapidly down the beach, and disappeared in the darkness without the convicts' attention having been in the least excited.

"You did well, Neb," said Harding, "but perhaps in not warning us you would have done still better!"

And, in speaking thus, Cyrus Harding thought of Herbert, whose recovery the removal had so seriously checked.

Neb ended his account. The convicts had not appeared at all on the beach. Not knowing the number of the island's inhabitants, they might suppose that Granite House was defended by a large party. They must have remembered that during the attack by the brig numerous shot had been fired both from the lower and upper rocks, and no doubt they did not wish to expose themselves. But the plateau of Prospect Heights was open to them, and not covered by the fire of Granite House. They gave themselves up, therefore, to their instinct of destruction—plundering, burning, devastating everything—and only retiring half an hour before the arrival of the colonists, whom they believed still confined in the corral.

On their retreat, Neb hurried out. He climbed the plateau at the risk of being perceived and fired at, tried to extinguish the fire which was consuming the buildings of the poultry-yard, and had struggled, though in vain, against it until the cart appeared at the edge of the wood.

Such had been these serious events. The presence of the convicts constituted a permanent source of danger to the settlers in Lincoln Island, until then so happy, and who might now expect still greater misfortunes.

Spilett remained in Granite House with Herbert and Pencroft, while Cyrus Harding, accompanied by Neb, proceeded to judge for himself of the extent of the disaster.

It was fortunate that the convicts had not advanced to the foot of Granite House. The workshop at the Chimneys would in that case not have escaped destruction. But after all, this evil would have been more easily reparable than the ruins accumulated on the plateau of Prospect Heights. Harding and Neb proceeded toward the Mercy, and ascended its left bank without meeting with any trace of the convicts; nor on the other side of the river, in the depths of the wood, could they perceive any suspicious indications.

Besides, it might be supposed that in all probability either the convicts knew of the return of the settlers to Granite House, by having seen them pass on the road from the corral, or, after the devastation of the plateau, they had penetrated into Jacamar Wood, following the course of the Mercy, and were thus ignorant of their return.

In the former case, they must have returned toward the corral, now without defenders, and which contained valuable stores.

In the latter, they must have regained their encampment, and would wait on opportunity to recommence the attack.

It was, therefore, possible to prevent them, but any enterprise to clear the island was now rendered difficult by reason of Herbert's condition. Indeed, their whole force would have been barely sufficient to cope with the convicts, and just now no one could leave Granite House.

The engineer and Neb arrived on the plateau. Desolation reigned everywhere. The fields had been trampled over; the ears of wheat, which were nearly full-grown, lay on the ground. The other plantations had not suffered less.

The kitchen-garden was destroyed. Happily, Granite House possessed a store of seed which would enable them to repair these misfortunes.

As to the wall and buildings of the poultry-yard and the onagers' stable, the fire had destroyed all. A few terrified creatures roamed over the plateau. The birds, which during the fire had taken refuge on the waters of the lake, had already returned to their accustomed spot, and were dabbling on the banks. Everything would have to be reconstructed.

Cyrus Harding's face, which was paler than usual, expressed an internal anger which he commanded with difficulty, but he did not utter a word. Once more he looked at his devastated fields, and at the smoke which still rose from the ruins, then he returned to Granite House.

The following days were the saddest of any that the colonists had passed on the island! Herbert's weakness visibly increased. It appeared that a more serious malady, the consequence of the profound physiological disturbance he had gone through, threatened to declare itself, and Gideon Spilett feared such an aggravation of his condition that he would be powerless to fight against it!

In fact, Herbert remained in an almost continuous state of drowsiness, and symptoms of delirium began to manifest themselves. Refreshing drinks were the only remedies at the colonists' disposal. The fever was not as yet very high, but it soon appeared that it would probably recur at regular intervals. Gideon Spilett first recognized this on the 6th of December.

The poor boy, whose fingers, nose, and ears had become extremely pale, was at first seized with slight shiverings, horripilations, and tremblings. His pulse was weak and irregular, his skin dry, his thirst intense. To this soon succeeded a hot fit; his face became flushed; his skin reddened; his pulse quick; then a profuse perspiration broke out after which the fever seemed to diminish. The attack had lasted nearly five hours.

Gideon Spilett had not left Herbert, who, it was only too certain, was now seized by an intermittent fever, and this fever must be cured at any cost before it should assume a more serious aspect.

"And in order to cure it," said Spilett to Cyrus Harding, "we need a febrifuge."

"A febrifuge—" answered the engineer. "We have neither Peruvian bark, nor sulphate of quinine."

"No," said Gideon Spilett, "but there are willows on the border of the lake, and the bark of the willow might, perhaps, prove to be a substitute for quinine."

"Let us try it without losing a moment," replied Cyrus Harding.

The bark of the willow has, indeed, been justly considered as a succedaneum for Peruvian bark, as has also that of the horse-chestnut tree, the leaf of the holly, the snake-root, etc. It was evidently necessary to make trial of this substance, although not so valuable as Peruvian bark, and to employ it in its natural state, since they had no means for extracting its essence.

Cyrus Harding went himself to cut from the trunk of a species of black willow, a few pieces of bark; he brought them back to Granite House, and reduced them to a powder, which was administered that same evening to Herbert.

The night passed without any important change. Herbert was somewhat delirious, but the fever did not reappear in the night, and did not return either during the following day.

Pencroft again began to hope. Gideon Spilett said nothing. It might be that the fever was not quotidian, but tertian, and that it would return next day. Therefore, he awaited the next day with the greatest anxiety.

It might have been remarked besides that during this period Herbert remained utterly prostrate, his head weak and giddy. Another symptom alarmed the reporter to the highest degree. Herbert's liver became congested, and soon a more intense delirium showed that his brain was also affected.

Gideon Spilett was overwhelmed by this new complication. He took the engineer aside.

"It is a malignant fever," said he.

"A malignant fever!" cried Harding. "You are mistaken, Spilett. A malignant fever does not declare itself spontaneously; its germ must previously have existed."

"I am not mistaken," replied the reporter. "Herbert no doubt contracted the germ of this fever in the marshes of the island. He has already had one attack; should a second come on and should we not be able to prevent a third, he is lost."

"But the willow bark?"

"That is insufficient," answered the reporter, "and the third attack of a malignant fever, which is not arrested by means of quinine, is always fatal."

Fortunately, Pencroft heard nothing of this conversation or he would have gone mad.

It may be imagined what anxiety the engineer and the reporter suffered during the day of the 7th of December and the following night.

Toward the middle of the day the second attack came on. The crisis was terrible. Herbert felt himself sinking. He stretched his arms toward Cyrus Harding, toward Spilett, toward Pencroft. He was so young to die! The scene was heart-rending. They were obliged to send Pencroft away.

The fit lasted five hours. It was evident that Herbert could not survive a third.

The night was frightful. In his delirium Herbert uttered words which went to the hearts of his companions. He struggled with the convicts, he called to Ayrton, he poured forth entreaties to that mysterious being—that powerful unknown protector—whose image was stamped upon his mind; then he again fell into a deep exhaustion which completely prostrated him. Several times Gideon Spilett thought that the poor boy was dead.

The next day, the 8th of December, was but a succession of the fainting fits. Herbert's thin hands clutched the sheets. They had administered further doses of pounded bark, but the reporter expected no result from it.

"If before to-morrow morning we have not given him a more energetic febrifuge," said the reporter, "Herbert will be dead."

Night arrived—the last night, it was too much to be feared, of the good, brave, intelligent boy, so far in advance of his years, and who was loved by all as their own child. The only remedy which existed against this terrible malignant fever, the only specific which could overcome it, was not to be found in Lincoln Island.

During the night of the 8th of December, Herbert was seized by a more violent delirium. His liver was fearfully congested, his brain affected, and already it was impossible for him to recognize any one.

Would he live until the next day, until that third attack which must infallibly carry him off? It was not probable. His strength was exhausted, and in the intervals of fever he lay as one dead.

Toward three o'clock in the morning Herbert uttered a piercing cry. He seemed to be torn by a supreme convulsion. Neb, who was near him, terrified, ran into the next room where his companions were watching.

Top, at that moment, barked in a strange manner.

All rushed in immediately and managed to restrain the dying boy, who was endeavoring to throw himself out of his bed, while Spilett, taking his arm, felt his pulse gradually quicken.

It was five in the morning. The rays of the rising sun began to shine in at the windows of Granite House. It promised to be a fine day, and this day was to be poor Herbert's last!

A ray glanced on the table placed near the bed.

Suddenly Pencroft, uttering a cry, pointed to the table.

On it lay a little oblong box, of which the cover bore these words:

SULPHATE OF QUININE.

XI

Gideon Spilett took the box and opened it. It contained nearly two hundred grains of a white powder, a few particles of which he carried to his lips. The extreme bitterness of the substance precluded all doubt; it was certainly the precious extract of quinine, that preeminent antifebrile.

This powder must be administered to Herbert without delay. How it came there might be discussed later.

"Some coffee!" said Spilett.

In a few moments Neb brought a cup of the warm infusion. Gideon Spilett threw into it about eighteen grains of quinine, and they succeeded in making Herbert drink the mixture.

There was still time, for the third attack of the malignant fever had not yet shown itself. How they longed to be able to add that it would not return!

Besides, it must be remarked, the hopes of all had now revived. The mysterious influence had been again exerted, and in a critical moment, when they had despaired of it.

In a few hours Herbert was much calmer. The colonists could now discuss this incident. The intervention of the stranger was more evident than ever. But how had he been able to penetrate during the night into Granite House? It was inexplicable, and, in truth, the proceedings of the genius of the island were not less mysterious than was that genius himself. During this day the sulphate of quinine was administered to Herbert every three hours.

The next day some improvement in Herbert's condition was apparent. Certainly, he was not out of danger, intermittent fevers being subject to frequent and dangerous relapses, but the most assiduous care was bestowed on him. And besides, the specific was at hand; nor, doubtless, was he who had brought it far distant! and the hearts of all were animated by returning hope.

This hope was not disappointed. Ten days after, on the 20th of December, Herbert's convalescence commenced.

He was still weak, and strict diet had been imposed upon him, but no access of fever supervened. And then, the poor boy submitted with such docility to all the prescriptions ordered him! He longed so to get well!

Pencroft was as a man who has been drawn up from the bottom of an abyss. Fits of joy approaching delirium seized him. When the time for the third attack had passed by, he nearly suffocated the reporter in his embrace. Since then, he always called him Dr. Spilett.

The real doctor, however, remained undiscovered.

"We will find him!" repeated the sailor.

Certainly, this man, whoever he was, might expect a somewhat too energetic embrace from the worthy Pencroft!

The month of December ended, and with it the year 1867, during which the colonists of Lincoln Island had of late been so severely tried. They commenced the year 1868 with magnificent weather, great heat, and a tropical temperature, delightfully cooled by the sea-breeze. Herbert's recovery progressed, and from his bed, placed near one of the windows of Granite House, he could inhale the fresh air, charged with ozone, which could not fail to restore his health. His appetite returned, and what numberless delicate, savory little dishes Neb prepared for him!

"It is enough to make one wish to have a fever oneself!" said Pencroft.

During all this time, the convicts did not once appear in the vicinity of Granite House. There was no news of Ayrton, and though the engineer and Herbert still had some hopes of finding him again, their companions did not doubt but that the unfortunate man had perished. However, this uncertainty could not last, and when once the lad should have recovered, the expedition, the result of which must be so important, would be undertaken. But they would have to wait a month, perhaps, for all the strength of the colony must be put into requisition to obtain satisfaction from the convicts.

However, Herbert's convalescence progressed rapidly. The congestion of the liver had disappeared, and his wounds might be considered completely healed.

During the month of January, important work was done on the plateau of Prospect Heights; but it consisted solely in saving as much as was possible from the devastated crops, either of corn or vegetables. The grain and the plants were gathered, so as to provide a new harvest for the approaching half-season. With regard to rebuilding the poultry-yard, wall, or stables, Cyrus Harding preferred to wait. While he and his companions were in pursuit of the convicts, the latter might very probably pay another visit to the plateau, and it would be useless to give them an opportunity of recommencing their work of destruction. When the island should be cleared of these miscreants, they would set about rebuilding. The young convalescent began to get up in the second week of January, at first for one hour a day, then two, then three. His strength visibly returned, so vigorous was his constitution. He was now eighteen years of age. He was tall, and promised to become a man of noble and commanding presence. From this time his recovery, while still requiring care—and Dr. Spilett was very strict—made rapid progress. Toward the end of the month, Herbert was already walking about on Prospect Heights, and the beach.

He derived, from several sea-baths, which he took in company with Pencroft and Neb, the greatest possible benefit. Cyrus Harding thought he might now settle the day for their departure, for which the 15th of February was fixed. The nights, very clear at this time of year, would be favorable to the researches they intended to make all over the island.

The necessary preparations for this exploration were now commenced, and were important, for the colonists had sworn not to return to Granite House until their twofold object had been achieved; on the one hand, to exterminate the convicts, and rescue Ayrton, if he was still living; on the other, to discover who it was that presided so effectually over the fortunes of the colony.

Of Lincoln Island, the settlers knew thoroughly all the eastern coast from Claw Cape to the Mandible capes, the extensive Tadorn's Fens, the neighborhood of Lake Grant, Jacamar Wood, between the road to the corral and the Mercy, the courses of the Mercy and Red Creek, and lastly, the spurs of Mount Franklin, among which the corral had been established.

They had explored, though only in an imperfect manner, the vast shore of Washington Bay from Claw Cape to Reptile End, the woody and marshy border of the west coast, and the interminable downs, ending at the open mouth of Shark Gulf. But they had in no way surveyed the woods which covered the Serpentine Peninsula, all to the right of the Mercy, the left bank of Falls River, and the wilderness of spurs and valleys which supported three quarters of the base of Mount Franklin, to the east, the north, and the west, and where doubtless many secret retreats existed. Consequently, many millions of acres of the island had still escaped their investigations.

It was, therefore, decided that the expedition should be carried through the Far West, so as to include all that region situated on the right of the Mercy.

It might, perhaps, be better worth while to go direct to the corral, where it might be supposed that the convicts had again taken refuge, either to pillage or to establish themselves there. But either the devastation of the corral would have been an accomplished fact by this time, and it would be too late to prevent it, or it had been the convicts' interest to entrench themselves there, and there would be still time to go and turn them out on their return.

Therefore, after some discussion, the first plan was adhered to, and the settlers resolved to proceed through the wood to Reptile End. They would make their way with their hatchets, and thus lay the first draft of a road which would place Granite House in communication with the end of the peninsula for a length of from sixteen to seventeen miles.

The cart was in good condition. The onagers, well rested, could go a long journey. Provisions, camp effects, a portable stove, and various utensils were packed in the cart, as also weapons and ammunition, carefully chosen from the now complete arsenal of Granite House. But it was necessary to remember that the convicts were, perhaps, roaming about the woods, and that in the midst of these thick forests a shot might quickly be fired and received. It was therefore resolved that the little band of settlers should remain together and not separate under any pretext whatever.

It was also decided that no one should remain at Granite House. Top and Jup themselves were to accompany the expedition; the inaccessible dwelling needed no guard. The 14th of February, eve of the departure, was consecrated entirely to repose, and thanksgiving addressed by the colonists to the Creator. A place in the cart was reserved for Herbert, who, though thoroughly convalescent, was still a little weak. The next morning, at daybreak, Cyrus Harding took the necessary measures to protect Granite House from any invasion. The ladders, which were formerly used for the ascent, were brought to the Chimneys and buried deep in the sand, so that they might be available on the return of the colonists, for the machinery of the lift had been taken to pieces, and nothing of the apparatus remained. Pencroft stayed the last in Granite House in order to finish this work, and he then lowered himself down by means of a double rope held below, and which, when once hauled down, left no communication between the upper landing and the beach.

The weather was magnificent.

"We shall have a warm day of it," said the reporter, laughing.

"Pooh! Dr. Spilett," answered Pencroft, "we shall walk under the shade of the trees and shan't even see the sun!"

"Forward!" said the engineer.

The cart was waiting on the beach before the Chimneys. The reporter made Herbert take his place in it during the first hours at least of the journey, and the lad was obliged to submit to his doctor's orders.

Neb placed himself at the onagers' heads. Cyrus Harding, the reporter, and the sailor, walked in front. Top bounded joyfully along. Herbert offered a seat in his vehicle to Jup, who accepted it without ceremony. The moment for departure had arrived, and the little band set out.

The cart first turned the angle of the mouth of the Mercy, then, having ascended the left bank for a mile, crossed the bridge, at the other side of which commenced the road to Port Balloon, and there the explorers, leaving this road on their left, entered the cover of the immense woods which formed the region of the Far West.

For the first two miles the widely scattered trees allowed the cart to pass with ease; from time to time it became necessary to cut away a few creepers and bushes, but no serious obstacle impeded the progress of the colonists.

The thick foliage of the trees threw a grateful shade on the ground. Deodars, Douglas firs, casuarinas, banksias, gum-trees, dragon-trees, and other well-known species, succeeded each other far as the eye could reach. The feathered tribes of the island were all represented—grouse, jacamars, pheasants, lories, as well as the chattering cockatoos, parrots, and paroquets. Agouties, kangaroos, and capybaras fled swiftly at their approach; and all this reminded the settlers of the first excursions they had made on their arrival at the island.

"Nevertheless," observed Cyrus Harding, "I notice that these creatures, both birds and quadrupeds, are more timid than formerly. These woods have, therefore, been recently traversed by the convicts, and we shall certainly find some traces of them."

And, in fact, in several places they could distinguish traces, more or less recent, of the passage of a band of men—here branches broken off the trees, perhaps to mark out the way; there the ashes of a fire, and footprints in clayey spots; but nothing which appeared to belong to a settled encampment.

The engineer had recommended his companions to refrain from hunting. The reports of the firearms might give the alarm to the convicts, who were, perhaps, roaming through the forest. Moreover, the hunters would necessarily ramble some distance from the cart, which it was dangerous to leave unguarded.

In the afterpart of the day, when about six miles from Granite House, their progress became much more difficult. In order to make their way through some thickets, they were obliged to cut down trees. Before entering such places Harding was careful to send in Top and Jup, who faithfully accomplished their commission, and when the dog and orang returned without giving any warning, there was evidently nothing to fear, either from convicts or wild beasts, two varieties of the animal kingdom, whose ferocious instincts placed them on the same level. On the evening of the first day the colonists encamped about nine miles from Granite House, on the border of a little stream falling into the Mercy, and of the existence of which they had till then been ignorant; it evidently, however, belonged to the hydrographical system to which the soil owed its astonishing fertility. The settlers made a hearty meal, for their appetites were sharpened, and measures were then taken that the night might be passed in safety. If the engineer had had only to deal with wild beasts, jaguars or others, he would have simply lighted fires all around his camp, which would have sufficed for its defense; but the convicts would be rather attracted than terrified by the flames, and it was, therefore, better to be surrounded by the profound darkness of night.

The watch was, however, carefully organized. Two of the settlers were to watch together, and every two hours it was agreed that they should be relieved by their comrades. And so, notwithstanding his wish to the contrary, Herbert was exempted from guard. Pencroft and Gideon Spilett in one party, the engineer and Neb in another, mounted guard in turns over the camp.

The night, however, was but of few hours. The darkness was due rather to the thickness of the foliage than to the disappearance of the sun. The silence was scarcely disturbed by the howling of jaguars and the chattering of the monkeys, the latter appearing to particularly irritate Master Jup. The night passed without incident, and on the next day, the 15th of February, the journey through the forest, tedious rather than difficult, was continued. This day they could not accomplish more than six miles, for every moment they were obliged to cut a road with their hatchets.

Like true settlers, the colonists spared the largest and most beautiful trees, which would besides have cost immense labor to fell, and the small ones only were sacrificed, but the result was that the road took a very winding direction, and lengthened itself by numerous detours.

During the day Herbert discovered several new specimens not before met with in the island, such as the tree-fern, with its leaves spread out like the waters of a fountain, locust-trees, on the long pods of which the onagers browsed greedily, and which supplied a sweet pulp of excellent flavor. There, too, the colonists again found groups of magnificent kauries, their cylindrical trunks, crowded with a cone of verdure, rising to a height of two hundred feet. These were the tree-kings of New Zealand, as celebrated as the cedars of Lebanon.

As to the fauna, there was no addition to those species already known to the hunters. Nevertheless, they saw, though unable to get near them, a couple of those large birds peculiar to Australia, a sort of cassowary, called emu, five feet in height, and with brown plumage, which belong to the tribe of waders. Top darted after them as fast as his four legs could carry him, but the emus distanced him with ease, so prodigious was their speed.

As to the traces left by the convicts, a few more were discovered. Some footprints found near an apparently recently extinguished fire were attentively examined by the settlers. By measuring them one after the other, according to their length and breadth, the marks of five men's feet were easily distinguished. The five convicts had evidently camped on this spot; but—and this was the object of so minute an examination—a sixth footprint could not be discovered, which in that case would have been that of Ayrton.

"Ayrton was not with them!" said Herbert.

"No," answered Pencroft, "and if he was not with them, it was because the wretches had already murdered him! but then these rascals have not a den to which they may be tracked like tigers!"

"No," replied the reporter, "it is more probable that they wander at random, and it is their interest to rove about until the time when they will be masters of the island!"

"The masters of the island!" exclaimed the sailor; "the masters of the island! . . ." he repeated, and his voice was choked, as if his throat was seized in an iron grasp. Then in a calmer tone, "Do you know, Captain Harding," said he, "what the ball is which I have rammed into my gun?"

"No, Pencroft!"

"It is the ball that went through Herbert's chest, and I promise you it won't miss its mark!"

But this just retaliation would not bring Ayrton back to life, and from the examination of the footprints left in the ground, they must, alas! conclude that all hopes of ever seeing him again must be abandoned.

That evening they encamped fourteen miles from Granite House, and Cyrus Harding calculated that they could not be more than five miles from Reptile End.

And indeed, the next day the extremity of the peninsula was reached, and the whole length of the forest had been traversed; but there was nothing to indicate the retreat in which the convicts had taken refuge, nor that, no less secret, which sheltered the mysterious unknown.

XII

The next day, the 18th of February, was devoted to the exploration of all that wooded region forming the shore from Reptile End to Falls River. The colonists were able to search this forest thoroughly, for, as it was comprised between the two shores of the Serpentine Peninsula, it was only from three to four miles in breadth. The trees, both by their height and their thick foliage, bore witness to the vegetative power of the soil, more astonishing here than in any other part of the island. One might have said that a corner from the virgin forests of America or Africa had been transported into this temperate zone. This led them to conclude that the superb vegetation found a heat in this soil, damp in its upper layer, but warmed in the interior by volcanic fires, which could not belong to a temperate climate. The most frequently occurring trees were kauries and eucalypti of gigantic dimensions.

But the colonists' object was not simply to admire the magnificent vegetation. They knew already that in this respect Lincoln Island would have been worthy to take the first rank in the Canary group, to which the first name given was that of the Happy Isles. Now, alas! their island no longer belonged to them entirely; others had taken possession of it, miscreants polluted its shores, and they must be destroyed to the last man.

No traces were found on the western coast, although they were carefully sought for. No more footprints, no more broken branches, no more deserted camps.

"This does not surprise me," said Cyrus Harding to his companions. "The convicts first landed on the island in the neighborhood of Flotsam Point, and they immediately plunged into the Far West forests, after crossing Tadorn's Fens. They then followed almost the same route that we took on leaving Granite House. This explains the traces we found in the wood. But, arriving on the shore, the convicts saw at once that they would discover no suitable retreat there, and it was then that, going northward again, they came upon the corral."

"Where they have perhaps returned," said Pencroft.

"I do not think so," answered the engineer, "for they would naturally suppose that our researches would be in that direction. The corral is only a storehouse to them, and not a definitive encampment."

"I am of Cyrus's opinion," said the reporter, "and I think that it is among the spurs of Mount Franklin that the convicts will have made their lair."

"Then, captain, straight to the corral!" cried Pencroft. "We must finish them off, and till now we have only lost time!"

"No, my friend," replied the engineer; "you forget that we have a reason for wishing to know if the Forests of the Far West do not contain some habitation. Our exploration has a double object, Pencroft. If, on the one hand, we have to chastise crime, we have, on the other, an act of gratitude to perform."

"That was well said, captain," replied the sailor, "but, all the same, it is my opinion that we shall not find the gentleman until he pleases."

And truly Pencroft only expressed the opinion of all. It was probable that the stranger's retreat was not less mysterious than was he himself.

That evening the cart halted at the mouth of Falls River. The camp was organized as usual, and the customary precautions were taken for the night. Herbert, become again the healthy and vigorous lad he was before his illness, derived great benefit from this life in the open air, between the sea-breezes and the vivifying air from the forests. His place was no longer in the cart, but at the head of the troop.

The next day, the 19th of February, the colonists, leaving the shore, where, beyond the mouth, basalts of every shape were so picturesquely piled up, ascended the river by its left bank. The road had been already partly cleared in their former excursions made from the corral to the west coast. The settlers were now about six miles from Mount Franklin.

The engineer's plan was this: To minutely survey the valley forming the bed of the river, and to cautiously approach the neighborhood of the corral; if the corral was occupied, to seize it by force; if it was not, to entrench themselves there and make it the center of the operations which had for their object the exploration of Mount Franklin.

This plan was unanimously approved by the colonists, for they were impatient to regain entire possession of their island.

They made their way then along the narrow valley separating two of the largest spurs of Mount Franklin. The trees, crowded on the river's bank, became rare on the upper slopes of the mountain. The ground was hilly and rough, very suitable for ambushes, and over which they did not venture without extreme precaution. Top and Jup skirmished on the flanks, springing right and left through the thick brushwood, and emulating each other in intelligence and activity. But nothing showed that the banks of the stream had been recently frequented—nothing announced either the presence or the proximity of the convicts. Toward five in the evening the cart stopped nearly 600 feet from the palisade. A semicircular screen of trees still hid it.

It was necessary to reconnoiter the corral, in order to ascertain if it was occupied. To go there openly, in broad daylight, when the convicts were probably in ambush, would be to expose themselves, as poor Herbert had done, to the firearms of the ruffians. It was better, then, to wait until night came on.

However, Gideon Spilett wished without further delay to reconnoiter the approaches to the corral, and Pencroft, who was quite out of patience, volunteered to accompany him.

"No, my friends," said the engineer, "wait till night. I will not allow one of you to expose himself in open day."

"But, captain—" answered the sailor, little disposed to obey.

"I beg of you, Pencroft," said the engineer.

"Very well!" replied the sailor, who vented his anger in another way, by bestowing on the convicts the worst names in his maritime vocabulary.

The colonists remained, therefore, near the cart, and carefully watched the neighboring parts of the forest.

Three hours passed thus. The wind had fallen, and absolute silence reigned under the great trees. The snapping of the smallest twig, a footstep on the dry leaves, the gliding of a body among the grass, would have been heard without difficulty. All was quiet. Besides, Top, lying on the grass, his head stretched out on his paws, gave no sign of uneasiness. At eight o'clock the day appeared far enough advanced for the reconnaissance to be made under favorable conditions. Gideon Spilett declared himself ready to set out accompanied by Pencroft. Cyrus Harding consented. Top and Jup were to remain with the engineer, Herbert, and Neb, for a bark or a cry at a wrong moment would give the alarm.

"Do not be imprudent," said Harding to the reporter and Pencroft; "you have not to gain possession of the corral, but only to find out whether it is occupied or not."

"All right," answered Pencroft.

And the two departed.

Under the trees, thanks to the thickness of their foliage, the obscurity rendered any object invisible beyond a radius of from thirty to forty feet. The reporter and Pencroft, halting at any suspicious sound, advanced with great caution.

They walked a little distance apart from each other so as to offer a less mark for a shot. And, to tell the truth, they expected every moment to hear a report. Five minutes after leaving the cart, Gideon Spilett and Pencroft arrived at the edge of the wood before the clearing beyond which rose the palisade.

They stopped. A few straggling beams still fell on the field clear of trees. Thirty feet distant was the gate of the corral, which appeared to be closed. This thirty feet, which it was necessary to cross from the wood to the palisade, constituted the dangerous zone, to borrow a ballistic term: in fact, one or more bullets fired from behind the palisade might knock over any one who ventured on to this zone. Gideon Spilett and the sailor were not men to draw back, but they knew that any imprudence on their part, of which they would be the first victims, would fall afterward on their companions. If they themselves were killed, what would become of Harding, Neb, and Herbert?

But Pencroft, excited at feeling himself so near the corral where he supposed the convicts had taken refuge, was about to press forward, when the reporter held him back with a grasp of iron.

"In a few minutes it will be quite dark," whispered Spilett in the sailor's ear, "then will be the time to act."

Pencroft, convulsively clasping the butt-end of his gun, restrained his energies, and waited, swearing to himself.

Soon the last of the twilight faded away. Darkness, which seemed as if it issued from the dense forest, covered the clearing. Mount Franklin rose like an enormous screen before the western horizon, and night spread rapidly over all, as it does in regions of low latitudes. Now was the time.

The reporter and Pencroft, since posting themselves on the edge of the wood, had not once lost sight of the palisade. The corral appeared to be absolutely deserted. The top of the palisade formed a line, a little darker than the surrounding shadow, and nothing disturbed its distinctness. Nevertheless, if the convicts were there, they must have posted one of their number to guard against any surprise.

Spilett grasped his companion's hand, and both crept toward the corral, their guns ready to fire.

They reached the gate without the darkness being illuminated by a single ray of light.

Pencroft tried to push open the gate, which, as the reporter and he had supposed, was closed. However, the sailor was able to ascertain that the outer bars had not been put up. It might, then, be concluded that the convicts were there in the corral, and that very probably they had fastened the gate in such a way that it could not be forced open.

Gideon Spilett and Pencroft listened.

Not a sound could be heard inside the palisade. The musmons and the goats, sleeping no doubt in their huts, in no way disturbed the calm of night.

The reporter and the sailor hearing nothing, asked themselves whether they had not better scale the palisades and penetrate into the corral. This would have been contrary to Cyrus Harding's instructions.

It is true that the enterprise might succeed, but it might also fail. Now, if the convicts were suspecting nothing, if they knew nothing of the expedition against them, if, lastly, there now existed a chance of surprising them, ought this chance to be lost by inconsiderately attempting to cross the palisades?

This was not the reporter's opinion. He thought it better to wait until all the settlers were collected together before attempting to penetrate into the corral. One thing was certain, that it was possible to reach the palisade without being seen, and also that it did not appear to be guarded. This point settled, there was nothing to be done but to return to the cart, where they would consult.

Pencroft probably agreed with this decision, for he followed the reporter without making any objection when the latter turned back to the wood.

In a few minutes the engineer was made acquainted with the state of affairs.

"Well," said he, after a little thought, "I now have reason to believe that the convicts are not in the corral."

"We shall soon know," said Pencroft, "when we have scaled the palisade."

"To the corral, my friends!" said Cyrus Harding.

"Shall we leave the cart in the wood?" asked Neb.

"No," replied the engineer, "it is our wagon of ammunition and provisions, and, if necessary, it would serve as an entrenchment."

"Forward, then!" said Gideon Spilett.

The cart emerged from the wood and began to roll noiselessly toward the palisade. The darkness was now profound, the silence as complete as when Pencroft and the reporter crept over the ground. The thick grass completely muffled their footsteps.

The colonists held themselves ready to fire. Jup, at Pencroft's orders, kept behind. Neb led Top in a leash, to prevent him from bounding forward.

The clearing soon came in sight. It was deserted. Without hesitating, the little band moved toward the palisade. In a short space of time the dangerous zone was passed. Neb remained at the onagers' heads to hold them. The engineer, the reporter, Herbert, and Pencroft, proceeded to the door, in order to ascertain if it was barricaded inside. It was open!

"What do you say now?" asked the engineer, turning to the sailor and Spilett.

Both were stupefied.

"I can swear," said Pencroft, "that this gate was shut just now!"

The colonists now hesitated. Were the convicts in the corral when Pencroft and the reporter made their reconnaissance? It could not be doubted, as the gate then closed could only have been opened by them. Were they still there, or had one of their number just gone out?

All these questions presented themselves simultaneously to the minds of the colonists, but how could they be answered?

At that moment, Herbert, who had advanced a few steps into the enclosure, drew back hurriedly, and seized Harding's hand.

"What's the matter?" asked the engineer.

"A light!"

"In the house?"

"Yes!"

All five advanced and indeed, through the window fronting them, they saw glimmering a feeble light. Cyrus Harding made up his mind rapidly. "It is our only chance," said he to his companions, "of finding the convicts collected in this house, suspecting nothing! They are in our power! Forward!" The colonists crossed through the enclosure, holding their guns ready in their hands. The cart had been left outside under the charge of Jup and Top, who had been prudently tied to it.

Cyrus Harding, Pencroft, and Gideon Spilett on one side, Herbert and Neb on the other, going along by the palisade, surveyed the absolutely dark and deserted corral.

In a few moments they were near the closed door of the house.

Harding signed to his companions not to stir, and approached the window, then feebly lighted by the inner light.

He gazed into the apartment.

On the table burned a lantern. Near the table was the bed formerly used by Ayrton.

On the bed lay the body of a man.

Suddenly Cyrus Harding drew back, and in a hoarse voice, "Ayrton!" he exclaimed.

Immediately the door was forced rather than opened, and the colonists rushed into the room.

Ayrton appeared to be asleep. His countenance showed that he had long and cruelly suffered. On his wrists and ankles could be seen great bruises.

Harding bent over him.

"Ayrton!" cried the engineer, seizing the arm of the man whom he had just found again under such unexpected circumstances.

At this exclamation Ayrton opened his eyes, and, gazing at Harding, then at the others,

"You!" he cried, "you?"

"Ayrton! Ayrton!" repeated Harding.

"Where am I?"

"In the house in the corral!"

"Alone?"

"Yes!"

"But they will come back!" cried Ayrton. "Defend yourselves! defend yourselves!"

And he fell back exhausted.

"Spilett," exclaimed the engineer, "we may be attacked at any moment. Bring the cart into the corral. Then, barricade the door, and all come back here."

Pencroft, Neb, and the reporter hastened to execute the engineer's orders. There was not a moment to be lost. Perhaps even now the cart was in the hands of the convicts!

In a moment the reporter and his two companions had crossed the corral and reached the gate of the palisade behind which Top was heard growling sullenly.

The engineer, leaving Ayrton for an instant, came out ready to fire. Herbert was at his side. Both surveyed the crest of the spur overlooking the corral. If the convicts were lying in ambush there, they might knock the settlers over one after the other.

At that moment the moon appeared in the east, above the black curtain of the forest, and a white sheet of light spread over the interior of the enclosure. The corral, with its clumps of trees, the little stream which watered it, its wide carpet of grass, was suddenly illuminated. From the side of the mountain, the house and a part of the palisade stood out white in the moonlight. On the opposite side toward the door, the enclosure remained dark.

A black mass soon appeared. This was the cart entering the circle of light, and Cyrus Harding could hear the noise made by the door, as his companions shut it and fastened the interior bars.

But, at that moment, Top, breaking loose, began to bark furiously and rush to the back of the corral, to the right of the house.

"Be ready to fire, my friends!" cried Harding.

The colonists raised their pieces and waited the moment to fire.

Top still barked, and Jup, running toward the dog, uttered shrill cries.

The colonists followed him, and reached the borders of the little stream, shaded by large trees. And there, in the bright moonlight, what did they see? Five corpses, stretched on the bank!

They were those of the convicts who, four months previously, had landed on Lincoln Island!

XIII

How had it happened? Who had killed the convicts? Was it Ayrton? No, for a moment before he was dreading their return.

But Ayrton was now in a profound stupor, from which it was no longer possible to rouse him. After uttering those few words he had again become unconscious, and had fallen back motionless on the bed.

The colonists, a prey to a thousand confused thoughts, under the influence of violent excitement, waited all night, without leaving Ayrton's house, or returning to the spot where lay the bodies of the convicts. It was very probable that Ayrton would not be able to throw any light on the circumstances under which the bodies had been found, since he himself was not aware that he was in the corral. But at any rate he would be in a position to give an account of what had taken place before this terrible execution. The next day Ayrton awoke from his torpor, and his companions cordially manifested all the joy they felt, on seeing him again, almost safe and sound, after a hundred and four days' separation.

Ayrton then in a few words recounted what had happened, or, at least, as much as he knew.

The day after his arrival at the corral, on the 10th of last November, at nightfall, he was surprised by the convicts, who had scaled the palisade. They bound and gagged him; then he was led to a dark cavern, at the foot of Mount Franklin, where the convicts had taken refuge.

His death had been decided upon, and the next day the convicts were about to kill him, when one of them recognized him and called him by the name which he bore in Australia. The wretches had no scruples as to murdering Ayrton! They spared Ben Joyce!

But from that moment Ayrton was exposed to the importunities of his former accomplices. They wished him to join them again, and relied upon his aid to enable them to gain possession of Granite House, to penetrate into that hitherto inaccessible dwelling, and to become masters of the island, after murdering the colonists!

Ayrton remained firm. The once convict, now repentant and pardoned, would rather die than betray his companions. Ayrton—bound, gagged, and closely watched—lived in this cave for four months.

Nevertheless the convicts had discovered the corral a short time after their arrival in the island, and since then they had subsisted on Ayrton's stores, but did not live at the corral.

On the 11th of November, two of the villains, surprised by the colonists' arrival, fired at Herbert, and one of them returned, boasting of having killed one of the inhabitants of the island; but he returned alone. His companion, as is known, fell by Cyrus Harding's dagger.

Ayrton's anxiety and despair may be imagined when he learned the news of Herbert's death. The settlers were now only four, and, as it seemed, at the mercy of the convicts. After this event, and during all the time that the colonists, detained by Herbert's illness, remained in the corral, the pirates did not leave their cavern, and even after they had pillaged the plateau of Prospect Heights, they did not think it prudent to abandon it.

The ill-treatment inflicted on Ayrton was now redoubled. His hands and feet still bore the bloody marks of the cords which bound him day and night. Every moment he expected to be put to death, nor did it appear possible that he could escape.

Matters remained thus until the third week of February. The convicts, still watching for a favorable opportunity, rarely quitted their retreat, and only made a few hunting excursions, either to the interior of the island, or the south coast.

Ayrton had no further news of his friends, and relinquished all hope of ever seeing them again. At last, the unfortunate man, weakened by ill-treatment, fell into a prostration so profound that sight and hearing failed him. From that moment, that is to say, since the last two days, he could give no information whatever of what had occurred.

"But, Captain Harding," he added, "since I was imprisoned in that cavern, how is it that I find myself in the corral?"

"How is it that the convicts are lying yonder dead, in the middle of the enclosure?" answered the engineer.

"Dead!" cried Ayrton, half rising from his bed, notwithstanding his weakness.

His companions supported him. He wished to get up, and with their assistance he did so. They then proceeded together toward the little stream.

It was now broad daylight.

There, on the bank, in the position in which they had been stricken by death in its most instantaneous form, lay the corpses of the five convicts!

Ayrton was astounded. Harding and his companions looked at him without uttering a word. On a sign from the engineer, Neb and Pencroft examined the bodies, already stiffened by the cold.

They bore no apparent trace of any wound.

Only, after carefully examining them, Pencroft found on the forehead of one, on the chest of another, on the back of this one, on the shoulder of that, a little red spot, a sort of scarcely visible bruise, the cause of which it was impossible to conjecture.

"It is there that they have been struck!" said Cyrus Harding.

"But with what weapon?" cried the reporter.

"A weapon, lightning-like in its effects, and of which we have not the secret!"

"And who has struck the blow?" asked Pencroft.

"The avenging power of the island," replied Harding, "he who brought you here, Ayrton, whose influence has once more manifested itself, who does for us all that which we cannot do for ourselves, and who, his will accomplished, conceals himself from us."

"Let us make search for him, then!" exclaimed Pencroft.

"Yes, we will search for him," answered Harding, "but we shall not discover this powerful being who performs such wonders, until he pleases to call us to him!"

This invisible protection, which rendered their own action unavailing, both irritated and piqued the engineer. The relative inferiority which it proved was of a nature to wound a haughty spirit. A generosity evinced in such a manner as to elude all tokens of gratitude, implied a sort of disdain for those on whom the obligation was conferred, which in Cyrus Harding's eyes marred, in some degree, the worth of the benefit.

"Let us search," he resumed, "and God grant that we may some day be permitted to prove to this haughty protector that he has not to deal with ungrateful people! What would I not give could we repay him, by rendering him in our turn, although at the price of our lives, some signal service!"

From this day, the thoughts of the inhabitants of Lincoln Island were solely occupied with the intended search. Everything incited them to discover the answer to this enigma, an answer which would only be the name of a man endowed with a truly inexplicable, and in some degree superhuman power.

In a few minutes, the settlers re-entered the house, where their influence soon restored to Ayrton his moral and physical energy.

Neb and Pencroft carried the corpses of the convicts into the forest, some distance from the corral, and buried them deep in the ground.

Ayrton was then made acquainted with the facts which had occurred during his seclusion. He learned Herbert's adventures, and through what various trials the colonists had passed. As to the settlers, they had despaired of ever seeing Ayrton again, and had been convinced that the convicts had ruthlessly murdered him.

"And now," said Cyrus Harding, as he ended his recital, "a duty remains for us to perform. Half of our task is accomplished, but although the convicts are no longer to be feared, it is not owing to ourselves that we are once more masters of the island."

"Well!" answered Gideon Spilett, "let us search all this labyrinth of the spurs of Mount Franklin. We will not leave a hollow, not a hole unexplored! Ah! if ever a reporter found himself face to face with a mystery, it is I who now speak to you, my friends!"

"And we will not return to Granite House until we have found our benefactor," said Herbert.

"Yes," said the engineer, "we will do all that it is humanly possible to do, but I repeat, we shall not find him until he himself permits us."

"Shall we stay at the corral?" asked Pencroft.

"We shall stay here," answered Harding. "Provisions are abundant, and we are here in the very center of the circle we have to explore. Besides, if necessary, the cart will take us rapidly to Granite House."

"Good!" answered the sailor. "Only I have a remark to make."

"What is it?"

"Here is the fine season getting on, and we must not forget that we have a voyage to make."

"A voyage?" said Gideon Spilett.

"Yes, to Tabor Island," answered Pencroft. "It is necessary to carry a notice there to point out the position of our island and say that Ayrton is here in case the Scotch yacht should come to take him off. Who knows if it is not already too late?"

"But, Pencroft," asked Ayrton, "how do you intend to make this voyage?"

"In the *Bonadventure.*"

"The *Bonadventure!*" exclaimed Ayrton. "She no longer exists."

"My *Bonadventure* exists no longer!" shouted Pencroft, bounding from his seat.

"No," answered Ayrton. "The convicts discovered her in her little harbor only eight days ago, they put to sea in her, and—"

"And?" said Pencroft, his heart beating.

"And not having Bob Harvey to steer her, they ran on the rocks, and the vessel went to pieces."

"Oh, the villains, the cutthroats, the infamous scoundrels!" exclaimed Pencroft.

"Pencroft," said Herbert, taking the sailor's hand, "we will build another *Bonadventure*—a larger one. We have all the ironwork—all the rigging of the brig at our disposal."

"But do you know," returned Pencroft, "that it will take at least five or six months to build a vessel of from thirty to forty tons?"

"We can take our time," said the reporter, "and we must give up the voyage to Tabor Island for this year."

"Oh, my *Bonadventure*! my poor *Bonadventure*!" cried Pencroft, almost broken-hearted at the destruction of the vessel of which he was so proud.

The loss of the *Bonadventure* was certainly a thing to be lamented by the colonists, and it was agreed that this loss should be repaired as soon as possible. This settled, they now occupied themselves with bringing their researches to bear on the most secret parts of the island.

The exploration was commenced at daybreak on the 19th of February, and lasted an entire week. The base of the mountain, with its spurs and their numberless ramifications, formed a labyrinth of valleys and elevations. It was evident that there, in the depths of these narrow gorges, perhaps even in the interior of Mount Franklin itself, was the proper place to pursue their researches. No part of the island could have been more suitable to conceal a dwelling whose occupant wished to remain unknown. But so irregular was the formation of the valleys that Cyrus Harding was obliged to conduct the exploration in a strictly methodical manner.

The colonists first visited the valley opening to the south of the volcano, and which first received the waters of Falls River. There Ayrton showed them the cavern where the convicts had taken refuge, and in which he had been imprisoned until his removal to the corral. This cavern was just as Ayrton had left it. They found there a considerable quantity of ammunition and provisions, conveyed thither by the convicts in order to form a reserve.

The whole of the valley bordering on the cave, shaded by fir and other trees, was thoroughly explored, and on turning the point of the southwestern spur, the colonists entered a narrower gorge similar to the picturesque columns of basalt on the coast. Here the trees were fewer. Stones took the place of grass. Goats and musmons gamboled among the rocks. Here began the barren part of the island. It could already be seen that, of the numerous valleys branching off at the base of Mount Franklin, three only were wooded and rich in pasturage like that of the corral, which bordered on the west on the Falls River valley, and on the east on the Red Creek valley. These two streams, which lower down became rivers by the absorption of several tributaries, were formed by all the springs of the mountain and thus caused the fertility of its southern part. As to the Mercy, it was more directly fed from ample springs concealed under the cover of Jacamar Wood, and it was by springs of this nature, spreading in a thousand streamlets, that the soil of the Serpentine Peninsula was watered.

Now, of these three well-watered valleys, either might have served as a retreat to some solitary who would have found there everything necessary for life. But the settlers had already explored them, and in no part had they discovered the presence of man.

Was it then in the depths of those barren gorges, in the midst of the piles of rock, in the rugged northern ravines, among the streams of lava, that this dwelling and its occupant would be found?

The northern part of Mount Franklin was at its base composed solely of two valleys, wide, not very deep, without any appearance of vegetation, strewn with masses of rock, paved with lava, and varied with great blocks of mineral. This region required a long and careful exploration. It contained a thousand cavities, comfortless no doubt, but perfectly concealed and difficult of access.

The colonists even visited dark tunnels, dating from the volcanic period, still black from the passage of the fire, and penetrated into the depths of the mountain. They traversed these somber galleries, waving lighted torches; they examined the smallest excavations; they sounded the shallowest depths, but all was dark and silent. It did not appear that the foot of man had ever before trodden these ancient passages, or that his arm had ever displaced one of these blocks, which remained as the volcano had cast them up above the waters, at the time of the submersion of the island.

However, although these passages appeared to be absolutely deserted, and the obscurity was complete, Cyrus Harding was obliged to confess that absolute silence did not reign there.

On arriving at the end of one of these gloomy caverns, extending several hundred feet into the interior of the mountain, he was surprised to hear a deep rumbling noise, increased in intensity by the sonorousness of the rocks.

Gideon Spilett, who accompanied him, also heard these distant mutterings, which indicated a revivification of the subterranean fires. Several times both listened, and they agreed that some chemical process was taking place in the bowels of the earth.

"Then the volcano is not totally extinct?" said the reporter.

"It is possible that since our exploration of the crater," replied Cyrus Harding, "some change has occurred. Any volcano, although considered extinct, may evidently again burst forth."

"But if an eruption of Mount Franklin occurred," asked Spilett, "would there not be some danger to Lincoln Island?"

"I do not think so," answered the reporter. "The crater, that is to say, the safety-valve, exists, and the overflow of smoke and lava, would escape, as it did formerly, by this customary outlet."

"Unless the lava opened a new way for itself toward the fertile parts of the island!"

"And why, my dear Spilett," answered Cyrus Harding, "should it not follow the road naturally traced out for it?"

"Well, volcanoes are capricious," returned the reporter.

"Notice," answered the engineer, "that the inclination of Mount Franklin favors the flow of water toward the valleys which we are exploring just now. To turn aside this flow, an earthquake would be necessary to change the mountain's center of gravity."

"But an earthquake is always to be feared at these times," observed Gideon Spilett.

"Always," replied the engineer, "especially when the subterranean forces begin to awake, as they risk meeting with some obstruction, after a long rest. Thus, my dear Spilett, an eruption would be a serious thing for us, and it would be better that the volcano should not have the slightest desire to wake up. But we could not prevent it, could we? At any rate, even if it should occur, I do not think Prospect Heights would be seriously threatened. Between them and the mountain, the ground is considerably depressed, and if the lava should ever take a course toward the lake, it would be cast on the downs and the neighboring parts of Shark Gulf."

"We have not yet seen any smoke at the top of the mountain, to indicate an approaching eruption," said Gideon Spilett.

"No," answered Harding, "not a vapor escapes from the crater, for it was only yesterday that I attentively surveyed the summit. But it is probable that at the lower part of the chimney, time may have accumulated rocks, cinders, hardened lava, and that this valve of which I spoke, may at any time become overcharged. But at the first serious effort, every obstacle will disappear, and you may be certain, my dear Spilett, that neither the island, which is the boiler, nor the volcano, which is the chimney, will burst under the pressure of gas. Nevertheless, I repeat, it would be better that there should not be an eruption."

"And yet we are not mistaken," remarked the reporter. "Mutterings can be distinctly heard in the very bowels of the volcano!"

"You are right," said the engineer, again listening attentively. "There can be no doubt of it. A commotion is going on there, of which we can neither estimate the importance nor the ultimate result."

Cyrus Harding and Spilett, on coming out, rejoined their companions, to whom they made known the state of affairs.

"Very well!" cried Pencroft, "the volcano wants to play his pranks! Let him try, if he likes! He will find his master!"

"Who?" asked Neb.

"Our good genius, Neb, our good genius, who will shut his mouth for him, if he so much as pretends to open it!"

As may be seen, the sailor's confidence in the tutelary deity of his island was absolute, and, certainly, the occult power, manifested until now in so many inexplicable ways, appeared to be unlimited; but also it knew how to escape the colonists' most minute researches, for, in spite of all their efforts, in spite of the more than zeal—the obstinacy—with which they carried on their exploration, the retreat of the mysterious being could not be discovered.

From the 19th to the 25th of February the circle of investigation was extended to all the northern region of Lincoln Island, whose most secret nooks were explored. The colonists even went the length of tapping every rock. The search was extended to the extreme verge of the mountain. It was explored thus to the very summit of the truncated cone terminating the first row of rocks, then to the upper ridge of the enormous hat, at the bottom of which opened the crater.

They did more; they visited the gulf, now extinct, but in whose depths the rumbling could be distinctly heard. However, no sign of smoke or vapor, no heating of the rock, indicated an approaching eruption. But neither there, nor in any other part of Mount Franklin, did the colonists find any traces of him of whom they were in search.

Their investigations were then directed to the downs. They carefully examined the high lava-cliffs of Shark Gulf from the base to the crest, although it was extremely difficult to reach even the level of the gulf. No one!—nothing!

Indeed, in these three words was summed up so much fatigue uselessly expended, so much energy producing no results, that somewhat of anger mingled with the discomfiture of Cyrus Harding and his companions.

It was now time to think of returning, for these researches could not be prolonged indefinitely. The colonists were certainly right in believing that the mysterious being did not reside on the surface of the island, and the wildest fancies haunted their excited imaginations. Pencroft and Neb, particularly, were not contented with the mystery, but allowed their imaginations to wander into the domain of the supernatural.

On the 25th of February the colonists re-entered Granite House, and by means of the double cord, carried by an arrow to the threshold of the door, they re-established communication between their habitation and the ground.

A month later they commemorated, on the 25th of March, the third anniversary of their arrival on Lincoln Island.

XIV

Three years had passed away since the escape of the prisoners from Richmond, and how often during those three years had they spoken of their country, always present in their thoughts!

They had no doubt that the civil war was at an end, and to them it appeared impossible that the just cause of the North had not triumphed. But what had been the incidents of this terrible war? How much blood had it not cost? How many of their friends must have fallen in the struggle? They often spoke of these things, without as yet being able to foresee the day when they would be permitted once more to see their country. To return thither, were it but for a few days, to renew the social link with the inhabited world, to establish a communication between their native land

and their island, then to pass the longest, perhaps the best, portion of their existence in this colony, founded by them, and which would then be dependent on their country, was this a dream impossible to realize?

There were only two ways of accomplishing it—either a ship must appear off Lincoln Island, or the colonists must themselves build a vessel strong enough to sail to the nearest land.

"Unless," said Pencroft, "our good genius himself provides us with the means of returning to our country."

And, really, had any one told Pencroft and Neb that a ship of 300 tons was waiting for them in Shark Gulf or at Port Balloon, they would not even have made a gesture of surprise. In their state of mind nothing appeared improbable.

But Cyrus Harding, less confident, advised them to confine themselves to fact, and more especially so with regard to the building of a vessel—a really urgent work, since it was for the purpose of depositing, as soon as possible, at Tabor Island a document indicating Ayrton's new residence.

As the *Bonadventure* no longer existed, six months at least would be required for the construction of a new vessel. Now winter was approaching, and the voyage would not be made before the following spring.

"We have time to get everything ready for the fine season," remarked the engineer, who was consulting with Pencroft about these matters. "I think, therefore, my friend, that since we have to rebuild our vessel it will be best to give her larger dimensions. The arrival of the Scotch yacht at Tabor Island is very uncertain. It may even be that, having arrived several months ago, she has again sailed after having vainly searched for some trace of Ayrton. Will it not then be best to build a ship which, if necessary, could take us either to the Polynesian Archipelago or to New Zealand? What do you think?"

"I think, captain," answered the sailor; "I think that you are as capable of building a large vessel as a small one. Neither the wood nor the tools are wanting. It is only a question of time."

"And how many months would be required to build a vessel of from 250 to 300 tons?" asked Harding.

"Seven or eight months at least," replied Pencroft. "But it must not be forgotten that winter is drawing near, and that in severe frost wood is difficult to work. We must calculate on several weeks' delay, and if our vessel is ready by next November we may think ourselves very lucky."

"Well," replied Cyrus Harding, "that will be exactly the most favorable time for undertaking a voyage of any importance, either to Tabor Island or to a more distant land."

"So it will, captain," answered the sailor. "Make out your plans then; the workmen are ready, and I imagine that Ayrton can lend us a good helping hand."

The colonists, having been consulted, approved the engineer's plan, and it was, indeed, the best thing to be done. It is true that the construction of a ship of from two to three hundred tons would be great labor, but the colonists had confidence in themselves, justified by their previous success.

Cyrus Harding then busied himself in drawing the plan of the vessel and making the model. During this time his companions employed themselves in felling and carting trees to furnish the ribs, timbers, and planks. The Forests of the Far West supplied the best oaks and elms. They took advantage of the opening already made on their last excursion to form a practicable road, which they named the Far West Road, and the trees were carried to the Chimneys, where the dockyard was established. As to the road in question, the choice of trees had rendered its direction somewhat capricious, but at the same time it facilitated the access to a large part of the Serpentine Peninsula.

It was important that the trees should be quickly felled and cut up, for they could not be used while yet green, and some time was necessary to allow them to get seasoned. The carpenters, therefore, worked vigorously during the month of April, which was troubled only by a few equinoctial gales of some violence. Master Jup aided them dexterously, either by climbing to the top of a tree to fasten the ropes or by lending his stout shoulders to carry the lopped trunks.

All this timber was piled up under a large shed, built near the Chimneys, and there awaited the time for use.

The month of April was tolerably fine, as October often is in the northern zone. At the same time other work was actively continued, and soon all trace of devastation disappeared from the plateau of Prospect Heights. The mill was rebuilt, and new buildings rose in the poultry-yard. It had appeared necessary to enlarge their dimensions, for the feathered population had increased considerably. The stable now contained five onagers, four of which were well broken, and allowed themselves to be either driven or ridden, and a little colt. The colony now possessed a plow, to which the onagers were yoked like regular Yorkshire or Kentucky oxen. The colonists divided their work, and their arms never tired. Then who could have enjoyed better health than these workers, and what good humor enlivened the evenings in Granite House as they formed a thousand plans for the future!

As a matter of course Ayrton shared the common lot in every respect, and there was no longer any talk of his going to live at the corral. Nevertheless he was still sad and reserved, and joined more in the work than in the pleasures of his companions. But he was a valuable workman at need—strong, skillful, ingenious, intelligent. He was esteemed and loved by all, and he could not be ignorant of it.

In the meanwhile the corral was not abandoned. Every other day one of the settlers, driving the cart or mounted on an onager, went to look after the flock of musmons and goats and bring back the supply of milk required by Neb. These excursions at the same time afforded opportunities for hunting. Therefore Herbert and Gideon Spilett, with Top in front, traversed more often than their companions the road to the corral, and with the capital guns which they carried, capybaras, agouties, kangaroos, and wild pigs for large game, ducks, grouse, jacamars, and snipe for small game, were never wanting in the house. The produce of the warren, of the oyster-bed, several turtles which were taken, excellent salmon which came up the Mercy, vegetables from the plateau, wild fruit from the forest, were riches upon riches, and Neb, the head cook, could scarcely by himself store them away.

The telegraphic wire between the corral and Granite House had of course been repaired, and it was worked whenever one or other of the settlers was at the corral and found it necessary to spend the night there. Besides, the island was safe now and no attacks were to be feared, at any rate from men.

However, that which had happened might happen again. A descent of pirates, or even of escaped convicts, was always to be feared. It was possible that companions or accomplices of Bob Harvey had been in the secret of his plans, and might be tempted to imitate him. The colonists, therefore, were careful to observe the sea around the island, and every day their telescope covered the horizon enclosed by Union and Washington bays. When they went to the corral they examined the sea to the west with no less attention, and by climbing the spur their gaze extended over a large section of the western horizon.

Nothing suspicious was discerned, but still it was necessary for them to be on their guard.

The engineer one evening imparted to his friends a plan which he had conceived for fortifying the corral. It appeared prudent to him to heighten the palisade and to flank it with a sort of blockhouse, which, if necessary, the settlers could hold against the enemy. Granite House might, by its very position, be considered impregnable; therefore the corral with its buildings, its stores, and the animals it contained, would always be the object of pirates, whoever they were, who might land on the island, and should the colonists be obliged to shut themselves up there, they ought also to be able to defend themselves without any disadvantage. This was a project which might be left for consideration, and they were, besides, obliged to put off its execution until the next spring.

About the 15th of May the keel of the new vessel lay along the dockyard, and soon the stem and stern-post, mortised at each of its extremities, rose almost perpendicularly. The keel, of good oak, measured 110 feet in length, this allowing a width of five-and-twenty feet to the midship beam. But this was all the carpenters could do before the arrival of the frosts and bad weather. During the following week they fixed the first of the stern timbers, but were then obliged to suspend work.

During the last days of the month the weather was extremely bad. The wind blew from the east, sometimes with the violence of a tempest. The engineer was somewhat uneasy on account of the dockyard sheds—which besides, he could not have established in any other place near to Granite House—for the islet only imperfectly sheltered the shore from the fury of the open sea, and in great storms the waves beat against the very foot of the granite cliff.

But, very fortunately, these fears were not realized. The wind shifted to the southeast, and there the beach of Granite House was completely covered by Flotsam Point.

Pencroft and Ayrton, the most zealous workmen at the new vessel, pursued their labor as long as they could. They were not men to mind the wind tearing at their hair, nor the rain wetting them to the skin, and a blow from a hammer is worth just as much in bad as in fine weather. But when a severe frost succeeded this wet period, the wood, its fibers acquiring the hardness of iron, became extremely difficult to work, and about the 10th of June ship-building was obliged to be entirely discontinued.

Cyrus Harding and his companions had not omitted to observe how severe was the temperature during the winters of Lincoln Island. The cold was comparable to that experienced in the States of New England, situated at almost the same distance from the equator. In the Northern Hemisphere, or at any rate in the part occupied by British America and the north of the United States, this phenomenon is explained by the flat conformation of the territories bordering on the pole, and on which there is no intumescence of the soil to oppose any obstacle to the north winds; here, in Lincoln Island, this explanation would not suffice.

"It has even been observed," remarked Harding one day to his companions, "that in equal latitudes the islands and coast regions are less tried by the cold than inland countries. I have often heard it asserted that the winters of Lombardy, for example, are not less rigorous than those of Scotland, which results from the sea restoring during the winter the heat which it received during the summer. Islands are, therefore, in a better situation for benefiting by this restitution."

"But then, Captain Harding," asked Herbert, "why does Lincoln Island appear to escape the common law?"

"That is difficult to explain," answered the engineer. "However, I should be disposed to conjecture that this peculiarity results from the situation of the island in the Southern Hemisphere, which, as you know, my boy, is colder than the Northern Hemisphere."

"Yes," said Herbert, "and icebergs are met with in lower latitudes in the south than in the north of the Pacific."

"That is true," remarked Pencroft, "and when I have been serving on board whalers I have seen icebergs off Cape Horn."

"The severe cold experienced in Lincoln Island," said Gideon Spilett, "may then perhaps be explained by the presence of floes or icebergs comparatively near to Lincoln Island."

"Your opinion is very admissible indeed, my dear Spilett," answered Cyrus Harding, "and it is evidently to the proximity of icebergs that we owe our rigorous winters. I would draw your attention also to an entirely physical cause, which renders the Southern colder than the Northern Hemisphere. In fact, since the sun is nearer to this hemisphere during the summer, it is necessarily more distant during the winter. This explains then the excess of temperature in the two seasons, for, if we find the winters very cold in Lincoln Island, we must not forget that the summers here, on the contrary, are very hot."

"But why, if you please, captain," asked Pencroft, knitting his brows, "why should our hemisphere, as you say, be so badly divided? It isn't just, that!"

"Friend Pencroft," answered the engineer, laughing, "whether just or not, we must submit to it, and here lies the reason for this peculiarity. The earth does not describe a circle around the sun, but an ellipse, as it must by the laws of rational mechanics. Now, the earth occupies one of the foci of the ellipse, and so at one point in its course it is at its apogee, that is, at its farthest from the sun, and at another point it is at its perigee, or nearest to the sun. Now it happens that it is during the winter of the southern countries that it is at its most distant point from the sun, and consequently, in a situation for those regions to feel the greatest cold. Nothing can be done to prevent that, and men, Pencroft, however learned they may be, can never change anything of the cosmographical order established by God Himself."

"And yet," added Pencroft, "the world is very learned. What a big book, captain, might be made with all that is known!"

"And what a much bigger book still with all that is not known!" answered Harding.

At last, for one reason or another, the month of June brought the cold with its accustomed intensity, and the settlers were often confined to Granite House. Ah! how wearisome this imprisonment was to them, and more particularly to Gideon Spilett.

"Look here," said he to Neb one day, "I would give you by notarial deed all the estates which will come to me some day, if you were a good-enough fellow to go, no matter where, and subscribe to some newspaper for me! Decidedly the thing that is most essential to my happiness is the knowing every morning what has happened the day before in other places than this!"

Neb began to laugh.

"'Pon my word," he replied, "the only thing I think about is my daily work!"

The truth was that indoors as well as out there was no want of work.

The colony of Lincoln Island was now at its highest point of prosperity, achieved by three years of continued hard work. The destruction of the brig had been a new source of riches. Without speaking of the complete rig which would serve for the vessel now on the stocks, utensils and tools of all sorts, weapons and ammunition, clothes and instruments, were now piled in the storerooms of Granite House. It had not even been necessary to resort again to the manufacture of the coarse felt materials. Though the colonists had suffered from cold during their first winter, the bad season might now come without their having any reason to dread its severity. Linen was plentiful also, and besides, they kept it with extreme care. From chloride of sodium, which is nothing else than sea salt, Cyrus Harding easily extracted the soda and chlorine. The soda, which it was easy to change into carbonate of soda, and the chlorine, of which he made chloride of lime, were employed for various domestic purposes, and especially in bleaching linen. Besides, they did not wash more than four times a year, as was done by families in the olden times, and it may be added, that Pencroft and Gideon Spilett, while waiting for the postman to bring him his newspaper, distinguished themselves as washermen.

So passed the winter months, June, July, and August. They were severe, and the average observations of the thermometer did not give more than eight degrees of Fahrenheit. It was therefore lower in temperature than the preceding winter. But then, what splendid fires blazed continually on the hearths of Granite House, the smoke marking the granite wall with long, zebra-like streaks! Fuel was not spared, as it grew naturally a few steps from them. Besides, the chips of the wood destined for the construction of the ship enabled them to economize the coal, which required more trouble to transport.

Men and animals were all well. Master Jup was a little chilly, it must be confessed. This was perhaps his only weakness, and it was necessary to make him a well-padded dressing-gown. But what a servant he was, clever, zealous, indefatigable, not indiscreet, not talkative, and he might have been with reason proposed as a model for all his biped brothers in the Old and New Worlds!

"As for that," said Pencroft, "when one has four hands at one's service, of course one's work ought to be done so much the better!"

And indeed the intelligent creature did it well.

During the seven months which had passed since the last researches made round the mountain, and during the month of September, which brought back fine weather, nothing was heard of the genius of the island. His power was not manifested in any way. It is true that it would have been superfluous, for no incident occurred to put the colonists to any painful trial.

Cyrus Harding even observed that if by chance the communication between the unknown and the tenants of Granite House had ever been established through the granite, and if Top's instinct had as it were felt it, there was no further sign of it during this period. The dog's growling had entirely ceased, as well as the uneasiness of the orang. The two friends—for they were so—no longer prowled around the opening of the inner well, nor did they bark or whine in that singular way which from the first the engineer had noticed. But could he be sure that this was all that was to be said about this enigma, and that he should never arrive at a solution? Could he be certain that some conjuncture would not occur which would bring the mysterious personage on the scene? Who could tell what the future might have in reserve?

At last the winter was ended, but an event, the consequences of which might be serious, occurred in the first days of the returning spring.

On the 7th of September, Cyrus Harding, having observed the crater, saw smoke curling around the summit of the mountain, its first vapors rising in the air.

XV

The colonists, warned by the engineer, left their work and gazed in silence at the summit of Mount Franklin.

The volcano had awoke, and the vapor had penetrated the mineral layer heaped at the bottom of the crater. But would the subterranean fires provoke any violent eruption? This was an event which could not be foreseen. However, even while admitting the possibility of an eruption, it was not probable that the whole of Lincoln Island would suffer from it. The flow of volcanic matter is not always disastrous, and the island had already undergone this trial, as was shown by the streams of lava hardened on the northern slopes of the mountain. Besides, from the shape of the crater—the opening broken in the upper edge—the matter would be thrown to the side opposite the fertile regions of the island.

However, the past did not necessarily answer for the future. Often, at the summit of volcanoes, the old craters close and new ones open. This had occurred in the two hemispheres—at Etna, Popocatepetl, at Orizaba—and on the eve of an eruption there is everything to be feared. In fact, an earthquake—a phenomenon which often accompanies volcanic eruptions—is enough to change the interior arrangement of a mountain, and to open new outlets for the burning lava.

Cyrus Harding explained these things to his companions, and, without exaggerating the state of things, he told them all the pros and cons. After all, they could not prevent it. It did not appear likely that Granite House would be threatened unless the ground was shaken by an earthquake. But the corral would be in great danger should a new crater open in the southern side of Mount Franklin.

From that day the smoke never disappeared from the top of the mountain, and it could even be perceived that it increased in height and thickness, without any flame mingling in its heavy volumes. The phenomenon was still concentrated in the lower part of the central crater.

However, with the fine days, work had been continued. The building of the vessel was hastened as much as possible, and, by means of the waterfall on the shore, Cyrus Harding managed to establish a hydraulic sawmill, which rapidly cut up the trunks of trees into planks and joists. The mechanism of this apparatus was as simple as those used in the rustic sawmills of Norway. A first horizontal movement to move the piece of wood, a second vertical movement to move the saw—this was all that was wanted; and the engineer succeeded by means of a wheel, two cylinders, and pulleys properly arranged. Toward the end of the month of September the skeleton of the vessel, which was to be rigged as a schooner, lay in the dockyard. The ribs were almost entirely completed, and, all the timbers having been sustained by a provisional band, the shape of the vessel could already be seen. The schooner, sharp in the bows, very slender in the after-part, would evidently be suitable for a long voyage, if wanted; but laying the planking would still take a considerable time. Very fortunately, the iron work of the pirate brig had been saved after the explosion. From the planks and injured ribs Pencroft and Ayrton had extracted the bolts and a large quantity of copper nails. It was so much work saved for the smiths, but the carpenters had much to do.

Ship-building was interrupted for a week for the harvest, the haymaking, and the gathering in of the different crops on the plateau. This work finished, every moment was devoted to finishing the schooner. When night came the workmen were really quite exhausted. So as not to lose any time they had changed the hours for their meals; they dined at twelve o'clock, and only had their supper when daylight failed them. They then ascended to Granite House, when they were always ready to go to bed.

Sometimes, however, when the conversation bore on some interesting subject the hour for sleep was delayed for a time. The colonists then spoke of the future, and talked willingly of the changes which a voyage in the schooner to inhabited lands would make in their situation. But always, in the midst of these plans, prevailed the thought of a subsequent return to Lincoln Island. Never would they abandon this colony, founded with so much labor and with such success, and to which a communication with America would afford a fresh impetus. Pencroft and Neb especially hoped to end their days there.

"Herbert," said the sailor, "you will never abandon Lincoln Island?"

"Never, Pencroft, and especially if you make up your mind to stay there."

"That was made up long ago, my boy," answered Pencroft. "I shall expect you. You will bring me your wife and children, and I shall make jolly chaps of your youngsters!"

"That's agreed," replied Herbert, laughing and blushing at the same time.

"And you, Captain Harding," resumed Pencroft enthusiastically, "you will be still the governor of the island! Ah, how many inhabitants could it support? Ten thousand at least!"

They talked in this way, allowing Pencroft to run on, and at last the reporter actually started a newspaper—the *New Lincoln Herald!*

So is man's heart. The desire to perform a work which will endure, which will survive him, is the origin of his superiority over all other living creatures here below. It is this which has established his dominion, and this it is which justifies it, over all the world.

After that, who knows if Jup and Top had not themselves their little dream of the future.

Ayrton silently said to himself that he would like to see Lord Glenarvan again and show himself to all restored.

One evening, on the 15th of October, the conversation was prolonged later than usual. It was nine o'clock. Already, long badly concealed yawns gave warning of the hour of rest, and Pencroft was proceeding toward his bed, when the electric bell, placed in the dining-room, suddenly rang.

All were there, Cyrus Harding, Gideon Spilett, Herbert, Ayrton, Pencroft, Neb. Therefore none of the colonists were at the corral.

Cyrus Harding rose. His companions stared at each other, scarcely believing their ears.

"What does that mean?" cried Neb. "Was it the devil who rang it?"

No one answered.

"The weather is stormy," observed Herbert. "Might not its influence of electricity—"

Herbert did not finish his phrase. The engineer, toward whom all eyes were turned, shook his head negatively.

"We must wait," said Gideon Spilett. "If it is a signal, whoever it may be who has made it, he will renew it."

"But who do you think it is?" cried Neb.

"Who?" answered Pencroft, "but he—"

The sailor's sentence was cut short by a new tinkle of the bell.

Harding went to the apparatus, and sent this question to the corral: "What do you want?"

A few moments later the needle, moving on the alphabetic dial, gave this reply to the tenants of Granite House:

"Come to the corral immediately."

"At last!" exclaimed Harding.

Yes! At last! The mystery was about to be unveiled. The colonists' fatigue had disappeared before the tremendous interest which was about to urge them to the corral, and all wish for rest had ceased. Without having uttered a word, in a few moments they had left Granite House, and were standing on the beach. Jup and Top alone were left behind. They could do without them.

The night was black. The new moon had disappeared at the same time as the sun. As Herbert had observed, great stormy clouds formed a lowering and heavy vault, preventing any star rays. A few lightning flashes, reflections from a distant storm, illuminated the horizon.

It was possible that a few hours later the thunder would roll over the island itself. The night was very threatening.

But however deep the darkness was, it would not prevent them from finding the familiar road to the corral.

They ascended the left bank of the Mercy, reached the plateau, passed the bridge over Creek Glycerine, and advanced through the forest.

They walked at a good pace, a prey to the liveliest emotions. There was no doubt but that they were now going to learn the long-searched-for answer to the enigma, the name of that mysterious being, so deeply concerned in their life, so generous in his influence, so powerful in his action! Must not this stranger have indeed mingled with their existence, have known the smallest details, have heard all that was said in Granite House, to have been able always to act in the very nick of time?

Every one, wrapped up in his own reflections, pressed forward. Under the arch of trees the darkness was such that even the edge of the road could not be seen. Not a sound in the forest. Both animals and birds, influenced by the heaviness of the atmosphere, remained motionless and silent. Not a breath disturbed the leaves. The footsteps of the colonists alone resounded on the hardened ground.

During the first quarter of an hour the silence was only interrupted by this remark from Pencroft:

"We ought to have brought a torch."

And by this reply from the engineer:

"We shall find one at the corral."

Harding and his companions had left Granite House at twelve minutes past nine. At forty-seven minutes past nine they had traversed three out of the five miles which separated the mouth of the Mercy from the corral.

At that moment sheets of lightning spread over the island and illumined the dark trees. The flashes dazzled and almost blinded them. Evidently the storm would not be long in bursting forth.

The flashes gradually became brighter and more rapid. Distant thunder growled in the sky. The atmosphere was stifling.

The colonists proceeded as if they were urged onward by some irresistible force.

At ten o'clock a vivid flash showed them the palisade, and as they reached the gate the storm burst forth with tremendous fury.

In a minute the corral was crossed, and Harding stood before the hut.

Probably the house was occupied by the stranger, since it was from thence that the telegram had been sent. However, no light shone through the window.

The engineer knocked at the door.

No answer.

Cyrus Harding opened the door, and the settlers entered the room, which was perfectly dark. A light was struck by Neb, and in a few moments the lantern was lighted and the light thrown into every corner of the room.

There was no one there. Everything was in the state in which it had been left.

"Have we been deceived by an illusion?" murmured Cyrus Harding.

No! that was not possible! The telegram had clearly said,

"Come to the corral immediately."

They approached the table specially devoted to the use of the wire. Everything was in order—the pile on the box containing it, as well as all the apparatus.

"Who came here the last time?" asked the engineer.

"I did, captain," answered Ayrton.

"And that was—"

"Four days ago."

"Ah! a note!" cried Herbert, pointing to a paper lying on the table.

On this paper were written these words in English:

"Follow the new wire."

"Forward!" cried Harding, who understood that the dispatch had not been sent from the corral, but from the mysterious retreat, communicating directly with Granite House by means of a supplementary wire joined to the old one.

Neb took the lighted lantern, and all left the corral. The storm then burst forth with tremendous violence. The interval between each lightning-flash and each thunder-clap diminished rapidly. The summit of the volcano, with its plume of vapor, could be seen by occasional flashes.

There was no telegraphic communication in any part of the corral between the house and the palisade; but the engineer, running straight to the first post, saw by the light of a flash a new wire hanging from the isolator to the ground.

"There it is!" said he.

This wire lay along the ground, and was surrounded with an isolating substance like a submarine cable, so as to assure the free transmission of the current. It appeared to pass through the wood and the southern spurs of the mountain, and consequently it ran toward the west.

"Follow it!" said Cyrus Harding.

And the settlers immediately pressed forward, guided by the wire.

The thunder continued to roar with such violence that not a word could be heard. However, there was no occasion for speaking, but to get forward as fast as possible.

Cyrus Harding and his companions then climbed the spur rising between the corral valley and that of Falls River, which they crossed at its narrowest part. The wire, sometimes stretched over the lower branches of the trees, sometimes lying on the ground, guided them surely. The engineer had supposed that the wire would perhaps stop at the bottom of the valley, and that the stranger's retreat would be there.

Nothing of the sort. They were obliged to ascend the southwestern spur, and re-descend on that arid plateau terminated by the strangely-wild basalt cliff. From time to time one of the colonists stooped down and felt for the wire with his hands; but there was now no doubt that the wire was running directly toward the sea. There, to a certainty, in the depths of those rocks, was the dwelling so long sought for in vain.

The sky was literally on fire. Flash succeeded flash. Several struck the summit of the volcano in the midst of the thick smoke. It appeared there as if the mountain was vomiting flame. At a few minutes to eleven the colonists arrived on the high cliff overlooking the ocean to the west. The wind had risen. The surf roared 500 feet below.

Harding calculated that they had gone a mile and a half from the corral.

At this point the wire entered among the rocks, following the steep side of a narrow ravine. The settlers followed it at the risk of occasioning a fall of the slightly-balanced rocks, and being dashed into the sea. The descent was extremely perilous, but they did not think of the danger; they were no longer masters of themselves, and an irresistible attraction drew them toward this mysterious place as the magnet draws iron.

Thus they almost unconsciously descended this ravine, which even in broad daylight would have been considered impracticable.

The stones rolled and sparkled like fiery balls when they crossed through the gleams of light. Harding was first—Ayrton last. On they went, step by step. Now they slid over the slippery rock; then they struggled to their feet and scrambled on.

At last the wire touched the rocks on the beach. The colonists had reached the bottom of the basalt cliff.

There appeared a narrow ridge, running horizontally and parallel with the sea. The settlers followed the wire along it. They had not gone a hundred paces when the ridge by a moderate incline sloped down to the level of the sea.

The engineer seized the wire and found that it disappeared beneath the waves.

His companions were stupefied.

A cry of disappointment, almost a cry of despair, escaped them! Must they then plunge beneath the water and seek there for some submarine cavern? In their excited state they would not have hesitated to do it.

The engineer stopped them.

He led his companions to a hollow in the rocks, and there,

"We must wait," said he. "The tide is high. At low water the way will be open."

"But what can make you think—" asked Pencroft.

"He would not have called us if the means had been wanting to enable us to reach him!"

Cyrus Harding spoke in a tone of such thorough conviction that no objection was raised. His remark, besides, was logical. It was quite possible that an opening, practicable at low water, though hidden now by the high tide, opened at the foot of the cliff.

There was some time to wait. The colonists remained silently crouching in a deep hollow. Rain now began to fall in torrents. The thunder was re-echoed among the rocks with a grand sonorousness.

The colonists' emotion was great. A thousand strange and extraordinary ideas crossed their brains, and they expected some grand and superhuman apparition, which alone could come up to the notion they had formed of the mysterious genius of the island.

At midnight, Harding carrying the lantern, descended to the beach to reconnoiter.

The engineer was not mistaken. The beginning of an immense excavation could be seen under the water. There the wire, bending at a right angle, entered the yawning gulf.

Cyrus Harding returned to his companions, and said simply,

"In an hour the opening will be practicable."

"It is there, then?" said Pencroft.

"Did you doubt it?" returned Harding.

"But this cavern must be filled with water to a certain height," observed Herbert.

"Either the cavern will be completely dry," replied Harding, "and in that case we can traverse it on foot, or it will not be dry, and some means of transport will be put at our disposal."

An hour passed. All climbed down through the rain to the level of the sea. There was now eight feet of the opening above the water. It was like the arch of a bridge, under which rushed the foaming water.

Leaning forward, the engineer saw a black object floating on the water. He drew it toward him. It was a boat, moored to some interior projection of the cave. This boat was iron-plated. Two oars lay at the bottom.

"Jump in!" said Harding.

In a moment the settlers were in the boat. Neb and Ayrton took the oars, Pencroft the rudder. Cyrus Harding in the bows, with the lantern, lighted the way.

The elliptical roof, under which the boat at first passed, suddenly rose; but the darkness was too deep, and the light of the lantern too slight, for either the extent, length, height, or depth of the cave to be ascertained. Solemn silence reigned in this basaltic cavern. Not a sound could penetrate into it, even the thunder peals could not pierce its thick sides.

Such immense caves exist in various parts of the world, natural crypts dating from the geological epoch of the globe. Some are filled by the sea; others contain entire lakes in their sides. Such is Fingal's Cave, in the island of Staffa, one of the Hebrides; such are the caves of Morgat, in the bay of Douarnenez, in Brittany, the caves of Bonifacio, in Corsica, those of Lyse-Fjord, in Norway; such are the immense Mammoth caverns in Kentucky, 500 feet in height, and more than twenty miles in length! In many parts of the globe, nature has excavated these caverns, and preserved them for the admiration of man.

Did the cavern which the settlers were now exploring extend to the center of the island? For a quarter of an hour the boat had been advancing, making detours, indicated to Pencroft by the engineer in short sentences, when all at once,

"More to the right!" he commanded.

The boat, altering its course, came up alongside the right wall. The engineer wished to see if the wire still ran along the side.

The wire was there fastened to the rock.

"Forward!" said Harding.

And the two oars, plunging into the dark waters, urged the boat onward.

On they went for another quarter of an hour, and a distance of half a mile must have been cleared from the mouth of the cave, when Harding's voice was again heard.

"Stop!" said he.

The boat stopped, and the colonists perceived a bright light illuminating the vast cavern, so deeply excavated in the bowels of the island, of which nothing had ever led them to suspect the existence.

At a height of a hundred feet rose the vaulted roof, supported on basalt shafts. Irregular arches, strange moldings, appeared on the columns erected by nature in thousands from the first epochs of the formation of the globe. The basalt pillars, fitted one into the other, measured from forty to fifty feet in height, and the water, calm in spite of the tumult outside, washed their base. The brilliant focus of light, pointed out by the engineer, touched every point of rocks, and flooded the walls with light.

By reflection the water reproduced the brilliant sparkles, so that the boat appeared to be floating between two glittering zones. They could not be mistaken in the nature of the irradiation thrown from the glowing nucleus, whose clear rays were shattered by all the angles, all the projections of the cavern. This light proceeded from an electric source, and its white color betrayed its origin. It was the sun of this cave, and it filled it entirely.

At a sign from Cyrus Harding the oars again plunged into the water, causing a regular shower of gems, and the boat was urged forward toward the light, which was now not more than half a cable's length distant.

At this place the breadth of the sheet of water measured nearly 350 feet, and beyond the dazzling center could be seen an enormous basaltic wall, blocking up any issue on that side. The cavern widened here considerably, the sea forming a little lake. But the roof, the side walls, the end cliff, all the prisms, all the peaks, were flooded with the electric fluid, so that the brilliancy belonged to them, and as if the light issued from them.

In the center of the lake a long cigar-shaped object floated on the surface of the water, silent, motionless. The brilliancy which issued from it escaped from its sides as from two kilns heated to a white heat. This apparatus, similar in shape to an enormous whale, was about 250 feet long, and rose about ten or twelve above the water.

The boat slowly approached it, Cyrus Harding stood up in the bows. He gazed, a prey to violent excitement. Then, all at once, seizing the reporter's arm,

"It is he! It can only be he!" he cried, "he!—"

Then, falling back on the seat, he murmured a name which Gideon Spilett alone could hear.

The reporter evidently knew this name, for it had a wonderful effect upon him, and he answered in a hoarse voice,

"He! an outlawed man!"

"He!" said Harding.

At the engineer's command the boat approached this singular floating apparatus. The boat touched the left side, from which escaped a ray of light through a thick glass.

Harding and his companions mounted on the platform. An open hatchway was there. All darted down the opening.

At the bottom of the ladder was a deck, lighted by electricity. At the end of this deck was a door, which Harding opened.

A richly-ornamented room, quickly traversed by the colonists, was joined to a library, over which a luminous ceiling shed a flood of light.

At the end of the library a large door, also shut, was opened by the engineer.

An immense saloon—a sort of museum, in which were heaped up, with all the treasures of the mineral world, works of art, marvels of industry—appeared before the eyes of the colonists, who almost thought themselves suddenly transported into a land of enchantment.

Stretched on a rich sofa they saw a man, who did not appear to notice their presence.

Then Harding raised his voice, and to the extreme surprise of his companions, he uttered these words,

"Captain Nemo, you asked for us! We are here."

XVI

At these words the reclining figure rose, and the electric light fell upon his countenance; a magnificent head, the forehead high, the glance commanding, beard white, hair abundant and falling over the shoulders.

His hand rested upon the cushion of the divan from which he had just risen. He appeared perfectly calm. It was evident that his strength had been gradually undermined by illness, but his voice seemed yet powerful, as he said in English, and in a tone which evinced extreme surprise,

"Sir, I have no name."

"Nevertheless, I know you!" replied Cyrus Harding.

Captain Nemo fixed his penetrating gaze upon the engineer, as though he were about to annihilate him.

Then, falling back amid the pillows of the divan,

"After all, what matters now?" he murmured; "I am dying!"

Cyrus Harding drew near the captain, and Gideon Spilett took his hand—it was of a feverish heat. Ayrton, Pencroft, Herbert, and Neb stood respectfully apart in an angle of the magnificent saloon, whose atmosphere was saturated with the electric fluid.

Meanwhile Captain Nemo withdrew his hand, and motioned the engineer and the reporter to be seated.

All regarded him with profound emotion. Before them they beheld that being whom they had styled the "genius of the island," the powerful protector whose intervention, in so many circumstances, had been so efficacious, the benefactor to whom they owed such a debt of gratitude! Their eyes beheld a man only, and a man at the point of death, where Pencroft and Neb had expected to find an almost supernatural being!

But how happened it that Cyrus Harding had recognized Captain Nemo? Why had the latter so suddenly risen on hearing this name uttered, a name which he had believed known to none?

The captain had resumed his position on the divan, and leaning on his arm, he regarded the engineer, seated near him.

"You know the name I formerly bore, sir?" he asked.

"I do," answered Cyrus Harding, "and also that of this wonderful submarine vessel—"

"The *Nautilus?*" said the captain, with a faint smile.

"The *Nautilus.*"

"But do you—do you know who I am?"

"I do."

"It is nevertheless many years since I have held any communication with the inhabited world; three long years have I passed in the depth of the sea, the only place where I have found liberty! Who then can have betrayed my secret?"

"A man who was bound to you by no tie, Captain Nemo, and who, consequently, cannot be accused of treachery."

"The Frenchman who was cast on board my vessel by chance sixteen years since?"

"The same."

"He and his two companions did not then perish in the maëlstrom, in the midst of which the *Nautilus* was struggling?"

"They escaped, and a book has appeared under the title of *Twenty Thousand Leagues Under the Sea,* which contains your history."

"The history of a few months only of my life!" interrupted the captain impetuously.

"It is true," answered Cyrus Harding, "but a few months of that strange life have sufficed to make you known—"

"As a great criminal, doubtless!" said Captain Nemo, a haughty smile curling his lips. "Yes, a rebel, perhaps an outlaw against humanity!"

The engineer was silent.

"Well, sir?"

"It is not for me to judge you, Captain Nemo," answered Cyrus Harding, "at any rate as regards your past life. I am, with the rest of the world, ignorant of the motives which induced you to adopt this strange mode of existence, and I cannot judge of effects without knowing their causes; but what I *do* know is, that a beneficent hand has constantly protected us since our arrival on Lincoln Island, that we all owe our lives to a good, generous, and powerful being, and that this being so powerful, good, and generous, Captain Nemo, is yourself!"

"It is I," answered the captain simply.

The engineer and the reporter rose. Their companions had drawn near, and the gratitude with which their hearts were charged was about to express itself in their gestures and words.

Captain Nemo stopped them by a sign, and in a voice which betrayed more emotion than he doubtless intended to show,

"Wait till you have heard all," he said.

And the captain, in a few concise sentences, ran over the events of his life.

His narrative was short, yet he was obliged to summon up his whole remaining energy to arrive at the end. He was evidently contending against extreme weakness. Several times Cyrus Harding entreated him to repose for a while, but he shook his head as a man to whom the morrow may never come, and when the reporter offered his assistance,

"It is useless," he said; "my hours are numbered."

Captain Nemo was an Indian, the Prince Dakkar. He was the son of a rajah of the then independent territory of Bundelkund and the nephew of the Indian hero Tippo-Saïb. His father sent him to Europe at the age of ten to receive a complete education and with the secret purpose that he prepare himself to struggle one day on equal terms with those whom he regarded as the oppressors of the country.

Between the ages of ten and thirty, Prince Dakkar, supremely gifted in spirit and intellect, took instruction in all fields. In the sciences, literature, and the arts he advanced his studies to an extensive and profound level.

Prince Dakkar traveled throughout Europe. His rank and his fortune made him much sought after, but the seductions of the world never attracted him. Though young and handsome, he remained serious and grave, consumed by the thirst for knowledge, with an implacable resentment burning in his heart.

For Prince Dakkar hated. He detested the one country in which he had never wished to set foot, the one country whose advances he consistently rejected: he hated England, and all the more because he also had reason to admire her.

This Indian embodied all the violent hatred of the conquered for the conquerer. In the eyes of the invaded, the invader could find no acceptance. The son of one of those rulers from whom the United Kingdom had been able to procure only a nominal servitude, this prince of the family of Tippo-Saïb was brought up with ideas of revenge and of reclaiming his country. He was filled with the inescapable love of his country burdened with English chains, and he wished never to set foot in the land which he cursed, the land to which India was enslaved.

Prince Dakkar became an artist nobly stirred by the marvels of art, a scholar to whom nothing of advanced science was unknown, a statesman formed in the courts of Europe. In the eyes of those who observed him only partially, he perhaps seemed to be one of those cosmopolitans, eager for knowledge but disdainful of action; or one of those opulent travelers—proud, platonic spirits who run about the world incessantly and have no country.

But he was neither of these. This artist, this scholar, this man remained Indian in his heart, Indian in his desire for vengeance, Indian in the hope that he cherished of one day being able to reclaim the rights of his country, to drive the foreigner from it, to give it back its independence.

Thus, Prince Dakkar returned to Bundelkund in 1849. He married an Indian noblewoman whose heart, like his, bled for the sorrows of their country. From this marriage he had two children, whom he cherished. But his domestic happiness could not make him forget India's enslavement. He waited for an opportunity, and one presented itself.

The weight of the English yoke had grown too heavy on the backs of the Hindoo population. Prince Dakkar spoke to the discontented in their own terms. He transmitted to them all the hate that he felt against the foreigner. He traveled not only through the still-independent countries of the Indian peninsula, but also through the regions directly subject to English administration. He recalled the great days of Tippo-Saïb, who had died heroically at Seringapatam in defense of his country.

In 1857, the great sepoy revolt broke out. Prince Dakkar was at the heart of it. He organized the immense uprising. He put all his talents and wealth in the service of this cause. He gave himself over entirely to it. He fought in the front lines. He risked his life like the most humble of those heroes who had risen to free their country. He was wounded ten times in twenty battles and had not found death when the last soldiers of independence fell before the bullets of the English.

Never had British power in India been so much in jeopardy, and if, as they had hoped, the sepoys had found help from outside, it could have ended British supremacy in Asia.

Thus the name of Prince Dakkar became reknowned. The hero who carried it did not hide. He fought openly. A price was put on his head, but no traitor delivered him to the English. His father, his mother, his wife, and his children nevertheless paid for him, even before he could know the dangers to which they were exposed because of him.

Right, once again, had been defeated by force. So, "civilization" never recedes. It persists. It finds its way. The sepoys were vanquished, and the country of the ancient rajahs fell under an even tighter grip of English domination.

Prince Dakkar, unable to find that death he courted, returned to the mountain fastnesses of Bundelkund. There, alone in the world, overcome by disappointment at the destruction of all his vain hopes, a prey to profound disgust for all human beings, filled with hatred of the civilized world, he realized the wreck of his fortune, assembled some score of his most faithful companions, and one day disappeared, leaving no trace behind.

Where, then, did he seek that liberty denied him upon the inhabited earth? Under the waves, in the depths of the ocean, where none could follow.

The warrior became the man of science. Upon a deserted island of the Pacific he established his dockyard, and there a submarine vessel was constructed from his designs. By methods which will at some future day be revealed he had rendered subservient the illimitable forces of electricity, which, extracted from inexhaustible sources, was employed for all the requirements of his floating equipage, as a moving, lighting, and heating agent. The sea, with its countless treasures, its myriads of fish, its numberless wrecks, its enormous mammalia, and not only all that nature supplied, but also all that man had lost in its depths, sufficed for every want of the prince and his crew—and thus was his most ardent desire accomplished, never again to hold communication with the earth. He named his submarine vessel the *Nautilus,* called himself simply Captain Nemo, and disappeared beneath the seas.

During many years this strange being visited every ocean, from pole to pole. Outcast of the inhabited earth, in these unknown worlds he gathered incalculable treasures. The millions lost in the Bay of Vigo, in 1702, by the galleons of Spain, furnished him with a mine of inexhaustible riches which he devoted always, anonymously, in favor of those nations who fought for the independence of their country.

For long, however, he had held no communication with his fellow-creatures, when, during the night of the 6th of November, 1866, three men were cast on board his vessel. They were a French professor, his servant, and a Canadian fisherman. These three men had been hurled overboard by a collision which had taken place between the *Nautilus* and the United States frigate *Abraham Lincoln,* which had chased her.

Captain Nemo learned from this professor that the *Nautilus,* taken now for a gigantic mammal of the whale species, now for a submarine vessel carrying a crew of pirates, was sought for in every sea.

He might have returned these three men to the ocean, from whence chance had brought them in contact with his mysterious existence. Instead of doing this he kept them prisoners, and during seven months they were enabled to behold all the wonders of a voyage of twenty thousand leagues under the sea.

One day, the 22nd of June, 1867, these three men, who knew nothing of the past history of Captain Nemo, succeeded in escaping in one of the *Nautilus*'s boats. But as at this time the *Nautilus* was drawn into the vortex of the Maëlstrom, off the coast of Norway, the captain naturally believed that the fugitives, engulfed in that frightful whirlpool, found their death at the bottom of the abyss. He was unaware that the Frenchman and his two companions had been miraculously cast on shore, that the fishermen of the Lofoten Islands had rendered them assistance, and that the professor, on his return to France, had published that work in which seven months of the strange and eventful navigation of the *Nautilus* were narrated and exposed to the curiosity of the public.

For a long time after this, Captain Nemo continued to live thus, traversing every sea. But one by one his companions died, and found their last resting-place in their cemetery of coral, in the bed of the Pacific. At last

Captain Nemo remained the solitary survivor of all those who had taken refuge with him in the depths of the ocean.

He was now sixty years of age. Although alone, he succeeded in navigating the *Nautilus* toward one of those submarine caverns which had sometimes served him as a harbor.

One of these ports was hollowed beneath Lincoln Island, and at this moment furnished an asylum to the *Nautilus.*

The captain had now remained there six years, navigating the ocean no longer, but awaiting death, and that moment when he should rejoin his former companions, when by chance he observed the descent of the balloon which carried the prisoners of the Confederates. Clad in his diving dress he was walking beneath the water at a few cables' lengths from the shore of the island, when the engineer had been thrown into the sea. Moved by a feeling of compassion the captain saved Cyrus Harding.

His first impulse was to fly from the vicinity of the five castaways; but his harbor refuge was closed, for in consequence of an elevation of the basalt, produced by the influence of volcanic action, he could no longer pass through the entrance of the vault. Though there was sufficient depth of water to allow a light craft to pass the bar, there was not enough for the *Nautilus,* whose draught of water was considerable.

Captain Nemo was compelled, therefore, to remain. He observed these men thrown without resources upon a desert island, but had no wish to be himself discovered by them. By degrees he became interested in their efforts when he saw them honest, energetic, and bound to each other by the ties of friendship. As if despite his wishes, he penetrated all the secrets of their existence. By means of the diving dress he could easily reach the well in the interior of Granite House, and climbing by the projections of rock to its upper orifice he heard the colonists as they recounted the past, and studied the present and future. He learned from them the tremendous conflict of America with America itself, for the abolition of slavery. Yes, these men were worthy to reconcile Captain Nemo with that humanity which they represented so nobly in the island.

Captain Nemo had saved Cyrus Harding. It was he also who had brought back the dog to the Chimneys, who rescued Top from the waters of the lake, who caused to fall at Flotsam Point the case containing so many things useful to the colonists, who conveyed the canoe back into the stream of the Mercy, who cast the cord from the top of Granite House at the time of the attack by the baboons, who made known the presence of

Ayrton upon Tabor Island, by means of the document enclosed in the bottle, who caused the explosion of the brig by the shock of a torpedo placed at the bottom of the canal, who saved Herbert from certain death by bringing the sulphate of quinine; and finally, it was he who had killed the convicts with the electric balls, of which he possessed the secret, and which he employed in the chase of submarine creatures. Thus were explained so many apparently supernatural occurrences, and which all proved the generosity and power of the captain.

Nevertheless, this noble misanthrope longed to benefit his protégés still further. There yet remained much useful advice to give them, and, his heart being softened by the approach of death, he invited, as we are aware, the colonists of Granite House to visit the *Nautilus,* by means of a wire which connected it with the corral. Possibly he would not have done this had he been aware that Cyrus Harding was sufficiently acquainted with his history to address him by the name of Nemo.

The captain concluded the narrative of his life. Cyrus Harding then spoke; he recalled all the incidents which had exercised so beneficent an influence upon the colony, and in the names of his companions and himself thanked the generous being to whom they owed so much.

But Captain Nemo paid little attention; his mind appeared to be absorbed by one idea, and without taking the proffered hand of the engineer,

"Now, sir," said he, "now that you know my history, your judgment!"

In saying this, the captain evidently alluded to an important incident witnessed by the three strangers thrown on board his vessel, and which the French professor had related in his work, causing a profound and terrible sensation. Some days previous to the flight of the professor and his two companions, the *Nautilus,* being chased by a frigate in the north of the Atlantic had hurled herself as a ram upon this frigate, and sunk her without mercy.

Cyrus Harding understood the captain's allusion, and was silent.

"It was an enemy's frigate," exclaimed Captain Nemo, transformed for an instant into the Prince Dakkar, "an enemy's frigate! It was she who attacked me—I was in a narrow and shallow bay—the frigate barred my way—and I sank her!"

A few moments of silence ensued; then the captain demanded,

"What think you of my life, gentlemen?"

Cyrus Harding extended his hand to the ci-devant prince and replied gravely, "Sir, your error was in supposing that the past can be resuscitated, and in contending against inevitable progress. It is one of those errors which some admire, others blame; which God alone can judge. He who is mistaken in an action which he sincerely believes to be right may be an enemy, but retains our esteem. Your error is one that we may admire, and your name has nothing to fear from the judgment of history, which does not condemn heroic folly, but its results."

The old man's breast swelled with emotion, and raising his hand to heaven,

"Was I wrong, or in the right?" he murmured.

Cyrus Harding replied, "All great actions return to God, from whom they are derived. Captain Nemo, we, whom you have succored, shall ever mourn your loss."

Herbert, who had drawn near the captain, fell on his knees and kissed his hand.

A tear glistened in the eyes of the dying man. "My child," he said, "may God bless you!"

XVII

Day had returned. No ray of light penetrated into the profundity of the cavern. It being high-water, the entrance was closed by the sea. But the artificial light, which escaped in long streams from the skylights of the *Nautilus* was as vivid as before, and the sheet of water shone around the floating vessel.

An extreme exhaustion now overcame Captain Nemo, who had fallen back upon the divan. It was useless to contemplate removing him to Granite House, for he had expressed his wish to remain in the midst of those marvels of the *Nautilus* which millions could not have purchased, and to wait there for that death which was swiftly approaching.

During a long interval of prostration, which rendered him almost unconscious, Cyrus Harding and Gideon Spilett attentively observed the condition of the dying man. It was apparent that his strength was gradually diminishing. That frame, once so robust, was now but the fragile tenement of a departing soul. All of life was concentrated in the heart and head.

The engineer and reporter consulted in whispers. Was it possible to render any aid to the dying man? Might his life, if not saved, be prolonged for some days? He himself had said that no remedy could avail, and he awaited with tranquillity that death which had for him no terrors.

"We can do nothing," said Gideon Spilett.

"But of what is he dying?" asked Pencroft.

"Life is simply fading out," replied the reporter.

"Nevertheless," said the sailor, "if we move him into the open air, and the light of the sun, he might perhaps recover."

"No, Pencroft," answered the engineer, "it is useless to attempt it. Besides, Captain Nemo would never consent to leave his vessel. He has lived for a dozen years on board the *Nautilus,* and on board the *Nautilus* he desires to die."

Without doubt Captain Nemo heard Cyrus Harding's reply, for he raised himself slightly, and in a voice more feeble, but always intelligible,

"You are right, sir," he said. "I shall die here—it is my wish; and therefore I have a request to make of you."

Cyrus Harding and his companions had drawn near the divan, and now arranged the cushions in such a manner as to better support the dying man.

They saw his eyes wander over all the marvels of this saloon, lighted by the electric rays which fell from the arabesques of the luminous ceiling. He surveyed, one after the other, the pictures hanging from the splendid tapestries of the partitions, the chef-d'oeuvres of the Italian, Flemish, French, and Spanish masters; the statues of marble and bronze on their pedestals; the magnificent organ, leaning against the after-partition; the aquarium, in which bloomed the most wonderful productions of the sea—marine plants, zoöphytes, chaplets of pearls of inestimable value; and, finally, his eyes rested on this device, inscribed over the pediment of the museum—the motto of the *Nautilus*—

MOBILIS IN MOBILI.

His glance seemed to rest fondly for the last time on these masterpieces of art and of nature, to which he had limited his horizon during a sojourn of so many years in the abysses of the seas.

Cyrus Harding respected the captain's silence, and waited till he should speak.

After some minutes, during which, doubtless, he passed in review his whole life, Captain Nemo turned to the colonists and said,

"You consider yourselves, gentlemen, under some obligations to me?"

"Captain, believe us that we would give our lives to prolong yours."

"Promise, then," continued Captain Nemo, "to carry out my last wishes, and I shall be repaid for all I have done for you."

"We promise," said Cyrus Harding.

And by this promise he bound both himself and his companions.

"Gentlemen," resumed the captain, "to-morrow I shall be dead."

Herbert was about to utter an exclamation, but a sign from the captain arrested him.

"To-morrow I shall die, and I desire no other tomb than the *Nautilus.* It is my grave! All my friends repose in the depths of the ocean; their resting-place shall be mine."

These words were received with profound silence.

"Pay attention to my wishes," he continued. "The *Nautilus* is imprisoned in this grotto, the entrance of which is blocked up; but, although egress is impossible, the vessel may at least sink in the abyss, and there bury my remains."

The colonists listened reverently to the words of the dying man.

"To-morrow, after my death, M. Harding," continued the captain, "yourself and companions will leave the *Nautilus,* for all the treasures it contains must perish with me. One token alone will remain with you of Prince Dakkar, with whose history you are now acquainted. That coffer yonder contains diamonds of the value of many millions, most of them mementoes of the time when, husband and father, I thought happiness possible for me, and a collection of pearls gathered by my friends and myself in the depths of the ocean. Of this treasure at a future day, you may make good use. In the hands of such men as yourself and your comrades, Captain Harding, money will never be a source of danger. From on high I shall still participate in your enterprises, and I fear not but that they will prosper."

After a few moments' repose, necessitated by his extreme weakness, Captain Nemo continued,

"To-morrow you will take the coffer, you will leave the saloon, of which you will close the door; then you will ascend on to the deck of the *Nautilus,* and you will lower the mainhatch so as entirely to close the vessel."

"It shall be done, captain," answered Cyrus Harding.

"Good. You will then embark in the canoe which brought you hither; but, before leaving the *Nautilus,* go to the stern and there open two large stop-cocks which you will find upon the water-line. The water will penetrate into the reservoirs, and the *Nautilus* will gradually sink beneath the water to repose at the bottom of the abyss."

And comprehending a gesture of Cyrus Harding, the captain added, "Fear nothing! You will but bury a corpse!"

Neither Cyrus Harding nor his companions ventured to offer any observation to Captain Nemo. He had expressed his last wishes, and they had nothing to do but to conform to them.

"I have your promise, gentlemen?" added Captain Nemo.

"You have, captain," replied the engineer.

The captain thanked the colonists by a sign, and requested them to leave him for some hours. Gideon Spilett wished to remain near him, in the event of a crisis coming on, but the dying man refused, saying, "I shall live until to-morrow, sir."

All left the saloon, passed through the library and the dining-room, and arrived forward, in the machine-room where the electrical apparatus was established, which supplied not only heat and light, but the mechanical power of the *Nautilus*.

The *Nautilus* was a masterpiece containing masterpieces with itself, and the engineer was struck with astonishment.

The colonists mounted the platform, which rose seven or eight feet above the water. There they beheld a thick glass lenticular covering, which protected a kind of large eye, from which flashed forth light. Behind this eye was apparently a cabin containing the wheels of the rudder, and in which was stationed the helmsman, when he navigated the *Nautilus* over the bed of the ocean, which the electric rays would evidently light up to a considerable distance.

Cyrus Harding and his companions remained for a time silent, for they were vividly impressed by what they had just seen and heard, and their hearts were deeply touched by the thought that he whose arm had so often aided them, the protector whom they had known but a few hours, was at the point of death.

Whatever might be the judgment pronounced by posterity upon the events of this, so to speak, extra-human existence, the character of Prince Dakkar would ever remain as one of those whose memory time can never efface.

"What a man!" said Pencroft. "Is it possible that he can have lived at the bottom of the sea? And it seems to me that perhaps he has not found peace there any more than elsewhere!"

"The *Nautilus,*" observed Ayrton, "might have enabled us to leave Lincoln Island and reach some inhabited country."

"Good Heavens!" exclaimed Pencroft, "I for one would never risk myself in such a craft. To sail on the seas, good, but under the seas, never!"

"I believe, Pencroft," answered the reporter, "that the navigation of a submarine vessel such as the *Nautilus* ought to be very easy, and that we should soon become accustomed to it. There would be no storms, no lee-shore to fear. At some feet beneath the surface the waters of the ocean are as calm as those of a lake."

"That may be," replied the sailor, "but I prefer a gale of wind on board a well-found craft. A vessel is built to sail on the sea, and not beneath it."

"My friends," said the engineer, "it is useless, at any rate as regards the *Nautilus,* to discuss the question of submarine vessels. The *Nautilus* is not ours, and we have not the right to dispose of it. Moreover, we could in no case avail ourselves of it. Independently of the fact that it would be impossible to get it out of this cavern, whose entrance is now closed by the uprising of the basaltic rocks, Captain Nemo's wish is that it shall be buried with him. His wish is our law, and we will fulfill it."

After a somewhat prolonged conversation, Cyrus Harding and his companions again descended to the interior of the *Nautilus.* There they took some refreshment and returned to the saloon.

Captain Nemo had somewhat rallied from the prostration which had overcome him, and his eyes shone with their wonted fire. A faint smile even curled his lips.

The colonists drew around him.

"Gentlemen," said the captain, "you are brave and honest men. You have devoted yourselves to the common weal. Often have I observed your conduct. I have esteemed you—I esteem you still! Your hand, Mr. Harding."

Cyrus Harding gave his hand to the captain, who clasped it affectionately.

"It is well!" he murmured.

He resumed,

"But enough of myself. I have to speak concerning yourselves, and this Lincoln Island, upon which you have taken refuge. You now desire to leave it?"

"To return, captain!" answered Pencroft quickly.

"To return, Pencroft?" said the captain, with a smile. "I know, it is true, your love for this island. You have helped to make it what it now is, and it seems to you a paradise!"

"Our project, captain," interposed Cyrus Harding, "is to annex it to the United States, and to establish for our shipping a port so fortunately situated in this part of the Pacific."

"Your thoughts are with your country, gentlemen," continued the captain; "your toils are for her prosperity and glory. You are right. One's native land!—there should one live! there die! And I die far from all I loved!"

"You have some last wish to transmit," said the engineer with emotion, "some souvenir to send to those friends you have left in the mountains of India?"

"No, Captain Harding; no friends remain to me! I am the last of my race, and to all whom I have known I have long been as are the dead—But to return to yourselves. Solitude, isolation, are painful things, and beyond human endurance. I die of having thought it possible to live alone! You should, therefore, dare all in the attempt to leave Lincoln Island, and see once more the land of your birth. I am aware that those wretches have destroyed the vessel you have built."

"We propose to construct a vessel," said Gideon Spilett, "sufficiently large to convey us to the nearest land; but if we should succeed, sooner or later we shall return to Lincoln Island. We are attached to it by too many recollections ever to forget it."

"It is here that we have known Captain Nemo," said Cyrus Harding.

"It is here only that we can make our home!" added Herbert.

"And here shall I sleep the sleep of eternity, if—" replied the captain.

He paused for a moment, and, instead of completing the sentence, said simply,

"Mr. Harding, I wish to speak with you—alone!"

The engineer's companions, respecting the wish, retired.

Cyrus Harding remained but a few minutes alone with Captain Nemo, and soon recalled his companions; but he said nothing to them of the private matters which the dying man had confided to him.

Gideon Spilett now watched the captain with extreme care. It was evident that he was no longer sustained by his moral energy, which had lost the power of reaction against his physical weakness.

The day closed without change. The colonists did not quit the *Nautilus* for a moment. Night arrived, although it was impossible to distinguish it from day in the cavern.

Captain Nemo suffered no pain, but he was visibly sinking. His noble features, paled by the approach of death, were perfectly calm. Inaudible words escaped at intervals from his lips, bearing upon various incidents of his checkered career. Life was evidently ebbing slowly and his extremities were already cold.

Once or twice more he spoke to the colonists who stood around him, and smiled on them with that last smile which continues after death.

At length, shortly after midnight, Captain Nemo by a supreme effort succeeded in folding his arms across his breast, as if wishing in that attitude to compose himself for death.

By one o'clock his glance alone showed signs of life. A dying light gleamed in those eyes once so brilliant. Then, murmuring the words, "God and my country!" he quietly expired.

Cyrus Harding, bending low, closed the eyes of him who had once been the Prince Dakkar, and was now not even Captain Nemo.

Herbert and Pencroft sobbed aloud. Tears fell from Ayrton's eyes. Neb was on his knees by the reporter's side, motionless as a statue.

Then Cyrus Harding, extending his hand over the forehead of the dead, said solemnly, "May his soul be with God!" Turning to his friends, he added, "Let us pray for him whom we have lost!"

Some hours later the colonists fulfilled the promise made to the captain by carrying out his dying wishes.

Cyrus Harding and his companions quitted the *Nautilus,* taking with them the only memento left them by their benefactor, the coffer which contained wealth amounting to millions.

The marvelous saloon, still flooded with light, had been carefully closed. The iron door leading on deck was then securely fastened in such a manner as to prevent even a drop of water from penetrating to the interior of the *Nautilus*.

The colonists then descended into the canoe, which was moored to the side of the submarine vessel.

The canoe was now brought around to the stern. There, at the water-line, were two large stop-cocks communicating with the reservoirs employed in the submersion of the vessel.

The stop-cocks were opened, the reservoirs filled, and the *Nautilus,* slowly sinking, disappeared beneath the surface of the lake.

But the colonists were yet able to follow its descent through the waves.

The powerful light it gave forth lighted up the translucent water, while the cavern became gradually obscure. At length this vast effusion of electric light faded away, and soon after the *Nautilus,* now the tomb of Captain Nemo, reposed in its ocean bed.

XVIII

At break of day the colonists regained in silence the entrance of the cavern, to which they gave the name of Dakkar Grotto, in memory of Captain Nemo. It was now low-water, and they passed without difficulty under the arcade, washed on the right by the sea.

The canoe was left here, carefully protected from the waves. As additional precaution, Pencroft, Neb, and Ayrton drew it up on a little beach which bordered one of the sides of the grotto, in a spot where it could run no risk of harm.

The storm had ceased during the night. The last low mutterings of the thunder died away in the west. Rain fell no longer, but the sky was yet obscured by clouds. On the whole, this month of October, the first of the southern spring, was not ushered in by satisfactory tokens, and the wind had a tendency to shift from one point of the compass to another, which rendered it impossible to count upon settled weather.

Cyrus Harding and his companions, on leaving Dakkar Grotto, had taken the road to the corral. On their way Neb and Herbert were careful to preserve the wire which had been laid down by the captain between the corral and the grotto, and which might at a future time be of service.

The colonists spoke but little on the road. The various incidents of the night of October 15th had left a profound impression on their minds. The unknown being whose influence had so effectually protected them, the man whom their imagination had endowed with supernatural powers, Captain Nemo, was no more. His *Nautilus* and he were buried in the depths of the abyss. To each one of them their existence seemed even more isolated than before. They had been accustomed to count upon the intervention of that power which existed no longer, and Gideon Spilett, and even Cyrus Harding, could not escape this impression. Thus they maintained a profound silence during their journey to the corral.

Toward nine in the morning the colonists arrived at Granite House.

It had been agreed that the construction of the vessel should be actively pushed forward, and Cyrus Harding more than ever devoted his time and labor to this object. It was impossible to divine what future lay before them. Evidently the advantage to the colonists would be great of having at their disposal a substantial vessel, capable of keeping the sea even in heavy weather, and large enough to attempt, in case of need, a voyage of some duration. Even if, when their vessel should be completed, the colonists should not resolve to leave Lincoln Island as yet, in order to gain either one of the Polynesian archipelagoes of the Pacific or the shores of New Zealand, they might at least, sooner or later, proceed to Tabor Island, to leave there the notice relating to Ayrton. This was a precaution rendered indispensable by the possibility of the Scotch yacht reappearing in those seas, and it was of the highest importance that nothing should be neglected on this point.

The works were then resumed. Cyrus Harding, Pencroft, and Ayrton, assisted by Neb, Gideon Spilett, and Herbert, except when unavoidably called off by other necessary occupations, worked without cessation. It was important that the new vessel should be ready in five months—that is to say, by the beginning of March—if they wished to visit Tabor Island before the equinoctial gales rendered the voyage impracticable. Therefore the carpenters lost not a moment. Moreover, it was unnecessary to manufacture rigging, that of the *Speedy* having been saved entire, so that the hull only of the vessel needed to be constructed.

The end of the year 1868 found them occupied by these important labors, to the exclusion of almost all others. At the expiration of two months and a half the ribs had been set up and the first planks adjusted. It was already evident that the plans made by Cyrus Harding were admirable, and that the vessel would behave well at sea.

Pencroft brought to the task a devouring energy, and would even grumble when one or the other abandoned the carpenter's axe for the gun of the hunter. It was nevertheless necessary to keep up the stores of Granite House, in view of the approaching winter. But this did not satisfy Pencroft. The brave, honest sailor was not content when the workmen were not at the dockyard. When this happened he grumbled vigorously, and, by way of venting his feelings, did the work of six men.

The weather was very unfavorable during the whole of the summer season. For some days the heat was overpowering, and the atmosphere, saturated with electricity, was only cleared by violent storms. It was rarely that the distant growling of the thunder could not be heard, like a low but incessant murmur, such as is produced in the equatorial regions of the globe.

The 1st of January, 1869, was signalized by a storm of extreme violence, and the thunder burst several times over the island. Large trees were struck by the electric fluid and shattered, and among others one of those gigantic nettle-trees which had shaded the poultry-yard at the southern extremity of the lake. Had this meteor any relation to the phenomenon going on in the bowels of the earth? Was there any connection between the commotion of the atmosphere and that of the interior of the earth? Cyrus Harding was inclined to think that such was the case, for the development of these storms was attended by the renewal of volcanic symptoms.

It was on the 3rd of January that Herbert, having ascended at daybreak to the plateau of Prospect Heights to harness one of the onagers, perceived an enormous bat-shaped cloud rolling from the summit of the volcano.

Herbert immediately apprised the colonists, who at once joined him in watching the summit of Mount Franklin.

"Ah!" exclaimed Pencroft, "those are not vapors this time! It seems to me that the giant is not content with breathing; he must smoke!"

This figure of speech employed by the sailor exactly expressed the changes going on at the mouth of the volcano. Already for three months had the crater emitted vapors more or less dense, but which were as yet produced only by an internal ebullition of mineral substances. But now the vapors were replaced by a thick smoke, rising in the form of a grayish column, more than three hundred feet in width at its base, and which spread like an immense mushroom to a height of from seven to eight hundred feet above the summit of the mountain.

"The fire is in the chimney," observed Gideon Spilett.

"And we can't put it out!" replied Herbert.

"The volcano ought to be swept," observed Neb, who spoke as if perfectly serious.

"Well said, Neb!" cried Pencroft, with a shout of laughter; "and you'll undertake the job, no doubt?"

Cyrus Harding attentively observed the dense smoke emitted by Mount Franklin, and even listened, as if expecting to hear some distant muttering. Then, turning toward his companions, from whom he had gone somewhat apart, he said,

"The truth is, my friends, we must not conceal from ourselves that an important change is going forward. The volcanic substances are no longer in a state of ebullition, they have caught fire, and we are undoubtedly menaced by an approaching eruption."

"Well, captain," said Pencroft, "we shall witness the eruption; and if it is a good one, we'll applaud it. I don't see that we need concern ourselves further about the matter."

"It may be so," replied Cyrus Harding, "for the ancient track of the lava is still open; and thanks to this, the crater has hitherto overflowed toward the north. And yet—"

"And yet, as we can derive no advantage from an eruption, it might be better it should not take place," said the reporter.

"Who knows?" answered the sailor. "Perhaps there may be some valuable substance in this volcano, which it will spout forth, and which we may turn to good account!"

Cyrus Harding shook his head with the air of a man who augured no good from the phenomenon whose development had been so sudden. He did not regard so lightly as Pencroft the results of an eruption. If the lava, in consequence of the position of the crater, did not directly menace the wooded and cultivated parts of the island, other complications might present themselves. In fact, eruptions are not unfrequently accompanied by earthquakes; and an island of the nature of Lincoln Island, formed of substances so varied, basalt on one side, granite on the other, lava on the north, rich soil on the south, substances which consequently could not be firmly attached to each other, would be exposed to the risk of disintegration. Although, therefore, the spreading of the volcanic matter might not constitute a serious danger, any movement of the terrestrial structure which should shake the island might entail the gravest consequences.

"It seems to me," said Ayrton, who had reclined so as to place his ear to the ground, "it seems to me that I can hear a dull, rumbling sound, like that of a wagon loaded with bars of iron."

The colonists listened with the greatest attention, and were convinced that Ayrton was not mistaken. The rumbling was mingled with a subterranean roar, which formed a sort of *rinforzando,* and died slowly away, as if some violent storm had passed through the profundities of the globe. But no explosion properly so termed, could be heard. It might therefore be concluded that the vapors and smoke found a free passage through the central shaft; and that the safety-valve being sufficiently large, no convulsion would be produced, no explosion was to be apprehended.

"Well, then!" said Pencroft, "are we not going back to work? Let Mount Franklin smoke, groan, bellow, or spout forth fire and flame as much as it pleases, that is no reason why we should be idle! Come, Ayrton, Neb, Herbert, Captain Harding, Mr. Spilett, every one of us must turn to at our work to-day! We are going to place the keelson, and a dozen pair of hands would not be too many. Before two months I want our new *Bonadventure*—for we shall keep the old name, shall we not?—to float on the waters of Port Balloon! Therefore there is not an hour to lose!"

All the colonists, their services thus requisitioned by Pencroft, descended to the dockyard, and proceeded to place the keelson, a thick mass of wood which forms the lower portion of a ship and unites firmly the timbers of the hull. It was an arduous undertaking, in which all took part.

They continued their labors during the whole of this day, the 3rd of January, without thinking further of the volcano, which could not, besides, be seen from the shore of Granite House. But once or twice, large shadows, veiling the sun, which described its diurnal arc through an extremely clear sky, indicated that a thick cloud of smoke passed between its disc and the island. The wind, blowing on the shore, carried all these vapors to the westward. Cyrus Harding and Gideon Spilett remarked these somber appearances, and from time to time discussed the evident progress of the volcanic phenomena, but their work went on without interruption. It was, besides, of the first importance from every point of view, that the vessel should be finished with the least possible delay. In presence of the eventualities which might arise, the safety of the colonists would be to a great extent secured by their ship. Who could tell that it might not prove some day their only refuge?

In the evening, after supper, Cyrus Harding, Gideon Spilett, and Herbert again ascended the plateau of Prospect Heights. It was already dark, and the obscurity would permit them to ascertain if flames or incandescent matter thrown up by the volcano were mingled with the vapor and smoke accumulated at the mouth of the crater.

"The crater is on fire!" said Herbert, who, more active than his companion, first reached the plateau.

Mount Franklin, distant about six miles, now appeared like a gigantic torch, around the summit of which turned fuliginous flames. So much smoke, and possibly scoriae and cinders were mingled with them, that their light gleamed but faintly amid the gloom of the night. But a kind of lurid brilliancy spread over the island, against which stood out confusedly the wooded masses of the heights. Immense whirlwinds of vapor obscured the sky, through which glimmered a few stars.

"The change is rapid!" said the engineer.

"That is not surprising," answered the reporter. "The reawakening of the volcano already dates back some time. You may remember, Cyrus, that the first vapors appeared about the time we searched the sides of the mountain to discover Captain Nemo's retreat. It was, if I mistake not, about the 15th of October."

"Yes," replied Herbert, "two months and a half ago!"

"The subterranean fires have therefore been smoldering for ten weeks," resumed Gideon Spilett, "and it is not to be wondered at that they now break out with such violence!"

"Do not you feel a certain vibration of the soil?" asked Cyrus Harding.

"Yes," replied Gideon Spilett, "but there is a great difference between that and an earthquake."

"I do not affirm that we are menaced with an earthquake," answered Cyrus Harding, "may God preserve us from that! No; these vibrations are due to the effervescence of the central fire. The crust of the earth is simply the shell of a boiler, and you know that such a shell, under the pressure of steam, vibrates like a sonorous plate. It is this effect which is being produced at this moment."

"What magnificent flames!" exclaimed Herbert.

At this instant a kind of bouquet of flames shot forth from the crater, the brilliancy of which was visible even through the vapors. Thousands of luminous sheets and barbed tongues of fire were cast in various directions. Some, extending beyond the dome of smoke, dissipated it, leaving behind an incandescent powder. This was accompanied by successive explosions, resembling the discharge of a battery of machine-guns.

Cyrus Harding, the reporter, and Herbert, after spending an hour on the plateau of Prospect Heights, again descended to the beach, and returned to Granite House. The engineer was thoughtful and preoccupied, so much so, indeed, that Gideon Spilett inquired if he apprehended any immediate danger, of which the eruption might directly or indirectly be the cause.

"Yes, and no," answered Cyrus Harding.

"Nevertheless," continued the reporter, "would not the greatest misfortune which could happen to us be an earthquake which would overturn the island? Now, I do not suppose that this is to be feared, since the vapors and lava have found a free outlet."

"True," replied Cyrus Harding, "and I do not fear an earthquake in the sense in which the term is commonly applied to convulsions of the soil provoked by the expansion of subterranean gases. But other causes may produce great disasters."

"How so, my dear Cyrus?"

"I am not certain. I must consider. I must visit the mountain. In a few days I shall learn more on this point."

Gideon Spilett said no more, and soon, in spite of the explosions of the volcano, whose intensity increased, and which were repeated by the echoes of the island, the inhabitants of Granite House were sleeping soundly.

Three days passed by—the 4th, 5th, and 6th of January. The construction of the vessel was diligently continued, and without offering further explanations the engineer pushed forward the work with all his energy. Mount Franklin was now hooded by a somber cloud of sinister aspect, and, amid the flames, vomiting forth incandescent rocks, some of which fell back into the crater itself. This caused Pencroft, who would only look at the matter in the light of a joke, to exclaim,

"Ah! the giant is playing at cup and ball; he is a conjurer."

In fact, the substances thrown up fell back again in to the abyss, and it did not seem that the lava, though swollen by the internal pressure, had yet risen to the orifice of the crater. At any rate, the opening on the northeast, which was partly visible, poured out no torrent upon the northern slope of the mountain.

Nevertheless, however pressing was the construction of the vessel, other duties demanded the presence of the colonists on various portions of the island. Before everything it was necessary to go to the corral, where the flocks of musmons and goats were enclosed, and replenish the provision of forage for those animals. It was accordingly arranged that Ayrton should proceed thither the next day, the 7th of January; and as he was sufficient for the task, to which he was accustomed, Pencroft and the rest were somewhat surprised on hearing the engineer say to Ayrton,

"As you are going to-morrow to the corral I will accompany you."

"But, Captain Harding," exclaimed the sailor, "our working days will not be many, and if you go also we shall be two pair of hands short!"

"We shall return to-morrow," replied Cyrus Harding, "but it is necessary that I should go to the corral. I must learn how the eruption is progressing."

"The eruption! always the eruption!" answered Pencroft, with an air of discontent. "An important thing, truly, this eruption! I trouble myself very little about it."

Whatever might be the sailor's opinion, the expedition projected by the engineer was settled for the next day. Herbert wished to accompany Cyrus Harding, but he would not vex Pencroft by his absence.

The next day, at dawn, Cyrus Harding and Ayrton, mounting the cart drawn by two onagers, took the road to the corral and set off at a round trot.

Above the forest were passing large clouds, to which the crater of Mount Franklin incessantly added fuliginous matter. These clouds, which rolled heavily in the air, were evidently composed of heterogeneous substances. It was not alone from the volcano that they derived their strange opacity and weight. Scoriae, in a state of dust, like powdered pumice-stone, and grayish ashes as small as the finest feculae, were held in suspension in the midst of their thick folds. These ashes are so fine that they have been observed in the air for whole months. After the eruption of 1783 in Iceland, for upward of a year the atmosphere was thus charged with volcanic dust through which the rays of the sun were only with difficulty discernible.

But more often this pulverized matter falls, and this happened on the present occasion. Cyrus Harding and Ayrton had scarcely reached the corral when a sort of black snow like fine gunpowder fell, and instantly changed the appearance of the soil. Trees, meadows, all disappeared beneath a covering several inches in depth. But, very fortunately, the wind blew from the northeast, and the greater part of the cloud dissolved itself over the sea.

"This is very singular, Captain Harding," said Ayrton.

"It is very serious," replied the engineer. "This powdered pumice-stone, all this mineral dust, proves how grave is the convulsion going forward in the lower depths of the volcano."

"But can nothing be done?"

"Nothing, except to note the progress of the phenomenon. Do you, therefore, Ayrton, occupy yourself with the necessary work at the corral. In the meantime I will ascend just beyond the source of Red Creek and examine the condition of the mountain upon its northern aspect. Then—"

"Well, Captain Harding?"

"Then we will pay a visit to Dakkar Grotto. I wish to inspect it. At any rate I will come back for you in two hours."

Ayrton then proceeded to enter the corral, and, while awaiting the engineer's return, busied himself with the musmons and goats which seemed to feel a certain uneasiness in presence of these first signs of an eruption.

Meanwhile Cyrus Harding ascended the crest of the eastern spur, passed Red Creek, and arrived at the spot where he and his companions had discovered a sulphurous spring at the time of their first exploration.

How changed was everything! Instead of a single column of smoke he counted thirteen, forced through the soil as if violently propelled by some piston. It was evident that the crust of the earth was subjected in this part of the globe to a frightful pressure. The atmosphere was saturated with gases and carbonic acid, mingled with aqueous vapors. Cyrus Harding felt the volcanic tufa with which the plain was strewn, and which was but pulverized cinders hardened into solid blocks by time, tremble beneath him, but he could discover no traces of fresh lava.

The engineer became more assured of this when he observed all the northern part of Mount Franklin. Pillars of smoke and flame escaped from the crater; a hail of scoriae fell on the ground; but no current of lava burst from the mouth of the volcano, which proved that the volcanic matter had not yet attained the level of the superior orifice of the central shaft.

"But I would prefer that it were so," said Cyrus Harding to himself. "At any rate, I should then know that the lava had followed its accustomed track. Who can say that it may not take a new course? But the danger does not consist in that! Captain Nemo foresaw it clearly! No, the danger does not lie there!"

Cyrus Harding advanced toward the enormous causeway whose prolongation enclosed the narrow Shark Gulf. He could now sufficiently examine on this side the ancient channels of the lava. There was no doubt in his mind that the most recent eruption had occurred at a far-distant epoch.

He then returned by the same way, listening attentively to the subterranean mutterings which rolled like long-continued thunder, interrupted by deafening explosions. At nine in the morning he reached the corral.

Ayrton awaited him.

"The animals are cared for, Captain Harding," said Ayrton.

"Good, Ayrton."

"They seem uneasy, Captain Harding."

"Yes, instinct speaks through them, and instinct is never deceived."

"Are you ready?"

"Take a lamp, Ayrton," answered the engineer; "we will start at once."

Ayrton did as desired. The onagers, unharnessed, roamed in the corral. The gate was secured on the outside, and Cyrus Harding, preceding Ayrton, took the narrow path which led westward to the shore.

The soil they walked upon was choked with the pulverized matter fallen from the cloud. No quadruped appeared in the woods. Even the birds had fled. Sometimes a passing breeze raised the covering of ashes, and the two colonists, enveloped in a whirlwind of dust, lost sight of each other. They were then careful to cover their eyes and mouths with handkerchiefs, for they ran the risk of being blinded and suffocated.

It was impossible for Cyrus Harding and Ayrton, with these impediments, to make rapid progress. Moreover, the atmosphere was close, as if the oxygen had been partly burned up, and had become unfit for respiration. At every hundred paces they were obliged to stop to take breath. It was therefore past ten o'clock when the engineer and his companion reached the crest of the enormous mass of rocks of basalt and porphyry which composed the northwest coast of the island.

Ayrton and Cyrus Harding commenced the descent of this abrupt declivity, following almost step for step the difficult path which, during that stormy night, had led them to Dakkar Grotto. In open day the descent was less perilous, and, besides, the bed of ashes which covered the polished surface of the rock enabled them to make their footing more secure.

The ridge at the end of the shore, about forty feet in height, was soon reached. Cyrus Harding recollected that this elevation gradually sloped toward the level of the sea. Although the tide was at present low, no beach could be seen, and the waves, thickened by the volcanic dust, beat upon the basaltic rocks.

Cyrus Harding and Ayrton found without difficulty the entrance to Dakkar Grotto, and paused for a moment at the last rock before it.

"The iron boat should be there," said the engineer.

"It is here, Captain Harding," replied Ayrton, drawing toward him the fragile craft, which was protected by the arch of the vault.

"On board, Ayrton!"

The two colonists stepped into the boat. A slight undulation of the waves carried it farther under the low arch of the crypt, and there Ayrton, with the aid of flint and steel, lighted the lamp. He then took the oars, and the lamp having been placed in the bow of the boat, so that its rays fell before them, Cyrus Harding took the helm and steered through the shades of the grotto.

The *Nautilus* was there no longer to illuminate the cavern with its electric light. Possibly it might not yet be extinguished, but no ray escaped from the depths of the abyss in which reposed all that was mortal of Captain Nemo.

The light afforded by the lamp, although feeble, nevertheless enabled the engineer to advance slowly, following the wall of the cavern. A deathlike silence reigned under the vaulted roof, or at least in the anterior portion, for soon Cyrus Harding distinctly heard the rumbling which proceeded from the bowels of the mountain.

"That comes from the volcano," he said.

Besides these sounds, the presence of chemical combinations was soon betrayed by their powerful odor, and the engineer and his companion were almost suffocated by sulphurous vapors.

"This is what Captain Nemo feared," murmured Cyrus Harding, changing countenance. "We must go to the end, notwithstanding."

"Forward!" replied Ayrton, bending to his oars and directing the boat toward the head of the cavern.

Twenty-five minutes after entering the mouth of the grotto the boat reached the extreme end.

Cyrus Harding then, standing up, cast the light of the lamp upon the walls of the cavern which separated it from the central shaft of the volcano. What was the thickness of this wall? It might be ten feet or a hundred feet—it was impossible to say. But the subterranean sounds were too perceptible to allow of the supposition that it was of any great thickness.

The engineer, after having explored the wall at a certain height horizontally, fastened the lamp to the end of an oar, and again surveyed the basaltic wall at a greater elevation.

There, through scarcely visible clefts and joinings, escaped a pungent vapor, which infected the atmosphere of the cavern. The wall was broken by large cracks, some of which extended to within two or three feet of the water's edge.

Cyrus Harding thought for a brief space. Then he said in a low voice, "Yes! the captain was right! The danger lies there, and a terrible danger!"

Ayrton said not a word, but, upon a sign from Cyrus Harding, resumed the oars, and half an hour later the engineer and he reached the entrance of Dakkar Grotto.

XIX

The next day, the 8th of January, after a day and night passed at the corral, where they left all in order, Cyrus Harding and Ayrton arrived at Granite House.

The engineer immediately called his companions together, and informed them of the imminent danger which threatened Lincoln Island, and from which no human power could deliver them.

"My friends," he said, and his voice betrayed the depth of his emotion, "our island is not among those which will endure while this earth endures. It is doomed to more or less speedy destruction, the cause of which it bears within itself, and from which nothing can save it."

The colonists looked at each other, then at the engineer. They did not clearly comprehend him.

"Explain yourself, Cyrus!" said Gideon Spilett.

"I will do so," replied Cyrus Harding, "or rather I will simply afford you the explanation which, during our few minutes of private conversation, was given me by Captain Nemo."

"Captain Nemo!" exclaimed the colonists.

"Yes, and it was the last service he desired to render us before his death!"

"The last service!" exclaimed Pencroft, "the last service! You will see that though he is dead he will render us others yet!"

"But what did the captain say?" inquired the reporter.

"I will tell you, my friends," said the engineer. "Lincoln Island does not resemble the other islands of the Pacific, and a fact of which Captain Nemo has made me cognizant must sooner or later bring about the subversion of its foundation."

"Nonsense! Lincoln Island, it can't be!" cried Pencroft, who, in spite of the respect he felt for Cyrus Harding, could not prevent a gesture of incredulity.

"Listen, Pencroft," resumed the engineer, "I will tell you what Captain Nemo communicated to me, and which I myself confirmed yesterday, during the exploration of Dakkar Grotto. This cavern stretches under the island as far as the volcano, and is only separated from its central shaft by the wall which terminates it. Now, this wall is seamed with fissures and clefts which already allow the sulphurous gases generated in the interior of the volcano to escape."

"Well?" said Pencroft, his brow suddenly contracting.

"Well, then, I saw that these fissures widen under the internal pressure from within, that the wall of basalt is gradually giving way, and that after a longer or shorter period it will afford a passage to the waters of the lake which fill the cavern."

"Good!" replied Pencroft, with an attempt at pleasantry. "The sea will extinguish the volcano, and there will be an end of the matter!"

"Not so!" said Cyrus Harding, "should a day arrive when the sea, rushing through the wall of the cavern, penetrates by the central shaft into the interior of the island to the boiling lava, Lincoln Island will that day be blown into the air—just as would happen to the island of Sicily were the Mediterranean to precipitate itself into Mount Etna."

The colonists made no answer to these significant words of the engineer. They now understood the danger by which they were menaced.

It may be added that Cyrus Harding had in no way exaggerated the danger to be apprehended. Many persons have formed an idea that it would be possible to extinguish volcanoes, which are almost always situated on the shores of a sea or lake, by opening a passage for the admission of the water. But they are not aware that this would be to incur the risk of blowing up a portion of the globe, like a boiler whose steam is suddenly expanded by intense heat. The water, rushing into a cavity whose temperature might be estimated at thousands of degrees, would be converted into steam with a sudden energy which no enclosure could resist.

It was not therefore doubtful that the island, menaced by a frightful and approaching convulsion, would endure only so long as the wall of Dakkar Grotto itself should endure. It was not even a question of months, nor of weeks, but of days; it might be of hours.

The first sentiment which the colonists felt was that of profound sorrow. They thought not so much of the peril which menaced themselves personally, but of the destruction of the island which had sheltered them, which they had cultivated, which they loved so well, and had hoped to render so flourishing. So much effort ineffectually expended, so much labor lost.

Pencroft could not prevent a large tear from rolling down his cheek, nor did he attempt to conceal it.

Some further conversation now took place. The chances yet in favor of the colonists were discussed; but finally it was agreed that there was not an hour to be lost, that the building and fitting of the vessel should be pushed forward with their utmost energy, and that this was the sole chance of safety for the inhabitants of Lincoln Island.

All hands, therefore, set to work on the vessel. What could it avail to sow, to reap, to hunt, to increase the stores of Granite House? The contents of the storehouse and outbuildings contained more than sufficient to provide the ship for a voyage, however long might be its duration. But it was imperative that the ship should be ready to receive them before the inevitable catastrophe should arrive.

Their labors were now carried on with feverish ardor. By the 23rd of January the vessel was half-decked over. Up to this time no change had taken place on the summit of the volcano. Vapor and smoke mingled with flames and incandescent stones were thrown up from the crater. But during the night of the 23rd, in consequence of the lava attaining the level of the first stratum of the volcano, the hat-shaped cone which formed over the latter disappeared. A frightful sound was heard. The colonists at first thought the island was rent asunder, and rushed out of Granite House.

This occurred about two o'clock in the morning.

The sky appeared on fire. The superior cone, a mass of rock a thousand feet in height, and weighing thousands of millions of pounds, had been thrown down upon the island, making it tremble to its foundation. Fortunately, this cone inclined to the north, and had fallen upon the plain of sand and tufa stretching between the volcano and the sea. The aperture of the crater being thus enlarged projected toward the sky a glare so intense that by the simple effect of reflection the atmosphere appeared red-hot. At the same time a torrent of lava, bursting from the new summit, poured out in long cascades, like water escaping from a vase too full, and a thousand tongues of fire crept over the sides of the volcano.

"The corral! the corral!" exclaimed Ayrton.

It was, in fact, toward the corral that the lava was rushing as the new crater faced the east, and consequently the fertile portions of the island, the springs of Red Creek and Jacamar Wood, were menaced with instant destruction.

At Ayrton's cry the colonists rushed to the onagers' stables. The cart was at once harnessed. All were possessed by the same thought—to hasten to the corral and set at liberty the animals it enclosed.

Before three in the morning they arrived at the corral. The cries of the terrified musmons and goats indicated the alarm which possessed them. Already a torrent of burning matter and liquefied minerals fell from the side of the mountain upon the meadows as far as the side of the palisade. The gate was burst open by Ayrton, and the animals, bewildered with terror, fled in all directions.

An hour afterward the boiling lava filled the corral, converting into vapor the water of the little rivulet which ran through it, burning up the house like dry grass, and leaving not even a post of the palisade to mark the spot where the corral once stood.

To contend against this disaster would have been folly—nay, madness. In presence of nature's grand convulsions man is powerless.

It was now daylight—the 24th of January. Cyrus Harding and his companions, before returning to Granite House, desired to ascertain the probable direction this inundation of lava was about to take. The soil sloped gradually from Mount Franklin to the east coast, and it was to be feared that, in spite of the thick Jacamar Wood, the torrent would reach the plateau of Prospect Heights.

"The lake will cover us," said Gideon Spilett.

"I hope so!" was Cyrus Harding's only reply.

The colonists were desirous of reaching the plain upon which the superior cone of Mount Franklin had fallen, but the lava arrested their progress. It had followed, on one side, the valley of Red Creek, and on the other that of Falls River, evaporating those watercourses in its passage. There was no possibility of crossing the torrent of lava; on the contrary, the colonists were obliged to retreat before it. The volcano, without its crown, was no longer recognizable, terminated as it was by a sort of flat table which replaced the ancient crater. From two openings in its southern and eastern sides an unceasing flow of lava poured forth, thus forming two distinct streams. Above the new crater a cloud of smoke and ashes, mingled with those of the atmosphere, massed over the island. Loud peals of thunder broke, and could scarcely be distinguished from the rumblings of the mountain, whose mouth vomited forth ignited rocks, which, hurled to more than a thousand feet, burst in the air like shells. Flashes of lightning rivaled in intensity the volcano's eruption.

Toward seven in the morning the position was no longer tenable by the colonists, who accordingly took shelter in the borders of Jacamar Wood. Not only did the projectiles begin to rain around them, but the lava, overflowing the bed of Red Creek, threatened to cut off the road to the corral. The nearest rows of trees caught fire, and their sap, suddenly transformed into vapor, caused them to explode with loud reports, while others, less moist, remained unhurt in the midst of the inundation.

The colonists had again taken the road to the corral. They proceeded but slowly, frequently looking back; but, in consequence of the inclination of the soil, the lava gained rapidly in the east, and as its lower waves became solidified, others, at boiling heat, covered them immediately.

Meanwhile, the principal stream of Red Creek Valley became more and more menacing. All this portion of the forest was on fire, and enormous wreaths of smoke rolled over the trees, whose trunks were already consumed by the lava.

The colonists halted near the lake, about half a mile from the mouth of Red Creek. A question of life or death was now to be decided.

Cyrus Harding, accustomed to the consideration of important crises, and aware that he was addressing men capable of hearing the truth, whatever it might be, then said,

"Either the lake will arrest the progress of the lava, and a part of the island will be preserved from utter destruction, or the stream will overrun the Forests of the Far West, and not a tree or plant will remain on the surface of the soil. We shall have no prospect but that of starvation upon these barren rocks—a death which will probably be anticipated by the explosion of the island."

"In that case," replied Pencroft, folding his arms and stamping his foot, "what's the use of working any longer on the vessel?"

"Pencroft," answered Cyrus Harding, "we must do our duty to the last!"

At this instant the river of lava, after having broken a passage through the noble trees it devoured in its course, reached the borders of the lake. At this point there was an elevation of the soil which, had it been greater, might have sufficed to arrest the torrent.

"To work!" cried Cyrus Harding.

The engineer's thought was at once understood. It might be possible to dam, as it were, the torrent, and thus compel it to pour itself into the lake.

The colonists hastened to the dockyard. They returned with shovels, picks, axes, and by means of banking the earth with the aid of fallen trees they succeeded in a few hours in raising an embankment three feet high and some hundreds of paces in length. It seemed to them, when they had finished, as if they had scarcely been working more than a few minutes.

It was not a moment too soon. The liquefied substances soon after reached the bottom of the barrier. The stream of lava swelled like a river about to overflow its banks, and threatened to demolish the sole obstacle which could prevent it from over-running the whole Far West. But the dam held firm, and after a moment of terrible suspense the torrent precipitated itself into Grant Lake from a height of twenty feet.

The colonists, without moving or uttering a word, breathlessly regarded this strife of the two elements.

What a spectacle was this conflict between water and fire! What pen could describe the marvelous horror of this scene—what pencil could depict it? The water hissed as it evaporated by contact with the boiling lava. The vapor whirled in the air to an immeasurable height, as if the valves of an immense boiler had been suddenly opened. But, however considerable might be the volume of water contained in the lake, it must eventually be absorbed, because it was not replenished, while the stream of lava, fed from an inexhaustible source, rolled on without ceasing new waves of incandescent matter.

The first waves of lava which fell in the lake immediately solidified and accumulated so as speedily to emerge from it. Upon their surface fell other waves, which in their turn became stone, but a step nearer the center of the lake. In this manner was formed a pier which threatened to gradually fill up the lake, which could not overflow, the water displaced by the lava being evaporated. The hissing of the water rent the air with a deafening sound, and the vapor, blown by the wind, fell in rain upon the sea. The pier became longer and longer, and the blocks of lava piled themselves one on another. Where formerly stretched the calm waters of the lake now appeared an enormous mass of smoking rocks, as if an upheaving of the soil had formed immense shoals. Imagine the waters of the lake aroused by a hurricane, then suddenly solidified by an intense frost, and some conception may be formed of the aspect of the lake three hours after the eruption of this irresistible torrent of lava.

This time water would be vanquished by fire.

Nevertheless it was a fortunate circumstance for the colonists that the effusion of lava should have been in the direction of Lake Grant. They had before them some days' respite. The plateau of Prospect Heights, Granite House, and the dockyard were for the moment preserved. And these few days it was necessary to employ in planking and carefully calking the vessel, and launching her. The colonists would then take refuge on board the vessel, content to rig her after she should be afloat on the waters. With the danger of an explosion which threatened to destroy the island there could be no security on shore. The walls of Granite House, once so sure a retreat, might at any moment fall in upon them.

During the six following days, from the 25th to the 30th of January, the colonists accomplished as much of the construction of their vessel as twenty men could have done. They hardly allowed themselves a moment's repose, and the glare of the flames which shot from the crater enabled them to work night and day. The flow of lava continued, but perhaps less abundantly. This was fortunate, for Lake Grant was almost entirely choked up, and if more lava should accumulate it would inevitably spread over the plateau of Prospect Heights, and thence upon the beach.

But if the island was thus partially protected on this side, it was not so with the western part.

In fact, the second stream of lava, which had followed the valley of Falls River, a valley of great extent, the land on both sides of the creek being flat, met with no obstacle. The burning liquid had then spread through the Forests of the Far West. At this period of the year, when the trees were dried up by a tropical heat, the forest caught fire instantaneously, in such a manner that the conflagration extended itself both by the trunks of the trees and by their higher branches, whose interlacement favored its progress. It even appeared that the current of flame spread more rapidly among the summits of the trees than the current of lava at their bases.

Thus it happened that the wild animals, jaguars, wild boars, capybaras, koalas, and game of every kind, mad with terror, had fled to the banks of the Mercy and to the Tadorn's Fens, beyond the road to Port Balloon. But the colonists were too much occupied with their task to pay any attention to even the most formidable of these animals. They had abandoned Granite House, and would not even take shelter at the Chimneys, but encamped under a tent, near the mouth of the Mercy.

Each day Cyrus Harding and Gideon Spilett ascended the plateau of Prospect Heights. Sometimes Herbert accompanied them, but never Pencroft, who could not bear to look upon the prospect of the island now so utterly devastated.

It was, in truth, a heart-rending spectacle. All the wooded part of the island was now completely bare. One single clump of green trees raised their heads at the extremity of Serpentine Peninsula. Here and there were a few grotesque blackened and branchless stumps. The side of the devastated forest was even more barren than Tadorn's Fens. The eruption of lava had been complete. Where formerly sprang up that charming verdure, the soil was now nothing but a savage mass of volcanic tufa. In the valleys of the Falls and Mercy rivers no drop of water now flowed toward the sea, and should Lake Grant be entirely dried up, the colonists would have no means of quenching their thirst. But, fortunately the lava had spared the southern corner of the lake, containing all that remained of the drinking water of the island. Toward the northwest stood out the rugged and well-defined outlines of the sides of the volcano, like a gigantic claw hovering over the island. What a sad and fearful sight, and how painful to the colonists, who, from a fertile domain covered with forests, irrigated by watercourses, and enriched by the produce of their toils, found themselves, as it were, transported to a desolate rock, upon which, but for their reserves of provisions, they could not even gather the means of subsistence!

"It is enough to break one's heart!" said Gideon Spilett, one day.

"Yes, Spilett," answered the engineer. "May God grant us the time to complete this vessel, now our sole refuge!"

"Do not you think, Cyrus, that the violence of the eruption has somewhat lessened? The volcano still vomits forth lava, but somewhat less abundantly, if I mistake not."

"It matters little," answered Cyrus Harding. "The fire is still burning in the interior of the mountain, and the sea may break in at any moment. We are in the condition of passengers whose ship is devoured by a conflagration which they cannot extinguish, and who know that sooner or later the flames must reach the powder-magazine. To work, Spilett, to work, and let us not lose an hour!"

During eight days more, that is to say until the 7th of February, the lava continued to flow, but the eruption was confined within the previous limits. Cyrus Harding feared above all lest the liquefied matter should overflow the shore, for in that event the dockyard could not escape. Moreover, about this time the colonists felt in the frame of the island vibrations which alarmed them to the highest degree.

It was the 20th of February. Yet another month must elapse before the vessel would be ready for sea. Would the island hold together till then? The intention of Pencroft and Cyrus Harding was to launch the vessel as soon as the hull should be complete. The deck, the upperworks, the interior woodwork, and the rigging might be finished afterward, but the essential point was that the colonists should have an assured refuge away from the island. Perhaps it might be even better to conduct the vessel to Port Balloon, that is to say, as far as possible from the center of eruption, for at the mouth of the Mercy, between the islet and the wall of granite, it would run the risk of being crushed in the event of any convulsion. All the exertions of the voyagers were therefore concentrated upon the completion of the hull.

Thus the 3rd of March arrived, and they might calculate upon launching the vessel in ten days.

Hope revived in the hearts of the colonists, who had, in this fourth year of their sojourn on Lincoln Island, suffered so many trials. Even Pencroft lost in some measure the somber taciturnity occasioned by the devastation and ruin of his domain. His hopes, it is true, were concentrated upon his vessel.

"We shall finish it," he said to the engineer, "we shall finish it, captain, and it is time, for the season is advancing and the equinox will soon be here. Well, if necessary, we must put in to Tabor Island to spend the winter. But think of Tabor Island after Lincoln Island. Ah, how unfortunate! who could have believed it possible?"

"Let us get on," was the engineer's invariable reply.

And they worked away without losing a moment.

"Master," asked Neb, a few days later, "do you think all this could have happened if Captain Nemo had been still alive?"

"Certainly, Neb," answered Cyrus Harding.

"I, for one, don't believe it!" whispered Pencroft to Neb.

"Nor I!" answered Neb seriously.

During the first week of March appearances again became menacing. Thousands of threads like glass, formed of fluid lava, fell like rain upon the island. The crater was again boiling with lava which overflowed the back of the volcano. The torrent flowed along the surface of the hardened tufa, and destroyed the few meager skeletons of trees which had withstood the first eruption. The stream, flowing this time toward the southwest shore of Lake Grant, stretched beyond Creek Glycerine, and invaded the plateau of Prospect Heights. This last blow to the work of the colonists was terrible. The mill, the buildings of the inner court, the stables, were all destroyed. The affrighted poultry fled in all directions. Top and Jup showed signs of the greatest alarm, as if their instinct warned them of an impending catastrophe. A large number of the animals of the island had perished in the first eruption. Those which survived found no refuge but Tadorn's Fens, save a few to which the plateau of Prospect Heights afforded asylum. But even this last retreat was now closed to them, and the lava-torrent, flowing over the edge of the granite wall, began to pour down upon the beach its cataracts of fire. The sublime horror of this spectacle passed all description. During the night it could only be compared to a Niagara of molten fluid, with its incandescent vapors above and its boiling masses below.

The colonists were driven to their last entrenchment, and although the upper seams of the vessel were not yet calked, they decided to launch her at once.

Pencroft and Ayrton therefore set about the necessary preparations for the launching, which was to take place the morning of the next day, the 9th of March.

But during the night of the 8th an enormous column of vapor escaping from the crater rose with frightful explosions to a height of more than three thousand feet. The wall of Dakkar Grotto had evidently given way under the pressure of gases, and the sea, rushing through the central shaft into the igneous gulf, was at once converted into vapor. But the crater could not afford a sufficient outlet for this vapor. An explosion, which might have been heard at a distance of a hundred miles, shook the air. Fragments of mountains fell into the Pacific, and, in a few minutes, the ocean rolled over the spot where Lincoln Island once stood.

XX

An isolated rock, thirty feet in length, twenty in breadth, scarcely ten from the water's edge, such was the only solid point which the waves of the Pacific had not engulfed.

It was all that remained of the structure of Granite House! The wall had fallen headlong and been then shattered to fragments, and a few of the rocks of the large room were piled one above another to form this point. All around had disappeared in the abyss; the inferior cone of Mount Franklin, rent asunder by the explosion; the lava jaws of Shark Gulf, the plateau of Prospect Heights, Safety Islet, the granite rocks of Port Balloon, the basalts of Dakkar Grotto, the long Serpentine Peninsula, so distant nevertheless from the center of the eruption. All that could now be seen of Lincoln Island was the narrow rock which now served as a refuge to the six colonists and their dog Top.

The animals had also perished in the catastrophe; the birds, as well as those representing the fauna of the island—all either crushed or drowned, and the unfortunate Jup himself had, alas! found his death in some crevice of the soil.

If Cyrus Harding, Gideon Spilett, Herbert, Pencroft, Neb, and Ayrton had survived, it was because, assembled under their tent, they had been hurled into the sea at the instant when the fragments of the island rained down on every side.

When they reached the surface they could only perceive, at half a cable's length, this mass of rocks, toward which they swam and on which they found footing.

On this barren rock they had now existed for nine days. A few provisions taken from the magazine of Granite House before the catastrophe, a little fresh water from the rain which had fallen in a hollow of the rock, was all that the unfortunate colonists possessed. Their last hope, the vessel, had been shattered to pieces. They had no means of quitting the reef; no fire, nor any means of obtaining it. It seemed that they must inevitably perish.

This day, the 18th of March, there remained only provisions for two days, although they limited their consumption to the bare necessaries of life. All their science and intelligence could avail them nothing in their present position. They were in the hand of God.

Cyrus Harding was calm, Gideon Spilett more nervous, and Pencroft, a prey to sullen anger, walked to and fro on the rock. Herbert did not for a moment quit the engineer's side, as if demanding from him that assistance he had no power to give. Neb and Ayrton were resigned to their fate.

"Ah, what a misfortune! what a misfortune!" often repeated Pencroft. "If we had but a walnut-shell to take us to Tabor Island! But we have nothing, nothing!"

"Captain Nemo did right to die," said Neb.

During the five ensuing days Cyrus Harding and his unfortunate companions husbanded their provisions with the most extreme care, eating only what would prevent them from dying of starvation. Their weakness was extreme. Herbert and Neb began to show symptoms of delirium.

Under these circumstances was it possible for them to retain even the shadow of a hope? No! What was their sole remaining chance? That a vessel should appear in sight of the rock? But they knew only too well from experience that no ships ever visited this part of the Pacific. Could they calculate that, by a truly providential coincidence, the Scotch yacht would arrive precisely at this time in search of Ayrton at Tabor Island? It was scarcely probable; and, besides, supposing she should come there, as the colonists had not been able to deposit a notice pointing out Ayrton's change of abode, the commander of the yacht, after having explored Tabor Island without results, would again set sail and return to lower latitudes.

No! no hope of being saved could be retained, and a horrible death, death from hunger and thirst, awaited them upon this rock.

Already they were stretched on the rock, inanimate, and no longer conscious of what passed around them. Ayrton alone, by a supreme effort, from time to time raised his head, and cast a despairing glance over the desert ocean.

But on the morning of the 24th of March Ayrton's arms were extended toward a point in the horizon; he raised himself, at first on his knees, then upright, and his hand seemed to make a signal.

A sail was in sight off the rock. She was evidently not without an object. The reef was the mark for which she was making in a direct line, under all steam, and the unfortunate colonists might have made her out some hours before if they had had the strength to watch the horizon.

"The *Duncan!*" murmured Ayrton—and fell back without sign of life.

When Cyrus Harding and his companions recovered consciousness, thanks to the attention lavished upon them, they found themselves in the cabin of a steamer, without being able to comprehend how they had escaped death.

A word from Ayrton explained everything.

"The *Duncan!*" he murmured.

"The *Duncan!*" exclaimed Cyrus Harding. And raising his hand to Heaven, he said, "Oh! Almighty God! mercifully hast Thou preserved us!"

It was, in fact, the *Duncan*, Lord Glenarvan's yacht, now commanded by Robert, son of Captain Grant, who had been dispatched to Tabor Island to find Ayrton, and bring him back to his native land after twelve years of expiation.

The colonists were not only saved, but already on the way to their native country.

"Captain Grant," asked Cyrus Harding, "who can have suggested to you the idea, after having left Tabor Island, where you did not find Ayrton, of coming a hundred miles farther northeast?"

"Captain Harding," replied Robert Grant, "it was in order to find, not only Ayrton, but yourself and your companions."

"My companions and myself?"

"Doubtless, at Lincoln Island."

"At Lincoln Island!" exclaimed in a breath Gideon Spilett, Herbert, Neb, and Pencroft, in the highest degree astonished.

"How could you be aware of the existence of Lincoln Island?" inquired Cyrus Harding, "it is not even named in the charts."

"I knew of it from a document left by you on Tabor Island," answered Robert Grant.

"A document!" cried Gideon Spilett.

"Without doubt, and here it is," answered Robert Grant, producing a paper which indicated the longitude and latitude of Lincoln Island, "the present residence of Ayrton and five American colonists."

"It is Captain Nemo!" cried Cyrus Harding, after having read the notice, and recognized that the handwriting was similar to that of the paper found at the corral.

"Ah!" said Pencroft, "it was then he who took our *Bonadventure* and hazarded himself alone to go to Tabor Island!"

"In order to leave this notice," added Herbert.

"I was then right in saying," exclaimed the sailor, "that even after his death the captain would render us a last service."

"My friends," said Cyrus Harding, in a voice of the profoundest emotion, "may the God of mercy have had pity on the soul of Captain Nemo, our benefactor."

The colonists uncovered themselves at these last words of Cyrus Harding, and murmured the name of Captain Nemo.

Then Ayrton, approaching the engineer, said simply, "Where should this coffer be deposited?"

It was the coffer which Ayrton had saved at the risk of his life, at the very instant that the island had been engulfed, and which he now faithfully handed to the engineer.

"Ayrton! Ayrton!" said Cyrus Harding, deeply touched. Then, addressing Robert Grant, "Sir," he added, "you left behind you a criminal; you find in his place a man who has become honest by penitence, and whose hand I am proud to clasp in mine."

Robert Grant was now made acquainted with the strange history of Captain Nemo and the colonists of Lincoln Island. Then, observation being taken of what remained of this shoal, which must henceforward figure on the charts of the Pacific, the order was given to make all sail.

A few weeks afterward the colonists landed in America, and found their country once more at peace after the terrible conflict in which right and justice had triumphed.

Of the treasures contained in the coffer left by Captain Nemo to the colonists of Lincoln Island, the larger portion was employed in the purchase of a vast territory in the State of Iowa. One pearl alone, the finest, was reserved from the treasure and sent to Lady Glenarvan in the name of the castaways restored to their country by the *Duncan*.

There, upon this domain, the colonists invited to labor, that is to say, to wealth and happiness, all those to whom they had hoped to offer the hospitality of Lincoln Island. There was founded a vast colony to which they gave the name of that island sunk beneath the waters of the Pacific. A river there was called the Mercy, a mountain took the name of Mount Franklin, a small lake was named Lake Grant, and the forests became the Forests of the Far West. It might have been an island on terra firma.

There, under the intelligent hands of the engineer and his companions, everything prospered. Not one of the former colonists of Lincoln Island was absent, for they had sworn to live always together. Neb was with his master; Ayrton was there ready to sacrifice himself for all; Pencroft was more a farmer than he had ever been a sailor; Herbert, who completed his studies under the superintendence of Cyrus Harding, and Gideon Spilett, who founded the *New Lincoln Herald*, the best-informed journal in the world.

There Cyrus Harding and his companions received at intervals visits from Lord and Lady Glenarvan, Captain John Mangles and his wife, the sister of Robert Grant, Robert Grant himself, Major McNab, and all those who had taken part in the history both of Captain Grant and Captain Nemo.

There, to conclude, all were happy, united in the present as they had been in the past; but never could they forget that island upon which they had arrived poor and friendless, that island which, during four years had supplied all their wants, and of which there remained but a fragment of granite washed by the waves of the Pacific, the tomb of him who had borne the name of Captain Nemo.

Journey to the Center of the Earth

Contents

I

My Uncle Makes a Great Discovery

Looking back to all that has occurred to me since that eventful day, I am scarcely able to believe in the reality of my adventures. They were truly so wonderful that even now I am bewildered when I think of them.

My uncle was a German, having married my mother's sister, an Englishwoman. Being very much attached to his fatherless nephew, he invited me to study under him in his home in the fatherland. This home was in a large town, and my uncle a professor of philosophy, chemistry, geology, mineralogy, and many other ologies.

One day, after passing some hours in the laboratory—my uncle being absent at the time—I suddenly felt the necessity of renovating the tissues—i.e., I was hungry, and was about to rouse up our old French cook, when my uncle, Professor Von Hardwigg, suddenly opened the street door, and came rushing upstairs.

Now Professor Hardwigg, my worthy uncle, is by no means a bad sort of man; he is, however, choleric and original. To bear with him means to obey; and scarcely had his heavy feet resounded within our joint domicile than he shouted for me to attend upon him.

"Harry—Harry—Harry—"

I hastened to obey, but before I could reach his room, jumping three steps at a time, he was stamping his right foot upon the landing.

"Harry!" he cried, in a frantic tone, "are you coming up?"

Now to tell the truth, at that moment I was far more interested in the question as to what was to constitute our dinner than in any problem of science; to me soup was more interesting than soda, an omelette more tempting than arithmetic, and an artichoke of ten times more value than any amount of asbestos.

But my uncle was not a man to be kept waiting; so adjourning therefore all minor questions, I presented myself before him.

He was a very learned man. Now most persons in this category supply themselves with information, as peddlers do with goods, for the benefit of others, and lay up stores in order to diffuse them abroad for the benefit of society in general. Not so my excellent uncle, Professor Hardwigg; he studied, he consumed the midnight oil, he pored over heavy tomes, and digested huge quartos and folios in order to keep the knowledge acquired to himself.

There was a reason, and it may be regarded as a good one, why my uncle objected to display his learning more than was absolutely necessary: he stammered; and when intent upon explaining the phenomena of the heavens, was apt to find himself at fault, and allude in such a vague way to sun, moon, and stars that few were able to comprehend his meaning. To tell the honest truth, when the right word would not come, it was generally replaced by a very powerful adjective.

In connection with the sciences there are many almost unpronounceable names—names very much resembling those of Welsh villages; and my uncle being very fond of using them, his habit of stammering was not thereby improved. In fact, there were periods in his discourse when he would finally give up and swallow his discomfiture—in a glass of water.

As I said, my uncle, Professor Hardwigg, was a very learned man; and I now add a most kind relative. I was bound to him by the double ties of affection and interest. I took deep interest in all his doings, and hoped some day to be almost as learned myself. It was a rare thing for me to be absent from his lectures. Like him, I preferred mineralogy to all the other sciences. My anxiety was to gain *real knowledge of the earth.* Geology and mineralogy were to us the sole objects of life, and in connection with these studies many a fair specimen of stone, chalk, or metal did we break with our hammers.

Steel rods, loadstone, glass pipes, and bottles of various acids were oftener before us than our meals. My uncle Hardwigg was once known to classify six hundred different geological specimens by their weight, hardness, fusibility, sound, taste, and smell.

He corresponded with all the great, learned, and scientific men of the age. I was, therefore, in constant communication with, at all events the letters of, Sir Humphry Davy, Captain Franklin, and other great men.

But before I state the subject on which my uncle wished to confer with me, I must say a word about his personal appearance. Alas! my readers will see a very different portrait of him at a future time, after he has gone through the fearful adventures yet to be related.

My uncle was fifty years old; tall, thin, and wiry. Large spectacles hid, to a certain extent, his vast, round, and goggle eyes, while his nose was irreverently compared to a thin file. So much indeed did it resemble that useful article, that a compass was said in his presence to have made considerable N deviation.

The truth being told, however, the only article really attracted to my uncle's nose was tobacco.

Another peculiarity of his was, that he always stepped a yard at a time, clenched his fists as if he were going to hit you, and was, when in one of his peculiar humors, very far from a pleasant companion.

It is further necessary to observe that he lived in a very nice house, in that very nice street, the Königstrasse at Hamburg. Though lying in the center of a town, it was perfectly rural in its aspect—half wood, half bricks, with old-fashioned gables—one of the few old houses spared by the great fire of 1842.

When I say a nice house, I mean a handsome house—old, tottering, and not exactly comfortable to English notions: a house a little off the perpendicular and inclined to fall into the neighboring canal; exactly the house for a wandering artist to depict; all the more that you could scarcely see it for ivy and a magnificent old tree which grew over the door.

My uncle was rich; his house was his own property, while he had a considerable private income. To my notion the best part of his possessions was his god-daughter, Gretchen. And the old cook, the young lady, the Professor, and I were the sole inhabitants.

I loved mineralogy, I love geology. To me there was nothing like pebbles—and if my uncle had been in a little less of a fury, we should have been the happiest of families. To prove the excellent Hardwigg's impatience, I solemnly declare that when the flowers in the drawing-room pots began to grow, he rose every morning at four o'clock to make them grow quicker by pulling the leaves.

Having described my uncle, I will now give an account of our interview.

He received me in his study; a perfect museum, containing every natural curiosity that can well be imagined—minerals, however, predominating. Every one was familiar to me, having been catalogued by my own hand. My uncle, apparently oblivious of the fact that he had summoned me to his presence, was absorbed in a book. He was particularly fond of early editions, tall copies, and unique works.

"Wonderful!" he cried, tapping his forehead. "Wonderful—wonderful!"

It was one of those yellow-leaved volumes now rarely found on stalls, and to me it appeared to possess but little value. My uncle, however, was in raptures.

He admired its binding, the clearness of its characters, the ease with which it opened in his hand, and repeated aloud, half-a-dozen times, that it was very, very old.

To my fancy he was making a great fuss about nothing, but it was not my province to say so. On the contrary, I professed considerable interest in the subject, and asked him what it was about.

"It is the Heims-Kringla of Snorre Tarleson," he said, "the celebrated Icelandic author of the twelfth century—it is a true and correct account of the Norwegian princes who reigned in Iceland."

My next question related to the language in which it was written. I hoped at all events it was translated into German. My uncle was indignant at the very thought, and declared he wouldn't give a penny for a translation. His delight was to have found the original work in the Icelandic tongue, which he declared to be one of the most magnificent and yet simple idioms in the world—while at the same time its grammatical combinations were the most varied known to students.

"About as easy as German?" was my insidious remark.

My uncle shrugged his shoulders.

"The letters at all events," I said, "are rather difficult of comprehension."

"It is a Runic manuscript, the language of the original population of Iceland, invented by Odin himself," cried my uncle, angry at my ignorance.

I was about to venture upon some misplaced joke on the subject, when a small scrap of parchment fell out of the leaves. Like a hungry man snatching at a morsel of bread the Professor seized it. It was about five inches by three and was scrawled over in the most extraordinary fashion.

The lines on page 762 are an exact facsimile of what was written on the venerable piece of parchment—and have wonderful importance, as they induced my uncle to undertake the most wonderful series of adventures which ever fell to the lot of human beings.

My uncle looked keenly at the document for some moments and then declared that it was Runic. The letters were similar to those in the book, but then what did they mean? This was exactly what I wanted to know.

Now as I had a strong conviction that the Runic alphabet and dialect were simply an invention to mystify poor human nature, I was delighted to find that my uncle knew as much about the matter as I did—which was nothing. At all events, the tremulous motion of his fingers made me think so.

"And yet," he muttered to himself, "it is old Icelandic, I am sure of it."

And my uncle ought to have known, for he was a perfect polyglot dictionary in himself. He did not pretend, like a certain learned pundit, to speak the two thousand languages and four thousand idioms made use of in different parts of the globe, but he did know all the more important ones.

It is a matter of great doubt to me now, to what violent measures my uncle's impetuosity might have led him, had not the clock struck two, and our old French cook called out to let us know that dinner was on the table.

"Bother the dinner!" cried my uncle.

But as I was hungry, I sallied forth to the dining-room, where I took up my usual quarters. Out of politeness I waited three minutes, but no sign of my uncle, the Professor. I was surprised. He was not usually so blind to the pleasure of a good dinner. It was the acme of German luxury—parsley soup, a ham omelette with sorrel trimmings, an oyster of veal stewed with prunes, delicious fruit, and sparkling Moselle. For the sake of poring over this musty old piece of parchment, my uncle forbore to share our meal. To satisfy my conscience, I ate for both.

The old cook and housekeeper was nearly out of her mind. After taking so much trouble, to find her master not appear at dinner was to her a sad disappointment—which, as she occasionally watched the havoc I was making on the viands, became also alarm. If my uncle were to come to table after all?

Suddenly, just as I had consumed the last apple and drunk the last glass of wine, a terrible voice was heard at no great distance. It was my uncle roaring for me to come to him. I made very nearly one leap of it—so loud, so fierce was his tone.

II
The Mysterious Parchment

"I declare" cried my uncle, striking the table fiercely with his fist, "I declare to you it is Runic—and contains some wonderful secret, which I must get at, at any price."

I was about to reply when he stopped me.

"Sit down," he said, quite fiercely, "and write to my dictation."

I obeyed.

"I will substitute," he said, "a letter of our alphabet for that of the Runic: we will then see what that will produce. Now, begin and make no mistakes."

The dictation commenced with the following incomprehensible result:

m.rnlls	Atvaar	unteief
sgtssmf	ccdrmi	atrateS
kt,samn	dt,iac	nuaect
emtnael	esreuel	.nscrc
eeutuc	niedrke	ieaabs
oseibo	Saodrrn	frantum
seecJde	rrilSa	Kediil

Scarcely giving me time to finish, my uncle snatched the document from my hands and examined it with the most rapt and deep attention.

"I should like to know what it means," he said, after a long period.

I certainly could not tell him, nor did he expect me to—his conversation being uniformly answered by himself.

"I declare it puts me in mind of a cryptograph," he cried, "unless, indeed, the letters have been written without any real meaning; and yet why take so much trouble? Who knows but I may be on the verge of some great discovery?"

My candid opinion was that it was all rubbish! But this opinion I kept carefully to myself, as my uncle's choler was not pleasant to bear. All this time he was comparing the book with the parchment.

"The manuscript volume and the smaller document are written in different hands," he said, "the cryptograph is of much later date than the book; there is an undoubted proof of the correctness of my surmise. [An irrefragable proof I took it to be.] The first letter is a double M, which was only added to the Icelandic language in the twelfth century—this makes the parchment two hundred years posterior to the volume."

The circumstances appeared very probable and very logical, but it was all surmise to me.

"To me it appears probable that this sentence was written by some owner of the book. Now who was the owner, is the next important question. Perhaps by great good luck it may be written somewhere in the volume."

With these words Professor Hardwigg took off his spectacles, and, taking a powerful magnifying glass, examined the book carefully.

On the fly leaf was what appeared to be a blot of ink, but on examination proved to be a line of writing almost effaced by time. This was what he sought; and, after some considerable time, he made out these letters:

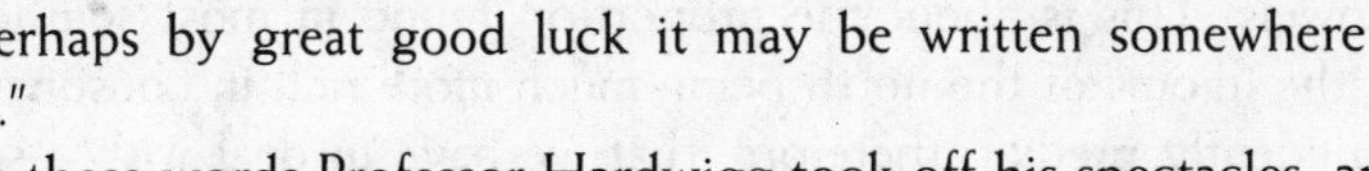

"Arne Saknussemm!" he cried in a joyous and triumphant tone, "that is not only an Icelandic name, but of a learned professor of the sixteenth century, a celebrated alchemist."

I bowed as a sign of respect.

"These alchemists," he continued, "Avicenna, Bacon, Lully, Paracelsus, were the true, the only learned men of the day. They made surprising discoveries. May not this Saknussemm, nephew mine, have hidden on this bit of parchment some astounding invention? I believe the cryptograph to have a profound meaning—which I must make out."

My uncle walked about the room in a state of excitement almost impossible to describe.

"It may be so, sir," I timidly observed, "but why conceal it from posterity, if it be a useful, a worthy discovery?"

"Why—how should I know? Did not Galileo make a secret of his discoveries in connection with Saturn? But we shall see. Until I discover the meaning of this sentence I will neither eat nor sleep."

"My dear uncle—" I began.

"Nor you neither," he added.

It was lucky I had taken double allowance that day.

"In the first place," he continued, "there must be a clue to the meaning. If we could find that, the rest would be easy enough."

I began seriously to reflect. The prospect of going without food and sleep was not a promising one, so I determined to do my best to solve the mystery. My uncle, meanwhile, went on with his soliloquy.

"The way to discover it is easy enough. In this document there are one hundred and thirty-two letters, giving seventy-nine consonants to fifty-three vowels. This is about the proportion found in most southern languages, the idioms of the north being much more rich in consonants. We may confidently predict, therefore, that we have to deal with a southern dialect."

Nothing could be more logical.

"Now," said Professor Hardwigg, "to trace the particular language."

"As Shakespeare says, 'that is the question,'" was my rather satirical reply.

"This man Saknussemm," he continued, "was a very learned man: now as he did not write in the language of his birthplace, he probably, like most learned men of the sixteenth century, wrote in Latin. If, however, I prove wrong in this guess, we must try Spanish, French, Italian, Greek, and even Hebrew. My own opinion, though, is decidedly in favor of Latin."

This proposition startled me. Latin was my favorite study, and it seemed sacrilege to believe this gibberish to belong to the country of Virgil.

"Barbarous Latin, in all probability," continued my uncle, "but still Latin."

"Very probably," I replied, not to contradict him.

"Let us see into the matter," continued my uncle; "here you see we have a series of one hundred and thirty-two letters, apparently thrown pell-mell upon paper, without method or organization. There are words which are composed wholly of consonants, such as *m.rnlls*, others which are nearly all vowels, the fifth, for instance, which is *unteief*, and one of the last *oseibo*. This appears an extraordinary combination. Probably we shall find that the phrase is arranged according to some mathematical plan. No doubt a certain sentence has been written out and then jumbled up—some plan to which some figure is the clue. Now, Harry, to show your English wit—what is that figure?"

I could give him no hint. My thoughts were indeed far away. While he was speaking I had caught sight of the portrait of my cousin Gretchen, and was wondering when she would return.

We were affianced, and loved one another very sincerely. But my uncle, who never thought even of such sublunary matters, knew nothing of this. Without noticing my abstraction, the Professor began reading the puzzling cryptograph all sorts of ways, according to some theory of his own. Presently, rousing my wandering attention, he dictated one precious attempt to me.

I mildly handed it over to him. It read as follows:

MMESSUNKASENRA. ICEFDOK.SEGNITTAMURTN
ECERTSERRETTE, ROTAIVSADUA, EDNECSEDSADNE
LACARTNIIIILUJSIRATRACSARBMUTABELEDMEK
MERETARCSILUCOYSLEFFENSNI.

I could scarcely keep from laughing, while my uncle, on the contrary, got in a towering passion, struck the table with his fist, darted out of the room, out of the house, and then taking to his heels was presently lost to sight.

III

An Astounding Discovery

"What is the matter?" cried the cook, entering the room; "when will master have his dinner?"

"Never."

"And, his supper?"

"I don't know. He says he will eat no more, neither shall I. My uncle has determined to fast and make me fast until he makes out this abominable inscription," I replied.

"You will be starved to death," she said.

I was very much of the same opinion, but not liking to say so, sent her away, and began some of my usual work of classification. But try as I might, nothing could keep me from thinking alternately of the stupid manuscript and of the pretty Gretchen.

Several times I thought of going out, but my uncle would have been angry at my absence. At the end of an hour, my allotted task was done. How to pass the time? I began by lighting my pipe. Like all other students, I delighted in tobacco; and, seating myself in the great armchair, I began to think.

Where was my uncle? I could easily imagine him tearing along some solitary road, gesticulating, talking to himself, cutting the air with his cane, and still thinking of the absurd bit of hieroglyphics. Would he hit upon some clue? Would he come home in better humor? While these thoughts were passing through my brain, I mechanically took up the execrable puzzle and tried every imaginable way of grouping the letters. I put them together by twos, by threes, fours, and fives—in vain. Nothing intelligible came out, except that the fourteenth, fifteenth, and sixteenth made *ice* in English; the eighty-fourth, eighty-fifth, and eighty-sixth, the word *sir;* then at last I seemed to find the Latin words *rota, mutabile, ira, nec, atra.*

"Ha! there seems to be some truth in my uncle's notion," thought I.

Then again I seemed to find the word *luco,* which means sacred wood. Then in the third line I appeared to make out *labiled,* a perfect Hebrew word, and at the last the syllables *mère, are, mer,* which were French.

It was enough to drive one mad. Four different idioms in this absurd phrase. What connection could there be between ice, sir, anger, cruel, sacred wood, changing, mother, are, and sea? The first and the last might, in a sentence connected with Iceland, mean sea of ice. But what of the rest of this monstrous cryptograph?

I was, in fact, fighting against an insurmountable difficulty; my brain was almost on fire; my eyes were strained with staring at the parchment; the whole absurd collection of letters appeared to dance before my vision in a number of black little groups. My mind was possessed with temporary hallucination—I was stifling. I wanted air. Mechanically I fanned myself with the document, of which now I saw the back and then the front.

Imagine my surprise when glancing at the back of the wearisome puzzle, the ink having gone through, I clearly made out Latin words, and among others *craterem* and *terrestre*.

I had discovered the secret!

It came upon me like a flash of lightning. I had got the clue. All you had to do to understand the document was to read it backward. All the ingenious ideas of the Professor were realized; he had dictated it rightly to me; by a mere accident I had discovered what he so much desired.

My delight, my emotion may be imagined; my eyes were dazzled and I trembled so that at first I could make nothing of it. One look, however, would tell me all I wished to know.

"Let me read," I said to myself, after drawing a long breath.

I spread it before me on the table, I passed my finger over each letter, I spelled it through; in my excitement I read it out.

What horror and stupefaction took possession of my soul. I was like a man who had received a knock-down blow. Was it possible that I really read the terrible secret, and it had really been accomplished! A man had dared to do—what?

No living being should ever know.

"Never!" cried I, jumping up. "Never shall my uncle be made aware of the dread secret. He would be quite capable of undertaking the terrible journey. Nothing would check him, nothing stop him. Worse, he would compel me to accompany him, and we should be lost forever. But no; such folly and madness cannot be allowed."

I was almost beside myself with rage and fury.

"My worthy uncle is already nearly mad," I cried aloud. "This would finish him. By some accident he may make the discovery; in which case, we are both lost. Perish the fearful secret—let the flames forever bury it in oblivion."

I snatched up book and parchment, and was about to cast them into the fire, when the door opened and my uncle entered.

I had scarcely time to put down the wretched documents before my uncle was by my side. He was profoundly absorbed. His thoughts were evidently bent on the terrible parchment. Some new combination had probably struck him while taking his walk.

He seated himself in his armchair, and with a pen began to make an algebraical calculation. I watched him with anxious eyes. My flesh crawled as it became probable that he would discover *the* secret.

His combinations I knew now were useless, I having discovered the one only clue. For three mortal hours he continued without speaking a word, without raising his head, scratching, rewriting, calculating over and over again. I knew that in time he must hit upon the right phrase. The letters of every alphabet have only a certain number of combinations. But then years might elapse before he would arrive at the correct solution.

Still time went on; night came, the sounds in the streets ceased—and still my uncle went on, not even answering our worthy cook when she called us to supper.

I did not dare to leave him, so waved her away, and at last fell asleep on the sofa.

When I awoke my uncle was still at work. His red eyes, his pallid countenance, his matted hair, his feverish hands, his hectically flushed cheeks, showed how terrible had been his struggle with the impossible, and what fearful fatigue he had undergone during that long sleepless night. It made me quite ill to look at him. Though he was rather severe with me, I loved him, and my heart ached at his sufferings. He was so overcome by one idea that he could not even get in a passion! All his energies were focused on one point. And I knew that by speaking one little word all this suffering would cease. I could not speak it.

My heart was, nevertheless, inclining toward him. Why, then, did I remain silent? In the interest of my uncle himself.

"Nothing shall make me speak," I muttered. "He will want to follow in the footsteps of the other! I know him well. His imagination is a perfect volcano, and to make discoveries in the interests of geology he would sacrifice his life. I will therefore be silent and strictly keep the secret I have discovered. To reveal it would be suicidal. He would not only rush, himself, to destruction, but drag me with him."

I crossed my arms, looked another way, and smoked—resolved never to speak.

When our cook wanted to go out to market, or on any other errand, she found the front door locked and the key taken away. Was this done purposely or not? Surely Professor Hardwigg did not intend the old woman and myself to become martyrs to his obstinate will. Were we to be starved to death? A frightful recollection came to my mind. Once we had fed on bits and scraps for a week while he sorted some curiosities. It gave me the cramp even to think of it!

I wanted my breakfast, and I saw no way of getting it. Still my resolution held good. I would starve rather than yield. But the cook began to take me seriously to task. What was to be done? She could not go out; and I dared not.

My uncle continued counting and writing; his imagination seemed to have translated him to the skies. He neither thought of eating nor drinking. In this way twelve o'clock came round. I was hungry, and there was nothing in the house. The cook had eaten the last bit of bread. This could not go on. It did, however, until two, when my sensations were terrible. After all, I began to think the document very absurd. Perhaps it might only be a gigantic hoax. Besides, some means would surely be found to keep my uncle back from attempting any such absurd expedition. On the other hand, if he did attempt anything so quixotic, I should not be compelled to accompany him. Another line of reasoning partially decided me. Very likely he would make the discovery himself when I should have suffered starvation for nothing. Under the influence of hunger this reasoning appeared admirable. I determined to tell all.

The question now arose as to how it was to be done. I was still dwelling on the thought, when he rose and put on his hat.

What! go out and lock us in? Never!

"Uncle," I began.

He did not appear even to hear me.

"Professor Hardwigg," I cried.

"What," he retorted, "did you speak?"

"How about the key?"

"What key—the key of the door?"

"No—of these horrible hieroglyphics?"

He looked at me from under his spectacles, and started at the odd expression of my face. Rushing forward, he clutched me by the arm and keenly examined my countenance. His very look was an interrogation.

I simply nodded.

With an incredulous shrug of the shoulders, he turned upon his heel. Undoubtedly he thought I had gone mad.

"I have made a very important discovery."

His eyes flashed with excitement. His hand was lifted in a menacing attitude. For a moment neither of us spoke. It is hard to say which was most excited.

"You don't mean to say that you have any idea of the meaning of the scrawl?"

"I do," was my desperate reply. "Look at the sentence as dictated by you."

"Well, but it means nothing," was the angry answer.

"Nothing if you read from left to right, but mark, if from right to left—"

"Backward!" cried my uncle, in wild amazement. "Oh most cunning Saknussemm; and I to be such a blockhead!"

He snatched up the document, gazed at it with haggard eye, and read it out as I had done.

It read as follows:

In Sneffels yoculis craterem kem delebat
Umbra Scartaris Julii intra calendas descende.
Audas viator, et terrestre centrum attinges,
Kod feci. Arne Saknussemm.

Which dog Latin being translated, reads as follows:

Descend into the crater of Yocul of Sneffels, which the shade of Scartaris caresses, before the kalends of July, audacious traveler, and you will reach the center of the earth. I did it.

Arne Saknussemm

My uncle leaped three feet from the ground with joy. He looked radiant and handsome. He rushed about the room wild with delight and satisfaction. He knocked over tables and chairs. He threw his books about until at last, utterly exhausted, he fell into his armchair.

"What's o'clock?" he asked.

"About three."

"My dinner does not seem to have done me much good," he observed. "Let me have something to eat. We can then start at once. Get my portmanteau ready."

"What for?"

"And your own," he continued. "We start at once."

My horror may be conceived. I resolved however to show no fear. Scientific reasons were the only ones likely to influence my uncle. Now, there were many against this terrible journey. The very idea of going down to the center of the earth was simply absurd. I determined therefore to argue the point after dinner.

My uncle's rage was now directed against the cook for having no dinner ready. My explanation however satisfied him, and having gotten the key, she soon contrived to get sufficient to satisfy our voracious appetites.

During the repast my uncle was rather gay than otherwise. He made some of those peculiar jokes which belong exclusively to the learned. As soon, however, as dessert was over, he called me to his study. We each took a chair on opposite sides of the table.

"Henry," he said, in a soft and winning voice; "I have always believed you ingenious, and you have rendered me a service never to be forgotten. Without you, this great, this wondrous discovery would never have been made. It is my duty, therefore, to insist on your sharing the glory."

"He is in a good humor," thought I; "I'll soon let him know my opinion of glory."

"In the first place," he continued, "you must keep the whole affair a profound secret. There is no more envious race of men than scientific discoverers. Many would start on the same journey. At all events, we will be the first in the field."

"I doubt your having many competitors," was my reply.

"A man of real scientific acquirements would be delighted at the chance. We should find a perfect stream of pilgrims on the traces of Arne Saknussemm, if this document were once made public."

"But, my dear sir, is not this paper very likely to be a hoax?" I urged.

"The book in which we find it is sufficient proof of its authenticity," he replied.

"I thoroughly allow that the celebrated Professor wrote the lines, but only, I believe, as a kind of mystification," was my answer.

Scarcely were the words out of my mouth, when I was sorry I had uttered them. My uncle looked at me with a dark and gloomy scowl, and I began to be alarmed for the results of our conversation. His mood soon changed, however, and a smile took the place of a frown.

"We shall see," he remarked, with decisive emphasis.

"But see, what is all this about Yocul, and Sneffels, and this Scartaris? I have never heard anything about them."

"The very point to which I am coming. I lately received from my friend Augustus Peterman, of Leipzig, a map. Take down the third atlas from the second shelf, series Z, plate 4."

I rose, went to the shelf, and presently returned with the volume indicated.

"This," said my uncle, "is one of the best maps of Iceland. I believe it will settle all your doubts, difficulties, and objections."

With a grim hope to the contrary, I stooped over the map.

IV

WE START ON THE JOURNEY

You see, the whole island is composed of volcanoes," said the Professor, "and remark carefully that they all bear the name of Yokul. The word is Icelandic, and means a glacier. In most of the lofty mountains of that region the volcanic eruptions come forth from icebound caverns. Hence the name applied to every volcano on this extraordinary island."

"But what does this word Sneffels mean?"

To this question I expected no rational answer. I was mistaken.

"Follow my finger to the western coast of Iceland, there you see Reykjavik, its capital. Follow the direction of one of its innumerable fjords or arms of the sea, and what do you see below the sixty-fifth degree of latitude?"

"A peninsula—very like a thighbone in shape."

"And in the center of it—?"

"A mountain."

"Well, that's Sneffels."

I had nothing to say.

"That is Sneffels—a mountain about five thousand feet in height, one of the most remarkable in the whole island, and certainly doomed to be the most celebrated in the world, for through its crater we shall reach the center of the earth."

"Impossible!" cried I, startled and shocked at the thought.

"Why impossible?" said Professor Hardwigg in his severest tones.

"Because its crater is choked with lava, by burning rocks—by infinite dangers."

"But if it be extinct?"

"That would make a difference."

"Of course it would. There are about three hundred volcanoes on the whole surface of the globe—but the greater number are extinct. Of these

Sneffels is one. No eruption has occurred since 1219—in fact it has ceased to be a volcano at all."

After this what more could I say? Yes—I thought of another objection.

"But what is all this about Scartaris and the kalends of July—?"

My uncle reflected deeply. Presently he gave forth the result of his reflections in a sententious tone.

"What appears obscure to you, to me is light. This very phrase shows how particular Saknussemm is in his directions. The Sneffels mountain has many craters. He is careful therefore to point the exact one which is the highway into the interior of the earth. He lets us know, for this purpose, that about the end of the month of June, the shadow of Mount Scartaris falls upon the one crater. There can be no doubt about the matter."

My uncle had an answer for everything.

"I accept all your explanations," I said, "and Saknussemm is right. He found out the entrance to the bowels of the earth, he has indicated correctly, but that he or anyone else ever followed up the discovery is madness to suppose."

"Why so, young man?"

"All scientific teaching, theoretical and practical, shows it to be impossible."

"I care nothing for theories," retorted my uncle.

"But is it not well known that heat increases one degree for every seventy feet you descend into the earth? Which gives a fine idea of the central heat. All the matters which composed the globe are in a state of incandescence; even gold, platinum, and the hardest rocks are in a state of fusion. What would become of us?"

"Don't be alarmed at the heat, my boy."

"How so?"

"Neither you nor anybody else know anything about the real state of the earth's interior. All modern experiments tend to explode the older theories. Were any such heat to exist, the upper crust of the earth would be shattered to atoms, and the world would be at an end."

A long, learned, and not uninteresting discussion followed, which ended in this wise:

"I do not believe in the dangers and difficulties which you, Henry, seem to multiply; and the only way to learn is, like Arne Saknussemm, to go and see."

"Well," cried I, overcome at last, "let us go and see. Though how we can do that in the dark is another mystery."

"Fear nothing. We shall overcome these, and many other difficulties. Besides, as we approach the center, I expect to find it luminous—"

"Nothing is impossible."

"And now that we have come to a thorough understanding, not a word to any living soul. Our success depends on secrecy and dispatch."

Thus ended our memorable conference, which roused a perfect fever in me. Leaving my uncle, I went forth like one possessed. Reaching the banks of the Elbe, I began to think. Was all I had heard really and truly possible? Was my uncle in his sober senses, and could the interior of the earth be reached? Was I the victim of a madman, or was he a discoverer of rare courage and grandeur of conception?

To a certain extent I was anxious to be off. I was afraid my enthusiasm would cool. I determined to pack up at once. At the end of an hour, however, on my way home, I found that my feelings had very much changed.

"I'm all abroad," I cried; " 'tis a nightmare—I must have dreamed it."

At this moment I came face to face with Gretchen, whom I warmly embraced.

"So you have come to meet me," she said; "how good of you. But what is the matter?"

Well, it was no use mincing the matter; I told her all. She listened with awe, and for some minutes she could not speak.

"Well?" I at last said, rather anxiously.

"What a magnificent journey. If I were only a man! A journey worthy of the nephew of Professor Hardwigg. I should look upon it as an honor to accompany him."

"My dear Gretchen, I thought you would be the first to cry out against this mad enterprise."

"No; on the contrary, I glory in it. It is magnificent, splendid—an idea worthy of my father. Henry Lawson, I envy you."

This was, as it were, conclusive. The final blow of all.

When we entered the house we found my uncle surrounded by workmen and porters, who were packing up. He was pulling and hauling at a bell.

"Where have you been wasting your time? Your portmanteau is not packed—my papers are not in order—the precious tailor has not brought my clothes, nor my gaiters—the key of my carpet bag is gone!"

I looked at him stupefied. And still he tugged away at the bell.

"We are really off, then?" I said.

"Yes—of course, and yet you go out for a stroll, unfortunate boy!"

"And when do we go?"

"The day after tomorrow, at daybreak."

I heard no more; but darted off to my little bedchamber and locked myself in. There was no doubt about it now. My uncle had been hard at work all the afternoon. The garden was full of ropes, rope ladders, torches, gourds, iron clamps, crowbars, alpenstocks, and pickaxes—enough to load ten men.

I passed a terrible night. I was called early the next day to learn that the resolution of my uncle was unchanged and irrevocable. I also found my cousin and affianced wife as warm on the subject as was her father.

Next day, at five o'clock in the morning, the post chaise was at the door. Gretchen and the old cook received the keys of the house; and, scarcely pausing to wish anyone good-by, we started on our adventurous journey into the center of the earth.

V

First Lessons in Climbing

At Altona, a suburb of Hamburg, is the Chief Station of the Kiel railway, which was to take us to the shores of the Belt. In twenty minutes from the moment of our departure we were in Holstein, and our carriage entered the station. Our heavy luggage was taken out, weighed, labeled, and placed in a huge van. We then took our tickets, and exactly at seven o'clock were seated opposite each other in a first-class railway carriage.

My uncle said nothing. He was too busy examining his papers, among which of course was the famous parchment, and some letters of introduction from the Danish consul, which were to pave the way to an introduction to the Governor of Iceland. My only amusement was looking out of the window. But as we passed through a flat though fertile country, this occupation was slightly monotonous. In three hours we reached Kiel, and our baggage was at once transferred to the steamer.

We had now a day before us, a delay of about ten hours. Which fact put my uncle in a towering passion. We had nothing to do but to walk about the pretty town and bay. At length, however, we went on board, and at half past ten were steaming down the Great Belt. It was a dark night, with a strong breeze and a rough sea, nothing being visible but the occasional fires on shore, with here and there a lighthouse. At seven in the morning we left Korsör, a little town on the western side of Seeland.

Here we took another railway, which in three hours brought us to the capital, Copenhagen, where, scarcely taking time for refreshment, my uncle hurried out to present one of his letters of introduction. It was to the director of the Museum of Antiquities, who, having been informed that we were tourists bound for Iceland, did all he could to assist us. One wretched hope sustained me now. Perhaps no vessel was bound for such distant parts.

Alas! a little Danish schooner, the *Valkyrie,* was to sail on the second of June for Reykjavik. The captain, M. Bjarne, was on board, and was rather surprised at the energy and cordiality with which his future passenger shook him by the hand. To him a voyage to Iceland was merely a matter of course. My uncle, on the other hand, considered the event of sublime importance. The honest sailor took advantage of the Professor's enthusiasm to double the fare.

"On Tuesday morning at seven o'clock be on board," said M. Bjarne, handing us our receipts.

"Excellent! Capital! Glorious!" remarked my uncle as we sat down to a late breakfast; "refresh yourself, my boy, and we will take a run through the town."

Our meal concluded, we went to the Kongens-Nye-Torw; to the king's magnificent palace; to the beautiful bridge over the canal near the Museum; to the immense cenotaph of Thorwaldsen with its hideous naval groups; to the castle of Rosenberg; and to all the other lions of the place—none of which my uncle even saw, so absorbed was he in his anticipated triumphs.

But one thing struck his fancy, and that was a certain singular steeple situated on the Island of Amak, which is the southeast quarter of the city of Copenhagen. My uncle at once ordered me to turn my steps that way, and accordingly we went on board the steam ferry boat which does duty on the canal, and very soon reached the noted dockyard quay.

In the first instance we crossed some narrow streets, where we met numerous groups of galley slaves, with particolored trousers, gray and yellow, working under the orders and the sticks of severe taskmasters, and finally reached the Vor-Frelser's-Kirk.

This church exhibited nothing remarkable in itself; in fact, the worthy Professor had only been attracted to it by one circumstance, which was, that its rather elevated steeple started from a circular platform, after which there was an exterior staircase, which wound round to the very summit.

"Let us ascend," said my uncle.

"But I never could climb church towers," I cried, "I am subject to dizziness in my head."

"The very reason why you should go up. I want to cure you of a bad habit."

"But my good sir—"

"I tell you to come. What is the use of wasting so much valuable time?"

It was impossible to dispute the dictatorial commands of my uncle. I yielded with a groan. On payment of a fee, a verger gave us the key. He, for one, was not partial to the ascent. My uncle at once showed me the way, running up the steps like a schoolboy. I followed as well as I could, though no sooner was I outside the tower, than my head began to swim. There was nothing of the eagle about me. The earth was enough for me, and no ambitious desire to soar ever entered my mind. Still things did not go badly until I had ascended 150 steps, and was near the platform, when I began to feel the rush of cold air. I could scarcely stand, when clutching the railings, I looked upward. The railing was frail enough, but nothing to those which skirted the terrible winding staircase, that appeared, from where I stood, to ascend to the skies.

"Now then, Henry."

"I can't do it!" I cried, in accents of despair.

"Are you, after all, a coward, sir?" said my uncle in a pitiless tone. "Go up, I say!"

To this there was no reply possible. And yet the keen air acted violently on my nervous system; sky, earth, all seemed to swim around, while the steeple rocked like a ship. My legs gave way like those of a drunken man. I crawled upon my hands and knees; I hauled myself up slowly, crawling like a snake. Presently I closed my eyes, and allowed myself to be dragged upward.

"Look around you," said my uncle in a stern voice, "heaven knows what profound abysses you may have to look down. This is excellent practice."

Slowly, and shivering all the while with cold, I opened my eyes. What then did I see? My first glance was upward at the cold fleecy clouds, which as by some optical delusion appeared to stand still, while the steeple, the weathercock, and our two selves were carried swiftly along. Far away on one side could be seen the grassy plain, while on the other lay the sea bathed in translucent light. The Sund, or Sound as we call it, could be discovered beyond the point of Elsinore, crowded with white sails, which, at that distance, looked like the wings of seagulls; while to the east could be made out the far-off coast of Sweden. The whole appeared a magic panorama.

But faint and bewildered as I was, there was no remedy for it. Rise and stand up I must. Despite my protestations my first lesson lasted quite an hour. When, nearly two hours later, I reached the bosom of mother earth, I was like a rheumatic old man bent double with pain.

"Enough for one day," said my uncle, rubbing his hands, "we will begin again tomorrow."

There was no remedy. My lessons lasted five days, and at the end of that period, I ascended blithely enough, and found myself able to look down into the depths below without even winking, and with some degree of pleasure.

VI
Our Voyage to Iceland

The hour of departure came at last. The night before, the worthy M. Thompson brought us the most cordial letters of introduction for Baron Trampe, Governor of Iceland, for M. Pictursson, coadjutor to the bishop, and for M. Finsen, mayor of the town of Reykjavik. In return, my uncle nearly crushed his hands, so warmly did he shake them.

On the second of the month, at two in the morning, our precious cargo of luggage was taken on board the good ship *Valkyrie.* We followed, and were very politely introduced by the captain to a small cabin with two standing bed places, neither very well ventilated nor very comfortable. But in the cause of science men are expected to suffer.

"Well, and have we a fair wind?" cried my uncle, in his most mellifluous accents.

"An excellent wind!" replied Captain Bjarne; "we shall leave the Sound, going free with all sails set."

A few minutes afterward, the schooner started before the wind, under all the canvas she could carry, and entered the channel. An hour later, the capital of Denmark seemed to sink into the waves, and we were at no great distance from the coast of Elsinore. My uncle was delighted; for myself, moody and dissatisfied, I appeared almost to expect a glimpse of the ghost of Hamlet.

"Sublime madman," thought I, "you doubtless would approve our proceedings. You might perhaps even follow us to the center of the earth, there to resolve your eternal doubts."

But no ghost or anything else appeared upon the ancient walls. The fact is, the castle is much later than the time of the heroic prince of Denmark. It is now the residence of the keeper of the Strait of the Sound, and through that Sound more than fifteen thousand vessels of all nations pass every year.

The castle of Kronborg soon disappeared in the murky atmosphere, as well as the tower of Helsinborg, which raises its head on the Swedish Bank. And here the schooner began to feel in earnest the breezes of the Kattegat. The *Valkyrie* was swift enough, but with all sailing boats there is the same uncertainty. Her cargo was coal, furniture, pottery, woolen clothing, and a load of corn. As usual, the crew was small, five Danes doing the whole of the work.

"How long will the voyage last?" asked my uncle.

"Well, I should think about ten days," replied the skipper, "unless, indeed, we meet with some northeast gales among the Faroe Islands."

"At all events, there will be no very considerable delay," cried the impatient Professor.

"No, M. Hardwigg," said the captain, "no fear of that. At all events, we shall get there some day."

Toward evening the schooner doubled Cape Skagen, the northernmost part of Denmark, crossed the Skagerrak during the night—skirted the extreme point of Norway through the gut of Cape Lindesnes, and then reached the Northern Seas. Two days later we were not far from the coast of Scotland, somewhere near what Danish sailors call Peterhead, and then the *Valkyrie* stretched out direct for the Faroe Islands, between Orkney and Shetland. Our vessel now felt the full force of the ocean waves, and the wind shifting, we with great difficulty made the Faroe Isles. On the eighth day, the captain made out Myganness, the westernmost of the isles, and from that moment headed directly for Portland, a cape on the southern shores of the singular island for which we were bound.

The voyage offered no incident worthy of record. I bore it very well, but my uncle to his great annoyance, and even shame, was remarkably seasick! This *mal de mer* troubled him the more that it prevented him from questioning Captain Bjarne as to the subject of Sneffels, as to the means of communication, and the facilities of transport. All these explanations he had to adjourn to the period of his arrival. His time, meanwhile, was spent lying in bed groaning, and dwelling anxiously on the hoped-for termination of the voyage. I didn't pity him.

On the eleventh day we sighted Cape Portland, over which towered Mount Myrdals Yokul, which, the weather being clear, we made out very readily. The cape itself is nothing but a huge mount of granite standing naked and alone to meet the Atlantic waves. The *Valkyrie* kept off the coast, steering to the westward. On all sides were to be seen whole "schools" of whales and sharks. After some hours we came in sight of a solitary rock in the ocean, forming a mighty vault, through which the foaming waves poured with intense fury. The islets of Westman appeared to leap from the ocean, being so low in the water as scarcely to be seen until you were right upon them. From that moment the schooner was steered to the westward in order to round Cape Reykjanes, the western point of Iceland.

My uncle, to his great disgust, was unable even to crawl on deck, so heavy a sea was on, and thus lost the first view of the Land of Promise. Forty-eight hours later, after a storm which drove us far to sea under bare poles, we came once more in sight of land, and were boarded by a pilot, who, after three hours of dangerous navigation, brought the schooner safely to an anchor in the bay of Faxa before Reykjavik.

My uncle came out of his cabin pale, haggard, thin, but full of enthusiasm, his eyes dilated with pleasure and satisfaction. Nearly the whole population of the town was on foot to see us land. The fact was, that scarcely any one of them but expected some goods by the periodical vessel.

Professor Hardwigg was in haste to leave his prison, or rather as he called it, his hospital; but before he attempted to do so, he caught hold of my hand, led me to the quarterdeck of the schooner, took my arm with his left hand, and pointed inland with his right, over the northern part of the bay, to where rose a high two-peaked mountain—a double cone covered with eternal snow.

"Behold," he whispered in an awe-stricken voice, "behold—Mount Snefels!"

Then without further remark, he put his finger to his lips, frowned darkly, and descended into the small boat which awaited us. I followed, and in a few minutes we stood upon the soil of mysterious Iceland!

Scarcely were we fairly on shore when there appeared before us a man of excellent appearance, wearing the costume of a military officer. He was, however, but a civil servant, a magistrate, the governor of the island—Baron Trampe. The Professor knew whom he had to deal with. He therefore handed him the letters, from Copenhagen, and a brief conversation in Danish followed, to which I of course was a stranger, and for a very good reason, for I did not know the language in which they conversed. I afterward heard, however, that Baron Trampe placed himself entirely at the beck and call of Professor Hardwigg.

My uncle was most graciously received by M. Finsen, the mayor, who as far as costume went, was quite as military as the governor, but also from character and occupation quite as pacific. As for his coadjutor, M. Pictursson, he was absent on an episcopal visit to the northern portion of the diocese. We were therefore compelled to defer the pleasure of being presented to him. His absence was, however, more than compensated by the presence of M. Fridriksson, professor of natural science in the college of Reykjavik, a man of invaluable ability. This modest scholar spoke no languages save Icelandic and Latin. When, therefore, he addressed himself to me in the language of Horace, we at once came to understand one another. He was, in fact, the only person that I did thoroughly understand during the whole period of my residence in this benighted island.

Out of three rooms of which his house was composed, two were placed at our service, and in a few hours we were installed with all our baggage, the amount of which rather astonished the simple inhabitants of Reykjavik.

"Now, Harry," said my uncle, rubbing his hands, "all goes well, the worse difficulty is now over."

"How the worse difficulty over?" I cried in fresh amazement.

"Doubtless. Here we are in Iceland. Nothing more remains but to descend into the bowels of the earth."

"Well, sir, to a certain extent you are right. We have only to go down—but, as far as I am concerned, that is not the question. I want to know how we are to get up again."

"That is the least part of the business, and does not in any way trouble me. In the meantime, there is not an hour to lose. I am about to visit the public library. Very likely I may find there some manuscripts from the hand of Saknussemm. I shall be glad to consult them."

"In the meanwhile," I replied, "I will take a walk through the town. Will you not likewise do so?"

"I feel no interest in the subject," said my uncle. "What for me is curious in this island, is not what is above the surface, but what is below."

I bowed by way of reply, put on my hat and furred cloak, and went out.

It was not an easy matter to lose oneself in the two streets of Reykjavik; I had therefore no need to ask my way. The town lies on a flat and marshy plain, between two hills. A vast field of lava skirts it on one side, falling away in terraces toward the sea. On the other hand is the large bay of Faxa, bordered on the north by the enormous glacier of Sneffels, and in which bay the *Valkyrie* was then the only vessel at anchor. Generally there were one or two English or French gunboats, to watch and protect the fisheries in offing. They were now, however, absent on duty.

The longest of the streets of Reykjavik runs parallel to the shore. In this street the merchants and traders live in wooden huts made with beams of wood, painted red—mere log huts, such as you find in the wilds of America. The other street, situated more to the west, runs toward a little lake between the residences of the bishop and the other personages not engaged in commerce.

I had soon seen all I wanted of these weary and dismal thoroughfares. Here and there was a strip of discolored turf, like an old worn-out bit of woolen carpet; and now and then a bit of kitchen garden, in which grew potatoes, cabbage, and lettuce, almost diminutive enough to suggest the idea of Lilliput.

In the center of the new commercial street, I found the public cemetery, enclosed by an earthen wall. Though not very large, it appeared not likely to be filled for centuries. From hence I went to the house of the Governor —a mere hut in comparison with the Mansion House of Hamburg—but a palace alongside the other Icelandic houses. Between the little lake and the town was the church, built in simple Protestant style, and composed of calcined stones, thrown up by volcanic action. I have not the slightest doubt that in high winds its red tiles were blown out, to the great annoyance of the pastor and congregation. Upon an eminence close at hand was the national school, in which were taught Hebrew, English, French, and Danish.

In three hours my tour was complete. The general impression upon my mind was sadness. No trees, no vegetation, so to speak—on all sides volcanic peaks—the huts of turf and earth—more like roofs than houses. Thanks to the heat of these residences, grass grows on the roof, which grass is carefully cut for hay. I saw but few inhabitants during my excursion, but I met a crowd on the beach, drying, salting, and loading codfish, the principal article of exportation. The men appeared robust but heavy; fair-haired like Germans, but of pensive mien—unhappy exiles from the greater part of humanity, who, like the Eskimos, are compelled to live within the limits of the Polar Circle.

Sometimes they gave vent to a convulsive laugh, but by no chance did they smile. Their costume consists of a coarse capote of black wool, known in Scandinavian countries as the "vadmel," a broad-brimmed hat, trousers of red serge, and a piece of leather tied with strings for a shoe—a coarse kind of moccasin. The women, though sad-looking and mournful, had rather agreeable features, without much expression. They wear a bodice and petticoat of somber vadmel. When unmarried they wear a little brown knitted cap over a crown of plaited hair; but when married, they cover their heads with a colored handkerchief, over which they tie a white scarf.

VII

Conversation and Discovery

When I returned, dinner was ready. This meal was devoured by my worthy relative with avidity and voracity. His shipboard diet had turned his interior into a perfect gulf. The repast, which was more

Danish than Icelandic, was in itself nothing, but the excessive hospitality of our host made us enjoy it doubly.

The conversation turned upon scientific matters, and M. Fridriksson asked my uncle what he thought of the public library.

"Library, sir?" cried my uncle; "it appears to me a collection of useless odd volumes, and a beggarly amount of empty shelves."

"What!" cried M. Fridriksson; "why, we have eight thousand volumes of most rare and valuable works—some in the Scandinavian language, besides all the new publications from Copenhagen."

"Eight thousand volumes, my dear sir—why, where are they?" cried my uncle.

"Scattered over the country, Professor Hardwigg. We are very studious, my dear sir, though we do live in Iceland. Every farmer, every laborer, every fisherman can both read and write—and we think that books instead of being locked up in cupboards, far from the sight of students, should be distributed as widely as possible. The books of our library are therefore, passed from hand to hand without returning to the library shelves perhaps for years."

"Then when foreigners visit you, there is nothing for them to see?"

"Well, sir, foreigners have their own libraries, and our first consideration is, that our humbler classes should be highly educated. Fortunately, the love of study is innate in the Icelandic people. In 1816 we founded a Literary Society and Mechanics' Institute; many foreign scholars of eminence are honorary members; we publish books destined to educate our people, and these books have rendered valuable services to our country. Allow me to have the honor, Professor Hardwigg, to enroll you as an honorary member?"

My uncle, who already belonged to nearly every literary and scientific institution in Europe, immediately yielded to the amiable wishes of good M. Fridriksson.

"And now," he said, after many expressions of gratitude and good will, "if you will tell me what books you expected to find, perhaps I may be of some assistance to you."

I watched my uncle keenly. For a minute or two he hesitated, as if unwilling to speak; to speak openly was, perhaps, to unveil his projects. Nevertheless, after some reflection, he made up his mind.

"Well, M. Fridriksson," he said in an easy, unconcerned kind of way. "I was desirous of ascertaining, if among other valuable works, you had any of the learned Arne Saknussemm."

"Arne Saknussemm!" cried the Professor of Reykjavik; "you speak of one of the most distinguished scholars of the sixteenth century, of the great naturalist, the great alchemist, the great traveler."

"Exactly so."

"One of the most distinguished men connected with Icelandic science and literature."

"As you say, sir—"

"A man illustrious above all."

"Yes, sir, all this is true, but his works?"

"We have none of them."

"Not in Iceland?"

"There are none in Iceland or elsewhere," answered the other, sadly.

"Why so?"

"Because Arne Saknussemm was persecuted for heresy, and in 1573 his works were publicly burnt at Copenhagen, by the hands of the common hangman."

"Very good! capital!" murmured my uncle, to the great astonishment of the worthy Icelander.

"You said, sir—"

"Yes, yes, all is clear, I see the link in the chain; everything is explained, and I now understand why Arne Saknussemm, put out of court, forced to hide his magnificent discoveries, was compelled to conceal beneath the veil of an incomprehensible cryptograph, the secret—"

"What secret?"

"A secret—which," stammered my uncle.

"Have you discovered some wonderful manuscript?" cried M. Fridriksson.

"No, no, I was carried away by my enthusiasm. A mere supposition."

"Very good, sir. But, really, to turn to another subject, I hope you will not leave our island without examining into its mineralogical riches."

"Well, the fact is, I am rather late. So many learned men have been here before me."

"Yes, yes, but there is still much to be done," cried M. Fridriksson.

"You think so," said my uncle, his eyes twinkling with hidden satisfaction.

"Yes, you have no idea how many unknown mountains, glaciers, volcanoes there are which remain to be studied. Without moving from where we sit, I can show you one. Yonder on the edge of the horizon, you see Sneffels."

"Oh yes, Sneffels," said my uncle.

"One of the most curious volcanoes in existence, the crater of which has been rarely visited."

"Extinct?"

"Extinct, any time these five hundred years," was the ready reply.

"Well," said my uncle, who dug his nails into his flesh, and pressed his knees tightly together to prevent himself leaping up with joy. "I have a great mind to begin my studies with an examination of the geological mysteries of this Mount Seffel—Feisel—what do you call it?"

"Sneffels, my dear sir."

This portion of the conversation took place in Latin, and I therefore understood all that had been said. I could scarcely keep my countenance when I found my uncle so cunningly concealing his delight and satisfaction. I must confess that his artful grimaces, put on to conceal his happiness, made him look like a new Mephistopheles.

"Yes, yes," he continued, "your proposition delights me. I will endeavor to climb to the summit of Sneffels, and, if possible, will descend into its crater."

"I very much regret," continued M. Fridriksson, "that my occupation will entirely preclude the possibility of my accompanying you. It would have been both pleasurable and profitable if I could have spared the time."

"No, no, a thousand times no," cried my uncle. "I do not wish to disturb the serenity of any man. I thank you, however, with all my heart. The presence of one so learned as yourself, would no doubt have been most useful, but the duties of your office and profession before everything."

In the innocence of his simple heart, our host did not perceive the irony of these remarks.

"I entirely approve your project," continued the Icelander, after some further remarks. "It is a good idea to begin by examining this volcano. You will make a harvest of curious observations. In the first place, how do you propose to get to Sneffels?"

"By sea. I shall cross the bay. Of course that is the most rapid route."

"Of course. But still it cannot be done."

"Why?"

"We have not an available boat in all Reykjavik," replied the other.

"What is to be done?"

"You must go by land along the coast. It is longer, but much more interesting."

"Then I must have a guide."

"Of course; and I have your very man."

"Somebody on whom I can depend."

"Yes, an inhabitant of the peninsula on which Sneffels is situated. He is a very shrewd and worthy man, with whom you will be pleased. He speaks Danish like a Dane."

"When can I see him—today?"

"No, tomorrow; he will not be here before."

"Tomorrow be it," replied my uncle with a deep sigh.

The conversation ended by compliments on both sides. During the dinner my uncle had learned much as to the history of Arne Saknussemm, the reasons for his mysterious and hieroglyphical document. He also became aware that his host would not accompany him on his adventurous expedition, and that next day we should have a guide.

VIII

THE EIDER-DOWN HUNTER—OFF AT LAST

That evening I took a brief walk on the shore near Reykjavik, after which I returned to an early sleep on my bed of coarse planks, where I slept the sleep of the just. When I awoke I heard my uncle speaking loudly in the next room. I rose hastily and joined him. He was talking in Danish with a man of tall stature, and of perfectly Herculean build. This man appeared to be possessed of very great strength. His eyes, which started rather prominently from a very large head, the face belonging to which was simple and naïve, appeared very quick and intelligent. Very long hair, which even in England would have been accounted exceedingly red, fell over his athletic shoulders. This native of Iceland was active and supple in appearance, though he scarcely moved his arms, being in fact one of those men who despise the habit of gesticulation common to southern people.

Everything in this man's manner revealed a calm and phlegmatic temperament. There was nothing indolent about him but his appearance spoke of tranquillity. He was one of those who never seemed to expect anything from anybody, who liked to work when he thought proper, and whose philosophy nothing could astonish or trouble.

I began to comprehend his character, simply from the way in which he listened to the wild and impassioned verbiage of my worthy uncle. While the excellent Professor spoke sentence after sentence, he stood with folded arms, utterly still, motionless to all my uncle's gesticulations. When he wanted to say No he moved his head from left to right; when he acquiesced he nodded, so slightly that you could scarcely see the undulation of his head. This economy of motion was carried to the length of avarice.

Judging from his appearance I should have been a long time before I had suspected him to be what he was, a mighty hunter. Certainly his manner was not likely to frighten the game. How, then, did he contrive to get at his prey?

My surprise was slightly modified when I knew that this tranquil and solemn personage, was only a hunter of the eider duck, the down of which is, after all, the greatest source of the Icelanders' wealth.

In the early days of summer, the female of the eider, a pretty sort of duck, builds its nest amid the rocks of the fjords—the name given to all narrow gulfs in Scandinavian countries—with which every part of the island is indented. No sooner has the eider duck made her nest than she lines the inside of it with the softest down from her breast. Then comes the hunter or trader, taking away the nest, the poor bereaved female begins her task over again, and this continues as long as any eider down is to be found.

When she can find no more, the male bird sets to work to see what he can do. As, however, his down is not so soft, and has therefore no commercial value, the hunter does not take the trouble to rob him of his nest lining. The nest is accordingly finished, the eggs are laid, the little ones are born, and next year the harvest of eider down is again collected.

Now, as the eider duck never selects steep rocks or aspects to build its nest, but rather sloping and low cliffs near to the sea, the Icelandic hunter can carry on his trade operations without much difficulty. He is like a farmer who has neither to plow, to sow, nor to harrow, only to collect his harvest.*

This grave, sententious, silent person, as phlegmatic as an Englishman on the French stage, was named Hans Bjelke. He had called upon us in consequence of the recommendation of M. Fridriksson. He was, in fact, our future guide. It struck me that had I sought the world over, I could not have found a greater contradiction to my impulsive uncle.

They, however, readily understand one another. Neither of them had any thought about money; one was ready to take all that was offered him, the other ready to offer anything that was asked. It may readily be conceived, then, that an understanding was soon come to between them.

Now, the understanding was, that he was to take us to the village of Stapi, situated on the southern slope of the peninsula of Sneffels, at the very foot of the volcano. Hans, the guide, told us the distance was about twenty-two miles, a journey which my uncle supposed would take about two days.

But when my uncle came to understand that they were Danish miles, of eight thousand yards each, he was obliged to be more moderate in his ideas, and, considering the horrible roads we had to follow, to allow eight or ten days for the journey.

Four horses were prepared for us, two to carry the baggage, and two to bear the important weight of myself and uncle. Hans declared that nothing ever would make him climb on the back of any animal. He knew every inch of that part of the coast, and promised to take us the very shortest way.

His engagement with my uncle was by no means to cease with our arrival at Stapi; he was further to remain in his service during the whole time required for the completion of his scientific investigations, at the fixed salary of three rix-dollars a week, being exactly fourteen shillings and twopence, minus one farthing, English currency. One stipulation, however,

* The birds, however, are not always so accommodating. They are found in the southern part of England as a winter visitant, but in the more northern part of our isle, and in the north of Scotland remain all the year. One of our ablest naturalists says: "Taking these nests is a regular business not unattended with risk, on account of the precipitous localities in which the eider duck often breeds." Again, "The eider is a shy, retiring bird, placing its nest on islands and rocks projecting well into the sea."

was made by the guide—the money was to be paid to him every Saturday night, failing which, his engagement was at an end.

The day of our departure was fixed. My uncle wished to hand the eider-down hunter an advance, but he refused in one emphatic word—

"*Efter.*"

Which being translated from Icelandic into plain English means—"After."

The treaty concluded, our worthy guide retired without another word.

"A splendid fellow," said my uncle; "only he little suspects the marvelous part he is about to play in the history of the world."

"You mean, then," I cried in amazement, "that he should accompany us?"

"To the interior of the earth, yes," replied my uncle. "Why not?"

There were yet forty-eight hours to elapse before we made our final start. To my great regret, our whole time was taken up in making preparations for our journey. All our industry and ability were devoted to packing every object in the most advantageous manner—the instruments on one side, the arms on the other, the tools here, and the provisions there. There were, in fact, four distinct groups.

The instruments were of course of the best manufacture:

1. A centigrade thermometer of Eizel, counting up to 150 degrees, which to me did not appear half enough—or too much. Too hot by half, if the degree of heat was to ascend so high—in which case we should certainly be cooked—not enough, if we wanted to ascertain the exact temperature of springs or metal in a state of fusion.

2. A *manometer* worked by compressed air, an instrument used to ascertain the upper atmospheric pressure on the level of the ocean. Perhaps a common barometer would not have done as well, the atmospheric pressure being likely to increase in proportion as we descended below the surface of the earth.

3. A first-class chronometer made by Boissonnas, of Geneva, set at the meridian of Hamburg, from which Germans calculate, as the English do from Greenwich, and the French from Paris.

4. Two compasses, one for horizontal guidance, the other to ascertain the dip.

5. A night glass.

6. Two Ruhmkorf's coils, which, by means of a current of electricity,

would ensure us a very excellent, easily carried, and certain means of obtaining light.

7. A voltaic battery on the newest principle.*

Our arms consisted of two rifles, with two revolving six-shooters. Why these arms were provided it was impossible for me to say. I had every, reason to believe that we had neither wild beasts nor savage natives to fear. My uncle, on the other hand, was quite as devoted to his arsenal as to his collection of instruments, and above all was very careful with his provision of fulminating or gun cotton, warranted to keep in any climate, and of which the expansive force was known to be greater than that of ordinary gunpowder.

Our tools consisted of two pickaxes, two crowbars, a silken ladder, three iron-shod Alpine poles, a hatchet, a hammer, a dozen wedges, some pointed pieces of iron, and a quantity of strong rope. You may conceive that the whole made a tolerable parcel, especially when I mention that the ladder itself was three hundred feet long!

Then there came the important question of provisions. The hamper was not very large but tolerably satisfactory, for I knew that in concentrated essence of meat and biscuit there was enough to last six months. The only liquid provided by my uncle was Schiedam. Of water, not a drop. We had, however, an ample supply of gourds, and my uncle counted on finding water, and enough to fill them, as soon as we commenced our downward journey.

My remarks as to the temperature, the quality, and even as to the possibility of none being found, remained wholly without effect.

To make up the exact list of our traveling gear—for the guidance of

* Thermometer (*thermos,* hot, and *metron,* measure); an instrument for measuring the temperature of the air. Manometer (*manos,* rare, and *metron,* measure), an instrument to show the density or rarity of gases. Chronometer (*chronos,* time, and *metron,* measure), a time measurer, or superior watch. Ruhmkorf's coil, an instrument for producing currents of induced electricity of great intensity. It consists of a coil of copper wire, insulated by being covered with silk, surrounded by another coil of fine wire, also insulated, in which a momentary current is induced when a current is passed through the inner coil from a voltaic battery. When the apparatus is in action, the gas becomes luminous, and produces a white and continued light. The battery and wire are carried in a leather bag, which the traveler fastens to his shoulders. The lantern is in front, and enables the benighted wanderer to see in the most profound obscurity. He may venture without fear of explosion into the midst of the most inflammable gases, and the lantern will burn beneath the deepest waters. M. Ruhmkorf, an able and learned chemist, discovered the induction coil. In 1864 he obtained the great French prize £2,000 for this ingenious application of electricity. A voltaic battery, so called from Volta, its designer, is an apparatus consisting of a series of metal plates arranged in pairs and subjected to the action of saline solutions for producing currents of electricity.

future travelers—I will add, that we carried a medicine and surgical chest with all apparatus necessary for wounds, fractures, and blows; lint, scissors, lancets—in fact, a perfect collection of horrible-looking instruments; a number of vials containing ammonia, alcohol, ether, Goulard water, aromatic vinegar, in fact—every possible and impossible drug; finally, all the materials for working the Ruhmkorf coil!

My uncle had also been careful to lay in a goodly supply of tobacco, several flasks of very fine gunpowder, boxes of tinder, besides a large belt crammed full of notes and gold. Good boots rendered watertight were to be found to the number of six in the tool box.

"My boy, with such clothing, with such boots, and such general equipment," said my uncle, in a state of rapturous delight, "we may hope to travel far."

It took a whole day to put all these matters in order. In the evening we dined with Baron Trampe, in company with the Mayor of Reykjavik, and Doctor Hyaltalin, the great medical man of Iceland. M. Fridriksson was not present, and I was afterward sorry to hear that he and the governor did not agree on some matters connected with the administration of the island. Unfortunately, the consequence was, that I did not understand a word that was said at dinner—a kind of semiofficial reception. One thing I can say, my uncle never left off speaking.

The next day our labor came to an end. Our worthy host delighted my uncle, Professor Hardwigg, by giving him a good map of Iceland, a most important and precious document for a mineralogist.

Our last evening was spent in a long conversation with M. Fridriksson, whom I liked very much—the more that I never expected to see him or anyone else again. After this agreeable way of spending an hour or so, I tried to sleep. In vain; with the exception of a few dozes, my night was miserable.

At five o'clock in the morning I was awakened from the only real half-hour's sleep of the night by the loud neighing of horses under my window. I hastily dressed myself and went down into the street. Hans was engaged in putting the finishing stroke to our baggage, which he did in a silent, quiet way that won my admiration, and yet he did it admirably well. My uncle wasted a great deal of breath in giving him directions, but worthy Hans took not the slightest notice of his words.

At six o'clock all our preparations were completed, and M. Fridriksson shook hands heartily with us. My uncle thanked him warmly, in the Icelandic language, for his kind hospitality, speaking truly from the heart.

As for myself I put together a few of my best Latin phrases and paid him the highest compliments I could. This fraternal and friendly duty performed, we sallied forth and mounted our horses.

As soon as we were quite ready, M. Fridriksson advanced, and by way of farewell, called after me in the words of Virgil—words which appeared to have been made for us, travelers starting for an uncertain destination:

"Et quacunque viam dederit fortuna sequamur."

("And whichsoever way thou goest, may fortune follow!")

IX

Our Start—We Meet with Adventures by the Way

The weather was overcast but settled, when we commenced our adventurous and perilous journey. We had neither to fear fatiguing heat nor drenching rain. It was, in fact, real tourist weather.

As there was nothing I liked better than horse exercise, the pleasure of riding through an unknown country caused the early part of our enterprise to be particularly agreeable to me.

I began to enjoy the exhilarating delight of traveling, a life of desire, gratification, and liberty. The truth is, that my spirits rose so rapidly, that I began to be indifferent to what had once appeared to be a terrible journey.

"After all," I said to myself, "what do I risk? Simply to take a journey through a curious country, to climb a remarkable mountain, and if the worst comes to the worst, to descend into the crater of an extinct volcano."

There could be no doubt that this was all this terrible Saknussemm had done. As to the existence of a gallery, or of subterraneous passages leading into the interior of the earth, the idea was simply absurd, the hallucination of a distempered imagination. All, then, that may be required of me I will do cheerfully, and will create no difficulty.

It was just before we left Reykjavik that I came to this decision.

Hans, our extraordinary guide, went first, walking with a steady, rapid, and unvarying step. Our two horses with the luggage followed of their own accord, without requiring whip or spur. My uncle and I came behind, cutting a very tolerable figure upon our small but vigorous animals.

Iceland is one of the largest islands in Europe. It contains thirty thousand square miles of surface, and has about seventy thousand inhabitants. Geographers have divided it into four parts, and we had to cross the southwest quarter which in the vernacular is called Sudvestr Fjordùngr.

Hans, on taking his departure from Reykjavik, had followed the line of the sea. We took our way through poor and sparse meadows, which made a desperate effort every year to show a little green. They very rarely succeeded in a good show of yellow.

The rugged summits of the rocky hills were dimly visible on the edge of the horizon through the misty fogs; every now and then some heavy flakes of snow showed conspicuous in the morning light, while certain lofty and pointed rocks were first lost in the gray low clouds, their summits clearly visible above, like jagged reefs rising from a troublous sea.

Every now and then a spur of rock came down through the arid ground, leaving us scarcely room to pass. Our horses, however, appeared not only well acquainted with the country, but by a kind of instinct, knew which was the best road. My uncle had not even the satisfaction of urging forward his steed by whip, spur, or voice. It was utterly useless to show any signs of impatience. I could not help smiling to see him look so big on his little horse; his long legs now and then touching the ground made him look like a six-footed centaur.

"Good beast, good beast," he would cry. "I assure you, Henry, that I begin to think no animal is more intelligent than an Icelandic horse. Snow, tempest, impracticable roads, rocks, icebergs—nothing stops him. He is brave; he is sober; he is safe; he never makes a false step; never glides or slips from his path. I dare to say that if any river, any fjord has to be crossed—and I have no doubt there will be many—you will see him enter the water without hesitation like an amphibious animal, and reach the opposite side in safety. We must not, however, attempt to hurry him; we must allow him to have his own way, and I will undertake to say that between us we shall do our ten leagues a day."

"We may do so," was my reply, "but what about our worthy guide?"

"I have not the slightest anxiety about him: that sort of people go ahead without knowing even what they are about. Look at Hans. He moves so little that it is impossible for him to become fatigued. Besides, if he were to complain of weariness, he could have the loan of my horse. I should have a violent attack of the cramp if I were not to have some sort of exercise. My arms are right—but my legs are getting a little stiff."

All this while we were already advancing at a rapid pace. The country we had reached was already nearly a desert. Here and there could be seen an isolated farm, some solitary *bur*, or Icelandic house, built of wood, earth, fragments of lava—looking like beggars on the highway of life. These wretched and miserable huts excited in us such pity that we felt half disposed to leave alms at every door. In this country there are no roads, paths are nearly unknown, and vegetation, poor as it was, slowly as it reached perfection, soon obliterated all traces of the few travelers who passed from place to place.

Nevertheless, this division of the province, situated only a few miles from the capital, is considered one of the best cultivated and most thickly peopled in all Iceland. What, then, must be the state of the less known and more distant parts of the island? After traveling fully half a Danish mile, we had met neither a farmer at the door of his hut, nor even a wandering shepherd with his wild and savage flock.

A few stray cows and sheep were only seen occasionally. What, then, must we expect when we come to the upheaved regions—to the districts broken and roughened from volcanic eruptions and subterraneous commotions?

We were to learn this all in good time. I saw, however, on consulting the map, that we avoided a good deal of this rough country, by following the winding and desolate shores of the sea. In reality, the great volcanic movement of the island, and all its attendant phenomena, is concentrated in the interior of the island; there, horizontal layers or strata of rocks, piled one upon the other, eruptions of basaltic origin, and streams of lava have given this country a kind of supernatural reputation.

Little did I expect, however, the spectacle which awaited us when we reached the peninsula of Sneffels, where agglomerations of nature's ruins form a kind of terrible chaos.

Some two hours or more after we had left the city of Reykjavik, we reached the little town called Aoalkirkja, or the principal church. It consists simply of a few houses—not what in England or Germany we should call a hamlet.

Hans stopped here one half-hour. He shared our frugal breakfast, answered Yes and No to my uncle's questions as to the nature of the road, and at last when asked where we were to pass the night, was as laconic as usual.

"Gardar!" was his one-worded reply.

I took occasion to consult the map, to see where Gardar was to be found. After looking keenly I found a small town of that name on the borders of the Hvalfjord, about four miles from Reykjavik. I pointed this out to my uncle, who made a very energetic grimace.

"Only four miles out of twenty-two? Why it is only a little walk."

He was about to make some energetic observation to the guide, but Hans, without taking the slightest notice of him, went in front of the horses, and walked ahead with the same imperturbable phlegm he had always exhibited.

Three hours later, still traveling over those apparently interminable and sandy prairies, we were compelled to go around the Kollafjord, an easier and shorter cut than crossing the gulfs. Shortly after we entered a place of communal jurisdiction called Ejulberg, and the clock of which would then have struck twelve, if any Icelandic church had been rich enough to possess so valuable and useful an article. These sacred edifices are, however, very much like these people, who do without watches—and never miss them.

Here the horses were allowed to take some rest and refreshment, then following a narrow strip of shore between high rocks and the sea, they took us without further halt to the Oalkirkja of Brantar, and after another mile to Saurboer Annexia, a chapel of ease, situated on the southern bank of the Hvalfjord.

It was four o'clock in the evening and we had traveled four Danish miles, about equal to twenty English.

The fjord was in this place about half a mile in width. The sweeping and broken waves came rolling in upon the pointed rocks; the gulf was surrounded by rocky walls—a mighty cliff, three thousand feet in height, remarkable for its brown strata, separated here and there by beds of tufa of a reddish hue. Now, whatever may have been the intelligence of our horses, I had not the slightest reliance upon them, as a means of crossing a stormy arm of the sea. To ride over salt water upon the back of a little horse seemed to me absurd.

"If they are really intelligent," I said to myself, "they will certainly not make the attempt. In any case, I shall trust rather to my own intelligence than theirs."

But my uncle was in no humor to wait. He dug his heels into the side of his steed, and made for the shore. His horse went to the very edge of the water, sniffed at the approaching wave, and retreated.

My uncle, who was, sooth to say, quite as obstinate as the beast he bestrode, insisted on his making the desired advance. This attempt was followed by a new refusal on the part of the horse which quietly shook his head. This demonstration of rebellion was followed by a volley of words and a stout application of whipcord; also followed by kicks on the part of the horse, which threw its head and heels upward and tried to throw his rider. At length the sturdy little pony, spreading out his legs, in a stiff and ludicrous attitude, got from under the Professor's legs, and left him standing with both feet on a separate stone, like the Colossus of Rhodes.

"Wretched animal!" cried my uncle, suddenly transformed into a foot passenger—and as angry and ashamed as a dismounted cavalry officer on the field of battle.

"Farja," said the guide, tapping him familiarly on the shoulder.

"What, a ferry boat!"

"Der," answered Hans, pointing to where lay the boat in question—"there."

"Well," I cried, quite delighted with the information; "so it is."

"Why did you not say so before," cried my uncle; "why not start at once?"

"Tidvatten," said the guide.

"What does he say?" I asked, considerably puzzled by the delay and the dialogue.

"He says tide," replied my uncle, translating the Danish word for my information.

"Of course I understand—we must wait till the tide serves."

"For bida?" asked my uncle.

"Ja," replied Hans.

My uncle frowned, stamped his feet, and then followed the horses to where the boat lay.

I thoroughly understood and appreciated the necessity for waiting, before crossing the fjord, for that moment when the sea at its highest point is in a state of slack water. As neither the ebb nor flow can then be felt, the ferry boat was in no danger of being carried out to sea, or dashed upon the rocky coast.

The favorable moment did not come until six o'clock in the evening.

Then my uncle, myself, and guide, two boatmen, and the four horses got into a very awkward flat-bottom boat. Accustomed as I had been to the steam ferry boats of the Elbe, I found the long oars of the boatmen but sorry means of locomotion. We were more than an hour in crossing the fjord; but at length the passage was concluded without accident.

Half an hour later we reached Gardar.

X

Traveling in Iceland—the Lepers

It ought, one would have thought, to have been night, even in the sixty-fifth parallel of latitude; but still the nocturnal illumination did not surprise me. For in Iceland, during the months of June and July, the sun never sets.

The temperature, however, was very much lower than I expected. I was cold, but even that did not affect me so much as ravenous hunger. Welcome indeed, therefore, was the hut which hospitably opened its doors to us.

It was merely the house of a peasant, but in the matter of hospitality, it was worthy of being the palace of a king. As we alighted at the door the master of the house came forward, held out his hand, and without any further ceremony, signaled to us to follow him.

We followed him, for to accompany him was impossible. A long, narrow, gloomy passage led into the interior of this habitation, made from beams roughly squared by the ax. This passage gave ingress to every room. The chambers were four in number—the kitchen, the workshop, where the weaving was carried on, the general sleeping chamber of the family, and the best room, to which strangers were especially invited. My uncle, whose lofty stature had not been taken into consideration when the house was built, contrived to knock his head against the beams of the roof.

We were introduced into our chamber, a kind of large room with a hard earthen floor, and lighted by a window, the panes of which were made of a sort of parchment from the intestines of sheep—very far from transparent.

The bedding was composed of dry hay thrown into two long red wooden boxes, ornamented with sentences painted in Icelandic. I really had no idea that we should be made so comfortable. There was one objection to the house, and that was, the very powerful odor of dried fish, of macerated meat, and of sour milk, which three fragrances combined did not at all suit my olfactory nerves.

As soon as we had freed ourselves from our heavy traveling costume, the voice of our host was heard calling to us to come into the kitchen, the only room in which the Icelanders ever make any fire, no matter how cold it may be.

My uncle, nothing loath, hastened to obey this hospitable and friendly invitation. I followed.

The kitchen chimney was made on an antique model. A large stone standing in the middle of the room was the fireplace; above, in the roof, was a hole for the smoke to pass through. This apartment was kitchen, parlor, and dining-room all in one.

On our entrance, our worthy host, as if he had not seen us before, advanced ceremoniously, uttered a word which means "be happy," and then kissed both of us on the cheek.

His wife followed, pronounced the same word, with the same ceremonial, then the husband and wife, placing their right hands upon their hearts, bowed profoundly.

This excellent Icelandic woman was the mother of nineteen children, who little and big, rolled, crawled, and walked about in the midst of volumes of smoke arising from the angular fireplace in the middle of the room. Every now and then I could see a fresh white head, and a slightly melancholy expression of countenance, peering at me through the vapor.

Both my uncle and myself, however, were very friendly with the whole party, and before we were aware of it, there were three or four of these little ones on our shoulders, as many on our boxes, and the rest hanging about our legs. Those who could speak kept crying out *sællvertu* in every possible and impossible key. Those who did not speak only made all the more noise.

This concert was interrupted by the announcement of supper. At this moment our worthy guide, the eider-duck hunter, came in after seeing to the feeding and stabling of the horses—which consisted in letting them loose to browse on the stunted green of the Icelandic prairies. There was little for them to eat, but moss and some very dry and innutritious grass; next day they were ready before the door, some time before we were.

"Welcome," said Hans.

Then tranquilly, with the air of an automaton, without any more expression in one kiss than another, he embraced the host and hostess and their nineteen children.

This ceremony concluded to the satisfaction of all parties, we all sat down to table, that is twenty-four of us, somewhat crowded. Those who were best off had only two juveniles on their knees.

As soon, however, as the inevitable soup was placed on the table, the natural taciturnity, common even to Icelandic babies, prevailed over all else. Our host filled our plates with a portion of lichen soup of Ice and moss, of by no means disagreeable flavor, an enormous lump of fish floating in sour butter. After that there came some skyr, a kind of curds and whey, served with biscuits and juniper-berry juice. To drink, we had blanda, skimmed milk with water. I was hungry, so hungry, that by way of dessert I finished up with a basin of thick oaten porridge.

As soon as the meal was over, the children disappeared, whilst the grown people sat around the fireplace, on which was placed turf, heather, cow dung, and dried fish-bones. As soon as everybody was sufficiently warm, a general dispersion took place, all retiring to their respective couches. Our hostess offered to pull off our stockings and trousers, according to the custom of the country, but as we graciously declined to be so honored, she left us to our bed of dry fodder.

Next day, at five in the morning, we took our leave of these hospitable peasants. My uncle had great difficulty in making them accept a sufficient and proper remuneration.

Hans then gave the signal to start.

We had scarcely got a hundred yards from Gardar, when the character of the country changed. The soil began to be marshy and boggy, and less favorable to progress. To the right, the range of mountains was prolonged indefinitely like a great system of natural fortifications, of which we skirted the glacis. We met with numerous streams and rivulets which it was necessary to ford, and that without wetting our baggage. As we advanced, the deserted appearance increased, and yet now and then we could see human shadows flitting in the distance. When a sudden turn of the track brought us within easy reach of one of these specters, I felt a sudden impulse of disgust at the sight of a swollen head, with shining skin, utterly without hair, and whose repulsive and revolting wounds could be seen through his rags. The unhappy wretches never came forward to beg; on the contrary, they ran away; not so quick, however, but that Hans was able to salute them with the universal *sællvertu*.

"Spetelsk," said he.

"A leper," explained my uncle.

The very sound of such a word caused a feeling of repulsion. The horrible affliction known as leprosy, which has almost vanished before the effects of modern science, is common in Iceland. It is not contagious but hereditary, so that marriage is strictly prohibited to these unfortunate creatures.

These poor lepers did not tend to enliven our journey, the scene of which was inexpressibly sad and lonely. The very last tufts of grassy vegetation appeared to die at our feet. Not a tree was to be seen, except a few stunted willows about as big as blackberry bushes. Now and then we watched a falcon soaring in the gray and misty air, taking his flight toward warmer and sunnier regions. I could not help feeling a sense of melancholy come over me. I sighed for my own native land, and wished to be back with Gretchen.

We were compelled to cross several little fjords, and at last came to a real gulf. The tide was at its height, and we were able to go over at once, and reach the hamlet of Alftanes, about a mile farther.

That evening, after fording the Alfa and the Heta, two rivers rich in trout and pike, we were compelled to pass the night in a deserted house, worthy of being haunted by all the fays of Scandinavian mythology. The King of Cold had taken up his residence there, and made us feel his presence all night.

The following day was remarkable by its lack of any particular incidents. Always the same damp and swampy soil; the same dreary uniformity; the same sad and monotonous aspect of scenery. In the evening, having accomplished the half of our projected journey, we slept at the Annexia of Krosolbt.

For a whole mile we had under our feet nothing but lava. This disposition of the soil is called *braun*: the crumbled lava on the surface was in some instances like ship cables stretched out horizontally, in others coiled up in heaps; an immense field of lava came from the neighboring mountains, all extinct volcanoes, but whose remains showed what once they had been. Here and there could be made out the steam from hot water springs.

There was no time, however, for us to take more than a cursory view of these phenomena. We had to go forward with what speed we might. Soon the soft and swampy soil again appeared under the feet of our horses, while at every hundred yards we came upon one or more small lakes. Our journey was now in a westerly direction; we had, in fact, swept around the great bay of Faxa, and the twin white summits of Sneffels rose to the clouds at a distance of less than five miles.

The horses now advanced rapidly. The accidents and difficulties of the soil no longer checked them. I confess that fatigue began to tell severely upon me; but my uncle was as firm and as hard as he had been on the first day. I could not help admiring both the excellent Professor and the worthy guide; for they appeared to regard this rugged expedition as a mere walk!

On Saturday, the 20th June, at six o'clock in the evening, we reached Budir, a small town picturesquely situated on the shore of the ocean; and here the guide asked for his money. My uncle settled with him immediately. It was now the family of Hans himself, that is to say, his uncles, his cousins-german, who offered us hospitality. We were exceedingly well received, and without taking too much advantage of the goodness of these worthy people, I should have liked very much to have rested with them after the fatigues of the journey. But my uncle, who did not require rest, had no idea of anything of the kind; and despite the fact that next day was Sunday, I was compelled once more to mount my steed.

The soil was again affected by the neighborhood of the mountains, whose granite peered out of the ground like tops of an old oak. We were skirting the enormous base of the mighty volcano. My uncle never took his eyes from off it; he could not keep from gesticulating, and looking at it with a kind of sullen defiance as much as to say "That is the giant I have made up my mind to conquer."

After four hours of steady traveling, the horses stopped of themselves before the door of the presbytery of Stapi.

XI

We Reach Mount Sneffels—the "Reykir"

Stapi is a town consisting of thirty huts, built on a large plain of lava, exposed to the rays of the sun, reflected from the volcano. It stretches its humble tenements along the end of a little fjord, surrounded by a basaltic wall of the most singular character.

Basalt, is a brown rock of igneous origin. It assumes regular forms, which astonish by their singular appearance. Here we found Nature proceeding geometrically, and working quite after a human fashion, as if she had employed the plummet line, the compass, and the rule. If elsewhere she produces grand artistic effects by piling up huge masses without order or connection—if elsewhere we see truncated cones, imperfect pyramids, with an odd succession of lines; here, as if wishing to give a lesson in regularity, and preceding the architects of the early ages, she had erected a severe order of architecture, which neither the splendors of Babylon nor the marvels of Greece ever surpassed.

I had often heard of the Giants' Causeway in Ireland, the Grotto of Fingal in one of the Hebrides, but the grand spectacle of a real basaltic formation had never yet come before my eyes.

This at Stapi gave us an idea of one in all its wonderful beauty and grace.

The wall of the fjord, like nearly the whole of the peninsula, consisted of a series of vertical columns, in height about thirty feet. These upright pillars of stone, of the finest proportions, supported an archivalt of horizontal columns which formed a kind of half-vaulted roof above the sea. At certain intervals, and below this natural basin, the eye was pleased and surprised by the sight of oval openings through which the outward waves came thundering in volleys of foam. Some banks of basalt, torn from their fastenings by the fury of the waves, lay scattered on the ground like the ruins of an ancient temple—ruins eternally young, over which the storms of ages swept without producing any perceptible effect!

This was the last stage of our journey. Hans had brought us along with fidelity and intelligence, and I began to feel somewhat more comfortable when I reflected that he was to accompany us still farther on our way.

When we halted before the house of the rector, a small and incommodious cabin, neither handsome nor more comfortable than those of his neighbors, I saw a man in the act of shoeing a horse, a hammer in his hand, and a leathern apron tied around his waist.

"Be happy," said the eider-down hunter, using his national salutation in his own language.

"*Good-dag*—good day!" replied the former, in excellent Danish.

"*Kyrkoherde,*" cried Hans, turning around and introducing him to my uncle.

"The rector," repeated the worthy Professor; "it appears, my dear Harry, that this worthy man is the rector, and is not above doing his own work."

During the speaking of these few words the guide intimated to the *Kyrkoberde* what was the true state of the case. The good man, ceasing from his occupation, gave a kind of halloo, upon which a tall woman, almost a giantess, came out of the hut. She was at least six feet high, which in that region is something considerable.

My first impression was one of horror. I thought she had come to give us the Icelandic kiss. I had, however, nothing to fear, for she did not even show much inclination to receive us into her house.

The room devoted to strangers appeared to me to be by far the worst in the presbytery; it was narrow, dirty, and offensive. There was, however, no choice about the matter. The rector had no notion of practicing the usual cordial and antique hospitality. Far from it. Before the day was over, I found we had to deal with a blacksmith, a fisherman, a hunter, a carpenter, anything but a clergyman. It must be said in his favor that we had caught him on a weekday; probably he appeared to greater advantage on the Sunday.

These poor priests receive from the Danish Government a most ridiculously inadequate salary, and collect one quarter of the tithe of their parish —not more than sixty marks current, or about £3 10s. sterling. Hence the necessity of working to live. In truth, we soon found that our host did not count civility among the cardinal virtues.

My uncle soon became aware of the kind of man he had to deal with. Instead of a worthy and learned scholar, he found a dull ill-mannered peasant. He therefore resolved to start on his great expedition as soon as possible. He did not care about fatigue, and resolved to spend a few days in the mountains.

The preparations for our departure were made the very next day after our arrival at Stapi; Hans now hired three Icelanders to take the place of the horses—which could no longer carry our luggage. When, however, these worthy islanders had reached the bottom of the crater, they were to go back and leave us to ourselves. This point was settled before they would agree to start.

On this occasion, my uncle partially confided in Hans, the eider-duck hunter, and gave him to understand that it was his intention to continue his exploration of the volcano to the last possible limits.

Hans listened calmly, and then nodded his head. To go there, or elsewhere, to bury himself in the bowels of the earth, or to travel over its summits, was all the same to him! As for me, amused and occupied by the incidents of travel, I had begun to forget the inevitable future; but now I was once more destined to realize the actual state of affairs. What was to be done? Run away? But if I really had intended to leave Professor Hardwigg to his fate, it should have been at Hamburg and not at the foot of Sneffels.

One idea above all others, began to trouble me: a very terrible idea, and one calculated to shake the nerves of a man even less sensitive than myself.

"Let us consider the matter," I said to myself; "we are going to ascend the Sneffels mountain. Well and good. We are about to pay a visit to the very bottom of the crater. Good, still. Others have done it and did not perish from that course.

"That, however, is not the whole matter to be considered. If a road does really present itself by which to descend into the dark and subterraneous bowels of Mother Earth, if this thrice unhappy Saknussemm has really told the truth, we shall be most certainly lost in the midst of the labyrinth of subterraneous galleries of the volcano. Now, we have no evidence to prove that Sneffels is really extinct. What proof have we that an eruption is not shortly about to take place? Because the monster has slept soundly since 1219, does it follow that he is never to wake?

"If he does wake, what is to become of us?"

These were questions worth thinking about, and upon them I reflected long and deeply. I could not lie down in search of sleep without dreaming of eruptions. The more I thought, the more I objected to be reduced to the state of dross and ashes.

I could stand it no longer; so I determined at last to submit the whole case to my uncle, in the most adroit manner possible, and under the form of some totally irreconcilable hypothesis.

I sought him. I laid before him my fears, and then drew back in order to let him get his passion over at his ease.

"I have been thinking about the matter," he said, in the quietest tone in the world.

What did he mean? Was he at last about to listen to the voice of reason? Did he think of suspending his projects? It was almost too much happiness to be true.

I however made no remark. In fact, I was only too anxious not to interrupt him, and allowed him to reflect at his leisure. After some moments he spoke out.

"I have been thinking about the matter," he resumed. "Ever since we have been at Stapi, my mind has been almost solely occupied with the grave question which has been submitted to me by yourself—for nothing would be unwiser and more inconsistent than to act with imprudence."

"I heartily agree with you, my dear uncle," was my somewhat hopeful rejoinder.

"It is now six hundred years since Sneffels has spoken, but though now reduced to a state of utter silence, he may speak again. New volcanic eruptions are always preceded by perfectly well-known phenomena. I have closely examined the inhabitants of this region; I have carefully studied the soil, and I beg to tell you emphatically, my dear Harry, there will be no eruption at present."

As I listened to his positive affirmations, I was stupefied and could say nothing.

"I see you doubt my word," said my uncle; "follow me."

I obeyed mechanically.

Leaving the presbytery, the Professor took a road through an opening in the basaltic rock, which led far away from the sea. We were soon in open country, if we could give such a name to a place all covered with volcanic deposits. The whole land seemed crushed under the weight of enormous stones—of trap, of basalt, of granite, of lava, and of all other volcanic substances.

I could see many spouts of steam rising in the air. These white vapors, called in the Icelandic language "reykir," come from hot water fountains, and indicate by their violence the volcanic activity of the soil. Now the sight of these appeared to justify my apprehension. I was, therefore, all the more surprised and mortified when my uncle thus addressed me.

"You see all this smoke, Harry, my boy?"

"Yes, sir."

"Well, as long as you see them thus, you have nothing to fear from the volcano."

"How can that be?"

"Be careful to remember this," continued the Professor. "At the approach of an eruption these spouts of vapor redouble their activity—to disappear altogether during the period of volcanic eruption; for the elastic fluids, no longer having the necessary tension, seek refuge in the interior of the crater, instead of escaping through the fissures of the earth. If, then, the steam remains in its normal or habitual state, if their energy does not increase, and if you add to this, the remark that the wind is not replaced by heavy atmospheric pressure and dead calm, you may be quite sure that there is no fear of any immediate eruption."

"But—"

"Enough, my boy. When science has sent forth her fiat—it is only to hear and obey."

I came back to the house quite downcast and disappointed. My uncle had completely defeated me with his scientific arguments. Nevertheless, I had still one hope, and that was, when once we were at the bottom of the crater, that it would be impossible in default of a gallery or tunnel, to descend any deeper; and this, despite all the learned Saknussemms in the world.

I passed the whole of the following night with a nightmare on my chest! and, after unheard-of miseries and tortures, found myself in the very depths of the earth, from which I was suddenly launched into planetary space, under the form of an eruptive rock!

Next day, the 23d June, Hans calmly awaited us outside the presbytery with his two companions loaded with provisions, tools, and instruments. Two iron-shod poles, two guns, and two large game bags, were reserved for my uncle and myself. Hans, who was a man who never forgot even the minutest precautions, had added to our baggage a large skin full of water, as an addition to our gourds. This assured us water for eight days.

It was nine o'clock in the morning when we were quite ready. The rector and his huge wife or servant, I never knew which, stood at the door to see us off. They appeared to be about to inflict on us the usual final kiss of the Icelanders. To our supreme astonishment their adieu took the shape of a formidable bill, in which they even counted the use of the pastoral house, really and truly the most abominable and dirty place I ever was in. The worthy couple cheated and robbed us like a Swiss innkeeper, and made us feel, by the sum we had to pay, the splendors of their hospitality.

My uncle, however, paid without bargaining. A man who had made up his mind to undertake a voyage into the interior of the earth, is not the man to haggle over a few miserable rix-dollars.

This important matter settled, Hans gave the signal for departure, and some few moments later we had left Stapi.

XII

The Ascent of Mount Sneffels

The huge volcano which was the first stage of our daring experiment is above five thousand feet high. Sneffels is the termination of a long range of volcanic mountains, of a different character to the system of the island itself. One of its peculiarities is its two huge pointed summits. From whence we started it was impossible to make out the real outlines of the peak against the gray field of sky. All we could distinguish was a vast dome of white, which fell downward from the head of the giant.

The commencement of the great undertaking filled me with awe. Now that we had actually started, I began to believe in the reality of the undertaking!

Our party formed quite a procession. We walked in single file, preceded by Hans, the imperturbable eider-duck hunter. He calmly led us by narrow paths where two persons could by no possibility walk abreast. Conversation was wholly impossible. We had all the more opportunity to reflect and admire the awful grandeur of the scene around.

Beyond the extraordinary basaltic wall of the fjord of Stapi we found ourselves making our way through fibrous turf, over which grew a scanty vegetation of grass, the residuum of the ancient vegetation of the swampy peninsula. The vast mass of this combustible, the field of which as yet is utterly unexplored, would suffice to warm Iceland for a whole century. This mighty turf pit, measured from the bottom of certain ravines, is often not less than seventy feet deep, and presents to the eye the view of successive layers of black burned-up rocky detritus, separated by thin streaks of porous sandstone.

The grandeur of the spectacle was undoubted, as well as its arid and deserted air.

As a true nephew of the great Professor Hardwigg, and despite my preoccupation and doleful fears of what was to come, I observed with great interest the vast collection of mineralogical curiosities spread out before me in this vast museum of natural history. Looking back to my recent studies, I went over in thought the whole geological history of Iceland.

This extraordinary and curious island must have made its appearance from out of the great world of waters at a comparatively recent date. Like the coral islands of the Pacific, it may, for aught we know, be still rising by slow and imperceptible degrees.

If this really be the case, its origin can be attributed to only one cause—that of the continued action of subterranean fires.

This was a happy thought.

If so, if this were true, away with the theories of Sir Humphry Davy; away with the authority of the parchment of Arne Saknussemm; the wonderful pretensions to discovery on the part of my uncle—and to our journey!

All must end in smoke.

Charmed with the idea, I began more carefully to look about me. A serious study of the soil was necessary to negate or confirm my hypothesis. I took in every item of what I saw, and I began to comprehend the succession of phenomena which had preceded its formation.

Iceland, being absolutely without sedimentary soil, is composed exclusively of volcanic tufa; that is to say, of an agglomeration of stones and of rocks of a porous texture. Long before the existence of volcanoes, it was composed of a solid body of massive trap rock lifted bodily and slowly out of the sea, by the action of the centrifugal force at work in the earth.

The internal fires, however, had not as yet burst their bounds and flooded the exterior cake of Mother Earth with hot and raging lava.

My readers must excuse this brief and somewhat pedantic geological lecture. But it is necessary to the complete understanding of what follows.

At a later period in the world's history, a huge and mighty fissure must, reasoning by analogy, have been dug diagonally from the southwest to the northeast of the island, through which by degrees flowed the volcanic crust. The great and wondrous phenomenon then went on without violence—the outpouring was enormous, and the seething fused matter, ejected from the bowels of the earth, spread slowly and peacefully in the form of vast level plains, or what are called mamelons or mounds.

It was at this epoch that the rocks called feldspars, syenites, and porphyries appeared.

But as a natural consequence of this overflow, the depth of the island increased. It can readily be believed what an enormous quantity of elastic fluids were piled up within its center, when at last it afforded no other openings, after the process of cooling the crust had taken place.

At length a time came when despite the enormous thickness and weight of the upper crust, the mechanical forces of the combustible gases below became so great, that they actually upheaved the weighty back and made for themselves huge and gigantic shafts. Hence the volcanoes which suddenly arose through the upper crust, and next the craters, which burst forth at the summit of these new creations.

It will be seen that the first phenomena in connection with the formation of the island were simply eruptive; to these, however, shortly succeeded the volcanic phenomena.

Through the newly formed openings, escaped the marvelous mass of basaltic stones with which the plain we were now crossing was covered. We were trampling our way over heavy rocks of dark gray color, which, while cooling, had been moulded into six-sided prisms. In the "back distance" we could see a number of flattened cones, which formerly were so many fire-vomiting mouths.

After the basaltic eruption was appeased and set at rest, the volcano, the force of which increased with that of the extinct craters, gave free passage to the fiery overflow of lava, and to the mass of cinders and pumice stone, now scattered over the sides of the mountain, like disheveled hair on the shoulders of a Bacchante.

Here, in a nutshell, I had the whole history of the phenomena from which Iceland arose. All take their rise in the fierce action of interior fires, and to believe that the central mass did not remain in a state of liquid fire, white hot, was simply and purely madness.

This being satisfactorily proved (Q.E.D.), what insensate folly to pretend to penetrate into the interior of the mighty earth!

This mental lecture delivered to myself while proceeding on a journey, did me good. I was quite reassured as to the fate of our enterprise; and therefore went, like a brave soldier mounting a bristling battery, to the assault of old Sneffels.

As we advanced, the road became every moment more difficult. The soil was broken and dangerous. The rocks broke and gave way under our feet, and we had to be scrupulously careful in order to avoid dangerous and constant falls.

Hans advanced as calmly as if he had been walking over Salisbury Plain; sometimes he would disappear behind huge blocks of stone, and we momentarily lost sight of him. There was a little period of anxiety and then there was a shrill whistle, just to tell us where to look for him.

Occasionally he would take it into his head to stop to pick up lumps of rock, and silently pile them up into small heaps, *in order that we might not lose our way on our return.*

He had no idea of the journey we were about to undertake.

At all events, the precaution was a good one; though how utterly useless and unnecessary—but I must not anticipate.

Three hours of terrible fatigue, walking incessantly, had only brought us to the foot of the great mountain. This will give some notion of what we had still to undergo.

Suddenly, however, Hans cried a halt—that is, he made signs to that effect—and a summary kind of breakfast was laid out on the lava before us. My uncle, who now was simply Professor Hardwigg, was so eager to advance, that he bolted his food like a greedy clown. This halt for refreshment was also a halt for repose. The Professor was therefore compelled to wait the good pleasure of his imperturbable guide, who did not give the signal for departure for a good hour.

The three Icelanders, who were as taciturn as their comrade, did not say a word; but went on eating and drinking very quietly and soberly.

From this, our first real stage, we began to ascend the slopes of the Sneffels volcano. Its magnificent snowy nightcap, as we began to call it, by an optical delusion very common in mountains, appeared to me to be close at hand; and yet how many long weary hours must elapse before we reached its summit! What unheard-of fatigue must we endure!

The stones on the mountain side, held together by no cement of soil, bound together by no roots or creeping herbs, gave way continually under our feet, and went rushing below into the plains, like a series of small avalanches.

In certain places the sides of this stupendous mountain were at an angle so steep that it was impossible to climb upward, and we were compelled to get around these obstacles as best we might.

Those who understand Alpine climbing will comprehend our difficulties. Often we were obliged to help each other along by means of our climbing poles.

I must say this for my uncle, that he stuck as close to me as possible. He never lost sight of me, and on many occasions his arm supplied me with firm and solid support. He was strong, wiry, and apparently insensible to fatigue. Another great advantage with him was that he had the innate sentiment of equilibrium—for he never slipped or failed in his steps. The

Icelanders, though heavily loaded, climbed with the agility of mountaineers.

Looking up, every now and then, at the height of the great volcano of Sneffels, it appeared to me wholly impossible to reach to the summit on that side; at all events, if the angle of inclination did not speedily change.

Fortunately, after an hour of unheard-of fatigues, and of gymnastic exercises that would have been trying to an acrobat, we came to a vast field of ice, which wholly surrounded the bottom of the cone of the volcano. The natives called it the tablecloth, probably from some such reason as the dwellers in the Cape of Good Hope call their mountain Table Mountain, and their roads Table Bay.

Here, to our mutual surprise, we found an actual flight of stone steps, which wonderfully assisted our ascent. This singular flight of stairs was, like everything else, volcanic. It had been formed by one of those torrents of stones cast up by the eruptions, and of which the Icelandic name is *stinâ*. If this singular torrent had not been checked in its descent by the peculiar shape of the flanks of the mountain, it would have swept into the sea, and would have formed new islands.

Such as it was, it served us admirably. The abrupt character of the slopes momentarily increased, but these remarkable stone steps, a little less difficult than those of the Egyptian pyramids, were the one simple natural means by which we were enabled to proceed.

About seven in the evening of that day, after having clambered up two thousand of these rough steps, we found ourselves overlooking a kind of spur or projection of the mountain—a sort of buttress upon which the conelike crater, properly so called, leaned for support.

The ocean lay beneath us at a depth of more than three thousand two hundred feet—a grand and mighty spectacle. We had reached the region of eternal snows.

The cold was keen, searching, and intense. The wind blew with extraordinary violence. I was utterly exhausted.

My worthy uncle, the Professor, saw clearly that my legs refused further service, and that, in fact, I was utterly exhausted. Despite his hot and feverish impatience, he decided, with a sigh, upon a halt. He called the eider-duck hunter to his side. That worthy, however, shook his head.

"Ofvanfor," was his sole spoken reply.

"It appears," says my uncle with a woebegone look, "that we must go higher."

He then turned to Hans, and asked him to give some reason for this decisive response.

"Mistour," replied the guide.

"Ja, mistour—yes, the mistour," cried one of the Icelandic guides in a terrified tone.

It was the first time he had spoken.

"What does this mysterious word signify?" I anxiously inquired.

"Look," said my uncle.

I looked down upon the plain below, and I saw a vast, a prodigious volume of pulverized pumice stone, of sand, of dust, rising to the heavens in the form of a mighty waterspout. It resembled the fearful phenomenon of a similar character known to the travelers in the desert of the great Sahara.

The wind was driving it directly toward that side of Sneffels on which we were perched. This opaque veil standing up between us and the sun projected a deep shadow on the flanks of the mountain. If this sand spout broke over us, we must all be infallibly destroyed, crushed in its fearful embraces. This extraordinary phenomenon, very common when the wind shakes the glaciers, and sweeps over the arid plains, is in the Icelandic tongue called "mistour."

"Hastigt, Hastigt!" cried our guide.

Now I certainly knew nothing of Danish, but I thoroughly understood that his gestures were meant to quicken us.

The guide turned rapidly in a direction which would take us to the back of the crater, all the while ascending slightly.

We followed rapidly, despite our excessive fatigue.

A quarter of an hour later Hans paused to enable us to look back. The mighty whirlwind of sand was spreading up the slope of the mountain to the very spot where we had proposed to halt. Huge stones were caught up, cast into the air, and thrown about as during an eruption. We were happily a little out of the direction of the wind, and therefore out of reach of danger. But for the precaution and knowledge of our guide, our dislocated bodies, our crushed and broken limbs, would have been cast to the wind, like dust from some unknown meteor.

Hans, however, did not think it prudent to pass the night on the bare side of the cone. We therefore continued our journey in a zigzag direction. The fifteen hundred feet which remained to be accomplished took us at least five hours. The turnings and windings, the no-thoroughfares, the marches and marches, turned that insignificant distance into at least three leagues. I never felt such misery, fatigue, and exhaustion in my life. I was ready to faint from hunger and cold. The rarefied air at the same time painfully acted upon my lungs.

At last, when I thought myself at my last gasp, about eleven at night, it being in that region quite dark, we reached the summit of Mount Sneffels! It was in an awful mood of mind, that despite my fatigue, before I descended into the crater which was to shelter us for the night, I paused to behold the sun rise at midnight on the very day of its lowest declension, and enjoyed the spectacle of its ghastly pale rays cast upon the isle which lay sleeping at our feet!

I no longer wondered at people traveling all the way from England to Norway to behold this magical and wondrous spectacle.

XIII
The Shadow of Scartaris

Our supper was eaten with ease and rapidity, after which everybody did the best he could for himself within the hollow of the crater. The bed was hard, the shelter unsatisfactory, the situation painful —laying in the open air, five thousand feet above the level of the sea!

Nevertheless, it has seldom happened to me to sleep so well as I did on that particular night. I did not even dream. So much for the effects of what my uncle called "wholesome fatigue."

Next day, when we awoke under the rays of a bright and glorious sun, we were nearly frozen by the keen air. I left my granite couch and made one of the party to enjoy a view of the magnificent spectacle which developed itself panorama-like, at our feet.

I stood upon the lofty summit of Mount Sneffels' southern peak. Thence I was able to obtain a view of the greater part of the island. The optical delusion, common to all lofty heights, raised the shores of the island, while the central portions appeared depressed. It was by no means too great a flight of fancy to believe that a giant picture was stretched out before me. I could see the deep valleys that crossed each other in every direction. I could see precipices looking like sides of wells, lakes that seemed to be changed into ponds, ponds that looked like puddles, and rivers that were transformed into petty brooks. To my right were glaciers upon glaciers, and multiplied peaks, topped with light clouds of smoke.

The undulation of these infinite numbers of mountains, whose snowy summits make them look as if covered by foam, recalled to my remembrance the surface of a storm-beaten ocean. If I looked toward the west, the ocean lay before me in all its majestic grandeur, a continuation as it were, of these fleecy hilltops.

Where the earth ended and the sea began it was impossible for the eye to distinguish.

I soon felt that strange and mysterious sensation which is awakened in the mind when looking down from lofty hilltops, and now I was able to do so without any feeling of nervousness, having fortunately hardened myself to that kind of sublime contemplation.

I wholly forgot who I was, and where I was. I became intoxicated with a sense of lofty sublimity, without thought of the abysses into which my daring was soon about to plunge me. I was presently, however, brought back to the realities of life by the arrival of the Professor and Hans, who joined me upon the lofty summit of the peak.

My uncle, turning in a westerly direction, pointed out to me a light cloud of vapor, a kind of haze, with a faint outline of land rising out of the waters.

"Greenland!" said he.

"Greenland?" cried I in reply.

"Yes," continued my uncle, who always when explaining anything spoke as if he were in a professor's chair; "we are not more than thirty-five leagues distant from that wonderful land. When the great annual breakup of the ice takes place, white bears come over to Iceland, carried by the floating masses of ice from the north. This, however, is a matter of little consequence. We are now on the summit of the great, the transcendent Sneffels, and here are its two peaks, north and south. Hans will tell you the name by which the people of Iceland call that on which we stand."

My uncle turned to the imperturbable guide, who nodded, and spoke as usual—one word.

"Scartaris."

My uncle looked at me with a proud and triumphant glance.

"A crater," he said, "you hear?"

I did hear, but I was totally unable to make reply.

The crater of Mount Sneffels represented an inverted cone, the gaping orifice apparently half a mile across; the depth indefinite feet. Conceive what this *hole* must have been like when full of flame and thunder and lightning. The bottom of the funnel-shaped hollow was about five hundred feet in circumference, by which it will be seen that the slope from the summit to the bottom was very gradual, and we were therefore clearly able to get there without much fatigue or difficulty. Involuntarily, I compared this crater to an enormous loaded cannon; and the comparison completely terrified me.

"To descend into the interior of a cannon," I thought to myself, "when perhaps it is loaded, and will go off at the least shock, is the act of a madman."

But there was no longer any opportunity for me to hesitate. Hans, with a perfectly calm and indifferent air, took his usual post at the head of the adventurous little band. I followed without uttering a syllable.

I felt like the lamb led to the slaughter.

In order to render the descent less difficult, Hans took his way down the interior of the cone in rather a zigzag fashion, making, as the sailors say, long tracks to the eastward, followed by equally long ones to the west. It was necessary to walk through the midst of eruptive rocks, some of which, shaken in their balance, went rolling down with thundering clamor to the bottom of the abyss. These continual falls awoke echoes of singular power and effect.

Many portions of the cone consisted of inferior glaciers. Hans, whenever he met with one of these obstacles, advanced with a great show of precaution, sounding the soil with his long iron pole in order to discover fissures and layers of deep soft snow. In many doubtful or dangerous places, it became necessary for us to be tied together by a long rope in order that should any one of us be unfortunate enough to slip, he would be supported by his companions. This connecting link was doubtless a prudent precaution, but not by any means unattended with danger.

Nevertheless, and despite all the manifold difficulties of the descent, along slopes with which our guide was wholly unacquainted, we made considerable progress without accident. One of our great parcels of rope slipped from one of the Iceland porters, and rushed by a short cut to the bottom of the abyss.

By midday we were at the end of our journey. I looked upward, and saw only the upper orifice of the cone, which served as a circular frame to a very small portion of the sky—a portion which seemed to me singularly beautiful. Should I ever again gaze on that lovely sunlit sky!

The only exception to this extraordinary landscape, was the Peak of Scartaris, which seemed lost in the great void of the heavens.

The bottom of the crater was composed of three separate shafts, through which, during periods of eruption, when Sneffels was in action, the great central furnace sent forth its burning lava and poisonous vapors. Each of these chimneys or shafts gaped open-mouthed in our path. I kept as far away from them as possible, not even venturing to take the faintest peep downward.

As for the Professor, after a rapid examination of their disposition and characteristics, he became breathless and panting. He ran from one to the other like a delighted schoolboy, gesticulating wildly, and uttering incomprehensible and disjointed phrases in all sorts of languages.

Hans, the guide, and his humbler companions seated themselves on some piles of lava and looked silently on. They clearly took my uncle for a lunatic; and—waited the result.

Suddenly the Professor uttered a wild, unearthly cry. At first I imagined he had lost his footing, and was falling headlong into one of the yawning gulfs. Nothing of the kind. I saw him, his arms spread out to their widest extent, his legs stretched apart, standing upright before an enormous pedestal, high enough and black enough to bear a gigantic statue of Pluto. His attitude and mine were that of a man utterly stupefied. But his stupefaction was speedily changed to the wildest joy.

"Harry! Harry! come here!" he cried; "make haste—wonderful—wonderful!"

Unable to understand what he meant, I turned to obey his commands. Neither Hans nor the other Icelanders moved a step.

"Look!" said the Professor, in something of the manner of the French general pointing out the pyramids to his army.

And fully partaking his stupefaction, if not his joy, I read on the eastern side of the huge block of stone, the same characters, half eaten away by the corrosive action of time, the name, to me a thousand times accursed—

"Arne Saknussemm!" cried my uncle, "now, unbeliever, do you begin to have faith?"

It was totally impossible for me to answer a single word. I went back to my pile of lava, in a state of silent awe. The evidence was unanswerable, overwhelming!

In a few moments, however, my thoughts were far away, back in my German home, with Gretchen and the old cook. What would I have given for one of my cousin's smiles, for one of the ancient domestic's omelettes, and for my own featherbed!

How long I remained in this state I know not. All I can say is, that when at last I raised my head from between my hands, there remained at the bottom of the crater only myself, my uncle, and Hans. The Icelandic porters had been dismissed and were now descending the exterior slopes of Mount Sneffels, on their way to Stapi. How heartily did I wish myself with them!

Hans slept tranquilly at the foot of a rock in a kind of rill of lava, where he had made himself a rough and ready bed. My uncle was walking about the bottom of the crater like a wild beast in a cage. I had no desire, neither had I the strength, to move from my recumbent position. Taking example by the guide, I gave way to a kind of painful somnolency, during which I seemed both to hear and feel continued heavings and shudderings in the mountain.

In this way we passed our first night in the interior of a crater.

Next morning, a gray, cloudy, heavy sky hung like a funeral pall over the summit of the volcanic cone. I did not notice it so much from the obscurity that reigned around us, as from the rage with which my uncle was devoured.

I fully understood the reason, and again a glimpse of hope made my heart leap with joy. I will briefly explain the cause.

Of the three openings which yawned beneath our steps, only one could have been followed by the adventurous Saknussemm. According to the words of the learned Icelander, it was only to be known by that one particular mentioned in the cryptograph, that the shadow of Scartaris fell upon it, just touching its mouth in the last days of the month of June.

We were, in fact, to consider the pointed peak as the stylus of an immense sun-dial, the shadow of which pointed on one given day, like the inexorable finger of fate, to the yawning chasm which led into the interior of the earth.

Now, as often happens in these regions, should the sun fail to burst through the clouds, no shadow. Consequently, no chance of discovering the right aperture. We had already reached the 25th June. If the kindly heavens would only remain densely clouded for six more days, we should have to put off our voyage of discovery for another year, when certainly there would be one person fewer in the party. I already had sufficient of the mad and monstrous enterprise.

It would be utterly impossible to depict the impotent rage of Professor Hardwigg. The day passed away, and not the faintest outline of a shadow could be seen at the bottom of the crater. Hans the guide never moved from his place. He must have been curious to know what we were about, if indeed he could believe we were about anything. As for my uncle, he never addressed a word to me. He was nursing his wrath to keep it warm! His eyes fixed on the black and foggy atmosphere, his complexion hideous with suppressed passion. Never had his eyes appeared so fierce, his nose so aquiline, his mouth so hard and firm.

On the 26th no change for the better. A mixture of rain and snow fell during the whole day. Hans very quietly built himself a hut of lava into which he retired like Diogenes into his tub. I took a malicious delight in watching the thousand little cascades that flowed down the side of the cone, carrying with them at times a stream of stones into the "vasty deep" below.

My uncle was almost frantic: to be sure it was enough to make even a patient man angry. He had reached to a certain extent the goal of his desires, and yet he was likely to be wrecked in port.

But if the heavens and the elements are capable of causing us much pain and sorrow, there are two sides to a medal. And there was reserved for Professor Hardwigg a brilliant and sudden surprise which was to compensate him for all his sufferings.

Next day the sky was still overcast, but on Sunday, the 28th, the last day but two of the month, with a sudden change of wind and a new moon there came a change of weather. The sun poured its beaming rays to the very bottom of the crater.

Each hillock, every rock, every stone, every asperity of the soil had its share of the luminous effulgence, and its shadow fed heavily on the soil. Among others, to his insane delight, the shadow of Scartaris was marked and clear, and moved slowly with the radiant star of day.

My uncle moved with it in a state of mental ecstasy.

At twelve o'clock exactly, when the sun had attained its highest altitude for the day, the shadow fell upon the edge of the central pit!

"Here it is," gasped the Professor in an agony of joy, "here it is—we have found it. Forward, my friends, into the interior of the earth."

I looked curiously at Hans to see what reply he would make to this terrific announcement.

"Forüt," said the guide tranquilly.

"Forward it is," answered my uncle, who was now in the seventh heaven of delight.

When we were quite ready, our watches indicated thirteen minutes past one!

XIV

THE REAL JOURNEY COMMENCES

Our real journey had now commenced.

Hitherto our courage and determination had overcome all difficulties. We were fatigued at times; and that was all. Now, unknown and fearful dangers we were about to encounter.

I had not as yet ventured to take a glimpse down the horrible abyss into which in a few minutes more I was about to plunge. The fatal moment had, however, at last arrived. I had still the option of refusing or accepting a share in this foolish and audacious enterprise. But I was ashamed to show more fear than the eider-duck hunter. Hans seemed to accept the difficulties of the journey so tranquilly, with such calm indifference, with such perfect recklessness of all danger, that I actually blushed to appear less of a man than he!

Had I been alone with my uncle, I should certainly have sat down and argued the point fully; but in the presence of the guide I held my tongue. I gave one moment to the thought of my charming cousin, and then I advanced to the mouth of the central shaft.

It measured about a hundred feet in diameter, which made about three hundred in circumference. I leaned over a rock which stood on its edge, and looked down. My hair stood on end, my teeth chattered, my limbs trembled. I seemed utterly to lose my center of gravity, while my head was in a sort of whirl, like that of a drunken man. There is nothing more powerful than this attraction toward an abyss. I was about to fall headlong into the gaping well, when I was drawn back by a firm and powerful hand. It was that of Hans. I had not taken lessons enough at the Frelser's-Kirk of Copenhagen in the art of looking down from lofty eminences without blinking!

However, few as the minutes were during which I gazed down this tremendous and even wondrous shaft, I had a sufficient glimpse of it to give me some idea of its physical conformation. Its sides, which were almost as perpendicular as those of a well, presented numerous projections which doubtless would assist our descent.

It was a sort of wild and savage staircase, without bannister or fence. A rope fastened above, near the surface, would certainly support our weight and enable us to reach the bottom, but how, when we had arrived at its utmost depth, were we to loosen it above? This was, I thought, a question of some importance.

My uncle, however, was one of those men who are nearly always prepared with expedients. He hit upon a very simple method of obviating this difficulty. He unrolled a cord about as thick as my thumb and at least four hundred feet in length. He allowed about half of it to go down the pit and catch in a hitch over a great block of lava which stood on the edge of the precipice. This done, he threw the second half after the first.

Each of us could now descend by catching the two cords in one hand. When about two hundred feet below, all the explorer had to do was to let go one end and pull away at the other, when the cord would come falling at his feet. In order to go down farther, all that was necessary was to continue the same operation.

This was a very excellent proposition, and no doubt, a correct one. Going down appeared to me easy enough; it was the coming up again that now occupied my thoughts.

"Now," said my uncle, as soon as he had completed this important preparation, "let us see about the baggage. It must be divided into three separate parcels, and each of us must carry one on his back. I allude to the more important and fragile articles."

My worthy and ingenious uncle did not appear to consider that we came under that denomination.

"Hans," he continued, "you will take charge of the tools and some of the provisions; you, Harry, must take possession of another third of the provisions and of the arms. I will load myself with the rest of the eatables, and with the more delicate instruments."

"But," I exclaimed, "our clothes, this mass of cord and ladders—who will undertake to carry them down?"

"They will go down of themselves."

"And how so?" I asked.

"You shall see."

My uncle was not fond of half measures, nor did he like anything in the way of hesitation. Giving his orders to Hans he had the whole of the nonfragile articles made up into one bundle; and the packet, firmly and solidly fastened, was simply pitched over the edge of the gulf.

I heard the moaning of the suddenly displaced air, and the noise of falling stones. My uncle leaning over the abyss followed the descent of his luggage with a perfectly self-satisfied air, and did not rise until it had completely disappeared from sight.

"Now then," he cried, "it is our turn."

I put it in good faith to any man of common sense—was it possible to hear this energetic cry without a shudder?

The Professor fastened his case of instruments on his back. Hans took charge of the tools, I of the arms. The descent then commenced in the following order: Hans went first, my uncle followed, and I went last. Our progress was made in profound silence—a silence only troubled by the fall of pieces of rock, which breaking from the jagged sides, fell with a roar into the depths below.

I allowed myself to slide, so to speak, holding frantically on the double cord with one hand and with the other keeping myself off the rocks by the assistance of my iron-shod pole. One idea was all the time impressed upon my brain. I feared that the upper support would fail me. The cord appeared to me far too fragile to bear the weight of three such persons as we were, with our luggage. I made as little use of it as possible, trusting to my own agility and doing miracles in the way of feats of dexterity and strength upon the projecting shelves and spurs of lava which my feet seemed to clutch as strongly as my hands.

The guide went first, I have said, and when one of the slippery and frail supports broke from under his feet, he had recourse to his usual monosyllabic way of speaking.

"Gifakt—"

"Attention—look out," repeated my uncle.

In about half an hour we reached a kind of small terrace formed by a fragment of rock projecting some distance from the sides of the shaft.

Hans now began to haul upon the cord on one side only, the other going as quietly upward as the other came down. It fell at last, bringing with it a shower of small stones, lava, and dust, a disagreeable kind of rain or hail.

While we were seated on this extraordinary bench I ventured once more to look downward. With a sigh I discovered that the bottom was still wholly invisible. Were we, then, going direct to the interior of the earth?

The performance with the cord recommenced, and a quarter of an hour later we had reached to the depth of another two hundred feet.

I have very strong doubts if the most determined geologist would, during that descent, have studied the nature of the different layers of earth around him. I did not trouble my head much about the matter; whether we were among the combustible carbon, silurians, or primitive soil, I neither knew nor cared to know.

Not so the inveterate Professor. He must have taken notes all the way down, for, at one of our halts, he began a brief lecture.

"The farther we advance," said he, "the greater is my confidence in the result. The disposition of these volcanic strata absolutely confirms the theories of Sir Humphry Davy. We are still within the region of the primordial soil, the soil in which took place the chemical operation of metals becoming inflamed by coming in contact with the air and water. I at once regret the old and now forever exploded theory of a central fire. At all events, we shall soon know the truth."

Such was the everlasting conclusion to which he came. I, however, was very far from being in humor to discuss the matter. I had something else to think of. My silence was taken for consent; and still we continued to go down.

At the expiration of three hours, we were, to all appearance, as far off as ever from the bottom of the well. When I looked upward, however, I could see that the upper orifice was every minute decreasing in size. The sides of the shaft were getting closer and closer together, we were approaching the regions of eternal night!

And still we continued to descend!

At length, I noticed that when pieces of stone were detached from the sides of this stupendous precipice, they were swallowed up with less noise than before. The final sound was sooner heard. We were approaching the bottom of the abyss!

As I had been very careful to keep account of all the changes of cord which took place, I was able to tell exactly what was the depth we had reached, as well as the time it had taken.

We had shifted the rope twenty-eight times, each operation taking a quarter of an hour, which in all made seven hours. To this had to be added twenty-eight pauses; in all ten hours and a half. We started at one, it was now, therefore, about eleven o'clock at night.

It does not require great knowledge of arithmetic to know that twenty-eight times two hundred feet makes five thousand six hundred feet in all (more than an English mile).

While I was making this mental calculation a voice broke the silence. It was the voice of Hans.

"Halt!" he cried.

I checked myself very suddenly, just at the moment when I was about to kick my uncle on the head.

"We have reached the end of our journey," said the worthy Professor in a satisfied tone.

"What, the interior of the earth?" said I, slipping down to his side.

"No, you stupid fellow! but we have reached the bottom of the well."

"And I suppose there is no farther progress to be made?" I hopefully exclaimed.

"Oh, yes, I can dimly see a sort of tunnel, which turns off obliquely to the right. At all events, we must see about that tomorrow. Let us sup now, and seek slumber as best we may."

I thought it time, but made no observations on that point. I was fairly launched on a desperate course, and all I had to do was to go forward hopefully and trustingly.

It was not even now quite dark, the light filtering down in a most extraordinary manner.

We opened the provision bag, ate a frugal supper, and each did his best to find a bed amid the pile of stones, dirt, and lava which had accumulated for ages at the bottom of the shaft.

I happened to grope out the pile of ropes, ladders, and clothes which we had thrown down; and upon them I stretched myself. After such a day's labor, my rough bed seemed as soft as down!

For a while I lay in a sort of pleasant trance.

Presently, after lying quietly for some minutes, I opened my eyes and looked upward. As I did so I made out a brilliant little dot, at the extremity of this long, gigantic telescope.

It was a star without scintillating rays. According to my calculation, must be β in the constellation of the Little Bear.

After this little bit of astronomical recreation, I dropped into a sound sleep.

XV

We Continue Our Descent

At eight o'clock the next morning, a faint kind of dawn of day awoke us. The thousand and one prisms of the lava, collected the light as it passed and brought it to us like a shower of sparks.

We were able with ease to see objects around us.

"Well, Harry, my boy," cried the delighted Professor, rubbing his hands together, "what say you now? Did you ever pass a more tranquil night in our house in the Königstrasse? No deafening sounds of cart wheels, no cries of hawkers, no bad language from boatmen or watermen!"

"Well, Uncle, we are quiet at the bottom of this well—but to me there is something terrible in this calm."

"Why," said the Professor hotly, "one would say you were already beginning to be afraid. How will you get on presently? Do you know, that as yet, we have not penetrated one inch into the bowels of the earth."

"What can you mean, sir?" was my bewildered and astonished reply.

"I mean to say that we have only just reached the soil of the island itself. This long vertical tube, which ends at the bottom of the crater of Sneffels, ceases here just about on a level with the sea."

"Are you sure, sir?"

"Quite sure. Consult the barometer."

It was quite true that the mercury, after rising gradually in the instrument, as long as our descent was taking place, had stopped precisely at twenty-nine degrees.

"You perceive," said the Professor, "we have as yet only to endure the pressure of air. I am curious to replace the barometer by the manometer."

The barometer, in fact, was about to become useless—as soon as the weight of the air was greater than what was calculated as above the level of the ocean.

"But," said I, "is it not very much to be feared that this ever-increasing pressure may not in the end turn out very painful and inconvenient?"

"No," said he. "We shall descend very slowly, and our lungs will be gradually accustomed to breathe compressed air. It is well known that aeronauts have gone so high as to be nearly without air at all—why, then, should we not accustom ourselves to breathe when we have, say, a little too much of it? For myself, I am certain I shall prefer it. Let us not lose a moment. Where is the packet which preceded us in our descent?"

I smilingly pointed it out to my uncle. Hans had not seen it, and believed it caught somewhere above us: "Huppe," as he phrased it.

"Now," said my uncle, "let us breakfast, and break fast like people who have a long day's work before them."

Biscuit and dried meat, washed down by some mouthfuls of water flavored with Schiedam, was the material of our luxurious meal.

As soon as it was finished, my uncle took from his pocket a notebook destined to be filled by memoranda of our travels. He had already placed his instruments in order, and this is what he wrote:

Monday, July 1st
Chronometer 8h. 17m. morning.
Barometer, 29 degrees.
Thermometer, 43° Fahr.
Direction, E.S.E.

This last observation referred to the obscure gallery, and was indicated to us by the compass.

"Now, Harry," cried the Professor, in an enthusiastic tone of voice, "we are truly about to take our first step into the interior of the earth; never before visited by man since the first creation of the world. You may consider, therefore, that at this precise moment our travels really commence."

As my uncle made this remark, he took in one hand the Ruhmkorf coil apparatus, which hung around his neck, and with the other he put the electric current into communication with the worm of the lantern. And a bright light at once illumined that dark and gloomy tunnel!

The effect was magical!

Hans, who carried the second apparatus, had it also put into operation. This ingenious application of electricity to practical purposes enabled us to move along by the light of an artificial day, amid even the flow of the most inflammable and combustible gases.

"Forward!" cried my uncle. Each took up his burden. Hans went first, my uncle followed, and I going third, we entered the somber gallery!

Just as we were about to engulf ourselves in this dismal passage, I lifted up my head, and through the tubelike shaft saw that Iceland sky I was never to see again!

Was it the last I should ever see of any sky?

The stream of lava flowing from the bowels of the earth in 1219 had forced itself a passage through the tunnel. It lined the whole of the inside with its thick and brilliant coating. The electric light added very greatly to the brilliancy of the effect.

The great difficulty of our journey now began. How were we to prevent ourselves from slipping down the steeply inclined plane? Happily some cracks, abrasures of the soil, and other irregularities, served the place of steps; and we descended slowly; allowing our heavy luggage to slip on before, at the end of a long cord.

But that which served as steps under our feet became in other places stalactites. The lava, very porous in certain places, took the form of little round blisters. Crystals of opaque quartz, adorned with limpid drops of natural glass suspended to the roof like lusters, seemed to take fire as we passed beneath them. One would have fancied that the genii of romance were illuminating their underground palaces to receive the sons of men.

"Magnificent, glorious!" I cried in a moment of involuntary enthusiasm, "what a spectacle, Uncle! Do you not admire these variegated shades of lava, which run through a whole series of colors, from reddish brown to pale yellow—by the most insensible degrees? And these crystals, they appear like luminous globes."

"You are beginning to see the charms of travel, Master Harry," cried my uncle. "Wait a bit, until we advance farther. What we have as yet discovered is nothing—onward, my boy, onward!"

It would have been a far more correct and appropriate expression, had he said, "let us slide," for we were going down an inclined plane with perfect ease. The compass indicated that we were moving in a southeasterly direction. The flow of lava had never turned to the right or the left. It had the inflexibility of a straight line.

Nevertheless, to my surprise, we found no perceptible increase in heat. This proved the theories of Humphry Davy to be founded on truth, and more than once I found myself examining the thermometer in silent astonishment.

Two hours after my departure it only marked fifty-four degrees Fahrenheit. I had every reason to believe from this that our descent was far more horizontal than vertical. As for discovering the exact depth to which we had attained, nothing could be easier. The Professor, as he advanced, measured the angles of deviation and inclination; but he kept the result of his observation to himself.

About eight o'clock in the evening, my uncle gave the signal for halting. Hans seated himself on the ground. The lamps were hung to fissures in the lava rock. We were now in a large cavern where air was not wanting. On the contrary, it abounded. What could be the cause of this—to what atmospheric agitation could be ascribed this draft? But this was a question which I did not care to discuss just then. Fatigue and hunger made me incapable of reasoning. An unceasing march of seven hours had not been kept up without great exhaustion. I was really and truly worn out; and delighted enough I was to hear the word Halt.

Hans laid out some provisions on a lump of lava, and we each supped with keen relish. One thing, however, caused us great uneasiness—our water reserve was already half exhausted. My uncle had full confidence in finding subterranean resources, but hitherto we had completely failed in so doing. I could not help calling my uncle's attention to the circumstance.

"And you are surprised at this total absence of springs?" he said.

"Doubtless—I am very uneasy on the point. We have certainly not enough water to last us five days."

"Be quite easy on that matter," continued my uncle. "I answer for it we shall find plenty of water—in fact, far more than we shall want."

"But when?"

"When we once get through this crust of lava. How can you expect springs to force their way through these solid stone walls?"

"But what is there to prove that this concrete mass of lava does not extend to the center of the earth? I don't think we have as yet done much in a vertical way."

"What puts that into your head, my boy?" asked my uncle mildly.

"Well, it appears to me that if we had descended very far below the level of the sea—we should find it rather hotter than we have."

"According to your system," said my uncle; "but what does the thermometer say?"

"Scarcely fifteen degrees by Reaumur, which is only an increase of nine since our departure."

"Well, and what conclusion does that bring you to?" inquired the Professor.

"The deduction I draw from this is very simple. According to the most exact observations, the augmentation of the temperature of the interior of the earth is one degree for every hundred feet. But certain local causes may considerably modify this figure. Thus at Yakoust in Siberia, it has been remarked that the heat increases a degree every thirty-six feet. The difference evidently depends on the conductibility of certain rocks. In the neighborhood of an extinct volcano, it has remarked that the elevation of temperature was only one degree in every five-and-twenty feet. Let us, then, go upon this calculation—which is the most favorable—and calculate."

"Calculate away, my boy."

"Nothing easier," said I, pulling out my notebook and pencil. "Nine times one hundred and twenty-five feet, make a depth of eleven hundred and twenty-five feet."

"Archimedes could not have spoken more geometrically."

"Well?"

"Well, according to my observations, we are at least ten thousand feet below the level of the sea."

"Can it be possible?"

"Either my calculation is correct, or there is no truth in figures."

The calculations of the Professor were perfectly correct. We were already six thousand feet deeper down in the bowels of the earth than anyone had ever been before. The lowest known depth to which man had hitherto penetrated was in the mines of Kitzbühl, in the Tirol, and those of Württemberg.

The temperature, which should have been eighty-one, was in this place only fifteen. This was a matter for serious consideration.

XVI

The Eastern Tunnel

The next day was Tuesday, the 2d of July—and at six o'clock in the morning we resumed our journey.

We still continued to follow the gallery of lava, a perfect natural pathway, as easy of descent as some of those inclined planes which, in very old German houses, serve the purpose of staircases. This went on until seventeen minutes past twelve, the precise instant at which we rejoined Hans, who, having been somewhat in advance, had suddenly stopped.

"At last," cried my uncle, "we have reached the end of the shaft."

I looked wonderingly about me. We were in the center of four cross paths—somber and narrow tunnels. The question now arose as to which it was wise to take; and this of itself was no small difficulty.

My uncle, who did not wish to appear to have any hesitation about the matter before myself or the guide, at once made up his mind. He pointed quietly to the eastern tunnel; and, without delay, we entered within its gloomy recesses.

Besides, had he entertained any feeling of hesitation it might have been prolonged indefinitely, for there was no indication by which to determine on a choice. It was absolutely necessary to trust to chance and good fortune!

The descent of this obscure and narrow gallery was very gradual and winding. Sometimes we gazed through a succession of arches, its course very like the aisles of a Gothic cathedral. The great artistic sculptors and builders of the Middle Ages might have here completed their studies with advantage. Many most beautiful and suggestive ideas of architectural beauty would have been discovered by them. After passing through this phase of the cavernous way, we suddenly came, about a mile farther on, upon a square system of arch, adopted by the early Romans, projecting from the solid rock, and keeping up the weight of the roof.

Suddenly we would come upon a series of low subterranean tunnels which looked like beaver holes, or the work of foxes—through whose narrow and winding ways we had literally to crawl!

The heat still remained at quite a supportable degree. With an involuntary shudder, I reflected on what the heat must have been when the volcano of Sneffels was pouring its smoke, flames, and streams of boiling lava

—all of which must have come up by the road we were now following. I could imagine the torrents of hot seething stone darting on, bubbling up with accompaniments of smoke, steam, and sulphurous stench!

"Only to think of the consequences," I mused, "if the old volcano were once more to set to work."

I did not communicate these rather unpleasant reflections to my uncle. He not only would not have understood them, but would have been intensely disgusted. His only idea was to go ahead. He walked, he slid, he clambered over piles of fragments, he rolled down heaps of broken lava, with an earnestness and conviction it was impossible not to admire.

At six o'clock in the evening, after a very wearisome journey, but one not so fatiguing as before, we had made six miles toward the southward, but had not gone more than a mile downward.

My uncle, as usual, gave the signal to halt. We ate our meal in thoughtful silence, and then retired to sleep.

Our arrangements for the night were very primitive and simple. A traveling rug, in which each rolled himself, was all our bedding. We had no necessity to fear cold or any unpleasant visit. Travelers who bury themselves in the wilds and depths of the African desert, who seek profit and pleasure in the forests of the New World, are compelled to take it in turn to watch during the hours of sleep; but in this region of the earth, absolute solitude and complete security reigned supreme.

We had nothing to fear either from savages or from wild beasts.

After a night's sweet repose, we awoke fresh and ready for action. There being nothing to detain us, we started on our journey. We continued to burrow through the lava tunnel as before. It was impossible to make out through what soil we were making way. The tunnel, moreover, instead of going down into the bowels of the earth, became absolutely horizontal.

I even thought, after some examination, that we were actually tending upward. About ten o'clock in the day this state of things became so clear that, finding the change very fatiguing, I was obliged to slacken my pace and finally come to a halt.

"Well," said the Professor quickly, "what is the matter?"

"The fact is, I am dreadfully tired," was my earnest reply.

"What," cried my uncle, "tired after a three hours' walk, and by so easy a road?"

"Easy enough, I dare say, but very fatiguing."

"But how can that be, when all we have to do is to go downward?"

"I beg your pardon, sir. For some time I have noticed that we are going upward."

"Upward," cried my uncle, shrugging his shoulders, "how can that be?"

"There can be no doubt about it. For the last half hour the slopes have been upward—and if we go on this way much longer we shall find ourselves back in Iceland."

My uncle shook his head with the air of a man who does not want to be convinced. I tried to continue the conversation. He would not answer me, but once more gave the signal for departure. His silence I thought was only caused by concentrated ill-temper.

However this might be, I once more took up my load, and boldly and resolutely followed Hans, who was now in advance of my uncle. I did not like to be beaten or even distanced. I was naturally anxious not to lose sight of my companions. The very idea of being left behind, lost in that terrible labyrinth, made me shiver as with the ague.

Besides, if the ascending path was more arduous and painful to clamber, I had one source of secret consolation and delight. It was to all appearance taking us back to the surface of the earth. That of itself was hopeful. Every step I took confirmed me in my belief, and I began to build castles in the air in relation to my marriage with my pretty little cousin.

About twelve o'clock there was a great and sudden change in the aspect of the rocky sides of the gallery. I first noticed it from the diminution of the rays of light which cast back the reflection of the lamp. From being coated with shining and resplendent lava, it became living rock. The sides were sloping walls, which sometimes became quite vertical.

We were now in what the geological professors call a state of transition, in the period of Silurian stones, so called because this specimen of early formation is very common in England in the counties formerly inhabited by the Celtic nation known as Silures.

"I can see, clearly now," I cried; "the sediment from the waters which once covered the whole earth formed during the second period of its existence these schists and these calcareous rocks. We are turning our backs on the granite rocks, and are like people from Hamburg who would go to Lübeck by way of Hanover."

I might just as well have kept my observations to myself. My geological enthusiasm got the better, however, of my cooler judgment, and Professor Hardwigg heard my observations.

"What is the matter now?" he said, in a tone of great gravity.

"Well," cried I, "do you not see these different layers of calcareous rocks and the first indication of slate strata?"

"Well; what then?"

"We have arrived at that period of the world's existence when the first plants and the first animals made their appearance."

"You think so?"

"Yes, look; examine and judge for yourself."

I induced the Professor with some difficulty to cast the light of his lamp on the sides of the long winding gallery. I expected some exclamation to burst from his lips. I was very much mistaken. The worthy Professor never spoke a word.

It was impossible to say whether he understood me or not. Perhaps it was possible that in his pride—my uncle and a learned professor—he did not like to own that he was wrong in having chosen the eastern tunnel, or was he determined at any price to go to the end of it? It was quite evident we had left the region of lava and that the road by which we were going could not take us back to the great crater of Mount Sneffels.

As we went along I could not help ruminating on the whole question, and asked myself if I did not lay too great a stress on these sudden and peculiar modifications of the earth's crust.

After all, I was very likely to be mistaken—and it was within the range of probability and possibility that we were not making our way through the strata of rocks which I believe I recognized piled on the lower layer of granite formation.

"At all events, if I am right," I thought to myself, "I must certainly find some remains of primitive plants, and it will be absolutely necessary to give way to such indubitable evidence. Let us have a good search."

I accordingly lost no opportunity of searching, and had not gone more than about a hundred yards, when the evidence I sought for cropped up in the most incontestable manner before my eyes. It was quite natural that I should expect to find these signs, for during the Silurian period the seas contained no fewer than fifteen hundred different animal and vegetable species. My feet, so long accustomed to the hard and arid lava soil, suddenly found themselves treading on a kind of soft dust, the remains of plants and shells.

Upon the walls themselves I could clearly make out the outline, as plain as a sun picture, of the fucus and the lycopodes. The worthy and excellent Professor Hardwigg could not of course make any mistake about the matter; but I believe he deliberately closed his eyes, and continued on his way with a firm and unalterable step.

I began to think that he was carrying his obstinacy a great deal too far. I could no longer act with prudence or composure. I stooped on a sudden and picked up an almost perfect shell, which had undoubtedly belonged to some animal very much resembling some of the present day. Having secured the prize, I followed in the wake of my uncle.

"Do you see this?" I said.

"Well," said the Professor, with the most imperturbable tranquillity, "it is the shell of a crustaceous animal of the extinct order of the trilobites; nothing more, I assure you."

"But," cried I, much troubled at his coolness, "do you draw no conclusion from it?"

"Well, if I may ask, what conclusion do you draw from it yourself?"

"Well, I thought—"

"I know, my boy, what you would say, and you are right, perfectly and incontestably right. We have finally abandoned the crust of lava and the road by which the lava ascended. It is quite possible that I may have been mistaken, but I shall be unable to discover my error until I get to the end of this gallery."

"You are quite right as far as that is concerned," I replied, "and I should highly approve of your decision, if we had not to fear the greatest of all dangers."

"And what is that?"

"Want of water."

"Well, my dear Henry, it can't be helped. We must put ourselves on rations."

And on he went.

⚒

XVII

Deeper and Deeper—the Coal Mine

In truth, we were compelled to put ourselves upon rations. Our supply would certainly last not more than three days. I found this out about supper time. The worst part of the matter was that, in what is called the transition rocks, it was hardly to be expected we should meet with water!

I had read of the horrors of thirst, and I knew that where we were, a brief trial of its sufferings would put an end to our adventures—and our lives! But it was utterly useless to discuss the matter with my uncle. He would have answered by some axiom from Plato.

During the whole of next day we proceeded on our journey through this interminable gallery, arch after arch, tunnel after tunnel. We journeyed without exchanging a word. We had become as mute and reticent as Hans, our guide.

The road had no longer an upward tendency; at all events if it had, it was not to be made out very clearly. Sometimes there could be no doubt that we were going downward. But this inclination was scarcely to be distinguished, and was by no means reassuring to the Professor, because the character of the strata was in no wise modified, and the transition character of the rocks became more and more marked.

It was a glorious sight to see how the electric light brought out the sparkles in the walls of calcareous rocks, and the old red sandstone. One might have fancied oneself in one of those deep cuttings in Devonshire, which have given their name to this kind of soil. Some magnificent specimens of marble projected from the sides of the gallery: some of an agate gray with white veins of variegated character, others of a yellow spotted color, with red veins; farther off might be seen samples of color in which cherry-tinted seams were to be found in all their brightest shades.

The greater number of these marbles were stamped with the marks of primitive animals. Since the previous evening, nature and creation had made considerable progress. Instead of the rudimentary trilobites, I perceived the remains of a more perfect order. Among others, the fish in which the eye of a geologist has been able to discover the first form of the reptile.

The Devonian seas were inhabited by a vast number of animals of this species, which were deposited in tens of thousands in the rocks of new formation.

It was quite evident to me that we were ascending the scale of animal life of which man forms the summit. My excellent uncle, the Professor, appeared not to take notice of these warnings. He was determined at any risk to proceed.

He must have been in expectation of one of two things; either that a vertical well was about to open under his feet, and thus allow him to continue his descent, or that some insurmountable obstacle would compel us to stop and go back by the road we had so long traveled. But evening came and, to my horror, neither hope was doomed to be realized!

On Friday, after a night when I began to feel the gnawing agony of thirst, and when in consequence appetite decreased, our little band rose and once more followed the turnings and windings, the ascents and descents, of this interminable gallery. All were silent and gloomy. I could see that even my uncle had ventured too far.

After about ten hours of further progress—a progress dull and monotonous to the last degree—I remarked that the reverberation and reflection of our lamps upon the sides of the tunnel had singularly diminished. The marble, the schist, the calcereous rocks, the red sandstone, had disappeared, leaving in their places a dark and gloomy wall, somber and without brightness. When we reached a remarkably narrow part of the tunnel, I leaned my left hand against the rock.

When I took my hand away, and happened to glance at it, it was quite black. We had reached the coal strata of the Central Earth.

"A coal mine!" I cried.

"A coal mine without miners," responded my uncle, a little severely.

"How can we tell?"

"I can tell," replied my uncle, in a sharp and doctorial tone. "I am perfectly certain that this gallery through successive layers of coal, was not cut by the hand of man. But whether it is the work of Nature or not is of little concern to us. The hour for our evening meal has come—let us sup."

Hans, the guide, occupied himself in preparing food. I had come to that point when I could no longer eat. All I cared about were the few drops of water which fell to my share. What I suffered it is useless to record. The guide's gourd, not quite half full, was all that was left for us three!

Having finished their repast, my two companions laid themselves down upon their rugs, and found in sleep a remedy for their fatigue and sufferings. As for me, I could not sleep, I lay counting the hours until morning.

The next morning, Saturday, at six o'clock, we started again. Twenty minutes later we suddenly came upon a vast excavation. From its mighty extent I saw at once that the hand of man could have had nothing to do with this coal mine; the vault above would have fallen in: as it was, it was only held together by some miracle of Nature.

This mighty natural cavern was about a hundred feet wide, by about a hundred and fifty high. The earth had evidently been cast apart by some violent subterranean commotion. The mass, giving way to some prodigious upheaving of Nature, had split in two, leaving the vast gap into which we inhabitants of the earth had penetrated for the first time.

The whole singular history of the coal period was written on those dark and gloomy walls. A geologist would have been able easily to follow the different phases of its formation. The seams of coal were separated by strata of sandstone, a compact clay, which appeared to be crushed down by the weight from above.

At that period of the world which preceded the secondary epoch, the earth was covered by a coating of enormous and rich vegetation, due to the double action of tropical heat and perpetual humidity. A vast atmospheric cloud of vapor surrounded the earth on all sides, preventing the rays of the sun from ever reaching it.

Hence the conclusion that these intense heats did not arise from this new source of caloric.

Perhaps even the star of day was not quite ready for its brilliant work—to illumine a universe. Climates did not as yet exist, and a level heat pervaded the whole surface of the globe—the same heat existing at the North Pole as at the equator.

Whence did it come? From the interior of the earth?

In spite of all the learned theories of Professor Hardwigg, a fierce and vehement fire certainly burned within the entrails of the great spheroid. Its action was felt even to the very topmost crust of the earth; the plants then in existence, being deprived of the vivifying rays of the sun, had neither buds, nor flowers, nor odor, but their roots drew a strong and vigorous life from the burning earth of early days.

There were but few of what may be called trees—only herbaceous plants, immense turfs, briers, mosses, rare families, which, however, in those days were counted by tens and tens of thousands.

It is entirely to this exuberant vegetation that coal owes its origin. The crust of the vast globe still yielded under the influence of the seething, boiling mass, which was forever at work beneath. Hence arose numerous fissures, and continual falling in of the upper earth. The dense mass of plants being beneath the waters, soon formed themselves into vast agglomerations.

Then came about the action of natural chemistry; in the depths of the ocean the vegetable mass at first became turf, then, thanks to the influence of gases and subterranean fermentation, they underwent the complete process of mineralization.

In this manner, in early days, were formed those vast and prodigious layers of coal, which an ever-increasing consumption must utterly use up in about three centuries more, if people do not find some more economic light than gas, and some cheaper motive power than steam.

All these reflections, the memories of my school studies, came to my mind while I gazed upon these mighty accumulations of coal, whose riches, however, are scarcely likely to be utilized. The working of these mines could only be carried out at an expense that would never yield a profit.

The matter, however, is scarcely worthy of consideration, when coal is scattered over the whole surface of the globe, within a few yards of the upper crust. As I looked at these untouched strata, therefore, I knew they would remain as long as the world lasts.

While we still continued our journey, I alone forgot the length of the road, by giving myself up wholly to these geological considerations. The temperature continued to be very much the same as while we were traveling amid the lava and schists. On the other hand my sense of smell was much affected by a very powerful odor. I immediately knew that the gallery was filled to overflowing with that dangerous gas the miners call fire damp, the explosion of which has caused such fearful and terrible accidents, making a hundred widows and hundreds of orphans in a single hour.

Happily, we were able to illume our progress by means of the Ruhmkorf apparatus. If we had been so rash and imprudent as to explore this gallery, torch in hand, a terrific explosion would have put an end to our travels, simply because no travelers would be left.

Our excursion through this wondrous coal mine in the very bowels of the earth lasted until evening. My uncle was scarcely able to conceal his impatience and dissatisfaction at the road continuing to advance in a horizontal direction.

The darkness, dense and opaque a few yards in advance and in the rear, rendered it impossible to make out what was the length of the gallery. For myself, I began to believe that it was simply interminable, and would go on in the same manner for months.

Suddenly, at six o'clock, we stood in front of a wall. To the right, to the left, above, below, nowhere was there any passage. We had reached a spot where the rocks said in unmistakable accents—No Thoroughfare.

I stood stupefied. The guide simply folded his arms. My uncle was silent.

"Well, well, so much the better," cried my uncle, at last, "I now know what we are about. We are decidedly not upon the road followed by Saknussemm. All we have to do is to go back. Let us take one night's good rest, and before three days are over, I promise you we shall have regained the point where the galleries divided."

"Yes, we may, if our strength lasts as long," I cried, in a lamentable voice.

"And why not?"

"Tomorrow, among us three, there will not be a drop of water. It is just gone."

"And your courage with it," said my uncle, speaking in a severe tone.

What could I say? I turned around on my side, and from sheer exhaustion fell into a heavy but troubled sleep. Dreams of water! And I awoke unrefreshed.

I would have bartered a diamond mine for a glass of pure spring water!

XVIII

The Wrong Road!

Next day, our departure took place at a very early hour. There was no time for the least delay. According to my account, we had five days' hard work to get back to the place where the galleries divided.

I can never tell all the sufferings we endured upon our return. My uncle bore them like a man who has been in the wrong—that is, with concentrated and suppressed anger; Hans, with all the resignation of his pacific character; and I—I confess that I did nothing but complain and despair. I had no heart for this bad fortune.

But there was one consolation. Defeat at the outset would probably upset the whole journey!

As I had expected from the first, our supply of water gave completely out on our first day's march. Our provision of liquids was reduced to our supply of Schiedam; but this horrible—nay, I will say it—this infernal liquor burnt the throat, and I could not even bear the sight of it. I found the temperature to be stifling. I was paralyzed with fatigue. More than once I was about to fall insensible to the ground. The whole party then halted, and the worthy Icelander and my excellent uncle did their best to console and comfort me. I could, however, plainly see that my uncle was contending painfully against the extreme fatigues of our journey, and the awful torture generated by the absence of water.

At length a time came when I ceased to recollect anything—when all was one awful, hideous, fantastic dream!

At last, on Tuesday, the seventh of the month of July, after crawling on our hands and knees for many hours, more dead than alive, we reached the point of junction between the galleries. I lay like a log, an inert mass of human flesh on the arid lava soil. It was then ten in the morning.

Hans and my uncle, leaning against the wall, tried to nibble away at some pieces of biscuit, while deep groans and sighs escaped from my scorched and swollen lips. Then I fell off into a kind of deep lethargy.

Presently I felt my uncle approach, and lift me up tenderly in his arms.

"Poor boy," I heard him say in a tone of deep commiseration.

I was profoundly touched by these words, being by no means accustomed to signs of womanly weakness in the Professor. I caught his trembling hands in mine and gave them a gentle pressure. He allowed me to do so without resistance, looking at me kindly all the time. His eyes were wet with tears.

I then saw him take the gourd which he wore at his side. To my surprise, or rather to my stupefaction, he placed it to my lips.

"Drink, my boy," he said.

Was it possible my ears had not deceived me? Was my uncle mad? I looked at him, with, I am sure, quite an idiotic expression. I would not understand him. I too much feared the counteraction of disappointment.

"Drink," he said again.

Had I heard aright? Before, however, I could ask myself the question a second time, a mouthful of water cooled my parched lips and throat—one mouthful, but I do believe it brought me back to life.

I thanked my uncle by clasping my hands. My heart was too full to speak.

"Yes," said he, "one mouthful of water, the very last—do you hear, my boy—the very last! I have taken care of it at the bottom of my bottle as the apple of my eye. Twenty times, a hundred times, I have resisted the fearful desire to drink it. But—no—no, Harry, I saved it for you."

"My dear uncle," I exclaimed, and the big tears rolled down my hot and feverish cheeks.

"Yes, my poor boy, I knew that when you reached this place, this crossroad in the earth, you would fall down half dead, and I saved my last drop of water in order to restore you."

"Thanks," I cried; "thanks from my heart."

As little as my thirst was really quenched, I had nevertheless partially recovered my strength. The contracted muscles of my throat relaxed—and the inflammation of my lips in some measure subsided. At all events, I was able to speak.

"Well," I said, "there can be no doubt now as to what we have to do. Water has utterly failed us; our journey is therefore at an end. Let us return."

While I spoke thus, my uncle evidently avoided my face: he held down his head; his eyes were turned in every possible direction but the right one.

"Yes," I continued, getting excited by my own words, "we must go back to Sneffels. May heaven give us strength to enable us once more to revisit the light of day. Would that we now stood on the summit of the crater."

"Go back," said my uncle, speaking to himself, "and must it be so?"

"Go back—yes, and without losing a single moment," I vehemently cried.

For some moments there was silence under that dark and gloomy vault.

"So, my dear Harry," said the Professor in a very singular tone of voice, "those few drops of water have not sufficed to restore your energy and courage."

"Courage!" I cried.

"I see that you are quite as downcast as before—and still give way to discouragement and despair."

What, then, was the man made of, and what other projects were entering his fertile and audacious brain!

"You are not discouraged, sir?"

"What! Give up just as we are on the verge of success?" he cried. "Never, never shall it be said that Professor Hardwigg retreated."

"Then we must make up our minds to perish," I cried with a helpless sigh.

"No, Harry, my boy, certainly not. Go, leave me, I am very far from desiring your death. Take Hans with you. *I will go on alone.*"

"You ask us to leave you?"

"Leave me, I say. I have undertaken this dangerous and perilous adventure. I will carry it to the end—or I will never return to the surface of Mother Earth. Go, Harry—once more I say to you—go!"

My uncle as he spoke was terribly excited. His voice, which before had been tender, almost womanly, became harsh and menacing. He appeared to be struggling with desperate energy against the impossible. I did not wish to abandon him at the bottom of that abyss, while, on the other hand, the instinct of preservation told me to fly.

Meanwhile, our guide was looking on with profound calmness and indifference. He appeared to be an unconcerned party, and yet he perfectly well knew what was going on between us. Our gestures sufficiently indicated the different roads each wished to follow—and which each tried to influence the other to undertake. But Hans appeared not to take the slightest interest in what was really a question of life and death for us all, but waited quite ready to obey the signal which should say go aloft, or to resume his desperate journey into the interior of the earth.

How then I wished with all my heart and soul that I could make him understand my words. My representations, my sighs and groans, the earnest accents in which I should have spoken would have convinced that cold, hard nature. Those fearful dangers and perils of which the stolid guide had no idea, I would have pointed them out to him—I would have, as it were, made him see and feel. Between us, we might have convinced the obstinate Professor. If the worse had come to the worst, we could have compelled him to return to the summit of Sneffels.

I quietly approached Hans. I caught his hand in mine. He never moved a muscle. I indicated to him the road to the top of the crater. He remained motionless. My panting form, my haggard countenance, must have indicated the extent of my sufferings. The Icelander gently shook his head and pointed to my uncle.

"Master," he said.

The word is Icelandic as well as English.

"The master!" I cried, beside myself with fury—"madman! no—I tell you he is not the master of our lives; we must fly! we must drag him with us! do you hear me? Do you understand me, I say?"

I have already explained that I held Hans by the arm. I tried to make him rise from his seat. I struggled with him and tried to force him away. My uncle now interposed.

"My good Henry, be calm," he said. "You will obtain nothing from my devoted follower; therefore, listen to what I have to say."

I folded my arms, as well as I could, and looked my uncle full in the face.

"This wretched want of water," he said, "is the sole obstacle to the success of my project. In the entire gallery, composed of lava, schist, and coal, it is true we found not one liquid in the western tunnel."

My sole reply was to shake my head with an air of incredulity.

"Listen to me to the end," said the Professor in his well-known lecturing voice. "While you lay yonder without life or motion, I undertook a reconnoitering journey into the conformation of this other gallery. I have discovered that it goes directly downward into the bowels of the earth, and in a few hours will take us to the old granitic formation. In this we shall undoubtedly find innumerable springs. The nature of the rock makes this a mathematical certainty, and instinct agrees with logic to say that it is so. Now, this is the serious proposition which I have to make to you. When Christopher Columbus asked of his men three days to discover the land of promise, his men ill, terrified, and hopeless, yet gave him three days—and the New World was discovered. Now I, the Christopher Columbus of this subterranean region, only ask of you one more day. If, when that time is expired, I have not found the water of which we are in search, I swear to you, I will give up my mighty enterprise and return to the earth's surface."

Despite my irritation and despair, I knew how much it cost my uncle to make this proposition, and to hold such conciliatory language. Under the circumstances, what could I do but yield?

"Well," I cried, "let it be as you wish, and may heaven reward your superhuman energy. But as, unless we discover water, our hours are numbered, let us lose no time, but go ahead."

XIX
The Western Gallery—a New Route

Our descent was now resumed by means of the second gallery. Hans took up his post in front as usual. We had not gone more than a hundred yards when the Professor carefully examined the walls.

"This is the primitive formation—we are on the right road—onward is our hope!"

When the whole earth got cool in the first hours of the world's morning, the diminution of the volume of the earth produced a state of dislocation in its upper crust, followed by ruptures, crevasses, and fissures. The passage was a fissure of this kind, through which, ages ago, had flowed the eruptive granite. The thousand windings and turnings formed an inextricable labyrinth through the ancient soil.

As we descended, successions of layers composing the primitive soil appeared with the utmost fidelity of detail. Geological science considers this primitive soil as the base of the mineral crust, and it has recognized that it is composed of three different strata or layers, all resting on the immovable rock known as granite.

No mineralogists had ever found themselves placed in such a marvelous position to study Nature in all her real and naked beauty. The sounding rod, a mere machine, could not bring to the surface of the earth the objects of value for the study of its internal structure, which we were about to see with our own eyes, to touch with our own hands.

Remember that I am writing this *after* the journey.

Across the streak of the rocks, colored by beautiful green tints, wound metallic threads of copper, of manganese, with traces of platinum and gold. I could not help gazing at these riches buried in the entrails of Mother Earth, and of which no man would have the enjoyment to the end of time! These treasures—mighty and inexhaustible, were buried in the morning of the earth's history, at such awful depths, that no crowbar or pickax will ever drag them from their tomb!

The light of our Ruhmkorf's coil, increased tenfold by the myriad of prismatic masses of rock, sent their jets of fire in every direction, and I could fancy myself traveling through a huge hollow diamond, the rays of which produced myriads of extraordinary effects.

Toward six o'clock, this festival of light began sensibly and visibly to decrease, and soon almost ceased. The sides of the gallery assumed a crystallized tint, with a somber hue; white mica began to commingle more freely with feldspar and quartz, to form what may be called the true rock—the stone which is hard above all, that supports, without being crushed, the four stories of the earth's soil.

We were walled by an immense prison of granite!

It was now eight o'clock, and still there was no sign of water. The sufferings I endured were horrible. My uncle now kept at the head of our little column. Nothing could induce him to stop. I, meanwhile, had but one real thought. My ear was keenly on the watch to catch the sound of a spring. But no pleasant sound of falling water fell upon my listening ear.

But at last the time came when my limbs refused to longer carry me. I contended heroically against the terrible tortures I endured, because I did not wish to compel my uncle to halt. To him I knew this would be the last fatal stroke.

Suddenly I felt a deadly faintness come over me. My eyes could no longer see; my knees shook. I gave one despairing cry—and fell!

"Help, help, I am dying!"

My uncle turned and slowly retraced his steps. He looked at me with folded arms, and then allowed one sentence to escape, in hollow accents, from his lips:

"All is over."

The last thing I saw was a face fearfully distorted with pain and sorrow; and then my eyes closed.

When I again opened them, I saw my companions lying near me, motionless, wrapped in their huge traveling rugs. Were they asleep or dead? For myself, sleep was wholly out of the question. My fainting fit over, I was wakeful as the lark. I suffered too much for sleep to visit my eyelids—the more, than I thought myself sick unto death—dying. The last works spoken by my uncle seemed to be buzzing in my ears—*all is over!* And it was probable that he was right. In the state of prostration to which I was reduced, it was madness to think of ever again seeing the light of day.

Above were miles upon miles of the earth's crust. As I thought of it, I could fancy the whole weight resting on my shoulders. I was crushed, annihilated! and exhausted myself in vain attempts to turn in my granite bed.

Hours upon hours passed away. A profound and terrible silence reigned around us—a silence of the tomb. Nothing could make itself heard through these gigantic walls of granite. The very thought was stupendous.

Presently, despite my apathy, despite the kind of deadly calm into which I was cast, something aroused me. It was a slight but peculiar noise. While I was watching intently, I observed that the tunnel was becoming dark. Then gazing through the dim light that remained, I thought I saw the Icelander taking his departure, lamp in hand.

Why had he acted thus? Did Hans the guide mean to abandon us? My uncle lay fast asleep—or dead. I tried to cry out, and arouse him. My voice, feebly issuing from my parched and fevered lips, found no echo in that fearful place. My throat was dry, my tongue stuck to the roof of my mouth. The obscurity had by this time become intense, and at last even the faint sound of the guide's footsteps was lost in the blank distance. My soul seemed filled with anguish, and death appeared welcome, only let it come quickly.

"Hans is leaving us," I cried. "Hans—Hans, if you are a man, come back."

These words were spoken to myself. They could not be heard aloud. Nevertheless, after the first few moments of terror were over, I was ashamed of my suspicions against a man who hitherto had behaved so admirably. Nothing in his conduct or character justified suspicion. Moreover, a moment's reflection reassured me. His departure could not be a flight. Instead of ascending the gallery, he was going deeper down into the gulf. Had he had any bad design, his way would have been upward.

This reasoning calmed me a little and I began to hope!

The good, and peaceful, and imperturbable Hans would certainly not have arisen from his sleep without some serious and grave motive. Was he bent on a voyage of discovery? During the deep, still silence of the night had he at last heard that sweet murmur about which we were all so anxious?

XX

Water, Where Is It? A Bitter Disappointment

During a long, long, weary hour, there crossed my wildly delirious brain all sorts of reasons as to what could have aroused our quiet and faithful guide. The most absurd and ridiculous ideas passed through my head, each more impossible than the other. I believe I was either half or wholly mad.

Suddenly, however, there arose, as it were from the depths of the earth, a voice of comfort. It was the sound of footsteps! Hans was returning.

Presently the uncertain light began to shine upon the walls of the passage, and then it came in view far down the sloping tunnel. At length Hans himself appeared.

He approached my uncle, placed his hand upon his shoulder, and gently awakened him. My uncle, as soon as he saw who it was, instantly arose.

"Well!" exclaimed the Professor.

"Vatten," said the hunter.

I did not know a single word of the Danish language, and yet by a sort of mysterious instinct I understood what the guide had said.

"Water, water!" I cried, in a wild and frantic tone, clapping my hands, and gesticulating like a madman.

"Water!" murmured my uncle, in a voice of deep emotion and gratitude. *"Hvar!"* ("Where?")

"Nedat." ("Below.")

"Where? below!" I understood every word. I had caught the hunter by the hands, and I shook them heartily, while he looked on with perfect calmness.

The preparations for our departure did not take long, and we were soon making a rapid descent into the tunnel.

An hour later we had advanced a thousand yards, and descended two thousand feet.

At this moment I heard an accustomed and well-known sound running along the floors of the granite rock—a kind of dull and sullen roar, like that of a distant waterfall.

During the first half-hour of our advance, not finding the discovered spring, my feelings of intense suffering appeared to return. Once more I began to lose all hope. My uncle, however, observing how downhearted I was again becoming, took up the conversation.

"Hans was right," he exclaimed enthusiastically; "that is the dull roaring of a torrent."

"A torrent," I cried, delighted at even hearing the welcome words.

"There's not the slightest doubt about it," he replied, "a subterranean river is flowing beside us."

I made no reply, but hastened on, once more animated by hope. I began not even to feel the deep fatigue which hitherto had overpowered me. We could hear it increasing in volume every moment. The torrent, which for a long time could be heard flowing over our heads, now ran distinctly along the left wall, roaring, rushing, spluttering, and still falling.

Several times I passed my hand across the rock hoping to find some trace of humidity—of the slightest percolation. Alas! in vain.

Again a half-hour passed in the same weary toil. Again we advanced.

It now became evident that the hunter, during his absence, had not been able to carry his researches any farther. Guided by an instinct peculiar to the dwellers in mountain regions and water finders, he "smelt" the living spring through the rock. Still he had not seen the precious liquid. He had neither quenched his own thirst, nor brought us one drop in his gourd.

Moreover, we soon made the disastrous discovery that, if our progress continued, we should soon be moving away from the torrent, the sound of which gradually diminished. We turned back. Hans halted at the precise spot where the sound of the torrent appeared nearest.

I could bear the suspense and suffering no longer, and seated myself against the wall, behind which I could hear the water seething and effervescing not two feet away. But a solid wall of granite still separated us from it!

Hans looked keenly at me, and, strange enough, for once I thought I saw a smile on his imperturbable face.

He rose from a stone on which he had been seated, and took up the lamp. I could not help rising and following. He moved slowly along the firm and solid granite wall. I watched him with mingled curiosity and eagerness. Presently he halted and placed his ear against the dry stone, moving slowly along and listening with the most extreme care and attention. I understood at once that he was searching for the exact spot where the torrent's roar was most plainly heard. This point he soon found in the lateral wall on the left side, about three feet above the level of the tunnel floor.

I was in a state of intense excitement. I scarcely dared believe what the eider-duck hunter was about to do. It was, however, impossible at a moment more not to both understand and applaud, and even to smother him in my embraces, when I saw him raise the heavy crowbar and commense an attack upon the rock itself.

"Saved," I cried.

"Yes," cried my uncle, even more excited and delighted than myself; "Hans is quite right. Oh, the worthy, excellent man! We should never have thought of such an idea."

And nobody else, I think, would have done so. Such a process, simple as it seemed, would most certainly not have entered our heads. Nothing could be more dangerous than to begin to work with pickaxes in that particular part of the globe. Supposing while he was at work a break-up were to take place, and supposing the torrent once having gained an inch were to take an ell, and come pouring bodily through the broken rock!

Not one of these dangers was chimerical. They were only too real. But at that moment no fear of falling in of the roof, or even if inundation was capable of stopping us. Our thirst was so intense that to quench it we would have dug below the bed of old Ocean itself.

Hans went quietly to work—a work which neither my uncle nor I would have undertaken at any price. Our impatience was so great that if we had once begun with pickax and crowbar, the rock would soon have split into a hundred fragments. The guide, on the contrary, calm, ready, moderate, wore away the hard rock by little steady blows of his instrument, making no attempt at a larger hole than about six inches. As I stood, I heard, or I thought I heard, the roar of the torrent momentarily increasing in loudness, and at times I almost felt the pleasant sensation of water upon my parched lips.

At the end of what appeared an age, Hans had made a hole which enabled his crowbar to enter two feet into the solid rock. He had been at work exactly an hour. It appeared a dozen. I was getting wild with impatience. My uncle began to think of using more violent measures. I had the greatest difficulty in checking him. He had indeed just got hold of his crowbar when a loud and welcome hiss was heard. Then a stream, or rather jet, of water burst through the wall and came out with such force as to hit the opposite side!

Hans, the guide, who was half upset by the shock, was scarcely able to keep down a cry of pain and grief. I understood his meaning when, plunging my hands into the sparkling jet, I myself gave a wild and frantic cry. The water was scalding hot!

"Boiling," I cried, in bitter disappointment.

"Well, never mind," said my uncle, "it will soon get cool."

The tunnel began to be filled by clouds of vapor, while a small stream ran away into the interior of the earth. In a short time we had some sufficiently cool to drink. We swallowed it in huge mouthfuls.

Oh what exalted delight—what rich and incomparable luxury! What was this water, whence did it come? To us what was that? The simple fact was—it was water; and, though still with a tingle of warmth about it, it brought back to the heart, that life which, but for it, must surely have faded away. I drank greedily, almost without tasting it.

When, however, I had almost quenched my ravenous thirst, I made a discovery.

"Why, it is ferruginous water."

"Most excellent stomachic," replied my uncle, "and highly mineralized. Here is a journey worth twenty to Spa."

"It's very good," I replied.

"I should think so. Water found six miles under ground. There is a peculiarly inky flavor to it, which is by no means disagreeable. Hans may congratulate himself on having made a rare discovery. What do you say, nephew, according to the usual custom of travelers, to name the stream after him?"

"Good," said I.

And the name of "Hansbach" was at once agreed upon.

Hans was not a bit more proud after hearing our determination than he was before. After having taken a very small modicum of the welcome refreshment, he had seated himself in a corner with his usual imperturbable gravity.

"Now," said I, "it is not worth while letting this water run to waste."

"What is the use," replied my uncle, "the source from which this river rises is inexhaustible."

"Never mind," I continued, "let us fill our goatskin and gourds, and then try to stop the opening up."

My advice, after some hesitation, was followed or attempted to be followed. Hans picked up all the broken pieces of granite he had knocked out, and using some tow he happened to have about him, tried to shut up the fissure he had made in the wall. All he did was to scald his hands. The pressure was too great, and all our attempts were utter failures.

"It is evident," I remarked, "that the upper surface of these springs is situated at a very great height above—as we may fairly infer from the great pressure of the jet."

"That is by no means doubtful," replied my uncle, "if this column of water is about thirty-two thousand feet high, the atmospheric pressure must be something enormous. But a new idea has just struck me."

"And what is that?"

"Why be at so much trouble to close this aperture?"

"Because—"

I hesitated and stammered, having no real reason.

"When our water bottles are empty, we are not at all sure that we shall be able to fill them," observed my uncle.

"I think that is very probable."

"Well, then, let this water run. It will, of course, naturally follow in our track, and will serve to guide and refresh us."

"I think the idea is a good one," I cried in reply, "and with this rivulet as a companion, there is no further reason why we should not succeed in our marvelous project."

"Ah, my boy," said the Professor, laughing, "after all, you are coming around."

"More than that, I am now confident of ultimate success. Forward."

"One moment, nephew mine. Let us begin by taking some hours of repose."

I had utterly forgotten that it was night. The chronometer, however, informed me of the fact. Soon we were sufficiently restored and refreshed, and had all fallen into a profound sleep.

XXI
Under the Ocean

By the next day we had forgotten our past sufferings. The first sensation I experienced was surprise at not being thirsty, and I actually asked myself the reason. The running stream, which flowed in rippling wavelets at my feet, was the satisfactory reply.

We breakfasted with a good appetite, and then drank our fill of the excellent water. I felt myself quite a new man, ready to go anywhere my uncle chose to lead. I began to think. Why should not a man as seriously convinced as my uncle, succeed, with so excellent a guide as worthy Hans, and so devoted a nephew as myself? These were the brilliant ideas which now invaded my brain. Had the proposition now been made to go back to the summit of Mount Sneffels, I should have declined the offer in a most indignant manner.

But fortunately there was no question of going up. We were about to descend farther into the interior of the earth.

"Let us be moving," I cried, awakening the echoes of the old world.

We resumed our march on Thursday at eight o'clock in the morning. The great granite tunnel going around by sinuous and winding ways, presented every now and then sharp turns, and in fact had all the appearance of a labyrinth. Its direction, however, was in general toward the southwest. My uncle made several pauses in order to consult his compass.

The gallery now began to trend downward in a horizontal direction, with about two inches of fall in every furlong. The murmuring stream flowed quietly at our feet. I could not but compare it to some familiar spirit, guiding us through the earth, and I dabbled my fingers in its tepid water, which sang like a naiad as we progressed. My good humor began to assume a mythological character.

As for my uncle he began to complain of the horizontal character of the road. His route he found began to be indefinitely prolonged, instead of "sliding down the celestial ray," according to his expression.

But we had no choice; and as long as our road led toward the center—however little progress we made, there was no reason to complain.

Moreover, from time to time the slopes were much greater, the naiad sang more loudly, and we began to dip downward in earnest.

As yet, however, I felt no painful sensation. I had not got over the excitement of the discovery of water.

That day and the next we did a considerable amount of horizontal and relatively very little vertical, traveling.

On Friday evening, the tenth of July, according to our estimation, we ought to have been thirty leagues to the southeast of Reykjavik, and about two leagues and a half deep. We now received a rather startling surprise.

Under our feet there opened a horrible well. My uncle was so delighted that he actually clapped his hands—as he saw how steep and sharp was the descent.

"Ah, ah!" he cried, in rapturous delight; "this will take us a long way. Look at the projections of the rock. Hah!" he exclaimed, "it's a fearful staircase!"

Hans, however, who in all our troubles had never given up the ropes, took care so to dispose of them as to prevent any accidents. Our descent then began, I dare not call it a perilous descent, for I was already too familiar with that sort of work to look upon it as anything but a very ordinary affair.

This well was a kind of narrow opening in the massive granite of the kind known as a fissure. The contradiction of the terrestrial scaffolding, when it suddenly cooled, had been evidently the cause. If it had ever served in former times as a kind of funnel through which passed the eruptive masses vomited by Sneffels, I was at a loss to explain how it had left no mark. We were, in fact, descending a spiral, something like those winding staircases in use in modern houses.

We were compelled every quarter of an hour or thereabouts to sit down in order to rest our legs. Our calves ached. We then seated ourselves on some projecting rock with our legs hanging over, and gossiped while we ate a mouthful—drinking still from the pleasantly warm running stream which had not deserted us.

It is scarcely necessary to say that in this curiously shaped fissure the Hansbach had become a cascade to the detriment of its size. It was still, however, sufficient, and more, for our wants. Besides we knew that, as soon as the declivity ceased to be so abrupt, the stream must resume its peaceful course. At this moment it reminded me of my uncle, his impatience and rage, while when it flowed more peacefully, I pictured to myself the placidity of the Icelandic guide.

During the whole of two days, the eleventh and twelfth of July, we followed the extraordinary spiral staircase of the fissure, penetrating two leagues farther into the crust of the earth, which put us five leagues below the level of the sea. On the eighth, however, at twelve o'clock in the day, the fissure suddenly assumed a much more gentle slope still trending in a southeast direction.

The road now became comparatively easy, and at the same time dreadfully monotonous. It would have been difficult for matters to have turned out otherwise. Our peculiar journey had no chance of being diversified by landscape and scenery. At all events, such was my idea.

At length, on Wednesday the fifteenth, we were actually seven leagues (twenty-one miles) below the surface of the earth, and fifty leagues distant from the mountain of Sneffels. Though, if the truth be told, we were very tired, our health had resisted all suffering, and was in a most satisfactory state. Our traveler's box of medicaments had not even been opened.

My uncle was careful to note every hour the indications of the compass, of the manometer, and of the thermometer, all which he afterward published in his elaborate philosophical and scientific account of our remarkable voyage. He was therefore able to glove an exact relation of the situation. When, therefore, he informed me that we were fifty leagues in a horizontal direction distant from our starting point, I could not suppress a loud exclamation.

"What is the matter now?" cried my uncle.

"Nothing very important, only an idea has entered my head," was my reply.

"Well, out with it, my boy."

"It is my opinion that if your calculations are correct we are no longer under Iceland."

"Do you think so?"

"We can easily find out," I replied, pulling out the map and compasses.

"You see," I said, after careful measurement, "that I am not mistaken. We are far beyond Cape Portland; and those fifty leagues to the southeast will take us into the open sea."

"Under the open sea," cried my uncle, rubbing his hands with a delighted air.

"Yes," I cried, "no doubt old ocean flows over our heads."

"Well, my dear boy, what can be more natural. Do you not know that in the neighborhood of Newcastle there are coal mines which have been worked far out under the sea?"

Now my worthy uncle, the Professor, no doubt regarded this discovery as a very simple fact, but to me the idea was by no means a pleasant one. And yet when one came to think the matter over seriously, what mattered it whether the plains and mountains of Iceland were suspended over our devoted heads, or the mighty billows of the Atlantic Ocean? The whole question rested on the solidity of the granite roof above us. However, I soon got used to the idea, for the passage now level, now running down, and still always to the southeast, kept going deeper and deeper into the profound abysses of Mother Earth.

Three days later, on the eighteenth day of July, on a Saturday, we reached a kind of vast grotto. My uncle here paid Hans his usual rix-dollars, and it was decided that the next day should be a day of rest.

XXII

SUNDAY BELOW GROUND

I awoke on Sunday morning without any sense of hurry and bustle attendant on an immediate departure. Though the day to be devoted to repose and reflection was spent under such strange circumstances, and in so wonderful a place, the idea was a pleasant one. Besides, we all began to get used to this kind of existence. I had almost ceased to think of the sun, of the moon, of the stars, of the trees, houses, and towns; in fact, about any terrestrial necessities. In our peculiar position we were far above such reflections.

The grotto was a vast and magnificent hall. Along its granitic soil the stream flowed placidly and pleasantly. So great a distance was it now from its fiery source that its water was scarcely lukewarm, and could be drunk without delay or difficulty.

After a frugal breakfast, the Professor made up his mind to devote some hours to putting his notes and calculations in order.

"In the first place," he said, "I have a good many to verify and prove, in order that we may know our exact position. I wish to be able on our return to the upper regions to make a map of our journey, a kind of vertical section of the globe, which will be, as it were, the profile of the expedition."

"That would indeed be a curious work, Uncle; but can you make your observations with anything like certainty and precision?"

"I can. I have never on one occasion failed to note with great care the angles and slopes. I am certain as to having made no mistake. Take the compass and examine how she points."

I looked at the instrument with care.

"East one quarter southeast."

"Very good," resumed the Professor, noting the observation, and going through some rapid calculations. "I make out that we have journeyed two hundred and fifty miles from the point of our departure."

"Then the mighty waves of the Atlantic are rolling over our heads?"

"Certainly."

"And at this very moment it is possible that fierce tempests are raging above, and that men and ships are battling against the angry blasts just over our heads?"

"It is quite within the range of possibility," rejoined my uncle, smiling.

"And that whales are playing in shoals, thrashing the bottom of the sea, the roof of our adamantine prison?"

"Be quite at rest on that point; there is no danger of their breaking through. But to return to our calculations. We are to the southeast, two hundred and fifty miles from the base of Sneffels, and, according to my preceding notes, I think we have gone sixteen leagues in a downward direction."

"Sixteen leagues—fifty miles!" I cried.

"I am sure of it."

"But this is the extreme limit allowed by science for the thickness of the earth's crust," I replied, referring to my geological studies.

"I do not contravene that assertion," was his quiet answer.

"And at this stage of our journey, according to all known laws on the increase of heat, there should be here a temperature of *fifteen hundred* degrees of Reaumur."

"There should be—you say, my boy."

"In which case this granite would not exist but in a state of fusion."

"But you perceive, my boy, that it is not so, and that facts, as usual, are very stubborn things, overruling all theories."

"I am forced to yield to the evidence of my senses, but I am nevertheless very much surprised."

"What heat does the thermometer really indicate?" continued the philosopher.

"Twenty-seven six-tenths."

"So that science is wrong by fourteen hundred and seventy-four degrees and four-tenths. According to which, it is demonstrated that the proportional increase in temperature is an exploded error. Humphry Davy here shines forth in all his glory. He is right, and I have acted wisely to believe him. Have you any answer to make to this statement?"

Had I chosen to have spoken, I might have said a great deal. I in no way admitted the theory of Humphry Davy—I still held out for the theory of proportional increase of heat, though I did not feel it.

I was far more willing to allow that this chimney of an extinct volcano was covered by lava of a kind refractory to heat—in fact a bad conductor—which did not allow the great increase of temperature to percolate through its sides. The hot water jet supported my view of the matter.

But without entering on a long and useless discussion, or seeking for new arguments to controvert my uncle, I contented myself with taking up facts as they were.

"Well, sir, I take for granted that all your calculations are correct, but allow me to draw from them a rigorous and definite conclusion."

"Go on, my boy—have your say," cried my uncle good-humoredly.

"At the place where we now are, under the latitude of Iceland, the terrestrial depth is about fifteen hundred and eighty-three leagues."

"Fifteen hundred eighty-three and a quarter."

"Well, suppose we say sixteen hundred in round numbers. Now, out of a voyage of sixteen hundred leagues we have completed sixteen."

"As you say, what then?"

"At the expense of a diagonal journey of no less than eighty-five leagues."

"Exactly."

"We have been twenty days about it."

"Exactly twenty days."

"Now sixteen is the hundredth part of our contemplated expedition. If we go on in this way we shall be two thousand days, that is about five years and a half going down."

The professor folded his arms, listened, but did not speak.

"Without counting that if a vertical descent of sixteen leagues costs us a horizontal of eighty-five, we shall have to go about eight thousand leagues to the southeast, and we must therefore come out somewhere in the circumference long before we can hope to reach the center."

"Bother your calculations," cried my uncle in one of his old rages. "On what basis do they rest? How do you know that this passage does not take us direct to the end we require? Moreover, I have in my favor, fortunately, a precedent. What I have undertaken to do, another has done, and he having succeeded, why should I not be equally successful?"

"I hope, indeed, you will, but still, I suppose I may be allowed to—"

"You are allowed to hold your tongue," cried Professor Hardwigg, "when you talk so unreasonably as this."

I saw at once that the old doctorial Professor was still alive in my uncle—and fearful to rouse his angry passions, I dropped the unpleasant subject.

"Now, then," be explained, "consult the manometer. What does that indicate?"

"A considerable amount of pressure."

"Very good. You see, then, that by descending slowly, and by gradually accustoming ourselves to the density of this lower atmosphere, we shall not suffer."

"Well, I suppose not, except it may be a certain amount of pain in the ears," was my rather grim reply.

"That, my dear boy, is nothing, and you will easily get rid of that source of discomfort by bringing the exterior air in communication with the air contained in your lungs."

"Perfectly," said I, for I had quite made up my mind in no wise to contradict my uncle. "I should fancy almost that I should experience a certain amount of satisfaction in making a plunge into this dense atmosphere. Have you taken note of how wonderfully sound is propagated?"

"Of course I have. There can be no doubt that a journey into the interior of the earth would be an excellent cure for deafness."

"But then, Uncle," I ventured mildly to observe, "this density will continue to increase."

"Yes—according to a law which, however, is scarcely defined. It is true that the intensity of weight will diminish just in proportion to the depth to which we go. You know very well that it is on the surface of the earth that its action is most powerfully felt, while on the contrary, in the very center of the earth bodies cease to have any weight at all."

"I know that is the case, but as we progress will not the atmosphere finally assume the density of water?"

"I know it; when placed under the pressure of seven hundred and ten atmospheres," cried my uncle with imperturbable gravity.

"And when we are still lower down?" I asked with natural anxiety.

"Well, lower down; the density will become even greater still."

"Then how shall we be able to make our way through this atmospheric fog?"

"Well, my worthy nephew, we must ballast ourselves by filling our pockets with stones," said Professor Hardwigg.

"Faith, Uncle, you have an answer for everything," was my only reply.

I began to feel that it was unwise of me to go any farther into the wide field of hypotheses for I should certainly have revived some difficulty, or rather impossibility, that would have enraged the Professor.

It was evident, nevertheless, that the air under a pressure which might be multiplied by thousands of atmospheres, would end by becoming perfectly solid, and that then admitting our bodies resisted the pressure, we should have to stop, in spite of all the reasonings in the world. Facts overcome all arguments.

But I thought it best not to urge this argument. My uncle would simply have quoted the example of Saknussemm. Supposing the learned Icelander's journey ever really to have taken place—there was one simple answer to be made:

In the sixteenth century neither the barometer nor the manometer had been invented—how, then, could Saknussemm have been able to discover when he did reach the center of the earth?

This unanswerable and learned objection I, however, kept to myself and, bracing up my courage, awaited the course of events—little aware of how adventurous yet were to be the incidents of our remarkable journey.

The rest of this day of leisure and repose was spent in calculation and conversation. I made it a point to agree with the Professor in everything; but I envied the perfect indifference of Hans, who, without taking any such trouble about the cause and effect, went blindly onward wherever destiny chose to lead him.

XXIII
Alone

It must in all truth be confessed, things as yet had gone on well, and I should have acted in bad taste to have complained. If the true medium of our difficulties did not increase, it was within the range of possibility that we might ultimately reach the end of our journey. Then what glory would be ours! I began in the newly aroused ardor of my soul to speak enthusiastically to the Professor. Well, was I serious? The whole state in which we existed was a mystery—and it was impossible to know whether or not I was in earnest.

For several days after our memorable halt, the slopes became more rapid—some were even of a most frightful character—almost vertical, so that we were forever going down into the solid interior mass. During some days, we actually descended a league and a half, even two leagues toward the center of the earth. The descents were sufficiently perilous, and while we were engaged in them we learned fully to appreciate the marvelous coolness of our guide, Hans. Without him we should have been wholly lost. The grave and impassible Icelander devoted himself to us with the most incomprehensible *sang-froid* and ease; and, thanks to him, many a dangerous pass was got over, where, but for him, we should inevitably have stuck fast.

His silence increased every day. I think that we began to be influenced by this peculiar trait in his character. It is certain that the inanimate objects by which you are surrounded have a direct action on the brain. It must be that a man who shuts himself up between four walls must lose the faculty of associating ideas and words. How many persons condemned to the horrors of solitary confinement have gone mad—simply because the thinking faculties have lain dormant!

During the two weeks that followed our last interesting conversation, there occurred nothing worthy of being especially recorded.

I have, while writing these memoirs, taxed my memory in vain for one incident of travel during this particular period.

But the next event to be related is terrible indeed. Its very memory, even now, makes my soul shudder, and my blood run cold.

It was on the seventh of August. Our constant and successive descents had taken us quite thirty leagues into the interior of the earth, that is to say that there were above us thirty leagues, nearly a hundred miles, of rocks, and oceans, and continents, and towns, to say nothing of living inhabitants. We were in a southeasterly direction, about two hundred leagues from Iceland.

On that memorable day the tunnel had begun to assume an almost horizontal course.

I was on this occasion walking on in front. My uncle had charge of one of the Ruhmkorf coils, I had possession of the other. By means of its light I was busy examining the different layers of granite. I was completely absorbed in my work.

Suddenly halting and turning around, I found that I was alone!

"Well," thought I to myself, "I have certainly been walking too fast—or else Hans and my uncle have stopped to rest. The best thing I can do is to go back and find them. Luckily, there is very little ascent to tire me."

I accordingly retraced my steps and, while doing so, walked for at least a quarter of an hour. Rather uneasy, I paused and looked eagerly around. Not a living soul. I called aloud. No reply. My voice was lost amid the myriad cavernous echoes it aroused!

I began for the first time to feel seriously uneasy. A cold shiver shook my whole body, and perspiration, chill and terrible, burst upon my skin.

"I must be calm," I said, speaking aloud, as boys whistle to drive away fear. "There can be no doubt that I shall find my companions. There cannot be two roads. It is certain that I was considerably ahead; all I have to do is to go back."

Having come to this determination I ascended the tunnel for at least half an hour, unable to decide if I had ever seen certain landmarks before. Every now and then I paused to discover if any loud appeal was made to me, well knowing that in that dense and intensified atmosphere I should hear it a long way off. But no. The most extraordinary silence reigned in this immense gallery. Only the echoes of my own footsteps could be heard.

At last I stopped. I could scarcely realize the fact of my isolation. I was quite willing to think that I had made a mistake, but not that I was lost. If I had made a mistake, I might find my way; if lost—I shuddered to think of it.

"Come, come," said I to myself, "since there is only one road, and they must come by it, we shall at last meet. All I have to do is still to go upward. Perhaps, however, not seeing me and forgetting I was ahead, they may have gone back in search of me. Still, even in this case, if I make haste, I shall get up to them. There can be no doubt about the matter."

But as I spoke these last words aloud, it would have been quite clear to any listener—had there been one—that I was by no means convinced of the fact. Moreover, in order to associate together these simple ideas and to reunite them under the form of reasoning, required some time. I could not all at once bring my brain to think.

Then another dread doubt fell upon my soul. After all, was I ahead? Of course I was. Hans was no doubt following behind preceded by my uncle. I perfectly recollected his having stopped for a moment to strap his baggage on his shoulder. I now remembered this trifling detail. It was, I believed, just at that very moment that I had determined to continue my route.

"Again," thought I, reasoning as calmly as was possible, "there is another sure means of not losing my way, a thread to guide me through the labyrinthine subterraneous retreat—one which I had forgotten—my faithful river."

This course of reasoning roused my drooping spirits, and I resolved to resume my journey without further delay. No time was to be lost.

It was at this moment that I had reason to bless the thoughtfulness of my uncle, when he refused to allow the eider-down hunter to close the orifices of the hot spring—that small fissure in the great mass of granite. This beneficent spring after having saved us from thirst during so many days would now enable me to regain the right road.

Having come to this mental decision, I made up my mind before I started upward, that ablution would certainly do me a great deal of good.

I stopped to plunge my hands and forehead in the pleasant water of the Hansbach stream, blessing its presence as a certain consolation.

Conceive my horror and stupefaction!—I was treading a hard, dusty, shingly road of granite. The stream on which I reckoned had wholly disappeared!

XXIV

Lost!

No words in any human language can depict my utter despair. I was literally buried alive; with no other expectation before me but to die in the slow horrible torture of hunger and thirst.

Mechanically I crawled about, feeling the dry and arid rock. Never to my fancy had I ever felt anything so dry.

But, I frantically asked myself, how had I lost the course of the flowing stream? There could be no doubt it had ceased to flow in the gallery on which I now was. Now I began to understand the cause of the strange silence which prevailed when last I tried if any appeal from my companions might perchance reach my ear.

It so happened that when I first took an imprudent step in the wrong direction, I did not perceive the absence of the all-important stream.

It was now quite evident that when we halted, another tunnel must have received the waters of the little torrent, and that I had unconsciously entered a different gallery. To what unknown depths had my companions gone? Where was I?

How to get back! Clue or landmark there was absolutely none! My feet left no signs on the granite and shingle. My brain throbbed with agony as I tried to discover the solution of this terrible problem. My situation, after all sophistry and reflection, had finally to be summed up in three awful words—

Lost! LOST! LOST!!!

Lost at a depth which, to my finite understanding, appeared to be immeasurable.

These thirty leagues of the crust of the earth weighed upon my shoulders like the globe on the shoulders of Atlas. I felt myself crushed by the awful weight. It was indeed a position to drive the sanest man to madness!

I tried to bring my thoughts back to the things of the world so long forgotten. It was with the greatest difficulty that I succeeded in doing so. Hamburg, the house on the Königstrasse, my dear cousin Gretchen—all that world which had before vanished like a shadow floated before my vivid imagination.

There they were before me, but how unreal. Under the influence of a terrible hallucination I saw the whole incidents of our journey pass before me like the scenes of a panorama. The ship and its inmates, Iceland, M. Fridriksson, and the great summit of Mount Sneffels! I said to myself that, if in my position I retained the most faint and shadowy outline of a hope, it would be a sure sign of approaching delirium. It were better to give way wholly to despair!

In fact, did I but reason with calmness and philosophy, what human power was there in existence able to take me back to the surface of the earth, and ready, too, to split asunder, to rend in twain those huge and mighty vaults which stand above my head? Who could enable me to find my road—and regain my companions?

Insensate folly and madness to entertain even a shadow of hope!

"Oh, Uncle!" was my despairing cry.

This was the only word of reproach which came to my lips; for I thoroughly understood how deeply and sorrowfully the worthy Professor would regret my loss, and how in his turn he would patiently seek for me.

When I at last began to resign myself to the fact that no further aid was to be expected from man, and knowing that I was utterly powerless to do anything for my own salvation, I kneeled with earnest fervor and asked assistance from Heaven. The remembrance of my innocent childhood, the memory of my mother, known only in my infancy, came welling forth from my heart. I had recourse to prayer. And little as I had a right to be remembered by Him whom I had forgotten in the hour of prosperity, and whom I so tardily invoked, I prayed earnestly and sincerely.

This renewal of my youthful faith brought about a much greater amount of calm, and I was enabled to concentrate all my strength and intelligence on the terrible realities of my unprecedented situation.

I had about me that which I had at first wholly forgotten—three days' provisions. Moreover, my water bottle was quite full. Nevertheless, the one thing which it was impossible to do was to remain alone. Try to find my companions I must, at any price. But which course should I take? Should I go upward or again descend? Doubtless it was right to retrace my steps in an upward direction.

By doing this with care and coolness, I must reach the point where I had turned away from the rippling stream. I must find the fatal bifurcation or fork. Once at this spot, once the river at my feet, I could, at all events, regain the awful crater of Mount Sneffels. Why had I not thought of this before? This, at last, was a reasonable hope of safety. The most important thing, then, to be done was to discover the bed of the Hansbach.

After a slight meal and a draft of water, I rose like a giant refreshed. Leaning heavily on my pole, I began the ascent of the gallery. The slope was very rapid and rather difficult. But I advanced hopefully and carefully, like a man who at last is to follow.

During one whole hour nothing happened to check my progress. As I advanced, I tried to recollect the shape of the tunnel—to recall to my memory projections of rocks—to persuade myself that I had followed certain winding routes before. But no one particular sign could I bring to mind, and I was soon forced to allow that this gallery would never take me back to the point at which I had separated myself from my companions. It was absolutely without issue—a mere blind alley in the earth.

The moment at length cane when, facing the solid rock, I knew my fate, and fell inanimate on the arid floor!

To describe the horrible state of despair and fear into which I then fell would now be vain and impossible. My last hope, the courage which had sustained me, drooped before the sight of this pitiless granite rock!

Lost in a vast labyrinth, the sinuosities of which spread in every direction, without guide, clue, or compass, I knew it was a vain and useless task to attempt flight. All that remained to me was to lie down and die. To lie down and die the most cruel and horrible of deaths!

In my state of mind, the idea came into my head that one day perhaps, when my fossil bones were found, their discovery so far below the level of the earth might give rise to solemn and interesting scientific discussions.

I tried to cry aloud, but hoarse, hollow, and inarticulate sounds alone could make themselves heard through my parched lips. I literally panted for breath.

In the midst of all these horrible sources of anguish and despair, a new horror took possession of my soul. My lamp, by falling down, had got out of order. I had no means of repairing it. Its light was already becoming paler and paler, and soon would expire.

With a strange sense of resignation and despair, I watched the luminous current in the coil getting less and less. A procession of shadows moved flashing along the granite wall. I scarcely dared to lower my eyelids, fearing to lose the last spark of this fugitive light. Every instant it seemed to me that it was about to vanish and to leave me forever—in utter darkness!

At last, one final trembling flame remained in the lamp; I followed it with all my power of vision; I gasped for breath; I concentrated upon it all the power of my soul, as upon the last scintillation of light I was ever destined to see: and then I was to be lost forever in Cimmerian and tenebrous shades.

A wild and plaintive cry escaped my lips. On earth during the most profound and comparatively complete darkness, light never allows a complete destruction and extinction of its power. Light is so diffuse, so subtle, that it permeates everywhere, and whatever little may remain, the retina of the eye will succeed in finding it. In this place nothing—not the faintest ray of light. It amazed me!

My head was now wholly lost. I raised my arm trying the effects of the feeling in getting against the cold stone wall. It was painful in the extreme. Madness must have taken possession of me. I knew not what I did. I began to run, to fly, rushing at haphazard in this inextricable labyrinth, always going downward, running wildly underneath the terrestrial crust, like an inhabitant of the subterranean furnaces, screaming, roaring, howling, until bruised by the pointed rocks, falling and picking myself up all covered with blood which dripped from my torn features, mad because this blood only trickled over my face, and watching always for this horrid wall which ever presented to me the fearful obstacle against which I could not dash my head.

Where was I going? It was impossible to say. I was perfectly ignorant of the matter.

Several hours passed in this way. After a long time, having utterly exhausted my strength, I fell a heavy inert mass along the side of the tunnel, and lost all consciousness of existence!

XXV
THE WHISPERING GALLERY

When at last I came back to a sense of life and being, my face was wet, but wet, as I soon knew, with tears. How long this state of insensibility lasted, it is quite impossible for me now to say. I had no means left to me of taking any account of time. Never since the creation of the world had such a solitude as mine existed. I was completely abandoned.

After my fall I lost much blood. I felt myself flooded with the life-giving liquid. My first sensation was perhaps a natural one. Why was I not dead? Because I was alive, there was something left to do. I tried to make up my mind to think no longer. As far as I was able, I drove away all ideas, and utterly overcome by pain and grief, I crouched against the granite wall.

I just commenced to feel the fainting coming on again, and the sensation that this was the last struggle before complete annihilation—when, on a sudden, a violent uproar reached my ears. It had some resemblance to the prolonged rumbling voice of thunder, and I clearly distinguished sonorous voices, lost one after the other, in the distant depths of the gulf.

Whence came this noise? Naturally, it was to be supposed from new phenomena which were taking place in the bosom of the solid mass of Mother Earth! The explosion of some gaseous vapors, or the fall of some solid, of the granitic or other rock.

Again I listened with deep attention. I was extremely anxious to hear if this strange and inexplicable sound was likely to be renewed! A whole quarter of an hour elapsed in painful expectation. Deep and solemn silence reigned in the tunnel. So still that I could hear the beatings of my own heart! I waited, waited, waited with a strange kind of hopefulness.

Suddenly my ear, which leaned accidentally against the wall, appeared to catch, as it were, the faintest echo of a sound. I thought that I heard vague, incoherent, and distant voices. I quivered all over with excitement and hope!

"It must be hallucination," I cried. "It cannot be! It is not true!"

But no! By listening more attentively, I really did convince myself that what I heard was truly the sound of human voices. To make any meaning out of the sound, however, was beyond my power. I was too weak even to hear distinctly. Still it was a positive fact that someone was speaking. Of that I was quite certain.

There was a moment of fear. A dread fell upon my soul that it might be my own words brought back to me by a distant echo. Perhaps without knowing it, I might have been crying aloud. I resolutely closed my lips, and once more placed my ear to the huge granite wall.

Yes, for certain. It was in truth the sound of human voices.

I now by the exercise of great determination dragged myself along the sides of the cavern, until I reached a point where I could hear more distinctly. But though I could detect the sound, I could only make out uncertain, strange, and incomprehensible words. They reached my ear as if they had been spoken in a low tone—murmured, as it were, afar off.

At last, I made out the word *förlorad* repeated several times in a tone betokening great mental anguish and sorrow.

What could this word mean, and who was speaking it? It must be either my uncle or the guide Hans! If, therefore, I could hear them, they must surely be able to hear me.

"Help," I cried at the top of my voice; "help, I am dying!"

I then listened with scarcely a breath: I panted for the slightest sound in the darkness—a cry, a sigh, a question! But silence reigned supreme. No answer came! In this way some minutes passed. A whole flood of ideas flashed through my mind. I began to fear that my voice, weakened by sickness and suffering, could not reach my companions who were in search of me.

"It must be them," I cried; "what other men can by possibility be buried a hundred miles below the level of the earth?" The mere supposition was preposterous.

I began, therefore, to listen again with the most breathless attention. As I moved my ears along the side of the place I was in, I found a mathematical point as it were, where the voices appeared to attain their maximum of intensity. The word *förlorad* again distinctly reached my ear. Then came again that rolling noise like thunder which had awakened me out of torpor.

"I begin to understand," I said to myself after some little time devoted to reflection; "it is not through the solid mass that the sound reaches my ears. The walls of my cavernous retreat are of solid granite, and the most fearful explosion would not make uproar enough to penetrate them. The sound must come along the gallery itself. The place I was in must possess some peculiar acoustic properties of its own."

Again I listened; and this time—yes, this time—I heard my name distinctly pronounced: cast as it were into space.

It was my uncle, the Professor, who was speaking. He was in conversation with the guide, and the word which had so often reached my ears, *förlorad*, was a Danish expression.

Then I understood it all. In order to make myself heard, I too must speak as it were along the side of the gallery which would carry the sound of my voice just as the wire carries the electric fluid from point to point.

But there was no time to lose. If my companions were only to remove a few feet from where they stood, the acoustic effect would be over, my Whispering Gallery would be destroyed. I again therefore crawled toward the wall, and said as clearly and distinctly as I could:

"Uncle Hardwigg."

I then awaited a reply.

Sound does not possess the property of traveling with such extreme rapidity. Besides, the density of the air at that depth from light and motion was very far from adding to the rapidity of circulation. Several seconds elapsed, which to my excited imagination, appeared ages; and these words reached my eager ears, and moved my wildly beating heart:

"Harry, my boy, is that you?"

A short delay between question and answer.

"Yes—yes."

"Where are you?"

"Lost!"

"And your lamp?"

"Out."

"But the guiding stream?"

"Is lost!"

"Keep your courage, Harry. We will do our best."

"One moment, my uncle," I cried; "I have no longer strength to answer your questions. But—for heaven's sake—do you—continue—to speak—to me!"

Absolute silence, I felt, would be annihilation.

"Keep up your courage," said my uncle. "As you are so weak, do not speak. We have been searching for you in all directions, both by going upward and downward in the gallery. My dear boy, I had begun to give over all hope—and you can never know what bitter tears of sorrow and regret I have shed. At last, supposing you to be still on the road beside the Hansbach, we again descended, firing off guns as signals. Now, however, that we have found you, and that our voices reach each other, it may be a long time before we actually meet. We are conversing by means of some extraordinary acoustic arrangement of the labyrinth. But do not despair, my dear boy. It is something gained even to hear each other."

While he was speaking, my brain was at work reflecting. A certain undefined hope, vague and shapeless as yet, made my heart beat wildly. In the first place, it was absolutely necessary for me to know one thing. I once more, therefore, leaned my head against the wall which I almost touched with my lips, and again spoke.

"Uncle."

"My boy," was his ready answer.

"It is of the utmost consequence that we should know how far we are asunder."

"That is not difficult."

"You have your chronometer at hand?" I asked.

"Certainly."

"Well, take it into your hand. Pronounce my name, noting exactly the second at which you speak. I will reply as soon as I hear your words—and you will then note exactly the moment at which my reply reaches you."

"Very good; and the mean time between my question and your answer will be the time occupied by my voice in reaching you."

"That is exactly what I mean, Uncle," was my eager reply.

"Are you ready?"

"Yes."

"Well, make ready, I am about to pronounce your name," said the Professor.

I applied my ear close to the sides of the cavernous gallery, and as soon as the word "Harry" reached my ear, I turned around and, placing my lips to the wall, repeated the sound.

"Forty seconds," said my uncle. "There has elapsed forty seconds between the two words. The sound, therefore, takes twenty seconds to ascend. Now, allowing a thousand and twenty feet for every second—we have twenty thousand four hundred feet—a league and a half and one-eighth."

These words fell on my soul like a kind of death knell.

"A league and a half," I muttered in a low and despairing voice.

"It shall be got over, my boy," cried my uncle in a cheery tone; "depend on us."

"But do you know whether to ascend or descend?" I asked faintly enough.

"We have to descend, and I will tell you why. You have reached a vast open space, a kind of bare crossroad, from which galleries diverge in every direction. That in which you are now lying must necessarily bring you to this point, for it appears that all these mighty fissures, these fractures of the globe's interior, radiate from the vast cavern which we at this moment occupy. Rouse yourself, then, have courage and continue your route. Walk if you can, if not drag yourself along—slide, if nothing else is possible. The slope, must be rather rapid—and you will find strong arms to receive you at the end of your journey. Make a start, like a good fellow."

These words served to rouse some kind of courage in my sinking frame.

"Farewell for the present, good uncle, I am about to take my departure. As soon as I start, our voices will cease to commingle. Farewell, then, until we meet again."

"Adieu, Harry—until we say Welcome." Such were the last words which reached my anxious ears before I commenced my weary and almost hopeless journey.

This wonderful and surprising conversation which took place through the vast mass of the earth's labyrinth, these words exchanged, the speakers being about five miles apart—ended with hopeful and pleasant expressions. I breathed one more prayer to Heaven, I sent up words of thanksgiving—believing in my inmost heart that He had led me to the only place where the voices of my friends could reach my ears.

This apparently astounding acoustic mystery is easily explainable by simple natural laws; it arose from the conductibility of the rock. There are many instances of this singular propagation of sound which are not perceptible in its less mediate positions. In the interior gallery of St. Paul's, and amid the curious caverns in Sicily, these phenomena are observable. The most marvelous of them all is known as the Ear of Dionysius.

These memories of the past, of my early reading and studies, came fresh into my thoughts. Moreover, I began to reason that if my uncle and I could communicate at so great a distance, no serious obstacle could exist between us. All I had to do was to follow the direction whence the sound had reached me; and, logically putting it, I must reach him if my strength did not fail.

I accordingly rose to my feet. I soon found, however, that I could not walk; that I must drag myself along. The slope, as I expected, was very rapid; but I allowed myself to slip down.

Soon the rapidity of the descent began to assume frightful proportions; and menaced a fearful fall. I clutched at the sides; I grasped at projections of rocks; I threw myself backward. All in vain. My weakness was so great I could do nothing to save myself.

Suddenly earth failed me.

I was first launched into a dark gloomy void. I then struck against the projecting asperities of a vertical gallery, a perfect well. My head bounded against a pointed rock, and I lost all knowledge of existence. As far as I was concerned, death had claimed me for his own.

XXVI
A Rapid Recovery

When I returned to the consciousness of existence, I found myself surrounded by a kind of semiobscurity, lying on some thick soft coverlets. My uncle was watching—his eyes fixed intently on my countenance, a grave expression on his face, a tear in his eye. At the first sigh which struggled from my bosom, he took hold of my hand. When he saw my eyes open and fix themselves upon his, he uttered a loud cry of joy.

"He lives! He lives!"

"Yes, my good uncle," I whispered.

"My dear boy," continued the grim Professor, clasping me to his heart, "you are saved!"

I was deeply and unaffectedly touched by the tone in which these words were uttered, and even more by the kindly care which accompanied them. The Professor, however, was one of those men who must be severely tried in order to induce any display of affection or gentle emotion. At this moment our friend Hans, the guide, joined us. He saw my hand in that of my uncle, and I venture to say that, taciturn as he was, his eyes beamed with lively satisfaction.

"God dag," he said.

"Good day, Hans, good day," I replied, in as hearty a tone as I could assume, "and now, Uncle, that we are together, tell me where we are. I have lost all idea of our position, as of everything else."

"Tomorrow, Harry, tomorrow," he replied. "Today you are far too weak. Your head is surrounded with bandages and poultices that must not be touched. Sleep, my boy, sleep, and tomorrow you will know all that you require."

"But," I cried, "let me know what o'clock it is—what day it is?"

"It is now eleven o'clock at night, and this is once more Sunday. It is now the ninth of the month of August. And I distinctly prohibit you from asking any more questions until the tenth of the same."

I was, if the truth were told, very weak indeed, and my eyes soon closed involuntarily. I did require a good night's rest, and I went off reflecting at the last moment that my perilous adventure in the interior of the earth, in total darkness, had lasted four days!

On the morning of the next day, at my awakening, I began to look around me. My sleeping place, made of all our traveling bedding, was in a charming grotto, adorned with magnificent stalagmites, glittering in all the colors of the rainbow, the floor of soft and silvery sand.

A dim obscurity prevailed. No torch, no lamp was lighted, and yet certain unexplained beams of light penetrated from without, and made their way through the opening of the beautiful grotto.

I, moreover, heard a vague and indefinite murmur, like the ebb and flow of the waves upon a strand, and sometimes I verily believed I could hear the sighing of the wind.

I began to believe that, instead of being awake, I must be dreaming. Surely, had not my brain been affected by my fall, and was not all that occurred during the last twenty-four hours the frenzied visions of madness? And yet after some reflection, a trial of my faculties, I came to the conclusion that I could not be mistaken. Eyes and ears could not surely both deceive me.

"It is a ray of blessed daylight," I said to myself, "which has penetrated through some mighty fissure in the rocks. But what is the meaning of this murmur of waves, this unmistakable moaning of the salt-sea billows? I can hear, too, plainly enough, the whistling of the wind. But can I be altogether mistaken? If my uncle, during my illness, has but carried me back to the surface of the earth! Has he, on my account, given up his wondrous expedition, or in some strange manner has it come to an end?"

I was puzzling my brain over these and other questions, when the Professor joined me.

"Good day, Harry," he cried in a joyous tone. "I fancy you are quite well."

"I am very much better," I replied, actually sitting up in my bed.

"I knew that would be the end of it, as you slept both soundly and tranquilly. Hans and I have each taken turn to watch, and every hour we have seen visible signs of amelioration."

"You must be right, Uncle," was my reply, "for I feel as if I could do justice to any meal you could put before me. I am really hungry."

"You shall eat, my boy, you shall eat. The fever has left you. Our excellent friend Hans has rubbed your wounds and bruises with I know not what ointment, of which the Icelanders alone possess the secret. And they have healed your bruises in the most marvelous manner. Ah, he's a wise fellow, is Master Hans."

While he was speaking, my uncle was placing before me several articles of food, which, despite his earnest injunctions, I readily devoured. As soon as the first rage of hunger was appeased, I overwhelmed him with questions, to which he now no longer hesitated to give answers.

I then learned, for the first time, that my providential fall had brought me to the bottom of an almost perpendicular gallery. As I came down, amidst a perfect shower of stones, the least of which falling on me would have crushed me to death, they came to the conclusion that I had carried with me an entire dislocated rock. Riding as it were on this terrible chariot, I was cast headlong into my uncle's arms. And into them I fell, insensible and covered with blood.

"It is indeed a miracle," was the Professor's final remark, "that you were not killed a thousand times over. But let us take care never to separate; for surely we should risk never meeting again."

"Let us take care never again to separate."

These words fell with a sort of chill upon my heart. The journey, then, was not over. I looked at my uncle with surprise and astonishment. My uncle, after an instant's examination of my countenance, said: "What is the matter, Harry?"

"I want to ask you a very serious question. You say that I am all right in health?"

"Certainly you are."

"And all my limbs are sound and capable of new exertion?" I asked.

"Most undoubtedly."

"But what about my head?" was my next anxious question.

"Well, your head, except that you have one or two contusions, is exactly where it ought to be—on your shoulders," said my uncle, laughing.

"Well, my own opinion is that my head is not exactly right. In fact, I believe myself slightly delirious."

"What makes you think so?"

"I will explain why I fancy I have lost my senses," I cried. "Have we not returned to the surface of Mother Earth?"

"Certainly not."

"Then truly I must be mad, for do I not see the light of day? do I not hear the whistling of the wind? and can I not distinguish the wash of a great sea?"

"And that is all that makes you uneasy?" said my uncle, with a smile.

"Can you explain?"

"I will not make any attempt to explain; for the whole matter is utterly inexplicable. But you shall see and judge for yourself. You will then find that geological science is as yet in its infancy—and that we are doomed to enlighten the world."

"Let us advance, then," I cried eagerly, no longer able to restrain my curiosity.

"Wait a moment, my dear Harry," he responded; "you must take precautions after your illness before going into the open air."

"The open air?"

"Yes, my boy. I have to warn you that the wind is rather violent—and I have no wish for you to expose yourself without necessary precautions."

"But I beg to assure you that I am perfectly recovered from my illness."

"Have just a little patience, my boy. A relapse would be inconvenient to all parties. We have no time to lose—as our approaching sea voyage may be of long duration."

"Sea voyage?" I cried, more bewildered than ever.

"Yes. You must take another day's rest, and we shall be ready to go on board by tomorrow," replied my uncle, with a peculiar smile.

"Go on board!" The words utterly astonished me.

Go on board—what and how? Had we come upon a river, a lake, had we discovered some inland sea? Was a vessel lying at anchor in some part of the interior of the earth?

My curiosity was worked up to the very highest pitch. My uncle made vain attempts to restrain me. When at last, however, he discovered that my feverish impatience would do more harm than good—and that the satisfaction of my wishes could alone restore me to a calm state of mind—he gave way.

I dressed myself rapidly—and then taking the precaution, to please my uncle, of wrapping myself in one of the coverlets, I rushed out of the grotto.

XXVII
The Central Sea

At first I saw absolutely nothing. My eyes, wholly unused to the effulgence of light, could not bear the sudden brightness; and I was compelled to close them. When I was able to reopen them, I stood still, far more stupefied than astonished. Not all the wildest effects of imagination could have conjured up such a scene!

"The sea—the sea," I cried.

"Yes," replied my uncle, in a tone of pardonable pride; "the Central Sea. No future navigator will deny the fact of my having discovered it; and hence of acquiring a right of giving it a name."

It was quite true. A vast, limitless expanse of water, the end of a lake if not of an ocean, spread before us, until it was lost in the distance. The shore, which was very much indented, consisted of a beautiful soft golden sand, mixed with small shells, the long deserted home of some of the creatures of a past age. The waves broke incessantly—and with a peculiarly sonorous murmur, to be found in underground localities. A slight frothy flake arose as the wind blew along the pellucid waters; and many a dash of spray was blown into my face. The mighty superstructure of rock which rose above to an inconceivable height left only a narrow opening—but where we stood, there was a large margin of strand. On all sides were capes and promontories and enormous cliffs, partially worn by the eternal breaking of the waves, through countless ages! And as I gazed from side to side, the mighty rocks faded away like a fleecy film of cloud.

It was in reality an ocean, with all the usual characteristics of an inland sea, only horribly wild—so rigid, cold, and savage.

One thing startled and puzzled me greatly. How was it that I was able to look upon that vast sheet of water instead of being plunged in utter darkness? The vast landscape before me was lit up like day. But there was wanting the dazzling brilliancy, the splendid irradiation of the sun; the pale cold illuminating power in this subterraneous region, from its trembling and flickering character, its clear dry whiteness, the very slight elevation of its temperature, its great superiority to that of the moon, was evidently electric; something in the nature of the aurora borealis, only that its phenomena were constant, and able to light up the whole of the ocean cavern.

The tremendous vault above our heads, the sky, so to speak, appeared to be composed of a conglomeration of nebulous vapors, in constant motion. I should originally have supposed that, under such an atmospheric pressure as must exist in that place, the evaporation of water could not really take place, and yet from the action of some physical law, which escaped my memory, there were heavy and dense clouds rolling along that mighty vault, partially concealing the roof. Electric currents produced astonishing play of light and shade in the distance, especially around the heavier clouds. Deep shadows were cast beneath, and then suddenly, between two clouds, there would come a ray of unusual beauty, and remarkable intensity. And yet it was not like the sun, for it gave no heat.

The effect was sad and excruciatingly melancholy. Instead of a noble firmament of blue, studded with stars, there was above me a heavy roof of granite, which seemed to crush me.

Gazing around, I began to think of the theory of the English captain who compared the earth to a vast hollow sphere in the interior of which the air is retained in a luminous state by means of atmospheric pressure, while two stars, Pluto and Proserpine, circled there in their mysterious orbits. After all, suppose the old fellow was right!

In truth, we were imprisoned—bound, as it were, in a vast excavation. Its width it was impossible to make out; the shore, on either hand, widening rapidly until lost to sight; while its length was equally uncertain. A haze on the distant horizon bounded our view. As to its height, we could see that it must be many miles to the roof. Looking upward, it was impossible to discover where the stupendous roof began. The lowest of the clouds must have been floating at an elevation of two thousand yards, a height greater than that of terrestrial vapors, which circumstance was doubtless owing to the extreme density of the air.

I use the word cavern in order to give an idea of the place. I cannot describe its awful grandeur; human language fails to convey an idea of its savage sublimity. Whether this singular vacuum had or had not been caused by the sudden cooling of the earth when in a state of fusion, I could not say. I had read of most wonderful and gigantic caverns—but none in any way like this.

The great grotto of Guachara, in Colombia, visited by the learned Humboldt; the vast and partially explored Mammoth Cave in Kentucky—what were these holes in the earth to that in which I stood in speechless admiration! with its vapory clouds, its electric light, and the mighty ocean slumbering in its bosom! Imagination, not description, can alone give an idea of the splendor and vastness of the cave.

I gazed at these marvels in profound silence. Words were utterly wanting to indicate the sensations of wonder I experienced. I seemed, as I stood upon that mysterious shore, as if I were some wandering inhabitant of a distant planet, present for the first time at the spectacle of some terrestrial phenomena belonging to another existence. To give body and existence to such new sensations would have required the coinage of new words—and here my feeble brain found itself wholly at fault. I looked on, I thought, I reflected, I admired, in a state of stupefaction not altogether unmingled with fear!

The unexpected spectacle restored some color to my pallid cheeks. I seemed to be actually getting better under the influence of this novelty. Moreover, the vivacity of the dense atmosphere reanimated my body by inflating my lungs with unaccustomed oxygen.

It will be readily conceived that after an imprisonment of forty-seven days, in a dark and miserable tunnel, it was with infinite delight that I breathed the saline air. It was like the genial, reviving of the salt sea waves.

My uncle had already got over the first surprise.

With the Latin poet Horace his idea was that—

Not to admire is all the art I know,
To make man happy and to keep him so.

"Well," he said, after giving me time thoroughly to appreciate the marvels of this underground sea, "do you feel strong enough to walk up and down?"

"Certainly," was my ready answer, "nothing would give me greater pleasure."

"Well then, my boy," he said, "lean on my arm, and we will stroll along the beach."

I accepted his offer eagerly, and we began to walk along the shores of this extraordinary lake. To our left were abrupt rocks, piled one upon the other—a stupendous titanic pile; down their sides leaped innumerable cascades, which at last, becoming limpid and murmuring streams, were lost in the waters of the lake. Light vapors, which rose here and and there, and floated in fleecy clouds from rock to rock, indicated hot springs, which also poured their superfluity into the vast reservoir at our feet.

Among them I recognized our old and faithful stream, the Hansbach, which, lost in the wild basin, seemed as if it had been flowing since the creation of the world.

"We shall miss our excellent friend," I remarked, with a deep sigh.

"Bah!" said my uncle testily, "what matters it. That or another, it is all the same."

I thought the remark ungrateful, and felt almost inclined to say so; but I forbore.

At this moment my attention was attracted by an unexpected spectacle. After we had gone about five hundred yards, we suddenly turned a steep promontory, and found ourselves close to a lofty forest! It consisted of straight trunks with tufted tops, in shape like parasols. The air seemed to have no effect upon these trees—which in spite of a tolerable breeze remained as still and motionless as if they had been petrified.

I hastened forward. I could find no name for these singular formations. Did they not belong to the two thousand and more known trees—or were we to make the discovery of a new growth? By no means. When we at last reached the forest, and stood beneath the trees, my surprise gave way to admiration.

In truth, I was simply in the presence of a very ordinary product of the earth, of singular and gigantic proportions. My uncle unhesitatingly called them by their real names.

"It is only," he said, in his coolest manner, "a forest of mushrooms."

On close examination I found that he was not mistaken. Judge of the development attained by this product of damp hot soils. I had heard that the *Lycoperdon giganteum* reaches nine feet in circumference, but here were white mushrooms, nearly forty feet high, and with tops of equal dimensions. They grew in countless thousands—the light could not make its way through their massive substance, and beneath them reigned a gloomy and mystic darkness.

Still I wished to go forward. The cold in the shades of this singular forest was intense. For nearly an hour we wandered about in this darkness visible. At length I left the spot, and once more returned to the shores of the lake, to light and comparative warmth.

But the amazing vegetation of subterraneous land was not confined to gigantic mushrooms. New wonders awaited us at every step. We had not gone many hundred yards, when we came upon a mighty group of other trees with discolored leaves—the common humble trees of Mother Earth, of an exorbitant and phenomenal size: lycopodes a hundred feet high; flowering ferns as tall as pines; gigantic grasses!

"Astonishing, magnificent, splendid!" cried my uncle; "here we have before us the whole flora of the second period of the world, that of transition. Behold the humble plants of our gardens, which in the first ages of the world were mighty trees. Look around you, my dear Harry. No botanist ever before gazed on such a sight!"

My uncle's enthusiasm, always a little more than was required, was now excusable.

"You are right, Uncle," I remarked. "Providence appears to have designed the preservation in this vast and mysterious hothouse of antediluvian plants, to prove the sagacity of learned men in figuring them so marvelously on paper."

"Well said, my boy—very well said; it is indeed a mighty hothouse. But you would also be within the bounds of reason and common sense, if you also added—a vast menagerie."

I looked rather anxiously around. If the animals were as exaggerated as the plants, the matter would certainly be serious.

"A menagerie?"

"Doubtless. Look at the dust we are treading underfoot—behold the bones with which the whole soil of the seashore in covered—"

"Bones," I replied, "yes, certainly, the bones of antediluvian animals."

I stooped down as I spoke, and picked up one or two singular remains, relics of a bygone age. It was easy to give a name to these gigantic bones, in some instances as big as trunks of trees.

"Here is, clearly, the lower jawbone of a mastedon," I cried, almost as warmly and enthusiastically as my uncle; "here are the molars of the dinotherium; here is a leg bone which belonged to the megatherium. You are right, Uncle, it is indeed a menagerie; for the mighty animals to which these bones once belonged, have lived and died on the shores of this subterranean sea, under the shadow of these plants. Look, yonder are whole skeletons—and yet—"

"And yet, nephew?" said my uncle, noticing that I suddenly came to a full stop.

"I do not understand the presence of such beasts in granite caverns, however vast and prodigious," was my reply.

"Why not?" said my uncle, with very much of his old professional impatience.

"Because it is well known that animal life only existed on earth during the secondary period, when the sedimentary soil was formed by the alluviums, and thus replaced the hot and burning rocks of the primitive age."

"I have listened to you earnestly and with patience, Harry, and I have a simple and clear answer to your objections: and that is, that this itself is a sedimentary soil."

"How can that be at such enormous depth from the surface of the earth?"

"The fact can be explained both simply and geologically. At a certain period, the earth consisted only of an elastic crust, liable to alternative upward and downward movements in virtue of the law of attraction. It is very probable that many a landslip took place in those days, and that large portions of sedimentary soil were cast into huge and mighty chasms."

"Quite possible," I dryly remarked. "But, Uncle, if these antediluvian animals formerly lived in these subterranean regions, what more likely that one of these huge monsters may at this moment be concealed behind one of yonder mighty rocks."

As I spoke, I looked keenly around, examining with care every point of the horizon; but nothing alive appeared to exist on these deserted shores.

I now felt rather fatigued, and told my uncle so. The walk and excitement were too much for me in my weak state. I therefore seated myself at the end of a promontory, at the foot of which the waves broke in incessant rolls. I looked around a bay formed by projections of vast granite rocks. At the extreme end was a little port protected by huge pyramids of stones. A brig and three or four schooners might have lain there with perfect ease. So natural did it seem, that every minute my imagination induced me to expect a vessel coming out under all sail and making for the open sea under the influence of a warm southerly breeze.

But the fantastic illusion never lasted more than a minute. We were the only living creatures in this subterranean world!

During certain periods there was an utter cessation of wind, when a silence deeper, more terrible than the silence of the desert fell upon these solitary and arid rocks—and seemed to hang like a leaden weight upon the waters of this singular ocean. I sought, amid the awful stillness, to penetrate through the distant fog, to tear down the veil which concealed the mysterious distance. What unspoken words were murmured by my trembling lips—what questions did I wish to ask and did not! Where did this sea end—to what did it lead? Should we ever be able to examine its distant shores?

But my uncle had no doubts about the matter. He was convinced that our enterprise would in the end be successful. For my part, I was in a state of painful indecision—I desired to embark on the journey and to succeed, and still I feared the result.

After we had passed an hour or more in silent contemplation of the wondrous spectacle, we rose and went down toward the bank on our way to the grotto, which I was not sorry to gain. After a slight repast, I sought refuge in slumber, and at length, after many and tedious struggles, sleep came over my weary eyes.

XXVIII

Launching the Raft

On the morning of the next day, to my great surprise, I awoke completely restored. I thought a bath would be delightful after my long illness and sufferings. So, soon after rising, I went and plunged into the waters of this new Mediterranean. The bath was cool, fresh, and invigorating.

I came back to breakfast with an excellent appetite. Hans, our worthy guide, thoroughly understood how to cook such eatables as we were able to provide; he had both fire and water at discretion, so that he was enabled slightly to vary the weary monotony of our ordinary repast.

Our morning meal was like a capital English breakfast, with coffee by way of a wind up. And never had this delicious beverage been so welcome and refreshing.

My uncle had sufficient regard for my state of health not to interrupt me in the enjoyment of the meal, but he was evidently delighted when I had finished.

"Now then," said he, "come with me. It is the height of the tide, and I am anxious to study its curious phenomena."

"What," I cried, rising in astonishment, "did you say the tide, Uncle?"

"Certainly I did."

"You do not mean to say," I replied, in a tone of respectful doubt, "that the influence of the sun and moon is felt here below."

"And pray why not? Are not all bodies influenced by the law of universal attraction? Why should this vast underground sea be exempt from the general law, the rule of the universe? Besides, there is nothing like that which is proved and demonstrated. Despite the great atmospheric pressure down here, you will notice that this inland sea rises and falls with as much regularity as the Atlantic itself."

As my uncle spoke, we reached the sandy shore, and saw and heard the waves breaking monotonously on the beach. They were evidently rising.

"This is truly the flood," I cried, looking at the water at my feet.

"Yes, my excellent nephew," replied my uncle rubbing his hands with the gusto of a philosopher, "and you see by these several streaks of foam that the tide rises at least ten or twelve feet."

"It is indeed marvelous."

"By no means," he responded; "on the contrary, it is quite natural."

"It may appear so in your eyes, my dear uncle," was my reply, "but the whole phenomena of the place appear to me to partake of the marvelous. It is almost impossible to believe that which I see. Who in his wildest dreams could have imagined that, beneath the crust of our earth, there could exist a real ocean, with ebbing and flowing tides, with its changes of winds, and even its storms. I for one should have laughed the suggestion to scorn."

"But, Harry, my boy, why not?" inquired my uncle, with a pitying smile; "is there any physical reason in opposition to it?"

"Well, if we give up the great theory of the central heat of the earth, I certainly can offer no reasons why anything should be looked upon as impossible."

"Then you will own," he added, "that the system of Sir Humphry Davy is wholly justified by what we have seen?"

"I allow that it is—and that point once granted, I certainly can see no reason for doubting the existence of seas and other wonders, even countries, in the interior of the globe."

"That is so—but of course these varied countries are uninhabited?"

"Well, I grant that it is more likely than not: still, I do not see why this sea should not have given shelter to some species of unknown fish."

"Hitherto we have not discovered any, and the probabilities are rather against our ever doing so," observed the Professor.

I was losing my skepticism in the presence of these wonders.

"Well, I am determined to solve the question. It is my intention to try my luck with my fishing line and hook."

"Certainly; make the experiment," said my uncle, pleased with my enthusiasm. "While we are about it, it will certainly be only proper to discover all the secrets of this extraordinary region."

"But, after all, where are we now?" I asked; "all this time I have quite forgotten to ask you a question, which, doubtless, your philosophical instruments have long since answered."

"Well," replied the Professor, "examining the situation from only one point of view, we are now distant three hundred and fifty leagues from Iceland."

"So much?" was my exclamation.

"I have gone over the matter several times, and am sure not to have made a mistake of five hundred yards," replied my uncle positively.

"And as to the direction—are we still going to the southeast?"

"Yes, with a western declination* of nineteen degrees, forty-two minutes, just as it is above. As for the inclination† I have discovered a very curious fact."

"What may that be, Uncle? Your information interests me."

"Why that the needle, instead of dipping toward the pole as it does on earth, in the northern hemisphere, has an upward tendency."

"This proves," I cried, "that the great point of magnetic attraction lies somewhere between the surface of the earth and the spot we have succeeded in reaching."

"Exactly, my observant nephew," exclaimed my uncle, elated and delighted, "and it is quite probable that if we succeed in getting toward the polar regions—somewhere near the seventy-third degree of latitude, where Sir James Ross discovered the magnetic pole, we shall behold the needle point directly upward. We have therefore discovered by analogy, that this great center of attraction is not situated at a very great depth."

"Well," said I, rather surprised, "this discovery will astonish experimental philosophers. It was never suspected."

"Science, great, mighty, and in the end, unerring," replied my uncle dogmatically, "science has fallen into many errors—errors which have

* The declination is the variation of the needle from the true meridian of a place.
† Inclination is the dip of the magnetic needle with a tendency to incline toward the earth.

been fortunate and useful rather than otherwise, for they have been the stepping stones to truth."

After some further discussion, I turned to another matter.

"Have you any idea of the depth we have reached?"

"We are now," continued the Professor, "exactly thirty-five leagues—above a hundred miles—down into the interior of the earth."

"So," said I, after measuring the distance on the map, "we are now beneath the Scottish Highlands, and have over our heads the lofty Grampian hills."

"You are quite right," said the Professor, laughing; "it sounds very alarming, the weight being heavy—but the vault which supports this vast mass of earth and rock is solid and safe; the mighty Architect of the Universe has constructed it of solid materials. Man, even in his highest flights of vivid and poetic imagination, never thought of such things! What are the finest arches of our bridges, what the vaulted roofs of our cathedrals, to that mighty dome above us, and beneath which floats an ocean with its storms and calms and tides!"

"I admire it all as much as you can, Uncle, and have no fear that our granite sky will fall upon our heads. But now that we have discussed matters of science and discovery, what are your future intentions? Are you not thinking of getting back to the surface of our beautiful earth?"

This was said more as a feeler than with any hope of success.

"Go back, nephew," cried my uncle in a tone of alarm, "you are not surely thinking of anything so absurd or cowardly. No, my intention is to advance and continue our journey. We have as yet been singularly fortunate, and henceforth I hope we shall be more so."

"But," said I, "how are we to cross yonder liquid plain?"

"It is not my intention to leap into it head foremost, or even to swim across it, like Leander over the Hellespont. But as oceans are, after all, only great lakes, inasmuch as they are surrounded by land, so does it stand to reason, that this central sea is circumscribed by granite surroundings."

"Doubtless," was my natural reply.

"Well, then, do you not think that when once we reach the other end, we shall find some means of continuing our journey?"

"Probably, but what extent do you allow to this internal ocean?"

"Well, I should fancy it to extend about forty or fifty leagues—more or less."

"But even supposing this approximation to be a correct one—what then?" I asked.

"My dear boy, we have no time for further discussion. We shall embark tomorrow."

I looked around with surprise and incredulity. I could see nothing in the shape of boat or vessel.

"What!" I cried, "we are about to launch out upon an unknown sea; and where, if I may ask, is the vessel to carry us?"

"Well, my dear boy, it will not be exactly what you would call a vessel. For the present we must be content with a good and solid raft."

"A raft," I cried, incredulously, "but down here a raft is as impossible of construction as a vessel—and I am at a loss to imagine—"

"My good Harry—if you were to listen instead of talking so much, you would hear," said my uncle, waxing a little impatient.

"I should hear?"

"Yes—certain knocks with the hammer, which Hans is now employing to make the raft. He has been at work for many hours."

"Making a raft?"

"Yes."

"But where has he found trees suitable for such a construction?"

"He found the trees all ready to his hand. Come, and you shall see our excellent guide at work."

More and more amazed at what I heard and saw, I followed my uncle like one in a dream.

After a walk of about a quarter of an hour, I saw Hans at work on the other side of the promontory which formed our natural port. A few minutes more and I was beside him. To my great surprise, on the sandy shore lay a half-finished raft. It was made from beams of a very peculiar wood, and a great number of limbs, joints, boughs, and pieces lay about, sufficient to have constructed a fleet of ships and boats.

I turned to my uncle, silent with astonishment and awe.

"Where did all this wood come from?" I cried; "what wood is it?"

"Well, there is pinewood, fir, and the palms of the northern regions, mineralized by the action of the sea," he replied, sententiously.

"Can it be possible?"

"Yes," said the learned Professor, "what you see is called fossil wood."

"But then," cried I, after reflecting for a moment, "like the lignites, it must be as hard and as heavy as iron, and therefore will certainly not float."

"Sometimes that is the case. Many of these woods have become true anthracites, but others again, like those you see before you, have only undergone one phase of fossil transformation. But there is no proof like demonstration," added my uncle, picking one or two of these precious waifs and casting them into the sea.

The piece of wood, after having disappeared for a moment, came to the surface and floated about with the oscillation produced by wind and tide.

"Are you convinced?" said my uncle, with a self-satisfied smile.

"I am convinced," I cried, "that what I see is incredible."

The fact was that my journey into the interior of the earth was rapidly changing all preconceived notions and day by day preparing me for the marvelous.

I should not have been surprised to have seen a fleet of native canoes afloat upon that silent sea.

The very next evening, thanks to the industry and ability of Hans, the raft was finished. It was about ten feet long and five feet wide. The beams, bound together with stout ropes, were solid and firm, and once launched by our united efforts, the improvised vessel floated tranquilly upon the waters of what the Professor had well named the Central Sea.

XXIX

On the Waters—a Raft Voyage

On the thirteenth of August we were up betimes. There was no time to be lost. We now had to inaugurate a new kind of locomotion, which would have the advantage of being rapid and not fatiguing.

A mast, made of two pieces of wood fastened together, to give additional strength, a yard made from another one, the sail a linen sheet from our bed. We were fortunately in no want of cordage, and the whole on trial appeared solid and seaworthy.

At six o'clock in the morning, when the eager and enthusiastic Professor gave the signal to embark, the victuals, the luggage, all our instruments, our weapons, and a goodly supply of sweet water, which we had collected from springs in the rocks, were placed on the raft.

Hans had, with considerable ingenuity, contrived a rudder, which enabled him to guide the floating apparatus with ease. He took the tiller, as a matter of course. The worthy man was as good a sailor as he was a guide and duck hunter. I then let go the painter which held us to the shore, the sail was brought to the wind, and we made a rapid offing.

Our sea voyage had at length commenced; and once more we were making for distant and unknown regions.

Just as we were about to leave the little port where the raft had been constructed, my uncle, who was very strong as to geographic nomenclature, wanted to give it a name, and among others suggested mine.

"Well," said I, "before you decide I have another to propose."

"Well, out with it."

"I should like to call it Gretchen. Port Gretchen will sound very well on our future map."

"Well then, Port Gretchen let it be," said the Professor.

And thus it was that the memory of my dear girl was attached to our adventurous and memorable expedition.

When we left the shore the wind was blowing from the northward and eastward. We went directly before the wind at a much greater speed than might have been expected from a raft. The dense layers of atmosphere at that depth had great propelling power and acted upon the sail with considerable force.

At the end of an hour, my uncle, who had been taking careful observations, was enabled to judge of the rapidity with which we moved. It was far beyond anything seen in the upper world.

"If," he said, "we continue to advance at our present rate, we shall have traveled at least thirty leagues in twenty-four hours. With a mere raft this is an almost incredible velocity."

I certainly was surprised, and without making any reply, went forward upon the raft. Already the northern shore was fading away on the edge of the horizon. The two shores appeared to separate more and more, leaving a wide and open space for our departure. Before me I could see nothing but the vast and apparently limitless sea—upon which we floated—the only living objects in sight.

Huge and dark clouds cast their gray shadows below—shadows which seemed to crush that colorless and sullen water by their weight. Anything more suggestive of gloom and of regions of nether darkness I never beheld. Silvery rays of electric light, reflected here and there upon some small spots of water, brought up luminous sparkles in the long wake of our cumbrous bark. Presently we were wholly out of sight of land; not a vestige could be seen, nor any indication of where we were going. So still and motionless did we seem without any distant point to fix our eyes on that but for the phosphoric light at the wake of the raft, I should have fancied that we were still and motionless.

But I knew that we were advancing at a very rapid rate.

About twelve o'clock in the day, vast collections of seaweed were discovered surrounding us on all sides. I was aware of the extraordinary vegetative power of these plants, which have been known to creep along the bottom of the great ocean, and stop the advance of large ships. But never were seaweeds ever seen, so gigantic and wonderful as those of the Central Sea. I could well imagine how, seen at a distance, tossing and heaving on the summit of the billows, the long lines of algæ have been taken for living things, and thus have been the fertile sources of the belief in sea serpents.

Our raft swept past great specimens of fucæ or seawrack, from three to four thousand feet in length, immense, incredibly long, looking like snakes that stretched out far beyond our horizon. It afforded me great amusement to gaze on their variegated ribbonlike endless lengths. Hour after hour passed without our coming to the termination of these floating weeds. If my astonishment increased, my patience was well nigh exhausted.

What natural force could possibly have produced such abnormal and extraordinary plants? What must have been the aspect of the globe, during the first centuries of its formation, when under the combined action of heat and humidity, the vegetable kingdom occupied its vast surface to the exclusion of everything else?

These were considerations of never-ending interest for the geologist and the philosopher.

All this while we were advancing on our journey; and at length night came; but as I had remarked the evening before, the luminous state of the atmosphere was in nothing diminished. Whatever was the cause, it was a phenomenon upon the duration of which we could calculate with certainty.

As soon as our supper had been disposed of, and some little speculative conversation indulged in, I stretched myself at the foot of the mast, and presently went to sleep.

Hans remained motionless at the tiller, allowing the raft to rise and fall on the waves. The wind being aft, and the sail square, all he had to do was to keep his oar in the center.

Ever since we had taken our departure from the newly named Port Gretchen, my worthy uncle had directed me to keep a regular log of our day's navigation, with instructions to put down even the most minute particulars, every interesting and curious phenomenon, the direction of the wind, our rate of sailing, the distance we went; in a word, every incident of our extraordinary voyage.

From our log, therefore, I tell the story of our voyage on the Central Sea.

Friday, August 14th. A steady breeze from the northwest. Raft progressing with extreme rapidity, and going perfectly straight. Coast still dimly visible about thirty leagues to leeward. Nothing to be seen beyond the horizon in front. The extraordinary intensity of the light neither increases nor diminishes. It is singularly stationary. The weather remarkably fine; that is to say, the clouds have ascended very high, and are light and fleecy, and surrounded by an atmosphere resembling silver in fusion.

Thermometer, + 32 degrees centigrade.

About twelve o'clock in the day our guide Hans having prepared and baited a hook, cast his line into the subterranean waters. The bait he used was a small piece of meat, by means of which he concealed his hook. Anxious as I was, I was for a long time doomed to disappointment. Were these waters supplied with fish or not? That was the important question. No—was my decided answer. Then there came a sudden and rather hard tug. Hans coolly drew it in, and with it a fish, which struggled violently to escape.

"A fish," cried my uncle, putting on his spectacles to examine it.

"It is a sturgeon!" I cried, "certainly a small sturgeon."

The Professor examined the fish carefully, noting every characteristic; and he did not coincide in my opinion. The fish had a flat head, round body, and the lower extremities covered with body scales; its mouth was wholly without teeth, the pectoral fins, which were highly developed, sprouted directly from the body, which properly speaking had no tail. The animal certainly belonged to the order in which naturalists class the sturgeon, but it differed from that fish in many essential particulars.

My uncle, after all, was not mistaken. After a long and patient examination, he said:

"This fish, my dear boy, belongs to a family which has been extinct for ages, and of which no trace has ever been found on earth, except fossil remains in the Devonian strata."

"You do not mean to say," I cried, "that we have captured a live specimen of a fish belonging to the primitive stock that existed before the deluge?"

"We have," said the Professor, who all this time was continuing his observations, "and you may see by careful examination that these fossil fish have no identity with existing species. To hold in one's hand, therefore, a living specimen of the order, is enough to make a naturalist happy for life."

"But," cried I, "to what family does it belong?"

"To the order of Ganoides—an order of fish having angular scales, covered with bright enamel—forming one of the family of the Cephalaspides, of the genus—"

"Well, sir," I remarked, as I noticed my uncle hesitated to conclude.

"To the genus Pterychtis—yes, I am certain of it. Still, though I am confident of the correctness of my surmise, this fish offers to our notice a remarkable peculiarity, never known to exist in any other fish but those which are the natives of subterranean waters, wells, lakes, in caverns, and such like hidden pools."

"And what may that be?"

"It is blind."

"Blind!" I cried, much surprised.

"Not only blind," continued the Professor, "but absolutely without organs of sight."

I now examined our discovery for myself. It was singular, to be sure, but it was really a fact. This, however, might be a solitary instance, I suggested. The hook was baited again and once more thrown into the water. This subterranean ocean must have been tolerably well supplied with fish, for in two hours we took a large number of Pterychtis, as well as other fish belonging to another supposed extinct family—the Dipterides (a genus of fish, furnished with two fins only, whence the name), though my uncle could not class it exactly. All, without exception, however, were blind. This unexpected capture enabled us to renew our stock of provisions in a very satisfactory way.

We were now convinced that this subterranean sea contained only fish known to us as fossil specimens—and fish and reptiles alike were all the more perfect the farther back they dated their origin.

We began to hope that we should find some of those Saurians which science has succeeded in reconstructing from bits of bone or cartilage.

I took up the telescope and carefully examined the horizon—looked over the whole sea; it was utterly and entirely deserted. Doubtless we were still too near the coast.

After an examination of the ocean, I looked upward, toward the strange and mysterious sky. Why should not one of the birds reconstructed by the immortal Cuvier flap his stupendous wings aloft in the dull strata of subterranean air? It would, of course, find quite sufficient food from the fish in the sea. I gazed for some time upon the void above. It was as silent and as deserted as the shores we had but lately left.

Nevertheless, though I could neither see nor discover anything, my imagination carried me away into wild hypotheses. I was in a kind of waking dream. I thought I saw on the surface of the water those enormous antediluvian turtles as big as floating islands. Upon those dull and somber shores passed a spectral row of the mammifers of early days, the great Leptotherium found in the cavernous hollow of the Brazilian hills, the Mesicotherium, a native of the glacial regions of Siberia.

Farther on, the pachydermatous Lophrodon, that gigantic tapir, which concealed itself behind rocks, ready to do battle for its prey with the Anoplotherium, a singular animal partaking of the nature of the rhinoceros, the horse, the hippopotamus, and the camel.

There was the giant Mastodon, twisting and turning his horrid trunk, with which he crushed the rocks of the shore to powder, while the Megatherium—his back raised like a cat in a passion, his enormous claws stretched out, dug into the earth for food, at the same time that he awoke the sonorous echoes of the whole place with his terrible roar.

Higher up still, the first monkey ever seen on the face of the globe clambered, gamboling and playing up in the granite hills. Still father away, ran the Pterodactyl, with the winged hand, gliding or rather sailing through the dense and compressed air like a huge bat.

Above all, near the leaden granite sky, were immense birds, more powerful than the casoar, giants to the ostrich, which spread their mighty wings and fluttered against the huge stone vault of the inland sea.

I thought, such was the effect of my imagination, that I saw this whole tribe of antediluvian creatures. I carried myself back to far ages, long before man existed—when, in fact, the earth was in too imperfect a state for him to live upon it.

My dream was of countless ages before the existence of man. The mammifers first disappeared, then the mighty birds, then the reptiles of the secondary period, presently the fish, the crustacea, the mollusks, and finally the vertebrata. The zoophytes of the period of transition in their turn sank into annihilation.

The whole panorama of the world's life before the historic period, seemed to be born over again, and mine was the only human heart that beat in this unpeopled world! There were no more seasons; there were no more climates; the natural heat of the world increased unceasingly, and neutralized that of the great radiant Sun.

Vegetation was exaggerated in an extraordinary manner. I passed like a shadow in the midst of brushwood as lofty as the giant trees of California, and trod underfoot the moist and humid soil, reeking with a rank and varied vegetation.

I leaned against the huge column-like trunks of giant trees, to which those of Canada were as ferns. Whole ages passed, hundreds upon hundreds of years were concentrated into a single day.

Next, unrolled before me like a panorama, came the great and wondrous series of terrestrial transformations. Plants disappeared; the granitic rocks lost all trace of solidity; the liquid state was suddenly substituted for that which had before existed. This was caused by intense heat acting on the organic matter of the earth. The waters flowed over the whole surface of the globe; they boiled; they were volatilized, or turned into vapor; a kind of steam cloud wrapped the whole earth, the globe itself becoming at last nothing but one huge sphere of gas, indescribable in color, between white heat and red, as big and as brilliant as the sun.

In the very center of this prodigious mass, fourteen hundred thousand times as large as our globe, I was whirled around in space, and brought into close conjunction with the planets. My body was subtilized, or rather became volatile, and commingled in a state of atomic vapor, with the prodigious clouds, which rushed forward like a mighty comet into infinite space!

What an extraordinary dream! Where would it finally take me? My feverish hand began to write down the marvelous details—details more like the imaginings of a lunatic than anything sober and real. I had during this period of hallucination forgotten everything—the Professor, the guide, and the raft on which we were floating. My mind was in a state of semioblivion.

"What is the matter, Harry?" said my uncle suddenly.

My eyes, which were wide opened like those of a somnambulist, were fixed upon him, but I did not see him, nor could I clearly make out anything around me.

"Take care, my boy," again cried my uncle, "you will fall into the sea."

As he uttered these words, I felt myself seized on the other side by the firm hand of our devoted guide. Had it not been for the presence of mind of Hans, I must infallibily have fallen into the waves and been drowned.

"Have you gone mad?" cried my uncle, shaking me on the other side.

"What—what is the matter?" I said at last, coming to myself.

"Are you ill, Henry?" continued the Professor in an anxious tone.

"No—no; but I have had an extraordinary dream. It, however, has passed away. All now seems well," I added, looking around me with strangely puzzled eyes.

"All right," said my uncle; "a beautiful breeze, a splendid sea. We are going along at a rapid rate, and if I am not out in my calculations we shall soon see land. I shall not be sorry to exchange the narrow limits of our raft for the mysterious strand of the subterranean ocean."

As my uncle uttered these words, I rose and carefully scanned the horizon. But the line of water was still confounded with the lowering clouds that hung aloft, and in the distance appeared to touch the edge of the water.

XXX

TERRIFIC SAURIAN COMBAT

Saturday, August 15th. The sea still retains its uniform monotony. The same leaden hue, the same eternal glare from above. No indication of land being in sight. The horizon appears to retreat before us, more and more as we advance.

My head, still dull and heavy from the effects of my extraordinary dream, which I cannot as yet banish from my mind.

The Professor, who has not dreamed, is, however, in one of his morose and unaccountable humors. Spends his time in scanning the horizon, at every point of the compass. His telescope is raised every moment to his eyes, and when he finds nothing to give any clue to our whereabouts, he assumes a Napoleonic attitude and walks anxiously.

I remarked that my uncle, the Professor, had a strong tendency to resume his old impatient character, and I could not but make a note of this disagreeable circumstance in my journal. I saw clearly that it had required all the influence of my danger and suffering, to extract from him one scintillation of humane feeling. Now that I was quite recovered, his original nature had conquered and obtained the upper hand.

And, after all, what had he to be angry and annoyed about, now more than at any other time? Was not the journey being accomplished under the most favorable circumstances? Was not the raft progressing with the most marvelous rapidity?

What, then, could be the matter? After one or two preliminary hems, I determined to inquire.

"You seem uneasy, Uncle," said I, when for about the hundredth time he put down his telescope and walked up and down, muttering to himself.

"No, I am not uneasy," he replied in a dry harsh tone, "by no means."

"Perhaps I should have said impatient," I replied, softening the force of my remark.

"Enough to make me so, I think."

"And yet we are advancing at a rate seldom attained by a raft," I remarked.

"What matters that?" cried my uncle. "I am not vexed at the rate we go at, but I am annoyed to find the sea so much vaster than I expected."

I then recollected that the Professor, before our departure, had estimated the length of this subterranean ocean as at most about thirty leagues. Now we had traveled at least over thrice that distance without discovering any trace of the distant shore. I began to understand my uncle's anger.

"We are not going down," suddenly exclaimed the Professor. "We are not progressing with our great discoveries. All this is utter loss of time. After all, I did not come from home to undertake a party of pleasure. This voyage on a raft over a pond annoys and wearies me."

He called this adventurous journey a party of pleasure, and this great inland sea a pond!

"But," argued I, "if we have followed the route indicated by the great Saknussemm, we cannot be going far wrong."

" 'That is the question,' as the great, the immortal Shakespeare, has it. Are we following the route indicated by that wondrous sage? Did Saknussemm ever fall in with this great sheet of water? If he did, did he cross it? I begin to fear that the rivulet we adopted for a guide has led us wrong."

"In any case, we can never regret having come thus far. It is worth the whole journey to have enjoyed this magnificent spectacle—it is something to have seen."

"I care nothing about seeing, nor about magnificent spectacles. I came down into the interior of the earth with an object, and that object I mean to attain. Don't talk to me about admiring scenery, or any other sentimental trash."

After this I thought it well to hold my tongue, and allow the Professor to bite his lips until the blood came, without further remark.

At six o'clock in the evening, our matter-of-fact guide, Hans, asked for his week's salary, and receiving his three rix-dollars put them carefully in his pocket. He was perfectly contended and satisfied.

Sunday, August 16th. Nothing new to record. The same weather as before. The wind has a slight tendency to freshen up, with signs of an approaching gale. When I awoke, my first observation was in regard to the intensity of the light. I keep on fearing, day after day, that the extraordinary electric phenomenon should become first obscured, and then go wholly out, leaving us in total darkness. Nothing, however, of the kind occurs. The shadow of the raft, its mast, and sails, is clearly distinguished on the surface of the water.

This wondrous sea is, after all, infinite in its extent. It must be quite as wide as the Mediterranean—or perhaps even as the great Atlantic Ocean. Why, after all, should it not be so?

My uncle has, on more than one occasion, tried deep-sea soundings. He tied the cross of one of our heaviest crowbars to the extremity of a cord, which he allowed to run out to the extent of two hundred fathoms. We had the greatest difficulty in hoisting in our novel kind of lead.

When the crowbar was finally dragged on board, Hans called my attention to some singular marks upon its surface. The piece of iron looked as if it had been crushed between two very hard substances.

I looked at our worthy guide with an inquiring glance.

"Tänder," said he.

Of course I was at a loss to understand. I turned around toward my uncle, absorbed in gloomy reflections. I had little wish to disturb him from his reveries. I accordingly turned once more toward our worthy Icelander.

Hans very quietly and significantly opened his mouth once or twice, as if in the act of biting, and in this way made me understand his meaning.

"Teeth!" cried I, with stupefaction, as I examined the bar of iron with more attention.

Yes. There can be no doubt about the matter. The indentations on the bar of iron are the marks of teeth! What jaws must the owner of such molars be possessed of! Have we, then, come upon a monster of unknown species, which still exists within the vast waste of waters—a monster more voracious than a shark, more terrible and bulky than the whale? I am unable to withdraw my eyes from the bar of iron, actually half crushed!

Is, then, my dream about to come true—a dread and terrible reality?

All day my thoughts were bent upon these speculations, and my imagination scarcely regained a degree of calmness and power of reflection until after a sleep of many hours.

This day, as on other Sundays, we observed as a day of rest and pious meditation.

Monday, August 17th. I have been trying to realize from memory the particular instincts of those antediluvian animals of the secondary period, which succeeding to the mollusca, to the crustacea, and to the fish, preceded the appearance of the race of mammifers. The generation of reptiles then reigned supreme upon the earth. These hideous monsters ruled everything in the seas of the secondary period, which formed the strata of which the Jura mountains are composed. Nature has endowed them with perfect organization. What a gigantic structure was theirs; what vast and prodigious strength they possessed!

The existing saurians, which include all such reptiles as lizards, crocodiles, and alligators, even the largest and most formidable of their class, are but feeble imitations of their mighty sires, the animals of ages long ago. If there were giants in the days of old, there were also gigantic animals.

I shuddered as I evolved from my mind the idea and recollection of these awful monsters. No eye of man had seen them in the flesh. They took their walks abroad upon the face of the earth thousands of ages before man came into existence, and their fossil bones, discovered in the limestone, have allowed us to reconstruct them anatomically, and thus to get some faint idea of the colossal formation.

I recollect once seeing in the great Museum of Hamburg the skeleton of one of these wonderful saurians. It measured no less than thirty feet from the nose to the tail. Am I, then, an inhabitant of the earth of the present day, destined to find myself face to face with a representative of this antediluvian family? I can scarcely believe it possible; can hardly believe it true. And yet these marks of powerful teeth upon the bar of iron! Can there be a doubt from their shape that the bite is the bite of a crocodile?

My eyes stare wildly and with terror upon the subterranean sea. Every moment I expect one of these monsters to rise from its vast cavernous depths.

I fancy that the worthy Professor in some measure shares my notions, if not my fears, for, after an attentive examination of the crowbar, he cast his eyes rapidly over the mighty and mysterious ocean.

"What could possess him to leave the land," I thought, "as if the depth of this water was of any importance to us. No doubt he has disturbed some terrible monster in his watery home, and perhaps we may pay dearly for our temerity."

Anxious to be prepared for the worst, I examined our weapons, and saw that they were in a fit state for use. My uncle looked on at me and nodded his head approvingly. He, too, has noticed what we have to fear.

Already the uplifting of the waters on the surface indicates that something is in motion below. The danger approaches. It comes nearer and nearer. It behooves us to be on the watch.

Tuesday, August 18th. Evening came at last, the hour when the desire for sleep caused our eyelids to be heavy. Night there is not, properly speaking, in this place, any more than there is in summer in the arctic regions. Hans, however, is immovable at the rudder. When he snatches a moment of rest I really cannot say. I take advantages of his vigilance to take some little repose.

But two hours after I was awakened from a heavy sleep by an awful shock. The raft appeared to have struck upon a sunken rock. It was lifted right out of the water by some wondrous and mysterious power, and then started off twenty fathoms distant.

"Eh, what is it?" cried my uncle starting up. "Are we shipwrecked, or what?"

Hans raised his hand and pointed to where, about two hundred yards off, a large black mass was moving up and down. I looked with awe. My worst fears were realized.

"It is a colossal monster!" I cried, clasping my hands.

"Yes," cried the agitated Professor, "and there yonder is a huge sea lizard of terrible size and shape."

"And farther on behold a prodigious crocodile. Look at his hideous jaws, and that row of monstrous teeth. Ha! he has gone."

"A whale! a whale!" shouted the Professor, "I can see her enormous fins. See, see, how she blows air and water!"

Two liquid columns rose to a vast height above the level of the sea, into which they fell with a terrific crash, waking up the echoes of that awful place. We stood still—surprised, stupefied, terror-stricken at the sight of this group of fearful marine monsters, more hideous in the reality than in my dream. They were of supernatural dimensions; the very smallest of the whole party could with ease have crushed our raft and ourselves with a single bite.

Hans, seizing the rudder which had flown out of his hand, puts it hard aweather in order to escape from such dangerous vicinity; but no sooner does he do so, than he finds he is flying from Scylla to Charybdis. To leeward is a turtle about forty feet wide, and a serpent quite as long, with an enormous and hideous head peering from out the waters.

Look which way we will, it is impossible for us to fly. The fearful reptiles advanced upon us; they turned and twisted about the raft with awful rapidity. They formed around our devoted vessel a series of concentric circles. I took up my rifle in desperation. But what effect can a rifle ball produce upon the armor scales with which the bodies of these horrid monsters are covered?

We remain still and dumb from utter horror. They advance upon us, nearer and nearer. Our fate appears certain, fearful, and terrible. On one side the mighty crocodile, on the other the great sea serpent. The rest of the fearful crowd of marine prodigies have plunged beneath the briny waves and disappeared!

I am about at all risks to fire, and try the effect of a shot. Hans, the guide, however, interfered by a sign to check me. The two hideous and ravenous monsters passed within fifty fathoms of the raft, and then made a rush at one another—their fury and rage preventing them from seeing us.

The combat commenced. We distinctly made out every action of the two hideous monsters.

But to my excited imagination the other animals appeared about to take part in the fierce and deadly struggle—the monster, the whale, the lizard, and the turtle. I distinctly saw them every moment. I pointed them out to the Icelander. But he only shook his head.

"Tva," he said.

"What—two only does he say? Surely he is mistaken," I cried in a tone of wonder.

"He is quite right," replied my uncle coolly and philosophically, examining the terrible duel with his telescope and speaking as if he were in a lecture room.

"How can that be?"

"Yes, it is so. The first of these hideous monsters has the snout of a porpoise, the head of a lizard, the teeth of a crocodile; and it is this that has deceived us. It is the most fearful of all antediluvian reptiles, the world-renowned Ichthyosaurus or great fish lizard."

"And the other?"

"The other is a monstrous serpent, concealed under the hard vaulted shell of the turtle, the terrible enemy of its fearful rival, the Plesiosaurus, or sea crocodile."

Hans was quite right. The two monsters only, disturbed the surface of the sea!

At last have mortal eyes gazed upon two reptiles of the great primitive ocean! I see the flaming red eyes of the Ichthyosaurus, each as big, or bigger than a man's head. Nature in its infinite wisdom had gifted this wondrous marine animal with an optical apparatus of extreme power, capable of resisting the pressure of the heavy layers of water which rolled over him in the depths of the ocean where he usually fed. It has by some authors truly been called the whale of the saurian race, for it is as big and quick in its motions as our king of the seas. This one measures not less than a hundred feet in length, and I can form some idea of his girth when I see him lift his prodigious tail out of the waters. His jaw is of awful size and strength, and according to the best-informed naturalists, it does not contain less than a hundred and eighty-two teeth.

The other was the mighty Plesiosaurus, a serpent with a cylindrical trunk, with a short stumpy tail, with fins like a bank of oars in a Roman galley.

Its whole body covered by a carapace or shell, and its neck, as flexible as that of a swan, rose more than thirty feet above the waves, a tower of animated flesh!

These animals attacked one another with inconceivable fury. Such a combat was never *seen* before by mortal eyes, and to us who did see it, it appeared more like the phantasmagoric creation of a dream than anything else. They raised mountains of water, which dashed in spray over the raft, already tossed to and fro by the waves. Twenty times we seemed on the point of being upset and hurled headlong into the waves. Hideous hisses appeared to shake the gloomy granite roof of that mighty cavern—hisses which carried terror to our hearts. The awful combatants held each other in a tight embrace. I could not make out one from the other. Still the combat could not last forever; and woe unto us, whichsoever became the victor.

One hour, two hours, three hours passed away, without any decisive result. The struggle continued with the same deadly tenacity, but without apparent result. The deadly opponents now approached, now drew away from the raft. Once or twice we fancied they were about to leave us altogether, but instead of that, they came nearer and nearer.

We crouched on the raft ready to fire at them at a moment's notice, poor as the prospect of hurting or terrifying them was. Still we were determined not to perish without a struggle.

Suddenly the Ichthyosaurus and the Plesiosaurus disappeared beneath the waves, leaving behind them a maelstrom in the midst of the sea. We were very nearly drawn down by the indraft of the water!

Several minutes elapsed before anything was again seen. Was this wonderful combat to end in the depths of the ocean? Was the last act of this terrible drama to take place without spectators?

It was impossible for us to say.

Suddenly, at no great distance from us, an enormous mass rises out of the waters—the head of the great Plesiosaurus. The terrible monster is now wounded unto death. I can see nothing now of his enormous body. All that could be distinguished was his serpent-like neck, which he twisted and curled in all the agonies of death. Now he struck the waters with it as if it had been a gigantic whip, and then again wriggled like a worm cut in two. The water was spurted up to a great distance in all directions. A great portion of it swept over our raft and nearly blinded us. But soon the end of the beast approached nearer and nearer; his movements slackened visibly; his contortions almost ceased; and at last the body of the mighty snake lay an inert, dead mass on the surface of the now calm and placid waters.

As for the Ichthyosaurus, has he gone down to his mighty cavern under the sea to rest, or will he reappear to destroy us?

This question remained unanswered. And we had breathing time.

XXXI
The Sea Monster

Wednesday, August 19th. Fortunately the wind, which at the present blows with great violence, has allowed us to escape from the scene of the unparalleled and extraordinary struggle. Hans with his usual imperturbable calm remained at the helm. My uncle, who for a short time had been withdrawn from his absorbing reverie by the novel incidents of this sea fight, fell back again apparently into a brown study. All this time, however, his eyes were fixed impatiently on the widespread ocean.

Our voyage now became monotonous and uniform. Dull as it has become, I have no desire to have it broken by any repetition of the perils and adventures of yesterday.

Thursday, August 20th. The wind is now N. N. E., and blows very irregularly. It has changed to fitful gusts. The temperature is exceedingly high. We are now progressing at the average rate of about ten miles and a half per hour.

About twelve o'clock a distant sound as of thunder fell upon our ears. I make a note of the fact without even venturing a suggestion as to its cause. It was one continued roar as of a sea falling over mighty rocks.

"Far off in the distance," said the Professor dogmatically, "there is some rock or some island against which the sea, lashed to fury by the wind, is breaking violently."

Hans, without saying a word, clambered to the top of the mast, but could make out nothing. The ocean was level in every direction as far as the eye could reach.

Three hours passed away without any sign to indicate what might be before us. The sound began to assume that of a mighty cataract.

I expressed my opinion on this point strongly to my uncle. He merely shook his head. I, however, am strongly impressed by a conviction that I am not wrong. Are we advancing toward some mighty waterfall which shall cast us into the abyss? Probably this mode of descending into the abyss may be agreeable to the Professor, because it would be something like the vertical descent he is so eager to make. I entertain a very different opinion.

Whatever be the truth, it is certain that not many leagues distant there must be some very extraordinary phenomenon, for as we advance the roar becomes something mighty and stupendous. Is it in the water, or in the air?

I cast hasty glances aloft at the suspended vapors, and I seek to penetrate their mighty depths. But the vault above is tranquil. The clouds, which are now elevated to the very summit, appear utterly still and motionless, and completely lost in the irradiation of electric light. It is necessary, therefore, to seek for the cause of this phenomenon elsewhere.

I examine the horizon, now perfectly calm, pure, and free from all haze. Its aspect still remains unchanged. But if this awful noise proceeds from a cataract—if, so to speak in plain English, this vast interior ocean is precipitated into a lower basin—if these tremendous roars are produced by the noise of falling waters, the current would increase in activity, and its increasing swiftness would give me some idea of the extent of the peril with which we are menaced. I consult the current. It simply does not exist: there is no such thing. An empty bottle cast into the water lies to leeward without motion.

About four o'clock Hans rises, clambers up the mast, and reaches the truck itself. From this elevated position his looks are cast around. They take in a vast circumference of the ocean. At last, his eyes remain fixed. His face expresses no astonishment, but his eyes slightly dilate.

"He has seen something at last," cried my uncle.

"I think so," I replied.

Hans came down, stood beside us, and pointed with his right hand to the south.

"Der nere," he said.

"There," replied my uncle.

And seizing his telescope, he looked at it with great attention for about a minute, which to me appeared an age. I knew not what to think or expect.

"Yes, yes," he cried in a tone of considerable surprise, "there it is."

"What?" I asked.

"A tremendous spurt of water rising out of the waves."

"Some other marine monster," I cried, already alarmed.

"Perhaps."

"Then let us steer more to the westward, for we know what we have to expect from antediluvian animals," was my eager reply.

"Go ahead," said my uncle.

I turned toward Hans. Hans was at the tiller steering with his usual imperturbable calm.

Nevertheless, if from the distance which separated us from this creature, a distance which must be estimated at not less than a dozen leagues, and this spurting of water proceeded from the pranks of some antediluvian animal, his dimensions must be something preternatural. To fly is, therefore, the course to be suggested by ordinary prudence. But we have not come into that part of the world to be prudent. Such is my uncle's determination.

We, accordingly, continued to advance. The nearer we come, the loftier is the spouting water. What monster can fill himself with such huge volumes of water, and then unceasingly spout them out in such lofty jets?

At eight o'clock in the evening, reckoning as above ground, where there is day and night, we are not more than two leagues from the mighty beast. Its long, black, enormous, mountainous body, lies on the top of the water like an island. But then sailors have been said to have gone ashore on sleeping whales, mistaking them for land. Is it illusion, or is it fear? Its length cannot be less than a thousand fathoms. What, then, is this cetaceous monster of which no Cuvier ever thought?

It is quite motionless and presents the appearance of sleep. The sea seems unable to lift him upward; it is rather the waves which break on his huge and gigantic frame. The waterspout, rising to a height of five hundred feet, breaks in spray with a dull, sullen roar.

We advance, like senseless lunatics, toward this mighty mass.

I honestly confess that I was abjectly afraid. I declared that I would go no farther. I threatened in my terror to cut the sheet of the sail. I attacked the Professor with considerable acrimony, calling him foolhardy, mad, I know not what. He made no answer.

Suddenly the imperturbable Hans once more pointed his finger to the menacing object.

"Holme!"

"An island!" cried my uncle.

"An island?" I replied, shrugging my shoulders at this poor attempt at deception.

"Of course it is," cried my uncle, bursting into a loud and joyous laugh.

"But the waterspout?"

"Geyser," said Hans.

"Yes, of course—a geyser," replied my uncle, still laughing, "a geyser like those common in Iceland. Jets like this are the great wonders of the country."

At first I would not allow that I had been so grossly deceived. What could be more ridiculous than to have an island for a marine monster? But kick as one may, one must yield to evidence, and I was finally convinced of my error. It was nothing, after all, but a natural phenomenon.

As we approached nearer and nearer, the dimensions of the liquid sheaf of waters became truly grand and stupendous. The island had, at a distance, presented the appearance of an enormous whale, whose head rose high above the waters. The geyser, a word the Icelanders pronounce *geysir*, and which signifies fury, rose majestically from its summit. Dull detonations are heard every now and then, and the enormous jet, taken as it were with sudden fury, shakes its plume of vapor, and bounds into the first layer of the clouds. It is alone. Neither spurts of vapor nor hot springs surround it, and the whole volcanic power of that region is concentrated in one sublime column. The rays of electric light mix with this dazzling sheaf, every drop as it falls assuming the prismatic colors of the rainbow.

"Let us go on shore," said the Professor, after some minutes of silence.

It is necessary, however, to take great precaution, in order to avoid the weight of falling waters, which would cause the raft to founder in an instant. Hans, however, steers admirably, and brings us to the other extremity of the island.

I was the first to leap on the rock. My uncle followed, while the eider-duck hunter remained still, like a man above any childish sources of astonishment. We were now walking on granite mixed with siliceous sandstone; the soil shivered under our feet like the sides of boilers in which overheated steam is forcibly confined. It is burning. We soon came in sight of the little central basin from which rose the geyser. I plunged a thermometer into the water which ran bubbling from the center, and it marked a heat of a hundred and sixty-three degrees!

This water, therefore, came from some place where the heat was intense. This was singularly in contradiction with the theories of Professor Hardwigg. I could not help telling him my opinion on the subject.

"Well," said he sharply, "and what does this prove against my doctrine?"

"Nothing," replied I dryly, seeing that I was running my head against a foregone conclusion.

Nevertheless, I am compelled to confess that until now we have been most remarkably fortunate, and that this voyage is being accomplished in most favorable conditions of temperature; but it appears evident, in fact, certain, that we shall sooner or later arrive at one of those regions where the central heat will reach its utmost limits, and will go far beyond all the possible gradations of thermometers.

Visions of the Hades of the ancients, believed to be in the center of the earth, floated through my imagination.

We shall, however, see what we shall see. That is the Professor's favorite phrase now. Having christened the volcanic island by the name of his nephew, the leader of the expedition turned away and gave the signal for embarkation.

I stood still, however, for some minutes, gazing upon the magnificent geyser. I soon was able to perceive that the upward tendency of the water was irregular; now it diminished in intensity, and then, suddenly, it regained new vigor, which I attributed to the variation of the pressure of the accumulated vapors in its reservoir.

At last we took our departure, going carefully around the projecting, and rather dangerous, rocks of the southern side. Hans had taken advantage of this brief halt to repair the raft. Not before it was required.

Before we took our final departure from the island, however, I made some observations to calculate the distance we had gone over, and I put them down in my journal. Since we left Port Gretchen, we had traveled two hundred and seventy leagues—more than eight hundred miles—on this great inland sea; we were, therefore, six hundred and twenty leagues from Iceland, and exactly under England.

XXXII

THE BATTLE OF THE ELEMENTS

Friday, August 21st. This morning the magnificent geyser had wholly disappeared. The wind had freshened up, and we were fast leaving the neighborhood of Harry's Island. Even the roaring sound of the mighty column was lost to the ear.

The weather, if, under the circumstances, we may use such an expression, is about to change very suddenly. The atmosphere is being gradually loaded with vapors, which carry with them the electricity formed by the constant evaporation of the saline waters; the clouds are slowly but sensibly falling toward the sea, and are assuming a dark-olive texture; the electric rays can scarcely pierce through the opaque curtain which has fallen like a drop scene before this wondrous theater, on the stage of which another and terrible drama is soon to be enacted. This time it is no fight of animals; it is the fearful battle of the elements.

I feel that I am very peculiarly influenced, as all creatures are on land when a deluge is about to take place.

The cumuli, a perfectly oval kind of cloud, piled upon the south, presented a most awful and sinister appearance, with the pitiless aspect often seen before a storm. The air is extremely heavy; the sea is comparatively calm.

In the distance, the clouds have assumed the appearance of enormous balls of cotton, or rather pods, piled one above the other in picturesque confusion. By degrees, they appear to swell out, break, and gain in number what they lose in grandeur; their heaviness is so great that they are unable to lift themselves from the horizon; but under the influence of the upper currents of air, they are gradually broken up, become much darker, and then present the appearance of one single layer of a formidable character; now and then a lighter cloud, still lit up from above, rebounds upon this gray carpet, and is lost in the opaque mass.

There can be no doubt that the entire atmosphere is saturated with electric fluid; I am myself wholly impregnated; my hairs literally stand on end as if under the influence of a galvanic battery. If one of my companions ventured to touch me, I think he would receive rather a violent and unpleasant shock.

About ten o'clock in the morning, the symptoms of the storm became more thorough and decisive; the wind appeared to soften down as if to take breath for a renewed attack; the vast funeral pall above us looked like a huge bag—like the cave of Aeolus, in which the storm was collecting its forces for the attack.

I tried all I could not to believe in the menacing signs of the sky, and yet I could not avoid saying, as it were involuntarily:

"I believe we are going to have bad weather."

The Professor made me no answer. He was in a horrible, in a detestable humor—to see the ocean stretching interminably before his eyes. On hearing my words he simply shrugged his shoulders.

"We shall have a tremendous storm," I said again, pointing to the horizon. "These clouds are falling lower and lower upon the sea, as if to crush it."

A great silence prevailed. The wind wholly ceased. Nature assumed a dead calm, and ceased to breathe. Upon the mast, where I noticed a sort of slight *ignis fatuus*, the sail hangs in loose heavy folds. The raft is motionless in the midst of a dark heavy sea—without undulation, without motion. It is as still as glass. But as we are making no progress, what is the use of keeping up the sail, which may be the cause of our perdition if the tempest should suddenly strike us without warning.

"Let us lower the sail," I said; "it is only an act of common prudence."

"No—no," cried my uncle, in an exasperated tone, "a hundred times, no. Let the wind strike us and do its worst, let the storm sweep us away where it will—only let me see the glimmer of some coast—of some rocky cliffs, even if they dash our raft into a thousand pieces. No! keep up the sail—no matter what happens."

These words were scarcely uttered when the southern horizon underwent a sudden and violent change. The long accumulated vapors were resolved into water, and the air required to fill up the void produced became a wild and raging tempest.

It came from the most distant corners of the mighty cavern. It raged from every point of the compass. It roared; it yelled; it shrieked with glee as of demons let loose. The darkness increased and became indeed darkness visible.

The raft rose and fell with the storm, and bounded over the waves. My uncle was cast headlong upon the deck. I with great difficulty dragged myself toward him. He was holding on with might and main to the end of a cable, and appeared to gaze with pleasure and delight at the spectacle of the unchained elements.

Hans never moved a muscle. His long hair driven hither and thither by the tempest and scattered wildly over his motionless face, gave him a most extraordinary appearance—for every single hair was illuminated by little sparkling sprigs.

His countenance presents the extraordinary appearance of an antediluvian man, a true contemporary of the megatherium.

Still the mast holds good against the storm. The sail spreads out and fills like a soap bubble about to burst. The raft rushes on at a pace impossible to estimate, but still less swiftly than the body of water displaced beneath it, the rapidity of which may be seen by the lines which fly right and left in the wake.

"The sail, the sail!" I cried, making a trumpet of my hands, and then endeavoring to lower it.

"Let it alone!" said my uncle, more exasperated than ever.

"Nej," said Hans, gently shaking his head.

Nevertheless, the rain formed a roaring cataract before this horizon of which we were in search, and to which we were rushing like madmen.

But before this wilderness of waters reached us, the mighty veil of cloud was torn in twain; the sea began to foam wildly; and the electricity, produced by some vast and extraordinary chemical action in the upper layer of cloud, is brought into play. To the fearful claps of thunder are added dazzling flashes of lightning, such as I had never seen. The flashes crossed one another, hurled from every side; while the thunder came pealing like an echo. The mass of vapor becomes incandescent; the hailstones which strike the metal of our boots and our weapons are actually luminous; the waves as they rise appear to be fire-eating monsters, beneath which seethes an intense fire, their crests surmounted by combs of flame.

My eyes are dazzled, blinded by the intensity of light, my ears are deafened by the awful roar of the elements. I am compelled to hold onto the mast, which bends like a reed beneath the violence of the storm, to which none ever before seen by mariners bore any resemblance.

Here my traveling notes become very incomplete, loose, and vague. I have only been able to make out one or two fugitive observations, jotted down in a mere mechanical way. But even their brevity, even their obscurity, show the emotions which overcame me.

Sunday, August 23rd. Where have we got to? In what region are we wandering? We are still carried forward with inconceivable rapidity.

The night has been fearful, something not to be described. The storm shows no signs of cessation. We exist in the midst of an uproar which has no name. The detonations as of artillery are incessant. Our ears literally bleed. We are unable to exchange a word, or hear each other speak.

The lightning never ceases to flash for a single instant. I can see the zigzags after a rapid dart strike the arched roof of this mightiest of mighty vaults. If it were to give way and fall upon us! Other lightnings plunge their forked streaks in every direction, and take the form of globes of fire, which explode like bombshells over a beleaguered city. The general crash and roar do not apparently increase; it has already gone far beyond what human ear can appreciate. If all the powder magazines in the world were to explode together, it would be impossible for us to hear worse noise.

There is a constant emission of light from the storm clouds; the electric matter is incessantly released; evidently the gaseous principles of the air are out of order; innumerable columns of water rush up like waterspouts, and fall back upon the surface of the ocean in foam.

Whither are we going? My uncle still lies at full length upon the raft, without speaking—without taking any note of time.

The heat increases. I look at the thermometer, to my surprise it indicates — *The exact figure is here rubbed out in my manuscript.*

Monday, August 24th. This terrible storm will never end. Why should not this state of the atmosphere, so dense and murky, once modified, again remain definitive?

We are utterly broken and harassed by fatigue. Hans remains just as usual. The raft runs to the southeast invariably. We have now already run two hundred leagues from the newly discovered island.

About twelve o'clock the storm became worse than ever. We are obliged now to fasten every bit of cargo tightly on the deck of the raft, or everything would be swept away. We tie ourselves to the mast, each man lashing the other. The waves drive over us, so that several times we are actually under water.

We had been under the painful necessity of abstaining from speech for three days and three nights. We opened our mouths, we moved our lips, but no sound came. Even when we placed our mouths to each other's ears it was the same.

The wind carried the voice away.

My uncle once contrived to get his head close to mine after several almost vain endeavors. He appeared to my nearly exhausted senses to articulate some word. I had a notion, more from intuition than anything else, that he said to me, "We are lost."

I took out my notebook, from which under the most desperate circumstances I never parted, and wrote a few words as legibly as I could:

"Take in sail."

With a deep sigh he nodded his head and acquiesced.

His head had scarcely time to fall back in the position from which he had momentarily raised it than a disk or ball of fire appeared on the very edge of the raft—our devoted, our doomed craft. The mast and sail are carried away bodily, and I see them swept away to a prodigious height like a kite.

We were frozen, actually shivered with terror. The ball of fire, half white, half azure-colored, about the size of a ten-inch bombshell, moved along, turning with prodigious rapidity to leeward of the storm. It ran about here, there, and everywhere, it clambered up one of the bulwarks of the raft, it leaped upon the sack of provisions, and then finally descended lightly, fell like a football, and landed on our powder barrel.

Horrible situation. An explosion of course was now inevitable.

By heaven's mercy, it is not so.

The dazzling disk moved on one side, it approached Hans, who looked at it with singular fixity; then it approached my uncle, who cast himself on his knees to avoid it; it came toward me, as I stood pale and shuddering in the dazzling light and heat; it pirouetted around my feet, which I endeavored to withdraw.

An odor of nitrous gas filled the whole air; it penetrated to the throat, to the lungs. I felt ready to choke.

Why is it that I cannot withdraw my feet? Are they riveted to the flooring of the raft?

No.

The fall of the electric globe has turned all the iron on board into loadstones—the instruments, the tools, the arms are clanging together with awful and horrible noise; the nails of my heavy boots adhere closely to the plate of iron incrustated in the wood. I cannot withdraw my foot. It is the old story over again of the mountain of adamant.

At last, by a violent and almost superhuman effort, I tear it away just as the ball which is still executing its gyratory motions is about to run around it and drag me with it—if—

Oh, what intense stupendous light! The globe of fire bursts—we are enveloped in cascades of living fire, which flood the space around with luminous matter.

Then all went out and darkness once more fell upon the deep! I had just time to see my uncle once more cast apparently senseless on the flooring of the raft, Hans at the helm, "spitting fire" under the influence of the electricity which seemed to have gone through him.

Whither are we going, I ask? and echo answers, Whither?

Tuesday, August 25th. I have just come out of a long fainting fit. The awful and hideous storm still continues; the lightning has increased in vividness, and pours out its fiery wrath like a brood of serpents let loose in the atmosphere.

Are we still upon the sea? Yes, and being carried along with incredible velocity.

We have passed under England, under the Channel, under France, probably under the whole extent of Europe.

Another awful clamor in the distance. This time it is certain that the sea is breaking upon the rocks at no great distance. Then—

XXXIII
OUR ROUTE REVERSED

Here ends what I call "My Journal" of our voyage on board the raft, which journal was happily saved from the wreck. I proceed with my narrative as I did before I commenced my daily notes.

What happened when the terrible shock took place, when the raft was cast upon the rocky shore, it would be impossible for me now to say. I felt myself precipitated violently into the boiling waves, and if I escaped from a certain and cruel death, it was wholly owing to the determination of the faithful Hans, who, clutching me by the arm, saved me from the yawning abyss.

The courageous Icelander then carried me in his powerful arms, far out of the reach of the waves, and laid me down upon a burning expanse of sand, where I found myself some time afterward in the company of my uncle, the Professor.

Then he quietly returned toward the fatal rocks, against which the furious waves were beating, in order to save any stray waifs from the wreck. This man was always practical and thoughtful. I could not utter a word; I was quite overcome with emotion; my whole body was broken and bruised with fatigue; it took hours before I was anything like myself.

Meanwhile, there fell a fearful deluge of rain, drenching us to the skin. Its very violence, however, proclaimed the approaching end of the storm. Some overhanging rocks afforded us a slight protection from the torrents.

Under this shelter, Hans prepared some food, which, however, I was unable to touch; and, exhausted by the three weary days and nights of watching, we fell into a deep and painful sleep. My dreams were fearful, but at last exhausted, Nature asserted her supremacy, and I slumbered.

Next day when I awoke the change was magical. The weather was magnificent. Air and sea, as if by mutual consent, had regained their serenity. Every trace of the storm, even the faintest, had disappeared. I was saluted on my awakening by the first joyous tones I had heard from the Professor for many a day. His gaiety, indeed, was something terrible.

"Well, my lad," he cried, rubbing his hands together, "have you slept soundly?"

Might it not have been supposed that we were in the old house on the Königstrasse; that I had just come down quietly to my breakfast; and that my marriage with Gretchen was to take place that very day? My uncle's coolness was exasperating.

Alas, considering how the tempest had driven us in an easterly direction, we had passed under the whole of Germany, under the city of Hamburg where I had been so happy, under the very street which contained all I loved and cared for in the world.

It was a positive fact that I was only separated from her by a distance of forty leagues. But these forty leagues were of hard, impenetrable granite!

All these dreary and miserable reflections passed through my mind before I attempted to answer my uncle's question.

"Why, what is the matter?" he cried. "Can you not say whether you have slept well or not?"

"I have slept very well," was my reply, "but every bone in my body aches. I suppose that will lead to nothing."

"Nothing at all, my boy. It is only the result of the fatigue of the last few days—that is all."

"You appear—if I may be allowed to say so—to be very jolly this morning," I said.

"Delighted, my dear boy, delighted. Was never happier in my life. We have at last reached the wished-for port."

"The end of our expedition?" cried I, in a tone of considerable surprise.

"No; but to the confines of that sea which I began to fear would never end but go around the whole world. We will now tranquilly resume our journey by land, and once again endeavor to dive into the center of the earth."

"My dear uncle," I began, in a hesitating kind of way, "allow me to ask you one question."

"Certainly, Harry; a dozen if you think proper."

"One will suffice. How about getting back?" I asked.

"How about getting back? What a question to ask. We have not as yet reached the end of our journey."

"I know that. All I want to know is how you propose we shall manage the return voyage?"

"In the most simple manner in the world," said the imperturbable Professor. "Once we reach the exact center of this sphere, either we shall find a new road by which to ascend to the surface, or we shall simply turn around and go back by the way we came. I have every reason to believe that while we are traveling forward, it will not close behind us."

"Then one of the first matters to see to will be to repair the raft," was my rather melancholy response.

"Of course. We must attend to that above all things," continued the Professor.

"Then comes the all-important question of provisions," I urged. "Have we anything like enough left to enable us to accomplish such great, such amazing, designs as you contemplate carrying out?"

"I have seen into the matter, and my answer is in the affirmative. Hans is a very clever fellow, and I have reason to believe that he has saved the greater part of the cargo. But the best way to satisfy your scruples is to come and judge for yourself."

Saying which, he led the way out of the kind of open grotto in which we had taken shelter. I had almost begun to hope that which I should rather have feared, and this was the impossibility of such a shipwreck leaving even the slightest signs of what it had carried as freight. I was, however, thoroughly mistaken.

As soon as I reached the shores of this inland sea, I found Hans standing gravely in the midst of a large number of things laid out in complete order. My uncle wrung his hands with deep and silent gratitude. His heart was too full for speech.

This man, whose superhuman devotion to his employers I not only never saw surpassed, nor even equaled, had been hard at work all the time we slept, and at the risk of his life had succeeded in saving the most precious articles of our cargo.

Of course, under the circumstances, we necessarily experienced several severe losses. Our weapons had wholly vanished. But experience had taught us to do without them. The provision of powder had, however, remained intact, after having narrowly escaped blowing us all to atoms in the storm.

"Well," said the Professor, who was now ready to make the best of everything, "as we have no guns, all we have to do is to give up all idea of hunting."

"Yes, my dear sir, we can do without them, but what about all our instruments?"

"Here is the manometer, the most useful of all, and which I gladly accept in lieu of the rest. With it alone I can calculate the depth as we proceed; by its means alone I shall be able to decide when we have reached the center of the earth. Ha, ha! but for this little instrument we might make a mistake, and run the risk of coming out at the antipodes!"

All this was said amid bursts of unnatural laughter.

"But the compass," I cried; "without that what can we do?"

"Here it is safe and sound!" he cried, with real joy, "ah, ah, and here we have the chronometer and the thermometers. Hans the hunter is indeed an invaluable man!"

It was impossible to deny this fact. As far as the nautical and other instruments were concerned, nothing was wanting. Then on further examination, I found ladders, cords, pickaxes, crowbars, and shovels, all scattered about on the shore.

There was, however, finally the most important question of all, and that was, provisions.

"But what are we to do for food?" I asked.

"Let us see to the commissariat department," replied my uncle gravely.

The boxes which contained our supply of food for the voyage were placed in a row along the strand, and were in a capital state of preservation; the sea had in every case respected their contents, and to sum up in one sentence, taking into consideration, biscuits, salt, meat, Schiedam, and dried fish, we could still calculate on having about four months' supply, if used with prudence and caution.

"Four months," cried the sanguine Professor in high glee. "Then we shall have plenty of time both to go and to come, and with what remains I undertake to give a grand dinner to my colleagues of the Johanneum."

I sighed. I should by this time have used myself to the temperament of my uncle, and yet this man astonished me more and more every day. He was the greatest human enigma I ever had known.

"Now," said he, "before we do anything else, we must lay in a stock of fresh water. The rain has fallen in abundance, and filled the hollows of the granite. There is a rich supply of water, and we have no fear of suffering from thirst, which in our circumstances is of the last importance. As for the raft, I shall recommend Hans to repair it to the best of his abilities; though I have every reason to believe we shall not require it again."

"How is that?" I cried, more amazed than ever at my uncle's style of reasoning.

"I have an idea, my dear boy; it is none other than this simple fact: we shall not come out by the same opening as that by which we entered."

I began to look at my uncle with vague suspicion. An idea had more than once taken possession of me; and this was, that he was going mad. And yet, little did I think how true and prophetic his words were doomed to be.

"And now," he said, "having seen to all these matters of detail, to breakfast."

I followed him to a sort of projecting cape, after he had given his last instructions to our guide. In this original position, with dried meat, biscuit, and a delicious cup of tea, we made a satisfactory meal—I may say one of the most welcome and pleasant I ever remember. Exhaustion, the keen atmosphere, the state of calm after so much agitation, all contributed to give me an excellent appetite. Indeed, it contributed very much to producing a pleasant and cheerful state of mind.

While breakfast was in hand, and between the sips of warm tea, I asked my uncle if he had any idea of how we now stood in relation to the world above.

"For my part," I added, "I think it will be rather difficult to determine."

"Well, if we were compelled to fix the exact spot," said my uncle, "it might be difficult, since during the three days of that awful tempest I could keep no account either of the quickness of our pace, or of the direction in which the raft was going. Still, we will endeavor to approximate the truth. We shall not, I believe, be so very far out."

"Well, if I recollect rightly," I replied, "our last observation was made at the geyser island."

"Harry's Island, my boy! Harry's Island. Do not decline the honor of having named it; given your name to an island discovered by us, the first human beings who trod it since the creation of the world!"

"Let it be so, then. At Harry's Island we had already gone over two hundred and seventy leagues of sea, and we were, I believe, about six hundred leagues, more or less, from Iceland."

"Good. I am glad to see that you remember so well. Let us start from that point, and let us count four days of storm, during which our rate of traveling must have been very great. I should say that our velocity must have been about eighty leagues to the twenty-four hours."

I agreed that I thought this a fair calculation. There were then three hundred leagues to be added to the grand total.

"Yes, and the Central Sea must extend at least six hundred leagues from side to side. Do you know, my boy, Harry, that we have discovered an inland lake larger than the Mediterranean?"

"Certainly, and we only know of its extent in one way. It may be hundreds of miles in length."

"Very likely."

"Then," said I, after calculating for some minutes, "if your previsions are right, we are at this moment exactly under the Mediterranean itself."

"Do you think so?"

"Yes, I am almost certain of it. Are we not nine hundred leagues distant from Reykjavik?"

"That is perfectly true, and a famous bit of road we have traveled, my boy. But why we should be under the Mediterranean more than under Turkey or the Atlantic Ocean can only be known when we are sure of not having deviated from our course; and of this we know nothing."

"I do not think we were driven very far from our course; the wind appears to me to have been always about the same. My opinion is that this shore must be situated to the southeast of Port Gretchen."

"Good—I hope so. It will, however, be easy to decide the matter by taking the bearings from our departure by means of the compass. Come along, and we will consult that invaluable invention."

The Professor now walked eagerly in the direction of the rock where the indefatigable Hans had placed the instruments in safety. My uncle was gay and lighthearted; he rubbed his hands, and assumed all sorts of attitudes. He was to all appearance once more a young man. Since I had known him, never had he been so amiable and pleasant. I followed him, rather curious to know whether I had made any mistake in my estimation of our position.

As soon as we had reached the rock, my uncle took the compass, placed it horizontally before him, and looked keenly at the needle.

As he had at first shaken it to give it vivacity, it oscillated considerably, and then slowly assumed its right position under the influence of the magnetic power.

The Professor bent his eyes curiously over the wondrous instrument. A violent start immediately showed the extent of his emotion.

He closed his eyes, rubbed them, and took another and a keener survey.

Then he turned slowly around to me, stupefaction depicted on his countenance.

"What is the matter?" said I, beginning to be alarmed.

He could not speak. He was too overwhelmed for words. He simply pointed to the instrument.

I examined it eagerly according to his mute directions, and a loud cry of surprise escaped my lips. The needle of the compass pointed due north—in the direction we expected was the south!

It pointed to the shore instead of to the high seas.

I shook the compass; I examined it with a curious and anxious eye. It was in a state of perfection. No blemish in any way explained the phenomenon. Whatever position we forced the needle into, it returned invariably to the same unexpected point.

It was useless attempting to conceal from ourselves the fatal truth.

There could be no doubt about it, unwelcome as was the fact, that during the tempest, there had been a sudden slant of wind, of which we had been unable to take any account, and thus the raft had carried us back to the shores we had left, apparently forever, so many days before!

XXXIV
A Voyage of Discovery

It would be altogether impossible for me to give any idea of the utter astonishment which overcame the Professor on making this extraordinary discovery. Amazement, incredulity, and rage were blended in such a way as to alarm me.

During the whole course of my life I had never seen a man at first so chapfallen; and then so furiously indignant.

The terrible fatigues of our sea voyage, the fearful dangers we had passed through, had all, all, gone for nothing. We had to begin them all over again.

Instead of progressing, as we fondly expected, during a voyage of so many days, we had retreated. Every hour of our expedition on the raft had been so much lost time!

Presently, however, the indomitable energy of my uncle overcame every other consideration.

"So," he said between his set teeth, "fatality will play me these terrible tricks. The elements themselves conspire to overwhelm me with mortification. Air, fire, and water combine their united efforts to oppose my passage. Well, they shall see what the earnest will of a determined man can do. I will not yield, I will not retreat even one inch; and we shall see who shall triumph in this great contest—man or nature."

Standing upright on a rock, irritated and menacing, Professor Hardwigg, like the ferocious Ajax, seemed to defy the fates. I, however, took upon myself to interfere, and to impose some sort of check upon such insensate enthusiasm.

"Listen to me, Uncle," I said in a firm but temperate tone of voice, "there must be some limit to ambition here below. It is utterly useless to struggle against the impossible. Pray listen to reason. We are utterly unprepared for a sea voyage; it is simple madness to think of performing a journey of five hundred leagues upon a wretched pile of beams, with a counterpane for a sail, a paltry stick for a mast, and a tempest to contend with. As we are totally incapable of steering our frail craft, we shall become the mere plaything of the storm, and it is acting the part of madmen if we, a second time, run any risk upon this dangerous and treacherous Central Sea."

These are only a few of the reasons and arguments I put together—

reasons and arguments which to me appeared unanswerable. I was allowed to go on without interruption for about ten minutes. The explanation to this I soon discovered. The Professor was not even listening, and did not hear a word of all my eloquence.

"To the raft!" he cried in a hoarse voice, when I paused for a reply.

Such was the result of my strenuous effort to resist his iron will. I tried again; I begged and implored him; I got into a passion; but I had to deal with a will more determined than my own. I seemed to feel like the waves which fought and battled against the huge mass of granite at our feet, which had smiled grimly for so many ages at their puny efforts.

Hans, meanwhile, without taking part in our discussion, had been repairing the raft. One would have supposed that he instinctively guessed at the further projects of my uncle.

By means of some fragments of cordage, he had again made the raft seaworthy.

While I had been speaking, he had hoisted a new mast and sail, the latter already fluttering and waving in the breeze.

The worthy Professor spoke a few words to our imperturbable guide, who immediately began to put our baggage on board and to prepare for our departure. The atmosphere was now tolerably clear and pure, and the northeast wind blew steadily and serenely. It appeared likely to last for some time.

What, then, could I do? Could I undertake to resist the iron will of two men? It was simply impossible if even I could have hoped for the support of Hans. This, however, was out of the question. It appeared to me that the Icelander had set aside all personal will and identity. He was a picture of abnegation.

I could hope for nothing from one so infatuated with and devoted to his master. All I could do, therefore, was to swim with the stream.

In a mood of stolid and sullen resignation, I was about to take my accustomed place on the raft when my uncle placed his hand upon my shoulder.

"There is no hurry, my boy," he said, "we shall not start until tomorrow."

I looked the picture of resignation to the dire will of fate.

"Under the circumstances," he said, "I ought to neglect no precautions. As fate has cast me upon these shores, I shall not leave without having completely examined them."

In order to understand this remark, I must explain that though we had been driven back to the northern shore, we had landed at a very different spot from that which had been our starting point.

Port Gretchen must, we calculated, be very much to the westward. Nothing, therefore, was more natural and reasonable than that we should reconnoiter this new shore upon which we had so unexpectedly landed.

"Let us go on a journey of discovery," I cried.

And leaving Hans to his important operation, we started on our expedition. The distance between the foreshore at high water and the foot of the rocks was considerable. It would take about half an hour's walking to get from one to the other.

As we trudged along, our feet crushed innumerable shells of every shape and size—once the dwelling place of animals of every period of creation.

I particularly noticed some enormous shells—carapaces (turtle and tortoise species) the diameter of which exceeded fifteen feet.

They had in past ages belonged to those gigantic glyptodons of the Pliocene period, of which the modern turtle is but a minute specimen. In addition, the whole soil was covered by a vast quantity of stony relics, having the appearance of flints worn by the action of the waves, and lying in successive layers one above the other. I came to the conclusion that in past ages the sea must have covered the whole district. Upon the scattered rocks, now lying far beyond its reach, the mighty waves of ages had left evident marks of their passage.

On reflection, this appeared to me partially to explain the existence of this remarkable ocean, forty leagues below the surface of the earth's crust. According to my new, and perhaps fanciful, theory, this liquid mass must be gradually lost in the deep bowels of the earth. I had also no doubt that this mysterious sea was fed by infiltration of the ocean above, through imperceptible fissures.

Nevertheless, it was impossible not to admit that these fissures must now be nearly chocked up, for if not, the cavern, or rather the immense and stupendous reservoir, would have been completely filled in a short space of time. Perhaps even this water, having to contend against the accumulated subterraneous fires of the interior of the earth, had become partially vaporized. Hence the explanation of those heavy clouds suspended over our heads, and the superabundant display of that electricity which occasioned such terrible storms in this deep and cavernous sea.

This lucid explanation of the phenomena we had witnessed appeared to me quite satisfactory. However great and mighty the marvels of Nature may seem to us, they are always to be explained by physical reasons. Everything is subordinate to some great law of Nature.

It now appeared clear that we were walking upon a kind of sedimentary soil, formed like all the soils of that period, so frequent on the surface of the globe, by the subsidence of the waters. The Professor, who was now in his element, carefully examined every rocky fissure. Let him only find an opening and it directly became important to him to examine its depth.

For a whole mile we followed the windings of the Central Sea, when suddenly an important change took place in the aspect of the soil. It seemed to have been rudely cast up, convulsionized, as it were, by a violent unheaving of the lower strata. In many places, hollows here and hillocks there attested great dislocations of some other period of the terrestrial mass.

We advanced with great difficulty over the broken masses of granite mixed with flint quartz, and alluvial deposits, when a large field, more even than a field, a plain of bones, appeared suddenly before our eyes! It looked like an immense cemetery, where generation after generation had mingled their mortal dust.

Lofty barrows of early remains rose at intervals. They undulated away to the limits of the distant horizon and were lost in a thick and brown fog.

On that spot, some three square miles in extent, was accumulated the whole history of animal life—scarcely one creature upon the comparatively modern soil of the upper and inhabited world had there existed.

Nevertheless, we were drawn forward by an all-absorbing and impatient curiosity. Our feet crushed with a dry and crackling sound the remains of those prehistoric fossils, for which the museums of great cities quarrel, even when they obtain only rare and curious morsels. A thousand such naturalists as Cuvier would not have sufficed to recompose the skeletons of the organic beings which lay in this magnificent osseous collection.

I was utterly confounded. My uncle stood for some minutes with his arms raised on high toward the thick granite vault which served us for a sky. His mouth was wide open; his eyes sparkled wildly behind his spectacles (which he had fortunately saved), his head bobbed up and down and from side to side, while his whole attitude and mien expressed unbounded astonishment.

He stood in the presence of an endless, wondrous, and inexhaustibly rich collection of antediluvian monsters, piled up for his own private and peculiar satisfaction.

Fancy an enthusiastic lover of books carried suddenly into the very midst of the famous library of Alexandria burned by the sacrilegious Omar, and which some miracle had restored to its pristine splendor! Such was something of the state of mind in which Uncle Hardwigg was now placed.

For some time he stood thus, literally aghast at the magnitude of his discovery.

But it was even a greater excitement when, darting wildly over this mass of organic dust, he caught up a naked skull and addressed me in a quivering voice:

"Harry, my boy—Harry—this is a human head!"

"A human head, Uncle!" I said, no less amazed and stupefied than himself.

"Yes, nephew. Ah! M. Milne-Edwards—ah! M. De Quatrefages—why are you not here where I am—I, Professor Hardwigg!"

XXXV

Discovery upon Discovery

In order fully to understand the exclamation made by my uncle, and his allusions to these illustrious and learned men, it will be necessary to enter into certain explanations in regard to a circumstance of the highest importance to paleontology, or the science of fossil life, which had taken place a short time before our departure from the upper regions of the earth.

On the 28th of March, 1863, some navigators under the direction of M. Boucher de Perthes, were at work in the great quarries of Moulin-Quignon, near Abbeville, in the department of the Somme, in France. While at work, they unexpectedly came upon a human jawbone buried fourteen feet below the surface of the soil. It was the first fossil of the kind that had ever been brought to the light of day. Near this unexpected human relic were found stone hatchets and carved flints, colored and clothed by time in one uniform brilliant tint of verdigris.

The report of this extraordinary and unexpected discovery spread not only all over France, but over England and Germany. Many learned men belonging to various scientific bodies, and noteworthy among others,

Messrs. Milne-Edwards and De Quatrefages, took the affair very much to heart, demonstrated the incontestable authenticity of the bone in question, and became—to use the phrase then recognized in England—the most ardent supporters of the "jawbone question."

To the eminent geologists of the United Kingdom who looked upon the fact as certain—Messrs. Falconer, Buck, Carpenter, and others—were soon united the learned men of Germany, and among those in the first rank, the most eager, the most enthusiastic, was my worthy uncle, Professor Hardwigg.

The authenticity of a human fossil of the Quaternary period seemed then to be incontestably demonstrated, and even to be admitted by the most skeptical.

This system or theory, call it what you will, had, it is true, a bitter adversary in M. Elie de Beaumont. This learned man, who holds such a high place in the scientific world, holds that the soil of Moulin-Quignon does not belong to the diluvium, but to a much less ancient strata, and, in accordance with Cuvier in this respect, he would by no means admit that the human species was contemporary with the animals of the Quaternary epoch. My worthy uncle, Professor Hardwigg, in concert with the great majority of geologists, had held firm, had disputed, discussed, and finally, after considerable talking and writing, M. Elie le Beaumont had been pretty well left alone in his opinions.

We were familiar with all the details of this discussion, but were far from being aware then that since our departure the matter had entered upon a new phase. Other similar jawbones, though belonging to individuals of varied types and very different natures, had been found in the movable gray sands of certain grottoes in France, Switzerland, and Belgium; together with arms, utensils, tools, bones of children, of men in the prime of life, and of old men. The existence of men in the Quaternary period became, therefore, more positive every day.

But this was far from being all. New remains, dug up from the Pliocene or Tertiary deposits, had enabled the more farseeing or audacious among learned men to assign even a far greater degree of antiquity to the human race. These remains, it is true, were not those of men; that is, were not the bones of men, but objects decidedly having served the human race: shinbones, thighbones of fossil animals, regularly scooped out, and in fact sculptured—bearing the unmistakable signs of human handiwork.

By means of these wondrous and unexpected discoveries, man ascended endless centuries in the scale of time; he, in fact, preceded the mastodon; became the contemporary of the *Elephas meridionalis*—the southern elephant; acquired an antiquity of over a hundred thousand years, since that is the date given by the most eminent geologists to the Pliocene period of the earth. Such was then the state of paleontologic science, and what we moreover knew sufficed to explain our attitude before this great cemetery of the plains of the Hardwigg Ocean.

It will now be easy to understand the Professor's mingled astonishment and joy when, on advancing about twenty yards, he found himself in the presence of, I may say face to face with, a specimen of the human race actually belonging to the Quaternary period!

It was indeed a human skull, perfectly recognizable. Had a soil of very peculiar nature, like that of the cemetery of St. Michel at Borleaux, preserved it during countless ages? This was the question I asked myself, but which I was wholly unable to answer. But this head with stretched and parchmenty skin, with the teeth whole, the hair abundant, was before our eyes as in life!

I stood mute, almost paralyzed with wonder and awe before this dread apparition of another age. My uncle, who on almost every occasion was a great talker, remained for a time completely dumbfounded. He was too full of emotion for speech to be possible. After a while, however, we raised up the body to which the skull belonged. We stood it on end. It seemed, to our excited imaginations, to look at us with its terrible hollow eyes.

After some minutes of silence, the man was vanquished by the Professor. Human instincts succumbed to scientific pride and exultation. Professor Hardwigg, carried away by his enthusiasm, forgot all the circumstances of our journey, the extraordinary position in which we were placed, the immense cavern which stretched far away over our heads. There can be no doubt that he thought himself at the Institution addressing his attentive pupils, for he put on his most doctorial style, waved his hand, and began:

"Gentlemen, I have the honor on this auspicious occasion to present to you a man of the Quaternary period of our globe. Many learned men have denied his very existence, while other able persons, perhaps of even higher authority, have affirmed their belief in the reality of his life. If the St. Thomases of paleontology were present, they would reverentially touch him with their fingers and believe in his existence, thus acknowledging their obstinate heresy. I know that science should be careful in relation to all discoveries of this nature. I am not without having heard of the many

Barnums and other quacks who have made a trade of such like pretended discoveries. I have, of course, heard of the discovery of the kneebones of Ajax, of the pretended finding of the body of Orestes by the Spartiates, and of the body of Asterius, ten spans long, fifteen feet—of which we read in Pausanias.

"I have read everything in relation to the skeleton of Trapani, discovered in the fourteenth century, and which many persons chose to regard as that of Polyphemus, and the history of the giant dug up during the sixteenth century in the environs of Palmyra. You are as well aware as I am, gentlemen, of the existence of the celebrated analysis made near Lucerne, in 1577, of the great bones which the celebrated Doctor Felix Plater declared belonged to a giant about nineteen feet high. I have devoured all the treatises of Cassanion, and all those memoirs, pamphlets, speeches, and replies published in reference to the skeleton of Teutobochus, king of the Cimbri, the invader of Gaul, dug out of a gravel pit in Dauphiné, in 1613. In the eighteenth century I should have denied, with Peter Campet, the existence of the preadamites of Scheuchzer. I have had in my hands the writing called Gigans—"

Here my uncle was afflicted by the natural infirmity which prevented him from pronouncing difficult words in public. It was not exactly stuttering, but a strange sort of constitutional hesitation.

"The writing named Gigans—" he repeated.

He, however, could get no further.

"Giganteo—"

Impossible! The unfortunate word would not come out. There would have been great laughter at the Institution, had the mistake happened there.

"Gigantosteology!" at last exclaimed Professor Hardwigg between two savage growls.

Having got over our difficulty, and getting more and more excited—

"Yes, gentlemen, I am well acquainted with all these matters, and know, also, that Cuvier and Blumenbach fully recognized in these bones the undeniable remains of mammoths of the Quaternary period. But after what we now see, to allow a doubt is to insult scientific inquiry. There is the body; you can see it; you can touch it. It is not a skeleton, it is a complete and uninjured body, preserved with an anthropological object."

I did not attempt to controvert this singular and astounding assertion.

"If I could but wash this corpse in a solution of sulphuric acid," continued my uncle, "I would undertake to remove all the earthy particles, and these resplendent shells, which are incrusted all over this body. But I am without this precious dissolving medium. Nevertheless, such as it is, this body will tell its own history."

Here the Professor held up the fossil body, and exhibited it with rare dexterity. No professional showman could have shown more activity.

"As on examination you will see," my uncle continued, "it is only about six feet in length, which is a long way from the pretended giants of early days. As to the particular race to which it belonged, it is incontestably Caucasian. It is of the white race, that is, of our own. The skull of this fossil being is a perfect ovoid without any remarkable or prominent development of the cheekbones, and without any projection of the jaw. It presents no indication of the prognathism which modifies the facial angle.* Measure the angle for yourselves, and you will find that it is just ninety degrees. But I will advance still farther on the road of inquiry and deduction, and I dare venture to say that this human sample or specimen belongs to the Japhetic family, which spread over the world from India to the uttermost limits of western Europe. There is no occasion, gentlemen, to smile at my remarks."

Of course nobody smiled. But the excellent Professor was so accustomed to beaming countenances at his lectures, that he believed he saw all his audience laughing during the delivery of his learned dissertation.

"Yes," he continued, with renewed animation, "this is a fossil man, a contemporary of the mastodons, with the bones of which this whole amphitheater is covered. But if I am called on to explain how he came to this place, how these various strata by which he is covered have fallen into this vast cavity, I can undertake to give you no explanation. Doubtless, if we carry ourselves back to the Quaternary epoch, we shall find that great and mighty convulsions took place in the crust of the earth; the continually cooling operation, through which the earth had to pass, produced fissures, landslips, and chasms, through which a large portion of the earth made its way. I come to no absolute conclusion, but there is the man, surrounded by the works of his hands, his hatchets and his carved flints, which belong to the stony period; and the only rational supposition is, that, like myself, he visited the center of the earth as a traveling tourist, a pioneer of science. At

* The facial angle is formed by two planes—one more or less vertical which is in a straight line with the forehead and the incisors; the other, horizontal, which passes through the organs of hearing, and the lower nasal bone. Prognathism, in anthropological language, means that particular projection of the jaw which modifies the facial angle.

all events, there can be no doubt of his great age, and of his being one of the oldest race of human beings."

The Professor with these words ceased his oration, and I burst forth into loud and "unanimous" applause. Besides, after all, my uncle was right. Much more learned men than his nephew would have found it rather hard to refute his facts and arguments.

Another circumstance soon presented itself. This fossilized body was not the only one in this vast plain of bones—the cemetery of an extinct world. Other bodies were found, as we trod the dusty plain, and my uncle was able to choose the most marvelous of these specimens in order to convince the most incredulous.

In truth, it was a surprising spectacle, the successive remains of generations and generations of men and animals confounded together in one vast cemetery. But a great question now presented itself to our notice, and one we were actually afraid to contemplate in all its bearings.

Had these once animated beings been buried so far beneath the soil by tremendous convulsion of Nature, after they had been earth to earth and ashes to ashes, or had they lived here below, in this subterranean world, under this factitious sky, borne, married, and given in marriage, and died at last, just like ordinary inhabitants of the earth?

Up to the present moment, marine monsters, fish, and such like animals had alone been seen alive!

The question, which rendered us rather uneasy, was a pertinent one. Were any of these men of the abyss wandering about the deserted shores of this wondrous sea of the center of the earth?

This was a question which rendered me very uneasy and uncomfortable. How, should they really be in existence, would they receive us men from above?

XXXVI

What Is It?

For a long and weary hour we tramped over this great bed of bones. We advanced regardless of everything, drawn on by ardent curiosity. What other marvels did this great cavern contain—what other wondrous treasures for the scientific man? My eyes were quite prepared for any number of surprises, my imagination lived in expectation of something new and wonderful.

The borders of the great Central Ocean had for some time disappeared behind the hills that were scattered over the ground occupied by the plain of bones. The imprudent and enthusiastic Professor, who did not care whether he lost himself or not, hurried me forward. We advanced silently, bathed in waves of electric fluid.

By reason of a phenomenon which I cannot explain, and thanks to its extreme diffusion, now complete, the light illumined equally the sides of every hill and rock. Its seat appeared to be nowhere, in no determined force, and produced no shade whatever.

The appearance presented was that of a tropical country at midday in summer—in the midst of the equatorial regions and under the vertical rays of the sun.

All signs of vapor had disappeared. The rocks, the distant mountains, some confused masses of far-off forests, assumed a weird and mysterious aspect under this equal distribution of the luminous fluid!

We resembled, to a certain extent, the mysterious personage in one of Hoffmann's fantastic tales—the man who lost his shadow.

After we had walked about a mile farther, we came to the edge of a vast forest, not, however, one of the vast mushroom forests we had discovered near Port Gretchen.

It was the glorious and wild vegetation of the Tertiary period, in all its superb magnificence. Huge palms, of a species now unknown, superb palmacites—a genus of fossil palms from the coal formation—pines, yews, cypress, and conifers or cone-bearing trees, the whole bound together by an inextricable and complicated mass of creeping plants.

A beautiful carpet of mosses and ferns grew beneath the trees. Pleasant brooks murmured beneath umbrageous boughs, little worthy of this name, for no shade did they give. Upon their borders grew small treelike shrubs, such as are seen in the hot countries on our own inhabited globe.

The one thing wanted in these plants, these shrubs, these trees—was color! Forever deprived of the vivifying warmth of the sun, they were vapid and colorless. All shade was lost in one uniform tint, of a brown and faded character. The leaves were wholly devoid of verdure, and the flowers, so numerous during the Tertiary period which gave them birth, were without color and without perfume, something like paper discolored by long exposure to the atmosphere.

My uncle ventured beneath the gigantic groves. I followed him, though not without a certain amount of apprehension. Since Nature had shown herself capable of producing such stupendous vegetable productions, why might we not meet with mammals (animals with breasts) as large, and therefore dangerous.

I particularly remarked, in the clearings left by trees that had fallen and been partially consumed by time, many leguminous (beanlike) shrubs, such as the maple and other eatable trees, dear to ruminating animals. Then there appeared confounded together and intermixed, the trees of such varied lands, specimens of the vegetation of every part of the globe; there was the oak near the palm tree, the Australian eucalyptus, an interesting class of the order *Myrtaceae*—leaning against the tall Norwegian pine, the poplar of the north, mixing its branches with those of the New Zealand kauris. It was enough to drive the most ingenious classifier of the upper regions out of his mind, and to upset all his received ideas about botany.

Suddenly I stopped short and restrained my uncle.

The extreme diffuseness of the light enabled me to see the smallest objects in the distant copses. I thought I saw—no, I really did see with my own eyes—immense, gigantic animals moving about under the mighty trees. Yes, they were truly gigantic animals, a whole herd of mastodons, not fossils, but living, and exactly like those discovered in 1801, on the marshy banks of the great Ohio, in North America.

Yes, I could see these enormous elephants, whose trunks were tearing down large boughs, and working in and out of the trees like a legion of serpents. I could hear the sounds of the mighty tusks uprooting huge trees!

The boughs crackled, and the whole masses of leaves and green branches went down the capacious throats of these terrible monsters!

That wondrous dream, when I saw the antehistorical times revivified, when the Tertiary and Quaternary periods passed before me, was now realized!

And there we were alone, far down in the bowels of the earth, at the mercy of its ferocious inhabitants!

My uncle paused, full of wonder and astonishment.

"Come," he said at last, when his first surprise was over, "come along, my boy, and let us see them nearer."

"No," replied I, restraining his efforts to drag me forward, "we are wholly without arms. What should we do in the midst of that flock of gigantic quadrupeds? Come away, Uncle, I implore you. No human creature can with impunity brave the ferocious anger of these monsters."

"No human creature," said my uncle, suddenly lowering his voice to a mysterious whisper, "you are mistaken, my dear Henry. Look! look yonder! It seems to me that I behold a human being—a being like ourselves—a man!"

I looked, shrugging my shoulders, decided to push incredulity to its very last limits. But whatever might have been my wish, I was compelled to yield to the weight of ocular demonstration.

Yes—not more than a quarter of a mile off, leaning against the trunk of an enormous tree, was a human being—a Proteus of these subterranean regions, a new son of Neptune keeping this innumerable herd of mastodons.

*Immanis pecoris custos, immanis ipse!**

Yes—it was no longer a fossil whose corpse we had raised from the ground in the great cemetery, but a giant capable of guiding and driving these prodigious monsters. His height was above twelve feet. His head, as big as the head of a buffalo, was lost in a mane of matted hair. It was indeed a huge mane, like those which belonged to the elephants of the earlier ages of the world.

In his hand was a branch of a tree, which served as a crook for this antediluvian shepherd.

We remained profoundly still, speechless with surprise.

But we might at any moment be seen by him. Nothing remained for us but instant flight.

"Come, come!" I cried, dragging my uncle along; and, for the first time, he made no resistance to my wishes.

A quarter of an hour later we were far away from that terrible monster!

Now that I think of the matter calmly, and that I reflect upon it dispassionately; now that months, years, have passed since this strange and unnatural adventure befell us—what am I to think, what am I to believe?

No, it is utterly impossible! Our ears must have deceived us, and our eyes have cheated us! we have not seen what we believed we had seen. No human being could by any possibility have existed in that subterranean world! No generation of men could inhabit the lower caverns of the globe

* The keeper of gigantic cattle, himself a giant!

without taking note of those who peopled the surface, without communication with them. It was folly, folly, folly! nothing else!

I am rather inclined to admit the existence of some animal resembling in structure the human race—of some monkey of the first geological epochs, like that discovered by M. Lartet in the ossiferous deposit of Sansan.

But this animal, or being, whichsoever it was, surpassed in height all things known to modern science. Never mind. However unlikely it may be, it might have been a monkey—but a man, a living man, and with him a whole generation of gigantic animals, buried in the entrails of the earth—it was too monstrous to be believed!

XXXVII

The Mysterious Dagger

During this time, we had left the bright and transparent forest far behind us. We were mute with astonishment, overcome by a kind of feeling which was next door to apathy. We kept running in spite of ourselves. It was a perfect flight, which resembled one of those horrible sensations we sometimes meet with in our dreams.

Instinctively we made our way toward the Central Sea, and I cannot now tell what wild thoughts passed through my mind, nor of what follies I might have been guilty, but for a very serious preoccupation which brought me back to practical life.

Though I was aware that we were treading on a soil quite new to us, I, however, every now and then noticed certain aggregations of rock, the shape of which forcibly reminded me of those near Port Gretchen.

This confirmed, moreover, the indications of the compass and our extraordinary and unlooked-for, as well as involuntary, return to the north of this great Central Sea. It was so like our starting point, that I could scarcely doubt the reality of our position. Streams and cascades fed in hundreds over the numerous projections of the rocks.

I actually thought I could see our faithful and monotonous Hans and the wonderful grotto in which I had come back to life after my tremendous fall.

Then, as we advanced still farther, the position of the cliffs, the appearance of a stream, the unexpected profile of a rock, threw me again into a state of bewildering doubt.

After some time, I explained my state of mental indecision to my uncle. He confessed to a similar feeling of hesitation. He was totally unable to make up his mind in the midst of this extraordinary but uniform panorama.

"There can be no doubt," I insisted, "that we have not landed exactly at the place whence we first took our departure; but the tempest has brought us above our starting point. I think, therefore, that if we follow the coast we shall once more find Port Gretchen."

"In that case," cried my uncle, "it is useless to continue our exploration. The very best thing we can do is to make our way back to the raft. Are you quite sure, Harry, that you are not mistaken?"

"It is difficult," was my reply, "to come to any decision, for all these rocks are exactly alike. There is no marked difference between them. At the same time, the impression on my mind is that I recognize the promontory at the foot of which our worthy Hans constructed the raft. We are, I am nearly convinced, near the little port: if this be not it," I added, carefully examining a creek which appeared singularly familiar to my mind.

"My dear Harry—if this were the case, we should find traces of our own footsteps, some signs of our passage; and I can really see nothing to indicate our having passed this way."

"But I see something," I cried, in an impetuous tone of voice, as I rushed forward and eagerly picked up something which shone in the sand under my feet.

"What is it?" cried the astonished and bewildered Professor.

"This," was my reply.

And I handed to my startled relative a rusty dagger, of singular shape.

"What made you bring with you so useless a weapon?" he exclaimed. "It was needlessly hampering yourself."

"I bring it? It is quite new to me. I never saw it before—are you sure it is not out of your collection?"

"Not that I know of," said the Professor, puzzled. "I have no recollection of the circumstance. It was never my property."

"This is very extraordinary," I said, musing over the novel and singular incident.

"Not at all. There is a very simple explanation, Harry. The Icelanders are known to keep up the use of these antiquated weapons, and this must have belonged to Hans, who has let it fall without knowing it."

I shook my head. That dagger had never been in the possession of the pacific and taciturn Hans. I knew him and his habits too well.

"Then what can it be—unless it be the weapon of some antediluvian warrior," I continued, "of some living man, a contemporary of that mighty shepherd from whom we have just escaped? But no—mystery upon mystery—this is no weapon of the stony epoch, nor even of the bronze period. It is made of excellent steel—"

Ere I could finish my sentence, my uncle stopped me short from entering upon a whole train of theories, and spoke in his most cold and decided tone of voice.

"Calm yourself, my dear boy, and endeavor to use your reason. This weapon, upon which we have fallen so unexpectedly, is a true *dague,* one of those worn by gentlemen in their belts during the sixteenth century. Its use was to give the *coup de grâce,* the final blow, to the foe who would not surrender. It is clearly of Spanish workmanship. It belongs neither to you, nor to me, nor to the eider-down hunter, nor to any of the living beings who may still exist so marvelously in the interior of the earth."

"What can you mean, Uncle?" I said, now lost in a host of surmises.

"Look closely at it," he continued; "these jagged edges were never made by the resistance of human blood and bone. The blade is covered with a regular coating of iron mold and rust, which is not a day old, not a year old, not a century old, but much more—"

The Professor began to get quite excited, according to custom, and was allowing himself to be carried away by his fertile imagination. I could have said something. He stopped me.

"Harry," he cried, "we are now on the verge of a great discovery. This blade of a dagger you have so marvelously discovered, after being abandoned upon the sand for more than a hundred, two hundred, even three hundred years, has been indented by someone endeavoring to carve an inscription on these rocks."

"But this poniard never got here of itself," I exclaimed, "it could not have twisted itself. Someone, therefore, must have preceded us upon the shores of this extraordinary sea."

"Yes, a man."

"But what man has been sufficiently desperate to do such a thing?"

"A man who has somewhere written his name with this very dagger—a man who has endeavored once more to indicate the right road to the interior of the earth. Let us look around, my boy. You know not the importance of your singular and happy discovery."

Prodigiously interested, we walked along the wall of rock, examining the smallest fissures, which might finally expand into the much wished-for gully or shaft.

We at last reached a spot where the shore became extremely narrow. The sea almost bathed the foot of the rocks, which were here very lofty and steep. There was scarcely a path wider than two yards at any point. At last, under a huge overhanging rock, we discovered the entrance of a dark and gloomy tunnel.

There, on a square tablet of granite, which had been smoothed by rubbing it with another stone, we could see two mysterious, and much worn letters, the two initials of the bold and extraordinary traveler who had preceded us on our adventurous journey.

"A. S.," cried my uncle; "you see I was right. Arne Saknussemm, always Arne Saknussemm!"

XXXVIII

NO OUTLET—BLASTING THE ROCK

Ever since the commencement of our marvelous journey, I had experienced many surprises, had suffered from many illusions. I thought that I was case-hardened against all surprises and could neither see nor hear anything to amaze me again.

I was like a man who, having been around the world, finds himself wholly *blasé* and proof against the marvelous.

When, however, I saw these two letters, which had been engraven three hundred years before, I stood fixed in an attitude of mute surprise.

Not only was there the signature of the learned and enterprising alchemist written in the rock, but I held in my hand the very identical instrument with which he had laboriously engraved it.

It was impossible, without showing an amount of incredulity scarcely becoming a sane man, to deny the existence of the traveler, and the reality of that voyage which I believed all along to have been a myth—the mystification of some fertile brain.

While these reflections were passing through my mind, my uncle, the Professor, gave way to an access of feverish and poetical excitement.

"Wonderful and glorious genius, great Saknussemm," he cried, "you have left no stone unturned, no resource omitted, to show to other mortals the way into the interior of our mighty globe, and your fellow creatures can find the trail left by your illustrious footsteps, three hundred years ago, at the bottom of these obscure subterranean abodes. You have been careful to secure for others the contemplation of these wonders and marvels of creation. Your name engraved at every important stage of your glorious journey leads the hopeful traveler directly to the great and mighty discovery to which you devoted such energy and courage. The audacious traveler, who shall follow your footsteps to the last, will doubtless find your initials engraved with your own hand upon the center of the earth. *I* will be that audacious traveler—*I*, too, will sign my name upon the very same spot, upon the central granite stone of this wondrous work of the Creator. But in justice to your devotion, to your courage, and to your being the first to indicate the road, let this cape, seen by you upon the shores of this sea discovered by you, be called, of all time, Cape Saknussemm."

This is what I heard, and I began to be roused to the pitch of enthusiasm indicated by those words. A fierce excitement roused me. I forgot everything. The dangers of the voyage and the perils of the return journey were now as nothing!

What another man had done in ages past could, I felt, be done again; I was determined to do it myself, and now nothing that man had accomplished appeared to me impossible.

"Forward—forward," I cried in a burst of genuine and hearty enthusiasm.

I had already started in the direction of the somber and gloomy gallery when the Professor stopped me; he, the man so rash and hasty, he, the man so easily roused to the highest pitch of enthusiasm, checked me, and asked me to be patient and show more calm.

"Let us return to our good friend, Hans," he said; "we will then bring the raft down to this place."

I must say that though I at once yielded to my uncle's request, it was not without dissatisfaction, and I hastened along the rocks of that wonderful coast.

"Do you know, my dear uncle," I said, as we walked along, "that we have been singularly helped by a concurrence of circumstances, right up to this very moment."

"So you begin to see it, do you, Harry?" said the Professor with a smile.

"Doubtless," I responded, "and strangely enough, even the tempest has been the means of putting us on the right road. Blessings on the tempest! It brought us safely back to the very spot from which fine weather would have driven us forever. Supposing we had succeeded in reaching the southern and distant shores of this extraordinary sea, what would have become of us? The name of Saknussemm would never have appeared to us, and at this moment we should have been cast away upon an inhospitable coast, probably without an outlet."

"Yes, Harry, my boy, there is certainly something providential in that wandering at the mercy of wind and waves toward the south: we have come back exactly north; and what is better still, we fall upon this great discovery of Cape Saknussemm. I mean to say, that it is more than surprising; there is something in it which is far beyond my comprehension. The coincidence is unheard of, marvelous!"

"What matter! It is not our duty to explain facts, but to make the best possible use of them."

"Doubtless, my boy; but if you will allow me—" said the really delighted Professor.

"Excuse me, sir, but I see exactly how it will be; we shall take the northern route; we shall pass under the northern regions of Europe, under Sweden, under Russia, under Siberia, and who knows where—instead of burying ourselves under the burning plains and deserts of Africa, or beneath the mighty waves of the ocean; and that is all, at this stage of our journey, that I care to know. Let us advance, and Heaven will be our guide!"

"Yes, Harry, you are right, quite right; all is for the best. Let us abandon this horizontal sea, which could never have led to anything satisfactory. We shall descend, descend, and everlastingly descend. Do you know, my dear boy, that to reach the interior of the earth we have only five thousand miles to travel!"

"Bah!" I cried, carried away by a burst of enthusiasm, "the distance is scarcely worth speaking about. The thing is to make a start."

My wild, mad, and incoherent speeches continued until we rejoined our patient and phlegmatic guide. All was, we found, prepared for an immediate departure. There was not a single parcel but what was in its proper place. We all took up our posts on the raft, and the sail being hoisted, Hans received his directions, and guided the frail bark toward Cape Saknussemm, as we had definitely named it.

The wind was very unfavorable to a craft that was unable to sail close to the wind. It was constructed to go before the blast. We were continually reduced to pushing ourselves forward by means of poles. On several occasions the rocks ran far out into deep water and we were compelled to make a long round. At last, after three long and weary hours of navigation, that is to say, about six o'clock in the evening, we found a place at which we could land.

I jumped on shore first. In my present state of excitement and enthusiasm, I was always first. My uncle and the Icelander followed. The voyage from the port to this point of the sea had by no means calmed me. It had rather produced the opposite effect. I even proposed to burn our vessel, that is to destroy our raft, in order to completely cut off our retreat. But my uncle sternly opposed this wild project. I began to think him particularly lukewarm and unenthusiastic.

"At any rate, my dear uncle," I said, "let us start without delay."

"Yes, my boy, I am quite as eager to do so as you can be. But, in the first place, let us examine this mysterious gallery, in order to find if we shall need to prepare and mend our ladders."

My uncle now began to see to the efficiency of our Ruhmkorf's coil, which would doubtless soon be needed; the raft, securely fastened to a rock, was left alone. Moreover, the opening into the new gallery was not twenty paces distant from the spot. Our little troop, with myself at the head, advanced.

The orifice, which was almost circular, presented a diameter of about five feet; the somber tunnel was cut in the living rock, and coated on the inside by the different material which had once passed through it in a state of fusion. The lower part was about level with the water, so that we were able to penetrate to the interior without difficulty.

We followed an almost horizontal direction; when, at the end of about a dozen paces, our further advance was checked by the interposition of an enormous block of granite rock.

"Accursed stone!" I cried furiously, on perceiving that we were stopped by what seemed an insurmountable obstacle.

In vain we looked to the right, in vain we looked to the left; in vain examined it above and below. There existed no passage, no sign of any other tunnel. I experienced the most bitter and painful disappointment. So enraged was I that I would not admit the reality of any obstacle. I stopped to my knees; I looked under the mass of stone. No hole, no interstice. I then looked above. The same barrier of granite! Hans, with the lamp, examined the sides of the tunnel in every direction. But all in vain! It was necessary to renounce all hope of passing through.

I had seated myself upon the ground. My uncle walked angrily and hopelessly up and down. He was evidently desperate.

"But," I cried, after some moments' thought, "what about Arne Saknussemm?"

"You are right," replied my uncle, "he can never have been checked by a lump of rock."

"No—ten thousand times no," I cried, with extreme vivacity. "This huge lump of rock, in consequence of some singular concussion, or process, one of those magnetic phenomena which have so often shaken the terrestrial crust, has in some unexpected way closed up the passage. Many and many years have passed away since the return of Saknussemm, and the fall of this huge block of granite. Is it not quite evident that this gallery was formerly the outlet for the pent-up lava in the interior of the earth, and that these eruptive matters then circulated freely? Look at these recent fissures in the granite roof; it is evidently formed of pieces of enormous stone, placed here as if by the hand of a giant, who had worked to make a strong and substantial arch. One day, after an unusually strong shock, the vast rock which stands in our way, and which was doubtless the key of a kind of arch, fell through to a level with the soil and has barred our further progress. We are right, then, in thinking that this is an unexpected obstacle, with which Saknussemm did not meet; and if we do not upset it in some way, we are unworthy of following in the footsteps of the great discoverer; and incapable of finding our way to the center of the earth!"

In this wild way I addressed my uncle. The zeal of the Professor, his earnest longing for success, had become part and parcel of my being. I wholly forgot the past; I utterly despised the future. Nothing existed for me upon the surface of this spheroid in the bosom of which I was engulfed, no towns, no country, no Hamburg, no Königstrasse, not even my poor

Gretchen, who by this time would believe me utterly lost in the interior of the earth!

"Well," cried my uncle, roused to enthusiasm by my words, "let us go to work with pickaxes, with crowbars, with anything that comes to hand—but down with these terrible walls."

"It is far too tough and too big to be destroyed by a pickax or crowbar," I replied.

"What then?"

"As I said, it is useless to think of overcoming such a difficulty by means of ordinary tools."

"What then?"

"What else but gunpowder, a subterranean mine? Let us blow up the obstacle that stands in our way."

"Gunpowder!"

"Yes; all we have to do is get rid of this paltry obstacle."

"To work, Hans, to work!" cried the Professor.

The Icelander went back to the raft, and soon returned with a huge crowbar, with which he began to dig a hole in the rock, which was to serve as a mine. It was by no means a slight task. It was necessary for our purpose to make a cavity large enough to hold fifty pounds of fulminating gun cotton, the expansive power of which is four times as great as that of ordinary gunpowder.

I had roused myself to an almost miraculous state of excitement. While Hans was at work, I actively assisted my uncle to prepare a long wick, made from damp gunpowder, the mass of which we finally enclosed in a bag of linen.

"We are bound to go through," I cried, enthusiastically.

"We are bound to go through," responded the Professor, tapping me on the back.

At midnight, our work as miners was completely finished; the charge of fulminating cotton was thrust into the hollow, and the match, which we had made of considerable length, was ready.

A spark was now sufficient to ignite this formidable engine, and to blow the rock to atoms!

"We will now rest until tomorrow."

It was absolutely necessary to resign myself to my fate, and to consent to wait for the explosion for six weary hours!

XXXIX

The Explosion and Its Results

The next day, which was the twenty-seventh of August, was a day celebrated in our wondrous, subterranean journey.

I never think of it even now, but I shudder with horror. My heart beats wildly at the very memory of that awful day.

From this time forward, our reason, our judgment, our human ingenuity, have nothing to do with the course of events. We are about to become the plaything of the great phenomena of the earth!

At six o'clock we were all up and ready. The dreaded moment was arriving when we were about to seek an opening into the interior of the earth by means of gunpowder. What would be the consequences of breaking through the crust of the earth?

I begged that it might be my duty to set fire to the mine. I looked upon it as an honor. This task once performed, I could rejoin my friends upon the raft, which had not been unloaded. As soon as we were all ready, we were to sail away to some distance to avoid the consequences of the explosion, the effects of which would certainly not be concentrated in the interior of the earth.

The slow match we calculated to burn for about ten minutes, more or less, before it reached the chamber in which the great body of powder was confined. I should therefore have plenty of time to reach the raft and put off to a safe distance.

I prepared to execute my self-allotted task—not, it must be confessed, without considerable emotion.

After a hearty repast, my uncle and the hunter-guide embarked on board the raft, while I remained alone upon the desolate shore.

I was provided with a lantern which was to enable me to set fire to the wick of the infernal machine.

"Go, my boy," said my uncle, "and Heaven be with you. But come back as soon as you can. I shall be all impatience."

"Be easy on that matter," I replied; "there is no fear of my delaying on the road."

Having said this, I advanced toward the opening of the somber gallery. My heart beat wildly. I opened my lantern and seized the extremity of the wick.

The Professor, who was looking on, held his chronometer in his hand.

"Are you ready?" cried he.

"Quite ready."

"Well, then, fire away!"

I hastened to put the light to the wick, which crackled and sparkled, hissing and spitting like a serpent; then, running as fast as I could, I returned to the shore.

"Get on board, my lad, and you, Hans, shove off," cried my uncle.

By a vigorous application of his pole Hans sent us flying over the water. The raft was quite twenty fathoms distant.

It was a moment of palpitating interest, of deep anxiety. My uncle, the Professor, never took his eyes off the chronometer.

"Only five minutes more," he said in a low tone, "only four, only three."

My pulse went a hundred to the minute. I could hear my heart beating.

"Only two, one! Now, then, mountains of granite, crumble beneath the power of man!"

What happened after that? As to the terrific roar of the explosion, I do not think I heard it. But the form of the rocks completely changed in my eyes—they seemed to be drawn aside like a curtain. I saw a fathomless, and bottomless abyss, which yawned beneath the turgid waves. The sea, which seemed suddenly to have gone mad, then became one great mountainous mass, upon the top of which the raft rose perpendicularly.

We were all thrown down. In less than a second the light gave place to the most profound obscurity. Then I felt all solid support give way not to my feet, but to the raft itself. I thought it was going bodily down to a tremendous well. I tried to speak, to question my uncle. Nothing could be heard but the roaring of the mighty waves. We clung together in utter silence.

Despite the awful darkness, despite the noise, the surprise, the emotion, I thoroughly understood what had happened.

Beyond the rock which had been blown up, there existed a mighty abyss. The explosion had caused a kind of earthquake in this soil, broken by fissures and rents. The gulf, thus suddenly thrown open, was about to swallow the inland sea, which, transformed into a mighty torrent, was dragging us with it.

Only one idea filled my mind. We were utterly and completely lost!

One hour, two hours—what more I cannot say, passed in this manner. We sat close together, elbow touching elbow, knee touching knee! We held one another's hands not to be thrown off the raft. We were subjected to the most violent shocks, whenever our sole dependence, a frail wooden raft, struck against the rocky sides of the channel. Fortunately for us, these concussions became less and less frequent, which made me fancy that the gallery was getting wider and wider. There could be now no doubt that we had chanced upon the road once followed by Saknussemm, but instead of going down in a proper manner, we had, through our own imprudence, drawn a whole sea with us!

These ideas presented themselves to my mind in a very vague and obscure manner. I felt rather than reasoned. I put my ideas together only confusedly, while spinning along like a man going down a waterfall. To judge by the air which, as it were, whipped my face, we must have been rushing at a perfectly lightning rate.

To attempt under these circumstances to light a torch was simply impossible, and the last remains of our electric machine, of our Ruhmkorf's coil, had been destroyed during the fearful explosion.

I was therefore very much confused to see at last a bright light shining close to me. The calm countenance of the guide seemed to gleam upon me. The clever and patient hunter had succeeded in lighting the lantern; and though, in the keen and thorough draft, the flame flickered and vacillated and was nearly put out, it served partially to dissipate the awful obscurity.

The gallery into which we had entered was very wide. I was, therefore, quite right in that part of my conjecture. The insufficient light did not allow us to see both of the walls at the same time. The slope of waters, which was carrying us away, was far greater than that of the most rapid river of America. The whole surface of the stream seemed to be composed of liquid arrows, darted forward with extreme violence and power. I can give no idea of the impression it made upon me.

The raft, at times, caught in certain whirlpools, and rushed forward, yet turned on itself all the time. How it did not upset I shall never be able to understand. When it approached the sides of the gallery, I took care to throw upon them the light of the lantern, and I was able to judge the rapidity of motion by looking at the projecting masses of rock, which as soon as seen were again invisible. So rapid was our progress that points of rock at a considerable distance one from the other appeared like portions of transverse lines, which enclosed us in a kind of net, like that of a line of telegraphic wires.

I believe we were now going at a rate of not less than a hundred miles an hour.

My uncle and I looked at one another with wild and haggard eyes; we clung convulsively to the stump of the mast, which, at the moment when the catastrophe took place, had snapped short off. We turned our backs as much as possible to the wind, in order not to be stifled by a rapidity of motion which nothing human could face and live.

And still the long monotonous hours went on. The situation did not change in the least, though a discovery I suddenly made seemed to complicate it very much.

When we had slightly recovered our equilibrium, I proceeded to examine our cargo. I then made the unsatisfactory discovery that the greater part of it had utterly disappeared.

I became alarmed, and determined to discover what were our resources. My heart beat at the idea, but it was absolutely necessary to know on what we had to depend. With this view, I took the lantern and looked around.

Of all our former collection of nautical and philosophical instruments, there remained only the chronometer and the compass. The adders and ropes were reduced to a small piece of rope fastened to the stump of the mast. Not a pickax, not a crowbar, not a hammer, and, far worse than all, no food—not enough for one day!

This discovery was a prelude to a certain and horrible death.

Seated gloomily on the raft, clasping the stump of the mast mechanically, I thought of all I had read as to sufferings from starvation.

I remembered everything that history had taught me on the subject, and I shuddered at the remembrance of the agonies to be endured.

Maddened at the prospects of enduring the miseries of starvation, I persuaded myself that I must be mistaken. I examined the cracks in the raft; I poked between the joints and beams; I examined every possible hole and corner. The result was—simply nothing!

Our stock of provisions consisted of nothing but a piece of dry meat and some soaked and half-moldy biscuits.

I gazed around me scared and frightened. I could not understand the awful truth. And yet of what consequence was it in regard to any new danger? Supposing that we had had provisions for months, and even for years, how could we ever get out of the awful abyss into which we were being hurled by the irresistible torrent we had let loose?

Why should we trouble ourselves about the sufferings and tortures to be endured from hunger when death stared us in the face under so many other swifter and perhaps even more horrid forms?

It was very doubtful, under the circumstances in which we were placed, if we should have time to die of innition.

But the human frame is singularly constituted.

I knew not how it was; but, from some singular hallucination of mind, I forgot the real, serious, and immediate danger to which we were exposed, to think of the menaces of the future, which appeared before us in all their naked terror. Besides, after all, suggested Hope, perhaps we might finally escape the fury of the raging torrent, and once more revisit the glimpse of the moon, on the surface of our beautiful Mother Earth.

How was it to be done? I had not the remotest idea. Where were we to come out? No matter, so that we did.

One chance in a thousand is always a chance, while death from hunger gave us not even the faintest glimpse of hope. It left to the imagination nothing but blank horror, without the faintest chance of escape!

I had the greatest mind to reveal all to my uncle, to explain to him the extraordinary and wretched position to which we were reduced, in order that, between the two, we might make a calculation to the exact space of time which remained for us to live.

It was, it appeared to me, the only thing to be done. But I had the courage to hold my tongue, to gnaw at my entrails like the Spartan boy. I wished to leave him all his coolness.

At this moment, the light of the lantern slowly fell, and at last went out!

The wick had wholly burnt to an end. The obscurity became absolute. It was no longer possible to see through the impenetrable darkness! There was one torch left, but it was impossible to keep it alight. Then, like a child, I shut my eyes, that I might not see the darkness.

After a great lapse of time, the rapidity of our journey increased. I could feel it by the rush of air upon my face. The slope of the waters was excessive. I began to feel that we were no longer going down a slope; we were falling. I felt as one does in a dream, going down bodily—falling; falling; falling!

I felt that the hands of my uncle and Hans were vigorously clasping my arms.

Suddenly, after a lapse of time scarcely appreciable, I felt something like a shock. The raft had not struck a hard body, but had suddenly been checked in its course. A waterspout, a liquid column of water, fell upon us. I felt suffocating. I was being drowned.

Still the sudden inundation did not last. In a few seconds I felt myself once more able to breathe. My uncle and Hans pressed my arms, and the raft carried us all three away.

XL
THE APE GIGANS

It is difficult for me to determine what was the real time, but I should suppose, by after calculation, that it must have been ten at night.

I lay in a stupor, a half dream, during which I saw visions of astounding character. Monsters of the deep were side by side with the mighty elephantine shepherd. Gigantic fish and animals seemed to form strange conjunctions.

The raft took a sudden turn, whirled around, entered another tunnel—this time illumined in a most singular manner. The roof was formed of porous stalactite, through which a moonlit vapor appeared to pass, casting its brilliant light upon our gaunt and haggard figures. The light increased as we advanced, while the roof ascended; until at last, we were once more in a kind of water cavern, the lofty dome of which disappeared in a luminous cloud!

A rugged cavern of small extent appeared to offer a halting place to our weary bodies.

My uncle and the guide moved as men in a dream. I was afraid to waken them, knowing the danger of such a sudden start. I seated myself beside them to watch.

As I did so, I became aware of something moving in the distance, which at once fascinated my eyes. It was floating, apparently, upon the surface of the water, advancing by means of what at first appeared paddles. I looked with glaring eyes. One glance told me that it was something monstrous.

But what?

It was the great "shark-crocodile" of the early writers on geology. About the size of an ordinary whale, with hideous jaws and two gigantic eyes, it advanced. Its eyes fixed on me with terrible sternness. Some indefinite warning told me that it had marked me for its own.

I attempted to rise—to escape, no matter where, but my knees shook under me; my limbs trembled violently; I almost lost my senses. And still the mighty monster advanced. My uncle and the guide made no effort to save themselves.

With a strange noise, like none other I had ever heard, the beast came on. His jaws were at least seven feet apart, and his distended mouth looked large enough to have swallowed a boatful of men.

We were about ten feet distant when I discovered that much of his body resembled that of a crocodile, his mouth was wholly that of a shark.

His twofold nature now became apparent. To snatch us up at a mouthful it was necessary for him to turn on his back, which motion necessarily caused his legs to kick up helplessly in the air.

I actually laughed even in the very jaws of death!

But next minute, with a wild cry, I darted away into the interior of the cavern, leaving my unhappy comrades to their fate! This cavern was deep and dreary. After about a hundred yards, I paused and looked around.

The whole floor, composed of sand and malachite, was strewn with bones, freshly gnawed bones of reptiles and fish, with a mixture of mammalia. My very soul grew sick as my body shuddered with horror. I had truly, according to the old proverb, fallen out of the frying pan into the fire. Some beast larger and more ferocious even than the shark-crocodile inhabited this den.

What could I do? The mouth of the cave was guarded by one ferocious monster, the interior was inhabited by something too hideous to contemplate. Flight was impossible!

One only resource remained, and that was to find some small hiding place to which the fearful denizens of the cavern could not penetrate. I gazed wildly around, and at last discovered a fissure in the rock, to which I rushed in the hope of recovering my scattered senses.

Crouching down, I waited shivering as in an ague fit. No man is brave in presence of an earthquake, or a bursting boiler, or an exploding torpedo. I could not be expected to feel much courage in the presence of the fearful fate that appeared to await me.

An hour passed. I heard all the time a strange rumbling outside the cave.

What was the fate of my unhappy companions? It was impossible for me to pause to inquire. My own wretched existence was all I could think of.

Suddenly a groaning, as of fifty bears in a fight, fell upon my ears—hisses, spitting, moaning, hideous to hear—and then I saw—

Never, were ages to pass over my head, shall I forget the horrible apparition.

It was the Ape Gigans!

Fourteen feet high, covered with coarse hair, of a blackish brown, the hair on the arms, from the shoulder to the elbow joints, pointing downward, while that from the wrist to the elbow pointed upward, it advanced. Its arms were as long as its body, while its legs were prodigious. It had thick, long, and sharply pointed teeth—like a mammoth saw.

It struck its breast as it came on smelling and sniffing, reminding me of the stories we read in our early childhood of giants who ate the flesh of men and little boys!

Suddenly it stopped. My heart beat wildly, for I was conscious that, somehow or other, the fearful monster had smelled me out and was peering about with his hideous eyes to try and discover my whereabouts.

My reading, which as a rule is a blessing, but which on this occasion, seemed momentarily to prove a curse, told me the real truth. It was the Ape Gigans, the antediluvian gorilla.

Yes! This awful monster, confined by good fortune to the interior of the earth, was the progenitor of the hideous monster of Africa.

He glared wildly about, seeking something—doubtless myself. I gave myself up for lost. No hope of safety or escape seemed to remain.

At this moment, just as my eyes appeared to close in death, there came a strange noise from the entrance of the cave; and turning, the gorilla evidently recognized some enemy more worthy his prodigious size and strength. It was the huge shark-crocodile, which perhaps having disposed of my friends, was coming in search of further prey.

The gorilla placed himself on the defensive, and clutching a bone some seven or eight feet in length, a perfect club, aimed a deadly blow at the hideous beast, which reared upward and fell with all its weight upon its adversary.

A terrible combat, the details of which it is impossible to give, now ensued. The struggle was awful and ferocious. I, however, did not wait to witness the result. Regarding myself as the object of contention, I determined to remove from the presence of the victor. I slid down from my hiding place, reached the ground, and gliding against the wall, strove to gain the open mouth of the cavern.

But I had not taken many steps when the fearful clamor ceased, to be followed by a mumbling and groaning which appeared to be indicative of victory.

I looked back and saw the huge ape, gory with blood, coming after me with glaring eyes, with dilated nostrils that gave forth two columns of heated vapor. I could feel his hot and fetid breath on my neck; and with a horrid jump—awoke from my nightmare sleep.

Yes—it was all a dream. I was still on the raft with my uncle and the guide.

The relief was not instantaneous, for under the influence of the hideous nightmare my senses had become numbed. After a while, however, my feelings were tranquilized. The first of my preceptions which returned in full force was that of hearing. I listened with acute and attentive ears. All was still as death. All I comprehended was silence. To the roaring of the waters, which had filled the gallery with awful reverberations, succeeded perfect peace.

After some little time my uncle spoke, in a low and scarcely audible tone:

"Harry, boy, where are you?"

"I am here," was my faint rejoinder.

"Well, don't you see what has happened? We are going upward."

"My dear uncle, what can you mean?" was my half-delirious reply.

"Yes, I tell you we are ascending rapidly. Our downward journey is quite checked."

I held out my hand, and, after some little difficulty, succeeded in touching the wall. My hand was in an instant covered with blood. The skin was torn from the flesh. We were ascending with extraordinary rapidity.

"The torch—the torch!" cried the Professor, wildly; "it must be lighted."

Hans, the guide, after many vain efforts, at last succeeded in lighting it, and the flame, having now nothing to prevent its burning, shed a tolerably clear light. We were enabled to form an approximate idea of the truth.

"It is just as I thought," said my uncle, after a moment of two of silent attention. "We are in a narrow well about four fathoms square. The waters of the great inland sea, having reached the bottom of the gulf, are now forcing themselves up the mighty shaft. As a natural consequence, we are being cast up on the summit of the waters."

"That I can see," was my lugubrious reply; "but where will this shaft end, and to what fall are we likely to be exposed?"

"Of that I am as ignorant as yourself. All I know is, that we should be prepared for the worst. We are going up at a fearfully rapid rate. As far as I can judge, we are ascending at the rate of two fathoms a second, of a hundred and twenty fathoms a minute, or rather more than three and a half leagues an hour. At this rate, our fate will soon be a matter of certainty."

"No doubt of it," was my reply. "The great concern I have now, however, is to know whether this shaft has any issue. It may end in a granite roof—in which case we shall be suffocated by compressed air, or dashed to atoms against the top. I fancy, already, that the air is beginning to be close and condensed. I have a difficulty in breathing."

This might be fancy, or it might be the effect of our rapid motion, but I certainly felt a great oppression of the chest.

"Henry," said the Professor, "I do believe that the situation is to a certain extent desperate. There remain, however, many chances of ultimate safety, and I have, in my own mind, been revolving them over, during your heavy but agitated sleep. I have come to this logical conclusion—whereas we may at any moment perish, so at any moment we may be saved! We need, therefore, prepare ourselves for whatever may turn up in the great chapter of accidents."

"But what would you have us do?" I cried. "Are we not utterly helpless?"

"No! While there is life there is hope. At all events, there is one thing we can do—eat, and thus obtain strength to face victory or death."

As he spoke, I looked at my uncle with a haggard glance. I had put off the fatal communication as long as possible. It was now forced upon me, and I must tell him the truth. Still I hesitated.

"Eat," I said, in a deprecating tone as if there were no hurry.

"Yes, and at once. I feel like a starving prisoner," he said, rubbing his yellow and shivering hands together.

And, turning around to the guide, he spoke some hearty, cheering words, as I judged from his tone, in Danish. Hans shook his head in a terribly significant manner. I tried to look unconcerned.

"What!" cried the Professor, "you do not mean to say that all our provisions are lost?"

"Yes," was my lowly spoken reply, as I held out something in my hand, "this morsel of dried meat is all that remains for us three."

My uncle gazed at me as if he could not fully appreciate the meaning of my words. The blow seemed to stun him by its severity. I allowed him to reflect for some moments.

"Well," said I, after a short pause, "what do you think now? Is there any chance of our escaping from our horrible subterranean dangers? Are we not doomed to perish in the great hollows of the center of the earth?"

But my pertinent questions brought no answer. My uncle either heard me not, or appeared not to do so.

And in this way a whole hour passed. Neither of us cared to speak. For myself, I began to feel the most fearful and devouring hunger. My companions, doubtless, felt the same horrible tortures, but neither of them would touch the wretched morsel of meat that remained. It lay there, a last remnant of all our great preparations for the mad and senseless journey!

I looked back with wonderment, to my own folly. Fully was I aware that, despite his enthusiasm, and the ever-to-be-hated scroll of Saknussemm, my uncle should never have started on his perilous voyage. What memories of the happy past, what previsions of the horrible future, now filled my brain!

XLI

Hunger

Hunger, prolonged, is temporary madness!

The brain is at work without its required food, and the most fantastic notions fill the mind. Hitherto I had never known what hunger really meant. I was likely to understand it now.

And yet, three months before I could tell my terrible story of starvation, as I thought it. As a boy I used to make frequent excursions in the neighborhood of the Professor's house.

My uncle always acted on system, and he believed that, in addition to the day of rest and worship, there should be a day of recreation. In consequence, I was always free to do as I liked on a Wednesday.

Now, as I had a notion to combine the useful and the agreeable, my favorite pastime was birds' nesting. I had one of the best collections of eggs in all the town. They were classified, and under glass cases.

There was a certain wood, which, by rising at early morn, and taking the cheap train, I could reach at eleven in the morning. Here I would botanize or geologize at my will. My uncle was always glad of specimens for his herbarium, and stones to examine. When I had filled my wallet, I proceeded to search for nests.

After about two hours of hard work, I, one day, sat down by a stream to eat my humble but copious lunch. How the remembrance of the spiced sausage, the wheaten loaf, and the beer, made my mouth water now! I would have given every prospect of worldly wealth for such a meal. But to my story.

While seated thus at my leisure, I looked up at the ruins of an old castle, at no great distance. It was the remains of an historical dwelling, ivy-clad, and now falling to pieces.

While looking, I saw two eagles circling about the summit of a lofty tower. I soon became satisfied that there was a nest. Now, in all my collection, I wanted eggs of the native eagle and the large owl.

My mind was made up. I would reach the summit of that tower, or perish in the attempt. I went nearer, and surveyed the ruins. The old staircase, years before, had fallen in. The outer walls were, however, intact. There was no chance that way, unless I looked to the ivy solely for support. This was, as I soon found out, futile.

There remained the chimney, which still went up to the top, and had once served to carry off the smoke from every story of the tower.

Up this I determined to venture. It was narrow, rough, and therefore the more easily climbed. I took off my coat and crept into the chimney. Looking up, I saw a small, light opening, proclaiming the summit of the chimney.

Up—up I went, for some time using my hands and knees, after the fashion of a chimney sweep. It was slow work, but, there being continual projections, the task was comparatively easy. In this way, I reached halfway. The chimney now became narrower. The atmosphere was close, and, at last, to end the matter, I stuck fast. I could ascend no higher.

There could be no doubt of this, and there remained no resource but to descend, and give up my glorious prey in despair. I yielded to fate and endeavored to descend. But I could not move. Some unseen and mysterious obstacle intervened and stopped me. In an instant the full horror of my situation seized me.

I was unable to move either way, and was doomed to a terrible and horrible death, that of starvation. In a boy's mind, however, there is an extraordinary amount of elasticity and hope, and I began to think of all sorts of plans to escape my gloomy fate.

In the first place, I required no food just at present, having had an excellent meal, and was therefore allowed time for reflection. My first thought was to try and move the mortar with my hand. Had I possessed a knife, something might have been done, but that useful instrument I had left in my coat pocket.

I soon found that all efforts of this kind were vain and useless, and that all I could hope to do was to wriggle downward.

But though I jerked and struggled, and strove to turn, it was all in vain. I could not move an inch, one way or the other. And time flew rapidly. My early rising probably contributed to the fact that I felt sleepy, and gradually gave way to the sensation of drowsiness.

I slept, and awoke in darkness, ravenously hungry.

Night had come, and still I could not move. I was tight bound, and did not succeed in changing my position an inch. I groaned aloud. Never since the days of my happy childhood, when it was a hardship to go from meal to meal without eating, had I really experienced hunger. The sensation was as novel as it was painful. I began now to lose my head and to scream and cry out in my agony. Something appeared, startled by my noise. It was a harmless lizard, but it appeared to me a loathsome reptile. Again I made the old ruins resound with my cries, and finally so exhausted myself that I fainted.

How long I lay in a kind of trance or sleep I cannot say, but when again I recovered consciousness it was day. How ill I felt, how hunger still gnawed at me, it would be hard to say. I was too weak to scream now, far too weak to struggle.

Suddenly I was startled by a roar.

"Are you here, Henry?" said the voice of my uncle; "are you there, my boy?"

I could only faintly respond, but I also made a desperate effort to turn. Some mortar fell. To this I owed my being discovered. When the search took place, it was easily seen that mortar and small pieces of stone had recently fallen from above. Hence my uncle's cry.

"Be calm," he cried, "if we pull down the whole ruin, you shall be saved."

They were delicious words, but I had little hope.

Soon however, about a quarter of an hour later, I heard a voice *above me,* at one of the upper fireplaces.

"Are you below or above?"

"Below," was my reply.

In an instant a basket was lowered with milk, a biscuit, and an egg. My uncle was fearful to be too ready with his supply of food. I drank the milk first, for thirst had nearly deadened hunger. I then, much refreshed, ate my bread and hard egg.

They were now at work at the wall. I could hear a pickax. Wishing to escape all danger from this terrible weapon, I made a desperate struggle, and the belt, which surrounded my waist and which had been hitched to a stone, gave way; I was free, and only escaped falling down by a rapid motion of my hands and knees.

In ten minutes more I was in my uncle's arms, after being two days and nights in that horrible prison. My occasional delirium prevented me from counting time.

I was weeks recovering from that awful starvation adventure; and yet what was that to the hideous sufferings I now endured?

After dreaming for some time, and thinking of this and other matters, I once more looked around me. We were still ascending with fearful rapidity. Every now and then the air appeared to check our respiration as it does that of aeronauts when the ascension of the balloon is too rapid. But if they feel a degree of cold in proportion to the elevation they attain in the atmosphere, we experienced quite a contrary effect. The heat began to increase in a most threatening and exceptional manner. I cannot tell exactly the mean, but I think it must have reached one hundred twenty-two degrees of Fahrenheit.

What was the meaning of this extraordinary change in the temperature? As far as we had hitherto gone, facts had proved the theories of Davy and of Lidenbrock to be correct. Until now, all the peculiar conditions of refractory rocks, of electricity, of magnetism, had modified the general laws of nature, and had created for us a moderate temperature; for the theory of the central fire, remained, in my eyes, the only explainable one.

Were we, then, going to reach a position in which these phenomena were to be carried out in all their rigor, and in which the heat would reduce the rocks to a state of fusion?

Such was my not unnatural fear, and I did not conceal the fact from my uncle. My way of doing so might be cold and heartless, but I could not help it.

"If we are not drowned, or smashed into pancakes, and if we do not die of starvation, we have the satisfaction of knowing that we must be burned alive."

My uncle, in presence of this brusque attack, simply shrugged his shoulders, and resumed his reflections—whatever they might be.

An hour passed away, and except that there was a slight increase in the temperature no incident modified the situation. My uncle at last, of his own accord, broke silence.

"Well, Henry, my boy," he said, in a cheerful way, "we must make up our minds."

"Make up our minds to what?" I asked, in considerable surprise.

"Well—to something. We must at whatever risk recruit our physical strength. If we make the fatal mistake of husbanding our little remnant of food, we may probably prolong our wretched existence a few hours—but we shall remain weak to the end."

"Yes," I growled, "to the end. That, however, will not keep us long waiting."

"Well, only let a chance of safety present itself—only allow that a moment of action be necessary—where shall we find the means of action if we allow ourselves to be reduced to physical weakness by inanition?"

"When this piece of meat is devoured, Uncle, what hope will there remain unto us?"

"None, my dear Henry, none. But will it do you any good to devour it with your eyes? You appear to me to reason like one without will or decision, like a being without energy."

"Then," cried I, exasperated to a degree which is scarcely to be explained, "you do not mean to tell me—that you—that you—have not lost all hope."

"Certainly not," replied the Professor with consummate coolness.

"You mean to tell me, Uncle, that we shall get out of this monstrous subterranean shaft?"

"While there is life there is hope. I beg to assert, Henry, that as long as a man's heart beats, as long as a man's flesh quivers, I do not allow that a being gifted with thought and will can allow himself to despair."

What a nerve! The man placed in a position like that we occupied must have been very brave to speak like this.

"Well," I cried, "what do you mean to do?"

"Eat what remains of the food we have in our hands; let us swallow the last crumb. It will be, heaven willing, our last repast. Well, never mind—instead of being exhausted skeletons, we shall be men."

"True," muttered I in a despairing tone, "let us take our fill."

"We must," replied my uncle, with a deep sigh, "call it what you will."

My uncle took a piece of the meat that remained, and some crusts of biscuit which had escaped the wreck. He divided the whole into three parts.

Each had one pound of food to last him as long as he remained in the interior of the earth.

Each now acted in accordance with his own private character.

My uncle, the Professor, ate greedily, but evidently without appetite, eating simply from some mechanical motion. I put the food inside my lips, and hungry as I was, chewed my morsel without pleasure, and without satisfaction.

Hans, the guide, just as if he had been eider-down hunting, swallowed every mouthful, as though it were a usual affair. He looked like a man equally prepared to enjoy superfluity or total want.

Hans, in all probability, was no more used to starvation than ourselves, but his hardy Icelandic nature had prepared him for many sufferings. As long as he received his three rix-dollars every Saturday night, he was prepared for anything.

The fact was, Hans never troubled himself about much except his money. He had undertaken to serve a certain man at so much per week, and no matter what evils befell his employer or himself, he never found fault or grumbled, so long as his wages were duly paid.

Suddenly my uncle roused himself. He had seen a smile on the face of our guide. I could not make it out.

"What is the matter?" said my uncle.

"Schiedam," said the guide, producing a bottle of his precious fluid.

We drank. My uncle and myself will own to our dying day that hence we derived strength to exist until the last bitter moment. That precious bottle of Hollands was in reality only half full; but, under the circumstances, it was nectar.

It took some minutes for myself and my uncle to form a decided opinion on the subject. The worthy Professor swallowed about half a pint and did not seem able to drink any more.

"Fortrafflig," said Hans, swallowing nearly all that was left.

"Excellent—very good," said my uncle, with as much gusto as if he had just left the steps of the club at Hamburg.

I had begun to feel as if there had been one gleam of hope. Now all thought of the future vanished!

We had consumed our last ounce of food, and it was five o'clock in the morning!

XLII

The Volcanic Shaft

Man's constitution is so peculiar that his health is purely a negative matter. No sooner is the rage of hunger appeased than it becomes difficult to comprehend the meaning of starvation. It is only when you suffer that you really understand.

As to anyone who has not endured privation having any notion of the matter, it is simply absurd.

With us, after a long fast, some mouthfuls of bread and meat, a little moldy biscuit and salt beef, triumphed over all our previous gloomy and saturnine thoughts.

Nevertheless, after this repast each gave way to his own reflections. I wonder what were those of Hans—the man of the extreme north, who was yet gifted with the fatalistic resignation of Oriental character. But the utmost stretch of the imagination would not allow me to realize the truth. As for my individual self, my thoughts had ceased to be anything but memories of the past, and were all connected with that upper world which I never should have left. I saw it all now, the beautiful house in the Königstrasse, my poor Gretchen, the good Martha; they all passed before my mind like visions of the past. Every time any of the lugubrious groanings which were to be distinguished in the hollows around fell upon my ears, I fancied I heard the distant murmur of the great cities above my head.

As for my uncle, always thinking of his science, he examined the nature of the shaft by means of a torch. He closely examined the different strata one above the other, in order to recognize his situation by geological theory. This calculation, or rather this estimation, could by no means be anything but approximate. But a learned man, a philosopher, is nothing if not a philosopher, when he keeps his ideas calm and collected; and certainly the Professor possessed this quality to perfection.

I heard him, as I sat in silence, murmuring words of geological science. As I understood his object and his meaning, I could not but interest myself despite my preoccupation in that terrible hour.

"Eruptive granite," he said to himself, "we are still in the primitive epoch. But we are going up—going up, still going up. But who knows? Who knows?"

Then he still hoped. He felt along the vertical sides of the shaft with his hand, and some few minutes later, he would go on again in the following style:

"This is gneiss. This is mocashites—siliceous mineral. Good again; this is the epoch of transition; at all events, we are close to them—and then, and then—"

What could the Professor mean? Could he, by any conceivable means, measure the thickness of the crust of the earth suspended above our heads? Did he possess any possible means of making any approximation to this calculation? No.

The manometer was wanting, and no summary estimation could take the place of it.

And yet, as we progressed, the temperature increased in the most extraordinary degree, and I began to feel as if I were bathed in a hot and burning atmosphere. Never before had I felt anything like it. I could only compare it to the hot vapor from an iron foundry, when the liquid iron is in a state of ebullition and runs over. By degrees, and one after the other, Hans, my uncle, and myself had taken off our coats and waistcoats. They were unbearable. Even the slightest garment was not only uncomfortable, but the cause of extreme suffering.

"Are we ascending to a living fire?" I cried; when, to my horror and astonishment, the heat became greater than before.

"No, no," said my uncle, "it is simply impossible, quite impossible."

"And yet," said I, touching the side of the shaft with my naked hand, "this wall is literally burning."

At this moment, feeling as I did that the sides of this extraordinary wall were red hot, I plunged my hands into the water to cool them. I drew them back with a cry of despair.

"The water is boiling!" I cried.

My uncle, the Professor, made no reply other than a gesture of rage and despair.

Something very like the truth had probably struck his imagination.

But I could take no share in either what was going on, or in his speculations. An invincible dread had taken possession of my brain and soul. I could only look forward to an immediate catastrophe, such a catastrophe as not even the most vivid imagination could have thought of. An idea, at first vague and uncertain, was gradually being changed to certainty.

I tremulously rejected it at first, but it forced itself upon me by degrees with extreme obstinacy. It was so terrible an idea that I scarcely dared to whisper it to myself.

And yet all the while certain, and as it were, involuntary observations determined my convictions. By the doubtful glare of the torch, I could make out some singular changes in the granite strata; a strange and terrible phenomenon was about to be produced, in which electricity played a part.

Then this boiling water, this terrible and excessive heat? I determined as a last resource to examine the compass.

The compass had gone mad!

Yes, wholly stark staring mad. The needle jumped from pole to pole with sudden and surprising jerks, ran around, or as it is said, boxed the compass, and then ran suddenly back again as if it had the vertigo.

I was aware that, according to the best acknowledged theories, it was a received notion that the mineral crust of the globe is never, and never has been, in a state of complete repose.

It is perpetually undergoing the modifications caused by the decomposition of internal matter, the agitation consequent on the flowing of extensive liquid currents, the excessive action of magnetism which tends to shake it incessantly, at a time when even the multitudinous beings on its surface do not suspect the seething process to be going on.

Still this phenomenon would not have alarmed me alone; it would not have aroused in my mind a terrible, an awful idea.

But other facts could not allow my self-delusion to last.

Terrible detonations, like Heaven's artillery, began to multiply themselves with fearful intensity. I could only compare them with the noise made by hundreds of heavily laden chariots being madly driven over a stone pavement. It was a continuous roll of heavy thunder.

And then the mad compass, shaken by the wild electric phenomena, confirmed me in my rapidly formed opinion. The mineral crust was about to burst, the heavy granite masses were about to rejoin, the fissure was about to close, the void was about to be filled up, and we poor atoms to be crushed in its awful embrace!

"Uncle, Uncle!" I cried, "we are wholly, irretrievably lost!"

"What, then, my young friend, is your new cause of terror and alarm?" he said in his calmest manner. "What fear you now?"

"What do I fear now!" I cried in fierce and angry tones. "Do you not see that the walls of the shaft are in motion? Do you not see that the solid granite masses are cracking? Do you not feel the terrible, torrid heat? Do you not observe the awful boiling water on which we float? Do you not remark this mad needle? Every sign and portent of an awful earthquake!"

My uncle coolly shook his head.

"An earthquake," he replied in the most calm and provoking tone.

"Yes."

"My nephew. I tell you that you are utterly mistaken," he continued.

"Do you not, can you not, recognize all the well-known symptoms—"

"Of an earthquake? By no means. I am expecting something far more important."

"My brain is strained beyond endurance—what, what do you mean?" I cried.

"An eruption, Harry."

"An eruption," I gasped. "We are, then, in the volcanic shaft of a crater in full action and vigor."

"I have every reason to think so," said the Professor in a smiling tone, "and I beg to tell you that it is the most fortunate thing that could happen to us."

The most fortunate thing! Had my uncle really and truly gone mad? What did he mean by these awful words—what did he mean by this terrible calm, this solemn smile?

"What!" cried I, in the height of my exasperation, "we are on the way to an eruption, are we? Fatality has cast us into a well of burning and boiling lava, of rocks on fire, of boiling water, in a word, filled with every kind of eruptive matter? We are about to be expelled, thrown up, vomited, spit out of the interior of the earth, in common with huge blocks of granite, with showers of cinders and scoriae, in a wild whirlwind of flame, and you say—the most fortunate thing which could happen to us."

"Yes," replied the Professor, looking at me calmly from under his spectacles, "it is the only chance which remains to us for ever escaping from the interior of the earth to the light of day."

It is quite impossible that I can put on paper a thousand strange, wild thoughts which followed this extraordinary announcement.

But my uncle was right, quite right, and never had he appeared to me so audacious and so convinced as when he looked me calmly in the face and spoke of the chances of an eruption—of our being cast upon Mother Earth once more through the gaping crater of a volcano!

Nevertheless, while we were speaking we were still ascending; we passed the whole night going up, or to speak more scientifically, in an ascensional motion. The fearful noise redoubled; I was ready to suffocate. I seriously believed that my last hour was approaching, and yet, so strange is imagination, all I thought of was some childish hypothesis or other. In such circumstances you do not choose your own thoughts. They overcome you.

It was quite evident that we were being cast upward by eruptive matter; under the raft there was a mass of boiling water, and under this was a heaving mass of lava, and an aggregate of rocks which, on reaching the summit of the water, would be dispersed in every direction.

That we were inside the chimney of a volcano there could no longer be the shadow of a doubt. Nothing more terrible could be conceived!

But on this occasion, instead of Sneffels, an old and extinct volcano, we were inside a mountain of fire in full activity. Several times I found myself asking, what mountain was it, and on what part of the world we should be shot out. As if it were of any consequence!

In the northern regions, there could be no reasonable doubt about that. Before it went decidedly mad, the compass had never made the slightest mistake. From the cape of Saknussemm, we had been swept away to the northward many hundreds of leagues. Now the question was, were we once more under Iceland—should we be belched forth on to the earth through the crater of Mount Hecla, should we reappear through one of the other seven fire tunnels of the island? Taking in my mental vision a radius of five hundred leagues to the westward, I could see under this parallel only the little-known volcanoes of the northwest coast of America.

To the east one only existed somewhere about the eightieth degree of latitude, the Esk, upon the island of Jan Mayen, not far from the frozen regions of Spitsbergen.

It was not craters that were wanting, and many of them were big enough to vomit a whole army; all I wished to know was the particular one toward which we were making with such fearful velocity.

I often think now of my folly: as if I should ever have expected to escape!

Toward morning, the ascending motion became greater and greater. If the degree of heat increased instead of decreasing, as we approached the surface of the earth, it was simply because the causes were local and wholly due to volcanic influence. Our very style of locomotion left in my mind no doubt upon the subject. An enormous force, a force of some hundred of combined atmospheres produced by vapors accumulated and long compressed in the interior of the earth, was hoisting us upward with irresistible power.

But though we were approaching the light of day, to what fearful dangers were we about to be exposed?

Instant death appeared the only fate which we could expect or contemplate.

Soon a dim, sepulchral light penetrated the vertical gallery, which became wider and wider. I could make out to the right and left long dark corridors like immense tunnels, from which awful and horrid vapors poured out. Tongues of fire, sparkling and crackling, appeared about to lick us up.

The hour had come!

"Look, Uncle, look!" I cried.

"Well, what you see are the great sulphurous flames. Nothing more common in connection with an eruption."

"But if they lap us around!" I angrily replied.

"They will not lap us around," was his quiet and serene answer.

"But it will be all the same in the end if they stifle us," I cried.

"We shall not be stifled. The gallery is rapidly becoming wider and wider, and if it be necessary, we will presently leave the raft and take refuge in some fissure in the rock."

"But the water, the water, which is continually ascending?" I despairingly replied.

"There is no longer any water, Harry," he answered, "but a kind of lava paste, which is heaving us up, in company with itself, to the mouth of the crater."

In truth, the liquid column of water had wholly disappeared to give place to dense masses of boiling eruptive matter. The temperature was becoming utterly insupportable, and a thermometer exposed to this atmosphere would have marked between one hundred and eighty-nine and one hundred ninety degrees Fahrenheit.

Perspiration rushed from every pore. But for the extraordinary rapidity of our ascent we should have been stifled.

Nevertheless, the Professor did not carry out his proposition of abandoning the raft; and he did quite wisely. Those few ill-joined beams offered, anyway, a solid surface—a support which elsewhere must have utterly failed us.

Toward eight o'clock in the morning a new incident startled us. The ascensional movement suddenly ceased. The raft became still and motionless.

"What is the matter now?" I said, querulously, very much startled by this change.

"A simple halt," replied my uncle.

"Is the eruption about to fail?" I asked.

"I hope not."

Without making any reply, I rose. I tried to look around me. Perhaps the raft, checked by some projecting rock, opposed a momentary resistance to the eruptive mass. In this case, it was absolutely necessary to release it as quickly as possible.

Nothing of the kind had occurred. The column of cinders, of scoriae, of broken rocks and earth, had wholly ceased to ascend.

"I tell you, Uncle, that the eruption has stopped," was my oracular decision.

"Ah," said my uncle, "you think so, my boy. You are wrong. Do not be in the least alarmed; this sudden moment of calm will not last long, be assured. It has already endured five minutes, and before we are many minutes older we shall be continuing our journey to the mouth of the crater."

All the time he was speaking the Professor continued to consult his chronometer, and he was probably right in his prognostics. Soon the raft resumed its motion, in a very rapid and disorderly way, which lasted two minutes or thereabout; and then again it stopped as suddenly as before.

"Good," said my uncle, observing the hour, "in ten minutes we shall start again."

"In ten minutes?"

"Yes—precisely. We have to do with a volcano, the eruption of which is intermittent. We are compelled to breathe just as it does."

Nothing could be more true. At the exact minute he had indicated, we were again launched on high with extreme rapidity. Not to be cast off the raft, it was necessary to hold on to the beams. Then the hoist again ceased.

Many times since have I thought of this singular phenomenon without being able to find for it any satisfactory explanation. Nevertheless, it appeared quite clear to me, that we were not in the principal chimney of the volcano, but in an accessory conduit, where we felt the counter shock of the great and principal tunnel filled by burning lava.

It is impossible for me to say how many times this maneuver was repeated. All that I can remember is, that on every ascensional motion, we were hoisted up with ever increasing velocity, as if we had been launched from a huge projectile. During the sudden halts we were nearly stifled; during moments of projection the hot air took away our breath.

I thought for a moment of the voluptuous joy of suddenly finding myself in the hyperbole regions with the cold thirty degrees below zero!

My exalted imagination pictured to itself the vast snowy plains of the arctic regions, and I was impatient to roll myself on the icy carpet of the North Pole.

By degrees my head, utterly overcome by a series of violent emotions, began to give way to hallucination. I was delirious. Had it not been for the powerful arms of Hans, the guide, I should have broken my head against the granite masses of the shaft.

I have, in consequence, kept no account of what followed for many hours. I have a vague and confused remembrance of continual detonations, of the shaking of the huge granitic mass, and of the raft going around like a spinning top. It floated on the stream of hot lava, amidst a falling cloud of cinders. The huge flames roaring, wrapped us around.

A storm of wind which appeared to be cast forth from an immense ventilator roused up the interior fires of the earth. It was a hot, incandescent blast!

At last I saw the figure of Hans as if enveloped in the huge halo of burning blaze, and no other sense remained to me but that sinister dread which the condemned victim may be supposed to feel when led to the mouth of a cannon, at the supreme moment when the shot is fired and his limbs are dispersed into empty space.

XLIII

Daylight at Last

When I opened my eyes I felt the hand of the guide clutching me firmly by the belt. With his other hand he supported my uncle. I was not grievously wounded, but bruised all over in the most remarkable manner.

After a moment I looked around, and found that I was lying down on the slope of a mountain not two yards from a yawning gulf into which I should have fallen had I made the slightest false step. Hans had saved me from death, while I rolled insensible on the flanks of the crater.

"Where are we?" dreamily asked my uncle, who literally appeared to be disgusted at having returned to earth.

The eider-down hunter simply shrugged his shoulders as a mark of total ignorance.

"In Iceland?" said I, not positively but interrogatively.

"*Nej,*" said Hans.

"How do you mean?" cried the Professor; "no—what are your reasons?"

"Hans is wrong," said I, rising.

After all the innumerable surprises of this journey, a yet more singular one was reserved to us. I expected to see a cone covered by snow, by extensive and wide-spread glaciers, in the midst of the arid deserts of the extreme northern regions, beneath the full rays of a polar sky, beyond the highest latitudes.

But contrary to all our expectations, I, my uncle, and the Icelander, were cast upon the slope of a mountain calcined by the burning rays of a sun which was literally baking us with its fires.

I could not believe my eyes, but the actual heat which affected my body allowed me no chance of doubting. We came out of the crater half naked, and the radiant star from which we had asked nothing for two months, was enough to be prodigal to us of light and warmth—a light and warmth we could easily have dispensed with.

When our eyes were accustomed to the light we had lost sight of so long, I used them to rectify the errors of my imagination. Whatever happened, we should have been at Spitsbergen, and I was in no humor to yield to anything but the most absolute proof.

After some delay, the Professor spoke.

"Hem!" he said in a hesitating kind of way, "it really does not look like Iceland."

"But supposing it were the island of Jan Mayen?" I ventured to observe.

"Not in the least, my boy. This is not one of the volcanoes of the north, with its hills of granite and its crown of snow."

"Nevertheless—"

"Look, look, my boy," said the Professor, as dogmatically as usual.

Right above our heads, at a great height, opened the crater of a volcano from which escaped, from one quarter of an hour to the other, with a very loud expression, a lofty jet of flame mingled with pumice stone, cinders, and lava. I could feel the convulsions of Nature in the mountain, which breathed like a huge whale, throwing up from time to time fire and air through its enormous vents.

Below, and floating along a slope of considerable angularity, the stream of eruptive matter spread away to a depth which did not give the volcano a height of three hundred fathoms.

Its base disappeared in a perfect forest of green trees, among which I perceived olives, fig trees, and vines loaded with rich grapes.

Certainly this was not the ordinary aspect of the Arctic regions. About that there could not be the slightest doubt.

When the eye was satisfied at its glimpse of this verdant expanse, it fell upon the waters of a lovely sea or beautiful lake, which made of this enchanted land an island of not many leagues in extent.

On the side of the rising sun was to be seen a little port, crowded with houses, and near which the boats and vessels of peculiar build were floating upon azure waves.

Beyond, groups of islands rose above the liquid plain, so numerous and close together as to resemble a vast beehive.

Toward the setting sun, some distant shores were to be made out on the edge of the horizon. Some presented the appearance of blue mountains of harmonious conformation; upon others, much more distant, there appeared a prodigiously lofty cone, above the summit of which hung dark and heavy clouds.

Toward the north, an immense expanse of water sparkled beneath the solar rays, occasionally allowing the extremity of a mast or the convexity of a sail bellying to the wind, to be seen.

The unexpected character of such a scene added an hundredfold to its marvelous beauties.

"Where can we be?" I asked, speaking in a low and solemn voice.

Hans shut his eyes with an air of indifference, and my uncle looked on without clearly understanding.

"Whatever this mountain may be," he said, at last, "I must confess it is rather warm. The explosions do not leave off, and I do not think it is worthwhile to have left the interior of a volcano and remain here to receive a huge piece of rock upon one's head. Let us carefully descend the mountain and discover the real state of the case. To confess the truth, I am dying of hunger and thirst."

Decidedly the Professor was no longer a truly reflective character. For myself, forgetting all my necessities, ignoring my fatigues and sufferings, I should have remained still for several hours longer—but it was necessary to follow my companions.

The slope of the volcano was very steep and slippery; we slid over piles of ashes, avoiding the streams of hot lava which glided about like fiery serpents. Still, while we were advancing, I spoke with extreme volubility, for my imagination was too full not to explode in words.

"We are in Asia!" I exclaimed; "we are on the coast of India, in the great Malay islands, in the center of Oceania. We have crossed the one half of the globe to come out right at the antipodes of Europe!"

"But the compass!" exclaimed my uncle; "explain that to me!"

"Yes—the compass," I said with considerable hesitation. "I grant that is a difficulty. According to it, we have always been going northward."

"Then it lied."

"Hem—to say it lied is rather a harsh word," was my answer.

"Then we are at the North Pole—"

"The Pole—no—well—well I give it up," was my reply.

The plain truth was, that there was no explanation possible. I could make nothing of it.

And all the while we were approaching this beautiful verdure, hunger and thirst tormented me fearfully. Happily, after two long hours' march, a beautiful country spread out before us, covered by olives, pomegranates, and vines, which appeared to belong to anybody and everybody.

In the state of destitution into which we had fallen, we were not particular to a grape.

What delight it was to press these delicious fruits to our lips, and to bite at grapes and pomegranates fresh from the vine. Not far off, near some fresh and mossy grass, under the delicious shade of some trees, I discovered a spring of fresh water, in which we voluptuously laved our faces, hands, and feet.

While we were all giving way to the delights of new-found pleasures, a little child appeared between two tufted olive trees.

"Ah," cried I, "an inhabitant of this happy country."

The little fellow was poorly dressed, weak, and suffering, and appeared terribly alarmed at our appearance. Half-naked, with tangled, matted, and ragged beards, we did look supremely ill-favored; and unless the country was a bandit land, we were not unlikely to alarm the inhabitants!

Just as the boy was about to take to his heels, Hans ran after him, and brought him back, despite his cries and kicks.

My uncle tried to look as gentle as possible, and then spoke in German.

"What is the name of this mountain, my friend?"

The child made no reply.

"Good," said my uncle, with a very positive air of conviction, "we are not in Germany."

He then made the same demand in English, of which language he was an excellent scholar.

The child shook its head and made no reply. I began to be considerably puzzled.

"Is he dumb?" cried the Professor, who was rather proud of his polyglot knowledge of languages, and made the same demand in French.

The boy only stared in his face.

"I must perforce try him in Italian," said my uncle, with a shrug.

"Dove noi siamo?"

"Yes, tell me where we are," I added impatiently and eagerly.

Again the boy remained silent.

"My fine fellow, do you or do you not mean to speak?" cried my uncle, who began to get angry. He shook him, and spoke another dialect of the Italian language.

"Come si noma questa isola?"—"What is the name of this island?"

"Stromboli," replied the rickety little shepherd, dashing away from Hans and disappearing in the olive groves.

We thought little enough about him.

Stromboli! What effect on the imagination did these few words produce! We were in the center of the Mediterranean, amidst the eastern archipelago of mythological memory, in the ancient Strongylos, where Æolus kept the wind and the tempest chained up. And those blue mountains, which rose toward the rising of the sun, were the mountains of Calabria.

And that mighty volcano which rose on the southern horizon was Etna, the fierce and celebrated Etna!

"Stromboli! Stromboli!" I repeated to myself.

My uncle played a regular accompaniment to my gestures and words. We were singing together like an ancient chorus.

Ah—what a journey—what a marvelous and extraordinary journey! Here we had entered the earth by one volcano, and we had come out by another. And this other was situated more than twelve hundred leagues from Sneffels, from that drear country of Iceland cast away on the confines of the earth. The wondrous chances of this expedition had transported us to the most harmonious and beautiful of earthly lands. We had abandoned the region of eternal snows for that of infinite verdure, and had left over our heads the gray fog of the icy regions to come back to the azure sky of Sicily!

After a delicious repast of fruits and fresh water, we again continued our journey in order to reach the port of Stromboli. To say how we had reached the island would scarcely have been prudent. The superstitious character of the Italians would have been at work, and we should have been called demons vomited from the infernal regions. It was therefore necessary to pass for humble and unfortunate shipwrecked travelers. It was certainly less striking and romantic, but it was decidedly safer.

As we advanced, I could hear my worthy uncle muttering to himself:

"But the compass. The compass most certainly marked north. This is a fact I cannot explain in any way."

"Well, the fact is," said I, with an air of disdain, "we must not explain anything. It will be much more easy."

"I should like to see a professor of the Johanneum Institution who is unable to explain a cosmic phenomenon—it would indeed be strange."

And speaking thus, my uncle, half naked, his leathern purse around his loins, and his spectacles upon his nose, became once more the terrible Professor of Mineralogy.

An hour after leaving the wood of olives, we reached the fort of San Vicenza, where Hans demanded the price of his thirteenth week of service. My uncle paid him, with very many warm shakes of the hand.

At that moment, if he did not indeed quite share our natural emotion, he allowed his feelings so far to give way as to indulge in an extraordinary expression for him.

With the tips of two fingers he gently pressed our hands and smiled.

XLIV

THE JOURNEY ENDED

This is the final conclusion of a narrative which will be probably disbelieved even by people who are astonished at nothing. I am, however, armed at all points against human incredulity.

We were kindly received by the Strombolite fishermen, who treated us as shipwrecked travelers. They gave us clothes and food. After a delay of forty-eight hours, on the 30th of September a little vessel took us to Messina, where a few days of delightful and complete repose restored us to ourselves.

On Friday, the 4th of October, we embarked in the *Volturus,* one of the postal packets of the Imperial Messagerie of France; and three days later we landed at Marseilles, having no other care on our minds but that of our precious but erratic compass. This inexplicable circumstance tormented me terribly. On the 9th of October, in the evening, we reached Hamburg.

What was the astonishment of Martha, what the joy of Gretchen! I will not attempt to define it.

"Now, then, Harry, that you really are a hero," she said, "there is no reason why you should ever leave me again."

I looked at her. She was weeping tears of joy.

I leave it to be imagined if the return of Professor Hardwigg made or did not make a sensation in Hamburg. Thanks to the indiscretion of Martha, the news of his departure for the interior of the earth had been spread over the whole world.

No one would believe it—and when they saw him come back in safety they believed it all the less.

But the presence of Hans and many stray scraps of information by degrees modified public opinion.

Then my uncle became a great man and I the nephew of a great man, which, at all events, is something. Hamburg gave a festival in our honor. A public meeting of the Johanneum Institution was held, at which the Professor related the whole story of his adventures, omitting only the facts in connection with the compass.

That same day he deposited in the archives of the town the document he had found written by Saknussemm, and he expressed his great regret that circumstances, stronger than his will, did not allow him to follow the Icelandic traveler's track into the very center of the earth. He was modest in his glory, but his reputation only increased.

So much honor necessarily created for him many envious enemies. Of course they existed, and as his theories, supported by certain facts, contradicted the system of science upon the question of central heat, he maintained his own views both with pen and speech against the learned of every country. Although I still believe in the theory of central heat, I confess that certain circumstances, hitherto very ill defined, may modify the laws of such natural phenomena.

At the moment when these questions were being discussed with interest, my uncle received a rude shock—one that he felt very much. Hans, despite everything he could say to the contrary, quitted Hamburg; the man to whom we owed so much would not allow us to pay our deep debt of gratitude. He was taken with nostalgia; a love for his Icelandic home.

"*Farvel,*" said he, one day, and with this one short word of adieu, he started for Reykjavik, which he soon reached in safety.

We were deeply attached to our brave eider-duck hunter. His absence will never cause him to be forgotten by those whose lives he saved, and I hope, at some not distant day, to see him again.

To conclude, I may say that our journey into the interior of the earth created an enormous sensation throughout the civilized world. It was translated and printed in many languages. All the leading journals published extracts from it, which were commentated, discussed, attacked, and supported with equal animation by those who believed in its episodes, and by those who were utterly incredulous.

Wonderful! My uncle enjoyed during his lifetime all the glory he deserved; and he was even offered a large sum of money, by Mr. Barnum, to exhibit himself in the United States; while I am credibly informed by a traveler that he is to be seen in waxwork at Madame Tussaud's!

But one care preyed upon his mind, a care which rendered him very unhappy. One fact remained inexplicable—that of the compass. For a learned man to be baffled by such an inexplicable phenomenon was very aggravating. But Heaven was merciful, and in the end my uncle was happy.

One day, while he put some minerals belonging to his collection in order, I fell upon the famous compass and examined it keenly.

For six months it had lain unnoticed and untouched.

I looked at it with curiosity, which soon became surprise. I gave a loud cry. The Professor, who was at hand, soon joined me.

"What is the matter?" he cried.

"The compass!"

"What then?"

"Why its needle points to the south and not to the north."

"My dear boy, you must be dreaming."

"I am not dreaming. See the poles are changed."

"Changed!"

My uncle put on his spectacles, examined the instrument, and leaped with joy, shaking the whole house.

A clear light fell upon our minds.

"Here it is!" he cried, as soon as he had recovered the use of his speech, "after we had once passed Cape Saknussemm, the needle of this compass pointed to the southward instead of the northward."

"Evidently."

"Our error is now easily explained. But to what phenomenon do we owe this alteration in the needle?"

"Nothing more simple."

"Explain yourself, my boy. I am on thorns."

"During the storm, upon the Central Sea, the ball of fire which made a magnet of the iron in our raft, turned our compass topsy-turvy."

"Ah!" cried the Professor, with a loud and ringing laugh, "it was a trick of that inexplicable electricity."

From that hour my uncle was the happiest of learned men, and I the happiest of ordinary mortals. For my pretty Virland girl, abdicating her position as ward, took her place in the house in King Street (Königstrasse) in the double quality of niece and wife.

We need scarcely mention that her uncle was the illustrious Professor Hardwigg, corresponding member of all the scientific, geographical, mineralogical, and geological societies of the five quarters of the globe.

Around the World in Eighty Days

Contents

I

In which Phileas Fogg and Passepartout accept each other, the one as master, the other as servant

Mr. Phileas Fogg lived, in 1872, at No. 7, Saville Row, Burlington Gardens, the house in which Sheridan died in 1814. He was one of the most noticeable members of the Reform Club, though he seemed always to avoid attracting attention; an enigmatical personage, about whom little was known, except that he was a polished man of the world. People said that he resembled Byron—at least that his head was Byronic; but he was a bearded, tranquil Byron, who might live on a thousand years without growing old.

Certainly an Englishman it was more doubtful whether Phileas Fogg was a Londoner. He was never seen on 'Change, nor at the Bank, nor in the counting-rooms of the "City"; no ships ever came into London docks of which he was the owner; he had no public employment; he had never been entered at any of the Inns of Court, either at the Temple, or Lincoln's Inn, or Gray's Inn; nor had his voice ever resounded in the Court of Chancery, or in the Exchequer, or the Queen's Bench, or the Ecclesiastical Courts. He certainly was not a manufacturer; nor was he a merchant or a gentleman farmer. His name was strange to the scientific and learned societies, and he never was known to take part in the sage deliberations of the Royal Institution or the London Institution, the Artisan's Association or the Institution of Arts and Sciences. He belonged, in fact, to none of the numerous societies which swarm in the English capital, from the Harmonic to that of the Entomologists, founded mainly for the purpose of abolishing pernicious insects.

Phileas Fogg was a member of the Reform, and that was all.

The way in which he got admission to this exclusive club was simple enough.

He was recommended by the Barings, with whom he had an open credit. His checks were regularly paid at sight from his account current, which was always flush.

Was Phileas Fogg rich? Undoubtedly. But those who knew him best could not imagine how he had made his fortune, and Mr. Fogg was the last person to whom to apply for the information. He was not lavish, nor, on the contrary, avaricious; for whenever he knew that money was needed for a noble, useful, or benevolent purpose, he supplied it quietly and sometimes anonymously. He was, in short, the least communicative of men. He talked very little and seemed all the more mysterious for his taciturn manner. His daily habits were quite open to observation; but whatever he did was so exactly the same thing that he had always done before, that the wits of the curious were fairly puzzled.

Had he traveled? It was likely, for no one seemed to know the world more familiarly; there was no spot so secluded that he did not appear to have an intimate acquaintance with it. He often corrected, with a few clear words, the thousand conjectures advanced by members of the club as to lost and unheard-of travelers, pointing out the true probabilities, and seeming as if gifted with a sort of second sight, so often did events justify his predictions. He must have traveled everywhere, at least in the spirit.

It was at least certain that Phileas Fogg had not absented himself from London for many years. Those who were honored by a better acquaintance with him than the rest, declared that nobody could pretend to have ever seen him anywhere else. His sole pastimes were reading the papers and playing whist. He often won at this game, which, as a silent one, harmonized with his nature; but his winnings never went into his purse, being reserved as a fund for his charities. Mr. Fogg played, not to win, but for the sake of playing. The game was in his eyes a contest, a struggle with a difficulty, yet a motionless, unwearying struggle, congenial to his tastes.

Phileas Fogg was not known to have either wife or children, which may happen to the most honest people; either relatives or near friends, which is certainly more unusual. He lived alone in his house in Saville Row, whither none penetrated. A single domestic sufficed to serve him. He breakfasted and dined at the club, at hours mathematically fixed, in the same room, at the same table, never taking his meals with other members, much less bringing a guest with him; and went home at exactly midnight, only to retire at once to bed. He never used the cozy chambers which the Reform provides for its favored members. He passed ten hours out of the twenty-four in Saville Row, either in sleeping or making his toilet. When he chose to take a walk it was with a regular step in the entrance hall with its mosaic flooring, or in the circular gallery with its dome supported by twenty red porphyry Ionic columns, and illumined by blue painted windows. When he breakfasted or dined all the resources of the club—its kitchens and pantries, its buttery and dairy—aided to crowd his table with their most succulent stores; he was served by the gravest waiters, in dress coats, and shoes with swan-skin soles, who proffered the viands in special porcelain, and on the finest linen; club decanters, of a lost mold, contained his sherry, his port, and his cinnamon-spiced claret; while his beverages were refreshingly cooled with ice, brought at great cost from the American lakes.

If to live in this style is to be eccentric, it must be confessed that there is something good in eccentricity!

The mansion in Saville Row, though not sumptuous, was exceedingly comfortable. The habits of its occupant were such as to demand but little from the sole domestic, but Phileas Fogg required him to be almost superhumanly prompt and regular. On this very 2nd of October he had dismissed James Forster, because that luckless youth had brought him shaving-water at eighty-four degrees Fahrenheit instead of eighty-six; and he was awaiting his successor, who was due at the house between eleven and half-past.

Phileas Fogg was seated squarely in his armchair, his feet close together like those of a grenadier on parade, his hands resting on his knees, his body straight, his head erect; he was steadily watching a complicated clock which indicated the hours, the minutes, the seconds, the days, the months, and the years. At exactly half-past eleven Mr. Fogg would, according to his daily habit, quit Saville Row, and repair to the Reform.

A rap at this moment sounded on the door of the cozy apartment where Phileas Fogg was seated, and James Forster, the dismissed servant, appeared.

"The new servant," said he.

A young man of thirty advanced and bowed.

"You are a Frenchman, I believe," asked Phileas Fogg, "and your name is John?"

"Jean, if monsieur pleases," replied the newcomer, "Jean Passepartout, a surname which has clung to me because I have a natural aptness for going out of one business into another. I believe I'm honest, monsieur, but, to be outspoken, I've had several trades. I've been an itinerant singer, a circus-rider, when I used to vault like Leotard, and dance on a rope like Blondin. Then I got to be a professor of gymnastics, so as to make better use of my talents; and then I was a sergeant fireman at Paris, and assisted at many a big fire. But I quitted France five years ago, and, wishing to taste the sweets of domestic life, took service as a valet here in England. Finding myself out of place, and hearing that Monsieur Phileas Fogg was the most exact and settled gentleman in the United Kingdom, I have come to monsieur in the hope of living with him a tranquil life, and forgetting even the name of Passepartout."

"Passepartout suits me," responded Mr. Fogg. "You are well recommended to me; I hear a good report of you. You know my conditions?"

"Yes, monsieur."

"Good. What time is it?"

"Twenty-two minutes after eleven," returned Passepartout, drawing an enormous silver watch from the depths of his pocket.

"You are too slow," said Mr. Fogg.

"Pardon me, monsieur, it is impossible——"

"You are four minutes too slow. No matter; it's enough to mention the error. Now from this moment, twenty-nine minutes after eleven, A.M., this Wednesday, October second, you are in my service."

Phileas Fogg got up, took his hat in his left hand, put it on his head with an automatic motion, and went off without a word.

Passepartout heard the street door shut once; it was his new master going out. He heard it shut again; it was his predecessor, James Forster, departing in his turn. Passepartout remained alone in the house in Saville Row.

II

In which Passepartout is convinced that he has at last found his ideal

"Faith," muttered Passepartout, somewhat flurried, "I've seen people at Madame Tussaud's as lively as my new master!"

Madame Tussaud's "people," let it be said, are of wax, and are much visited in London; speech is all that is wanting to make them human.

During his brief interview with Mr. Fogg, Passepartout had been carefully observing him. He appeared to be a man about forty years of age, with fine, handsome features, and a tall, well-shaped figure; his hair and whiskers were light, his forehead compact and unwrinkled, his face rather pale, his teeth magnificent. His countenance possessed in the highest degree what physiognomists call "repose in action," a quality of those who act rather than talk. Calm and phlegmatic, with a clear eye, Mr. Fogg seemed a perfect type of that English composure which Angelica Kauffmann has so skillfully represented on canvas. Seen in the various phases of his daily life, he gave the idea of being perfectly well-balanced, as exactly regulated as a Leroy chronometer. Phileas Fogg was, indeed, exactitude personified, and this was betrayed even in the expression of his very hands and feet; for in men, as well as in animals, the limbs themselves are expressive of the passions.

He was so exact that he was never in a hurry, was always ready, and was economical alike of his steps and his motions. He never took one step too many, and always went to his destination by the shortest cut; he made no superfluous gestures, and was never seen to be moved or agitated. He was the most deliberate person in the world, yet always reached his destination at the exact moment.

He lived alone, and so to speak, outside of every social relation; and as he knew that in this world account must be taken of friction, and that friction retards, he never rubbed against anybody.

As for Passepartout, he was a true Parisian of Paris. Since he had abandoned his own country for England, taking service as a valet, he had in vain searched for a master after his own heart. Passepartout was by no means one of those pert dunces depicted by Molière, with a bold gaze and a nose held high in the air; he was an honest fellow, with a pleasant face, lips a trifle protruding, soft-mannered and serviceable, with a good round head, such as one likes to see on the shoulders of a friend. His eyes were blue, his complexion rubicund, his figure almost portly and well-built, his body muscular and his physical powers fully developed by the exercises of his younger days. His brown hair was somewhat tumbled; for while the ancient sculptors are said to have known eighteen methods of arranging Minerva's tresses, Passepartout was familiar with but one of dressing his own: three strokes of a large-tooth comb completed his toilet.

It would be rash to predict how Passepartout's lively nature would agree with Mr. Fogg. It was impossible to tell whether the new servant would turn out as absolutely methodical as his master required: experience alone could solve the question. Passepartout had been a sort of vagrant in his early years, and now yearned for repose; but so far he had failed to find it, though he had already served in ten English houses. But he could not take root in any of these; with chagrin he found his masters invariably whimsical and irregular, constantly running about the country, or on the look-out for adventure. His last master, young Lord Longferry, Member of Parliament, after passing his nights in the Haymarket taverns, was too often brought home in the morning on policemen's shoulders. Passepartout, desirous of respecting the gentleman whom he served, ventured a mild remonstrance on such conduct; which being ill-received, he took his leave. Hearing that Mr. Phileas Fogg was looking for a servant, and that his life was one of unbroken regularity, that he neither traveled nor stayed from home overnight, he felt sure that this would be the place he was after. He presented himself, and was accepted, as has been seen.

At half-past eleven, then, Passepartout found himself alone in the house in Saville Row. He began its inspection without delay, scouring it from cellar to garret. So clean, well-arranged, solemn a mansion pleased him; it seemed to him like a snail's shell, lighted and warmed by gas, which sufficed for both these purposes. When Passepartout reached the second story he recognized at once the room which he was to inhabit, and he was well satisfied with it. Electric bells and speaking tubes afforded communication with the lower stories; while on the mantel stood an electric clock, precisely like that in Mr. Fogg's bedchamber, both beating the same second at the same instant. "That's good, that'll do," said Passepartout to himself.

He suddenly observed, hung over the clock, a card which, upon inspection, proved to be a program of the daily routine of the house. It comprised all that was required of the servant, from eight in the morning, exactly at which hour Phileas Fogg rose, till half-past eleven, when he left the house for the Reform Club—all the details of service, the tea and toast at twenty-three minutes past eight, the shaving-water at thirty-seven minutes past nine, and the toilet at twenty minutes before ten. Everything was regulated and foreseen that was to be done from half-past eleven A.M. till midnight, the hour at which the methodical gentleman retired.

Mr. Fogg's wardrobe was amply supplied and in the best taste. Each pair of trousers, coat, and vest bore a number, indicating the time of year and season at which they were in turn to be laid out for wearing; and the same system was applied to the master's shoes. In short, the house in Saville Row, which must have been a very temple of disorder and unrest under the illustrious but dissipated Sheridan, was coziness, comfort, and method idealized. There was no study, nor were there books, which would have been quite useless to Mr. Fogg; for at the Reform two libraries, one of general literature and the other of law and politics, were at his service. A moderate-sized safe stood in his bedroom, constructed so as to defy fire as well as burglars; but Passepartout found neither arms nor hunting weapons anywhere; everything betrayed the most tranquil and peaceable habits.

Having scrutinized the house from top to bottom, he rubbed his hands, a broad smile overspread his features, and he said joyfully, "This is just what I wanted! Ah, we shall get on together, Mr. Fogg and I! What a domestic and regular gentleman! A real machine; well, I don't mind serving a machine."

III

In which a conversation takes place which seems likely to cost Phileas Fogg dear

Phileas Fogg, having shut the door of his house at half-past eleven, and having put his right foot before his left five hundred and seventy-five times, and his left foot before his right five hundred and seventy-six times, reached the Reform Club, an imposing edifice in Pall Mall, which could not have cost less than three millions. He repaired at once to the dining-room, the nine windows of which open upon a tasteful garden, where the trees were already gilded with an autumn coloring; and took his place at the habitual table, the cover of which had already been laid for him. His breakfast consisted of a side-dish, a broiled fish with Reading sauce, a scarlet slice of roast beef garnished with mushrooms, a rhubarb and gooseberry tart, and a morsel of Cheshire cheese, the whole being washed down with several cups of tea, for which the Reform is famous. He rose at thirteen minutes to one, and directed his steps toward the large hall, a sumptuous apartment adorned with lavishly-framed paintings. A flunky handed him an uncut *Times,* which he proceeded to cut with a skill which betrayed familiarity with this delicate operation. The perusal of this paper absorbed Phileas Fogg until a quarter before four, whilst the *Standard,* his next task, occupied him till the dinner hour. Dinner passed as breakfast had done, and Mr. Fogg reappeared in the reading-room and sat down to the *Pall Mall* at twenty minutes before six. Half-an-hour later several members of the Reform came in and drew up to the fireplace, where a coal fire was steadily burning. They were Mr. Fogg's usual partners at whist: Andrew Stuart, an engineer; John Sullivan and Samuel Fallentin, bankers; Thomas Flanagan, a brewer; and Gauthier Ralph, one of the directors of the Bank of England; all rich and highly respectable personages, even in a club which comprises the princes of English trade and finance.

"Well, Ralph," said Thomas Flanagan, "what about that robbery?"

"Oh," replied Stuart; "the bank will lose the money."

"On the contrary," broke in Ralph, "I hope we may put our hands on the robber. Skillful detectives have been sent to all the principal ports of America and the Continent, and he'll be a clever fellow if he slips through their fingers."

"But have you got the robber's description?" asked Stuart.

"In the first place, he is no robber at all," returned Ralph, positively.

"What! a fellow who makes off with fifty-five thousand pounds, no robber?"

"No."

"Perhaps he's a manufacturer, then."

"The *Daily Telegraph* says that he is a gentleman."

It was Phileas Fogg, whose head now emerged from behind his newspapers, who made this remark. He bowed to his friends, and entered into the conversation. The affair which formed its subject, and which was town talk, had occurred three days before at the Bank of England. A package of bank-notes, to the value of fifty-five thousand pounds, had been taken from the principal cashier's table, that functionary being at the moment engaged in registering the receipt of three shillings and sixpence. Of course he could not have his eyes everywhere. Let it be observed that the Bank of England reposes a touching confidence in the honesty of the public. There are neither guards nor gratings to protect its treasures; gold, silver, bank-notes are freely exposed, at the mercy of the first comer. A keen observer of English customs relates that, being in one of the rooms of the Bank one day, he had the curiosity to examine a gold ingot weighing some seven or eight pounds. He took it up, scrutinized it, passed it to his neighbor, he to the next man, and so on until the ingot, going from hand to hand, was transferred to the end of a dark entry; nor did it return to its place for half-an-hour. Meanwhile, the cashier had not so much as raised his head. But in the present instance things had not gone so smoothly. The package of notes not being found when five o'clock sounded from the ponderous clock in the "drawing office," the amount was passed to the account of profit and loss. As soon as the robbery was discovered, picked detectives hastened off to Liverpool, Glasgow, Havre, Suez, Brindisi, New York, and other ports, inspired by the proffered reward of two thousand pounds, and five per cent. on the sum that might be recovered. Detectives were also charged with narrowly watching those who arrived at or left London by rail, and a judicial examination was at once entered upon.

There were real grounds for supposing, as the *Daily Telegraph* said, that the thief did not belong to a professional band. On the day of the robbery a well-dressed gentleman of polished manners, and with a well-to-do air, had been observed going to and fro in the paying-room, where the crime was committed. A description of him was easily procured and sent to the detectives; and some hopeful spirits, of whom Ralph was one, did not despair of his apprehension. The papers and clubs were full of the affair, and everywhere people were discussing the probabilities of a successful pursuit; and the Reform Club was especially agitated, several of its members being Bank officials.

Ralph would not concede that the work of the detectives was likely to be in vain, for he thought that the prize offered would greatly stimulate their zeal and activity. But Stuart was far from sharing this confidence; and as they placed themselves at the whist-table, they continued to argue the matter. Stuart and Flanagan played together, while Phileas Fogg had Fallentin for his partner. As the game proceeded the conversation ceased, excepting between the rubbers, when it revived again.

"I maintain," said Stuart, "that the chances are in favor of the thief, who must be a shrewd fellow."

"Well, but where can he fly to?" asked Ralph. "No country is safe for him."

"Pshaw!"

"Where could he go, then?"

"Oh, I don't know that. The world is big enough."

"It was once," said Phileas Fogg, in a low tone. "Cut, sir," he added, handing the cards to Thomas Flanagan.

The discussion fell during the rubber, after which Stuart took up its thread.

"What do you mean by 'once'? Has the world grown smaller?"

"Certainly," returned Ralph. "I agree with Mr. Fogg. The world *has* grown smaller, since a man can now go round it ten times more quickly than a hundred years ago. And that is why the search for this thief will be more likely to succeed."

"And also why the thief can get away more easily."

"Be so good as to play, Mr. Stuart," said Phileas Fogg.

But the incredulous Stuart was not convinced, and when the hand was finished, said eagerly: "You have a strange way, Ralph, of proving that the world has grown smaller. So, because you can go round it in three months——"

"In eighty days," interrupted Phileas Fogg.

"That is true, gentlemen," added John Sullivan. "Only eighty days, now that the section between Rothal and Allahabad, on the Great Indian Peninsula Railway, has been opened. Here is the estimate made by the *Daily Telegraph*:

From London to Suez via Mont Cenis and Brindisi, by rail and steamboats	7	days
From Suez to Bombay, by steamer	13	"
From Bombay to Calcutta, by rail	3	"
From Calcutta to Hong Kong, by steamer	13	"
From Hong Kong to Yokohama (Japan), by steamer	6	"
From Yokohama to San Francisco, by steamer	22	"
From San Francisco to New York, by rail	7	"
From New York to London, by steamer and rail	9	"
Total	80	days

"Yes, in eighty days!" exclaimed Stuart, who in his excitement made a false deal. "But that doesn't take into account bad weather, contrary winds, shipwrecks, railway accidents, and so on."

"All included," returned Phileas Fogg, continuing to play despite the discussion.

"But suppose the Hindoos or Indians pull up the rails," replied Stuart; "suppose they stop the trains, pillage the luggage-vans, and scalp the passengers!"

"All included," calmly retorted Fogg; adding, as he threw down the cards, "Two trumps."

Stuart, whose turn it was to deal, gathered them up, and went on: "You are right theoretically, Mr. Fogg, but practically——"

"Practically also, Mr. Stuart."

"I'd like to see you do it in eighty days."

"It depends on you. Shall we go?"

"Heaven preserve me! But I would wager four thousand pounds that such a journey, made under these conditions, is impossible."

"Quite possible, on the contrary," returned Mr. Fogg.

"Well, make it, then!"

"The journey round the world in eighty days?"

"Yes."

"I should like nothing better."

"When?"

"At once. Only I warn you that I shall do it at your expense."

"It's absurd!" cried Stuart, who was beginning to be annoyed at the persistency of his friend. "Come, let's go on with the game."

"Deal over again, then," said Phileas Fogg. "There's a false deal."

Stuart took up the pack with a feverish hand; then suddenly put them down again.

"Well, Mr. Fogg," said he, "it shall be so; I will wager the four thousand on it."

"Calm yourself, my dear Stuart," said Fallentin. "It's only a joke."

"When I say I'll wager," returned Stuart, "I mean it."

"All right," said Mr. Fogg; and turning to the others he continued: "I have a deposit of twenty thousand at the Barings which I will willingly risk upon it."

"Twenty thousand pounds!" cried Sullivan. "Twenty thousand pounds, which you would lose by a single accidental delay!"

"The unforeseen does not exist," quietly replied Phileas Fogg.

"But, Mr. Fogg, eighty days are only the estimate of the least possible time in which the journey can be made."

"A well-used minimum suffices for everything."

"But, in order not to exceed it, you must jump mathematically from the trains upon the steamers, and from the steamers upon the trains again."

"I will jump—mathematically."

"You are joking."

"A true Englishman doesn't joke when he is talking about so serious a thing as a wager," replied Phileas Fogg, solemnly. "I will bet twenty thousand pounds against anyone who wishes, that I will make the tour of the world in eighty days or less; in nineteen hundred and twenty hours, or a hundred and fifteen thousand two hundred minutes. Do you accept?"

"We accept," replied Messrs. Stuart, Fallentin, Sullivan, Flanagan, and Ralph, after consulting each other.

"Good," said Mr. Fogg. "The train leaves for Dover at a quarter before nine. I will take it."

"This very evening?" asked Stuart.

"This very evening," returned Phileas Fogg. He took out and consulted a pocket almanac, and added, "As to-day is Wednesday, the second of October, I shall be due in London, in this very room of the Reform Club, on Saturday, the twenty-first of December, at a quarter before nine P.M.; or else the twenty thousand pounds, now deposited in my name at Baring's, will belong to you, in fact and in right, gentlemen. Here is a check for the amount."

A memorandum of the wager was at once drawn up and signed by the six parties, during which Phileas Fogg preserved a stoical composure. He certainly did not bet to win, and had only staked the twenty thousand pounds, half of his fortune, because he foresaw that he might have to expend the other half to carry out this difficult, not to say unattainable, project. As for his antagonists, they seemed much agitated; not so much by the value of their stake, as because they had some scruples about betting under conditions so difficult to their friend.

The clock struck seven, and the party offered to suspend the game so that Mr. Fogg might make his preparations for departure.

"I am quite ready now," was his tranquil response. "Diamonds are trumps: be so good as to play, gentlemen."

IV

In which Phileas Fogg astounds Passepartout, his servant

Having won twenty guineas at whist, and taken leave of his friends, Phileas Fogg, at twenty-five minutes past seven, left the Reform Club.

Passepartout, who had conscientiously studied the program of his duties, was more than surprised to see his master guilty of the inexactness of appearing at this unaccustomed hour; for, according to rule, he was not due in Saville Row until precisely midnight.

Mr. Fogg repaired to his bedroom, and called out, "Passepartout!"

Passepartout did not reply. It could not be he who was called; it was not the right hour.

"Passepartout!" repeated Mr. Fogg, without raising his voice.

Passepartout made his appearance.

"I've called you twice," observed his master.

"But it is not midnight," responded the other, showing his watch.

"I know it; I don't blame you. We start for Dover and Calais in ten minutes."

A puzzled grin overspread Passepartout's round face; clearly he had not comprehended his master.

"Monsieur is going to leave home?"

"Yes," returned Phileas Fogg. "We are going round the world."

Passepartout opened wide his eyes, raised his eyebrows, held up his hands, and seemed about to collapse, so overcome was he with stupefied astonishment.

"Round the world!" he murmured.

"In eighty days," responded Mr. Fogg. "So we haven't a moment to lose."

"But the trunks?" gasped Passepartout, unconsciously swaying his head from right to left.

"We'll have no trunks; only a carpet-bag, with two shirts and three pairs of stockings for me, and the same for you. We'll buy our clothes on the way. Bring down my mackintosh and traveling-cloak, and some stout shoes, though we shall do little walking. Make haste!"

Passepartout tried to reply, but could not. He went out, mounted to his own room, fell into a chair, and muttered: "That's good, that is! And I, who wanted to remain quiet!"

He mechanically set about making the preparations for departure. Around the world in eighty days! Was his master a fool! No. Was this a joke, then? They were going to Dover; good. To Calais; good again. After all, Passepartout, who had been away from France five years, would not be sorry to set foot on his native soil again. Perhaps they would go as far as Paris, and it would do his eyes good to see Paris once more. But surely a gentleman so chary of his steps would stop there; no doubt—but, then, it was none the less true that he was going away, this so domestic person hitherto!

By eight o'clock Passepartout had packed the modest carpet-bag, containing the wardrobes of his master and himself; then, still troubled in mind, he carefully shut the door of his room, and descended to Mr. Fogg.

Mr. Fogg was quite ready. Under his arm might have been observed a red-bound copy of "Bradshaw's Continental Railway Steam Transit and General Guide," with its time-tables showing the arrival and departure of steamers and railways. He took the carpet-bag, opened it, and slipped into it a goodly roll of Bank of England notes, which would pass wherever he might go.

"You have forgotten nothing?" asked he.

"Nothing, monsieur."

"My mackintosh and cloak?"

"Here they are."

"Good. Take this carpet-bag," handing it to Passepartout. "Take good care of it, for there are twenty thousand pounds in it."

Passepartout nearly dropped the bag, as if the twenty thousand pounds were in gold, and weighed him down.

Master and man then descended, the street door was double-locked, and at the end of Saville Row they took a cab and drove rapidly to Charing Cross. The cab stopped before the railway station at twenty minutes past eight. Passepartout jumped off the box and followed his master, who, after paying the cabman, was about to enter the station, when a poor beggar-woman, with a child in her arms, her naked feet smeared with mud, her head covered with a wretched bonnet, from which hung a tattered feather, and her shoulders shrouded in a ragged shawl, approached, and mournfully asked for alms.

Mr. Fogg took out the twenty guineas he had just won at whist, and handed them to the beggar, saying, "Here, my good woman. I'm glad that I met you;" and passed on.

Passepartout had a moist sensation about the eyes; his master's action touched his susceptible heart.

Two first-class tickets for Paris having been speedily purchased, Mr. Fogg was crossing the station to the train, when he perceived his five friends of the Reform.

"Well, gentlemen," said he, "I'm off, you see; and if you will examine my passport when I get back, you will be able to judge whether I have accomplished the journey agreed upon.

"Oh, that would be quite unnecessary, Mr. Fogg," said Ralph politely. "We will trust your word, as a gentleman of honor."

"You do not forget when you are due in London again?" asked Stuart.

"In eighty days; on Saturday, the twenty-first of December, 1872, at a quarter before nine P.M. Good-bye, gentlemen."

Phileas Fogg and his servant seated themselves in a first-class carriage at twenty minutes before nine; five minutes later the whistle screamed, and the train slowly glided out of the station.

The night was dark, and a fine, steady rain was falling. Phileas Fogg, snugly ensconced in his corner, did not open his lips. Passepartout, not yet recovered from his stupefaction, clung mechanically to the carpet-bag, with its enormous treasure.

Just as the train was whirling through Sydenham, Passepartout suddenly uttered a cry of despair.

"What's the matter?" asked Mr. Fogg.

"Alas! In my hurry—I—I forgot——"

"What?"

"To turn off the gas in my room!"

"Very well, young man," returned Mr. Fogg, coolly; "it will burn—at your expense."

V

In which a new species of funds, unknown to the moneyed men, appears on 'Change

Phileas Fogg rightly suspected that his departure from London would create a lively sensation at the West End. The news of the bet spread through the Reform Club, and afforded an exciting topic of conversation to its members. From the Club it soon got into the papers throughout England. The boasted "tour of the world" was talked about, disputed, argued with as much warmth as if the subject were another Alabama claim. Some took sides with Phileas Fogg, but the large majority shook their heads and declared against him; it was absurd, impossible, they declared, that the tour of the world could be made, except theoretically and on paper, in this minimum of time, and with the existing means of traveling. The *Times, Standard, Morning Post,* and *Daily News,* and twenty other highly respectable newspapers scouted Mr. Fogg's project as madness; the *Daily Telegraph* alone hesitatingly supported him. People in general thought him a lunatic, and blamed his Reform Club friends for having accepted a wager which betrayed the mental aberration of its proposer.

Articles no less passionate than logical appeared on the question, for geography is one of the pet subjects of the English; and the columns devoted to Phileas Fogg's venture were eagerly devoured by all classes of readers. At first some rash individuals, principally of the gentler sex, espoused his cause, which became still more popular when the *Illustrated London News* came out with his portrait, copied from a photograph in the Reform Club. A few readers of the *Daily Telegraph* even dared to say, "Why not, after all? Stranger things have come to pass."

At last a long article appeared, on the 7th of October, in the bulletin of the Royal Geographical Society, which treated the question from every point of view, and demonstrated the utter folly of the enterprise.

Everything, it said, was against the travelers, every obstacle imposed alike by man and by nature. A miraculous agreement of the times of departure and arrival, which was impossible, was absolutely necessary to his success. He might, perhaps, reckon on the arrival of trains at the designated hours, in Europe, where the distances were relatively moderate; but when he calculated upon crossing India in three days, and the United States in seven, could he rely beyond misgiving upon accomplishing his task? There were accidents to machinery, the liability of trains to run off the line, collisions, bad weather, the blocking up by snow—were not all these against Phileas Fogg? Would he not find himself, when traveling by steamer in winter, at the mercy of the winds and fogs? Is it uncommon for the best ocean steamers to be two or three days behind time? But a single delay would suffice to fatally break the chain of communication; should Phileas Fogg once miss, even by an hour, a steamer, he would have to wait for the next, and that would irrevocably render his attempt vain.

This article made a great deal of noise, and being copied into all the papers, seriously depressed the advocates of the rash tourist.

Everybody knows that England is the world of betting men, who are of a higher class than mere gamblers; to bet is in the English temperament. Not only the members of the Reform, but the general public, made heavy wagers for or against Phileas Fogg, who was set down in the betting books as if he were a race-horse. Bonds were issued, and made their appearance on 'Change; "Phileas Fogg bonds" were offered at par or at a premium, and a great business was done in them. But five days after the article in the bulletin of the Geographical Society appeared, the demand began to subside: "Phileas Fogg" declined. They were offered by packages, at first of five, then of ten, until at last nobody would take less than twenty, fifty, a hundred!

Lord Albemarle, an elderly paralytic gentleman, was now the only advocate of Phileas Fogg left. This noble lord, who was fastened to his chair, would have given his fortune to be able to make the tour of the world, if it took ten years; and he bet five thousand pounds on Phileas Fogg. When the folly as well as the uselessness of the adventure was pointed out to him, he contented himself with replying, "If the thing is feasible, the first to do it ought to be an Englishman."

The Fogg party dwindled more and more, everybody was going against him, and the bets stood a hundred and fifty and two hundred to one; and a week after his departure an incident occurred which deprived him of backers at any price.

The commissioner of police was sitting in his office at nine o'clock one evening, when the following telegraphic dispatch was put into his hands:

Suez to London

Rowan, Commissioner of Police, Scotland Yard:
I've found the bank robber, Phileas Fogg. Send without delay warrant of arrest to Bombay.

Fix, Detective.

The effect of this dispatch was instantaneous. The polished gentleman disappeared to give place to the bank robber. His photograph, which was hung with those of the rest of the members at the Reform Club, was minutely examined, and it betrayed, feature by feature, the description of the robber which had been provided to the police. The mysterious habits of Phileas Fogg were recalled; his solitary ways, his sudden departure; and it seemed clear that, in undertaking a tour around the world on the pretext of a wager, he had had no other end in view than to elude the detectives, and throw them off his track.

VI

In which Fix, the detective, betrays a very natural impatience

The circumstances under which this telegraphic dispatch about Phileas Fogg was sent were as follows:

The steamer *Mongolia,* belonging to the Peninsular and Oriental Company, built of iron, of two thousand eight hundred tons burden, and five hundred horse-power, was due at eleven o'clock A.M. on Wednesday, the 9th of October, at Suez. The *Mongolia* plied regularly between Brindisi and Bombay via the Suez Canal, and was one of the fastest steamers belonging to the company, always making more than ten knots an hour between Brindisi and Suez, and nine and a half between Suez and Bombay.

Two men were promenading up and down the wharves, among the crowd of natives and strangers who were sojourning at this once straggling village—now, thanks to the enterprise of M. Lesseps, a fast-growing town. One was the British consul at Suez, who, despite the prophecies of the English Government, and the unfavorable predictions of Stephenson, was in the habit of seeing, from his office window, English ships daily passing to and fro on the great canal, by which the old roundabout route from England to India by the Cape of Good Hope was abridged by at least a half. The other was a small, slight-built personage, with a nervous, intelligent face, and bright eyes peering out from under eyebrows which he was incessantly twitching. He was just now manifesting unmistakable signs of impatience, nervously pacing up and down, and unable to stand still for a moment. This was Fix, one of the detectives who had been dispatched from England in search of the bank robber; it was his task to narrowly watch every passenger who arrived at Suez, and to follow up all who seemed to be suspicious characters, or bore a resemblance to the description of the criminal, which he had received two days before from the police headquarters at London. The detective was evidently inspired by the hope of obtaining the splendid reward which would be the prize of success, and awaited with a feverish impatience, easy to understand, the arrival of the steamer *Mongolia*.

"So you say, consul," asked he for the twentieth time, "that this steamer is never behind time?"

"No, Mr. Fix," replied the consul. "She was bespoken yesterday at Port Said, and the rest of the way is of no account to such a craft. I repeat that the *Mongolia* has been in advance of the time required by the company's regulations, and gained the prize awarded for excess of speed."

"Does she come directly from Brindisi?"

"Directly from Brindisi; she takes on the Indian mails there, and she left there Saturday at five P.M. Have patience, Mr. Fix; she will not be late. But really I don't see how, from the description you have, you will be able to recognize your man, even if he is on board the *Mongolia*."

"A man rather feels the presence of these fellows, consul, than recognizes them. You must have a scent for them, and a scent is like a sixth sense which combines hearing, seeing, and smelling. I've arrested more than one of these gentlemen in my time, and if my thief is on board, I'll answer for it, he'll not slip through my fingers."

"I hope so, Mr. Fix, for it was a heavy robbery."

"A magnificent robbery, consul; fifty-five thousand pounds! We don't often have such windfalls. Burglars are getting to be so contemptible nowadays! A fellow gets hung for a handful of shillings!"

"Mr. Fix," said the consul, "I like your way of talking, and hope you'll succeed; but I fear you will find it far from easy. Don't you see, the description which you have there has a singular resemblance to an honest man?"

"Consul," remarked the detective, dogmatically, "great robbers *always* resemble honest folks. Fellows who have rascally faces have only one course to take, and that is to remain honest; otherwise they would be arrested offhand. The artistic thing is, to unmask honest countenances; it's no light task, I admit, but a real art."

Mr. Fix evidently was not wanting in a tinge of self-conceit.

Little by little the scene on the quay became more animated; sailors of various nations, merchants, shipbrokers, porters, fellahs, bustled to and fro as if the steamer were immediately expected. The weather was clear, and slightly chilly. The minarets of the town loomed above the houses in the pale rays of the sun. A jetty pier, some two thousand yards long, extended into the roadstead. A number of fishing-smacks and coasting boats, some retaining the fantastic fashion of ancient galleys, were discernible on the Red Sea.

As he passed among the busy crowd, Fix, according to habit, scrutinized the passers-by with a keen, rapid glance.

It was now half-past ten.

"The steamer doesn't come!" he exclaimed, as the port clock struck.

"She can't be far off now," returned his companion.

"How long will she stop at Suez?"

"Four hours; long enough to get in her coal. It is thirteen hundred and ten miles from Suez to Aden, at the other end of the Red Sea, and she has to take in a fresh coal supply."

"And does she go from Suez directly to Bombay?"

"Without putting in anywhere."

"Good," said Fix. "If the robber is on board he will no doubt get off at Suez, so as to reach the Dutch or French colonies in Asia by some other route. He ought to know that he would not be safe an hour in India, which is English soil."

"Unless," objected the consul, "he is exceptionally shrewd. An English criminal, you know, is always better concealed in London than anywhere else."

This observation furnished the detective food for thought, and meanwhile the consul went away to his office. Fix, left alone, was more impatient than ever, having a presentiment that the robber was on board the *Mongolia*. If he had indeed left London intending to reach the New World he would naturally take the route via India, which was less watched and more difficult to watch than that of the Atlantic. But Fix's reflections were soon interrupted by a succession of sharp whistles, which announced the arrival of the *Mongolia*. The porters and fellahs rushed down the quay, and a dozen boats pushed off from the shore to go and meet the steamer. Soon her gigantic hull appeared passing along between the banks, and eleven o'clock struck as she anchored in the road. She brought an unusual number of passengers, some of whom remained on deck to scan the picturesque panorama of the town, while the greater part disembarked in the boats, and landed on the quay.

Fix took up a position, and carefully examined each face and figure which made its appearance. Presently one of the passengers, after vigorously pushing his way through the importunate crowd of porters, came up to him and politely asked if he could point out the English consulate, at the same time showing a passport which he wished to have visaed. Fix instinctively took the passport, and with a rapid glance read the description of its bearer. An involuntary motion of surprise nearly escaped him, for the description in the passport was identical with that of the bank robber which he had received from Scotland Yard.

"Is this your passport?" asked he.

"No, it's my master's."

"And your master is——"

"He stayed on board."

"But he must go to the consul's in person, so as to establish his identity."

"Oh, is that necessary?"

"Quite indispensable."

"And where is the consulate?"

"There, on the corner of the square," said Fix, pointing to a house two hundred steps off.

"I'll go and fetch my master, who won't be much pleased, however, to be disturbed."

The passenger bowed to Fix, and returned to the steamer.

VII

Which once more demonstrates the uselessness of passports as aids to detectives

The detective passed down the quay, and rapidly made his way to the consul's office, where he was at once admitted to the presence of that official.

"Consul," said he, without preamble, "I have strong reasons for believing that my man is a passenger on the *Mongolia*." And he narrated what had just passed concerning the passport.

"Well, Mr. Fix," replied the consul; "I shall not be sorry to see the rascal's face; but perhaps he won't come here—that is, if he is the person you suppose him to be. A robber doesn't quite like to leave traces of his flight behind him; and, besides, he is not obliged to have his passport countersigned.

"If he is as shrewd as I think he is, consul, he will come."

"To have his passport visaed?"

"Yes. Passports are only good for annoying honest folks, and aiding in the flight of rogues. I assure you it will be quite the thing for him to do; but I hope you will not visa the passport."

"Why not? If the passport is genuine I have no right to refuse."

"Still, I must keep this man here until I can get a warrant to arrest him from London."

"Ah, that's your look-out. But I cannot——"

The consul did not finish his sentence, for as he spoke a knock was heard at the door, and two strangers entered, one of whom was the servant whom Fix had met on the quay. The other, who was his master, held out his passport with the request that the consul would do him the favor to visa it. The consul took the document and carefully read it, whilst Fix observed, or rather devoured, the stranger with his eyes from a corner of the room.

"You are Mr. Phileas Fogg?" said the consul, after reading the passport.

"I am."

"And this man is your servant?"

"He is; a Frenchman, named Passepartout."

"You are from London?"

"Yes."

"And you are going——"

"To Bombay."

"Very good, sir. You know that a visa is useless, and that no passport is required?"

"I know it, sir," replied Phileas Fogg; "but I wish to prove, by your visa, that I came by Suez."

"Very well, sir."

The consul proceeded to sign and date the passport, after which he added his official seal. Mr. Fogg paid the customary fee, coldly bowed, and went out, followed by his servant.

"Well?" queried the detective.

"Well, he looks and acts like a perfectly honest man," replied the consul.

"Possibly; but that is not the question. Do you think, consul, that this phlegmatic gentleman resembles, feature by feature, the robber whose description I have received?"

"I concede that; but then, you know, all descriptions——"

"I'll make certain of it," interrupted Fix. "The servant seems to me less mysterious than the master; besides, he's a Frenchman, and can't help talking. Excuse me for a little while, consul."

Fix started off in search of Passepartout.

Meanwhile Mr. Fogg, after leaving the consulate, repaired to the quay, gave some orders to Passepartout, went off to the *Mongolia* in a boat, and descended to his cabin. He took up his note-book, which contained the following memoranda:—

Left London, Wednesday, October 2nd, at 8:45 P.M.

Reached Paris, Thursday, October 3rd, at 7:20 A.M.

Left Paris, Thursday, at 8:40 A.M.

Reached Turin by Mont Cenis, Friday, October 4th, at 6:35 A.M.

Left Turin, Friday, at 7:20 A.M.

Arrived at Brindisi, Saturday, October 5th, at 4 P.M.

Sailed on the *Mongolia*, Saturday, at 5 P.M.

Reached Suez, Wednesday, October 9th, at 11 A.M.

Total of hours spent, $158\frac{1}{2}$; or, in days, six days and a half.

These dates were inscribed in an itinerary divided into columns, indicating the month, the day of the month, and the day for the stipulated and actual arrivals at each principal point—Paris, Brindisi, Suez, Bombay, Calcutta, Singapore, Hong Kong, Yokohama, San Francisco, New York, and London—from the 2nd of October to the 21st of December; and giving a space for setting down the gain made or the loss suffered on arrival at each locality. This methodical record thus contained an account of everything needed, and Mr. Fogg always knew whether he was behindhand or in advance of his time. On this Friday, October 9th, he noted his arrival at Suez, and observed that he had as yet neither gained nor lost. He sat down quietly to breakfast in his cabin, never once thinking of inspecting the town, being one of those Englishmen who are wont to see foreign countries through the eyes of their domestics.

VIII

In which Passepartout talks rather more, perhaps, than is prudent

Fix soon rejoined Passepartout, who was lounging and looking about on the quay, as if he did not feel that he, at least, was obliged not to see anything.

"Well, my friend," said the detective, coming up with him, "is your passport visaed?"

"Ah, it's you, is it, monsieur?" responded Passepartout. "Thanks, yes, the passport is all right."

"And you are looking about you?"

"Yes; but we travel so fast that I seem to be journeying in a dream. So this is Suez?"

"Yes."

"In Egypt?"

"Certainly, in Egypt."

"And in Africa?"

"In Africa."

"In Africa!" repeated Passepartout. "Just think, monsieur, I had no idea that we should go farther than Paris; and all that I saw of Paris was between twenty minutes past seven and twenty minutes before nine in the morning, between the Northern and the Lyons stations, through the windows of a car, and in a driving rain! How I regret not having seen once more Père la Chaise and the circus in the Champs Elysées!"

"You are in a great hurry, then?"

"I am not, but my master is. By the way, I must buy some shoes and shirts. We came away without trunks, only with a carpet-bag."

"I will show you an excellent shop for getting what you want."

"Really, monsieur, you are very kind."

And they walked off together, Passepartout chatting volubly as they went along.

"Above all," said he; "don't let me lose the steamer."

"You have plenty of time; it's only twelve o'clock."

Passepartout pulled out his big watch. "Twelve!" he exclaimed; "why it's only eight minutes before ten."

"Your watch is slow."

"My watch? A family watch, monsieur, which has come down from my great-grandfather! It doesn't vary five minutes in the year, it's a perfect chronometer, look you."

"I see how it is," said Fix. "You have kept London time, which is two hours behind that of Suez. You ought to regulate your watch at noon in each country."

"I regulate my watch? Never!"

"Well, then, it will not agree with the sun."

"So much the worse for the sun, monsieur. The sun will be wrong, then!"

And the worthy fellow returned the watch to its fob with a defiant gesture. After a few minutes' silence, Fix resumed: "You left London hastily, then?"

"I rather think so! Last Friday at eight o'clock in the evening, Monsieur Fogg came home from his club, and three-quarters of an hour afterward we were off."

"But where is your master going?"

"Always straight ahead. He is going round the world."

"Round the world?" cried Fix.

"Yes, and in eighty days! He says it is on a wager; but, between us, I don't believe a word of it. That wouldn't be common sense. There's something else in the wind."

"Ah! Mr. Fogg is a character, is he?"

"I should say he was."

"Is he rich?"

"No doubt, for he is carrying an enormous sum in brand-new bank-notes with him. And he doesn't spare the money on the way, either: he has offered a large reward to the engineer of the *Mongolia* if he gets us to Bombay well in advance of time."

"And you have known your master a long time?"

"Why, no; I entered his service the very day we left London."

The effect of these replies upon the already suspicious and excited detective may be imagined. The hasty departure from London soon after the robbery; the large sum carried by Mr. Fogg; his eagerness to reach distant countries; the pretext of an eccentric and foolhardy bet—all confirmed Fix in his theory. He continued to pump poor Passepartout, and learned that he really knew little or nothing of his master, who lived a solitary existence in London, was said to be rich, though no one knew whence came his riches, and was mysterious and impenetrable in his affairs and habits. Fix felt sure that Phileas Fogg would not land at Suez, but was really going on to Bombay.

"Is Bombay far from here?" asked Passepartout.

"Pretty far. It is a ten days' voyage by sea."

"And in what country is Bombay?"

"India."

"In Asia?"

"Certainly."

"The deuce! I was going to tell you—there's one thing that worries me—my burner!"

"What burner?"

"My gas-burner, which I forgot to turn off, and which is at this moment burning—at my expense. I have calculated, monsieur, that I lose two shillings every four and twenty hours, exactly sixpence more than I earn; and you will understand that the longer our journey——"

Did Fix pay any attention to Passepartout's trouble about the gas? It is not probable. He was not listening, but was cogitating a project. Passepartout and he had now reached the shop, where Fix left his companion to make his purchases, after recommending him not to miss the steamer, and hurried back to the consulate. Now that he was fully convinced Fix had quite recovered his equanimity.

"Consul," said he, "I have no longer any doubt. I have spotted my man. He passes himself off as an odd stick, who is going round the world in eighty days."

"Then he's a sharp fellow," returned the consul, "and counts on returning to London after putting the police of the two continents off his track."

"We'll see about that," replied Fix.

"But are you not mistaken?"

"I am not mistaken."

"Why was this robber so anxious to prove, by the visa, that he had passed through Suez?"

"Why? I have no idea; but listen to me."

He reported in a few words the most important parts of his conversation with Passepartout.

"In short," said the consul, "appearances are wholly against this man. And what are you going to do?"

"Send a dispatch to London for a warrant of arrest to be dispatched instantly to Bombay, take passage on board the *Mongolia*, follow my rogue to India, and there, on English ground, arrest him politely, with my warrant in my hand, and my hand on his shoulder."

Having uttered these words with a cool, careless air, the detective took leave of the consul, and repaired to the telegraph office, whence he sent the dispatch which we have seen to the London police office. A quarter of an hour later found Fix, with a small bag in his hand, proceeding on board the *Mongolia*; and ere many moments longer, the noble steamer rode out at full steam upon the waters of the Red Sea.

IX

In which the Red Sea and the Indian Ocean prove propitious to the designs of Phileas Fogg

The distance between Suez and Aden is precisely thirteen hundred and ten miles, and the regulations of the company allow the steamers one hundred and thirty-eight hours in which to traverse it. The *Mongolia*, thanks to the vigorous exertions of the engineer, seemed likely, so rapid was her speed, to reach her destination considerably within that time. The greater part of the passengers from Brindisi were bound for India—some for Bombay, others for Calcutta by way of Bombay, the nearest route thither, now that a railway crosses the Indian peninsula. Among the passengers was a number of officials and military officers of various grades, the latter being either attached to the regular British forces, or commanding the Sepoy troops and receiving high salaries ever since the central government has assumed the powers of the East India Company: for the sub-lieutenants get 280*l*., brigadiers, 2400*l*., and generals of division, 4,000*l*. What with the military men, a number of rich young Englishmen on their travels, and the hospitable efforts of the purser, the time passed quickly on the *Mongolia*. The best of fare was spread upon the cabin tables at breakfast, lunch, dinner, and the eight o'clock supper, and the ladies scrupulously changed their toilets twice a day; and the hours were whiled away, when the sea was tranquil, with music, dancing, and games.

But the Red Sea is full of caprice, and often boisterous, like most long and narrow gulfs. When the wind came from the African or Asian coast the *Mongolia*, with her long hull, rolled fearfully. Then the ladies speedily disappeared below; the pianos were silent; singing and dancing suddenly ceased. Yet the good ship ploughed straight on, unretarded by wind or wave, toward the straits of Bab-el-Mandeb. What was Phileas Fogg doing all this time? It might be thought that, in his anxiety, he would be constantly watching the changes of the wind, the disorderly raging of the billows—every chance, in short, which might force the *Mongolia* to slacken her speed, and thus interrupt his journey. But if he thought of these possibilities, he did not betray the fact by any outward sign.

Always the same impassible member of the Reform Club, whom no incident could surprise, as unvarying as the ship's chronometers, and seldom having the curiosity even to go upon the deck, he passed through the memorable scenes of the Red Sea with cold indifference; did not care to recognize the historic towns and villages which, along its borders, raised their picturesque outlines against the sky; and betrayed no fear of the dangers of the Arabic Gulf, which the old historians always spoke of with horror, and upon which the ancient navigators never ventured without propitiating the gods by ample sacrifices. How did this eccentric personage pass his time on the *Mongolia*? He made his four hearty meals every day, regardless of the most persistent rolling and pitching on the part of the steamer; and he played whist indefatigably, for he had found partners as enthusiastic in the game as himself. A tax-collector, on the way to his post at Goa; the Rev. Decimus Smith, returning to his parish at Bombay; and a brigadier-general of the English army, who was about to rejoin his brigade at Benares, made up the party, and, with Mr. Fogg, played whist by the hour together in absorbing silence.

As for Passepartout, he, too, had escaped seasickness, and took his meals conscientiously in the forward cabin. He rather enjoyed the voyage, for he was well fed and well lodged, took a great interest in the scenes through which they were passing, and consoled himself with the delusion that his master's whim would end at Bombay. He was pleased, on the day after leaving Suez, to find on deck the obliging person with whom he had walked and chatted on the quays.

"If I am not mistaken," said he, approaching this person with his most amiable smile, "you are the gentleman who so kindly volunteered to guide me at Suez?"

"Ah! I quite recognize you. You are the servant of the strange Englishman——"

"Just so, Monsieur——"

"Fix."

"Monsieur Fix," resumed Passepartout, "I'm charmed to find you on board. Where are you bound?"

"Like you, to Bombay."

"That's capital! Have you made this trip before?"

"Several times. I am one of the agents of the Peninsula Company."

"Then you know India?"

"Why—yes," replied Fix, who spoke cautiously.

"A curious place, this India?"

"Oh, very curious. Mosques, minarets, temples, fakirs, pagodas, tigers, snakes, elephants! I hope you will have ample time to see the sights."

"I hope so, Monsieur Fix. You see, a man of sound sense ought not to spend his life jumping from a steamer upon a railway train, and from a railway train upon a steamer again, pretending to make the tour of the world in eighty days! No; all these gymnastics, you may be sure, will cease at Bombay."

"And Mr. Fogg is getting on well?" asked Fix, in the most natural tone in the world.

"Quite well, and I too. I eat like a famished ogre; it's the sea air."

"But I never see your master on deck."

"Never; he hasn't the least curiosity."

"Do you know, Mr. Passepartout, that this pretended tour in eighty days may conceal some secret errand—perhaps a diplomatic mission?"

"Faith, Monsieur Fix, I assure you I know nothing about it, nor would I give half-a-crown to find out."

After this meeting, Passepartout and Fix got into the habit of chatting together, the latter making it a point to gain the worthy man's confidence. He frequently offered him a glass of whisky or pale ale in the steamer barroom, which Passepartout never failed to accept with graceful alacrity, mentally pronouncing Fix the best of good fellows.

Meanwhile the *Mongolia* was pushing forward rapidly; on the 13th, Mocha, surrounded by its ruined walls whereon date-trees were growing, was sighted, and on the mountains beyond were espied vast coffee-fields. Passepartout was ravished to behold this celebrated place, and thought that, with its circular walls and dismantled fort, it looked like an immense coffee cup and saucer. The following night they passed through the Strait of Bab-el-Mandeb, which means in Arabic "The Bridge of Tears," and the next day they put in at Steamer Point, north-west of Aden harbor, to take in coal. This matter of fueling steamers is a serious one at such distances from the coal mines; it costs the Peninsular Company some eight hundred thousand pounds a year. In these distant seas, coal is worth three or four pounds sterling a ton.

The *Mongolia* had still sixteen hundred and fifty miles to traverse before reaching Bombay, and was obliged to remain four hours at Steamer Point to coal up. But this delay, as it was foreseen, did not affect Phileas Fogg's program; besides, the *Mongolia*, instead of reaching Aden on the morning of the 15th, when she was due, arrived there on the evening of the 14th, a gain of fifteen hours.

Mr. Fogg and his servant went ashore at Aden to have the passport again visaed; Fix, unobserved, followed them. The visa procured, Mr. Fogg returned on board to resume his former habits; while Passepartout, according to custom, sauntered about among the mixed population of Somanlis, Banyans, Parsees, Jews, Arabs, and Europeans who comprise the twenty-five thousand inhabitants of Aden. He gazed with wonder upon the fortifications which make this place the Gibraltar of the Indian Ocean, and the vast cisterns where the English engineers were still at work, two thousand years after the engineers of Solomon.

"Very curious, *very* curious," said Passepartout to himself, on returning to the steamer. "I see that it is by no means useless to travel, if a man wants to see something new." At six P.M. the *Mongolia* slowly moved out of the roadstead, and was soon once more on the Indian Ocean. She had a hundred and sixty-eight hours in which to reach Bombay, and the sea was favorable, the wind being in the north-west, and all sails aiding the engine. The steamer rolled but little, the ladies, in fresh toilets, reappeared on deck, and the singing and dancing were resumed. The trip was being accomplished most successfully, and Passepartout was enchanted with the congenial companion which chance had secured him in the person of the delightful Fix. On Sunday, October 20th, toward noon, they came in sight of the Indian coast: two hours later the pilot came on board. A range of hills lay against the sky in the horizon, and soon the rows of palms which adorn Bombay came distinctly into view. The steamer entered the road formed by the islands in the bay, and at half-past four she hauled up at the quays of Bombay.

Phileas Fogg was in the act of finishing the thirty-third rubber of the voyage, and his partner and himself having, by a bold stroke, captured all thirteen of the tricks, concluded this fine campaign with a brilliant victory.

The *Mongolia* was due at Bombay on the 22nd; she arrived on the 20th. This was again to Phileas Fogg of two days since his departure from London, and he calmly entered the fact in the itinerary, in the column of gains.

X

In which Passepartout is only too glad to get off with the loss of his shoes

Everybody knows that the great reversed triangle of land, with its base in the north and its apex in the south, which is called India, embraces fourteen hundred thousand square miles, upon which is spread unequally a population of one hundred and eighty millions of souls. The British Crown exercises a real and despotic dominion over the larger portion of this vast country, and has a governor-general stationed at Calcutta, governors at Madras, Bombay, and in Bengal, and a lieutenant-governor at Agra.

But British India, properly so called, only embraces seven hundred thousand square miles, and a population of from one hundred to one hundred and ten millions of inhabitants. A considerable portion of India is still free from British authority; and there are certain ferocious rajahs in the interior who are absolutely independent. The celebrated East India Company was all-powerful from 1756, when the English first gained a foothold on the spot where now stands the city of Madras, down to the time of the great Sepoy insurrection. It gradually annexed province after province, purchasing them of the native chiefs, whom it seldom paid, and appointed the governor-general and his subordinates, civil and military. But the East India Company has now passed away, leaving the British possessions in India directly under the control of the Crown. The aspect of the country, as well as the manners and distinctions of race, is daily changing.

Formerly one was obliged to travel in India by the old cumbrous methods of going on foot or on horseback, in palanquins or unwieldy coaches; now, fast steamboats ply on the Indus and the Ganges, and a great railway, with branch lines joining the main line at many points on its route, traverses the peninsula from Bombay to Calcutta in three days. This railway does not run in a direct line across India. The distance between Bombay and Calcutta, as the bird flies, is only from one thousand to eleven hundred miles; but the deflections of the road increase this distance by more than a third.

The general route of the Great Indian Peninsula Railway is as follows:—Leaving Bombay, it passes through Salcette, crossing to the continent opposite Tannah, goes over the chain of the Western Ghauts, runs thence north-east as far as Burhampoor, skirts the nearly independent territory of Bundelcund, ascends to Allahabad, turns thence eastwardly, meeting the Ganges at Benares, then departs from the river a little, and, descending south-eastward by Burdivan and the French town of Chandernagor, has its terminus at Calcutta.

The passengers of the *Mongolia* went ashore at half-past four P.M.; at exactly eight the train would start for Calcutta.

Mr. Fogg, after bidding good-bye to his whist partners, left the steamer, gave his servant several errands to do, urged it upon him to be at the station promptly at eight, and, with his regular step, which beat to the second, like an astronomical clock, directed his steps to the passport office. As for the wonders of Bombay—its famous city hall, its splendid library, its forts and docks, its bazaars, mosques, synagogues, its Armenian churches, and the noble pagoda on Malebar Hill with its two polygonal towers—he cared not a straw to see them. He would not deign to examine even the masterpieces of Elephanta, or the mysterious hypogea, concealed southeast from the docks, or those fine remains of Buddhist architecture, the Kanherian grottoes of the island of Salcette.

Having transacted his business at the passport office, Phileas Fogg repaired quietly to the railway station, where he ordered dinner. Among the dishes served up to him, the landlord especially recommended a certain giblet of "native rabbit," on which he prided himself.

Mr. Fogg accordingly tasted the dish, but, despite its spiced sauce, found it far from palatable. He rang for the landlord, and on his appearance, said, fixing his clear eyes upon him, "Is this rabbit, sir?"

"Yes, my lord," the rogue boldly replied, "rabbit from the jungles."

"And this rabbit did not mew when he was killed?"

"Mew, my lord! what, a rabbit mew! I swear to you——"

"Be so good, landlord, as not to swear, but remember this: cats were formerly considered, in India, as sacred animals. That was a good time."

"For the cats, my lord?"

"Perhaps for the travelers as well!"

After which Mr. Fogg quietly continued his dinner. Fix had gone on shore shortly after Mr. Fogg, and his first destination was the headquarters of the Bombay police. He made himself known as a London detective, told his business at Bombay, and the position of affairs relative to the supposed robber, and nervously asked if a warrant had arrived from London. It had not reached the office; indeed, there had not yet been time for it to arrive. Fix was sorely disappointed, and tried to obtain an order of arrest from the director of the Bombay police. This the director refused, as the matter concerned the London office, which alone could legally deliver the warrant. Fix did not insist, and was fain to resign himself to await the arrival of the important document; but he was determined not to lose sight of the mysterious rogue as long as he stayed in Bombay. He did not doubt for a moment, any more than Passepartout, that Phileas Fogg would remain there, at least until it was time for the warrant to arrive.

Passepartout, however, had no sooner heard his master's orders on leaving the *Mongolia*, than he saw at once that they were to leave Bombay as they had done Suez and Paris, and that the journey would be extended at least as far as Calcutta, and perhaps beyond that place. He began to ask himself if this bet that Mr. Fogg talked about was not really in good earnest, and whether his fate was not in truth forcing him, despite his love of repose, around the world in eighty days!

Having purchased the usual quota of shirts and shoes, he took a leisurely promenade about the streets, where crowds of people of many nationalities—Europeans, Persians with pointed caps, Banyas with round turbans, Sindes with square bonnets, Parsees with black mitres, and long-robed Armenians—were collected. It happened to be the day of a Parsee festival. These descendants of the sect of Zoroaster—the most thrifty, civilized, intelligent, and austere of the East Indians, among whom are counted the richest native merchants of Bombay—were celebrating a sort of religious carnival, with processions and shows, in the midst of which Indian dancing-girls, clothed in rose-colored gauze, looped up with gold and silver, danced airily, but with perfect modesty, to the sound of viols and the clanging of tambourines. It is needless to say that Passepartout watched these curious ceremonies with staring eyes and gaping mouth, and that his countenance was that of the greenest booby imaginable.

Unhappily for his master, as well as himself, his curiosity drew him unconsciously farther off than he intended to go. At last, having seen the Parsee carnival wind away in the distance, he was turning his steps toward the station, when he happened to espy the splendid pagoda on Malebar Hill, and was seized with an irresistible desire to see its interior. He was quite ignorant that it is forbidden to Christians to enter certain Indian temples, and that even the faithful must not go in without first leaving their shoes outside the door. It may be said here that the wise policy of the British Government severely punishes a disregard of the practices of the native religions.

Passepartout, however, thinking no harm, went in like a simple tourist, and was soon lost in admiration of the splendid Brahmin ornamentation which everywhere met his eyes, when of a sudden he found himself sprawling on the sacred flagging. He looked up to behold three enraged priests, who forthwith fell upon him, tore off his shoes, and began to beat him with loud, savage exclamations. The agile Frenchman was soon upon his feet again, and lost no time in knocking down two of his long-gowned adversaries with his fists and a vigorous application of his toes; then, rushing out of the pagoda as fast as his legs could carry him, he soon escaped the third priest by mingling with the crowd in the streets.

At five minutes before eight, Passepartout, hatless, shoeless, and having in the squabble lost his package of shirts and shoes, rushed breathlessly into the station.

Fix, who had followed Mr. Fogg to the station, and saw that he was really going to leave Bombay, was there, upon the platform. He had resolved to follow the supposed robber to Calcutta, and farther, if necessary. Passepartout did not observe the detective, who stood in an obscure corner; but Fix heard him relate his adventures in a few words to Mr. Fogg.

"I hope that this will not happen again," said Phileas Fogg, coldly, as he got into the train. Poor Passepartout, quite crestfallen, followed his master without a word. Fix was on the point of entering another carriage, when an idea struck him which induced him to alter his plan.

"No, I'll stay," muttered he. "An offense has been committed on Indian soil. I've got my man."

Just then the locomotive gave a sharp screech, and the train passed out into the darkness of the night.

XI

In which Phileas Fogg secures a curious means of conveyance at a fabulous price

The train had started punctually. Among the passengers were a number of officers, Government officials, and opium and indigo merchants, whose business called them to the eastern coast. Passepartout rode in the same carriage with his master, and a third passenger occupied a seat opposite to them. This was Sir Francis Cromarty, one of Mr. Fogg's whist partners on the *Mongolia*, now on his way to join his corps at Benares. Sir Francis was a tall, fair man of fifty, who had greatly distinguished himself in the last Sepoy revolt. He made India his home, only paying brief visits to England at rare intervals; and was almost as familiar as a native with the customs, history, and character of India and its people. But Phileas Fogg, who was not traveling, but only describing a circumference, took no pains to inquire into these subjects; he was a solid body, traversing an orbit around the terrestrial globe, according to the laws of rational mechanics. He was at this moment calculating in his mind the number of hours spent since his departure from London, and, had it been in his nature to make a useless demonstration, would have rubbed his hands for satisfaction. Sir Francis Cromarty had observed the oddity of his traveling companion—although the only opportunity he had for studying him had been while he was dealing the cards, and between two rubbers—and questioned himself whether a human heart really beat beneath this cold exterior, and whether Phileas Fogg had any sense of the beauties of nature. The brigadier-general was free to mentally confess, that, of all the eccentric persons he had ever met, none was comparable to this product of the exact sciences.

Phileas Fogg had not concealed from Sir Francis his design of going around the world, nor the circumstances under which he set out; and the general only saw in the wager a useless eccentricity and a lack of sound commonsense. In the way this strange gentleman was going on, he would leave the world without having done any good to himself or anybody else.

An hour after leaving Bombay the train had passed the viaducts and the island of Salcette, and had got into the open country. At Callyan they reached the junction of the branch line which descends toward south-eastern India by Kandallah and Pounah; and, passing Pauwell, they entered the defiles of the mountains, with their basalt bases, and their summits crowned with thick and verdant forests. Phileas Fogg and Sir Francis Cromarty exchanged a few words from time to time, and now Sir Francis, reviving the conversation, observed, "Some years ago, Mr. Fogg, you would have met with a delay at this point which would probably have lost you your wager."

"How so, Sir Francis?"

"Because the railway stopped at the base of these mountains, which the passengers were obliged to cross in palanquins or on ponies to Kandallah, on the other side."

"Such a delay would not have deranged my plans in the least," said Mr. Fogg. "I have constantly foreseen the likelihood of certain obstacles."

"But, Mr. Fogg," pursued Sir Francis, "you run the risk of having some difficulty about this worthy fellow's adventure at the pagoda." Passepartout, his feet comfortably wrapped in his traveling-blanket, was sound asleep, and did not dream that anybody was talking about him. "The Government is very severe upon that kind of offense. It takes particular care that the religious customs of the Indians should be respected, and if your servant were caught——"

"Very well, Sir Francis," replied Mr. Fogg; "if he had been caught he would have been condemned and punished, and then would have quietly returned to Europe. I don't see how this affair could have delayed his master."

The conversation fell again. During the night the train left the mountains behind, and passed Nassik, and the next day proceeded over the flat, well-cultivated country of the Khandeish, with its straggling villages, above which rose the minarets of the pagodas. This fertile territory is watered by numerous small rivers and limpid streams, mostly tributaries of the Godavery.

Passepartout, on waking and looking out, could not realize that he was actually crossing India in a railway train. The locomotive, guided by an English engineer and fed with English coal, threw out its smoke upon cotton, coffee, nutmeg, clove, and pepper plantations, while the steam curled in spirals around groups of palm-trees, in the midst of which were seen picturesque bungalows, viharis (a sort of abandoned monasteries), and marvelous temples enriched by the exhaustless ornamentation of Indian architecture. Then they came upon vast tracts extending to the horizon, with jungles inhabited by snakes and tigers, which fled at the noise of the train; succeeded by forests penetrated by the railway, and still haunted by elephants which, with pensive eyes, gazed at the train as it passed. The travelers crossed, beyond Malligaum, the fatal country so often stained with blood by the sectaries of the goddess Kali. Not far off rose Ellora, with its graceful pagodas, and the famous Aurungabad, capital of the ferocious Aureng-Zeb, now the chief town of one of the detached provinces of the kingdom of the Nizam. It was thereabouts that Feringhea, the Thuggee chief, king of the stranglers, held his sway. These ruffians, united by a secret bond, strangled victims of every age in honor of the goddess Death, without ever shedding blood; there was a period when this part of the country could scarcely be traveled over without corpses being found in every direction. The English Government has succeeded in greatly diminishing these murders, though the Thuggees still exist, and pursue the exercise of their horrible rites.

At half-past twelve the train stopped at Burhampoor, where Passepartout was able to purchase some Indian slippers, ornamented with false pearls, in which, with evident vanity, he proceeded to incase his feet. The travelers made a hasty breakfast and started off for Assurghur, after skirting for a little the banks of the small river Tapty, which empties into the Gulf of Cambray, near Surat.

Passepartout was now plunged into absorbing reverie. Up to his arrival at Bombay, he had entertained hopes that their journey would end there; but now that they were plainly whirling across India at full speed, a sudden change had come over the spirit of his dreams. His old vagabond nature returned to him; the fantastic ideas of his youth once more took possession of him. He came to regard his master's project as intended in good earnest, believed in the reality of the bet, and therefore in the tour of the world, and the necessity of making it without fail within the designated period. Already he began to worry about possible delays, and accidents which might happen on the way. He recognized himself as being personally interested in the wager, and trembled at the thought that he might have been the means of losing it by his unpardonable folly of the night before. Being much less cool-headed than Mr. Fogg, he was much more restless, counting and recounting the days passed over, uttering maledictions when the train stopped, and accusing it of sluggishness, and mentally blaming Mr. Fogg for not having bribed the engineer. The worthy fellow was ignorant that, while it was possible by such means to hasten the rate of a steamer, it could not be done on the railway.

The train entered the defiles of the Sutpour Mountains, which separate the Khandeish from Bundelcund, toward evening. The next day Sir Francis Cromarty asked Passepartout what time it was; to which, on consulting his watch, he replied that it was three in the morning. This famous timepiece, always regulated on the Greenwich meridian, which was now some seventy-seven degrees westward, was at least four hours slow. Sir Francis corrected Passepartout's time, whereupon the latter made the same remark that he had done to Fix; and upon the general insisting that the watch should be regulated in each new meridian, since he was constantly going eastward, that is in the face of the sun, and therefore the days were shorter by four minutes for each degree gone over, Passepartout obstinately refused to alter his watch, which he kept at London time. It was an innocent delusion which could harm no one.

The train stopped, at eight o'clock, in the midst of a glade some fifteen miles beyond Rothal, where there were several bungalows, and workmen's cabins. The conductor, passing along the carriages, shouted, "Passengers will get out here!"

Phileas Fogg looked at Sir Francis Cromarty for an explanation; but the general could not tell what meant a halt in the midst of this forest of dates and acacias.

Passepartout, not less surprised, rushed out and speedily returned, crying: "Monsieur, no more railway!"

"What do you mean?" asked Sir Francis.

"I mean to say that the train isn't going on."

The general at once stepped out, while Phileas Fogg calmly followed him, and they proceeded together to the conductor.

"Where are we?" asked Sir Francis.

"At the hamlet of Kholby."

"Do we stop here?"

"Certainly. The railway isn't finished."

"What! not finished?"

"No. There's still a matter of fifty miles to be laid from here to Allahabad, where the line begins again."

"But the papers announced the opening of the railway throughout."

"What would you have, officer? The papers were mistaken."

"Yet you sell tickets from Bombay to Calcutta," retorted Sir Francis, who was growing warm.

"No doubt," replied the conductor; "but the passengers know that they must provide means of transportation for themselves from Kholby to Allahabad."

Sir Francis was furious. Passepartout would willingly have knocked the conductor down, and did not dare to look at his master.

"Sir Francis," said Mr. Fogg, quietly, "we will, if you please, look about for some means of conveyance to Allahabad."

"Mr. Fogg, this is a delay greatly to your disadvantage."

"No, Sir Francis; it was foreseen."

"What! You knew that the way——"

"Not at all; but I knew that some obstacle or other would sooner or later arise on my route. Nothing, therefore, is lost. I have two days, which I have already gained, to sacrifice. A steamer leaves Calcutta for Hong Kong at noon, on the 25th. This is the 22nd, and we shall reach Calcutta in time."

There was nothing to say to so confident a response.

It was but too true that the railway came to a termination at this point. The papers were like some watches, which have a way of getting too fast, and had been premature in their announcement of the completion of the line. The greater part of the travelers were aware of this interruption, and leaving the train, they began to engage such vehicles as the village could provide—four-wheeled palkigharis, wagons drawn by zebus, carriages that looked like perambulating pagodas, palanquins, ponies, and what not.

Mr. Fogg and Sir Francis Cromarty, after searching the village from end to end, came back without having found anything.

"I shall go afoot," said Phileas Fogg.

Passepartout, who had now rejoined his master, made a wry grimace, as he thought of his magnificent, but too frail Indian shoes. Happily he too had been looking about him, and, after a moment's hesitation, said, "Monsieur, I think I have found a means of conveyance."

"What?"

"An elephant! An elephant that belongs to an Indian who lives but a hundred steps from here."

"Let's go and see the elephant," replied Mr. Fogg.

They soon reached a small hut, near which, enclosed within some high palings, was the animal in question. An Indian came out of the hut, and, at their request, conducted them within the enclosure. The elephant, which its owner had reared, not for a beast of burden, but for warlike purposes, was half domesticated. The Indian had begun already, by often irritating him, and feeding him every three months on sugar and butter, to impart to him a ferocity not in his nature, this method being often employed by those who train the Indian elephants for battle. Happily, however, for Mr. Fogg, the animal's instruction in this direction had not gone far, and the elephant still preserved his natural gentleness. Kiouni—this was the name of the beast—could doubtless travel rapidly for a long time, and, in default of any other means of conveyance, Mr. Fogg resolved to hire him. But elephants are far from cheap in India, where they are becoming scarce; the males, which alone are suitable for circus shows, are much sought, especially as but few of them are domesticated. When, therefore, Mr. Fogg proposed to the Indian to hire Kiouni, he refused point-blank. Mr. Fogg persisted, offering the excessive sum of ten pounds an hour for the loan of the beast to Allahabad. Refused. Twenty pounds? Refused also. Forty pounds? Still refused. Passepartout jumped at each advance; but the Indian declined to be tempted. Yet the offer was an alluring one, for, supposing it took the elephant fifteen hours to reach Allahabad, his owner would receive no less than six hundred pounds sterling.

Phileas Fogg, without getting in the least flurried, then proposed to purchase the animal outright, and at first offered a thousand pounds for him. The Indian, perhaps thinking he was going to make a great bargain, still refused.

Sir Francis Cromarty took Mr. Fogg aside, and begged him to reflect before he went any further; to which the gentleman replied that he was not in the habit of acting rashly, that a bet of twenty thousand pounds was at stake, that the elephant was absolutely necessary to him, and that he would secure him if he had to pay twenty times his value. Returning to the Indian, whose small, sharp eyes, glistening with avarice, betrayed that with him it was only a question of how great a price he could obtain, Mr. Fogg offered first twelve hundred, then fifteen hundred, eighteen hundred, two thousand pounds. Passepartout, usually so rubicund, was fairly white with suspense.

At two thousand pounds the Indian yielded.

"What a price, good heaven!" cried Passepartout, "for an elephant!"

It only remained now to find a guide, which was comparatively easy. A young Parsee, with an intelligent face, offered his services, which Mr. Fogg accepted, promising so generous a reward as to materially stimulate his zeal. The elephant was led out and equipped. The Parsee, who was an accomplished elephant driver, covered his back with a sort of saddle-cloth, and attached to each of his flanks some curiously uncomfortable howdahs.

Phileas Fogg paid the Indian with some bank-notes which he extracted from the famous carpet-bag, a proceeding that seemed to deprive poor Passepartout of his vitals. Then he offered to carry Sir Francis to Allahabad, which the brigadier gratefully accepted, as one traveler the more would not be likely to fatigue the gigantic beast. Provisions were purchased at Kholby, and while Sir Francis and Mr. Fogg took the howdahs on either side, Passepartout got astride the saddle-cloth between them. The Parsee perched himself on the elephant's neck, and at nine o'clock they set out from the village, the animal marching off through the dense forest of palms by the shortest cut.

XII

In which Phileas Fogg and his companions venture across the Indian forests, and what ensued

In order to shorten the journey, the guide passed to the left of the line where the railway was still in process of being built. This line, owing to the capricious turnings of the Vindhia Mountains, did not pursue a straight course. The Parsee, who was quite familiar with the roads and paths in the district, declared that they would gain twenty miles by striking directly through the forest.

Phileas Fogg and Sir Francis Cromarty, plunged to the neck in the peculiar howdahs provided for them, were horribly jostled by the swift trotting of the elephant, spurred on as he was by the skillful Parsee; but they endured the discomfort with true British phlegm, talking little, and scarcely able to catch a glimpse of each other. As for Passepartout, who was mounted on the beast's back, and received the direct force of each concussion as he trod along, he was very careful, in accordance with his master's advice, to keep his tongue from between his teeth, as it would otherwise have been bitten off short. The worthy fellow bounced from the elephant's neck to his rump, and vaulted like a clown on a spring-board; yet he laughed in the midst of his bouncing, and from time to time took a piece of sugar out of his pocket, and inserted it in Kiouni's trunk, who received it without in the least slackening his regular trot.

After two hours the guide stopped the elephant, and gave him an hour for rest, during which Kiouni, after quenching his thirst at a neighboring spring, set to devouring the branches and shrubs round about him. Neither Sir Francis nor Mr. Fogg regretted the delay, and both descended with a feeling of relief. "Why, he's made of iron!" exclaimed the general, gazing admiringly on Kiouni.

"Of forged iron," replied Passepartout, as he set about preparing a hasty breakfast.

At noon the Parsee gave the signal of departure. The country soon presented a very savage aspect. Copses of dates and dwarf-palms succeeded the dense forests; then vast, dry plains, dotted with scanty shrubs, and sown with great blocks of syenite. "All this portion of Bundelcund, which is little frequented by travelers, is inhabited by a fanatical population, hardened in the most horrible practices of the Hindoo faith. The English have not been able to secure complete dominion over this territory, which is subjected to the influence of rajahs, whom it is almost impossible to reach in their inaccessible mountain fastnesses. The travelers several times saw bands of ferocious Indians, who, when they perceived the elephant striding across country, made angry and threatening motions. The Parsee avoided them as much as possible. Few animals were observed on the route; even the monkeys hurried from their path with contortions and grimaces which convulsed Passepartout with laughter.

In the midst of his gaiety, however, one thought troubled the worthy servant. What would Mr. Fogg do with the elephant, when he got to Allahabad? Would he carry him on with him? Impossible! The cost of transporting him would make him ruinously expensive. Would he sell him, or set him free? The estimable beast certainly deserved some consideration. Should Mr. Fogg choose to make him, Passepartout, a present of Kiouni, he would be very much embarrassed; and these thoughts did not cease worrying him for a long time.

The principal chain of the Vindhias was crossed by eight in the evening, and another halt was made on the northern slope, in a ruined bungalow. They had gone nearly twenty-five miles that day, and an equal distance still separated them from the station of Allahabad.

The night was cold. The Parsee lit a fire in the bungalow with a few dry branches, and the warmth was very grateful. The provisions purchased at

Kholby sufficed for supper, and the travelers ate ravenously. The conversation, beginning with a few disconnected phrases, soon gave place to loud and steady snores. The guide watched Kiouni, who slept standing, bolstering himself against the trunk of a large tree. Nothing occurred during the night to disturb the slumberers, although occasional growls from panthers and chatterings of monkeys broke the silence; the more formidable beasts made no cries or hostile demonstration against the occupants of the bungalow. Sir Francis slept heavily, like an honest soldier overcome with fatigue. Passepartout was wrapped in uneasy dreams of the bouncing of the day before. As for Mr. Fogg, he slumbered as peacefully as if he had been in his serene mansion in Saville Row.

The journey was resumed at six in the morning; the guide hoped to reach Allahabad by evening. In that case, Mr. Fogg would only lose a part of the forty-eight hours saved since the beginning of the tour. Kiouni, resuming his rapid gait, soon descended the lower spurs of the Vindhias, and toward noon they passed by the village of Kallenger, on the Cani, one of the branches of the Ganges. The guide avoided inhabited places, thinking it safer to keep to the open country, which lies along the first depressions of the basin of the great river. Allahabad was now only twelve miles to the north-east. They stopped under a clump of bananas, the fruit of which, as healthy as bread and as succulent as cream, was amply partaken of and appreciated.

At two o'clock the guide entered a thick forest which extended several miles; he preferred to travel under cover of the woods. They had not as yet had any unpleasant encounters, and the journey seemed on the point of being successfully accomplished, when the elephant, becoming restless, suddenly stopped.

It was then four o'clock.

"What's the matter?" asked Sir Francis, putting out his head.

"I don't know, officer," replied the Parsee, listening attentively to a confused murmur which came through the thick branches.

The murmur soon became more distinct; it now seemed like a distant concert of human voices accompanied by brass instruments. Passepartout was all eyes and ears. Mr. Fogg patiently waited without a word. The Parsee jumped to the ground, fastened the elephant to a tree, and plunged into the thicket. He soon returned, saying—

"A procession of Brahmins is coming this way. We must prevent their seeing us, if possible."

The guide unloosed the elephant and led him into a thicket, at the same time asking the travelers not to stir. He held himself ready to bestride the animal at a moment's notice, should flight become necessary; but he evidently thought that the procession of the faithful would pass without perceiving them amid the thick foliage, in which they were wholly concealed.

The discordant tones of the voices and instruments drew nearer, and now droning songs mingled with the sound of the tambourines and cymbals. The head of the procession soon appeared beneath the trees, a hundred paces away; and the strange figures who performed the religious ceremony were easily distinguished through the branches. First came the priests, with mitres on their heads, and clothed in long lace robes. They were surrounded by men, women, and children, who sang a kind of lugubrious psalm, interrupted at regular intervals by the tambourines and cymbals; while behind them was drawn a car with large wheels, the spokes of which represented serpents entwined with each other. Upon the car, which was drawn by four richly caparisoned zebus, stood a hideous statue with four arms, the body colored a dull red, with haggard eyes, disheveled hair, protruding tongue, and lips tinted with betel. It stood upright upon the figure of a prostrate and headless giant.

Sir Francis, recognizing the statue, whispered, "The goddess Kali; the goddess of love and death."

"Of death, perhaps," muttered back Passepartout, "but of love—that ugly old hag? Never!"

The Parsee made a motion to keep silence.

A group of old fakirs were capering and making a wild ado around the statue; these were striped with ochre, and covered with cuts whence their blood issued drop by drop—stupid fanatics, who, in the great Indian ceremonies, still throw themselves under the wheels of Juggernaut. Some Brahmins, clad in all the sumptuousness of Oriental apparel, and leading a woman who faltered at every step, followed. This woman was young, and as fair as a European. Her head and neck, shoulders, ears, arms, hands, and toes, were loaded down with jewels and gems—with bracelets, earrings, and rings; while a tunic bordered with gold, and covered with a light muslin robe betrayed the outline of her form.

The guards who followed the young woman presented a violent contrast to her, armed as they were with naked sabres hung at their waists, and long damascened pistols, and bearing a corpse on a palanquin. It was the body of an old man, gorgeously arrayed in the habiliments of a rajah, wearing, as in life, a turban embroidered with pearls, a robe of tissue of silk and gold, a scarf of cashmere sewed with diamonds, and the magnificent weapons of a Hindoo prince. Next came the musicians and a rearguard of capering fakirs, whose cries sometimes drowned the noise of the instruments; these closed the procession.

Sir Francis watched the procession with a sad countenance, and, turning to the guide, said, "A suttee."

The Parsee nodded, and put his finger to his lips. The procession slowly wound under the trees, and soon its last ranks disappeared in the depths of the wood. The songs gradually died away; occasionally cries were heard in the distance, until at last all was silence again.

Phileas Fogg had heard what Sir Francis said, and, as soon as the procession had disappeared, asked: "What is a 'suttee'?"

"A suttee," returned the general, "is a human sacrifice, but a voluntary one. The woman you have just seen will be burned to-morrow at the dawn of day."

"Oh, the scoundrels!" cried Passepartout, who could not repress his indignation.

"And the corpse?" asked Mr. Fogg.

"Is that of the prince, her husband," said the guide; "an independent rajah of Bundelcund."

"Is it possible," resumed Phileas Fogg, his voice betraying not the least emotion, "that these barbarous customs still exist in India, and that the English have been unable to put a stop to them?"

"These sacrifices do not occur in the larger portion of India," replied Sir Francis; "but we have no power over these savage territories, and especially here in Bundelcund. The whole district north of the Vindhias is the theatre of incessant murders and pillage."

"The poor wretch!" exclaimed Passepartout, "to be burned alive!"

"Yes," returned Sir Francis, "burned alive. And if she were not, you cannot conceive what treatment she would be obliged to submit to from her relatives. They would shave off her hair, feed her on a scanty allowance of rice, treat her with contempt; she would be looked upon as an unclean creature, and would die in some corner, like a scurvy dog. The prospect of so frightful an existence drives these poor creatures to the sacrifice much more than love or religious fanaticism. Sometimes, however, the sacrifice is really voluntary, and it requires the active interference of the Government to prevent it. Several years ago, when I was living at Bombay, a young widow asked permission of the governor to be burned along with her husband's body; but, as you may imagine, he refused. The woman left the town, took refuge with an independent rajah, and there carried out her self-devoted purpose."

While Sir Francis was speaking, the guide shook his head several times, and now said: "The sacrifice which will take place to-morrow at dawn is not a voluntary one."

"How do you know?"

"Everybody knows about this affair in Bundelcund."

"But the wretched creature did not seem to be making any resistance," observed Sir Francis.

"That was because they had intoxicated her with fumes of hemp and opium."

"But where are they taking her?"

"To the pagoda of Pillaji, two miles from here; she will pass the night there."

"And the sacrifice will take place——"

"To-morrow, at the first light of dawn."

The guide now led the elephant out of the thicket, and leaped upon his neck. Just at the moment that he was about to urge Kiouni forward with a peculiar whistle, Mr. Fogg stopped him, and, turning to Sir Francis Cromarty, said, "Suppose we save this woman."

"Save the woman, Mr. Fogg!"

"I have yet twelve hours to spare; I can devote them to that."

"Why, you are a man of heart!"

"Sometimes," replied Phileas Fogg, quietly; "when I have the time."

XIII

In which Passepartout receives a new proof that fortune favors the brave

The project was a bold one, full of difficulty, perhaps impracticable. Mr. Fogg was going to risk life, or at least liberty, and therefore the success of his tour. But he did not hesitate, and he found in Sir Francis Cromarty an enthusiastic ally.

As for Passepartout, he was ready for anything that might be proposed. His master's idea charmed him; he perceived a heart, a soul, under that icy exterior. He began to love Phileas Fogg.

There remained the guide: what course would he adopt? Would he not take part with the Indians? In default of his assistance, it was necessary to be assured of his neutrality.

Sir Francis frankly put the question to him.

"Officers," replied the guide, "I am a Parsee, and this woman is a Parsee. Command me as you will."

"Excellent," said Mr. Fogg.

"However," resumed the guide; "it is certain, not only that we shall risk our lives, but horrible tortures, if we are taken."

"That is foreseen," replied Mr. Fogg. "I think we must wait till night before acting."

"I think so," said the guide.

The worthy Indian then gave some account of the victim, who, he said, was a celebrated beauty of the Parsee race, and the daughter of a wealthy Bombay merchant. She had received a thoroughly English education in that city, and, from her manners and intelligence, would be thought a European. Her name was Aouda. Left an orphan, she was married against her will to the old rajah of Bundelcund; and, knowing the fate that awaited her, she escaped, was retaken, and devoted by the rajah's relatives, who had an interest in her death, to the sacrifice from which it seemed she could not escape.

The Parsee's narrative only confirmed Mr. Fogg and his companions in their generous design. It was decided that the guide should direct the elephant toward the pagoda of Pillaji, which he accordingly approached as quickly as possible. They halted, half-an-hour afterward, in a copse, some five hundred feet from the pagoda, where they were well concealed; but they could hear the groans and cries of the fakirs distinctly.

They then discussed the means of getting at the victim. The guide was familiar with the pagoda of Pillaji, in which, as he declared, the young woman was imprisoned. Could they enter any of its doors while the whole party of Indians was plunged in a drunken sleep, or was it safer to attempt to make a hole in the walls? This could only be determined at the moment and the place themselves; but it was certain that the abduction must be made that night, and not when, at break of day, the victim was led to her funeral pyre. Then no human intervention could save her.

As soon as night fell, about six o'clock, they decided to make a reconnaissance around the pagoda. The cries of the fakirs were just ceasing; the Indians were in the act of plunging themselves into the drunkenness caused by liquid opium mingled with hemp, and it might be possible to slip between them to the temple itself.

The Parsee, leading the others, noiselessly crept through the wood, and in ten minutes they found themselves on the banks of a small stream, whence, by the light of the rosin torches, they perceived a pyre of wood, on the top of which lay the embalmed body of the rajah, which was to be burned with his wife. The pagoda, whose minarets loomed above the trees in the deepening dusk, stood a hundred steps away.

"Come!" whispered the guide.

He slipped more cautiously than ever through the brush, followed by his companions; the silence around was only broken by the low murmuring of the wind among the branches.

Soon the Parsee stopped on the borders of the glade, which was lit up by the torches. The ground was covered by groups of the Indians, motionless in their drunken sleep; it seemed a battle-field strewn with the dead. Men, women, and children lay together.

In the background, among the trees, the pagoda of Pillaji loomed indistinctly. Much to the guide's disappointment, the guards of the rajah, lighted by torches, were watching at the doors and marching to and fro with naked sabres; probably the priests, too, were watching within.

The Parsee, now convinced that it was impossible to force an entrance to the temple, advanced no farther, but led his companions back again. Phileas Fogg and Sir Francis Cromarty also saw that nothing could be attempted in that direction. They stopped, and engaged in a whispered colloquy.

"It is only eight now," said the brigadier, "and these guards may also go to sleep."

"It is not impossible," returned the Parsee.

They lay down at the foot of a tree, and waited.

The time seemed long; the guide ever and anon left them to take an observation on the edge of the wood, but the guards watched steadily by the glare of the torches, and a dim light crept through the windows of the pagoda.

They waited till midnight; but no change took place among the guards, and it became apparent that their yielding to sleep could not be counted on. The other plan must be carried out; an opening in the walls of the pagoda must be made. It remained to ascertain whether the priests were watching by the side of their victim as assiduously as were the soldiers at the door.

After a last consultation, the guide announced that he was ready for the attempt, and advanced, followed by the others. They took a roundabout way, so as to get at the pagoda on the rear. They reached the walls about half-past twelve, without having met anyone; here there was no guard, nor were there either windows or doors.

The night was dark. The moon, on the wane, scarcely left the horizon, and was covered with heavy clouds; the height of the trees deepened the darkness.

It was not enough to reach the walls; an opening in them must be accomplished, and to attain this purpose the party only had their pocketknives. Happily the temple walls were built of brick and wood, which could be penetrated with little difficulty; after one brick had been taken out, the rest would yield easily.

They set noiselessly to work, and the Parsee on one side and Passepartout on the other began to loosen the bricks so as to make an aperture two feet wide. They were getting on rapidly, when suddenly a cry was heard in the interior of the temple, followed almost instantly by other cries replying from the outside. Passepartout and the guide stopped. Had they been heard? Was the alarm being given? Common prudence urged them to retire, and they did so, followed by Phileas Fogg and Sir Francis. They again hid themselves in the wood, and waited till the disturbance, whatever it might be, ceased, holding themselves ready to resume their attempt without delay. But awkwardly enough, the guards now appeared at the rear of the temple, and there installed themselves, in readiness to prevent a surprise.

It would be difficult to describe the disappointment of the party, thus interrupted in their work. They could not now reach the victim; how, then, could they save her? Sir Francis shook his fists, Passepartout was beside himself, and the guide gnashed his teeth with rage. The tranquil Fogg waited, without betraying any emotion.

"We have nothing to do but to go away," whispered Sir Francis.

"Nothing but to go away," echoed the guide.

"Stop," said Fogg. "I am only due at Allahabad to-morrow before noon."

"But what can you hope to do?" asked Sir Francis. "In a few hours it will be daylight, and——"

"The chance which now seems lost may present itself at the last moment."

Sir Francis would have liked to read Phileas Fogg's eyes.

What was this cool Englishman thinking of? Was he planning to make a rush for the young woman at the very moment of the sacrifice, and boldly snatch her from her executioners?

This would be utter folly, and it was hard to admit that Fogg was such a fool. Sir Francis consented, however, to remain to the end of this terrible drama. The guide led them to the rear of the glade, where they were able to observe the sleeping groups.

Meanwhile Passepartout, who had perched himself on the lower branches of a tree, was resolving an idea which had at first struck him like a flash, and which was now firmly lodged in his brain.

He had commenced by saying to himself, "What folly!" and then he repeated, "Why not, after all? It's a chance—perhaps the only one; and with such sots!" Thinking thus, he slipped, with the suppleness of a serpent, to the lowest branches, the ends of which bent almost to the ground.

The hours passed, and the lighter shades now announced the approach of day, though it was not yet light. This was the moment. The slumbering multitude became animated, the tambourines sounded, songs and cries arose; the hour of the sacrifice had come. The doors of the pagoda swung open, and a bright light escaped from its interior, in the midst of which Mr. Fogg and Sir Francis espied the victim. She seemed, having shaken off the stupor of intoxication, to be striving to escape from her executioner. Sir Francis's heart throbbed; and convulsively seizing Mr. Fogg's hand, found in it an open knife. Just at this moment the crowd began to move.

The young woman had again fallen into a stupor caused by the fumes of hemp, and passed among the fakirs, who escorted her with their wild, religious cries.

Phileas Fogg and his companions, mingling in the rear ranks of the crowd, followed; and in two minutes they reached the banks of the stream, and stopped fifty paces from the pyre, upon which still lay the rajah's corpse. In the semi-obscurity they saw the victim, quite senseless, stretched out beside her husband's body. Then a torch was brought, and the wood, soaked with oil, instantly took fire.

At this moment Sir Francis and the guide seized Phileas Fogg, who, in an instant of mad generosity, was about to rush upon the pyre. But he had quickly pushed them aside, when the whole scene suddenly changed. A cry of terror arose. The whole multitude prostrated themselves, terror-stricken, on the ground.

The old rajah was not dead, then, since he rose of a sudden, like a spectre, took up his wife in his arms, and descended from the pyre in the midst of the clouds of smoke, which only heightened his ghostly appearance.

Fakirs and soldiers and priests, seized with instant terror, lay there with their faces on the ground, not daring to lift their eyes and behold such a prodigy.

The inanimate victim was borne along by the vigorous arms which supported her, and which she did not seem in the least to burden. Mr. Fogg and Sir Francis stood erect, the Parsee bowed his head, and Passepartout was, no doubt, scarcely less stupefied.

The resuscitated rajah approached Sir Francis and Mr. Fogg, and, in an abrupt tone, said, "Let us be off!"

It was Passepartout himself, who had slipped upon the pyre in the midst of the smoke and, profiting by the still overhanging darkness, had delivered the young woman from death! It was Passepartout who, playing his part with a happy audacity, had passed through the crowd amid the general terror.

A moment after all four of the party had disappeared in the woods, and the elephant was bearing them away at a rapid pace. But the cries and noise, and a ball which whizzed through Phileas Fogg's hat, apprised them that the trick had been discovered.

The old rajah's body, indeed, now appeared upon the burning pyre; and the priests, recovered from their terror, perceived that an abduction had taken place. They hastened into the forest, followed by the soldiers, who fired a volley after the fugitives; but the latter rapidly increased the distance between them, and ere long found themselves beyond the reach of the bullets and arrows.

XIV

In which Phileas Fogg descends the whole length of the beautiful Valley of the Ganges without ever thinking of seeing it

The rash exploit had been accomplished; and for an hour Passepartout laughed gaily at his success. Sir Francis pressed the worthy fellow's hand, and his master said, "Well done!" which, from him, was high commendation; to which Passepartout replied that all the credit of the affair belonged to Mr. Fogg. As for him, he had only been struck with a "queer" idea; and he laughed to think that for a few moments he, Passepartout, the ex-gymnast, ex-sergeant fireman, had been the spouse of a charming woman, a venerable, embalmed rajah! As for the young Indian woman, she had been unconscious throughout of what was passing, and now, wrapped up in a traveling-blanket, was reposing in one of the howdahs.

The elephant, thanks to the skillful guidance of the Parsee, was advancing rapidly through the still darksome forest, and, an hour after leaving the pagoda, had crossed a vast plain. They made a halt at seven o'clock, the young woman being still in a state of complete prostration. The guide made her drink a little brandy and water, but the drowsiness which stupefied her could not yet be shaken off. Sir Francis, who was familiar with the effects of the intoxication produced by the fumes of hemp, reassured his companions on her account. But he was more disturbed at the prospect of her future fate. He told Phileas Fogg that, should Aouda remain in India, she would inevitably fall again into the hands of her executioners. These fanatics were scattered throughout the country, and would, despite the English police, recover their victim at Madras, Bombay, or Calcutta. She would only be safe by quitting India for ever.

Phileas Fogg replied that he would reflect upon the matter.

The station at Allahabad was reached about ten o'clock, and the interrupted line of railway being resumed, would enable them to reach Calcutta in less than twenty-four hours. Phileas Fogg would thus be able to arrive in time to take the steamer which left Calcutta the next day, October 25th, at noon, for Hong Kong.

The young woman was placed in one of the waiting-rooms of the station, whilst Passepartout was charged with purchasing for her various articles of toilet, a dress, shawl, and some furs; for which his master gave him unlimited credit. Passepartout started off forthwith, and found himself in the streets of Allahabad, that is, the "City of God," one of the most venerated in India, being built at the junction of the two sacred rivers, Ganges and Jumna, the waters of which attract pilgrims from every part of the peninsula. The Ganges, according to the legends of the Ramayana, rises in heaven, whence owing to Brahma's agency, it descends to the earth.

Passepartout made it a point, as he made his purchases, to take a good look at the city. It was formerly defended by a noble fort, which has since become a state prison; its commerce has dwindled away, and Passepartout in vain looked about him for such a bazaar as he used to frequent in Regent Street. At last he came upon an elderly, crusty Jew, who sold second-hand articles, and from whom he purchased a dress of Scotch stuff, a large mantle, and a fine otter-skin pelisse, for which he did not hesitate to pay seventy-five pounds. He then returned triumphantly to the station.

The influence to which the priests of Pillaji had subjected Aouda began gradually to yield, and she became more herself, so that her fine eyes resumed all their soft Indian expression.

When the poet-king, Ucaf Uddaul, celebrates the charms of the queen of Ahmehnagara, he speaks thus:

"Her shining tresses, divided in two parts, encircle the harmonious contour of her white and delicate cheeks, brilliant in their glow and freshness. Her ebony brows have the form and charm of the bow of Kama, the god of love, and beneath her long silken lashes the purest reflections and a celestial light swim, as in the sacred lakes of Himalaya, in the black pupils of her great clear eyes. Her teeth, fine, equal, and white, glitter between her smiling lips like dewdrops in a passion-flower's half-enveloped breast. Her delicately formed ears, her vermilion hands, her little feet, curved and tender as the lotus-bud, glitter with the brilliancy of the loveliest pearls of Ceylon, the most dazzling diamonds of Golconda. Her narrow and supple waist, which a hand may clasp around, sets forth the outline of her rounded figure and the beauty of her bosom, where youth in its flower displays the wealth of its treasures; and beneath the silken folds of her tunic she seems to have been modeled in pure silver by the godlike hand of Vicvarcarma, the immortal sculptor."

It is enough to say, without applying this poetical rhapsody to Aouda, that she was a charming woman, in all the European acceptation of the phrase. She spoke English with great purity, and the guide had not exaggerated in saying that the young Parsee had been transformed by her bringing up.

The train was about to start from Allahabad, and Mr. Fogg proceeded to pay the guide the price agreed upon for his service, and not a farthing more; which astonished Passepartout, who remembered all that his master owed to the guide's devotion. He had, indeed, risked his life in the adventure at Pillaji, and if he should be caught afterward by the Indians, he would with difficulty escape their vengeance. Kiouni, also, must be disposed of. What should be done with the elephant, which had been so dearly purchased? Phileas Fogg had already determined this question.

"Parsee," said he to the guide, "you have been serviceable and devoted. I have paid for your service, but not for your devotion. Would you like to have this elephant? He is yours."

The guide's eyes glistened.

"Your honor is giving me a fortune!" cried he.

"Take him, guide," returned Mr. Fogg, "and I shall still be your debtor."

"Good!" exclaimed Passepartout; "take him, friend. Kiouni is a brave and faithful beast." And, going up to the elephant, he gave him several lumps of sugar, saying, "Here, Kiouni, here, here."

The elephant grunted out his satisfaction, and, clasping Passepartout around the waist with his trunk, lifted him as high as his head. Passepartout, not in the least alarmed, caressed the animal, which replaced him gently on the ground.

Soon after, Phileas Fogg, Sir Francis Cromarty, and Passepartout, installed in a carriage with Aouda, who had the best seat, were whirling at full speed toward Benares. It was a run of eighty miles, and was accomplished in two hours. During the journey, the young woman fully recovered her senses. What was her astonishment to find herself in this carriage, on the railway, dressed in European habiliments, and with travelers who were quite strangers to her! Her companions first set about fully reviving her with a little liquor, and then Sir Francis narrated to her what had passed, dwelling upon the courage with which Phileas Fogg had not hesitated to risk his life to save her, and recounting the happy sequel of the venture, the result of Passepartout's rash idea. Mr. Fogg said nothing; while Passepartout, abashed, kept repeating that "it wasn't worth telling."

Aouda pathetically thanked her deliverers, rather with tears than words; her fine eyes interpreted her gratitude better than her lips. Then, as her thoughts strayed back to the scene of the sacrifice, and recalled the dangers which still menaced her, she shuddered with terror.

Phileas Fogg understood what was passing in Aouda's mind, and offered, in order to reassure her, to escort her to Hong Kong, where she might remain safely until the affair was hushed up—an offer which she eagerly and gratefully accepted. She had, it seems, a Parsee relation, who was one of the principal merchants of Hong Kong, which is wholly an English city, though on an island on the Chinese coast.

At half-past twelve the train stopped at Benares. The Brahmin legends assert that this city is built on the site of the ancient Casi, which, like Mahomet's tomb, was once suspended between heaven and earth; though the Benares of to-day, which the Orientalists call the Athens of India, stands quite unpoetically on the solid earth. Passepartout caught glimpses of its brick houses and clay huts, giving an aspect of desolation to the place, as the train entered it.

Benares was Sir Francis Cromarty's destination, the troops he was rejoining being encamped some miles northward of the city. He bade adieu to Phileas Fogg, wishing him all success, and expressing the hope that he would come that way again in a less original but more profitable fashion. Mr. Fogg lightly pressed him by the hand. The parting of Aouda, who did not forget what she owed to Sir Francis, betrayed more warmth; and, as for Passepartout, he received a hearty shake of the hand from the gallant general.

The railway, on leaving Benares, passed for a while along the valley of the Ganges. Through the windows of their carriage the travelers had glimpses of the diversified landscape of Behar, with its mountains clothed in verdure, its fields of barley, wheat, and corn, its jungles peopled with green alligators, its neat villages and its still thickly-leaved forests. Elephants were bathing in the waters of the sacred river, and groups of Indians, despite the advanced season and chilly air, were performing solemnly their pious ablutions. These were fervent Brahmins, the bitterest foes of

Buddhism, their deities being Vishnu, the solar god, Shiva, the divine impersonation of natural forces, and Brahma, the supreme ruler of priests and legislators. What would these divinities think of India, anglicized as it is to-day, with steamers whistling and scudding along the Ganges, frightening the gulls which float upon its surface, the turtles swarming along its banks, and the faithful dwelling upon its borders?

The panorama passed before their eyes like a flash, save when the steam concealed it fitfully from the view; the travelers could scarcely discern the fort of Chupenie, twenty miles south-westward from Benares, the ancient stronghold of the rajahs of Behar; or Ghazipur and its famous rose-water factories; or the tomb of Lord Cornwallis, rising on the left bank of the Ganges; the fortified town of Buxar, or Patna, a large manufacturing and trading place, where is held the principal opium market of India; or Monghir, a more than European town, for it is as English as Manchester or Birmingham, with its iron foundries, edge-tool factories, and high chimneys puffing clouds of black smoke heavenward.

Night came on; the train passed on at full speed, in the midst of the roaring of the tigers, bears, and wolves which fled before the locomotive; and the marvels of Bengal, Golconda, ruined Gour, Murshedabad, the ancient capital, Burdwan, Hugly, and the French town of Chandernagor, where Passepartout would have been proud to see his country's flag flying, were hidden from their view in the darkness.

Calcutta was reached at seven in the morning, and the packet left for Hong Kong at noon; so that Phileas Fogg had five hours before him.

According to his journal, he was due at Calcutta on the 25th of October, and that was the exact date of his actual arrival. He was therefore neither behindhand nor ahead of time. The two days gained between London and Bombay had been lost, as has been seen, in the journey across India. But it is not to be supposed that Phileas Fogg regretted them.

XV

In which the bag of bank-notes disgorges some thousands of pounds more

The train entered the station, and Passepartout, jumping out first, was followed by Mr. Fogg, who assisted his fair companion to descend. Phileas Fogg intended to proceed at once to the Hong Kong steamer, in order to get Aouda comfortably settled for the voyage. He was unwilling to leave her while they were still on dangerous ground.

Just as he was leaving the station a policeman came up to him, and said, "Mr. Phileas Fogg?"

"I am he."

"Is this man your servant?" added the policeman, pointing to Passepartout.

"Yes."

"Be so good, both of you, as to follow me."

Mr. Fogg betrayed no surprise whatever. The policeman was a representative of the law, and law is sacred to an Englishman. Passepartout tried to reason about the matter, but the policeman tapped him with his stick, and Mr. Fogg made him a signal to obey.

"May this young lady go with us?" asked he.

"She may," replied the policeman.

Mr. Fogg, Aouda, and Passepartout were conducted to a "palki-gari," a sort of four-wheeled carriage, drawn by two horses, in which they took their places and were driven away. No one spoke during the twenty minutes which elapsed before they reached their destination. They first passed through the "black town," with its narrow streets, its miserable, dirty huts, and squalid population; then through the "European town," which presented a relief in its bright brick mansions, shaded by cocoanut-trees and bristling with masts, where, although it was early morning, elegantly dressed horsemen and handsome equipages were passing back and forth.

The carriage stopped before a modest-looking house, which, however, did not have the appearance of a private mansion. The policeman having requested his prisoners—for so, truly, they might be called—to descend, conducted them into a room with barred windows, and said: "You will appear before Judge Obadiah at half-past eight."

He then retired, and closed the door.

"Why, we are prisoners!" exclaimed Passepartout, falling into a chair.

Aouda, with an emotion she tried to conceal, said to Mr. Fogg: "Sir, you must leave me to my fate! It is on my account that you receive this treatment; it is for having saved me!"

Phileas Fogg contented himself with saying that it was impossible. It was quite unlikely that he should be arrested for preventing a suttee. The complainants would not dare present themselves with such a charge. There was some mistake. Moreover, he would not in any event abandon Aouda, but would escort her to Hong Kong.

"But the steamer leaves at noon!" observed Passepartout, nervously.

"We shall be on board by noon," replied his master, placidly.

It was said so positively, that Passepartout could not help muttering to himself, "Parbleu, that's certain! Before noon we shall be on board." But he was by no means reassured.

At half-past eight the door opened, the policeman appeared, and, requesting them to follow him, led the way to an adjoining hall. It was evidently a court-room, and a crowd of Europeans and natives already occupied the rear of the apartment.

Mr. Fogg and his two companions took their places on a bench opposite the desks of the magistrate and his clerk. Immediately after, Judge Obadiah, a fat, round man, followed by the clerk, entered. He proceeded to take down a wig which was hanging on a nail, and put it hurriedly on his head.

"The first case," said he; then, putting his hand to his head, he exclaimed, "Heh! This is not my wig!"

"No, your worship," returned the clerk, "it is mine."

"My dear Mr. Oysterpuff, how can a judge give a wise sentence in a clerk's wig?"

The wigs were exchanged.

Passepartout was getting nervous, for the hands on the face of the big clock over the judge seemed to go around with terrible rapidity.

"The first case," repeated Judge Obadiah.

"Phileas Fogg?" demanded Oysterpuff.

"I am here," replied Mr. Fogg.

"Passepartout?"

"Present!" responded Passepartout.

"Good," said the judge. "You have been looked for, prisoners, for two days on the trains from Bombay."

"But of what are we accused?" asked Passepartout, impatiently.

"You are about to be informed."

"I am an English subject, sir," said Mr. Fogg, "and I have the right——"

"Have you been ill-treated?"

"Not at all."

"Very well; let the complainants come in."

A door was swung open by order of the judge and three Indian priests entered.

"That's it," muttered Passepartout; "these are the rogues who were going to burn our young lady."

The priests took their places in front of the judge, and the clerk proceeded to read in a loud voice, a complaint of sacrilege against Phileas Fogg and his servant, who were accused of having violated a place held consecrated by the Brahmin religion.

"You hear the charge?" asked the judge.

"Yes, sir," replied Mr. Fogg, consulting his watch, "and I admit it."

"You admit it?"

"I admit it, and I wish to hear these priests admit, in their turn, what they were going to do at the pagoda of Pillaji."

The priests looked at each other; they did not seem to understand what was said.

"Yes," cried Passepartout, warmly; "at the pagoda of Pillaji, where they were on the point of burning their victim."

The judge stared with astonishment, and the priests were stupefied.

"What victim?" said Judge Obadiah. "Burn whom? In Bombay itself?"

"Bombay?" cried Passepartout.

"Certainly. We are not talking of the pagoda of Pillaji, but of the pagoda of Malebar Hill, at Bombay."

"And as a proof," added the clerk, "here are the desecrator's very shoes, which he left behind him.

Whereupon he placed a pair of shoes on his desk.

"My shoes!" cried Passepartout, in his surprise permitting this imprudent exclamation to escape him.

The confusion of master and man, who had quite forgotten the affair at Bombay, for which they were now detained at Calcutta, may be imagined.

Fix, the detective, had foreseen the advantage which Passepartout's escapade gave him, and, delaying his departure for twelve hours, had consulted the priests of Malebar Hill. Knowing that the English authorities dealt very severely with this kind of misdemeanor, he promised them a goodly sum in damages, and sent them forward to Calcutta by the next train. Owing to the delay caused by the rescue of the young widow, Fix and the priests reached the Indian capital before Mr. Fogg and his servant, the magistrates having been already warned by a dispatch to arrest them should they arrive. Fix's disappointment when he learned that Phileas Fogg had not made his appearance in Calcutta, may be imagined. He made up his mind that the robber had stopped somewhere on the route and taken refuge in the southern provinces. For twenty-four hours Fix watched the station with feverish anxiety; at last he was rewarded by seeing Mr. Fogg and Passepartout arrive, accompanied by a young woman, whose presence he was wholly at a loss to explain. He hastened for a policeman; and this was how the party came to be arrested and brought before Judge Obadiah.

Had Passepartout been a little less preoccupied, he would have espied the detective ensconced in a corner of the court-room, watching the proceedings with an interest easily understood; for the warrant had failed to reach him at Calcutta, as it had done at Bombay and Suez.

Judge Obadiah had unfortunately caught Passepartout's rash exclamation, which the poor fellow would have given the world to recall.

"The facts are admitted?" asked the judge.

"Admitted," replied Mr. Fogg, coldly.

"Inasmuch," resumed the judge, "as the English law protects equally and sternly the religions of the Indian people, and as the man Passepartout has admitted that he violated the sacred pagoda of Malebar Hill, at Bombay, on the 20th of October, I condemn the said Passepartout to imprisonment for fifteen days and a fine of three hundred pounds."

"Three hundred pounds!" cried Passepartout, startled at the largeness of the sum.

"Silence!" shouted the constable.

"And inasmuch," continued the judge, "as it is not proved that the act was not done by the connivance of the master with the servant, and as the master in any case must be held responsible for the acts of his paid servant, I condemn Phileas Fogg to a week's imprisonment and a fine of one hundred and fifty pounds."

Fix rubbed his hands softly with satisfaction; if Phileas Fogg could be detained in Calcutta a week, it would be more than time for the warrant to arrive. Passepartout was stupefied. This sentence ruined his master. A wager of twenty thousand pounds lost, because he, like a precious fool, had gone into that abominable pagoda!

Phileas Fogg, as self-composed as if the judgment did not in the least concern him, did not even lift his eyebrows while it was being pronounced. Just as the clerk was calling the next case, he rose, and said, "I offer bail."

"You have that right," returned the judge.

Fix's blood ran cold, but he resumed his composure when he heard the judge announce that the bail required for each prisoner would be one thousand pounds.

"I will pay it at once," said Mr. Fogg, taking a roll of bank-bills from the carpet-bag, which Passepartout had by him, and placing them on the clerk's desk.

"This sum will be restored to you upon your release from prison," said the judge. "Meanwhile, you are liberated on bail."

"Come!" said Phileas Fogg to his servant.

"But let them at least give me back my shoes!" cried Passepartout, angrily.

"Ah, these are pretty dear shoes!" he muttered, as they were handed to him. "More than a thousand pounds apiece; besides, they pinch my feet."

Mr. Fogg, offering his arm to Aouda, then departed, followed by the crestfallen Passepartout. Fix still nourished hopes that the robber would not, after all, leave the two thousand pounds behind him, but would decide to serve out his week in jail, and issued forth on Mr. Fogg's traces. That gentleman took a carriage, and the party were soon landed on one of the quays.

The *Rangoon* was moored half a mile off in the harbor, its signal of departure hoisted at the mast-head. Eleven o'clock was striking; Mr. Fogg was an hour in advance of time. Fix saw them leave the carriage and push off in a boat for the steamer, and stamped his feet with disappointment.

"The rascal is off, after all!" he exclaimed. "Two thousand pounds sacrificed! He's as prodigal as a thief! I'll follow him to the end of the world if necessary; but at the rate he is going on, the stolen money will soon be exhausted."

The detective was not far wrong in making this conjecture. Since leaving London, what with traveling expenses, bribes, the purchase of the elephant, bails, and fines, Mr. Fogg had already spent more than five thousand pounds on the way, and the percentage of the sum recovered from the bank robber, promised to the detectives, was rapidly diminishing.

XVI

In which Fix does not seem to understand in the least what is said to him

The *Rangoon*—one of the Peninsular and Oriental Company's boats plying in the Chinese and Japanese seas—was a screw steamer, built of iron, weighing about seventeen hundred and seventy tons, and with engines of four hundred horse-power. She was as fast, but not as well fitted up, as the *Mongolia*, and Aouda was not as comfortably provided for on board of her as Phileas Fogg could have wished. However, the trip from Calcutta to Hong Kong only comprised some three thousand five hundred miles, occupying from ten to twelve days, and the young woman was not difficult to please.

During the first days of the journey Aouda became better acquainted with her protector, and constantly gave evidence of her deep gratitude for what he had done. The phlegmatic gentleman listened to her, apparently at least, with coldness, neither his voice nor his manner betraying the slightest emotion; but he seemed to be always on the watch that nothing should be wanting to Aouda's comfort. He visited her regularly each day at certain hours, not so much to talk himself as to sit and hear her talk. He treated her with the strictest politeness, but with the precision of an automaton, the movements of which had been arranged for this purpose. Aouda did not quite know what to make of him, though Passepartout had given her some hints of his master's eccentricity, and made her smile by telling her of the wager which was sending him around the world. After all, she owed Phileas Fogg her life, and she always regarded him through the exalting medium of her gratitude.

Aouda confirmed the Parsee guide's narrative of her touching history. She did, indeed, belong to the highest of the native races of India. Many of the Parsee merchants have made great fortunes there by dealing in cotton;

and one of them, Sir Jametsee Jeejeebhoy, was made a baronet by the English government. Aouda was a relative of this great man, and it was his cousin, Jeejeeh, whom she hoped to join at Hong Kong. Whether she would find a protector in him she could not tell; but Mr. Fogg essayed to calm her anxieties, and to assure her that everything would be mathematically—he used the very word—arranged. Aouda fastened her great eyes, "clear as the sacred lakes of the Himalaya," upon him; but the intractable Fogg, as reserved as ever, did not seem at all inclined to throw himself into this lake.

The first few days of the voyage passed prosperously, amid favorable weather and propitious winds, and they soon came in sight of the great Andaman, the principal of the islands in the Bay of Bengal, with its picturesque Saddle Peak, two thousand four hundred feet high, looming above the waters. The steamer passed along near the shores, but the savage Papuans, who are in the lowest scale of humanity, but are not, as has been asserted, cannibals, did not make their appearance.

The panorama of the islands, as they steamed by them, was superb. Vast forests of palms, arecs, bamboo, teakwood, of the gigantic mimosa, and tree-like ferns covered the foreground, while behind, the graceful outlines of the mountains were traced against the sky; and along the coasts swarmed by thousands the precious swallows whose nests furnish a luxurious dish to the tables of the Celestial Empire. The varied landscape afforded by the Andaman Islands was soon passed, however, and the *Rangoon* rapidly approached the Straits of Malacca, which give access to the China seas.

What was detective Fix, so unluckily drawn on from country to country, doing all this while? He had managed to embark on the *Rangoon* at Calcutta without being seen by Passepartout, after leaving orders that, if the warrant should arrive, it should be forwarded to him at Hong Kong; and he hoped to conceal his presence to the end of the voyage. It would have been difficult to explain why he was on board without awaking Passepartout's suspicions, who thought him still at Bombay. But necessity impelled him, nevertheless, to renew his acquaintance with the worthy servant, as will be seen.

All the detective's hopes and wishes were now centerd on Hong Kong; for the steamer's stay at Singapore would be too brief to enable him to take any steps there. The arrest must be made at Hong Kong, or the robber would probably escape him for ever. Hong Kong was the last English ground on which he would set foot; beyond, China, Japan, America offered to Fogg an almost certain refuge. If the warrant should at last make its appearance at Hong Kong, Fix could arrest him and give him into the hands of the local police, and there would be no further trouble. But beyond Hong Kong, a simple warrant would be of no avail; an extradition warrant would be necessary, and that would result in delays and obstacles, of which the rascal would take advantage to elude justice.

Fix thought over these probabilities during the long hours which he spent in his cabin, and kept repeating to himself, "Now, either the warrant will be at Hong Kong, in which case I shall arrest my man, or it will not be there; and this time it is absolutely necessary that I should delay his departure. I have failed at Bombay, and I have failed at Calcutta: if I fail at Hong Kong, my reputation is lost. Cost what it may, I *must succeed!* But how shall I prevent his departure, if that should turn out to be my last resource?"

Fix made up his mind that, if worse came to worst, he would make a confidant of Passepartout, and tell him what kind of a fellow his master really was. That Passepartout was not Fogg's accomplice, he was very certain. The servant, enlightened by his disclosure, and afraid of being himself implicated in the crime, would doubtless become an ally of the detective. But this method was a dangerous one, only to be employed when everything else had failed. A word from Passepartout to his master would ruin all. The detective was therefore in a sore strait. But suddenly a new idea struck him. The presence of Aouda on the *Rangoon*, in company with Phileas Fogg, gave him new material for reflection.

Who was this woman? What combination of events had made her Fogg's traveling companion? They had evidently met somewhere between Bombay and Calcutta; but where? Had they met accidentally, or had Fogg gone into the interior purposely in quest of this charming damsel? Fix was fairly puzzled. He asked himself whether there had not been a wicked elopement; and this idea so impressed itself upon his mind that he determined to make use of the supposed intrigue. Whether the young woman were married or not, he would be able to create such difficulties for Mr. Fogg at Hong Kong, that he could not escape by paying any amount of money.

But could he even wait till they reached Hong Kong? Fogg had an abominable way of jumping from one boat to another, and, before anything could be effected, might get full under weigh again for Yokohama.

Fix decided that he must warn the English authorities, and signal the *Rangoon* before her arrival. This was easy to do, since the steamer stopped at Singapore, whence there is a telegraphic wire to Hong Kong. He finally resolved, moreover, before acting more positively, to question Passepartout. It would not be difficult to make him talk; and, as there was no time to lose, Fix prepared to make himself known.

It was now the 30th of October, and on the following day the *Rangoon* was due at Singapore.

Fix emerged from his cabin and went on deck. Passepartout was promenading up and down in the forward part of the steamer. The detective rushed forward with every appearance of extreme surprise, and exclaimed, "You here, on the *Rangoon*?"

"What, Monsieur Fix, are you on board?" returned the really astonished Passepartout, recognizing his crony of the *Mongolia*. "Why, I left you at Bombay, and here you are, on the way to Hong Kong! Are you going round the world too?"

"No, no," replied Fix; "I shall stop at Hong Kong—at least for some days."

"Hum!" said Passepartout, who seemed for an instant perplexed. "But how is it I have not seen you on board since we left Calcutta?"

"Oh, a trifle of seasickness—I've been staying in my berth. The Gulf of Bengal does not agree with me as well as the Indian Ocean. And how is Mr. Fogg?"

"As well and as punctual as ever, not a day behind time! But, Monsieur Fix, you don't know that we have a young lady with us."

"A young lady?" replied the detective, not seeming to comprehend what was said.

Passepartout thereupon recounted Aouda's history, the affair at the Bombay pagoda, the purchase of the elephant for two thousand pounds, the rescue, the arrest and sentence of the Calcutta court, and the restoration of Mr. Fogg and himself to liberty on bail. Fix, who was familiar with the last events, seemed to be equally ignorant of all that Passepartout related; and the latter was charmed to find so interested a listener.

"But does your master propose to carry this young woman to Europe?"

"Not at all. We are simply going to place her under the protection of one of her relatives, a rich merchant at Hong Kong."

"Nothing to be done there," said Fix to himself, concealing his disappointment. "A glass of gin, Mr. Passepartout?"

"Willingly, Monsieur Fix. We must at least have a friendly glass on board the *Rangoon*."

XVII

Showing what happened on the voyage from Singapore to Hong Kong

The detective and Passepartout met often on deck after this interview, though Fix was reserved, and did not attempt to induce his companion to divulge any more facts concerning Mr. Fogg. He caught a glimpse of that mysterious gentleman once or twice; but Mr. Fogg usually confined himself to the cabin, where he kept Aouda company, or according to his inveterate habit, took a hand at whist.

Passepartout began very seriously to conjecture what strange chance kept Fix still on the route that his master was pursuing. It was really worth considering why this certainly very amiable and complacent person, whom he had first met at Suez, had then encountered on board the *Mongolia*, who disembarked at Bombay, which he announced at his destination, and now turned up so unexpectedly on the *Rangoon*, was following Mr. Fogg's tracks step by step. What was Fix's object? Passepartout was ready to wager his Indian shoes—which he religiously preserved—that Fix would also leave Hong Kong at the same time with them, and probably on the same steamer.

Passepartout might have cudgeled his brain for a century without hitting upon the real object which the detective had in view. He could never have imagined that Phileas Fogg was being tracked as a robber around the globe. But as it is in human nature to attempt the solution of every mystery, Passepartout suddenly discovered an explanation of Fix's movements, which was in truth far from unreasonable. Fix, he thought, could only be an agent of Mr. Fogg's friends at the Reform Club, sent to follow him up, and to ascertain that he really went around the world as had been agreed upon.

"It's clear!" repeated the worthy servant to himself, proud of his shrewdness. "He's a spy sent to keep us in view! That isn't quite the thing, either, to be spying Mr. Fogg, who is so honorable a man! Ah, gentlemen of the Reform, this shall cost you dear!"

Passepartout, enchanted with his discovery, resolved to say nothing to his master, lest he should be justly offended at this mistrust on the part of his adversaries. But he determined to chaff Fix, when he had the chance, with mysterious allusions, which, however, need not betray his real suspicions.

During the afternoon of Wednesday, October 30th, the *Rangoon* entered the Strait of Malacca, which separates the peninsula of that name from Sumatra. The mountainous and craggy islets intercepted the beauties of this noble island from the view of the travelers. The *Rangoon* weighed anchor at Singapore the next day at four A.M., to receive coal, having gained half a day on the prescribed time of her arrival. Phileas Fogg noted this gain in his journal, and then, accompanied by Aouda, who betrayed a desire for a walk on shore, disembarked.

Fix, who suspected Mr. Fogg's every movement, followed them cautiously, without being himself perceived; while Passepartout, laughing in his sleeve at Fix's maneuvers, went about his usual errands.

The island of Singapore is not imposing in aspect, for there are no mountains; yet its appearance is not without attractions. It is a park checkered by pleasant highways and avenues. A handsome carriage, drawn by a sleek pair of New Holland horses, carried Phileas Fogg and Aouda into the midst of rows of palms with brilliant foliage, and of clove-trees whereof the cloves form the heart of a half-open flower. Pepper plants replaced the prickly hedges of European fields; sago-bushes, large ferns with gorgeous branches, varied the aspect of this tropical clime; while nutmeg-trees in full foliage filled the air with a penetrating perfume. Agile and grinning bands of monkeys skipped about in the trees, nor were tigers wanting in the jungles.

After a drive of two hours through the country, Aouda and Mr. Fogg returned to the town, which is a vast collection of heavy-looking, irregular houses, surrounded by charming gardens rich in tropical fruits and plants; and at ten o'clock they re-embarked, closely followed by the detective, who had kept them constantly in sight.

Passepartout, who had been purchasing several dozen mangoes—a fruit as large as good-sized apples, of a dark-brown color outside and a bright red within, and whose white pulp, melting in the mouth, affords gourmands a delicious sensation—was waiting for them on deck. He was only too glad to offer some mangoes to Aouda, who thanked him very gracefully for them.

At eleven o'clock the *Rangoon* rode out of Singapore harbor, and in a few hours the high mountains of Malacca, with their forests inhabited by the most beautifully-furred tigers in the world, were lost to view. Singapore is distant some thirteen hundred miles from the island of Hong Kong, which is a little English colony near the Chinese coast. Phileas Fogg hoped to accomplish the journey in six days, so as to be in time for the steamer which would leave on the 6th of November for Yokohama, the principal Japanese port.

The *Rangoon* had a large quota of passengers, many of whom disembarked at Singapore, among them a number of Indians, Ceylonese, Chinamen, Malays, and Portuguese, mostly second-class travelers.

The weather, which had hitherto been fine, changed with the last quarter of the moon. The sea rolled heavily, and the wind at intervals rose almost to a storm, but happily blew from the south-west, and thus aided the steamer's progress. The captain as often as possible put up his sails, and under the double action of steam and sail the vessel made rapid progress along the coasts of Anam and Cochin China. Owing to the defective construction of the *Rangoon*, however, unusual precautions became necessary in unfavorable weather; but the loss of time which resulted from this cause, while it nearly drove Passepartout out of his senses, did not seem to affect his master in the least. Passepartout blamed the captain, the engineer, and the crew, and consigned all who were connected with the ship to the land where the pepper grows. Perhaps the thought of the gas, which was remorselessly burning at his expense in Saville Row, had something to do with his hot impatience.

"You are in a great hurry, then," said Fix to him one day, "to reach Hong Kong?"

"A very great hurry!"

"Mr. Fogg, I suppose, is anxious to catch the steamer for Yokohama?"

"Terribly anxious."

"You believe in this journey around the world, then?"

"Absolutely. Don't you, Mr. Fix?"

"I? I don't believe a word of it."

"You're a sly dog!" said Passepartout, winking at him.

This expression rather disturbed Fix, without his knowing why. Had the Frenchman guessed his real purpose? He knew not what to think. But how could Passepartout have discovered that he was a detective? Yet, in speaking as he did, the man evidently meant more than he expressed.

Passepartout went still further the next day; he could not hold his tongue.

"Mr. Fix," said he, in a bantering tone; "shall we be so unfortunate as to lose you when we get to Hong Kong?"

"Why," responded Fix, a little embarrassed, "I don't know; perhaps——"

"Ah, if you would only go on with us! An agent of the Peninsular Company, you know, can't stop on the way! You were only going to Bombay, and here you are in China. America is not far off, and from America to Europe is only a step."

Fix looked intently at his companion, whose countenance was as serene as possible, and laughed with him. But Passepartout persisted in chaffing him by asking him if he made much by his present occupation.

"Yes, and no," returned Fix; "there is good and bad luck in such things. But you must understand that I don't travel at my own expense."

"Oh, I am quite sure of that!" cried Passepartout, laughing heartily.

Fix, fairly puzzled, descended to his cabin and gave himself up to his reflections. He was evidently suspected; somehow or other the Frenchman had found out that he was a detective. But had he told his master? What part was he playing in all this: was he an accomplice or not? Was the game, then, up? Fix spent several hours turning these things over in his mind, sometimes thinking that all was lost, then persuading himself that Fogg was ignorant of his presence, and then undecided what course it was best to take.

Nevertheless, he preserved his coolness of mind, and at last resolved to deal plainly with Passepartout. If he did not find it practicable to arrest Fogg at Hong Kong, and if Fogg made preparations to leave that last foothold of English territory, he, Fix, would tell Passepartout all. Either the servant was the accomplice of his master, and in this case the master knew of his operations, and he should fail; or else the servant knew nothing about the robbery, and then his interest would be to abandon the robber.

Such was the situation between Fix and Passepartout. Meanwhile Phileas Fogg moved about above them in the most majestic and unconscious indifference. He was passing methodically in his orbit around the world, regardless of the lesser stars which gravitated around him. Yet there was nearby what the astronomers would call a disturbing star, which might have produced an agitation in this gentleman's heart. But no! the charms of Aouda failed to act, to Passepartout's great surprise; and the disturbances, if they existed, would have been more difficult to calculate than those of Uranus which led to the discovery of Neptune.

It was every day an increasing wonder to Passepartout, who read in Aouda's eyes the depths of her gratitude to his master. Phileas Fogg, though brave and gallant, must be, he thought, quite heartless. As to the sentiment which this journey might have awakened in him, there was clearly no trace of such a thing; while poor Passepartout existed in perpetual reveries.

One day he was leaning on the railing of the engine-room, and was observing the engine, when a sudden pitch of the steamer threw the screw out of the water. The steam came hissing out of the valves; and this made Passepartout indignant.

"The valves are not sufficiently charged!" he exclaimed. "We are not going. Oh, these English! If this was an American craft, we should blow up, perhaps, but we should at all events go faster!"

XVIII

In which Phileas Fogg, Passepartout, and Fix go each about his business

The weather was bad during the latter days of the voyage. The wind, obstinately remaining in the north-west, blew a gale, and retarded the steamer. The *Rangoon* rolled heavily, and the passengers became impatient of the long, monstrous waves which the wind raised before their path. A sort of tempest arose on the 3rd of November, the squall knocking the vessel about with fury, and the waves running high. The *Rangoon* reefed all her sails, and even the rigging proved too much, whistling and shaking amid the squall. The steamer was forced to proceed slowly, and the captain estimated that she would reach Hong Kong twenty hours behind time, and more if the storm lasted.

Phileas Fogg gazed at the tempestuous sea, which seemed to be struggling especially to delay him, with his habitual tranquillity. He never changed countenance for an instant, though a delay of twenty hours, by making him too late for the Yokohama boat, would almost inevitably cause the loss of the wager. But this man of nerve manifested neither impatience nor annoyance; it seemed as if the storm were a part of his program, and had been foreseen. Aouda was amazed to find him as calm as he had been from the first time she saw him.

Fix did not look at the state of things in the same light. The storm greatly pleased him. His satisfaction would have been complete had the *Rangoon* been forced to retreat before the violence of wind and waves. Each delay filled him with hope, for it became more and more probable that Fogg would be obliged to remain some days at Hong Kong; and now the heavens themselves became his allies, with the gusts and squalls. It mattered not that they made him sea-sick—he made no account of this inconvenience; and whilst his body was writhing under their effects, his spirit bounded with hopeful exultation.

Passepartout was enraged beyond expression by the unpropitious weather. Everything had gone so well till now! Earth and sea had seemed to be at his master's service; steamers and railways obeyed him; wind and steam united to speed his journey. Had the hour of adversity come? Passepartout was as much excited as if the twenty thousand pounds were to come from his own pocket. The storm exasperated him, the gale made him furious, and he longed to lash the obstinate sea into obedience. Poor fellow! Fix carefully concealed from him his own satisfaction, for, had he betrayed it, Passepartout could scarcely have restrained himself from personal violence.

Passepartout remained on deck as long as the tempest lasted, being unable to remain quiet below, and taking it into his head to aid the progress of the ship by lending a hand with the crew. He overwhelmed the captain, officers, and sailors, who could not help laughing at his impatience, with all sorts of questions. He wanted to know exactly how long the storm was going to last; whereupon he was referred to the barometer, which seemed to have no intention of rising. Passepartout shook it, but with no perceptible effect; for neither shaking nor maledictions could prevail upon it to change its mind.

On the 4th, however, the sea became more calm, and the storm lessened its violence; the wind veered southward, and was once more favorable. Passepartout cleared up with the weather. Some of the sails were unfurled, and the *Rangoon* resumed its most rapid speed. The time lost could not, however, be regained. Land was not signaled until five o'clock on the morning of the 6th; the steamer was due on the 5th. Phileas Fogg was twenty-four hours behindhand, and the Yokohama steamer would, of course, be missed.

The pilot went on board at six, and took his place on the bridge, to guide the *Rangoon* through the channels to the port of Hong Kong. Passepartout longed to ask him if the steamer had left for Yokohama; but he dared not, for he wished to preserve the spark of hope, which still remained, till the last moment. He had confided his anxiety to Fix, who—the sly rascal!—tried to console him by saying that Mr. Fogg would be in time if he took the next boat; but this only put Passepartout in a passion.

Mr. Fogg, bolder than his servant, did not hesitate to approach the pilot, and tranquilly ask him if he knew when a steamer would leave Hong Kong for Yokohama.

"At high tide to-morrow morning," answered the pilot.

"Ah!" said Mr. Fogg, without betraying any astonishment.

Passepartout, who heard what passed, would willingly have embraced the pilot, while Fix would have been glad to twist his neck.

"What is the steamer's name?" asked Mr. Fogg.

"The *Carnatic.*"

"Ought she not to have gone yesterday?"

"Yes, sir; but they had to repair one of her boilers, and so her departure was postponed till to-morrow."

"Thank you," returned Mr. Fogg, descending mathematically to the saloon.

Passepartout clasped the pilot's hand and shook it heartily in his delight, exclaiming, "Pilot, you are the best of good fellows!"

The pilot probably does not know to this day why his responses won him this enthusiastic greeting. He remounted the bridge, and guided the steamer through the flotilla of junks, tankas, and fishing-boats which crowd the harbor of Hong Kong.

At one o'clock the *Rangoon* was at the quay, and the passengers were going ashore.

Chance had strangely favored Phileas Fogg, for, had not the *Carnatic* been forced to lie over for repairing her boilers, she would have left on the 6th of November, and the passengers for Japan would have been obliged to await for a week the sailing of the next steamer. Mr. Fogg was, it is true, twenty-four hours behind his time; but this could not seriously imperil the remainder of his tour.

The steamer which crossed the Pacific from Yokohama to San Francisco made a direct connection with that from Hong Kong, and it could not sail until the latter reached Yokohama; and if Mr. Fogg was twenty-four hours late on reaching Yokohama, this time would no doubt be easily regained in the voyage of twenty-two days across the Pacific. He found himself, then, about twenty-four hours behindhand, thirty-five days after leaving London.

The *Carnatic* was announced to leave Hong Kong at five the next morning. Mr. Fogg had sixteen hours in which to attend to his business there, which was to deposit Aouda safely with her wealthy relative.

On landing, he conducted her to a palanquin, in which they repaired to the Club Hotel. A room was engaged for the young woman, and Mr. Fogg, after seeing that she wanted for nothing, set out in search of her cousin Jeejeeh. He instructed Passepartout to remain at the hotel until his return, that Aouda might not be left entirely alone.

Mr. Fogg repaired to the Exchange, where, he did not doubt, every one would know so wealthy and considerable a personage as the Parsee merchant. Meeting a broker, he made the inquiry, to learn that Jeejeeh had left China two years before, and, retiring from business with an immense fortune, had taken up his residence in Europe—in Holland, the broker thought, with the merchants of which country he had principally traded. Phileas Fogg returned to the hotel, begged a moment's conversation with Aouda, and, without more ado, apprised her that Jeejeeh was no longer at Hong Kong, but probably in Holland.

Aouda at first said nothing. She passed her hand across her forehead, and reflected a few moments. Then, in her sweet, soft voice, she said: "What ought I to do, Mr. Fogg?"

"It is very simple," responded the gentleman. "Go on to Europe."

"But I cannot intrude——"

"You do not intrude, nor do you in the least embarrass my project. Passepartout!"

"Monsieur."

"Go to the *Carnatic*, and engage three cabins."

Passepartout, delighted that the young woman, who was very gracious to him, was going to continue the journey with them, went off at a brisk gait to obey his master's order.

XIX

In which Passepartout takes a too great interest in his master, and what comes of it

Hong Kong is an island which came into the possession of the English by the treaty of Nankin, after the war of 1842; and the colonizing genius of the English has created upon it an important city and an excellent port. The island is situated at the mouth of the Canton River, and is separated by about sixty miles from the Portuguese town of Macao, on the opposite coast. Hong Kong has beaten Macao in the struggle for the Chinese trade, and now the greater part of the transportation of Chinese goods finds its depôt at the former place. Docks, hospitals, wharves, a Gothic cathedral, a Government house, macadamized streets give to Hong Kong the appearance of a town in Kent or Surrey transferred by some strange magic to the antipodes.

Passepartout wandered, with his hands in his pockets, toward the Victoria port, gazing as he went at the curious palanquins and other modes of conveyance, and the groups of Chinese, Japanese, and Europeans who passed to and fro in the streets. Hong Kong seemed to him not unlike Bombay, Calcutta, and Singapore, since, like them, it betrayed everywhere the evidence of English supremacy. At the Victoria port he found a confused mass of ships of all nations: English, French, American, and Dutch, men-of-war and trading vessels, Japanese and Chinese junks, sempas, tankas, and flower-boats, which formed so many floating parterres. Passepartout noticed in the crowd a number of the natives who seemed very old and were dressed in yellow. On going into a barber's to get shaved he learned that these ancient men were all at least eighty years old, at which age they are permitted to wear yellow, which is the Imperial color. Passepartout, without exactly knowing why, thought this very funny.

On reaching the quay where they were to embark on the *Carnatic,* he was not astonished to find Fix walking up and down. The detective seemed very much disturbed and disappointed.

"This is bad," muttered Passepartout, "for the gentlemen of the Reform Club!" He accosted Fix with a merry smile, as if he had not perceived that gentleman's chagrin. The detective had, indeed, good reasons to inveigh against the bad luck which pursued him. The warrant had not come! It was certainly on the way, but as certainly it could not now reach Hong Kong for several days; and this being the last English territory on Mr. Fogg's route, the robber would escape, unless he could manage to detain him.

"Well, Monsieur Fix," said Passepartout, "have you decided to go on with us as far as America?"

"Yes," returned Fix, through his set teeth.

"Good!" exclaimed Passepartout, laughing heartily. "I knew you could not persuade yourself to separate from us. Come and engage your berth."

They entered the steamer office and secured cabins for four persons. The clerk, as he gave them the tickets, informed them that, the repairs on the *Carnatic* having been completed, the steamer would leave that very evening, and not next morning as had been announced.

"That will suit my master all the better," said Passepartout. "I will go and let him know."

Fix now decided to make a bold move; he resolved to tell Passepartout all. It seemed to be the only possible means of keeping Phileas Fogg several days longer at Hong Kong. He accordingly invited his companion into a tavern which caught his eye on the quay. On entering, they found themselves in a large room handsomely decorated, at the end of which was a large camp-bed furnished with cushions. Several persons lay upon this bed in a deep sleep. At the same tables which were arranged about the room some thirty customers were drinking English beer, porter, gin, and brandy; smoking, the while, long red clay pipes stuffed with little balls of opium mingled with essence of rose. From time to time one of the smokers, overcome with the narcotic, would slip under the table, whereupon the waiters, taking him by the head and feet, carried and laid him upon the bed. The bed already supported twenty of these stupefied sots.

Fix and Passepartout saw that they were in a smoking-house haunted by those wretched, cadaverous, idiotic creatures, to whom the English merchants sell every year the miserable drug called opium, to the amount of one million four hundred thousand pounds—thousands devoted to one of the most despicable vices which afflict humanity! The Chinese Government has in vain attempted to deal with the evil by stringent laws. It passed gradually from the rich, to whom it was at first exclusively reserved, to the lower classes, and then its ravages could not be arrested. Opium is smoked everywhere, at all times, by men and women, in the Celestial Empire; and, once accustomed to it, the victims cannot dispense with it, except by suffering horrible bodily contortions and agonies. A great smoker can smoke as many as eight pipes a day; but he dies in five years. It was in one of these dens that Fix and Passepartout, in search of a friendly glass, found themselves. Passepartout had no money, but willingly accepted Fix's invitation in the hope of returning the obligation at some future time.

They ordered two bottles of port, to which the Frenchman did ample justice, while Fix observed him with close attention. They chatted about the journey, and Passepartout was especially merry at the idea that Fix was going to continue it with them. When the bottles were empty, however, he rose to go and tell his master of the change in the time of the sailing of the *Carnatic*.

Fix caught him by the arm, and said, "Wait a moment."

"What for, Mr. Fix?"

"I want to have a serious talk with you."

"A serious talk!" cried Passepartout, drinking up the little wine that was left in the bottom of his glass. "Well, we'll talk about it to-morrow; I haven't time now."

"Stay! What I have to say concerns your master."

Passepartout, at this, looked attentively at his companion. Fix's face seemed to have a singular expression. He resumed his seat.

"What is it that you have to say?"

Fix placed his hand upon Passepartout's arm, and, lowering his voice, said, "You have guessed who I am?"

"Parbleu!" said Passepartout, smiling.

"Then I'm going to tell you everything——"

"Now that I know everything, my friend! Ah! that's very good. But go on, go on. First, though, let me tell you that those gentlemen have put themselves to a useless expense."

"Useless!" said Fix. "You speak confidently. It's clear that you don't know how large the sum is."

"Of course I do," returned Passepartout. "Twenty thousand pounds."

"Fifty-five thousand!" answered Fix, pressing his companion's hand.

"What!" cried the Frenchman. "Has Monsieur Fogg dared—fifty-five thousand pounds! Well, there's all the more reason for not losing an instant," he continued, getting up hastily.

Fix pushed Passepartout back in his chair, and resumed: "Fifty-five thousand pounds; and if I succeed, I get two thousand pounds. If you'll help me, I'll let you have five hundred of them."

"Help you?" cried Passepartout, whose eyes were standing wide open.

"Yes; help me keep Mr. Fogg here for two or three days."

"Why, what are you saying? Those gentlemen are not satisfied with following my master and suspecting his honor, but they must try to put obstacles in his way! I blush for them!"

"What do you mean?"

"I mean that it is a piece of shameful trickery. They might as well waylay Mr. Fogg and put his money in their pockets!"

"That's just what we count on doing."

"It's a conspiracy, then," cried Passepartout, who became more and more excited as the liquor mounted in his head, for he drank without perceiving it. "A real conspiracy! And gentlemen, too. Bah!"

Fix began to be puzzled.

"Members of the Reform Club!" continued Passepartout. "You must know, Monsieur Fix, that my master is an honest man, and that, when he makes a wager, he tries to win it fairly!"

"But who do you think I am?" asked Fix, looking at him intently.

"Parbleu! An agent of the members of the Reform Club, sent out here to interrupt my master's journey. But, though I found you out some time ago, I've taken good care to say nothing about it to Mr. Fogg."

"He knows nothing, then?"

"Nothing," replied Passepartout, again emptying his glass.

The detective passed his hand across his forehead, hesitating before he spoke again. What should he do? Passepartout's mistake seemed sincere, but it made his design more difficult. It was evident that the servant was not the master's accomplice, as Fix had been inclined to suspect.

"Well," said the detective to himself, "as he is not an accomplice, he will help me."

He had no time to lose: Fogg must be detained at Hong Kong, so he resolved to make a clean breast of it.

"Listen to me," said Fix abruptly. "I am not, as you think, an agent of the members of the Reform Club——"

"Bah!" retorted Passepartout, with an air of raillery.

"I am a police detective, sent out here by the London office."

"You, a detective?"

"I will prove it. Here is my commission."

Passepartout was speechless with astonishment when Fix displayed this document, the genuineness of which could not be doubted.

"Mr. Fogg's wager," resumed Fix, "is only a pretext, of which you and the gentlemen of the Reform are dupes. He had a motive for securing your innocent complicity."

"But why?"

"Listen. On the 28th of last September a robbery of fifty-five thousand pounds was committed at the Bank of England by a person whose description was fortunately secured. Here is this description; it answers exactly to that of Mr. Phileas Fogg."

"What nonsense!" cried Passepartout, striking the table with his fist. "My master is the most honorable of men!"

"How can you tell? You know scarcely anything about him. You went into his service the day he came away; and he came away on a foolish pretext, without trunks, and carrying a large amount in bank-notes. And yet you are bold enough to assert that he is an honest man!"

"Yes, yes," repeated the poor fellow, mechanically.

"Would you like to be arrested as his accomplice?"

Passepartout, overcome by what he had heard, held his head between his hands, and did not dare to look at the detective. Phileas Fogg, the savior of Aouda, that brave and generous man, a robber! And yet how many presumptions there were against him! Passepartout essayed to reject the suspicions which forced themselves upon his mind; he did not wish to believe that his master was guilty.

"Well, what do you want of me?" said he, at last, with an effort.

"See here," replied Fix; "I have tracked Mr. Fogg to this place, but as yet I have failed to receive the warrant of arrest for which I sent to London. You must help me to keep him here in Hong Kong——"

"I! But I——"

"I will share with you the two thousand pounds reward offered by the Bank of England."

"Never!" replied Passepartout, who tried to rise, but fell back, exhausted in mind and body.

"Mr. Fix," he stammered; "even should what you say be true—if my master is really the robber you are seeking for—which I deny—I have been, am, in his service; I have seen his generosity and goodness; and I will never betray him—not for all the gold in the world. I come from a village where they don't eat that kind of bread!"

"You refuse?"

"I refuse."

"Consider that I've said nothing," said Fix; "and let us drink."

"Yes; let us drink!"

Passepartout felt himself yielding more and more to the effects of the liquor. Fix, seeing that he must, at all hazards, be separated from his master, wished to entirely overcome him. Some pipes full of opium lay upon the table. Fix slipped one into Passepartout's hand. He took it, put it between his lips, lit it, drew several puffs, and his head, becoming heavy under the influence of the narcotic, fell upon the table.

"At last!" said Fix, seeing Passepartout unconscious. "Mr. Fogg will not be informed of the *Carnatic*'s departure; and, if he is, he will have to go without this cursed Frenchman!

And, after paying his bill, Fix left the tavern.

XX

In which Fix comes face to face with Phileas Fogg

While these events were passing at the opium-house, Mr. Fogg, unconscious of the danger he was in of losing the steamer, was quietly escorting Aouda about the streets of the English quarter, making the necessary purchases for the long voyage before them. It was all very well for an Englishman like Mr. Fogg to make the tour of the world with a carpet-bag; a lady could not be expected to travel comfortably under such conditions. He acquitted his task with characteristic serenity, and invariably replied to the remonstrances of his fair companion, who was confused by his patience and generosity—

"It is in the interest of my journey—a part of my program."

The purchases made, they returned to the hotel, where they dined at a sumptuously served *table-d'hôte*; after which Aouda, shaking hands with her protector after the English fashion, retired to her room for rest. Mr. Fogg absorbed himself throughout the evening in the perusal of the *Times* and *Illustrated London News*.

Had he been capable of being astonished at anything, it would have been not to see his servant return at bed-time. But, knowing that the steamer was not to leave for Yokohama until the next morning, he did not disturb himself about the matter. When Passepartout did not appear the next morning to answer his master's bell, Mr. Fogg, not betraying the least vexation, contented himself with taking his carpet-bag, calling Aouda, and sending for a palanquin.

It was then eight o'clock; at half-past nine, it being then high tide, the *Carnatic* would leave the harbor. Mr. Fogg and Aouda got into the palanquin, their luggage being brought after on a wheelbarrow, and half-an-hour later stepped upon the quay whence they were to embark. Mr. Fogg then learned that the *Carnatic* had sailed the evening before. He had expected to find not only the steamer, but his domestic, and was forced to give up both; but no sign of disappointment appeared on his face, and he merely remarked to Aouda, "It is an accident, madam; nothing more."

At this moment a man who had been observing him attentively approached. It was Fix, who, bowing, addressed Mr. Fogg: "Were you not, like me, sir, a passenger by the *Rangoon*, which arrived yesterday?"

"I was, sir," replied Mr. Fogg coldly. "But I have not the honor——"

"Pardon me; I thought I should find your servant here."

"Do you know where he is, sir?" asked Aouda anxiously.

"What!" responded Fix, feigning surprise. "Is he not with you?"

"No," said Aouda. "He has not made his appearance since yesterday. Could he have gone on board the *Carnatic* without us?"

"Without you, madam?" answered the detective. "Excuse me, did you intend to sail in the *Carnatic*?"

"Yes, sir."

"So did I, madam, and I am excessively disappointed. The *Carnatic*, its repairs being completed, left Hong Kong twelve hours before the stated time, without any notice being given; and we must now wait a week for another steamer."

As he said "a week" Fix felt his heart leap for joy. Fogg detained at Hong Kong a week! There would be time for the warrant to arrive, and fortune at last favored the representative of the law. His horror may be imagined when he heard Mr. Fogg say, in his placid voice, "But there are other vessels besides the *Carnatic*, it seems to me, in the harbor of Hong Kong."

And, offering his arm to Aouda, he directed his steps toward the docks in search of some craft about to start. Fix, stupefied, followed; it seemed as if he were attached to Mr. Fogg by an invisible thread. Chance, however, appeared really to have abandoned the man it had hitherto served so well. For three hours Phileas Fogg wandered about the docks, with the determination, if necessary, to charter a vessel to carry him to Yokohama; but he could only find vessels which were loading or unloading, and which could not therefore set sail. Fix began to hope again.

But Mr. Fogg, far from being discouraged, was continuing his search, resolved not to stop if he had to resort to Macao, when he was accosted by a sailor on one of the wharves.

"Is your honor looking for a boat?"

"Have you a boat ready to sail?"

"Yes, your honor; a pilot-boat—No. 43—the best in the harbor."

"Does she go fast?"

"Between eight and nine knots the hour. Will you look at her?"

"Yes."

"Your honor will be satisfied with her. Is it for a sea excursion?"

"No; for a voyage."

"A voyage?"

"Yes; will you agree to take me to Yokohama?"

The sailor leaned on the railing, opened his eyes wide, and said, "Is your honor joking?"

"No. I have missed the *Carnatic,* and I must get to Yokohama by the 14th at the latest, to take the boat for San Francisco."

"I am sorry," said the sailor; "but it is impossible."

"I offer you a hundred pounds per day, and an additional reward of two hundred pounds if I reach Yokohama in time."

"Are you in earnest?"

"Very much so."

The pilot walked away a little distance, and gazed out to sea, evidently struggling between the anxiety to gain a large sum and the fear of venturing so far. Fix was in mortal suspense.

Mr. Fogg turned to Aouda and asked her, "You would not be afraid, would you, madam?"

"Not with you, Mr. Fogg," was her answer.

The pilot now returned, shuffling his hat in his hands.

"Well, pilot?" said Mr. Fogg.

"Well, your honor," replied he; "I could not risk myself, my men, or my little boat of scarcely twenty tons on so long a voyage at this time of year. Besides, we could not reach Yokohama in time, for it is sixteen hundred and sixty miles from Hong Kong."

"Only sixteen hundred," said Mr. Fogg.

"It's the same thing."

Fix breathed more freely.

"But," added the pilot; "it might be arranged another way."

Fix ceased to breathe at all.

"How?" asked Mr. Fogg.

"By going to Nagasaki, at the extreme south of Japan, or even to Shanghai, which is only eight hundred miles from here. In going to Shanghai we should not be forced to sail wide of the Chinese coast, which would be a great advantage, as the currents run northward, and would aid us."

"Pilot," said Mr. Fogg. "I must take the American steamer at Yokohama, and not at Shanghai or Nagasaki."

"Why not?" returned the pilot. "The San Francisco steamer does not start from Yokohama. It puts in at Yokohama and Nagasaki, but it starts from Shanghai."

"You are sure of that?"

"Perfectly."

"And when does the boat leave Shanghai?"

"On the 11th, at seven in the evening. We have, therefore, four days before us, that is ninety-six hours; and in that time, if we had good luck and a south-west wind, and the sea was calm, we could make those eight hundred miles to Shanghai."

"And you could go——"

"In an hour; as soon as provisions could be got aboard and the sails put up."

"It is a bargain. Are you the master of the boat?"

"Yes; John Bunsby, master of the *Tankadere.*"

"Would you like some earnest-money?"

"If it would not put your honor out——"

"Here are two hundred pounds on account. Sir," added Phileas Fogg, turning to Fix, "if you would like to take advantage——"

"Thanks, sir; I was about to ask the favor."

"Very well. In half-an-hour we shall go on board."

"But poor Passepartout?" urged Aouda, who was much disturbed by the servant's disappearance.

"I shall do all I can to find him," replied Phileas Fogg.

While Fix, in a feverish, nervous state, repaired to the pilot-boat the others directed their course to the police-station at Hong Kong. Phileas Fogg there gave Passepartout's description, and left a sum of money to be spent in the search for him. The same formalities having been gone through at the French consulate, and the palanquin having stopped at the hotel for the luggage, which had been sent back there, they returned to the wharf.

It was now three o'clock; and pilot-boat No. 43, with its crew on board, and its provisions stored away, was ready for departure.

The *Tankadere* was a neat little craft of twenty tons, as gracefully built as if she were a racing yacht. Her shining copper sheathing, her galvanized ironwork, her deck, white as ivory, betrayed the pride taken by John Bunsby in making her presentable. Her two masts leaned a trifle backward; she carried brigantine, foresail, storm-jib, and standing-jib, and was well rigged for running before the wind; and she seemed capable of brisk speed, which, indeed, she had already proved by gaining several prizes in pilot-boat races. The crew of the *Tankadere* was composed of John Bunsby, the master, and four hardy mariners, who were familiar with the Chinese seas. John Bunsby himself, a man of forty-five or thereabouts, vigorous, sunburnt, with a sprightly expression of the eye, and energetic and self-reliant countenance, would have inspired confidence in the most timid.

Phileas Fogg and Aouda went on board, where they found Fix already installed. Below deck was a square cabin, of which the walls bulged out in the form of cots, above a circular divan; in the center was a table provided with a swinging lamp. The accommodation was confined, but neat.

"I am sorry to have nothing better to offer you," said Mr. Fogg to Fix, who bowed without responding.

The detective had a feeling akin to humiliation in profiting by the kindness of Mr. Fogg.

"It's certain," thought he, "though rascal as he is, he is a polite one!"

The sails and the English flag were hoisted at ten minutes past three. Mr. Fogg and Aouda, who were seated on deck, cast a last glance at the quay, in the hope of espying Passepartout. Fix was not without his fears lest chance should direct the steps of the unfortunate servant, whom he had so badly treated, in this direction; in which case an explanation the reverse of satisfactory to the detective must have ensued. But the Frenchman did not appear, and, without doubt, was still lying under the stupefying influence of the opium.

John Bunsby, master, at length gave the order to start, and the *Tankadere*, taking the wind under her brigantine, foresail, and standing-jib, bounded briskly forward over the waves.

XXI

In which the master of the *Tankadere* runs great risk of losing a reward of two hundred pounds

This voyage of eight hundred miles was a perilous venture, on a craft of twenty tons, and at that season of the year, the Chinese seas are usually boisterous, subject to terrible gales of wind, and especially during the equinoxes; and it was now early November.

It would clearly have been to the master's advantage to carry his passengers to Yokohama, since he was paid a certain sum per day; but he would have been rash to attempt such a voyage, and it was imprudent even to attempt to reach Shanghai. But John Bunsby believed in the *Tankadere,* which rode on the waves like a seagull; and perhaps he was not wrong.

Late in the day they passed through the capricious channels of Hong Kong, and the *Tankadere,* impelled by favorable winds, conducted herself admirably.

"I do not need, pilot," said Phileas Fogg, when they got into the open sea, "to advise you to use all possible speed."

"Trust me, your honor. We are carrying all the sail the wind will let us. The poles would add nothing, and are only used when we are going into port."

"It's your trade, not mine, pilot, and I confide in you."

Phileas Fogg, with body erect and legs wide apart, standing like a sailor, gazed without staggering at the swelling waters. The young woman, who was seated aft, was profoundly affected as she looked out upon the ocean, darkening now with the twilight, on which she had ventured in so frail a vessel. Above her head rustled the white sails, which seemed like great white wings. The boat, carried forward by the wind, seemed to be flying in the air.

Night came. The moon was entering her first quarter, and her insufficient light would soon die out in the mist on the horizon. Clouds were rising from the east, and already overcast a part of the heavens.

The pilot had hung out his lights, which was very necessary in these seas crowded with vessels bound landward; for collisions are not uncommon occurrences, and, at the speed she was going the least shock would shatter the gallant little craft.

Fix, seated in the bow, gave himself up to meditation. He kept apart from his fellow-travelers, knowing Mr. Fogg's taciturn tastes; besides, he did not quite like to talk to the man whose favors he had accepted. He was thinking, too, of the future. It seemed certain that Fogg would not stop at Yokohama, but would at once take the boat for San Francisco; and the vast extent of America would ensure him impunity and safety. Fogg's plan appeared to him the simplest in the world. Instead of sailing directly from England to the United States, like a common villain, he had traversed three-quarters of the globe, so as to gain the American continent more surely; and there, after throwing the police off his track, he would quietly enjoy himself with the fortune stolen from the bank. But, once in the United States, what should he, Fix, do? Should he abandon this man? No, a hundred times no! Until he had secured his extradition, he would not lose sight of him for an hour. It was his duty, and he would fulfill it to the end. At all events, there was one thing to be thankful for; Passepartout was not with his master; and it was above all important, after the confidences Fix had imparted to him, that the servant should never have speech with his master.

Phileas Fogg was also thinking of Passepartout, who had so strangely disappeared. Looking at the matter from every point of view, it did not seem to him impossible that, by some mistake, the man might have embarked on the *Carnatic* at the last moment; and this was also Aouda's opinion, who regretted very much the loss of the worthy fellow to whom she owed so much. They might then find him at Yokohama; for if the *Carnatic* was carrying him thither, it would be easy to ascertain if he had been on board.

A brisk breeze arose about ten o'clock; but, though it might have been prudent to take in a reef, the pilot, after carefully examining the heavens, let the craft remain rigged as before. The *Tankadere* bore sail admirably, as she drew a great deal of water, and everything was prepared for high speed in case of a gale.

Mr. Fogg and Aouda descended into the cabin at midnight, having been already preceded by Fix, who had lain down on one of the cots. The pilot and crew remained on deck all night.

At sunrise the next day, which was November 8th, the boat had made more than one hundred miles. The log indicated a mean speed of between eight and nine miles. The *Tankadere* still carried all sail, and was accomplishing her greatest capacity of speed. If the wind held as it was, the chances would be in her favor. During the day she kept along the coast, where the currents were favorable; the coast, irregular in profile, and visible sometimes across the clearings, was at most five miles distant. The sea was less boisterous, since the wind came off land—a fortunate circumstance for the boat, which would suffer, owing to its small tonnage, by a heavy surge on the sea.

The breeze subsided a little toward noon, and set in from the southwest. The pilot put up his poles, but took them down again within two hours, as the wind freshened up anew.

Mr. Fogg and Aouda, happily unaffected by the roughness of the sea, ate with a good appetite, Fix being invited to share their repast, which he accepted with secret chagrin. To travel at this man's expense and live upon his provisions was not palatable to him. Still, he was obliged to eat, and so he ate.

When the meal was over, he took Mr. Fogg apart, and said, "Sir,"—this "sir" scorched his lips, and he had to control himself to avoid collaring this "gentleman,"—"sir, you have been very kind to give me a passage on this boat. But, though my means will not admit of my expending them as freely as you, I must ask to pay my share——"

"Let us not speak of that, sir," replied Mr. Fogg.

"But, if I insist——"

"No, sir," repeated Mr. Fogg, in a tone which did not admit of a reply. "This enters into my general expenses."

Fix, as he bowed, had a stifled feeling, and going forward, where he ensconced himself, did not open his mouth for the rest of the day.

Meanwhile they were progressing famously, and John Bunsby was in high hope. He several times assured Mr. Fogg that they would reach Shanghai in time; to which that gentleman responded that he counted upon it. The crew set to work in good earnest, inspired by the reward to be gained. There was not a sheet which was not tightened, not a sail which was not vigorously hoisted; not a lurch could be charged to the man at the helm. They worked as desperately as if they were contesting in a Royal Yacht regatta.

By evening, the log showed that two hundred and twenty miles had been accomplished from Hong Kong, and Mr. Fogg might hope that he would be able to reach Yokohama without recording any delay in his journal; in which case, the only misadventure which had overtaken him since he left London would not seriously affect his journey.

The *Tankadere* entered the Straits of Fo-Kien, which separate the island of Formosa from the Chinese coast, in the small hours of the night, and crossed the Tropic of Cancer. The sea was very rough in the straits, full of eddies formed by the counter currents, and the chopping waves broke her course, whilst it became very difficult to stand on deck.

At daybreak the wind began to blow hard again, and the heavens seemed to predict a gale. The barometer announced a speedy change, the mercury rising and falling capriciously; the sea also, in the southeast, raised long surges which indicated a tempest. The sun had set the evening before in a red mist, in the midst of the phosphorescent scintillations of the ocean.

John Bunsby long examined the threatening aspect of the heavens, muttering indistinctly between his teeth. At last he said in a low voice to Mr. Fogg, "Shall I speak out to your honor?"

"Of course."

"Well, we are going to have a squall."

"Is the wind north or south?" asked Mr. Fogg quietly.

"South. Look! a typhoon is coming up."

"Glad it's a typhoon from the south, for it will carry us forward."

"Oh, if you take it that way," said John Bunsby, "I've nothing more to say." John Bunsby's suspicions were confirmed. At a less advanced season of the year the typhoon, according to a famous meteorologist, would have passed away like a luminous cascade of electric flame; but in the winter equinox, it was to be feared that it would burst upon them with great violence.

The pilot took his precautions in advance. He reefed all sail, the pole-masts were dispensed with; all hands went forward to the bows. A single triangular sail, of strong canvas, was hoisted as a storm-jib, so as to hold the wind from behind. Then they waited.

John Bunsby had requested his passengers to go below; but this imprisonment in so narrow a space, with little air, and the boat bouncing in the gale, was far from pleasant. Neither Mr. Fogg, Fix, nor Aouda consented to leave the deck.

The storm of rain and wind descended upon them toward eight o'clock. With but its bit of sail, the *Tankadere* was lifted like a feather by a wind, an idea of whose violence can scarcely be given. To compare her speed to four times that of a locomotive going on full steam would be below the truth.

The boat scudded thus northward during the whole day, borne on by monstrous waves, preserving always, fortunately, a speed equal to theirs. Twenty times she seemed almost to be submerged by these mountains of water which rose behind her; but the adroit management of the pilot saved her. The passengers were often bathed in spray, but they submitted to it philosophically. Fix cursed it, no doubt; but Aouda, with her eyes fastened upon her protector, whose coolness amazed her, showed herself worthy of him, and bravely weathered the storm. As for Phileas Fogg, it seemed just as if the typhoon were a part of his program.

Up to this time the *Tankadere* had always held her course to the north; but toward evening the wind, veering three-quarters, bore down from the north-west. The boat, now lying in the trough of the waves, shook and rolled terribly; the sea struck her with fearful violence. At night the tempest increased in violence. John Bunsby saw the approach of darkness and the rising of the storm with dark misgivings. He thought awhile, and then asked his crew if it was not time to slacken speed. After a consultation he approached Mr. Fogg, and said, "I think, your honor, that we should do well to make for one of the ports on the coast."

"I think so too."

"Ah!" said the pilot. "But which one?"

"I know of but one," returned Mr. Fogg tranquilly.

"And that is——"

"Shanghai."

The pilot, at first, did not seem to comprehend; he could scarcely realize so much determination and tenacity. Then he cried, "Well—yes! Your honor is right. To Shanghai!"

So the *Tankadere* kept steadily on her northward track.

The night was really terrible; it would be a miracle if the craft did not founder. Twice it would have been all over with her if the crew had not been constantly on the watch. Aouda was exhausted, but did not utter a complaint. More than once Mr. Fogg rushed to protect her from the violence of the waves.

Day reappeared. The tempest still raged with undiminished fury; but the wind now returned to the south-east. It was a favorable change, and the *Tankadere* again bounded forward on this mountainous sea, though the waves crossed each other, and imparted shocks and countershocks which would have crushed a craft less solidly built. From time to time the coast was visible through the broken mist, but no vessel was in sight. The *Tankadere* was alone upon the sea.

There were some signs of a calm at noon, and these became more distinct as the sun descended toward the horizon. The tempest had been as brief as terrific. The passengers, thoroughly exhausted, could now eat a little, and take some repose.

The night was comparatively quiet. Some of the sails were again hoisted, and the speed of the boat was very good. The next morning at dawn they espied the coast, and John Bunsby was able to assert that they were not one hundred miles from Shanghai. A hundred miles, and only one day to traverse them! That very evening Mr. Fogg was due at Shanghai, if he did not wish to miss the steamer to Yokohama. Had there been no storm, during which several hours were lost, they would be at this moment within thirty miles of their destination.

The wind grew decidedly calmer, and happily the sea fell with it. All sails were now hoisted, and at noon the *Tankadere* was within forty-five miles of Shanghai. There remained yet six hours in which to accomplish that distance. All on board feared that it could not be done, and everyone —Phileas Fogg, no doubt, excepted—felt his heart beat with impatience. The boat must keep up an average of nine miles an hour, and the wind was becoming calmer every moment! It was a capricious breeze, coming from the coast, and after it passed the sea became smooth. Still, the *Tankadere* was so light, and her fine sails caught the fickle zephyrs so well, that, with the aid of the current, John Bunsby found himself at six o'clock not more than ten miles from the mouth of the Shanghai River. Shanghai itself is situated at least twelve miles up the stream. At seven they were still three miles from Shanghai. The pilot swore an angry oath; the reward of two hundred pounds was evidently on the point of escaping him. He looked at Mr. Fogg. Mr. Fogg was perfectly tranquil; and yet his whole fortune was at this moment at stake.

At this moment, also, a long black funnel crowned with wreaths of smoke, appeared on the edge of the waters. It was the American steamer, leaving for Yokohama at the appointed time.

"Confound her!" cried John Bunsby, pushing back the rudder with a desperate jerk.

"Signal her!" said Phileas Fogg quietly.

A small brass cannon stood on the forward deck of the *Tankadere,* for making signals in the fogs. It was loaded to the muzzle; but just as the pilot was about to apply a red-hot coal to the touch-hole, Mr. Fogg said, "Hoist your flag!"

The flag was run up at half-mast, and, this being the signal of distress, it was hoped that the American steamer, perceiving it, would change her course a little, so as to succour the pilot-boat.

"Fire!" said Mr. Fogg. And the booming of the little cannon resounded in the air.

XXII

In which Passepartout finds out that, even at the antipodes, it is convenient to have some money in one's pocket

The *Carnatic,* setting sail from Hong Kong at half-past six on the 7th of November, directed her course at full steam toward Japan. She carried a large cargo and a well-filled cabin of passengers. Two state-rooms in the rear were, however, unoccupied—those which had been engaged by Phileas Fogg.

The next day a passenger with a half-stupefied eye, staggering gait, and disordered hair, was seen to emerge from the second cabin, and to totter to a seat on deck.

It was Passepartout; and what had happened to him was as follows: Shortly after Fix left the opium den, two waiters had lifted the unconscious Passepartout, and had carried him to the bed reserved for the smokers. Three hours later, pursued even in his dreams by a fixed idea, the poor fellow awoke, and struggled against the stupefying influence of the narcotic. The thought of a duty unfulfilled shook off his torpor, and he hurried from the abode of drunkenness. Staggering and holding himself up by keeping against the walls, falling down, and creeping up again, and irresistibly impelled by a kind of instinct, he kept crying out, "The *Carnatic!* the *Carnatic!*"

The steamer lay puffing alongside the quay, on the point of starting. Passepartout had but few steps to go; and, rushing upon the plank, he crossed it, and fell unconscious on the deck, just as the *Carnatic* was moving off. Several sailors, who were evidently accustomed to this sort of scene, carried the poor Frenchman down into the second cabin, and Passepartout did not wake until they were one hundred and fifty miles away from China. Thus he found himself the next morning on the deck of the *Carnatic*, and eagerly inhaling the exhilarating sea-breeze. The pure air sobered him. He began to collect his senses, which he found a difficult task; but at last he recalled the events of the evening before, Fix's revelation, and the opium-house.

"It is evident," said he to himself, "that I have been abominably drunk! What will Mr. Fogg say? At least I have not missed the steamer, which is the most important thing."

Then, as Fix occurred to him: "As for that rascal, I hope we are well rid of him, and that he has not dared, as he proposed, to follow us on board the *Carnatic*. A detective on the track of Mr. Fogg, accused of robbing the Bank of England! Pshaw! Mr. Fogg is no more a robber than I am a murderer."

Should he divulge Fix's real errand to his master? Would it do to tell the part the detective was playing? Would it not be better to wait until Mr. Fogg reached London again, and then impart to him that an agent of the metropolitan police had been following him around the world, and have a good laugh over it? No doubt; at least, it was worth considering. The first thing to do was to find Mr. Fogg, and apologize for his singular behavior.

Passepartout got up and proceeded, as well as he could with the rolling of the steamer, to the after-deck. He saw no one who resembled either his master or Aouda. "Good!" muttered he; "Aouda has not got up yet, and Mr. Fogg has probably found some partners at whist."

He descended to the saloon. Mr. Fogg was not there. Passepartout had only, however, to ask the purser the number of his master's state-room. The purser replied that he did not know any passenger by the name of Fogg.

"I beg your pardon," said Passepartout persistently. "He is a tall gentleman, quiet, and not very talkative, and has with him a young lady——"

"There is no young lady on board," interrupted the purser. "Here is a list of the passengers; you may see for yourself."

Passepartout scanned the list, but his master's name was not upon it. All at once an idea struck him.

"Ah! am I on the *Carnatic*?"

"Yes."

"On the way to Yokohama?"

"Certainly."

Passepartout had for an instant feared that he was on the wrong boat; but, though he was really on the *Carnatic,* his master was not there.

He fell thunderstruck on a seat. He saw it all now. He remembered that the time of sailing had been changed, that he should have informed his master of that fact, and that he had not done so. It was his fault, then, that Mr. Fogg and Aouda had missed the steamer. Yes, but it was still more the fault of the traitor who, in order to separate him from his master, and detain the latter at Hong Kong, had inveigled him into getting drunk! He now saw the detective's trick; and at this moment Mr. Fogg was certainly ruined, his bet was lost, and he himself perhaps arrested and imprisoned! At this thought Passepartout tore his hair. Ah, if Fix ever came within his reach, what a settling of accounts there would be!

After his first depression, Passepartout became calmer, and began to study his situation. It was certainly not an enviable one. He found himself on the way to Japan, and what should he do when he got there? His pocket was empty; he had not a solitary shilling—not so much as a penny. His passage had fortunately been paid for in advance; and he had five or six days in which to decide upon his future course. He fell to at meals with an appetite, and ate for Mr. Fogg, Aouda, and himself. He helped himself as generously as if Japan were a desert, where nothing to eat was to be looked for.

At dawn on the 13th the *Carnatic* entered the port of Yokohama. This is an important way-station in the Pacific, where all the mail-steamers, and those carrying travelers between North America, China, Japan, and the Oriental islands, put in. It is situated in the bay of Yeddo, and at but a short distance from that second capital of the Japanese Empire, and the residence of the Tycoon, the civil Emperor, before the Mikado, the spiritual Emperor, absorbed his office in his own. The *Carnatic* anchored at the quay near the custom-house, in the midst of a crowd of ships bearing the flags of all nations.

Passepartout went timidly ashore on this so curious territory of the Sons of the Sun. He had nothing better to do than, taking chance for his guide, to wander aimlessly through the streets of Yokohama. He found himself at first in a thoroughly European quarter, the houses having low fronts, and being adorned with verandas, beneath which he caught glimpses of neat peristyles. This quarter occupied, with its streets, squares, docks, and warehouses, all the space between the "promontory of the Treaty" and the river. Here, as at Hong Kong and Calcutta, were mixed crowds of all races—Americans and English, Chinamen and Dutchmen, mostly merchants ready to buy or sell anything. The Frenchman felt himself as much alone among them as if he had dropped down in the midst of Hottentots.

He had, at least, one resource—to call on the French and English consuls at Yokohama for assistance. But he shrank from telling the story of his adventures, intimately connected as it was with that of his master; and, before doing so, he determined to exhaust all other means of aid. As chance did not favor him in the European quarter, he penetrated that inhabited by the native Japanese, determined, if necessary, to push on to Yeddo.

The Japanese quarter of Yokohama is called Benten, after the goddess of the sea, who is worshipped on the islands round about. There Passepartout beheld beautiful fir and cedar groves, sacred gates of a singular architecture, bridges half hid in the midst of bamboos and reeds, temples shaded by immense cedar-trees, holy retreats where were sheltered Buddhist priests and sectaries of Confucius, and interminable streets, where a perfect harvest of rose-tinted and red-cheeked children, who looked as if they had been cut out of Japanese screens, and who were playing in the midst of short-legged poodles and yellowish cats, might have been gathered.

The streets were crowded with people. Priests were passing in processions, beating their dreary tambourines; police and custom-house officers with pointed hats encrusted with lac, and carrying two sabres hung to their waists; soldiers, clad in blue cotton with white stripes, and bearing guns; the Mikado's guards, enveloped in silken doublets, hauberks, and coats of mail; and numbers of military folk of all ranks—for the military profession is as much respected in Japan as it is despised in China—went hither and thither in groups and pairs. Passepartout saw, too, begging friars, long-robed pilgrims, and simple civilians, with their warped and jet-black hair, big heads, long busts, slender legs, short stature, and complexions varying from copper-color to a dead white, but never yellow, like the Chinese, from whom the Japanese widely differ. He did not fail to observe the curious equipages—carriages and palanquins, barrows supplied with sails, and litters made of bamboo; nor the women—whom he thought not especially handsome—who took little steps with their little feet, whereon they wore canvas shoes, straw sandals, and clogs of worked wood, and who displayed tight-looking eyes, flat chests, teeth fashionably blackened, and gowns crossed with silken scarfs, tied in an enormous knot behind—an ornament which the modern Parisian ladies seem to have borrowed from the dames of Japan.

Passepartout wandered for several hours in the midst of this motley crowd, looking in at the windows of the rich and curious shops, the jewelery establishments glittering with quaint Japanese ornaments, the restaurants decked with streamers and banners, the tea-houses, where the odorous beverage was being drunk with "saki," a liquor concocted from the fermentation of rice, and the comfortable smoking-houses, where they were puffing, not opium, which is almost unknown in Japan, but a very fine, stringy tobacco. He went on till he found himself in the fields, in the midst of vast rice plantations. There he saw dazzling camelias expanding themselves, with flowers which were giving forth their last colors and perfumes, not on bushes, but on trees; and within bamboo enclosures, cherry, plum, and apple trees, which the Japanese cultivate rather for their blossoms than their fruit, and which queerly-fashioned grinning scarecrows protected from the sparrows, pigeons, ravens, and other voracious birds. On the branches of the cedars were perched large eagles; amid the foliage of the weeping willows were herons, solemnly standing on one leg; and on every hand were crows, ducks, hawks, wild birds, and a multitude of cranes, which the Japanese consider sacred, and which to their minds symbolize long life and prosperity.

As he was strolling alone, Passepartout espied some violets among the shrubs.

"Good!" said he; "I'll have some supper."

But, on smelling them, he found that they were odorless.

"No chance there," thought he.

The worthy fellow had certainly taken good care to eat as hearty a breakfast as possible before leaving the *Carnatic*; but as he had been walking about all day, the demands of hunger were becoming importunate. He observed that the butchers' stalls contained neither mutton, goat, nor pork; and knowing also that it is a sacrilege to kill cattle, which are preserved solely for farming, he made up his mind that meat was far from plentiful in Yokohama—nor was he mistaken; and in default of butcher's meat, he could have wished for a quarter of wild boar or deer, a partridge, or some quails, some game or fish, which, with rice, the Japanese eat almost exclusively. But he found it necessary to keep up a stout heart, and to postpone the meal he craved till the following morning. Night came, and Passepartout re-entered the native quarter, where he wandered through the streets, lit by vari-colored lanterns, looking on at the dancers who were executing skillful steps and boundings, and the astrologers who stood in the open air with their telescopes. Then he came to the harbor, which was lit up by the rosin torches of the fishermen, who were fishing from their boats.

The streets at last became quiet, and the patrol, the officers of which, in their splendid costumes, and surrounded by their suites, Passepartout thought seemed like ambassadors, succeeded the bustling crowd. Each time a company passed, Passepartout chuckled, and said to himself: "Good! another Japanese embassy departing for Europe!"

XXIII

In which Passepartout's nose becomes outrageously long

The next morning poor, jaded, famished Passepartout said to himself that he must get something to eat at all hazards, and the sooner he did so the better. He might, indeed, sell his watch; but he would have starved first. Now or never he must use the strong, if not melodious voice which nature had bestowed upon him. He knew several French and English songs, and resolved to try them upon the Japanese, who must be lovers of music, since they were for ever pounding on their cymbals, tam-tams, and tambourines, and could not but appreciate European talent.

It was, perhaps, rather early in the morning to get up a concert, and the audience, prematurely aroused from their slumbers, might not, possibly, pay their entertainer with coin bearing the Mikado's features. Passepartout therefore decided to wait several hours; and, as he was sauntering along, it occurred to him that he would seem rather too well dressed for a wandering artist. The idea struck him to change his garments for clothes more in harmony with his project; by which he might also get a little money to satisfy the immediate cravings of hunger. The resolution taken, it remained to carry it out.

It was only after a long search that Passepartout discovered a native dealer in old clothes, to whom he applied for an exchange. The man liked the European costume, and ere long Passepartout issued from his shop accoutred in an old Japanese coat, and a sort of one-sided turban, faded with long use. A few small pieces of silver, moreover, jingled in his pocket.

"Good!" thought he. "I will imagine I am at the Carnival!"

His first care, after being thus "Japanesed," was to enter a tea-house of modest appearance, and upon half a bird and a little rice, to breakfast like a man for whom dinner was as yet a problem to be solved.

"Now," thought he, when he had eaten heartily, "I mustn't lose my head. I can't sell this costume again for one still more Japanese. I must consider how to leave this country of the Sun, of which I shall not retain the most delightful of memories, as quickly as possible.

It occurred to him to visit the steamers which were about to leave for America. He would offer himself as a cook or servant, in payment of his passage and meals. Once at San Francisco, he would find some means of going on. The difficulty was, how to traverse the four thousand seven hundred miles of the Pacific which lay between Japan and the New World.

Passepartout was not the man to let an idea go begging, and directed his steps toward the docks. But, as he approached them, his project, which at first had seemed so simple, began to grow more and more formidable to his mind. What need would they have of a cook or servant on an American steamer, and what confidence would they put in him, dressed as he was? What references could he give?

As he was reflecting in this wise, his eyes fell upon an immense placard which a sort of clown was carrying through the streets. This placard, which was in English, read as follows:

ACROBATIC JAPANESE TROUPE,

HONORABLE WILLIAM BATULCAR, PROPRIETOR,

LAST REPRESENTATIONS,

PRIOR TO THEIR DEPARTURE TO THE UNITED STATES,

OF THE LONG NOSES! LONG NOSES!

UNDER THE DIRECT PATRONAGE OF THE GOD TINGOU!

GREAT ATTRACTION!

"The United States!" said Passepartout; "that's just what I want!"

He followed the clown, and soon found himself once more in the Japanese quarter. A quarter of an hour later he stopped before a large cabin, adorned with several clusters of streamers, the exterior walls of which were designed to represent, in violent colors and without perspective, a company of jugglers.

This was the Honorable William Batulcar's establishment. That gentleman was a sort of Barnum, the director of a troupe of mountebanks, jugglers, clowns, acrobats, equilibrists, and gymnasts, who, according to the placard, was giving his last performances before leaving the Empire of the Sun for the States of the Union.

Passepartout entered and asked for Mr. Batulcar, who straightway appeared in person.

"What do you want?" said he to Passepartout, whom he at first took for a native.

"Would you like a servant, sir?" asked Passepartout.

"A servant!" cried Mr. Batulcar, caressing the thick gray beard which hung from his chin. "I already have two who are obedient and faithful, have never left me, and serve me for their nourishment—and here they are," added he, holding out his two robust arms, furrowed with veins as large as the strings of a bass-viol.

"So I can be of no use to you?"

"None."

"The devil! I should so like to cross the Pacific with you!"

"Ah!" said the Honorable Mr. Batulcar. "You are no more a Japanese than I am a monkey! Why are you dressed up in that way?"

"A man dresses as he can."

"That's true. You are a Frenchman, aren't you?"

"Yes; a Parisian of Paris."

"Then you ought to know how to make grimaces?"

"Why," replied Passepartout, a little vexed that his nationality should cause this question; "we Frenchmen know how to make grimaces, it is true—but not any better than the Americans do."

"True. Well, if I can't take you as a servant, I can as a clown. You see, my friend, in France they exhibit foreign clowns, and in foreign parts French clowns."

"Ah!"

"You are pretty strong, eh?"

"Especially after a good meal."

"And you can sing?"

"Yes," returned Passepartout, who had formerly been wont to sing in the streets.

"But can you sing standing on your head, with a top spinning on your left foot, and a sabre balanced on your right?"

"Humph! I think so," replied Passepartout, recalling the exercises of his younger days.

"Well, that's enough," said the Honorable William Batulcar.

The engagement was concluded there and then.

Passepartout had at last found something to do. He was engaged to act in the celebrated Japanese troupe. It was not a very dignified position, but within a week he would be on his way to San Francisco.

The performance, so noisily announced by the Honorable Mr. Batulcar, was to commence at three o'clock, and soon the deafening instruments of a Japanese orchestra resounded at the door. Passepartout, though he had not been able to study or rehearse a part, was designated to lend the aid of his sturdy shoulders in the great exhibition of the "human pyramid," executed by the Long Noses of the god Tingou. This "great attraction" was to close the performance.

Before three o'clock the large shed was invaded by the spectators, comprising Europeans and natives, Chinese and Japanese, men, women, and children, who precipitated themselves upon the narrow benches and into the boxes opposite inside, and were vigorously performing on their gongs, tam-tams, flutes, bones, tambourines, and immense drums.

The performance was much like all acrobatic displays; but it must be confessed that the Japanese are the first equilibrists in the world.

One, with a fan and some bits of paper, performed the graceful trick of the butterflies and the flowers; another traced in the air, with the odorous smoke of his pipe, a series of blue words, which composed a compliment to the audience; while a third juggled with some lighted candles, which he extinguished successively as they passed his lips, and relit again without interrupting for an instant his juggling. Another reproduced the most singular combinations with a spinning-top; in his hands the revolving tops seemed to be animated with a life of their own in their interminable whirling; they ran over pipe-stems, the edges of sabres, wires, and even hairs stretched across the stage; they turned around on the edges of large glasses, crossed bamboo ladders, dispersed into all the corners, and produced strange musical effects by the combination of their various pitches of tone. The jugglers tossed them in the air, threw them like shuttlecocks with wooden battledores, and yet they kept on spinning; they put them into their pockets, and took them out still whirling as before.

It is useless to describe the astonishing performances of the acrobats and gymnasts. The turning on ladders, poles, balls, barrels, &c., was executed with wonderful precision.

But the principal attraction was the exhibition of the Long Noses, a show to which Europe is as yet a stranger.

The Long Noses form a peculiar company, under the direct patronage of the god Tingou. Attired after the fashion of the Middle Ages, they bore upon their shoulders a splendid pair of wings; but what especially distinguished them was the long noses which were fastened to their faces, and the uses which they made of them. These noses were made of bamboo, and were five, six, and even ten feet long, some straight, others curved, some ribboned, and some having imitation warts upon them. It was upon these appendages, fixed tightly on their real noses, that they performed their gymnastic exercises. A dozen of these sectaries of Tingou lay flat upon their backs, while others, dressed to represent lightning-rods, came and frolicked on their noses, jumping from one to another, and performing the most skillful leapings and somersaults.

As a last scene, a "human pyramid" had been announced, in which fifty Long Noses were to represent the Car of Juggernaut. But, instead of forming a pyramid by mounting each other's shoulders, the artists were to group themselves on top of the noses. It happened that the performer who had hitherto formed the base of the Car had quitted the troup, and as, to fill this part, only strength and adroitness were necessary, Passepartout had been chosen to take his place.

The poor fellow really felt sad when—melancholy reminiscence of his youth!—he donned his costume, adorned with vari-colored wings, and fastened to his natural feature a false nose six feet long. But he cheered up when he thought that this nose was winning him something to eat.

He went upon the stage, and took his place beside the rest who were to compose the base of the Car of Juggernaut. They all stretched themselves on the floor, their noses pointing to the ceiling. A second group of artists disposed themselves on these long appendages, then a third above these, then a fourth, until a human monument reaching to the very cornices of the theatre soon arose on top of the noses. This elicited loud applause in the midst of which the orchestra was just striking up a deafening air, when the pyramid tottered, the balance was lost, one of the lower noses vanished from the pyramid, and the human monument was shattered like a castle built of cards!

It was Passepartout's fault. Abandoning his position, clearing the footlights without the aid of his wings, and clambering up to the right-hand gallery, he fell at the feet of one of the spectators, crying, "Ah, my master! my master!"

"You here?"

"Myself."

"Very well; then let us go to the steamer, young man!"

Mr. Fogg, Aouda, and Passepartout passed through the lobby of the theatre to the outside, where they encountered the Honorable Mr. Batulcar, furious with rage. He demanded damages for the "breakage" of the pyramid; and Phileas Fogg appeased him by giving him a handful of banknotes.

At half-past six, the very hour of departure, Mr. Fogg and Aouda, followed by Passepartout, who in his hurry had retained his wings, and nose six feet long, stepped upon the American steamer.

XXIV

During which Mr. Fogg and party cross the Pacific Ocean

What happened when the pilot-boat came in sight of Shanghai will be easily guessed. The signals made by the *Tankadere* had been seen by the captain of the Yokohama steamer, who, espying the flag at half-mast, had directed his course toward the little craft. Phileas Fogg, after paying the stipulated price of his passage to John Bunsby, and rewarding that worthy with the additional sum of five hundred and fifty pounds, ascended the steamer with Aouda and Fix; and they started at once for Nagasaki and Yokohama.

They reached their destination on the morning of the 14th of November. Phileas Fogg lost no time in going on board the *Carnatic,* where he learned, to Aouda's great delight—and perhaps to his own, though he betrayed no emotion—that Passepartout, a Frenchman, had really arrived on her the day before.

The San Francisco steamer was announced to leave that very evening, and it became necessary to find Passepartout, if possible, without delay. Mr. Fogg applied in vain to the French and English consuls, and, after wandering through the streets a long time, began to despair of finding his missing servant. Chance, or perhaps a kind of presentiment, at last led him into the Honorable Mr. Batulcar's theatre. He certainly would not have recognized Passepartout in the eccentric mountebank's costume; but the latter, lying on his back, perceived his master in the gallery. He could not help starting, which so changed the position of his nose as to bring the "pyramid" pell-mell upon the stage.

All this Passepartout learned from Aouda, who recounted to him what had taken place on the voyage from Hong Kong to Shanghai on the *Tankadere,* in company with one Mr. Fix.

Passepartout did not change countenance on hearing this name. He thought that the time had not yet arrived to divulge to his master what had taken place between the detective and himself; and in the account he gave of his absence, he simply excused himself for having been overtaken by drunkenness, in smoking opium at a tavern in Hong Kong.

Mr. Fogg heard this narrative coldly, without a word; and then furnished his man with funds necessary to obtain clothing more in harmony with his position. Within an hour the Frenchman had cut off his nose and parted with his wings, and retained nothing about him which recalled the sectary of the god Tingou.

The steamer which was about to depart from Yokohama to San Francisco belonged to the Pacific Mail Steamship Company, and was named the *General Grant.* She was a large paddle-wheel steamer of two thousand five hundred tons, well equipped and very fast. The massive walking-beam rose and fell above the deck; at one end a piston-rod worked up and down; and at the other was a connecting-rod which, in changing the rectilinear motion to a circular one, was directly connected with the shaft of the paddles. The *General Grant* was rigged with three masts, giving a large capacity for sails, and thus materially aiding the steam power. By making twelve miles an hour, she would cross the ocean in twenty-one days. Phileas Fogg was therefore justified in hoping that he would reach San Francisco by the 2nd of December, New York by the 11th, and London on the 20th—thus gaining several hours on the fatal date of the 21st of December.

There was a full complement of passengers on board, among them

English, many Americans, a large number of Coolies on their way to California, and several East Indian officers, who were spending their vacation in making the tour of the world. Nothing of moment happened on the voyage; the steamer, sustained on its large paddles, rolled but little, and the Pacific almost justified its name. Mr. Fogg was as calm and taciturn as ever. His young companion felt herself more and more attached to him by other ties than gratitude; his silent but generous nature impressed her more than she thought; and it was almost unconsciously that she yielded to emotions which did not seem to have the least effect upon her protector. Aouda took the keenest interest in his plans, and became impatient at any incident which seemed likely to retard his journey.

She often chatted with Passepartout, who did not fail to perceive the state of the lady's heart; and, being the most faithful of domestics, he never exhausted his eulogies of Phileas Fogg's honesty, generosity, and devotion. He took pains to calm Aouda's doubts of a successful termination of the journey, telling her that the most difficult part of it had passed, that now they were beyond the fantastic countries of Japan and China, and were fairly on their way to civilized places again. A railway train from San Francisco to New York, and a transatlantic steamer from New York to Liverpool, would doubtless bring them to the end of this impossible journey around the world within the period agreed upon.

On the ninth day after leaving Yokohama, Phileas Fogg had traversed exactly one half of the terrestrial globe. The *General Grant* passed, on the 23rd of November, the one hundred and eightieth meridian, and was at the very antipodes of London. Mr. Fogg had, it is true, exhausted fifty-two of the eighty days in which he was to complete the tour, and there were only twenty-eight left. But, though he was only half-way by the difference of meridians, he had really gone over two-thirds of the whole journey; for he had been obliged to make long circuits from London to Aden, from Aden to Bombay, from Calcutta to Singapore, and from Singapore to Yokohama. Could he have followed without deviation the fiftieth parallel, which is that of London, the whole distance would only have been about twelve thousand miles; whereas he would be forced, by the irregular methods of locomotion, to traverse twenty-six thousand, of which he had, on the 23rd of November, accomplished seventeen thousand five hundred. And now the course was a straight one, and Fix was no longer there to put obstacles in their way!

It happened also, on the 23rd of November, that Passepartout made a joyful discovery. It will be remembered that the obstinate fellow had insisted on keeping his famous family watch at London time, and on regarding that of the countries he had passed through as quite false and unreliable. Now, on this day, though he had not changed the hands, he found that his watch exactly agreed with the ship's chronometers. His triumph was hilarious. He would have liked to know what Fix would say if he were aboard!

"The rogue told me a lot of stories," repeated Passepartout, "about the meridians, the sun, and the moon! Moon, indeed! moonshine more likely! If one listened to that sort of people, a pretty sort of time one would keep! I was sure that the sun would some day regulate itself by my watch!"

Passepartout was ignorant that, if the face of his watch had been divided into twenty-four hours, like the Italian clocks, he would have no reason for exultation; for the hands of his watch would then, instead of as now indicating nine o'clock in the morning, indicate nine o'clock in the evening, that is the twenty-first hour after midnight—precisely the difference between London time and that of the one hundred and eightieth meridian. But if Fix had been able to explain this purely physical effect, Passepartout would not have admitted, even if he had comprehended it. Moreover, if the detective had been on board at that moment, Passepartout would have joined issue with him on a quite different subject, and in an entirely different manner.

Where was Fix at that moment?

He was actually on board the *General Grant*.

On reaching Yokohama, the detective, leaving Mr. Fogg, whom he expected to meet again during the day, had repaired at once to the English consulate, where he at last found the warrant of arrest. It had followed him from Bombay, and had come by the *Carnatic*, on which steamer he himself was supposed to be. Fix's disappointment may be imagined when he reflected that the warrant was now useless. Mr. Fogg had left English ground, and it was now necessary to procure his extradition!

"Well," thought Fix, after a moment of anger, "my warrant is not good here, but it will be in England. The rogue evidently intends to return to his country, thinking he has thrown the police off his track. Good! I will follow him across the Atlantic. As for the money, Heaven grant there may be some left! But the fellow has already spent in traveling, rewards, trials, bail, elephants, and all sorts of charges, more than five thousand pounds. Yet, after all, the Bank is rich!"

His course decided on, he went on board the *General Grant*, and was there when Mr. Fogg and Aouda arrived. To his utter amazement, he recognized Passepartout, despite his theatrical disguise. He quickly concealed himself in his cabin, to avoid an awkward explanation, and hoped—thanks to the number of passengers—to remain unperceived by Mr. Fogg's servant.

On that very day, however, he met Passepartout face to face on the forward deck. The latter, without a word, made a rush for him, grasped him by the throat, and, much to the amusement of a group of Americans, who immediately began to bet on him, administered to the detective a perfect volley of blows, which proved the great superiority of French over English pugilistic skill.

When Passepartout had finished, he found himself relieved and comforted. Fix got up in a somewhat rumpled condition, and, looking at his adversary, coldly said, "Have you done?"

"For this time—yes."

"Then let me have a word with you."

"But I——"

"In your master's interest."

Passepartout seemed to be vanquished by Fix's coolness, for he quietly followed him, and they sat down aside from the rest of the passengers.

"You have given me a thrashing," said Fix. "Good. I expected it. Now, listen to me. Up to this time I have been Mr. Fogg's adversary. I am now in his game."

"Aha!" cried Passepartout; "you are convinced he is an honest man?"

"No," replied Fix coldly, "I think him a rascal. Sh! don't budge, and let me speak. As long as Mr. Fogg was on English ground, it was for my interest to detain him there until my warrant of arrest arrived. I did everything I could to keep him back. I sent the Bombay priests after him, I got you intoxicated at Hong Kong, I separated you from him, and I made him miss the Yokohama steamer."

Passepartout listened, with closed fists.

"Now," resumed Fix, "Mr. Fogg seems to be going back to England. Well, I will follow him there. But hereafter I will do as much to keep obstacles out of his way as I have done up to this time to put them in his path. I've changed my game, you see, and simply because it was for my interest to change it. Your interest is the same as mine; for it is only in

England that you will ascertain whether you are in the service of a criminal or an honest man."

Passepartout listened very attentively to Fix, and was convinced that he spoke with entire good faith.

"Are we friends?" asked the detective.

"Friends?—no," replied Passepartout; "but allies, perhaps. At the least sign of treason, however, I'll twist your neck for you."

"Agreed," said the detective quietly.

Eleven days later, on the 3rd of December, the *General Grant* entered the bay of the Golden Gate, and reached San Francisco

Mr. Fogg had neither gained nor lost a single day.

XXV

In which a slight glimpse is had of San Francisco

It was seven in the morning when Mr. Fogg, Aouda, and Passepartout set foot upon the American continent, if this name can be given to the floating quay upon which they disembarked. These quays, rising and falling with the tide, thus facilitate the loading and unloading of vessels. Alongside them were clippers of all sizes, steamers of all nationalities, and the steamboats, with several decks rising one above the other, which ply on the Sacramento and its tributaries. There were also heaped up the products of a commerce which extends to Mexico, Chile, Peru, Brazil, Europe, Asia, and all the Pacific islands.

Passepartout, in his joy on reaching at last the American continent, thought he would manifest it by executing a perilous vault in fine style; but, tumbling upon some worm-eaten planks, he fell through them. Put out of countenance by the manner in which he thus "set foot" upon the New World, he uttered a loud cry, which so frightened the innumerable cormorants and pelicans that are always perched upon these movable quays, that they flew noisily away.

Mr. Fogg, on reaching shore, proceeded to find out at what hour the first train left for New York, and learned that this was at six o'clock P.M.; he had, therefore, an entire day to spend in the Californian capital. Taking a carriage at a charge of three dollars, he and Aouda entered it, while Passepartout mounted the box beside the driver, and they set out for the International Hotel.

From his exalted position Passepartout observed with much curiosity the wide streets, the low, evenly ranged houses, the Anglo-Saxon Gothic churches, the great docks, the palatial wooden and brick warehouses, the numerous conveyances, omnibuses, horse-cars, and upon the side-walks, not only Americans and Europeans, but Chinese and Indians. Passepartout was surprised at all he saw. San Francisco was no longer the legendary city of 1849—a city of banditti, assassins, and incendiaries, who had flocked hither in crowds in pursuit of plunder; a paradise of outlaws, where they gambled with gold-dust, a revolver in one hand and a bowie-knife in the other: it was now a great commercial emporium.

The lofty tower of its City Hall overlooked the whole panorama of the streets and avenues, which cut each other at right angles, and in the midst of which appeared pleasant, verdant squares, while beyond appeared the Chinese quarter, seemingly imported from the Celestial Empire in a toy-box. Sombreros and red shirts and plumed Indians were rarely to be seen; but there were silk hats and black coats everywhere worn by a multitude of nervously active, gentlemanly-looking men. Some of the streets—especially Montgomery Street, which is to San Francisco what Regent Street is to London, the Boulevard des Italiens to Paris, and Broadway to New York—were lined with splendid and spacious stores, which exposed in their windows the products of the entire world.

When Passepartout reached the International Hotel, it did not seem to him as if he had left England at all.

The ground floor of the hotel was occupied by a large bar, a sort of restaurant freely open to all passers-by, who might partake of dried beef, oyster soup, biscuits, and cheese, without taking out their purses. Payment was made only for the ale, porter, or sherry which was drunk. This seemed "very American" to Passepartout. The hotel refreshment-rooms were comfortable, and Mr. Fogg and Aouda, installing themselves at a table, were abundantly served on diminutive plates by Negroes of darkest hue.

After breakfast, Mr. Fogg, accompanied by Aouda, started for the English consulate to have his passport visaed. As he was going out, he met Passepartout, who asked him if it would not do well, before taking the train, to purchase some dozens of Enfield rifles and Colt's revolvers. He had been listening to stories of attacks upon the trains by the Sioux and

Pawnees. Mr. Fogg thought it a useless precaution, but told him to do as he thought best, and went on to the consulate.

He had not proceeded two hundred steps, however, when, "by the greatest chance in the world," he met Fix. The detective seemed wholly taken by surprise. What! Had Mr. Fogg and himself crossed the Pacific together, and not met on the steamer! At least Fix felt honored to behold once more the gentleman to whom he owed so much, and as his business recalled him to Europe, he should be delighted to continue the journey in such pleasant company.

Mr. Fogg replied that the honor would be his; and the detective—who was determined not to lose sight of him—begged permission to accompany them in their walk about San Francisco—a request which Mr. Fogg readily granted.

They soon found themselves in Montgomery Street, where a great crowd was collected; the side-walks, street, horse-car rails, the shop-doors, the windows of the houses, and even the roofs, were full of people. Men were going about carrying large posters, and flags and streamers were floating in the wind; while loud cries were heard on every hand.

"Hurrah for Camerfield!"

"Hurrah for Mandiboy!"

It was a political meeting; at least so Fix conjectured, who said to Mr. Fogg, "Perhaps we had better not mingle with the crowd. There may be danger in it."

"Yes," returned Mr. Fogg; "and blows, even if they are political, are still blows."

Fix smiled at this remark; and in order to be able to see without being jostled about, the party took up a position on the top of a flight of steps situated at the upper end of Montgomery Street. Opposite them, on the other side of the street, between a coal wharf and a petroleum warehouse, a large platform had been erected in the open air, toward which the current of the crowd seemed to be directed.

For what purpose was this meeting? What was the occasion of this excited assemblage? Phileas Fogg could not imagine. Was it to nominate some high official—a governor or member of Congress? It was not improbable, so agitated was the multitude before them.

Just at this moment there was an unusual stir in the human mass. All the hands were raised in the air. Some, tightly closed, seemed to disappear suddenly in the midst of the cries—an energetic way, no doubt, of casting a vote. The crowd swayed back, the banners and flags wavered, disappeared an instant, then reappeared in tatters. The undulations of the human surge reached the steps, while all the heads floundered on the surface like a sea agitated by a squall. Many of the black hats disappeared, and the greater part of the crowd seemed to have diminished in height.

"It is evidently a meeting," said Fix, "and its object must be an exciting one. I should not wonder if it were about the Alabama, despite the fact that that question is settled."

"Perhaps," replied Mr. Fogg simply.

"At least, there are two champions in presence of each other, the Honorable Mr. Camerfield and the Honorable Mr. Mandiboy."

Aouda, leaning upon Mr. Fogg's arm, observed the tumultuous scene with surprise, while Fix asked a man near him what the cause of it all was. Before the man could reply, a fresh agitation arose; hurrahs and excited shouts were heard; the staffs of the banners began to be used as offensive weapons; and fists flew about in every direction. Thumps were exchanged from the tops of the carriages and omnibuses which had been blocked up in the crowd. Boots and shoes went whirling through the air, and Mr. Fogg thought he even heard the crack of revolvers mingling in the din. The rout approached the stairway, and flowed over the lower step. One of the parties had evidently been repulsed; but the mere lookers-on could not tell whether Mandiboy or Camerfield had gained the upper hand.

"It would be prudent for us to retire," said Fix, who was anxious that Mr. Fogg should not receive any injury, at least until they got back to London. "If there is any question about England in all this, and we were recognized, I fear it would go hard with us."

"An English subject——" began Mr. Fogg.

He did not finish his sentence; for a terrific hubbub now arose on the terrace behind the flight of steps where they stood, and there were frantic shouts of, "Hurrah for Mandiboy! Hip, hip, hurrah!"

It was a band of voters coming to the rescue of their allies, and taking the Camerfield forces in flank. Mr. Fogg, Aouda, and Fix found themselves between two fires; it was too late to escape. The torrent of men, armed with loaded canes and sticks, was irresistible. Phileas Fogg and Fix were roughly hustled in their attempts to protect their fair companion; the former, as cool as ever, tried to defend himself with the weapons which nature has placed at the end of every Englishman's arm, but in vain. A big brawny fellow with a red beard, flushed face, and broad shoulders, who seemed to be the chief of the band, raised his clenched fist to strike Mr. Fogg, whom he would have given a crushing blow, had not Fix rushed in and received it in his stead. An enormous bruise immediately made its appearance under the detective's silk hat, which was completely smashed in.

"Yankee!" exclaimed Mr. Fogg, darting a contemptuous look at the ruffian.

"Englishman!" returned the other. "We will meet again!"

"When you please."

"What is your name?"

"Phileas Fogg. And yours?"

"Colonel Stamp Proctor."

The human tide now swept by, after overturning Fix, who speedily got upon his feet again, though with tattered clothes. Happily, he was not seriously hurt. His traveling overcoat was divided into two unequal parts, and his trousers resembled those of certain Indians, which fit less compactly than they are easy to put on. Aouda had escaped unharmed, and Fix alone bore marks of the fray in his black and blue bruise.

"Thanks," said Mr. Fogg to the detective, as soon as they were out of the crowd.

"No thanks are necessary," replied Fix; "but let us go."

"Where?"

"To a tailor's."

Such a visit was, indeed, opportune. The clothing of both Mr. Fogg and Fix was in rags, as if they had themselves been actively engaged in the contest between Camerfield and Mandiboy. An hour after, they were once more suitably attired, and with Aouda returned to the International Hotel.

Passepartout was waiting for his master, armed with half-a-dozen six-barreled revolvers. When he perceived Fix, he knit his brows; but Aouda having, in a few words, told him of their adventure, his countenance resumed its placid expression. Fix evidently was no longer an enemy, but an ally; he was faithfully keeping his word.

Dinner over, the coach which was to convey the passengers and their luggage to the station drew up to the door. As he was getting in, Mr. Fogg said to Fix, "You have not seen this Colonel Proctor again?"

"No."

"I will come back to America to find him," said Phileas Fogg calmly. "It would not be right for an Englishman to permit himself to be treated in that way, without retaliating."

The detective smiled, but did not reply. It was clear that Mr. Fogg was one of those Englishmen who, while they do not tolerate dueling at home, fight abroad when their honor is attacked.

At a quarter before six the travelers reached the station, and found the train ready to depart. As he was about to enter it, Mr. Fogg called a porter, and said to him: "My friend, was there not some trouble to-day in San Francisco?"

"It was a political meeting, sir," replied the porter.

"But I thought there was a great deal of disturbance in the streets."

"It was only a meeting assembled for an election."

"The election of a general-in-chief, no doubt?" asked Mr. Fogg.

"No, sir; of a justice of the peace."

Phileas Fogg got into the train, which started off at full speed.

XXVI

In which Phileas Fogg and party travel by the Pacific Railroad

"From ocean to ocean"—so say the Americans; and these four words compose the general designation of the "great trunk line" which crosses the entire width of the United States. The Pacific Railroad is, however, really divided into two distinct lines: the Central Pacific, between San Francisco and Ogden, and the Union Pacific, between Ogden and Omaha. Five main lines connect Omaha with New York.

New York and San Francisco are thus united by an uninterrupted metal ribbon, which measures no less than three thousand seven hundred and eighty-six miles. Between Omaha and the Pacific the railway crosses a territory which is still infested by Indians and wild beasts, and a large tract which the Mormons, after they were driven from Illinois in 1845, began to colonize.

The journey from New York to San Francisco consumed, formerly, under the most favorable conditions, at least six months. It is now accomplished in seven days.

It was in 1862 that, in spite of the Southern members of Congress, who wished a more southerly route, it was decided to lay the road between the forty-first and forty-second parallels. President Lincoln himself fixed the end of the line at Omaha, in Nebraska. The work was at once commenced, and pursued with true American energy; nor did the rapidity with which it went on injuriously affect its good execution. The road grew, on the prairies, a mile and a half a day. A locomotive, running on the rails laid down the evening before, brought the rails to be laid on the morrow, and advanced upon them as fast as they were put in position.

The Pacific Railroad is joined by several branches in Iowa, Kansas, Colorado, and Oregon. On leaving Omaha, it passes along the left bank of the Platte River as far as the junction of its northern branch, follows its southern branch, crosses the Laramie territory and the Wahsatch Mountains, turns the Great Salt Lake, and reaches Salt Lake City, the Mormon capital, plunges into the Tuilla Valley, across the American Desert, Cedar and Humboldt Mountains, the Sierra Nevada, and descends, via Sacramento, to the Pacific—its grade, even on the Rocky Mountains, never exceeding one hundred and twelve feet to the mile.

Such was the road to be traversed in seven days, which would enable Phileas Fogg—at least, so he hoped—to take the Atlantic steamer at New York on the 11th for Liverpool.

The car which he occupied was a sort of long omnibus on eight wheels, and with no compartments in the interior. It was supplied with two rows of seats, perpendicular to the direction of the train on either side of an aisle which conducted to the front and rear platforms. These platforms were found throughout the train, and the passengers were able to pass from one end of the train to the other. It was supplied with saloon cars, balcony cars, restaurants, and smoking cars; theatre cars alone were wanting, and they will have these some day.

Books and news dealers, sellers of edibles, drinkables, and cigars, who seemed to have plenty of customers, were continually circulating in the aisles.

The train left Oakland station at six o'clock. It was already night, cold and cheerless, the heavens being overcast with clouds which seemed to threaten snow. The train did not proceed rapidly; counting the stoppages, it did not run more than twenty miles an hour, which was a sufficient speed, however, to enable it to reach Omaha within its designated time.

There was but little conversation in the car, and soon many of the passengers were overcome with sleep. Passepartout found himself beside the detective; but he did not talk to him. After recent events, their relations with each other had grown somewhat cold; there could no longer be mutual sympathy or intimacy between them. Fix's manner had not changed; but Passepartout was very reserved, and ready to strangle his former friend on the slightest provocation.

Snow began to fall an hour after they started, a fine snow, however, which happily could not obstruct the train; nothing could be seen from the windows but a vast, white sheet, against which the smoke of the locomotive had a grayish aspect.

At eight o'clock a steward entered the car and announced that the time for going to bed had arrived; and in a few minutes the car was transformed into a dormitory. The backs of the seats were thrown back, bedsteads carefully packed were rolled out by an ingenious system, berths were suddenly improvised, and each traveler had soon at his disposition a comfortable bed, protected from curious eyes by thick curtains. The sheets were clean and the pillows soft. It only remained to go to bed and sleep—which everybody did—while the train sped on across the State of California.

The country between San Francisco and Sacramento is not very hilly. The Central Pacific, taking Sacramento for its starting-point, extends eastward to meet the road from Omaha. The line from San Francisco to Sacramento runs in a north-easterly direction, along the American River, which empties into San Pablo Bay. The one hundred and twenty miles between these cities were accomplished in six hours, and toward midnight, while fast asleep, the travelers passed through Sacramento; so that they saw nothing of that important place, the seat of the State government, with its fine quays, its broad streets, its noble hotels, square, and churches.

The train, on leaving Sacramento, and passing the junction, Roclin, Auburn, and Colfax, entered the range of the Sierra Nevada. Cisco was reached at seven in the morning; and an hour later the dormitory was transformed into an ordinary car, and the travelers could observe the picturesque beauties of the mountain region through which they were steaming. The railway track wound in and out among the passes, now approaching the mountain sides, now suspended over precipices, avoiding abrupt angles by bold curves, plunging into narrow defiles, which seemed to have no outlet. The locomotive, its great funnel emitting a weird light, with its sharp bell, and its cow-catcher extended like a spur, mingled its shrieks and bellowings with the noise of torrents and cascades, and twined its smoke among the branches of the gigantic pines.

There were few or no bridges or tunnels on the route. The railway turned around the sides of the mountains, and did not attempt to violate nature by taking the shortest cut from one point to another.

The train entered the State of Nevada through the Carson Valley about nine o'clock, going always north-easterly; and at midday reached Reno, where there was a delay of twenty minutes for breakfast.

From this point the road, running along Humboldt River, passed northward for several miles by its banks; then it turned eastward, and kept by the river until it reached the Humboldt Range, nearly at the extreme eastern limit of Nevada.

Having breakfasted, Mr. Fogg and his companions resumed their places in the car, and observed the varied landscape which unfolded itself as they passed along: the vast prairies, the mountains lining the horizon, and the creeks with their frothy, foaming streams. Sometimes a great herd of buffaloes, massing together in the distance, seemed like a movable dam. These innumerable multitudes of ruminating beasts often form an insurmountable obstacle to the passage of the trains; thousands of them have been seen passing over the track for hours together, in compact ranks. The locomotive is then forced to stop and wait till the road is once more clear.

This happened, indeed, to the train in which Mr. Fogg was traveling. About twelve o'clock a troop of ten or twelve thousand head of buffalo encumbered the track. The locomotive, slackening in speed, tried to clear the way with its cow-catcher; but the mass of animals was too great. The buffaloes marched along with a tranquil gait, uttering now and then deafening bellowings. There was no use of interrupting them, for, having taken a particular direction, nothing can moderate and change their course; it is a torrent of living flesh which no dam could contain.

The travelers gazed on this curious spectacle from the platforms; but Phileas Fogg, who had the most reason of all to be in a hurry, remained in his seat, and waited philosophically until it should please the buffaloes to get out of the way.

Passepartout was furious at the delay they occasioned, and longed to discharge his arsenal of revolvers upon them.

"What a country!" cried he. "Mere cattle stop the trains, and go by in a procession, just as if they were not impeding travel! Parbleu! I should like to know if Mr. Fogg foresaw *this* mishap in his program! And here's an engineer who doesn't dare to run the locomotive into this herd of beasts!"

The engineer did not try to overcome the obstacle, and he was wise. He would have crushed the first buffaloes, no doubt, with the cow-catcher; but the locomotive, however powerful, would soon have been checked, the train would inevitably have been thrown off the track, and would then have been helpless.

The best course was to wait patiently, and regain the lost time by greater speed when the obstacle was removed. The procession of buffaloes lasted three full hours, and it was night before the track was clear. The last ranks of the herd were now passing over the rails, while the first had already disappeared below the southern horizon.

It was eight o'clock when the train passed through the defiles of the Humboldt Range, and half-past nine when it penetrated Utah, the region of the Great Salt Lake, the singular colony of the Mormons.

XXVII

In which Passepartout undergoes, at a speed of twenty miles an hour, a course of Mormon history

During the night of the 5th of December, the train ran south-easterly for about fifty miles; then rose an equal distance in a north-easterly direction, toward the Great Salt Lake.

Passepartout, about nine o'clock, went out upon the platform to take the air. The weather was cold, the heavens gray, but it was not snowing. The sun's disc, enlarged by the mist, seemed an enormous ring of gold, and Passepartout was amusing himself by calculating its value in pounds sterling, when he was diverted from this interesting study by a strange-looking personage who made his appearance on the platform.

This personage, who had taken the train at Elko, was tall and dark, with black moustaches, black stockings, a black silk hat, a black waistcoat, black trousers, a white cravat, and dog-skin gloves. He might have been taken for a clergyman. He went from one end of the train to the other, and affixed to the door of each car a notice written in manuscript.

Passepartout approached and read one of these notices, which stated that Elder William Hitch, Mormon missionary, taking advantage of his presence on train No. 48, would deliver a lecture on Mormonism in car No. 117, from eleven to twelve o'clock; and that he invited all who were desirous of being instructed concerning the mysteries of the religion of the "Latter Day Saints" to attend.

"I'll go," said Passepartout to himself. He knew nothing of Mormonism except the custom of polygamy, which is its foundation.

The news spread quickly through the train, which contained about one hundred passengers, thirty of whom, at most, attracted by the notice, esconced themselves in car No. 117. Passepartout took one of the front seats. Neither Mr. Fogg nor Fix cared to attend.

At the appointed hour Elder William Hitch rose, and, in an irritated voice, as if he had already been contradicted, said, "I tell you that Joe Smith is a martyr, that his brother Hiram is a martyr; and that the persecutions of the United States government against the prophets will also make a martyr of Brigham Young. Who dares to say the contrary?"

No one ventured to gainsay the missionary, whose excited tone contrasted curiously with his naturally calm visage. No doubt his anger arose from the hardships to which the Mormons were actually subjected. The government had just succeeded, with some difficulty, in reducing these independent fanatics to its rule. It had made itself master of Utah, and subjected that territory to the laws of the Union, after imprisoning Brigham Young on a charge of rebellion and polygamy. The disciples of the prophet had since redoubled their efforts, and resisted, by words at least, the authority of Congress. Elder Hitch, as is seen, was trying to make proselytes on the very railway trains.

Then, emphasizing his words with his loud voice and frequent gestures, he related the history of the Mormons from Biblical times: how that, in Israel, a Mormon prophet of the tribe of Joseph published the annals of the new religion, and bequeathed them to his son Mormon; how, many centuries later, a translation of this precious book, which was written in Egyptian, was made by Joseph Smith, Junior, a Vermont farmer, who revealed himself as a mystical prophet in 1825; and how, in short, the celestial messenger appeared to him in an illuminated forest, and gave him the annals of the Lord.

Several of the audience, not being much interested in the missionary's narrative, here left the car; but Elder Hitch, continuing his lecture, related how Smith, Junior, with his father, two brothers, and a few disciples, founded the church of the "Latter Day Saints," which, adopted not only in America, but in England, Norway and Sweden, and Germany, counts many artisans, as well as men engaged in the liberal professions, among its members; how a colony was established in Ohio, a temple erected there at a cost of two hundred thousand dollars, and a town built at Kirkland; how Smith became an enterprising banker, and received from a simple mummy showman a papyrus scroll written by Abraham and several famous Egyptians.

The Elder's story became somewhat wearisome, and his audience grew gradually less, until it was reduced to twenty passengers. But this did not disconcert the enthusiast, who proceeded with the story of Joseph Smith's bankruptcy in 1837, and how his ruined creditors gave him a coat of tar and feathers; his reappearance some years afterward, more honorable and honored than ever, at Independence, Missouri, the chief of a flourishing colony of three thousand disciples, and his pursuit thence by outraged Gentiles, and retirement into the Far West.

Ten hearers only were now left, among them honest Passepartout, who was listening with all his ears. Thus he learned that, after long persecutions, Smith reappeared in Illinois, and in 1839 founded a community at Nauvoo, on the Mississippi, numbering twenty-five thousand souls, of which he became mayor, chief justice, and general-in-chief; that he announced himself, in 1843, as a candidate for the Presidency of the United States; and that finally, being drawn into ambuscade at Carthage, he was thrown into prison, and assassinated by a band of men disguised in masks.

Passepartout was now the only person left in the car, and the Elder, looking him full in the face, reminded him that, two years after the assassination of Joseph Smith, the inspired prophet, Brigham Young, his successor, left Nauvoo for the banks of the Great Salt Lake, where, in the midst of that fertile region, directly on the route of the emigrants who crossed Utah on their way to California, the new colony, thanks to the polygamy practiced by the Mormons, had flourished beyond expectation.

"And this," added Elder William Hitch, "this is why the jealousy of Congress has been aroused against us! Why have the soldiers of the Union invaded the soil of Utah? Why has Brigham Young, our chief, been imprisoned, in contempt of all justice? Shall we yield to force? Never! Driven from Vermont, driven from Illinois, driven from Ohio, driven from Missouri, driven from Utah, we shall yet find some independent territory on which to plant our tents. And you, my brother," continued the Elder, fixing his angry eye upon his single auditor, "will you not plant yours there, too, under the shadow of our flag?"

"No!" replied Passepartout courageously, in his turn retiring from the car, and leaving the Elder to preach to vacancy.

During the lecture the train had been making good progress, and toward half-past twelve it reached the north-west border of the Great Salt Lake. Thence the passengers could observe the vast extent of this interior sea, which is also called the Dead Sea, and into which flows an American Jordan. It is a picturesque expanse, framed in lofty crags in large strata, encrusted with white salt—a superb sheet of water, which was formerly of larger extent than now, its shores having encroached with the lapse of time, and thus at once reduced its breadth and increased its depth.

The Salt Lake, seventy miles long and thirty-five wide, is situated three miles eight hundred feet above the sea. Quite different from Lake Asphaltite, whose depression is twelve hundred feet below the sea, it contains considerable salt, and one quarter of the weight of its water is solid matter, its specific weight being 1170, and, after being distilled, 1000. Fishes are of course unable to live in it, and those which descend through the Jordan, the Weber, and other streams, soon perish.

The country around the lake was well cultivated, for the Mormons are mostly farmers; while ranches and pens for domesticated animals, fields of wheat, corn, and other cereals, luxuriant prairies, hedges of wild rose, clumps of acacias and milk-wort, would have been seen six months later. Now the ground was covered with a thin powdering of snow.

The train reached Ogden at two o'clock, where it rested for six hours. Mr. Fogg and his party had time to pay a visit to Salt Lake City, connected with Ogden by a branch road; and they spent two hours in this strikingly American town, built on the pattern of other cities of the Union, like a checker-board, "with the sombre sadness of right angles," as Victor Hugo expresses it. The founder of the City of the Saints could not escape from the taste for symmetry which distinguishes the Anglo-Saxons. In this strange country, where the people are certainly not up to the level of their institutions, everything is done "squarely"—cities, houses, and follies.

The travelers, then, were promenading, at three o'clock, about the streets of the town built between the banks of the Jordan and the spurs of the Wahsatch Range. They saw few or no churches, but the prophet's mansion, the court-house, and the arsenal, blue-brick houses with verandas and porches, surrounded by gardens bordered with acacias, palms, and locusts. A clay and pebble wall, built in 1853, surrounded the town; and in the principal street were the market and several hotels adorned with pavilions. The place did not seem thickly populated. The streets were almost deserted, except in the vicinity of the Temple, which they only reached after having traversed several quarters surrounded by palisades. There were many women, which was easily accounted for by the "peculiar institution" of the Mormons; but it must not be supposed that all the Mormons are polygamists. They are free to marry or not, as they please; but it is worth noting that it is mainly the female citizens of Utah who are anxious to marry, as, according to the Mormon religion, maiden ladies are not admitted to the possession of its highest joys. These poor creatures seemed to be neither well off nor happy. Some—the more well-to-do, no doubt—wore short, open, black silk dresses, under a hood or modest shawl; others were habited in Indian fashion.

Passepartout could not behold without a certain fright these women, charged, in groups, with conferring happiness on a single Mormon. His common sense pitied, above all, the husband. It seemed to him a terrible thing to have to guide so many wives at once across the vicissitudes of life, and to conduct them, as it were, in a body to the Mormon paradise, with the prospect of seeing them in the company of the glorious Smith, who doubtless was the chief ornament of that delightful place, to all eternity. He felt decidedly repelled from such a vocation, and he imagined—perhaps he was mistaken—that the fair ones of Salt Lake City cast rather alarming glances on his person. Happily, his stay there was but brief. At four the party found themselves again at the station, took their places in the train, and the whistle sounded for starting. Just at the moment, however, that the locomotive wheels began to move, cries of "Stop! stop!" were heard.

Trains, like time and tide, stop for no one. The gentleman who uttered the cries was evidently a belated Mormon. He was breathless with running. Happily for him, the station had neither gates nor barriers. He rushed along the track, jumped on the rear platform of the train, and fell exhausted into one of the seats.

Passepartout, who had been anxiously watching this amateur gymnast, approached him with lively interest, and learned that he had taken flight after an unpleasant domestic scene.

When the Mormon had recovered his breath, Passepartout ventured to ask him politely how many wives he had; for, from the manner in which he had decamped, it might be thought that he had twenty at least.

"One, sir," replied the Mormon, raising his arms heavenward—"one, and that was enough!"

XXVIII

In which Passepartout does not succeed in making anybody listen to reason

The train, on leaving Great Salt Lake at Ogden, passed northward for an hour as far as Weber River, having completed nearly nine hundred miles from San Francisco. From this point it took an easterly direction toward the jagged Wahsatch Mountains. It was in the section included between this range and the Rocky Mountains that the American engineers found the most formidable difficulties in laying the road, and that the government granted a subsidy of forty-eight thousand dollars per mile, instead of sixteen thousand allowed for the work done on the plains. But the engineers, instead of violating nature, avoided its difficulties by winding around, instead of penetrating the rocks. One tunnel only, fourteen thousand feet in length, was pierced in order to arrive at the great basin.

The track up to this time had reached its highest elevation at the Great Salt Lake. From this point it described a long curve, descending toward Bitter Creek Valley, to rise again to the dividing ridge of the waters between the Atlantic and the Pacific. There were many creeks in this mountainous region, and it was necessary to cross Muddy Creek, Green Creek, and others, upon culverts.

Passepartout grew more and more impatient as they went on, while Fix longed to get out of this difficult region, and was more anxious than Phileas Fogg himself to be beyond the danger of delays and accidents, and set foot on English soil.

At ten o'clock at night the train stopped at Fort Bridger station, and twenty minutes later entered Wyoming Territory, following the valley of Bitter Creek throughout. The next day, December 7th, they stopped for a quarter of an hour at Green River station. Snow had fallen abundantly during the night, but, being mixed with rain, it had half melted, and did not interrupt their progress. The bad weather, however, annoyed Passepartout; for the accumulation of snow, by blocking the wheels of the cars, would certainly have been fatal to Mr. Fogg's tour.

"What an idea!" he said to himself. "Why did my master make this journey in winter? Couldn't he have waited for the good season to increase his chances?"

While the worthy Frenchman was absorbed in the state of the sky and the depression of the temperature, Aouda was experiencing fears from a totally different cause.

Several passengers had got off at Green River, and were walking up and down the platforms; and among these Aouda recognized Colonel Stamp Proctor, the same who had so grossly insulted Phileas Fogg at the San Francisco meeting. Not wishing to be recognized, the young woman drew back from the window, feeling much alarm at her discovery. She was attached to the man who, however coldly, gave her daily evidences of the most absolute devotion. She did not comprehend, perhaps, the depth of the sentiment with which her protector inspired her, which she called gratitude, but which, though she was unconscious of it, was really more than that. Her heart sank within her when she recognized the man whom Mr. Fogg desired, sooner or later, to call to account for his conduct. Chance alone, it was clear, had brought Colonel Proctor on this train; but there he was, and it was necessary, at all hazards, that Phileas Fogg should not perceive his adversary.

Aouda seized a moment when Mr. Fogg was asleep to tell Fix and Passepartout whom she had seen.

"That Proctor on this train!" cried Fix. "Well, reassure yourself, madam; before he settles with Mr. Fogg, he has got to deal with me! It seems to me that I was the more insulted of the two."

"And besides," added Passepartout, "I'll take charge of him, colonel as he is."

"Mr. Fix," resumed Aouda, "Mr. Fogg will allow no one to avenge him. He said that he would come back to America to find this man. Should he perceive Colonel Proctor, we could not prevent a collision which might have terrible results. He must not see him."

"You are right, madam," replied Fix; "a meeting between them might ruin all. Whether he were victorious or beaten, Mr. Fogg would be delayed, and——"

"And," added Passepartout, "that would play the game of the gentlemen of the Reform Club. In four days we shall be in New York. Well, if my master does not leave this car during those four days, we may hope that chance will not bring him face to face with this confounded American. We must, if possible, prevent his stirring out of it."

The conversation dropped. Mr. Fogg had just woke up, and was looking out of the window. Soon after Passepartout, without being heard by his master or Aouda, whispered to the detective, "Would you really fight for him?"

"I would do anything," replied Fix, in a tone which betrayed determined will, "to get him back living to Europe!"

Passepartout felt something like a shudder shoot through his frame, but his confidence in his master remained unbroken.

Was there any means of detaining Mr. Fogg in the car, to avoid a meeting between him and the colonel? It ought not to be a difficult task, since that gentleman was naturally sedentary and little curious. The detective, at least, seemed to have found a way; for, after a few moments, he said to Mr. Fogg, "These are long and slow hours, sir, that we are passing on the railway."

"Yes," replied Mr. Fogg; "but they pass."

"You were in the habit of playing whist," resumed Fix, "on the steamers."

"Yes; but it would be difficult to do so here. I have neither cards nor partners."

"Oh, but we can easily buy some cards, for they are sold on all the American trains. And as for partners, if madam plays——"

"Certainly, sir," Aouda quickly replied; "I understand whist. It is part of an English education."

"I myself have some pretensions to playing a good game. Well, here are three of us, and a dummy——"

"As you please, sir," replied Phileas Fogg, heartily glad to resume his favorite pastime—even on the railway.

Passepartout was dispatched in search of the steward, and soon returned with two packs of cards, some pins, counters, and a shelf covered with cloth.

The game commenced. Aouda understood whist sufficiently well, and even received some compliments on her playing from Mr. Fogg. As for the detective, he was simply an adept, and worthy of being matched against his present opponent.

"Now," thought Passepartout, "we've got him. He won't budge."

At eleven in the morning the train had reached the dividing ridge of the waters at Bridger Pass, seven thousand five hundred and twenty-four feet above the level of the sea, one of the highest points attained by the track in crossing the Rocky Mountains. After going about two hundred miles, the travelers at last found themselves on one of those vast plains which extend to the Atlantic, and which nature has made so propitious for laying the iron road.

On the declivity of the Atlantic basin the first streams, branches of the North Platte River, already appeared. The whole northern and eastern horizon was bounded by the immense semicircular curtain which is formed by the southern portion of the Rocky Mountains, the highest being Laramie Peak. Between this and the railway extended vast plains, plentifully irrigated. On the right rose the lower spurs of the mountainous mass which extends southward to the sources of the Arkansas River, one of the great tributaries of the Missouri.

At half-past twelve the travelers caught sight for an instant of Fort Halleck, which commands that section; and in a few more hours the Rocky Mountains were crossed. There was reason to hope, then, that no accident would mark the journey through this difficult country. The snow had ceased falling, and the air became crisp and cold. Large birds, frightened by the locomotive, rose and flew off in the distance. No wild beast appeared on the plain. It was a desert in its vast nakedness.

After a comfortable breakfast, served in the car, Mr. Fogg and his partners had just resumed whist, when a violent whistling was heard, and the train stopped. Passepartout put his head out of the door, but saw nothing to cause the delay; no station was in view.

Aouda and Fix feared that Mr. Fogg might take it into his head to get out; but that gentleman contented himself with saying to his servant, "See what is the matter."

Passepartout rushed out of the car. Thirty or forty passengers had already descended, amongst them Colonel Stamp Proctor.

The train had stopped before a red signal which blocked the way. The engineer and conductor were talking excitedly with a signal-man, whom the station-master at Medicine Bow, the next stopping-place, had sent on before. The passengers drew around and took part in the discussion, in which Colonel Proctor, with his insolent manner, was conspicuous.

Passepartout, joining the group, heard the signal-man say, "No! you can't pass. The bridge at Medicine Bow is shaky, and would not bear the weight of the train."

This was a suspension-bridge thrown over some rapids, about a mile from the place where they now were. According to the signal-man, it was in a ruinous condition, several of the iron wires being broken; and it was impossible to risk the passage. He did not in any way exaggerate the condition of the bridge. It may be taken for granted that, rash as the Americans usually are, when they are prudent there is good reason for it.

Passepartout, not daring to apprise his master of what he heard, listened with set teeth, immovable as a statue.

"Hum!" cried Colonel Proctor; "but we are not going to stay here, I imagine, and take root in the snow?"

"Colonel," replied the conductor, "we have telegraphed to Omaha for a train, but it is not likely that it will reach Medicine Bow in less than six hours."

"Six hours!" cried Passepartout.

"Certainly," returned the conductor. "Besides, it will take us as long as that to reach Medicine Bow on foot."

"But it is only a mile from here," said one of the passengers.

"Yes, but it's on the other side of the river."

"And can't we cross that in a boat?" asked the colonel.

"That's impossible. The creek is swelled by the rains. It is a rapid, and we shall have to make a circuit of ten miles to the north to find a ford."

The colonel launched a volley of oaths, denouncing the railway company and the conductor; and Passepartout, who was furious, was not disinclined to make common cause with him. Here was an obstacle, indeed, which all his master's bank-notes could not remove.

There was a general disappointment among the passengers, who, without reckoning the delay, saw themselves compelled to trudge fifteen miles over a plain covered with snow. They grumbled and protested, and would certainly have thus attracted Phileas Fogg's attention if he had not been completely absorbed in his game.

Passepartout found that he could not avoid telling his master what had occurred, and, with hanging head he was turning toward the car, when the engineer—a true Yankee, named Forster—called out, "Gentlemen, perhaps there is a way, after all, to get over."

"On the bridge?" asked a passenger.

"On the bridge."

"With our train?"

"With our train."

Passepartout stopped short, and eagerly listened to the engineer.

"But the bridge is unsafe," urged the conductor.

"No matter," replied Forster; "I think that by putting on the very highest speed we might have a chance of getting over."

"The devil!" muttered Passepartout.

But a number of the passengers were at once attracted by the engineer's proposal, and Colonel Proctor was especially delighted, and found the plan a very feasible one. He told stories about engineers leaping their trains over rivers without bridges, by putting on full steam; and many of those present avowed themselves of the engineer's mind.

"We have fifty chances out of a hundred of getting over," said one.

"Eighty! ninety!"

Passepartout was astounded, and, though ready to attempt anything to get over Medicine Creek, thought the experiment proposed a little too American. "Besides," thought he, "there's still a more simple way, and it does not even occur to any of these people! Sir," said he aloud to one of the passengers, "the engineer's plan seems to me a little dangerous, but——"

"Eighty chances!" replied the passenger, turning his back on him.

"I know it," said Passepartout, turning to another passenger, "but a simple idea——"

"Ideas are no use," returned the American, shrugging his shoulders, "as the engineer assures us that we can pass."

"Doubtless," urged Passepartout, "we can pass, but perhaps it would be more prudent——"

"What! Prudent!" cried Colonel Proctor, whom this word seemed to excite prodigiously. "At full speed, don't you see, at full speed!"

"I know—I see," repeated Passepartout; "but it would be, if not more prudent, since that word displeases you, at least more natural——"

"Who! What! What's the matter with this fellow?" cried several.

The poor fellow did not know to whom to address himself.

"Are you afraid?" asked Colonel Proctor.

"I afraid! Very well; I will show these people that a Frenchman can be as American as they!"

"All aboard!" cried the conductor.

"Yes, all aboard!" repeated Passepartout, and immediately. "But they can't prevent me from thinking that it would be more natural for us to cross the bridge on foot, and let the train come after!"

But no one heard this sage reflection, nor would anyone have acknowledged its justice. The passengers resumed their places in the cars. Passepartout took his seat without telling what had passed. The whist-players were quite absorbed in their game.

The locomotive whistled vigorously; the engineer, reversing the steam, backed the train for nearly a mile—retiring, like a jumper, in order to take a longer leap. Then, with another whistle, he began to move forward; the train increased its speed, and soon its rapidity became frightful; a prolonged screech issued from the locomotive; the piston worked up and down twenty strokes to the second. They perceived that the whole train, rushing on at the rate of a hundred miles an hour, hardly bore upon the rails at all.

And they passed over! It was like a flash. No one saw the bridge. The train leaped, so to speak, from one bank to the other, and the engineer could not stop it until it had gone five miles beyond the station. But scarcely had the train passed the river, when the bridge, completely ruined, fell with a crash into the rapids of Medicine Bow.

XXIX

In which certain incidents are narrated which are only to be met with on American railroads

The train pursued its course, that evening, without interruption, passing Fort Saunders, crossing Cheyenne Pass, and reaching Evans Pass. The road here attained the highest elevation of the journey, eight thousand and ninety-one feet above the level of the sea. The travelers had now only to descend to the Atlantic by limitless plains, leveled by nature. A branch of the "grand trunk" led off southward to Denver, the capital of

Colorado. The country round about is rich in gold and silver, and more than fifty thousand inhabitants are already settled there.

Thirteen hundred and eighty-two miles had been passed over from San Francisco, in three days and three nights; four days and nights more would probably bring them to New York. Phileas Fogg was not as yet behind-hand.

During the night Camp Walbach was passed on the left; Lodge Pole Creek ran parallel with the road, marking the boundary between the territories of Wyoming and Colorado. They entered Nebraska at eleven, passed near Sedgwick, and touched at Julesburg, on the southern branch of the Platte River.

It was here that the Union Pacific Railroad was inaugurated on the 23rd of October, 1867, by the chief engineer, General Dodge. Two powerful locomotives, carrying nine cars of invited guests, amongst whom was Thomas C. Durant, vice-president of the road, stopped at this point; cheers were given, the Sioux and Pawnees performed an imitation Indian battle, fireworks were let off, and the first number of the *Railway Pioneer* was printed by a press brought on the train. Thus was celebrated the inauguration of this great railroad, a mighty instrument of progress and civilization, thrown across the desert, and destined to link together cities and towns which do not yet exist. The whistle of the locomotive, more powerful than Amphion's lyre, was about to bid them rise from American soil.

Fort McPherson was left behind at eight in the morning, and three hundred and fifty-seven miles had yet to be traversed before reaching Omaha. The road followed the capricious windings of the southern branch of the Platte River, on its left bank. At nine the train stopped at the important town of North Platte, built between the two arms of the river, which rejoin each other around it and form a single artery—a large tributary whose waters empty into the Missouri a little above Omaha.

The one hundred and first meridian was passed.

Mr. Fogg and his partners had resumed their game; no one—not even the dummy—complained of the length of the trip. Fix had begun by winning several guineas, which he seemed likely to lose; but he showed himself a not less eager whist-player than Mr. Fogg. During the morning, chance distinctly favored that gentleman. Trumps and honors were showered upon his hands.

Once, having resolved on a bold stroke, he was on the point of playing a spade, when a voice behind him said, "I should play a diamond."

Mr. Fogg, Aouda, and Fix raised their heads, and beheld Colonel Proctor.

Stamp Proctor and Phileas Fogg recognized each other at once.

"Ah! it's you, is it, Englishman?" cried the colonel; "it's you who are going to play a spade!"

"And who plays it," replied Phileas Fogg coolly, throwing down the ten of spades.

"Well, it pleases me to have it diamonds," replied Colonel Proctor, in an insolent tone.

He made a movement as if to seize the card which had just been played, adding, "You don't understand anything about whist."

"Perhaps I do, as well as another," said Phileas Fogg, rising.

"You have only to try, son of John Bull," replied the colonel.

Aouda turned pale, and her blood ran cold. She seized Mr. Fogg's arm and gently pulled him back. Passepartout was ready to pounce upon the American, who was staring insolently at his opponent. But Fix got up, and going to Colonel Proctor said, "You forget that it is I with whom you have to deal, sir; for it was I whom you not only insulted, but struck!"

"Mr. Fix," said Mr. Fogg, "pardon me, but this affair is mine, and mine only. The colonel has again insulted me, by insisting that I should not play a spade, and he shall give me satisfaction for it."

"When and where you will," replied the American, "and with whatever weapon you choose."

Aouda in vain attempted to retain Mr. Fogg; as vainly did the detective endeavor to make the quarrel his. Passepartout wished to throw the colonel out of the window, but a sign from his master checked him. Phileas Fogg left the car, and the American followed him upon the platform.

"Sir," said Mr. Fogg to his adversary, "I am in a great hurry to get back to Europe, and any delay whatever will be greatly to my disadvantage."

"Well, what's that to me?" replied Colonel Proctor.

"Sir," said Mr. Fogg, very politely, "after our meeting at San Francisco, I determined to return to America and find you as soon as I had completed the business which called me to England."

"Really!"

"Will you appoint a meeting for six months hence?"

"Why not ten years hence?"

"I say six months," returned Phileas Fogg, "and I shall be at the place of meeting promptly."

"All this is an evasion," cried Stamp Proctor. "Now or never!"

"Very good. You are going to New York?"

"No."

"To Chicago?"

"No."

"To Omaha?"

"What difference is it to you? Do you know Plum Creek?"

"No," replied Mr. Fogg.

"It's the next station. The train will be there in an hour, and will stop there ten minutes. In ten minutes several revolver-shots could be exchanged."

"Very well," said Mr. Fogg. "I will stop at Plum Creek."

"And I guess you'll stay there too," added the American insolently.

"Who knows?" replied Mr. Fogg, returning to the car as coolly as usual. He began to reassure Aouda, telling her that blusterers were never to be feared, and begged Fix to be his second at the approaching duel, a request which the detective could not refuse. Mr. Fogg resumed the interrupted game with perfect calmness.

At eleven o'clock the locomotive's whistle announced that they were approaching Plum Creek station. Mr. Fogg rose, and, followed by Fix, went out upon the platform. Passepartout accompanied him, carrying a pair of revolvers. Aouda remained in the car, as pale as death.

The door of the next car opened, and Colonel Proctor appeared on the platform, attended by a Yankee of his own stamp as his second. But just as the combatants were about to step from the train, the conductor hurried up, and shouted, "You can't get off, gentlemen!"

"Why not?" asked the colonel.

"We are twenty minutes late, and we shall not stop."

"But I am going to fight a duel with this gentleman."

"I am sorry," said the conductor; "but we shall be off at once. There's the bell ringing now."

The train started.

"I'm really very sorry, gentlemen," said the conductor. "Under any other circumstances I should have been happy to oblige you. But, after all, as you have not had time to fight here, why not fight as we go along?"

"That wouldn't be convenient, perhaps, for this gentleman," said the colonel, in a jeering tone.

"It would be perfectly so," replied Phileas Fogg.

"Well, we are really in America," thought Passepartout, "and the conductor is a gentleman of the first order!"

So muttering, he followed his master.

The two combatants, their seconds, and the conductor passed through the cars to the rear of the train. The last car was only occupied by a dozen passengers, whom the conductor politely asked if they would not be so kind as to leave it vacant for a few moments, as two gentlemen had an affair of honor to settle. The passengers granted the request with alacrity, and straightaway disappeared on the platform.

The car, which was some fifty feet long, was very convenient for their purpose. The adversaries might march on each other in the aisle, and fire at their ease. Never was duel more easily arranged. Mr. Fogg and Colonel Proctor, each provided with two six-barreled revolvers, entered the car. The seconds, remaining outside, shut them in. They were to begin firing at the first whistle of the locomotive. After an interval of two minutes, what remained of the two gentlemen would be taken from the car.

Nothing could be more simple. Indeed, it was all so simple that Fix and Passepartout felt their hearts beating as if they would crack. They were listening for the whistle agreed upon, when suddenly savage cries resounded in the air, accompanied by reports which certainly did not issue from the car where the duelists were. The reports continued in front and the whole length of the train. Cries of terror proceeded from the interior of the cars.

Colonel Proctor and Mr. Fogg, revolvers in hand, hastily quitted their prison, and rushed forward where the noise was most clamorous. They then perceived that the train was attacked by a band of Sioux.

This was not the first attempt of these daring Indians, for more than once they had waylaid trains on the road. A hundred of them had, according to their habit, jumped upon the steps without stopping the train, with the ease of a clown mounting a horse at full gallop.

The Sioux were armed with guns, from which came the reports, to which the passengers, who were almost all armed, responded by revolver-shots.

The Indians had first mounted the engine, and half stunned the engineer and stoker with blows from their muskets. A Sioux chief, wishing to stop the train, but not knowing how to work the regulator, had opened wide instead of closing the steam-valve, and the locomotive was plunging forward with terrific velocity.

The Sioux had at the same time invaded the cars, skipping like enraged monkeys over the roofs, thrusting open the doors, and fighting hand to hand with the passengers. Penetrating the baggage-car, they pillaged it, throwing the trunks out of the train. The cries and shots were constant.

The travelers defended themselves bravely; some of the cars were barricaded, and sustained a siege, like moving forts, carried along at a speed of a hundred miles an hour.

Aouda behaved courageously from the first. She defended herself like a true heroine with a revolver, which she shot through the broken windows whenever a savage made his appearance. Twenty Sioux had fallen mortally wounded to the ground, and the wheels crushed those who fell upon the rails as if they had been worms. Several passengers, shot or stunned, lay on the seats.

It was necessary to put an end to the struggle, which had lasted for ten minutes, and which would result in the triumph of the Sioux if the train was not stopped. Fort Kearney station, where there was a garrison, was only two miles distant; but, that once passed, the Sioux would be masters of the train between Fort Kearney and the station beyond.

The conductor was fighting beside Mr. Fogg, when he was shot and fell. At the same moment he cried, "Unless the train is stopped in five minutes, we are lost!"

"It shall be stopped," said Phileas Fogg, preparing to rush from the car.

"Stay, monsieur," cried Passepartout, "I will go."

Mr. Fogg had not time to stop the brave fellow, who, opening a door unperceived by the Indians, succeeded in slipping under the car; and while the struggle continued, and the balls whizzed across each other over his head, he made use of his old acrobatic experience, and with amazing agility worked his way under the cars, holding on to the chains, aiding himself by the brakes and edges of the sashes, creeping from one car to another with marvelous skill, and thus gaining the forward end of the train.

There, suspended by one hand between the baggage-car and the tender, with the other he loosened the safety chains; but, owing to the traction, he would never have succeeded in unscrewing the yoking-bar, had not a violent concussion jolted this bar out. The train, now detached from the engine, remained a little behind, whilst the locomotive rushed forward with increased speed.

Carried on by the force already acquired, the train still moved for several minutes; but the brakes were worked, and at last they stopped, less than a hundred feet from Kearney station.

The soldiers of the fort, attracted by the shots, hurried up; the Sioux had not expected them, and decamped in a body before the train entirely stopped.

But when the passengers counted each other on the station platform several were found missing; among others the courageous Frenchman, whose devotion had just saved them.

XXX

In which Phileas Fogg simply does his duty

Three passengers—including Passepartout—had disappeared. Had they been killed in the struggle? Were they taken prisoners by the Sioux? It was impossible to tell.

There were many wounded, but none mortally. Colonel Proctor was one of the most seriously hurt; he had fought bravely, and a ball had entered his groin. He was carried into the station with the other wounded passengers, to receive such attention as could be of avail.

Aouda was safe; and Phileas Fogg, who had been in the thickest of the fight, had not received a scratch. Fix was slightly wounded in the arm. But Passepartout was not to be found, and tears coursed down Aouda's cheeks.

All the passengers had got out of the train, the wheels of which were stained with blood. From the tires and spokes hung ragged pieces of flesh. As far as the eye could reach on the white plain behind, red trails were visible. The last Sioux were disappearing in the south, along the banks of the Republican River.

Mr. Fogg, with folded arms, remained motionless. He had a serious decision to make. Aouda, standing near him, looked at him without speaking, and he understood her look. If his servant was a prisoner, ought he not to risk everything to rescue him from the Indians? "I will find him, living or dead," said he quietly to Aouda.

"Ah, Mr.—Mr. Fogg!" cried she, clasping his hands and covering them with tears.

"Living," added Mr. Fogg, "if we do not lose a moment."

Phileas Fogg, by this resolution, inevitably sacrificed himself; he pronounced his own doom. The delay of a single day would make him lose the steamer at New York, and his bet would be certainly lost. But as he thought, "It is my duty," he did not hesitate.

The commanding officer of Fort Kearney was there. A hundred of his soldiers had placed themselves in a position to defend the station, should the Sioux attack it.

"Sir," said Mr. Fogg to the captain, "three passengers have disappeared."

"Dead?" asked the captain.

"Dead or prisoners; that is the uncertainty which must be solved. Do you propose to pursue the Sioux?"

"That's a serious thing to do, sir," returned the captain. "These Indians may retreat beyond the Arkansas, and I cannot leave the fort unprotected."

"The lives of three men are in question, sir," said Phileas Fogg.

"Doubtless; but can I risk the lives of fifty men to save three?"

"I don't know whether you can, sir; but you ought to do so."

"Nobody here," returned the other, "has a right to teach me my duty."

"Very well," said Mr. Fogg, coldly. "I will go alone."

"You, sir!" cried Fix, coming up; "you go alone in pursuit of the Indians?"

"Would you have me leave this poor fellow to perish—him to whom every one present owes his life? I shall go."

"No, sir, you shall not go alone," cried the captain, touched in spite of himself. "No! you are a brave man. Thirty volunteers!" he added, turning to the soldiers.

The whole company started forward at once. The captain had only to pick his men. Thirty were chosen, and an old sergeant placed at their head.

"Thanks, captain," said Mr. Fogg.

"Will you let me go with you?" asked Fix.

"Do as you please, sir. But if you wish to do me a favor, you will remain with Aouda. In case anything should happen to me——"

A sudden pallor overspread the detective's face. Separate himself from the man whom he had so persistently followed step by step! Leave him to wander about in this desert! Fix gazed attentively at Mr. Fogg, and, despite his suspicions and of the struggle which was going on within him, he lowered his eyes before that calm and frank look.

"I will stay," said he.

A few moments after, Mr. Fogg pressed the young woman's hand, and, having confided to her his precious carpet-bag, went off with the sergeant and his little squad. But, before going, he had said to the soldiers, "My friends, I will divide five thousand dollars among you, if we save the prisoners."

It was then a little past noon.

Aouda retired to a waiting-room, and there she waited alone, thinking of the simple and noble generosity, the tranquil courage of Phileas Fogg. He had sacrificed his fortune, and was now risking his life, all without hesitation, from duty, in silence.

Fix did not have the same thoughts, and could scarcely conceal his agitation. He walked feverishly up and down the platform, but soon resumed his outward composure. He now saw the folly of which he had been guilty in letting Fogg go alone. What! This man, whom he had just followed around the world, was permitted now to separate himself from him! He began to accuse and abuse himself, and, as if he were director of police, administered to himself a sound lecture for his greenness.

"I have been an idiot!" he thought, "and this man will see it. He has gone, and won't come back! But how is it that I, Fix, who have in my pocket a warrant for his arrest, have been so fascinated by him? Decidedly, I am nothing but an ass!"

So reasoned the detective, while the hours crept by all too slowly. He did not know what to do. Sometimes he was tempted to tell Aouda all; but he could not doubt how the young woman would receive his confidences. What course should he take? He thought of pursuing Fogg across the vast white plains; it did not seem impossible that he might overtake him. Footsteps were easily printed on the snow! But soon, under a new sheet, every imprint would be effaced.

Fix became discouraged. He felt a sort of insurmountable longing to abandon the game altogether. He could now leave Fort Kearney station, and pursue his journey homeward in peace.

Toward two o'clock in the afternoon, while it was snowing hard, long whistles were heard approaching from the east. A great shadow, preceded by a wild light, slowly advanced, appearing still larger through the mist, which gave it a fantastic aspect. No train was expected from the east, neither had there been time for the succor asked for by telegraph to arrive; the train from Omaha to San Francisco was not due till the next day. The mystery was soon explained.

The locomotive, which was slowly approaching with deafening whistles, was that which, having been detached from the train, had continued its route with such terrific rapidity, carrying off the unconscious engineer and stoker. It had run several miles, when, the fire becoming low for want of fuel, the steam had slackened; and it had finally stopped an hour after, some twenty miles beyond Fort Kearney. Neither the engineer nor the stoker was dead, and, after remaining for some time in their swoon, had come to themselves. The train had then stopped. The engineer, when he found himself in the desert, and the locomotive without cars, understood what had happened. He could not imagine how the locomotive had become separated from the train; but he did not doubt that the train left behind was in distress.

He did not hesitate what to do. It would be prudent to continue on to Omaha, for it would be dangerous to return to the train, which the Indians might still be engaged in pillaging. Nevertheless, he began to rebuild the fire in the furnace; the pressure again mounted, and the locomotive returned, running backward to Fort Kearney. This it was which was whistling in the mist.

The travelers were glad to see the locomotive resume its place at the head of the train. They could now continue the journey so terribly interrupted.

Aouda, on seeing the locomotive come up, hurried out of the station, and asked the conductor, "Are you going to start?"

"At once, madam."

"But the prisoners—our unfortunate fellow-travelers——"

"I cannot interrupt the trip," replied the conductor. "We are already three hours behind time."

"And when will another train pass here from San Francisco?"

"To-morrow evening, madam."

"To-morrow evening! But then it will be too late! We must wait——"

"It is impossible," responded the conductor. "If you wish to go, please get in."

"I will not go," said Aouda.

Fix had heard this conversation. A little while before, when there was no prospect of proceeding on the journey, he had made up his mind to leave Fort Kearney; but now that the train was there, ready to start, and he had only to take his seat in the car, an irresistible influence held him back. The station platform burned his feet, and he could not stir. The conflict in his mind again began; anger and failure stifled him. He wished to struggle on to the end.

Meanwhile the passengers and some of the wounded, among them Colonel Proctor, whose injuries were serious, had taken their places in the train. The buzzing of the overheated boiler was heard, and the steam was escaping from the valves. The engineer whistled, the train started, and soon disappeared, mingling its white smoke with the eddies of the densely falling snow.

The detective had remained behind.

Several hours passed. The weather was dismal, and it was very cold. Fix sat motionless on a bench in the station; he might have been thought asleep. Aouda, despite the storm, kept coming out of the waiting-room, going to the end of the platform, and peering through the tempest of snow, as if to pierce the mist which narrowed the horizon around her, and to hear, if possible, some welcome sound. She heard and saw nothing. Then she would return, chilled through, to issue out again after the lapse of a few moments, but always in vain.

Evening came, and the little band had not returned. Where could they be? Had they found the Indians, and were they having a conflict with them, or were they still wandering amid the mist? The commander of the fort was anxious, though he tried to conceal his apprehensions. As night approached, the snow fell less plentifully, but it became intensely cold. Absolute silence rested on the plains. Neither flight of bird nor passing of beast troubled the perfect calm.

Throughout the night Aouda, full of sad forebodings, her heart stifled with anguish, wandered about on the verge of the plains. Her imagination carried her far off, and showed her innumerable dangers. What she suffered through the long hours it would be impossible to describe.

Fix remained stationary in the same place, but did not sleep. Once a man approached and spoke to him, and the detective merely replied by shaking his head.

Thus the night passed. At dawn the half-extinguished disc of the sun rose above a misty horizon; but it was now possible to recognize objects two miles off. Phileas Fogg and the squad had gone southward; in the south all was still vacancy. It was then seven o'clock.

The captain, who was really alarmed, did not know what course to take.

Should he send another detachment to the rescue of the first? Should he sacrifice more men, with so few chances of saving those already sacrificed? His hesitation did not last long, however. Calling one of his lieutenants, he was on the point of ordering a reconnaissance, when gunshots were heard.

Was it a signal? The soldiers rushed out of the fort, and half-a-mile off they perceived a little band returning in good order.

Mr. Fogg was marching at their head, and just behind him were Passepartout and the other two travelers, rescued from the Sioux.

They had met and fought the Indians ten miles south of Fort Kearney. Shortly before the detachment arrived, Passepartout and his companions had begun to struggle with their captors, three of whom the Frenchman had felled with his fists, when his master and the soldiers hastened up to their relief.

All were welcomed with joyful cries. Phileas Fogg distributed the reward he had promised to the soldiers, while Passepartout, not without reason, muttered to himself, "It must certainly be confessed that I cost my master dear!"

Fix, without saying a word, looked at Mr. Fogg, and it would have been difficult to analyze the thoughts which struggled within him. As for Aouda, she took her protector's hand and pressed it in her own, too much moved to speak.

Meanwhile, Passepartout was looking about for the train; he thought he should find it there, ready to start for Omaha, and he hoped that the time lost might be regained.

"The train! the train!" cried he.

"Gone," replied Fix.

"And when does the next train pass here?" said Phileas Fogg.

"Not till this evening."

"Ah!" returned the impassible gentleman quietly.

XXXI

In which Fix the detective considerably furthers the interests of Phileas Fogg

Phileas Fogg found himself twenty hours behind time. Passepartout, the involuntary cause of this delay, was desperate. He had ruined his master!

At this moment the detective approached Mr. Fogg, and, looking him intently in the face, said—

"Seriously, sir, are you in great haste?"

"Quite seriously."

"I have a purpose in asking," resumed Fix. "Is it absolutely necessary that you should be in New York on the 11th, before nine o'clock in the evening, the time that the steamer leaves for Liverpool?"

"It is absolutely necessary."

"And, if your journey had not been interrupted by these Indians, you would have reached New York on the morning of the 11th?"

"Yes; with eleven hours to spare before the steamer left."

"Good! you are therefore twenty hours behind. Twelve from twenty leaves eight. You must regain eight hours. Do you wish to try to do so?"

"On foot?" asked Mr. Fogg.

"No; on a sledge," replied Fix. "On a sledge with sails. A man has proposed such a method to me."

It was the man who had spoken to Fix during the night, and whose offer he had refused.

Phileas Fogg did not reply at once; but Fix having pointed out the man, who was walking up and down in front of the station, Mr. Fogg went up to him. An instant after, Mr. Fogg and the American, whose name was Mudge, entered a hut built just below the fort.

There Mr. Fogg examined a curious vehicle, a kind of frame on two long beams, a little raised in front like the runners of a sledge, and upon which there was room for five or six persons. A high mast was fixed on the frame, held firmly by metallic lashings, to which was attached a large brigantine sail. This mast held an iron stay upon which to hoist a jib-sail. Behind, a sort of rudder served to guide the vehicle. It was, in short, a sledge rigged like a sloop. During the winter, when the trains are blocked up by the snow, these sledges make extremely rapid journeys across the frozen plains from one station to another. Provided with more sail than a cutter, and with the wind behind them, they slip over the surface of the prairies with a speed equal if not superior to that of the express trains.

Mr. Fogg readily made a bargain with the owner of this land-craft. The wind was favorable, being fresh, and blowing from the west. The snow had hardened, and Mudge was very confident of being able to transport Mr. Fogg in a few hours to Omaha. Thence the trains eastward run frequently to Chicago and New York. It was not impossible that the lost time might yet be recovered; and such an opportunity was not to be rejected.

Not wishing to expose Aouda to the discomforts of traveling in the open air, Mr. Fogg proposed to leave her with Passepartout at Fort Kearney, the servant taking upon himself to escort her to Europe by a better route and under more favorable conditions. But Aouda refused to separate from Mr. Fogg, and Passepartout was delighted with her decision; for nothing could induce him to leave his master while Fix was with him.

It would be difficult to guess the detective's thoughts. Was his conviction shaken by Phileas Fogg's return, or did he still regard him as an exceedingly shrewd rascal, who, his journey around the world completed, would think himself absolutely safe in England? Perhaps Fix's opinion of Phileas Fogg was somewhat modified; but he was nevertheless resolved to do his duty, and to hasten the return of the whole party to England as much as possible.

At eight o'clock the sledge was ready to start. The passengers took their places on it, and wrapped themselves up closely in their traveling-cloaks. The two great sails were hoisted, and under the pressure of the wind the sledge slid over the hardened snow with a velocity of forty miles an hour.

The distance between Fort Kearney and Omaha, as the birds fly, is at most two hundred miles. If the wind held good, the distance might be traversed in five hours; if no accident happened the sledge might reach Omaha by one o'clock.

What a journey! The travelers, huddled close together, could not speak for the cold, intensified by the rapidity at which they were going. The sledge sped on as lightly as a boat over the waves. When the breeze came skimming the earth, the sledge seemed to be lifted off the ground by its sails. Mudge, who was at the rudder, kept in a straight line, and by a turn of his hand checked the lurches which the vehicle had a tendency to make. All the sails were up, and the jib was so arranged as not to screen the brigantine. A topmast was hoisted, and another jib, held out to the wind, added its force to the other sails. Although the speed could not be exactly estimated, the sledge could not be going at less than forty miles an hour.

"If nothing breaks," said Mudge, "we shall get there!"

Mr. Fogg had made it for Mudge's interest to reach Omaha within the time agreed on, by the offer of a handsome reward.

The prairie, across which the sledge was moving in a straight line, was as flat as a sea. It seemed like a vast frozen lake. The railroad which ran through this section ascended from the south-west to the north-west by Great Island, Columbus, an important Nebraska town, Schuyler, and Fremont, to Omaha. It followed throughout the right bank of the Platte River. The sledge, shortening this route, took a chord of the arc described by the railway. Mudge was not afraid of being stopped by the Platte River, because it was frozen. The road, then, was quite clear of obstacles, and Phileas Fogg had but two things to fear—an accident to the sledge, and a change or calm in the wind.

But the breeze, far from lessening its force, blew as if to bend the mast, which, however, the metallic lashings held firmly. These lashings, like the chords of a stringed instrument, resounded as if vibrated by a violin bow. The sledge slid along in the midst of a plaintively intense melody.

"Those chords give the fifth and the octave," said Mr. Fogg.

These were the only words he uttered during the journey. Aouda, cozily packed in furs and cloaks, was sheltered as much as possible from the attacks of the freezing wind. As for Passepartout, his face was as red as the sun's disc when it sets in the mist, and he laboriously inhaled the biting air. With his natural buoyancy of spirits, he began to hope again. They would reach New York on the evening, if not on the morning, of the 11th, and there were still some chances that it would be before the steamer sailed for Liverpool.

Passepartout even felt a strong desire to grasp his ally, Fix, by the hand. He remembered that it was the detective who procured the sledge, the only means of reaching Omaha in time; but, checked by some presentiment, he kept his usual reserve. One thing, however, Passepartout would never forget, and that was the sacrifice which Mr. Fogg had made, without hesitation, to rescue him from the Sioux. Mr. Fogg had risked his fortune and his life. No! His servant would never forget that!

While each of the party was absorbed in reflections so different, the sledge flew fast over the vast carpet of snow. The creeks it passed over were not perceived. Fields and streams disappeared under the uniform whiteness. The plain was absolutely deserted. Between the Union Pacific road and the branch which unites Kearney with Saint Joseph it formed a great uninhabited island. Neither village, station, nor fort appeared. From time to time they sped by some phantom-like tree, whose white skeleton twisted and rattled in the wind. Sometimes flocks of wild birds rose, or bands of gaunt, famished, ferocious prairie-wolves ran howling after the sledge. Passepartout, revolver in hand, held himself ready to fire on those which came too near. Had an accident then happened to the sledge, the travelers, attacked by these beasts, would have been in the most terrible danger; but it held on its even course, soon gained on the wolves, and ere long left the howling band at a safe distance behind.

About noon Mudge perceived by certain landmarks that he was crossing the Platte River. He said nothing, but he felt certain that he was now within twenty miles of Omaha. In less than an hour he left the rudder and furled his sails, whilst the sledge, carried forward by the great impetus the wind had given it, went on half a mile further with its sails unspread.

It stopped at last, and Mudge, pointing to a mass of roofs white with snow, said: "We have got there!"

Arrived! Arrived at the station which is in daily communication, by numerous trains, with the Atlantic seaboard!

Passepartout and Fix jumped off, stretched their stiffened limbs, and aided Mr. Fogg and the young woman to descend from the sledge. Phileas Fogg generously rewarded Mudge, whose hand Passepartout warmly grasped, and the party directed their steps to the Omaha railway station.

The Pacific Railroad proper finds its terminus at this important Nebraska town. Omaha is connected with Chicago by the Chicago and Rock Island Railroad, which runs directly east, and passes fifty stations.

A train was ready to start when Mr. Fogg and his party reached the station, and they only had time to get into the cars. They had seen nothing of Omaha; but Passepartout confessed to himself that this was not to be regretted, as they were not traveling to see the sights.

The train passed rapidly across the State of Iowa, by Council Bluffs, Des Moines, and Iowa City. During the night it crossed the Mississippi at Davenport, and by Rock Island entered Illinois. The next day, which was the 10th, at four in the evening, it reached Chicago, already risen from its ruins, and more proudly seated than ever on the borders of its beautiful Lake Michigan.

Nine hundred miles separated Chicago from New York; but trains are not wanting at Chicago. Mr. Fogg passed at once from one to the other, and the locomotive of the Pittsburg, Fort Wayne, and Chicago Railway left at full speed, as if it fully comprehended that that gentleman had no time to lose. It traversed Indiana, Ohio, Pennsylvania, and New Jersey like a flash, rushing through towns with antique names, some of which had streets and car-tracks, but as yet no houses. At last the Hudson came into view; and at a quarter-past eleven in the evening of the 11th, the train stopped in the station on the right bank of the river, before the very pier of the Cunard line.

The *China*, for Liverpool, had started three-quarters of an hour before!

XXXII

In which Phileas Fogg engages in a direct struggle with bad fortune

The *China*, in leaving, seemed to have carried off Phileas Fogg's last hope. None of the other steamers were able to serve his projects. The *Pereire*, of the French Transatlantic Company, whose admirable steamers are equal to any in speed and comfort, did not leave until the 14th; the Hamburg boats did not go directly to Liverpool or London, but to Havre; and the additional trip from Havre to Southampton would render Phileas Fogg's last efforts of no avail. The Inman steamer did not depart till the next day, and could not cross the Atlantic in time to save the wager.

Mr. Fogg learned all this in consulting his "Bradshaw," which gave him the daily movements of the transatlantic steamers.

Passepartout was crushed; it overwhelmed him to lose the boat by three-quarters of an hour. It was his fault, for, instead of helping his master, he had not ceased putting obstacles in his path! And when he recalled all the incidents of the tour, when he counted up the sums expended in pure loss and on his own account, when he thought that the immense stake, added to the heavy charges of this useless journey, would completely ruin Mr. Fogg, he overwhelmed himself with bitter self-accusations. Mr. Fogg, however, did not reproach him; and, on leaving the Cunard pier, only said: "We will consult about what is best to-morrow. Come."

The party crossed the Hudson in the Jersey City ferry-boat, and drove in a carriage to the St. Nicholas Hotel, on Broadway. Rooms were engaged, and the night passed, briefly to Phileas Fogg, who slept profoundly, but very long to Aouda and the others, whose agitation did not permit them to rest.

The next day was the 12th of December. From seven in the morning of the 12th, to a quarter before nine in the evening of the 21st, there were nine days, thirteen hours, and forty-five minutes. If Phileas Fogg had left in the *China,* one of the fastest steamers on the Atlantic, he would have reached Liverpool, and then London, within the period agreed upon.

Mr. Fogg left the hotel alone, after giving Passepartout instructions to await his return, and inform Aouda to be ready at an instant's notice. He proceeded to the banks of the Hudson, and looked about among the vessels moored or anchored in the river, for any that were about to depart. Several had departure signals, and were preparing to put to sea at morning tide; for in this immense and admirable port there is not one day in a hundred that vessels do not set out for every quarter of the globe. But they were mostly sailing vessels, of which, of course, Phileas Fogg could make no use.

He seemed about to give up all hope, when he espied, anchored at the Battery, a cable's length off at most, a trading vessel, with a screw, well-shaped, whose funnel, puffing a cloud of smoke, indicated that she was getting ready for departure.

Phileas Fogg hailed a boat, got into it, and soon found himself on board the *Henrietta,* iron-hulled, wood-built above. He ascended to the deck, and asked for the captain, who forthwith presented himself. He was a man of fifty, a sort of sea-wolf, with big eyes, a complexion of oxidized copper, red hair and thick neck, and a growling voice.

"The captain?" asked Mr. Fogg.

"I am the captain."

"I am Phileas Fogg, of London."

"And I am Andrew Speedy, of Cardiff."

"You are going to put to sea?"

"In an hour."

"You are bound for——"

"Bordeaux."

"And your cargo?"

"No freight. Going in ballast."

"Have you any passengers?"

"No passengers. Never have passengers. Too much in the way."

"Is your vessel a swift one?"

"Between eleven and twelve knots. The *Henrietta,* well known."

"Will you carry me and three other persons to Liverpool?"

"To Liverpool? Why not to China?"

"I said Liverpool."

"No!"

"No?"

"No. I am setting out for Bordeaux, and shall go to Bordeaux."

"Money is no object?"

"None."

The captain spoke in a tone which did not admit of a reply.

"But the owners of the *Henrietta*——" resumed Phileas Fogg.

"The owners are myself," replied the captain. "The vessel belongs to me."

"I will freight it for you."

"No."

"I will buy it of you."

"No."

Phileas Fogg did not betray the least disappointment; but the situation was a grave one. It was not at New York as at Hong Kong, nor with the captain of the *Henrietta* as with the captain of the *Tankedere.* Up to this time money had smoothed away every obstacle. Now money failed.

Still, some means must be found to cross the Atlantic on a boat, unless by balloon—which would have been venturesome, besides not being capable of being put in practice. It seemed that Phileas Fogg had an idea, for he said to the captain, "Well, will you carry me to Bordeaux?"

"No, not if you paid me two hundred dollars."

"I offer you two thousand."

"Apiece?"

"Apiece."

"And there are four of you?"

"Four."

Captain Speedy began to scratch his head. There were eight thousand dollars to gain, without changing his route; for which it was well worth conquering the repugnance he had for all kinds of passengers. Besides, passengers at two thousand dollars are no longer passengers, but valuable merchandise. "I start at nine o'clock," said Captain Speedy, simply. "Are you and your party ready?"

"We will be on board at nine o'clock," replied, no less simply, Mr. Fogg.

It was half-past eight. To disembark from the *Henrietta,* jump into a hack, hurry to the St. Nicholas, and return with Aouda, Passepartout, and even the inseparable Fix, was the work of a brief time, and was performed by

Mr. Fogg with the coolness which never abandoned him. They were on board when the *Henrietta* made ready to weigh anchor.

When Passepartout heard what this last voyage was going to cost, he uttered a prolonged "Oh!" which extended throughout his vocal gamut.

As for Fix, he said to himself that the Bank of England would certainly not come out of this affair well indemnified. When they reached England, even if Mr. Fogg did not throw some handfuls of bank-bills into the sea, more than seven thousand pounds would have been spent!

XXXIII

In which Phileas Fogg shows himself equal to the occasion

An hour after, the *Henrietta* passed the lighthouse which marks the entrance of the Hudson, turned the point of Sandy Hook, and put to sea. During the day she skirted Long Island, passed Fire Island, and directed her course rapidly eastward.

At noon the next day, a man mounted the bridge to ascertain the vessel's position. It might be thought that this was Captain Speedy. Not the least in the world. It was Phileas Fogg, Esquire. As for Captain Speedy, he was shut up in his cabin under lock and key, and was uttering loud cries, which signified an anger at once pardonable and excessive.

What had happened was very simple. Phileas Fogg wished to go to Liverpool, but the captain would not carry him there. Then Phileas Fogg had taken passage for Bordeaux, and, during the thirty hours he had been on board, had so shrewdly managed with his bank-notes that the sailors and stokers, who were only an occasional crew, and were not on the best terms with the captain, went over to him in a body. This was why Phileas Fogg was in command instead of Captain Speedy; why the captain was a prisoner in his cabin; and why, in short, the *Henrietta* was directing her course toward Liverpool. It was very clear, to see Mr. Fogg manage the craft, that he had been a sailor.

How the adventure ended will be seen anon. Aouda was anxious, though she said nothing. As for Passepartout, he thought Mr. Fogg's maneuver simply glorious. The captain had said "between eleven and twelve knots," and the *Henrietta* confirmed his prediction.

If, then—for there were "ifs" still—the sea did not become too boisterous, if the wind did not veer around to the east, if no accident happened to the boat or its machinery, the *Henrietta* might cross the three thousand miles from New York to Liverpool in the nine days, between the 12th and the 21st of December. It is true that, once arrived, the affair on board the *Henrietta*, added to that of the Bank of England, might create more difficulties for Mr. Fogg than he imagined or could desire.

During the first days, they went along smoothly enough. The sea was not very unpropitious, the wind seemed stationary in the north-east, the sails were hoisted, and the *Henrietta* ploughed across the waves like a real transatlantic steamer.

Passepartout was delighted. His master's last exploit, the consequences of which he ignored, enchanted him. Never had the crew seen so jolly and dexterous a fellow. He formed warm friendships with the sailors, and amazed them with his acrobatic feats. He thought they managed the vessel like gentlemen, and that the stokers fired up like heroes. His loquacious good-humor infected every one. He had forgotten the past, its vexations and delays. He only thought of the end, so nearly accomplished; and sometimes he boiled over with impatience, as if heated by the furnaces of the *Henrietta*. Often, also, the worthy fellow revolved around Fix, looking at him with a keen, distrustful eye; but he did not speak to him, for their old intimacy no longer existed.

Fix, it must be confessed, understood nothing of what was going on. The conquest of the *Henrietta*, the bribery of the crew, Fogg managing the boat like a skilled seaman, amazed and confused him. He did not know what to think. For, after all, a man who began by stealing fifty-five thousand pounds might end by stealing a vessel; and Fix was not unnaturally inclined to conclude that the *Henrietta*, under Fogg's command, was not going to Liverpool at all, but to some part of the world where the robber, turned into a pirate, would quietly put himself in safety. The conjecture was at least a plausible one, and the detective began to seriously regret that he had embarked in the affair.

As for Captain Speedy, he continued to howl and growl in his cabin; and Passepartout, whose duty it was to carry him his meals, courageous as he was, took the greatest precautions. Mr. Fogg did not seem even to know that there was a captain on board.

On the 13th they passed the edge of the Banks of Newfoundland, a dangerous locality; during the winter, especially, there are frequent fogs and heavy gales of wind. Ever since the evening before, the barometer, suddenly falling, had indicated an approaching change in the atmosphere; and during the night the temperature varied, the cold became sharper, and the wind veered to the south-east.

This was a misfortune. Mr. Fogg, in order not to deviate from his course, furled his sails and increased the force of the steam; but the vessel's speed slackened, owing to the state of the sea, the long waves of which broke against the stern. She pitched violently, and this retarded her progress. The breeze little by little swelled into a tempest, and it was to be feared that the *Henrietta* might not be able to maintain herself upright on the waves.

Passepartout's visage darkened with the skies, and for two days the poor fellow experienced constant fright. But Phileas Fogg was a bold mariner, and knew how to maintain headway against the sea; and he kept on his course, without even decreasing his steam. The *Henrietta,* when she could not rise upon the waves, crossed them, swamping her deck, but passing safely. Sometimes the screw rose out of the water, beating its protruding end, when a mountain of water raised the stern above the waves; but the craft always kept straight ahead.

The wind, however, did not grow as boisterous as might have been feared; it was not one of those tempests which burst, and rush on with a speed of ninety miles an hour. It continued fresh, but, unhappily, it remained obstinately in the south-east, rendering the sails useless.

The 16th of December was the seventy-fifth day since Phileas Fogg's departure from London, and the *Henrietta* had not yet been seriously delayed. Half of the voyage was almost accomplished, and the worst localities had been passed. In summer, success would have been well-nigh certain. In winter, they were at the mercy of the bad season. Passepartout said nothing; but he cherished hope in secret, and comforted himself with the reflection that, if the wind failed them, they might still count on the steam.

On this day the engineer came on deck, went up to Mr. Fogg, and began to speak earnestly with him. Without knowing why—it was a presentiment, perhaps—Passepartout became vaguely uneasy. He would have given one of his ears to hear with the other what the engineer was saying.

He finally managed to catch a few words, and was sure he heard his master say, "You are certain of what you tell me?"

"Certain, sir," replied the engineer. "You must remember that, since we started, we have kept up hot fires in all our furnaces, and though we had coal enough to go on short steam from New York to Bordeaux, we haven't enough to go with all steam from New York to Liverpool.

"I will consider," replied Mr. Fogg.

Passepartout understood it all; he was seized with mortal anxiety. The coal was giving out! "Ah, if my master can get over that," muttered he, "he'll be a famous man!" He could not help imparting to Fix what he had overheard.

"Then you believe that we really are going to Liverpool?"

"Of course."

"Ass!" replied the detective, shrugging his shoulders and turning on his heel.

Passepartout was on the point of vigorously resenting the epithet, the reason of which he could not for the life of him comprehend; but he reflected that the unfortunate Fix was probably very much disappointed and humiliated in his self-esteem, after having so awkwardly followed a false scent around the world, and refrained.

And now what course would Phileas Fogg adopt? It was difficult to imagine. Nevertheless he seemed to have decided upon one, for that evening he sent for the engineer, and said to him, "Feed all the fires until the coal is exhausted."

A few moments after, the funnel of the *Henrietta* vomited forth torrents of smoke. The vessel continued to proceed with all steam on; but on the 18th, the engineer, as he had predicted, announced that the coal would give out in the course of the day.

"Do not let the fires go down," replied Mr. Fogg. "Keep them up to the last. Let the valves be filled."

Toward noon Phileas Fogg, having ascertained their position, called Passepartout, and ordered him to go for Captain Speedy. It was as if the honest fellow had been commanded to unchain a tiger. He went to the poop, saying to himself, "He will be like a madman!"

In a few moments, with cries and oaths, a bomb appeared on the poop-deck. The bomb was Captain Speedy. It was clear that he was on the point of bursting. "Where are we?" were the first words his anger permitted him to utter. Had the poor man been apoplectic, he could never have recovered from his paroxysm of wrath.

"Where are we?" he repeated, with purple face.

"Seven hundred and seven miles from Liverpool," replied Mr. Fogg, with imperturbable calmness.

"Pirate!" cried Captain Speedy.

"I have sent for you, sir—"

"Pickaroon!"

"—Sir," continued Mr. Fogg, "to ask you to sell me your vessel."

"No! By all the devils, no!"

"But I shall be obliged to burn her."

"Burn the *Henrietta!*"

"Yes; at least the upper part of her. The coal has given out."

"Burn my vessel!" cried Captain Speedy, who could scarcely pronounce the words. "A vessel worth fifty thousand dollars!"

"Here are sixty thousand," replied Phileas Fogg, handing the captain a roll of bank-bills. This had a prodigious effect on Andrew Speedy. An American can scarcely remain unmoved at the sight of sixty thousand dollars. The captain forgot in an instant his anger, his imprisonment, and all his grudges against his passenger. The *Henrietta* was twenty years old; it was a great bargain. The bomb would not go off after all. Mr. Fogg had taken away the match.

"And I shall still have the iron hull," said the captain in a softer tone.

"The iron hull and the engine. Is it agreed?"

"Agreed."

And Andrew Speedy, seizing the bank-notes, counted them and consigned them to his pocket.

During this colloquy, Passepartout was as white as a sheet, and Fix seemed on the point of having an apoplectic fit. Nearly twenty thousand pounds had been expended, and Fogg left the hull and engine to the captain, that is, near the whole value of the craft! It was true, however, that fifty-five thousand pounds had been stolen from the bank.

When Andrew Speedy had pocketed the money, Mr. Fogg said to him, "Don't let this astonish you, sir. You must know that I shall lose twenty thousand pounds, unless I arrive in London by a quarter before nine on the evening of the 21st of December. I missed the steamer at New York, and as you refused to take me to Liverpool——"

"And I did well!" cried Andrew Speedy; "for I have gained at least forty thousand dollars by it!" He added, more sedately, "Do you know one thing, Captain——"

"Fogg."

"Captain Fogg, you've got something of the Yankee about you."

And, having paid his passenger what he considered a high compliment, he was going away, when Mr. Fogg said, "The vessel now belongs to me?"

"Certainly, from the keel to the truck of the masts—all the wood, that is."

"Very well. Have the interior seats, bunks, and frames pulled down, and burn them."

It was necessary to have dry wood to keep the steam up to the adequate pressure, and on that day the poop, cabins, bunks, and the spare deck were sacrificed. On the next day, the 19th of December, the masts, rafts, and spars were burned; the crew worked lustily, keeping up the fires. Passepartout hewed, cut, and sawed away with all his might. There was a perfect rage for demolition.

The railings, fittings, the greater part of the deck, and top sides disappeared on the 20th, and the *Henrietta* was now only a flat hulk. But on this day they sighted the Irish coast and Fastnet Light. By ten in the evening they were passing Queenstown. Phileas Fogg had only twenty-four hours more in which to get to London; that length of time was necessary to reach Liverpool, with all steam on. And the steam was about to give out altogether!

"Sir," said Captain Speedy, who was now deeply interested in Mr. Fogg's project, "I really commiserate you. Everything is against you. We are only opposite Queenstown."

"Ah," said Mr. Fogg, "is that place where we see the lights Queenstown?"

"Yes."

"Can we enter the harbor?"

"Not under three hours. Only at high tide."

"Stay," replied Mr. Fogg calmly, without betraying in his features that by a supreme inspiration he was about to attempt once more to conquer ill-fortune.

Queenstown is the Irish port at which the transatlantic steamers stop to put off the mails. These mails are carried to Dublin by express trains always held in readiness to start; from Dublin they are sent on to Liverpool by the most rapid boats, and thus gain twelve hours on the Atlantic steamers.

Phileas Fogg counted on gaining twelve hours in the same way. Instead of arriving at Liverpool the next evening by the *Henrietta*, he would be there by noon, and would therefore have time to reach London before a quarter before nine in the evening.

The *Henrietta* entered Queenstown Harbor at one o'clock in the morning, it then being high tide; and Phileas Fogg, after being grasped heartily by the hand by Captain Speedy, left that gentleman on the leveled hulk of his craft, which was still worth half what he had sold it for.

The party went on shore at once. Fix was greatly tempted to arrest Mr. Fogg on the spot; but he did not. Why? What struggle was going on within him? Had he changed his mind about "his man"? Did he understand that he had made a grave mistake? He did not, however, abandon Mr. Fogg. They all got upon the train, which was just ready to start, at half-past one; at dawn of day they were in Dublin; and they lost no time in embarking on a steamer which, disdaining to rise upon the waves, invariably cut through them.

Phileas Fogg at last disembarked on the Liverpool quay, at twenty minutes before twelve, December 21st. He was only six hours distant from London.

But at this moment Fix came up, put his hand upon Mr. Fogg's shoulder and, showing his warrant, said, "You are really Phileas Fogg?"

"I am."

"I arrest you in the Queen's name!"

XXXIV

In which Phileas Fogg at last reaches London

Phileas Fogg was in prison. He had been shut up in the custom-house, and he was to be transferred to London the next day.

Passepartout, when he saw his master arrested, would have fallen upon Fix had he not been held back by some policemen. Aouda was thunderstruck at the suddenness of an event which she could not understand. Passepartout explained to her how it was that the honest and courageous Fogg was arrested as a robber. The young woman's heart revolted against so heinous a charge, and when she saw that she could attempt or do nothing to save her protector, she wept bitterly.

As for Fix, he had arrested Mr. Fogg because it was his duty, whether Mr. Fogg were guilty or not.

The thought then struck Passepartout, that he was the cause of this new misfortune! Had he not concealed Fix's errand from his master? When Fix revealed his true character and purpose, why had he not told Mr. Fogg? If the latter had been warned, he would no doubt have given Fix proof of his innocence, and satisfied him of his mistake; at least, Fix would not have continued his journey at the expense and on the heels of his master, only to arrest him the moment he set foot on English soil. Passepartout wept till he was blind, and felt like blowing his brains out.

Aouda and he had remained, despite the cold, under the portico of the custom-house. Neither wished to leave the place; both were anxious to see Mr. Fogg again.

That gentleman was really ruined, and that at the moment when he was about to attain his end. This arrest was fatal. Having arrived at Liverpool at twenty minutes before twelve on the 21st of December, he had till a quarter before nine that evening to reach the Reform Club, that is, nine hours and a quarter; the journey from Liverpool to London was six hours.

If anyone, at this moment, had entered the custom-house, he would have found Mr. Fogg seated, motionless, calm, and without apparent anger, upon a wooden bench. He was not, it is true, resigned; but this last blow failed to force him into an outward betrayal of any emotion. Was he being devoured by one of those secret rages, all the more terrible because contained, and which only burst forth, with an irresistible force, at the last moment? No one could tell. There he sat, calmly waiting—for what? Did he still cherish hope? Did he still believe, now that the door of this prison was closed upon him, that he would succeed?

However that may have been, Mr. Fogg carefully put his watch upon the table, and observed its advancing hands. Not a word escaped his lips, but his look was singularly set and stern. The situation, in any event, was a terrible one, and might be thus stated: If Phileas Fogg was honest he was ruined; if he was a knave, he was caught.

Did escape occur to him? Did he examine to see if there were any practicable outlet from his prison? Did he think of escaping from it? Possibly; for once he walked slowly around the room. But the door was locked, and the window heavily barred with iron rods. He sat down again, and drew his journal from his pocket. On the line where these words were written, "December 21st, Saturday, Liverpool," he added, "80th day, 11:40 A.M.," and waited.

The custom-house clock struck one. Mr. Fogg observed that his watch was two hours too fast.

Two hours! Admitting that he was at this moment taking an express train, he could reach London and the Reform Club by a quarter before nine, P.M. His forehead slightly wrinkled.

At thirty-three minutes past two he heard a singular noise outside, then a hasty opening of doors. Passepartout's voice was audible, and immediately after that of Fix. Phileas Fogg's eyes brightened for an instant.

The door swung open, and he saw Passepartout, Aouda, and Fix, who hurried toward him.

Fix was out of breath, and his hair was in disorder. He could not speak. "Sir," he stammered, "Sir—forgive me—a most—unfortunate resemblance—robber arrested three days ago—you—are free!"

Phileas Fogg was free! He walked to the detective, looked him steadily in the face, and with the only rapid motion he had ever made in his life, or which he ever would make, drew back his arms, and with the precision of a machine, knocked Fix down.

"Well hit!" cried Passepartout. "Parbleu! that's what you might call a good application of English fists!"

Fix, who found himself on the floor, did not utter a word. He had only received his deserts. Mr. Fogg, Aouda, and Passepartout left the custom-house without delay, got into a cab, and in a few moments descended at the station.

Phileas Fogg asked if there was an express train about to leave for London. It was forty minutes past two. The express train had left thirty-five minutes before.

Phileas Fogg then ordered a special train.

There were several rapid locomotives on hand; but the railway arrangements did not permit the special train to leave until three o'clock.

At that hour Phileas Fogg, having stimulated the engineer by the offer of a generous reward, at last set out toward London with Aouda and his faithful servant.

It was necessary to make the journey in five hours and a half; and this would have been easy on a clear road throughout. But there were forced delays, and when Mr. Fogg stepped from the train at the terminus, all the clocks in London were striking ten minutes before nine.*

Having made the tour of the world, he was behindhand five minutes. He had lost the wager!

XXXV

In which Phileas Fogg does not have to repeat his orders to Passepartout twice

The dwellers in Saville Row would have been surprised, the next day, if they had been told that Phileas Fogg had returned home. His doors and windows were still closed; no appearance of change was visible.

After leaving the station, Mr. Fogg gave Passepartout instructions to purchase some provisions, and quietly went to his domicile.

He bore his misfortune with his habitual tranquillity. Ruined! And by the blundering of the detective! After having steadily traversed that long journey, overcome a hundred obstacles, braved many dangers, and still found time to do some good on his way, to fail near the goal by a sudden event which he could not have foreseen, and against which he was unarmed; it was terrible! But a few pounds were left of the large sum he had carried with him. There only remained of his fortune the twenty thousand pounds deposited at the Barings, and this amount he owed to his friends of the Reform Club. So great had been the expense of his tour, that, even had he won, it would not have enriched him; and it is probable that he had not sought to enrich himself, being a man who rather laid wagers for honor's sake than for the stake proposed. But this wager totally ruined him.

Mr. Fogg's course, however, was fully decided upon; he knew what remained for him to do.

A room in the house in Saville Row was set apart for Aouda, who was overwhelmed with grief at her protector's misfortune. From the words which Mr. Fogg dropped, she saw that he was meditating some serious project.

Knowing that Englishmen governed by a fixed idea sometimes resort to

* A somewhat remarkable eccentricity on the part of the London clocks!—Translator.

the desperate expedient of suicide, Passepartout kept a narrow watch upon his master, though he carefully concealed the appearance of so doing.

First of all, the worthy fellow had gone up to his room, and had extinguished the gas-burner, which had been burning for eighty days. He had found in the letter-box a bill from the gas company, and he thought it more than time to put a stop to this expense, which he had been doomed to bear.

The night passed. Mr. Fogg went to bed, but did he sleep? Aouda did not once close her eyes. Passepartout watched all night, like a faithful dog, at his master's door.

Mr. Fogg called him in the morning, and told him to get Aouda's breakfast, and a cup of tea and a chop for himself. He desired Aouda to excuse him from breakfast and dinner, as his time would be absorbed all day in putting his affairs to rights. In the evening he would ask permission to have a few moments' conversation with the young lady.

Passepartout, having received his orders, had nothing to do but obey them. He looked at his imperturbable master, and could scarcely bring his mind to leave him. His heart was full, and his conscience tortured by remorse; for he accused himself more bitterly than ever of being the cause of the irretrievable disaster. Yes! if he had warned Mr. Fogg, and had betrayed Fix's projects to him, his master would certainly not have given the detective passage to Liverpool, and then——

Passepartout could hold in no longer.

"My master! Mr. Fogg!" he cried, "why do you not curse me? It was my fault that——"

"I blame no one," returned Phileas Fogg, with perfect calmness. "Go!"

Passepartout left the room, and went to find Aouda, to whom he delivered his master's message.

"Madam," he added, "I can do nothing myself—nothing! I have no influence over my master; but you, perhaps——"

"What influence could I have?" replied Aouda. "Mr. Fogg is influenced by no one. Has he ever understood that my gratitude to him is overflowing? Has he ever read my heart? My friend, he must not be left alone an instant! You say he is going to speak with me this evening?"

"Yes, madam; probably to arrange for your protection and comfort in England."

"We shall see," replied Aouda, becoming suddenly pensive.

Throughout this day (Sunday) the house in Saville Row was as if uninhabited, and Phileas Fogg, for the first time since he had lived in that house, did not set out for his club when Westminster clock struck half-past eleven.

Why should he present himself at the Reform? His friends no longer expected him there. As Phileas Fogg had not appeared in the saloon on the evening before (Saturday, the 21st of December, at a quarter before nine), he had lost his wager. It was not even necessary that he should go to his bankers for the twenty thousand pounds; for his antagonists already had his check in their hands, and they had only to fill it out and send it to the Barings to have the amount transferred to their credit.

Mr. Fogg, therefore, had no reason for going out, and so he remained at home. He shut himself up in his room, and busied himself putting his affairs in order. Passepartout continually ascended and descended the stairs. The hours were long for him. He listened at his master's door, and looked through the keyhole, as if he had a perfect right so to do, and as if he feared that something terrible might happen at any moment. Sometimes he thought of Fix, but no longer in anger. Fix, like all the world, had been mistaken in Phileas Fogg, and had only done his duty in tracking and arresting him; while he, Passepartout——. This thought haunted him, and he never ceased cursing his miserable folly.

Finding himself too wretched to remain alone, he knocked at Aouda's door, went into her room, seated himself, without speaking, in a corner, and looked ruefully at the young woman. Aouda was still pensive.

About half-past seven in the evening Mr. Fogg sent to know if Aouda would receive him, and in a few moments he found himself alone with her.

Phileas Fogg took a chair, and sat down near the fireplace, opposite Aouda. No emotion was visible on his face. Fogg returned was exactly the Fogg who had gone away; there was the same calm, the same impassibility.

He sat several minutes without speaking; then, bending his eyes on Aouda, "Madam," said he, "will you pardon me for bringing you to England?"

"I, Mr. Fogg!" replied Aouda, checking the pulsations of her heart.

"Please let me finish," returned Mr. Fogg. "When I decided to bring you far away from the country which was so unsafe for you, I was rich, and counted on putting a portion of my fortune at your disposal; then your existence would have been free and happy. But now I am ruined."

"I know it, Mr. Fogg," replied Aouda; "and I ask you in my turn, will you forgive me for having followed you, and—who knows?—for having, perhaps, delayed you, and thus contributed to your ruin?"

"Madam, you could not remain in India, and your safety could only be assured by bringing you to such a distance that your persecutors could not take you."

"So, Mr. Fogg," resumed Aouda, "not content with rescuing me from a terrible death, you thought yourself bound to secure my comfort in a foreign land?"

"Yes, madam; but circumstances have been against me. Still, I beg to place the little I have left at your service."

"But what will become of you, Mr. Fogg?"

"As for me, madam," replied the gentleman, coldly, "I have need of nothing."

"But how do you look upon the fate, sir, which awaits you?"

"As I am in the habit of doing."

"At least," said Aouda, "want should not overtake a man like you. Your friends——"

"I have no friends, madam."

"Your relatives——"

"I have no longer any relatives."

"I pity you, then, Mr. Fogg, for solitude is a sad thing, with no heart to which to confide your griefs. They say, though, that misery itself, shared by two sympathetic souls, may be borne with patience."

"They say so, madam."

"Mr. Fogg," said Aouda, rising and seizing his hand, "do you wish at once a kinswoman and friend? Will you have me for your wife?"

Mr. Fogg, at this, rose in his turn. There was an unwonted light in his eyes, and a slight trembling of his lips. Aouda looked into his face. The sincerity, rectitude, firmness, and sweetness of this soft glance of a noble woman, who could dare all to save him to whom she owed all, at first astonished, then penetrated him. He shut his eyes for an instant, as if to avoid her look. When he opened them again, "I love you!" he said, simply. "Yes, by all that is holiest, I love you, and I am entirely yours!"

"Ah!" cried Aouda, pressing his hand to her heart.

Passepartout was summoned and appeared immediately. Mr. Fogg still held Aouda's hand in his own; Passepartout understood, and his big, round face became as radiant as the tropical sun at its zenith.

Mr. Fogg asked him if it was not too late to notify the Reverend Samuel Wilson, of Marylebone Parish, that evening.

Passepartout smiled his most genial smile, and said, "Never too late."

It was five minutes past eight.

"Will it be for to-morrow, Monday?"

"For to-morrow, Monday," said Mr. Fogg, turning to Aouda.

"Yes; for to-morrow, Monday," she replied.

Passepartout hurried off as fast as his legs could carry him.

XXXVI

In which Phileas Fogg's name is once more at a premium on 'Change

It is time to relate what a change took place in English public opinion, when it transpired that the real bank-robber, a certain James Strand, had been arrested, on the 17th of December, at Edinburgh. Three days before, Phileas Fogg had been a criminal, who was being desperately followed up by the police; now he was an honorable gentleman, mathematically pursuing his eccentric journey around the world.

The papers resumed their discussion about the wager; all those who had laid bets, for or against him, revived their interest, as if by magic; the "Phileas Fogg bonds" again became negotiable, and many new wagers were made. Phileas Fogg's name was once more at a premium on 'Change.

His five friends of the Reform Club passed these three days in a state of feverish suspense. Would Phileas Fogg, whom they had forgotten, reappear before their eyes! Where was he at this moment? The 17th of December, the day of James Strand's arrest, was the seventy-sixth since Phileas Fogg's departure, and no news of him had been received. Was he dead? Had he abandoned the effort, or was he continuing his journey along the route agreed upon? And would he appear on Saturday, the 21st of December, at a quarter before nine in the evening, on the threshold of the Reform Club saloon?

The anxiety in which, for three days, London society existed, cannot be described. Telegrams were sent to America and Asia for news of Phileas

Fogg. Messengers were dispatched to the house in Saville Row morning and evening. No news. The police were ignorant of what had become of the detective, Fix, who had so unfortunately followed up a false scent. Bets increased, nevertheless, in number and value. Phileas Fogg, like a race-horse, was drawing near his last turning-point. The bonds were quoted, no longer at a hundred below par, but at twenty, at ten, and at five; and paralytic old Lord Albemarle bet even in his favor.

A great crowd was collected in Pall Mall and the neighboring streets on Saturday evening; it seemed like a multitude of brokers permanently established around the Reform Club. Circulation was impeded, and everywhere disputes, discussions, and financial transactions were going on. The police had great difficulty in keeping back the crowd, and as the hour when Phileas Fogg was due approached, the excitement rose to its highest pitch.

The five antagonists of Phileas Fogg had met in the great saloon of the club. John Sullivan and Samuel Fallentin, the bankers, Andrew Stuart, the engineer, Gauthier Ralph, the director of the Bank of England, and Thomas Flanagan, the brewer, one and all waited anxiously.

When the clock indicated twenty minutes past eight, Andrew Stuart got up, saying, "Gentlemen, in twenty minutes the time agreed upon between Mr. Fogg and ourselves will have expired."

"What time did the last train arrive from Liverpool?" asked Thomas Flanagan.

"At twenty-three minutes past seven," replied Gauthier Ralph; "and the next does not arrive till ten minutes after twelve."

"Well, gentlemen," resumed Andrew Stuart, "if Phileas Fogg had come in the seven twenty-three train, he would have got here by this time. We can, therefore, regard the bet as won."

"Wait; don't let us be too hasty," replied Samuel Fallentin. "You know that Mr. Fogg is very eccentric. His punctuality is well known; he never arrives too soon, or too late; and I should not be surprised if he appeared before us at the last minute."

"Why," said Andrew Stuart nervously, "if I should see him, I should not believe it was he."

"The fact is," resumed Thomas Flanagan, "Mr. Fogg's project was absurdly foolish. Whatever his punctuality, he could not prevent the delays which were certain to occur; and a delay of only two or three days would be fatal to his tour."

"Observe, too," added John Sullivan, "that we have received no intelligence from him, though there are telegraphic lines all along his route."

"He has lost, gentlemen," said Andrew Stuart—"he has a hundred times lost! You know, besides, that the *China*—the only steamer he could have taken from New York to get here in time—arrived yesterday. I have seen a list of the passengers, and the name of Phileas Fogg is not among them. Even if we admit that fortune has favored him, he can scarcely have reached America. I think he will be at least twenty days behindhand, and that Lord Albemarle will lose a cool five thousand."

"It is clear," replied Gauthier Ralph; "and we have nothing to do but to present Mr. Fogg's check at the Barings to-morrow."

At this moment, the hands of the club clock pointed to twenty minutes to nine.

"Five minutes more," said Andrew Stuart.

The five gentlemen looked at each other. Their anxiety was becoming intense; but, not wishing to betray it, they readily assented to Mr. Fallentin's proposal of a rubber.

"I wouldn't give up my four thousand of the bet," said Andrew Stuart, as he took his seat, "for three thousand nine hundred and ninety-nine."

The clock indicated eighteen minutes to nine.

The players took up their cards, but could not keep their eyes off the clock. Certainly, however secure they felt, minutes had never seemed so long to them!

"Seventeen minutes to nine," said Thomas Flanagan, as he cut the cards which Ralph handed to him.

Then there was a moment of silence. The great saloon was perfectly quiet; but the murmurs of the crowd outside were heard, with now and then a shrill cry. The pendulum beat the seconds, which each player eagerly counted, as he listened, with mathematical regularity.

"Sixteen minutes to nine!" said John Sullivan, in a voice which betrayed his emotion.

One minute more, and the wager would be won. Andrew Stuart and his partners suspended their game. They left their cards, and counted the seconds.

At the fortieth second, nothing. At the fiftieth, still nothing.

At the fifty-fifth, a loud cry was heard in the street, followed by applause, hurrahs, and some fierce growls.

The players rose from their seats.

At the fifty-seventh second the door of the saloon opened; and the pendulum had not beat the sixtieth second when Phileas Fogg appeared, followed by an excited crowd who had forced their way through the club doors, and in his calm voice, said, "Here I am, gentlemen!"

XXXVII

In which it is shown that Phileas Fogg gained nothing by his tour around the world, unless it were happiness

Yes; Phileas Fogg in person.

The reader will remember that at five minutes past eight in the evening about five and twenty hours after the arrival of the travelers in London—Passepartout had been sent by his master to engage the services of the Reverend Samuel Wilson in a certain marriage ceremony, which was to take place the next day.

Passepartout went on his errand enchanted. He soon reached the clergyman's house, but found him not at home. Passepartout waited a good twenty minutes, and when he left the reverend gentleman, it was thirty-five minutes past eight. But in what a state he was! With his hair in disorder, and without his hat, he ran along the street as never man was seen to run before, overturning passers-by, rushing over the side-walk like a waterspout.

In three minutes he was in Saville Row again, and staggered breathlessly into Mr. Fogg's room.

He could not speak.

"What is the matter?" asked Mr. Fogg.

"My master!" gasped Passepartout—"marriage—impossible——"

"Impossible?"

"Impossible—for to-morrow."

"Why so?"

"Because to-morrow—is Sunday!"

"Monday," replied Mr. Fogg.

"No—to-day—is Saturday."

"Saturday? Impossible!"

"Yes, yes, yes, yes!" cried Passepartout. "You have made a mistake of one day! We arrived twenty-four hours ahead of time; but there are only ten minutes left!"

Passepartout had seized his master by the collar, and was dragging him along with irresistible force.

Phileas Fogg, thus kidnapped, without having time to think, left his house, jumped into a cab, promised a hundred pounds to the cabman, and, having run over two dogs and overturned five carriages, reached the Reform Club.

The clock indicated a quarter before nine when he appeared in the great saloon.

Phileas Fogg had accomplished the journey around the world in eighty days!

Phileas Fogg had won his wager of twenty thousand pounds!

How was it that a man so exact and fastidious could have made this error of a day? How came he to think that he had arrived in London on Saturday, the twenty-first day of December, when it was really Friday, the twentieth, the seventy-ninth day only from his departure?

The cause of the error is very simple.

Phileas Fogg had, without suspecting it, gained one day on his journey, and this merely because he had traveled constantly *eastward*; he would, on the contrary, have lost a day had he gone in the opposite direction, that is, *westward*.

In journeying eastward he had gone toward the sun, and the days therefore diminished for him as many times four minutes as he crossed degrees in this direction. There are three hundred and sixty degrees, multiplied by four minutes, gives precisely twenty-four hours—that is, the day unconsciously gained. In other words, while Phileas Fogg, going eastward, saw the sun pass the meridian *eighty* times, his friends in London only saw it pass the meridian *seventy-nine* times. This is why they awaited him at the Reform Club on Saturday, and not Sunday, as Mr. Fogg thought.

And Passepartout's famous family watch, which had always kept London time, would have betrayed this fact, if it had marked the days as well as the hours and minutes!

Phileas Fogg, then, had won the twenty thousand pounds; but as he had spent nearly nineteen thousand on the way, the pecuniary gain was small. His object was, however, to be victorious, and not to win money. He divided the one thousand pounds that remained between Passepartout and the unfortunate Fix, against whom he cherished no grudge. He deducted, however, from Passepartout's share the cost of the gas which had burned in his room for nineteen hundred and twenty hours, for the sake of regularity.

That evening, Mr. Fogg, as tranquil and phlegmatic as ever, said to Aouda: "Is our marriage still agreeable to you?"

"Mr. Fogg," replied she, "it is for me to ask that question. You were ruined, but now you are rich again."

"Pardon me, madam; my fortune belongs to you. If you had not suggested our marriage, my servant would not have gone to the Reverend Samuel Wilson's, I should not have been apprised of my error, and——"

"Dear Mr. Fogg!" said the young woman.

"Dear Aouda!" replied Phileas Fogg.

It need not be said that the marriage took place forty-eight hours after, and that Passepartout, glowing and dazzling, gave the bride away. Had he not saved her, and was he not entitled to this honor?

The next day, as soon as it was light, Passepartout rapped vigorously at his master's door. Mr. Fogg opened it, and asked, "What's the matter, Passepartout?"

"What is it, sir? Why, I've just this instant found out——"

"What?"

"That we might have made the tour of the world in only seventy-eight days."

"No doubt," returned Mr. Fogg, "by not crossing India. But if I had not crossed India, I should not have saved Aouda; she would not have been my wife, and——"

Mr. Fogg quietly shut the door.

Phileas Fogg had won his wager, and had made his journey around the world in eighty days. To do this he had employed every means of conveyance—steamers, railways, carriages, yachts, trading-vessels, sledges, elephants. The eccentric gentleman had throughout displayed all his marvelous qualities of coolness and exactitude. But what then? What had he really gained by all this trouble? What had he brought back from this long and weary journey?

Nothing, say you? Perhaps so; nothing but a charming woman, who, strange as it may appear, made him the happiest of men!

Truly, would you not for less than that make the tour around the world?